EVERYMAN'S LIBRARY

EVERYMAN,
I WILL GO WITH THEE,
AND BE THY GUIDE,
IN THY MOST NEED
TO GO BY THY SIDE

MIGUEL de CERVANTES

Don Quixote

Translated from the Spanish by P. A. Motteux

with an Introduction by
A. J. Close

E V E R Y M A N ' S   L I B R A R Y

First included in Everyman's Library, 1906
Introduction, Bibliography and Chronology © David Campbell
Publishers Ltd., 1991
Printed from the Nonesuch edition

ISBN 1-85715-003-1

A CIP catalogue record for this book is available from the
British Library

Published by David Campbell Publishers Ltd., 79 Berwick Street,
London W1V 3PF

Distributed by Random House (UK) Ltd.,
20 Vauxhall Bridge Road, London SW1V 2SA

DON QUIXOTE

INTRODUCTION

Miguel de Cervantes Saavedra was born in Alcalá de Henares, near Madrid, in 1547. His father was a poor surgeon with a numerous family. Little is known for certain about his education, save that he completed it at a humanist academy in Madrid. In 1569, he suddenly left Spain for Italy, and, by 1570, had enlisted in the Spanish army. In 1571 he took part in the historic sea battle of Lepanto, which he describes in the prologue to *Don Quixote* Part II as 'the most glorious occasion seen by centuries past or present or to be seen in those to come'. In the battle he sustained wounds which left him permanently maimed in the left hand. After further military action in the Mediterranean, he was captured by Berber corsairs while returning from Naples to Spain by sea. He spent the next five years in captivity in Algiers; contemporary records testify to his fortitude and kindness to fellow captives during that ordeal, and also, to his defiant courage, displayed by four unsuccessful escape attempts. This 'heroic' decade of Cervantes' life, from 1570 to 1580, is recalled in the Captive's story in *Don Quixote* Part I, Chapters 39–42.

Ransomed in 1580, he returned to Spain, settled in Madrid, and began a moderately successful literary career, in which he wrote poetry, published a pastoral romance, *La Galatea* (1585), and had some twenty to thirty plays performed without, as he puts it, 'offerings of cucumbers or other throwable matter'. Then, in 1587, he was forced by penury to undertake more aggravating and humdrum occupations: commissioner of food supplies for the Armada expedition, and subsequently, tax-collector. The latter job led to his imprisonment in 1597 as a result of a shortfall in the revenues due to the Spanish Treasury. This misfortune was not due to Cervantes' dishonesty, but to the bankruptcy of the Sevillian banker with whom he had deposited the collected tax-money. Cervantes confesses to having 'engendered' *Don Quixote* in a prison (Prologue to Part I); and tradition has it that he refers to this three-month internment.

When, around 1600, he took up writing once again, he had been made painfully aware of the huge success of the school of drama led by Lope de Vega – the cause, on his own admission, of the reluctance of actor-managers to buy his plays. In *Don Quixote* I, 48, he delivers a severe, though measured and reasoned, attack on the New Comedy's violations of the rules of art, placing them on the same footing as the excesses of the romances of chivalry – his principal target in *Don Quixote*. One perceives some measure of personal resentment in this censure, and also in the prologue to Part I, which wittily satirizes the snobbish and pedantic pretensions of contemporary writers (including Lope de Vega, by allusion), and bears witness to Cervantes' general sense, around this time, of artistic standards cheapened, outlets blocked and opportunities lost to luckier rivals during his enforced period of literary inconspicuousness.

The enthusiastic reception of Part I, after its publication in 1605, mellowed Cervantes and spurred him to unchecked literary activity until his death – a gloriously creative old age in which he completed *Don Quixote* Part II (1615), his twelve *Exemplary Novels* (1613), a collection of comedies and farces (1615), and a long, satiric fantasy, in verse, about contemporary poetry, *The Voyage to Parnassus* (1614), amongst works unfinished or unpublished. *Persiles and Sigismunda*, a Byzantine romance, was posthumously published in 1617. In this period, he lived in Madrid, famous, widely admired and prominent in literary academies. Towards the end, the patronage of the Archbishop of Toledo and the Count of Lemos somewhat alleviated his chronic poverty. Something may be inferred about his character from his prologues, which are minor works of art in themselves. Typically, they show him affably conversing with friends, including the reader in this category. Their tone is self-deprecating, intimate, anecdotal, jocular; the Prologue to *Don Quixote* I shows him, unforgettably, in a dithering quandary, cheek on hand, elbow on desk, not knowing how to proceed until rescued by his facetious counsellor. Its theme is, in effect, 'how I learnt to stop worrying about the need to write this prologue'. In the preface to Part II, similarly bantering, he sends the reader off as emissary to Avellaneda –

the man who, under this pseudonym, published a continuation of Part I a year before the publication of Cervantes' own Part II – with a couple of jokes about madmen and dogs, the second one cheerfully vulgar. Both jokes carry disparaging implications about his rival's leaden wit. Considering the provocation that Cervantes had received, his tone is relatively mild; and the humorous tone of this preface carries over into the chapters of Part II which allude to Avellaneda's novel (notably, Chapters 59, 70, 72). These allusions presumably date from the moment of composition when Cervantes became aware of the publication of his rival's book. The moving prologue to *Persiles*, written when Cervantes was on his deathbed, contains his farewell to life, and specifically, to laughter and friends. His priorities are revealing. The spirit of all these prefaces is reflected in *Don Quixote* itself, marked by humorous self-consciousness, conviviality, festival gaiety and a kind of innocence. This is a world, like that of Boccaccio's *Decameron*, where care has been banished in a mood of civilized, communal fun.

Something should be said about the society and culture in which *Don Quixote* was written. The Spain of Philip III (1598–1621) had to cope with the financial exhaustion to which it had been brought by the imperialistic policies of Philip II (1556–98). So it curbed military adventures abroad. However, the court, based in Madrid from 1606, extravagantly belied this retrenchment. Powerful court favourites ran the country for the colourless monarch, enriching themselves in the process; and their spectacular rises and falls gave proof of the precariousness of fortune. People swarmed to Madrid from the impoverished provinces in order to seek preferment at court or service in noble households. Another important provider of livings in a country where industry and commerce were in decline was the Church, rich with its lands and tithes. Art – painting, theatre, literature – flourished; the Inquisition may have checked intellectual inquiry, but it did not curb creativity. By its policy of enforced religious unity, Spain avoided the religious conflicts that shook its European neighbours. However, it experienced a different kind of dissension, originating from the socially stigmatized, hence disaffected, descendants of converted Jews and Moors. This was a society hyperconscious of honour, caste and status; the gentry pursued a life of dignified idleness, while those lower down the social pyramid sought unscrupulously to scramble up. Gold and silver from the Indies, while they stoked inflation and hence had a deleterious effect on Spanish commerce, created a new *parvenu* class, determined to buy status with money. Widespread religious fervour, propagated by the Counter-Reformation, contrasted with the violence and dissolution of *mores*. In the literature of the age, *desengaño*, disenchantment with worldly vanity, is an insistent theme.

Faced with the social ills of a nation in decline, Cervantes adopts a reticent and restrained attitude. It is very unlikely that he intended the politico-historical message that has been discerned in *Don Quixote*: alleged symbol of the nation's incapacity to measure its ambitions to its means. While Cervantes offers a grandiose and sweeping picture of the society around him, its tone is mellow and picturesque, rather than caustic. Yet the moral themes which run through the novel and are centred individually on Don Quixote and Sancho – the folly of building castles in the air, of empty posturings of honour, of opportunistic social climbing; the ideals of fair justice and zealous government – obviously have wider social implications.

*

Any attempt to interpret *Don Quixote* must take account of the literary principles which motivate it and explain its central place in Cervantes' literary career. It is, in basic conception, a debunking parody of Spanish romances of chivalry. This genre, which had been immensely popular in Spain in the sixteenth century, was effectively launched by *Amadís of Gaul* (1508), a late, sophisticated offshoot of the corpus of medieval prose romances celebrating the deeds of the knights of the Round Table. *Amadís* is, in effect, the Spanish equivalent of Sir Thomas Malory's *Le Morte d'Arthur*; familiarity with Malory's book gives a quite good idea of the contents of *Amadís*. It dresses up the medieval code of chivalry in fabulous garb:

marvellous adventures in a largely legendary setting of forests, palaces, castles and tourneys, with a cast of giants, enchanters, damsels in distress, dwarfs and princesses, whose qualities of beauty, bloodthirstiness and chivalry and so forth are invariably superlative. Despite the obviously escapist gratifications that it offers, *Amadís* is a work of considerable literary merit, duly acknowledged by Cervantes in *Don Quixote* I, 6. It has strongly drawn central characters, a poetic tone and a reflective theme about the vanity of worldly ambitions. In Europe, it would remain popular for over two centuries, and in Spain, it generated a spate of sequels and imitations, many of which, like *Amadís* itself, were heavy tomes in several books or parts. The addicts of this mass of literature comprised all classes. Their diversity and degrees of taste and discrimination (or lack of them) are well represented in *Don Quixote*, which seeks to cure this readership's condition by precise diagnosis and prescription, as well as by the shock treatment of parody.

Cervantes' objections to the romances reflect the prevailing spirit of the times, when the combined influence of the Counter-Reformation and neoclassical literary theory was pressing literature and the arts to become didactic and academic. They are based on aesthetic principles of reason, harmony, taste and exemplariness, and more specifically, on the need to strike a just balance, in epic fiction, between the demands of the marvellous and those of verisimilitude. They are formulated in *Don Quixote* I, 47, by Cervantes' spokesman, the Canon of Toledo, who, besides censuring chivalry books, also offers a detailed blueprint for the kind of romance which might replace them. Towards the end of his career, Cervantes fulfilled it by writing *Persiles and Sigismunda*, an epic tale of a pilgrimage to Rome by two chaste, faithful lovers. It is piteous, grave and lofty in tone, ingeniously labyrinthine in structure and plot, deeply pious, and illustrative of man's relation to Providence. Cervantes probably judged it his masterpiece.

The interpolated tales in *Don Quixote* I are somewhat similar to *Persiles* in character. They represent the literary species – the romantic *novela* or episode – which Cervantes cultivates assiduously throughout his career. Integral to it are peripeties and crises which imperil or save life, love and honour: capture by pirates, shipwrecks, escapes; compromising flights from home by girls pursuing or pursued; providential reunions and wondrous recognitions. The tone is sentimental, exemplary and decorous; the status of the principals genteel; and the discourse courtly and rhetorical. Though no longer to our taste, these tales are well told, and reveal Cervantes' mastery of narrative technique in *all* the forms known to his age, not just the comic genres. Indeed, the handling of suspense, pace, style, effects of dramatic immediacy, and interweaving of strands of plot in his romantic fiction – for example, the interpolated stories of Cardenio and Dorotea (*Don Quixote* I, 23–4, 27–9, 36) – have notable repercussions on his comic fiction, manifest in the fact that the comic and the romantic strands are inseparably intermeshed in *Don Quixote*, particularly Part I. One might be tempted to suppose, given Cervantes' denunciations of the improbabilities of chivalric romance, that these interpolations are offered to us tongue-in-cheek. One must set aside the suggestion, except in the case of the pastoral interludes of Part I (Chapters 12–14 and 50–51), where irony at the expense of the pastoral convention is a notable, though not a predominant feature. The fact that the coincidences of the Captive's tale, for example, are set in a historical and contemporary world, full of autobiographical significance, mark their *possibility* for Cervantes, hence their difference from a kind of fiction where 'a lad of sixteen stabs a giant as big as a tower and splits him in two as if he were made of sugar paste' (*Don Quixote* I, 47). In sum, Cervantes' standpoint in attacking chivalry books is that of a writer strongly drawn to heroic romance, and indignant about the massive proliferation of an inferior species of it which has lowered public taste and queered his own pitch.

*

Anyone who reads *Don Quixote* for the first time inevitably has some preconceptions about it, beginning with the dictionary definition of 'quixotic' and with the plethora of modern re-creations of Cervantes' story and his heroes in films, music, ballet, painting, novels. The reader will doubtless know that it concerns a country squire from a village somewhere in La Mancha, who goes mad as a result of reading chivalry books and comes to believe that they are historically true and that he can become a knight such as they depict, with all the ensuing glory and perquisites. Mounted on bony Rozinante, clad in makeshift armour, and accompanied by Sancho Panza as his squire, this *hidalgo* goes through the countryside in search of adventure, interpreting the commonplace objects and travellers that he meets – windmills, flocks of sheep, a funeral cortège, a chain of galley slaves – as perpetrators or victims of some dreadful wrong that must be righted. Out of the resulting merry confusions Cervantes has somehow wrought a great and complex novel which posterity has found to be profound, enigmatic and inspiring.

How and why is it that an old book, with such a simple theme, written in a culture so remote from our own, has had such a powerful and lasting impact? Let us begin by answering these questions as they have affected practising novelists.

For about a hundred years after its publication, *Don Quixote* was widely appreciated in Europe as a broad, coarse-grained work of burlesque comedy, as may be inferred from the nature of its principal imitations, Avellaneda's *El Quijote* and Samuel Butler's *Hudibras* (1663). It was not placed on the pedestal of classic status until the eighteenth century. The process began in England, around 1740, and spread to France, Germany and Spain. Two of the greatest English novels of the century, Fielding's *Joseph Andrews* (1742) and Sterne's *Tristram Shandy* (1759), are heavily and explicitly indebted to Cervantes. Both feature the character type of the 'amiable humorist' (Parson Adams and Uncle Toby, respectively), whose eccentric hobbyhorse makes him, like Don Quixote, at once absurd and lovable; both imitate, and also complicate, Cervantes' whimsical and burlesque style of narration, which pokes playful fun at the conventions of fiction. Though the Age of the Enlightenment reveals a more refined appreciation of the finer shades of Cervantes' novel, it persists, broadly speaking, with the view of *Don Quixote* entertained by its first readers: namely, that it is a burlesque, satiric and corrective work, admirable for its urbanity, good taste, rationality and verisimilitude.

DON QUIXOTE

Don Quixote's apotheosis came around 1800, when the German Romantic generation took it as a model for the 'Romantic' genre par excellence – the novel – overturning the Enlightenment view of it in the process. The Romantics admired it for its poetry, its bitter-sweet attitude to medieval chivalry, its profound irony, and its mythic universality, exemplified by its treatment of the theme of the opposition between ideal and real. They brought about a lasting change in the valuation of Cervantes' novel, whose effects may be seen in the exploitation and expansion of the Quixote theme in many major novels of the nineteenth century: Dickens' *The Pickwick Papers* (1836–7), Melville's *Moby-Dick* (1853), Flaubert's *Madame Bovary* (1856–7), Dostoevsky's *The Idiot* (1868), Mark Twain's *The Adventures of Huckleberry Finn* (1885), Galdós' *Fortunata and Jacinta* (1886–7). Preserving Cervantes' epic and detailed panorama of contemporary life, and something like his central narrative theme of the forging and loss of illusions, these novelists filled the canvas with much grander and more sombre designs. Thus, Melville's Captain Ahab, pursuing universal evil in the form of the White Whale, exhibits a Quixotic sense of mission infused with Shakespearian frenzy; his sordid crew of savages and social outcasts are latter-day crusaders, symbols of the common man's capacity to scale heights of idealism and heroism; life's material flux, symbolized by the waves traversed by the *Pequod*, is a screen for transcendental Ideas – or perhaps figments – that man is doomed to pursue, perishing in the attempt. Though twentieth-century novelists have rendered *Don Quixote* somewhat less sustained and concerted homage than their predecessors, they nonetheless include a long and impressive list of *aficionados*: Unamuno, Gide, Thomas Mann, Kafka, Hašek, Nabokov, Borges, Carlos Fuentes, Milan Kundera, Graham Greene. The lessons that they tend to draw from *Don Quixote* are twofold. One concerns the self-reflexive and self-questioning nature of art, in relation to its own premises, enabling conventions and mimetic purposes (cf. Gide's *The Counterfeiters*, or Borges' story of Pierre Menard in *Fictions*). The other has been formulated thus in the epilogue to Milan Kundera's *The Book of Laughter and Forgetting*: 'When Don

Quixote went out into the world, that world turned into a mystery before his eyes. That is the legacy of the first European novel to the entire subsequent history of the novel. The novelist teaches its reader to comprehend the world as a question.'

Thus, the enthusiasm that Cervantes has inspired amongst practising novelists since about 1740 is due to his having created a story which both anticipates the formal features of a novel, as the genre was conceived in the eighteenth and nineteenth centuries, and also displays something of the potency of a myth about origins. From Fielding onwards, Cervantes' book has had the status of the Old Testament in relation to the New: an inspiringly prophetic symbol which each epoch can treat as a prefiguration of its own concerns and re-create accordingly. Moreover, since 1800, the artistic re-creation of *Don Quixote* has tended to lead and inspire academic interpretation, rather than the other way around. Thus, the above-quoted words of Milan Kundera, which typify one kind of novelistic inflection of the Quixote theme from Unamuno onwards, coincide with a dominant view of *Don Quixote* amongst Cervantine critics in the twentieth century: the idea that it dramatizes, ironically and non-committally, the collision of viewpoints and ideologies in a world where the certitudes of faith and tradition-sanctioned truth are beginning to come under attack.

Whence this capacity to strike so resonant a chord, with such diverse overtones? One can think of many features of *Don Quixote* which contain it: the quasi-epic nature of the hero's rebellion against the social order and common sense; his elusive switching between crazy heroics, specious semi-lucidity, and genuine wisdom; the softening of sensibility towards 'alienation', generally understood, since the eighteenth century; Cervantes' non-committal irony; above all, perhaps, his tendency to dissolve specific social reference in situations which, like Sancho's governorship, blend fantasy, fable, legend and clownish comedy, and thus achieve a kind of universality. In what follows, I shall concentrate on those features which explain *Don Quixote*'s immediate appeal to the ordinary reader, and potently elicit his or her identification with the story, in a way neatly pinpointed by Dr Johnson's remark about Quixote and Sancho: 'very few readers, amidst their mirth or their pity, can deny that they have admitted visions of the same kind, though they have not perhaps expected events equally strange, or by means equally inadequate'.

*

Don Quixote embodies literary heroism, not in its customarily noble and fulfilled form, but in one which, by its chronic fallibility, matches the ordinary mortal's wry sense about such heroism: 'real life's not like that'. This, precisely, is Cervantes' point about chivalric romances. Moreover, that wry perception does not merely apply to the gap between fiction and reality, but also to that which separates any individual's flattering self-image from the real state of affairs. Cervantes' feat, in drawing the character of his hero, consists in making the two gaps coincide, so that one becomes a metaphor of the other. The hero's madness has an implicit representativeness – not deliberately intended symbolism – which, beyond its immediate reference to chivalry books, evokes the monsters of unreason repeatedly ridiculed in Cervantes' writings: vainglory, literary affectation, crackbrained ambition, empty heroics, superstition, love's blindness, the passions of anger, envy and revenge – all symptoms of the insatiable desire and failure of self-knowledge that are the lot of fallen human nature. This power of analogy becomes increasingly apparent as *Don Quixote* unfolds, throwing up more and more cases parallel or antithetical to the central one: Sancho, the pathological figures of Cardenio or Anselmo, sundry precious and love-lorn shepherds, the Knight of the Green Cloak and others. Cervantes' technique of treating the 'episodes' of *Don Quixote* – that is, the stories not centred on Quixote and Sancho – as loose mirror-images of the hero's experience emphasizes these connections. It is, for example, scarcely a coincidence that the feature of knight-errantry most heavily emphasized and caricatured in Don Quixote – gratuitous belligerence inspired by vainglory – directly corresponds to the vice which, perhaps above all others, attracts Cervantes' censure as a moralist: acts of revenge motivated by a regard for personal honour. Two episodes in *Don Quixote* Part II – that of the 'braying' villagers (II, 25 and 27) and that featuring the Catalan outlaw Roque Guinart (II, 60) – are replicas of Don Quixote's experience in this respect. Now, we, as readers of *Don Quixote*, are the more disposed to make this kind of connection between the hero's behaviour and our own experience because this behaviour embodies, first and foremost, the states of mind of a compulsive *reader*.

The hero's primordial motive is reader's make-believe exaggerated to the point where the 'willing suspension of belief' has passed into total abandonment of it. This motive, which involves the dynamic assumptions that imagination equals reality and imitation equals doing or being, is brilliantly developed. Don Quixote's aim is to *be* a hero of chivalric romance, that is, of a chivalric *history*, since the romances, for him, are true histories (I, 1). Accordingly, he has only to imitate them for all that happens in them to happen to him. Implicitly believing other people's fictions, he logically believes his own; so he is able simultaneously to admit that Dulcinea is an idealized figment and to request Sancho to deliver a love-letter to her (I, 25). Arguing the historical truth of chivalry books with the Canon of Toledo (I, 49), he disconcerts his opponent with his erudite confusion of fact and legend, putting on the same level an historical tourney of 1434, the love of Tristan and Isolde and the wooden peg with which Pierre of Provence guided his wooden horse through the air. Let us now consider the adventure of the fulling-mills (I, 20) – a finely observed study, not just of reader's make-believe, but also of trying, and failing, to keep face.

Don Quixote and Sancho find themselves at night in a wild and solitary woodland somewhere in the foothills of the Sierra Morena. It is pitch dark; the leaves rustle with sinister softness in the wind; from somewhere there resounds a dreadful pounding and clanking which seem to herald a perilous adventure. Rashly drawing the moral before the event, Don Quixote invites Sancho to contemplate in him a knight destined to eclipse all the heroes immortalized by fame, and so intrepid that he is fired by circumstances which would have made Mars quake. As Amadís did just prior to his battle with a dreadful dragon (*Amadís of Gaul*, Chapter 73), Don Quixote tells Sancho that, should he not return, Sancho is to wait three days, then journey back to Dulcinea to tell her that her true knight died in attempting feats which might make him worthy to call himself hers. The speech's orotund style, its messianic overtones, its evocation of a revived Golden Age of chivalry, the hero's mad intrepidity and his request to Sancho – all these are reminiscent of the world of chivalry books. And, as we have seen, Cervantes artfully contrives circumstances which are atmospherically consonant with that world, and make the hero's response to danger seem authentically heroic. Yet the reader cannot help feeling that Don Quixote's speech strikes the wrong note and offers too many hostages to fortune. Amadís, his model in this adventure and a paragon of modesty, would have cringed at the very idea of permitting himself such bombast. That is to say, Cervantes has caused his hero to imitate the style of chivalry books plausibly and solemnly, while overdoing the heroic note, with the result that he incurs melodramatic pomposity and strikes a pose of fatuous arrogance in circumstances expressly designed to show him up. In the world of Amadís, all is providentially arranged to ensure that the reader's expectations of heroic achievement are fulfilled. The world of Don Quixote is governed by a quite different dispensation, Sod's Law, which ensures that such expectations are regularly frustrated by outcomes which are banal, normal and naturally caused. Thus does Cervantes provoke the sense that the hero gets it nearly right while simultaneously getting it dreadfully wrong.

There is a further, subtler reason for this impression. Though Don Quixote, in his self-glorifying speech, is deliberately trying to enact the hero's part, he is implicitly deflected from this path by self-preening fantasies of what it would be like to be Amadís in this kind of situation, and to be regarded and extolled in the appropriate terms. Pompous forecasts about the hero, such as Don Quixote makes about himself, regularly occur in chivalry books; yet they are delivered by the narrator, by the Merlin-figure who presides over the hero's

destiny, by anyone but the hero himself. Don Quixote, impro-
vising a chivalric romance by word and deed, and projecting
himself in the star role, amalgamates all these discourses in
one, acting as hero, narrator and reader simultaneously. The
reader's viewpoint is primordial here; Don Quixote's fatuous
arrogance in this scene is psychologically attributable to it.

The sequel to his fanfare of self-praise is a chain of events
designed to flatten it and cause initial tantalizing suspense to
crumple in anticlimax. These events are: Sancho's tearful,
cowardly and undignified entreaties to his master to desist
from his enterprise; his sly trick of hobbling Rozinante; his
artlessly meandering shaggy-dog story; his contorted attempts
to relieve himself of his fear-induced burden without attracting attention or leaving his master's side; above all, by the
discovery of the cause of the horrendous din on the following
morning – the alternate beating of six fulling-mill paddles.
Throughout all this, the frustrated and exasperated Don
Quixote tries to maintain a pose of haughty superiority: his
interventions in the shaggy-dog story are crushingly sardonic;
his reaction to Sancho's defecation combines disgusted prim-
ness with pained reproof of his servant's disrespect. However,
the pomposity collapses absurdly with the discovery of the
fulling-mills, and more specifically, with its immediate sequel.
Don Quixote, raising his eyes to his servant's face, sees it
puffed out with mirth and cannot repress a giggle. This
triggers Sancho's uninhibited guffaws, together with his mischievous mimicry of his master's boasting. Don Quixote vents
his mortification by delivering his servant two blows with his
lance, and then, in an understandably petty and natural way,
tries to recoup by bluster and reprimand the esteem that he
has lost by failure to match deeds to promises. My point is
that, despite the fantastic abnormality of Don Quixote's
delusions, the vividness and force with which he exhibits the
familiar psychology of make-believe and 'pride before a fall'
fully justify Dr Johnson's observation.

The eery scene-setting and the hero's self-glorifying speech
in the chapter just considered are good examples of Cervantes'
mock-grave burlesque technique – a feature of *Don Quixote*
that was much admired in eighteenth-century England. As we

have seen, the mock-gravity not only affects the hero's character and style, but also the narrator's ironic empathy towards his viewpoint, reflected in the initial or outer appearances of the world around him, seemingly so propitious to heroic action. It also affects the tone and persona that the narrator adopts in order to relate the story; we might characterize this narrative style as sustained jocular whimsy, which, by its blend of arch fulsomeness and familiar irreverence, creates a playful complicity between author and reader and hints continually at the innocent preposterousness of the subject matter. A good, brief example of this is the sentence which describes the discovery of the fulling-mills: 'there, patent and exposed to view was the very unmistakable cause of that horrendous and dreadful din, which had kept them in such fearful suspense all night. It was, if it doesn't irritate and upset you, reader, six fulling-mill paddles, which caused the din by their alternate blows.' Here, Cervantes recaptures the tone of his portentous scene-setting before making, with an ironic wink at the reader, an apologetic blow for delivering so little after promising so much.

Cervantes' main strategy, as narrator of *Don Quixote*, follows the same procedure. On the one hand, he matches the hero's expectation that the chronicle of his deeds must perforce be 'grandiloquent, lofty, notable, magnificent and true' (II, 3), and he does this by adopting the manner of the scrupulous historian and the epic poet. Thus, he intervenes in the story with precious dawn-descriptions (II, 14), emotional apostrophes to the hero or the reader or abstract personifications (II, 17, 44), gravely scrupulous debates about the reliability of 'sources' (II, 24), the Virgilian valediction to his quill at the end of the novel. At the same time, he ridiculously subverts this pomposity by various kinds of flippancy, notably his attribution of a thoroughly unworthy status to the 'chronicler', Cide Hamete Benengeli. Near the beginning of Part I, in Chapter 9, Cervantes describes with a splendid flourish how he discovered, in a street bazaar in Toledo, Benengeli's Arabic manuscript, containing the punctilious record of Don Quixote's heroic deeds. This spoof sends up the familiar pretence in medieval prose romances that the story is based on the chronicle of a sage, recorded in an occult tongue on yellowed parchments preserved in some recondite vault. According to this, Cervantes is simply the editor (or 'second author') of the translated chronicle recorded by Benengeli, the 'first author'. The pretence is clearly preposterous. Benengeli is a deformation of the Arabic for 'aubergine-like'; a popular expression linking Toledans to aubergines explains this 'etymology' (see II, 2). As a *morisco*, member of a despised ethnic community, he has most unsuitable credentials for hymning a Spanish hero, and indeed, even for qualifying as a historian. For how can a member of a race of liars possibly be veridical? This question reminds us of what we already know: that the book in our hands is a comic fiction, composed by Miguel de Cervantes. So, Cervantes' apparent effacement of responsibility for his story is a form of self-advertisement; significantly, the novel ends, as it began, in a strongly *self*-assertive way: 'For me alone was Don Quixote born, and I for him; his were the deeds and mine the words; we are inseparably united ...' But let us return to mock-gravity as it affects Don Quixote's character, since it is largely responsible for the novel's notorious ambiguity.

Cervantes hits upon this method by virtue of the fact that he criticizes chivalric romances from a viewpoint internal to Romance in general: intimate with its techniques and conventions, responsive to its style and atmosphere. So, Don Quixote's imitation of his models tends constantly to expand at the periphery, drawing in any high style or theme that has some affinity with them. The florid dawn-description that he attributes to his future chronicler in I, 2, as he sets forth on his first sally, is sedulously copied, so Cervantes assures us, from chivalry books. In fact, it is a fulsome reproduction of the precious clichés that Cervantes had himself employed in *La Galatea* in the appropriate contexts; no doubt Cervantes mentally associated them with a determinate species of 'purple' topic, which might appear in various genres (epic, pastoral, lyric poetry), without being peculiar to any one in particular. What gives the passage an undeniably parodic air is its combination of deliberately exaggerated preciosity and utter incongruity to the hero's early morning ride over the monotonous plain of Montiel. Thus, it creates the general impression that Cervantes wants to achieve – that of 'imitating their language as closely as he could' – without in fact employing the means that these words suggest. This passage is typical of Cervantes' parodic technique in *Don Quixote*, which is unusual in two respects. It depends less on a detailed relation of caricature between the imitation and the model, than on a relation of incongruity between it and the real state of affairs, and less on the mimicry of stylistic mannerisms (e.g. the chivalric archaisms and formulae which spatter the hero's discourse in the early chapters of Part I), than on the extrapolation from chivalry books of typical adventures and principles of conduct (fighting giants, righting wrongs, succouring damsels in distress, and so forth). In terms of style, generally understood, the hero plays free and eclectic variations on his chivalric theme.

Thus, Don Quixote's description of two armies in battle array (I, 18), which, again, purports to imitate his favourite literature most scrupulously, contains unmistakable echoes of the description of Turnus' armies in *Aeneid* Book VI. And in his improvised story of the Knight of the Lake (I, 50), he launches into an exuberantly lyrical pastiche of the descriptions of the Bowers of Bliss or enchanted palaces that are to be found, not in chivalry books, but in Ariosto's *Orlando Furioso*, in Spanish pastoral romances and in Cervantes' own *Persiles*: Elysian fields, a delightful forest, a crystal brook running over pearly pebbles and golden sand, a castle made entirely of precious stones and metals. The same eclecticism may be found in the hero's eccentric rationale of his chivalric enterprise, which often presses into service, elegantly but incongruously, the topics and argumentation of Renaissance humanism. Examples of this are: the oration on the virtues of the Golden Age (I, 11); the exposition of the merits of imitation, considered as a path to excellence in the arts (I, 25); the Aristotelian casuistry about the need to err on the side of rashness rather than cowardice (II, 17). Don Quixote is capable, too, of tuning this erudition in a lucid key, and does so increasingly in Part II, where, in his 'lucid intervals', he covers most of the significant items of the epoch's moral/social agenda: honour and lineages

(II, 6), fame (II, 8), education (II, 16), the duties of marriage (II, 19 and 22), the conditions of the just war (II, 27) and, above all, government (II, 42–3).

The epithet 'ingenious' in the novel's title, and Cervantes' description of his brainchild (the hero) as 'dry, wizened, capricious, and full of diverse notions never imagined by anyone else' (prologue to Part I), helps us to understand why he characterizes Don Quixote in this way. A mischievous, bookish vein of humour in Cervantes makes him revel in depicting this crazily inventive reader, who is capable of generating such well-concerted nonsense, such exuberant flights of fancy, such widely nourished and elegant, but always idiosyncratic wisdom. By this means Cervantes found an ingenious solution for a problem which vexed Spanish novelists around 1600 and is posed with particular acuteness in Spain's classical picaresque novel, *Guzmán of Alfarache*: how to incorporate, without impropriety, eloquently expressed, didactic matter in a work of comic fiction. By this means too Cervantes found a satisfying outlet for mixed motives in himself: a frustrated poet-in-prose whose flights of fantasy or lyricism in his serious works are often curbed by puritanical and self-critical scruples. Don Quixote's madness gives his creator licence to indulge his naughty penchant with a clear conscience, appeasing the puritan in him with the thought: all is well, I'm only joking.

Freely embroidered around its chivalric theme, Don Quixote's character is, in many ways, an exaggeration or misapplication of heroic or romantic traits of a general kind, rather than of chivalric traits in particular. For example, his excesses of gallantry, intrepidity and rhetorical effusion are often reminiscent of those of the heroes of Lope de Vega's theatre. This generality of reference, with its mix of stylishness, learning and madness, makes his imitation of chivalry accessible to us, multiplying the connections that we can discover, instead of limiting them, as parody normally does. It is also responsible for creating disconcerting correspondences between Don Quixote's mad attitudes and forms of behaviour which Cervantes invites us seriously to admire. The Don has much in common with the hero of Cervantes' Byzantine romance,

Persiles: compassion for victims of persecution, prudish chastity, an enthusiastic sensibility, a tourist's curiosity, didacticism and more besides. What, for Cervantes, makes Don Quixote's behaviour unambiguously comic – outside his 'lucid intervals' – is its violation of the principle of decorum and the artificial literariness of his motivation. However, for us, things are much less clear. The stylishness of Don Quixote's imitation, and the passage of time, have blurred the indecorum; his residual good sense and good intentions leave us uncertain where to draw the line between his lucidity and madness. If we add to all this the factors which have already been mentioned in connection with *Don Quixote*'s mythic suggestiveness, the result is the notorious ambiguity that the novel holds for its modern readers.

The conversations between Don Quixote and Sancho are the core of the novel and the principal scene of its inner drama: the long, slow process by which Don Quixote's and Sancho's delusions – respectively, about chivalry and Dulcinea, and about the governorship of an island – are built up, modified and eroded. Cervantes' motive in giving the conversations such prominence is his desire to project the two central personages as 'characters': that is, bundles of idiosyncrasies. Hence the extraordinary shift that he effects, in the development of prose fiction, from incident to dialogue. His primary model consists of the master/servant dialogues of sixteenth-century Spanish comedy, in which, typically, the master's elevated posturings of passion and honour are met by the servant's quips, objections and concern for his belly and self-preservation. The exchanges between Quixote and Sancho are notable for their domestic and intimate quality, suggested, for example, by the continuous ironic references to a shared past and each other's familiar mannerisms, or by the ripples of altercation which disguise underlying sympathy and dependence. They pit Quixote's delusions against down-to-earth simple-mindedness and credulity – Sancho's chief traits – and not, as is sometimes said, against down-to-earth common sense. As a result, the ironic incongruities in the relationship – the radical mismatch between Quixote's high-mindedness and Sancho's thoroughly prosaic and plebeian conception of their mission – are never consistently perceived from a viewpoint within it. What keeps the pair together, despite this seemingly total incompatibility, is the affectionate innocence common to both men; and this, together with the ties that bind master to servant, both from the same village, account for the sympathy and loyalty that they express for each other, memorably and movingly, in the Duke's palace (II, 32 and 33).

A principal source of the interest of these conversations lies in the exquisite perceptiveness with which Cervantes shows the two heroes' delusions continually shifting in response to recent and cumulative experience. As the prospect of achievement recedes or draws nearer, so the barometer of morale rises or falls, and changes take place in their attitudes to each other and the world. A felicitous example of this is a passage of conversation which occurs just after the disastrous battle with the sheep (I, 18), which Don Quixote took to be armies. Showing very poor timing, he consoles Sancho with a little homily on the swings and roundabouts of fortune, ending with the admonition not to be so despondent about misfortunes which do not directly affect *him*. Since Sancho has just discovered the loss of his saddle-bags and is inwardly vowing to return home, the homily provokes a sarcastic reaction from him, which sharpens still further when Don Quixote acknowledges that, if the saddle-bags have gone, so have their provisions. Sancho retorts: 'Only if . . . there were any shortage round here of those herbs that you claim to know about, with which unfortunate knights errant like you make up for such deficiencies.' Here Sancho taunts his master with his previous claim that, as a knight-errant, he is *ex officio* an expert herbalist, and therefore has no need of sustenance, on his wanderings, beyond what grows by the wayside (see I, 10). Instead of rounding on his cheeky servant, as one might expect, Don Quixote reacts with unprecedented humility, mildness, self-mocking humour and Biblical wisdom:

All the same . . . I would rather have a hunk of bread or some coarse bran bread and a brace of smoked sardines than all the herbs described by Dioscorides, even it it were in Dr Laguna's illustrated edition. But anyway, get on your ass, good Sancho, and follow me, for

God, provider of all things, won't fail us, especially as we're so much employed in his service, for he doesn't fail the flies of the air nor the worms of the ground nor the tadpoles of the water, and he is so merciful that he causes his sun to shine on good and bad alike and his rain to fall on the just and the unjust.

The passage represents a small turning-point for both men. For Sancho, it is a nadir of disillusionment in Part I, bringing an erosion of his initial confidence in his master. When such insubordination recurs, particularly in Part II, it is a concomitant of the recognition of his master's madness and the emptiness of his promises. Yet its sporadic nature betrays its shallowness; credulity, affection or covetous hope soon reassert their grip (see, e.g., II, 28 and 33). For Don Quixote, the passage is a turning-point because it anticipates the peaceableness and recurrent lucidity which characterize his conduct in Part II. Yet at this stage, such enlightenment is far away. Even very late in Part II, the revival of old enthusiams is capable of making him revert to original type, just as Sancho does.

The passage is also significant because it exemplifies the quality of 'everydayness' which the novel extols and to which Quixote and Sancho, in the last act of their drama, wisely return. At the outset, everyday reality seems to be represented by the dregs of society: crafty innkeepers 'more thieving than Cacchus', boorish mule-drovers, prostitutes and so forth. Though such stereotype figures of sixteenth-century Spanish comedy continue to provide an important element in Don Quixote's world thereafter, they tend to be outnumbered by characters – and the corresponding settings – of a more humdrum and realistic, or even of a romantic and picturesque, variety. An example of the humdrum category is that poor country barber, attacked by Don Quixote for having supposedly usurped Mambrino's helmet (I, 21); when the fateful encounter occurs, the barber in question is travelling by ass to a nearby village in order to shave one man and bleed another, and is wearing a basin on his head to protect his new hat from a shower of rain. *Don Quixote* insistently implies that this prosaic level of existence, on which men 'eat and sleep and die in their beds and make their wills before dying' (I, 6), is valuable and important, and that any life-style, whether lived or literary, which fails to adjust to it is perversely out of proportion. As we have just seen, the hero's first moment of wisdom in Part I occurs when, rejecting literary fare, he links bread and sardines to the Gospel according to St Matthew and the Christian virtue of humility. His last and crowning act of wisdom is to realize, on his deathbed, that concerns for his soul, his estate and his dependants is paramount, and with this realization, to consign dreams of glory and Dulcinea to oblivion. And Sancho's finest moment is his declaration, in his speech of abdication from the governorship (II, 53), that a scythe in his hand, *gazpacho*, a shepherd's coat and hemp sandals suit him better than a governor's sceptre, with its attendant cares and perquisites.

As we have noted, Don Quixote and Sancho undergo a continuous process of evolution, and yet remain fundamentally true to type. Though this might seem perfectly natural, we should refrain from explaining either the process of evolution or the continuity entirely in terms of natural psychology. Cervantes' two heroes are larger-than-life figures, exaggerated in two opposite directions for comic effect, and endowed with many traits or functions which are the product of artistic stylization rather than observation of how people normally behave. The paradoxical development of Don Quixote in Part II is a striking illustration of this, and to understand it, we need to take account of this Part's changed purpose and atmosphere.

Part II transpires in holiday mood; the season is springtime/ early summer; this is a rural world largely removed from urban and courtly bustle; it teems with entertainers, people in costume, adventurers, outcasts. The abrasive comedy of Part I, with its insistent reference to chivalry books, has become mellower and less polemical. The types that Don Quixote and Sancho meet, though picturesque in the manner described, are more in touch with public, contemporary affairs than their precursors of Part I. They meet the outlaw Roque Guinart (II, 60), actors of the troupe of Angulo el Malo (II, 11), various dignitaries of Barcelona during their triumphal visit to the city (II, 61 ff.), a member of the recently exiled *morisco* community, returning illegally to recover his buried treasure and find his daughter (II, 54). Now, the general reason for this topicality of reference is the invasion of Don Quixote's world by Benengeli's readership; a feature of Part II which gives it an extraordinary self-reflexiveness. In accordance with the story's original premise that it is based on the historical doings of a contemporary Manchegan knight, Don Quixote and Sancho learn, in early Part II, of the publication of their 'chronicle' (i.e. Part I), and of its reception, merits and defects (II, 2–3). From this point on, they meet a succession of characters who have read Benengeli's 'chronicle' and acclaim them as the heroes recorded in it. The purpose of all these encounters is implicitly celebratory: the theme of Part II, particularly from Chapter 30 onwards, may fairly be said to be the universal popularity of Quixote and Sancho and their book. The chapter just mentioned marks the point at which the two heroes arrive at the country seat of a duke and duchess in Aragon, who actively show their delight in meeting the subjects of Benengeli's chronicle by playing a series of elaborate hoaxes on them, matched to their expectations. And from Chapter 59 the theme acquires a sharper focus: it is the superiority of Benengeli's book, and his *real* heroes, to the fraudulent imitations attributable to Avellaneda.

Now, this celebratory spirit, combining or contrasting with Don Quixote's increased lucidity, creates two contradictory tendencies in Part II and gives it a somewhat paradoxical aspect. On the one hand, it contributes to the impression that society is drawing nearer to the two heroes and *vice versa*. For reasons already stated, 'society' now constitutes a large literary fan club, whose attitudes towards its two idols include friendliness, hospitality, affability, curiosity, partial respect and discreetly dissimulated mirth and astonishment – rather different from the derision and pity shown towards the heroes in Part I. Quixote and Sancho, particularly the former, reciprocate this movement of approximation. In Part II, Cervantes not only emphasizes the hero's lucidity, but also the process by which he adjusts to chastening experience. Thus, in Chapter 11, he beholds an apparition which, like the fantasmagorical cortège in Part I, Chapter 19, seems really to herald an adventure: a cart driven by an ugly devil, bearing the figure of Death, an angel with painted wings, an emperor and other marvellous personifications. He issues the customary challenge, and receives a reasonable explanation for the prodigy: this is a company of actors travelling to a nearby locality to stage a religious play as part of the festival of Corpus Christi. His urbanely lucid reaction to this explanation is pointedly different from what we have come to expect, and marks a small but significant step towards the recovery of sanity: 'one must set one's hand to appearances in order to be disabused of false assumptions'. Pointed contrasts like this keep being forced on us in Part II. Even the dives into blatant lunacy are less obdurate and aggressive than before: partly because they are often the result of other people's plausible trickery; partly because they are qualified by doubt, bafflement, mild deference to the scepticism of others, even irony. This is particularly true of the whole business of Dulcinea's 'enchantment', initiated by Sancho when he tricks his master into thinking that a rustic wench is Dulcinea in enchanted guise (II, 10). Cervantes hints that cumulative defeats and, subsequently, disappointment over the tardiness or possibility of Dulcinea's disenchantment, induce a general improvement in the hero's wits and, at the end, his terminal illness.

Now let us consider the other side of the paradox. The impression of a progressive improvement in the hero's condition is disconcertingly checked by the previously mentioned events at the Duke's palace (II, 30 ff.). By putting the limelight on the artistry with which the hoaxes are executed by the Duke's servants, and reducing Quixote and Sancho to credulous foils, Cervantes diverts attention from the process of the hero's disillusionment, not putting him or it stage-centre again until he gets him out of stately homes and on the open road. In effect, in the Duke's palace, Quixote and Sancho are treated as something like court fools: a spectacle to which the modern reader is liable to react with some distaste. In part the reaction is understandable; it is supported by Cide Hamete's accusation against the Duke and Duchess of having carried the joke too far (II, 70). Yet, in making this criticism, Cervantes doubtless felt no reservations about the principle on which these practical jokes are based, merely about the manner and degree of implementation. He would surely not have devoted so much space to them – 'the best adventures that this great history contains' (end of II, 33) – had he not expected the reader to share the high estimation that these words imply. He doubtless saw Part II as being, in a full sense, a sequel to Part I, continuing and developing its major themes. This entails the vigorous survival of the burlesque framework of Don Quixote's delusions, which change in their outward form – from extrovert dynamism to passive credulity – but do not collapse until the very end, despite the process of erosion that is initiated from early Part II. Since the hoaxes that are devised by the Duke's servants are reminiscent of the festival pageants, the masques and farces in which Don Quixote and Sancho often appeared in seventeenth-century Spain, Cervantes would have probably regarded them, not as a symptom of aristocratic frivolity, but as a tribute by the whole community of *Don Quixote*'s readers to its two protagonists. As an act of homage made by *readers*, it is also an interpretation of where the novel's entertainment value essentially lies.

This brings us back to our point of departure. By giving the act of reading such prominence in the fictional world of *Don Quixote*, and by making its principal subject and object – the hero – so paradoxical a figure, Cervantes positively invites *readings* of his book: a seventeenth-century reading, according to which we laugh *with* society *against* the hero; a nineteenth-century reading, which feels *with* the hero *against* society; and a twentieth-century reading, which affirms that the novel permits both options, and others, simultaneously. My purpose here is not to adjudicate or even to say whether adjudication is valid; it is merely to explain how such polysemic virtuality is made possible.

A. J. Close

SELECT BIBLIOGRAPHY

CERVANTES, *Exemplary Stories*, trans. C. A. Jones, Penguin Books, 1972. Contains six of Cervantes' best-known *novelas*.

RILEY, E. C., *Don Quixote*, Allen and Unwin, 1986. A good, general coverage with excellent bibliography.

— *Cervantes's Theory of the Novel*, Clarendon Press, 1962. Classic study of Cervantes' relation to Renaissance literary theory.

BYRON, WILLIAM, *Cervantes: A Biography*, Cassell, 1979. A lively, detailed and colourful, if somewhat over-written treatment.

McKENDRICK, MELVEENA, *Cervantes*, Little, Brown, Boston, Mass., 1980. A lucid and scholarly 'life and works'.

ENTWISTLE, W. J., *Cervantes*, Clarendon Press, 1940, and reprints 1965 and 1967. Succinct and readable 'life and works', though the judgements are now somewhat out of date.

ELLIOTT, J. H., *Imperial Spain, 1469–1716*, 1963. A classic study of the history of this period.

MANN, THOMAS, 'Voyage with *Don Quixote*' in *Cervantes*, ed. Lowry Nelson, Prentice Hall, Englewood Cliffs, NJ, 1969.

WILLIAMSON, EDWIN, *The Half-Way House of Fiction: 'Don Quixote' and Arthurian Romance*, Clarendon Press, 1984.

PARKER, A. A., *Literature and the Delinquent*, Edinburgh University Press, 1967. Influential study of the Spanish picaresque novel, which has a general connection with *Don Quixote*.

CLOSE, A. J., *Don Quixote*, Cambridge University Press, 1990.

One may group together a number of influential essays or works which deal in general with Cervantes' relation to the subsequent development of the novel: ERICH AUERBACH, 'The Enchanted Dulcinea', in *Mimesis. The Representation of Reality in Western Literature*, Princeton University Press, Princeton, NJ, 1953; also in LOWRY NELSON, *Cervantes* (cited above); IAN WATT, *The Rise of the Novel*, Penguin Books, 1983; HARRY LEVIN, 'The Example of Cervantes' and 'Cervantes and *Moby Dick*' in *Contexts of Criticism*, Harvard University Press, Cambridge, Mass., 1957; LIONEL TRILLING, 'Manners, Morals, and the Novel' in *The Liberal Imagination*, Mercury Books, 1961; RENÉ GIRARD, *Deceit, Desire, and the Novel*, Johns Hopkins University Press, Baltimore, Md, 1966; ROBERT ALTER, *Partial Magic: The Novel as a Self-Conscious Genre*, University of California Press, Berkeley, Cal., 1975; M. BAKHTIN, *The Dialogic Imagination*, ed. M. Holquist, University of Texas Press, Austin, Texas, 1981.

CHRONOLOGY

DATE	AUTHOR'S LIFE	LITERARY CONTEXT
1547	Born at Alcalá de Henares to Rodrigo de Cervantes, a surgeon, and Leonor de Cortinas.	Rabelais: *Fourth Book*.
1553		
1554		*Lazarillo de Tormes*.
1555		
1556		
1557		
1558		
1559		First Spanish Index.
1563		
1565		
1568	Studies at López de Hoyos' academy in Madrid; writes verses on death of Philip II's wife, Isabel de Valois.	Gascoigne: *Jocasta*. Wilmot: *Tancred and Gismund*. Second edition of Vasari's *Lives of the Artists*.
1569	Wounds Antonio de Sigura in a duel? Goes to Rome, enters service of Cardinal Acquaviva.	St Teresa of Avila: *Libro de su vida*.
1571	Aboard the galley *Marquesa*, fights valiantly in sea battle of Lepanto against Turks.	
1572	Involved in naval expeditions to Navarino and (1573) Tunis.	
1574		
1575	Returning from Naples to Spain by sea, is captured by Berber corsairs and taken to Algiers; during captivity (until 1580) makes four escape attempts; his resolution recorded in Diego de Haedo's *History of Algiers* (1612).	Tasso: *Jerusalem Liberated*.
1576		Castiglione's *The Book of the Courtier* banned by the Spanish Inquisition.
1577		St Teresa: *The Abodes*.
1578		St John of the Cross: *Spiritual Song of Love*. Ronsard: *Sonnets pour Hélène*.

HISTORICAL EVENTS
Deaths of François I and Henry VIII.

Accession of Catholic Queen Mary of England, who marries Philip of Spain
(1554).

Smithfield Fires, burning of English Protestants.
Charles V abdicates from Spanish throne; is succeeded by Philip II.
Spanish forces defeat French at Battle of St Quentin.
Accession of Elizabeth I of England.

Close of Council of Trent.
Malta withstands Turkish siege.
Outbreak of Eighty Years War between Spain and its Flemish colonies.
Mary Stuart flees from Scotland.

Revolt of *moriscos* in province of Granada.

Allied fleet under Don John of Austria, representing Spain, inflicts crushing
defeat on Turks at Lepanto.

Massacre of French Huguenots on St Bartholomew's Eve. Dutch rebels
conquer Holland and Zeeland.
Accession of Henry III and new outbreak of civil war in France.

Sack of Antwerp by Spanish troops. End of French Civil War. Titian: *Pietà*.

Sir Francis Drake circumnavigates globe. Birth of Rubens. El Greco active
in Toledo.
King Sebastian of Portugal killed at Battle of Alcazarquivir.

DATE	AUTHOR'S LIFE	LITERARY CONTEXT
1579		Spenser: *The Shepherd's Calendar*.
1580	Ransomed by Trinitarian friars; returns to Madrid; literary activity as poet and dramatist until 1587.	
1581	In Portugal at court of Philip II; is entrusted with secret commission to Oran.	
1582	Liaison (to 1584 approximately) with Ana Franca de Rojas; birth of Isabel de Saavedra.	Fernando de Herrera's poems published.
1583		Léon: *De Los Nombres de Cristo* (to 1585); *La Perfecta Casada*.
1584	Marries Catalina de Salazar.	
1585	Publishes his pastoral romance *La Galatea*; lives with Catalina in Esquivias.	Death of Pierre de Ronsard, leader of the French Pléiade.
1587	Departs for Seville; acts as commissioner of supplies for Armada expedition; end of first phase of literary career.	
1588		Montaigne: *Essays*.
1589		Earliest likely date for Shakespeare's composition of his first plays (*Henry VI, Part 1*, *The Taming of the Shrew*).
1590	Applies to Council of the Indies for employment in America in recognition of his military services; request refused: 'let him seek preferment over here'.	Spenser: *The Faerie Queene*. Marlowe: *Tamburlaine the Great*. Sidney: *Arcadia*.
1592	Briefly imprisoned in Castro del Río on order of magistrate of Écija, alleging illegal sale of wheat; released on appeal; contract with Rodrigo Osorio to write six plays.	Kyd: *The Spanish Tragedy*. Marlowe's *Edward II* and *Doctor Faustus* performed. *Arden of Feversham* printed. Mariana: *Historiae de Rebus Hispaniae* (to 1605).
1593		Shakespeare: *Venus and Adonis*.
1594	Obtains commission to collect tax arrears in province of Granada.	Spenser: *Amoretti* and *Epithalamion*. Shakespeare: *The Rape of Lucrece*, *Love's Labour's Lost*, *Romeo and Juliet* (to 1595).
1595	Bankruptcy of Sevillian banker with whom he had deposited tax revenues.	Sidney: *Defence of Poesy*. Ralegh: *The Discovery of the Empire of Guiana*.

CHRONOLOGY

HISTORICAL EVENTS

Formation of Dutch United Provinces. The Corral de la Cruz built in Madrid.
Philip II annexes Portugal.

Northern provinces of the Netherlands renounce their allegiance to Philip II and invite the duc d'Alençon to be their sovereign.

The Corral del Principe built in Madrid.

Completion of El Escorial. Assassination of William of Orange.
Queen Elizabeth sends troops to aid Dutch rebels; outbreak of war of succession in France. El Greco: *Burial of Count Orgaz*.

Execution of Mary Stuart. Drake's raid on Cadiz.

Defeat of Spanish Armada.
Assassination of Henry III of France; accession of Henry of Navarre.

Revolt in Aragon.

Philip II fails in his attempt to drive Henry of Navarre from French throne. Tintoretto: *Last Supper*.

War between the Turks and the Hapsburgs.
Henry IV enters Paris: 'Paris is well worth a mass.'

DATE	AUTHOR'S LIFE	LITERARY CONTEXT
1595 *cont*		Shakespeare: *A Midsummer Night's Dream* (to 1596).
1597	Due to auditors' error, imprisoned in Seville for shortfall in tax moneys due to the Treasury; in this internment *Don Quixote* was supposedly engendered.	Bacon: First edition of *Essays*. Shakespeare: *Henry IV* Parts I & II (to 1598).
1598	Writes burlesque ode on Philip II's funeral monument in Seville, later citing it as 'principal honour of my writings'.	Lope de Vega: *La Arcadia*. Marlowe: *Hero and Leander*. Shakespeare: *As You Like It*, *Much Ado About Nothing* (to 1600).
1599		Mateo Alemán: *Guzmán de Alfarache* Part I. Shakespeare: *Henry V*, *Julius Caesar*. *The Passionate Pilgrim*.
1600	About this time, departure from Seville and beginning of second phase of literary career.	Shakespeare: *Hamlet*. Charron: *Concerning Wisdom*. *England's Helicon*. Birth of Calderón de la Barca.
1601		
1602	Tangles with Treasury over missing tax moneys; busy in composition of *Don Quixote*.	
1603		
1604		First Part of *Comedies* of Lope de Vega published. Shakespeare: *Othello*.
1605	Publishes *Don Quixote* I; re-edition in Madrid; pirate editions in Lisbon and Valencia; Don Quixote and Sancho appear as carnival figures in popular festivities.	Quevedo writes (approximate date) first of his satiric *Visions*. Shakespeare: *King Lear*. Jonson: *Volpone*.
1606	About this time, composition of *The Dog's Colloquy*, *The Illustrious Scullery Maid*, *Licentiate Glass* (*novelas*), and appearance of two earlier *novelas*, *Rinconete and Cortadillo* and *The Jealous Extremaduran*, in a miscellany compiled for the Archbishop of Seville; (to 1607) moves back to Madrid.	Shakespeare: *Macbeth*, *Antony and Cleopatra*.

CHRONOLOGY

DATE	AUTHOR'S LIFE	LITERARY CONTEXT
1607	Thomas Shelton translates *Don Quixote* 'in the space of forty days'.	Tourneur's *The Revenger's Tragedy* printed.
1608	Third edition of *Don Quixote* from press of Juan de la Cuesta in Madrid.	Lope de Vega: *Peribanez*. Beaumont and Fletcher: *Philaster*.
1609	Joins Congregation of Slaves of Blessed Sacrament; attendance at literary academies in Madrid; estrangement from his daughter Isabel after her marriage to Luis de Molina; Richer's French version of excerpts from *Don Quixote*.	François de Sales: *Introduction to the Devout Life*. Lope de Vega: *New Art of Writing Plays for the Theatre*. Shakespeare: *Sonnets*. Donne's 'The Expiration' printed; 'Liturgic' and 'On the Annunciation' written.
1610	Disappointed in hopes of accompanying retinue of Count of Lemos to Naples; composes *The Little Gipsy Girl* (*novela*); (about now) at work on *Don Quixote* II and *Persiles*.	Jonson: *The Alchemist*, which mentions *Don Quixote* in Act IV. Shakespeare: *The Winter's Tale*. Beaumont and Fletcher: *The Maid's Tragedy*.
1611		Authorized Version of Bible in English. Tourneur: *The Atheist's Tragedy*. Donne's first *Anniversary*. Shakespeare: *Cymbeline*, *The Tempest*.
1612	European diffusion of *Don Quixote* I marked by Shelton's English translation.	Góngora's major poems circulate in Madrid. Lope de Vega: *Fuente Ovejuna*. Webster: *The White Devil*.
1613	Publication of *Exemplary Novels*; dedicatory refers to Count of Lemos' patronage; becomes novice of Franciscan Tertiaries.	
1614	*Voyage to Parnassus*; Avellaneda's *El Quijote*; Oudin's French translation of *Don Quixote* I.	Webster: *The Duchess of Malfi*. Ralegh: *The History of the World*. Jonson: *Bartholomew Fair*.
1615	Publishes *Don Quixote* II and *Eight Comedies and Farces*; moral approbation preceding *Don Quixote* II by licentiate Márquez Torres contrasts Cervantes' poverty and low status in Spain with his high reputation in France: 'Does Spain not enrich such a man and maintain him from the public purse?'	

CHRONOLOGY

HISTORICAL EVENTS

Landings at Jamestown, Virginia. Monteverdi: *Orfeo*.

Champlain founds Quebec. Plantation of Ulster by Protestant English and Scots begins.

Twelve Years truce between Spain and United Provinces; decree of expulsion of Spanish *moriscos*. Galileo's experiments with the telescope confirm the Copernican theory. Kepler draws up 'Laws of Planetary Motion'. Henry Hudson discovers river named after him.

Galileo publishes first major astronomical observations; assassination of Henry IV. Regency of Marie de'Medici. In England, Parliament submits the Petition of Grievances. Sir Thomas Roe sails up the Amazon. Monteverdi: *Vespers*.

The Inquisition in Rome begins investigating Galileo. Gustavus Adolphus becomes king of Sweden.

Rubens: *The Toilet of Venus*.

French States-General dissolved (does not meet again until 1789). Spilbergen sails round the world. Napier of Merchiston discovers logarithms. El Greco: *The Assumption of the Virgin*. Harvey's discovery of circulation of blood.

DON QUIXOTE

DATE	AUTHOR'S LIFE	LITERARY CONTEXT
1616	Dedicates *Persiles* to Count of Lemos; mentions works unfinished at death, including *La Galatea* Part II and *Weeks in the Garden* (probably a collection of *novelas*). 'Farewell jests, farewell witticisms, farewell merry friends, for I am dying and hoping soon to see you happy in the life to come.' Dies on 22 April.	Death of Shakespeare. Jonson: *The Devil is an Ass*, *Epigrams*, *The Frost*. Chapman completes his English translation of Homer.
1617	Posthumous publication of *Persiles and Sigismunda*; French translation of *Exemplary Novels*.	
1618		Góngora: *Pyramus and Thisbe*.

CHRONOLOGY

Rise to power of Cardinal Richelieu. Ralegh released from the Tower of London to lead an expedition to Guiana; on his return he is executed (1618).

Start of Thirty Years War in Europe; fall of Duke of Lerma.

VOLUME ONE

THE AUTHOR'S DEDICATION
OF THE FIRST PART

To the Duke of Bejar

Marquis of Gibraleon, Count of Benalcazar and Bañares,
Viscount of the Town of Alcocer, and Lord of the
Towns of Capilla, Curiel and Burguillos

T RUSTING *in the favourable reception and honour
your Excellency accords to all kinds of books, as a
Prince so well disposed to welcome the liberal arts, more
especially those which, out of nobility, are not abased to the
service and profit of the vulgar, I have decided to publish
the* Ingenious Gentleman Don Quixote de la Mancha *under
the shelter of your Excellency's most Illustrious name, begging you with the respect I owe to such greatness to receive
him graciously under your protection; so that, although
naked of that precious adornment of elegance and erudition
in which works composed in the houses of the learned usually go clothed, in your shadow he may safely venture to
appear before the judgment of some who, undeterred by
their own ignorance, are in the habit of condemning the
works of others with more rigour than justice. For when
your excellency's wisdom takes account of my good intentions, I trust that you will not disdain the poverty of so
humble an offering.*

MIGUEL DE CERVANTES SAAVEDRA

CONTENTS

The Author's Preface to the Reader, p. 6.

PART I · BOOK I

PART I · BOOK II

PART I · BOOK III

CONTENTS

PART I · BOOK III (*continued*)

PART I · BOOK IV

CONTENTS

THE AUTHOR'S PREFACE TO
THE READER

YOU may depend upon my bare Word, Reader, without any farther Security, that I cou'd wish this Offspring of my Brain were as ingenious, sprightly, and accomplish'd as your self could desire; but the Mischief on't is, Nature will have its Course: Every Production must resemble its Author, and my barren and unpolish'd Understanding can produce nothing but what is very dull, very impertinent, and extravagant beyond Imagination. You may suppose it the Child of Disturbance, engendered in some dismal Prison,* where Wretchedness keeps its Residence, and every dismal Sound its Habitation. Rest and Ease, a convenient Place, pleasant Fields and Groves, murmuring Springs, and a sweet Repose of Mind, are Helps that raise the Fancy, and impregnate even the most barren Muses with Conceptions that fill the World with Admiration and Delight. Some Parents are so blinded by a Fatherly Fondness, that they mistake the very Imperfections of their Children for so many Beauties; and the Folly and Impertinence of the brave Boy, must pass upon their Friends and Acquaintance for Wit and Sense. But I, who am only a Step-Father, disavow the Authority of this modern and prevalent Custom; nor will I earnestly beseech you, with Tears in my Eyes, which is many a poor Author's Case, dear Reader, to pardon or dissemble my Child's Faults; for what Favour can I expect from you, who are neither his Friend nor Relation? You have a Soul of your own, and the Privilege of Freewill, whoever you be, as well as the proudest He that struts in a gaudy Outside: You are a King by your own Fire-side, as much as any Monarch in his Throne: You have Liberty and Property, which set you above Favour or Affection, and may therefore freely like or dislike this History, according to your Humour.

* The Author is said to have wrote this satyrical Romance in a Prison.

6

I had a great Mind to have expos'd it as naked as it was born, without the Addition of a Preface, or the numberless Trumpery of commendatory Sonnets, Epigrams, and other Poems that usually usher in the Conceptions of Authors: For I dare boldly say, that tho' I bestow'd some Time in writing the Book, yet it cost me not half so much Labour as this very Preface. I very often took up my Pen, and as often laid it down, and could not for my Life think of any thing to the Purpose. Sitting once in a very studious Posture, with my Paper before me, my Pen in my Ear, my Elbow on the Table, and my Cheek on my Hand, considering how I should begin; a certain Friend of mine, an ingenious Gentleman, and of a merry Disposition, came in and surpriz'd me. He ask'd me what I was so very intent and thoughtful upon? I was so free with him as not to mince the Matter, but told him plainly I had been puzzling my Brain for a Preface to Don Quixote, and had made my self so uneasy about it, that I was now resolv'd to trouble my Head no further either with Preface or Book, and even to let the Atchievements of that noble Knight remain unpublish'd: For, continu'd I, why shou'd I expose my self to the Lash of the old Legislator, the Vulgar? They will say I have spent my youthful Days very finely, to have nothing to recommend my grey Hairs to the World but a dry, insipid Legend, not worth a Rush, wanting good Language as well as Invention, barren of Conceits or pointed Wit, and without either Quotations in the Margin, or Annotations at the End, which other Books, tho' never so fabulous and profane, have to set 'em off. Other Authors can pass upon the Publick, by stuffing their Books from Aristotle, Plato, and the whole Company of ancient Philosophers; thus amusing their Readers into a great Opinion of their prodigious Reading. Plutarch and Cicero are slurr'd on the Publick for as orthodox Doctors as St Thomas, or any of the Fathers. And then the Method of these Moderns is so wonderfully agreeable and full of Variety, that they cannot fail to please. In one Line, they will describe you a whining amorous

7

Coxcomb, and the next shall be some dry Scrap of a Homily, with such ingenious Turns as cannot chuse but ravish the Reader. Now I want all these Embellishments and Graces: I have neither marginal Notes nor critical Remarks; I do not so much as know what Authors I follow, and consequently can have no formal Index, as 'tis the Fashion now, methodically strung on the Letters of the Alphabet, beginning with Aristotle, and ending with Xenophon, or Zoilus, or Zeuxis; which last two are commonly cramm'd into the same Piece, tho' one of them was a famous Painter, and t'other a saucy Critick. I shall want also the pompous Preliminaries of commendatory Verses sent to me by the Right Honourable my Lord such a one, by the Honourable the Lady such a one, or the most ingenious Mr such a one; tho' I know I might have them at an easy Rate from two or three Brothers of the Quill of my Acquaintance, and better, I'm sure, than the best Quality in Spain can compose.

In short, my Friend, said I, the Great Don Quixote may lie buried in the musty Records of La Mancha, 'till Providence has order'd some better Hand to fit him out as he ought to be; for I must own my self altogether uncapable of the Task; besides, I am naturally lazy, and love my Ease too well to take the Pains of turning over Authors for those Things which I can express as well without it. And these are the Considerations that made me so thoughtful when you came in. The Gentleman, after a long and loud Fit of Laughing, rubbing his Forehead; O' my Conscience, Friend, said he, your Discourse has freed me from a Mistake that has a great while impos'd upon me: I always took you for a Man of Sense, but now I am sufficiently convinc'd to the contrary. What! puzzled at so inconsiderable a Trifle! A Business of so little Difficulty confound a Man of such deep Sense and searching Thought as once you seem'd to be!

I am sorry, Sir, that your lazy Humour and poor Understanding should need the Advice I am about to give you, which will presently solve all your Objections and Fears concerning

8

the publishing of the renoun'd Don Quixote, the Luminary and Mirrour of all Knight-Errantry. Pray, Sir, said I, be pleas'd to instruct me in whatever you think may remove my Fears, or solve my Doubts. The first Thing you object, reply'd he, is your Want of commendatory Copies from Persons of Figure and Quality: There is nothing sooner help'd; 'tis but taking a little Pains in writing them your self, and clapping whose Name you please to 'em, you may father 'em on Prester John of the Indies, or on the Emperor of Trapizonde, whom I know to be most celebrated Poets: But suppose they were not, and that some presuming pedantick Criticks might snarle, and deny this notorious Truth, value it not two Farthings; and tho' they shou'd convict you of Forgery, you are in no Danger of losing the Hand with which you wrote them.*

As to marginal Notes and Quotations from Authors for your History, 'tis but dropping here and there some scatter'd Latin Sentences that you have already by rote, or may have with little or no Pains. For Example, in treating of Liberty and Slavery, clap me in, Non bene pro toto libertas venditur auro; *and, at the same Time, make* Horace, *or some other Author, vouch it in the Margin. If you treat of the Power of Death, come round with this Close,*† Pallida mors æquo pulsat pede pauperum tabernas, Regumque turres. *If of loving our Enemies, as Heaven enjoins, you may, if you have the least Curiosity, presently turn to the divine Precept, and say,* Ego autem dico vobis, diligite inimicos vestros; *or if you discourse of bad Thoughts, bring in this Passage,* De corde exeunt cogitationes malæ. *If the Uncertainty of Friendship be your Theme,* Cato *offers you his old Couplet with all his Heart;* Donec eris felix multos numerabis amicos: Tempora si fuerint nubila, solus eris. *And so proceed. These Scraps*

---

* He lost his left Hand (*izquierda*) in the Sea-Fight at *Lepanto* against the *Turks*.   † This Quotation from *Horace*, and the following from Scripture, are omitted in *Shelton's* Translation; as is also this and another ingenious Preface of the Author's in that of *Stevens*, many of whose Notes indeed I have made use of.

9

of Latin *will at least gain you the Credit of a great Grammarian, which, I'll assure you, is no small Accomplishment in this Age. As to Annotations or Remarks at the End of your Book, you may safely take this Course. If you have Occasion for a Giant in your Piece, be sure you bring in* Goliah, *and on this very* Goliah (*who will not cost you one Farthing*) *you may spin out a swingeing Annotation. You may say,* The Giant *Goliah, or Goliat, was a Philistine, whom David* the Shepherd slew with the thundering Stroke of a Pebble in the Valley of *Terebinthus: Vide* Kings, *in such a Chapter, and such a Verse, where you may find it written. If not satisfy'd with this, you would appear a great Humanist, and would shew your Knowledge in Geography, take some Occasion to draw the River* Tagus *into your Discourse, out of which you may fish a most notable Remark.* The River *Tagus, say you,* was so call'd from a certain King of *Spain.* It takes its Rise from such a Place, and buries its Waters in the Ocean, kissing first the Walls of the famous City of *Lisbon*; and some are of Opinion that the Sands of this River are Gold, *&c. If you have Occasion to talk of Robbers, I can presently give you the History of* Cacus, *for I have it by Heart. If you would descant upon Whores or Women of the Town, there is the Bishop of* Mondoñedo,* *who can furnish you with* Lamia, Lais *and* Flora, *Courtesans, whose Acquaintance will be very much to your Reputation.* Ovid's Medea *can afford you a good Example of Cruelty.* Calypso *from* Homer, *and* Circe *out of* Virgil, *are famous Instances for Witchcraft or Inchantment. Would you treat of Valiant Commanders?* Julius Cæsar *has writ his Commentaries on Purpose; and* Plutarch *can furnish you with a thousand* Alexanders. *If you would mention Love, and have but three Grains of* Italian, *you may find* Leon *the* Jew *ready to serve you most abundantly. But if you would keep nearer Home, 'tis but examining* Fonseca *of Divine Love, which you have here in your Study; and you need go no farther for all that can be said on that copious*

* Guevara.

*Subject. In short, 'tis but quoting these Authors in your Book,
and let me alone to make large Annotations; I'll engage to
croud your Margins sufficiently, and scribble you four or five
Sheets to boot at the End of your Book. And for the Citation
of so many Authors, 'tis the easiest Thing in Nature. Find
out one of these Books with an alphabetical Index, and without any farther Ceremony, remove it* verbatim *into your own:
And tho' the World won't believe you have Occasion for such
Lumber, yet there are Fools enough to be thus drawn into an
Opinion of the Work; at least, such a flourishing Train of
Attendants will give your Book a fashionable Air, and recommend it to Sale; for few Chapmen will stand to examine it,
and compare the Authorities upon the Compter, since they can
expect nothing but their Labour for their Pains. But after
all, Sir, if I know any thing of the Matter, you have no Occasion for any of these Things; for your Subject being a Satyr
on Knight-Errantry, is so absolutely new, that neither* Aristotle, St Basil, *nor* Cicero *ever dreamt or heard of it. Those
fabulous Extravagancies have nothing to do with the impartial Punctuality of true History; nor do I find any Business
you can have either with Astrology, Geometry, or Logick,
and I hope you are too good a Man to mix Sacred Things with
Profane. Nothing but pure Nature is your Business; her you
must consult, and the closer you can imitate, your Picture is
the better. And since this Writing of your's aims at no more
than to destroy the Authority and Acceptance the Books of
Chivalry have had in the World, and among the Vulgar, you
have no need to go begging Sentences of Philosophers, Passages out of Holy Writ, Poetical Fables, Rhetorical Orations,
or Miracles of Saints. Do but take care to express your self
in a plain, easy Manner, in well-chosen, significant, and decent Terms, and to give an harmonious and pleasing Turn
to your Periods: Study to explain your Thoughts, and set
them in the truest Light, labouring, as much as possible, not
to leave 'em dark nor intricate, but clear and intelligible: Let
your diverting Stories be express'd in diverting Terms, to*

*kindle Mirth in the Melancholick, and heighten it in the Gay:
Let Mirth and Humour be your superficial Design, tho' laid
on a solid Foundation, to challenge Attention from the Ignorant, and Admiration from the Judicious; to secure your Work
from the Contempt of the graver Sort, and deserve the Praises
of Men of Sense; keeping your Eye still fix'd on the principal
End of your Project, the Fall and Destruction of that monstrous Heap of ill-contriv'd Romances, which, tho' abhorr'd
by many, have so strangely infatuated the greater Part of
Mankind. Mind this, and your Business is done.*

    *I listen'd very attentively to my Friend's Discourse, and
found it so reasonable and convincing, that without any
Reply, I took his Advice, and have told you the Story by
way of Preface; wherein you may see, Gentlemen, how happy
I am in so ingenious a Friend, to whose seasonable Counsel
you are all oblig'd for the Omission of all this pedantick
Garniture in the History of the Renowned Don* Quixote de la
Mancha, *whose Character among all the Neighbours about*
Montiel *is, that he was the most chaste Lover, and the most
valiant Knight, that has been known in those Parts these
many Years. I will not urge the Service I have done you by
introducing you into so considerable and noble a Knight's
Acquaintance, but only beg the Favour of some small Acknowledgment for recommending you to the Familiarity of
the famous* Sancho Pança *his Squire, in whom, in my
Opinion, you will find united and describ'd all
the Squirelike Graces which are scatter'd up
and down in the whole Bead-roll of Books of
Chivalry. And now I take my Leave,
intreating you not to forget
your humble Servant.*

THE LIFE & ATCHIEVEMENTS OF THE RENOWN'D DON QUIXOTE DE LA MANCHA: PART I · BOOK I ·

I: THE QUALITY AND WAY OF LIVING OF THE RE-NOWN'D DON QUIXOTE DE LA MANCHA

A T a certain Village in *La Mancha*,* which I shall not name, there liv'd not long ago one of those old-fashion'd Gentlemen who are never with-out a Lance upon a Rack, an old Target, a lean Horse, and a Greyhound. His Diet consisted more of Beef† than Mutton; and with minc'd Meat on most Nights, Lentils on *Fridays*, Eggs and Bacon‡ on *Saturdays*, and a Pigeon extraordinary on *Sundays*, he consumed three Quarters of his Revenue: The rest was laid out in a Plush-Coat, Velvet-Breeches, with Slippers of the same, for Holidays; and a Suit of the very best home-spun Cloth, which he bestowed on himself for Working-days. His whole Family was a Housekeeper something turn'd of Forty, a Niece not Twenty, and a Man that serv'd him in

---

* *A small Territory partly in the Kingdom of* Arragon, *and partly in* Castile; *it is a Liberty within itself, distinct from all the Country about.* † *Beef being cheaper in* Spain *than Mutton.* ‡ *Strictly,* Sorrow *for his Sops, on* Saturdays. Duelos y Quebrantos; *in English,* Gruntings and Groanings. *He that can tell what Sort of Edible the Author means by those Words,* Erit mihi magnus Apollo. Cæsar Oudin, *the famous* French *Travel-ler, Negotiator, Translator and Dictionary-maker, will have it to be* Eggs and Bacon, *as above. Our Translator and Dictionary-maker,* Stevens, *has it,* Eggs and Collops, (*I suppose he means* Scotch-Collops) *but that's too good a Dish to mortify withal. Signor* Sobrino's Spanish *Dictionary says,* Duelos y Quebrantos *is* Pease-Soup. *Mr* Jarvis *translates it an* Amlet (Aumulette *in* French) *which* Boyer *says is a* Pancake *made of Eggs, tho' I always understood* Aumulette *to be a* Bacon-froise (*or rather* Bacon-fryze, *from its being* fry'd, *from* frit *in* French). *Some will have it to mean* Brains *fry'd with Eggs, which, we are told by Mr* Jarvis, *the Church allows in poor Countries in Defect of Fish. Others have guest it to mean some windy kind of Diet, as* Peas, Herbs, &c. *which are apt to occasion Cholicks, as if one should say,* Greens and Gripes on Saturdays. *To conclude, the 'forecited Author of the new Translation (if a Translator may be call'd an Author) absolutely says,* Duelos y Quebrantos *is a* Cant-Phrase *for some Fasting-Day-Dish in use in* la Mancha. *After all these learned Disquisi-tions, Who knows but the Author means a Dish of* Nichils!

the House and in the Field, and could saddle a Horse, and handle the Pruning-Hook. The Master himself was nigh fifty Years of Age, of a hale and strong Complexion, lean-body'd, and thin-fac'd, an early Riser, and a Lover of Hunting. Some say his Sirname was *Quixada*, or *Quesada* (for Authors differ in this Particular): However, we may reasonably conjecture he was call'd *Quixada* (*i.e.* Lanthorn-Jaws) tho' this concerns us but little, provided we keep strictly to the Truth in every Point of this History.

You must know then, that when our Gentleman had nothing to do (which was almost all the Year round) he pass'd his Time in reading Books of Knight-Errantry; which he did with that Application and Delight, that at last he in a manner wholly left off his Country-Sports, and even the Care of his Estate; nay, he grew so strangely besotted with those Amusements, that he sold many Acres of Arable-Land to purchase Books of that kind; by which means he collected as many of them as were to be had: But among them all, none pleas'd him like the Works of the famous *Feliciano de Sylva*; for the Clearness of his Prose, and those intricate Expressions with which 'tis interlac'd, seem'd to him so many Pearls of Eloquence, especially when he came to read the Challenges, and the amorous Addresses, many of them in this extraordinary Stile. "The Reason of your unreasonable "Usage of my Reason, does so enfeeble my Reason, that I "have Reason to expostulate with your Beauty:" And this, "The sublime Heavens, which with your Divinity divinely "fortify you with the Stars, and fix you the Deserver of the "Desert that is deserv'd by your Grandeur." These, and such like Expressions, strangely puzzled the poor Gentleman's Understanding, while he was breaking his Brain to unravel their Meaning, which *Aristotle* himself could never have found, though he should have been rais'd from the Dead for that very Purpose.

He did not so well like those dreadful Wounds which Don *Belianis* gave and received; for he considered that all the Art of Surgery could never secure his Face and Body from being strangely disfigured with Scars. However, he highly commended the Author for concluding his Book with a Promise to finish that unfinishable Adventure; and many times he had a Desire to put Pen to Paper, and faithfully and literally finish it himself; which he had certainly done, and doubtless with good Success, had not his Thoughts been wholly engrossed in much more important Designs.

He would often dispute with the Curate* of the Parish, a Man of Learning, that had taken his Degrees at *Ciguenza*,† who was the better Knight *Palmerin* of *England*,‡ or *Amadis de Gaul*? But Master *Nicholas*, the Barber§ of the same Town, would say, that none of 'em could compare with the *Knight of the Sun*; and that if any one came near him, 'twas certainly Don *Galaor*, the Brother of *Amadis de Gaul*; for he was a Man of a most commodious Temper, neither was he so finical, nor such a puling whining Lover as his Brother; and as for Courage, he was not a jot behind him.

In fine, he gave himself up so wholly to the reading of Romances, that a-Nights he would pore on 'till 'twas Day, and a-Days he would read on 'till 'twas Night; and thus by sleeping little, and reading much, the Moisture of his Brain was exhausted to that Degree, that at last he lost the Use of his Reason. A world of disorderly Notions, pick'd out of his Books, crouded into his Imagination; and now his Head was full of nothing but Inchantments, Quarrels, Battles, Challenges, Wounds, Complaints, Amours, Torments, and abundance of Stuff and Impossibilities; insomuch, that all the Fables and fantastical Tales which he read, seem'd to him now as true as the most authentick Histories. He would say, that the *Cid Ruydiaz*‖ was a very brave Knight, but not worthy to stand in Competition with the *Knight of the Burning Sword*, who with a single Backstroke had cut in

---

* *In* Spain *the Curate is the Head Priest in the Parish, and he that has the Cure of Souls: Thus* el Cura *means the* Rector, *or, as the Vulgar has it, the* Parson; *but the first not being commonly used, and the last seeming too gross, I chuse to make it* Curate, *those who have read the former Translations being us'd to the Word.*   † *An University in* Spain. ‡ England *seems to have been often made the Scene of Chivalry; for besides this* Palmerin, *we find Don* Florando *of* England, *and some others, not to mention* Amadis's *Mistress, the Princess* Oriana *of* England. § *The* Barber *in Country Towns in* Spain *is also the* Surgeon.   ‖ Cid Ruydiaz *a famous Spanish Commander, of whom many Fables are written.*

sunder two fierce and mighty Giants. He liked yet better *Bernardo del Carpio*, who at *Roncesvalles* depriv'd of Life the inchanted *Orlando*, having lifted him from the Ground, and choak'd him in the Air, as *Hercules* did *Antæus* the Son of the Earth.

As for the Giant *Morgante*, he always spoke very civil Things of him; for though he was one of that monstrous Brood, who ever were intolerably proud and brutish, he still behav'd himself like a civil and well-bred Person.

But of all Men in the World he admir'd *Rinaldo of Mont-alban*, and particularly his sallying out of his Castle to rob all he met; and then again when Abroad* he carried away the Idol of *Mahomet*, which was all massy Gold, as the History says: But he so hated that Traitor *Galalon*,† that for the Pleasure of kicking him handsomely, he would have given up his House-keeper; nay, and his Niece into the bargain.

Having thus lost his Understanding, he unluckily stumbled upon the oddest Fancy that ever enter'd into a Mad-man's Brain; for now he thought it convenient and necessary, as well for the Increase of his own Honour, as the Service of the Publick, to turn Knight-Errant, and roam through the whole World arm'd Cap-a-pee, and mounted on his Steed, in quest of Adventures; that thus imitating those Knight-Errants of whom he had read, and following their Course of Life, redressing all manner of Grievances, and exposing himself to Danger on all Occasions, at last, after a happy Conclusion of his Enterprizes, he might purchase everlasting Honour and Renown. Transported with these agreeable De-lusions, the poor Gentleman already grasp'd in Imagination the Imperial Sceptre of *Trapizonde*, and, hurry'd away by his mighty Expectations, he prepares with all Expedition to take the Field.

The first Thing he did was to scour a Suit of Armour that had belong'd to his Great-Grandfather, and had lain Time out of Mind carelesly rusting in a Corner: But when he had clean'd and repair'd it as well as he could, he perceiv'd

* *In* Barbary, Oudin *says*. † Galalon, *the* Spaniards *say*, *betray'd the* French *Army at* Roncesvalles.

there was a material Piece wanting; for instead of a complete Helmet, there was only a single Head-piece: However, his Industry supply'd that Defect, for with some Pasteboard he made a kind of Half-Beaver, or Vizor, which being fitted to the Head-piece, made it look like an entire Helmet. Then, to know whether it were Cutlass-Proof, he drew his Sword, and tried its Edge upon the Pasteboard Vizor; but with the very first Stroke he unluckily undid in a Moment what he had been a whole Week a doing. He did not like its being broke with so much Ease, and therefore to secure it from the like Accident, he made it a-new, and fenc'd it with thin Plates of Iron, which he fix'd on the Inside of it so artificially, that at last he had Reason to be satisfy'd with the Solidity of the Work; and so, without any farther Experiment, he resolv'd it should pass to all Intents and Purposes for a full and sufficient Helmet.

The next Moment he went to view his Horse, whose Bones stuck out like the Corners of a *Spanish* Real, being a worse Jade than *Gonela's, qui tantum pellis & ossa fuit*; however, his Master thought, that neither *Alexander's Bucephalus*, nor the *Cid's Babieca* could be compared with him. He was four Days considering what Name to give him; for, as he argu'd with himself, there was no Reason that a Horse bestrid by so famous a Knight, and withal so excellent in himself, should not be distinguish'd by a particular Name; and therefore he studied to give him such a one as should demonstrate as well what kind of Horse he had been before his Master was a Knight-Errant, as what he was now; thinking it but just, since the Owner chang'd his Profession, that the Horse should also change his Title, and be dignify'd with another; a good big Word, such a one as should fill the Mouth, and seem consonant with the Quality and Profession of his Master. And thus after many Names which he devis'd, rejected, chang'd, lik'd, dislik'd, and pitch'd upon again, he concluded to call him *Rozinante*;* a Name, in his Opinion, lofty, sounding, and significant of what he had been before, and also of what he was now; in a Word, a Horse *before* or above all the vulgar Breed of Horses in the World.

When he had thus given his Horse a Name so much to his

Satisfaction, he thought of chusing one for himself; and having seriously ponder'd on the Matter eight whole Days more, at last he determin'd to call himself Don *Quixote*. Whence the Author of this most authentick History draws this Inference, That his right Name was *Quixada*, and not *Quesada*, as others obstinately pretend. And observing, that the valiant *Amadis*, not satisfy'd with the bare Appellation of *Amadis*, added to it the Name of his Country, that it might grow more famous by his Exploits, and so stil'd himself *Amadis de Gaul*; so he, like a true Lover of his native Soil, resolv'd to call himself Don *Quixote de la Mancha*; which Addition, to his thinking, denoted very plainly his Parentage and Country, and consequently would fix a lasting Honour on that Part of the World.

And now his Armour being scour'd, his Head-Piece improv'd to a Helmet, his Horse and himself new nam'd, he perceiv'd he wanted nothing but a Lady, on whom he might bestow the Empire of his Heart; for he was sensible that a Knight-Errant without a Mistress, was a Tree without either Fruit or Leaves, and a Body without a Soul. Should I, said he to himself, by good or ill Fortune chance to encounter some Giant, as 'tis common in Knight-Errantry, and happen to lay him prostrate on the Ground, transfix'd with my Lance, or cleft in two, or, in short, overcome him, and have him at my Mercy, would it not be proper to have some Lady, to whom I may send him as a Trophy of my Valour? Then when he comes into her Presence, throwing himself at her Feet, he may thus make his humble Submission: "Lady, "I am the Giant *Caraculiambro*, Lord of the Island of "*Malindrania*, vanquish'd in single Combat by that never- "deservedly-enough-extoll'd Knight-Errant Don *Quixote de* "*la Mancha*, who has commanded me to cast my self most "humbly at your Feet, that it may please your Honour to "dispose of me according to your Will." Oh! how elevated was the Knight with the Conceit of this imaginary Submis-

---

* Rozin *commonly means an ordinary Horse*; Ante *signifies* before *and* formerly. *Thus the Word* Rozinante *may imply, that he was* formerly *an ordinary Horse, and also, that he is now an Horse that claims the* Precedence *from all other ordinary Horses.*

sion of the Giant; especially having withal bethought him-self of a Person, on whom he might confer the Title of his Mistress! Which, 'tis believ'd, happen'd thus: Near the Place where he lived, dwelt a good likely Country Lass, for whom he had formerly had a sort of an Inclination, though 'tis believ'd, she never heard of it, nor regarded it in the least. Her Name was *Aldonza Lorenzo*, and this was she whom he thought he might entitle to the Sovereignty of his Heart: Upon which he studied to find her out a new Name, that might have some Affinity with her old one, and yet at the same time sound somewhat like that of a Princess, or Lady of Quality: So at last he resolved to call her *Dulcinea*, with the Addition of *del Toboso*, from the Place where she was born; a Name, in his Opinion, sweet, harmonious, extra-ordinary, and no less significative than the others which he had devis'd.

II: OF DON QUIXOTE'S FIRST SALLY

THESE Preparations being made, he found his Designs ripe for Action, and thought it now a Crime to deny himself any longer to the injur'd World, that wanted such a Deliverer; the more when he consider'd what Grievances he was to redress, what Wrongs and Injuries to remove, what Abuses to correct, and what Duties to discharge. So one Morning before Day, in the greatest Heat of *July*, without acquainting any one with his Design, with all the Secrecy imaginable, he arm'd himself Cap-a-pee, lac'd on his ill-contriv'd Helmet, brac'd on his Target, grasp'd his Lance, mounted *Rozinante*, and at the private Door of his Back-yard sally'd out into the Fields, wonderfully pleas'd to see with how much Ease he had succeeded in the Beginning of his Enterprize. But he had not gone far e'er a terrible Thought alarm'd him, a Thought that had like to have made him renounce his great Undertaking; for now it came into his Mind, that the Honour of Knighthood had not yet been conferr'd upon him, and therefore, according to the Laws of Chivalry, he neither could, nor ought to appear in Arms against any profess'd Knight: Nay, he also consider'd, that tho' he were already knighted, it would become him to wear white Armour, and not to adorn his Shield with any *Device*, till he had deserved one by some extraordinary Demonstration of his Valour.

These Thoughts stagger'd his Resolution; but his Folly prevailing more than any Reason, he resolv'd to be dubb'd a Knight by the first he should meet, after the Example of several others, who, as his distracting Romances inform'd him, had formerly done the like. As for the other Difficulty about wearing white Armour, he propos'd to overcome it, by scouring his own at Leisure 'till it should look whiter than Ermin. And having thus dismiss'd these busy Scruples, he very calmly rode on, leaving it to his Horse's Discretion to go which Way he pleas'd; firmly believing, that in this consisted the very Being of Adventures. And as he thus went on, I cannot but believe, said he to himself, that when the History of my famous Atchievements shall be given to the World, the learned Author will begin it in this very Manner, when he comes to give an Account of this my early setting out: "Scarce had the ruddy-colour'd *Phœbus* "begun to spread the golden Tresses of his lovely Hair "over the vast Surface of the earthly Globe, and scarce "had those feather'd Poets of the Grove, the pretty painted "Birds, tun'd their little Pipes, to sing their early Wel- "comes in soft melodious Strains to the beautiful *Aurora*, "who having left her jealous Husband's Bed, display'd her "rosy Graces to mortal Eyes from the Gates and Balconies "of the *Manchegan* Horizon, when the renowned Knight "Don *Quixote de la Mancha*, disdaining soft Repose, for- "sook the voluptuous Down, and mounting his famous Steed "*Rozinante*, enter'd the ancient and celebrated Plains of "*Montiel*.*" This was indeed the very Road he took; and then proceeding, "O happy Age! O fortunate Times! cry'd "he, decreed to usher into the World my famous Atchieve- "ments; Atchievements worthy to be engraven on Brass, "carv'd in Marble, and delineated in some Masterpiece of "Painting, as Monuments of my Glory, and Examples for "Posterity! And thou venerable Sage, wise Enchanter, "whatever be thy Name; thou whom Fate has ordained "to be the Compiler of this rare History, forget not, I be- "seech thee, my trusty *Rozinante*, the eternal Companion "of all my Adventures." After this, as if he had been really in Love; "O Princess *Dulcinea*, cry'd he, Lady of this cap- "tive Heart, much Sorrow and Woe you have doom'd me "to in banishing me thus, and imposing on me your rigorous "Commands, never to appear before your beauteous Face! "Remember, Lady, that loyal Heart your Slave, who for "your Love submits to so many Miseries." To these ex- travagant Conceits, he added a world of others, all in Imita- tion, and in the very Stile of those, which the reading of Romances had furnish'd him with; and all this while he rode so softly, and the Sun's Heat increas'd so fast, and

---

* Montiel, *a proper Field to inspire Courage, being the Ground upon which* Henry the Bastard *slew his legitimate Brother Don* Pedro, *whom our brave* Black Prince Edward *had set upon the Throne of* Spain.

was so violent, that it would have been sufficient to have melted his Brains had he had any left.

He travell'd almost all that Day without meeting any Adventure worth the Trouble of relating; which put him into a kind of Despair; for he desir'd nothing more than to encounter immediately some Person on whom he might try the Vigour of his Arm.

Some Authors say, that his first Adventure was that of the Pass called *Puerto Lapice*; others, that of the Wind-mills; but all that I could discover of Certainty in this Matter, and that I meet with in the Annals of *La Mancha*, is, that he travelled all that Day; and towards the Evening, he and his Horse being heartily tir'd, and almost famish'd, Don *Quixote* looking about him, in hopes to discover some Castle, or at least some Shepherd's Cottage, there to repose and refresh himself, at last, near the Road which he kept, he espy'd an Inn, as welcome a Sight to his longing Eyes, as if he had discover'd a Star directing him to the Gate, nay, to the Palace of his Redemption. Thereupon hast'ning towards the Inn with all the speed he could, he got thither just at the close of the Evening. There stood by Chance at the Inn-door two young Female Adventurers, *alias* Common Wenches, who were going to *Sevil* with some Carriers, that happen'd to take up their Lodging there that very Evening: And, as whatever our Knight-Errant saw, thought, or imagin'd, was all of a romantick Cast, and appear'd to him altogether after the Manner of the Books that had perverted his Imagination, he no sooner saw the Inn, but he fancy'd it to be a Castle fenc'd with four Towers, and lofty Pinnacles glittering with Silver, together with a deep Moat, Draw-Bridge, and all those other Appurtenances peculiar to such kind of Places.

Therefore when he came near it, he stopp'd awhile at a Distance from the Gate, expecting that some Dwarf wou'd appear on the Battlements, and sound his Trumpet to give notice of the Arrival of a Knight; but finding that no Body came, and that *Rozinante* was for making the best of his Way to the Stable, he advanc'd to the Inn-door, where spying the two young Doxies, they seem'd to him two beautiful Damsels, or graceful Ladies, taking the Benefit of the fresh Air at the Gate of the Castle. It happen'd also at the very Moment, that a Swineherd getting together his Hogs (for, without begging Pardon, so they are call'd*) from the Stubble-field, winded his Horn; and Don *Quixote* presently imagin'd this was the wish'd-for Signal, which some Dwarf gave to notify his Approach; therefore with the greatest Joy in the World he rode up to the Inn. The Wenches, affrighted at the Approach of a Man cas'd in Iron, and arm'd with a Lance and Target, were for running into their Lodging; but Don *Quixote* perceiving their Fear by their Flight, lifted up the Pasteboard Beaver of his Helmet, and discovering his wither'd dusty Face, with comely Grace and grave Delivery accosted them in this Manner: "I beseech ye, Ladies, do not fly, nor fear "the least Offence: The Order of Knighthood, which I pro- "fess, does not permit me to countenance or offer Injuries "to any one in the Universe, and least of all to Virgins of "such high Rank as your Presence denotes." The Wenches look'd earnestly upon him, endeavouring to get a Glimpse of his Face, which his ill-contriv'd Beaver partly hid; but when they heard themselves stiled *Virgins*, a Thing so out of the Way of their Profession, they could not forbear laughing outright; which Don *Quixote* resented as a great Affront. "Give me leave to tell ye, Ladies, cry'd he, that "Modesty and Civility are very becoming in the Fair Sex; "whereas Laughter without Ground is the highest Piece "of Indiscretion: However, added he, I do not presume to "say this to offend you, or incur your Displeasure; no, "Ladies, I assure you I have no other Design but to do you "Service." This uncommon Way of Expression, join'd to the Knight's scurvy Figure, increas'd their Mirth; which incens'd him to that Degree, that this might have carry'd

* *In the Original* (que sin perdon assi se llaman). *This Parenthesis relating to Hogs, is left out by* Stevens, *and other Translators, but judiciously retain'd by* Jarvis, *who observes, that our Author thereby ridicules the affected Delicacy of the* Spaniards *and* Italians, *who look upon it as ill Manners to name the Word* Hog *or* Swine, *as too gross an Image. The Reader will find the like Excuse repeated at every mention of the Word* Hog.

23

Things to an Extremity, had not the Inn-keeper luckily
appear'd at that Juncture. He was a Man whose Burden of
Fat inclin'd him to Peace and Quietness, yet when he had
observ'd such a strange Disguise of human Shape in his odd
Armour and Equipage, he could hardly forbear keeping the
Wenches Company in their Laughter; but having the Fear
of such a warlike Appearance before his Eyes, he resolv'd to
give him good Words, and therefore accosted him civilly:
Sir Knight, said he, if your Worship be dispos'd to alight,
you will fail of nothing here but of a Bed; as for all other
Accommodations, you may be supply'd to your Mind. Don
Quixote observing the Humility of the Governor of the
Castle, (for such the Inn-keeper and Inn seem'd to him)
Senior *Castellano*, said he, the least Thing in the World
suffices me; for Arms are the only Things I value, and Combat is my Bed of Repose. The Inn-keeper thought he had
call'd him *Castellano*,* as taking him to be one of the true
Castilians, whereas he was indeed of *Andalusia*, nay, of the
Neighbourhood of *St Lucar*, no less thievish than *Cacus*,
or less mischievous than a Truant-Scholar, or Court-Page,
and therefore he made him this Reply; "At this rate, Sir
"Knight, your Bed might be a Pavement, and your Rest to
"be still awake; you may then safely alight, and I dare
"assure you, you can hardly miss being kept awake all the
"Year long in this House, much less one single Night."
With that he went and held Don *Quixote's* Stirrup, who
having not broke his Fast that Day, dismounted with no
small Trouble or Difficulty. He immediately desir'd the
Governor (that is, the Inn-keeper) to have special Care of
his Steed, assuring him, that there was not a better in the
Universe; upon which the Inn-keeper view'd him narrowly,
but could not think him to be half so good as Don *Quixote*
said: However, having set him up in the Stable, he came
back to the Knight to see what he wanted, and found him
pulling off his Armour by the Help of the good-natur'd
Wenches, who had already reconcil'd themselves to him;
but though they had eas'd him of his Corslet and Back-plate,

* Castellano *signifies both a Constable or Governor of a Castle, and an
Inhabitant of the Kingdom of* Castile *in Spain.*

they could by no means undo his Gorget, nor take off his ill-contriv'd Beaver, which he had ty'd so fast with green Ribbons, that 'twas impossible to get it off without cutting them; now he would by no means permit that, and so was forc'd to keep on his Helmet all Night, which was one of the most pleasant Sights in the World: And while his Armour was taking off by the two kind Lasses, imagining them to be Persons of Quality, and Ladies of that Castle, he very gratefully made them the following Compliment, [in Imitation of an old Romance.]

> *There never was on Earth a Knight*
> *So waited on by Ladies fair,*
> *As once was he, Don* Quixote *hight,*
> *When first he left his Village dear:*
> *Damsels t'undress him ran with Speed,*
> *And Princesses to dress his Steed.*

O *Rozinante*! for that is my Horse's Name, Ladies, and mine Don *Quixote de la Mancha*; I never thought to have discover'd it, 'till some Feats of Arms atchiev'd by me in your Service, had made me better known to your Ladyships; but Necessity forcing me to apply to present Purpose that Passage of the ancient Romance of Sir *Lancelot*, which I now repeat, has extorted the Secret from me before its Time; yet a Day will come, when you shall command, and I obey, and then the Valour of my Arm shall evince the Reality of my Zeal to serve your Ladyships.

The two Females, who were not used to such rhetorical Speeches, could make no Answer to this; they only ask'd him whether he would eat any thing? That I will with all my Heart, cry'd Don *Quixote*, whatever it be, for I am of Opinion nothing can come to me more seasonably. Now, as Ill-luck would have it, it happen'd to be *Friday*, and there was nothing to be had at the Inn but some Pieces of Fish, which is called *Abadexo* in *Castile*, *Bacallao* in *Andalusia*, *Curadillo* in some Places, and in others *Truchuela* or *Little Trout*, though after all 'tis but *Poor Jack*: So they ask'd him whether he could eat any of that *Truchuela*, because they had no other Fish to give him. Don *Quixote* imagining

25

they meant a small Trout, told them, that provided there were more than one, 'twas the same Thing to him, they would serve him as well as a great one; for, continued he, 'tis all one to me whether I am paid a Piece of Eight in one single Piece, or in eight small Reals, which are worth as much: Besides, 'tis probable these *Small Trouts* may be like Veal, which is finer Meat than Beef; or like the Kid, which is better than the Goat. In short, let it be what it will, so it comes quickly, for the Weight of Armour and the Fatigue of Travel are not to be supported without recruiting Food. Thereupon they laid the Cloth at the Inn-door, for the Benefit of the fresh Air, and the Landlord brought him a Piece of that Salt-fish, but ill-water'd, and as ill-dres'd; and as for the Bread, 'twas as mouldy and brown as the Knight's Armour: But 'twould have made one laugh to have seen him eat; for having his Helmet on, with his Beaver lifted up, 'twas impossible for him to feed himself without Help, so that one of those Ladies had that Office; but there was no giving him Drink that Way, and he must have gone without it, had not the Inn-keeper bored a Cane, and setting one End of it to his Mouth, pour'd the Wine in at the other; all which the Knight suffer'd patiently, because he would not cut the Ribbons that fasten'd his Helmet.

While he was at Supper, a Sow-gelder happen'd to sound his Cane-Trumpet, or Whistle of Reeds, four or five times as he came near the Inn; which made Don *Quixote* the more positive of his being in a famous Castle, where he was entertain'd with Musick at Supper, that the *Poor Jack* was young *Trout*, the Bread of the finest Flour, the Wenches Great Ladies, and the Inn-keeper the Governor of the Castle; which made him applaud himself for his Resolution, and his setting out on such an Account. The only Thing that vex'd him was, that he was not yet dubb'd a Knight; for he fansy'd he could not lawfully undertake any Adventure till he had receiv'd the Order of Knighthood.

III: AN ACCOUNT OF THE PLEASANT METHOD
TAKEN BY DON QUIXOTE TO BE
DUBB'D A KNIGHT

DON *Quixote's* Mind being disturb'd with that Thought, he abridg'd even his short Supper: And as soon as he had done, he call'd his Host, then shut him and himself up in the Stable, and falling at his Feet, I will never rise from this Place, cry'd he, most valorous Knight, till you have graciously vouchsafed to grant me a Boon, which I will now beg of you, and which will redound to your Honour and the Good of Mankind. The Inn-keeper, strangely at a Loss to find his Guest at his Feet, and talking at this rate, endeavour'd to make him rise, but all in vain, till he had promis'd to grant him what he ask'd. I expected no less from your great Magnificence, Noble Sir, reply'd Don *Quixote*, and therefore I make bold to tell you, that the Boon which I beg, and you generously condescend to grant me, is, that To-morrow you will be pleased to bestow the Honour of Knighthood upon me. This Night I will watch my Armour in the Chapel of your Castle, and then in the Morning you shall gratify me, as I passionately desire, that I may be duly qualify'd to seek out Adventures in every Corner of the Universe, to relieve the Distress'd, according to the Laws of Chivalry, and the Inclinations of Knight-Errants like my self. The Inn-keeper, who, as I said, was a sharp Fellow, and had already a shrewd Suspicion of the Disorder in his Guest's Understanding, was fully convinc'd of it when he heard him talk after this manner; and, to make Sport that Night, resolv'd to humour him in his Desires, telling him he was highly to be commended for his Choice of such an Employment, which was altogether worthy a Knight of the first Order, such as his gallant Deportment discover'd him to be: That he himself had in his Youth follow'd that honourable Profession, ranging through many Parts of the World in search of Adventures, without so much as forgetting to visit the *Percheles* of

27

Malaga,* the Isles of *Riaran*, the Compass of *Sevil*, the Quicksilver-House of *Segovia*, the Olive Field of *Valencia*, the Circle of *Granada*, the Wharf of *St Lucar*, the *Potro* of *Cordova*,† the Hedge-Taverns of *Toledo*, and divers other Places, where he had exercised the Nimbleness of his Feet and the Subtility of his Hands, doing Wrongs in Abundance, soliciting many Widows, undoing some Damsels, bubbling young Heirs,‡ and in a Word, making himself famous in most of the Courts of Judicature in *Spain*, till at length he retired to this Castle, where he liv'd on his own Estate and those of others, entertaining all Knights-Errant of what Quality or Condition soever, purely for the great Affection he bore them, and to partake of what they got in Recompence of his Good-will. He added, That his Castle at present had no Chapel where the Knight might keep the Vigil of his Arms, it being pull'd down in order to be new-built; but that he knew they might lawfully be watch'd in any other Place in a Case of Necessity, and therefore he might do it that Night in the Court-yard of the Castle; and in the Morning (God willing) all the necessary Ceremonies should be perform'd, so that he might assure himself he should be dubb'd a Knight, nay, as much a Knight as any one in the World could be. He then ask'd Don *Quixote* whether he had any Money? Not a Cross, reply'd the Knight, for I never read in any History of Chivalry that any Knight-Errant ever carry'd Money about him. You are mistaken, cry'd the Inn-keeper; for admit the Histories are silent in this Matter, the Authors thinking it needless to mention

---

* *These are all Places noted for Rogueries and disorderly Doings.* † *A Square in the City of* Cordova, *where a Fountain gushes out from the Mouth of a Horse, near which is also a Whipping-post. The* Spanish *Word* Potro *signifies a Colt or young Horse.* ‡ *Pieces of Roguery not unlike some of these, are to be met with in Don* Belianis *of Greece, and not disapprov'd of by the Hero of that Romance. In Allusion to this, Don* Quixote's *Host brags of divers Wonders he had perform'd this way; and this was a strong Precedent, nor could our Knight object to any Example fetch'd from his Favourite Don* Belianis's *approv'd History. So that this Passage in* Cervantes, *which has been thought very faulty, as being too gross and open, appears from hence to be not only excusable, but very judicious, and directly to his Purpose of exposing those Authors, and their numberless Absurdities.*

28

Things so evidently necessary as Money and clean Shirts, yet there is no Reason to believe the Knights went without either; and you may rest assur'd, that all the Knight-Errants, of whom so many Histories are full, had their Purses well lin'd to supply themselves with Necessaries, and carry'd also with them some Shirts, and a small Box of Salves to heal their Wounds; for they had not the Conveniency of Surgeons to cure 'em every Time they fought in Fields and Desarts, unless they were so happy as to have some Sage or Magician for their Friend to give them present Assistance, sending them some Damsel or Dwarf through the Air in a Cloud, with a small Bottle of Water of so great a Virtue, that they no sooner tasted a Drop of it, but their Wounds were as perfectly cured as if they had never receiv'd any. But when they wanted such a Friend in former Ages, the Knights thought themselves oblig'd to take care, that their Squires should be provided with Money and other Necessaries, as Lint and Salves to dress their Wounds; and if those Knights ever happen'd to have no Squires, which was but very seldom, then they carry'd those Things behind them in a little Bag,* as if it had been something of greater Value, and so neatly fitted to their Saddle, that it was hardly seen; for had it not been upon such an Account, the carrying of Wallets was not much allow'd among Knight-Errants. I must therefore advise you, continu'd he, nay, I might even charge and command you, as you are shortly to be my Son in Chivalry, never from this Time forwards to ride without Money, nor without the other Necessaries of which I spoke to you, which you will find very beneficial when you least expect it. Don *Quixote* promis'd to perform very punctually all his Injunctions; and so they dispos'd every thing in order to his Watching his Arms in a great Yard that adjoin'd to the Inn. To which Purpose the Knight, having got them all together, laid them in a Horse-trough close by a Well in that Yard; then bracing his Target and grasping his Lance, just as it drew dark, he began to walk about by the Horse-trough with a graceful

* *Of striped Stuff, which every one carries, in* Spain, *when they are travelling.*

Deportment. In the mean while the Inn-keeper acquainted all those that were in the House with the Extravagancies of his Guest, his Watching his Arms, and his Hopes of being made a Knight. They all admir'd very much at so strange a kind of Folly, and went on to observe him at a Distance; where they saw him sometimes walk about with a great deal of Gravity, and sometimes lean on his Lance, with his Eyes all the while fix'd upon his Arms. 'Twas now un-doubted Night, but yet the Moon did shine with such a Brightness, as might almost have vy'd with that of the Planet which lent it her; so that the Knight was wholly expos'd to the Spectators View. While he was thus employ'd, one of the Carriers who lodg'd in the Inn came out to water his Mules, which he could not do without removing the Arms out of the Trough. With that Don *Quixote*, who saw him make towards him, cry'd out to him aloud, O thou, whoe'er thou art, rash Knight, that prepares to lay thy Hands on the Arms of the most valorous Knight-Errant that ever wore a Sword, take heed; do not audaciously attempt to profane them with a Touch, lest instant Death be the too sure Re-ward of thy Temerity. But the Carrier never regarded these dreadful Threats; and laying hold on the Armour by the Straps, without any more ado threw it a good way from him; though it had been better for him to have let it alone; for Don *Quixote* no sooner saw this, but lifting up his Eyes to Heaven, and addressing his Thoughts, as it seem'd, to his Lady *Dulcinea*, Assist me, Lady, cry'd he, in the first Oppor-tunity that offers it self to your faithful Slave; nor let your Favour and Protection be deny'd me in this first Trial of my Valour! Repeating such-like Ejaculations, he let slip his Tar-get, and lifting up his Lance with both his Hands, he gave the Carrier such a terrible Knock on his inconsiderate Head with his Lance, that he laid him at his Feet in a woful Condition; and had he back'd that Blow with another, the Fellow would certainly have had no need of a Surgeon. This done, Don *Quixote* took up his Armour, laid it again in the Horse-trough, and then walk'd on backwards and forwards with as great Unconcern as he did at first.

Soon after another Carrier, not knowing what had hap-

pen'd, came also to water his Mules, while the first yet lay
on the Ground in a Trance; but as he offer'd to clear the
Trough of the Armour, Don *Quixote*, without speaking a
Word, or imploring any one's Assistance, once more dropp'd
his Target, lifted up his Lance, and then let it fall so heavily
on the Fellow's Pate, that without damaging his Lance, he
broke the Carrier's Head in three or four Places. His Outcry soon alarm'd and brought thither all the People in the
Inn, and the Landlord among the rest; which Don *Quixote*
perceiving, Thou Queen of Beauty (cry'd he, bracing on his
Shield, and drawing his Sword) thou Courage and Vigour of
my weaken'd Heart, now is the Time when thou must enliv-
en thy adventurous Slave with the Beams of thy Greatness,
while this Moment he is engaging in so terrible an Adventure! With this, in his Opinion, he found himself supply'd
with such an Addition of Courage, that had all the Carriers
in the World at once attack'd him, he would undoubtedly
have fac'd them all. On the other Side, the Carriers, enrag'd
to see their Comrades thus us'd, though they were afraid to
come near, gave the Knight such a Volley of Stones, that he
was forc'd to shelter himself as well as he could under the
Covert of his Target, without daring to go far from the Horse-
trough, lest he should seem to abandon his Arms. The Inn-
keeper call'd to the Carriers as loud as he could to let him
alone; that he had told them already he was mad, and consequently the Law would acquit him, though he should kill
'em. Don *Quixote* also made yet more Noise, calling 'em false
and treacherous Villains, and the Lord of the Castle base
and unhospitable, and a discourteous Knight, for suffering
a Knight-Errant to be so abus'd. I would make thee know
(cry'd he) what a perfidious Wretch thou art, had I but receiv'd the Order of Knighthood; but for you, base, ignominious Rabble! fling on, do your worst; come on, draw nearer
if you dare, and receive the Reward of your Indiscretion and
Insolence. This he spoke with so much Spirit and Undaunted-
ness, that he struck a Terror into all his Assailants; so that
partly through Fear, and partly through the Inn-keeper's
Perswasions, they gave over flinging Stones at him; and he,
on his Side, permitted the Enemy to carry off their Wounded,

and then return'd to the Guard of his Arms as calm and compos'd as before.

The Inn-keeper, who began somewhat to disrelish these
mad Tricks of his Guest, resolv'd to dispatch him forthwith,
and bestow on him that unlucky Knighthood, to prevent
farther Mischief: So coming to him, he excus'd himself for
the Insolence of those base Scoundrels, as being done without
his Privity or Consent; but their Audaciousness, he said, was
sufficiently punished. He added, that he had already told
him there was no Chapel in his Castle; and that indeed there
was no need of one to finish the rest of the Ceremony of
Knighthood, which consisted only in the Application of the
Sword to the Neck and Shoulders, as he had read in the
Register of the Ceremonies of the Order; and that this might
be perform'd as well in a Field as any where else: That he
had already fulfill'd the Obligation of watching his Arms,
which requir'd no more than Two Hours Watch, whereas
he had been Four Hours upon the Guard. Don *Quixote*, who
easily believ'd him, told him he was ready to obey him, and
desir'd him to make an End of the Business as soon as possible, for if he were but Knighted, and should see himself once
attack'd, he believ'd he should not leave a Man alive in the
Castle, except those whom he should desire him to spare for
his Sake.

Upon this the Inn-keeper, lest the Knight should proceed
to such Extremities, fetch'd the Book in which he us'd to
set down the Carriers Accounts for Straw and Barley; and
having brought with him the two kind Females, already
mentioned, and a Boy that held a Piece of lighted Candle in
his Hand, he order'd Don *Quixote* to kneel: Then reading
in his *Manual*, as if he had been repeating some pious Oration, in the midst of his Devotion he lifted up his Hand, and
gave him a good Blow on the Neck, and then a gentle Slap
on the Back with the Flat of his Sword, still mumbling some
Words between his Teeth in the Tone of a Prayer. After
this he ordered one of the Wenches to gird the Sword about
the Knight's Waist; which she did with much Solemnity,
and, I may add, Discretion, considering how hard a Thing
it was to forbear laughing at every Circumstance of the Cere-

mony: 'Tis true, the Thoughts of the Knight's late Prowess, did not a little contribute to the Expression of her Mirth. As she girded on his Sword, Heav'n, cry'd the kind Lady, make your Worship a lucky Knight, and prosper you wherever you go. Don *Quixote* desir'd to know her Name, that he might understand to whom he was indebted for the Favour she had bestow'd upon him, and also make her Partaker of the Honour he was to acquire by the Strength of his Arm. To which the Lady answer'd with all Humility, that her Name was *Tolosa*, a Cobler's Daughter, that kept a Stall among the little Shops of *Sanchobinaya* at *Toledo*; and that whenever he pleas'd to command her, she would be his humble Servant. Don *Quixote* begg'd of her to do him the Favour to add hereafter the Title of Lady to her Name, and for his Sake to be call'd from that Time the Lady *Tolosa*; which she promis'd to do. Her Companion having buckl'd on his Spurs, occasion'd the like Conference between them; and when he had ask'd her Name, she told him she went by the Name of *Miller*, being the Daughter of an honest Miller of *Antequera*. Our new Knight intreated her also to stile her self the Lady *Miller*, making her new Offers of Service. These extraordinary Ceremonies (the like never seen before) being thus hurried over in a kind of Post-haste, Don *Quixote* could not rest till he had taken the Field in quest of Adventures; therefore having immediately saddled his *Rozinante*, and being mounted, he embrac'd the Inn-keeper, and return'd him so many Thanks at so extravagant a rate, for the Obligation he had laid upon him in dubbing him a Knight, that 'tis impossible to give a true Relation of 'em all: To which the Inn-keeper, in haste to get rid of him, return'd as rhetorical, though shorter, Answers; and, without stopping his Horse for the Reckoning, was glad with all his Heart to see him go.

AURORA began to usher in the Morn, when Don *Quixote* sally'd out of the Inn, so well pleas'd, so gay and so overjoy'd to find himself knighted, that he infus'd the same Satisfaction into his Horse, who seem'd ready to burst his Girths for Joy. But calling to mind the Admonitions which the Inn-keeper had given him, concerning the Provision of necessary Accommodations in his Travels, particularly Money and clean Shirts, he resolv'd to return home to furnish himself with them, and likewise get him a Squire, designing to entertain as such a labouring Man, his Neighbour, who was poor and had a Charge of Children, but yet very fit for the Office. With this Resolution he took the Road which led to his own Village; and *Rozinante*, that seem'd to know his Will by Instinct, began to carry him a round Trot so briskly, that his Heels seem scarcely to touch the Ground. The Knight had not travell'd far, when he fansy'd he heard an effeminate Voice complaining in a Thicket on his right Hand. "I thank Heaven" (said he when he heard the Cries) "for favouring me so soon with "an Opportunity to perform the Duty of my Profession, and "reap the Fruit of my Desires! For these Complaints are "certainly the Moans of some distressed Creature who wants "my present Help." Then turning to that Side with all the Speed which *Rozinante* could make, he no sooner came into the Wood but he found a Mare ty'd to an Oak, and to another a young Lad about fifteen Years of Age, naked from the Waist upwards. This was he who made such a lamentable Outcry; and not without Cause, for a lusty Country-fellow was strapping him soundly with a Girdle, at every Stripe putting him in mind of a Proverb, *Keep your Mouth shut, and your Eyes open, Sirrah.* Good Master, cry'd the Boy, I'll do so no more; as I hope to be sav'd, I'll never do so again! Indeed, Master, hereafter I'll take more Care of your Goods. Don *Quixote* seeing this, cry'd, in an angry Tone, "Discourteous Knight, "'tis an unworthy Act to strike a Person who is not able to

"defend himself: Come, bestride thy Steed, and take thy
"Lance," (for the Farmer had something that look'd like
one leaning to the same Tree to which his Mare was ty'd)
"then I'll make thee know thou hast acted the Part of a
"Coward." The Country-fellow, who gave himself for lost
at the Sight of an Apparition in Armour brandishing his
Lance at his Face, answer'd him in mild and submissive
Words: "Sir Knight, cry'd he, this Boy, whom I am chas-
"tising, is my Servant, employ'd by me to look after a Flock
"of Sheep, which I have not far off; but he is so heedless,
"that I lose some of 'em every Day. Now, because I correct
"him for his Carelesness or his Knavery, he says I do it out
"of Covetousness, to defraud him of his Wages; but, upon
"my Life and Soul, he belies me." "What! the Lie in my
"Presence, you saucy Clown (cry'd Don *Quixote*); by the
"Sun that shines I have a good mind to run thee through
"the Body with my Lance. Pay the Boy this Instant, with-
"out any more Words, or, by the Power that rules us all, I'll
"immediately dispatch, and annihilate thee: Come, unbind
"him this Moment." The Country-man hung down his Head,
and without any further Reply unbound the Boy; who being
ask'd by Don *Quixote* what his Master ow'd him? told him
'twas nine Months Wages, at seven Reals a Month. The
Knight having cast it up, found it came to sixty-three Reals
in all; which he order'd the Farmer to pay the Fellow immediately, unless he intended to lose his Life that very Moment. The poor Country-man trembling for Fear, told him,
that, as he was on the Brink of Death, by the Oath he had
sworn (by the by he had not sworn at all) he did not owe
the Lad so much; for there was to be deducted for three
Pair of Shoes which he had bought him, and a Real for his
being let Blood twice when he was sick. That may be, reply'd Don *Quixote*; but set the Price of the Shoes and the
Bleeding against the Stripes which you have given him without Cause: For if he has us'd the Shoe-leather which you
paid for, you have in Return misus'd and impair'd his Skin
sufficiently; and if the Surgeon let him Blood when he was
sick, you have drawn Blood from him now he is in health;
so that he owes you nothing on that Account. The worst is,

Sir Knight, cry'd the Farmer, that I have no Money about me; but let *Andrew* go home with me, and I'll pay him every Piece out of hand. What! I go home with him, cry'd the Youngster, the Devil a-bit, Sir! Not I, truly, I know better Things; for he'd no sooner have me by himself, but he'd flea me alive like another St *Bartholomew*. He will never dare to do it, reply'd Don *Quixote*; I command him, and that's sufficient to restrain him: Therefore provided he will swear by the Order of Knighthood which has been conferr'd upon him, that he will duly observe this Regulation, I will freely let him go, and then thou art secure of thy Money. Good Sir, take heed what you say, cry'd the Boy; for my Master is no Knight, nor ever was of any Order in his Life: He's *John Haldudo*, the rich Farmer of *Quintinar*. This signifies little, answer'd Don *Quixote*, for there may be Knights among the *Haldudo's*; besides, the brave Man carves out his Fortune, and every Man is the Son of his own Works. That's true, Sir, quoth *Andrew*; but of what Works can this Master of mine be the Son, who denies me my Wages, which I have earn'd with the Sweat of my Brows? I do not deny to pay thee thy Wages, honest *Andrew*, cry'd the Master; be but so kind as to go along with me, and by all the Orders of Knighthood in the World, I swear, I'll pay thee every Piece, as I said, nay and perfum'd to boot.* "You may spare "your Perfume, said Don *Quixote*; do but pay him in Reals, "and I am satisfy'd; but be sure you perform your Oath; "for if you fail, I my self swear by the same Oath to return "and find you out, and punish you, though you should hide "your self as close as a Lizard. And if you would be in- "form'd who 'tis that lays these Injunctions on you, that you "may understand how highly it concerns you to observe "'em, know, I am the valorous Don *Quixote de la Mancha*, "the Righter of Wrongs, the Revenger and Redresser of "Grievances; and so farewel: But remember what you have

* *To pay or return a Thing perfum'd, is a* Spanish *Expression, signify-ing it shall be done to Content or with Advantage to the Receiver.* Jarvis *says it is used here as a Satire on the effeminate Custom of wearing every thing perfum'd, insomuch that the very Money in their Pockets was scented.*

"promis'd and sworn, as you will answer the Contrary at
"your Peril." This said, he clapp'd Spurs to *Rozinante*, and
quickly left the Master and the Man a good Way behind him.

The Country-man, who follow'd him with both his Eyes,
no sooner perceived that he was pass'd the Woods, and quite
out of Sight, but he went back to his Boy *Andrew*. Come,
Child, said he, I will pay thee what I owe thee, as that
Righter of Wrongs, and Redresser of Grievances has ordered me. Ay, quoth *Andrew*, on my Word, you'll do well
to fulfil the Commands of that good Knight, whom Heaven
grant long to live; for he is so brave a Man, and so just a
Judge, that adad if you don't pay me he'll come back and
make his Words good. I dare swear as much, answer'd the
Master; and to shew thee how much I love thee, I am willing
to increase the Debt, that I may enlarge the Payment. With
that he caught the Youngster by the Arm, and ty'd him
again to the Tree; where he handled him so unmercifully,
that scarce any Signs of Life were left in him. Now call
your Righter of Wrongs, Mr *Andrew*, cry'd the Farmer, and
you shall see he'll ne'er be able to undo what I have done;
though I think 'tis but a Part of what I ought to do, for I
have a good Mind to flea you alive, as you said I would, you
Rascal. However, he unty'd him at last, and gave him Leave
to go and seek out his Judge, in order to have his Decree
put in Execution. *Andrew* went his ways not very well
pleas'd you may be sure, yet fully resolv'd to find out the
valorous Don *Quixote de la Mancha*, and give him an exact
Account of the whole Transaction, that he might pay the
Abuse with sevenfold Usury: In short, he crept off sobbing
and weeping, while his Master staid behind laughing. And
in this Manner was this Wrong redressed by the valorous
Don *Quixote de la Mancha*.

In the mean time, being highly pleased with himself and
what had happen'd, imagining he had given a most fortunate
and noble Beginning to his Feats of Arms, as he went on towards his Village, "O most beautiful of Beauties," said he
with a low Voice, "*Dulcinea del Toboso!* well may'st thou
"deem thy self most happy, since 'twas thy good Fortune
"to captivate and hold a willing Slave to thy Pleasure so

"valorous and renowned a Knight as is, and ever shall be,
"Don *Quixote de la Mancha*; who, as all the World knows,
"had the Honour of Knighthood bestow'd on him but Yes-
"terday, and this Day redressed the greatest Wrong and
"Grievance that ever Injustice could design, or Cruelty
"commit: This Day has he wrested the Scourge out of the
"Hands of that Tormenter, who so unmercifully treated a
"tender Infant, without the least Occasion given." Just as
he had said this, he found himself at a Place where four
Roads met; and this made him presently bethink of those
Cross-ways which often us'd to put Knights-Errant to a
Stand, to consult with themselves which Way they should
take: And that he might follow their Example, he stopp'd
a-while, and after he had seriously reflected on the Matter,
gave *Rozinante* the Reins, subjecting his own Will to that
of his Horse, who pursuing his first Intent, took the Way
that led to his own Stable.

Don *Quixote* had not gone above two Miles, but he discover'd a Company of People riding towards him, who prov'd
to be Merchants of *Toledo*, that were going to buy Silks in
Murcia. They were six in all, every one screen'd with an
Umbrella, besides four Servants on Horse-back, and three
Muleteers* on Foot. The Knight no sooner perceiv'd 'em,
but he imagined this to be some new Adventure; and because he was resolv'd to imitate as much as possible the
Passages which he had read in his Books, he was pleas'd to
represent this to himself as such a particular Adventure as
he had a singular Desire to meet with; and so, with a dreadful Grace and Assurance, fixing himself in his Stirrups,
couching his Lance, and covering his Breast with his Target,
he posted himself in the Middle of the Road, expecting the
coming up of the supposed Knights-Errant. As soon as they
came within hearing, with a loud Voice and haughty Tone,
"Hold, cry'd he, let all Mankind stand, nor hope to pass on
"further, unless all Mankind acknowledge and confess, that
"there is not in the Universe a more beautiful Damsel than
"the Empress of *La Mancha*, the peerless *Dulcinea del*

* *Mule-Boys, who conduct Travellers through* Spain, *and bring back the Mules, and take Care of 'em all the Way.*

"*Toboso.*" At those Words the Merchants made a Halt, to view the unaccountable Figure of their Opponent; and easily conjecturing, both by his Expression and Disguise, that the poor Gentleman had lost his Senses, they were willing to understand the Meaning of that strange Confession which he would force from them; and therefore one of the Company, who lov'd and understood Rallery, having Discretion to manage it, undertook to talk to him. "Signor Cavalier, "cry'd he, we do not know this worthy Lady you talk of; "but be pleased to let us see her, and then if we find her "possess'd of those matchless Charms, of which you assert "her to be the Mistress, we will freely, and without the "least Compulsion, own the Truth which you would extort "from us." "Had I once shew'd you that Beauty, reply'd "Don *Quixote*, What Wonder would it be to acknowledge "so notorious a Truth? The Importance of the thing lies "in obliging you to believe it, confess it, affirm it, swear it, "and maintain it, without seeing her; and therefore make "this Acknowledgment this very Moment, or know, 'tis "with me you must join in Battle, ye proud and unreason- "able Mortals. Come one by one, as the Laws of Chivalry "require, or all at once, according to the dishonourable "Practice of Men of your Stamp; here I expect you all my "single self, and will stand the Encounter, confiding in the "Justice of my Cause." "Sir Knight,* reply'd the Mer- "chant, I beseech you, in the Name of all the Princes here "present, that for the Discharge of our Consciences, which "will not permit us to affirm a thing we never heard or saw, "and which, besides, tends so much to the Dishonour of the "Empresses and Queens of *Alcaria* and *Estremadura*, your "Worship will vouchsafe to let us see some Portraiture of "that Lady, though 'twere no bigger than a Grain of Wheat; "for by a small Sample we may judge of the whole Piece, "and by that Means rest secure and satisfy'd, and you con- "tented and appeas'd. Nay, I verily believe, that we all find "our selves already so inclinable to comply with you, that "though her Picture should represent her to be blind of one

---

* *Now the Merchant finds him to be a Knight-Errant, he calls him* Sir Knight: *Before, it was only* Signor Cavalier.

39

"Eye, and distilling Vermillion and Brimstone at the other,
"yet, to oblige you, we should be ready to say in her Favour
"whatever your Worship desires." "Distil, ye infamous
"Scoundrels, reply'd Don *Quixote*, in a burning Rage! Distil,
"say you? Know, that nothing distils from her but Amber
"and Civet: Neither is she defective in her Make or Shape,
"but more streight than a *Guadaramian* Spindle.* But you
"shall all severely pay for the horrid Blasphemy which thou
"hast utter'd against the transcendent Beauty of my incom-
"parable Lady." Saying this, with his Lance couch'd, he
ran so furiously at the Merchant who thus provok'd him,
that had not good Fortune so order'd it, that *Rozinante*
should stumble and fall in the midst of his Career, the audacious Trifler had paid dear for his Rallery: But as *Rozinante*
fell, he threw down his Master, who roll'd and tumbled a
good way on the Ground, without being able to get upon his
Legs, though he us'd all his Skill and Strength to effect it, so
encumber'd he was with his Lance, Target, Spurs, Helmet,
and the Weight of his rusty Armour. However, in this helpless Condition he play'd the Heroe with his Tongue; "Stay,
"cry'd he, Cowards, Rascals, do not fly! 'Tis not through
"my Fault that I lie here, but through that of my Horse, ye
"Poltroons!"

One of the Grooms, who was none of the best-natur'd
Creatures, hearing the overthrown Knight thus insolently
treat his Master, could not bear it without returning him
an Answer on his Ribs; and therefore coming up to him, as
he lay wallowing, he snatch'd his Lance, and having broke
it to pieces, he so belabour'd Don *Quixote's* Sides with one
of them, that, in spite of his Arms, he thrash'd him like a
Wheat-sheaf. His Master indeed call'd to him not to lay
him on so vigorously, and to let him alone; but the Fellow,
whose Hand was in, would not give over Rib-roasting the
Knight, till he had tir'd out his Passion and himself; and

---

* As streight as a Spindle, is a Spanish Simile, and Guadarama is a noted
Place for making them, says Stevens. Guadarama is a small Town nine
Leagues from Madrid, seated at the Foot of the Mountain: Near it stands
the Escurial. Jarvis says, the Rocks of this Hill are so streight, and per-
pendicular, that they are called the Spindles.

therefore running to the other Pieces of the broken Lance, he fell to it again without ceasing, 'till he had splinter'd them all on the Knight's Iron Inclosure. He, on his Side, notwithstanding all this Storm of Bastinadoes, lay all the while bellowing, threatning Heaven and Earth, and those villainous Ruffians, as he took them to be. At last the Mule-driver was tir'd, and the Merchants pursu'd their Journey, sufficiently furnish'd with Matter of Discourse at the poor Knight's Expence. When he found himself alone, he try'd once more to get on his Feet; but if he cou'd not do it when he had the Use of his Limbs, how should he do it now, bruis'd and batter'd as he was? But yet for all this, he esteem'd himself a happy Man, being still persuaded, that his Misfortune was one of those Accidents common in Knight-Errantry, and such a one as he cou'd wholly attribute to the Falling of his Horse; nor could he possibly get up, so sore and mortify'd as his Body was all over.

DON *Quixote* perceiving that he was not able
to stir, resolv'd to have recourse to his usual
Remedy, which was to bethink himself what
Passage in his Books might afford him some
Comfort: And presently his Folly brought to
his Remembrance the Story of *Baldwin* and
the Marquess of *Mantua*, when *Charlot* left the former
wounded on the Mountain; a Story learn'd and known by
little Children, not unknown to young Men and Women,
celebrated, and even believ'd, by the old, and yet not a jot
more authentick than the Miracles of *Mahomet*. This seem'd
to him as if made on purpose for his present Circumstances,
and therefore he fell a rolling and tumbling up and down,
expressing the greatest Pain and Resentment, and breathing
out, with a languishing Voice, the same Complaints which
the wounded *Knight of the Wood* is said to have made:

> *Alas! where are you, Lady dear,*
> *That for my Woe you do not moan?*
> *You little know what ails me here,*
> *Or are to me disloyal grown!*

Thus he went on with the Lamentations in that Romance,
till he came to these Verses:

> *O thou, my Uncle and my Prince,*
> *Marquess of* Mantua, *noble Lord!*——

When kind Fortune so order'd it, that a Ploughman, who
liv'd in the same Village, and near his House, happen'd to
pass by, as he came from the Mill with a Sack of Wheat. The
Fellow seeing a Man lie at his full Length on the Ground,
ask'd him who he was, and why he made such a sad Complaint? Don *Quixote*, whose distemper'd Brain presently
represented to him the Country-man for the Marquess of
Mantua, his imaginary Uncle, made him no Answer, but
went on with the Romance, giving him an Account of his
Misfortunes, and of the Loves of his Wife, and the Emperor's

Son, just as the Book relates 'em. The Fellow star'd, much
amaz'd to hear a Man talk such accountable Stuff; and taking off the Vizor of his Helmet, broken all to pieces with
Blows bestow'd upon't by the Mule-driver, he wip'd off the
Dust that cover'd his Face, and presently knew the Gentleman. Master *Quixada*! cry'd he, (for so he was properly
call'd when he had the right Use of his Senses, and had
not yet from a sober Gentleman transform'd himself into a
wand'ring Knight) how came you in this Condition? But the
other continu'd his Romance, and made no Answers to all
the Questions the Country-man put to him, but what follow'd
in course in the Book: Which the good Man perceiving, he
took off the batter'd Adventurer's Armour, as well as he
could, and fell a searching for his Wounds; but finding no
sign of Blood, or any other Hurt, he endeavour'd to set him
upon his Legs; and at last, with a great deal of Trouble, he
heav'd him upon his own Ass, as being the more easy and
gentle Carriage: He also got all the Knight's Arms together,
not leaving behind so much as the Splinters of his Lance; and
having ty'd 'em up, and laid 'em on *Rozinante*, which he
took by the Bridle, and his Ass by the Halter, he led 'em all
towards the Village, and trudg'd a-foot himself very pensive, while he reflected on the Extravagancies which he
heard Don *Quixote* utter. Nor was Don *Quixote* himself less
melancholy, for he felt himself so bruis'd and mortify'd,
that he could hardly sit on the Ass; and now and then he
breath'd such grievous Sighs, as seem'd to pierce the very
Skies, which mov'd his compassionate Neighbour once more
to intreat him to declare to him the Cause of his Grief: But one
would have imagin'd the Devil prompted him with Stories,
that had some resemblance of his Circumstances; for in that
Instant, wholly forgetting *Baldwin*, he bethought himself
of the Moor *Abindarez*, whom *Rodrigo de Narvaez*, Alcayde
of *Antequera*, took and carried Prisoner to his Castle; so that
when the Husband-man ask'd him how he did, and what
ail'd him? he answered Word for Word as the Prisoner *Abindarez* reply'd to *Rodrigo de Narvaez*, in the *Diana* of *George
de Monte-mayor*, where that Adventure is related; applying
it so properly to his Purpose, that the Country-man wish'd

himself at the Devil rather than within the hearing of such strange Nonsense; and being now fully convinc'd, that his Neighbour's Brains were turn'd, he made all the haste he could to the Village, to be rid of his troublesome Impertin-encies. Don *Quixote* in the mean time thus went on: You must know, Don *Rodrigo de Narvaez*, that this beautiful *Xerifa*, of whom I gave you an Account, is at present the most lovely *Dulcinea del Toboso*, for whose Sake I have done, still do, and will atchieve the most famous Deeds of Chivalry that ever were, are, or ever shall be seen in the Universe. Good Sir, reply'd the Husband-man, as I'm a Sinner, I am not Don *Rodrigo de Narvaez*, nor the Marquess of *Mantua*, but *Pedro Alonso* by Name, your Worship's Neighbour; nor are you *Baldwin*, nor *Abindaraez*, but only that worthy Gentleman Senior *Quixada*. I know very well who I am, answer'd Don *Quixote*; and what's more, I know, that I may not only be the Persons I have named, but also the Twelve Peers of *France*, nay, and the Nine Worthies all in One; since my Atchievements will outrival not only the famous Exploits which made any of 'em singly illustrious, but all their mighty Deeds accumulated together.

Thus discoursing, they at last got near their Village about Sun-set; but the Country-man staid at some Distance till 'twas dark, that the distressed Gentleman might not be seen so scurvily mounted, and then he led him home to his own House, which he found in great Confusion. The Curate and the Barber of the Village, both of 'em Don *Quixote's* inti-mate Acquaintance, happen'd to be there at that Juncture, as also the House-keeper, who was arguing with 'em: What do you think, pray good Doctor *Perez*, said she, (for this was the Curate's Name) what do you think of my Master's Mischance? Neither he, nor his Horse, nor his Target, Lance, nor Armour have been seen these six Days. What shall I do, Wretch that I am! I dare lay my Life, and 'tis as sure as I am a living Creature, that those cursed Books of Errantry, which he us'd to be always poring upon, have set him besides his Senses; for now I remember, I have heard him often mutter to himself, that he had a mind to turn Knight-Errant, and jaunt up and down the World to find out Adventures. May *Satan* and *Barabbas* e'en take all such Books that have thus crackt the best Head-piece in all *La Mancha*! His Niece said as much, addressing herself to the Barber: You must know, Mr *Nicholas*, quoth she, (for that was his Name) that many times my Uncle would read you those unconscionable Books of Disventures for eight and forty Hours together; then away he'd throw you his Book, and drawing his Sword, he'd fall a fencing against the Walls; and when he had tir'd himself with cutting and slashing, he would cry, he had kill'd four Giants as big as any Steeples; and the Sweat which he put himself into, he would say, was the Blood of the Wounds he had received in the Fight; then would he swallow you a huge Jug of cold Water, and presently he'd be as quiet and as well as e'er he was in his Life; and he said, that this same Water was a sort of precious Drink brought him by the Sage *Esquife**★** a great Magician, and his special Friend. Now 'tis I who am the Cause of all this Mischief, for not giving you timely Notice of my Uncle's Raving, that you might have put a Stop to it, ere 'twas too late, and have burnt all these excommunicated Books; for there are I don't know how many of them that deserve as much to be burn'd as those of the rankest Hereticks. I am of your Mind, said the Curate; and verily to Morrow shall not pass over before I have fairly brought 'em to a Trial, and condemn'd 'em to the Flames, that they may not minister Occasion to such as would read 'em, to be perverted after the Example of my good Friend. The Countryman, who with Don *Quixote* stood without, listening to all this Discourse, now perfectly understood by this the Cause of his Neighbour's Disorder; and therefore, without any more ado, he call'd out aloud, Here! House! open the Gates there, for the Lord *Baldwin*, and the Lord Marquess of *Mantua*, who is coming sadly wounded; and for the Moorish Lord *Abindaraez*, whom the valorous Don *Rodrigo de Narvaez*, Alcayde of *Antequera*, brings Prisoner. At which Words they all got out of Doors; and the one finding it to be her Uncle, and the other to be her Master, and the rest their Friend,

★ *She means* Alquife, *a famous Enchanter in* Amadis de Gaul *and* Don Belianis *of* Greece, *Husband to the no less famous* Urganda *the Sorceress*.

who had not yet alighted from the Ass, because indeed he was not able, they all ran to embrace him: To whom Don *Quixote*; Forbear, said he, for I am sorely hurt, by reason that my Horse fail'd me; carry me to Bed, and if it be possible let the Enchantress *Urganda* be sent for to cure my Wounds. Now, in the name of Mischief, qouth the House-keeper, see whether I did not guess right, on which Foot my Master halted? Come, get you to Bed, I beseech you; and, my Life for your's, we'll take care to cure you without sending for that same *Urganda*. A hearty Curse, and the Curse of Curses, I say it again and again a hundred times, light upon those Books of Chivalry that have put you in this Pickle. Thereupon they carry'd him up to his Bed, and search'd for his Wounds, but could find none; and then he told them he was only bruis'd, having had a dreadful Fall from his Horse *Rozinante* while he was fighting ten Giants, the most outragious and audacious that ever could be found upon the Face of the Earth. How! cry'd the Curate, have we Giants too in the Dance?* Nay then, by the Holy Sign of the Cross, I'll burn 'em all by To-morrow Night. Then did they ask the Don a thousand Questions; but to every one he made no other Answer, but that they should give him something to eat, and then leave him to his Repose, a thing which was to him of the greatest Importance. They comply'd with his Desires; and then the Curate inform'd himself at large in what Condition the Country-man had found him; and having had a full Account of every Particular, as also of the Knight's extravagant Talk, both when the Fellow found him, and as he brought him home, this increas'd the Curate's Desire of effecting what he had resolv'd to do the next Morning: At which Time he call'd upon his Friend, Mr *Nicholas* the Barber, and went with him to Don *Quixote's* House.

* *Alluding to a Passage* in Amadis, *where several Giants are mix'd with Ladies and Knights at* Constantinople *in a Dance.*

VI: OF THE PLEASANT AND CURIOUS SCRUTINY WHICH THE CURATE AND THE BARBER MADE OF THE LIBRARY OF OUR INGENIOUS GENTLEMAN

THE Knight was yet asleep, when the Curate came attended by the Barber, and desir'd his Niece to let him have the Key of the Room where her Uncle kept his Books, the Authors of his Woes: She readily consented; and so in they went, and the House-keeper with 'em. There they found above a hundred large Volumes neatly bound, and a good Number of small ones: As soon as the House-keeper had spy'd 'em out, she ran out of the Study, and return'd immediately with a Holy-water Pot and a Sprinkler: Here Doctor, cry'd she, pray sprinkle every Creek and Corner in the Room, lest there should lurk in it some one of the many Sorcerers these Books swarm with, who might chance to bewitch us, for the Ill-will we bear 'em, in going about to send 'em out of the World. The Curate could not forbear smiling at the good Woman's Simplicity; and desir'd the Barber to reach him the Books one by one, that he might peruse the Title-pages, for perhaps they might find some among 'em, that might not deserve to be committed to the Flames. Oh, by no means, cry'd the Niece, spare none of them, they all helpt some how or other to crack my Uncle's Brain. I fansy we had best throw 'em all out at the Window in the Yard, and lay 'em together in a Heap, and then set 'em o'fire, or else carry 'em into the Back-yard, and there make a Pile of 'em, and burn 'em, and so the Smoak will offend no Body: The House-keeper join'd with her, so eagerly bent they were both upon the Destruction of those poor Innocents; but the Curate would not condescend to those irregular Proceedings, and resolv'd first to read at least the Title-page of every Book.

The first that Mr *Nicholas* put into his Hands was *Amadis de Gaul*, in four Volumes.* There seems to me some Mystery

* *Hence it appears, that only the first four Books of* Amadis *were thought genuine by* Cervantes. *The subsequent Volumes, to the Number of twenty-one, are condemn'd hereby as spurious.*

in this Book's being the first taken down (cry'd the Curate, as soon as he had look'd upon't) for I have heard 'tis the first Book of Knight-Errantry that ever was printed in *Spain*, and the Model of all the rest; and therefore I am of Opinion, that, as the first Teacher and Author of so pernicious a Sect, it ought to be condemn'd to the Fire without Mercy. I beg a Reprieve for him, cry'd the Barber, for I have been told 'tis the best Book that has been written in that Kind; and therefore, as the only good thing of that sort, it may deserve a Pardon. Well then, reply'd the Curate, for this Time let him have it. Let's see that other, which lies next to him. These, said the Barber, are the Exploits of *Esplandian*, the lawfully begotten Son of *Amadis de Gaul*. Verily, said the Curate, the Father's Goodness shall not excuse the Want of it in the Son: Here, good Mistress House-keeper, open that Window, and throw it into the Yard, and let it serve as a Foundation to that Pile we are to set a blazing presently. She was not slack in her Obedience; and thus poor Don *Esplandian* was sent headlong into the Yard, there patiently to wait the Time of his fiery Trial. To the next, cry'd the Curate. This, said the Barber, is *Amadis of Greece*; and I'm of Opinion, that all those that stand on this Side are of the same Family. Then let 'em all be sent packing into the Yard, reply'd the Curate; for rather than lose the Pleasure of burning Queen *Pintiquiniestra*,* and the Shepherd *Darinel*† with his Eclogues, and the confounded unintelligible Discourses of the Author, I think I should burn my own Father along with 'em, if I met him in the Disguise of a Knight-Errant. I am of your Mind, cry'd the Barber; and I too, said the Niece: Nay, then, quoth the old Female, let 'em come, and down with 'em all into the Yard. They were deliver'd to her accordingly, and many they were; so that to save her self the Labour of carrying 'em down Stairs, she fairly sent them flying out at the Window.

* *A terrible fighting Giantess in* Amadis de Gaul, *and one of the most ridiculous Characters imaginable.*   † *A ridiculous Buffoon, in love with an Empress*, ibid.

What overgrown Piece of Lumber* have we here? cry'd
the Curate. *Olivante de Laura*, return'd the Barber. The
same Author wrote *The Garden of Flowers*; and, to deal ingenuously with you, I cannot well tell which of the two
Books has most Truth in it, or, to speak more properly, less
Lies: But this I know for certain, that he shall march into
the Backyard like a nonsensical arrogant Block-head as he is.

The next, cry'd the Barber, is *Florismart of Hyrcania*.
How! my Lord *Florismart*, is he here? reply'd the Curate:
Nay then truly he shall e'en follow the rest to the Yard, in
spite of his wonderful Birth and incredible Adventures; for
his rough, dull, and insipid Stile deserves no better Usage.
Come, toss him into the Yard, and this other too, good Mistress. With all my heart, quoth the Governess; and straight
she was as good as her Word.

Here's the noble Don *Platir*, cry'd the Barber. 'Tis an old
Book, replied the Curate, and I can think of nothing in him
that deserves a Grain of Pity: Away with him, without any
more Words; and down he went accordingly.

Another Book was open'd, and it prov'd to be *The Knight
of the Cross*. The holy Title, cry'd the Curate, might in
some measure atone for the Badness of the Book; but then,
as the Saying is, *The Devil lurks behind the Cross!* To the
Flames with him.

Then the Barber taking down another Book, cry'd, here's
The Mirrour of Knighthood. Oh! I have the Honour to know
him, reply'd the Curate. There you will find the Lord
Rinalde of Montalban, with his Friends and Companions,
all of them greater Thieves than *Cacus*, together with the
Twelve Peers of *France*, and that faithful Historian *Turpin*.
Truly, I must needs say, I am only for condemning them to
perpetual Banishment, at least because their Story contains
something of the famous *Boyardo's*† Invention, out of which
the Christian Poet *Ariosto* also spun his Web: Yet, if I happen to meet with him in this bad Company, and speaking in
any other Language than his own, I'll shew him no manner

---

* *What Tun of an Author*, &c. *Quien es esse* Tonel, *&c.? in the Original.*
† *A famous* Italian *Poet, Author of several Canto's of* Orlando Inamorato,
from whom Ariosto *borrow'd a great Part of his* Orlando Furioso.

of Favour; but if he talks in his own native Tongue, I'll treat him with all the Respect imaginable.* I have him at home in *Italian*, said the Barber, but I cannot understand him. Neither is it any great Matter, whether you do or not,† reply'd the Curate; and I could willingly have excus'd the good Captain who translated it that Trouble of attempting to make him speak *Spanish*, for he has depriv'd him of a great deal of his primitive Graces; a Misfortune incident to all those who presume to translate Verses, since their utmost Wit and Industry can never enable 'em to preserve the native Beauties and Genius that shine in the Original. For this Reason I am for having not only this Book, but likewise all those which we shall find here, treating of *French* Affairs,‡ laid up and deposited in some dry Vault, till we have maturely determined what ought to be done with 'em; yet give me Leave to except one *Barnardo del Carpio*, that must be somewhere here among the rest, and another, call'd *Roncesvalles*; for whenever I meet with 'em I will certainly deliver 'em up into the Hands of the House-keeper, who shall toss them into the Fire. The Barber gave his Approbation to every Particular, well knowing that the Curate was so good a Christian, and so great a Lover of Truth, that he would not have utter'd a Falsity for all the World. Then opening another Volume, he found it to be *Palmerin de Oliva*, and the next to that *Palmerin of England*. Ha! have I found you? cry'd the Curate. Here, take that *Oliva*, let him be torn to pieces, then burnt, and his Ashes scatter'd in the Air; but let *Palmerin of England* be preserved as a singular Relique of Antiquity; and let such a costly Box be made for him as *Alexander* found among the Spoils of *Darius*, which he devoted to inclose *Homer's* Works: For I must tell you, Neighbour, that Book deserves particular Respect for two things; first, for its own Excellencies; and, secondly, for the sake of its Author, who is said to have been a learned King of *Portugal*: Then all the Adventures of the Castle of *Miraguarda* are well and art-

---

* *I will put him upon my Head, in the Original: A Mark of Honour and Respect.* † *It is plain from hence, that* Cervantes *did not relish* Ariosto's *Extravagancies.* ‡ *Meaning the common Subject of Romances, the Scene of which lay in* France, *under* Charlemayne *and the* Paladins.

50

fully manag'd, the Dialogue very courtly and clear, and the Decorum strictly observed in every Character, with equal Propriety and Judgment. Therefore, Mr *Nicholas*, continu'd he, with Submission to your better Advice, this and *Amadis de Gaul* shall be exempted from the Fire; and let all the rest be condemn'd without any further Enquiry or Examination. By no means, I beseech you, return'd the Barber, for this which I have in my Hands is the famous Don *Bellianis*. Truly, cry'd the Curate, he, with his Second, Third, and Fourth Parts, had need of a Dose of *Rhubarb* to purge his excessive Choler: Besides, his Castle of Fame should be demolish'd, and a Heap of other Rubbish remov'd; in order to which I give my Vote to grant 'em the Benefit of a Reprieve; and as they shew Signs of Amendment, so shall Mercy or Justice be us'd towards 'em: In the mean time, Neighbour, take 'em into Custody, and keep them safe at home; but let none be permitted to converse with them. Content, cry'd the Barber; and to save himself the Labour of looking on any more Books of that kind, he bid the House-keeper take all the great Volumes, and throw them into the Yard. This was not spoken to one stupid or deaf, but to one who had a greater mind to be burning them, than weaving the finest and largest Web:* So that laying hold on no less than eight Volumes at once, she presently made 'em leap towards the Place of Execution: But as she went too eagerly to work, taking more Books than she could conveniently carry, she happen'd to drop one at the Barber's Feet, which he took up out of Curiosity to see what it was, and found it to be the History of the famous Knight *Tirante the White*. Good-lack-a-day, cry'd the Curate, is *Tirante the White* here? Oh! pray, good Neighbour, give it me by all means, for I promise my self to find in it a Treasure of Delight, and a Mine of Recreation. There we have that valorous Knight Don *Kyrie-Eleison*† of *Montalban*, with his Brother *Thomas* of *Montalban*, and the Knight

---

* *A conceal'd Piece of Satire on the Laziness and Want of good House-wifery of the* Spanish Women. † *Most of these Names are significative, and are Qualities personify'd: As* Kyrie-Eleison, *Greek for* Lord have Mercy upon us; Alano *is a* Mastiff-Dog; Plazerdemivida, *Pleasure of my Life;* Reposada, *sedate and staid.*

Fonseca; the Combat between the valorous *Detriante* and *Alano*; the dainty and witty Conceits of the Damsel *Plazerde-mivida*, with the Loves and Guiles of the Widow *Reposada*; together with the Lady Empress, that was in love with *Hippolito* her Gentleman-Usher. I vow and protest to you, Neighbour, continu'd he, that in its Way there is not a bet-ter Book in the World: Why here your Knights eat and drink, sleep and die natural Deaths in their Beds, nay, and make their last Wills and Testaments; with a world of other things, of which all the rest of these sort of Books don't say one Syllable. Yet after all, I must tell you, that for wilfully taking the Pains to write so many foolish things, the worthy Author fairly deserves to be sent to the Galleys for all the Days of his Life. Take it home with you and read it, and then tell me whether I have told you the Truth or no. I believe you, reply'd the Barber; but what shall we do with all these smaller Books that are left? Certainly, reply'd the Curate, these cannot be Books of Knight-Errantry, they are too small; you'll find they are only Poets: And so opening one, it happen'd to be the *Diana of Montemayor*; which made him say (believing all the rest to be of that Stamp) these do not deserve to be punish'd like the others, for they neither have done, nor can do that Mischief which those Stories of Chivalry have done, being generally ingenious Books, that can do no Body any Prejudice. Oh! good Sir, cry'd the Niece, burn 'em with the rest, I beseech you; for should my Uncle get cur'd of his Knight-Errant Frenzy, and betake himself to the Reading of these Books, we should have him turn Shepherd, and so wander thro' the Woods and Fields; nay, and what would be worse yet, turn Poet, which they say is a catching and an incurable Disease. The Gentlewoman is in the Right, said the Curate, and it will not be amiss to remove that Stumbling-block out of our Friend's Way; and since we began with the *Diana of Montemayor*, I am of Opinion we ought not to burn it, but only take out that Part of it which treats of the Magician *Felicia*, and the inchanted Water, as also all the longer Poems; and let the Work escape with its Prose, and the Honour of being the First of that Kind. Here's another *Diana*, quoth the Barber, the second of that Name, by *Salmantino*; (of *Salamanca*) nay, and a third too, by *Gil Polo*. Pray, said the Curate, let *Salmantino* increase the Number of the Criminals in the Yard; but as for that by *Gil Polo*, preserve it as charily as if *Apollo* himself had wrote it; and go on as fast as you can, I beseech you, good Neighbour, for it grows late. Here, quoth the Barber, I've a Book called the *Ten Books of the Fortunes of Love*, by *Anthony de Lofraco*, a *Sardinian* Poet. Now, by my holy Orders, cry'd the Curate, I do not think since *Apollo* was *Apollo*, the Muses Muses, and the Poets Poets, there was ever a more comical, more whimsical Book. Of all the Works of the Kind commend me to this, for in its way 'tis certainly the best and most singular that ever was publish'd, and he that never read it, may safely think he never in his Life read any thing that was pleasant. Give it me, Neighbour, continu'd he, for I'm more glad to have found it, than if any one had given me a Cassock of the best *Florence Serge*. With that he laid it aside with extraordinary Satisfaction, and the Barber went on: These that follow, cry'd he, are *The Shepherd of Iberia*, *The Nymphs of Enares*, and *The Cure of Jealousy*. Take 'em Jayler, quoth the Curate, and never ask me why, for then we shall ne'er have done. The next, said the Barber, is *The Shepherd of Filida*. He's no Shepherd, return'd the Curate, but a very discreet Courtier; keep him as a precious Jewel. Here's a bigger, cry'd the Barber, call'd, *The Treasure of divers Poems*. Had there been fewer of 'em, said the Curate, they would have been more esteem'd. 'Tis fit the Book should be prun'd and clear'd of several Trifles that disgrace the rest: Keep it however, because the Author is my Friend, and for the sake of his other more heroick and lofty Productions. Here's a Book of Songs by *Lopez Maldonado*, cry'd the Barber. He's also my particular Friend, said the Curate: His Verses are very well lik'd when he reads them himself; and his Voice is so excellent, that they charm us whenever he sings 'em. He seems indeed to be somewhat too long in his Eclogues; but can we ever have too much of a good thing? Let him be preserv'd among the best. What's the next Book? The *Galatea of Miguel de Cervantes*, reply'd the Barber. That *Cervantes* has been my intimate Acquaintance these many Years,

53

cry'd the Curate; and I know he has been more conversant with Misfortunes than with Poetry. His Book indeed has I don't know what that looks like a good Design; he aims at something, but concludes nothing: Therefore we must stay for the Second Part, which he has promis'd us;* perhaps he may make us Amends, and obtain a full Pardon, which is denied him for the present; till that Time keep him close Prisoner at your House. I will, quoth the Barber: But see, I have here three more for you, *The Araucana of Don Alonso de Ercilla*, *The Austirada of Juan Ruffo*, a Magistrate of *Cordoua*, and the *Monserrato* of *Christopher de Virves*, a *Valencian* Poet. These, cry'd the Curate, are the best heroick Poems we have in *Spanish*, and may vie with the most celebrated of *Italy*: Reserve 'em as the most valuable Performances which *Spain* has to boast of in Poetry.

At last the Curate grew so tir'd with prying into so many Volumes, that he ordered all the rest to be burnt at a venture.† But the Barber shew'd him one which he had open'd by Chance ere the dreadful Sentence was pass'd. Truly, said the Curate, who saw by the Title 'twas *The Tears of Angelica*, I should have wept my self, had I caus'd such a Book to share the Condemnation of the rest; for the Author was not only one of the best Poets in *Spain*, but in the whole World, and translated some of *Ovid's* Fables with extraordinary Success.

* Cervantes *never perform'd this Promise.*   † *In the Original*, à Carga Cerrada (*Inside and Contents unknown*) a Mercantile Phrase used in their Bills of Lading.

VII: DON QUIXOTE'S SECOND SALLY IN QUEST OF ADVENTURES

WHILE they were thus employed, Don Quixote in a raving Fit began to talk aloud to himself: Here, here, valorous Knights, cry'd he, now's the Time that you must exert the Strength of your mighty Arms; for lo! the Courtiers bear away the Honour of the Tournament. This amazing Outcry call'd away the Inquisitors from any further Examination of the Library; and therefore the House-keeper and the Niece being left to their own Discretion, 'tis thought *The Carolea*, and *Leo of Spain*, with the *Deeds of the Emperor*, written by Don *Lewis d' Avila*, which to be sure were Part of the Collection, were committed to the Flames unseen and unheard, without any legal Trial; a Fate which perhaps they might have escap'd, had the Curate been there to have weigh'd what might have been urg'd in their Defence.

When they came into Don *Quixote's* Chamber, they found him risen out of his Bed as mad as ever he was, tearing his Throat, and making a heavy Bustle, laying about him with his Sword back-stroke and fore-stroke, as broad awake as if he had never slept. They ran in upon him, caught him in their Arms, and carry'd him to Bed again by main Force; where, after he was somewhat quiet and settled, turning himself to the Curate, Certainly, cry'd he, my Lord Archbishop *Turpin*, 'tis a great Dishonour to us who are call'd the Twelve Peers, to suffer the Knights of the Court to bear away the Honour of the Tournament without any further Opposition, after we the Knight-Adventurers had carry'd it for three Days before. Be pacify'd, my good Friend, reply'd the Curate; Fortune may have yet a better Success in Reserve for you, and they who lose to Day may win to Morrow: At present think on your Health, for doubtless you must needs be now extremely tir'd, if not very much wounded. Wounded! reply'd Don *Quixote*, No; but as for being bruis'd, I will not deny it, for that base-born Knight Don *Orlando* has batter'd all my Limbs with the Trunk of an Oak, out of meer Envy,

55

because he sees that I only dare rival his Exploits: But may I no more be called *Rinaldo of Montalban*, if, in spite of his Inchantments, I do not make him severely pay for this as soon as I can leave my Bed; and therefore let my Dinner be brought in, for 'tis what I want most at this Juncture, and then let me alone to revenge this Abuse. Accordingly they brought him some Victuals, which when he had eaten, he fell asleep again, and they left him, all of them strangely amaz'd at his uncommon Madness. That Night the House-keeper burnt all the Books, not only those in the Yard, but all those that were in the House; and several suffer'd in the general Calamity, that deserv'd to have been treasur'd up in everlasting Archives, had not their Fate and the Remiss-ness of the Inquisitors order'd it otherwise. And thus they verify'd the Proverb, *That the Good often fare the worse for the Bad*.

One of the Expedients which the Curate and the Barber bethought themselves of, in order to their Friend's Recovery, was to stop up the Door of the Room where his Books lay, that he might not find it, nor miss them when he rose; for they hop'd the Effect would cease when they had taken away the Cause; and they order'd, that if he enquir'd about it, they should tell him, that a certain Inchanter had carry'd away Study, Books and all. Two Days after, Don *Quixote* being got up, the first thing he did was to go visit his darling Books; and as he could not find the Study in the Place where he had left it, he went up and down, and look'd for it in every Room. Sometimes he came to the Place where the Door us'd to stand, and then stood feeling and groping about a good while, then cast his Eyes, and star'd on every Side, without speaking a Word. At last, after a long Deliberation, he thought fit to ask his House-keeper which was the Way to his Study? What Study, (answer'd the Woman, according to her Instructions) or rather, what Nothing is it you look for? Alas! here's neither Study nor Books in the House now, for the Devil is run away with them all. No, 'twas not the Devil, said the Niece, but a Conjurer, or an Inchanter, as they call 'em, who, since you went, came hither one Night mounted on a Dragon o'th' Top of a Cloud, and then alight-

ing, went into your Study, where what he did, he and the
Devil best can tell, for a while after, he flew out at the Roof
of the House, leaving it all full of Smoke; and when we went
to see what he had done, we could neither find the Books,
nor so much as the very Study; only the House-keeper and I
very well remember, that when the old Thief went away,
he cry'd out aloud, That out of a private Grudge which he
bore in his Mind to the Owner of those Books, he had done
the House a Mischief, as we should soon perceive; and then
I think he call'd himself the Sage *Muniaton*. Not *Muniaton*,
but *Freston** you should have said, cry'd Don *Quixote*. Truly,
quoth the Niece, I can't tell whether it was *Freston* or *Fris-
ton*, but sure I am that his Name ended with a *ton*. 'Tis so,
return'd Don *Quixote*, for he is a famous Necromancer, and
my mortal Enemy, and bears me a great deal of Malice; for
seeing by his Art, that in spite of all his Spells, in Process of
Time I shall fight and vanquish in single Combat a Knight
whose Interest he espouses, therefore he endeavours to do
me all manner of Mischief; but I dare assure him, that he
strives against the Stream, nor can his Power reverse the
first Decrees of Fate. Who doubts of that? cry'd the Niece:
But, dear Uncle, what makes you run your self into these
Quarrels? Had not you better stay at home, and live in Peace
and Quietness, than go rambling up and down like a Vagabond, and seeking for better Bread than is made of Wheat,
without once so much as considering, That many go to seek
Wool, and come home shorn themselves? Oh, good Niece,
reply'd Don *Quixote*, how ill thou understandest these Matters! Know, that before I'll suffer my self to be shorn, I'll
tear and pluck off the Beards of all those audacious Mortals,
that shall attempt to profane the Tip of one single Hair
within the Verge of these Mustachoes. To this neither the
Niece nor the Governess thought fit to make any Reply, for
they perceiv'd the Knight to grow angry. Full fifteen Days
did our Knight remain quietly at home, without betraying
the least Sign of his Desire to renew his Rambling; during
which time there pass'd a great deal of pleasant Discourse
between him and his two Friends the Curate and the Barber;

* *An Enchanter in Don* Belianis *of* Greece.

while he maintain'd, that there was nothing the World stood so much in need of as Knights-Errant; wherefore he was resolv'd to revive the Order: In which Disputes Mr Curate sometimes contradicted him, and sometimes submitted; for had he not now and then given way to his Fancies, there would have been no conversing with him.

In the mean time Don *Quixote* earnestly sollicited one of his Neighbours, a Country-Labourer, and a good honest Fellow, if we may call a poor Man honest, for he was poor indeed, poor in Purse, and poor in Brains; and, in short, the Knight talk'd so long to him, ply'd him with so many Arguments, and made him so many fair Promises, that at last the poor silly Clown consented to go along with him, and become his Squire. Among other Inducements to entice him to do it willingly, Don *Quixote* forgot not to tell him, that 'twas likely such an Adventure would present it self, as might secure him the Conquest of some Island in the Time that he might be picking up a Straw or two, and then the Squire might promise himself to be made Governor of the Place. Allur'd with these large Promises, and many others, *Sancho Pança* (for that was the Name of the Fellow) forsook his Wife and Children to be his Neighbour's Squire.

This done, Don *Quixote* made it his Business to furnish himself with Money; to which Purpose, selling one House, mortgaging another, and losing by all, he at last got a pretty good Sum together. He also borrowed a Target of a Friend, and having patch'd up his Head-piece and Beaver as well as he could, he gave his Squire Notice of the Day and Hour when he intended to set out, that he might also furnish himself with what he thought necessary; but above all he charg'd him to provide himself with a Wallet; which *Sancho* promis'd to do, telling him he wou'd also take his Ass along with him, which being a very good one, might be a great Ease to him, for he was not us'd to travel much a-foot. The mentioning of the Ass made the noble Knight pause a while; he mus'd and ponder'd whether he had ever read of any Knight-Errant, whose Squire us'd to ride upon an Ass; but he could not remember any Precedent for it: However, he gave him Leave at last to bring his Ass, hoping to mount him more honourably with the first Opportunity, by unhorsing the next discourteous Knight he should meet. He also furnished himself with Shirts, and as many other Necessaries as he could conveniently carry, according to the Innkeeper's Injunctions. Which being done, *Sancho Pança*, without bidding either his Wife or Children good-by; and Don *Quixote*, without taking any more Notice of his House-keeper or of his Niece, stole out of the Village one Night, not so much as suspected by any Body, and made such haste, that by Break of Day they thought themselves out of Reach, should they happen to be pursued. As for *Sancho Pança*, he rode like a Patriarch, with his Canvas Knapsack, or Wallet, and his Leathern Bottle, having a huge Desire to see himself Governour of the Island, which his Master had promised him.

Don *Quixote* happen'd to strike into the same Road which he took the Time before, that is, the Plains of *Montiel*, over which he travell'd with less Inconveniency than when he went alone, by reason it was yet early in the Morning; at which Time the Sun-beams being almost parallel to the Surface of the Earth, and not directly darted down, as in the Middle of the Day, did not prove so offensive. As they jogg'd on, I beseech your Worship, Sir Knight-Errant, quoth *Sancho* to his Master, be sure you don't forget what you promis'd me about the Island; for I dare say I shall make shift to govern it, let it be never so big. You must know, Friend *Sancho*, reply'd *Don Quixote*, that it has been the constant Practice of Knight-Errants in former Ages, to make their Squires Governours of the Islands or Kingdoms they conquer'd: Now I am not only resolv'd to keep up that laudable Custom, but even to improve it, and outdo my Predecessors in Generosity: For whereas sometimes, or rather most commonly, other Knights delayed rewarding their Squires till they were grown old, and worn out with Service, bad Days, worse Nights, and all manner of hard Duty, and then put them off with some Title, either of Count, or at least Marquess of some Valley or Province, of great or small Extent; now, if thou and I do but live, it may happen, that before we have pass'd six Days together, I may conquer some Kingdom, having many other Kingdoms annexed to its Imperial Crown; and this would fall out most luckily for thee; for then would I presently crown thee King of one of them. Nor do thou imagine this to be a mighty Matter; for so strange Accidents and Revolutions, so sudden and so unforeseen, attend the Profession of Chivalry, that I might easily give thee a great deal more than I have promised. Why, should this come to pass, quoth *Sancho Pança*, and I be made a King by some such Miracle, as your Worship says, then happy be lucky, my *Whither-d'ye-go Mary Gutierez* wou'd be at least a Queen, and my Children Infantas and Princes, an't like your Worship. Who doubts of that? cry'd Don *Quixote*: I doubt of it, reply'd *Sancho Pança*; for I can't help believing, that though it should rain Kingdoms down upon the Face of the Earth, not one of them would sit well upon *Mary Gutierez's* Head; for I must needs tell you, she's not worth two Brass Jacks to make a Queen of: No, Countess would be better for her, an't please you; and that too, God help her, will be as much as she can handsomely manage. Re-commend the Matter to Providence, return'd Don *Quixote*, 'twill be sure to give what is most expedient for thee; but yet disdain to entertain inferiour Thoughts, and be not tempted to accept less than the Dignity of a Vice-Roy. No more I won't, Sir, quoth *Sancho*, especially since I have so rare a Master as your Worship, who will take care to give me whatever may be fit for me, and what I may be able to deal with.

VIII: OF THE GOOD SUCCESS WHICH THE VALOR-
OUS DON QUIXOTE HAD IN THE MOST TERRI-
FYING AND NEVER-TO-BE-IMAGIN'D ADVENTURE
OF THE WIND-MILLS, WITH OTHER TRANSAC-
TIONS WORTHY TO BE TRANSMITTED
TO POSTERITY

As they were thus discoursing, they discover'd some thirty or forty Wind-mills, that are in that Plain; and as soon as the Knight had spy'd them, Fortune, cry'd he, directs our Affairs better than we our selves could have wish'd: Look yonder, Friend *Sancho*, there are at least thirty outrageous Giants, whom I intend to encounter; and having depriv'd them of Life, we will begin to enrich our selves with their Spoils: For they are lawful Prize; and the Extirpation of that cursed Brood will be an acceptable Service to Heaven. What Giants, quoth *Sancho Pança*? Those whom thou see'st yonder, answer'd Don *Quixote*, with their long-extended Arms; some of that detested Race have Arms of so immense a Size, that sometimes they reach two Leagues in Length. Pray look better, Sir, quoth *Sancho*; those things yonder are no Giants, but Wind-mills, and the Arms you fancy, are their Sails, which being whirl'd about by the Wind, make the Mill go. 'Tis a Sign, cry'd Don *Quixote*, thou art but little acquainted with Adventures! I tell thee, they are Giants; and therefore if thou art afraid, go aside and say thy Prayers, for I am resolv'd to engage in a dreadful unequal Combat against them all. This said, he clapp'd Spurs to his Horse *Rozinante*, without giving Ear to his Squire *Sancho*, who bawl'd out to him, and assur'd him, that they were Wind-mills, and no Giants. But he was so fully possess'd with a strong Conceit of the contrary, that he did not so much as hear his Squire's Outcry, nor was he sensible of what they were, although he was already very near them: Far from that, Stand, Cowards, cry'd he as loud as he could; stand your Ground, ignoble Creatures, and fly not basely from a single Knight, who dares encounter you all. At the same Time the Wind rising, the Mill-Sails began to move, which, when Don *Quixote* spy'd, Base Miscreants, cry'd he, though you move more Arms than the Giant *Briareus*, you shall pay for your Arrogance. He most devoutly recommended himself to his Lady *Dulcinea*, imploring her Assistance in this perilous Adventure; and so covering himself with his Shield, and couching his Lance, he rush'd with *Rozinante's* utmost Speed upon the first Wind-mill he could come at, and running his Lance into the Sail, the Wind whirl'd it about with such Swiftness, that the Rapidity of the Motion presently broke the Lance into Shivers, and hurl'd away both Knight and Horse along with it, till down he fell rolling a good Way off in the Field. *Sancho Pança* ran as fast as his Ass could drive to help his Master, whom he found lying, and not able to stir, such a Blow he and *Rozinante* had receiv'd. Mercy o'me! cry'd *Sancho*, did not I give your Worship fair Warning? Did not I tell you they were Wind-mills, and that no Body could think otherwise, unless he had also Wind-mills in his Head? Peace, Friend *Sancho*, reply'd Don *Quixote*: There is nothing so subject to the Inconstancy of Fortune as War. I am verily perswaded, that cursed Necromancer *Freston*, who carry'd away my Study and my Books, has transform'd these Giants into Wind-mills, to deprive me of the Honour of the Victory; such is his inveterate Malice against me: But in the End, all his pernicious Wiles and Stratagems shall prove ineffectual against the prevailing Edge of my Sword. *Amen*, say I, reply'd *Sancho*; and so heaving him up again upon his Legs, once more the Knight mounted poor *Rozinante*, that was half Shoulder-slipp'd with his Fall.

This Adventure was the Subject of their Discourse, as they made the best of their Way towards the Pass of *Lapice*;* for Don *Quixote* took that Road, believing he could not miss of Adventures in one so mightily frequented. However, the Loss of his Lance was no small Affliction to him; and as he was making his Complaint about it to his Squire, I have read,

* *A Pass in the Mountains, such as they call* Puerto Seco, *a dry Port, where the King's Officers levy the Tolls and Customs upon Passengers and Goods.*

said he, Friend *Sancho*, that a certain *Spanish* Knight, whose
Name was *Diego Perez de Vargas*, having broken his Sword
in the Heat of an Engagement, pull'd up by the Roots a huge
Oak-Tree, or at least tore down a massy Branch, and did such
wonderful Execution, crushing and grinding so many *Moors*
with it that Day, that he won himself and his Posterity the
Sirname of *The Pounder*,* or *Bruiser*. I tell thee this, because
I intend to tear up the next Oak, or Holm-Tree we meet;
with the Trunk whereof I hope to perform such wondrous
Deeds, that thou wilt esteem thy self particularly happy in
having had the Honour to behold them, and been the ocular
Witness of Atchievements which Posterity will scarce be
able to believe. Heaven grant you may, cry'd *Sancho*: I believe it all, because your Worship says it. But, an't please
you, sit a little more upright in your Saddle; you ride sideling
methinks; but that, I suppose, proceeds from your being
bruis'd by the Fall. It does so, reply'd Don *Quixote*; and if I
do not complain of the Pain, 'tis because a Knight-Errant
must never complain of his Wounds, though his Bowels were
dropping out through 'em. Then I've no more to say, quoth
Sancho; and yet, Heaven knows my Heart, I shou'd be glad
to hear your Worship hone a little now and then when something ails you: For my Part, I shall not fail to bemoan my
self when I suffer the smallest Pain, unless indeed it can be
proved, that the Rule of not complaining extends to the
Squires as well as Knights. Don *Quixote* could not forbear
smiling at the Simplicity of his Squire; and told him, he gave
him Leave to complain not only when he pleas'd, but as
much as he pleas'd, whether he had any Cause or no; for he
had never yet read any thing to the contrary in any Books of
Chivalry. *Sancho* desir'd him, however, to consider, that
'twas high Time to go to Dinner; but his Master answer'd
him, that he might eat whenever he pleas'd; as for himself, he was not yet dispos'd to do it. *Sancho* having thus
obtain'd Leave, fix'd himself as orderly as he cou'd upon his
Ass; and taking some Victuals out of his Wallet, fell to mun-
ching lustily as he rode behind his Master; and ever and anon
he lifted his Bottle to his Nose, and fetch'd such hearty Pulls,

* Machuca, *from* Machucar, *to pound in a Mortar.*

that it would have made the best pamper'd Vintner in *Mal-aga* a-dry to have seen him. While he thus went on stuffing and swilling, he did not think in the least of all his Master's great Promises; and was so far from esteeming it a Trouble to travel in quest of Adventures, that he fancy'd it to be the greatest Pleasure in the World, though they were never so dreadful.

In fine, they pass'd that Night under some Trees; from one of which Don *Quixote* tore a wither'd Branch, which in some sort was able to serve him for a Lance, and to this he fix'd the Head or Spear of his broken Lance. But he did not sleep all that Night, keeping his Thoughts intent on his dear *Dulcinea*, in Imitation of what he had read in Books of Chivalry, where the Knights pass that Time, with-out Sleep, in Forests and Desarts, wholly taken up with the entertaining Thoughts of their absent Mistresses. As for *San-cho*, he did not spend the Night at that idle Rate; for having his Paunch well stuff'd with something more substantial than Dandelion-Water, he made but one Nap of it; and had not his Master wak'd him, neither the sprightly Beams which the Sun darted on his Face, nor the Melody of the Birds, that chearfully on every Branch welcom'd the smiling Morn, wou'd have been able to have made him stir. As he got up, to clear his Eye-sight, he took two or three long-winded Swigs at his friendly Bottle for a Morning's Draught: But he found it somewhat lighter than it was the Night before; which Misfortune went to his very Heart, for he shrewdly mistrusted that he was not in a way to cure it of that Dis-temper as soon as he could have wish'd. On the other side, Don *Quixote* wou'd not break Fast, having been feasting all Night on the more delicate and savoury Thoughts of his Mistress; and therefore they went on directly towards the Pass of *Lapice*, which they discover'd about Three a-Clock. When they came near it, Here it is, Brother *Sancho*, said Don *Quixote*, that we may wanton, and as it were, thrust our Arms up to the very Elbows, in that which we call Adven-tures. But let me give thee one necessary Caution; Know, that tho' thou should'st see me in the greatest Extremity of Danger, thou must not offer to draw thy Sword in my

Defence, unless thou findest me assaulted by base Plebeians and vile Scoundrels; for in such a Case thou may'st assist thy Master: But if those with whom I am fighting are Knights, thou must not do it; for the Laws of Chivalry do not allow thee to encounter a Knight, till thou art one thy self. Never fear, quoth *Sancho*; I'll be sure to obey your Worship in that, I'll warrant you; for I've ever lov'd Peace and Quietness, and never car'd to thrust my self into Frays and Quarrels: And yet I don't care to take Blows at any one's Hands neither; and shou'd any Knight offer to set upon me first, I fancy I shou'd hardly mind your Laws; for all Laws, whether of God or Man, allow one to stand in his own Defence if any offer to do him a Mischief. I agree to that, reply'd Don *Quixote*; but as for helping me against any Knights, thou must set Bounds to thy natural Impulses. I'll be sure to do it, quoth *Sancho*; ne'er trust me if I don't keep your Commandment as well as I do the Sabbath.

As they were talking, they spy'd coming towards them two Monks of the Order of St *Benedict* mounted on two Dromedaries, for the Mules on which they rode were so high and stately, that they seem'd little less. They wore Riding-Masks, with Glasses at the Eyes, against the Dust, and Umbrella's to shelter them from the Sun. After them came a Coach, with four or five Men on Horseback, and two Muleteers on Foot. There prov'd to be in the Coach a *Biscayan* Lady, who was going to *Seville* to meet her Husband, that was there in order to embark for the *Indies*, to take Possession of a considerable Post. Scarce had Don *Quixote* perceiv'd the Monks, who were not of the same Company, though they went the same Way, but he cry'd to his Squire, Either I am deceiv'd, or this will prove the most famous Adventure that ever was known; for without all question those two black Things that move towards us must be some Necromancers, that are carrying away by Force some Princess in that Coach; and 'tis my Duty to prevent so great an Injury. I fear me this will prove a worse Jobb than the Windmills, quoth *Sancho*. 'Slife, Sir, don't you see these are *Benedictin* Friars, and 'tis likely the Coach belongs to some Travellers that are in't: Therefore once more take Warning, and don't you be led away by the Devil. I have already told thee *Sancho*, reply'd Don *Quixote*, thou art miserably ignorant in Matters of Adventures: What I say is true, and thou shalt find it so presently. This said, he spurr'd on his Horse, and posted himself just in the midst of the Road where the Monks were to pass. And when they came within Hearing, Curs'd Implements of Hell, cry'd he in a loud and haughty Tone, immediately release those high-born Princesses whom you are violently conveying away in the Coach, or else prepare to meet with instant Death, as the just Punishment of your pernicious Deeds. The Monks stopp'd their Mules, no less astonish'd at the Figure, than at the Expressions of the Speaker. Sir Knight, cry'd they, we are no such Persons as you are pleas'd to term us, but religious Men, of the Order of St *Benedict*, that travel about our Affairs; and are wholly ignorant whether or no there are any Princesses carry'd away by Force in that Coach. I'm not to be deceiv'd with fair Words, reply'd Don *Quixote*; I know you well enough, perfidious Caitiffs; and immediately, without expecting their Reply, he set Spurs to *Rozinante*, and ran so furiously, with his Lance couch'd, against the first Monk, that if he had not prudently flung himself off to the Ground, the Knight wou'd certainly have laid him either dead, or grievously wounded. The other observing the discourteous Usage of his Companion, clapp'd his Heels to his over-grown Mule's Flanks, and scour'd o'er the Plain as if he had been running a Race with the Wind. *Sancho Pança* no sooner saw the Monk fall, but he nimbly skipp'd off his Ass, and running to him, began to strip him immediately. But then the two Muleteers, who waited on the Monks, came up to him, and ask'd why he offer'd to strip him? *Sancho* told them, that this belong'd to him as lawful Plunder, being the Spoils won in Battle by his Lord and Master Don *Quixote*. The Fellows, with whom there was no jesting, not knowing what he meant by his Spoils and Battle, and seeing Don *Quixote* at a good Distance in deep Discourse by the Side of the Coach, fell both upon poor *Sancho*, threw him down, tore his Beard from his Chin, trampled on his Guts, thump'd and maul'd him in every Part of his Carcase, and there left him sprawling without Breath or Motion. In the mean while the Monk, fear'd out of his Wits, and as pale as a Ghost, got upon his Mule again as fast as he cou'd, and spurr'd after his Friend, who staid for him at a Distance, expecting the Issue of this strange Adventure; but being unwilling to stay to see the End of it, they made the best of their Way, making more Signs of the Cross than if the Devil had been posting after them.

Don *Quixote*, as I said, was all that while engaged with the Lady in the Coach. Lady, cry'd he, your Discretion is now at Liberty to dispose of your beautiful self as you please; for the presumptuous Arrogance of those who attempted to enslave your Person lies prostrate in the Dust, overthrown by this my strenuous Arm: And that you may not be at a Loss for the Name of your Deliverer, know I am call'd Don *Quixote de la Mancha*, by Profession a Knight-Errant and Adventurer, Captive to that peerless Beauty Donna *Dulcinea del Toboso*: Nor do I desire any other Recompence for the Service I have done you, but that you return to *Toboso* to present your selves to that Lady, and let her know what I have done to purchase your Deliverance. To this strange Talk, a certain *Biscayan*, the Lady's Squire, Gentleman-Usher, or what you'll please to call him, who rode along with the Coach, listen'd with great Attention; and perceiving that Don *Quixote* not only stopp'd the Coach, but would have it presently go back to *Toboso*, he bore briskly up to him, and laying hold on his Lance, *Get gone*, cry'd he to him in bad *Spanish*, and worse *Biscayan*,* *Get gone thou Knight, and Devil go with thou; or by he who me create, if thou do not leave the Coach, me kill thee now so sure as me be a Biscayan.* Don *Quixote*, who made shift to understand him well enough, very calmly made him this Answer: Wert thou a Gentleman,† as thou art not, ere this I would have chastis'd thy Insolence and Temerity, thou inconsiderable Mortal. What! me no Gentleman? reply'd the *Biscayan*; I swear

---

* *The* Biscainers *generally speak broken* Spanish, *as is imitated in the Original; wherefore the* English *is render'd accordingly.* † Cavallero in Spanish *signifies a* Gentleman *as well as a* Knight; *and being here used, is to be suppos'd to have caus'd the Difference betwixt Don* Quixote *and the* Biscainer.

thou be Liar, as me be Christian. If thou throw away Lance,
and draw Sword, me will make no more of thee than Cat
does of Mouse: Me will shew thee me be *Biscayan*, and
Gentleman by Land, Gentleman by Sea, Gentleman in spite
of Devil; and thou lye if thou say contrary. I'll try Titles
with you, as the Man said, reply'd Don *Quixote*; and with
that throwing away his Lance, he drew his Sword, grasp'd
his Target, and attack'd the *Biscayan*, fully bent on his
Destruction. The *Biscayan* seeing him come on so furiously,
would gladly have alighted, not trusting to his Mule, which
was one of those scurvy Jades that are let out to Hire; but all
he had Time to do was only to draw his Sword, and snatch
a Cushion out of the Coach to serve him instead of a Shield;
and immediately they assaulted one another with all the
Fury of mortal Enemies. The By-standers did all they could
to prevent their Fighting; but 'twas in vain, for the *Biscayan*
swore in his Gibberish he would kill his very Lady, and all
those who presum'd to hinder him, if they would not let
him fight. The Lady in the Coach being extremely affrighted at these Passages, made her Coachman drive out of
Harm's-way, and at a Distance was an Eye-witness of the
furious Combat. At the same time the *Biscayan* let fall such
a mighty Blow on Don *Quixote's* Shoulder over his Target,
that had not his Armour been Sword-proof he would have
cleft him down to the very Waist. The Knight feeling the
Weight of that unmeasurable Blow, cry'd out aloud, Oh!
Lady of my Soul, *Dulcinea*! Flower of all Beauty, vouchsafe to succour your Champion in this dangerous Combat,
undertaken to set forth your Worth. The breathing out of
this short Prayer, the griping fast of his Sword, the covering of himself with his Shield, and the charging of his
Enemy, was but the Work of a Moment; for Don *Quixote*
was resolv'd to venture the Fortune of the Combat all upon
one Blow. The *Biscayan*, who read his Design in his dreadful Countenance, resolv'd to face him with equal Bravery,
and stand the terrible Shock, with up-lifted Sword, and
cover'd with the Cushion, not being able to manage his jaded
Mule, who defying the Spur, and not being cut out for such
Pranks, would move neither to the Right nor to the Left.

While Don *Quixote*, with his Sword aloft, was rushing upon the wary *Biscayan*, with a full Resolution to cleave him asunder, all the Spectators stood trembling with Terror and Amazement, expecting the dreadful Event of those prodigious Blows which threaten'd the two desperate Combatants: The Lady in the Coach, with her Women, were making a thousand Vows and Offerings to all the Images and Places of Devotion in *Spain*, that Providence might deliver them and the Squire out of the great Danger that threaten'd them.

But here we must deplore the abrupt End of this History, which the Author leaves off just at the very Point when the Fortune of the Battle is going to be decided, pretending that he could find nothing more recorded of Don *Quixote's* wondrous Atchievements than what he had already related. However, the second Undertaker of this Work could not believe, that so curious a History could lie for ever inevitably buried in Oblivion; or that the Learned of *La Mancha* were so regardless of their Country's Glory, as not to preserve in their Archives, or at least in their Closets, some Memoirs, as Monuments of this famous Knight; and therefore he wou'd not give over inquiring after the Continuation of this pleasant History, till at last he happily found it, as the next Book will inform the Reader.

Part I Book II

I: THE EVENT OF THE MOST STUPENDIOUS COMBAT BETWEEN THE BRAVE BIS-CAYAN AND THE VALOROUS DON QUIXOTE

IN the First Book of this History, we left the valiant *Biscayan* and the renowned Don *Quixote* with their Swords lifted up, and ready to discharge on each other two furious and most terrible Blows, which had they fall'n directly, and met with no Opposition, would have cut and divided the two Combatants from Head to Heel, and have split 'em like a Pomgranate: But, as I said before, the Story remain'd imperfect; neither did the Author inform us where we might find the remaining Part of the Relation. This vex'd me extremely, and turn'd the Pleasure, which the Perusal of the Beginning had afforded me, into Disgust, when I had Reason to despair of ever seeing the rest. Yet, after all, it seem'd to me no less impossible than unjust, that so valiant a Knight should have been destitute of some learned Person to record his incomparable Exploits; a Misfortune which never attended any of his Predecessors, I mean the Knights-Adventurers, each of whom was always provided with one or two learned Men, who were always at hand to write not only their wondrous Deeds, but also to set down their Thoughts and childish petty Actions, were they never so hidden. Therefore, as I could not imagine that so worthy a Knight should be so unfortunate, as to want that which has been so profusely lavish'd even on such a one as *Platyr*,* and others of that Stamp; I cou'd not induce my self to be-lieve, that so admirable a History was ever left unfinish'd, and rather chose to think that Time, the Devourer of all things, had hid or consum'd it. On the other Side, when I consider'd that several modern Books were found in his Study, as *The Cure of Jealousy*, and *The Nymphs and Shep-*

* *A second-rate Knight in* Palmerin *of* England.

herds of Henares, I had reason to think, that the History of our Knight could be of no very ancient Date; and that, had it never been continu'd, yet his Neighbours and Friends could not have forgot the most remarkable Passages of his Life. Full of this Imagination, I resolv'd to make it my Business to make a particular and exact Inquiry into the Life and Miracles of our renown'd *Spaniard*, Don *Quixote*, that refulgent Glory and Mirrour of the Knighthood of *La Mancha*, and the first who in these deprav'd and miserable Times devoted himself to the neglected Profession of Knight-Errantry, to redress Wrongs and Injuries, to relieve Widows, and defend the Honour of Damsels; such of them, I mean, who in former Ages rode up and down over Hills and Dales with Whip in Hand, mounted on their Palfreys, with all their Virginity about them, secure from all manner of Danger, and who, unless they happen'd to be ravish'd by some boistrous Villain or huge Giant, were sure, at fourscore Years of Age, (all which Time they never slept one Night under a Roof) to be decently lain in their Graves, as pure Virgins as the Mothers that bore 'em. For this Reason and many others, I say, our gallant Don *Quixote* is worthy everlasting and universal Praise: Nor ought I to be deny'd my due Commendation for my indefatigable Care and Diligence, in seeking and finding out the Continuation of this delightful History; though, after all, I must confess, that had not Providence, Chance, or Fortune, as I will now inform you, assisted me in the Discovery, the World had been depriv'd of two Hours Diversion and Pleasure, which 'tis likely to afford to those who will read it with Attention. One Day, being in the *Alcana*† at *Toledo*, I saw a young Lad offer to sell a Parcel of old written Papers to a Shopkeeper. Now I being apt to take up the least Piece of written or printed Papers that lies in my way, though 'twere in the Middle of the Street, cou'd not forbear laying my Hands

---

* *The River that runs through* Madrid, *says the Author of the new Translation: But he mistakes;* Henares *runs by the University of* Alcala (*i.e.* Complutum) *in* Old Castile, *and therefore much celebrated by* Spanish *Poets bred in that University. They call it* Henarius *in Latin.*

The River that runs by Madrid, *and which is in* New Castile, *is call'd* Manzanares, *in Lat.* Manzanarius.

† *An Exchange; a Place full of Shops.*

THE COMBAT WITH THE BISCAYAN

on one of the Manuscripts, to see what it was, and I found it
to be written in *Arabick*, which I cou'd not read. This made
me look about to see whether I cou'd find e'er a *Morisco**
that understood *Spanish*, to read it for me, and give me some
Account of it; nor was it very difficult to meet with an Interpreter there; for had I wanted one for a better and more
ancient Tongue,† that Place would have infallibly supply'd
me. 'Twas my good Fortune to find one immediately; and
having informed him of my Desire, he no sooner read some
Lines, but he began to laugh. I ask'd him what he laugh'd
at? At a certain Remark here in the Margin of the Book, said
he. I pray'd him to explain it; whereupon still laughing, he
did it in these Words: *This* Dulcinea del Toboso, *so often
mention'd in this History, is said to have had the best Hand
at salting of Pork of any Woman in all* La Mancha. I was
surprized when I heard him name *Dulcinea del Toboso*, and
presently imagin'd that those old Papers contain'd the History of Don *Quixote*. This made me press him to read the
Title of the Book; which he did, turning it thus *extempore*
out of *Arabick*; *The History of Don* Quixote de la Mancha;
written by Cid Hamet Benengeli, *an* Arabian *Historiographer*. I was so overjoy'd when I heard the Title, that I
had much ado to conceal it; and presently taking the Bargain
out of the Shop-keeper's Hand, I agreed with the young Man
for the Whole, and bought that for half a *Real*, which he
might have sold me for twenty times as much, had he but
guess'd at the Eagerness of his Chapman. I immediately
withdrew with my Purchase to the Cloister of the Great
Church, taking the *Moor* with me; and desir'd him to translate me all those Papers that treated of Don *Quixote*, without adding or omitting the least Word, offering him any
reasonable Satisfaction. He ask'd me but two *Arrobes*‡ of
Raisins, and two Bushels of Wheat, and promis'd me to do
it faithfully with all Expedition: In short, for the quicker
Dispatch, and the greater Security, being unwilling to let
such a lucky Prize go out of my Hands, I took the *Moor* to

* A Morisco *is one of the Race of the* Moors.   † *Meaning some* Jew,
to interpret the Hebrew *or* Chaldee.   ‡ *An* Arroba *is about* 32 lb.
Weight.

my own House, where in less than six Weeks he finish'd the whole Translation.

Don *Quixote's* Fight with the *Biscayan* was exactly drawn on one of the Leaves of the first Quire, in the same Posture as we left them, with their Swords lifted up over their Heads, the one guarding himself with his Shield, the other with his Cushion. The *Biscayan's* Mule was pictur'd so to the Life, that with half an Eye you might have known it to be an hir'd Mule. Under the *Biscayan* was written Don *Sancho de Aspetia*, and under *Rozinante* Don *Quixote*. *Rozinante* was so admirably delineated, so slim, so stiff, so lean, so jaded, with so sharp a Ridge-bone, and altogether so like one wasted with an incurable Consumption, that any one must have owned at first Sight, that no Horse ever better deserved that Name. Not far off stood *Sancho Pança*** holding his Ass by the Halter; at whose Feet there was a Scroll, in which was written *Sancho Canças*:† And if we may judge of him by his Picture, he was thick and short, paunch-belly'd, and long-haunch'd; so that in all likelihood for this Reason he is sometimes called *Pança* and sometimes *Cança* in the History. There were some other Niceties to be seen in that Piece, but hardly worth Observation, as not giving any Light into this true History, otherwise they had not pass'd unmention'd; for none can be amiss so they be authentick. I must only acquaint the Reader, that if any Objection is to be made as to the Veracity of this, 'tis only that the Author is an *Arabian*, and those of that Country are not a little addicted to Lying: But yet, if we consider that they are our Enemies, we shou'd sooner imagine, that the Author has rather suppress'd the Truth, than added to the real Worth of our Knight; and I am the more inclinable to think so, because 'tis plain, that where he ought to have enlarg'd on his Praises, he maliciously chooses to be silent; a Proceeding unworthy of an Historian, who ought to be exact, sincere, and impartial; free from Passion, and not to be biass'd either by Interest, Fear, Resentment, or Affection to deviate from Truth, which is the Mother of History, the Preserver and Eternizer of great Actions, the professed Enemy of Oblivion, the

* *Paunch.* † *Haunches, or rather Thigh-bones.*

Witness of Things pass'd, and the Director of future Times. As for this History, I know 'twill afford you as great Variety as you cou'd wish, in the most entertaining Manner; and if in any Point it falls short of your Expectation, I am of Opinion 'tis more the Fault of the Infidel* its Author, than the Subject: And so let us come to the Second Book, which, according to our Translation, began in this Manner.

Such were the bold and formidable Looks of the two enraged Combatants, that with up-lifted Arms, and with destructive Steel, they seem'd to threaten Heaven, Earth, and the infernal Mansions; while the Spectators seem'd wholly lost in Fear and Astonishment. The cholerick *Biscayan* discharg'd the first Blow, and that with such a Force, and so desperate a Fury, that had not his Sword turn'd in his Hand, that single Stroke had put an End to the dreadful Combat, and all our Knight's Adventures. But Fate, that reserv'd him for greater Things, so order'd it, that his Enemy's Sword turn'd in such a Manner, that tho' it struck him on the left Shoulder, it did him no other Hurt than to disarm that Side of his Head, carrying away with it a great Part of his Helmet and one Half of his Ear, which like a dreadful Ruin fell together to the Ground. Assist me ye Powers! But it is in vain: The Fury which then engross'd the Breast of our Heroe of *La Mancha* is not to be express'd; Words wou'd but wrong it; for what Colour of Speech can be lively enough to give but a slight Sketch or faint Image of his unutterable Rage? Exerting all his Valour, he rais'd himself upon his Stirrups, and seem'd even greater than himself; and at the same Instant griping his Sword fast with both Hands, he discharg'd such a tremendous Blow full on the *Biscayan's* Cushion and his Head, that in spite of so good a Defence, as if a whole Mountain had fallen upon him, the Blood gush'd out at his Mouth, Nose, and Ears, all at once; and he totter'd so in his Saddle, that he had fallen to the Ground immediately, had he not caught hold of the Neck of his Mule: But the dull Beast it self being rous'd out of its Stupidity with that terrible Blow, began to run about the Fields; and the

---

* Galgo in *the Original, which properly means a Grey-hound, but here it means any Dog. In* Spain *they call the Moors* Dogs.

Biscayan, having lost his Stirrups and his Hold, with two or three Winces the Mule shook him off, and threw him on the Ground. Don *Quixote* beheld the Disaster of his Foe with the greatest Tranquillity and Unconcern imaginable; and seeing him down, slipp'd nimbly from his Saddle, and running to him, set the Point of his Sword to his Throat, and bid him yield, or he would cut off his Head. The *Biscayan* was so stunn'd, that he could make him no Reply; and Don *Quixote* had certainly made good his Threats, so provok'd was he, had not the Ladies in the Coach, who with great Uneasiness and Fear beheld these sad Transactions, hasten'd to beseech Don *Quixote* very earnestly to spare his Life. Truly, beautiful Ladies, said the victorious Knight, with a great deal of Loftiness and Gravity, I am willing to grant your Request; but upon Condition that this same Knight shall pass his Word of Honour to go to *Toboso*, and there present himself in my Name before the peerless Lady *Donna Dulcinea*, that she may dispose of him as she shall see convenient. The Lady, who was frighted almost out of her Senses, without considering what Don *Quixote* enjoyn'd, or enquiring who the Lady *Dulcinea* was, promised in her Squire's Behalf a punctual Obedience to the Knight's Commands. Let him live then, reply'd Don *Quixote*, upon your Word, and owe to your Intercession that Pardon which I might justly deny his Arrogance.

SANCHO PANÇA was got up again before this, not much the better for the Kicks and Thumps bestow'd on his Carcase by the Monks Grooms; and seeing his Master engag'd in Fight, he went devoutly to Prayers, beseeching Heaven to grant him Victory, and that he might now win some Island, in order to his being made Governour of it, according to his Promise. At last, perceiving the Danger was over, the Combat at an End, and his Master ready to mount again, he ran in all Haste to help him; but ere the Knight put his Foot in the Stirrup, *Sancho* fell on his Knees before him, and kissing his Hand, An't please your Worship, cry'd he, my good Lord Don *Quixote*, I beseech you make me Governour of the Island you have won in this dreadful and bloody Fight; for tho' it were never so great, I find my self able to govern it as well as the best He that ever went about to govern an Island in this World. Brother *Sancho*, reply'd Don *Quixote*, these are no Adventures of Islands; these are only Rencounters on the Road, where little is to be got besides a broken Head, or the Loss of an Ear: Therefore have Patience, and some Adventure will offer it self, which will not only enable me to prefer thee to a Government, but even to something more considerable. *Sancho* gave him a World of Thanks; and having once more kiss'd his Hand, and the Skirts of his Coat of Armour, he help'd him to get upon *Rozinante*; and then leaping on his Ass, he follow'd the Heroe, who, without taking Leave of those in the Coach, put on a good round Pace, and rode into a Wood, that was not far off. *Sancho* made after him as fast as his Ass wou'd trot; but finding that *Rozinante* was like to leave him behind, he was forc'd to call to his Master to stay for him. Don *Quixote* accordingly check'd his Horse, and soon gave *Sancho* Leisure to overtake him. Methinks, Sir, said the fearful Squire, as soon as he came up with him, it won't be amiss for us to betake our selves to some Church, to get out of Harm's-way;

for if that same Man whom you've fought with should do otherwise than well, I dare lay my Life they'll get a Warrant from the holy Brotherhood,* and have us taken up; which if they do, on my Word 'twill go hard with us ere we can get out of their Clutches. Hold thy Tongue, cry'd Don *Quixote*: Where didst thou ever read, or find that a Knight-Errant was ever brought before any Judge for the Homicides which he committed? I can't tell what you mean by your *Homilies*, repl'yd *Sancho*; I don't know that ever I saw one in my born Days, not I: But well I wot, that the Law lays hold on those that goes to murder one another in the Fields; and as for your what d'ye call 'ems, I've nothing to say to 'em. Then be not afraid, good *Sancho*, cry'd Don *Quixote*; for I wou'd deliver thee out of the Hands of the *Chaldeans*, and with much more Ease out of those of the holy Brotherhood. But come, tell me truly, Dost thou believe that the whole World can boast of another Knight that may pretend to rival me in Valour? Didst thou ever read in History, that any other ever shew'd more Resolution to undertake, more Vigour to attack, more Breath to hold out, more Dexterity and Activity to strike, and more Art and Force to overthrow his Enemies? Not I, by my Troth, reply'd *Sancho*, I never did meet with any Thing like you in History, for I neither can read nor write; but that which I dare wager is, That I never in my Life serv'd a bolder Master than your Worship: Pray Heaven this same Boldness mayn't bring us to what I bid you beware of. All I've to put you in mind of now is, that you get your Ear dress'd, for you lose a deal of Blood; and by good Luck I've here some Lint and a little white Salve in my Wallet. How needless would all this have been, cry'd Don *Quixote*, had I but bethought my self of making a small Bottle full of the Balsam of *Fierabrass*? a single Drop of which would have spar'd us a great deal of Time and Medicaments. What is that same Balsam, an't please you? cry'd *Sancho*. A Balsam, answer'd Don *Quixote*, of which I've the Receipt in my Head; he that has some of it may defy Death it self, and dally with all manner of Wounds: Therefore when I have

---

* *An Institution spread thro' all* Spain, *to suppress Robbers, and make the Roads safe to Travellers.*

made some of it, and given it thee, if at any Time thou
happen'st to see my Body cut in two by some unlucky Back-
stroke, as 'tis common among us Knights-Errant, thou hast
no more to do but to take up nicely that Half of me which
is fall'n to the Ground, and clap it exactly to the other Half
on the Saddle before the Blood's congeal'd, always taking
care to lay it just in its proper Place; then thou shalt give
me two Draughts of that Balsam, and thou shalt immediately
see me become whole, and sound as an Apple. If this be true,
quoth *Sancho*, I'll quit you of your Promise about the Island
this Minute of an Hour, and will have nothing of your Worship for what Service I have done, and am to do you, but
the Receipt of that same Balsam; for, I dare say, let me go
wherever I will, 'twill be sure to yield me three good *Reals*
an Ounce; and thus I shall make shift to pick a pretty good
Livelihood out of it. But stay though, continu'd he, does the
Making stand your Worship in much, Sir? Three Quarts of
it, reply'd Don *Quixote*, may be made for less than three
Reals. Body of me, cry'd *Sancho*, why don't you make some
out of Hand, and teach me how to make it? Say no more,
Friend *Sancho*, return'd Don *Quixote*; I intend to teach thee
much greater Secrets, and design thee nobler Rewards; but
in the mean time dress my Ear, for it pains me more than
I could wish. *Sancho* then took his Lint and Ointment out
of his Wallet; but when Don *Quixote* perceived the Vizor
of his Helmet was broken, he had like to have run stark-
staring mad; straight laying hold on his Sword, and lifting
up his Eyes to Heaven, By the Great Creator of the Universe,
cry'd he, by every Syllable contain'd in the Four holy Even-
gelists, I swear to lead a Life like the Great Marquess of
Mantua, when he made a Vow to revenge the Death of his
Cousin *Baldwin*, which was, never to eat Bread on a Table-
cloth, never to lie with the dear Partner of his Bed, and
other Things, which, though they are now at present slipp'd
out of my Memory, I comprize in my Vow no less than if I
had now mention'd 'em; and this I bind my self to, till I have
fully reveng'd my self on him that has done me this Injury.

Good your Worship, cry'd *Sancho*, (amaz'd to hear him
take such a horrid Oath) think on what you're doing; for if

that same Knight has done as you bid him, and has gone
and cast himself before my Lady *Dulcinea del Toboso*, I don't
see but you and he are quit; and the Man deserves no further Punishment, unless he does you some new Mischief.
'Tis well observ'd, reply'd Don *Quixote*; and therefore as
to the Point of Revenge, I revoke my Oath; but I renew and
confirm the rest, protesting solemnly to lead the Life I mention'd, 'till I have by Force of Arms despoil'd some Knight
of as good a Helmet as mine was. Neither do thou fansy,
Sancho, that I make this Protestation lightly, or make a
Smoke of Straw: No, I have a laudable Precedent for it, the
Authority of which will sufficiently justify my Imitation; for
the very same thing happen'd about *Mambrino's* Helmet,
which cost *Sacripante* so dear.* Good Sir, quoth *Sancho*,
let all such Cursing and Swearing go to the Devil; there's
nothing can be worse for your Soul's Health, nay for your
Bodily Health neither. Besides, suppose we should not this
good while meet any one with a Helmet on, what a sad Case
should we then be in? Will your Worship then keep your
Oath in spite of so many Hardships, such as to lie rough for
a Month together, far from any inhabited Place, and a thousand other idle Penances which that mad old Marquess of
Mantua punish'd himself with by his Vow. Do but consider,
that we may ride I don't know how long upon this Road
without meeting any arm'd Knight to pick a Quarrel with;
for here are none but Carriers and Waggoners, who are so
far from wearing any Helmets, that 'tis ten to one whether
they ever heard of such a Thing in their Lives. Thou art
mistaken, Friend *Sancho*, reply'd Don *Quixote*; for we shall
not be two Hours this Way without meeting more Men in
Arms than there were at the Siege of *Albraca*, to carry off
the fair *Angelica*.† Well then, let it be so, quoth *Sancho*;
and may we have the Luck to come off well, and quickly win
that Island which costs me so dear, and then I don't matter
what befalls me. I have already bid thee not trouble thy
self about this Business, *Sancho*, said Don *Quixote*; for shou'd
we miss of an Island, there is either the Kingdom of *Den-*

* *The Story is in* Ariosto's Orlando Furioso. † *Meaning King* Marsilio,
and the Thiry-two Kings his Tributaries, with all their Forces. Ariosto.

mark, or that of *Sobradisa,** as fit for thy Purpose as a Ring to thy Finger; and what ought to be no small Comfort to thee, they are both upon *Terra Firma.*† But we'll talk of this in its proper Season: At this Time I'd have thee see whether thou hast any thing to eat in thy Wallet, that we may afterwards seek for some Castle, where we may lodge this Night, and make the Balsam I told thee; for I protest my Ear smarts extremely. I have here an Onion, reply'd the Squire, a Piece of Cheese, and a few stale Crusts of Bread; but sure such coarse Fare is not for such a brave Knight as your Worship. Thou art grosly mistaken, Friend *Sancho,* answer'd Don *Quixote:* Know, that 'tis the Glory of Knights-Errant to be whole Months without Eating: and when they do, they fall upon the first Thing they meet with, though it be never so homely. Hadst thou but read as many Books as I have done, thou hadst been better inform'd as to that Point; for tho' I think I have read as many Histories of Chivalry in my Time as any other Man, I never cou'd find that the Knights-Errant ever eat, unless it were by meer Accident, or when they were invited to great Feasts and royal Banquets; at other Times they indulg'd themselves with little other Food besides their Thoughts. Though it is not to be imagin'd they could live without supplying the Exigencies of human Nature, as being after all no more than mortal Men, yet 'tis likewise to be suppos'd, that as they spent the greatest Part of their Lives in Forests and Desarts, and always destitute of a Cook, consequently their usual Food was but such coarse Country Fare as thou now offerest me. Never then make thy self uneasy about what pleases me, Friend *Sancho,* nor pretend to make a new World, nor to unhinge the very Constitution and ancient Customs of Knight-Errantry. I beg your Worship's Pardon, cry'd *Sancho*; for as I was never bred a Scholar, I may chance to have miss'd in some main Point of your Laws of Knighthood; but from this Time forward I'll be sure to stock my Wallet with all Sorts of dry Fruits for you, because your Worship's a Knight; as for

* *A fictitious Kingdom* in Amadis de Gaul.   † *In Allusion to the famous* Firm Island, in Amadis de Gaul, *the Land of Promise to the faithful Squires of Knights-Errant.*

my self, who am none, I'll provide good Poultry and other substantial Victuals. I don't say, *Sancho*, reply'd Don *Quixote*, that a Knight-Errant is oblig'd to feed altogether upon Fruit; I only mean, that this was their common Food, together with some Roots and Herbs, which they found up and down the Fields, of all which they had a perfect Knowledge, as I my self have. 'Tis a good Thing to know those Herbs, cry'd *Sancho*; for I am much mistaken, or that kind of Knowledge will stand us in good stead ere long. In the mean time, continu'd he, here's what good Heaven has sent us: With that he pull'd out the Provision he had, and they fell to heartily together. But their Impatience to find out a Place where they might be harbour'd that Night, made 'em shorten their sorry Meal, and mount again, for fear of being benighted: So away they put on in Search of a Lodging. But the Sun and their Hopes fail'd them at once, as they came to a Place where some Goat-herds had set up some small Huts; and therefore they concluded to take up their Lodging there that Night. This was as great a Mortification to *Sancho*, who was altogether for a good Town, as it was a Pleasure to his Master, who was for sleeping in the open Field, as believing, that as often as he did it, he confirm'd his Title to Knighthood by a new Act of Possession.

III: WHAT PASS'D BETWEEN DON QUIXOTE
AND THE GOAT-HERDS

THE Knight was very courteously receiv'd by the
Goat-herds; and as for *Sancho*, after he had set
up *Rozinante* and his Ass as well as he cou'd,
he presently repair'd to the attractive Smell of
some Pieces of Kid's Flesh which stood boiling in
a Kettle over the Fire. The hungry Squire wou'd
immediately have try'd whether they were fit to be remov'd
out of the Kettle into the Stomach, but was not put to that
Trouble; for the Goat-herds took 'em off the Fire, and spread
some Sheep-skins on the Ground, and soon got their rural
Feast ready; and chearfully invited his Master and him to
partake of what they had. Next, with some coarse Compliment, after the Country way, they desir'd Don *Quixote* to
sit down on a Trough with the Bottom upwards; and then
six of 'em, who were all that belong'd to that Fold, squatted
'em down round the Skins, while *Sancho* stood to wait upon
his Master, and give him Drink in a Horn-Cup, which the
Goat-herds us'd. But he seeing his Man stand behind, said
to him, That thou may'st understand, *Sancho*, the Benefits
of Knight-Errantry, and how the meanest Retainers to it
have a fair Prospect of being speedily esteem'd and honour'd
by the World, 'tis my Pleasure that thou sit thee down by
me, in the Company of these good People; and that there
be no Difference now observ'd between thee and me, thy
natural Lord and Master; that thou eat in the same Dish,
and drink in the same Cup: For it may be said of Knight-
Errantry, as of Love, that it makes all Things equal. I thank
your Worship, cry'd *Sancho*; but yet I must needs own, had
I but a good deal of Meat before me, I'd eat it as well, or
rather better, standing, and by my self, than if I sat by an
Emperor; and, to deal plainly and truly with you, I had rather
munch a Crust of brown Bread and an Onion in a Corner,
without any more a-do or Ceremony, than feed upon Turkey
at another Man's Table, where one is fain to sit mincing and
chewing his Meat an Hour together, drink little, be always
wiping his Fingers and his Chops, and never dare to cough

nor sneeze, though he has never so much a Mind to it, nor do a many things which a Body may do freely by one's self: Therefore, good Sir, change those Tokens of your Kindness, which I have a Right to by being your Worship's Squire, into something that may do me more Good. As for these same Honours, I heartily thank you as much as if I had accepted 'em, but yet I give up my Right to 'em from this Time to the World's End. Talk no more, reply'd Don *Quixote*, but sit thee down, for the Humble shall be exalted; and so pulling him by the Arms, he forc'd him to sit by him.

All this while the Goat-herds, who did not understand this Jargon of Knights-Errant, Chivalry, and Squires, fed heartily, and said nothing, but star'd upon their Guests; who very fairly swallow'd whole Luncheons as big as their Fists with a mighty Appetite. The first Course being over, they brought in the second, consisting of dry'd Acorns, and half a Cheese as hard as a Brick: Nor was the Horn idle all the while, but went merrily round up and down so many times, sometimes full, and sometimes empty, like the two Buckets of a Well, that they made shift at last to drink off one of the two Skins of Wine which they had there. And now Don *Quixote* having satisfy'd his Appetite, he took a Handful of Acorns, and looking earnestly upon 'em; O happy Age, cry'd he, which our first Parents call'd the Age of Gold! not because Gold, so much ador'd in this Iron-Age, was then easily pur-chas'd, but because those two fatal Words, Mine and Thine, were Distinctions unknown to the People of those fortunate Times; for all Things were in common in that holy Age: Men, for their Sustenance, needed only to lift their Hands, and take it from the sturdy Oak, whose spreading Arms liberally invited them to gather the wholsome savoury Fruit; while the clear Springs, and silver Rivulets, with luxuriant Plenty, offer'd them their pure refreshing Water. In hollow Trees, and in the Clefts of Rocks, the labouring and industrious Bees erected their little Commonwealths, that Men might reap with Pleasure and with Ease the sweet and fertile Harvest of their Toils. The tough and strenuous Cork-Trees did of themselves, and without other Art than their native Liber-ality, dismiss and impart their broad light Bark, which serv'd to cover those lowly Huts, propp'd up with rough-hewn Stakes, that were first built as a Shelter against the Inclemencies of the Air: All then was Union, all Peace, all Love and Friendship in the World: As yet no rude Plough-share presum'd with Violence to pry into the pious Bowels of our Mother Earth, for she without Compulsion kindly yielded from every Part of her fruitful and spacious Bosom, whatever might at once satisfy, sustain and indulge her frugal Children. Then was the Time when innocent beautiful young Shepherdesses went tripping o'er the Hills and Vales: Their lovely Hair sometimes plaited, sometimes loose and flowing, clad in no other Vestment but what was necessary to cover decently what Modesty would always have conceal'd: The *Tyrian* Die, and the rich glossy Hue of Silk, martyr'd and dissembled into every Colour, which are now esteem'd so fine and magnificent, were unknown to the innocent Plainness of that Age; yet bedeck'd with more becoming Leaves and Flowers, they may be said to outshine the proudest of the vain-dressing Ladies of our Age, array'd in the most magnificent Garbs and all the most sumptuous Adornings which Idleness and Luxury have taught succeeding Pride: Lovers then express'd the Passion of their Souls in the unaffected Language of the Heart, with the native Plainness and Sincerity in which they were conceiv'd, and divested of all that artificial Contexture, which enervates what it labours to enforce: Imposture, Deceit and Malice had not yet crept in, and impos'd themselves unbrib'd upon Mankind in the Disguise of Truth and Simplicity: Justice, unbiass'd either by Favour or Interest, which now so fatally pervert it, was equally and impartially dispensed; nor was the Judges Fancy Law, for then there were neither Judges, nor Causes to be judg'd; the modest Maid might walk where-ever she pleas'd alone, free from the Attacks of lewd lascivious Importuners. But in this degenerate Age, Fraud and a Legion of Ills infecting the World, no Virtue can be safe, no Honour be secure; while wanton Desires, diffus'd into the Hearts of Men, corrupt the strictest Watches, and the closest Retreats; which, though as intricate and unknown as the Labyrinth of *Crete*, are no Security for Chastity. Thus that Primitive Innocence

84

being vanish'd, and Oppression daily prevailing, there was a Necessity to oppose the Torrent of Violence: For which Reason the Order of Knighthood-Errant was instituted, to defend the Honour of Virgins, protect Widows, relieve Orphans, and assist all the Distress'd in general. Now I my self am one of this Order, honest Friends; and though all People are oblig'd by the Law of Nature to be kind to Persons of My Order; yet since you, without knowing any thing of this Obligation, have so generously entertain'd me, I ought to pay you my utmost Acknowledgment; and, accordingly, return you my most hearty Thanks for the same.

All this long Oration, which might very well have been spar'd, was owing to the Acorns that recall'd the Golden Age to our Knight's Remembrance, and made him thus hold forth to the Goat-herds, who devoutly listen'd, but edify'd little, the Discourse not being suited to their Capacities. *Sancho*, as well as they, was silent all the while, eating Acorns, and frequently visiting the second Skin of Wine, which for Coolness-sake was hung upon a neighbouring Cork-Tree. As for Don *Quixote*, he was longer, and more intent upon his Speech than upon his Supper. When he had done, one of the Goat-herds addressing himself to him, Sir Knight, said he, that you may be sure you are heartily welcome, we'll get one of our Fellows to give us a Song; he is just a coming: A good notable young Lad he is, I'll say that for him, and up to the Ears in Love. He's a Scholard, and can read and write; and plays so rarely upon the *Rebeck*,* that 'tis a Charm but to hear him. No sooner were the Words out of the Goat-herd's Mouth, but they heard the Sound of the Instrument he spoke of, and presently appear'd a good comely young Man of about two and twenty Years of Age. The Goat-herds ask'd him if he had supp'd? and he having told them he had, Then, dear *Antonio*, says the first Speaker, pr'ythee sing us a Song, to let this Gentleman, our Guest, see that we have those among us who know somewhat of Musick, for all we live amidst Woods and Mountains. We have told him of thee already; therefore pr'ythee make our Words good, and sing us the Ditty thy Uncle the Pre-

* *A Fiddle, with only three Strings, us'd by Shepherds.*

bendary made of thy Love, that was so liked in our Town.
With all my Heart, reply'd *Antonio*; and so without any
further Intreaty, sitting down on the Stump of an Oak, he
tun'd his Fiddle, and very handsomely sung the following
Song.

ANTONIO'S AMOROUS COMPLAINT

Tho' Love ne'er prattles at your Eyes,
(The Eyes those silent Tongues of Love)
Yet sure, Olalia, *you're my Prize:*
For Truth, with Zeal, ev'n Heaven can move.

I think, my Love you only try,
Ev'n while I fear you've seal'd my Doom:
So, though involv'd in Doubts I lie,
Hope sometimes glimmers thro' the Gloom.

A Flame so fierce, so bright, so pure,
No Scorn can quench, or Art improve:
Thus like a Martyr I endure;
For there's a Heaven to crown my Love.

In Dress and Dancing I have strove
My proudest Rivals to outvy.
In Serenades I've breath'd my Love,
When all Things slept but Love and I.

I need not add, I speak your Praise
Till every Nymph's Disdain I move:
Tho' thus a thousand Foes I raise,
'Tis sweet to praise the Fair I love.

Teresa *once your Charms debas'd,*
But I her Rudeness soon reprov'd:
In vain her Friend my Anger fac'd;
For then I fought for her I lov'd.

Dear cruel Fair, why then so coy?
How can you so much Love withstand?
Alas! I crave no lawless Joy,
But with my Heart would give my Hand.

Soft, easy, strong is Hymen's *Tye:*
Oh! then no more the Bliss refuse.
Oh! wed me, or I swear to die,
Or linger wretched and recluse.

Here *Antonio* ended his Song; Don *Quixote* intreated him to sing another, but *Sancho Pança*, who had more mind to sleep than to hear the finest Singing in the World, told his Master, there is enough. Good Sir, quoth he, your Worship had better go and lie down where you are to take your Rest this Night; besides, these good People are tir'd with their Day's Labour, and rather want to go to sleep, than to sit up all Night to hear Ballads. I understand thee, *Sancho*, cry'd Don *Quixote*; and indeed I thought thy frequent visiting the Bottle would make thee fonder of Sleep than of Musick. Make us thankful, cry'd *Sancho*, we all lik'd the Wine well enough. I do not deny it, reply'd Don *Quixote*; but go thou and lay thee down where thou pleasest; as for me, it better becomes a Man of my Profession to wake than to sleep: Yet stay and dress my Ear before thou goest, for it pains me extremely. Thereupon one of the Goat-herds beholding the Wound, as *Sancho* offer'd to dress it, desir'd the Knight not to trouble himself, for he had a Remedy that would quickly cure him; and then fetching a few Rosemary Leaves, which grew in great plenty thereabout, he bruis'd them, and mix'd a little Salt among 'em, and having apply'd the Medicine to the Ear, he bound it up, assuring him, he needed no other Remedy; which in a little time prov'd very true.

IV: THE STORY WHICH A YOUNG GOAT-
HERD TOLD TO THOSE THAT WERE
WITH DON QUIXOTE

A YOUNG Fellow, who us'd to bring 'em Provisions from the next Village, happen'd to come while this was doing, and addressing himself to the Goat-herds, Hark ye, Friends, said he, d'ye hear the News? What News, cry'd one of the Company? That fine Shepherd and Scholar *Chrysostome* dy'd this Morning, answer'd the other; and they say 'twas for Love of that devilish untoward Lass *Marcella*, rich *William's* Daughter, that goes up and down the Country in the Habit of a Shepherdess. For *Marcella*, cry'd one of the Goat-herds? I say for her, reply'd the Fellow, and what's more, 'tis reported, he had order'd by his Will, they should bury him in the Fields like any Heathen *Moor*, just at the Foot of the Rock, hard by the Cork-Tree-Fountain, where they say he had the first Sight of her. Nay, he has likewise order'd many other strange Things to be done, which the Heads of the Parish won't allow of, for they seem to be after the Way of the Pagans. But *Ambrose*, the other Scholar, who likewise apparell'd himself like a Shepherd, is resolv'd to have his Friend *Chrysostome's* Will fulfill'd in every Thing, just as he has order'd it. All the Village is in an Uproar. But after all, 'tis thought *Ambrose* and his Friends will carry the Day; and to Morrow Morning he is to be buried in great State where I told you: I fancy 'twill be worth seeing; howsoever, be it what it will, I'll e'en go and see it, even tho' I could not get back again to Morrow. We'll all go, cry'd the Goat-herds, and cast Lots who shall tarry to look after the Goats. Well said, *Peter*, cry'd one of the Goat-herds; but as for casting of Lots, I'll save you that Labour, for I'll stay my self, not so much out of Kindness to you neither, or want of Curiosity, as because of the Thorn in my Toe, that will not let me go. Thank you, however, quoth *Peter*. Don *Quixote*, who heard all this, intreated *Peter* to tell him who the Deceased was, and also to give him a short Account of the Shepherdess.

Peter made answer, That all he knew of the Matter was, That the Deceased was a wealthy Gentleman, who lived not far off, that he had been several Years at the University of *Salamanca*, and then came home mightily improv'd in his Learning. But above all, quoth he, 'twas said of him, that he had great Knowledge in the Stars, and whatsoever the Sun and Moon do in the Skies; for he would tell us to a tittle the Clip of the Sun and Moon. We call it an Eclipse, cry'd Don *Quixote*, and not a Clip, when either of those two great Luminaries are darken'd. He wou'd also (continu'd *Peter*, who did not stand upon such nice Distinctions) foretel when the Year wou'd be plentiful or *estil*. You wou'd say *steril*, cry'd Don *Quixote*, *Steril* or *Estil*, reply'd the Fellow, that's all one to me: But this I say, that his Parents and Friends, being rul'd by him, grew woundy rich in a short Time; for he would tell 'em, This Year sow Barley, and no Wheat: In this you may sow Pease, and no Barley: Next Year will be a good Year for Oil: The three after that, you shan't gather a Drop; and whatsoever he said wou'd certainly come to pass. That Science, said Don *Quixote*, is call'd Astrology. I don't know what you call it, answer'd *Peter*, but I know he knew all this, and a deal more. But, in short, within some few Months after he had left the Versity, on a certain Morning we saw him come dress'd for all the World like a Shepherd, and driving his Flock, having laid down the long Gown, which he us'd to wear as a Scholar. At the same time one *Ambrose*, a great Friend of his, who had been his Fellow-Scholar also, took upon him to go like a Shepherd, and keep him Company, which we all did not a little marvel at. I had almost forgot to tell you how he that's dead was a mighty Man for making of Verses, insomuch that he commonly made the *Carols* which we sung on *Christmas-Eve*; and the Plays which the young Lads in our Neighbourhood enacted on *Corpus Christi* Day, and every one wou'd say, that no body cou'd mend 'em. Somewhat before that Time *Chrysostome's* Father died, and left him a deal of Wealth, both in Land, Money, Cattle, and other Goods, whereof the young Man remain'd dissolute Master; and in troth he deserv'd it all, for he was as good-natur'd a Soul as e'er trod on Shoe of

Leather; mighty good to the Poor, a main Friend to all
honest People, and had a Face like a Blessing. At last it came
to be known, that the Reason of his altering his Garb in
that Fashion, was only that he might go up and down after
that Shepherdess *Marcella*, whom our Comrade told you of
before, for he was fallen mightily in love with her. And
now I'll tell you such a thing you never heard the like in
your born Days, and may'nt chance to hear of such another
while you breathe, tho' you were to live as long as *Sarnah*.
Say *Sarah*, cry'd Don *Quixote*; who hated to hear him
blunder thus. The *Sarna*, or the *Itch*, (for that's all one
with us, quoth *Peter*) lives long enough too; but if you go
on thus, and make me break off my Tale at every Word,
we an't like to have done this Twelve-month. Pardon me,
Friend, reply'd Don *Quixote*; I only spoke to make thee
understand that there's a Difference between *Sarna* and
Sarah: However, thou say'st well; for the *Sarna* (that is,
the *Itch*) lives longer than *Sarah*; therefore pray make an
end of thy Story, for I will not interrupt thee any more.
Well then, quoth *Peter*, you must know, good Master of
mine, that there liv'd near us one *William*, a Yeoman, who
was richer yet than *Chrysostome's* Father; now he had no
Child in the versal World but a Daughter; her Mother dy'd
in Child-bed of her (rest her Soul) and was as good a Woman
as ever went upon two Legs: Methinks I see her yet standing
afore me, with that bless'd Face of hers, the Sun on one
Side, and the Moon on the t'other. She was a main House-
wife, and did a deal of good among the Poor; for which I
dare say she is at this Minute in Paradise. Alas! her Death
broke old *William's* Heart, he soon went after her, poor
Man, and left all to his little Daughter, that *Marcella* by
Name, giving charge of her to her Uncle, the Parson of our
Parish. Well, the Girl grew such a fine Child, and so like
her Mother, that it us'd to put us in mind of her every Foot:
However, 'twas thought she'd make a finer Woman yet;
and so it happen'd indeed; for, by that Time she was Fourteen or Fifteen Years of Age, no Man set his Eyes on her,
that did not bless Heaven for having made her so handsome;
so that most Men fell in Love with her, and were ready to

run mad for her. All this while her Uncle kept her up very
close: Yet the Report of her great Beauty and Wealth spread
far and near, insomuch, that she had I don't know how many
Sweet-hearts, almost all the young Men in our Town ask'd
her of her Uncle; nay, from I don't know how many Leagues
about us, there flock'd whole Droves of Suitors, and the
very best in the Country too, who all begg'd and su'd, and
teaz'd her Uncle to let them have her. But though he'd have
been glad to have got fairly rid of her, as soon as she was
fit for a Husband, yet wou'd not he advise or marry her
against her Will; for he's a good Man, I'll say that for him,
and a true Christian every Inch of him, and scorns to keep
her from marrying to make a Benefit of her Estate; and, to
his Praise be it spoken, he has been mainly commended for't
more than once, when the People of our Parish meet together. For I must tell you, Sir Errant, that here in the
Country, and in our little Towns, there's not the least Thing
can be said or done, but People will talk and find Fault: But
let Busy-bodies prate as they please, the Parson must have
been a good Body indeed, who cou'd bring his whole Parish
to give him a good Word, especially in the Country. Thou'rt
in the right, cry'd Don *Quixote*, and therefore go on, honest
Peter, for the Story is pleasant, and thou tell'st it with a
Grace. May I never want God's Grace, quoth *Peter*, for that's
most to the Purpose. But for our Parson, as I told you before,
he was not for keeping his Niece from Marrying, and therefore he took care to let her know of all those that wou'd
have taken her to Wife, both what they were, and what
they had, and he was at her, to have her pitch upon one
of 'em for a Husband; yet wou'd she never answer otherwise, but that she had no mind to wed as yet, as finding
her self too young for the Burden of Wedlock. With these
and such like Come-offs, she got her Uncle to let her alone,
and wait till she thought fit to choose for her self: For
he was wont to say, That Parents are not to bestow their
Children where they bear no liking; and in that he spoke
like an honest Man. And thus it happen'd, that when we
least dreamt of it, that coy Lass, finding her self at Liberty,
wou'd needs turn Shepherdess, and neither her Uncle, nor

all those of the Village who advis'd her against it, cou'd
work any Thing upon her, but away she went to the Fields
to keep her own Sheep with the other young Lasses of the
Town. But then 'twas ten times worse; for no sooner was
she seen abroad, when I can't tell how many spruce Gallants,
both Gentlemen and rich Farmers, chang'd their Garb for
Love of her, and follow'd her up and down in Shepherd's
Guise. One of 'em, as I have told you, was this same *Chrysostome*, who now lies dead, of whom 'tis said, he not only
lov'd, but worshipp'd her. Howsoever, I wou'd not have
you think or surmise, because *Marcella* took that Course of
Life, and was as it were under no manner of keeping, that
she gave the least Token of Naughtiness or light Behaviour;
for she ever was, and is still so coy, and so watchful to keep
her Honour pure and free from evil Tongues, that among
so many Wooers who suitor her, there's not one can make
his brags of having the least hope of ever speeding with her.
For though she does not shun the Company of Shepherds,
but uses 'em courteously, so far as they behave themselves
handsomly; yet whensoever any one of them does but offer
to break his Mind to her, be it never so well meant, and
only in order to marry, she casts him away from her, as
with a Sling, and will never have any more to say to him.

And thus this fair Maiden does more harm in this Country,
than the Plague wou'd do; for her Courteousness and fair
Looks draw-on every body to love her; but then her dogged
stubborn Coyness breaks their Hearts, and makes 'em ready
to hang themselves; and all they can do, poor Wretches, is to
make a heavy Complaint, and call her cruel, unkind, ungrateful, and a World of such Names, whereby they plainly
shew what a sad Condition they are in: Were you but to
stay here some Time, you'd hear these Hills and Vallies
ring again with the doleful Moans of those she has deny'd,
who yet can't for the Blood of 'em give over sneaking after
her. We have a Place not far off, where there are some
two Dozen of Beech-trees, and on 'em all you may find I don't
know how many *Marcella's* cut in the smooth Bark. On
some of 'em there's a Crown carv'd over the Name, as much
as to say that *Marcella* bears away the Crown, and deserves

the Garland of Beauty. Here sighs one Shepherd, there
another whines; here is one singing doleful Ditties, there
another is wringing his Hands and making woful Complaints.
You shall have one lay him down at Night at the Foot of a
Rock, or some Oak, and there lie weeping and wailing without a Wink of Sleep, and talking to himself till the Sun finds
him the next Morning; you shall have another lie stretch'd
upon the hot sandy Ground, breathing his sad Lamentations
to Heaven, without heeding the sultry Heat of the Summer-
Sun. And all this while the hard-hearted *Marcella* ne'er
minds any one of 'em, and does not seem to be the least concern'd for 'em. We are all mightily at a Loss to know what
will be the End of all this Pride and Coyness, who shall
be the happy Man that shall at last tame her, and bring her
to his Lure. Now because there's nothing more certain than
all this, I am the more apt to give Credit to what our Comrade has told us, as to the Occasion of *Chrysostome's* Death;
and therefore I would needs have you go and see him laid
in's Grave to Morrow; which I believe will be worth your
while, for he had many Friends, and 'tis not half a League
to the Place where 'twas his Will to be bury'd. I intend to
be there, answer'd Don *Quixote*, and in the mean time I
return thee many Thanks for the extraordinary Satisfaction
this Story has afforded me. Alas! Sir Knight, reply'd the
Goat-herd, I have not told you half the Mischiefs this proud
Creature hath done here, but to Morrow may-hap we shall
meet some Shepherd by the Way that will be able to tell
you more. Mean while it won't be amiss for you to take
your rest in one of the Huts; for the open Air is not good
for your Wound, tho' what I've put to it is so special a Medicine that there's not much need to fear but 'twill do well
enough. *Sancho*, who was quite out of Patience with the
Goat-herd's long Story, and wish'd him at the Devil for his
Pains, at last prevail'd with him to lie down in *Peter's* Hutt,
where Don *Quixote*, in Imitation of *Marcella's* Lovers, devoted the Remainder of the Night to amorous Expostulations
with his Dear *Dulcinea*. As for *Sancho*, he laid himself down
between *Rozinante* and his Ass, and slept it out, not like a
disconsolate Lover, but like a Man that had been soundly
kick'd and bruis'd in the Morning. 93

V: A CONTINUATION OF THE STORY
OF MARCELLA

SCARCE had Day begun to appear from the Balconies of the East, when five of the Goat-herds got up, and having wak'd Don *Quixote*, ask'd him if he held his Resolution of going to the Funeral, whither they were ready to bear him Company. Thereupon the Knight, who desir'd nothing more, presently arose, and order'd *Sancho* to get *Rozinante* and the Ass ready immediately; which he did with all Expedition, and then they set forwards. They had not yet gone a Quarter of a League before they saw advancing towards them, out of a cross Path, six Shepherds clad in black Skins, their Heads crown'd with Garlands of *Cypress* and bitter *Rose-bay-tree*, with long Holly-Staves in their Hands. Two Gentlemen on Horseback, attended by three young Lads on Foot, came immediately after 'em: As they drew near, they saluted one another civilly, and after the usual Question, Which Way d'ye travel? they found they were all going the same Way to see the Funeral, and so they all join'd Company. I fancy, *Senior Vivaldo*, said one of the Gentlemen, addressing himself to the other, we shall not think our Time mis-spent in going to see this famous Funeral; for it must of necessity be very extraordinary, according to the Account which these Men have given us of the dead Shepherd and his murdering Mistress. I am so far of your Opinion, answer'd *Vivaldo*, that I would not only stay one Day, but a whole Week, rather than miss the Sight. This gave Don *Quixote* Occasion to ask them what they had heard concerning *Chrysostome* and *Marcella*? One of the Gentlemen made Answer, That having met that Morning with those Shepherds, they could not forbear inquiring of them, why they wore such a mournful Dress? Whereupon one of 'em acquainted 'em with the sad Occasion, by relating the Story of a certain Shepherdess, nam'd *Marcella*, no less Lovely than Cruel, whose Coyness and Disdain has made a World of unfortunate Lovers, and caus'd the Death of that *Chrysostome*, to whose Funeral they were going. In short, he repeated to Don *Quixote* all that *Peter* had told him the

Night before. After this, *Vivaldo* ask'd the Knight why he travell'd so compleatly Arm'd in so peaceable a Country? My Profession, answer'd the Champion, does not permit me to ride otherwise. Luxurious Feasts, Sumptuous Dresses, and Downy Ease were invented for Effeminate Courtiers; but Labour, Vigilance and Arms are the Portion of those whom the World calls Knights-Errant, of which Number I have the Honour to be One, though the most Unworthy, and the Meanest of the Fraternity. He needed to say no more to satisfy 'em his Brains were out of Order; however, that they might the better understand the Nature of his Folly, *Vivaldo* ask'd him, what he meant by a Knight-Errant? Have you not read then, cry'd Don *Quixote*, the Annals and History of *Britain*, where are Recorded the famous Deeds of King *Arthur*, who, according to an ancient Tradition in that Kingdom, never dy'd, but was turn'd into a Crow by Inchantment, and shall one Day resume his former Shape, and recover his Kingdom again. For which Reason since that Time, the People of *Great-Britain* dare not offer to kill a Crow. In this good King's Time, the most noble Order of the Knights of the round Table was first instituted, and then also the Amours between Sir *Lancelot* of the *Lake* and Queen *Guinever* were really transacted, as that History relates; they being manag'd and carry'd on by the Mediation of that honourable Matron the Lady *Quintaniona*. Which produc'd that excellent History in Verse so sung and celebrated here in *Spain*.

> *There never was on Earth a Knight*
> *So waited on by Ladies fair,*
> *As once was he Sir* Lancelot *hight,*
> *When first he left his Country dear:*

And the rest, which gives so delightful an Account both of his Loves and Feats of Arms. From that time the Order of Knight-Errantry began by degrees to dilate and extend it self into most Parts of the World. Then did the Great *Amadis de Gaul* signalize himself by heroick Exploits, and so did his Offspring to the fifth Generation. The valorous *Felixmart* of *Hyrcania* then got immortal Fame, and that undaunted Knight *Tirante* the *White*, who never can be applauded to

95

his Worth. Nay, had we but liv'd a little sooner, we might have been bless'd with the Conversation of that invincible Knight of our modern Times, the valorous Don *Belianis* of *Greece*. And this, Gentlemen, is that Order of Chivalry, which, as much a Sinner as I am, I profess, with a due Observance of the Laws which those brave Knights observ'd before me; and for that Reason I chuse to wander through these solitary Desarts, seeking Adventures, fully resolv'd to expose my Person to the most formidable Dangers which Fortune can obtrude on me, that by the Strength of my Arm I may relieve the Weak and the Distressed.

After all this Stuff, you may be sure the Travellers were sufficiently convinc'd of Don *Quixote's* Frenzy. Nor were they less surpriz'd than were all those who had hitherto discover'd so unaccountable a Distraction in one who seem'd a rational Creature. However, *Vivaldo*, who was of a gay Disposition, had no sooner made the Discovery, but he resolv'd to make the best Advantage of it, that the Shortness of the Way wou'd allow him.

Therefore, to give him further Occasion to divert 'em with his Whimsies, Methinks, Sir Knight-Errant, said he to him, you have taken up one of the strictest and most mortifying Professions in the World. I don't think but that a *Carthusian* Friar has a better Time on't than You have. Perhaps, answer'd Don *Quixote*, the Profession of a *Carthusian* may be as Austere, but I am within two Fingers Breadth of doubting, whether it may be as Beneficial to the World as ours. For, if we must speak the Truth, the Soldier, who puts his Captain's Command in Execution, may be said to do as much at least as the Captain who commanded him. The Application is easy: For, while those religious Men have nothing to do, but with all Quietness and Security to say their Prayers for the Prosperity of the World, We Knights, like Soldiers, execute what they do but pray for, and procure those Benefits to Mankind, by the Strength of our Arms, and at the Hazard of our Lives, for which they only interceed. Nor do we do this shelter'd from the Injuries of the Air, but under no other Roof than that of the wide Heavens, expos'd to Summer's scorching Heat, and Winter's pinching

Cold. So that we may justly style our selves the Ministers of Heaven, and the Instruments of its Justice upon Earth; and as the Business of War is not to be compass'd without vast Toil and Labour, so the religious Soldier must undoubtedly be preferr'd before the religious Monk, who living still quiet and at Ease, has nothing to do but to pray for the Afflicted and Distressed. However, Gentlemen, do not imagine I wou'd insinuate as if the Profession of a Knight-Errant was a State of Perfection equal to that of a holy Recluse: I would only infer from what I've said, and what I my self endure, that Ours without question is more laborious, more subject to the Discipline of heavy Blows, to Maceration, to the Penance of Hunger and Thirst, and in a Word, to Rags, to Want and Misery. For if you find that some Knights-Errant have at last by their Valour been rais'd to Thrones and Empires, you may be sure it has been still at the Expence of much Sweat and Blood. And had even those happier Knights been depriv'd of those assisting Sages and Inchanters, who help'd 'em in all Emergencies, they wou'd have been strangely disappointed of their mighty Expectations. I am of the same Opinion, reply'd *Vivaldo*. But one Thing among many others, which I can by no means approve in your Profession, is, that when you are just going to engage in some very hazardous Adventure, where your Lives are evidently to be much endanger'd, you never once remember to commend your selves to God, as every good Christian ought to do on such Occasions, but only recommend your selves to your Mistresses, and that with as great Zeal and Devotion as if you worshipp'd no other Deity; a thing, which in my Opinion, strongly relishes of Paganism. Sir, reply'd Don *Quixote*, there's no altering that Method; for shou'd a Knight-Errant do otherwise, he wou'd too much deviate from the Ancient and Establish'd Customs of Knight-Errantry, which inviolably oblige him just in the Moment when he is rushing on, and giving Birth to some dubious Atchievement, to have his Mistress still before his Eyes, still present to his Mind, by a strong and lively Imagination, and with soft, amorous and energetick Looks imploring her Favour and Protection in that perilous Circumstance. Nay, if no body can overhear him, he's oblig'd to whisper, or speak between his Teeth, some short Ejaculations, to recommend himself with all the Fervency imaginable to the Lady of his Wishes, and of this we have innumerable Examples in History. Nor are you for all this to imagine that Knights-Errant omit Recommending themselves to Heaven, for they have Leisure enough to do it even in the midst of the Combat.

Sir, reply'd *Vivaldo*, you must give me Leave to tell you, I am not yet throughly satisfy'd in this Point: For I have often observ'd in my Reading, that two Knights-Errant, having first talk'd a little together, have fallen out presently, and been so highly provok'd, that having turn'd their Horses Heads to gain Room for the Career, they have wheel'd about, and then with all Speed run full Tilt at one another, hastily recommending themselves to their Mistresses in the midst of their Career; and the next Thing has commonly been, that one of them has been thrown to the Ground over the Crupper of his Horse, fairly run thro' and thro' with his Enemy's Lance; and the other forc'd to catch hold of his Horse's Main to keep himself from falling. Now I can't apprehend how the Knight that was slain had any Time to recommend himself to Heaven, when his Business was done so suddenly. Methinks those hasty Invocations, which in his Career were directed to his Mistress, shou'd have been directed to Heaven, as every good Christian wou'd have done. Besides, I fancy every Knight-Errant has not a Mistress to Invoke, nor is every one of 'em in Love. Your Conjecture is wrong, reply'd Don *Quixote*; a Knight-Errant cannot be without a Mistress; 'tis not more essential for the Skies to have Stars, than 'tis to us to be in Love. Insomuch, that I dare affirm, that no History ever made mention of any Knight-Errant, that was not a Lover; for were any Knight free from the Impulses of that generous Passion, he wou'd not be allow'd to be a lawful Knight; but a mis-born Intruder, and one who was not admitted within the Pale of Knighthood at the Door, but leap'd the Fence, and stole in like a Robber and a Thief. Yet, Sir, reply'd the other, I'm much mistaken, or I have read that Don *Galaor*, the Brother of *Amadis*, never had any certain Mistress to recommend himself to, and yet for all that, he was not the less esteem'd. One Swallow never makes a Summer, answer'd Don *Quixote*. Besides, I know, that Knight was privately very much in Love; and as for his making his Addresses, wherever he met with Beauty, this was an Effect of his natural Inclination, which he cou'd not easily restrain. But after all, 'tis an undeniable Truth, that he had a Favourite Lady, whom he had Crown'd Empress of his Will; and to her he frequently recommended himself in private, for he did not a little value himself upon his Discretion and Secrecy in Love. Then, Sir, said *Vivaldo*, since 'tis so much the Being of Knight-Errantry to be in Love, I presume, You, who are of that Profession, cannot be without a Mistress. And therefore, if you do not set up for Secrecy as much as Don *Galaor* did, give me Leave to beg of you in the Name of all the Company, that you will be pleas'd so far to oblige us, as to let us know the Name and Quality of your Mistress, the Place of her Birth, and the Charms of her Person. For without doubt, the Lady cannot but esteem her self happy in being known to all the World to be the Object of the Wishes of a Knight so accomplish'd as your self. With that Don *Quixote* breathing out a deep Sigh, I cannot tell, said he, whether this lovely Enemy of my Repose, is the least affected with the World's being informed of her Power over my Heart; all I dare say, in compliance with your Request is, that her Name is *Dulcinea*, her Country *La Mancha*, and *Toboso* the happy Place which she honours with her Residence. As for her Quality, it cannot be less than Princess, seeing she is my Mistress and my Queen. Her Beauty transcends all the united Charms of her whole Sex; even those Chimerical Perfections, which the hyperbolical Imaginations of Poets in Love have assign'd to their Mistresses, cease to be incredible Descriptions when apply'd to her, in whom all those miraculous Endowments are most divinely centred. The curling Locks of her bright flowing Hair are purest Gold; her smooth Forehead the *Elysian* Plain; her Brows are two Celestial Bows; her Eyes two glorious Suns; her Cheeks two Beds of Roses; her Lips are Coral; her Teeth are Pearl; her Neck is Alabaster; her Breasts Marble; her Hands Ivory; and Snow wou'd lose its Whiteness near her Bosom. Then for the Parts which Modesty has veil'd, my Imagination, not to wrong 'em, chuses to lose it self in silent Admiration; for Nature boasts nothing that may give an Idea of their incomparable Worth. Pray, Sir, cry'd *Vivaldo*, oblige us with an Account of her Parentage, and the Place of her Birth, to compleat the Description. Sir, re-ply'd Don *Quixote*, she is not descended from the ancient *Curtius's*, *Caius's*, nor *Scipio's* of *Rome*, nor from the more modern *Colonna's*, nor *Ursini's*; nor from the *Moncada's*, and *Requesens's* of *Catalonia*; nor from the *Rebilla's*, and *Villanova's* of *Valencia*; nor from the *Palafoxes*, *Nucas*, *Rocabertis*, *Corellas*, *Lunas*, *Alagones*, *Urreas*, *Foze's*, or *Gurrea's* of *Arragon*; nor from the *Cerda's*, *Manriquez's*, *Mendoza's*, and *Gusmans* of *Castile*; nor from the *Alen-castro's*, *Palla's*, and *Menezes* of *Portugal*; but she derives her Great Original from the Family of *Toboso* in *La Mancha*, a Race, which tho' it be modern, is sufficient to give a noble Beginning to the most illustrious Progenies of succeeding Ages. And let no Man presume to contradict me in this, un-less it be upon these Conditions, which *Zerbin* fix'd at the Foot of *Orlando's* Armour,

> *Let none but he these Arms displace,*
> *Who dares* Orlando's *Fury face.*

I draw my Pedigree from the *Cachopines* of *Laredo*, reply'd *Vivaldo*, yet I dare not make any Comparisons with the *Toboso's* of *La Mancha*; tho' to deal sincerely with you, 'tis a Family I never heard of till this Moment. 'Tis strange, said Don *Quixote*, you shou'd never have heard of it before.

All the rest of the Company gave great Attention to this Discourse; and even the very Goat-herds and Shepherds were now fully convinc'd that Don *Quixote's* Brains were turn'd topsy-turvy. But *Sancho Pança* believ'd every Word that dropp'd from his Master's Mouth to be Truth, as having known him, from his Cradle, to be a Man of Sincerity. Yet that which somewhat stagger'd his Faith, was this Story of *Dulcinea* of *Toboso*; for he was sure he had never heard before of any such Princess, nor even of the Name, tho' he liv'd hard by *Toboso*.

As they went on thus discoursing, they saw, upon the hollow Road between the neighbouring Mountains, about twenty Shepherds more, all accouter'd in black Skins with Garlands on their Heads, which, as they afterwards perceiv'd, were all of Yew or Cypress; six of 'em carry'd a Bier cover'd with several sorts of Boughs and Flowers: Which one of the Goat-herds espying, Those are they, cry'd he, that are carrying poor *Chrysostome* to his Grave; and 'twas in yonder Bottom that he gave Charge they should bury his Corps. This made 'em all double their Pace, that they might get thither in Time; and so they arriv'd just as the Bearers had set down the Bier upon the Ground, and four of them had begun to open the Ground with their Spades, just at the Foot of a Rock. They all saluted each other courteously, and condol'd their mutual Loss; and then Don *Quixote*, with those who came with him, went to view the Bier; where they saw the dead Body of a young Man in Shepherd's Weeds all strew'd over with Flowers. The Deceas'd seem'd to be about thirty Years old; and, dead as he was, 'twas easily perceiv'd that both his Face and Shape were extraordinary handsome. Within the Bier were some few Books and several Papers, some open, and the rest folded up. This doleful Object so strangely fill'd all the Company with Sadness, that not only the Beholders, but also the Gravemakers, and all the mourning Shepherds remain'd a long Time silent; till at last one of the Bearers, addressing himself to one of the rest, Look, *Ambrose*, cry'd he, whether this be the Place which *Chrysostome* meant, since you must needs have his Will so punctually perform'd? This is the very Place, answer'd the other: There it was that my unhappy Friend many times told me the sad Story of his cruel Fortune; there it was that he first saw that mortal Enemy of Mankind; there it was that he made the first Discovery of his Passion, no less innocent than violent; there it was that the relentless *Marcella* last deny'd, shunn'd him, and drove him to that Extremity of Sorrow and Despair that hasten'd the sad Catastrophe of his tragical and miserable Life; and there it was, that, in Token of so many Misfortunes, he desir'd to be committed to the Bowels of eternal Oblivion.

Then addressing himself to Don *Quixote* and the rest of the Travellers, This Body, Gentlemen, said he, which here you now behold, was once enliven'd by a Soul which Heaven had enrich'd with the greatest Part of its most valuable Graces. This is the Body of that *Chrysostome* who was unrivall'd in Wit, matchless in Courteousness, incomparable in Gracefulness, a Phœnix in Friendship, generous and magnificent without Ostentation, prudent and grave without Pride, modest without Affectation, pleasing and complaisant without Meanness: In a Word, the first in every esteemable Qualification, and second to none in Misfortune: He lov'd well, and was hated; he ador'd, and was disdain'd; he begg'd Pity of Cruelty it self; he strove to move obdurate Marble; pursu'd the Wind; made his Moans to solitary Desarts; was constant to Ingratitude; and for the Recompense of his Fidelity, became a Prey to Death in the Flower of his Age, thro' the Barbarity of a Shepherdess, whom he strove to immortalize by his Verse; as these Papers which are here deposited might testify, had he not commanded me to sacrifice 'em to the Flames, at the same time that his Body was committed to the Earth.

Shou'd you do so, cry'd *Vivaldo*, you wou'd appear more cruel to 'em than their exasperated unhappy Parent. Consider, Sir, 'tis not consistent with Discretion, nor even with Justice, so nicely to perform the Request of the Dead, when 'tis repugnant to Reason. *Augustus Cæsar* himself wou'd have forfeited his Title to Wisdom, had he permitted that to have been effected which the divine *Virgil* had order'd by his Will. Therefore, Sir, now that you resign your Friend's Body to the Grave, do not hurry thus the noble and only Remains of that dear unhappy Man to a worse Fate, the Death of Oblivion. What, tho' he has doom'd 'em to perish in the Height of his Resentment, you ought not indiscreetly to be their Executioner; but rather reprieve and redeem 'em from eternal Silence, that they may live, and, flying thro' the World, transmit to all Ages the dismal Story of your Friend's Virtue and *Marcella's* Ingratitude, as a Warning to others, that they may avoid such tempting Snares and inchanting Destructions; for not only to me, but to all here present is

well known the History of your enamour'd and desperate
Friend: We are no Strangers to the Friendship that was
between you, as also to *Marcella's* Cruelty which occasion'd
his Death. Last Night being inform'd that he was to be buried
here to-day, mov'd not so much by Curiosity as Pity, we are
come to behold with our Eyes that which gave us so much
Trouble to hear. Therefore, in the Name of all the Company,
like me, deeply affected with a Sense of *Chrysostome's* extraordinary Merit, and his unhappy Fate, and desirous to
prevent such deplorable Disasters for the future, I beg that
you will permit me to save some of these Papers, whatever
you resolve to do with the rest. And so, without expecting
an Answer, he stretch'd out his Arm, and took out those
Papers which lay next to his Hand. Well, Sir, said *Ambrose*,
you have found a Way to make me submit, and you may keep
those Papers; but for the rest, nothing shall make me alter
my Resolution of burning 'em. *Vivaldo* said no more; but
being impatient to see what those Papers were, which he had
rescued from the Flames, he open'd one of 'em immediately
and read the Title of it, which was, *The Despairing Lover*.
That, said *Ambrose*, was the last Piece my dear Friend ever
wrote; and therefore, that you may all hear to what a sad
Condition his unhappy Passion had reduc'd him, read it aloud,
I beseech you, Sir, while the Grave is making. With all my
Heart, reply'd *Vivaldo*: And so the Company, having the
same Desire, presently gather'd round about him, and he
read the following Lines.

VI: THE UNFORTUNATE SHEPHERD'S VERSES, AND OTHER UNEXPECTED MATTERS

THE DESPAIRING LOVER

Relentless Tyrant of my Heart,
Attend, and hear thy Slave impart
The matchless Story of his Pain.
In vain I labour to conceal
What my extorted Groans reveal;
Who can be rack'd, and not complain?

But oh! who duly can express
Thy Cruelty, and my Distress?
No human Art, no human Tongue.
Then Fiends assist, and Rage infuse!
A raving Fury be my Muse,
And Hell inspire the dismal Song!

Owls, Ravens, Terrors of the Night,
Wolves, Monsters, Fiends, with dire Affright,
Join your dread Accents to my Moans!
Join, howling Winds, your sullen Noise;
Thou, grumbling Thunder, join thy Voice;
Mad Seas, your Roar, and Hell, thy Groans.

Tho' still I moan in dreary Caves,
To desart Rocks, and silent Graves,
My loud Complaints shall wander far;
Born by the Winds they shall survive,
By pitying Ecchoes kept alive,
And fill the World with my Despair.

Love's deadly Cure is fierce Disdain,
Distracting Fear a dreadful Pain,
And Jealousy a matchless Woe;
Absence is Death, yet while it kills,
I live with all these mortals Ills,
Scorn'd, jealous, loath'd, and absent too.

No Dawn of Hope e'er chear'd my Heart,
No pitying Ray e'er sooth'd my Smart,
All, all the Sweets of Life are gone;

Then come Despair, and frantick Rage,
With instant Fate my Pain asswage,
  And end a thousand Deaths by one.

But ev'n in Death let Love be crown'd,
My fair Destruction guiltless found,
  And I be thought with Justice scorn'd:
Thus let me fall unlov'd, unbless'd,
With all my Load of Woes oppress'd,
  And even too wretched to be mourn'd.

O! thou, by whose destructive Hate,
I'm hurry'd to this doleful Fate,
  When I'm no more, thy Pity spare!
I dread thy Tears; oh spare 'em then——
But oh! I rave, I was too vain,
  My Death can never cost a Tear.

Tormented Souls, on you I call,
Hear one more wretched than you all;
  Come howl as in redoubled Flames.
Attend me to th'eternal Night,
No other Dirge, or Fun'ral Rite,
  A poor despairing Lover claims.

And thou my Song, sad Child of Woe,
When Life is gone, and I'm below,
  For thy lost Parent cease to grieve.
With Life and thee my Woes increase,
And shou'd they not by dying cease,
  Hell has no Pain like these I leave.

These Verses were well approv'd by all the Company;
only *Vivaldo* observ'd, that the Jealousies and Fears of which
the Shepherd complain'd, did not very well agree with what
he had heard of *Marcella's* unspotted Modesty and Reservedness. But *Ambrose*, who had been always privy to the most
secret Thoughts of his Friend, inform'd him, that the unhappy *Chrysostome* wrote those Verses when he had torn
himself from his ador'd Mistress, to try whether Absence,
the common Cure of Love, would relieve him, and mitigate
his Pain. And as every thing disturbs an absent Lover, and

nothing is more usual than for him to torment himself with a thousand Chimeras of his own Brain, so did *Chrysostome* perplex himself with Jealousies and Suspicions, which had no Ground but in his distracted Imagination; and therefore whatever he said in those uneasy Circumstances, could never affect, or in the least prejudice *Marcella's* virtuous Character, upon whom, setting aside her Cruelty, and her disdainful Haughtiness, Envy itself cou'd never fix the least Reproach. *Vivaldo* being thus convinc'd, they were going to read another Paper, when they were unexpectedly prevented by a kind of Apparition that offer'd itself to their View. 'Twas *Marcella* herself, who appear'd at the Top of the Rock, at the Foot of which they were digging the Grave; but so beautiful, that Fame seem'd rather to have lessen'd than to have magnify'd her Charms: Those who had never seen her before, gaz'd on her with silent Wonder and Delight; nay, those who us'd to see her every Day seem'd no less lost in Admiration than the rest. But scarce had *Ambrose* spy'd her, when, with Anger and Indignation in his Heart, he cry'd out, What mak'st thou there, thou fierce, thou cruel Basilisk of these Mountains? Com'st thou to see whether the Wounds of this murder'd Wretch will bleed afresh at thy Presence? or com'st thou thus mounted aloft, to glory in the fatal Effects of thy native Inhumanity, like another *Nero* at the Sight of flaming *Rome*? or is it to trample on this unfortunate Corps, as *Tarquin's* ungrateful Daughter did her Father's? Tell us quickly why thou com'st, and what thou yet desirest? for since I know that *Chrysostome's* whole Study was to serve and please thee while he liv'd, I'm willing to dispose all his Friends to pay thee the like Obedience now he's dead. I come not here to any of those ungrateful Ends, *Ambrose*, reply'd *Marcella*; but only to clear my Innocence, and shew the Injustice of all those who lay their Misfortunes and *Chrysostome's* Death to My Charge: Therefore I intreat you all who are here at this Time to hear me a little, for I shall not need to use many Words to convince People of Sense of an evident Truth. Heav'n, you're pleas'd to say, has made me beautiful, and that to such a Degree, that you are forc'd, nay, as it were compell'd to love me, in spite of your Endeavours to the contrary; and for the sake of that Love, you say I ought to love You again. Now, tho' I am sensible, that whatever is beautiful is lovely, I cannot conceive, that what is lov'd for being handsome, shou'd be bound to love that by which 'tis lov'd, meerly because 'tis lov'd. He that loves a beautiful Object may happen to be ugly; and as what is ugly deserves not to be lov'd, it would be ridiculous to say, I love you because you are handsome, and therefore you must love me again tho' I am ugly. But suppose two Persons of different Sexes are equally handsome, it does not follow, that their Desires should be alike and reciprocal; for all Beauties do not kindle Love; some only recreate the Sight, and never reach, nor captivate the Heart. Alas! should whatever is beautiful beget Love, and enslave the Mind, Mankind's Desires would ever run confus'd and wandering, without being able to fix their determinate Choice: For as there is an infinite Number of beautiful Objects, the Desires would consequently be also infinite; whereas, on the contrary, I have heard, that true Love is still confin'd to one, and voluntary and unforc'd. This being granted, why would you have me force my Inclinations for no other Reason but that you say you love me? Tell me, I beseech you, had Heaven form'd me as ugly as it has made me beautiful, could I justly complain of You for not loving me? Pray consider also, that I do not possess those Charms by Choice; such as they are, they were freely bestow'd on me by Heaven: And as the Viper is not to be blam'd for the Poison with which she kills, seeing 'twas assign'd her by Nature; so I ought not to be censur'd for that Beauty which I derive from the same Cause: For Beauty in a virtuous Woman is but like a distant Flame, or a sharp-edg'd Sword, and only burns and wounds those who approach too near it. Honour and Virtue are the Ornaments of the Soul, and that Body that's destitute of 'em cannot be esteem'd beautiful, tho' it be naturally so. If then Honour be one of those Endowments which most adorn the Body, why should she that's belov'd for her Beauty, expose herself to the Loss of it, meerly to gratify the loose Desires of one, who for his own selfish Ends uses all the Means imaginable to make her lose it? I was born free, and that

I might continue so, I retir'd to these solitary Hills and Plains, where Trees are my Companions, and clear Fountains my Looking-glasses. With the Trees and with the Waters I communicate my Thoughts, and my Beauty. I am a distant Flame, and a Sword far off: Those whom I have attracted with my Sight, I have undeceiv'd with my Words; and if Hope be the Food of Desire, as I never gave any Encouragement to *Chrysostome*, nor to any other, it may well be said, 'twas rather his own Obstinacy than my Cruelty that shorten'd his Life. If you tell me that his Intentions were honest, and therefore ought to have been comply'd with; I answer, that when, at the very Place where his Grave is making, he discover'd his Passion, I told him, I was resolv'd to live and die single, and that the Earth alone should reap the Fruit of my Reservedness, and enjoy the Spoils of my Beauty; and if, after all the Admonitions I gave him, he would persist in his obstinate Pursuit, and sail against the Wind, what Wonder is't he should perish in the Waves of his Indiscretion? Had I ever encourag'd him, or amus'd him with ambiguous Words, then I had been false; and had I gratify'd his Wishes, I had acted contrary to my better Resolves: He persisted, tho' I had given him a due Caution, and he despair'd without being hated. Now I leave you to judge, whether I ought to be blam'd for his Sufferings? If I have deceiv'd any one, let him complain; if I have broke my Promise to any one, let him despair; if I encourage any one, let him presume; if I entertain any one, let him boast: But let no Man call me Cruel nor Murderer, 'till I either deceive, break my Promise, encourage, or entertain him. Heaven has not yet been pleas'd to shew whether 'tis its Will I should love by Destiny; and 'tis vain to think I will ever do it by Choice: So let this general Caution serve every one of those who make their Addresses to me for their own Ends. And if any one hereafter dies on my Account, let not their Jealousy, nor my Scorn or Hate, be thought the Cause of their Death; for she who never pretended to love, cannot make any one jealous, and a free and generous Declaration of our fix'd Resolution, ought not to be accounted Hate or Disdain. In short, let him that calls me a Tigress, and a Basilisk, avoid

108

me as a dangerous Thing; and let him that calls me ungrateful, give over serving me: I assure 'em I will never
seek nor pursue 'em. Therefore let none hereafter make it
their Business to disturb my Ease, nor strive to make me
hazard among Men the Peace I now enjoy, which I am persuaded is not to be found with them. I have Wealth enough;
I neither love nor hate any one: The innocent Conversation
of the neighbouring Shepherdesses, with the Care of my
Flocks, help me to pass away my Time, without either
coquetting with this Man, or practising Arts to ensnare that
other. My Thoughts are limited by these Mountains; and
if they wander further, 'tis only to admire the Beauty of
Heaven, and thus by Steps to raise my Soul towards her
original Dwelling.

As soon as she had said this, without expecting any Answer,
she left the Place, and ran into the Thickest of the adjoining Wood, leaving all that heard her charm'd with her Discretion as well as with her Beauty.

However, so prevalent were the Charms of the latter,
that some of the Company, who were desperately struck,
could not forbear offering to follow her, without being the
least deterr'd by the solemn Protestations which they had
heard her make that very Moment. But Don *Quixote* perceiving their Design, and believing he had now a fit Opportunity to exert his Knight-Errantry; Let no Man, cry'd he,
of what Quality or Condition soever, presume to follow the
fair *Marcella*, under the Penalty of incurring my furious
Displeasure. She has made it appear, by undeniable Reasons,
that she was not guilty of *Chrysostome's* Death; and has
positively declar'd her firm Resolution never to condescend
to the Desires of any of her Admirers: For which Reason,
instead of being importun'd and persecuted, she ought to be
esteem'd and honour'd by all good Men, as being perhaps
the only Woman in the World that ever liv'd with such a
virtuous Reservedness. Now, whether it were that Don
Quixote's Threats terrify'd the amorous Shepherds, or that
Ambrose's Persuasion prevail'd with 'em to stay and see their
Friend interr'd, none of the Shepherds left the Place, till the
Grave being made, and the Papers burnt, the Body was de-

posited into the Bosom of the Earth, not without many Tears from all the Assistants. They cover'd the Grave with a great Stone till a Monument was made, which *Ambrose* said he design'd to have set up there, with the following Epitaph upon it.

CHRYSOSTOME'S EPITAPH

Here of a wretched Swain
The frozen Body's laid,
Kill'd by the cold Disdain
Of an ungrateful Maid.
Here first Love's Pow'r he try'd,
Here first his Pains express'd;
Here first he was deny'd,
Here first he chose to rest.
You who the Shepherd mourn,
From coy Marcella *fly;*
Who Chrysostome *cou'd scorn,*
May all Mankind destroy.

The Shepherds strew'd the Grave with many Flowers and Boughs; and every one having condol'd a while with his Friend *Ambrose*, they took their Leave of him, and departed. *Vivaldo* and his Companion did the like; as did also Don *Quixote*, who was not a Person to forget himself on such Occasions: He likewise bid Adieu to the kind Goat-herds, that had entertain'd him, and to the two Travellers who desir'd him to go with 'em to *Seville*, assuring him there was no Place in the World more fertile in Adventures, every Street and every Corner there producing some. Don *Quixote* return'd them Thanks for their kind Information; but told 'em he neither would, nor ought to go to *Seville*, till he had clear'd all those Mountains of the Thieves and Robbers which he heard very much infested all those Parts. Thereupon the Travellers, being unwilling to divert him from so good a Design, took their Leaves of him once more, and pursu'd their Journey, sufficiently supply'd with Matter to discourse on from the Story of *Marcella* and *Chrysostome*, and Don *Quixote's* Follies. As for him, he resolv'd to find out the Shepherdess *Marcella*, if possible, to offer her his Service to protect her to the utmost of his Power: But he happen'd to be cross'd in his Designs, as you shall hear in the Sequel of this true History; for here ends the second Book.

Part I Book III

I: GIVING AN ACCOUNT OF DON QUIXOTE'S UNFORTUNATE RENCOUNTER WITH CERTAIN BLOODY-MINDED AND WICKED YANGUESIAN* CARRIERS

T HE Sage *Cid Hamet Benengeli* relates, that when Don *Quixote* had taken Leave of all those that were at *Chrysostome's* Funeral, he and his Squire went after *Marcella* into the Wood; and having rang'd it above two Hours without being able to find her, they came at last to a Meadow, whose springing Green, water'd with a delightful and refreshing Rivulet, invited, or rather pleasingly forc'd 'em to alight and give way to the Heat of the Day, which began to be very violent: So leaving the Ass and *Rozinante* to graze at large, they ransack'd the Wallet; and without Ceremony the Master and the Man fell to, and fed lovingly on what they found. Now *Sancho* had not taken care to tie up *Rozinante*, knowing him to be a Horse of that Sobriety and Chastity, that all the Mares in the Pastures of *Cordova* could not have rais'd him to attempt an indecent thing. But either Fortune, or the Devil, who seldom sleeps, so order'd it, that a good Number of *Galician* Mares, belonging to some *Yanguesian* Carriers, were then feeding in the same Valley, it being the Custom of those Men, about the hottest time of the Day, to stop wherever they meet with Grass and Water to refresh their Cattle: Nor could they have found a fitter Place than that where Don *Quixote* was. *Rozinante*, as I said before, was chaste and modest; however, he was Flesh and Blood; so that as soon as he had smelt the Mares, forsaking his natural Gravity and Reserv'dness, without asking his Master's Leave, away he trots it briskly to make 'em sensible of his little Necessities: But they, who it seems had more mind to feed than to be merry, receiv'd their Gallant so rudely with

* *Carriers of the Kingdom of* Galicia, *commonly so call'd.*

their Heels and Teeth, that in a Trice they broke his Girts and threw down his Saddle, and left him disrob'd of all his Equipage. And for an Addition to his Misery, the Carriers perceiving the Violence that was offer'd to their Mares, flew to their Relief with Poles and Pack-staves, and so belabour'd poor *Rozinante* that he soon sunk to the Ground under the Weight of their unmerciful Blows.

Don *Quixote* and *Sancho*, perceiving at a Distance the ill Usage of *Rozinante*, ran with all Speed to his Rescue; and as they came near the Place, panting, and almost out of Breath, Friend *Sancho*, cry'd Don *Quixote*, I perceive these are no Knights, but only a Pack of Scoundrels and Fellows of the lowest Rank; I say it, because thus thou may'st lawfully help me to revenge the Injury they have done *Rozinante* before our Faces. What a Devil d'ye talk of Revenge, quoth *Sancho*? We are like to revenge our selves finely! You see they are above twenty, and we are but two; nay, perhaps but one and a half. I alone am worth a hundred, reply'd Don *Quixote*; then, without any more Words, he drew his Sword, and flew upon the *Yanguesians*. *Sancho*, encourag'd by his Master's Example, did the like; and with the first Blow which Don *Quixote* gave one of 'em, he cut thro' his leathern Doublet, and gave him a deep Slash in the Shoulder. The *Yanguesians*, seeing themselves thus rudely handled, betook themselves to their Leavers and Pack-staves, and then All at once surrounding the valiant Knight and his trusty Squire, they charg'd 'em and laid on with great Fury. At the second Round, down they settled poor *Sancho*, and then Don *Quixote* himself, who, as Chance would have it, fell at the Feet of *Rozinante*, that had not yet recover'd his Legs; neither could the Knight's Courage nor his Skill avail against the Fury of a Number of rustical Fellows arm'd with Pack-staves. The *Yanguesians* fearing the ill Consequences of the Mischief they had done, made all the Haste they could to be gone, leaving our two Adventurers in a woful Condition. The first that came to himself was *Sancho Pança*, who, finding himself near his Master, call'd to him thus, with a weak and doleful Voice; Ah Master! Master! Sir, Sir Knight! What's the Matter, Friend *Sancho*? ask'd the Knight, in

the same feeble and lamenting Tone. I could wish, reply'd
Sancho, that your Worship would help me to two good
Draughts of the Liquor you talk on, if you have any by you;
perhaps 'tis as good to cure broken Bones, as 'tis to heal outward Wounds. Oh! that I had some of it here now, cry'd
Don *Quixote*; we could not then be said to want any thing:
But I swear to thee, honest *Sancho*, by the Faith of a Knight-
Errant, within these two Days (if no other Disaster prevent
me) I will have some at my Disposal, or it shall hardly escape
my Hands. Two Days, Sir! reply'd *Sancho*: Why, pray how
many Days do you think 'twill be before we are able to stir
our Feet? As for my self, answer'd the bruis'd Don *Quixote*,
I must own I cannot set a certain Term to the Days of our
Recovery; but 'tis I who am the fatal Cause of all this Mischief; for I ought not to have drawn my Sword against a
Company of Fellows, upon whom the Honour of Knighthood
was never conferr'd; and I do not doubt but that the Lord
of Hosts suffer'd this Punishment to befal me for transgressing
thus the Laws of Chivalry. Therefore, Friend *Sancho*, observe what I am going to tell thee, for it is a thing that highly
concerns the Welfare of us both: 'Tis, that for the future,
whenever thou perceiv'st us to be any ways abus'd by such
inferior Fellows, thou art not to expect I should offer to draw
my Sword against them; for I will not do it in the least: No,
do thou then draw, and chastise 'em as thou think'st fit: But
if any Knights come to take their Parts, then will I be sure
to step between thee and Danger, and assault 'em with the
utmost Vigour and Intrepidity. Thou hast already had a
thousand Proofs of the Greatness of my Valour, and the prevailing Strength of my most dreadful Arm; (so arrogant the
Knight was grown since his Victory over the bold *Biscayan*)
but *Sancho* was not so well pleas'd with his Master's Admonitions, but that he thought fit to answer him. Sir, says
he, I am a peaceful Man, a harmless quiet Fellow, d'ye see;
I can make Shift to pass by an Injury as well as any Man, as
having a Wife to maintain, and Children to bring up: And
therefore pray take this from me by the way of Advice, (for
I'll not offer to command my Master) that I will not in any
wise draw my Sword neither against Knight nor Clown, not I.

I freely forgive all Mankind, high and low, rich and poor, Lords and Beggars, whatever Wrongs they ever did or may do me, without the least Exception. *Sancho* (said his Master, hearing this) I heartily wish I had Breath enough to answer thee effectually, or that the Pain which I feel in one of my short Ribs would leave me but for so long as might serve to convince thee of thy Error. Come, suppose, thou silly Wretch, that the Gale of Fortune, which has hitherto been so contrary to us, should at last turn favourable, swelling the Sails of our Desires, so that we might with as much Security as Ease arrive at some of those Islands which I have promis'd thee; what would become of thee, if, after I had conquer'd one of 'em, I were to make thee Lord of it? Thou wouldst certainly be found not duly qualify'd for that Dignity, as having abjur'd all Knighthood, all Thoughts of Honour, and all Intention to revenge Injuries, and defend thy own Dominions. For thou must understand, that in Kingdoms and Provinces newly conquer'd, the Hearts and Minds of the Inhabitants are never so thoroughly subdu'd, or wedded to the Interests of their new Sovereign, but that there is reason to fear, they will endeavour to raise some Commotions to change the face of Affairs, and, as Men say, once more try their Fortune. Therefore 'tis necessary that the new Possessor have not only Understanding to govern, but also Valour to attack his Enemies, and defend himself on all Occasions. I would I had had that Understanding and Valour you talk of, quoth *Sancho*; but now, Sir, I must be free to tell you, I have more need of a Surgeon, than of a Preacher. Pray try whether you can rise, and we'll help *Rozinante*, tho' he does not deserve it; for he's the chief Cause of all this Beating. For my Part, I could never have believ'd the like of him before, for I always took him for as chaste and sober a Person as my self. In short, 'tis a true Saying, that *a Man must eat a Peck of Salt with his Friend, before he knows him;* and I find *there's nothing sure in this World:* For, who would have thought, after the dreadful Slashes you gave to that Knight-Errant, such a terrible Shower of Bastinadoes would so soon have fallen upon our Shoulders? As for thine, reply'd Don *Quixote*, I doubt they are us'd to endure such sort of Showers; but mine, that were nurs'd in soft Linnen, will most certainly be longer sensible of this Misfortune; and were it not that I imagine, (but why do I say imagine?) were it not that I am positively sure that all these Inconveniences are inseparable from the Profession of Chivalry, I wou'd abandon my self to Grief, and die of meer Despair on this very spot. I beseech you, Sir, quoth *Sancho*, since these Rubs are the Vails of your Trade of Knighthood, tell me whether they use to come often, or whether we may look for 'em at set times: For, I fancy, if we meet but with two such Harvests more, we shall never be able to reap the third, unless God of his infinite Mercy assist us. Know, Friend *Sancho*, return'd Don *Quixote*, that the Life of Knights-Errant is subject to a thousand Hazards and Misfortunes: But on the other side, they may at any time suddenly become Kings and Emperors, as Experience has demonstrated in many Knights, of whose Histories I have a perfect Knowledge. And I could tell thee now (would my Pain suffer me) of some of 'em who have rais'd themselves to those high Dignities only by the Valour of their Arm; and those very Knights, both before and after their Advancement, were involv'd in many Calamities: For, the valorous *Amadis de Gaul* saw himself in the Power of his mortal Enemy *Archelaus* the Inchanter, of whom 'tis credibly reported, that when he held him Prisoner, he gave him above two hundred Stripes with his Horse-Bridle, after he had ty'd him to a Pillar in the Court-yard of his House. There is also a secret Author of no little Credit relates, That the Knight of the Sun being taken in a Trap in a certain Castle, was hurry'd to a deep Dungeon, where, after they had bound him Hand and Foot, they forcibly gave him a Clyster of Snow-water and Sand, which would probably have cost him his Life, had he not been assisted in that Distress by a wise Magician, his particular Friend. Thus I may well bear my Misfortune patiently, since those which so many greater Persons have endur'd may be said to outdo it: For, I would have thee to know, that those Wounds that are given with the Instruments and Tools which a Man happens to have in his Hand, do not really disgrace the Person struck. We read it expresly in the Laws of Duels, *That if a Shoemaker strikes another*

Man with his Last which he held in his Hand, tho' it be of *Wood, as a Cudgel is, yet the Party who was struck with it* *shall not be said to have been cudgell'd.* I tell thee this, that thou may'st not think we are in the least dishonour'd, tho' we have been horribly beaten in this Rencounter; for the Weapons which those Men us'd were but the Instruments of their Profession, and not one of 'em, as I very well remember, had either Tuck, or Sword, or Dagger. They gave me no Leisure, quoth *Sancho*, to examine things so narrowly; for I had no sooner laid my Hand on my Cutlass,* but they cross'd my Shoulders with such a wooden Blessing, as settl'd me on the Ground without Sense or Motion, where you see me lie, and where I don't trouble my Head whether it be a Disgrace to be mawl'd with Cudgels or with Packstaves: Let 'em be what they will, I am only vex'd to feel them so heavy on my Shoulders, where I am afraid they are imprinted as deep as they are in my Mind. For all this, reply'd Don *Quixote*, I must inform thee, Friend *Sancho*, that there is no Remembrance which Time will not deface, nor no Pain to which Death will not put a Period. Thank you for nothing, quoth *Sancho*! What worse can befal us, than to have only Death to trust to? Were our Affliction to be cur'd with a Plaister or two, a Man might have some Patience; but, for ought I see, all the Salves in an Hospital won't set us on our best Legs again. Come, no more of this, cry'd Don *Quixote*; take Courage, and make a Virtue of Necessity; for 'tis what I am resolv'd to do. Let's see how it fares with *Rozinante*; for if I am not mistaken, the poor Creature has not been the least Sufferer in this Adventure. No wonder at that, quoth *Sancho*, seeing he's a Knight-Errant too; I rather wonder, how my Ass has escap'd so well, while we have far'd so ill. In our Disasters, return'd Don *Quixote*, Fortune leaves always some Door open to come at a Remedy. I say it, *Sancho*, because that little Beast may now supply the want of *Rozinante*, to carry me to some Castle, where I may get cur'd of my Wounds. Nor do I

---

* Tizona: *The Romantic Name of the Sword, which the* Spanish *General* Roderick Diaz de Bivar *used against the* Moors. Titio *Lat. for a* Firebrand (*from whence* Tison *in French*) *and thence* Tizona *in Spanish; and* (*if I mistake not*) Rinald *of* Montaubaris Whinyard *was call'd* Flamberge.

esteem this kind of Riding dishonourable, for I remember, that the good old *Silenus*, Tutor and Governor to the Jovial God of Wine, rode very fairly on a goodly Ass, when he made his Entry into the City with a hundred Gates. Ay, quoth *Sancho*, 'twill do well enough, cou'd you ride as fairly on your Ass, as he did on his; but there's a deal of Difference between Riding and being laid cross the Pannel like a pack of Rubbish. The Wounds which are receiv'd in Combat, said Don *Quixote*, rather add to our Honour, than deprive us of it; therefore, good *Sancho*, trouble me with no more Replies, but, as I said, endeavour to get up, and lay me as thou pleasest upon thy Ass, that we may leave this Place ere Night steal upon us. But, Sir, cry'd *Sancho*, I have heard you say, that 'tis a common thing among you Knights-Errant to sleep in Fields and Desarts the best part of the Year, and that you look upon it to be a very happy kind of Life. That is to say, reply'd Don *Quixote*, when we can do no better, or when we are in Love; and this is so true, that there have been Knights who have dwelt on Rocks, expos'd to the Sun, and other Inclemencies of the Sky, for the space of two Years, without their Lady's Knowledge: One of those was *Amadis*, when, assuming the Name of *The Lovely Obscure*, he inhabited the *Bare Rock*, either Eight Years, or Eight Months, I can't now punctually tell which of the two; for I don't thoroughly remember that Passage. Let it suffice that there he dwelt, doing Penance, for I don't know what Unkindness his Lady *Oriana* had shew'd him. But setting these Discourses aside, pr'ythee dispatch, lest some Mischief befal thy Ass, as it has done *Rozinante*. That would be the Devil indeed, reply'd *Sancho*, and so breathing out some thirty Lamentations, threescore Sighs, and a hundred and twenty Plagues and Poxes on those that had decoy'd him thither, he at last got upon his Legs, yet not so but that he went stooping, with his Body bent like a *Turk's* Bow, not being able to stand upright. Yet in this crooked Posture he made a shift to harness his Ass, who had not forgot to take his Share of Licentiousness that Day. After this, he help'd up *Rozinante*, who, could his Tongue have express'd his Sorrows, would certainly not have been behind-hand with *Sancho* and his Master. After many bitter Oh's, and screw'd Faces, *Sancho* laid Don *Quixote* on the Ass, ty'd *Rozinante* to its Tail, and then leading the Ass by the Halter, he took the nearest Way that he could guess to the high Road; to which he luckily came, before he had travell'd a short League, and then he discover'd an Inn; which, in spite of all he could say, Don *Quixote* was pleas'd to mistake for a Castle. *Sancho* swore bloodily 'twas an Inn, and his Master was as positive of the contrary. In short, their Dispute lasted so long, that before they could decide it they reach'd the Inn-door, where *Sancho* straight went in, with all his Train, without troubling himself any further about the Matter.

II: WHAT HAPPEN'D TO DON QUIXOTE IN THE INN WHICH HE TOOK FOR A CASTLE

THE Inn-keeper, seeing Don *Quixote* lying quite a-thwart the Ass, ask'd *Sancho* what ail'd him? *Sancho* answer'd, 'Twas nothing, only his Master had got a Fall from the Top of a Rock to the Bottom, and had bruis'd his Sides a little. The Inn-keeper had a Wife, very different from the common sort of Hostesses, for she was of a charitable Nature, and very compassionate of her Neighbour's Affliction; which made her immediately take care of Don *Quixote*, and call her Daughter (a good handsome Girl) to set her helping-hand to his Cure. One of the Servants in the Inn was an *Asturian* Wench, a Broad-fac'd, Flat-headed, Saddle-nos'd Dowdy; blind of one Eye, and t'other almost out: However, the Activity of her Body supply'd all other Defects. She was not above three Feet high from her Heels to her Head; and her Shoulders, which somewhat loaded her, as having too much Flesh upon 'em, made her look downwards oftner than she could have wish'd. This charming Original likewise assisted the Mistress and the Daughter; and with the latter, help'd to make the Knight's Bed, and a sorry one it was; the Room where it stood was an old gambling Cock-loft, which by manifold Signs seem'd to have been, in the Days of Yore, a Repository for chopp'd Straw. Somewhat further, in a Corner of that Garret, a Carrier had his Lodging; and tho' his Bed was nothing but the Pannels and Coverings of his Mules, 'twas much better than that of Don *Quixote*, which only consisted of four rough-hewn Boards laid upon two uneven Tressels, a Flock-bed, that, for Thinness, might well have pass'd for a Quilt, and was full of Knobs and Bunches, which had they not peep'd out thro' many a Hole, and shewn themselves to be of Wool, might well have been taken for Stones: The rest of that extraordinary Bed's Furniture was a Pair of Sheets, which rather seem'd to be of Leather than of Linen Cloth, and a Coverlet whose every individual Thread you might have told, and never have miss'd one in the Tale.

In this ungracious Bed was the Knight laid to rest his be-labour'd Carcase, and presently the Hostess and her Daughter anointed and plaister'd him all over, while *Maritornes* (for that was the Name of the *Asturian* Wench) held the Candle. The Hostess, while she greas'd him, wondering to see him so bruis'd all over, I fancy, said she, those Bumps look much more like a dry Beating than a Fall. 'Twas no dry Beating, Mistress, I promise you, quoth *Sancho*, but the Rock had I know not how many cragged Ends and Knobs, whereof every one gave my Master a Token of its Kindness. And by the way, forsooth, continu'd he, I beseech you save a little of that same Tow and Ointment for me too, for I don't know what's the Matter with my Back, but I fancy I stand mainly in want of a little greasing too. What, I suppose You fell too, quoth the Landlady. Not I, quoth *Sancho*, but the very Fright that I took to see my Master tumble down the Rock, has so wrought upon my Body, that I'm as sore as if I had been sadly mawl'd. It may well be as you say, cry'd the Inn-keeper's Daughter; for I have dream'd several Times that I have been falling from the Top of a high Tower without ever coming to the Ground; and, when I wak'd, I have found my self as out of order, and as bruis'd, as if I had fall'n in good earnest. That's e'en my Case, Mistress, quoth *Sancho*; only ill Luck would have it so, that I should find my self e'en almost as batter'd and bruis'd as my Lord Don *Quixote*, and yet all the while be as broad awake as I am now. How do you call this same Gentleman, quoth *Maritornes*? He's Don *Quixote de la Mancha*, reply'd *Sancho*; and he is a Knight-Errant, and one of the primest and stoutest that ever the Sun shin'd on. A Knight-Errant, cry'd the Wench, pray what's that? Heigh-day! cry'd *Sancho*, does the Wench know no more of the World than that comes to? Why, a Knight-Errant is a Thing which in two Words you see well Cud-gell'd, and then an Emperor. To Day there's not a more wretched Thing upon the Earth, and yet to Morrow he'll have you two or three Kingdoms to give away to his Squire. How comes it to pass then, quoth the Landlady, that thou who art this Great Person's Squire, hast not yet got thee at least an Earldom? Fair and softly goes far, reply'd *Sancho*.

Why, we have not been a Month in our Gears, so that we have not yet encounter'd any Adventure worth the naming: Besides, many a time we look for one thing, and light on another. But if my Lord Don *Quixote* happens to get well again, and I 'scape remaining a Cripple, I'll not take the best Title in the Land for what I am sure will fall to my Share.

Here Don *Quixote*, who had listen'd with great Attention to all these Discourses, rais'd himself up in his Bed with much ado, and taking the Hostess in a most obliging Manner by the Hand, Believe me, said he, beautiful Lady, you may well esteem it a Happiness that you have now the Opportunity to entertain My Person in your Castle. Self-praise is unworthy a Man of Honour, and therefore I shall say no more of my self, but my Squire will inform you who I am; only thus much let me add, That I will eternally preserve your Kindness in the Treasury of my Remembrance, and study all Occasions to testify my Gratitude. And I wish, continu'd he, the Powers above had so dispos'd my Fate, that I were not already Love's devoted Slave, and captivated by the Charms of the disdainful Beauty who engrosses all my softer Thoughts; for then would I be proud to sacrifice my Liberty to this beautiful Damsel. The Hostess, her Daughter, and the kind-hearted *Maritornes* star'd on one another, quite at a Loss for the Meaning of this high-flown Language, which they understood full as well as if it had been *Greek*. Yet, conceiving these were Words of Compliment and Courtship, they look'd upon him, and admir'd him as a Man of another World: And so, having made him such Returns as Innkeeper's Breeding cou'd afford, they left him to his Rest; only *Maritornes* staid to rub down *Sancho*, who wanted her Help no less than his Master.

Now you must know, that the Carrier and she had agreed to pass the Night together; and she had given him her Word, that as soon as all the People in the Inn were in Bed, she wou'd be sure to come to him, and be at his Service. And 'tis said of this good-natur'd Thing, that whenever she had pass'd her Word in such Cases, she was sure to make it good, tho' she had made the Promise in the midst of a Wood, and without any Witness at all: For she stood much upon her

Gentility, tho' she undervalu'd her self so far as to serve in an Inn; often saying, that nothing but Crosses and Necessity cou'd have made her stoop to it.

Don *Quixote's* hard, scanty, beggarly, miserable Bed was the first of the four in that wretched Apartment; next to that was *Sancho's* Kennel, which consisted of nothing but a Bed-Mat and a Coverlet, that rather seem'd shorn Canvas than a Rug. Beyond these two Beds was that of the Carrier, made, as we have said, of the Pannels and Furniture of two of the best of twelve Mules which he kept, every one of 'em goodly Beasts, and in special good Case; for he was one of the richest Muleteers of *Arevalo*, as the *Moorish* Author of this History relates, who makes particular mention of him, as having been acquainted with him; nay, some don't stick to say, he was somewhat a-kin to him. However it be, it appears, that *Cid Mahomet Benengeli* was a very exact Historian, since he takes Care to give us an Account of Things that seem so inconsiderable and trivial. A laudable Example which those Historians should follow, who usually relate Matters so concisely, that we have scarcely a Smack of 'em, leaving the most essential Part of the Story drown'd in the Bottom of the Ink-horn, either through Neglect, Malice, or Ignorance. A thousand Blessings then be given to the curious Author of *Tablante* of *Ricamonte*, and to that other indefatigable Sage who recorded the Atchievements of Count *Tomillas*; for they have describ'd even the most minute and trifling Circumstances with as ingular Preciseness. But to return to our Story, you must know, that after the Carrier had visited his Mules, and given them their second Course,* he laid himself down upon his Pannels, in Expectation of the most punctual *Maritornes's* kind Visit. By this Time *Sancho*, duly greas'd and anointed, was crept into his Sty, where he did all he could to sleep, but his aking Ribs did all they could to prevent him. As for the Knight, whose Sides were in as bad Circumstances as his Squire's, he lay with both his Eyes open like a Hare. And now was every Soul in the Inn gone to Bed, not any Light to be seen, except

* *In* Spain *they get up in the Night to dress their Cattle, and give 'em their Barley and Straw, which serves for Hay and Oats.*

that of a Lamp which hung in the middle of the Gate-way. This general Tranquillity setting Don *Quixote's* Thoughts at work, offer'd to his Imagination one of the most absurd Follies that ever crept into a distemper'd Brain from the Perusal of romantick Whimsies. Now he fancy'd himself to be in a famous Castle, (for, as we have already said, all the Inns he lodg'd in seem'd no less than Castles to Him) and that the Inn-keeper's Daughter (consequently Daughter to the Lord of the Castle) strangely captivated with his graceful Presence and Gallantry, had promis'd him the Pleasure of her Embraces, as soon as her Father and Mother were gone to Rest. This Chimera disturb'd him, as if it had been a real Truth; so that he began to be mightily perplex'd, reflecting on the Danger to which his Honour was expos'd: But at last his Virtue overcame the powerful Temptation, and he firmly resolv'd not to be guilty of the least Infidelity to his Lady *Dulcinea del Toboso*, tho' Queen *Genever* her self, with her trusty Matron *Quintaniona* should join to decoy him into the alluring Snare.

While these wild Imaginations work'd in his Brain, the gentle *Maritornes* was mindful of her Assignation, and with soft and wary Steps, bare-foot, and in her Smock, with her Hair gather'd up in a Fustian Coif, stole into the Room, and felt about for her beloved Carrier's Bed: But scarce had she got to the Door, when Don *Quixote*, whose Ears were on the Scout, was sensible that something was coming in; and therefore having rais'd himself in his Bed, sore and wrapp'd up in Plaisters, as he was, he stretch'd out his Arms to receive his fancy'd Damsel, and caught hold of *Maritornes* by the Wrist, as she was, with her Arms stretch'd, groping her Way to her *Paramour*; he pull'd her to him, and made her sit down by his Bed's-side, she not daring to speak a Word all the while. Now, as he imagin'd her to be the Lord of the Castle's Daughter, her Smock, which was of the coarsest Canvas, seem'd to him of the finest Holland; and the Glass-Beads about her Wrist, precious Oriental Pearls; her Hair, that was almost as rough as a Horse's Mane, he took to be soft flowing Threads of bright curling Gold; and her Breath, that had a stronger *Hogoe* than stale Venison, was to him a grateful Compound of the most fragrant Perfumes of *Arabia*. In short, flattering Imagination transform'd her into the Likeness of those romantick Beauties, one of whom, as he remember'd to have read, came to pay a private Visit to a wounded Knight, with whom she was desperately in Love; and the poor Gentleman's obstinate Folly had so infatuated his outward Sense, that his Feeling and his Smell could not in the least undeceive him, and he thought he had no less than a balmy *Venus* in his Arms, while he hugg'd a fulsome Bundle of Deformities, that would have turn'd any Man's Stomach but a sharp-set Carrier's. Therefore clasping her still closer, with a soft and amorous Whisper; Oh! thou most lovely Temptation, cry'd he, Oh! that I now might but pay a warm Acknowledgment for the mighty Blessing which your extravagant Goodness would lavish on me; yes, most beautiful Charmer, I would give an Empire to purchase your more desirable Embraces: But Fortune, Madam, Fortune, that Tyrant of my Life, that unrelenting Enemy to the truly Deserving, has maliciously hurry'd and rivetted me to this Bed, where I lie so bruis'd and macerated, that, tho' I were eager to gratify your Desires, I should at this dear unhappy Minute be doom'd to Impotence: Nay, to that unlucky Bar Fate has added a yet more invincible Obstacle; I mean my plighted Faith to the unrival'd *Dulcinea del Toboso*, the sole Mistress of my Wishes, and absolute Sovereign of my Heart. Oh! did not this oppose my present Happiness, I could never be so dull and insensible a Knight as to lose the Benefit of this extraordinary Favour which you have now condescended to offer me.

Poor *Maritornes* all this while sweated for Fear and Anxiety, to find her self thus lock'd in the Knight's Arms; and without either understanding, or willing to understand his florid Excuses, she did what she could to get from him, and sheer off, without speaking a Word. On the other side, the Carrier, whose lewd Thoughts kept him awake, having heard his trusty Lady when she first came in, and listen'd ever since to the Knight's Discourse, began to be afraid that she had made some other Assignation; and so, without any more ado, he crept softly to Don *Quixote's* Bed, where he listen'd a while to hear what would be the End of all this

Talk, which he could not understand: But perceiving at last by the struggling of his faithful *Maritornes*, that 'twas none of her Fault, and that the Knight strove to detain her against her Will, he could by no means bear his Familiarity; and therefore taking it in mighty Dudgeon, he up with his Fist, and hit the enamour'd Knight such a swinging Blow on the Jaws, that his Face was all over Blood in a Moment. And not satisfy'd with this, he got o'top of the Knight, and with his splay Feet betrampled him, as if he had been trampling a Hay-mow. With that the Bed, whose Foundations were none of the best, sunk under the additional Load of the Carrier, and fell with such a Noise, that it wak'd the Inn-keeper, who presently suspects it to be one of *Maritornes's* nightly Skirmishes; and therefore having call'd her aloud, and finding that she did not answer, he lighted a Lamp, and made to the Place where he heard the Bustle. The Wench, who heard him coming, knowing him to be of a passionate Nature, was scar'd out of her Wits, and fled for Shelter to *Sancho's* Sty, where he lay Snoring to some Tune: There she pigg'd in, and slunk under the Coverlet, where she lay snug, and truss'd up as round as an Egg. Presently her Master came in, in a mighty Heat: Where's this damn'd Whore, cry'd he? I dare say, this is one of her Pranks. By this, *Sancho* awak'd; and feeling that unusual Lump, which almost overlaid him, he took it to be the Night-Mare, and began to lay about him with his Fists, and thump'd the Wench so unmercifully, that at last Flesh and Blood were no longer able to bear it; and forgetting the Danger she was in, and her dear Reputation, she paid him back his Thumps as fast as her Fists could lay 'em on, and soon rous'd the drowsy Squire out of his Sluggishness, whether he would or no: Who finding himself thus pommell'd, by he did not know who, he bustled up in his Nest, and catching hold of *Maritornes*, they began the most pleasant Skirmish in the World. When the Carrier perceiving, by the Light of the Inn-keeper's Lamp, the dismal Condition that his dear Mistress was in, presently took her Part; and leaving the Knight, whom he had more than sufficiently mawl'd, flew at the Squire, and paid him confoundedly. On the other hand, the Inn-keeper, who took the Wench to be the Cause of all this Hurly-burly, cuff'd and kick'd, and kick'd and cuff'd her over and over again: And so there was a strange Multiplication of Fisticuffs and Drubbings. The Carrier pommell'd *Sancho*, *Sancho* mawl'd the Wench, the Wench belabour'd the Squire, and the Innkeeper thrash'd her again: And all of 'em laid on with such Expedition, that you would have thought they had been afraid of losing Time. But the best Jest was, that in the Heat of the Fray the Lamp went out, so that being now in the Dark, they ply'd one another at a Venture; they struck and tore, all went to Rack, while Nails and Fists flew about without Mercy.

There happen'd to lodge that Night in the Inn one of the Officers belonging to that Society which they call the Old holy Brotherhood of *Toledo*, whose chief Office is to look after Thieves and Robbers. Being wak'd with the heavy Bustle, he presently jump'd out of his Bed, and with his short Staff in one Hand, and a Tin-Box with his Commission in't in the other, he grop'd out his Way; and being enter'd the Room in the dark, cry'd out, I charge ye all to keep the Peace: I am an Officer of the holy Brotherhood. The first he popp'd his Hand upon happen'd to be the poor batter'd Knight, who lay upon his Back, at his full Length, without any Feeling, upon the Ruins of his Bed. The Officer, having caught him by the Beard, presently cry'd out, I charge you to aid and assist me: But finding he could not stir, tho' he grip'd him hard, he presently imagin'd him to be dead, and murder'd by the rest in the Room. With that he bawl'd out to have the Gates of the Inn shut. Here's a Man murder'd, cry'd he; look that no body makes his Escape. These Words struck all the Combatants with such a Terror, that as soon as they reach'd their Ears, they gave over, and left the Argument undecided. Away stole the Inn-keeper to his own Room, the Carrier to his Pannels, and the Wench to her Kennel; only the unfortunate Knight, and his as unfortunate Squire, remain'd where they lay, not being able to stir; while the Officer, having let go Don *Quixote's* Beard, went out for a Light, in order to apprehend the suppos'd Murderers: But the Inn-keeper having wisely put out the Lamp in the Gate-

way, as he sneak'd out of the Room, the Officer was oblig'd
to repair to the Kitchen-Chimney, where with much ado,
puffing and blowing a long while amidst the Embers, he at
last made shift to get a Light.

III: A FURTHER ACCOUNT OF THE INNUMERABLE HARDSHIPS WHICH THE BRAVE DON QUIXOTE, AND HIS WORTHY SQUIRE SANCHO, UNDERWENT IN THE INN, WHICH THE KNIGHT UN-LUCKILY TOOK FOR A CASTLE

DON *Quixote*, who by this Time was come to himself, began to call *Sancho* with the same lamentable Tone as the Day before, when he had been beaten by the Carriers in the Meadow. *Sancho*, cry'd he, Friend *Sancho*, art thou asleep? art thou asleep, Friend *Sancho*? Sleep! reply'd *Sancho*, mightily out of Humour, may Old Nick rock my Cradle then. Why, how the Devil should I sleep, when all the Imps of Hell have been tormenting me to Night? Nay, thou'rt in the right, answer'd Don *Quixote*, for either I have no Skill in these Matters, or this Castle is inchanted. Hear what I say to thee, but first swear thou wilt never reveal it till after my Death. I swear it, quoth *Sancho*. I am thus cautious, said Don *Quixote*, because I hate to take away the Reputation of any Person. Why, quoth *Sancho*, I tell you again, I swear never to speak a Word of the Matter while you live; and I wish I may be at liberty to talk on't to Morrow. Why, cry'd Don *Quixote*! Have I done thee so much Wrong, *Sancho*, that thou would'st have me die so soon? Nay, 'tis not for that neither, quoth *Sancho*; but because I can't abide to keep things long, for fear they should grow mouldy. Well, let it be as thou pleasest, said Don *Quixote*: For I dare trust greater Concerns to thy Courtesy and Affection. In short, know, that this very Night there happen'd to me one of the strangest Adventures that can be imagin'd; for the Daughter of the Lord of this Castle came to me, who is one of the most engaging and most beautiful Damsels that ever Nature has been proud to boast of: What could I not tell thee of the Charms of her Shape and Face, and the Perfections of her Mind! What could I not add of other hidden Beauties, which I condemn to Silence and Oblivion, lest I endanger my Allegiance and Fidelity to my Lady *Dulcinea del Toboso*! I will only tell thee, That the Heavens envying the inestimable Happiness which Fortune had thrown into my Hand; or rather, because this Castle is inchanted, it happen'd, that in the midst of the most tender and passionate Discourses that pass'd between us, the prophane Hand of some mighty Giant, which I could not see, nor imagine whence it came, hit me such a dreadful Blow on the Jaws, that they are still embru'd with Blood; after which the discourteous Wretch, presuming on my present Weakness, did so barbarously bruise me, that I feel my self in a worse Condition now than I did Yesterday, after the Carriers had so roughly handled me for *Rozinante's* Incontinency: From which I conjecture, that the Treasure of this Damsel's Beauty is guarded by some inchanted *Moor*, and not reserv'd for Me.

Nor for me neither, quoth *Sancho*; for I have been Ribroasted by above four Hundred *Moors*, who have hammer'd my Bones in such guise, that I may safely say, the Assault and Battery made on my Body by the Carriers Poles and Packstaves, were but Ticklings and Stroakings with a Feather to this.* But, Sir, pray tell me, d'ye call this such a pleasant Adventure, when we are so lamentably pounded after it? And yet your Hap may well be accounted better than mine, seeing you've hugg'd that fair Maiden in your Arms. But I, what have I had, I pray you, but the heaviest Blows that e'er fell on a poor Man's Shoulders? Woe's me, and the Mother that bore me, for I neither am, nor ever mean to be a Knight-Errant, and yet, of all the Misadventures, the greater Part falls still to my Lot. What, hast thou been beaten as well as I, said Don *Quixote*? What a Plague, cry'd *Sancho*, ha'n't I been telling you so all this while? Come, never let it trouble thee, Friend *Sancho*, reply'd Don *Quixote*; for I'll immediately make the precious Balsam, that will cure thee in the twinkling of an Eye.

By this time the Officer, having lighted his Lamp, came into the Room, to see who it was that was murder'd. *Sancho* seeing him enter in his Shirt, a Napkin wrapp'd about his Head like a Turbant, and the Lamp in his Hand, he being

* *In the Original*, were Tarts and Cheese-cakes to this: Tortas y pan pintado.

also an ugly ill-look'd Fellow; Sir, quoth the Squire to his Master, pray see whether this be not the inchanted *Moor*, that's come again to have t'other Bout with me, and try whether he has not left some Place unbruis'd* for him now to mawl as much as the rest. It cannot be the *Moor*, reply'd Don *Quixote*; for Persons inchanted are to be seen by no body. If they don't suffer themselves to be seen, quoth *Sancho*, at least they suffer themselves to be felt: If not, let my Carcase bear Witness. So might mine, cry'd Don *Quixote*: Yet this is no sufficient Reason to prove, that what we see is the inchanted *Moor*.

While they were thus arguing, the Officer advanc'd, and wonder'd to hear two Men talk so calmly to one another there: Yet finding the unfortunate Knight lying in the same deplorable Posture as he left him, stretch'd out like a Corps, bloody, bruis'd, and beplaister'd, and not able to stir himself; How is't, honest Fellow, quoth he to the Champion, how do you find your self? Were I your Fellow, reply'd Don *Quixote*, I would have a little more Manners than you have, you Blockhead, you; is that Your way of approaching Knights-Errant in this Country? The Officer could not bear such a Reprimand from one who made so scurvy a Figure, and lifting up the Lamp, Oil and all, hit Don *Quixote* such a Blow on the Head with it, that he had Reason to fear he had made Work for the Surgeon, and therefore stole presently out of the Room, under the Protection of the Night. Well, Sir, quoth *Sancho*, d'you think now 'twas the inchanted *Moor*, or no? For my Part, I think he keeps the Treasure you talk of for others, and reserves only Kicks, Cuffs, Thumps and Knocks for your Worship and my self. I am now convinc'd, answer'd Don *Quixote*: Therefore let's wave that Resentment of these Injuries, which we might

---

* Left some Place unbruis'd, etc. *The new Translation has it,* Left something at the Bottom of the Inkhorn; *which is indeed what* Cervantes *literally says,* Si se dexò algo en el tintero. *But as no English Reader wou'd understand this, and many more of the like Phrases (without Notes at least) I have thought proper to deviate sometimes from the very Words of the Original. To leave something at the Bottom of the Inkhorn, is to leave a History, or any other Book imperfect, or partly unwritten; here it alludes to the* unbruis'd *Places of* Sancho's *Body.*

otherwise justly shew; for considering these Inchanters can make themselves invisible when they please, 'tis needless to think of Revenge. But, I pr'ythee rise, if thou can'st, *Sancho*, and desire the Governour of the Castle to send me some Oil, Salt, Wine and Rosemary, that I may make my healing Balsam; for truly I want it extremely, so fast the Blood flows out of the Wound which the Fantasm gave me just now.

Sancho then got up as fast as his aking Bones wou'd let him, and with much ado made shift to crawl out of the Room to look for the Inn-keeper, and stumbling by the Way on the Officer, who stood heark'ning to know what Mischief he had done; Sir, quoth he to him, for Heaven's sake, do so much as help us to a little Oil, Salt, Wine, and Rosemary, to make a Med'cine for one of the best Knights-Errant that e'er trod on Shoe of Leather, who lies yonder grievously wounded by the inchanted *Moor* of this Inn. The Officer hearing him talk at that Rate, took him to be out of his Wits; and it beginning to be Day-light, he open'd the Inn-Door, and told the Inn-keeper what *Sancho* wanted. The Host presently provided the desir'd Ingredients, and *Sancho* crept back with 'em to his Master, whom he found holding his Head, and sadly complaining of the Pain which he felt there; tho' after all, the Lamp had done him no more Harm than only raising of two huge Bumps; for that which he fancy'd to be Blood, was only Sweat, and the Oil of the Lamp that had liquor'd his Hair and Face.

The Knight took all the Ingredients, and having mix'd 'em together, he had 'em set o'er the Fire, and there kept 'em boiling till he thought they were enough. That done, he ask'd for a Vial to put this precious Liquor in: But there being none to be got, the Inn-keeper presented him with an old earthen Jug, and Don *Quixote* was forc'd to be contented with that. Then he mumbled over the Pot above Fourscore *Paternoster's*, and as many *Ave-Maria's*, *Salve Regina's*, and *Credo's*, making the Sign of the Cross at every Word by way of Benediction. At which Ceremony, *Sancho*, the Inn-keeper, and the Officer were present; for as for the Carrier, he was gone to look after his Mules, and took no manner of Notice of what was pass'd. This blessed Medicine being made, Don *Quixote* resolv'd to make an immediate Experiment of it on himself; and to that Purpose he took off a good Draught of the Overplus, which the Pot wou'd not hold: But he had scarce gulp'd it down, when it set him a vomiting so violently, that you wou'd have thought he'd have cast up his Heart, Liver and Guts; and his reaching and straining put him into such a Sweat, that he desired to be cover'd up warm, and left to his Repose. With that they left him, and he slept three whole Hours; and then waking, found himself so wonderfully eas'd, that he made no Question but he had now the right Balsam of *Fierabrass*; and therefore he thought he might safely undertake all the most dangerous Adventures in the World, without the least Hazard of his Person.

Sancho, encourag'd by the wonderful Effect of the Balsam on his Master, begg'd that he would be pleas'd to give him leave to sip up what was left in the Pot, which was no small Quantity; and the Don having consented, honest *Sancho* lifted it up with both his Hands, and with a strong Faith, and better Will, pour'd every Drop down his Throat. Now the Man's Stomach not being so nice as his Master's, the Drench did not set him a vomiting after that Manner; but caus'd such a Wambling in his Stomach, such a bitter Loathing, Kecking, and Reaching, and such grinding Pangs, with cold Sweats and Swoonings, that he verily believ'd his last Hour was come, and in the midst of his Agony gave both the Balsam and him that made it to the Devil. Friend, said Don *Quixote*, seeing him in that Condition, I began to think all this Pain befalls thee, only because thou hast not receiv'd the Order of Knighthood; for 'tis my Opinion, this Balsam ought to be us'd by no Man that is not a profess'd Knight. What a Plague did you mean then by letting me drink it? quoth *Sancho*; a Murrain on me, and all my Generation, why did you not tell me this before? At length the Dose began to work to some Purpose, and forc'd its Way at both Ends so copiously, that both his Bed-Mat and Coverlet were soon made unfit for any further Use; and all the while he strain'd so hard, that not only himself but the Standers by thought he would have dy'd. This dreadful Hurricane lasted about two Hours; and then too, instead of finding himself as free from Pain as his Master, he felt himself as feeble, and so far spent, that he was not able to stand.

But Don *Quixote*, as we have said, found himself in an excellent Temper; and his active Soul loathing an inglorious Repose, he presently was impatient to depart to perform the Duties of his adventurous Profession: For he thought those Moments that were trifled away in Amusements, or other Concerns, only a Blank in Life; and all Delays a depriving distress'd Persons, and the World in general, of his needed Assistance. The Confidence which he reposed in his Balsam, heighten'd, if possible, his Resolution; and thus carry'd away by his eager Thoughts, he saddl'd *Rozinante* himself, and then put the Pannel upon the Ass, and his Squire upon the Pannel, after he had help'd him to huddle on his Cloaths: That done, he mounted his Steed; and having spy'd a Javelin that stood in a Corner, he seiz'd and appropriated it to himself, to supply the Want of his Lance. Above twenty People that were in the Inn stood Spectators of all these Transactions; and among the rest, the Inn-keeper's Daughter, from whom Don *Quixote* had not Power to withdraw his Eyes, breathing out at every Glance a deep Sigh from the very Bottom of his Heart; which those who had seen him so mortify'd the Night before, took to proceed from the Pain of his Bruises.

And now being ready to set forwards, he call'd for the Master of the House, and with a grave Delivery, My Lord Governour, cry'd he, the Favours I have receiv'd in your Castle are so great and extraordinary, that they bind my grateful Soul to an eternal Acknowledgment: Therefore that I may be so happy as to discharge Part of the Obligation, think if there be e'er a proud Mortal breathing on whom you desire to be reveng'd for some Affront or other Injury, and acquaint me with it now, and by my Order of Knighthood, which binds me to protect the Weak, relieve the Oppressed, and punish the Bad, I promise you I'll take effectual Care, that you shall have ample Satisfaction to the utmost of your Wishes. Sir Knight, answer'd the Inn-keeper with an austere Gravity, I shall not need your Assistance to revenge any Wrong that may have been offer'd to My Person; for I would have you to understand, that I am able to do my self Justice, whenever any Man presumes to do me Wrong: Therefore all the Satisfaction I desire is, that you will pay your Reckoning for Horse-Meat and Man's-Meat, and all your Expences in my Inn. How! cry'd Don *Quixote*, is this an Inn? Yes, answer'd the Host, and one of the most noted, and of the best Repute upon the Road. How strangely have I been mistaken then! cry'd Don *Quixote*; upon my Honour I took it for a Castle, and a considerable one too: But if it be an Inn, and not a Castle, all I have to say is, that you must excuse me from paying any thing; for I would by no Means break the Laws which we Knights-Errant are bound to observe; nor was it ever known, that they ever paid in any Inn whatsoever; for this is the least Recompence that can be allow'd 'em for the intolerable Labours they endure Day and Night, Winter and Summer, o'Foot and o'Horse-back, pinch'd with Hunger, choak'd with Thirst, and expos'd to all the Injuries of the Air, and all the Inconveniences in the World. I've nothing to do with all this, cry'd the Inn-keeper: Pay your Reckoning, and don't trouble me with your foolish Stories of a Cock and a Bull; I can't afford to keep House at that Rate. Thou art both a Fool and a Knave of an Inn-keeper, reply'd Don *Quixote*: And with that clapping Spurs to *Rozinante*, and brandishing his Javelin at his Host, he rode out of the Inn without any Opposition, and got a good way from it, without so much as once looking behind him to see whether his Squire came after him.

The Knight being march'd off, there remain'd only the Squire, who was stopp'd for the Reckoning. However he swore bloodily he would not pay a Cross; for the selfsame Law that acquitted the Knight acquitted the Squire. This put the Inn-keeper into a great Passion, and made him threaten *Sancho* very hard, telling him if he would not pay him by fair Means, he would have him laid by the Heels that Moment. *Sancho* swore by his Master's Knighthood, he would sooner part with his Life than his Money on such an Account; nor should the Squires in After-Ages ever have Occasion to upbraid him with giving so ill a Precedent, or breaking their Rights. But as ill Luck would have it, there happen'd to be in the Inn four *Segovia* Clothiers, three *Cordoua* Point-makers, and two *Seville* Hucksters, all brisk, gamesome, arch Fellows; who agreeing all in the same Design, encompass'd *Sancho*, and pull'd him off his Ass, while one of 'em went and got a Blanket. Then they put the unfortunate Squire into it, and observing the Roof of the Place they were in, to be somewhat too low for their Purpose, they carry'd him into the Back-Yard, which had no Limits but the Sky, and there they toss'd him for several times together in the Blanket, as they do Dogs on *Shrove-Tuesday*. Poor *Sancho* made so grievous an Out-cry all the while, that his Master heard him, and imagin'd those Lamentations were of some Person in Distress, and consequently the Occasion of some Adventure: But having at last distinguish'd the Voice, he made to the Inn with a broken Gallop; and finding the Gates shut, he rode about to see whether he might not find some other Way to get in. But he no sooner came to the Back-yard Wall, which was none of the highest, when he was an Eye-witness of the scurvy Trick that was put upon his Squire. There he saw him ascend and descend, and frolick and caper in the Air with so much Nimbleness and Agility, that 'tis thought the Knight himself could not have forborn Laughing, had he been any thing less angry. He did his best to get over the Wall, but alas! he was so bruis'd, that he could not so much as alight from his Horse. This made him fume and chafe, and vent his Passion in a thousand Threats and Curses, so strange and various that 'tis impossible to repeat 'em. But the more he storm'd, the more they toss'd and laugh'd; *Sancho* on his Side begging, and howling, and threatning, and damning to as little Purpose as his Master, for 'twas Weariness alone could make the Tossers give over. Then they charitably put an End to his high Dancing, and set him upon his Ass again, carefully wrapp'd in his Mantle. But *Maritornes's* tender Soul made her pity a male Creature in such Tribulation; and thinking he had danc'd and tumbled enough to be a-dry, she was so generous as to help him to a Draught of Water, which she purposely drew from the Well that Moment, that it might be the cooler. *Sancho* clapp'd the Pot to his Mouth, but his Master made him desist: Hold,

hold, cry'd he, Son *Sancho*, drink no Water, Child, 'twill kill thee: Behold I have here the most holy Balsam, two Drops of which will cure thee effectually. Ha, (reply'd *Sancho*, shaking his Head, and looking sourly on the Knight with a Side-Face) have you again forgot that I'm no Knight? or would you have me cast up the few Guts I've left since Yesternight's Jobb? Keep your Brewings for your self in the Devil's Name, and let Me alone. With that he lifted up the Jug to his Nose, but finding it to be meer Element, he spirted out again the little he had tasted, and desir'd the Wench to help him to some better Liquor: So she went and fetch'd him Wine to make him Amends, and paid for't too out of her own Pocket; for to give the Devil his Due, 'twas said of her, that tho' she was somewhat too free of her Favours, yet she had something of Christianity in her. As soon as *Sancho* had tipp'd off his Wine, he visited his Ass's Ribs twice or thrice with his Heels, and free Egress being granted him, he troop'd off, mightily tickled with the Thoughts of having had his Ends; and got off shot-free, tho' at the Expence of his Shoulders, his usual Sureties: 'Tis true, the Inn-keeper kept his Wallet for the Reckoning; but the poor Squire was so dismay'd, and in such haste to be gone, that he never miss'd it. The Host was for shutting the Inn-Doors after him, for fear of the worst; but the Tossers would not let him, being a sort of Fellows that would not have matter'd Don *Quixote* a Straw, tho' he had really been one of the Knights of the Round-Table.

IV: OF THE DISCOURSE BETWEEN THE KNIGHT AND THE SQUIRE, WITH OTHER MATTERS WORTH RELATING

SANCHO overtook his Master, but so pale, so dead-hearted, and so mortify'd, that he was hardly able to sit his Ass. My dear *Sancho*, said Don *Quixote*, seeing him in that Condition, I am now fully convinc'd that this Castle, or Inn, is inchanted: For what could they be that made themselves such barbarous Sport with thee, but Spirits and People of the other World? And I the rather believe this, seeing, that when I look'd over the Wall, and saw thee thus abus'd, I strove to get over it but could not stir, nor by any Means alight from *Rozinante*. For, by my Honour, could I either have got over the Wall or dismounted, I would have reveng'd thee so effectually on those discourteous Wretches, that they should never have forgot the Severity of their Punishment, though for once I had infringed the Laws of Chivalry; which, as I have often inform'd thee, do not permit any Knight to lay Hands on one that is not Knighted, unless it be in his own Defence, and in case of great Necessity. Nay, quoth *Sancho*, I would have paid 'em home my self, whether Knight or no Knight, but 'twas not in my Power; and yet I dare say, those that made themselves so merry with my Carcase were neither Spirits nor inchanted Folks, as you will have it, but meer Flesh and Blood as we be. I'm sure they call'd one another by their Christian Names and Sir-Names, while they made me vault and frisk in the air: One was call'd *Pedro Martinez*, t'other *Tenorio Hernandez*; and as for our Dog of a Host, I heard 'em call him *Juan Palomeque* the Left-handed. Then pray don't you fancy, that your not being able to get over the Wall, nor to alight, was some Inchanter's Trick. 'Tis a Folly to make many Words; 'tis as plain as the Nose in a Man's Face, that these same Adventures which we hunt for up and down, are like to bring us at last into a Peck of Troubles, and such a plaguy deal of Mischief, that we shan't be able to set one Foot afore t'other. The short and the long is, I take it to be the wisest Course to jog home and look after our Harvest, and not run rambling from *Ceca* to *Meca*,* lest *we leap out of the Frying-pan into the Fire*, or, *out of God's Blessing into the warm Sun*. Poor *Sancho*, cry'd Don *Quixote*, how ignorant thou art in Matters of Chivalry! Come, say no more, and have Patience: A Day will come when thou shalt be convinc'd how honourable a Thing it is to fol- low this Employment. For, tell me, what Satisfaction in this World, what Pleasure can equal that of vanquishing and triumphing over one's Enemy? None, without Doubt. It may be so for ought I know, quoth *Sancho*, though I know nothing of the Matter. However, this I may venture to say, that ever since we have turn'd Knights-Errant, (your Worship I mean, for 'tis not for such Scrubs as my self to be nam'd the same Day with such Folk) the Devil of any Fight you have had the better in, unless it be that with the *Biscayan*; and in that too you came off with the Loss of one Ear and the Vizor of your Helmet. And what have we got ever since, pray, but Blows, and more Blows; Bruises, and more Bruises? besides this tossing in a Blanket, which fell all to my Share, and for which I can't be reveng'd because they were Hobgoblins that serv'd me so forsooth, though I hugely long to be even with 'em, that I may know the Pleasure you say there is in vanquishing one's Enemy. I find, *Sancho*, cry'd Don *Quixote*, thou and I are both sick of the same Disease; but I will endeavour with all Speed to get me a Sword made with so much Art, that no sort of Inchantment shall be able to hurt whosoever shall wear it; and perhaps Fortune may put into my Hand that which *Amadis de Gaul* wore when he styl'd himself, *The Knight of the Burning Sword*, which was one of the best Blades that ever was drawn by Knight: For, besides the Virtue I now mention'd, it had an Edge like a Razor, and would enter the strongest Armour that ever was tempered or inchanted. I'll lay any thing, quoth *Sancho*, when you've found this Sword, 'twill prove just such another Help to me as your Balsam; that is to say, 'twill stand no

* Ceca *was a Place of Devotion among the* Moors, *in the City of* Cordova, *to which they us'd to go in Pilgrimage from other Places, as* Meca *is among the* Turks: *Whence the Proverb comes to signify* Sauntring about to no Purpose. A *Banter upon* Popish *Pilgrimages.*

body in any stead but your dubb'd Knights, let the poor Devil of a Squire shift how he can. Fear no such thing, reply'd Don *Quixote*; Heaven will be more propitious to thee than thou imaginest.

Thus they went on discoursing, when Don *Quixote*, perceiving a thick Cloud of Dust arise right before 'em in the Road, the Day is come, said he, turning to his Squire, the Day is come, *Sancho*, that shall usher in the Happiness which Fortune has reserv'd for me: This Day shall the Strength of my Arm be signaliz'd by such Exploits as shall be transmitted even to the latest Posterity. See'st thou that Cloud of Dust, *Sancho*? It is raised by a prodigious Army marching this Way, and composed of an infinite Number of Nations. Why then, at this Rate, quoth *Sancho*, there should be two Armies; for yonder's as great a Dust on t'other Side: With that Don *Quixote* look'd, and was transported with Joy at the Sight, firmly believing that two vast Armies were ready to engage each other in that Plain: For his Imagination was so crowded with those Battles, Inchantments, surprizing Adventures, amorous Thoughts, and other Whimsies which he had read of in Romances, that his strong Fancy chang'd every thing he saw into what he desir'd to see; and thus he could not conceive that the Dust was only rais'd by two large Flocks of Sheep that were going the same Road from different Parts, and could not be discern'd till they were very near: He was so positive that they were two Armies, that *Sancho* firmly believ'd him at last. Well Sir, quoth the Squire, what are we to do I beseech you? What should we do, reply'd Don *Quixote*, but assist the weaker and the injur'd Side? For know, *Sancho*, that the Army which now moves towards us is commanded by the Great *Alifanfaron*, Emperor of the vast Island of *Taprobana*: The other that advances behind us is his Enemy, the King of the *Garamantians*, *Pentapolin with the naked Arm*; so call'd, because he always enters into the Battle with his right Arm bare.* Pray Sir, quoth *Sancho*, why are these two Great Men going together by the Ears? The Occasion of their Quarrel is this, answer'd Don *Quixote*, *Alifanfaron*, a strong *Pagan*, is in Love with *Pentapolin's*

* *Alluding to the Story of* Scanderbeg *King of* Epirus.

Daughter, a very beautiful Lady and a Christian: Now her Father refuses to give her Marriage to the Heathen Prince, unless he abjure his false Belief and embrace the Christian Religion. Burn my Beard, said *Sancho*, if *Pentapolin* ben't in the right on't; I'll stand by him, and help him all I may. I commend thy Resolution, reply'd Don *Quixote*, 'tis not only lawful but requisite; for there's no Need of being a Knight to fight in such Battles. I guess'd as much, quoth *Sancho*: But where shall we leave my Ass in the mean time, that I may be sure to find him again after the Battle; for I fancy you never heard of any Man that ever charg'd upon such a Beast. 'Tis true, answer'd Don *Quixote*, and therefore I would have thee turn him loose, though thou wert sure never to find him again; for we shall have so many Horses after we have got the Day, that even *Rozinante* himself will be in Danger of being chang'd for another. Then mounting to the top of a Hillock, whence they might have seen both the Flocks, had not the Dust obstructed their Sight, Look yonder *Sancho*, cry'd Don *Quixote*! that Knight whom thou see'st in the gilded Arms, bearing in his Shield a crown'd Lion couchant at the Feet of a Lady, is the valiant *Laurealco*, Lord of the silver Bridge. He in the Armour powder'd with Flowers of Gold, bearing three Crows *Argent* in a Field *Azure*, is the formidable *Micocolembo*, Great Duke of *Quiracia*. That other of a Gigantick Size that marches on his Right, is the undaunted *Brandabarbaran* of *Boliche*, Sovereign of the three *Arabia's*; he's array'd in a Serpents-skin, and carries instead of a Shield a huge Gate, which they say belong'd to the Temple which *Sampson* pull'd down at his Death, when he reveng'd himself upon his Enemies. But cast thy Eyes on this Side, *Sancho*, and at the Head of t'other Army see the ever victorious *Timonel* of *Carcaiona*, Prince of *New Biscay*, whose Armour is quarter'd *Azure*, *Vert*, *Or*, and *Argent*, and who bears in his Shield a Cat *Or*, in a Field *Gules*, with these four Letters, *MIAU*, for a Motto, being the Beginning of his Mistress's Name, the beautiful *Miaulina*, Daughter to *Alpheniquen* Duke of *Algarva*. That other monstrous Load upon the Back of yonder wild Horse, with Arms as white as Snow, and a Shield without any *Device*, is a *Frenchman*, new-created

Knight, call'd *Pierre Papin*, Baron of *Utrick*: He whom you see pricking that py'd Courser's Flanks with his arm'd Heels, is the mighty Duke of *Nervia*, *Espartafilardo* of the Wood, bearing in his Shield a Field of pure Azure, powder'd with *Asparagus* (*Esparrago**) with this Motto in *Castilian*, *Rastrea mi suerte*; *Thus trails*, or *drags my Fortune*. And thus he went on, naming a great Number of others in both Armies, to every one of whom his fertile Imagination assign'd Arms, Colours, *Impresses* and *Motto's*, as readily as if they had really been that Moment extant before his Eyes. And then proceeding without the least Hesitation; That vast Body, said he, that's just opposite to us, is compos'd of several Nations. There you see those who drink the pleasant Stream of the famous *Xanthus*: There the Mountaineers that till the *Massilian*† Fields: Those that sift the pure Gold of *Arabia Fælix*: Those that inhabit the renown'd and delightful Banks of *Thermodoon*. Yonder, those who so many Ways sluice and drain the golden *Pactolus* for its precious Sand. The *Numidians*, unsteady, and careless of their Promises. The *Persians*, excellent Archers. The *Medes* and *Parthians*, who fight flying. The *Arabs*, who have no fix'd Habitations. The *Scythians*, cruel and savage, though fair-complexion'd. The sooty *Ethiopians*, that bore their Lips; and a thousand other Nations whose Countenances I know, tho' I have forgotten their Names. On the other Side, come those whose Country is water'd with the Crystal Streams of *Betis*, shaded with Olive-Trees. Those who bathe their Limbs in the rich Flood of the golden *Tagus*. Those whose Mansions are lav'd by the profitable Stream of the divine *Genile*. Those who range the verdant *Tartesian* Meadows. Those who indulge their luxurious Temper in the delicious Pastures of *Xerez*. The

---

* *The Gingle between the Duke's Name* Espartafilardo *and* Esparrago (*his Arms*) *is a Ridicule upon the foolish Quibbles so frequent in Heraldry; and probably this whole Catalogue is a Satire upon several great Names and sounding Titles in Spain, whose Owners were arrant Beggars. The trailing of his Fortune may allude to the Word* Esparto, *a sort of Rush they make Ropes with. Or perhaps he was without a Mistress, to which the Sparagrass may allude: For, in Spain they have a Proverb,* Solo comes el Esparrago: *As solitary as Sparagrass, because every one of 'em springs up by it self.* † *This is an Imitation of* Homer's *Catalogue of Ships.*

wealthy Inhabitants of the *Mancha*, crown'd with golden
Ears of Corn. The ancient Offspring of the *Goths*, cas'd in
Iron. Those who wanton in the lazy Current of *Pisverga*.
Those who feed their numerous Flocks in the ample Plains
where the *Guadiana*, so celebrated for its hidden Course,
pursues its wand'ring Race. Those who shiver with Extremity of Cold, on the woody *Pyrenean* Hills, or on the
hoary Tops of the snowy *Apennine*. In a Word, all that
Europe includes within its spacious Bounds, half a World in
an Army. 'Tis scarce to be imagin'd how many Countries he
ran over, how many Nations he enumerated, distinguishing
every one by what is peculiar to 'em, with an incredible Vivacity of Mind, and that still in the puffy Style of his fabulous
Books. *Sancho* listen'd to all this Romantick Muster-Roll as
mute as a Fish, with Amazement; all that he could do was
now and then to turn his Head on this Side and t'other Side,
to see if he could discern the Knights and Giants whom his
Master nam'd. But at length not being able to discover any;
why, cry'd he, you had as good tell me it snows; the Devil
of any Knight, Giant, or Man can I see, of all those you
talk of now; who knows but all this may be Witchcraft and
Spirits, like Yesternight? How, reply'd Don *Quixote*! Dost
thou not hear their Horses neigh, their Trumpets sound,
and their Drums beat? Not I, quoth *Sancho*, I prick up my
Ears like a Sow in the Beans, and yet I can hear nothing but
the Bleating of Sheep. *Sancho* might justly say so indeed,
for by this time the two Flocks were got very near 'em. Thy
Fear disturbs thy Senses, said Don *Quixote*, and hinders thee
from hearing and seeing right: But 'tis no Matter; withdraw
to some Place of Safety, since thou art so terrify'd; for I alone
am sufficient to give the Victory to that Side which I shall
favour with my Assistance. With that he couch'd his Lance,
clapp'd Spurs to *Rozinante*, and rush'd like a Thunder-bolt
from the Hillock into the Plain. *Sancho* bawl'd after him as
loud as he could; Hold, Sir, cry'd *Sancho*; for Heav'ns sake
come back. What do you mean? As sure as I am a Sinner those
you're going to maul are nothing but poor harmless Sheep.
Come back, I say. Woe be to him that begot me! Are you
mad, Sir? There are no Giants, no Knights, no Cats, no As-

paragus-Gardens, no golden Quarters, no what d'ye call 'ems. Does the Devil possess you? You're leaping over the Hedge before you come at the Stile. You're taking the wrong Sow by the Ear. Oh that I was ever born to see this Day! But Don *Quixote* still riding on, deaf and lost to good Advice, out-roar'd his expostulating Squire. Courage, brave Knights, cry'd he; march up, fall on, all you who fight under the Standard of the valiant *Pentapolin* with the naked Arm: Follow me, and you shall see how easily I will revenge him on that Infidel *Alifanfaron* of *Taprobana*; and so saying, he charg'd the Squadron of Sheep with that Gallantry and Resolution, that he pierc'd, broke, and put it to Flight in an Instant, charging through and through, not without a great Slaughter of his mortal Enemies, whom he laid at his Feet, biting the Ground and wallowing in their Blood. The Shep-herds seeing their Sheep go to Rack, call'd out to him; till finding fair Means ineffectual, they unloos'd their Slings, and began to ply him with Stones as big as their Fists. But the Champion disdaining such a distant War, spite of their Showers of Stones, rush'd among the routed Sheep, tramp-ling both the Living and the Slain in a most terrible Manner, impatient to meet the General of the Enemy, and end the War at once. Where, where art thou, cry'd he, proud *Ali-fanfaron*? Appear! See here a single Knight who seeks thee every where, to try now, Hand to Hand, the boasted Force of thy strenuous Arm, and deprive thee of Life, as a due Punishment for the unjust War which thou hast audaciously wag'd with the valiant *Pentapolin*. Just as he had said this, while the Stones flew about his Ears, one unluckily lit upon his small Ribs, and had like to have buried two of the shortest deep in the middle of his Body. The Knight thought himself slain, or at least desperately wounded; and therefore calling to mind his precious Balsam, and pulling out his Earthen Jug, he clapp'd it to his Mouth: But before he had swallow'd a sufficient Dose, *souse* comes another of those bitter Almonds that spoil'd his Draught, and hit him so pat upon the Jug, Hand and Teeth, that it broke the first, maim'd the second, and struck out three or four of the last. These two Blows were so violent, that the boisterous Knight falling from his

Horse, lay upon the Ground as quiet as the Slain; so that the Shepherds, fearing he was kill'd, got their Flock together with all Speed, and carrying away their Dead, which were no less than seven Sheep, they made what Haste they could out of Harm's way, without looking any farther into the Matter.

All this while *Sancho* stood upon the Hill, where he was mortify'd upon the Sight of this mad Adventure. There he stamp'd and swore, and bann'd his Master to the bottomless Pit; he tore his Beard for Madness, and curs'd the Moment he first knew him: But seeing him at last knock'd down, and settl'd, the Shepherds being scamper'd, he thought he might venture to come down; and found him in a very ill Plight, tho' not altogether senseless. Ah! Master, quoth he, this comes of not taking my Counsel. Did not I tell you 'twas a Flock of Sheep, and no Army? Friend *Sancho*, reply'd Don *Quixote*, know 'tis an easy Matter for Necromancers to change the Shapes of Things as they please: Thus that malicious Inchanter, who is my inveterate Enemy, to deprive me of the Glory which he saw me ready to acquire, while I was reaping a full Harvest of Laurels, transform'd in a Moment the routed Squadrons into Sheep. If thou wilt not believe me, *Sancho*, yet do one thing for my sake; do but take thy Ass, and follow those suppos'd Sheep at a Distance, and I dare engage thou shalt soon see 'em resume their former Shapes, and appear such as I describ'd 'em. But stay, do not go yet, for I want thy Assistance: Draw near, and see how many Cheek-Teeth and others I want, for by the dreadful Pain in my Jaws and Gums, I fear there's a total Dilapidation in my Mouth. With that the Knight open'd his Mouth as wide as he could, while the Squire gap'd to tell his Grinders, with his Snout almost in his Chaps; but just in that fatal Moment the Balsam that lay wambling and fretting in Don *Quixote's* Stomach, came up with an unlucky *Hickup*; and with the same Violence that the Powder flies out of a Gun, all that he had in his Stomach discharg'd it self upon the Beard, Face, Eyes, and Mouth of the officious Squire. *Santa Maria*, cry'd poor *Sancho*, what will become of me! My Master is a dead Man! He's vomiting his very

Heart's Blood! But he had hardly said this, when the Colour, Smell, and Taste soon undeceiv'd him; and finding it to be his Master's loathsome Drench, it caus'd such a sudden rumbling in his Maw, that before he could turn his Head he unladed the whole Cargo of his Stomach full in his Master's Face, and put him in as delicate a Pickle as he was him-self. *Sancho* having thus paid him in his own Coin, half blinded as he was, ran to his Ass, to take out something to clean himself and his Master: But when he came to look for his Wallet, and found it missing, not rememb'ring till then that he had unhappily left it in the Inn, he was ready to run quite out of his Wits: He storm'd and stamp'd, and curs'd him worse than before, and resolv'd with himself to let his Master go to the Devil, and e'en trudge home by him-self, tho' he was sure to lose his Wages, and his Hopes of being Governor of the promis'd Island.

Thereupon Don *Quixote* got up with much ado, and clap-ping his Left-Hand before his Mouth, that the rest of his loose Teeth might not drop out, he laid his Right-Hand on *Rozinante's* Bridle; (for such was the Good-nature of the Creature, that he had not budg'd a Foot from his Master) then he crept along to Squire *Sancho*, that stood lolling on his Ass's Pannel, with his Face in the Hollow of both his Hands, in a doleful moody melancholy Fit. Friend *Sancho*, said he, seeing him thus abandon'd to Sorrow, learn of Me, that one Man is no more than another, if he do no more than what another does. All these Storms and Hurricanes are but Arguments of the approaching Calm: Better Success will soon follow our past Calamities: Good and bad Fortune have their Vicissitudes; and 'tis a Maxim, That nothing violent can last long: And therefore we may well promise our selves a speedy Change in our Fortune, since our Afflictions have extended their Reign beyond the usual stint: Besides, thou ought'st not to afflict thy self so much for Misfortunes, of which thou hast no Share, but what Friendship and Humanity bid thee take. How, quoth *Sancho*! Have I no other Share in them! Was not he that was toss'd in the Blanket this Morning the Son of my Father? And did not the Wallet, and all that was in't, which I have lost, belong to the Son of my Mother?

How, ask'd Don *Quixote*, hast thou lost thy Wallet? I don't know, said *Sancho*, whether 'tis lost or no, but I'm sure I can't tell what's become of it. Nay then, reply'd Don *Quixote*, I find we must fast to Day. Ay marry must we, quoth *Sancho*, unless you take Care to gather in these Fields some of those Roots and Herbs which I've heard you say you know, and which use to help such unlucky Knights-Errant as your self at a dead Lift. For all that, cry'd Don *Quixote*, I would rather have at this time a good Luncheon of Bread, or a Cake and two Pilchards Heads, than all the Roots and Simples in *Dioscorides's* Herbal, and Doctor *Laguna's* Supplement and Commentary: I pray thee therefore get upon thy Ass, good *Sancho*, and follow me once more; for God's Providence, that relieves every Creature, will not fail Us, especially since we are about a Work so much to his Service: Thou seest he even provides for the little flying Insects in the Air, the Worm-lings in the Earth, and the Spawnlings in the Water; and, in his infinite Mercy, he makes his Sun shine on the Right-eous, and on the Unjust, and rains upon the Good and the Bad. Many Words won't fill a Bushel, quoth *Sancho*, inter-rupting him; you would make a better Preacher than a Knight-Errant, or I'm plaguily out. Knights-Errant, reply'd Don *Quixote*, ought to know all Things: There have been such in former Ages, that have deliver'd as ingenious and learned a Sermon or Oration at the Head of an Army, as if they had taken their Degrees at the University of *Paris*: From which we may infer, that the Lance never dull'd the Pen, nor the Pen the Lance. Well then, quoth *Sancho*, for once let it be as you'd have it; let's e'en leave this unlucky Place, and seek out a Lodging; where, I pray God, there may be neither Blankets, nor Blanket-heavers, nor Hobgoblins, nor inchanted *Moors*; for before I'll be hamper'd as I've been, may I be curs'd with Bell, Book and Candle, if I don't give the Trade to the Devil. Leave all Things to Providence, reply'd Don *Quixote*, and for once lead which Way thou pleasest, for I leave it wholly to thy Discretion to provide us a Lodging. But first, I pray thee, feel a little how many Teeth I want in my upper Jaw on the Right-side, for there I feel most Pain. With that *Sancho* feeling with his Finger

in the Knight's Mouth; Pray, Sir, quoth he, how many Grinders did your Worship use to have on that Side? Four, answer'd
Don *Quixote*, besides the Eye-Tooth, all of 'em whole and
sound. Think well on what you say, cry'd *Sancho*. I say four,
reply'd Don *Quixote*, if there were not five; for I never in
all my Life have had a Tooth drawn, or dropp'd out, or rotted
by the Worm, or loosen'd by Rheum. Bless me, quoth *Sancho*!
Why, you have in this nether Jaw on this Side but two Grinders and a Stump; and in that Part of your upper Jaw, never
a Stump, and never a Grinder; alas! all's levell'd there as
smooth as the Palm of one's Hand. Oh unfortunate Don
Quixote! cry'd the Knight, I had rather have lost an Arm,
so it were not my Sword-Arm; for a Mouth without Cheek-
Teeth, is like a Mill without a Mill-stone, *Sancho*; and every
Tooth in a Man's Head is more valuable than a Diamond.
But we that profess this strict Order of Knight-Errantry, are
all subject to these Calamities; and therefore since the Loss
is irretrievable, mount, my trusty *Sancho*, and go thy own
Pace; I'll follow thee. *Sancho* obey'd, and led the Way, still
keeping the Road they were in; which being very much
beaten, promis'd to bring him soonest to a Lodging. Thus pacing along very softly, for Don *Quixote's* Gums and Ribs would
not suffer him to go faster; *Sancho*, to divert his uneasy
Thoughts, resolv'd to talk to him all the while of one Thing
or other, as the next Chapter will inform you.

V: OF THE WISE DISCOURSE BETWEEN SANCHO
AND HIS MASTER; AS ALSO OF THE ADVENTURE
OF THE DEAD CORPS, AND OTHER FAMOUS
OCCURRENCES

NOW, Sir, quoth *Sancho*, I can't help think-ing, but that all the Mishaps that have be-fall'n us of late, are a just Judgment for the grievous Sin you've committed against the Order of Knighthood, in not keeping the Oath you swore, Not to eat Bread at Board, nor to have a merry Bout with the Queen, and the Lord knows what more, 'till you had won *What d'ye call him*, the *Moor's** Helmet, I think you nam'd him. Truly, answer'd Don *Quixote*, thou'rt much in the right, *Sancho*; and to deal ingeniously with thee, I wholly forgot that: And now thou may'st certainly assure thy self, thou wert toss'd in a Blanket for not rememb'ring to put me in Mind of it. However, I will take Care to make due Atonement; for Knight-Errantry has Ways to conciliate all sorts of Matters. Why, quoth *Sancho*, did I ever swear to mind you of your Vow? 'Tis nothing to the Purpose, reply'd Don *Quixote*, whether thou swor'st or no: Let it suffice, that I think thou art not very clear from being accessary to the Breach of my Vow; and therefore to prevent the Worst, there will be no Harm in providing for a Remedy. Hark you then, cry'd *Sancho*, be sure you don't forget your Atonement, as you did your Oath, lest those confounded Hobgoblins come and mawl Me, and mayhap You too, for being a stubborn Sinner.

Insensibly Night overtook 'em before they could discover any Lodging; and, which was worse, they were almost Hunger-starv'd, all their Provision being in the Wallet which *Sancho* had unluckily left behind; and to compleat their Dis-tress, there happen'd to them an Adventure, or something that really look'd like one.

While our benighted Travellers went on dolefully in the Dark, the Knight very hungry, and the Squire very sharp

* Melandrino.

set, what shou'd they see moving towards them but a great
Number of Lights, that appear'd like so many wand'ring
Stars. At this strange Apparition, down sunk *Sancho's* Heart
at once, and even Don *Quixote* himself was not without some
Symptoms of Surprize. Presently the one pull'd to him his
Ass's Halter, the other his Horse's Bridle, and both made a
Stop. They soon perceiv'd that the Lights made directly towards them, and the nearer they came the bigger they appear'd. At the terrible Wonder *Sancho* shook and shiver'd
every Joint like one in a Palsy, and Don *Quixote's* Hair stood
up on End: However, heroically shaking off the Amazement
which that Sight stamp'd upon his Soul, *Sancho*, said he, this
must doubtless be a great and most perilous Adventure, where
I shall have Occasion to exert the whole Stock of my Courage
and Strength. Woe's me, quoth *Sancho*, shou'd this happen
to be another Adventure of Ghosts, as I fear it is, where shall
I find Ribs to endure it? Come all the Fiends in Hell, cry'd
Don *Quixote*, I will not suffer 'em to touch a Hair of thy Head.
If they insulted thee lately, know there was then between
thee and me a Wall, over which I could not climb; but now
we are in the open Field, where I shall have Liberty to make
use of my Sword. Ay, quoth *Sancho*, you may talk; but shou'd
they bewitch you as they did before, what the Devil would
it avail us to be in the open Field? Come, *Sancho*, reply'd Don
Quixote, be of good Cheer; the Event will soon convince thee
of the Greatness of my Valour. Pray Heav'n it may, quoth
Sancho; I'll do my best. With that they rode a little out of
the Way, and gazing earnestly at the Lights, they soon discover'd a great Number of Persons all in White. At the dreadful Sight, all poor *Sancho's* shuffling Courage basely deserted
him; his Teeth began to chatter as if he had been in an Ague
Fit, and as the Objects drew nearer his Chattering increas'd.
And now they could plainly distinguish about twenty Men
on Horse-back, all in White, with Torches in their Hands,
follow'd by a Herse cover'd over with Black, and six Men in
deep Mourning, whose Mules were also in Black down to
their very Heels. Those in White mov'd slowly, murmuring
from their Lips something in a low and lamentable Tone.
This dismal Spectacle, at such a Time at Night, in the Midst

of such a vast Solitude, was enough to have shipwreck'd the
Courage of a stouter Squire than *Sancho*, and even of his
Master, had he been any other than Don *Quixote*: But as his
Imagination straight suggested to him, that this was one of
those Adventures of which he had so often read in his Books
of Chivalry, the Herse appear'd to him to be a Litter, where
lay the Body of some Knight either slain or dangerously
wounded, the Revenge of whose Misfortunes was reserv'd
for his prevailing Arm: And so without any more ado, couching his Lance, and seating himself firm in his Saddle, he
posted himself in the Middle of the Road, where the Company were to pass. As soon as they came near, Stand, cry'd
he to 'em in a haughty Tone, whoever you be, and tell me
who you are, whence ye come, whither ye go, and what you
carry in that Litter? For there's all the Reason in the World
to believe, that you have either done, or receiv'd a great deal
of Harm; and 'tis requisite I should be inform'd of the Matter,
in order either to punish you for the Ill you have committed,
or else to revenge you of the Wrong you have suffer'd. Sir,
answer'd one of the Men in White, we are in haste; the Inn
is a great Way off, and we cannot stay to answer so many
Questions; and with that spurring his Mule, he mov'd forwards. But Don *Quixote*, highly dissatisfy'd with the Reply,
laid hold on the Mule's Bridle and stopp'd him: Stay, cry'd
he, proud discourteous Knight, mend your Behaviour, and
give me instantly an Account of what I ask'd of ye, or here I
defy ye all to mortal Combat. Now the Mule, that was shy
and skittish, being thus rudely seiz'd by the Bridle, was presently scar'd, and rising up on her hinder Legs, threw her
Rider to the Ground. Upon this one of the Footmen that
belong'd to the Company gave Don *Quixote* ill Language;
which so incens'd him, that being resolv'd to be reveng'd
upon 'em all, in a mighty Rage he flew at the next he met,
who happen'd to be one of the Mourners. Him he threw to
the Ground very much hurt; and then turning to the rest
with a wonderful Agility, he fell upon 'em with such Fury,
that he presently put 'em all to flight. You wou'd have
thought *Rozinante* had Wings at that Time, so active and so
fierce he then approv'd himself.

It was not indeed for Men unarm'd, and naturally fearful, to maintain the Field against such an Enemy; no Wonder then if the Gentlemen in White were immediately dispers'd: Some ran one Way, some another, crossing the Plain with their lighted Torches: You wou'd now have taken them for a Parcel of frolicksome Masqueraders gamboling and scouring on a Carnaval Night. As for the Mourners, they, poor Men, were so muffled up in their long cumbersome Cloaks, that not being able to make their Party good, nor defend themselves, they were presently routed, and ran away like the rest, the rather, for that they thought 'twas no mortal Creature, but the Devil himself, that was come to fetch away the dead Body which they were accompanying to the Grave.* All the while *Sancho* was lost in Admiration and Astonishment, charm'd with the Sight of his Master's Valour; and now concluded him to be the formidable Champion he boasted himself.

After this the Knight, by the Light of a Torch that lay burning upon the Ground, perceiving the Man who was thrown by his Mule lying near it, he rode up to him, and setting his Lance to his Throat, Yield, cry'd he, and beg thy Life, or thou dy'st. Alas, Sir, cry'd t'other; what need you ask me to yield? I am not able to stir, for one of my Legs is broken; and I beseech you, if you are a Christian, do not kill me. I am a Master of Arts, and in holy Orders; 'twould be a heinous Sacrilege to take away my Life. What a Devil brought you hither then, if you are a Clergyman, cry'd Don *Quixote*? What else but my ill Fortune, reply'd the Supplicant? A worse hovers over thy Head, cry'd Don *Quixote*, and threatens thee, if thou do'st not answer this Moment to every particular Question I ask. I will, I will, Sir, reply'd the other; and first I must beg your Pardon for saying I was a Master of Arts, for I have yet but taken my Batchelor's Degree. My Name is *Alonso Lopez*: I am of *Alcovendas*, and came now from the Town of *Baeça*, with eleven other Clergymen, the same that now ran away with the Torches. We were going to *Segovia* to bury the Corps of a Gentleman of that Town, who dy'd at *Baeça*, and lies now in yonder Herse.

* *The Author seems here to have intended a Ridicule on those Funeral Solemnities.*

And who kill'd him? ask'd Don *Quixote*. Heaven, with a pestilential Fever, answer'd the other. If it be so, said Don *Quixote*, I am discharg'd of revenging his Death. Since Heaven did it, there is no more to be said; had it been its Pleasure to have taken me off so, I too must have submitted. I would have you inform'd, reverend Sir, that I am a Knight of *La Mancha*, my Name Don *Quixote*; my Employment is to visit all Parts of the World in quest of Adventures, to right and relieve injur'd Innocence, and punish Oppression. Truly, Sir, reply'd the Clergyman, I do not understand how you can call that to right and relieve Men, when you break their Legs: You've made that crooked which was right and straight before; and Heaven knows whether it can ever be set right as long as I live. Instead of relieving the Injur'd, I fear you have injur'd me past Relief; and while you seek Adventures, you have made me meet with a very great Mis-adventure.* All things, reply'd Don *Quixote*, are not bless'd alike with a prosperous Event, good Mr Batchelor: You shou'd have taken Care not to have thus gone a Proces-sioning in these desolate Plains, at this suspicious Time of Night, with your white Surplices, burning Torches and sable Weeds, like Ghosts and Goblins, that went about to scare People out of their Wits: For I could not omit doing the Duty of my Profession, nor would I have forborn attacking you, though you had really been all *Lucifer's* infernal Crew; for such I took you to be, and till this Moment cou'd have no better Opinion of you. Well, Sir, said the Batchelor, since my bad Fortune has so order'd it, I must desire you, as you are a Knight-Errant, who have made mine so ill an Errand, to help me to get from under my Mule, for it lies so heavy upon me, that I cannot get my Foot out of the Stirrup. Why did not you acquaint me sooner with your Grievances, cry'd Don *Quixote*? I might have talk'd on till to Morrow Morning and never have thought on't. With that

* *The Author's making the Batchelor quibble so much, under such impro-per Circumstances, was properly design'd as a Ridicule upon the younger Students of the Universities, who are so apt to run into an Affectation that way, and to mistake it for Wit; as also upon the Dramatic Writers, who frequently make their Heroes, in their greatest Distresses, guilty of the like Absurdity.*

he call'd *Sancho*, who made no great Haste, for he was much
better employ'd in rifling a Load of choice Provisions, which
the holy Men carry'd along with 'em on a Sumpter-Mule.
He had spread his Coat on the Ground, and having laid on
it as much Food as it would hold, he wrapp'd it up like a
Bag, and laid the Booty on his Ass; and then away he ran
to his Master, and help'd him to set the Batchelor upon his
Mule: After which he gave him his Torch, and Don *Quixote*
bade him follow his Company, and excuse him for his Mistake, though, all Things consider'd, he could not avoid doing
what he had done. And, Sir, quoth *Sancho*, if the Gentlemen would know who 'twas that so well thresh'd their
Jackets, you may tell 'em 'twas the famous Don *Quixote de la
Mancha*, otherwise call'd *The Knight of the woeful Figure*.

When the Batchelor was gone, Don *Quixote* ask'd *Sancho*
why he call'd him the Knight of the woeful Figure? I'll tell
you why, quoth *Sancho*; I have been staring upon you this
pretty while by the Light of that unlucky Priest's Torch,
and may I ne'er stir if e'er I set Eyes on a more dismal
Figure in my Born-days; and I can't tell what should be the
Cause on't, unless your being tir'd after this Fray, or the
Want of your Worship's Teeth. That's not the Reason, cry'd
Don *Quixote*; no, *Sancho*, I rather conjecture, that the Sage
who is commission'd by Fate to register my Atchievements,
thought it convenient I should assume a new Appellation,
as all the Knights of yore; for one was call'd the Knight
of the Burning Sword, another of the Unicorn, a third of
the Phœnix, a fourth the Knight of the Damsels, another
of the Griffin, and another the Knight of Death; by which
By-names and Distinctions they were known all over the
Globe. Therefore, doubtless, that learned Sage, my Historian, has inspired thee with the Thought of giving me that
additional Appellation of the Knight of the woeful Figure:
And accordingly I assume the Name, and intend henceforwards to be distinguish'd by that Denomination. And that
it may seem the more proper, I will with the first Opportunity have a most woeful Face painted on my Shield. O'my
Word, quoth *Sancho*, you may e'en save the Money, and
instead of having a woeful Face painted, you need no more

but only shew your own. I'm but in jest, as a Body may say, but what with the want of your Teeth, and what with Hunger, you look so queerly and so woefully, that no Painter can draw you a Figure so fit for your Purpose as your Worship's. This merry Conceit of *Sancho* extorted a Smile from his Master's austere Countenance: However, he persisted in his Resolution about the Name and the Picture; and after a Pause, a sudden Thought disturbing his Conscience, *Sancho*, cry'd he, I am afraid of being excommunicated for having laid violent Hands upon a Man in Holy Orders, *Juxta illud; Si quis suadente Diabolo*, &c.* But yet, now I think better on't, I never touch'd him with my Hands, but only with my Lance; besides, I did not in the least suspect I had to do with Priests, whom I honour and revere as every good Catholick and faithful Christian ought to do, but rather took 'em to be evil Spirits. Well, let the Worst come to the Worst, I remember what befel the *Cid Ruy-Dias*, when he broke to Pieces the Chair of a King's Ambassador in the Pope's Presence, for which he was excommunicated; which did not hinder the worthy *Rodrigo de Vivar* from behaving himself that Day like a valorous Knight, and a Man of Honour.

This said, Don *Quixote* was for visiting the Herse, to see whether what was in it were only dead Bones: But *Sancho* would not let him; Sir, quoth he, you are come off now with a whole Skin, and much better than you have done hitherto. Who knows but these same Fellows that are now scamper'd off, may chance to bethink themselves what a Shame it is for 'em to have suffer'd themselves to be thus routed by a single Man, and so come back, and fall upon us all at once; then we shall have Work enough upon our Hands. The Ass is in good Case: There's a Hill not far off, and our Bellies cry Cupboard. Come, let's e'en get out of Harm's-way, *and not let the Plough stand to catch a Mouse*, as the Saying is; *To the Grave with the Dead, and the Living to the Bread*. With that he put on a Dog-trot with his Ass, and his Master, bethinking himself that he was in the right, put on after him without replying.

* Canon. 72. Distinct. 134.

After they had rid a little Way, they came to a Valley that lay sculking between two Hills; there they alighted, and *Sancho* having open'd his Coat and spread it on the Grass, with the Provision which he had bundl'd up in it, our two Adventurers fell to; and their Stomachs being sharpen'd with the Sauce of Hunger, they eat their Breakfast, Dinner, Afternoon's Luncheon, and Supper, all at the same Time, feasting themselves with Variety of cold Meats, which you may be sure were the best that could be got, the Priests, who had brought it for their own eating, being like the rest of their Coat, none of the worst Stewards for their Bellies, and knowing how to make much of themselves.

But now they began to grow sensible of a very great Misfortune, and such a Misfortune as was bemoan'd by poor *Sancho*, as one of the saddest that ever could befal him; for they found they had not one Drop of Wine or Water to wash down their Meat and quench their Thirst, which now scorch'd and choaked 'em worse than Hunger had pinch'd 'em before. However, *Sancho* considering they were in a Place where the Grass was fresh and green, said to his Master ———what you shall find in the following Chapter.

VI: OF A WONDERFUL ADVENTURE ATCHIEV'D BY THE VALOROUS DON QUIXOTE DE LA MANCHA; THE LIKE NEVER COMPASS'D WITH LESS DANGER BY ANY OF THE MOST FAMOUS KNIGHTS IN THE WORLD

THE Grass is so fresh (quoth *Sancho*, half choak'd with Thirst) that I dare lay my Life we shall light on some Spring or Stream hereabouts; therefore, Sir, let's look, I beseech you, that we may quench this confounded Drought that plagues our Throats ten times worse than Hunger did our Guts. Thereupon Don *Quixote* leading *Rozinante* by the Bridle, and *Sancho* his Ass by the Halter, after he had laid up the Reversion of their Meal, they went feeling about, only guided by their Guess; for 'twas so dark they scarce could see their Hands. They had not gone above two hundred Paces before they heard a Noise of a great Water-fall; which was to them the most welcome Sound in the World: But then listening with great Attention to know on which side the grateful Murmur came, they on a sudden heard another kind of Noise that strangely allay'd the Pleasure of the first, especially in *Sancho*, who was naturally fearful, and pusillanimous. They heard a terrible Din of obstreperous Blows, struck Regularly, and a more dreadful rattling of Chains and Irons, which together with the roaring of the Waters, might have fill'd any other Heart but Don *Quixote's* with Terror and Amazement. Add to this the Horrors of a dark Night and Solitude, in an unknown Place, the loud rustling of the Leaves of some lofty Trees, under which Fortune brought 'em at the same unlucky Moment, the Whistling of the Wind, which concurr'd with the other dismaying Sounds; the Fall of the Waters, the thundering Thumps and the Clinking of Chains aforesaid. The worst too was, that the Blows were redoubled without ceasing, the Wind blow'd on, and Daylight was far distant. But then it was, Don *Quixote*, secur'd by his Intrepidity (his inseparable Companion) mounted his *Rozinante*, brac'd his Shield, brandish'd his Lance, and shew'd a Soul unknowing Fear, and superior to Danger and Fortune. Know, *Sancho*, cry'd he, I was born in this Iron Age, to restore the Age of Gold, or the Golden Age, as some chuse to call it. I am the Man for whom Fate has reserv'd the most dangerous and formidable Attempts, the most stupendious and glorious Adventures, and the most valorous Feats of Arms. I am the Man who must revive the Order of the Round-Table, the twelve Peers of *France*, and the nine Worthies, and efface the Memory of your *Platyrs*, your *Tablantes*, your *Olivantes*, and your *Tirantes*. Now must your Knights of the Sun, your *Belianis's*, and all the numerous Throng of famous Heroes, and Knights-Errant of former Ages, see the Glory of all their most dazzling Actions eclips'd and darken'd by more Illustrious Exploits. Do but observe, O thou my faithful Squire, what a *Multifarious Assemblage* of Terrors surrounds us! A horrid Darkness, a doleful Solitude, a confus'd rustling of Leaves, a dismal rattling of Chains, a howling of the Winds, an astonishing Noise of Cataracts, that seem to fall with a boist'rous Rapidity from the steep Mountains of the Moon, a terrible Sound of redoubled Blows, still wounding our Ears like furious Thunder-claps, and a dead and universal Silence of those things that might buoy up the sinking Courage of frail Mortality. In this extremity of Danger, *Mars* himself might tremble with the Affright: Yet I, in the midst of all these unutterable Alarms, still remain undaunted and unshaken. These are but Incentives to my Valour, and but animate my Heart the more; it grows too big and mighty for my Breast, and leaps at the approach of this threatning Adventure, as formidable as 'tis like to prove. Come, girt *Rozinante* straighter, and then Providence protect thee: Thou may'st stay for me here; but if I do not return in three Days, go back to our Village; and from thence, for my sake, to *Toboso*, where thou shalt say to my incomparable Lady *Dulcinea*, That her faithful Knight fell a Sacrifice to Love and Honour, while he attempted Things that might have made him worthy to be call'd her Adorer.

When *Sancho* heard his Master talk thus, he fell a weeping in the most pitiful manner in the World. Pray Sir, cry'd he, why will you thus run your self into Mischief? What need you go about this rueful Misventure? 'Tis main dark, and there's ne'er a living Soul sees us; we have nothing to do but to sheer off, and get out of Harm's way, though we were not to drink a drop these three Days. Who is there to take notice of our Flinching? I've heard our Parson, whom you very well know, say in his Pulpit, That he who seeks Danger, perishes therein: And therefore we should not tempt Heaven by going about a Thing that we cannot compass but by a Miracle. Is't not enough, think you, that it has preserv'd you from being toss'd in a Blanket, as I was, and made you come off safe and sound from among so many Goblins that went with the dead Man? If all this won't work upon that hard Heart of yours, do but think of Me, and rest your self assur'd, that when once you've left your poor *Sancho*, he'll be ready to give up the Ghost for very Fear, to the next that will come for't: I left my House and Home, my Wife, Children, and all to follow You, hoping to be the better for't, and not the worse; but as Covetousness breaks the *Sack*, so has it broke Me and my Hopes; for while I thought my self Cocksure of that Unlucky and Accurs'd Island, which you so often promis'd me, in lieu thereof you drop me here in a strange Place. Dear Master, don't be so hard-hearted; and if you won't be persuaded not to meddle with this ungracious Adventure, do but put it off till Day-break, to which, according to the little Skill I learn'd when a Shepherd, it can't be above three Hours; for the Muzzle of the lesser Bear is just over our Heads, and makes Midnight in the Line of the left Arm. How, can'st thou see the Muzzle of the Bear, ask'd Don *Quixote*? There's not a Star to be seen in the Sky. That's true, quoth *Sancho*; but Fear is sharp-sighted, and can see things under Ground, and much more in the Skies. Let Day come, or not come, 'tis all one to Me, cry'd the Champion; it shall never be recorded of Don *Quixote*, that either Tears or Intreaties could make him neglect the Duty of a Knight. Then, *Sancho*, say no more; for Heaven that has inspir'd me with a Resolution of attempting this dreadful Adventure, will certainly take care of me and thee: Come quickly, girt my Steed, and stay here for me; for you will shortly hear of me again, either alive or dead.

Sancho finding his Master obstinate, and neither to be mov'd with Tears nor good Advice, resolv'd to try a Trick of Policy to keep him there till Daylight: And accordingly, while he pretended to fasten the Girths, he slily ty'd *Rozinante's* hinder-Legs with his Ass's Halter, without being so much as suspected: So that when Don *Quixote* thought to have mov'd forwards he found his Horse would not go a Step without leaping, though he spurr'd him on smartly. *Sancho* perceiving his Plot took; look you, Sir, quoth he, Heaven's o'my side, and won't let *Rozinante* budge a Foot forwards; and now if you'll still be spurring him, I dare pawn my Life, 'twill be but striving against the Stream; or, as the Saying is, but kicking against the Pricks. Don *Quixote* fretted and chaf'd, and rav'd, and was in a desperate Fury, to find his Horse so stubborn; but at last, observing that the more he spurr'd and gall'd his Sides, the more resty he prov'd, he, though unwillingly, resolv'd to have Patience till 'twas light. Well, said he, since *Rozinante* will not leave this Place, I must tarry in't till the Dawn, though its slowness will cost me some Sighs. You shall not need to sigh nor be melancholy, quoth *Sancho*, for I'll undertake to tell you Stories till it be Day, unless your Worship had rather get off your Horse, and take a Nap upon the green Grass, as Knights-Errant are wont, that you may be the fresher, and the better able in the Morning to go through that monstrous Adventure that waits for you. What do'st thou mean by this alighting and sleeping, reply'd Don *Quixote*? Think'st thou I am one of those Carpet-Knights that abandon themselves to Sleep and lazy Ease, when Danger is at hand? No, sleep Thou, Thou art born to sleep; or do what thou wilt. As for my self, I know what I have to do. Good Sir, quoth *Sancho*, don't put your self into a Passion, I meant no such Thing, not I: Saying this, he clapp'd one of his Hands upon the Pommel of *Rozinante's* Saddle and t'other upon the Crupper, and thus he stood embracing his Master's left Thigh, not daring to budge an Inch, for fear of the Blows that dinn'd continually in his Ears. Don *Quixote* then thought fit to claim his Promise, and desired him to tell some of his Stories to help pass away the Time. Sir, quoth *Sancho*, I'm wofully

frighted, and have no Heart to tell Stories; however, I'll
do my best; and now I think on't there's one come into my
Head, which if I can but hit on't right, and nothing happen
to put me out, is the best Story you ever heard in your Life;
therefore listen, for I'm going to begin. In the Days of yore,
when it was as it was, Good betide us all, and Evil to him
that Evil seeks. And here, Sir, you are to take notice that
they of old did not begin their Tales in an ordinary Way;
for 'twas a Saying of a wise Man whom they call'd *Cato*,
the *Roman Tonsor*,* that said, Evil to him that Evil seeks,
which is as pat for your Purpose as a Ring for the Finger,
that you may neither meddle nor make, nor seek Evil and
Mischief for the nonce, but rather get out of Harm's way,
for no Body forces us to run into the Mouth of all the Devils
in Hell that wait for us yonder. Go on with the Story,
Sancho, cry'd Don *Quixote*, and leave the rest to My Discretion. I say then, quoth *Sancho*, that in a Country-Town
in *Estremadura*, there liv'd a certain Shepherd, Goat-herd
I should have said; which Goat-herd, as the Story has it,
was called *Lope Ruyz*; and this *Lope Ruyz* was in Love
with a Shepherdess, whose Name was *Toralva*, the which
Shepherdess, whose Name was *Toralva*, was the Daughter
of a wealthy Grazier, and this wealthy Grazier —— If
thou goest on at this rate, cry'd Don *Quixote*, and mak'st
so many needless Repetitions, thou'lt not have told thy
Story these two Days. Pr'ythee tell it concisely, and like a
Man of Sense, or let it alone. I tell it you, quoth *Sancho*,
as all Stories are told in our Country, and I can't for the
Blood of me tell it any other way, nor is it fit I should alter
the Custom. Why then tell it how thou wilt, reply'd Don
Quixote, since my ill Fortune forces me to stay and hear
thee. Well then, Dear Sir, quoth *Sancho*, as I was saying,
this same Shepherd, Goat-herd I should have said, was
woundily in Love with that same Shepherdess *Toralva*,
who was a well-truss'd, round, crummy, strapping Wench,
coy and froppish, and somewhat like a Man, for she had a
kind of Beard on her upper Lip; methinks I see her now
standing before me. Then I suppose thou knew'st her, said

* A *Mistake for* Cato *the* Roman Censor.

Don *Quixote*. Not I, answer'd *Sancho*, I ne'er set Eyes on her in my Life; but he that told me the Story said this was so true, that I might vouch it for a real Truth, and even swear I had seen it all my self. Well, —— but, as you know, Days go and come, and Time and Straw makes Medlars ripe; so it happen'd, that after several Days coming and going, the Devil, who seldom lies dead in a Ditch, but will have a Finger in every Pye, so brought it about, that the Shepherd fell out with his Sweetheart, insomuch that the Love he bore her turn'd into Dudgeon and Ill-will; and the Cause was, by report of some mischievous Tale-carriers that bore no good Will to either Party, for that the Shepherd thought her no better than she should be, a little loose i'the Hilts, and free of her Hips.* Thereupon being grievous in the Dumps about it, and now bitterly hating her, he e'en resolv'd to leave that Country to get out of her Sight: For now, as every Dog has his Day, the Wench perceiving he came no longer a Suitering to her, but rather toss'd his Nose at her, and shunn'd her, she began to love him and doat upon him like any thing. That's the Nature of Women, cry'd Don *Quixote*, not to Love when we Love them, and to Love when we Love them not. But go on ——— The Shepherd then gave her the slip, continu'd *Sancho*, and driving his Goats before him, went trudging through *Estremadura*, in his Way to *Portugal*. But *Toralva*, having a long Nose, soon smelt his Design, and then what does she do, think ye, but comes after him bare-foot and bare-legg'd, with a Pilgrim's Staff in her Hand, and a Wallet at her Back, wherein they say she carry'd a Piece of a Looking-Glass, half a Comb, a broken Pot with Paint, and I don't know what other Trinkums Trankums to prink her self up. But let her carry what she wou'd, 'tis no Bread and Butter of mine; the short and the long is, That they say the Shepherd with his Goats got at last to the River *Guadiana*, which happen'd to be overflow'd at that time, and what's worse than ill Luck,

---

* *In the Original it runs*, She gave him a certain quantity of little Jealousies, above Measure, and within the prohibited Degrees: *Alluding to certain Measures not to be exceeded* (in Spain) *on pain of Forfeiture and corporal Punishment, as Swords above such a Standard*, &c.

there was neither Boat nor Bark to ferry him over; which vex'd him the more because he perceiv'd *Toralva* at his Heels, and he fear'd to be teaz'd and plagu'd with her Weeping and Wailing. At last he spy'd a Fisher-man, in a little Boat, but so little it was, that it would carry but one Man and one Goat at a time. Well, for all that, he call'd to the Fisher-man, and agreed with him to carry him and his three hundred Goats over the Water. The Bargain being struck, the Fisher-man came with his Boat, and carry'd over one Goat; then he row'd back and fetch'd another Goat, and after that another Goat. Pray Sir, quoth *Sancho*, be sure you keep a good Account how many Goats the Fisher-man ferries over; for if you happen but to miss one, my Tale's at an end, and the Devil a Word I have more to say. Well then, whereabouts was I? —— Ho! I ha't —— Now the Landing-Place on the other side was very Muddy and Slippery, which made the Fisher-man be a long while in going and coming; yet for all that, he took Heart o'Grace, and made shift to carry over one Goat, then another, and then another. Come, said Don *Quixote*, we'll suppose he has landed them all on the other side of the River; for as thou goest on One by One we shall not have done these twelve Months. Pray, let me go on in my own Way, quoth *Sancho*. How many Goats are got over already? Nay, how the Devil can I tell, reply'd Don *Quixote*! There it is! quoth *Sancho*; Did not I bid you keep Count? On my Word the Tale is at an end, and now you may go whistle for the rest. Ridiculous, cry'd Don *Quixote*: Pr'ythee is there no going on with the Story unless I know exactly how many Goats are wafted over? No marry is there not, quoth *Sancho*, for as soon as you answer'd, that you could not tell, the rest of the Story quite and clean slipp'd out of my Head; and Troth 'tis a thousand Pities, for 'twas a special one. So then, cry'd Don *Quixote*, the Story's ended. Ay marry is it, quoth *Sancho*, 'tis no more to be fetch'd to Life than my dead Mother. Upon my Honour, cry'd Don *Quixote*, a most extraordinary Story, and told and concluded in as extraordinary a manner! 'Tis a Nonesuch I assure ye; though truly I expected no less from a Man of such uncommon Parts. Alas! poor *Sancho*, I am afraid this dreadful Noise has turn'd thy Brain. That may well be, quoth *Sancho*; but as for my Story I'm sure there's nothing more to be said, for where you lose the Account of the Goats, there it ends. Let it be so, reply'd Don *Quixote*; but now let's try whether *Rozinante* be in Humour to march: With that he gave *Rozinante* two Spurs, and the high-mettled Jade answer'd with one Bound, and then stood stock still, not having the Command of his hind Legs.

Much about this Time, whether it were the Coolness of the Night, or that *Sancho* had eaten some loosening Food at Supper, or, which seems more probable, that Nature, by a regular Impulse, gave him notice of her Desire to perform a certain Function that follows the third Concoction; it seems, honest *Sancho* found himself urg'd to do that which no body could do for him: But such were his Fears that he durst not for his Life stir the breadth of a Straw from his Master; yet to think of bearing the intolerable Load that press'd him so, was to him as great an Impossibility. In this perplexing Exigency, (with leave be it spoken) he could find no other Expedient but to take his Right Hand from the Crupper of the Saddle, and softly untying his Breeches, let 'em drop down to his Heels; having done this, he as silently took up his Shirt, and expos'd his Posteriors, which were none of the least, to the open Air: But the main Point was how to ease himself of this terrible Burden without making a Noise; to which purpose he clutch'd his Teeth close, screw'd up his Face, shrunk up his Shoulders, and held in his Breath as much as possible: Yet see what Misfortunes attend the best projected Undertakings! When he had almost compass'd his Design, he could not hinder an obstreperous Sound, very different from those that caus'd his Fear, from unluckily bursting out. Hark! cry'd Don *Quixote*, who heard it, what Noise is that, *Sancho*? Some new Adventures I'll warrant you, quoth *Sancho*, for ill Luck, you know, seldom comes alone. Having pass'd off the Thing thus, he e'en ventur'd t'other Strain, and did it so cleverly, that without the least Rumour or Noise, his Business was done effectually, to the unspeakable Ease of his Body and Mind.

But Don *Quixote* having the Sense of Smelling as perfect as that of Hearing, and *Sancho* standing so very near, or rather tack'd to him, certain Fumes, that ascended perpendicularly, began to regale his Nostrils with a Smell not so grateful as Amber. No sooner the unwelcome Steams disturb'd him, but having recourse to the common Remedy, he stopp'd his Nose, and then, with a snuffling Voice, *Sancho*, said he, thou art certainly in great bodily Fear. So I am, quoth *Sancho*; but what makes your Worship perceive it now more than you did before? Because, reply'd Don *Quixote*, thou smellest now more unsavourily than thou didst before. Hoh! that may be, quoth *Sancho*: But who's Fault's that? You may e'en thank your self for't. Why do you lead me a Wild-goose Chace, and bring me at such unseasonable Hours to such dangerous Places? You know I an't us'd to't. Pr'ythee, said Don *Quixote*, still holding his Nose, get thee three or four Steps from me; and for the future take more care, and know your Distance; for I find, my Familiarity with thee has bred Contempt. I warrant, quoth *Sancho*, you think I have been doing something I should not have done. Come, say no more, cry'd Don *Quixote*, the more thou stir, the worse 'twill be.

This Discourse, such as it was, serv'd them to pass away the Night; and now *Sancho*, seeing the Morning arise, thought it time to unty *Rozinante's* Feet, and do up his Breeches; and he did both with so much Caution that his Master suspected nothing. As for *Rozinante*, he no sooner felt himself at Liberty, but he seem'd to express his Joy by pawing the Ground; for, with his Leave be it spoken, he was a Stranger to Curvetting and Prancing. Don *Quixote* also took it as a good Omen, that his Steed was now ready to move, and believ'd it was a Signal given him by kind Fortune, to animate him to give Birth to the approaching Adventure.

Now had *Aurora* display'd her rosy Mantle over the blushing Skies, and dark Night withdrawn her Sable Veil; all Objects stood confess'd to human Eyes, and Don *Quixote* could now perceive he was under some tall Chesnut-Trees, whose thick spreading Boughs diffus'd an awful Gloom around the Place, but he could not yet discover whence proceeded the dismal Sound of those incessant Strokes. Therefore, being resolv'd to find it out, once more he took his Leave of *Sancho*, with the same Injunctions as before; adding withal, that he should not trouble himself about the Recompence of his Services, for he had taken care of that in his Will, which he had providently made before he left home; but if he came off victorious from this Adventure, he might most certainly expect to be gratify'd with the Promis'd Island. *Sancho* could not forbear blubbering again to hear these tender Expressions of his Master, and resolv'd not to leave him till he had finish'd this Enterprize. And from that deep Concern, and this nobler Resolution to attend him, the Author of this History infers, That the Squire was something of a Gentleman by Descent, or at least the Offspring of the old Christians.* Nor did his Good-nature fail to move his Master more than he was willing to shew, at a Time when it behov'd him to shake off all softer Thoughts; for now he rode towards the Place whence the Noise of the Blows and the Water seem'd to come, while *Sancho* trudg'd after him, leading by the Halter the inseparable Companion of his good and bad Fortune.

After they had gone a pretty way under a pleasing Covert of Chesnut-Trees, they came into a Meadow adjoining to certain Rocks, from whose Top there was a great Fall of Waters. At the Foot of those Rocks they discover'd certain old illcontriv'd Buildings, that rather look'd like Ruins than inhabited Houses; and they perceiv'd that the terrifying Noise of the Blows, which yet continued, issu'd out of that Place. When they came nearer, even patient *Rozinante* himself started at the dreadful Sound; but being hearten'd and pacify'd by his Master, he was at last prevail'd with to draw nearer and nearer with wary Steps; the Knight recommending himself all the way most devoutly to his *Dulcinea*, and now and then also to Heaven, in short Ejaculations. As for *Sancho*, he stuck close to his Master, peeping all the way through *Rozinante's* Legs, to see if he could perceive what he dreaded to find out. When a little farther, at the doubling of the Point of a Rock, they plainly discover'd (kind Reader, do not take it amiss) Six huge Fulling-Mill Hammers, which

* *In Contradistinction to the* Jewish *or* Moorish *Families, of which there were many in* Spain.

interchangeably thumping several Pieces of Cloth, made the terrible Noise that caus'd all Don *Quixote's* Anxieties and *Sancho's* Tribulation that Night.

Don *Quixote* was struck dumb at this unexpected Sight, and was ready to drop from his Horse with Shame and Confusion. *Sancho* star'd upon him, and saw him hang down his Head, with a desponding dejected Countenance, like a Man quite dispirited with this cursed Disappointment. At the same Time he look'd upon *Sancho*, and seeing by his Eyes, and his Cheeks swell'd with Laughter, that he was ready to burst, he could not forbear laughing himself in spight of all his Vexation; so that *Sancho* seeing his Master begin, immediately gave a Loose to his Mirth, and broke out into such a Fit of Laughing, that he was forc'd to hold his Sides with both his Knuckles, for fear of bursting his aking Paunch. Four times he ceas'd, and four times renew'd his obstreperous Laughing; which Sauciness Don *Quixote* began to resent with great Indignation; and the more when *Sancho*, in a jeering Tone, presum'd to ridicule him with his own Words, repeating part of the vain Speech he made when first they heard the Noise; *Know*, Sancho, *I was born in this Iron Age to restore the Age of Gold. I am the Man for whom Heaven has reserv'd the most dangerous and glorious Adventures*, &c. Thus he went on, till his Master, dreadfully inrag'd at his Insolence, hit him two such Blows on the Shoulders with his Lance, that had they fallen upon his Head they had sav'd Don *Quixote* the trouble of paying him his Wages, whatever he must have done to his Heirs. Thereupon *Sancho*, finding his Jest turn'd to Earnest, begg'd Pardon with all Submission: Mercy, good your Worship, cry'd he, spare my Bones I beseech you! I meant no harm, I did but joke a little. And because You joke, I do not, cry'd Don *Quixote*. Come hither, good Mr Jester, you who pretend to rally, tell me, had this been a dangerous Adventure, as well as it proves only a false Alarm, have I not shewn Resolution enough to undertake and finish it? Am I, who am a Knight, bound to know the Meaning of every Mechanick Noise, and distinguish between Sound and Sound? Besides, it might happen, as really it is, that I had never seen a Fulling-Mill before, tho' thou, like a base Scoundrel as thou art, wert born and brought up among such mean Implements of Drudgery. But let the six Fulling-Hammers be transform'd into so many Giants, and then set them at me one by one, or all together; and if I do not lay 'em at my Feet with their Heels upwards, then I'll give thee Leave to exercise thy ill-bred Railery as much as thou pleasest.

Good your Worship, quoth *Sancho*, talk no more on't, I beseech you; I confess I carry'd the Jest too far. But now all's hush'd and well; pray tell me in sober Sadness, as you hope to speed in all Adventures, and come off safe and sound as from this, don't you think but that the Fright we were in, I mean that I was in, would be a good Subject for People to make Sport with? I grant it, answer'd Don *Quixote*, but I would not have it told; for all People are not so discreet as to place Things, or look upon 'em in the Position in which they should be consider'd. I'll say that for you, quoth *Sancho*, you've shewn you understand how to place Things in their right Position, when aiming at my Head, you hit my Shoulders; had not I duck'd a little o'one side I had been in a fine Condition! But let that pass, 'twill wash out in the Bucking. I've heard my Grannam say, That Man loves thee well who makes thee to weep. Good Masters may be hasty sometimes with a Servant, but presently after a hard Word or two they commonly give him a Pair of cast Breeches: What they give after a Basting, Heaven knows; all I can tell is, that Knights-Errant, after Bastinadoes, give you some cast Island, or some old-fashion'd Kingdom upon the main Land.

Fortune, said Don *Quixote*, will perhaps order ev'ry thing thou hast said to come to pass; therefore, *Sancho*, I pr'ythee think no more of my Severity; thou know'st a Man cannot always command the first Impulse of his Passions. On the other side, let me advise thee not to be so saucy for the future, and not to assume that strange Familiarity with me which is so unbecoming in a Servant. I protest, in such a vast number of Books of Knight-Errantry as I have read, I never found that any Squire was ever allow'd so great a Freedom of Speech with his Master as thou takest with me; and truly I look upon it to be a great Fault in us both; in thee for disrespecting me, and in me for not making my self be more respected.

Gandalin, *Amadis de Gaule's* Squire, tho' he was Earl of the Firm Island, yet never spoke to his Master but with Cap in Hand, his Head bow'd, and his Body half bent, after the Turkish manner. But what shall we say of *Gasabal*, Don *Galaor's* Squire, who was such a strict Observer of Silence, that, to the Honour of his marvellous Taciturnity, he gave the Author occasion to mention his Name but once in that voluminous authentick History? From all this, *Sancho*, I would have thee make this Observation, That there ought to be a Distance kept between the Master and the Man, the Knight and the Squire. Therefore, once more I tell thee, let's live together for the future more according to the due Decorum of our respective Degrees, without giving one another any further Vexation on this Account; for after all, 'twill always be the worse for you on whatsoever Occasion we happen to disagree. As for the Rewards I promis'd you, they will come in due Time; and should you be disappointed that way, you have your Salary to trust to, as I have told you.

You say very well, quoth *Sancho*; but now Sir, suppose no Rewards should come, and I should be forc'd to stick to my Wages, I'd fain know how much a Squire-Errant us'd to earn in the Days of yore? Did they go by the Month, or by the Day, like our Labourers? I don't think, reply'd Don *Quixote*, they ever went by the Hire, but rather that they trusted to their Master's Generosity. And if I have assign'd thee Wages in my Will, which I left seal'd up at home, 'twas only to prevent the worst, because I do not know yet what Success I may have in Chivalry in these deprav'd Times; and I would not have my Soul suffer in the other World for such a trifling Matter; for there is no State of Life so subject to Dangers as that of a Knight-Errant. Like enough, quoth *Sancho*, when meerly the Noise of the Hammers of a Fulling-Mill is able to trouble and disturb the Heart of such a valiant Knight as your Worship! But you may be sure I'll not hereafter so much as offer to open my Lips to jibe or joke at your Doings, but always stand in Awe of you, and honour you as my Lord and Master. By doing so, reply'd Don *Quixote*, thy Days shall be long on the Face of the Earth; for next to our Parents we ought to respect our Masters, as if they were our Fathers.

VII: OF THE HIGH ADVENTURE AND CONQUEST OF MAMBRINO'S HELMET, WITH OTHER EVENTS RELATING TO OUR INVINCIBLE KNIGHT

At the same Time it began to rain, and *Sancho* would fain have taken Shelter in the Fulling-Mills; but Don *Quixote* had conceiv'd such an Antipathy against 'em for the Shame they had put upon him, that he would by no Means be prevail'd with to go in; and turning to the right Hand he struck into a High-way, where they had not gone far before he discover'd a Horse-man, who wore upon his Head something that glitter'd like Gold. The Knight had no sooner spy'd him, but turning to his Squire, *Sancho*, cry'd he, I believe there's no Proverb but what is true; they are all so many Sentences and Maxims drawn from Experience, the universal Mother of Sciences: For Instance, that Saying, That where one Door shuts, another opens: Thus Fortune, that last Night deceiv'd us with the false Prospect of an Adventure, this Morning offers us a real one to make us amends; and such an Adventure, *Sancho*, that if I do not gloriously succeed in it, I shall have now no Pretence to an Excuse, no Darkness, no unknown Sounds to impute my Disappointment to: In short, in all Probability yonder comes the Man who wears on his Head *Mambrino's* Helmet,* and thou know'st the Vow I have made. Good Sir, quoth *Sancho*, mind what you say, and take heed what you do; for I would willingly keep my Carcase and the Case of my Understanding from being pounded, mash'd, and crush'd with Fulling-Hammers. Hell take the Blockhead, cry'd Don *Quixote*, is there no Difference between a Helmet and a Fulling-Mill? I don't know, saith *Sancho*; but I'm sure, were I suffer'd to speak my Mind now as I was wont, mayhaps I would give you such main Reasons, that your self should see you're wide of the Matter. How can I be mistaken, thou eternal Misbeliever, cry'd Don *Quixote*? Do'st thou not see that Knight that comes riding up directly towards us upon a Dapple grey Steed, with

---

* Mambrino, *a Saracen of great Valour, who had a golden Helmet, which* Rinaldo *took from him. See* Orlando Furioso, Canto I.

a Helmet of Gold on his Head? I see what I see, reply'd *Sancho*, and the Devil of any thing I can spy but a Fellow on such another grey Ass as mine is, with something that glisters o'Top of his Head. I tell thee, that's *Mambrino's* Helmet, reply'd Don *Quixote*: Do Thou stand at a Distance, and leave Me to deal with him; thou shalt see, that without trifling away so much as a Moment in needless Talk, I'll finish this Adventure, and possess my self of the desir'd Helmet. I shall stand at a Distance, you may be sure, quoth *Sancho*; but I wish this may'nt prove another blue Bout, and a worse Jobb than the Fulling-Mills. I have warn'd you already, Fellow, said Don *Quixote*, not so much as to name the Fulling-Mills; dare but once more to do it, nay, but to think on't, and I vow to—I say no more, but I'll full and pound your Dog'sship into Jelly. These Threats were more than sufficient to pad-lock *Sancho's* Lips, for he had no Mind to have his Master's Vow fulfill'd at the Expence of his Bones.

Now the Truth of the Story was this; There were in that Part of the Country two Villages, one of which was so little, that it had not so much as a Shop in't, nor any Barber; so that the Barber of the greater Village serv'd also the smaller. And thus a Person happening to have Occasion to be let Blood, and another to be shav'd, the Barber was going thither with his Brass Bason, which he had clapp'd upon his Head to keep his Hat, that chanc'd to be a new one, from being spoil'd by the Rain; and as the Bason was new-scour'd, it made a glittering Show a great way off. As *Sancho* had well observ'd, he rode upon a grey Ass, which Don *Quixote* as easily took for a Dapple-grey Steed, as he took the Barber for a Knight, and his Brass Bason for a Golden Helmet; his distracted Brain easily applying ev'ry Object to his romantick Ideas. There-fore when he saw the poor imaginary Knight draw near, he fix'd his Lance, or Javelin, to his Thigh, and without staying to hold a Parley with his thoughtless Adversary, flew at him as fiercely as *Rozinante* would gallop, resolv'd to pierce him through and through; crying out in the midst of his Career, Caitiff, Wretch, defend thy self, or immediately surrender that which is so justly my Due. The Barber, who as he peace-ably went along saw that terrible Apparition come thund'ring upon him at unawares, had no other Way to avoid being run through with his Lance, but to throw himself off from his Ass to the Ground; and then as hastily getting up, he took to his Heels and ran o'er the Fields swifter than the Wind, leaving his Ass and his Bason behind him. Don *Quixote* finding himself thus Master of the Field, and of the Bason; The Miscreant, cry'd he, who has left this Helmet, has shewn himself as prudent as the Beaver, who finding himself hotly pursu'd by the Hunters, to save his Life, tears and cut off with his Teeth that for which his natural Instinct tells him he was follow'd. Then he order'd *Sancho* to take up the Helmet. On my Word, quoth *Sancho*, having taken it up, 'tis a special Bason, and as well worth a Piece of Eight as a Thief is worth a Halter. With that he gave it to his Master, who presently clapp'd it on his Head, turning it every way to find out the Beaver or Vizor; and at last seeing it had none, Doubtless, said he, the Pagan for whom this famous Helmet was first made, had a Head of a prodigious Size; but the worst is, that there's at least one Half of it wanting. *Sancho* could not forbear smiling to hear his Master call the Barber's Bason a Helmet, and had not his Fear dash'd his Mirth, he had certainly laugh'd outright. What does the Fool grin at now? cry'd Don *Quixote*. I laugh, said he, to think what a hugeous Jolt-head he must needs have had who was the Owner of this same Helmet, that looks for all the World like a Barber's Bason. I fancy, said Don *Quixote*, this inchanted Helmet has fallen by some strange Accident into the Hands of some Person, who, not knowing the Value of it, for the Lucre of a little Money, finding it to be of pure Gold, melted one Half, and of the other made this Head-piece, which, as thou say'st, has some Resemblance of a Barber's Bason: But to Me, who know the Worth of it, the Metamorphosis signifies little; for as soon as ever I come to some Town where there's an Armourer, I will have it alter'd so much for the better, that then even the Helmet which the God of Smiths made for the God of War shall not deserve to be compar'd with it. In the mean time I'll wear it as it is; 'tis better than nothing, and will serve at least to save part of my Head from the violent Encounter of a Stone. Ay, that it will, quoth *Sancho*, so 'tis not hurl'd out of a Sling, as were those at the Battle between the two Armies, when they hit you that confounded Dowse o' the Chops, that saluted your Worship's Cheek-Teeth, and broke the Pot about your Ears in which you kept that blessed Drench that made me bring up my Guts. True, cry'd Don *Quixote*, there I lost my precious Balsam indeed; but I do not much repine at it, for thou knowest I have the Receipt in my Memory. So have I too, quoth *Sancho*, and shall have while I have Breath to draw; but if ever I make any of that Stuff, or taste it again, may I give up the Ghost with it: Besides, I don't intend ever to do any thing that may give Occasion for the Use of it: For, my fix'd Resolution is, with all my five Senses, to preserve my self from hurting and from being hurt, by any body. As to being toss'd in a Blanket again, I've nothing to say to that, for there's no Remedy for Accidents but Patience it seems: So if it ever be my Lot to be serv'd so again, I'll e'en shrink up my Shoulders, hold my Breath, and shut my Eyes, and then happy be lucky, let the Blanket and Fortune e'en toss on to the End o' the Chapter.

Truly, said Don *Quixote*, I am afraid thou'rt no good Christian, *Sancho*, thou never forget'st Injuries. Let me tell thee, 'tis the Part of noble and generous Spirits to pass by Trifles. Where art thou lame? which of thy Ribs is broken? or what Part of thy Skull is bruis'd? that thou can'st never think on that Jest without Malice: For, after all, 'twas nothing but a Jest, a harmless Piece of Pastime; had I look'd upon it otherwise, I had return'd to that Place before this Time, and had made more noble Mischief in revenge of the Abuse, than ever the incens'd *Grecians* did at *Troy*, for the Detention of their *Helen*, that fam'd Beauty of the ancient World, who however had she liv'd in our Age, or had my *Dulcinea* adorn'd her's, would have found her Charms out-rivall'd by my Mistress's Perfections: And saying this, he heav'd up a deep Sigh. Well then, quoth *Sancho*, I'll not rip up old Sores; let it go for a Jest, since there's no revenging it in Earnest. But what shall we do with this Dapple-grey Steed that's so like a grey Ass? You see that same poor Devil Errant has left it to shift for it self, poor thing, and by his Haste to rub off, I don't think he means to come back for it, and, by my Beard,

the grey Beast is a special one. 'Tis not My Custom, reply'd
Don *Quixote*, to plunder those whom I overcome; nor is it
usual among us Knights, for the Victor to take the Horse of
his vanquish'd Enemy and let him go afoot, unless his own
Steed be kill'd or disabled in the Combat: Therefore, *Sancho*, leave the Horse, or the Ass, whatever thou pleasest to
call it, the Owner will be sure to come for't as soon as he sees
us gone. I've a huge Mind to take him along with us, quoth
Sancho, or at least to exchange him for my own, which is not
so good. What, are the Laws of Knight-Errantry so strict,
that a Man must not exchange one Ass for another? At least
I hope they'll give me Leave to swop one Harness for another. Truly, *Sancho*, reply'd Don *Quixote*, I am not so very
certain as to this last Particular, and therefore, till I am better
inform'd, I give thee leave to exchange the Furniture, if thou
hast absolutely Occasion for't. I've so much Occasion for't,
quoth *Sancho*, that tho' 'twere for my own very self I could
not need it more. So without any more ado, being author-
iz'd by his Master's Leave, he made *Mutatio Caparum*, (a
Change of Caparisons) and made his own Beast three Parts
in four better* for his new Furniture. This done, they break-
fasted upon what they left at Supper, and quench'd their
Thirst at the Stream that turn'd the Fulling-Mills, towards
which they took care not to cast an Eye, for they abominated
the very Thoughts of 'em. Thus their Spleen being eas'd,
their cholerick and melancholick Humours asswag'd, up
they got again, and never minding their Way, were all
guided by *Rozinante's* Discretion, the Depositary of his
Master's Will, and also of the Ass's, that kindly and sociably
always follow'd his Steps where-ever he went. Their Guide
soon brought 'em again into the high Road, where they kept
on a slow Pace, not caring which Way they went.

As they jogg'd on thus, quoth *Sancho* to his Master, Pray
Sir, will you give me leave to talk to you a little? For since
you have laid that bitter Command upon me, to hold my
Tongue, I've had four or five quaint Conceits that have rot-

---

* *Literally leaving him better by a* Tierce *and* Quint; *alluding to the
Game of* Piquet, *in which a* Tierce *or a* Quint *may be gain'd by putting
out bad Cards, and taking in better.*

ted in my Gizzard, and now I've another at my Tongue's End that I would not for any thing should miscarry. Say it, cry'd Don *Quixote*, but be short, for no Discourse can please when too long.

Well then, quoth *Sancho*, I've been thinking to my self of late how little is to be got by hunting up and down those barren Woods and strange Places, where, tho' you compass the hardest and most dangerous Jobbs of Knight-Errantry, yet no living Soul sees or hears on't, and so 'tis every bit as good as lost; and therefore methinks 'twere better (with Submission to your Worship's better Judgment be it spoken) that we e'en went to serve some Emperor, or other Great Prince that's at War; for there you might shew how stout, and how wond'rous strong and wise you be; which, being perceiv'd by the Lord we shall serve, he must needs reward each of us according to his Deserts; and there you'll not want a learned Scholar to set down all your high Deeds, that they may never be forgotten: As for mine I say nothing, since they are not to be nam'd the same Day with your Worship's; and yet I dare avouch, that if any Notice be taken in Knight-Errantry of the Feats of Squires, mine will be sure to come in for a Share. Truly, *Sancho*, reply'd Don *Quixote*, there is some Reason in what thou say'st; but first of all 'tis requisite that a Knight-Errant should spend some Time in various Parts of the World, as a Probationer in quest of Adventures, that by atchieving some extraordinary Exploits, his Renown may diffuse it self through neighbouring Climes and distant Nations: So when he goes to the Court of some Great Monarch, his Fame flying before him as his Harbinger, secures him such a Reception, that the Knight has scarce reach'd the Gates of the Metropolis of the Kingdom, when he finds himself attended and surrounded by admiring Crouds, pointing and crying out, There, there rides the Knight of the Sun, or of the Serpent, or whatever other Title the Knight takes upon him: That's he, they'll cry, who vanquish'd in single Combat the huge Giant *Brocabruno*, Sir-nam'd *Of the Invincible Strength*: This is he that freed the Great *Mamaluco* of *Persia* from the Inchantment that had kept him confin'd for almost nine hundred Years together. Thus, as they relate

his Atchievements with loud Acclamations, the spreading
Rumour at last reaches the King's Palace, and the Monarch
of that Country being desirous to be inform'd with his own
Eyes, will not fail to look out of his Window. As soon as he
sees the Knight, knowing him by his Arms, or the Device on
his Shield, he'll be oblig'd to say to his Attendants, My Lords
and Gentlemen, haste all of you, as many as are Knights, go
and receive the Flower of Chivalry that's coming to our
Court. At the King's Command, away they all run to intro-
duce him; the King himself meets him half way on the Stairs,
where he embraces his valorous Guest, and kisses his Cheek:
Then taking him by the Hand, he leads him directly to the
Queen's Apartment; where the Knight finds her attended
by the Princess her Daughter, who must be one of the most
beautiful and most accomplish'd Damsels in the whole Compass of the Universe. At the same time Fate will so dispose
of every thing, that the Princess shall gaze on the Knight,
and the Knight on the Princess, and each shall admire one
another as Persons rather Angelical than Human; and then
by an unaccountable Charm they shall both find themselves
caught and entangl'd in the inextricable Net of Love, and
wond'rously perplex'd for want of an Opportunity to discover their amorous Anguish to one another. After this, doubtless, the Knight is conducted by the King to one of the richest Apartments in the Palace; where, having taken off his
Armour, they will bring him a rich scarlet Vestment lin'd
with Ermins; and if he look'd so graceful cas'd in Steel, how
lovely will he appear in all the heightning Ornaments of
Courtiers! Night being come, he shall sup with the King, the
Queen, and the Princess; and shall all the while be feasting
his Eyes with the Sight of the Charmer, yet so as no Body
shall perceive it; and she will repay him his Glances with
as much Discretion; for, as I have said, she is a most accomplish'd Person. After Supper a surprizing Scene is unexpectedly to appear: Enter first an ill-favour'd little Dwarf, and
after him a fair Damsel between two Giants, with the Offer
of a certain Adventure so contriv'd by an ancient Necromancer, and so difficult to be perform'd, that he who shall
undertake and end it with Success, shall be esteem'd the best

176

Knight in the World. Presently 'tis the King's Pleasure that all his Courtiers should attempt it; which they do, but all of them unsuccessfully; for the Honour is reserv'd for the valorous Stranger, who effects that with Ease which the rest essay'd in vain; and then the Princess shall be over-joy'd, and esteem her self the most happy Creature in the World, for having bestow'd her Affections on so deserving an Object. Now by the happy Appointment of Fate, this King, or this Emperor, is at War with one of his Neighbours as powerful as himself; and the Knight being inform'd of this, after he has been some few Days at Court, offers the King his Service; which is accepted with Joy, and the Knight courteously kisses the King's Hand in acknowledgment of so great a Favour. That Night the Lover takes his Leave of the Princess at the Iron Grate before her Chamber-Window looking into the Garden, where he and she have already had several Interviews, by means of the Princess's Confident, a Damsel who carries on the Intrigue between them. The Knight sighs, the Princess swoons, the Damsel runs for cold Water to bring her to Life again, very uneasy also because the Morning-Light approaches, and she would not have them discover'd, lest it should reflect on her Lady's Honour. At last the Princess revives, and gives the Knight her lovely Hand to kiss thro' the Iron Grate; which he does a thousand and a thousand times, bathing it all the while with his Tears. Then they agree how to transmit their Thoughts with Se-crecy to each other, with a mutual Intercourse of Letters, during this fatal Absence. The Princess prays him to return with all the Speed of a Lover; the Knight promises it with repeated Vows, and a thousand kind Protestations. At last, the fatal Moment being come that must tear him from all he loves, and from his very self, he seals once more his Love on her soft snowy Hand, almost breathing out his Soul, which mounts to his Lips, and even would leave its Body to dwell there; and then he is hurry'd away by the fearful Confi-dent. After this cruel Separation he retires to his Chamber, throws himself on his Bed; but Grief will not suffer Sleep to close his Eyes. Then rising with the Sun, he goes to take his Leave of the King and the Queen: He desires to pay his

Compliment of Leave to the Princess, but he is told she is indispos'd; and as he has Reason to believe that his departing is the Cause of her Disorder, he is so griev'd at the News, that he is ready to betray the Secret of his Heart; which the Princess's Confident observing, she goes and acquaints her with it, and finds the lovely Mourner bath'd in Tears, who tells her, that the greatest Affliction of her Soul is her not knowing whether her charming Knight be of Royal Blood: But the Damsel pacifies her, assuring her that so much Gal, lantry, and such noble Qualifications, were unquestionably deriv'd from an Illustrious and Royal Original. This comforts the afflicted Fair, who does all she can to compose her Looks, lest the King or the Queen should suspect the Cause of their Alteration; and so some Days after she appears in publick as before. And now the Knight having been absent for some Time, meets, fights, and overcomes the King's Enemies, takes I don't know how many Cities, wins I don't know how many Battles, returns to Court, and appears before his Mistress laden with Honour. He visits her privately as before, and they agree that he shall demand her of the King her Father in Marriage, as the Reward of all his Services; but the King will not grant his Suit, as being unacquainted with his Birth: However, whether it be that the Princess suffers her self to be privately carry'd away, or that some other Means are us'd, the Knight marries her, and in a little Time the King is very well pleas'd with the Match; for now the Knight appears to be the Son of a mighty King of I can't tell you what Country, for I think 'tis not in the Map. Some Time after the Father dies, the Princess is Heiress, and thus in a Trice our Knight comes to be King. Having thus compleated his Happiness, his next Thoughts are to gratify his Squire, and all those who have been instrumental in his Advancement to the Throne: Thus he marries his Squire to one of the Princess's Damsels, and most probably to her Favourite, who had been privy to the Amours, and who is Daughter to one of the most consider- able Dukes in the Kingdom.

That's what I've been looking for all this while, quoth *Sancho*; give me but that, and let the World rub, there I'll stick; for every Tittle o' this will come to pass, and be your

Worship's Case as sure as a Gun, if you'll but take upon
ye that same Nick-name of *The Knight of the woeful Figure*.
Most certainly, *Sancho*, reply'd Don *Quixote*; for by the
same Steps, and in that very manner, Knights-Errant have
always proceeded to ascend to the Throne: Therefore our
chief Business is to find out some Great Potentate, either
among the Christians or the Pagans, that is at War with
his Neighbours, and has a fair Daughter. But we shall have
Time enough to enquire after that; for, as I have told thee,
we must first purchase Fame in other Places, before we presume to go to Court. Another Thing makes me more uneasy:
Suppose we have found out a King and a Princess, and I have
fill'd the World with the Fame of my unparallel'd Atchievements, yet cannot I tell how to find out that I am of Royal
Blood, though it were but second Cousin to an Emperor:
For, 'tis not to be expected that the King will ever consent
that I shall wed his Daughter 'till I have made this out by
authentick Proofs, tho' my Service deserve it never so much;
and thus for want of a Punctilio, I am in danger of losing
what my Valour so justly merits. 'Tis true, indeed, I am a
Gentleman, and of a noted ancient Family, and possess'd of
an Estate of a hundred and twenty Crowns a Year; nay, perhaps the learned Historiographer who is to write the History
of my Life, will so improve and beautify my Genealogy, that
he will find me to be the fifth, or sixth at least, in Descent
from a King: For, *Sancho*, there are two sorts of Originals
in the World; some who sprung from mighty Kings and
Princes, by little and little have been so lessen'd and obscur'd,
that the Estates and Titles of the following Generations have
dwindled to nothing, and ended in a Point like a Pyramid;
others, who from mean and low Beginnings still rise and
rise, till at last they are rais'd to the very Top of human
Greatness: So vast the Difference is, that those who were
Something are now Nothing, and those that were Nothing
are now Something. And therefore who knows but that I
may be one of those whose Original is so illustrious; which
being handsomely made out, after due Examination, ought
undoubtedly to satisfy the King, my Father-in-law. But even
supposing he were still refractory, the Princess is to be so

desperately in love with me, that she will marry me with-
out his Consent, tho' I were a Son of the meanest Water-
Carrier; and if her tender Honour scruples to bless me against
her Father's Will, then it may not be amiss to put a pleasing
Constraint upon her, by conveying her by Force out of the
Reach of her Father, to whose Persecutions either Time or
Death will be sure to put a Period.

Ay, quoth *Sancho*, your rake-helly Fellows have a Saying
that's pat to your Purpose, *Ne'er cringe nor creep, for what
you by Force may reap*; tho' I think 'twere better said, *A
Leap from a Hedge is better than the Prayer of a good Man.**
No more to be said, if the King your Father-in-law won't
let you have his Daughter by fair Means, ne'er stand Shall
I, Shall I, but fairly and squarely run away with her. All the
Mischief that I fear is only, that while you're making your
Peace with him, and waiting after a dead Man's Shoes, as
the Saying is, the poor Dog of a Squire is like to go long bare-
foot, and may go hang himself for any Good you'll be able
to do him, unless the Damsel, *Go-between*, who's to be his
Wife, run away too with the Princess, and he solace himself with her till a better Time comes; for I don't see but
that the Knight may clap up the Match between us without any more ado. That's most certain, answer'd Don *Quixote*.
Why then, quoth *Sancho*, let's e'en take our Chance, and let
the World rub. May Fortune crown our Wishes, cry'd Don
Quixote, and let him be a Wretch who thinks himself one.
Amen, say I, quoth *Sancho*; for I'm one of your old Christians, and that's enough to qualify me to be an Earl. And
more than enough, said Don *Quixote*; for tho' thou wer't
not so well descended, being a King I could bestow Nobility
on thee, without putting thee to the Trouble of buying it, or
doing me the least Service; and making thee an Earl, Men
must call thee My Lord, tho' it grieve 'em never so much.
And do you think, quoth *Sancho*, I would not become my
Equality main well? Thou should'st say Quality, said Don
Quixote, and not *Equality*. Ev'n as you will, return'd *Sancho*:
But, as I was saying, I should become an Earldom rarely; for
I was once Beadle to a Brotherhood, and the Beadle's Gown

* *Better to rob than to ask Charity.*

180

did so become me, that every Body said I had the Presence of
a Warden. Then how do you think I shall look with a Duke's
Robes on my Back, all bedawb'd with Gold and Pearl like
any foreign Count? I believe we shall have Folks come a
hundred Leagues to see me. Thou wilt look well enough,
said Don *Quixote*; but then thou must shave that rough bushy
Beard of thine at least ev'ry other Day, or People will read
thy Beginning in thy Face as soon as they see thee. Why then,
quoth *Sancho*, 'tis but keeping a Barber in my House; and
if needs be, he shall trot after me where-ever I go, like a
Grandee's Master of the Horse. How cam'st thou to know,
said Don *Quixote*, that Grandees have their Masters of the
Horse to ride after 'em? I'll tell you, quoth *Sancho*: Some
Years ago I happen'd to be about a Month among your Court-
folks, and there I saw a little Dandiprat riding about, who,
they said, was a Hugeous Great Lord: There was a Man a
Horseback that follow'd him close where-ever he went, turning and stopping as he did, you'd have thought he had been
ty'd to his Horse's Tail. With that I ask'd why that Hind-
man did not ride by the other, but still came after him thus?
And they told me he was Master of his Horses, and that the
Grandees have always such kind of Men at their Tail; and
I mark'd this so well, that I han't forgot it since. Thou art
in the right, said Don *Quixote*; and thou may'st as reasonably have thy Barber attend thee in this manner. Customs
did not come up all at once, but rather started up and were
improv'd by Degrees; so thou may'st be the first Earl that
rode in State with his Barber behind him; and this may be
said to justify thy Conduct, that 'tis an Office of more Trust
to shave a Man's Beard than to saddle a Horse. Well, quoth
Sancho, leave the Business of the Cut-beard to me, and do
but take care you be a King and I an Earl. Never doubt it,
reply'd Don *Quixote*; and with that looking about, he discover'd —— what the next Chapter will tell you.

VIII: HOW DON QUIXOTE SET FREE MANY MISER-ABLE CREATURES, WHO WERE CARRYING, MUCH AGAINST THEIR WILLS, TO A PLACE THEY DID NOT LIKE

CID *Hamet Benengeli*, an *Arabian* and *Manche-gan* Author, relates in this most grave, high-sounding, minute, soft and humorous History, That after this Discourse between the re-nown'd Don *Quixote* and his Squire *Sancho Pança*, which we have laid down at the End of the Seventh Chapter, the Knight lifting up his Eyes, saw about twelve Men a-foot, trudging in the Road, all in a Row, one behind another, like Beads upon a String, being link'd together by the Neck to a huge Iron Chain, and manacl'd besides. They were guarded by two Horsemen, arm'd with Carbines, and two Men afoot, with Swords and Javelins. As soon as *Sancho* spy'd 'em, Look ye, Sir, cry'd he, here's a Gang of Wretches hurry'd away by main Force to serve the King in the Gallies. How, reply'd Don *Quixote*! Is it possible the King will force any Body? I don't say so, answer'd *San-cho*; I mean these are Rogues whom the Law has sentenc'd for their Misdeeds, to row in the King's Gallies. However, reply'd Don *Quixote*, they are forc'd, because they do not go of their own free Will. Sure enough, quoth *Sancho*. If it be so, said Don *Quixote*, they come within the Verge of My Office, which is to hinder Violence and Oppression, and succour all People in Misery. Ay, Sir, quoth *Sancho*, but neither the King nor Law offer any Violence to such wicked Wretches, they have but their Deserts. By this the Chain of Slaves came up, when Don *Quixote*, in very civil Terms, desir'd the Guards to inform him why these poor People were led along in that manner? Sir, answer'd one of the Horse-men, they are Criminals condemn'd to serve the King in his Gallies: That's all I've to say to you, and you need enquire no further. Nevertheless, Sir, reply'd Don *Quixote*, I have a great Desire to know in few Words the Cause of their Mis-fortune, and I will esteem it an extraordinary Favour, if you will let me have that Satisfaction. We've here the Copies and Certificates of their several Sentences, said the other Horseman, but we can't stand to pull 'em out and read 'em now; you may draw near and examine the Men your self: I suppose they themselves will tell you why they are condemn'd; for they are such honest People, they are not asham'd to boast of their Rogueries. With this Permission, which Don *Quixote* wou'd have taken of himself had they deny'd it him, he rode up to the Chain, and ask'd the first, For what Crimes he was in these miserable Circumstances? The Gally-Slave answer'd him, That 'twas for being in Love. What, only for being in Love, cry'd Don *Quixote*! Were all those that are in Love to be thus us'd, I my self might have been long since in the Gallies. Ay, but, reply'd the Slave, my Love was not of that sort which you conjecture: I was so desperately in Love with a Basket of Linen, and embrac'd it so close, that had not the Judge taken it from me by Force, I wou'd not have parted with it willingly. In short, I was taken in the Fact, and so there was no need to put me to the Rack, 'twas prov'd so plain upon me. So I was committed, try'd, condemn'd, had the gentle Lash; and besides that, was sent, for three Years, to be an Element-dasher, and there's an End of the Business. An Element-dasher, cry'd Don *Quixote*, what do you mean by that? A Gally-Slave, answer'd the Criminal, who was a young Fellow, about four and twenty Years old, and said he was born at *Piedra Hita*.

Then Don *Quixote* examined the second, but he was so sad and desponding, that he would make no Answer; however, the first Rogue inform'd the Knight of his Affairs: Sir, said he, this *Canary-Bird* keeps us Company for having sung too much. Is't possible, cry'd Don *Quixote*! Are Men sent to the Gallies for Singing? Ay, marry, are they, quoth the arch Rogue; for there's nothing worse than to sing in Anguish. How, cry'd Don *Quixote*! That contradicts the Saying, *Sing away Sorrow, cast away Care*. Ay, but with Us the Case is different, reply'd the Slave, He that Sings in Disaster, Weeps all his Life after. This is a Riddle which I cannot unfold, cry'd Don *Quixote*. Sir, said one of the Guards, *Singing in Anguish*, among these Jail Birds, means to confess upon the

Rack: This Fellow was put to the Torture, and confess'd
his Crime, which was stealing of Cattle; and because he
squeak'd, or *sung*, as they call it, he was condemn'd to the
Gallies for Six Years, besides a Hundred Jirks with a Cat
of Nine Tails that have whisk'd and powder'd his Shoulders
already. Now the Reason why he goes thus mopish and out
o'sorts, is only because his Comrogues jeer and laugh at him
continually for not having had the Courage to deny: As if it
had not been as easy for him to have said *No* as *Yes*; or as
if a Fellow, taken up on Suspicion, were not a lucky Rogue,
when there is no positive Evidence can come in against him
but his own Tongue; and in my Opinion they're somewhat
in the right. I think so too, said Don *Quixote*.

Thence addressing himself to the third, And You, said he,
what have You done? Sir, answer'd the Fellow, readily and
pleasantly enough, I must Mow the great Meadow for five
Years together, for want of twice five Ducats. I will give
twenty with all my Heart, said Don *Quixote*, to deliver thee
from that Misery. Thank you for nothing, quoth the Slave;
'tis just like the Proverb, *After Meat comes Mustard*; or,
like Money to a starving Man at Sea, when there are no
Victuals to be bought with it: Had I had the twenty Ducats
you offer me before I was try'd, to have greas'd the Clerk's
[or Recorder's] Fist, and have whetted my Lawyer's Wit,
I might have been now at *Toledo* in the Market-Place of
Zocodover, and not have been thus led along like a Dog in a
String. But Heaven is powerful, *Basta*; I say no more.

Then passing to the fourth, who was a venerable old Don,
with a grey Beard that reach'd to his Bosom, he put the
same Question to him; whereupon the poor Creature fell a
weeping, and was not able to give him an Answer: So the
next behind him lent him a Tongue. Sir, said he, this honest
Person goes to the Gallies for four Years, having taken his
Progress through the Town in State, and rested at the usual
Stations. That is, quoth *Sancho*, as I take it, after he had
been expos'd to publick Shame.* Right, reply'd the Slave;

---

* *Instead of the Pillory, in* Spain, *they carry that sort of Malefactors
on an Ass, and in a particular Habit, along the Streets, the Crier going
before, and proclaiming their Crime.*

and all this he's condemn'd to for being a Broker of Human Flesh: For, to tell you the Truth, the Gentleman is a Pimp, and, besides that, he has a smack of Conjuring. If it were not for that Addition of Conjuring, cry'd Don *Quixote*, he ought not to have been sent to the Gallies, purely for being a Pimp, unless it were to be General of the Gallies: For, the Profession of a Bawd, Pimp, or Messenger of Love, is not like other common Employments, but an Office that requires a great deal of Prudence and Sagacity; an Office of Trust and Weight, and most highly necessary in a well-regulated Commonwealth; nor should it be executed but by civil well-descended Persons of good natural Parts, and of a liberal Education. Nay, 'twere requisite there should be a Comptroller and Surveyor of the Profession, as there are of others; and a certain and settled Number of 'em, as there is of Exchange-Brokers. This wou'd be a Means to prevent an infinite Number of Mischiefs that happen ev'ry Day, because the Trade or Profession is follow'd by poor ignorant Pretenders, silly waiting Women, young giddy-brain'd Pages, shallow Footmen, and such raw, unexperienc'd sort of People, who in unexpected Turns and Emergencies stand with their Fingers in their Mouths, know not their Right Hand from their Left, but suffer themselves to be surpriz'd, and spoil all for want of quickness of Invention either to conceal, carry on, or bring off a Thing artificially. Had I but Time I would point out what sort of Persons are best qualified to be chosen Professors of this most necessary Employment in the Commonwealth; however, at some fitter Season I will inform those of it who may remedy this Disorder. All I have to say now, is, That the Grief I had to see these venerable grey Hairs in such Distress, for having follow'd that no less useful than ingenious Vocation of Pimping, is now lost in my Abhorrence of his additional Character of a Conjurer; tho' I very well know that no Sorcery in the World can affect or force the Will, as some ignorant credulous Persons fondly imagine: For our Will is a Free Faculty, and no Herb nor Charms can constrain it. As for Philtres and such-like Compositions which some silly Women and designing Pretenders make, they are nothing but certain Mixtures and poisonous Preparations, that make those who take them run mad;

tho' the Deceivers labour to persuade us they can make one Person love another; which, as I've said, is an impossible thing, our Will being a free, uncontroulable Power. You say very well, Sir, cry'd the old Coupler; and, upon my Honour, I protest I am wholly innocent, as to the Imputation of Witchcraft. As for the Business of Pimping, I cannot deny it, but I never took it to be a Criminal Function; for my Intention was, that all the World should taste the Sweets of Love, and enjoy each other's Society, living together in Friendship and in Peace, free from those Griefs and Jars that unpeople the Earth. But my harmless Design has not been so happy as to prevent my being sent now to a Place whence I never expect to return, stooping as I do under the heavy Burden of old Age, and being grievously afflicted with the Strangury, which scarce affords me a Moment's respite from Pain. This said, the reverend Procurer burst out afresh into Tears and Lamentations, which melted *Sancho's* Heart so much, that he pull'd a Piece of Money out of his Bosom and gave it to him as an Alms.

Then Don *Quixote* turn'd to the fifth, who seem'd to be nothing at all concern'd. I go to serve his Majesty, said he, for having been somewhat too familiar with two of my Cousin-Germans, and two other kind-hearted Virgins that were Sisters; by which means I have multiply'd my Kind, and begot so odd and intricate a Medley of Kindred, that 'twould puzzle a Convocation of Casuists to resolve their Degrees of Consanguinity. All this was prov'd upon me. I had no Friends, and what was worse, no Money, and so was like to have swung for't: However, I was only condemn'd to the Gallies for six Years, and patiently submitted to't. I feel my self yet young, to my Comfort; so if my Life does but hold out, all will be well in Time. If you will be pleas'd to bestow something upon poor Sinners, Heaven will reward you; and when we pray, we will be sure to remember you, that your Life may be as long and prosperous, as your Presence is goodly and noble. This brisk Spark appear'd to be a Student by his Habit, and some of the Guards said he was a fine Speaker, and a good Latinist.

After him came a Man about thirty Years old, a clever, well-set, handsome Fellow, only he squinted horribly with

one Eye: He was strangely loaded with Irons; a heavy Chain
clogg'd his Leg, and was so long, that he twisted it about his
Waist like a Girdle: He had a Couple of Collars about his
Neck, the one to link him to the rest of the Slaves, and the
other, one of those Iron-Ruffs which they call a *Keep-Friend*,
or a *Friend's Foot*; from whence two Irons went down to his
Middle, and to their two Bars were rivetted a Pair of Manacles that grip'd him by the Fists, and were secur'd with a
large Padlock; so that he could neither lift his Hands to his
Mouth, nor bend down his Head towards his Hands. Don
Quixote enquiring why he was worse hamper'd with Irons
than the rest? Because he alone has done more Rogueries
than all the rest, answer'd one of the Guards. This is such a
Reprobate, such a Devil of a Fellow, that no Gaol nor Fetters
will hold him; we are not sure he's fast enough, for all he's
chain'd so. What sort of Crimes then has he been guilty of,
ask'd Don *Quixote*, that he is only sent to the Gallies? Why,
answer'd the Keeper, he is condemn'd to ten Years Slavery,
which is no better than a Civil Death: But I need not stand
to tell you any more of him, but that he is that notorious
Rogue *Gines de Passamonte*, alias *Ginesillo de Parapilla*.
Hark you, Sir, cry'd the Slave, fair and softly; what a Pox
makes you give a Gentleman more Names than he has? *Gines*
is my Christian-Name, and *Passamonte* my Sir-Name, and not
Ginesillo, nor *Parapilla*, as you say. Blood! let every Man
mind what he says, or it may prove the worse for him. Don't
you be so saucy, Mr Crack-rope, cry'd the Officer to him, or I
may chance to make you keep a better Tongue in your Head.
'Tis a Sign, cry'd the Slave, that a Man's fast, and under the
Lash; but one Day or other some body shall know whether
I'm call'd *Parapilla* or no. Why, Mr Slip-string, reply'd the
Officer, do not People call you by that Name? They do,
answer'd *Gines*, but I'll make 'em call me otherwise, or I'll
fleece and bite them worse than I care to tell you now. But
you, Sir, who are so inquisitive, added he, turning to Don
Quixote, if you've a mind to give us any thing, pray do it
quickly, and go your Ways; for I don't like to stand here
answering Questions; Broil me! I am *Gines de Passamonte*,
I am not asham'd of my Name. As for my Life and Con-

187

versation, there's an Account of 'em in Black and White, written with this numerical Hand of mine. There he tells you true, said the Officer, for he has written his own History himself, without omitting a Tittle of his Roguish Pranks; and he has left the Manuscript in Pawn in the Prison for two Hundred *Reals*: Ay, said *Gines*, and will redeem it, burn me! tho' it lay there for as many Ducats. Then it must be an extraordinary Piece, cry'd Don *Quixote*. So extraordinary, reply'd *Gines*, that it far out-does not only *Lazarillo de Tormes*, but whatever has been, and shall be written in that kind: For mine's true every Word, and no invented Stories can compare with it for Variety of Tricks and Accidents. What's the Title of the Book, ask'd Don *Quixote*? *The Life of* Gines de Passamonte, answer'd t'other. Is it quite finish'd, ask'd the Knight? How the Devil can it be finish'd and I yet living? reply'd the Slave. There's in it every material Point from my Cradle, to this my last going to the Gallies. Then it seems you have been there before, said Don *Quixote*. To serve God and the King I was some four Years there once before, reply'd *Gines*: I already know how the Biscuit and the Bull's-Pizzle agree with my Carcase: It does not grieve me much to go there again, for there I shall have Leisure to give a finishing Stroke to my Book. I have the Devil knows what to add; and in our *Spanish* Gallies there is always Leisure and idle Time enough o'Conscience: Neither shall I want so much for what I've to insert, for I know it all by Heart.

Thou seem'st to be a witty Fellow, said Don *Quixote*. You should have said unfortunate too, reply'd the Slave; for the Bitch Fortune is still unkind to Men of Wit. You mean to such wicked Wretches as your self, cry'd the Officer. Look you, Mr Commissary, said *Gines*, I have already desir'd you to use good Language; the Law did not give us to your keeping for you to abuse us, but only to conduct us where the King has Occasion for us. Let every Man mind his own Business, and give good Words, or hold his Tongue; for by the Blood —— I'll say no more, Murder will out; there will be a Time when some People's Rogueries may come to Light, as well as those of other Folks. With that the Officer, provok'd by the Slave's Threats, held up his Staff to strike him;

but Don *Quixote* stepp'd between 'em, and desir'd him not to do it, and to consider, that the Slave was the more to be excus'd for being too free of his Tongue, since he had ne'er another Member at Liberty. Then addressing himself to all the Slaves, My dearest Brethren, cry'd he, I find, by what I gather from your own Words, that tho' you deserve Punishment for the several Crimes of which you stand convicted, yet you suffer Execution of the Sentence by Constraint, and meerly because you cannot help it. Besides, 'tis not unlikely but that this Man's want of Resolution upon the Rack, the other's want of Money, the third's want of Friends and Favour, and, in short, the Judges perverting and wresting the Law to your great Prejudice, may have been the Cause of your Misery. Now, as Heaven has sent Me into the World to relieve the Distress'd, and free suffering Weakness from the Tyranny of Oppression, according to the Duty of my Profession of Knight-Errantry, these Considerations induce me to take you under my Protection —— But because 'tis the Part of a prudent Man not to use Violence where fair Means may be effectual, I desire you, Gentlemen of the Guard, to release these poor Men, there being People enough to serve his Majesty in their Places; for 'tis a hard Case to make Slaves of Men whom God and Nature made free; and you have the less Reason to use these Wretches with Severity, seeing they never did you any Wrong. Let 'em answer for their Sins in the other World; Heaven is just, you know, and will be sure to punish the Wicked, as 'twill certainly reward the Good. Consider besides, Gentlemen, that 'tis neither a Christian-like, nor an honourable Action, for Men to be the Butchers and Tormenters of one another; principally, when no Advantage can arise from it. I chuse to desire this of you, with so much Mildness, and in so peaceable a manner, Gentlemen, that I may have Occasion to pay you a thankful Acknowledgment, if you will be pleas'd to grant so reasonable a Request: But if you provoke me by Refusal, I must be oblig'd to tell ye, that this Lance, and this Sword, guided by this invincible Arm, shall force you to yield that to my Valour which you deny to my civil Intreaties.

A very good Jest indeed, cry'd the Officer, what a Devil

makes you dote at such a Rate? would you have us set at Liberty the King's Prisoners, as if We had Authority to do it, or You to command it? Go, go about your Business, good Sir Errant, and set your Bason right upon your empty Pate; and pray don't meddle any further in what does not concern you, for those who'll play with Cats must expect to be scratch'd.

Thou art a Cat, and Rat, and a Coward to boot, cry'd Don *Quixote*; and with that he attack'd the Officer with such a sudden and surprizing Fury, that before he had any Time to put himself into a Posture of Defence, he struck him down dangerously wounded with his Lance, and as Fortune had order'd it, this happen'd to be the Horse-man who was arm'd with a Carbine. His Companions stood astonish'd at such a bold Action, but at last fell upon the Champion with their Swords and Darts, which might have prov'd fatal to him, had not the Slaves laid hold of this Opportunity to break the Chain, in order to regain their Liberty: For, the Guards perceiving their Endeavours to get loose, thought it more material to prevent 'em, than to be fighting a Mad-man: But, as he press'd them vigorously on one side, and the Slaves were opposing them and freeing themselves on the other, the Hurly-burly was so great, and the Guards so perplex'd, that they did nothing to the Purpose. In the mean time *Sancho* was helping *Gines de Passamonte* to get off his Gives, which he did sooner than can be imagin'd; and then that active Desperado having seiz'd the wounded Officer's Sword and Carbine, he join'd with Don *Quixote*, and some-times aiming at the one, and sometimes at the other, as if he had been ready to shoot 'em, yet still without letting off the Piece, the other Slaves at the same time pouring Vollies of Stone-shot at the Guards, they betook themselves to their Heels, leaving Don *Quixote* and the Criminals Masters of the Field. *Sancho*, who was always for taking Care of the main Chance, was not at all pleas'd with this Victory; for he guess'd that the Guards who were fled, would raise a Hue and Cry, and soon be at their Heels with the whole *Posse* of the Holy Brotherhood, and lay 'em up for a Rescue and Rebellion. This made him advise his Master to get out of the Way as fast as he could, and hide himself in the neighbouring Mountains. I hear you, answer'd Don *Quixote* to this Motion of his Squire, and I know what I have to do. Then calling to him all the Slaves, who by this time had uncas'd the Keeper to his Skin, they gather'd about him to know his Pleasure, and he spoke to them in this manner: 'Tis the Part of generous Spirits to have a grateful Sense of the Benefits they receive, no Crime being more odious than Ingratitude. You see, Gentlemen, what I have done for your sakes, and you cannot but be sensible how highly you're oblig'd to me. Now all the Recompence I require is only, that every one of you, loaden with that Chain from which I have freed your Necks, do instantly repair to the City of *Toboso*; and there presenting your selves before the Lady *Dulcinea del Toboso*, tell her, that her faithful Votary, the Knight of the *Woeful Countenance*, commanded you to wait on her, and assure her of his profound Veneration. Then you shall give her an exact Account of every Particular relating to this famous Atchievement, by which you once more taste the Sweets of Liberty; which done, I give you leave to seek your Fortunes where you please.

To this the Ring-leader and Master-thief, *Gines de Passamonte*, made Answer for all the rest, What you would have us to do, said he, our noble Deliverer, is absolutely impracticable and impossible; for we dare not be seen all together for the World. We must rather part and sculk some one Way, some another, and lie snug in Creeks and Corners under Ground, for fear of those damn'd Man-hounds that will be after us with a Hue and Cry; therefore all we can, and ought to do in this Case, is to change this Compliment and Homage which you'd have us pay to the Lady *Dulcinea del Toboso*, into a certain Number of *Ave Maries* and *Creeds*, which we will say for your Worship's Benefit; and this may be done by Night or by Day, walking or standing, and in War as well as in Peace: But to imagine we will return to our Flesh-pots of *Egypt*, that is to say, take up our Chains again, and lug 'em the Devil knows whither, is as unreasonable as to think 'tis Night now at Ten a-Clock in the Morning. 'Sdeath, to expect this from us, is to expect Pears from an Elm-Tree. Now, by my Sword, reply'd Don *Quixote*, Sir Son of a Whore, Sir *Ginesillo de Parapilla*, or whatever be your Name, you your self, alone, shall go to *Toboso*, like a Dog that has scalded his Tail, with the whole Chain about your Shoulders. *Gines*, who was naturally very cholerick, judging by Don *Quixote's* Extravagance in freeing them, that he was not very wise, wink'd on his Companions, who, like Men that understood Signs, presently fell back to the Right and Left, and pelted Don *Quixote* with such a Shower of Stones, that all his Dexterity to cover himself with his Shield was now ineffectual, and poor *Rozinante* no more obey'd the Spur, than if he had been only the Statue of a Horse. As for *Sancho*, he got behind his Ass, and there shelter'd himself from the Vollies of Flints that threaten'd his Bones, while his Master was so batter'd, that in a little time he was thrown out of his Saddle to the Ground. He was no sooner down, but the Student leap'd on him, took off the Bason from his Head, gave him three or four Thumps o'the Shoulders with it, and then gave it so many Knocks against the Stones, that he almost broke it to Pieces. After this, they stripp'd him of his upper Coat, and had robb'd him of his Hose too, but that his Greaves hinder'd them. They also eas'd *Sancho* of his upper Coat, and left him in his Doublet;* then having divided the Spoils, they shifted every one for himself, thinking more how to avoid being taken up and link'd again in the Chain, than of trudging with it to my Lady *Dulcinea del Toboso*. Thus the Ass, *Rozinante*, *Sancho*, and Don *Quixote*, remain'd indeed Masters of the Field, but in an ill Condition: The Ass hanging his Head, and pensive, shaking his Ears now and then, as if the Vollies of Stones had still whizz'd about 'em; *Rozinante* lying in a desponding manner, for he had been knock'd down as well as his unhappy Rider; *Sancho* uncas'd to his Doublet, and trembling for fear of the Holy Brotherhood; and Don *Quixote* fill'd with sullen Regret, to find himself so barbarously us'd by those whom he had so highly oblig'd.

* En pelota, *which really signifies* Stark-naked, *as* Sobrino *explains it in* French, tout nud. *But it can hardly mean so here, as the Reader will soon see, especially if, according to* Stevens's Dictionary, Pelota *was a sort of Garment us'd in former Times in* Spain, *not known at present.*

IX: WHAT BEFELL THE RENOWN'D DON QUIX-OTE IN THE SIERRA MORENA (BLACK MOUN-TAIN) BEING ONE OF THE RAREST ADVENTURES IN THIS AUTHENTICK HISTORY

DON *Quixote* finding himself so ill treated, said to his Squire; *Sancho,* I have always heard it said, That to do a Kindness to Clowns, is like throwing Water into the Sea.* Had I given Ear to thy Advice, I had prevented this Mis-fortune: But since the Thing is done, 'tis need-less to repine; this shall be a Warning to me for the future. That is, quoth *Sancho,* when the Devil's blind: But since you say, you had 'scap'd this Mischief had you believ'd me, good Sir, believe me now, and you'll 'scape a greater; for I must tell you, that those of the Holy Brotherhood don't stand in awe of Your Chivalry, nor do they care a Straw for all the Knights-Errant in the World. Methinks I already hear their Arrows whizzing about my Ears.† Thou art naturally a Coward, *Sancho,* cry'd Don *Quixote;* nevertheless, that thou may'st not say I am obstinate, and never follow thy Advice, I will take thy Counsel, and for once convey my self out the Reach of this dreadful Brotherhood, that so strangely alarms thee; but upon this Condition, that thou never tell any mor-tal Creature, neither while I live, nor after my Death, that I withdrew my self from this Danger through Fear, but meerly to comply with thy Intreaties: For if thou ever presume to say otherwise, thou wilt belye me; and from this Time to that Time, and from that Time to the World's End, I give thee the Lye, and thou lyest, and shalt lye in thy Throat, as often as thou say'st, or but think'st to the contrary. Therefore do not offer to reply; for should'st thou but surmise, that I would avoid any Danger, and especially this which seems to give some Occasion or Colour for Fear, I would certainly stay here, though unattended and alone, and expect and face not only the Holy Brotherhood, which thou dread'st so much, but also

* *It is Labour lost, because they are ungrateful.*   † *The Troopers of the Holy Brotherhood ride with Bows, and shoot Arrows.*

the Fraternity or twelve Heads of the Tribes of *Israel*, the seven *Maccabees*, *Castor* and *Pollux*, and all the Brothers and Brotherhoods in the Universe. An't please your Worship, quoth *Sancho*, to withdraw is not to run away, and to stay is no wise Action, when there's more Reason to fear than to hope; 'tis the Part of a wise Man to keep himself to Day for to Morrow, and not venture all his Eggs in one Basket. And for all I'm but a Clown, or a Bumpkin, as you may say, yet I'd have you to know I know what's what, and have always taken care of the main Chance; therefore don't be asham'd of being rul'd by me, but e'en get o'Horseback an you're able: Come, I'll help you, and then follow Me; for my Mind plaguily misgives me, that now one Pair of Heels will stand us in more stead than two Pair of Hands.

Don *Quixote*, without any Reply, made shift to mount *Rozinante*, and *Sancho* on his Ass led the Way to the neighbouring mountainous Desart called *Sierra Morena*,* which the crafty Squire had a Design to cross over, and get out at the farthest End, either at *Viso*, or *Almadovar del Campo*, and in the mean time to lurk in the craggy and almost inaccessible Retreats of that vast Mountain, for fear of falling into the Hands of the Holy Brotherhood. He was the more eager to steer this Course, finding that the Provision which he had laid on his Ass had escap'd plundering, which was a kind of Miracle, considering how narrowly the Gally-Slaves had search'd every where for Booty. 'Twas Night before our two Travellers got to the Middle and most desart Part of the Mountain; where *Sancho* advis'd his Master to stay some Days, at least as long as their Provisions lasted; and accordingly that Night they took up their Lodging between two Rocks, among a great Number of Cork-Trees: But Fortune, which, according to the Opinion of those that have not the Light of true Faith, guides, appoints, and contrives all things as it pleases, directed *Gines de Passamonte* (that Master-Rogue, who, Thanks be to Don *Quixote's* Force and Folly,

* Sierra, *tho'* Spanish *for a Mountain, properly means (not a* Chain, *but) a* Saw, *from Latin* Serra, *because of its Ridges rising and falling like the Teeth of a Saw. This Mountain (call'd* Morena *from its Moorish or swarthy Colour) parts the Kingdom of* Castile *from the Province of* Andaluzia.

had been put in a Condition to do him a Mischief) to this very Part of the Mountain, in order to hide himself till the Heat of the Pursuit, which he had just Cause to fear, were over. He discover'd our Adventurers much about the Time that they fell asleep; and as wicked Men are always ungrateful, and urgent Necessity prompts many to do Things, at the very Thoughts of which they perhaps would start at other Times, *Gines*, who was a Stranger both to Gratitude and Humanity, resolv'd to ride away with *Sancho's* Ass; for as for *Rozinante*, he look'd upon him as a thing that would neither sell nor pawn: So while poor *Sancho* lay snoring, he spirited away his darling Beast, and made such haste, that before Day he thought himself and his Prize secure from the unhappy Owner's Pursuit.

Now *Aurora* with her smiling Face return'd to enliven and cheer the Earth, but alas! to grieve and affright *Sancho* with a dismal Discovery: For he had no sooner open'd his Eyes, but he miss'd his Ass; and finding himself depriv'd of that dear Partner of his Fortunes, and best Comfort in his Peregrinations, he broke out into the most pitiful and sad Lamentations in the World; insomuch that he wak'd Don *Quixote* with his Moans. O dear Child of my Bowels, cry'd he, born and bred under my Roof, my Childrens Play-fellow, the Comfort of my Wife, the Envy of my Neighbours, the Ease of my Burdens, the Staff of my Life, and in a Word, half my Maintenance; for with Six and twenty *Maravedis*, which were daily earn'd by thee, I made shift to keep half my Family. Don *Quixote*, who easily guess'd the Cause of these Complaints, strove to comfort him with kind condoling Words, and learn'd Discourses upon the Uncertainty of human Happiness: But nothing prov'd so effectual to asswage his Sorrow, as the Promise which his Master made him of drawing a Bill of Exchange on his Niece for three Asses out of five which he had at Home, payable to *Sancho Pança*, or his Order; which prevailing Argument soon dry'd up his Tears, hush'd his Sighs and Moans, and turn'd his Complaints into Thanks to his generous Master for so unexpected a Favour.

And now, as they wander'd further in these Mountains, Don *Quixote* was transported with Joy to find himself where he might flatter his Ambition with the Hopes of fresh Adventures to signalize his Valour; for these vast Desarts made him call to mind the wonderful Exploits of other Knights-Errant, perform'd in such Solitudes. Fill'd with those airy Notions, he thought on nothing else: But *Sancho* was for more substantial Food; and now thinking himself quite out of the Reach of the Holy Brotherhood, his only Care was to fill his Belly with the Relicks of the Clerical Booty; and thus sitting sideling, as Women do, upon his Beast,* he slily took out now one Piece of Meat, then another, and kept his Grinders going faster than his Feet. Thus plodding on, he would not have given a Rush to have met with any other Adventure.

While he was thus employ'd, he observ'd, that his Master endeavour'd to take up something that lay on the Ground with the End of his Lance: This made him run to help him to lift up the Bundle, which prov'd to be a Portmanteau, and the Seat of a Saddle, that were half, or rather quite rotted with lying expos'd to the Weather. The Portmanteau was somewhat heavy; and Don *Quixote* having order'd *Sancho* to see what it contain'd, though it was shut with a Chain and a Padlock, he easily saw what was in it through the Cracks, and pull'd out four fine Holland Shirts, and other clean and fashionable Linnen, besides a considerable Quantity of Gold ty'd up in a Handkerchief. Bless my Eye-sight,

---

* *It is scarce twenty Lines since* Sancho *lost his Ass, as Mr. Jarvis observes, and here he is upon his Back again. The best Excuse for this evident Blunder, adds that Gentleman, is* Horace's *aliquando bonus dormitat* Homerus. *Upon which Occasion the same Gentleman, in his Preface, asks, But what if* Cervantes *made this seeming Slip on Purpose for a Bait to tempt the minor Criticks; in the same manner as, in another Place, he made the Princess of* Micomicon *land at* Ossuna, *which is no Sea-Port? As by that he introduc'd a fine Satire on an eminent Spanish Historian of his Time, who had describ'd it as such in his History; so by this he might have only taken Occasion to reflect on a parallel Incident in* Ariosto, *where* Brunelo, *at the Siege of* Albraca, *steals a Horse from between the Legs of* Sacripante King of Circassia. *It is, adds this judicious Critick, the very Defence the Author makes for it himself, in the fourth Chapter of the second Part, where, by the way, both the* Italian *and old* English *Translators have preserv'd the Excuse, tho' by their altering the Text they had taken away the Occasion of it.*

quoth *Sancho*; and now Heaven I thank thee for sending us such a lucky Adventure once in our Lives: With that, groping further in the Portmanteau, he found a Table-Book richly Bound. Give me that, said Don *Quixote*, and do Thou keep the Gold. Heaven reward your Worship, quoth *Sancho*, kissing his Master's Hand, and at the same time clapping up the Linnen and the other Things into the Bag where he kept the Victuals. I fancy, said Don *Quixote*, that some Person, having lost his Way in these Mountains, has been met by Robbers, who have murder'd him, and bury'd his Body some-where hereabouts. Sure your Worship's mistaken, answer'd *Sancho*; for had they been Highwaymen, they would never have left such a Booty behind them. Thou art in the right, reply'd Don *Quixote*; and therefore I cannot imagine what it must be. But stay, I will examine the Table-Book, perhaps we shall find something written in that, which will help us to discover what I would know. With that he open'd it, and the first thing he found was the following rough Draught of a Sonnet, fairly enough written to be read with Ease; so he read it aloud, that *Sancho* might know what was in it as well as himself:

THE RESOLVE

A SONNET

Love is a God ne'er knows our Pain,
Or Cruelty's his darling Attribute;
Else he'd ne'er force me to complain,
And to his Spite my raging Pain impute.

But sure if Love's a God, he must
Have Knowledge equal to his Pow'r;
And 'tis a Crime to think a God unjust:
Whence then the Pains that now my Heart devour?

From Phyllis? *No: Why do I pause?*
Such cruel Ills ne'er boast so sweet a Cause;
Nor from the Gods such Torments we do bear,
Let Death then quickly be my Cure:
When thus we Ills unknown endure,
'Tis shortest to despair.

The De'il of any thing can be pick'd out o' this, quoth *Sancho*, unless you can tell who that same *Phyll* is. I did not read *Phyll*, but *Phyllis*, said Don *Quixote*. O then, mayhap, the Man has lost his Philly-foal. *Phyllis*, said Don *Quixote*, is the Name of a Lady that's belov'd by the Author of this Sonnet, who truly seems to be a tolerable Poet,* or I've but little Judgment. Why then, quoth *Sancho*, belike your Worship understands how to make Verses too? That I do, answer'd Don *Quixote*, and better than thou imagin'st, as thou shalt see, when I shall give thee a Letter written all in Verse to carry to my Lady *Dulcinea del Toboso*: For, I must tell thee, Friend *Sancho*, all the Knights-Errant, or at least the greatest Part of 'em, in former Times were great Poets, and as great Musicians; those Qualifications, or to speak better, those two Gifts, or Accomplishments, being almost inseparable from amorous Adventures: Though I must confess the Verses of the Knights in former Ages are not altogether so polite, nor so adorn'd with Words, as with Thoughts and Inventions.

Good Sir, quoth *Sancho*, look again into the Pocket-Book, mayhap you will find somewhat that will inform you of what you'd know. With that Don *Quixote* turning over the Leaf, here's some Prose, cry'd he, and I think 'tis the Sketch of a Love-Letter. O! good your Worship, quoth *Sancho*, read it out by all means; for I mightily delight in hearing of Love-Stories.

Don *Quixote* read it aloud, and found what follows:

The Falshood of your Promises, and my Despair, hurry me from you for ever; and you shall sooner hear the News of my Death, than the Cause of my Complaints. You have forsaken me, ungrateful Fair, for one more wealthy indeed, but not more deserving than your abandon'd Slave. Were Virtue esteem'd a Treasure equal to its Worth by your unthinking Sex, I must presume to say, I should have no Reason to envy the Wealth of others, and no Misfortune to bewail. What your Beauty has rais'd, your Actions have destroy'd; the first made me mistake you for an Angel, but the last convince me you're a very Woman. However, O! too lovely Disturber of

* Cervantes *himself*.

*my Peace, may uninterrupted Rest and downy Ease engross
your happy Hours; and may forgiving Heav'n still keep your
Husband's Perfidiousness conceal'd, lest it should cost your
repenting Heart a Sigh for the Injustice you have done to so
faithful a Lover, and so I should be prompted to a Revenge
which I do not desire to take. Farewel.*

This Letter, quoth Don *Quixote*, does not give us any further Insight into the Things we would know; all I can infer
from it is, that the Person who wrote it was a betray'd Lover:
And so turning over the remaining Leaves, he found several
other Letters and Verses, some of which were legible, and
some so scribbl'd, that he could make nothing of them. As
for those he read, he could meet with nothing in 'em but
Accusations, Complaints and Expostulations, Distrusts and
Jealousies, Pleasures and Discontents, Favours and Disdain,
the one highly valu'd, the other as mournfully resented. And
while the Knight was poring on the Table-Book, *Sancho* was
rummaging the Portmanteau, and the Seat of the Saddle,
with that Exactness, that he did not leave a Corner un-
search'd, nor a Seam unripp'd, nor a single Lock of Wool
unpick'd; for the Gold he had found, which was above an
hundred Ducats, had but whetted his greedy Appetite, and
made him wild for more. Yet though this was all he could
find, he thought himself well paid for the more than *Her-
culean* Labours he had undergone; nor could he now repine
at his being toss'd in a Blanket, the straining and griping
Operation of the Balsam, the Benedictions of the Pack-staves
and Leavers, the Fisticuffs of the lewd Carrier, the Loss of
his Cloak, his dear Wallet, and of his dearer Ass, and all the
Hunger, Thirst, and Fatigue which he had suffer'd in his
kind Master's Service. On the other Side, the Knight of the
woeful Figure strangely desired to know who was the Owner
of the Portmanteau, guessing by the Verses, the Letter, the
Linen, and the Gold, that he was a Person of Worth, whom
the Disdain and Unkindness of his Mistress had driven to
Despair. At length, however, he gave over the Thoughts of
it, discovering no body through that vast Desart; and so he
rode on, wholly guided by *Rozinante's* Discretion, which
always made the grave sagacious Creature chuse the plainest

and smoothest Way; the Master still firmly believing, that in those woody uncultivated Forests he should infallibly start some wonderful Adventure.

And indeed, while these Hopes possess'd him, he spy'd upon the Top of a stony Crag just before him a Man that skipp'd from Rock to Rock, over Briars and Bushes, with wonderful Agility. He seem'd to him naked from the Waist upwards, with a thick black Beard, his Hair long, and strangely tangled, his Head, Legs, and Feet bare; on his Hips a Pair of Breeches, that appear'd to be of sad-colour'd Velvet, but so tatter'd and torn, that they discover'd his Skin in many Places. These Particulars were observ'd by Don *Quixote* while he pass'd by; and he follow'd him, endeavouring to overtake him, for he presently guess'd this was the Owner of the Portmanteau. But *Rozinante*, who was naturally slow and phlegmatick, was in too weak a Case besides to run Races with so swift an Apparition: Yet the Knight of the *woeful Figure* resolv'd to find out that unhappy Creature, though he were to bestow a whole Year in the Search; and to that Intent he order'd *Sancho* to beat one Side of the Mountain, while he hunted the other. In good sooth, quoth *Sancho*, your Worship must excuse me as to that; for if I but offer to stir an Inch from you I'm almost frighted out of my seven Senses: And let this serve you hereafter for a Warning, that you may not send me a Nail's Breadth from your Presence. Well, said the Knight, I will take thy Case into Consideration; and it does not displease me, *Sancho*, to see thee thus rely upon my Valour, which I dare assure thee shall never fail thee, though thy very Soul should be scar'd out of thy Body. Follow me therefore Step by Step, with as much Haste as is consistent with good-Speed; and let thy Eyes pry every where while we search every Part of this Rock, where 'tis probable we may meet with that wretched Mortal, who doubtless is the Owner of the Portmanteau.

Odsnigs, Sir, quoth *Sancho*, I had rather get out of his Way; for should we chance to meet him, and he lay Claim to the Portmanteau, 'tis a plain Case I shall be forc'd to part with the Money: And therefore I think it much better, without making so much ado, to let me keep it *bona fide*, till we can light on the right Owner some more easy Way, and without dancing after him; which mayn't happen 'till we have spent all the Money; and in that Case I'm free from the Law, and he may go whistle for't. Thou art mistaken, *Sancho*, cry'd Don *Quixote*, for seeing we have some Reason to think, that we know who is the Owner, we are bound in Conscience to endeavour to find him out, and restore it to him; the rather, because should we not now strive to meet him, yet the strong Presumption we have that the Goods belong to him, would make us Possessors of 'em *mala fide*, and render us as guilty as if the Party whom we suspect to have lost the Things were really the right Owner: Therefore, Friend *Sancho*, do not think much of searching for him, since if we find him out, 'twill extreamly ease my Mind. With that he spurr'd *Rozinante*; and *Sancho*, not very well pleas'd, follow'd him, comforting himself however with the Hopes of the three Asses which his Master had promis'd him. So when they had rode over the greatest Part of the Mountain, they came to a Brook, where they found a Mule lying dead, with her Saddle and Bridle about her, and herself half devour'd by Beasts and Birds of Prey; which Discovery further confirm'd them in their Suspicion, that the Man who fled so nimbly from them, was the Owner of the Mule and Portmanteau. Now as they paus'd and ponder'd upon this, they heard a Whistling like that of some Shepherd keeping his Flocks; and presently after, upon their Left Hand, they spy'd a great Number of Goats with an old Herdsman after them, on the Top of the Mountain. Don *Quixote* call'd out to him, and desir'd him to come down; but the Goat-herd, instead of answering him, ask'd 'em in as loud a Tone how they came thither into those Desarts, where scarce any living Creatures resorted except Goats, Wolves, and other Wild Beasts? *Sancho* told him, they would satisfy him as to that Point if he would come where they were. With that the Goat-herd came down to 'em; and seeing them look upon the dead Mule, That dead Mule, said the old Fellow, has lain in that very Place this six Months; but pray tell me, good People, have you not met the Master of it by the Way? We have met no Body, answer'd Don *Quixote*; but we found a Portmanteau and a Saddle-Cushion not far from this Place. I have seen it too, quoth the Goat-herd, but I never durst meddle with it, nor so much as come near it, for fear of some Misdemeanour, lest I should be charg'd with having stol'n somewhat out of it: For who knows what might happen? The Devil is subtle, and some-times lays Baits in our Way to tempt us, or Blocks to make us stumble. 'Tis just so with me, Gaffer, quoth *Sancho*, for I saw the Portmanteau too, d'ye see, but the Devil a Bit would I come within a Stone's throw of it; no, there I found it, and there I left it, i'faith, it shall e'en lie there still for me. He that steals a Bell-weather shall be discover'd by the Bell. Tell me, honest Friend, ask'd Don *Quixote*, do'st thou know who is the Owner of those Things? All I know of the Matter, answer'd the Goat-herd, is, that 'tis now six Months, little more or less, since to a certain Sheepfold, some three Leagues off, there came a young well-featur'd proper Gentleman in good Cloaths, and under him this same Mule that now lies dead here, with the Cushion and Cloak-bag, which you say you met, but touch'd not. He ask'd us which was the most desart and least frequented Part of these Mountains? and we told him this where we are now; and in that we spoke the plain Truth, for should you venture to go but half a League further, you would hardly be able to get back again in haste; and I marvel how you could get even thus far; for there's neither High-way nor Foot-path that may direct a Man this Way. Now as soon as the young Gentleman had heard our Answer, he turn'd about his Mule, and made to the Place we shew'd him, leaving us all with a hugeous liking to his Comeliness, and strangely marvelling at his Demand, and at the Haste he made towards the Middle of the Mountain. After that we heard no more of him in a great while, till one Day by Chance one of the Shepherds coming by, he fell upon him without saying why or wherefore, and beat him with-out Mercy: After that he went to the Ass that carry'd our Victuals, and taking away all the Bread and Cheese that was there, he tripp'd back again to the Mountain with wond'rous Speed. Hearing this, a good Number of us together resolv'd to find him out; and when we had spent the best Part of two Days in the thickest of the Forest, we found him at last lurking in the Hollow of a huge Cork-Tree, from whence he came forth to meet us as mild as could be. But then he was so alter'd, his Face was so disfigur'd, wan, and Sun-burnt, that had it not been for his Attire, which we made shift to know again, tho' 'twas all in Rags and Tatters, we could not have thought it had been the same Man. He saluted us courteously, and told us in few Words, mighty handsomly put together, that we were not to marvel to see him in that manner, for that it behov'd him so to be, that he might fulfil a certain Penance enjoin'd him for the great Sins he had committed. We pray'd him to tell us who he was, but he would by no means do it: We likewise desir'd him to let us know where we might find him, that whensoever he wanted Victuals we might bring him some, which we told him we would be sure to do, for otherwise he would be starv'd in that barren Place; requesting him, that if he did not like that Motion neither, he would at least-wise come and ask us for what he wanted, and not take it by Force as he had done. He thank'd us heartily for our Offer, and begg'd Pardon for that Injury, and promis'd to ask it henceforwards as an Alms, without setting upon any one. As for his Place of Abode, he told us he had none certain, but where-ever Night caught him, there he lay: And he ended his Discourse with such bitter Moans, that we must have had Hearts of Flint, had we not had a Feeling of 'em, and kept him Company therein; chiefly considering we beheld him so strangely alter'd from what we had seen him before; for, as I said, he was a very fine comely young Man, and by his Speech and Behaviour we could guess him to be well born, and a Court-like sort of a Body: For tho' we were but Clowns, yet such was his genteel Behaviour, that we could not help being taken with it. Now as he was talking to us, he stopp'd of a sudden as if he had been struck dumb, fixing his Eyes steadfastly on the Ground; whereat we all stood in a Maze. After he had thus star'd a good while, he shut his Eyes, then open'd 'em again, bit his Lips, knit his Brows, clutch'd his Fists; and then rising from the Ground, whereon he had thrown himself a little before, he flew at the Man that stood next to him with such a Fury, that if we had not pull'd him off by main Force, he would have bit and thump'd him to Death; and all the while he cry'd out, *Ah! Traitor* Ferdinand, *here, here thou shalt pay for the Wrong thou hast done me; I must rip up that false Heart of thine;* and a deal more he added, all in Dispraise of that same *Ferdinand.* After that he flung from us without saying a Word, leaping over the Bushes and Brambles at such a strange rate, that 'twas impossible for us to come at him; from which we gather'd, that his Madness comes on him by Fits, and that some one call'd *Ferdinand* had done him an ill Turn, that had brought the poor young Man to this pass. And this has been confirm'd since that many and many Times; for when he's in his right Senses he'll come and beg for Victuals, and thank us for it with Tears; but when he is in his mad Fit, he will beat us though we proffer him Meat civilly: And to tell you the Truth, Sirs, added the Goat-herd, I and four others, of whom two are my Men, and the other two my Friends, Yesterday agreed to look for him till we should find him out, either by fair Means or by Force to carry him to *Almodovar* Town, that's but eight Leagues off; and there we'll have him cur'd if possible, or at least we shall learn what he is when he comes to his Wits, and whether he has any Friends to whom he may be sent back. This is all I know of the Matter; and I dare assure you, that the Owner of those Things which you saw in the Way is the self same Body that went so nimbly by you, for Don *Quixote* had by this Time acquainted the Goat-herd of his having seen that Man skipping among the Rocks.

The Knight was wonderfully concern'd when he had heard the Goat-herd's Story, and renew'd his Resolution of finding out that distracted Wretch, whatever Time and Pains it might cost him. But Fortune was more propitious to his Desires than he could reasonably have expected: For just as they were speaking they spy'd him right against the Place where they stood, coming towards 'em out of the Cleft of a Rock, muttering somewhat to himself, which they could not well have understood had they stood close by him, much less could they guess his Meaning at that Distance. His Apparel was such as has already been said, only Don *Quixote* observ'd, when he drew nearer, that he had on a Shamoy Waistcoat

torn in many Places, which yet the Knight found to be perfum'd with Amber; and by this, as also by the rest of his
Cloaths, and other Conjectures, he judg'd him to be a Man
of some Quality. As soon as the unhappy Creature came near
'em, he saluted 'em very civilly, but with a hoarse Voice. Don
Quixote return'd his Civilities, and alighting from *Rozinante*,
accosted him in a very graceful Manner, and hugg'd him close
in his Arms, as if he had been one of his intimate Acquaintance. The other, whom we may venture to call *the Knight
of the ragged Figure*, as well as Don *Quixote the Knight of
the woeful Figure*, having got loose from that Embrace, could
not forbear stepping back a little, and laying his Hands on
the Companion's Shoulders, he stood staring in his Face,
as if he had been striving to call to mind whether he had
known him before, probably wondering as much to behold
Don *Quixote's* Countenance, Armour, and strange Figure, as
Don *Quixote* did to see his tatter'd Condition: But the first
that open'd his Mouth after this Pause was the ragged Knight,
as you shall find by the Sequel of the Story.

THE History relates, that Don *Quixote* listen'd with great Attention to the disast'rous Knight of the Mountain, who made him the following Compliment. Truly, Sir, whoever you be (for I have not the Honour to know you) I'm much oblig'd to you for your Expressions of Civility and Friendship; and I cou'd wish I were in a Condition to convince you otherwise than by Words of the deep Sense I have of 'em: But my bad Fortune leaves me nothing to return for so many Favours, but unprofitable Wishes. Sir, answer'd Don *Quixote*, I've so hearty a Desire to serve you, that I was fully resolv'd not to depart these Mountains till I had found you out, that I might know from your self, whether the Discontents that have urg'd you to make Choice of this unusual Course of Life, might not admit of a Remedy; for if they do, assure your self I will leave no Means untry'd, till I have purchas'd you that Ease which I heartily wish you: Or if your Disasters are of that fatal Kind, that exclude you for ever from the Hopes of Comfort or Relief, then will I mingle Sorrows with you, and by sharing your Load of Grief, help you to bear the oppressing Weight of Affliction: For 'tis the only Comfort of the Miserable to have Partners in their Woes. If then good Intentions may plead Merit, or a grateful Requital, let me intreat you, Sir, by that generous Nature that shoots through the Gloom with which Adversity has clouded your graceful Outside; nay, let me conjure you by the darling Object of your Wishes, to let me know who you are, and what strange Misfortunes have urg'd you to withdraw from the Converse of your Fellow-Creatures, to bury your self alive in this horrid Solitude, where you linger out a wretched Being, a Stranger to Ease, to all Mankind, and even to your very self. And I solemnly swear, added Don *Quixote*, by the Order of Knighthood, of which I am an unworthy Professor, that if you so far gratify my Desires, I will assist you to the utmost of my Capacity, either by remedying your Disaster,

if 'tis not past Redress; or, at least, I will become your Partner in Sorrow, and strive to ease it by a Society in Sadness.

The Knight of the Wood hearing the Knight of the *woeful
Figure* talk at that rate, look'd upon him stedfastly for a long
Time, and view'd and review'd him from Head to Foot; and
when he had gaz'd a great while upon him, Sir, cry'd he, if
you have any thing to eat, for Heaven's Sake give it me, and
when my Hunger is abated, I shall be better able to comply
with your Desires, which your great Civilities and undeserv'd
Offers oblige me to satisfy. *Sancho* and the Goat-herd hearing this, presently took out some Victuals, the one out of his
Bag, the other out of his Scrip, and gave it to the ragged
Knight to allay his Hunger, who immediately fell on with
that greedy Haste, that he seem'd rather to devour than
feed; for he us'd no Intermission between Bit and Bit, so
greedily he chopp'd them up: And all the Time he was eating,
neither he, nor the By-standers, spoke the least Word. When
he had asswag'd his voracious Appetite, he beckon'd to Don
Quixote and the rest to follow him; and, after he had brought
'em to a neighbouring Meadow, he laid himself at his Ease
on the Grass, where the rest of the Company sitting down
by him, neither he nor they having yet spoke a Word since
he fell to eating, he began in this manner:

Gentlemen, said he, if you intend to be informed of my
Misfortunes, you must promise me beforehand not to cut off
the Thread of my doleful Narration with any Questions, or
any other Interruption; for in the very Instant that any of
you does it, I shall leave off abruptly, and will not afterwards go on with the Story. This Preamble put Don *Quixote*
in Mind of *Sancho's* ridiculous Tale, which by his Neglect
in not telling the Goats, was brought to an untimely Conclusion. I only use this Precaution, added the ragged Knight,
because I would be quick in my Relation; for the very Remembrance of my former Misfortune proves a new one to
me, and yet I promise you I'll endeavour to omit nothing
that's material, that you may have as full an Account of my
Disasters as I am sensible you desire. Thereupon Don *Quixote*,
for himself and the rest, having promis'd him uninterrupted
Attention, he proceeded in this manner: My Name is *Car-*

denio, the Place of my Birth one of the best Cities in *Anda-lusia*; my Descent noble,* my Parents wealthy: But my Misfortunes are so great, that they have doubtless fill'd my Relations with the deepest of Sorrows; nor are they to be remedy'd with Wealth, for Goods of Fortune avail but little against the Anger of Heaven. In the same Town dwelt the charming *Lucinda*, the most beautiful Creature that ever Nature fram'd, equal in Descent and Fortune to my self, but more happy and less constant. I lov'd, nay ador'd her almost from her Infancy; and from her tender Years she bless'd me with as kind Return as is suitable with the innocent Freedom of that Age. Our Parents were conscious of that early Friendship; nor did they oppose the Growth of this inoffensive Passion, which they perceiv'd could have no other Consequences than a happy Union of our Families by Marriage; a thing which the Equality of our Births and Fortunes did indeed of it self almost invite us to. Afterwards our Loves so grew up with our Years, that *Lucinda's* Father, either judging our usual Familiarity prejudicial to his Daughter's Honour, or for some other Reasons, sent to desire me to discontinue my frequent Visits to his House: But this Restraint prov'd but like that which was us'd by the Parents of that loving *Thisbe*, so celebrated by the Poets, and but added Flames to Flames, and Impatience to Desires. As our Tongues were now debarr'd their former Privilege, we had Recourse to our Pens, which assum'd the greater Freedom to disclose the most hidden Secrets of our Hearts; for the Presence of the beloved Object often heightens a certain Awe and Bashfulness, that disorders, confounds and strikes dumb even the most passionate Lover. How many Letters have I writ to that lovely Charmer! How many soft moving Verses have I address'd to her! What kind, yet honourable Returns have I receiv'd from her! the mutual Pledges of our secret Love, and the innocent Consolations of a violent Passion. At length, languishing and wasting with Desire, depriv'd of that reviving Comfort of my Soul, I resolv'd to remove those Bars with which her Father's Care and decent Caution obstructed my only Happiness, by demanding her of him in Marriage:

* *In Spain all the Gentry are call'd Noble.*

208

He very civilly told me, that he thank'd me for the Honour I did him, but that I had a Father alive, whose Consent was to be obtain'd as well as his, and who was the most proper Person to make such a Proposal. I thank'd him for his civil Answer, and thought it carry'd some Shew of Reason, not doubting but my Father would readily consent to the Proposal. I therefore immediately went to wait on him, with a Design to beg his Approbation and Assistance. I found him in his Chamber with a Letter open'd before him, which, as soon as he saw me, he put into my Hand, before I could have time to acquaint him with my Business. *Cardenio*, said he, you'll see by this Letter the extraordinary Kindness that Duke *Ricardo* has for you. I suppose I need not tell you, Gentlemen, that this Duke *Ricardo* is a Grandee of *Spain*, most of whose Estate lies in the best Part of *Andalusia*. I read the Letter, and found it contain'd so kind and advantageous an Offer, that my Father could not but accept of it with Thankfulness: For the Duke intreated him to send me to him with all speed, that I might be the Companion of his eldest Son, promising withal to advance me to a Post answerable to the good Opinion he had of me. This unexpected News struck me dumb; but my Surprize and Disappointment were much greater, when I heard my Father say to me, *Cardenio*, you must get ready to be gone in two Days: In the mean time give Heaven Thanks for opening you a Way to that Preferment which I am sensible you deserve. After this he gave me several wise Admonitions both as a Father and a Man of Business, and then he left me. The Day fix'd for my Journey quickly came; however, the Night that preceded it, I spoke to *Lucinda* at her Window, and told her what had happen'd. I also gave her Father a Visit, and inform'd him of it too, beseeching him to preserve his good Opinion of me, and defer the bestowing of his Daughter till I had been with Duke *Ricardo*, which he kindly promis'd me: And then *Lucinda* and I, after an Exchange of Vows and Protestations of eternal Fidelity, took our Leaves of each other with all the Grief which two tender and passionate Lovers can feel at a Separation.

I left the Town, and went to wait upon the Duke, who

receiv'd and entertain'd me with that extraordinary Kindness and Civility that soon rais'd the Envy of his greatest
Favourites. But he that most endearingly caress'd me, was
Don *Ferdinand*, the Duke's second Son, a young, airy, handsome, generous Gentleman, and of a very amorous Disposition; he seem'd to be overjoy'd at my coming, and in a most
obliging manner told me, he would have me one of his most
intimate Friends. In short, he so really convinc'd me of his
Affection, that tho' his elder Brother gave me many Testimonies of Love and Esteem, yet could I easily distinguish between their Favours. Now, as 'tis common for Bosom Friends
to keep nothing secret from each other, Don *Ferdinand* relying as much on my Fidelity, as I had Reason to depend on
his, reveal'd to me his most private Thoughts; and among
the rest, his being in Love with the Daughter of a very rich
Farmer, who was his Father's Vassal. The Beauty of that
lovely Country-maid, her Virtue, her Discretion, and the
other Graces of her Mind, gain'd her the Admiration of all
those who approach'd her; and those uncommon Endowments had so charm'd the Soul of Don *Ferdinand*, that finding
it absolutely impossible to corrupt her Chastity, since she
would not yield to his Embraces as a Mistress, he resolv'd to
marry her. I thought my self oblig'd by all the Ties of Gratitude and Friendship, to dissuade him from so unsuitable a
Match; and therefore I made use of such Arguments as might
have diverted any one but so confirm'd a Lover from such
an unequal Choice. At last, finding 'em all ineffectual, I resolv'd to inform the Duke his Father with his Intentions: But
Don *Ferdinand* was too clear-sighted not to read my Design
in my great Dislike of his Resolutions, and dreading such a
Discovery, which he knew my Duty to his Father might well
warrant, in spight of our Intimacy, since I look'd upon such
a Marriage as highly prejudicial to them both, he made it
his Business to hinder me from betraying his Passion to his
Father, assuring me, there would be no need to reveal it to
him. To blind me the more effectually, he told me he was
willing to try the Power of Absence, that common Cure of
Love, thereby to wear out and lose his unhappy Passion; and
that in order to this, he would take a Journey with me to

my Father's House, pretending to buy Horses in our Town, where the best in the World are bred. No sooner had I heard this plausible Proposal but I approv'd it, sway'd by the Interest of my own Love, that made me fond of an Opportunity to see my absent *Lucinda*. I have heard since, that Don *Ferdinand* had already been bless'd by his Mistress, with all the Liberty of boundless Love, upon a Promise of Marriage, and that he only waited an opportunity to discover it with Safety, being afraid of incurring his Father's Indignation. But as what we call Love in young Men, is too often only an irregular Passion, and boiling Desire, that has no other Object than sensual Pleasure, and vanishes with Enjoyment, while real Love, fixing it self on the Perfections of the Mind, is still improving and permanent; as soon as Don *Ferdinand* had accomplish'd his lawless Desires, his strong Affection slacken'd, and his hot Love grew cold: So that if at first his proposing to try the Power of Absence was only a Pretence, that he might get rid of his Passion, there was nothing now which he more heartily coveted, that he might thereby avoid fulfilling his Promise. And therefore having obtain'd the Duke's Leave, away we posted to my Father's House, where Don *Ferdinand* was entertain'd according to his Quality; and I went to visit my *Lucinda*, who by a thousand innocent Endearments, made me sensible, that her Love, like mine, was rather heighten'd than weaken'd by Absence, if any thing could heighten a Love so great and so perfect. I then thought my self oblig'd, by the Laws of Friendship, not to conceal the Secrets of my Heart from so kind and intimate a Friend, who had so generously entrusted me with his; and therefore, to my eternal Ruin, I unhappily discover'd to him my Passion. I prais'd *Lucinda's* Beauty, her Wit, her Virtue, and prais'd 'em so like a Lover, so often, and so highly, that I rais'd in him a great Desire to see so accomplish'd a Lady; and, to gratify his Curiosity, I shew'd her to him by the Help of a Light, one Evening, at a low Window, where we us'd to have our amorous Interviews. She prov'd but too charming, and too strong a Temptation to Don *Ferdinand*; and her prevailing Image made so deep an Impression on his Soul, that 'twas sufficient to blot out of his Mind all those Beauties that had till then

employ'd his wanton Thoughts: He was struck dumb with
Wonder and Delight, at the Sight of the ravishing Apparition; and, in short, to see her, and to love her, prov'd with
him the same thing: And when I say to love her, I need not
add to Desperation, for there's no loving her but to an Extreme. If her Face made him so soon take Fire, her Wit quickly set him all in a Flame. He often importun'd me to communicate to him some of her Letters, which I indeed would ne'er
expose to any Eyes but my own; but unhappily one Day he
found one, wherein she desired me to demand her of her
Father, and to hasten the Marriage. It was penn'd with that
Tenderness and Discretion, that when he had read it, he presently cry'd out, that the amorous Charms which were scatter'd and divided among other Beauties, were all divinely
center'd in *Lucinda*, and in *Lucinda* alone. Shall I confess a
shameful Truth? *Lucinda's* Praises, tho' never so deserv'd,
did not sound pleasantly to my Ears out of Don *Ferdinand's*
Mouth. I began to entertain I know not what Distrusts and
jealous Fears, the rather, because he would be still improving
the least Opportunity of talking of her, and insensibly turning
the Discourse he held of other Matters, to make her the Subject, tho' never so far fetch'd, of our constant Talk. Not that
I was apprehensive of the least Infidelity from *Lucinda*: Far
from it, she gave me daily fresh Assurances of her inviolable Affection: But I fear'd every thing from my malignant Stars, and
Lovers are commonly industrious to make themselves uneasy.

It happen'd one Day, that *Lucinda*, who took great Delight in reading Books of Knight-Errantry, desir'd me to lend
her the Romance of *Amadis de Gaul* ——

Scarce had *Cardenio* mention'd Knight-Errantry, when
Don *Quixote* interrupted him: Sir, said he, had you but told
me, when you first mention'd the Lady *Lucinda*, that she
was an Admirer of Books of Knight-Errantry, there had been
no need of using any Amplification to convince me of her being a Person of uncommon Sense: Yet, Sir, had she not us'd
those mighty Helps, those infallible Guides to Sense, tho'
indulgent Nature had strove to bless her with the richest
Gifts she can bestow, I might justly enough have doubted
whether her Perfections could have gain'd her the Love of

a Person of your Merit: But now you need not employ your Eloquence to set forth the Greatness of her Beauty, the Excellence of her Worth, or the Depth of her Sense: For, from this Account which I have of her taking great Delight in reading Books of Chivalry, I dare pronounce her to be the most beautiful, nay, the most accomplish'd Lady in the Universe: And I heartily could have wish'd that with *Amadis de Gaul* you had sent her the worthy Don *Rugel* of *Greece*; for I am certain the Lady *Lucinda* would have been extreamly delighted with *Darayda* and *Garaya*, as also with the discreet Shepherd *Darinel*, and those admirable Verses of his *Bucolicks*, which he sung and repeated with so good a Grace: But a Time may yet be found to give her the Satisfaction of reading those Master-pieces, if you will do me the Honour to come to my House; for there I may supply you with above three hundred Volumes, which are my Soul's greatest Delight, and the darling Comfort of my Life; though now I remember my self, I have just Reason to fear there's not one of 'em left in my Study, Thanks to the malicious Envy of wicked Inchanters. I beg your Pardon for giving you this Interruption, contrary to my Promise; but when I hear the least mention made of Knight-Errantry, it is no more in my Power to forbear speaking, than 'tis in the Sun-beams not to warm, or in those of the Moon not to impart her natural Humidity; and therefore, Sir, I beseech you to go on.

While Don *Quixote* was running on with this impertinent Digression, *Cardenio* hung down his Head on his Breast with all the Signs of a Man lost in Sorrow: Nor could Don *Quixote* with repeated Intreaties perswade him to look up, or answer a Word. At last, after he had stood thus a considerable while, he rais'd his Head, and suddenly breaking Silence, " I am positively convinc'd," cry'd he, "nor shall any Man in the "World ever perswade me to the contrary; and he's a Block-"head who says, that great Villain Mr *Elisabat*,* never lay "with Queen *Madasima*."

---

* Elisabat *is a skilful Surgeon in* Amadis de Gaul, *who performs wonderful Cures; and Queen* Madasima *is Wife to* Gantasis, *and makes a great Figure in the aforesaid Romance. They travel and lie together in Woods and Desarts, without any Imputation on her Honour.*

'Tis false, cry'd Don *Quixote*, in a mighty Heat; by all the Powers above, 'tis all Scandal and base Detraction to say this of Queen *Madasima*. She was a most noble and virtuous Lady; nor is it to be presum'd that so great a Princess would ever debase her self so far as to fall in Love with a Quack. Whoever dares to say she did, lyes like an arrant Villain; and I'll make him acknowledge it either a-Foot or a-Horseback, arm'd or unarm'd, by Night or by Day, or how he pleases. *Cardenio* very earnestly fix'd his Eyes on Don *Quixote*, while he was thus defying him, and taking Queen *Madasima's* Part, as if she had been his true and lawful Princess; and being provok'd by these Abuses into one of his mad Fits, he took up a great Stone that lay by him, and hit Don *Quixote* such a Blow on his Breast with it, that it beat him down backwards. *Sancho* seeing his Lord and Master so roughly handled, fell upon the mad Knight with his clench'd Fists; but he beat him off at the first Onset, and laid him at his Feet with a single Blow, and then fell a trampling on his Guts, like a Baker in a Dough-trough. Nay, the Goat-herd, who was offering to take *Sancho's* Part, had like to have been serv'd in the same manner. So the ragged Knight having tumbled 'em one over another, and beaten 'em handsomely, left 'em, and ran into the Wood without the least Opposition.

Sancho got up when he saw him gone; and being very much out of Humour to find himself so roughly handled without any manner of Reason, began to pick a Quarrel with the Goat-herd, railing at him for not fore-warning them of the Ragged Knight's mad Fits, that they might have stood upon their Guard. The Goat-herd answer'd, he had given 'em Warning at first, and if he could not hear, 'twas no Fault of his. To this *Sancho* reply'd, and the Goat-herd made a Rejoinder, till from *Pro's* and *Cons* they fell to a warmer way of disputing, and went to Fisty-cuffs together, catching one another by the Beards, and tugging, haling, and belabouring one another so unmercifully, that had not Don *Quixote* parted 'em, they would have pull'd one another's Chins off. *Sancho*, in great Wrath, still keeping his Hold, cry'd to his Master, Let me alone, Sir Knight of the *woeful Figure*: This is no dubb'd Knight, but an ordinary Fellow like my self; I may be reveng'd on him for the Wrong he has done me; let me box it out, and fight him fairly Hand to Fist like a Man. Thou may'st fight him as he's thy Equal, answer'd Don *Quixote*, but thou oughtest not to do it, since he has done us no Wrong. After this he pacify'd 'em, and then addressing himself to the Goat-herd, he ask'd him whether it were possible to find out *Cardenio* again, that he might hear the End of his Story? The Goat-herd answer'd, that, as he already told him, he knew of no settled Place he us'd, but that if they made any Stay thereabouts, he might be sure to meet with him, mad or sober, some time or other.

XI: OF THE STRANGE THINGS THAT HAPPEN'D TO THE VALIANT KNIGHT OF LA MANCHA IN THE BLACK MOUNTAIN; AND OF THE PENANCE HE DID THERE, IN IMITATION OF BELTENEBROS, OR THE LOVELY OBSCURE

DON *Quixote* took Leave of the Goat-herd, and having mounted *Rozinante*, commanded *Sancho* to follow him, which he did, but with no very good Will, his Master leading him into the roughest and most craggy Part of the Mountain. Thus they travell'd for a while without speaking a Word to each other. *Sancho*, almost dead, and ready to burst for want of a little Chat, waited with great Impatience till his Master should begin, not daring to speak first, since his strict Injunction of Silence. But at last, not being able to keep his Word any longer, Good your Worship, quoth he, give me your Blessing and Leave to be gone, I beseech you, that I may go home to my Wife and Children, where I may talk till I am weary, and no Body can hinder me; for I must needs tell you, that for you to think to lead me a Jaunt through Hedge and Ditch, over Hills and Dales, by Night and by Day, without daring to open my Lips, is to bury me alive. Could Beasts speak, as they did in *Æsop's* Time, 'twould not have been half so bad with me; for then might I have communed with my Ass as I pleas'd, and have forgot my ill Fortune:* But to trot on in this Fashion, all the Days of my Life, after Adventures, and to light of nothing but Thumps, Kicks, Cuffs, and be toss'd in a Blanket, and after all, forsooth, to have a Man's Mouth sew'd up, without daring to speak one's Mind, I say't again, no living Soul can endure it. I understand thee, *Sancho*, answer'd Don *Quixote*, thou lingerest with Impatience to exercise thy talking Faculty. Well, I am willing to free thy Tongue from this Restraint that so cruelly pains thee, upon Condition, that the Time of

---

* *See Note on the preceding Chapter but one. The* Spaniards *vulgarly call* Æsop Giosopete, *as* Cervantes *does here. The* French *too, according to* Oudin, *commonly call* Æsop Isopet.

this Licence shall not extend beyond that of our Continuance in these Mountains. A Match, quoth *Sancho*, let's make Hay while the Sun shines, I'll talk whilst I may; what I may do hereafter Heaven knows best! And so beginning to take the Benefit of his Privilege, Pray Sir, quoth he, what Occasion had you to take so hotly the Part of Queen *Magimasa*, or what d'ye call her? What a Devil was it to you, whether that same Master *Abbot** were her Friend in a Corner, or no? Had you taken no Notice of what was said, as you might well have done, seeing 'twas no Business of yours, the Mad-man wou'd have gone on with his Story, you had miss'd a good Thump on the Breast, and I had 'scap'd some five or six good Dowses on the Chaps, besides the trampling of my Pud-dings. Upon my Honour, Friend *Sancho*, reply'd Don *Quixote*, didst thou but know, as well as I do, what a Virtuous and Eminent Lady Queen *Madasima* was, thou would'st say I had a great deal of Patience, seeing I did not strike that pro-fane Wretch on the Mouth, out of which such Blasphemies proceeded: For, in short, 'twas the highest piece of Detrac-tion to say, That a Queen was scandalously familiar with a Barber-Surgeon: For the Truth of the Story is, that this Mas-ter *Elisabat*, of whom the Madman spoke, was a Person of extraordinary Prudence and Sagacity, and Physician to that Queen, who also made use of his Advice in Matters of Im-portance; but to say she gave him up her Honour, and pros-tituted her self to the Embraces of a Man of such an inferior Degree, was an impudent, groundless, and slanderous Accusa-tion, worthy the severest Punishment: Neither can I believe that *Cardenio* knew what he said, when he charg'd the Queen with that debasing Guilt: For, 'tis plain, that his raving Fit had disorder'd the Seat of his Understanding. Why, there it is, quoth *Sancho*; who but a Madman wou'd have minded what a Madman said? What if the Flint that hit you on the Breast had dash'd out your Brains? We had been in a dainty Pickle for taking the Part of that same Lady, with a Pease-cod on her. Nay, and *Cardenio* wou'd have come off too had

---

* Sancho, *remembring only the latter part of Master* Elisabat's *Name, pleasantly calls him* Abad, *which is* Spanish *for an Abbot.* Abad, *as* Oudin *observes, sounds like the End of* Elisabat.

he knock'd you on the Head; for the Law has nothing to do with Madmen. *Sancho*, reply'd Don *Quixote*, we Knights-Errant are oblig'd to vindicate the Honour of Women of what Quality soever, as well against Madmen as against Men in their Senses; much more Queens of that Magnitude and extraordinary Worth, as Queen *Madasima*, for whose rare Endowments I have a peculiar Veneration; for she was a most Beautiful Lady, Discreet and Prudent to Admiration, and behaved her self with an exemplary Patience in all her Misfortunes. 'Twas then that the Company and wholsome Counsels of Master *Elisabat* prov'd very useful to alleviate the Burden of her Afflictions: From which the ignorant and ill-meaning Vulgar took Occasion to suspect and rumour, that she was guilty of an unlawful Commerce with him. But I say once more, they lye, and lye a thousand times, whoever they be, that shall presumptuously report, or hint, or so much as think or surmise so base a Calumny.

Why, quoth *Sancho*, I neither say, nor think, one way nor the t'other, not I: Let them that say it, eat the Lye, and swallow it with their Bread. If they lay together, they have answer'd for it before now. I never thrust my Nose into other Mens Porridge. It is no Bread and Butter of mine: Every Man for himself, and God for us all, say I; for he that buys and lyes, finds it in his Purse. Let him that owns the Cow, take her by the Tail. Naked came I into the World, and naked must I go out. Many think to find Flitches of Bacon, and find not so much as the Racks to lay 'em on: But who can hedge in a Cuckow? Little said is soon amended. It's a Sin to belye the Devil: But Misunderstanding brings Lyes to Town, and there's no padlocking of Peoples Mouths; for a close Mouth catches no Flies.

Bless me! cry'd Don *Quixote*, what a Catalogue of musty Proverbs hast thou run through! What a heap of frippery Ware hast thou threaded together, and how wide from the Purpose! Pr'ythee have done, and for the future let thy whole Study be to spur thy Ass; nor do thou concern thy self with things that are out of thy Sphere; and with all thy five Senses remember this, That whatsoever I do, have done, and shall do, is no more than what is the Result of mature Consideration, and strictly conformable to the Laws of Chivalry, which I understand better than all the Knights that ever profess'd Knight-Errantry. Ay, ay, Sir, quoth *Sancho*, but pray, is't a good Law of Chivalry that says we shall wander up and down over Bushes and Briers, in this rocky Wilderness, where there's neither Foot-path nor Horse-way; running after a Madman, who, if we may light on him again, may chance to make an end of what he has begun, not of his Tale of a roasted Horse, I mean, but of belabouring you and me thoroughly, and squeezing out my Guts at both Ends? Once more I pr'ythee have done, said Don *Quixote*: I have Business of greater Moment than the finding this frantick Man; it is not so much that Business that detains me in this barren and desolate Wild, as a Desire I have to perform a certain Heroick Deed that shall immortalize my Fame, and make it fly to the remotest Regions of the Habitable Globe; nay, it shall seal and confirm me the most compleat and absolute Knight-Errant in the World. But is not this same Adventure very dangerous, ask'd *Sancho*? Not at all, reply'd Don *Quixote*, tho' as Fortune may order it, our Expectations may be baffled by disappointing Accidents: But the main thing consists in thy Diligence. My Diligence, quoth *Sancho*? I mean, said Don *Quixote*, that if thou return'st with all the Speed imaginable from the Place whither I design to send thee, my Pain will soon be at an end, and my Glory begin. And because I do not doubt thy Zeal for advancing thy Master's Interest, I will no longer conceal my Design from thee: Know then, my most faithful Squire, that *Amadis de Gaul* was one of the most accomplish'd Knights-Errant, nay, I should not have said, he was one of them, but the most perfect, the chief, and Prince of them all. And let not the *Belianises*, nor any others, pretend to stand in Competition with him for the Honour of Priority; for, to my Knowledge, should they attempt it, they would be egregiously in the wrong. I must also inform thee, that when a Painter studies to excel and grow famous in his Art, he takes care to imitate the best Originals; which Rule ought likewise to be observ'd in all other Arts and Sciences that serve for the Ornament of well-regulated Commonwealths. Thus he that is ambitious of gaining the Reputation of a prudent and patient Man, ought to propose to himself to imitate *Ulysses*, in whose Person and Troubles *Homer* has admirably delineated a perfect Pattern and Prototype of Wisdom and Heroick Patience. So *Virgil*, in his *Æneas*, has given the World a rare Example of Filial Piety, and of the Sagacity of a valiant and experienc'd General; both the *Greek* and *Roman* Poets representing their Heroes not such as they really were, but such as they should be, to remain Examples of Virtue to ensuing Ages. In the same manner, *Amadis* having been the Polar Star and Sun of valorous and amorous Knights, 'tis him we ought to set before our Eyes as our great Exemplar, all of us that fight under the Banner of Love and Chivalry; for 'tis certain that the Adventurer who shall emulate him best, shall consequently arrive nearest to the Perfection of Knight-Errantry. Now, *Sancho*, I find that among the things which most display'd that Champion's Prudence and Fortitude, his Constancy and Love, and his other Heroick Virtues, none was more remarkable than his retiring from his disdainful *Oriana*, to do Penance on the *Poor Rock*, changing his Name into that of *Beltenebros*, or *The Lovely Obscure*, a Title certainly most significant, and adapted to the Life which he then intended to lead. So I am resolv'd to imitate him in this, the rather because I think it a more easy Task than it would be to copy his other Atchievements, such as cleaving the Bodies of Giants, cutting off the Heads of Dragons, killing dreadful Monsters, routing whole Armies, dispersing Navies, and breaking the Force of Magick Spells. And since these Mountainous Wilds offer me so fair an Opportunity, I see no Reason why I should neglect it, and therefore I'll lay hold on it now. Very well, quoth *Sancho*; but pray, Sir, what is it that you mean to do in this Fag-end of the World? Have I not already told thee, answer'd Don *Quixote*, that I intend to copy *Amadis* in his Madness, Despair, and Fury? Nay, at the same time I will imitate the valiant *Orlando Furioso's* Extravagance, when he ran mad, after he had found the unhappy Tokens of the fair *Angelica's* dishonourable Commerce with *Medoro* at the Fountain; at which time, in his frantick Despair, he tore up Trees by the Roots, troubled the Waters of the clear

Fountains, slew the Shepherds, destroy'd their Flocks, fir'd their Huts, demolish'd Houses, drove their Horses before him, and committed a hundred thousand other Extravagancies worthy to be recorded in the eternal Register of Fame. Not that I intend however in all things to imitate *Roldan*, or *Orlando*, or *Rotoland*, (for he had all those Names) but only to make choice of such frantick Effects of his amorous Despair, as I shall think most essential and worthy Imitation. Nay, perhaps I shall wholly follow *Amadis*, who, without launching out into such destructive and fatal Ravings, and only expressing his Anguish in Complaints and Lamentations, gain'd nevertheless a Renown equal, if not superior to that of the greatest Heroes. Sir, quoth *Sancho*, I dare say the Knights who did these Penances had some Reason to be mad; but what need have You to be mad too? What Lady has sent you a packing, or so much as slighted you? When did you ever find that my Lady *Dulcinea del Toboso* did otherwise than she should do, with either *Moor*** or *Christian*? Why, there's the Point, cry'd Don *Quixote*; in this consists the singular Perfection of my Undertaking: For, mark me, *Sancho*, for a Knight-Errant to run mad upon any just Occasion, is neither strange nor meritorious; no, the Rarity is to run mad without a Cause, without the least Constraint or Necessity: There's a refin'd and exquisite Passion for you, *Sancho*! for thus my Mistress must needs have a vast Idea of my Love, since she may guess what I shou'd perform in the *Wet*, if I do so much in the *Dry*.† But besides, I have but too just a Motive to give a loose to my raving Grief, considering the long Date of my Absence from my ever Supreme Lady *Dulcinea del Toboso*; for as the Shepherd in *Matthias Ambrosio* has it,

> *Poor Lovers, absent from the Darling Fair,*
> *All Ills not only dread, but bear.*

Then do not lavish any more Time in striving to divert me from so rare, so happy, and so singular an Imitation. I am

---

* Sancho *says* Moro *for* Medoro, *in his blundering Way.* † *A profane Allusion to a Text in Scripture,* Luke xxiii. 31. *For if they do these Things in a Green Tree, What shall be done in the Dry? So here Don Quixote's Meaning is — My Mistress may guess what I wou'd do where Occasion shou'd be given me, since I can do so much without any.*

mad, and will be mad, 'till thy Return with an Answer to the
Letter which thou must carry from me to the Lady *Dulcinea*;
and if it be as favourable as my unshaken Constancy deserves,
then my Madness and my Penance shall end; but if I find she
repays my Vows and Services with ungrateful Disdain, then
will I be emphatically mad, and screw up my Thoughts to
such an Excess of Distraction, that I shall be insensible of the
Rigour of my relentless Fair. Thus what Return soever she
makes to my Passion, I shall be eas'd one way or other of the
anxious Thoughts that now divide my Soul; either entertaining the welcome News of her reviving Pity with Demonstrations of Sense, or else shewing my Insensibility of her Cruelty
by the Height of my Distraction. But in the mean time, *Sancho*, tell me, hast thou carefully preserved *Mambrino's* Helmet? I saw thee take it up t'other Day, after that Monster of
Ingratitude had spent his Rage in vain Endeavours to break
it; which by the way argues the most excellent Temper of
the Metal. Body of me, quoth *Sancho*, Sir Knight of the *woeful
Figure*, I can no longer bear to hear you run on at this rate:
Why, this were enough to make any Man believe that all
your bragging and bouncing of your Knight-Errantry, your
winning of Kingdoms, and bestowing of Islands, and Heaven
knows what, upon your Squire, are meer flim-flam Stories,
and nothing but Shams and Lies: For who the Devil can hear
a Man call a Barber's Bason a Helmet, nay, and stand to't,
and vouch it four Days together, and not think him that says
it, to be stark mad, or without Brains? I have the Bason safe
enough here in my Pouch, and I'll get it mended for my own
Use, if ever I have the Luck to get home to my Wife and Children. Now as I love bright Arms, cry'd Don *Quixote*, I swear
thou art the shallowest, silliest, and most stupid Fellow of a
Squire that ever I heard or read of in my Life. How is it possible for thee to be so dull of Apprehension, as not to have
learnt in all this time that thou hast been in my Service, that
all the Actions and Adventures of us Knights-Errant seem to
be meer Chimera's, Follies and Impertinencies? Not that they
are so indeed, but either thro' the officious Care, or else thro'
the Malice and Envy of those Enchanters that always haunt
and persecute us unseen, and by their Fascinations change

the Appearance of our Actions into what they please, according to their Love or Hate. This is the very Reason why that which I plainly perceive to be *Mambrino's* Helmet, seems to thee to be only a Barber's Bason, and perhaps another Man may take it to be something else. And in this I can never too much admire the Prudence of the Sage who espouses my Interests, in making that inestimable Helmet seem a Bason; for did it appear in its proper Shape, its tempting Value would raise me as many Enemies as there are Men in the Universe, all eager to snatch from me so desireable a Prize: But so long as it shall seem to be nothing else but a Barber's Bason, Men will not value it; as is manifest from the Fellow's leaving it behind him on the Ground; for had he known what it really was, he would sooner have parted with his Life. Keep it safe then, *Sancho*, for I have no need of it at present; far from it, I think to put off my Armour, and strip my self as naked as I came out of my Mother's Womb, in case I determine to imitate *Orlando's* Fury, rather than the Penance of *Amadis*.

This Discourse brought 'em to the Foot of a high Rock that stood by it self, as if it had been hewn out, and divided from the rest; by the Skirt of it glided a purling Stream, that softly took its winding Course through an adjacent Meadow. The verdant Freshness of the Grass, the Number of wild Trees, Plants, and Flowers, that feasted the Eyes in that pleasant Solitude, invited the Knight of the *woeful Figure* to make Choice of it to perform his amorous Penance; and therefore as soon as he had let his ravish'd Sight rove a while o'er the scatter'd Beauties of the Place, he took Possession of it with the following Speech, as if he had utterly lost the small Share of Reason he had left. Behold, O Heavens! cry'd he, the Place which an unhappy Lover has chosen to bemoan the deplorable State to which you have reduc'd him: Here shall my flowing Tears swell the liquid Veins of this Crystal Rill, and my deep Sighs perpetually move the Leaves of these shady Trees, in Testimony of the Anguish and Pain that harrows up my Soul. Ye Rural Deities, whoever ye be, that make these unfrequented Desarts your Abode, hear the Complaints of an unfortunate Lover, whom a tedious Absence, and some slight Impressions of a jealous Mistrust, have driven to these Regions of Despair, to bewail his rigorous Destiny, and deplore the distracting Cruelty of that ungrateful Fair, who is the Perfection of all Human Beauty. Ye pitying *Napœan* Nymphs and *Dryades*, silent Inhabitants of the Woods and Groves, assist me to lament my Fate, or at least attend the mournful Story of my Woes; so may no designing beastly Satyrs, those just Objects of your Hate, ever have Power to interrupt your Rest —— Oh *Dulcinea del Toboso*! Thou Sun that turn'st my gloomy Night to Day! Glory of my Pain! North-Star of my Travels, and reigning Planet that controll'st my Heart! Pity, I conjure thee, the unparallel'd Distress to which thy Absence has reduc'd the faithfullest of Lovers, and grant to my Fidelity that kind Return which it so justly claims! So may indulgent Fate shower on thee all the Blessings thou ever canst desire, or Heavens grant! —— Ye lonesome Trees, under whose spreading Branches I come to linger out the gloomy Shadow of a tedious Being; let the soft Language of your rustling Leaves, and the kind nodding of your springing Boughs, satisfy me that I am welcome to your shady Harbours. O thou my trusty Squire, the inseparable Companion of my Adventures, diligently observe what thou shalt see me do in this lonely Retreat, that thou may'st inform the dear Cause of my Ruin with every Particular. As he said this, he alighted, and presently taking off his Horse's Bridle and Saddle, Go, *Rozinante*, saith he, giving the Horse a Clap on the Posteriors, he that has lost his Freedom gives thee thine, thou Steed as renown'd for thy extraordinary Actions, as for thy Misfortunes; go rear thy awful Front where-e'er thou pleasest, secure that neither the *Hippogryphon* of *Astolpho*, nor the renown'd *Frontino*, which *Bradamante* purchas'd at so high a Price, could ever be thought thy Equals.

Well fare him, cry'd *Sancho*, that sav'd me the Trouble of sending my Ass to Grass too: Poor Thing, had I him here, he should not want two or three Claps on the Buttocks, nor a fine Speech in his Praise neither, while I took off his Pannel. But stay, were he here, what Need wou'd there be to strip him of his Harness? Alas, he never had any Thing to do with these mad Pranks of Love, no more than my self, who was his Master when Fortune pleas'd. But d'ye hear me, now I think on't,

Sir Knight of the *woeful Figure*, if your Worship is resolv'd to be mad, and send me away in good Earnest, we must e'en clap the Saddle again on *Rozinante's* Back; for to tell you the Truth, I'm but a sorry Foot-man, and if I don't ride home, I don't know when I shall be able to come back again. Do as thou think'st fit for that, *Sancho*, answer'd Don *Quixote*, for I design thou shalt set forward about three Days hence. In the mean while thou shalt be a Witness of what I will do for my Lady's Sake, that thou may'st give her an Account of it. Bless my Eye-sight, quoth *Sancho*, what can I see more than I've seen already? Thou hast seen nothing yet, answer'd Don *Quixote*; thou must see me throw away my Armour, tear my Cloaths, knock my Head against the Rocks, and do a thousand other Things of that Kind, that will fill thee with Astonishment. For Goodness-sake, Sir, quoth *Sancho*, take heed how you quarrel with those ungracious Rocks; you may chance to get such a Crack o'the Crown at the very first Rap, as may spoil your Penance at one Dash. No, I don't like that Way by no Means; if you must needs be knocking your Noddle, to go through stitch with this ugly Jobb, seeing 'tis all but a Mockery, or as it were between Jest and Earnest, why can't you as well play your Tricks on something that's softer than these unconscionable Stones: You may run your Head against Water, or rather against Cotton, or the Stuffing of *Rozinante's* Saddle; and then let me alone with the rest: I'll be sure to tell my Lady *Dulcinea*, that you bebump'd your Poll against the Point of a Rock that's harder than a Diamond.

I thank thee for thy Good-will, dear *Sancho*, reply'd Don *Quixote*: But I assure thee, that all these seeming Extravagancies that I must run through, are no Jests: Far from it, they must be all perform'd seriously and solemnly; for otherwise we should transgress the Laws of Chivalry, that forbid us to tell Lyes upon Pain of Degradation; now to pretend to do one Thing, and effect another, is an Evasion, which I esteem to be as bad as Lying. Therefore the Blows which I must give my self on the Head, ought to be real, substantial, sound ones, without any Trick, or mental Reservation; for which Reason I would have thee leave me some Lint and Salve, since Fortune has depriv'd us of the Sovereign Balsam which we lost. 'Twas a worse Loss to lose the Ass, quoth *Sancho*, for with him we've lost Bag and Baggage, Lint and all: But no more of your damn'd Drench, if you love me; the very Thoughts on't are enough not only to turn my Stomach, but my Soul, such a Rumbling I feel in my Wem at the Name on't. Then as for the three Days you'd have me to loiter here to mind your mad Tricks, you had as good make Account they're already over; for I hold them for done, unsight unseen, and will tell Wonders to my Lady: Wherefore write you your Letter, and send me going with all haste; for let me be hang'd if I don't long already to be back, to take you out of this Purgatory wherein I leave you.

Dost thou only call it Purgatory, *Sancho*? cry'd Don *Quixote*; call it Hell rather, or something worse, if there be in Nature a Term expressive of a more wretched State. Nay, not so neither, quoth *Sancho*, I would not call it Hell; because, as I heard our Parson say, *There's no Retention* out of Hell*. Retention, cry'd Don *Quixote*! what dost thou mean by that Word? Why, quoth *Sancho*, Retention is Retention; it is, that whosoever is in Hell never comes, nor can come out of it: Which shan't be your Case this Bout, if I can stir my Heels, and have but Spurs to tickle *Rozinante's* Flanks, till I come to my Lady *Dulcinea*; for I will tell her such strange Things of your Magotty Tricks, your Folly and your Madness, for indeed they are no better, that I'll lay my Head to a Hazle-Nut, I'll make her as supple as a Glove, tho' I found her at first as tough-hearted as a Cork; and when I've wheedled an Answer out of her, all full of sweet honey Words, away will I whisk it back to you, cutting the Air as swift as a Witch upon a Broomstick, and free you out of your Purgatory; for a Purgatory I will have it to be in spight of Hell, nor shall you gainsay me in that Fancy; for, as I've told you before, there's some Hopes of your Retention out of this Place.

Well, be it so, said the Knight of the *woeful Figure*: But how shall I do to write this Letter? And the Order for the three Asses, added *Sancho*? I'll not forget it, answer'd Don *Quixote*; but since we have here no Paper, I must be obliged to write on the Leaves or Bark of Trees, or on Wax, as they

* No Redemption *he means*.

did in ancient Times; yet now I consider on't, we are here as ill provided with Wax as with Paper: But stay, now I remember, I have *Cardenio's* Pocket-Book, which will supply that Want in this Exigence, and then thou shalt get the Letter fairly transcrib'd at the first Village where thou canst meet with a School-master; or for want of a School-master, thou may'st get the Clerk of the Parish to do it; but by no Means give it to any Notary or Scrivener to be written out; for they commonly write such confounded Hands, that the Devil himself would scarce be able to read it. Well, quoth *Sancho*, but what shall I do for want of your Name to it? Why, answer'd Don *Quixote*, *Amadis* never us'd to subscribe his Letters. Ay, reply'd *Sancho*, but the Bill of Exchange for the three Asses must be sign'd; for should I get it copy'd out afterwards, they'd say it is not your Hand, and so I shall go without the Asses. I'll write and sign the Order for 'em in the Table-Book, answer'd Don *Quixote*; and as soon as my Niece sees the Hand, she'll never scruple the Delivery of the Asses: And as for the Love-Letter, when thou get'st it transcrib'd, thou must get it thus under-written, *Yours till Death, The Knight of the woeful Figure.* 'Tis no Matter whether the Letter and Subscription be written by the same Hand or no; for, as I remember, *Dulcinea* can neither read nor write, nor did she ever see any of my Letters, nay, not so much as any of my Writing in her Life: For my Love and her's have always been purely Platonick, never extending beyond the lawful Bounds of a modest Look; and that too so very seldom, that I dare safely swear, that tho' for these twelve Years she has been dearer to my Soul than Light to my Eyes, yet I never saw her four Times in my Life; and perhaps of those few Times that I have seen her, she has scarce perceiv'd once that I beheld her: So strictly and so discreetly *Lorenzo Corchuelo* her Father, and *Aldonza Nogales* her Mother, have kept and educated her. Heigh-day, quoth *Sancho*! did you ever hear the like! And is my Lady *Dulcinea del Toboso*, at last the Daughter of *Lorenzo Corchuelo*, she that's otherwise call'd *Aldonza Lorenzo*? The same, answer'd Don *Quixote*; and 'tis she that merits to be the Sovereign Mistress of the Universe. Udsdiggers, quoth *Sancho*, I know her full well; 'tis a strapping Wench, i'faith,

and pitches the Bar with e'er a lusty young Fellow in our Parish. By the Mass, 'tis a notable, strong-built, sizable, sturdy,
manly Lass, and one that will keep her Chin out of the Mire,
I warrant her; nay, and hold the best Knight-Errant to't that
wears a Head, if ever he venture upon her. Body o'me, what
a Pair of Lungs and a Voice she has when she sets up her
Throat! I saw her one Day pearch'd up o' Top of our Steeple
to call to some Plough-men that were at work in a Fallow-
Field; and tho' they were half a League off, they heard her
as plain as if they had been in the Church-yard under her.
The best of her is, that she's neither coy nor frumpish, she's
a tractable Lass, and fit for a Courtier, for she'll play with
you like a Kitten, and jibes and jokes at every Body. And now
in good Truth, Sir Knight of the *woeful Figure*, you may e'en
play as many Gambols as you please; you may run mad, you
may hang your self for her Sake; there's no Body but will say
you e'en took the wisest Course, tho' the Devil himself should
carry you away a Pick-a-pack. Now am I e'en wild to be gone,
tho' 'twere for nothing else but to see her, for I have not seen
her this many a Day: I fancy I shall hardly know her again,
for a Woman's Face strangely alters by her being always in
the Sun, and drudging and moiling in the open Fields. Well,
I must needs own I've been mightily mistaken all along: For
I durst have sworn this Lady *Dulcinea* had been some great
Princess with whom you were in Love, and such a one as deserved those rare Gifts you bestowed on her, as the *Biscayan*,
the Galley-Slaves, and many others that for ought I know you
may have sent her before I was your Squire. I can't chuse
but laugh to think how my Lady *Aldonza Lorenzo* (my Lady
Dulcinea del Toboso I should have said) would behave her
self should any of those Men which you have sent, or may
send to her, chance to go and fall down o'their Marrow-bones
before her: For 'tis ten to one they may happen to find her
a carding of Flax, or threshing in the Barn, and then how
finely balk'd they'll be! As sure as I'm alive they must needs
think the Devil ow'd 'em a Shame; and she her self will but
flout 'em, and mayhap be somewhat nettl'd at it.

I have often told thee, *Sancho*, said Don *Quixote*, and I tell
thee again, that thou ought'st to bridle or immure thy sawcy

prating Tongue; for tho' thou art but a dull-headed Dunce, yet now and then thy ill-manner'd Jests bite too sharp. But that I may at once make thee sensible of thy Folly and my Discretion, I will tell thee a short Story. A handsome, brisk, young, rich Widow, and withal no Prude, happen'd to fall in Love with a well-set, lusty *Lay-Brother*.* His *Superior* hearing of it, took Occasion to go to her, and said to her, by way of charitable Admonition, I mightily wonder, *Madam*, how a Lady of your Merit, so admir'd for Beauty and for Sense, and withal so rich, could make so ill a Choice, and dote on a mean, silly, despicable Fellow, as I hear you do, while we have in our House so many Masters of Art, Batche-lors, and Doctors of Divinity, among whom your Ladyship may pick and chuse, as you wou'd among Pears, and say, This I like, That I don't like. But she soon answer'd the officious grave Gentleman: Sir, said she, with a Smile, you are much mistaken, and think altogether after the old out-of-fashion Way, if you imagine I have made so ill a Choice; for tho' you fancy the Man's a Fool, yet as to what I take him for, he knows as much, or rather more Philosophy than *Aristotle* himself. So, *Sancho*, as to the Use which I make of the Lady *Dulcinea*, she is equal to the greatest Princesses in the World. Pr'ythee tell me, Dost thou think the Poets, who every one of 'em celebrate the Praises of some Lady or other, had all real Mistresses? Or that the *Amaryllis's*, the *Phyllis's*, the *Sylvia's*, the *Diana's*, the *Galatea's*, the *Alida's*, and the like, which you shall find in so many Poems, Romances, Songs and Ballads, upon every Stage, and even in every Barber's Shop, were Creatures of Flesh and Blood, and Mistresses to those that did and do celebrate 'em? No, no, never think it; for I dare assure thee, the greatest Part of 'em were nothing but the meer Imaginations of the Poets, for a Ground-work to exercise their Wits upon, and give to the World Occasion to look on the Authors as Men of an amorous and gallant Dis-position: And so 'tis sufficient for me to imagine, that *Aldonza Lorenzo* is beautiful and chaste; as for her Birth and Parent-

---

* Motillon, *a Lay-Brother, or Servant in a Convent or College, so call'd from* Motile, *a cropp'd Head; his Hair being cropp'd short, he has no Crown like those in Orders.*

age, they concern me but little; for there's no need to make
an Enquiry about a Woman's Pedigree, as there is of us Men,
when some Badge of Honour is bestowed on us; and so she's
to me the greatest Princess in the World: For thou ought'st
to know, *Sancho*, if thou know'st it not already, that there
are but two things that chiefly excite us to love a Woman,
an attractive Beauty, and unspotted Fame. Now these two
Endowments are happily reconcil'd in *Dulcinea*; for as for
the one, she has not her Equal, and few can vie with her
in the other: But to cut off all Objections at once, I imagine,
that All I say of her is really so, without the least Addition
or Diminution: I fancy her to be just such as I would have
her for Beauty and Quality. *Helen* cannot stand in Competition with her; *Lucretia* cannot rival her; and all the Heroines
which Antiquity has to boast, whether *Greeks*, *Romans* or
Barbarians, are at once out-done by her incomparable Perfections. Therefore let the World say what it will; should
the Ignorant Vulgar foolishly censure me, I please my self
with the Assurances I have of the Approbation of Men of the
strictest Morals, and the nicest Judgment. Sir, quoth *Sancho*,
I knock under: You've Reason o'your Side in all you say,
and I own my self an Ass. Nay, I'm an Ass to talk of an Ass;
for 'tis ill talking of Halters i'th' House of a Man that was
hang'd. But where's the Letter all this while, that I may be
jogging? With that Don *Quixote* pull'd out the Table-Book,
and retiring a little aside, he very seriously began to write
the Letter; which he had no sooner finish'd, but he call'd
Sancho, and order'd him to listen while he read it over to
him, that he might carry it as well in his Memory as in his
Pocket-Book, in case he should have the ill Luck to lose it by
the Way; for so cross was Fortune to him, that he fear'd
every Accident. But, Sir, said *Sancho*, write it over twice or
thrice there in the Book, and give it me, and then I'll be sure
to deliver the Message safe enough I warrant ye: For 'tis a
Folly to think I can get it by Heart; alas, my Memory is so
bad, that many times I forget my own Name! But yet for all
that read it out to me, I beseech you, for I've a hugeous Mind
to hear it. I dare say, 'tis as fine as tho' 'twere in Print. Well
then, listen, said Don *Quixote*.

A LETTER TO LADY DULCINEA

DON *QUIXOTE DE LA MANCHA*

to

DULCINEA DEL TOBOSO

High and Sovereign Lady!

He that is stabb'd to the Quick with the Poinard of Absence, and wounded to the Heart with Love's most piercing Darts, sends you that Health which he wants himself, sweetest Dulcinea del Toboso.* *If your Beauty reject me, if your Virtue refuse to raise my fainting Hopes, if your Disdain exclude me from Relief, I must at last sink under the Pressure of my Woes, tho' much inur'd to Sufferings: for my Pains are not only too violent, but too lasting. My trusty Squire* Sancho *will give you an exact Account of the Condition to which Love and You have reduc'd me, too beautiful Ingrate! If you relent at last, and pity my Distress, then I may say I live, and you preserve what's yours. But if you abandon me to Despair, I must patiently submit, and by ceasing to breathe, satisfy Your Cruelty and My Passion.*

Yours till Death,

The Knight of the Woeful Figure.

By the Life of my Father, quoth *Sancho*, if I ever saw a finer Thing in my born Days! How neatly and roundly you tell her your Mind, and how cleverly you bring in at last, *The Knight of the Woful Figure!* Well, I say't again in good Earnest, you're a Devil at every Thing; and there's no kind of Thing in the 'versal World but what you can turn your Hand to. A Man ought to have some Knowledge of every Thing, answer'd Don *Quixote*, if he would be duly qualify'd for the Employment I profess. Well then, quoth *Sancho*, do so much as write the Warrant for the three Asses on the other Side of that Leaf; and pray write it mighty plain, that they may know 'tis your Hand at first Sight. I will, said Don *Quixote*, and with that he wrote it accordingly, and then read it in this Form:

* Dulcissima Dulcinea.

My dear Niece,

Upon Sight of this my first Bill of Asses, be pleas'd to deliver three of the five which I left at Home in your Custody to Sancho Pança, *my Squire, for the like Number receiv'd of him here in Tale; and This, together with his Receipt, shall be your Discharge. Given* in the very Bowels of* Sierra Morena, *the 22d of* August, *in the present Year.*

'Tis as it should be, quoth *Sancho*; there only wants your Name at the Bottom. There's no need to set my Name, answer'd Don *Quixote*; I'll only set the two first Letters of it, and 'twill be as valid as if 'twere written at length, tho' 'twere not only for three Asses, but for three hundred. I dare take your Worship's Word, quoth *Sancho*; and now I'm going to saddle *Rozinante*, and then you shall give me your Blessing; for I intend to set out presently, without seeing any of your mad Tricks; and I will relate, that I saw you perform so many, that she can desire no more. Nay, said Don *Quixote*, I will have thee stay a while, *Sancho*, and see me stark naked; 'tis also absolutely necessary thou shouldst see me practise some twenty or thirty mad Gamboles; I shall have dispatch'd 'em in less than Half an Hour: And when thou hast been an Eye-witness of that Essay, thou may'st with a safe Conscience swear thou hast seen me play a thousand more; for I dare assure thee, for thy Encouragement, thou never canst exceed the Number of those I shall perform. Good Sir, quoth *Sancho*, as you love me don't let me stay to see you naked; 'twill grieve me so to the Heart, that I shall cry my Eyes out; and I have blubber'd and howl'd but too much since Yesternight for the Loss of my Ass; my Head's so sore with it, I a'n't able to cry any longer: But if you'll needs have me see some of your Anticks, pray do 'em in your Cloaths out of Hand, and let 'em be such as are most to the Purpose; for the sooner I go, the sooner I shall come back; and the Way to be gone, is not to stay here. I long to bring you an Answer to your Heart's Content: And I'll be sure to do't, or let the Lady *Dulcinea* look to't; for if she does not answer as she shou'd do, I protest

* *In the Original it is* Fecha, *i.e.* Done; *for the King of* Spain *writes,* Done at our Court, &c. *as the King of* England *does,* Given, &c.

232

solemnly I'll force an Answer out of her Guts by Dint of good
Kicks and Fisticuffs: For 'tis not to be endured, that such a
notable Knight-Errant as your Worship is, should thus run
out of his Wits without knowing why or wherefore, for such
a ——— Odsbobs, I know what I know; she had not best provoke me to speak it out; for, by the Lord, I shall let fly, and
out with it all by Wholesale, tho' it spoil the Market.*

I protest, *Sancho*, said Don *Quixote*, I think thou art as mad
as my self. Nay, not so mad neither, reply'd *Sancho*, but somewhat more cholerick. But talk no more of that: Let's see,
How will you do for Victuals when I'm gone? Do you mean to
do like t'other Mad-man yonder, rob upon the Highway, and
snatch the Goat-herds Victuals from 'em by main Force?
Never let that trouble thy Head, reply'd Don *Quixote*; for
tho' I had all the Dainties that can feast a luxurious Palate, I
would feed upon nothing but the Herbs and Fruits which this
Wilderness will afford me; for the Singularity of my present
Task consists in fasting, and half starving my self, and in the
Performance of other Austerities. But there's another Thing
come into my Head, quoth *Sancho*; How shall I do to find the
Way hither again, 'tis such a By-place? Take good Notice of
it before-hand, said Don *Quixote*, and I'll endeavour to keep
hereabouts till thy Return: Besides, about the Time when I
may reasonably expect thee back, I'll be sure to watch on the
Top of yonder high Rock for thy coming. But now I bethink
my self of a better Expedient; thou shalt cut down a good
Number of Boughs, and strew 'em in the Way as thou ridest
along, till thou get'st to the Plains, and this will serve thee to
find me again at thy Return, like *Perseus's* Clue to the Labyrinth in *Crete*.

I'll go about it out of hand, quoth *Sancho*. With that he
went and cut down a Bundle of Boughs, then came and ask'd
his Master's Blessing, and, after a Shower of Tears shed on
both Sides, mounted *Rozinante*, which Don *Quixote* very
seriously recommended to his Care, charging him to be as ten-

---

* Sancho *here, by threatning to blurt out something, gives a kind of sly
Prophecy of the* Dulcinea *he intended to palm upon his Master's Folly,
and prepares the Reader for that gross Imposition, of enchanting the three
Princesses and their Palfries, into three Country Wenches upon Asses.*

233

der of that excellent Steed as of his own Person. After that he set forward towards the Plains, strewing several Boughs as he rid, according to Order. His Master importun'd him to stay and see him do two or three of his antick Postures before he went, but he could not prevail with him: However, before he was got out of Sight he consider'd of it, and rode back. Sir, quoth he, I've thought better of it and believe I had best take your Advice, that I may swear with a safe Conscience I have seen you play your mad Tricks; therefore I would see you do one of 'em at least, tho' I think I've seen you do a very great one already, I mean your staying by your self in this Desart.

I had advis'd thee right, said Don *Quixote*; and therefore stay but while a Man may repeat the Creed,* and I will shew thee what thou would'st see. With that, slipping off his Breeches, and stripping himself naked to the Waist, he gave two or three Frisks in the Air, and then pitching on his Hands, he fetch'd his Heels over his Head twice together; and as he tumbled with his Legs aloft, discover'd such Rarities, that *Sancho* e'en made Haste to turn his Horse's Head, that he might no longer see 'em, and rode away full satisfy'd, that he might swear his Master was mad; and so we will leave him to make the best of his Way till his Return, which will be more speedy than might be imagin'd.

* *A Proverb to express Brevity in* Romish *Countries, where they huddle the* Credo *over so fast, that they have done before one wou'd think they were got half through.*

XII: A CONTINUATION OF THE REFIN'D EXTRAVA-GANCIES BY WHICH THE GALLANT KNIGHT OF LA MANCHA CHOSE TO EXPRESS HIS LOVE IN THE SIERRA MORENA

THE History relates, that as soon as the Knight of the *woeful Figure* saw himself alone, after he had taken his Frisks and Leaps naked as he was, the Prelude to his amorous Penance, he ascended the Top of a high Rock, and there began seriously to consider with himself what Resolution to take in that nice Dilemma, which had already so perplex'd his Mind; that is, whether he should imitate *Orlando* in his wild ungovernable Fury, or *Amadis* in his melancholy Mood. To which Purpose, reasoning with himself, I do not much wonder, said he, at *Orlando's* being so very valiant, considering he was inchanted in such a manner, that he could not be slain but by the Thrust of a long Pin through the Bottom of his Foot, which he sufficiently secur'd, always wearing seven Iron Soles to his Shoes; and yet this avail'd him nothing against *Bernardo del Carpio*, who understanding what he depended upon, squeez'd him to Death between his Arms at *Roncevalles*. But setting aside his Valour, let us examine his Madness; for that he was Mad, is an unquestionable Truth; nor is it less certain, that his Frenzy was occasion'd by the Assurances he had that the fair *Angelica* had resign'd herself up to the unlawful Embraces of *Medor*, that young *Moor* with curl'd Locks, who was Page to *Agramant*. Now, after all, seeing he was too well convinc'd of his Lady's Infidelity, 'tis not to be admir'd he should run Mad: But how can I imitate him in his Furies, if I cannot imitate him in their Occasion? For I dare swear my *Dulcinea del Toboso* never saw a downright *Moor* in his own Garb since she first beheld Light, and that she is at this present speaking as right as the Mother that bore her: So that I should do her a great Injury, should I entertain any dishonourable Thoughts of her Behaviour, and fall into such a kind of Madness as that of *Orlando Furioso*. On the other Side I find, that *Amadis de Gaul*,

without punishing himself with such a Distraction, or expressing his Resentments in so boisterous and raving a manner, got as great a Reputation for being a Lover as any one
whatsoever: For what I find in History as to his abandoning
himself to Sorrow, is only this: He found himself disdain'd,
his Lady *Oriana* having charg'd him to get out of her Sight,
and not to presume to appear in her Presence till she gave
him Leave; and this was the true Reason why he retir'd to
the *poor Rock* with the Hermit, where he gave up himself
wholly to Grief, and wept a Deluge of Tears, till pitying
Heaven at last commiserating his Affliction, sent him Relief
in the Height of his Anguish. Now then, since this is true,
as I know it is, what need have I to tear off my Cloaths,
to rend and root up these harmless Trees, or trouble the
clear Water of these Brooks, that must give me Drink when
I am thirsty? No, long live the Memory of *Amadis de Gaul*,
and let him be the great Exemplar which Don *Quixote de la
Mancha* chuses to imitate in all Things that will admit of a
Parallel. So may it be said of the living Copy, as was said of
the dead Original, That if he did not perform great Things,
yet no Man was more ambitious of undertaking 'em than he;
and tho' I am not disdain'd nor discarded by *Dulcinea*, yet
'tis sufficient that I am absent from her. Then 'tis resolv'd!
And now ye famous Actions of the great *Amadis* occur to my
Remembrance, and be my trusty Guides to follow his Example. This said, he call'd to mind, that the chief Exercise of
that Heroe in his Retreat was Prayer: To which purpose, our
modern *Amadis* presently went and made himself a Rosary
of Galls or Acorns instead of Beads; but he was extreamly
troubled for want of an Hermit to hear his Confession, and
comfort him in his Affliction. However, he entertain'd himself with his amorous Contemplations, walking up and down
the Meadow, and writing some poetical Conceptions in the
smooth Sand, and upon the Barks of Trees, all of 'em expressive of his Sorrows, and the Praises of *Dulcinea*; but unhappily none were found entire and legible but these Stanzas
that follow.

Ye lofty Trees with spreading Arms,
The Pride and Shelter of the Plain;
Ye humbler Shrubs, and flow'ry Charms,
Which here in springing Glory reign!
If my Complaint may Pity move,
Hear the sad Story of my Love!
While with me here you pass your Hours,
Should you grow faded with my Cares,
I'll bribe you with refreshing Show'rs,
You shall be water'd with my Tears.
Distant, tho' present in Idea,
I mourn my absent Dulcinea
Del Toboso.

Love's truest Slave despairing chose
This lonely Wild, this desart Plain,
The silent Witness of the Woes
Which he, tho' guiltless, must sustain.
Unknowing why those Pains he bears,
He groans, he raves, and he despairs:
With ling'ring Fires Love racks my Soul,
In vain I grieve, in vain lament;
Like tortur'd Fiends I weep, I howl,
And burn, yet never can repent.
Distant, tho' present in Idea,
I mourn my absent Dulcinea
Del Toboso.

While I thro' Honour's thorny Ways,
In search of distant Glory rove,
Malignant Fate my Toil repays
With endless Woes, and hopeless Love.
Thus I on barren Rocks despair,
And curse my Stars, yet bless my Fair.
Love arm'd with Snakes has left his Dart,
And now does like a Fury rave,
And scourge and sting in every Part,
And into Madness lash his Slave.
Distant, tho' present in Idea,
I mourn my absent Dulcinea
Del Toboso.

This Addition of *Del Toboso* to the Name of *Dulcinea*, made those who found these Verses laugh heartily; and they imagin'd, that when Don *Quixote* made them, he was afraid those who should happen to read 'em would not understand on whom they were made, should he omit to mention the Place of his Mistress's Birth and Residence: And this was indeed the true Reason, as he himself afterwards confess'd. With this Employment did our disconsolate Knight beguile the tedious Hours; sometimes also he express'd his Sorrows in Prose, sigh'd to the Winds, and call'd upon the *Sylvan* Gods, the *Fauns*, the *Naïdes*, the Nymphs of the adjoining Groves, and the mournful *Echo*, imploring their Attention and Condolement with repeated Supplications: At other Times he employ'd himself in gathering Herbs for the Support of languishing Nature, which decay'd so fast, what with his slender Diet, and what with his studied Anxiety and Intenseness of thinking, that had *Sancho* staid but three Weeks from him, whereas by good Fortune he stay'd but three Days, the Knight of the *woeful Figure* would have been so disfigur'd, that his Mother would never have known the Child of her own Womb.

But now 'tis necessary we should leave him a while to his Sighs, his Sobs, and his amorous Expostulations, and see how *Sancho Pança* behav'd himself in his Embassy. He made all the Haste he could to get out of the Mountain; and then taking the direct Road to *Toboso*, the next Day he arriv'd near the Inn where he had been toss'd in a Blanket. Scarce had he descry'd the fatal Walls, but a sudden Shivering seiz'd his Bones, and he fancy'd himself to be again dancing in the Air; so that he had a good Mind to have rode farther before he baited, tho' it was Dinner-time, and his Mouth water'd strangely at the Thoughts of a hot Bit of Meat, the rather, because he had liv'd altogether upon cold Victuals for a long while. This greedy Longing drew him near the Inn, in spite of his Aversion to the Place; but yet when he came to the Gate he had not the Courage to go in, but stopp'd there, not knowing whether he had best enter or no. While he sat musing, two Men happen'd to come out, and believing they knew him, Look, Master Doctor, cry'd one to the other, is not that

Sancho Pança, whom the House-keeper told us her Master had inveigl'd to go along with him? The same, answer'd the other; and more than that, he rides on Don *Quixote's* Horse. Now these two happen'd to be the Curate and the Barber, who had brought his Books to a Trial, and pass'd Sentence on 'em; therefore they had no sooner said this, but they call'd to *Sancho*, and ask'd him where he had left his Master? The trusty Squire presently knew 'em, and having no mind to discover the Place and Condition he left his Master in, told 'em, He was taken up with certain Business of great Consequence at a certain Place, which he durst not discover for his Life. How! *Sancho*, cry'd the Barber, you must not think to put us off with a flim-flam Story; if you won't tell us where he is, we shall believe you have murther'd him, and robb'd him of his Horse; therefore either satisfy us where you've left him, or we'll have you laid by the Heels. Look you, Neighbour, quoth *Sancho*, I a'n't afraid of Words, d'ye see: I am neither a Thief nor a Man-slayer; I kill no Body, so no Body kill me; I leave every Man to fall by his own Fortune, or by the Hand of him that made him. As for my Master, I left him frisking and doing Penance in the midst of yon Mountain, to his Heart's Content. After this, without any further Intreaty, he gave 'em a full Account of that Business, and of all their Adventures; how he was then going from his Master to carry a Letter to my Lady *Dulcinea del Toboso*, *Lorenzo Corchuelo's* Daughter, with whom he was up to the Ears in Love. The Curate and Barber stood amaz'd, hearing all these Particulars; and though they already knew Don *Quixote's* Madness but too well, they wonder'd more and more at the Increase of it, and at so strange a Cast and Variety of Extravagance. Then they desir'd *Sancho* to shew them the Letter. He told 'em 'twas written in a Pocket-Book, and that his Master had order'd him to get it fairly transcrib'd upon Paper at the next Village he should come at. Whereupon the Curate promising to write it out very fairly himself, *Sancho* put his Hand into his Bosom to give him the Table-Book; but though he fumbl'd a great while for it, he could find none of it; he search'd and search'd again, but it had been in vain tho' he had search'd till Dooms-day, for he came away from Don *Quixote* without it. This put him into a cold Sweat, and made him turn as pale as Death: He fell a searching all his Cloaths, turn'd his Pockets Inside outwards, fumbl'd in his Bosom again: But being at last convinc'd he had it not about him, he fell a raving and stamping, and cursing himself like a Mad-man; he rent his Beard from his Chin with both Hands; befisted his own forgetful Skull, and his blubber Cheeks, and gave himself a bloody Nose in a Moment. The Curate and the Barber ask'd him what was the Matter with him, and why he punish'd himself at that strange rate? I deserve it all, quoth *Sancho*, like a Blockhead as I am, for losing at one Cast no less than three Asses, of which the least was worth a Castle. How so, quoth the Barber? Why, cry'd *Sancho*, I've lost that same Table-Book, wherein was written *Dulcinea's* Letter, and a Bill of Exchange drawn by my Master upon his Niece for three of the five Asses which he has at Home; and with that he told 'em how he had lost his own Ass. But the Curate cheer'd him up, and promis'd him to get another Bill of Exchange from his Master written upon Paper, whereas that in the Table-Book not being in due Form, would not have been accepted. With that *Sancho* took Courage, and told 'em, if it were so, he car'd not a Straw for *Dulcinea's* Letter; for he knew it almost all by Rote. Then pry'thee let's hear it, said the Barber, and we'll see and write it. In order to this *Sancho* paus'd, and began to study for the Words; presently he fell a scratching his Head, stood first upon one Leg, and then upon another, gaped sometimes upon the Skies, sometimes upon the Ground; at length, after he had gnaw'd away the Top of his Thumb, and quite tir'd out the Curate and Barber's Patience: Before *George*, cry'd he, Mr Doctor, I believe the Devil's in't; for may I be choak'd if I can remember a Word of this confounded Letter, but only, that there was at the Beginning, *High and Subterrane Lady*: Sovereign, or Super-humane Lady, you would say, quoth the Barber. Ay, ay, quoth *Sancho*, you're in the right —— But stay, now I think, I can remember some of that which follow'd: Ho! I have it, I ha't now—— *He that is wounded, and wants Sleep, sends you the Dagger——which he wants himself—— that stabb'd him to the Heart—— and the hurt Man does kiss your Ladyship's Hand——* and at last, after a hundred Hums and Haws, *Sweetest* Dulcinea del Toboso: And thus he went on rambling a good while with I don't know what more of *Fainting*, and *Relief*, and *Sinking*, till at last he ended with *Yours till Death, The Knight of the woeful Figure.* The Curate and the Barber were mightily pleased with *Sancho's* excellent Memory; insomuch, that they desir'd him to repeat the Letter twice or thrice more, that they might also get it by Heart, and write it down; which *Sancho* did very freely, but every Time he made many odd Alterations and Additions as pleasant as the first. Then he told 'em many other things of his Master, but spoke not a Word of his own being toss'd in a Blanket at that very Inn. He also told 'em, that if he brought a kind Answer from the Lady *Dulcinea*, his Master would forthwith set out to see and make himself an Emperor, or at least a King; for so they two had agreed between themselves, he said; and that after all, 'twas a mighty easy Matter for his Master to become one, such was his Prowess, and the Strength of his Arm: Which being done, his Master would marry him to one of the Empress's Damsels; and that fine Lady was to be Heiress to a large Country on the main Land, but not to any Island, or Islands, for he was out of Conceit with them. Poor *Sancho* spoke all this so seriously, and so feelingly, ever and anon wiping his Nose, and stroaking his Beard, that now the Curate and the Barber were more surpriz'd than they were before, considering the prevalent Influences of Don *Quixote's* Folly upon that silly credulous Fellow. However, they did not think it worth their while to undeceive him yet, seeing this was only a harmless Delusion, that might divert them a while; and therefore they exhorted him to pray for his Master's Health, and long Life, seeing it was no impossible thing, but that he might in Time become an Emperor as he said, or at least an Archbishop, or somewhat else equivalent to it.

But pray, good Mr Doctor, ask'd *Sancho*, should my Master have no Mind to be an Emperor, and take a Fancy to be an Archbishop, I would fain know what your Archbishops-Errant are wont to give their Squires? Why, answer'd the Curate, they use to give 'em some Parsonage, or *Sine Cure*, or some such other Benefice, or Church-Living, which, with the Profits of the Altar, and other Fees, brings them in a handsome Revenue. Ay, but, says *Sancho*, to put in for that, the Squire must be a Single Man, and know how to answer, and assist at Mass at least; and how shall I do then, seeing I have the ill Luck to be marry'd? Nay, and besides I don't so much as know the first Letter of my Christ-Cross-Row. What will become of me, should it come into my Master's Head to make himself an Archbishop, and not an Emperor, as 'tis the Custom of Knights-Errant? Don't let that trouble thee, Friend *Sancho*, said the Barber, we'll talk to him about it, and advise him, nay, urge it to him as a Point of Conscience to be an Emperor, and not an Archbishop, which will be better for Him, by reason he has more Courage than Learning.

Troth, I'm of your Mind, quoth *Sancho*, though he's such a Head-piece, that I dare say he can turn himself to any thing: Nevertheless, I mean to make it the Burden of my Prayers, that Heaven may direct him to that which is best for Him, and what may enable him to reward Me most. You speak like a wise Man, and a good Christian, said the Curate: But all we have to do at present, is to see how we shall get your Master to give over that severe unprofitable Penance which he has undertaken; and therefore let's go in to consider about it, and also to eat our Dinner, for I fancy 'tis ready by this Time. Do you two go in if you please, quoth *Sancho*, but as for me, I had rather stay without; and anon I'll tell you why I don't care to go in a-Doors: However, pray send me out a Piece of hot Victuals to eat here, and some Provender for *Rozinante*. With that they went in, and a while after the Barber brought him out some Meat; and returning to the Curate, they consulted how to compass their Design. At last the latter luckily bethought himself of an Expedient that seem'd most likely to take, as exactly fitting Don *Quixote's* Humour; which was, that he shou'd disguise himself in the Habit of a Damsel-Errant, and the Barber should alter his Dress as well as he could, so as to pass for his Squire, or Gentleman-Usher. In that Equipage, added he, we will go to Don *Quixote*, and feigning my self to be a distress'd Damsel, I'll beg a Boon of him, which he, as a valorous Knight-Errant, will not fail to promise me. By this Means I will engage him to go with me to redress a very great Injury done me by a *false and discourteous Knight*, beseeching him not to desire to see my Face, nor ask me any thing about my Circumstances, till he has reveng'd me of that wicked Knight. This Bait will take, I dare engage, and by this Stratagem we'll decoy him back to his own House, where we'll try to cure him of his romantick Frenzy.

XIII: HOW THE CURATE AND BARBER PUT THEIR DESIGN IN EXECUTION; WITH OTHER THINGS WORTHY TO BE RECORDED IN THIS IMPORTANT HISTORY

THE Curate's Project was so well lik'd by the Barber, that they instantly put it into Practice. First they borrowed a complete Woman's Apparel of the Hostess, leaving her in Pawn a new Cassock of the Curate's; and the Barber made himself a long Beard with a grizzl'd Ox's Tail, in which the Inn-keeper us'd to hang his Combs. The Hostess being desirous to know what they intended to do with those Things, the Curate gave her a short Account of Don *Quixote's* Distraction, and their Design. Whereupon the Inn-keeper and his Wife presently guess'd this was their romantick Knight, that made the precious Balsam; and accordingly they told 'em the whole Story of Don *Quixote's* lodging there, and of *Sancho's* being toss'd in a Blanket. Which done, the Hostess readily fitted out the Curate at such a Rate, that 'twould have pleas'd any one to have seen him; for she dress'd him up in a Cloth Gown trimm'd with Borders of black Velvet, the Breadth of a Span, all pink'd and jagg'd; and a Pair of green Velvet Bodice, with Sleeves of the same, and fac'd with white Sattin; which Accoutrements probably had been in Fashion in old King *Bamba's** Days. The Curate would not let her encumber his Head with a Woman's Head-Geer, but only clapp'd upon his Crown a white quilted Cap which he us'd to wear a-Nights, and bound his Forehead with one of his Garters, that was of black Taffety, making himself a kind of Muffler and Vizard-Mask with the other: Then he half bury'd his Head under his Hat, pulling it down to squeeze in his Ears; and as the broad Brim flapp'd down over his Eyes, it seem'd a kind of Umbrella. This done, he wrapp'd his Cloak about him, and seated himself on his Mule, Side-ways like a Woman: Then the Barber clapp'd on his Ox-Tail Beard, half

* *An ancient* Gothick *King of* Spain, *concerning whom several Fables are written; wherefore the* Spaniards, *to express any Thing exceeding old, say it was in Being in His Time; as in* England *we say a Thing is as old as* Paul's, *and the like.*

red and half grizzl'd, which hung from his Chin down to his Waist; and having mounted his Mule, they took Leave of their Host and Hostess, as also of the good-condition'd *Maritornes*, who vow'd, tho' she was a Sinner, to tumble her Beads, and say a Rosary to the good Success of so arduous and truly Christian an Undertaking.

But scarce were they got out of the Inn, when the Curate began to be troubled with a Scruple of Conscience about his putting on Woman's Apparel, being apprehensive of the Indecency of the Disguise in a Priest, though the Goodness of his Intention might well warrant a Dispensation from the Strictness of Decorum: Therefore he desired the Barber to change Dresses, for that in his Habit of a Squire he should less profane his own Dignity and Character, to which he ought to have a greater Regard than to Don *Quixote*; withal assuring the Barber, that unless he consented to this Exchange, he was absolutely resolv'd to go no further, though 'twere to save Don *Quixote's* Soul from Hell. *Sancho* came up with 'em just upon their Demur, and was ready to split his Sides with laughing at the Sight of these strange Masqueraders. In short, the Barber consented to be the Damsel, and to let the Curate be the Squire. Now while they were thus changing Sexes, the Curate offer'd to tutor him how to behave himself in that female Attire, so as to be able to wheedle Don *Quixote* out of his Penance: But the Barber desir'd him not to trouble himself about that Matter, assuring him, that he was well enough vers'd in Female Affairs to be able to act a Damsel without any Directions: However, he said he would not now stand fiddling and managing his Pins to prink himself up, seeing it would be time enough to do that when they came near Don *Quixote's* Hermitage; and therefore having folded up his Cloaths, and the Curate his Beard, they spurr'd on, while their Guide *Sancho* entertain'd 'em with a Relation of the mad tatter'd Gentleman whom they had met in the Mountain; however, without mentioning a Word of the Portmanteau or the Gold; for, as much a Fool as he was, he lov'd Money, and knew how to keep it when he had it, and was wise enough to keep his own Counsel.

They got the next Day to the Place were *Sancho* had

strew'd the Boughs to direct him to Don *Quixote*; and therefore he advis'd them to put on their Disguises, if 'twere, as
they told him, that their Design was only to make his Master
leave that wretched kind of Life, in order to become an
Emperor. Thereupon they charg'd him on his Life not to take
the least Notice who they were. As for *Dulcinea's* Letter,
if Don *Quixote* ask'd him about it, they order'd him to say
he had deliver'd it; but that by reason she could neither
write nor read, she had sent him her Answer by Word of
Mouth; which was, That on Pain of her Indignation, he
should immediately put an End to his severe Penance, and
repair to her Presence. This, they told *Sancho*, together with
what they themselves design'd to say, was the only Way
to oblige his Master to leave the Desert, that he might prosecute his Design of making himself an Emperor; assuring
him they would take care he should not entertain the least
Thought of an Archbishoprick.

Sancho listen'd with great Attention to all these Instructions, and treasur'd 'em up in his Mind, giving the Curate
and the Barber a world of Thanks for their good Intention of
advising his Master to become an Emperor, and not an Archbishop; for, as he said, he imagin'd in his simple Judgment, that
an Emperor-Errant was ten times better than an Archbishop-
Errant, and could reward his Squire a great deal better.

He likewise added, That he thought it would be proper
for him to go to his Master somewhat before them, and give
him an Account of his Lady's kind Answer; for, perhaps,
that alone would be sufficient to fetch him out of that Place,
without putting 'em to any further Trouble. They lik'd this
Proposal very well, and therefore agreed to let him go, and
wait there till he came back to give them an Account of his
Success. With that *Sancho* rode away, and struck into the
Clefts of the Rock, in order to find out his Master, leaving
the Curate and the Barber by the Side of a Brook, where
the neighbouring Hills, and some Trees that grew along its
Banks, combin'd to make a cool and pleasant Shade. There
they shelter'd themselves from the scorching Beams of the
Sun, that commonly shines intolerably hot in those Parts at
that Time, being about the Middle of *August*, and hardly

246

three o'Clock in the Afternoon. While they quietly refresh'd
themselves in that delightful Place, where they agreed to
stay till *Sancho's* Return, they heard a Voice, which though
unattended with any Instrument, ravish'd their Ears with
its melodious Sound: And what increas'd their Surprize, and
their Admiration, was to hear such artful Notes, and such
delicate Musick, in so unfrequented and wild a Place, where
scarce any Rusticks ever straggl'd, much less such skilful
Songsters, as the Person whom they heard unquestionably
was; for though the Poets are pleas'd to fill the Fields and
Woods with Swains and Shepherdesses, that sing with all
the Sweetness and Delicacy imaginable, yet 'tis well enough
known that those Gentlemen deal more in Fiction than in
Truth, and love to embellish the Descriptions they make,
with Things that have no Existence but in their own Brain.
Nor could our two list'ning Travellers think it the Voice of
a Peasant, when they began to distinguish the Words of the
Song, for they seem'd to relish more of a courtly Style than
a rural Composition. These were the Verses.

A SONG

1

What makes me languish and complain?
                              O 'tis Disdain!
What yet more fiercely tortures me?
                              'Tis Jealousy.
How have I my Patience lost?
                              By Absence *crost.*
  Then Hopes farewel, there's no Relief;
  I sink beneath oppressing Grief;
  Nor can a Wretch, without Despair,
  Scorn, Jealousy, *and* Absence *bear.*

2

What in my Breast this Anguish drove?
                              Intruding Love.
Who cou'd such mighty Ills create?
                              Blind Fortune's *Hate.*
What cruel Pow'rs my Fate approve?
                              The Powers above.

Then let me bear, and cease to moan;
'Tis glorious thus to be undone:
When These invade, Who dares oppose?
Heaven, Love and Fortune are my Foes.

3

Where shall I find a speedy Cure?

Death is sure.

No milder Means to set me free?

Inconstancy.

Can nothing else my Pains asswage?

Distracting Rage.

What Die or Change? Lucinda lose?
O let me rather Madness chuse!
But judge, ye Gods, what we endure,
When Death or Madness are a Cure!

The Time, the Hour, the Solitariness of the Place, the
Voice and agreeable Manner with which the unseen Musician
sung, so fill'd the Hearers Minds with Wonder and Delight,
that they were all Attention; and when the Voice was silent,
they continu'd so too a pretty while, watching with list'ning
Ears to catch the expected Sounds, expressing their Satisfaction best by that dumb Applause. At last, concluding the
Person would sing no more, they resolv'd to find out the
charming Songster; but as they were going so to do, they
heard the wish'd-for Voice begin another Air, which fix'd
'em where they stood till it had sung the following Sonnet:

A SONNET

O Sacred Friendship, Heaven's Delight,
Which tir'd with Man's unequal Mind,
Took to thy native Skies thy Flight,
    While scarce thy Shadow's left behind!

From thee, diffusive Good, below,
    Peace and her Train of Joys we trace;
But Falshood with dissembl'd Show
    Too oft usurps thy sacred Face.

> *Bless'd* Genius, *then resume thy Seat!*
> *Destroy Imposture and Deceit,*
>> *Which in thy Dress confound the Ball!*
> *Harmonious Peace and Truth renew,*
> *Shew the false Friendship from the true,*
>> *Or Nature must to* Chaos *fall.*

This Sonnet concluded with a deep Sigh, and such doleful Throbs, that the Curate and the Barber now out of Pity, as well as Curiosity before, resolv'd instantly to find out who this mournful Songster was. They had not gone far, when by the Side of a Rock they discover'd a Man, whose Shape and Aspect answer'd exactly to the Description *Sancho* had given 'em of *Cardenio*. They observ'd he stopp'd short as soon as he spy'd them, yet without any Signs of Fear; only he hung down his Head, like one abandon'd to Sorrow, never so much as lifting up his Eyes to mind what they did. The Curate, who was a good and a well-spoken Man, presently guessing him to be the same of whom *Sancho* had given them an Account, went towards him, and addressing himself to him with great Civility and Discretion, earnestly intreated him to forsake this Desart, and a Course of Life so wretched and forlorn, which endanger'd his Title to a better, and from a wilful Misery might make him fall into greater and everlasting Woes. *Cardenio* was then free from the Distraction that so often disturb'd his Senses; yet seeing two Persons in a Garb wholly different from that of those few Rusticks who frequented those Desarts, and hearing 'em talk as if they were no Strangers to his Concerns, he was somewhat surpriz'd at first; however, having look'd upon 'em earnestly for some time, Gentlemen, said he, whoever ye be, I find Heaven, pitying my Misfortunes, has brought ye to these solitary Regions, to retrieve me from this frightful Retirement, and recover me to the Society of Men: But because you do not know how unhappy a Fate attends me, and that I never am free from one Affliction but to fall into a greater, you perhaps take me for a Man naturally endow'd with a very small Stock of Sense, and, what's worse, for one of those Wretches who are altogether depriv'd of Reason. And indeed I cannot blame any

249

one that entertains such Thoughts of me; for even I my self am convinc'd, that the bare Remembrance of my Disasters often distracts me to that Degree, that losing all Sense of Reason and Knowledge, I unman my self for the Time, and launch into those Extravagancies which nothing but Height of Frenzy and Madness would commit: And I am the more sensible of my being troubl'd with this Distemper, when People tell me what I have done during the Violence of that terrible Accident, and give me too certain Proofs of it. And after all, I can alledge no other Excuse but the Cause of my Misfortune, which occasion'd that frantick Rage, and therefore tell the Story of my hard Fate to as many as have the Patience to hear it; for Men of Sense perceiving the Cause, will not wonder at the Effects; and though they can give me no Relief, yet at least they will cease to condemn me; for a bare Relation of my Wrongs must needs make 'em lose their Resentments of the Effects of my Disorder into a Compassion of my miserable Fate. Therefore, Gentlemen, if you come here with that Design, I beg that before you give your selves the Trouble of reproving or advising me, you will be pleas'd to attend to the Relation of my Calamities; for perhaps when you have heard it, you will think 'em past Redress, and so will save your selves the Labour you would take. The Curate and the Barber, who desir'd nothing more than to hear the Story from his own Mouth, were extremely glad of his Proffer; and having assur'd him they had no Design to aggravate his Miseries with pretending to remedy 'em, nor would they cross his Inclinations in the least, they intreated him to begin his Relation.

The unfortunate *Cardenio* then began his Story, and went on with the first Part of it, almost in the same Words, as far as when he related it to Don *Quixote* and the Goat-herd, when the Knight, out of superstitious Niceness to observe the Decorum of Chivalry, gave an Interruption to the Relation, by quarrelling about Master *Elizabat*, as we have already said. Then he went on with that Passage concerning the Letter sent him by *Lucinda*, which Don *Ferdinand* had unluckily found, happening to be by, to open the Book of *Amadis de Gaul* first, when *Lucinda* sent it back to *Cardenio*

250

with that Letter in it between the Leaves; which *Cardenio* told 'em was as follows:

LUCINDA *TO* CARDENIO

I Discover in you every Day so much Merit, that I am oblig'd, or rather forc'd, to esteem you more and more. If you think this Acknowledgment to your Advantage, make that use of it which is most consistent with Your Honour and Mine. I have a Father that knows you, and is too kind a Parent ever to obstruct my Designs, when he shall be satisfy'd with their being Just and Honourable: So that 'tis now Your Part to shew you love me, as you pretend, and I believe.

This Letter, continu'd *Cardenio*, made me resolve once more to demand *Lucinda* of her Father in Marriage, and was the same that increas'd Don *Ferdinand's* Esteem for her, by that Discovery of her Sense and Discretion, which so inflam'd his Soul, that from that Moment he secretly resolv'd to destroy my Hopes e'er I could be so happy as to crown them with Success. I told that Perfidious Friend what *Lucinda's* Father had advis'd me to do, when I had rashly ask'd her for my Wife before, and that I durst not now impart this to my Father, lest he should not readily consent I should marry yet. Not but that he knew, that her Quality, Beauty, and Virtue were sufficient to make her an Ornament to the noblest House in *Spain*, but because I was apprehensive he would not let me marry till he saw what the Duke would do for me. Don *Ferdinand*, with a pretended Officiousness, proffer'd me to speak to my Father, and perswade him to treat with *Lucinda's*. Ungrateful Man! Deceitful Friend! Ambitious *Marius*! Cruel *Catiline*! Wicked *Sylla*! Perfidious *Galalon*! Faithless *Vellido*! Malicious *Julian*!* Treacherous, Covetous *Judas*! Thou all those fatal hated Men in one, false *Ferdinand*! What Wrongs had that fond confiding Wretch done thee, who thus to thee unbosom'd all his Cares, all the Delights, and Secrets of his Soul? What Injury did I ever utter, or Advice did I ever give, which were not all directed to advance thy Honour and

---

* Julian. *Count* Julian *brought the* Moors *into* Spain, *because King* Rodrigo *had ravish'd his Daughter.* Galalon *and* Vellido *are explain'd elsewhere.* Marius, Catiline, *&c. are well known.*

Profit? But, oh! I rave, unhappy Wretch! I should rather accuse the Cruelty of my Stars, whose fatal Influence pours Mischiefs on me, which no earthly Force can resist, or human Art prevent. Who would have thought that Don *Ferdinand*, whose Quality and Merit entitl'd him to the lawful Possession of Beauties of the highest Rank, and whom I had engag'd by a thousand endearing Marks of Friendship and Services, should forfeit thus his Honour and his Truth, and lay such a treacherous Design to deprive me of all the Happiness of my Life? But I must leave expostulating, to end my Story. The Traitor *Ferdinand* thinking his Project impracticable, while I stay'd near *Lucinda*, bargain'd for six fine Horses the same Day he promis'd to speak to my Father, and presently desired me to ride away to his Brother for Money to pay for 'em. Alas! I was so far from suspecting his Treachery, that I was glad of doing him a Piece of Service. Accordingly I went that very Evening to take my Leave of *Lucinda*, and to tell her what Don *Ferdinand* had promised to do. She bid me return with all the Haste of an expecting Lover, not doubting but our lawful Wishes might be crown'd, as soon as my Father had spoke for me to be her's. When she had said this, I mark'd her trickling Tears, and a sudden Grief so obstructed her Speech, that though she seem'd to strive to tell me something more, she could not give it Utterance. This unusual Scene of Sorrow strangely amaz'd and mov'd me; yet because I would not murder Hope, I chose to attribute this to the Tenderness of her Affection, and Unwillingness to part with me. In short, away I went, bury'd in deep Melancholy, and full of Fears and Imaginations, for which I could give no manner of Reason. I deliver'd Don *Ferdinand's* Letter to his Brother, who receiv'd me with all the Kindness imaginable, but did not dispatch me as I expected. For, to my Sorrow, he enjoyn'd me to tarry a whole Week, and to take Care the Duke might not see me, his Brother having sent for Money unknown to his Father: But this was only a Device of false *Ferdinand's*; for his Brother did not want Money, and might have dispatch'd me immediately, had he not been privately desir'd to delay my Return.

This was so displeasing an Injunction, that I was ready

to come away without the Money, not being able to live so
long absent from my *Lucinda*, principally considering in what
Condition I had left her. Yet at last I forc'd my self to stay,
and my Respect for my Friend prevail'd over my Impatience:
But e'er four tedious Days were expired, a Messenger brought
me a Letter, which I presently knew to be *Lucinda's* Hand.
I open'd it with trembling Hands, and an aking Heart, justly
imagining it was no ordinary Concern that could urge her to
send thither to me: And before I read it, I ask'd the Messenger who had given it him? He answer'd me, "That going
"by accidentally in the Street about Noon in our Town, a
"very handsome Lady, all in Tears, had call'd him to her
"Window, and with great Precipitation, Friend, said she,
"if you be a Christian, as you seem to be, for Heaven's sake
"take this Letter, and deliver it with all speed into the Per-
"son's own Hand to whom 'tis directed: I assure you in this
"you'll do a very good Action; and that you may not want
"Means to do it, take what's wrapp'd up in this; and saying
"so, she threw me a Handkerchief, wherein I found a hun-
"dred Reals, this Gold Ring which you see, and the Letter
"which I now brought you: Which done, I having made her
"Signs to let her know I would do as she desir'd, without
"so much as staying for an Answer, she went from the Grate.
"This Reward, but much more that beautiful Lady's Tears,
"and earnest Prayers, made me post away to you that very
"Minute, and so in sixteen Hours I have travell'd eighteen
"long Leagues." While the Messenger spoke, I was seiz'd
with sad Apprehensions of some fatal News; and such a Trembling shook my Limbs, that I could scarce support my fainting
Body. However, taking Courage, at last I read the Letter;
the Contents of which were these:

Don Ferdinand, *according to his Promise, has desired your
Father to speak to mine; but he has done that for himself which
you had engag'd him to do for you: For, he has demanded
me for his Wife; and my Father, allur'd by the Advantages
which he expects from such an Alliance, has so far consented,
that two Days hence the Marriage is to be perform'd, and
with such Privacy, that only Heaven and some of the Family
are to be Witnesses. Judge of the Affliction of my Soul by that*

253

Concern which I guess fills your own; and therefore haste to me, my Dear Cardenio. *The Issue of this Business will shew how much I love you: And grant, propitious Heaven, this may reach your Hands e'er mine is in Danger of being join'd with his who keeps his Promise so ill.*

I had no sooner read the Letter, added *Cardenio*, but away I flew, without waiting for my Dispatch; for then I too plainly discover'd Don *Ferdinand's* Treachery, and that he had only sent me to his Brother to take the Advantage of my Absence. Revenge, Love, and Impatience gave me Wings, so that I got home privately the next Day, just when it grew duskish, in good Time to speak with *Lucinda*; and leaving my Mule at the honest Man's House who brought me the Letter, I went to wait upon my Mistress, whom I luckily found at the Window,* the only Witness of our Loves. She presently knew me, and I her, but she did not welcome me as I expected, nor did I find her in such a Dress as I thought suitable to our Circumstances. But what Man has Assurance enough but to pretend to know thoroughly the Riddle of a Woman's Mind, and who could ever hope to fix her mutable Nature? *Cardenio*, said *Lucinda* to me, my Wedding-Cloaths are on, and the perfidious *Ferdinand*, with my covetous Father, and the rest, stay for me in the Hall, to perform the Marriage-Rites; but they shall sooner be Witnesses of my Death than of my Nuptials. Be not troubled, my Dear *Cardenio*; but rather strive to be present at that Sacrifice. I promise thee, if Entreaties and Words cannot prevent it, I have a Dagger that shall do me Justice; and my Death, at least, shall give thee undeniable Assurances of my Love and Fidelity. Do, Madam, cry'd I to her with Precipitation, and so disorder'd that I did not know what I said, let your Actions verify your Words: Let us leave nothing unattempted may serve our common Interests; and I assure you, if my Sword does not defend them well, I will turn it upon my own Breast, rather than out-live my Disappointment. I cannot tell whether *Lucinda* heard me, for she was call'd away in great Haste, the Bridegroom

* A la rexa, *at the Iron Grate. In* Spain *the Lovers make their Courtship at a low Window that has a Grate before it, having seldom Admission into the House till the Parents on both sides have agreed.*

impatiently expecting her. My Spirit forsook me when she left me, and my Sorrow and Confusion cannot be express'd. Methought I saw the Sun set for ever; and my Eyes and my Senses partaking of my Distraction, I could not so much as spy the Door to go into the House, and seem'd rooted to the Place where I stood. But at last, the Consideration of my Love having rous'd me out of this stupifying Astonishment, I got into the House without being discover'd, every thing being there in a Hurry; and going into the Hall, I hid my self behind the Hangings, where two Pieces of Tapestry met, and gave me Liberty to see, without being seen. Who can describe the various Thoughts, the Doubts, the Fears, the Anguish that perplex'd and toss'd my Soul while I stood waiting there! Don *Ferdinand* enter'd the Hall, not like a Bridegroom, but in his usual Habit, with only a Cousin-German of *Lucinda's*, the rest were the People of the House: Some time after came *Lucinda* her self, with her Mother, and two Waiting-Women. I perceiv'd she was as richly dress'd as was consistent with her Quality, and the Solemnity of the Ceremony; but the Distraction that possess'd me, lent me no Time to note particularly the Apparel she had on: I only mark'd the Colours, that were Carnation and White, and the Splendor of the Jewels that enrich'd her Dress in many Places; but nothing equall'd the Lustre of her Beauty that adorn'd her Person much more than all those Ornaments. Oh Memory! thou fatal Enemy of my Ease, why dost thou now so faithfully represent to the Eyes of my Mind *Lucinda's* incomparable Charms? Why dost thou not rather shew me what she did then, that, mov'd by so provoking a Wrong, I may endeavour to revenge it, or at least to die. Forgive me these tedious Digressions, Gentlemen! Alas! my Woes are not such as can or ought to be related with Brevity; for to me every Circumstance seems worthy to be enlarg'd upon.

The Curate assured *Cardenio*, that they attended every Word with a mournful Pleasure, that made them greedy of hearing the least Passage. With that *Cardenio* went on. All Parties being met, said he, the Priest enter'd, and taking the young Couple by the Hands, he ask'd *Lucinda* whether she were willing to take Don *Ferdinand* for her wedded Hus-

band? With that, I thrust out my Head from between the two
Pieces of Tapestry, list'ning with anxious Heart to hear her
Answer, upon which depended my Life and Happiness. Dull,
heartless Wretch that I was! Why did I not then shew my
self? Why did I not call to her aloud? Consider what thou
dost, *Lucinda*, thou art mine, and canst not be another Man's:
Nor canst thou speak now the fatal Yes, without injuring
Heaven, thy Self, and Me, and murdering thy *Cardenio*! And
thou perfidious *Ferdinand*, who darest to violate all Rights,
both Human and Divine, to rob me of my Treasure; canst thou
hope to deprive me of the Comfort of my Life with Impunity?
Or think'st thou that any Consideration can stifle my Resentments, when my Honour and my Love lie at stake? Fool that
I am! now that 'tis too late, and Danger is far distant, I say
what I should have done, and not what I did then: After I've
suffer'd the Treasure of my Soul to be stolen, I exclaim against
the Thief whom I might have punish'd for the base Attempt,
had I had but so much Resolution to revenge, as I have now
to complain. Then let me rather accuse my faint Heart that
durst not do me right, and let me die here like a Wretch,
void both of Sense and Honour, the Outcast of Society and
Nature. The Priest stood waiting for *Lucinda's* Answer a
good while before she gave it; and all that Time I expected
she would have pull'd out her Dagger, or unloos'd her Tongue
to plead her former Engagement to Me. But, alas! to my
eternal Disappointment, I heard her at last, with a feeble
Voice, pronounce the fatal Yes; and then Don *Ferdinand*
saying the same, and giving her the Ring, the Sacred Knot
was ty'd which Death alone can dissolve. Then did the faithless Bridegroom advance to embrace his Bride; but she laying
her Hand upon her Heart, in that very Moment swoon'd away
in her Mother's Arms. Oh what Confusion seiz'd me, what
Pangs, what Torments rack'd me, seeing the Falshood of *Lucinda's* Promises, all my Hopes shipwrack'd, and the only
Thing that made me wish to live, for ever ravish'd from me!
Confounded, and despairing, I look'd upon my self as abandon'd by Heaven to the Cruelty of my Destiny; and the Violence of my Griefs stifling my Sighs, and denying a Passage to
my Tears, I felt my self transfix'd with killing Anguish, and

burning with jealous Rage and Vengeance! In the mean Time
the whole Company was troubled at *Lucinda's* Swooning;
and as her Mother unclasp'd her Gown before, to give her
Air, a folded Paper was found in her Bosom, which Don *Ferdinand* immediately snatch'd; then stepping a little aside, he
open'd it and read it by the Light of one of the Tapers: And
as soon as he had done, he as it were let himself fall upon
a Chair, and there he sate with his Hand upon the side of his
Face, with all the Signs of Melancholy and Discontent, as
unmindful of his Bride as if he had been insensible of her
Accident. For my own part, seeing all the House thus in an
Uproar, I resolv'd to leave the hated Place, without caring
whether I were seen or not, and in case I were seen, I resolv'd
to act such a desperate Part in punishing the Traitor *Ferdinand*, that the World should at once be inform'd of his
Perfidiousness, and the Severity of my just Resentment: But
my Destiny, that preserv'd me for greater Woes (if greater
can be) allow'd me then the Use of that small Remainder of
my Senses, which afterwards quite forsook me: So that I left
the House, without revenging my self on my Enemies, whom
I could easily have sacrific'd to my Rage in this unexpected
Disorder; and I chose to inflict upon my self, for my Credulity,
the Punishment which their Infidelity deserv'd. I went to
the Messenger's House where I had left my Mule, and without so much as bidding him Adieu, I mounted, and left the
Town like another *Lot*, without turning to give it a parting
Look; and as I rode along the Fields, Darkness and Silence
round me, I vented my Passion in Execrations against the
treacherous *Ferdinand*, and in as loud Complaints of *Lucinda's* Breach of Vows and Ingratitude. I call'd her cruel, ungrateful, false, but above all, covetous and sordid, since the
Wealth of my Enemy was what had induc'd her to forgo
her Vows to me: But then again, said I to my self, 'tis no
strange thing for a young Lady, that was so strictly educated,
to yield herself up to the Guidance of her Father and Mother
who had provided her a Husband of that Quality and Fortune.
But yet with Truth and Justice she might have pleaded that
she was mine before. In fine, I concluded that Ambition had
got the better of her Love, and made her forget her Promises

to *Cardenio*. Thus abandoning my self to these tempestuous Thoughts, I rode on all that Night, and about Break of Day I struck into one of the Passes that leads into these Mountains; where I wander'd for three Days together without keeping any Road, till at last coming to a certain Valley that lies somewhere hereabouts, I met some Shepherds, of whom I enquir'd the Way to the most craggy and inaccessible Part of these Rocks. They directed me, and I made all the Haste I could to get thither, resolv'd to linger out my hated Life far from the Converse of false ungrateful Mankind. When I came among these Desarts, my Mule, through Weariness and Hunger, or rather to get rid of so useless a Load as I was, fell down dead, and I my self was so weak, so tir'd and dejected, being almost famish'd, and withal destitute and careless of Relief, that I soon laid my self down, or rather fainted on the Ground, where I lay a considerable while, I don't know how long, extended like a Corpse. When I came to my self again, I got up, and cou'd not perceive I had any Appetite to eat: I found some Goat-herds by me, who, I suppose, had given me some Sustenance, tho' I was not sensible of their Relief: For, they told me in what a wretched Condition they found me, staring, and talking so strangely, that they judg'd I had quite lost my Senses. I have indeed since that had but too much Cause to think that my Reason sometimes leaves me, and that I commit those Extravagancies which are only the Effects of senseless Rage and Frenzy; tearing my Cloaths, howling through these Desarts, filling the Air with Curses and Lamentations, and idly repeating a thousand times *Lucinda's* Name; all my Wishes at that Time being to breathe out my Soul with the dear Word upon my Lips; and when I come to my self, I am commonly so weak, and so weary, that I am scarce able to stir. As for my Place of Abode, 'tis usually some hollow Cork-Tree, into which I creep at Night; and there some few Goat-herds, whose Cattle browse on the neighbouring Mountains, out of Pity and Christian Charity, sometimes leave some Victuals for the Support of my miserable Life: For, even when my Reason is absent, Nature performs its animal Functions, and Instinct guides me to satisfy it. Sometimes these good People meet me in my lucid Intervals, and chide me for taking

that from 'em by Force and Surprize, which they are always
so ready to give me willingly; for which Violence I can make
no other Excuse, but the Extremity of my Distraction. Thus
must I drag a miserable Being, 'till Heaven, pitying my Afflictions, will either put a Period to my Life, or blot out of my
Memory perjur'd *Lucinda's* Beauty and Ingratitude, and *Ferdinand's* Perfidiousness. Could I but be so happy e'er I die,
I might then hope to be able, in Time, to compose my frantick
Thoughts: But if I must despair of such a Favour, I have no
other Way but to recommend my Soul to Heaven's Mercy; for
I am not able to extricate my Body or my Mind out of that
Misery in which I have unhappily plung'd my self.

Thus, Gentlemen, I have given you a faithful Account of
my Misfortunes. Judge now whether 'twas possible I should
relate 'em with less Concern. And pray do not lose Time to
prescribe Remedies to a Patient who will make use of none:
I will, and can have no Health without *Lucinda*; since she
forsakes me, I must die: She has convinc'd me, by her Infidelity, that she desires my Ruin; and by my unparallel'd Sufferings to the last, I will strive to convince her I deserv'd
a better Fate. Let me then suffer on, and may I be the only
unhappy Creature whom Despair could not relieve, while
the Impossibility of receiving Comfort brings Cure to so many
other Wretches!

Here *Cardenio* made an End of his mournful Story; and
just as the Curate was preparing to give him some proper
Consolation, he was prevented by the doleful Accents of another Complaint that engag'd 'em to new Attention. But the
Account of that Adventure is reserv'd for the Fourth Book
of this History; for our Wise and Judicious Historian, *Cid
Hamet Benengeli*, puts here a Period to the Third.

Part I Book IV

I: THE PLEASANT NEW ADVENTURE THE
CURATE AND BARBER MET WITH
IN SIERRA MORENA, OR
BLACK MOUNTAIN

OST fortunate and happy was the Age that usher'd into the World that most daring Knight Don *Quixote de la Mancha*! For from his generous Resolution to revive and restore the ancient Order of Knight-Errantry, that was not only wholly neglected, but almost lost and abolish'd, our Age, barren in it self of pleasant Recreations, derives the Pleasure it reaps from his true History, and the various Tales and Episodes thereof, in some respects, no less pleasing, artful and authentic, than the History itself. We told you that as the Curate was preparing to give *Cardenio* some seasonable Consolation, he was prevented by a Voice, whose doleful Complaints reach'd his Ears. O Heavens, cry'd the unseen Mourner, is it possible I have at last found out a Place that will afford a private Grave to this miserable Body, whose Load I so repine to bear? Yes, if the Silence and Solitude of these Desarts do not deceive me, here I may die conceal'd from Human Eyes. Ah me! Ah wretched Creature! To what Extremity has Affliction driven me, reduc'd to think these hideous Woods and Rocks a kind Retreat! 'Tis true indeed, I may here freely complain to Heaven, and beg for that Relief which I might ask in vain of false Mankind: For 'tis vain, I find to seek below either Counsel, Ease, or Remedy. The Curate and his Company, who heard all this distinctly, justly conjectur'd they were very near the Person who thus express'd his Grief, and therefore rose to find him out. They had not gone about twenty Paces, before they spy'd a Youth in a Country Habit, sitting at the Foot of a Rock behind an Ash-tree; but they cou'd not well see his Face, being bow'd almost upon his Knees, as he sat washing his Feet in a

Rivulet that glided by. They approach'd him so softly that he did not perceive 'em: And, as he was gently padling in the clear Water, they had time to discern that his Legs were as white as Alabaster, and so taper, so curiously proportion'd, and so fine that nothing of the kind could appear more beautiful. Our Observers were amaz'd at this Discovery, rightly imagining that such tender Feet were not us'd to trudge in rugged ways, or measure the Steps of Oxen at the Plough, the common Employments of People in such Apparel; and therefore the Curate, who went before the rest, whose Curiosity was heighten'd by this Sight, beckon'd to 'em to step aside, and hide themselves behind some of the little Rocks that were by; which they did, and from thence making a stricter Observation, they found he had on a grey double-skirted Jerkin, girt tight about his Body with a Linen-Towel. He wore also a pair of Breeches, and Gamashes of grey Cloth, and a grey Huntsman's Cap on his Head. His Gamashes were now pull'd up to the middle of his Leg, which really seem'd to be of Snowy Alabaster. Having made an end of washing his beauteous Feet, he immediately wiped them with a Handkerchief, which he pull'd out from under his Cap; and with that, looking up, he discover'd so charming a Face, so accomplish'd a Beauty, that *Cardenio* could not forbear saying to the Curate, that since this was not *Lucinda*, 'twas certainly no Human Form, but an Angel. And then the Youth taking off his Cap, and shaking his Head, an incredible quantity of lovely Hair flow'd down upon his Shoulders, and not only cover'd 'em, but almost all his Body; by which they were now convinc'd, that what they at first took to be a Country Lad, was a Young Woman, and one of the most beautiful Creatures in the World. *Cardenio* was not less surpriz'd than the other two, and once more declar'd, that no Face could vie with hers but *Lucinda's*. To part her dishevel'd Tresses, she only us'd her slender Fingers, and at the same time discover'd so fine a pair of Arms, and Hands, so white and lovely, that our three admiring Gazers grew more impatient to know who she was, and mov'd forwards to accost her. At the Noise they made, the pretty Creature started; and peeping thro' her Hair, which she hastily remov'd from before her Eyes with both her Hands,

she no sooner saw three Men coming towards her, but in a
mighty Fright she snatch'd up a little Bundle that lay by her,
and fled as fast as cou'd, without so much as staying to put on
her Shoes, or do up her Hair. But alas! scarce had she gone six
Steps, when her tender Feet not being able to endure the
rough Encounter of the Stones, the poor affrighted Fair fell
on the hard Ground; so that those from whom she fled, hast'n-
ing to help her; Stay, Madam, cry'd the Curate, whoever you
be, you have no reason to fly; We have no other Design but to
do you service. With that, approaching her, he took her by
the Hand, and perceiving she was so disorder'd with Fear and
Confusion, that she cou'd not answer a Word; he strove to
compose her Mind with kind Expressions. Be not afraid,
Madam, continu'd he; tho' your Hair has betray'd what your
Disguise conceal'd from us, we are but the more dispos'd to
assist you, and do you all manner of service. Then pray tell us
how we may best do it. I imagine it was no slight Occasion
that made you obscure your singular Beauty under so unworthy a Disguise, and venture into this Desart, where it was
the greatest Chance in the World that e'er you met with us.
However, we hope it is not impossible to find a Remedy for
your Misfortunes; since there are none which Reason and
Time will not at last surmount: And therefore, Madam, if you
have not absolutely renounc'd all human Comfort, I beseech
you tell us the Cause of your Affliction, and assure your self we
do not ask this out of meer Curiosity, but a real Desire to serve
you, and either to condole or asswage your Grief.

While the Curate endeavour'd thus to remove the trembling Fair-one's Apprehension, she stood amaz'd, staring,
without speaking a Word, sometimes upon one, sometimes
upon another, like one scarce well awake, or like an ignorant
Clown who happens to see some strange Sight. But at last
the Curate having given her time to recollect herself, and
persisting in his earnest and civil Intreaties, she fetch'd a
deep Sigh, and then unclosing her Lips, broke Silence in this
manner. Since this Desart has not been able to conceal me,
and my Hair has betray'd me, 'twould be needless now for
me to dissemble with you; and since you desire to hear the
Story of my Misfortunes, I cannot in Civility deny you, after

all the obliging Offers you have been pleas'd to make me: But yet, Gentlemen, I am much affraid, what I have to say will but make you sad, and afford you little Satisfaction; for you will find my Disasters are not to be remedy'd. There's one thing that troubles me yet more; it shocks my Nature to think I must be forc'd to reveal to you some Secrets which I had design'd to have bury'd in my Grave: But yet considering the Garb and the Place you've found me in, I fancy 'twill be better for me to tell you all than to give you occasion to doubt of my past Conduct and my present Designs by an affected Reserv-edness. The disguis'd Lady having made this Answer, with a modest Blush and extraordinary Discretion, the Curate and his Company, who now admir'd her the more for her Sense, renew'd their kind Offers and pressing Solicitations; and then they modestly let her retire a Moment to some Distance to put herself in decent Order. Which done, she return'd, and being all seated on the Grass, after she had us'd no small Violence to smother her Tears, she thus began her Story.

I was born in a certain Town of *Andaluzia*, from which a Duke takes his Title, that makes him a Grandee of *Spain*. This Duke has two Sons, the Eldest Heir to his Estate and as it may be presum'd, of his Virtues; the Youngest Heir to no-thing I know of, but the Treachery of *Vellido*,* and the De-ceitfulness of *Galalon*.† My Father, who is one of his Vassals, is but of low degree; but so very rich, that had Fortune equall'd his Birth to his Estate, he cou'd have wanted nothing more, and I, perhaps, had never been so miserable; for I verily believe, my not being of noble Blood is the chief Occasion of my Ruin. True it is my Parents are not so meanly born, as to have any cause to be asham'd of their Original, nor so high as to alter the Opinion I have that my Misfortune proceeds from their Lowness. 'Tis true, they have been Farmers from Father to Son, yet without any Mixture or Stain of infamous or scandalous Blood. They are old rusty‡ Christians (as we call our true primitive *Spaniards*) and the Antiquity of their

* *Who murder'd* Sancho *King of* Castile, *as he was easing himself, at the Siege of* Zamora.   † *Who betray'd the French Army at* Roncesvalles.
‡ Ranciosos *in the Original: a Metaphor taken from rusty* Bacon, *yellow and mouldy, as it were with Age. 'Tis a Farmer's Daughter speaks this.*

Family, together with their large Possessions, and the Port they live in, raises 'em much above their Profession, and has by little and little almost universally gain'd them the Name of Gentlemen, setting 'em, in a Manner, equal to many such in the World's Esteem. As I am their only Child, they ever lov'd me with all the Tenderness of indulgent Parents; and their great Affection made 'em esteem themselves happier in their Daughter, than in the peaceable Enjoyment of their large Estate. Now as it was my good Fortune to be possessed of their Love, they were pleas'd to trust me with their Substance. The whole House and Estate was left to my Management, and I took such care not to abuse the Trust repos'd in me, that I never forfeited their good Opinion of my Discretion. The time I had to spare from the Care of the Family, I commonly employ'd in the usual Exercises of young Women, sometimes making Bone-lace, or at my Needle, and now and then reading some good Book, or playing on the Harp; having experienc'd that Musick was very proper to recreate the wearied Mind: And this was the innocent Life I led. I have not descended to these Particulars out of vain Ostentation, but meerly that when I come to relate my Misfortunes, you may observe I do not owe 'em to my ill Conduct. While I thus liv'd the Life of a Nun, unseen, as I thought, by any Body but our own Family, and never leaving the House but to go to Church, which was commonly betimes in the Morning, and always with my Mother, and so close hid in a Veil that I cou'd scarce find my way; notwithstanding all the Care that was taken to keep me from being seen, 'twas unhappily rumour'd abroad that I was handsome, and to my eternal Disquiet, Love intruded into my peaceful Retirement. Don *Ferdinand*, second Son to the Duke I've mention'd, had a Sight of me —— Scarce had *Cardenio* heard Don *Ferdinand* nam'd, but he chang'd Colour, and betray'd such a Disorder of Body and Mind, that the Curate and the Barber were afraid he wou'd have fallen into one of those frantick Fits that often us'd to take him; but by good Fortune it did not come to that, and he only set himself to look stedfastly on the Country Maid, presently guessing who she was; while She continu'd her Story, without taking any notice of the Alteration of his Countenance.

No sooner had he seen me, said she, but, as he since told me, he felt in his Breast that violent Passion of which he afterwards gave me so many Proofs. But not to tire you with a needless Relation of every Particular, I will pass over all the Means he us'd to inform me of his Love: He purchas'd the Good-will of all our Servants with private Gifts: He made my Father a thousand kind Offers of Service: Every Day seem'd a Day of Rejoicing in our Neighbourhood, every Evening usher'd in some Serenade, and the continual Musick was even a Disturbance in the Night. He got an infinite number of Love-Letters transmitted to me, I don't know by what means, every one full of the tenderest Expressions, Promises, Vows, and Protestations. But all this assiduous Courtship was so far from inclining my Heart to a kind Return, that it rather mov'd my Indignation; insomuch that I look'd upon Don *Ferdinand* as my greatest Enemy, and one wholly bent on my Ruin: Not but that I was well enough pleas'd with his Gallantry, and took a secret Delight in seeing myself thus courted by a Person of his Quality. Such Demonstrations of Love are never altogether displeasing to Women, and the most Disdainful, in spight of all their Coyness, reserve a little Complaisance in their Hearts for their Admirers. But the Disproportion between our Qualities was too great to suffer me to entertain any reasonable Hopes, and his Gallantry too singular not to offend me. Besides, my Father, who soon made a right Construction of Don *Ferdinand's* Pretensions, with his prudent Admonitions concur'd with the Sense I ever had of my Honour, and banish'd from my Mind all favourable Thoughts of his Addresses. However, like a kind Parent, perceiving I was somewhat uneasy, and imagining the flattering Prospect of so advantageous a Match might still amuse me, he told me one Day he reposed the utmost trust in my Virtue, esteeming it the strongest Obstacle he could oppose to Don *Ferdinand's* dishonourable Designs; yet if I wou'd marry, to rid me at once of his unjust Pursuit, and prevent the ruin of my Reputation, I shou'd have liberty to make my own choice of a suitable Match, either in our own Town or the Neighbourhood; and that he wou'd do for me whatever cou'd be expected from a loving Father. I humbly thank'd him for his Kindness, and told him, that as I had never yet had any

Thoughts of Marriage, I wou'd try to rid my self of Don *Ferdinand* some other way. Accordingly I resolv'd to shun him with so much Precaution, that he shou'd never have the Opportunity to speak to me: But all my Reservedness, far from tiring out his Passion, strengthened it the more. In short, Don *Ferdinand*, either hearing or suspecting I was to be marry'd, thought of a Contrivance to cross a Design that was likely to cut off all his Hopes. One Night therefore, when I was in my Chamber, no Body with me but my Maid, and the Door double lock'd and bolted, that I might be secur'd against the Attempts of Don *Ferdinand*, whom I took to be a Man who wou'd stick at nothing to compass his Designs, unexpectedly I saw him just before me; which amazing Sight so suppriz'd me, that I was struck dumb, and fainted away with Fear. So I had not power to call for Help, nor do I believe he wou'd have given me time to have done it, had I attempted it; for he presently ran to me, and taking me in his Arms, while I was sinking with the Fright, he spoke to me in such endearing Terms, and with so much Address, and pretended Tenderness and Sincerity, that I did not dare to cry out when I came to my self. His Sighs, and yet more his Tears, seem'd to me undeniable Proofs of his vow'd Integrity; and I being but young, bred up in perpetual Retirement, from all Society but my virtuous Parents, and unexperienc'd in those Affairs, in which even the most knowing are apt to be mistaken, my Reluctancy abated by Degrees, and I began to have some Sense of Compassion, yet none but what was consistent with my Honour. However, when I was pretty well recover'd from my first Fright, my former Resolution return'd; and then, with more Courage then I thought I shou'd have had, My Lord, said I, if at the same time that you offer me your Love, and give me such strange Demonstrations of it, you wou'd also offer me Poison, and Leave to take my Choice, I wou'd soon resolve which to accept, and convince you by my Death, that my Honour is dearer to me than my Life. To be plain, I can have no good Opinion of a Presumption that endangers my Reputation; and unless you leave me this Moment, I will so effectually make you know how much you are mistaken in me, that if you have but the least sense of Honour left, you'll repent the driving me to that Extremity

as long as you live. I was born your Vassal, but not your Slave;
nor does the Greatness of your Birth privilege you to injure
your Inferiors, or exact from me more than the Duties which
all Vassals pay; That excepted, I do not esteem my self less
in my low Degree, than you have Reason to value your self
in your high Rank. Do not then think to awe or dazzle me
with your Grandeur, or fright or force me into a base Compliance; I am not to be tempted with Titles, Pomp, and Equipage; nor weak enough to be moved with vain Sighs and false
Tears. In short, my Will is wholly at my Father's Disposal,
and I will not entertain any Man as a Lover, but by his
Appointment. Therefore, my Lord, if you wou'd have me
believe you so sincerely love me, give over your vain and injurious Pursuit; suffer me peaceably to enjoy the Benefits of
Life in the free Possession of my Honour, the Loss of which
for ever imbitters all Life's Sweets; and since you cannot be
my Husband, do not expect from me that Affection which
I cannot pay to any other. What do you mean, charming
Dorothea? cry'd the perfidious Lord. Cannot I be yours by
the sacred Title of Husband? Who can hinder me, if you'll
but consent to bless me on those Terms? Too happy if I have
no other Obstacle to surmount. I am yours this Moment,
beautiful *Dorothea*; see, I give you here my Hand to be yours,
and yours alone for ever: And let all-seeing Heaven, and this
Holy Image here on your Oratory, witness the solemn Truth.

Cardenio hearing her call herself *Dorothea*, was now fully
satisfied she was the Person whom he took her to be: However, he would not interrupt her Story, being impatient to
hear the End of it; only addressing himself to her, Is then
your Name *Dorothea*, Madam, cry'd he? I have heard of a
Lady of that Name, whose Misfortunes have a great Resemblance with yours. But proceed I beseech you, and when you
have done, I may perhaps surprize you with an Account of
things that have some Affinity with those you relate. With
that *Dorothea* made a stop to study *Cardenio's* Face, and his
wretched Attire; and then earnestly desir'd him, if he knew
any thing that concern'd her, to let her know it presently;
telling him, that all the Happiness she had left, was only the
Courage to bear with Resignation all the Disasters that might

befall her, well assur'd that no new one could make her more unfortunate than she was already. Truly, Madam, reply'd *Cardenio*, I would tell you all I know, were I sure my Conjectures were true; but so far as I may judge by what I have heard hitherto, I don't think it material to tell it you yet, and I shall find a more proper time to do it. Then *Dorothea* resuming her Discourse, Don *Ferdinand*, said she, repeated his Vows of Marriage in the most serious manner; and giving me his Hand, plighted me his Faith with the most binding Words, and sacred Oaths. But before I would let him engage himself thus, I advis'd him to have a care how he suffer'd an unruly Passion to get the Ascendant over his Reason, to the endangering of his future Happiness. My Lord, said I, let not a few transitory and imaginary Charms, which cou'd never excuse such an Excess of Love, hurry you to your Ruin: Spare your noble Father the Shame and Displeasure of seeing you marry'd to a Person so much below your Birth; and do not rashly do a thing of which you may repent, and that may make my Life uncomfortable. I added several other Reasons to dissuade him from that hasty Match, but they were all unregarded. Don *Ferdinand*, deaf to every thing but to his Desires, engag'd and bound himself like an inconsiderate Lover, who sacrifices all things to his Passion, or rather like a Cheat, who does not value a Breach of Vows. When I saw him so obstinate, I began to consider what I had to do. I am not the first, thought I to my self, whom Marriage has rais'd to unhop'd for Greatness, and whose Beauty alone has supply'd her want of Birth and Merit: Thousands besides Don *Ferdinand* have married meerly for Love, without any regard to the Inequality of Wealth or Birth. The Opportunity was fair and tempting; and as Fortune is not always favourable, I thought it an imprudent thing to let it slip. Thought I to myself, while she kindly offers me a Husband who assures me of an inviolable Affection, why should I by an unreasonable Denial make myself an Enemy of such a Friend? and then there was one thing more; I apprehended it would be dangerous to drive him to despair by an ill-tim'd Refusal: Nor could I think myself safe alone in his Hands, lest he should resolve to satisfy his Passion by Force; which done, he

might think himself free from performing a Promise which
I wou'd not accept, and then I should be left without either
Honour or an Excuse; for it would be no easy matter to perswade my Father, and the censorious World, that this Nobleman was admitted into my Chamber without my Consent.
All these Reasons, which in a Moment offer'd themselves in
my Mind, shook my former Resolves; and Don *Ferdinand's*
Sighs, his Tears, his Vows, and the sacred Witnesses by
which he swore, together with his graceful Mien, his extraordinary Accomplishments, and the Love which I fancy'd I
read in all his Actions, help'd to bring on my Ruin, as I believe they would have prevail'd with any one's Heart as free
and as well guarded as was mine. Then I call'd my Maid to
be Witness of Don *Ferdinand's* Vows and sacred Engagements, which he reiterated to me, and confirm'd with new
Oaths and solemn Promises; he call'd again on Heaven, and
on many particular Saints, to witness his Sincerity, wishing
a thousand Curses might fall on him, in case he ever violated
his Word. Again he sigh'd, again he wept, and mov'd me more
and more with fresh Marks of Affection; and the treacherous
Maid having left the Room, the perfidious Lord presuming
on my Weakness, compleated his pernicious Design. The Day
which succeeded that unhappy Night, had not yet begun to
dawn, when Don *Ferdinand*, impatient to be gone, made all
the haste he cou'd to leave me. For after the Gratifications
of Brutish Appetite are past, the greatest Pleasure then is, to
get rid of that which entertain'd it. He told me, though not
with so great a shew of Affection, nor so warmly as before,
that I might rely on his Honour and on the Sincerity of his Vows
and Promises; and as a further Pledge, he pull'd off a Ring of
great Value from his Finger, and put it upon mine. In short,
he went away; and my Maid, who, as she confess'd it to me,
had let him in privately, took care to let him out into the
street by break of day, while I remain'd so strangely concern'd
at the Thoughts of all these Passages, that I cannot well tell
whether I was sorry or pleased. I was in a manner quite distracted, and either forgot or had not the Heart to chide my
Maid for her Treachery, not knowing yet whether she had
done me Good or Harm. I had told Don *Ferdinand* before he

went, that seeing I was now his own, he might make use of
the same means to come again to see me, till he found it convenient to do me the Honour of owning me publickly for his Wife:
But he came to me only the next Night, and from that time I
never cou'd see him more, neither at Church nor in the Street,
though for a whole Month together I tir'd myself endeavouring to find him out; being credibly inform'd he was still near
us, and went a Hunting almost every Day. I leave you to think
with what Uneasiness I pass'd those tedious Hours, when I
perceiv'd his Neglect, and had reason to suspect his Breach
of Faith. So unexpected a Slight which I look'd upon as the
most sensible Affliction that cou'd befal me, had like to have
quite overwhelm'd me. Then it was that I found my Maid
had betray'd me; I broke out into severe Complaints of her
Presumption, which I had smother'd till that time. I exclaim'd
against Don *Ferdinand*, and exhausted my Sighs and Tears
without asswaging my Sorrow. What was worse, I found my
self oblig'd to set a Guard upon my very Looks, for fear my
Father and Mother shou'd inquire into the Cause of my Discontent, and so occasion my being guilty of shameful Lies and Evasions to conceal my more shameful Disaster. But at last I perceiv'd 'twas in vain to dissemble, and I gave a loose to my Resentments; for I could no longer hold when I heard that Don
Ferdinand was marry'd in a neighbouring Town to a young
Lady of rich and noble Parentage, and extreamly handsome,
whose Name is *Lucinda*. *Cardenio* hearing *Lucinda* nam'd,
felt his former Disorder, but by good Fortune it was not so
violent as it us'd to be, and he only shrug'd up his Shoulders,
bit his Lips, knit his Brows, and a little while after let fall
a shower of Tears, which did not hinder *Dorothea* from going
on. This News, continued she, instead of freezing up my
Blood with Grief and Astonishment, fill'd me with burning
Rage. Despair took possession of my Soul, and in the Transports of my Fury I was ready to run raving thro' the Streets,
and publish Don *Ferdinand's* Disloyalty, tho' at the Expence
of my Reputation. I don't know whether a remainder of
Reason stop't these violent Motions, but I found my self
mightily eas'd as soon as I had pitch'd upon a Design that
presently came into my Head. I discover'd the Cause of my

Grief to a young Country Fellow that serv'd my Father, and desir'd him to lend me a Suit of Man's Apparel, and to go along with me to the Town where I heard Don *Ferdinand* was. The Fellow us'd the best Arguments he had to hinder me from so strange an Undertaking; but finding I was inflexible in my Resolution, he assur'd me he was ready to serve me. Thereupon I put on this Habit which you see, and taking with me some of my own Cloaths, together with some Gold and Jewels, not knowing but I might have occasion for 'em, I set out that very Night, attended with that Servant and many anxious Thoughts, without so much as acquainting my Maid with my Design. To tell you the truth, I did not well know my self what I went about; for as there could be no Remedy, Don *Ferdinand* being actually marry'd to another, What could I hope to get by seeing him, unless it were the wretched Satisfaction of upbraiding him with his Infidelity? In two Days and a half we got to the Town; where the first thing I did was to enquire where *Lucinda's* Father liv'd. That single Question produc'd a great deal more than I desir'd to hear; for the first Man I address'd my self to, shew'd me the House, and inform'd me of all that happen'd at *Lucinda's* Marriage; which it seems was grown so publick, that it was the Talk of the whole Town. He told me how *Lucinda* swoon'd away as soon as she had answer'd the Priest, that she was contented to be Don *Ferdinand's* Wife; and how after he had approach'd to open her Stays to give her more room to breathe, he found a Letter under her own Hand, wherein she declar'd she could not be Don *Ferdinand's* Wife, because she was already contracted to a considerable Gentleman of the same Town, whose Name was *Cardenio*; and that she had only consented to that Marriage in obedience to her Father. He also told me, that it appear'd by the Letter, and a Dagger which was found about her, that she design'd to have kill'd herself after the Ceremony was over; and that Don *Ferdinand*, enrag'd to see himself thus deluded, would have kill'd her himself with that very Dagger, had he not been prevented by those that were present. He added, 'twas reported, that upon this Don *Ferdinand* immediately left the Town: and that *Lucinda* did not come to herself till the next Day; and then she told her

271

Parents, that she was really *Cardenio's* Wife, and that he and she were contracted before she had seen Don *Ferdinand*. I heard also that this *Cardenio* was present at the Wedding; and that as soon as he saw her married, which was a Thing he never could have believed, he left the Town in despair, leaving a Letter behind him full of Complaints of *Lucinda's* Breach of Faith, and to inform his Friends of his Resolution to go to some place where they should never hear of him more. This was all the Discourse of the Town when I came thither, and soon after we heard that *Lucinda* also was missing, and that her Father and Mother were grieving almost to Distraction, not being able to learn what was become of her. For my part, this News revived my Hopes, having Reason to be pleas'd to find Don *Ferdinand* unmarry'd, I flatter'd my self that Heaven had perhaps prevented his second Marriage to make him sensible of his violating the first, and to touch his Conscience, in order to his acquitting himself of his Duty like a Christian, and a Man of Honour. So I strove to beguile my Cares with an imaginary Prospect of a far distant Change of Fortune, amusing my self with vain Hopes that I might not sink under the Load of Affliction, but prolong Life; tho' this was only a lengthening of my Sorrows, since I have now but the more Reason to wish to be eas'd of the Trouble of living. But while I staid in that Town, not knowing what I had best to do, seeing I cou'd not find Don *Ferdinand*, I heard a Crier publickly describe my Person, my Cloaths, and my Age, in the open Street, promising a considerable Reward to any that cou'd bring Tidings of *Dorothea*. I also heard that 'twas rumour'd I was run away from my Father's House with the Servant who attended me; and *that* Report touch'd my Soul as much as Don *Ferdinand's* Perfidiousness; for thus I saw my Reputation wholly lost, and that too for a Subject so base and so unworthy of my nobler Thoughts. Thereupon I made all the haste I could to get out of the Town with my Servant, who even then, to my thinking, began by some Tokens to betray a faultering in the Fidelity he had promised me. Dreading to be discover'd, we reach'd the most desart part of this Mountain that Night: But, as 'tis a common saying, that Misfortunes seldom come alone, and the End of one Disaster is often the Beginning of a greater, I was no sooner got to that Place, where I thought my self safe, but the Fellow, whom I had hitherto found to be modest and respectful, now rather incited by his own Villany, than my Beauty, and the Opportunity which that Place offered, than by any Thing else, had the Impudence to talk to me of Love; and seeing I answer'd him with Anger and Contempt, he would no longer lose Time in clownish Courtship, but resolv'd to use Violence to compass his wicked Design. But just Heaven, which seldom or never fails to succour just Designs, so assisted mine, and his brutish Passion so blinded him, that not perceiving he was on the Brink of a steep Rock, I easily push'd him down; and then without looking to see what was become of him, and with more Nimbleness than cou'd be expected from my Surprize and Weariness, I ran into the thickest part of the Desart to secure my self. The next Day I met a Country-man, who took me to his House amidst these Mountains, and employed me ever since in the nature of his Shepherd. There I have continu'd some Months, making it my Business to be as much as possible in the Fields, the better to conceal my Sex: But notwithstanding all my Care and Industry, he at last discover'd I was a Woman; which made him presume to importune me with beastly Offers: So that Fortune not favouring me with the former Opportunity of freeing my self, I left his House, and chose to seek a Sanctuary among these Woods and Rocks, there with Sighs and Tears to beseech Heaven to pity me, and to direct and relieve me in this forlorn Condition; or at least to put an end to my miserable Life, and bury in this Desart the very Memory of an unhappy Creature, who, more thro' ill Fortune then ill Intent, has given the idle World occasion to be too busy with her Fame.

II: AN ACCOUNT OF THE BEAUTIFUL DOROTHEA'S DISCRETION, WITH OTHER PLEASANT PASSAGES

THIS, Gentlemen, continued *Dorothea*, is the true Story of my tragical Adventures; and now be you Judges whether I had Reason to make the Complaint you overheard, and whether so unfortunate and hopeless a Creature be in a Condition to admit of Comfort. I have only one Favour to beg of you; be pleas'd to direct me to some Place where I may pass the rest of my Life secure from the Search and Inquiry of my Parents; not but their former Affection is a sufficient Warrant for my kind Reception, could the Sense I have of the Thoughts they must have of my past Conduct permit me to return to 'em; but when I think they must believe me guilty, and can now have nothing but my bare Word to assure them of my Innocence, I can never resolve to stand their Sight. Here *Dorothea* stopt, and the Blushes that over-spread her Cheeks were certain Signs of the Discomposure of her Thoughts, and the unfeigned Modesty of her Soul. Those who had heard her Story were deeply mov'd with Compassion for her hard Fate, and the Curate would not delay any longer to give her some charitable Comfort and Advice. But scarce had he begun to speak, when *Cardenio*, addressing himself to her, interrupted him; How Madam, said he, taking her by the Hand, are you then the beautiful *Dorothea*, the only Daughter of the rich *Cleonardo*? *Dorothea* was strangely surprized to hear her Father nam'd, and by one in so tatter'd a Garb. And pray who are you, Friend,* said she to him, that know so well my Father's Name? for I think I did not mention it once throughout the whole Relation of my Afflictions. I am *Cardenio*, reply'd the other, that unfortunate Person, whom *Lucinda*, as you told us, declar'd to be her Husband: I am that miserable *Cardenio*, whom the Perfidiousness of the Man who has reduc'd you to this deplorable Condition, has also brought to this wretched State, to Rags, to Nakedness, to Despair, nay to Madness itself, and all Hardships and Want of human Comforts; only enjoying the

---

* Y quien sois vos, hermano, *i.e.* and pray who are you, Brother. *It is the Spanish way of Speaking. We say*, Friend; *the French the same*, Mon Amy.

Privilege of Reason by short Intervals, to feel and bemoan my Miseries the more. I am the Man, fair *Dorothea*, who was the unhappy Eye-witness of Don *Ferdinand's* unjust Nuptials, and who heard my *Lucinda* give her Consent to be his Wife; that heartless Wretch, who, unable to bear so strange a Disappointment, lost in Amazement and Trouble, flung out of the House, without staying to know what would follow her Trance, and what the Paper that was taken out of her Bosom would produce. I abandon'd my self to Despair, and having left a Letter with a Person whom I charg'd to deliver it into *Lucinda's* own Hands, I hasten'd to hide myself from the World in this Desart, resolv'd to end there a Life, which from that Moment I had abhorr'd as my greatest Enemy. But Fortune has preserv'd me, I see, that I may venture it upon a better Cause; for from what you have told us now, which I have no Reason to doubt, I am embolden'd to hope that Providence may yet reserve us both to a better Fate than we durst have expected; Heaven will restore you Don *Ferdinand*, who cannot be *Lucinda's*, and to me *Lucinda*, who cannot be Don *Ferdinand's*. For my part, tho' my Interests were not link'd with yours, as they are, I have so deep a Sense of your Misfortunes, that I would expose my self to any Dangers to see you righted by Don *Ferdinand*: And here, on the Word of a Gentleman, and a Christian, I vów and promise not to forsake you till he has done you Justice, and to oblige him to do it at the Hazard of my Life, should Reason and Generosity prove ineffectual to force him to be blest with you. *Dorothea*, ravish'd with Joy, and not knowing how to express a due Sense of *Cardenio's* obliging Offers, would have thrown herself at his Feet, had he not civilly hinder'd it. At the same Time the Curate discreetly speaking for 'em both, highly applauded *Cardenio* for his generous Resolution, and comforted *Dorothea*. He also very heartily invited 'em to his House, where they might furnish themselves with Necessaries, and consult together how to find out Don *Ferdinand*, and bring *Dorothea* home to her Father; which kind Offer they thankfully accepted. Then the Barber, who had been silent all this while, put in for a Share, and handsomly assur'd them, he would be very ready to do 'em all the Service that might lie in his

Power. After these Civilities, he acquainted 'em with the De-sign that had brought the Curate and him to that Place; and gave 'em an Account of Don *Quixote's* strange kind of Mad-ness, and of their staying there for his Squire. *Cardenio* hear-ing him mentioned, remember'd something of the Scuffle he had with them both, but only as if it had been a Dream; so that tho' he told the Company of it, he could not let them know the Occasion. By this Time they heard some Body call, and by the Voice they knew it was *Sancho Panza*, who not finding 'em where he had left 'em, tore his very Lungs with hollow-ing. With that they all went to meet him; which done, they ask'd him what was become of Don *Quixote*? Alas, answer'd *Sancho*, I left him yonder, in an ill Plight: I found him in his Shirt, lean, pale, and almost starv'd, sighing and whining for his Lady *Dulcinea*. I told him, how that she'd have him come to her presently to *Toboso*, where she look'd for him out of Hand; yet for all this he wou'd not budge a Foot, but e'en told me he was resolv'd he wou'd ne'er set Eyes on her sweet Face again, till he had done some Feats that might make him worthy of her Goodness: So that, added *Sancho*, if he leads this Life any longer, I fear me my poor Master is never like to be an Emperor, as he is bound in Honour to be, nay not so much as an Archbishop, which is the least Thing he can come off with; therefore, good Sir, see and get him away by all Means I be-seech you. The Curate bid him be of good Cheer, for they would take care to make him leave that Place whether he would or not; and then turning to *Cardenio* and *Dorothea*, he informed 'em of the Design which he and the Barber had laid in order to his Cure, or at least to get him home to his House. *Dorothea*, whose Mind was much eas'd with the Prospect of better Fortune, kindly undertook to act the distressed Lady herself, which she said she thought wou'd become her better than the Barber, having a Dress very proper for that Purpose; besides she had read many Books of Chivalry, and knew how the distress'd Ladies us'd to express themselves when they came to beg some Knight-Errant's Assistance. This is obliging, Madam, said the Curate, and we want nothing more: So let's to work as fast as we can; we may now hope to succeed, since you thus happily facilitate the Design. Presently *Dorothea* took out of her Bundle a Petticoat of very rich Stuff, and a Gown of very fine green Silk; also a Necklace, and several other Jewels out of a Box; and with these in an Instant she so adorned herself, and appear'd so beautiful and glorious, that they all stood in Admiration that Don *Ferdinand* should be so injudicious to slight so accomplish'd a Beauty. But he that admir'd her most was *Sancho Panza*; for he thought he had ne'er set Eyes on so fine a Creature, and perhaps he thought right: Which made him earnestly ask the Curate, who that fine Dame was, and what Wind had blown her thither among the Woods and Rocks? Who that fine Lady, *Sancho*? answer'd the Curate; she's the only Heiress in a direct Line to the vast Kingdom of *Micomicon*: Mov'd by the Fame of your Master's great Exploits, that spreads it self over all *Guinea*, she comes to seek him out, and beg a Boon of him; that is, to redress a Wrong which a wicked Giant has done her. Why that's well, quoth *Sancho*: a happy Seeking and a happy Finding. Now if my Master be but so lucky as to right that Wrong, by killing that Son of a Whore of a Giant you tell me of, I'm a made Man: Yes he will kill him, that he will, if he can but come at him, and he ben't a Hobgoblin; for my Master can do no good with Hobgoblins. But Mr Curate, an't please you, I have a Favour to ask of you, I beseech you put my Master out of Conceit with all Archbishopricks, for that's what I dread; and therefore to rid me of my Fears, put it into his Head to clap up a Match with this same Princess; for by that Means 'twill be past his Power to make himself Arch-bishop, and he'll come to be Emperor, and I a great Man as sure as a Gun. I have thought well of the Matter, and I find it is not at all fitting he should be an Archbishop for my Good; for what should I get by it? I an't fit for Church Preferment, I am a married Man; and now for me to go to trouble my Head with getting a Licence to hold Church-Livings, 'twould be an endless Piece of Business: Therefore 'twill be better for him to marry out of hand this same Princess, whose Name I can't tell, for I never heard it. They call her the Princess *Micomicona*, said the Curate; for her Kingdom being call'd *Micomicon*, 'tis a clear Case she must be call'd so. Like enough, quoth *Sancho*; for I have known several Men in my Time go by the

Names of the Places where they were born, as *Pedro de Alcala*, *Juan de Ubeda*, *Diego de Valladolid*; and mayhap the like is done in *Guinea*, and the Queens go by the Name of their Kingdoms. 'Tis well observ'd, reply'd the Curate: As for the Match, I'll promote it to the utmost of my Power. *Sancho* was heartily pleas'd with this Promise; and on the other Side, the Curate was amaz'd to find the poor Fellow so strangely infected with his Master's mad Notions, as to rely on his becoming an Emperor. By this Time *Dorothea* being mounted on the Curate's Mule, and the Barber having clapp'd on his Ox-tail Beard, nothing remain'd but to order *Sancho* to shew 'em the Way, and to renew their Admonitions to him, lest he shou'd seem to know 'em, and to spoil the Plot, which if he did, they told him 'twould be the Ruin of all his Hopes and his Master's Empire. As for *Cardenio*, he did not think fit to go with 'em, having no Business there; besides, he could not tell but that Don *Quixote* might remember their late Fray. The Curate likewise not thinking his Presence necessary, resolv'd to stay to keep *Cardenio* Company; so after he had once more given *Dorothea* her Cue, she and the Barber went before with *Sancho*, while the two others followed on Foot at a Distance.

Thus they went on for about three Quarters of a League, and then among the Rocks they spy'd Don *Quixote*, who had by this Time put on his Clothes, tho' not his Armour. Immediately *Dorothea*, understanding he was the Person, whipp'd her Palfry, and when she drew near Don *Quixote*, her Squire alighted and took her from her Saddle. When she was upon her Feet, she gracefully advanc'd towards the Knight, and, with her Squire, falling on her Knees before him, in spite of his Endeavours to hinder her; Thrice valorous and invincible Knight, said she, never will I rise from this Place, till your Generosity has granted me a Boon, which shall redound to your Honour, and the Relief of the most disconsolate and most injur'd Damsel that the Sun ever saw: And indeed if your Valour and the Strength of your formidable Arm be answerable to the Extent of your immortal Renown, you are bound by the Laws of Honour, and the Knighthood which you profess, to succour a distress'd Princess, who, led by the resounding Fame of your marvellous and redoubted

Feats of Arms, comes from the remotest Regions, to implore your Protection. I cannot, said Don *Quixote*, make you any Answer, most beautiful Lady, nor will I hear a Word more, unless you vouchsafe to rise. Pardon me, noble Knight, reply'd the petitioning Damsel; my Knees shall first be rooted here, unless you will courteously condescend to grant me the Boon which I humbly request. I grant it then, Lady, said Don *Quixote*, provided it be nothing to the Disservice of my King, my Country, and that Beauty who keeps the Key of my Heart and Liberty. It shall not tend to the Prejudice or Detriment of any of these, cry'd the Lady. With that *Sancho* closing up to his Master, and whispering him in the Ear, Grant it, Sir, quoth he, grant it, I tell ye; 'tis but a Trifle next to nothing, only to kill a great Looby of a Giant; and she that asks this, is the high and mighty Princess *Micomicona*, Queen of the huge Kingdom of *Micomicon* in *Ethiopia*. Let her be what she will, reply'd Don *Quixote*, I will discharge my Duty, and obey the Dictates of my Conscience, according to the Rules of my Profession. With that turning to the Damsel, Rise Lady, I beseech you, cry'd he; I grant you the Boon which your singular Beauty demands. Sir, said the Lady, the Boon I have to beg of your magnanimous Valour, is, that you will be pleased to go with me instantly whither I shall conduct you, and promise me not to engage in any other Adventure, till you have reveng'd me on a Traitor who usurps my Kingdom, contrary to all Laws both Human and Divine. I grant you all this, Lady, quoth Don *Quixote*; and therefore from this Moment shake off all desponding Thoughts that sit heavy upon your Mind, and study to revive your drooping Hopes; for by the Assistance of Heaven, and my strenuous Arm, you shall see yourself restor'd to your Kingdom, and seated on the Throne of your Ancestors, in spite of all the Traitors that dare oppose your Right. Let us then hasten our Performance; Delay always breeds Danger; and to protract a great Design is often to ruin it. The thankful Princess, to speak her grateful Sense of his Generosity, strove to kiss the Knight's Hand; however, he who was in every thing the most gallant and courteous of all Knights, would, by no Means, admit of such a Submission; but having gently raised her up,

279

he embrac'd her with an awful Grace and Civility, and then call'd to *Sancho* for his Arms. *Sancho* went immediately, and having fetch'd 'em from a Tree, where they hung like Trophies, arm'd his Master in a Moment. And now the Champion being compleatly accoutred, Come on, said he, let us go and vindicate the Rights of this dispossessed Princess. The Barber was all this while upon his Knees, and had enough to do to keep himself from laughing, and his Beard from falling, which, if it had dropp'd off, as it threatn'd, wou'd have betray'd his Face and their whole Plot at once. But being reliev'd by Don *Quixote's* Haste to put on his Armour, he rose up, and taking the Princess by the Hand, they both together set her upon her Mule. Then the Knight mounted his *Rozinante*, and the Barber got on his Beast. Only poor *Sancho* was forced to foot it, which made him fetch many a heavy Sigh for the Loss of his dear Dapple: However, he bore his Crosses patiently, seeing his Master in so fair a way of being next door to an Emperor; for he did not question but he would marry that Princess, and so be, at least, King of *Micomicon*. But yet it griev'd him, to think his Master's Dominions were to be in the Land of the Negroes, and that, consequently, the People, over whom he was to be Governor, were all to be black. But he presently bethought himself of a good Remedy for that: What care I, quoth he, tho' they be Blacks? Best of all; 'tis but loading a Ship with 'em, and having 'em into *Spain*, where I shall find Chapmen enow to take 'em off my Hands, and pay me ready Money for 'em; and so I'll raise a good round Sum, and buy me a Title or an Office to live upon frank and easy all the Days of my Life. Hang him that has no Shifts, say I; 'tis a sorry Goose that will not baste herself. Why what if I am not so Book-learn'd as other Folks, sure I've a Headpiece good enough to know how to sell thirty or ten thousand Slaves in the turn of a Hand.* Let 'em e'en go higgledy-piggledy, little and great. What tho' they be as black as the Devil in Hell, let me alone to turn 'em into white and yellow Boys: I think I know how to lick my own Fingers. Big with these Imaginations, *Sancho* trudg'd along so pleas'd

* *Literally*, While one may say, take away those Straws; en quitame alla essas pajas, *i.e. in a Moment.*

and light-hearted, that he forgot his Pain of travelling afoot. *Cardenio* and the Curate had beheld the pleasant Scene thro' the Bushes, and were at a loss what they should do to join Companies. But the Curate, who had a contriving Head, at last bethought himself of an Expedient; and pulling out a Pair of Scissars, which he us'd to carry in his Pocket, he snip'd off *Cardenio's* Beard in a Trice; and having pull'd off his black Cloak and a sad-colour'd Riding-Coat which he had on, he equip'd *Cardenio* with 'em, while he himself remained in his Doublet and Breeches. In which new Garb *Cardenio* was so strangely alter'd, that he wou'd not have known himself in a Looking-Glass. This done, they made to the High-way, and there stay'd till Don *Quixote* and his Company were got clear of the Rocks and bad ways, which did not permit Horsemen to go so fast as those on foot. When they came near, the Curate look'd very earnestly upon Don *Quixote*, as one that was in a Study whether he might not know him; and then, like one that had made a Discovery, he ran towards the Knight with open Arms, crying out, Mirrour of Chivalry, my noble Countryman Don *Quixote de la Mancha*! the Cream and Flower of Gentility! the Shelter and Relief of the Afflicted, and Quintessence of Knight-Errantry! How overjoy'd am I to have found you! At the same time he embrac'd his left Leg. Don *Quixote* admiring what Adorer of his heroick Worth this should be, look'd on him earnestly; and at last calling him to mind, would have alighted to have paid him his Respects, not a little amaz'd to meet him there. But the Curate hindring him, Reverend Sir, cry'd the Knight, I beseech you let me not be so rude as to sit on Horse-back, while a Person of your Worth and Character is on foot. Sir, reply'd the Curate, you shall by no means alight: Let your Excellency be pleas'd to keep your Saddle, since thus mounted you every Day atchieve the most stupendous Feats of Arms and Adventures that were ever seen in our Age. 'Twill be Honour enough for an unworthy Priest, like me, to get up behind some of your Company, if they will permit me; and I will esteem it as great a Happiness as to be mounted upon *Pegasus*, or the *Zebra*,* or

* Zebra, Stevens *says, is a Beast in* Africk, *shap'd like a Horse, hard to be tam'd, wonderfull fleet, and will hold its course all Day.*

the *Fleet-Mare* of the famous Moor *Musaraque*, who to this Hour lies inchanted in the dreary Cavern of *Zulema*, not far distant from the great *Compluto*.* Truly, good Sir, I did not think of this, answer'd Don *Quixote*; but I suppose my Lady the Princess will be so kind as to command her Squire to lend you his Saddle, and to ride behind himself, if his Mule be us'd to carry double. I believe it will, cry'd the Princess; and my Squire, I suppose, will not stay for my Commands to offer his Saddle, for he is too courteous and well-bred to suffer an Ecclesiastical Person to go afoot, when we may help him to a Mule. Most certainly, cry'd the Barber; and with that dis-mounting, he offer'd the Curate his Saddle, which was ac-cepted without much Intreaty. By ill Fortune the Mule was a hir'd Beast, and consequently unlucky; so as the Barber was getting up behind the Curate, the resty Jade gave two or three Jerks with her hinder Legs, that had they met with Master *Nicolas's* Scull or Ribs, he would have bequeath'd his Rambling after Don *Quixote* to the Devil. However, he flung himself nimbly off, and was more afraid than hurt; but yet as he fell his Beard drop'd off, and being presently sensible of that Accident he cou'd not think of any better Shift than to clap both his Hands before his Cheeks, and cry out he had broke his Jaw-bone. Don *Quixote* was amaz'd to see such an overgrown Bush of Beard lie on the Ground without Jaws and bloodless. Bless me, cry'd he, what an amazing Miracle is this! Here's a Beard as cleverly taken off by Accident, as if a Bar-ber had mow'd it. The Curate perceiving the Danger they were in of being discover'd, hastily caught up the Beard, and running to the Barber, who lay all the while roaring and com-plaining, he pull'd his Head close to his own Breast, and then muttering certain Words, which he said were a Charm ap-propriated to the fastning on of fal'n Beards, he fix'd it on again so handsomely, that the Squire was presently then as bearded and as well as ever he was before; which rais'd Don *Quixote's* Admiration, and made him engage the Curate to teach him the Charm at his Leisure, not doubting but its Vir-tue extended further than to the fastning on of Beards, since 'twas impossible that such a one cou'd be torn off without

* *An University of* Spain, *now call'd* Alcala de Henares.

fetching away Flesh and all; and consequently such a sudden Cure might be beneficial to him upon Occasion. And now every thing being set to rights, they agreed that the Curate shou'd ride first by himself, and then the other two by turns relieving one another, sometimes riding, sometimes walking, till they came to their Inn, which was about two Leagues off. So Don *Quixote*, the Princess and the Curate being mounted, and *Cardenio*, the Barber, and *Sancho* ready to move forwards on foot, the Knight addressing himself to the distress'd Damsel, Now, Lady, said he, let me intreat your Greatness to tell me which Way we must go, to do you Service. The Curate, before she cou'd answer, thought fit to ask her a Question, that might the better enable her to make a proper Reply. Pray, Madam, said he, towards what Country is it your Pleasure to take your Progress? Is it not towards the Kingdom of *Micomicon*? I am very much mistaken if that be not the Part of the World whither you desire to go. The Lady having her Cue, presently understood the Curate, and answer'd that he was in the right. Then, said the Curate, your Way lies directly through the Village where I live, from whence we have a strait Road to *Carthagena*, where you may conveniently take Shipping; and if you have a fair Wind and good Weather, you may in something less than nine Years reach the vast Lake *Meona*, I mean the *Palus Mæotis*, which lies somewhat more than a hundred Days Journey from your Kingdom. Surely, Sir, reply'd the Lady, you are under a Mistake; for 'tis not quite two Years since I left the Place; and besides, we have had very little fair Weather all the while, and yet I am already got hither, and have so far succeeded in my Designs, as to have obtain'd the Sight of the Renowned Don *Quixote de la Mancha*, the Fame of whose Atchievements reach'd my Ears as soon as I landed in *Spain*, and mov'd me to find him out, to throw my self under his Protection, and commit the Justice of my Cause to his invincible Valour. No more, Madam, I beseech you, cry'd Don *Quixote*; spare me the Trouble of hearing my self prais'd, for I mortally hate whatever may look like Adulation; and tho' your Compliments may deserve a better Name, my Ears are too modest to be pleas'd with any such Discourse; 'tis my Study to deserve and

to avoid Applause. All I will venture to say, is, that whether I have any Valour or no, I am wholly at your Service, even at the Expence of the last Drop of my Blood; and therefore waving all these Matters till a fit Opportunity, I would gladly know of this Reverend Clergyman what brought him hither, unattended by any of his Servants, alone, and so slenderly cloath'd, for I must confess I am not a little surpriz'd to meet him in this Condition. To tell you the Reason in few Words, answer'd the Curate, you must know, that Mr *Nicholas*, our Friend and Barber, went with me to *Sevile*, to receive some Money which a Relation of mine sent me from the *Indies*, where he has been settled these many Years; neither was it a small Sum, for 'twas no less than seventy thousand Pieces of Eight, and all of due Weight, which is no common thing, you may well judge: But upon the Road hereabouts we met four Highwaymen that robb'd us of all we had, even to our very Beards, so that the poor Barber was forc'd to get him a Chin-Periwig. And for that young Gentleman whom you see there (continued he, pointing to *Cardenio*) after they had stripp'd him to his Shirt, they transfigur'd him as you see.*
Now every Body hereabouts says, that those who robb'd us were certainly a Pack of Rogues condemn'd to the Gallies, who as they were going to Punishment, were rescu'd by a single Man, not far from this Place, and that with so much Courage, that in spite of the King's Officer and his Guards, he alone set 'em all at Liberty. Certainly that Man was either mad, or as great a Rogue as any of 'em; for wou'd anyone that had a Grain of Sense or Honesty, have let loose a Company of Wolves among Sheep, Foxes among innocent Poultry, and Wasps among the Honey-Pots? he has hinder'd publick Justice from taking its Course, broke his Allegiance to his lawful Sovereign, disabled the Strength of his Gallies, rebelled against him, and oppos'd his Officers in contempt of the Law, and alarm'd the holy Brotherhood, that had lain quiet so long; nay, what is yet worse, he has endangered his Life upon Earth, and his Salvation hereafter. *Sancho* had given the Curate an Account of the Adventure of the Gally-Slaves, and this made him lay it on thick in the Relation, to try how Don

* *The Priest had clipp'd of* Cardenio's *Beard in haste.*

Quixote would bear it. The Knight chang'd Colour at every Word, not daring to confess he was the pious Knight-Errant who had deliver'd those worthy Gentlemen out of Bondage. These, said the Curate, by way of Conclusion, were the Men that reduc'd us to this Condition; and may Heaven in Mercy forgive him that freed 'em from the Punishment they so well deserv'd.

III: THE PLEASANT STRATAGEMS US'D TO FREE THE ENAMOUR'D KNIGHT FROM THE RIGOROUS PENANCE WHICH HE HAD UNDERTAKEN

SCARCE had the Curate made an end, when *Sancho* addressing himself to him, Faith and Troth, quoth he, Master Curate, he that did that rare Job was my Master his own self, and that not for want of fair Warning; for I bid him have a care what he did, and told him over and over, 'twould be a grievous Sin to put such a Gang of wicked Wretches out of Durance, and that they all went to the Gallies for their Roguery. You buffle-headed Clown, cry'd Don *Quixote*, Is it for a Knight-Errant when he meets with People laden with Chains, and under Oppression, to examine whether they are in those Circumstances for their Crimes, or only thro' Misfortune? We are only to relieve the Afflicted, to look on their Distress, and not on their Crimes. I met a Company of poor Wretches, who went along sorrowful, dejected and link'd together like the Beads of a Rosary; thereupon I did what my Conscience and my Profession oblig'd me to. And what has any Man to say to this? If any one dares say otherwise, saving this reverend Clergyman's Presence and the holy Character he bears, I say, he knows little of Knight-Errantry, and lies like a Son of a Whore, and a base-born Villain; and this I will make him know more effectually, with the convincing Edge of my Sword! This said with a grim Look, he fix'd himself in his Stirrups, and pull'd his Helm over his Brows; for the Bason, wh ich he took to be *Mambrino's* Helmet, hung at his Saddle Bow, in order to have the Damage repair'd which it had receiv'd from the Gally-Slaves. Thereupon *Dorothea*, by this Time well acquainted with his Temper, seeing him in such a Passion, and that every Body, except *Sancho Panza*, made a Jest of him, resolv'd with her Native Sprightliness and Address, to carry on the Humour. I beseech you, Sir, cry'd she, remember the Promise you have made me, and that you cannot engage in any Adventure whatsoever, till you have perform'd that we are going about. Therefore pray asswage your Anger; for had Master Curate known the Gally-Slaves were

286

rescu'd by your invincible Arm, I'm sure he wou'd rather have stitch'd up his Lips, or bit off his Tongue, than have spoken a Word, that should make him incur your Displeasure. Nay, I assure you, cry'd the Curate, I wou'd sooner have twitch'd off one of my Mustachoes into the Bargain. I am satisfy'd, Madam, cry'd Don *Quixote*, and for your sake the Flame of my just Indignation is quench'd; nor will I be induc'd to engage in any Quarrel, till I have fulfill'd my Promise to your Highness. Only in recompence of my good Intentions, I beg you will give us the Story of your Misfortunes, if this will not be too great a Trouble to you; and let me know who and what, and how many are the Persons of whom I must have due and full Satisfaction on your behalf. I am very willing to do it, reply'd *Dorothea*; but yet I fear a Story like mine, consisting wholly of Afflictions and Disasters, will prove but a tedious Entertainment. Never fear that, Madam, cry'd Don *Quixote*. Since then it must be so, said *Dorothea*, be pleas'd to lend me your Attention. With that *Cardenio* and the Barber gather'd up to her, to hear what kind of Story she had provided so soon; *Sancho* also hung his Ears upon her Side-Saddle, being no less deceived in her than his Master; and the Lady having seated herself well on her Mule, after coughing once or twice, and other Preparations, very gracefully began her Story.

First, Gentlemen, said she, you must know my Name is ——here she stopp'd short, and cou'd not call to mind the Name the Curate had given her; whereupon finding her at a Nonplus, he made haste to help her out. 'Tis not at all strange, said he, Madam, that you shou'd be so discomposed by your Disasters, as to stumble at the very beginning of the Account you are going to give of them; extreme Affliction often distracts the Mind to that Degree, and so deprives us of Memory, that sometimes we for a while can scarce think on our very Names: No wonder then, that the Princess *Micomicona*, Lawful Heiress to the vast Kingdom of *Micomicon*, disorder'd with so many Misfortunes and perplexed with so many various Thoughts for the Recovery of her Crown, should have her Imagination and Memory so incumber'd; but I hope you will now recollect yourself, and be able to proceed. I hope so

287

too, said the Lady, and I will try to go thro' with my Story, without any further Hesitation. Know, then, Gentlemen, that the King my Father, who was call'd *Tinacrio* the Sage, having great Skill in the Magic Art, understood by his profound Knowledge in that Science, that Queen *Xaramilla*, my Mother, should die before him, that he himself should not survive her long, and I should be left an Orphan. But he often said, that this did not so much trouble him, as the Foresight he had by his Speculations, of my being threatn'd with great Misfortunes, which wou'd be occasion'd by a certain Giant, Lord of a great Island near the Confines of my Kingdom; his Name *Pandafilando*, sirnam'd *of the gloomy Sight*; because tho' his Eye-balls are seated in their due Place, yet he affects to squint and look askew on purpose to fright those on whom he stares. My Father, I say, knew that this Giant, hearing of his Death wou'd one Day invade my Kingdom with a powerful Army, and drive me out of my Territories, without leaving me so much as the least Village for a Retreat; tho' he knew withal that I might avoid that Extremity, if I wou'd but consent to marry him; but as he found out by his Art, he had Reason to think I never wou'd incline to such a Match. And indeed I never had any Thoughts of marrying this Giant, nor really any other Giant in the World, how unmeasurably Great and Mighty soever he were. My Father therefore charg'd me patiently to bear my Misfortunes, and abandon my Kingdom to *Pandafilando* for a Time, without offering to keep him out by Force of Arms, since this wou'd be the best means to prevent my own Death and the Ruin of my Subjects, considering the Impossibility of withstanding the devilish Force of the Giant. But withal, he order'd me to direct my Course towards *Spain*, where I shou'd be sure to meet with a powerful Champion, in the Person of a Knight-Errant, whose Fame should at that Time be spread over all the Kingdom; and his Name, my Father said, should be, if I forget not, Don *Azote*,* or Don *Gigote*. An't please you, Foresooth, quoth *Sancho*, you wou'd say Don *Quixote*, otherwise call'd the Knight of the *woful Figure*. You are right, answer'd *Doro-*

* *Don Azote, is Don Horse-whip; and Don Gigote Don Hash or Minc'd-Meat: wilful Mistakes upon Likeness of the Words.*

thea, and my Father also describ'd him, and said he should be a tall thin fac'd Man, and that on his right Side, under the left Shoulder, or somewhere thereabouts, he should have a tawny Mole over-grown with a Tuft of Hair, not much unlike that of a Horse's Mane. With that Don *Quixote* calling for his Squire to come to him; Here, said he, *Sancho*, help me off with my Clothes, for I'm resolv'd to see whether I be the Knight of whom the Negromantick King has prophesy'd. Pray Sir, why wou'd you pull off your Cloaths, cry'd *Doro-thea*? To see whether I have such a Mole about me as your Father mention'd, reply'd the Knight. Your Worship need not strip to know that, quoth *Sancho*; for to my Knowledge, you've just such a Mark as my Lady says, on the Small of your Back, which betokens you to be a strong-body'd Man. That's enough, said *Dorothea*; Friends may believe one another without such a strict Examination; and whether it be on the Shoulder or on the Back-bone, 'tis not very material. In short, I find my Father aim'd right in all his Predictions, and so do I in recommending my self to Don *Quixote*, whose Stature and Appearance so well agree with my Father's Description, and whose Renown is so far spread, not only in *Spain*, but over all *La Mancha*,* that I had no sooner landed at *Ossuna*, but the Fame of his Prowess reach'd my Ears; so that I was satis-fy'd in my self he was the Person in quest of whom I came. But pray, Madam, cry'd Don *Quixote*, how did you do to land at *Ossuna*, since 'tis no Sea-port Town? Doubtless, Sir, (said the Curate, before *Dorothea* cou'd answer for her self) the Princess wou'd say, that after she landed at *Malaga*, the first place where she heard of your Feats of Arms, was *Ossuna*. That's what I wou'd have said, reply'd *Dorothea*. 'Tis easily understood, said the Curate; then pray let your Majesty be pleas'd to go on with your Story. I've nothing more to add,

---

* *This whimsical Anti-climax, says* Jarvis, *puts one in mind of the In-stances of that Figure in the* Art of Sinking in Poetry, *especially this:*

> Under the *Tropicks* is our Language spoke,
> And Part of *Flanders* hath receiv'd our Yoke.

Pope *and* Swift's *Miscellanies, Vol.* III. *p.* 57.

Shelton *taking it perhaps for an Error of the Press, has put* Æthiopia *for* La Mancha.

answer'd *Dorothea*, but that Fortune has at last so far favour'd me, as to make me find the noble Don *Quixote*, by whose
Valour I look upon my self as already restor'd to the Throne
of my Ancestors; since he has so courteously, and magnani-
mously vouchsaf'd to grant me the Boon I begg'd, to go with
me wheresoever I shall guide him. For all I have to do is, to
shew him this *Pandafilando* of *the gloomy Sight*, that he may
slay him, and restore that to me of which he has so unjustly
depriv'd me. For all this will certainly be done with the
greatest ease in the World, since 'twas foretold by *Tinacrio*
the Sage, my good and Royal Father, who has also left a Prediction written either in *Chaldæan* or *Greek* Characters (for
I cannot read 'em) which denotes, that after the Knight of
the Prophecy has cut off the Giant's Head, and restor'd me
to the Possession of my Kingdom, if he shou'd ask me to marry
him, I shou'd by no means refuse him, but instantly put him
in Possession of my Person and Kingdom. Well Friend *Sancho*
(said Don *Quixote* hearing this, and turning to the Squire)
what think'st thou now? Dost thou not hear how Matters go?
Did not I tell thee as much before! See now, whether we
have not a Kingdom which we may command, and a Queen
whom we may espouse. Ah marry have you, reply'd *Sancho*,
and a Pox take the Son of a Whore, I say, that will not wed
and bed her Majesty's Grace as soon as Master *Pandafilando's*
Wind-pipes are slit. Look what a dainty Bit she is! ha! wou'd
I never had a worse Flea in my Bed! With that to shew his
Joy, he cut a couple of Capers in the Air; and turning to *Dorothea*, laid hold on her Mule by the Bridle, and flinging himself
down on his Knees, begg'd she would be graciously pleas'd
to let him kiss her Hand, in token of his owning her for his
Sovereign Lady. There was none of the Beholders, but was
ready to burst for Laughter, having a Sight of the Master's
Madness, and the Servant's Simplicity. In short, *Dorothea*
was obliged to comply with his Intreaties, and promis'd to
make him a Grandee, when Fortune should favour her with
the Recovery of her lost Kingdom. Whereupon *Sancho* gave
her his Thanks, in such a Manner as oblig'd the Company to
a fresh Laughter. Then going on with her Relation, Gentlemen, said she, this is my History; and among all my Misfor-

tunes, this only has escap'd a Recital, That not one of the numerous Attendants I brought from my Kingdom has surviv'd the Ruins of my Fortune, but this good Squire with the long Beard: The rest ended their Days in a great Storm, which dash'd our Ship to pieces in the very Sight of the Harbour; and he and I had been Sharers in their Destiny, had we not laid hold of two Planks, by which Assistance we were driven to Land, in a Manner altogether miraculous, and agreeable to the whole Series of my Life, which seems, indeed, but one continued Miracle. And if in any Part of my Relation I have been tedious, and not so exact as I should have been, you must impute it to what Master Curate observ'd to you, in the beginning of my Story, that continual Troubles oppress the Senses, and weaken the Memory. Those Pains and Afflictions, be they ever so intense and difficult, said Don *Quixote*, shall never deter me (most virtuous and high-born Lady) from adventuring for your Service, and enduring whatever I shall suffer in it: And therefore I again ratify the Assurances I've given you, and swear that I will bear you Company, tho' to the end of the World, in search of this implacable Enemy of yours, till I shall find him; whose insulting Head, by the Help of Heaven, and my own invincible Arm, I am resolv'd to cut off, with the Edge of this (I will not say good) Sword; a Curse on *Gines de Passamonte*, who took away my own! this he spoke murmering to himself, and then prosecuted his Discourse in this Manner: And after I have divided it from the Body, and left you quietly possess'd of your Throne, it shall be left at your own Choice to dispose of your Person, as you shall think convenient: For as long as I shall have my Memory full of her Image, my Will captivated, and my Understanding wholly subjected to Her, whom I now forbear to name, 'tis impossible I should in the least deviate from the Affection I bear to her, or be induc'd to think of marrying, tho' it were a Phænix.

The Close of Don *Quixote's* Speech, which related to his not marrying, touch'd *Sancho* so to the quick, that he cou'd not forbear bawling out his Resentments: Body o' me, Sir Don *Quixote*, cry'd he, you are certainly out of your Wits, or how is it possible you shou'd stick at striking a Bargain with so great a Lady as this is? D'you think, Sir, Fortune will put such dainty Bits in your Way at every Corner? Is my Lady *Dulcinea* handsomer, d'you think? No marry is she not half so handsome: I cou'd almost say she's not worthy to tie this Lady's Shoe-latchets: I am likely indeed to get the Earldom I have fed my self with hopes of, if you spend your Time in fishing for Mushrooms in the Bottom of the Sea. Marry, marry out of hand, or *Old Nick* take you for me; Lay hold of the Kingdom which is ready to leap into your Hands; and as soon as you are a King, e'en make me a Marquis, or a Peer of the Land, and afterwards let Things go at Sixes and Sevens, 'twill be all a Case to *Sancho*. Don *Quixote*, quite divested of all Patience, at the Blasphemies which were spoken against his Lady *Dulcinea*, cou'd bear with him no longer; and therefore, without so much as a Word to give him notice of his Displeasure, gave him two such Blows with his Lance, that poor *Sancho* measur'd his length on the Ground, and had certainly there breath'd his last, had not the Knight desisted, through the Persuasions of *Dorothea*. Think'st thou (said he, after a considerable Pause) most infamous Peasant, that I shall always have leisure and disposition to put up thy Affronts; and that thy whole Business shall be to study new Offences, and mine to give thee new Pardons? Dost thou not know, excommunicated Traitor (for certainly Excommunication is the least Punishment can fall upon thee, after such Profanations of the peerless *Dulcinea's* Name) and art thou not assur'd, vile Slave and ignominious Vagabond, that I shou'd not have Strength sufficient to kill a Flea, did not she give Strength to my Nerves, and infuse Vigour into my Sinews? Speak, thou Villain with the Viper's Tongue; Who do'st thou imagine has restor'd the Queen to her Kingdom, cut off the Head of a Giant, and made thee a Marquis (for I count all this as done already) but the Power of *Dulcinea*, who makes use of my Arm, as the Instrument of her Act in me? She fights and overcomes in me; and I live and breathe in her, holding Life and Being from her. Thou base-born Wretch! art thou not possess'd of the utmost Ingratitude, thou who seest thy self exalted, from the very Dregs of the Earth, to Nobility and Honour, and yet dost repay so great a Benefit with Obloquies against the Person of thy Benefactress.

Sancho was not so mightily hurt, but he cou'd hear what his Master said well enough; wherefore getting upon his Legs in all haste, he ran for shelter behind *Dorothea's* Palfry, and being got thither, Hark you, Sir, cry'd he to him, if you have no Thought of marrying this same Lady, 'tis a clear Case that the Kingdom will never be yours; and if it be not, what good can you be able to do me? Then let any one judge whether I have not cause to complain. Therefore, good your Worship, marry her once for all, now we have her here rain'd down, as it were, from Heaven to us, and you may after keep Company with my Lady *Dulcinea*; for I guess you'll not be the only King in the World, that has kept a Miss or two in a Corner. As for Beauty, d'you see, I'll not meddle nor make; for (if I must say the Truth) I like both the Gentlewomen well enough in Conscience; tho, now I think on't, I have never seen the Lady *Dulcinea*. How, not seen her, blasphemous Traitor, reply'd Don *Quixote*, when just now thou brought'st me a Message from her! I say, answer'd *Sancho*, I have not seen her so leisurely as to take notice of her Features and good Parts one by one; but yet, as I saw 'em at a Blush, and all at once, methought I had no reason to find fault with 'em. Well, I pardon thee now, quoth Don *Quixote*, and thou must excuse me for what I have done to thee; for the first Motions are not in our Power. I perceive that well enough, said *Sancho*, and that's the reason my first Motions are always in my Tongue; and I can't for my Life help speaking what comes uppermost. However, Friend *Sancho*, said Don *Quixote*, thou had'st best think before thou speakest; for the Pitcher never goes so oft to the Well — I need say no more. Well, what must be must be, answer'd *Sancho*, there's somebody above who sees all, and will one Day judge which has most to answer for, whether I for speaking amiss, or you for doing so. No more of this, *Sancho*, said *Dorothea*, but run, and kiss your Lord's Hands, and beg his Pardon; and for the Time to come, be more advis'd and cautious how you run into the Praise or Dispraise of any Person; but especially take care you do not speak ill of that Lady of *Toboso*, whom I do not know, tho' I am ready to do her any Service; and for your own Part, trust in Heaven; for you shall infallibly have a Lordship, which shall enable you to live like a Prince. *Sancho* shrugg'd up his Shoulders, and in a sneaking Posture went and ask'd his Master for his Hand, which he held out to him with a grave Countenance; and after the Squire had kiss'd the back of it, the Knight gave him his Blessing, and told him he had a Word or two with him, bidding him come nearer, that he might have the better convenience of speaking to him. *Sancho* did as his Master commanded, and going a little from the Company with him; Since thy Return, said Don *Quixote*, applying himself to him, I have neither had Time nor Opportunity to enquire into the Particulars of thy Embassy, and the Answer thou hast brought; and therefore since Fortune has now befriended us with Convenience and Leisure, deny me not the Satisfaction thou may'st give me by the Rehearsal of thy News. Ask what you will, cry'd *Sancho*, and you shall not want for an Answer; but good your Worship, for the Time to come, I beseech you don't be too hasty. What Occasion hast thou, *Sancho*, to make this Request, reply'd Don *Quixote*? Reason good enough truly, said *Sancho*; for the Blows you gave me e'en now, were rather given me on Account of the Quarrel which the Devil stirr'd up between your Worship and me t'other Night, than for your Dislike of any Thing which was spoken against my Lady *Dulcinea*. Pr'ythee, *Sancho*, cry'd Don *Quixote*, be careful of falling again into such irreverent Expressions; for they provoke me to Anger, and are highly offensive. I pardon'd thee then for being a Delinquent, but thou art sensible that a new Offence must be attended with a new Punishment. As they were going on in such Discourse as this, they saw at a distance a Person riding up to 'em on an Ass, who, as he came near enough to be distinguish'd, seem'd to be a Gipsy by his Habit. But *Sancho Panza*, who, whenever he got Sight of any Asses, follow'd them with his Eyes and his Heart, as one whose Thoughts were ever fix'd on his own, had scarce given him half an Eye, but he knew him to be *Gines de Passamonte*, and by the Looks of the Gipsy found out the Visage of his Ass; as really it was the very same which *Gines* had got under him; who, to conceal himself from the Knowledge of the Publick, and have the better Opportunity of making a good Market of his Beast, had cloth'd himself like a Gipsy; the Cant of that sort of People, as well as the Languages of other Countries, being as natural and familiar to him as his own. *Sancho* saw him and knew him; and scarce had he seen and taken notice of him, when he cried out as loud as his Tongue would permit him: Ah; thou Thief *Genesillo*, leave my Goods and Chattels behind thee; get off from the Back of my own dear Life: Thou hast nothing to do with my poor Beast, without whom I can't enjoy a Moment's Ease: Away from my Dapple, away from my Comfort; take to thy Heels thou Villain; hence thou Hedge-bird, leave what is none of thine. He had no Occasion to use so many Words; for *Gines* dismounted as soon as he heard him speak, and taking to his Heels, got from 'em, and was out of Sight in an Instant. *Sancho* ran immediately to his Ass, and embrac'd him: How hast thou done, cry'd he, since I saw thee, my Darling and Treasure, my dear Dapple, the Delight of my Eyes, and my Dearest Companion? And then he stroak'd and slabber'd him with Kisses, as if the Beast had been a rational Creature. The Ass, for his part, was as silent as cou'd be, and gave *Sancho* the Liberty of as many Kisses as he pleas'd, without the Return of so much as one Word to the many Questions he had put to him. At sight of this the rest of the Company came up with him, and paid their Compliments of Congratulation to *Sancho* for the Recovery of his Ass, especially Don *Quixote*, who told him, that tho' he had found his Ass again, yet would not he revoke the Warrant he had giv'n him for the three Asses; for which Favour *Sancho* return'd him a Multitude of Thanks.

While they were travelling together, and discoursing after this Manner, the Curate address'd himself to *Dorothea*, and gave her to understand, that she had excellently discharg'd herself of what she had undertaken, as well in the Management of the History itself, as in her Brevity, and adapting her Stile to the particular Terms made use of in Books of Knight-Errantry. She return'd for answer, that she had frequently convers'd with such Romances, but that she was ignorant of the Situation of the Provinces, and the Sea-Ports, which occasion'd the Blunder she had made, by saying that she landed

at *Ossuna.* I perceiv'd it, reply'd the Curate, and therefore
I put in what you heard, which brought Matters to rights
again. But is it not an amazing Thing, to see how ready this
unfortunate Gentleman is to give Credit to these fictitious
Reports, only because they have the Air of the extravagant
Stories in Books of Knight-Errantry? *Cardenio* said, that he
thought this so strange a Madness, that he did not believe the
Wit of Man with all the Liberty of Invention and Fiction,
capable of hitting so extraordinary a Character. The Gentleman, reply'd the Curate, had some Qualities in him, ev'n as
surprizing in a Mad-man, as his unparallel'd Frenzy: For,
take him but off from his romantick Humour, discourse with
him of any other Subject, you will find him to handle it with
a great deal of Reason, and shew himself, by his Conversation, to have very clear and entertaining Conceptions: Insomuch that if Knight-Errantry bears no relation to his Discourse, there is no Man but will esteem him for his Vivacity
of Wit, and Strength of Judgment. While they were thus
discoursing, Don *Quixote*, prosecuting his Converse with his
Squire; *Sancho*, said he, let us lay aside all Manner of Ani-
mosity, let us forget and forgive Injuries;* and answer me
as speedily as thou can'st, without any Remains of thy last
Displeasure, how, when, and where didst thou find my Lady
Dulcinea? What was she doing when thou first pay'dst thy
Respects to her? How didst thou express thyself to her? What
Answer was she pleas'd to make thee? What Countenance
did she put on at the Perusal of my Letter? Who transcrib'd
it fairly for thee? and every Thing else which has any relation to this Affair, without Addition, Lies or Flattery. On
the other side, take care thou losest not a Tittle of the whole
Matter, by abreviating it, lest thou rob me of Part of that
Delight which I propose to myself from it. Sir, answer'd *San-*

* *In the Original* Spanish *it is*—Echemos pelillos a la mar: *i.e. literally,
Let us throw small little Hairs into the Sea; but figuratively, Let us renew
our Friendship and forget past Differences:* Renouons, &c. *says* Sobrino,
in his French *Exposition of that Phrase. And* Oudin *translates it in* French
—Mettons toutes nos Disputes soubs le pied, *Let us put all Disputes under
our Feet; tho' he owns it can't be translated properly into* French, *unless
by saying* jettons à vau l'eau, *Let us make a Wreck of all Disputes, i.e.
drown 'em.*

cho, if I must speak the Truth, and nothing but the Truth, no body copy'd out the Letter for me; for I carry'd none at all. That's right, cry'd Don *Quixote*, for I found the Pocket-Book, in which it was written, two Days after thy Departure, which occasion'd exceeding Grief in me, because I knew not what thou could'st do, when thou found'st thyself without the Letter; and I could not but be induc'd to believe that thou would'st have return'd, in order to take it with thee. I had certainly done so, reply'd *Sancho*, were it not for this Head of mine, which kept it in Remembrance ever since your Worship read it to me, and help'd me to say it over to a Parish-Clerk, who writ it out for me Word for Word so purely, that he swore, tho' he had written out many a Letter of Excommunication in his Time, he never in all the Days of his Life had read or seen any Thing so well spoken as it was. And do'st thou still retain the Memory of it, my dear *Sancho*, cry'd Don *Quixote*? Not I, quoth *Sancho*; for as soon as I had giv'n it her, and your Turn was serv'd, I was very willing to forget it. But if I remember any thing, 'tis what was on the Top; and it was thus; *High and Subterrene*, I wou'd say *Sovereign Lady*; and at the Bottom, *Yours until Death, the Knight of the woful Figure*; and I put between these two Things, three hundred *Souls* and *Lives* and *Pigsnyes*.

IV: THE PLEASANT DIALOGUE BETWEEN DON QUIXOTE AND HIS SQUIRE CONTINU'D, WITH OTHER ADVENTURES

ALL this is mighty well, said Don *Quixote*, proceed therefore: You arriv'd, and how was that Queen of Beauty then employ'd? On my Conscience thou found'st her stringing of Orient Pearls, or embroidering some curious Device in Gold for me her Captive Knight; was it not so, my *Sancho*? No faith, answer'd the Squire, I found her winnowing a Parcel of Wheat very seriously in the Back-yard. Then said the Don, you may rest assur'd, that every Corn of that Wheat was a Grain of Pearl, since she did it the Honour of touching it with her divine Hand. Didst thou observe the Quality of the Wheat, was it not of the finest Sort? Very indifferent, I thought, said the Squire. Well, this, at least, you must allow; it must make the finest whitest Bread, if sifted by her white Hands: But go on; when you deliver'd my Letter, did she kiss it? Did she treasure it in her Bosom, or what Ceremony did she use worthy such a Letter? How did she behave herself? Why truly, Sir, answer'd *Sancho*, when I offer'd her the Letter, she was very busy handling her Sieve; and, pr'ythee honest Friend, said she, do so much as lay that Letter down upon the Sack there; I can't read it till I have winnow'd out what's in my Hands. O unparallel'd Discretion! cry'd Don *Quixote*, she knew that a Perusal requir'd Leisure, and therefore deferr'd it for her more pleasing and private Hours. But oh! my Squire; while she was thus employed, what Conferences past? What did she ask about her Knight, and what did you reply? Say all, say all, my dearest *Sancho*, let not the smallest Circumstance 'scape thy Tongue; speak all that Thought can frame, or Pen describe. Her Questions were easily answer'd, Sir, said *Sancho*, for she ask'd me none at all: I told her indeed, in what a sad Pickle I had left you for her Sake, naked to the Waste; that you eat and slept like the brute Beasts; that you wou'd let a Razor as soon touch your Throat as your Beard; that you were still blubbering and crying, or swearing and cursing your Fortune. There you mistook, reply'd Don *Quixote*, I rather bless my Fortune, and always shall, while Life affords me Breath, since I am thought to merit the Esteem of so high a Lady as *Dulcinea del Toboso*. There you hit it, said *Sancho*, she is a high Lady indeed, Sir, for she's taller than I am by a Foot and a half.* Why, how now, *Sancho*, said the Knight, hast thou measured with her! Ah marry did I, Sir, said the Squire; for you must know that she desir'd me to lend her a hand in lifting a Sack of Wheat on an Ass; so we buckl'd about it, and I came so close to her, that I found she was taller than I by a full Span at least. Right, answer'd Don *Quixote*, but thou art also conscious that the uncommon Stature of her Person is adorn'd with innumerable Graces and Endowments of Soul! but *Sancho*, when you approach'd the charming She, did not an Aromatick Smell strike thy Sense, a Scent so odoriferous, pleasing and sweet, that I want a Name for it; sweet as—— you understand me, as the richest Fragrancy diffus'd around a Perfumer's Magazine of Odours? this, at least, you must grant me. I did indeed feel a sort of Scent a little unsavoury, said *Sancho*, somewhat vigorous or so; for I suppose she had wrought hard, and sweat somewhat plentifully. 'Tis false, answer'd the Knight, thy smelling has been debauch'd by thy own Scent, or some Canker in thy Nose; if thou could'st tell the Scent of opening Roses, fragrant Lilies, or the choicest Amber, then thou might'st guess at her's. Cry Mercy, Sir, said *Sancho*, it may be so indeed, for I remember that I myself have smelt very oft just as Madam *Dulcinea* did then, and that she shou'd smell like me, is no such wondrous Thing neither, since there's never a Barrel the better Herring of us. But now, said the Knight, supposing the Corn winnow'd and dispatch'd to the Mill; what did she after she had read my Letter? Your Letter, Sir! answer'd *Sancho*, your Letter was not read at all, Sir; as for her Part, she said, she cou'd neither read nor write, and she would trust no Body else, lest they should tell Tales, and so she cunningly tore your Letter. She said, that what

* Coto *in* Spanish, *which* Sobrino *says is but a Handful, so says* Stevens *in his Dictionary, tho' he translates it in this Place a Cubit.* Oudin *says it is the Breadth of four Fingers, and the Height of the Thumb when rais'd up in clenching the Fist.*

I told her by word of Mouth of your Love and Penance was enough: To make short now, she gave her Service to you, and said she had rather see you than hear from you; and she pray'd you, if ever you lov'd her, upon Sight of me, forth-with to leave your Madness among the Bushes here, and come strait to *Toboso* (if you be at leisure) for she has something to say to you, and has a huge Mind to see you: She had like to burst with laughing, when I call'd you the Knight of the *Woful Figure*. She told me the *Biscayan* whom you maul'd so was there, and that he was a very honest Fellow; but that she heard no News at all of the Gally-Slaves.

Thus far all goes well, said Don *Quixote*; but tell me pray, what Jewel did she present you at your Departure, as a Re-ward for the News you brought? For 'tis a Custom of ancient standing among Knights and Ladies-Errant, to bestow on Squires, Dwarfs, or Damsels, who bring them good News of their Ladies or Servants, some precious Jewel as a grateful Reward of their welcome Tidings. Ah, Sir, said *Sancho*, that was the Fashion in the Days of Yore; and a very good Fashion I take it: But all the Jewels *Sancho* got, was a Luncheon of Bread and a Piece of Cheese, which she handed to me over the Wall, when I was taking my Leave, by the same Token (I hope there's no ill Luck in't) the Cheese was made of Sheep's Milk. 'Tis strange, said Don *Quixote*, for she is liberal, even to Pro-fuseness; and if she presented thee not a Jewel, she certainly had none about her at that Time; but what is deferr'd is not lost, Sleeves are good after Easter.* I shall see her, and Matters shall be accommodated. Know'st thou, *Sancho*, what raises my Astonishment? 'tis thy sudden Return; for proportioning thy short Absence to the length of thy Journey, *Toboso* being, at least, thirty Leagues distant, thou must have ridden on the Wind; certainly the sagacious Enchanter, who is my Guard-ian and Friend (for doubtless such a one there is and ought to be, or I shou'd not be a true Knight-Errant) certainly, I say, that wise Magician has further'd thee on thy Journey un-

---

* *A proverbial Expression, signifying that* a good thing is always season-able. *The* Spaniards, *for the sake of Warmth, wear Sleeves in Winter, 'till about* Easter: *But if the Weather continues cold, Sleeves may be proper after* Easter.

awares; for there are Sages of such incredible Power, as to take up a Knight-Errant sleeping in his Bed, and waken him next Morning a thousand Leagues from the Place where he fell asleep. By this Power Knights-Errant succour one another in their most dangerous Exigents, when and where they please; for Instance, suppose me fighting in the Mountains of *Armenia* with some hellish Monster, some dreadful Spright, or fierce Gigantick Knight, where perhaps I am like to be worsted (such a Thing may happen) when just in the very Crisis of my Fate, when I least expect it, behold on the Top of a flying Cloud, or riding in a flaming Chariot, another Knight, my Friend, who but a Minute before was in *England* perhaps; he sustains me, delivers me from Death, and returns that Night to his own Lodging, where he sups with a very good Appetite after his Journey, having rid you two or three thousand Leagues that Day: And all this perform'd by the Industry and Wisdom of these knowing Magicians, whose only Business and Charge is glorious Knight-Errantry. Some such expeditious Power, I believe, *Sancho*, though hidden from you, has promoted so great a Dispatch in your late Journey. I believe, indeed (answer'd *Sancho*) that there was Witchcraft in the Case, for *Rozinante* went without a Spur all the Way, and was as mettlesom as though he had been a Gipsy's Ass with Quicksilver in his Ears. Quicksilver! You Coxcomb, said the Knight, ay, and a Troop of Devils besides; and they are the best Horse-coursers in Nature, you must know, for they must needs go whom the Devil drives; but no more of that. What is thy Advice as to my Lady's Commands to visit her? I know her Power should regulate my Will; but then my Honour, *Sancho*, my solemn Promise has engag'd me to the Princess's Service that comes with us, and the Law of Arms confines me to my Word: Love draws me one, and Glory t'other way; on this side *Dulcinea's* strict Commands, on the other my promis'd Faith; but—'tis resolv'd. I'll travel Night and Day, cut off this Giant's Head, and having settl'd the Princess in her Dominions, will presently return to see that Sun which enlightens my Senses: She will easily condescend to excuse my Absence, when I convince her 'twas for her Fame and Glory; since the past, present, and future Success of my victorious

Arms depends wholly on the gracious Influences of her Favour, and the Honour of being her Knight. Oh sad, oh sad! said
Sancho, I doubt your Worship's Head is much the worse for
wearing: Are you mad, Sir, to take so long a Voyage for nothing? Why don't you catch at this Preferment that now offers,
where a fine Kingdom is the Portion, twenty thousand Leagues
round, they say; nay, bigger than *Portugal* and *Castile* both
together — Good your Worship! hold your Tongue, I wonder
you are not asham'd — take a Fool's Council for once, marry
her by the first Priest you meet, here's our own Curate can do
the Job most curiously:* Come Master, I have Hair enough
in my Beard to make a Counsellor, and my Advice is as fit for
you, as your Shoe for your Foot; a Bird in Hand is worth two
in the Bush; and

> *He that will not when he may,*
> *When he wou'd, he shall have nay.*

Thou advisest me thus, answer'd Don *Quixote*, that I may
be able to promote thee according to my Promise; but that I
can do without marrying this Lady: For I shall make this the
Condition of entring into Battle: That after my Victory, without marrying the Princess, she shall leave Part of her Kingdom at my Disposal, to gratify whom I please; and who can
claim any such Gratuity but thyself? That's plain, answer'd
Sancho, but pray, Sir, take care that you reserve some Part
near the Sea-side for me; that if the Air does not agree with
me, I may transport my black Slaves, make my Profit of them,
and go live somewhere else; so that I would have you resolve
upon it presently, leave the Lady *Dulcinea* for the present,
and go kill this same Giant, and make an End of that Business
first; for I dare swear 'twill yield you a good Market. I am
fix'd in thy Opinion (said Don *Quixote*) but I admonish thee
not to whisper to any Person the least Hint of our Conference;
for since *Dulcinea* is so cautious and secret, 'tis proper that I
and mine should follow her Example. Why the Devil then,
said *Sancho*, should you send every Body you overcome packing to Madam *Dulcinea*, to fall down before her, and tell her

* *As if 'twas done with* Pearl, *in the Original:* lo harà de perlas, *i.e. to
a Nicety.*

they came from you to pay their Obedience, when this tells all the World that she's your Mistress as much as if they had it under your own Hand? How dull of Apprehension and stupid thou art, said the Knight; hast thou not Sense to find that all this redounds to her greater Glory? Know that in Proceedings of Chivalry, a Lady's Honour is calculated from the Number of her Servants, whose Services must not tend to any Reward, but the Favour of her Acceptance, and the pure Honour of performing them for her Sake, and being call'd her Servants. I have heard our Curate, answer'd Sancho, preach up this Doctrine of loving for Love's sake, and that we ought to love our Maker so for his own Sake, without either Hope of Good, or Fear of Pain; tho' for my Part I would love and serve him for what I could get. Thou art an unaccountable Fellow, cry'd Don Quixote: thou talk'st sometimes with so much Sense, that one would imagine thee to be something of a Scholar. A Scholard, Sir, answer'd Sancho, lack a-day, I don't know, as I'm a honest Man, a Letter in the Book. Master Nicholas seeing them so deep in Discourse, call'd to them to stop and drink at a little Fountain by the Road: Don Quixote halted, and Sancho was very glad of the Interruption, his Stock of Lies being almost spent, and he stood in Danger besides of being trapp'd in his Words, for he had never seen Dulcinea, though he knew she liv'd at Toboso. Cardenio by this had chang'd his Clothes for those Dorothea wore, when they found her in the Mountains; and though they made but an ordinary Figure, they look'd much better than those he had put off.* They all stopp'd at the Fountain, and fell aboard the Curate's Provision, which was but a Snap among so many, for they were all very hungry. While they sat refreshing themselves, a young Lad, travelling that way, observ'd them, and, looking earnestly on the whole Company, ran suddenly and fell down before Don Quixote, addressing him in a very doleful Manner. Alas, good Sir, said he, don't you know me? don't you remember poor Andrew whom you caus'd to be unty'd from the Tree? With that the Knight knew him; and raising him up, turn'd to the Company, That

---

* These must be the ragged Apparel Cardenio wore before he was drest in the Priest's short Cassock and Cloak.

you may all know, said he, of how great Importance, to the redressing of Injuries, punishing Vice, and the universal Benefit of Mankind, the Business of Knight-Errantry may be, you must understand, that riding through a Desart some Days ago, I heard certain lamentable Screeks and Out-cries: Prompted by the Misery of the Afflicted, and borne away by the Zeal of my Profession I follow'd the Voice, and found this Boy, whom you all see, bound to a great Oak; I'm glad he's present, because he can attest the Truth of my Relation. I found him as I told you, bound to an Oak, naked from the Waste upwards, and a bloody-minded Peasant scourging his Back unmercifully with the Reins of a Bridle. I presently demanded the Cause of his severe Chastisement? The rude Fellow answer'd, that he had Liberty to punish his own Servant, whom he thus us'd for some Faults that argu'd him more Knave than Fool. Good Sir, said the Boy, he can lay nothing to my Charge, but demanding my Wages. His Master made some Reply, which I would not allow as a just Excuse, and order'd him immediately to unbind the Youth, and took his Oath that he would take him home and pay him all his Wages upon the Nail, in good and lawful Coin. Is not this literally true, *Andrew*? Did you not mark besides, with what Face of Authority I commanded, and with how much Humility he promis'd to obey all I impos'd, commanded and desir'd? Answer me, Boy, and tell boldly all that pass'd to this worthy Company, that it may appear how necessary the Vocation of Knights-Errant is up and down the high Roads.

All you have said is true enough, answer'd *Andrew*, but the Business did not end after that Manner you and I hop'd it would. How? said the Knight, has not the Peasant paid you? Ay, he has paid me with a Vengeance, said the Boy, for no sooner was your Back turn'd, but he ty'd me again to the same Tree, and lash'd me so cursedly, that I look'd like St *Bartholomew* flea'd alive; and at every Blow he had some Joke or another to laugh at you; and had he not laid on me as he did, I fancy I could not have help'd laughing myself. At last he left me in so pitiful Case, that I was forc'd to crawl to an Hospital, where I have lain ever since to get cur'd, so wofully the Tyrant had lash'd me. And now I may thank You for this, for had you rid on your Journey, and neither meddl'd nor made, seeing no Body sent for you, and 'twas none of your Business, my Master, perhaps, had been satisfy'd with giving me ten or twenty Lashes, and after that would have paid me what he ow'd me; but you was so huffy, and call'd him so many Names, that it made him mad, and so he vented all his Spite against You upon My poor Back, as soon as yours was turn'd, insomuch that I fear I shall never be my own Man again. The Miscarriage, answer'd the Knight, is only charge-able on my Departure before I saw my Orders executed; for I might, by Experience, have remembred, that the Word of a Peasant is regulated, not by Honour, but Profit. But you re-member, *Andrew*, how I swore if he disobey'd, that I would return and seek him through the Universe, and find him, tho' hid in a Whale's Belly. Ah, Sir, answer'd *Andrew*, but that's no Cure for my sore Shoulders. You shall be redress'd, an-swer'd the Knight, starting fiercely up, and commanding *Sancho* immediately to bridle *Rozinante*, who was baiting as fast as the rest of the Company. *Dorothea* ask'd what he in-tended to do? he answer'd, that he intended to find out the Villain and punish him severely for his Crimes, then force him to pay *Andrew* his Wages to the last *Maravedi*,* in spite of all the Peasants in the Universe. She then desir'd him to remember his Engagement to her, which with-held him from any new Atchievement till that was finish'd; that he must therefore suspend his Resentments till his Return from her Kingdom. 'Tis but just and reasonable, said the Knight, and therefore *Andrew* must wait with Patience my Return; but when I do return, I do hereby ratify my former Oath and Pro-mise, never to rest till he be fully satisfy'd and paid. I dare not trust to that, answer'd *Andrew*; but if you'll bestow on me as much Money as will bear my Charges to *Seville*, I shall thank your Worship more than for all the Revenge you tell me of: Give me a Snap to eat, and a Bit in my Pocket, and so Heaven be wi'ye and all other Knights-Errant, and may they prove as arrant Fools in their own Business as they have been in mine.

   Sancho took a Crust of Bread and a Slice of Cheese, and reaching it to *Andrew*, there Friend, said he, there's some-

* *Near the Value of a Farthing.*

thing for thee; on my Word, we have all of us a Share of thy Mischance. What Share? said *Andrew*. Why the curs'd Mischance of parting with this Bread and Cheese to thee; for my Head to a Half-penny, I may live to want it; for thou must know, Friend of mine, that we, the Squires of Knights-Errant, often pick our Teeth without a Dinner, and are subject to many other things, which are better felt than told. *Andrew* snatch'd at the Provender, and seeing no likelihood of any more, he made his Leg and march'd off. But looking over his Shoulder at Don *Quixote*, Hark-ye, you Sir Knight-Errant, cry'd he, if ever you meet me again in your Travels, which I hope you never shall; though I were torn in Pieces, don't trouble me with your plaguy Help, but mind your own Business; and so fare you well, with a Curse upon you and all the Knights-Errant that ever were born. The Knight thought to chastise him, but the Lad was too nimble for any there, and his Heels carry'd him off; leaving Don *Quixote* highly incens'd at his Story, which mov'd the Company to hold their Laughter, lest they should raise his Anger to a dangerous Height.

V: WHAT BEFEL DON QUIXOTE AND HIS COMPANY AT THE INN

WHEN they had eaten plentifully, they left that Place, and travell'd all that Day and the next, without meeting any thing worth Notice, till they came to the Inn, which was so frightful a Sight to poor *Sancho*, that he wou'd willingly not have gone in, but could by no Means avoid it. The Inn-keeper, the Hostess, her Daughter, and *Maritornes*, met Don *Quixote* and his Squire with a very hearty Welcome: The Knight receiv'd them with a Face of Gravity and Approbation, bidding them prepare him a better Bed than their last Entertainment afforded him. Sir, said the Hostess, pay us better than you did then, and you shall have a Bed for a Prince; and upon the Knight's Promise that he would, she provided him a tolerable Bed, in the large Room where he lay before: He presently undress'd, and being heartily craz'd in Body, as well as in Mind, he went to Bed. He was scarcely got to his Chamber, when the Hostess flew suddenly at the Barber, and catching him by the Beard, on my Life, said she, you shall use my Tail no longer for a Beard; pray, Sir, give me my Tail, my Husband wants it to stick his Thing into, his Comb I mean, and my Tail I will have, Sir. The Barber held Tug with her till the Curate advis'd him to return it, telling him that he might now undisguise himself, and tell Don *Quixote*, that after the Gally-Slaves had pillag'd him, he fled to that Inn; and if he shou'd ask for the Princess's Squire, he shou'd pretend that he was dispatch'd to her Kingdom before her, to give her Subjects an Account of her Arrival, and of the Power she brought to free them all from Slavery. The Barber thus school'd, gave the Hostess her Tail, with the other Trinkets which he had borrow'd to decoy Don *Quixote* out of the Desart. *Dorothea's* Beauty, and *Cardenio's* handsome shape surpriz'd every Body. The Curate bespoke Supper, and the Host, being pretty secure of his Reckoning, soon got them a tolerable Entertainment. They would not disturb the Knight, who slept very soundly, for his Distemper wanted Rest more than Meat; but they divert-

ed themselves with the Hostess's Account of his Encounter
with the Carriers, and of *Sancho's* being toss'd in a Blanket.
Don *Quixote's* unaccountable Madness was the principal Subject of their Discourse, upon which the Curate insisting, and
arguing it to proceed from his reading Romances, the Inn-
keeper took him up. Sir, said he, you can't make me of your
Opinion; for in my Mind, it is the pleasantest Reading that
ever was. I have now in the House two or three Books of
that kind, and some other Pieces, that really have kept me,
and many others, alive. In Harvest-time, a great many of the
Reapers come to drink here in the Heat of the Day, and he
that can read best among us takes up one of these Books; and
all the rest of us, sometimes Thirty or more, sit round about
him, and listen with such Pleasure, that we think neither
of Sorrow nor Care; as for my own Part, when I hear the
mighty Blows and dreadful Battles of these Knights-Errant,
I have half a mind to be one myself, and am rais'd to such
a Life and Briskness, that I frighten away old Age; I could
sit and hear them from Morning till Night. I wish you wou'd
Husband, said the Hostess, for then we should have some
Rest; for at all other Times you are so out of Humour and so
snappish, that we lead a hellish Life with you. That's true
enough, said *Maritornes*; and for my part, I think there are
mighty pretty Stories in those Books, especially that one about
the young Lady who is hugg'd so sweetly by her Knight
under the Orange-tree, when the Damsel watches lest somebody comes, and stands with her Mouth watering all the
while; and a thousand such Stories, which I would often
forego my Dinner and Supper to hear. And what think you of
this Matter, young Miss, said the Curate to the Inn-keeper's
Daughter? Alack-a-day, Sir, said she, I don't understand
those Things, and yet I love to hear 'em: but I don't like
that frightful ugly fighting that so pleases my Father. Indeed
the sad Lamentations of the poor Knights, for the Loss of their
Mistresses, sometimes make me cry like any Thing. I suppose
then, young Gentlewoman, said *Dorothea*, you will be tender-
hearted, and will never let a Lover die for you. I don't know
what may happen, as to that, said the Girl; but this I know,
that I will never give any Body reason to call me Tygress and

Lioness, and I don't know how many other ugly Names, as those Ladies are often call'd, and I think they deserve yet worse, so they do; for they can neither have Soul nor Conscience to let such fine Gentlemen die or run mad for a Sight of them? What signifies all their Fiddling and Coyness? If they are civil Women, why don't they marry 'em, for that's all their Knights would be at? Hold your prating, Mistress, said the Hostess, How came you to know all this? 'Tis not for such as you to talk of these Matters. The Gentleman only ask'd me a Question, said she, and it would be uncivil not to answer him. Well, said the Curate, do me the Favour, good Landlord, to bring out these Books that I may have a Sight of them.

With all my Heart, said the Inn-keeper; and with that stepping to his Chamber, he open'd a little Portmantle that shut with a Chain, and took out three large Volumes, with a parcel of Manuscripts in a fair legible Letter: The Title of the First was Don *Cirongilio* of *Thrace*; the Second *Felixmarte* of *Hircania*; and the Third was the History of the great Captain *Gonçalo Hernandez de Corduba*, and the Life of *Diego Garcia de Paredes*, bound together.* The Curate reading the Titles, turn'd to the Barber, and told him, they wanted now Don *Quixote's* House-keeper and his Niece. I shall do as well with the Books, said the Barber, for I can find the Way to the Back-yard, or the Chimney, there's a good Fire that will do their Business. Business! said the Inn-keeper, I hope you wou'd not burn my Books. Only two of them, said the Curate, this same Don *Cirongilio* and his Friend *Felixmarte*. I hope, Sir, said the Host, they are neither Hereticks nor Flegmaticks. Schismaticks you mean, said the Barber; I mean so, said the Inn-keeper; and if you must burn any, let it be this of *Gonçalo Hernandez* and *Diego Garcia*, for you should sooner burn one of my Children than the others. These Books, honest Friend, said the Curate, that you appear so concern'd for, are senseless Rhapsodies of Falshoods and Folly; and this

* *There were such famous Leaders, as the Great Captain, who conquer'd* Naples *for King* Ferdinand *of* Spain, *and* Diego Garcia *before him; but Authors have added such monstrous Fables to their true Actions, that there is no more believing any of them, than the Fables of* Guy *of* Warwick, *or the like romantick Heroes, as may appear by what the Curate speaks in their Praise.*

309

which you so despise is a true History, and contains a true
Account of two celebrated Men; the first by his Bravery and
Courage purchas'd immortal Fame, and the Name of the great
General, by the universal Consent of Mankind. The other,
Diego Garcia de Paredes, was of Noble Extraction, and born
in *Truxillo* a Town of *Estremadura*, and was a Man of singular Courage, and such mighty Strength, that with one of his
Hands he could stop a Mill-wheel in its most rapid Motion;
and with his single Force defended the Passage of a Bridge
against a great Army. Several other great Actions are related
in the Memoirs of his Life, but all with so much Modesty and
unbiass'd Truth, that they easily pronounce him his own
Historiographer; and had they been written by any one else,
with Freedom and Impartiality, they might have eclips'd your
Hectors, *Achilles's*, and *Orlando's*, with all their Heroick Exploits. That's a fine Jest, faith, said the Inn-keeper, my Father
could have told you another Tale, Sir. Holding a Mill-wheel?
why, is that such a mighty Matter! Odds fish, do but turn over
a Leaf of *Felixmarte* there; you'll find how with one single
Back-stroke he cut five swingeing Giants off by the Middle,
as if they had been so many Bean-cods, of which the Children
make little Puppet-Friars;* and read how at another Time he
charg'd a most mighty and powerful Army of above a Million
and Six hundred thousand fighting Men, all arm'd Cap-a-pee,
and routed them all like so many Sheep. And what can you
say of the Worthy *Cirongilio* of *Thrace*? who, as you may read
there, going by Water one Day, was assaulted by a fiery Serpent in the Middle of the River; he presently leap'd nimbly
upon her Back, and hanging by her scaly Neck, grasp'd her
Throat fast with both his Arms, so that the Serpent finding
herself almost strangl'd, was forc'd to dive into the Water to
save herself, and carry'd the Knight, who would not quit his
Hold, to the very Bottom, where he found a stately Palace,
and such pleasant Gardens, that 'twas a Wonder; and straight
the Serpent turn'd into a very old Man, and told him such

---

* *Children, in Spain, we are told, make Puppets, resembling Friars, out
of Bean-cods, by breaking as much of the upper end as to discover part
of the first Bean, which is to represent the bald Head, and letting the broken
Cod hang back like a Cowl.*

Things as were never heard nor spoken. —— Now a Fig for your great Captain, and your *Diego Garcia*. *Dorothea* hearing this, said softly to *Cardenio*, that the Host was capable of making a Second Part to Don *Quixote*. I think so too, cry'd *Cardenio*, for 'tis plain he believes every Tittle contain'd in those Books, nor can all the *Carthusian* Friars in the World persuade him otherwise. I tell thee, Friend (said the Curate) there were never any such Persons, as your Books of Chivalry mention, upon the Face of the Earth; your *Felixmarte* of *Hircania*, and your *Cirongilio* of *Thrace*, are all but Chimera's and Fictions of idle and luxuriant Wits, who wrote them for the same Reason that you read them, because they had nothing else to do. *Sir* (said the Inn-keeper) *you must Angle with another Bait, or you'll catch no Fish,** *I know what's what, as well as another; I can tell where my own Shoe pinches me; and you must not think, Sir, to catch old Birds with Chaff;* a pleasant Jest, faith, that you should pretend to persuade me now that these notable Books are Lies and Stories; why Sir, are they not in Print? Are they not publish'd according to Order? Licens'd by Authority from the Privy-Conncil? And do you think that they would permit so many Untruths to be printed, and such a Number of Battles and Enchantments to set us all a madding? I have told you already (Friend) reply'd the Curate, that this is licens'd for our Amusement in our idle Hours; for the same Reason that Tennis, Billiards, Chess, and other Recreations are tolerated, that Men may find a Pastime for those Hours they cannot find Employment for. Neither could the Government foresee this Inconvenience from such Books, that you urge, because they could not reasonably suppose any rational Person would believe their Absurdities. And were this a proper time, I could say a great deal in favour of such Writings, and how, with some Regulations, they might be made both instructive and diverting; but I design, upon the first Opportunity, to communicate my Thoughts on this Head to some that may redress it: In the mean time, honest Land-

---

* *In the Original, what's in Italick runs thus,* A otro perro con esse huesso, &c. *i.e.* To another Dog, with this Bone; *as if I did not know how many make five, nor where my own Shoe pinches; don't think, Sir, to feed me with Pap; for, before God, I'm no Suckling.*

lord, you may put up your Books, and believe them true if you please, and much good may they do you. And I wish you may never halt of the same Foot as your Guest Don Quixote. There's no fear of that, said the Inn-keeper, for I never design to turn Knight-Errant, because I find the Customs that supported that Noble Order are quite out of Doors.

About the Middle of their Discourse enter'd Sancho, who was very uneasy at hearing that Knights-Errant were out of Fashion, and Books of Chivalry full of nothing but Folly and Fiction; he resolv'd, however (in spight of all their Contempt of Chivalry) still to stick by his Master; and if his intended Expedition fail'd of Success, then to return to his Family and Plough. As the Inn-keeper was carrying away the Books, the Curate desir'd his leave to look over those Manuscripts which appear'd in so fair a Character; he reach'd them to him, to the Number of eight Sheets, on one of which there was written in a large Hand, *The Novel of the Curious Impertinent.* The Title, said the Curate, promises something, perhaps it may be worth reading through: Your Reverence, said the Inn-keeper, may be worse employ'd; for that Novel has receiv'd the Approbation of several ingenious Guests of mine who have read it, and who would have begg'd it of me; but I would by no means part with it, till I deliver it to the Owner of this Portmantle, who left it here with these Books and Papers; I may, perhaps, see him again, and restore them honestly; for I am as much a Christian as my Neighbours, though I am an Inn-keeper. But I hope (said the Curate) if it pleases me you won't deny me a Copy of it. Nay, as to that Matter, said the Host, we shan't fall out. *Cardenio* having by this perus'd it a little, recommended it to the Curate, and intreated him to read it for the Entertainment of the Company. The Curate would have excus'd himself, by urging the unseasonable time of Night, and that Sleep was then more proper, especially for the Lady; a pleasant Story, said *Dorothea,* will prove the best Repose for some Hours to me; for my Spirits are not compos'd enough to allow me to rest, tho' I want it. Mr *Nicholas* and *Sancho* join'd in the Request. To please ye then, and satisfy my own Curiosity, said the Curate, I'll begin, if you'll but give your Attention.

VI: THE NOVEL OF THE CURIOUS
IMPERTINENT

ANSELMO and *Lothario*, considerable Gentlemen of *Florence*, the capital City of *Tuscany* in *Italy*, were so eminent for their Friendship, that they were called nothing but the *Two Friends*. They were both young and unmarried, of the same Age and Humour, which did not a little concur to the Continuance of their mutual Affection, tho', of the two, *Anselmo* was the most amourously inclin'd, and *Lothario* the greater Lover of Hunting; yet they lov'd one another above all other Considerations; and mutually quitted their own Pleasure for their Friend's; and their very Wills, like the different Motions of a well regulated Watch, were always subservient to their Unity, and still kept time with one another. *Anselmo*, at last, fell desperately in love with a beautiful Lady of the same City; so eminent for her Fortune and Family, that he resolv'd, by the Consent of his Friend (for he did nothing without his Advice) to demand her in Marriage. *Lothario* was the Person employ'd in this Affair, which he manag'd with that Address, that in few Days he put his Friend into Possession of *Camilla*, for that was the Lady's Name; and this so much to their Satisfaction, that he receiv'd a thousand Acknowledgments from both, for the equal Happiness they deriv'd from his Endeavours. *Lothario*, as long as the Nuptials lasted, was every Day at *Anselmo's*, and did all he could to add to the Sports and Diversions of the Occasion. But as soon as the new-marry'd Pair had receiv'd the Congratulation of their Friends, and the nuptial Ceremonies were over, *Lothario* retir'd, with the rest of their Acquaintance, and forbore his Visits, because he prudently imagin'd, that it was not at all proper to be so frequent at his Friend's House after Marriage as before; for tho' true Friendship entirely banishes all Suspicion and Jealousy, yet the Honour of a married Man is of so nice and tender a Nature, that it has been sometimes sully'd by the Conversation of the nearest Relations, and therefore more liable to suffer from that of a Friend. *Anselmo* observ'd this Remissness of *Lothario*; and, fond as he was of

his Wife, shew'd by his tender Complaints how much it affected him. He told him, that if he could have believed he
must have lost so dear a Correspondence by Marriage; as
much as he lov'd, he would never have paid so great a Price
for the Satisfaction of his Passion; and that he would never
for the idle Reputation of a cautious Husband, suffer so tender
and agreeable a Name to be lost, as that of *The Two Friends*,
which before his Marriage, they had so happily obtain'd, and
therefore he begg'd him, if that were a Term lawful to be
us'd betwixt them two, to return to his former Familiarity
and Freedom of Conversation; assuring him, that his Wife's
Will and Pleasure were entirely form'd by his; and that being
acquainted with their antient and strict Friendship, she was
equally surpriz'd at so unexpected a Change. *Lothario* reply'd
to these endearing Persuasions of his Friend, with such Prudence and Discretion, that he convinced him of the Sincerity
of his Intentions in what he had done; and so in Conclusion
they agreed that *Lothario* should dine twice a Week at his
House, besides Holy-days. Yet *Lothario's* Compliance with
this Resolution being only not to disoblige his Friend, he design'd to observe it no farther than he should find it consistent
with *Anselmo's* Honour, whose Reputation was as dear to him
as his own; and he us'd to tell him, that the Husband of a
beautiful Wife ought to be as cautious of the Friends whom he
carry'd home to her himself, as other Female Acquaintance
and Visitants. For a Friend's or Relation's House often renders
the Contrivance of those things easy and not suspected, which
could not be compass'd either in the Church, the Markets, or
at publick Entertainments and Places of resort, which no Man
can entirely keep a Woman from frequenting. To this *Lothario* said also, that every marry'd Man ought to have some
Friend to put him in mind of the Defects of his Conduct; for
a Husband's Fondness many times makes him either not see,
or at least, for fear of displeasing his Wife, not command or
forbid her what may be advantageous or prejudicial to his
Reputation. In all which, a Friend's Warning and Advice
might supply him with a proper Remedy. But where shall we
find a Friend so qualify'd with Wisdom and Truth as *Anselmo*
demands? I must confess I cannot tell, unless it were *Lothario*,

whose Care of his Friend's Honour made him so cautious as not to comply with his promis'd visiting Days, lest the malicious Observers should give a scandalous Censure of the frequent Admission of so well qualify'd a Gentleman, both for his Wit, Fortune, Youth and Address, to the House of a Lady of so celebrated a Beauty as *Camilla*: For tho' his Virtue was sufficiently known to check the Growth of any malignant Report, yet he would not suffer his Friend's Honour nor his own, to run the Hazard of being call'd in question; which made him spend the greatest part of those Days, he had by Promise devoted to his Friend's Conversation, in other Places and Employments; yet excusing his Absence so agreeably, that *Anselmo* could not deny the Reasonableness of what he alledg'd. And thus the Time pass'd away in pathetick Accusations of Want of Love and Friendship on one side, and plausible Excuses on the other.

I know very well, said *Anselmo*, walking one Day in the Fields with his Friend, that of all the Favours and Benefits for which Heaven commands my Gratitude, as the Advantage of my Birth, Fortune and Nature; the greatest and most obliging is the Gift of such a Wife, and such a Friend; being both of you Pledges of so great Value, that tho' 'tis impossible for me to raise my Esteem and Love equal to your Deserts, yet is no Man capable of having a greater. And yet while I am in Possession of all that can or usually does make a Man happy, I live the most discontented Life in the World. I am not able to tell you when my Misery began, which now inwardly torments me with so strange, extravagant, and singular a Desire, that I never reflect on it, but I wonder at my self, and condemn and curb my Folly, and would fain hide my Desires even from my self: And yet I have receiv'd no more Advantage from this private Confusion, than if I had publish'd my Extravagance to all the World. Since therefore 'tis evident that it will at last break out, dear *Lothario*, I would have it go no farther than thy known Fidelity and Secrecy; for that and my own Industry (which as my Friend thou wilt turn to my Assistance) will quickly, I hope, free me from the Anguish it now gives me, and restore me that Tranquillity of which my own Folly has now depriv'd me.

Lothario stood in great suspence, unable to guess at the Consequence of so strange and prolix an Introduction. In vain he rack'd his Imagination for the Causes of his Friend's Affliction, the Truth was the last thing he cou'd think of; but no longer to remain in doubt, he told *Anselmo*, that he did his Friendship a particular injury, in not coming directly to the Point in the discovery of his Thoughts to him, since his Counsels might enable him to support, and, perhaps, to lose or compass such importunate Desires,

'Tis very true, reply'd *Anselmo*, and with that Assurance I must inform you, that the Desire that gives me so much Pain, is to know whether *Camilla* be really as Virtuous as I think her. Nor can this be made evident but by such a Trial, that, like Gold by the Fire, the Standard and Degree of her Worth be discover'd. For, in my Opinion, no Woman has more Virtue than she retains, after the Force of the most earnest Solicitations. *Casta est quam nemo rogavit:** And she only may be said to be chaste, who has withstood the Force of Tears, Vows, Promises, Gifts, and all the Importunities of a Lover that is not easily deny'd: For where's the Praise of a Woman's Virtue whom no Body has ever endeavour'd to corrupt? Where is the Wonder if a Wife be reserv'd, when she has no Temptation nor Opportunity of being otherwise, especially if she have a jealous Husband, with whom the least Suspicion goes for a Reality, and who therefore punishes the least Appearance with Death. Now I can never so much esteem her who owes her Virtue meerly to Fear or want of Opportunity of being False, as I would one who victoriously surmounts all the Assaults of a vigorous and watchful Lover, and yet retains her Virtue intire and unshaken. These, and many other Reasons, which I could urge to strengthen my Opinion, make me desire that my *Camilla's* Virtue may pass through the fiery Trial of vigorous Solicitations and Addresses, and these offer'd by a Gallant, who may have Merit enough to deserve her good Opinion; and if, as I am confident she will, she be able to resist so agreeable a Temptation, I shall think my self the most happy Man in the World, and attain to the height and utmost Aim of my Desires, and shall say, that a *Virtuous Woman is fallen to*

* *The Nymph may be chaste that has never been Try'd.*

my Lot, of whom the Wise Man says, *Who can find her?* If she yields, I shall, at least, have the Satisfaction of finding my Opinion of Women justify'd; and not be impos'd on by a foolish Confidence, that abuses most Men; which Consideration will be sufficient to make me support the Grief I shall derive from so expensive an Experiment. And assuring my self, that nothing which you can say can disswade me from my Resolution, I desire that you your self, my dear Friend, would be the Person to put my Design in Execution. I will furnish you with Opportunities enough of making your Addresses, in which I would have you omit nothing you may suppose likely to prevail with, and work upon a Woman of Quality, who is modest, virtuous, reserv'd, and discreet by Nature. The most prevailing Reason that makes me choose you for this Affair above all others, is, because if she should prove so frail, as to be overcome by Addresses and Importunities, the Victory will not cost me so dear, since I am secur'd from *your* taking that Advantage, of which *another* might make no Scruple. And so my Honour will remain untouch'd, and the intended Injury a Secret, in the Virtue of thy Silence; for I know my Friend so well, that Death and the Grave will as soon divulge my Affairs. Wherefore if you would give me Life indeed, and deliver me from the most perplexing Torment of Doubt, you will immediately begin this Amorous Assault, with all that Warmth, Assiduity, and Courage, I expect from that Confidence I put in your Friendship.

Lothario gave so great an Attention to *Anselmo's* Reasons, that he gave him no other Interruption, than what we mention'd. But, now finding his Discourse was at an end, full of Amazement at the Extravagance of the Proposal, he thus reply'd, Could I, my dear *Anselmo*, persuade my self that what you have said were any more than a piece of Rallery, I should not have been so long silent; no, I should have interrupted you at the beginning of your Speech. Sure you know neither your self nor me, *Anselmo*, or you would never have employ'd me on such an Affair, if you had not thought me as much alter'd from what I was, as you seem to be; for as the Poet has it, *usque ad aras; A true Friend ought to desire nothing of his Friend that is offensive to Heaven.* But should a Man so far exert his Friendship, as to deviate a little from the Severity of Religion, in compliance to his Friend, no trifling Motives can excuse the Transgression, but such only as concern, at least, his Friend's Life and Honour. Which therefore of these, *Anselmo*, is in danger, to warrant my undertaking so detestable a Thing as you desire? Neither, I dare engage: On the contrary, you would make me the Assaulter of both, in which my own is included; for to rob you of your Reputation, is to take away your Life, since an infamous Life is worse than Death; and by making me the guilty Instrument of this, as you would have me, you make me worse than a dead Man, by the Murder of my Reputation. Therefore I desire you would hear with Patience what I have to urge against your extravagant Desire, and I shall afterwards hear your Reply, without Interruption. *Anselmo* having promis'd his Attention, *Lothario* proceeded in this manner. In my Opinion, you are not unlike the *Moors*, who are incapable of being convinc'd of the Error of their Religion, by Scripture, speculative Reasons, or those drawn immediately from the Articles of our Faith; and will yield to nothing but Demonstrations, as evident as those of the Mathematicks, and which can as little be deny'd, as when we say, *If from two equal Parts, we take away two equal Parts, the Parts that remain are also equal.* And when they do not understand this Proposition, which they seldom do, we are oblig'd by Operation, to make it yet more plain and obvious to their Senses; and yet all this Labour will at last prove ineffectual to the convincing them of the Verities of our Religion. The same must be my Method with you, since your strange Desire is so very foreign to all manner of Reason, that I very much fear I shall spend my Time and Labour in vain, in endeavouring to convince you of your own Folly, for I can afford it no other Name. Nay, did I not love you as I do, I should leave you to the Prosecution of your own odd Humour, which certainly tends to your Ruin. But to lay your Folly a little more open, you bid me, *Anselmo*, attempt a Woman of Honour, cautious of her Reputation, and one who is not much inclin'd to Love; for all these good Qualifications you allow'd her. If therefore you already know your Wife is possess'd of all these Advantages of Prudence, Discretion, Honour, and Reservedness, what have you more to enquire after? And if you believe, as I my self do, that she will be impregnable to all my Assaults; what greater and better Names will you give her, than she already deserves? Either you pretend to think better of her, than really you do, or else you desire you know not what your-self. But then if you do not believe her as virtuous as you pre-tend, why would you put it to the Trial, why do you not rather use her as you think she deserves? On the other Hand, if she be as good as you profess you believe her, why would you go to tempt Truth and Goodness it self, without any reasonable Prospect of Advantage? For when the Trial is over, she will be but the same virtuous Woman she was before. Wherefore 'tis allow'd that it is the effect of Temerity, and want of Reason, to attempt what is likely to produce nothing but Danger and Detriment to the Undertaker, especially, when there is no necessity for it, and when we may easily foresee the Folly of the Undertaking. There are but these Motives to incite us to difficult Attempts, Religion, Interest, or both together. The first makes the Saints endeavour to lead Angelick Lives in these frail Bodies. The Second makes us expose ourselves to the Hazards of long Voyages and Travels in pursuit of Riches. The Third Motive is compounded of both, and prompts us to act as well for the Honour of God, as for our own particular Glory and Interests; as for Example, the daring Adventures of the valiant Soldier, who, urg'd by his Duty to God, his Prince, and his Country, fiercely runs into the midst of a dreadful Breach, unterrify'd with any Consider-ations of the Danger that threatens him. These are things done every Day, and let them be never so dangerous, they bring Honour, Glory, and Profit, to those that attempt them. But by the Project you design to reduce to an Experiment, you will never obtain either the Glory of Heaven, Profit or Reputation; For should the Experiment answer your Expec-tation, it will make no Addition, either to your Content, Hon-our, or Riches; but if it disappoint your Hopes, it makes you the most miserable Man alive. And the imaginary Advantage of no Man's knowing your Disgrace will soon vanish, when you consider, that to know it your self, will be enough to

319

supply you perpetually with all the tormenting Thoughts in the World. A Proof of this is what the famous Poet *Ludovico Tansilo*, at the end of his first Part of St *Peter's Tears*,* says, in these Words:

> Shame, Grief, Remorse in Peter's Breast increase,
> Soon as the blushing Morn his Crime betrays.
> When most unseen, then most himself he sees,
> And with due Horror all his Soul surveys.
>
> For a great Spirit needs no cens'ring Eyes
> To wound his Soul, when conscious of a Fault;
> But self-condemn'd and e'en self-punish'd lies,
> And dreads no Witness like upbraiding Thought.

So that your boasted Secrecy, far from alleviating your Grief, will only serve to increase it: and if your Eyes do not express it by outward Tears, they will flow from your very Heart in Blood. So wept that simple Doctor, who, as our Poet tells us, made that Experiment on the brittle Vessel, which the more prudent *Reynoldus* excus'd himself from doing. This, indeed, is but a Poetical Fiction, but yet the Moral which it enforces is worthy being observ'd and imitated. And accordingly I hope you will discover the strange Mistake into which you would run, principally when you have heard what I have farther to say to you.

Suppose, *Anselmo*, you had a Diamond, as valuable, in the Judgment of the best Jewellers, as such a Stone could be, would you not be satisfy'd with their Opinion, without trying its Hardness on the Anvil? You must own, that should it be Proof against your Blows, it would not be one Jot the more valuable than really it was before your foolish Trial; but should it happen to break, as well it might, the Jewel were then entirely lost, as well as the Sense and Reputation of the Owner. This precious Diamond, my Friend, is your *Camilla*, for so she ought to be esteemed in all Men's Opinions as well as your own; why then would you imprudently put her in danger of falling, since your Trial will add no greater

* *This Poem, written Originally in* Italian, *is translated into* Spanish *by* Juan Sedeno, *and into* French *by* Malherbe.

Value to her than she has already? But if she should prove
frail, reflect with yourself on the Unhappiness of your Condition, and how justly you might complain of your being the
Cause of both Her Ruin and your own. Consider, that as a
modest and honest Woman is the most valuable Jewel in the
World, so all Women's Virtue and Honour consist in the
Opinion and Reputation they maintain with other People,
and since that of your Wife is perfect, both in your own and
all other Mens Opinion, why will you go, to no purpose, to
call the reality of it in question? You must remember, my
Friend, that the Nature of Women is, at best, but weak and
imperfect; and for that reason we should be so far from casting Rubs in its way, that we ought, with all imaginable Care,
to remove every Appearance that might hinder its Course to
that Perfection it wants, which is *Virtue*.

If you believe the Naturalists, the *Ermine* is a very white
little Creature; when the Hunters have found its Haunts, they
surround it almost with Dirt and Mire, towards which the
Ermine being forc'd to fly, rather than sully its native White
with Dirt, it suffers itself to be taken, preferring its Colour
to its Liberty and Life. The virtuous Woman is our *Ermine*,
whose Chastity is whiter than Snow; but to preserve its Colour
unsully'd, you must observe just a contrary Method: The Addresses and Services of an importunate Lover, are the Mire
into which you should never drive a Woman; for 'tis ten to
one she will not be able to free her self and avoid it, being but
too apt to stumble into it; and therefore That should be always
remov'd, and only the Candour and Beauty of Virtue, and the
Charms of a good Fame and Reputation plac'd before her. A
good Woman is also not unlike a Mirrour of Crystal, which
will infallibly be dimm'd and stain'd by breathing too much
upon it: She must rather be us'd like the Reliques of Saints,
ador'd but not touch'd; or like a Garden of curious tender
Flowers, that may at a distance gratify the Eye, but are not
permitted by the Master to be trampled on or touch'd by every
Beholder. I shall add but a few Verses out of a late new Play,
very fit for our present Purpose, where a prudent old Man
advis'd his Neighbour, that had a Daughter, to lock her up
close; and gives these Reasons for it, besides several others:

Since nothing is frailer than Woman and Glass,
He that wou'd expose 'em to fall is an Ass;
And sure the rash Mortal is yet more unwise,
Who on Bodies so ticklish Experiments tries.
With Ease both are damag'd; then keep that with Care
Which no Art can restore, nor no Solder repair.
Fond Man take my Counsel, watch what is so frail;
For, where Danaes lie, Golden Show'rs will prevail.

All I have hitherto urg'd relates only to You, I may now at last be allow'd to consider what regards my self; and if I am tedious I hope you will pardon me; for to draw you out of the Labyrinth into which you have run yourself, I am forc'd on that Prolixity: You call me Friend, yet, which is absolutely inconsistent with Friendship, you would rob me of my Honour; nay, you stop not here, but would oblige me to destroy yours. First, That you would rob me of mine is evident; for what will *Camilla* think, when I make a Declaration of Love to her, but that I am a perfidious Villain, that make no scruple of violating the most sacred Laws of Friendship, and who sacrifice the Honour and Reputation of my Friend to a criminal Passion: Secondly, That I destroy yours is as evident; for when she sees me take such a Liberty with her, she will imagine that I have discovered some Weakness in her, that has given me assurance to make her so guilty a Discovery, by which she esteeming herself injur'd in her Honour, *you* being the principal part of her, must of necessity be affected with the Affronts *she* receives. For this is the Reason why the Husband, though never so deserving, cautious and careful, suffers the Infamy of a scandalous Name if his Wife goes astray; whereas in reason he ought rather to be an Object of Compassion than Contempt, seeing the Misfortune proceeds from the Vice and Folly of the Wife, not his own Defects. But since the Reason and Justice of the Man's suffering for his Wife's Transgression may be serviceable to you, I'll give you the best Account of it I can; and pray do not think me tedious, since this is meant for your Good. When Woman was given to Man, and Marriage first ordain'd in Paradise, Man and Wife were made and pronounc'd *one Flesh*; the Husband therefore being of a piece with the Wife, whatever affects her affects him, as a Part of her; tho', as I have said, he has been no Occasion of it: For as the whole Body is affected by the Pain of any Part, as the Head will share the Pain of the Foot, tho' it never caus'd that Pain, so is the Husband touch'd with his Wife's Infamy, because she is Part of him. And since all worldly Honours and Dishonours are deriv'd from Flesh and Blood, and the scandalous Baseness of an unfaithful Wife proceeds from the same Principle, it necessarily follows, that the Husband, tho' no Party in the Offence, and intirely ignorant and innocent of it, must have his Share of the Infamy. Let what I have said, my dear *Anselmo*, make you sensible of the Danger into which you would run, by endeavouring thus to disturb the happy Tranquillity and Repose that your Wife at present enjoys; and for how vain a Curiosity, and extravagant a Caprice, you would rouse and awake those peccant Humours which are now lull'd asleep by the Power of an unattempted Chastity. Reflect farther, how small a Return you can expect from so hazardous a Voyage, and such valuable Commodities as you venture; for the Treasure you will lose is so great, and ought to be so dear, that all Words are too inexpressive to shew how much you ought to esteem it. But if all I have said be too weak to destroy your foolish Resolve, employ some other Instrument of your Disgrace and Ruin; for, tho' I should lose your Friendship, a Loss which I must esteem the greatest in the World, I will have no Hand in an Affair so prejudicial to your Honour.

Lothario said no more, and *Anselmo* discovering a desponding Melancholy in his Face, remain'd a great while silent and confounded. At last, I have, said he, my Friend, listen'd to your Discourse, as you might observe, with all the Attention in Nature, and every part of what you have said convinces me of the Greatness of your Wisdom and Friendship; and I must own, that if I suffer my Desires to prevail over your Reasons, I shun the Good and pursue the Evil. But yet, my Friend, you ought, on the other side, to reflect, that my Distemper is not much unlike that of those Women, who sometimes long for Coals, Lime, nay, some things that are loathsome to the very sight; and therefore some little Arts should be us'd to endeavour my Cure, which might easily be effected, if you would but consent to solicit *Camilla*, though it were but weakly and remissly; for I am sure she will not be so frail to surrender at the first Assault, which yet will be sufficient to give me the Satisfaction I desire; And in this you will fulfil the Duty of our Friendship, in restoring me to Life, and securing my Honour, by your powerful and perswasive Reasons. And you are indeed bound as my Friend to do thus much to secure me from betraying my Defects, and Follies to a Stranger, which would hazard that Reputation, which you have taken so much Pains to preserve; since I am so bent on this Experiment, that if you refuse me, I shall certainly apply myself elsewhere: And though a while your Reputation may suffer in *Camilla's* Opinion, yet when she has once prov'd triumphant, you may cure that Wound, and recover her good Opinion, by a sincere Discovery of your Design. Wherefore I conjure you to comply with my Importunity, in spite of all the Obstacles that may present themselves to you, since what I desire is so little, and the Pleasure I shall derive from it so great: For as I have promis'd, your very first Attempt shall satisfy me as much as if you had gone through the whole Experiment.

Lothario plainly saw that *Anselmo's* Resolution was too much fix'd for any thing he cou'd say to alter it, and finding that he threaten'd to betray his Folly to a Stranger, if he persisted in a Refusal; to avoid greater Inconveniencies, he resolv'd to seem to comply with his Desires, privately designing to satisfy *Anselmo's* Caprice, without giving *Camilla* any Trouble; and therefore he desir'd him to break the Matter to no body else, since he would himself undertake it, and begin as soon as he pleas'd. *Anselmo* embrac'd him with all the Love and Tenderness imaginable, and was as prodigal of his Thanks, as if the very Promise had been the greatest Obligation that could be laid on him. They immediately agreed on the next Day for the Trial, at which time *Anselmo* should give him the Opportunity of being alone with her, and Gold and Jewels to present her with. He advis'd him to omit no Point of Gallantry, as Serenades and Songs, and Verses in her Praise; offering to make 'em himself, if *Lothario* would not be at the Trouble. But *Lothario* promis'd him to do all himself, tho' his Design was far different from *Anselmo's*.

Matters being thus adjusted, they return'd to *Anselmo's*

House, where they found the Beautiful *Camilla* sad with Concern for the Absence of her Husband beyond his usual Hour. *Lothario* left him there, and retir'd home, as pensive how to come off handsomely in this ridiculous Affair, as he had left *Anselmo* pleas'd and contented with his undertaking it. But that Night, he contriv'd a Way of imposing on *Anselmo* to his Satisfaction, without offending *Camilla*. So next Day he goes to *Anselmo's*, and was receiv'd by *Camilla* with a Civility and Respect answerable to the uncommon Friendship she knew was between him and her Husband. Dinner being over, *Anselmo* desir'd his Friend to keep his Lady company till his return from an extraordinary Affair, that would require his Absence about an Hour and half. *Camilla* desir'd him not to go; *Lothario* offer'd to go with him; but he pleaded peculiar Business, intreated his Friend to stay, and injoin'd his Wife not to leave him alone till his return. In short, he knew so well how to counterfeit a Necessity for his Absence, 'tho that Necessity proceeded only from his own Folly, that no one cou'd perceive it was feign'd. And so he left them together, without any one to observe their Actions, all the Servants being retir'd to Dinner.

Thus *Lothario* found himself enter'd the Lists, his Adversary before him terribly arm'd with a thousand piercing Beauties, sufficient to overcome all the Men she should encounter, which gave him cause enough to fear his own Fate. The first thing he did in this first Onset, was to lean his Head carelessly on his Hand, and beg her leave to take a Nap in his Chair, till his Friend came back: *Camilla* told him she thought he might rest with more ease on the Couch* in the next Room; he declared himself satisfy'd with the Place where he was, and so slept till his Friend came back. *Anselmo* finding his Wife in her Chamber, and *Lothario* asleep at his return, concluded that he had given them time enough both for Discourse, and Repose; and therefore waited with a great deal of Impatience for his Friend's awaking, that they might retire, and he might acquaint him with his Success. *Lothario* at last

---

* Estrado. *A Space of the Visiting-Rooms of Ladies, rais'd a Foot above the Floor of the rest of the Room, cover'd with Carpets or Mats, on which the Ladies sit on Cushions laid along by the Wall, or low Stools.*

awak'd, and going out with his Friend, he answer'd his Enquiry to this purpose, That he did not think it convenient to proceed farther, at that Time, than some general Praise of her Wit and Beauty, which would best prepare his Way for what he might do hereafter, and dispose her to give a more easy and willing Ear to what he should say to her: As the Devil, by laying a pleasing and apparent Good at first before us, insinuates himself into our Inclinations so that he generally gains his Point before we discover the Cloven-Foot, if his Disguise pass on us in the beginning. *Anselmo* was extremely satisfy'd with what *Lothario* said, and promis'd him every Day as good an Opportunity; and tho' he could not go every Day abroad, yet he would manage his Conduct so well, that *Camilla* should have no cause of Suspicion. He took care to do as he said. But *Lothario* wilfully lost the frequent Opportunities he gave him; however, he sooth'd him still with Assurances, that his Lady was inflexible, her Virtue not to be surmounted, and that she had threatned to discover his Attempts to her Husband, if he ever presum'd to be so Insolent again; so far was she from giving the least Hope or Encouragement. Thus far 'tis well, said *Anselmo*, but yet *Camilla* has resisted nothing but Words, we must now see what Proof she is against more substantial Temptations. To-morrow I will furnish you with two thousand Crowns in Gold, to present her with; and as a farther Bait, you shall have as much more for Jewels. For Women, especially if they are handsome, naturally love to go gayly and richly drest, be they never so chaste and virtuous; and if she have Power to overcome this Temptation, I'll give you no farther Trouble. Since I have begun this Adventure, reply'd *Lothario*, I will make an end of it, tho' I am sure her Repulses will tire out my Patience, and her Virtue overcome any Temptation, and baffle my Endeavours.

The next Day *Anselmo* deliver'd him the four thousand Crowns, and with them as many perplexing Thoughts, not knowing how to supply his Invention with some new Story to amuse his Friend. However at last he resolv'd to return the Money, with Assurance that *Camilla* was as unmov'd with Presents, as with Praise, and as untouch'd with Promises as with Vows and Sighs of Love; and therefore all farther Attempts wou'd be but a fruitless Labour. This was his Intention; but Fortune that meddl'd too much in these Affairs disappointed his Designs. For *Anselmo* having left him alone with his Wife one Day as he us'd to do, privately convey'd himself into the Closet, and thro' the Chinks of the Door set himself to observe what they did; he found that for one half Hour *Lothario* said not one Word to *Camilla*, from whence he concluded that all the Addresses, Importunities and Repulses, with which he had amus'd him were pure Fictions. But, that he might be fully satisfy'd in the Truth of his Surmise, coming from his Covert he took his Friend aside, and enquired of him what *Camilla* had then said to him, and how he now found her inclin'd? *Lothario* reply'd, that he would make no farther tryal of her, since her Answer had now been so severe and awful, that he durst not for the future venture upon a Discourse so evidently her Aversion.

Ah! *Lothario! Lothario!* cry'd *Anselmo*, is it thus that you keep your Promises? Is this what I should expect from your Friendship? I observ'd you through that Door, and found that you said not a Word to *Camilla*; and from thence I am very well satisfy'd, that you have only impos'd on me all the Answers and Relations you have made. Why did you hinder me from employing some other, if you never intended to satisfy my Desire? *Anselmo* said no more, but this was enough to confound *Lothario*, and cover him with Shame for being found in a Lye. Therefore to appease his Friend, he swore to him, from that Time forward, to set in good earnest about the Matter, and that so effectually, that he himself, if he wou'd again give himself the Trouble of observing him, should find proof enough of his Sincerity. *Anselmo* believ'd him; and to give him the better Opportunity, he engag'd a Friend of his to send for him, with a great deal of Importunity, to come to his House at a Village near the City, where he meant to spend eight Days, to take away all Apprehension and Fear from both his Friend and his Wife.

Was ever Man so unhappy as *Anselmo*, who industriously contriv'd the Plot of his own Ruin and Dishonour? He had a very good Wife, and possess'd her in quiet, without any other Man's mingling in his Pleasures; her Thoughts were bounded with her own House, and her Husband, the only earthly Good she hoped or thought on, and her only Pleasure and Desire; his Will the Rule of hers, and Measure of her Conduct. When he possess'd Love, Honour, Beauty and Discretion, without Pain or Toil, what shou'd provoke him to seek with so much Danger and Hazard of what he had already, that which was not to be found in Nature! He that aims at Things impossible, ought justly to lose those Advantages which are within the Bounds of Possibility, as the Poet sings:

I

In Death I seek for Life,
In a Disease for Health,
For Quietness in Strife,
In Poverty for Wealth,
   And constant Truth in an inconstant Wife.

2

But sure the Fates disdain
My mad Desires to please,
Nor shall I e'er obtain
What others get with Ease,
   Since I demand what no Man e'er cou'd gain.

The next Day *Anselmo* went out of Town; having first in- form'd *Camilla*, that his Friend *Lothario* would look after his Affairs, and keep her Company in his Absence, and desir'd her to make as much of him as of himself. His Lady, like a discreet Woman, begg'd him to consider how improper a Thing it was for any other to take his Place in his Absence; and told him, that if he doubted her Ability in managing her House, he should try her but this time, and she question'd not but he would find she had Capacity to acquit herself to his Satisfac- tion in greater Matters. *Anselmo* reply'd, that it was her Duty not to dispute, but obey his Command; To which she return'd, that she would comply, tho' much against her Will. In short, her Husband left the Town: *Lothario*, the next Day, was re- ceiv'd at her House with all the Respect that could be paid a Friend so dear to her Husband; but yet with so much Caution, that she never permitted herself to be left alone with him but kept perpetually some of her Maids in the Room, and chiefly *Leonela*, for whom she had a particular Love, as having been bred in her Father's House with her from her Infancy.

Lotario said nothing to her the three first Days, notwithstanding he might have found an Opportunity when the Servants were gone to Dinner; for tho' the prudent *Camilla* had order'd *Leonela* to dine before her, that she might have no Occasion to go out of the Room; yet she, who had other Affairs to employ her Thoughts, more agreeable to her Inclinations (to gratify which that was usually the only convenient time she could find) was not so very punctually obedient to her Lady's Commands, but that she sometimes left them together. *Lotario* did not yet make use of these Advantages, as I have said, being aw'd by the Virtue and Modesty of *Camilla*. But this Silence which she thus impos'd on *Lotario*, had at last a quite contrary Effect. For though he said nothing, his Thoughts were active, his Eyes were employ'd to see and survey the outward Charms of a Form so perfect, that 'twas enough to fire the most cold, and soften the most obdurate Heart. In these Intervals of Silence, he consider'd how much she deserv'd to be belov'd; and these Considerations by little and little undermin'd and assaulted the Faith which he ow'd to his Friend. A thousand times he resolv'd to leave the City and retire where *Anselmo* should never see him, and where he should never more behold the dangerous Face of *Camilla*; but the extreme Pleasure he found in seeing her, soon destroy'd so feeble a Resolve. When he was alone he wou'd accuse his want of Friendship and Religion, and run into frequent Comparisons betwixt himself and *Anselmo*, which generally concluded that *Anselmo's* Folly and Madness was greater than his Breach of Faith; and that, wou'd Heaven as easily excuse his Intentions as Man, he had no cause to fear any Punishment for the Crime he was going to commit. In fine, *Camilla's* Beauty, and the Opportunity given him by the Husband himself, wholly vanquish'd his Faith and Friendship. And now having an Eye only to the means of obtaining that Pleasure, to which he was prompted with so much Violence; after he had spent the three first Days of *Anselmo's* Absence, in a Conflict betwixt Love and Virtue, he attempted,

by all means possible, to prevail with *Camilla*, and discover'd
so much Passion in his Words and Actions, that *Camilla*, surpriz'd with the unexpected Assault, flung from him out of
the Room, and retir'd with haste to her Chamber. Hope is
always born with Love, nor did this Repulse in the least dis-
courage *Lothario* from farther Attempts on *Camilla*, who by
this appear'd more charming, and more worthy his Pursuit.
She, on the other hand, knew not what to do upon the
Discovery of that in *Lothario*, which she never cou'd have
imagin'd. The Result of her Reflections was this, that since
she cou'd not give him any Opportunity of speaking to her
again, without the Hazard of her Reputation and Honour,
she wou'd send a Letter to her Husband to solicit his Return
to his House. The Letter she sent by a Messenger that very
Night; and it was to this purpose.

VII: IN WHICH THE HISTORY OF THE CURIOUS IMPERTINENT IS PURSU'D

As 'tis very improper to leave an Army without a General, and a Garrison without its Governor; so to me it seems much more imprudent to leave a young marry'd Woman without her Husband; especially when there are no Affairs of Consequence to plead for his Absence. I find my self so ill in your's, and so impatient, and unable to endure it any longer, that if you come not home very quickly, I shall be oblig'd to return to my Father's, tho' I leave your House without any one to look after it: For the Person to whom you have intrusted the Care of your Family, has, I believe, more Regard to his own Pleasure than your Concerns. You are wise and prudent, and therefore I shall say no more, nor is it convenient I shou'd.

Anselmo was not a little satisfy'd at the Receipt of this Letter, which assur'd him that Lothario had begun the Attempt, which she had repell'd according to his Hopes; and therefore he sent her Word not to leave his House, assuring her it shou'd not be long before he return'd. Camilla was surpriz'd with his Answer, and more perplex'd than before, being equally afraid of going to her Father, and of staying at home; in the first she disobey'd her Husband, in the latter ran the Risque of her Honour. The worst Resolution prevail'd, which was to stay at her own House, and not avoid Lothario's Company, lest it shou'd give some Cause of Suspicion to her Servants. And now she repented her writing to Anselmo, lest he shou'd suspect that Lothario had observ'd some Indiscretion in her, that made him lose the Respect due to her, and gave him Assurance to offer at the corrupting her Virtue: But confiding in Heaven and her own Innocence, which she thought Proof against all Lothario's Attempts, she resolv'd to make no Answer to whatever he should say to her, and never more to trouble her Husband with Complaints, for fear of engaging him in Disputes and Quarrels with his Friend. For that Reason she consider'd how she might best excuse him to Anselmo, when he shou'd examine the Cause of her writing to him in that Manner. With a Resolution so innocent and dangerous, the next Day she gave ear to all that *Lothario* said; and he gave the Assault with such Force and Vigour, that *Camilla's* Constancy could not stand the Shock unmov'd, and her Virtue cou'd do no more than guard her Eyes from betraying that tender Compassion, of which his Vows and Intreaties, and all his Sighs and Tears had made her Heart sensible. *Lothario* discover'd this with an infinite Satisfaction, and no less Addition to his Flame; and found that he ought to make use of this Opportunity of *Anselmo's* Absence, with all his Force and Importunity, to win so valuable a Fortress. He began with the powerful Battery of the Praise of her Beauty, which being directly pointed on the Weakest Part of Woman, her Vanity, with the greatest Ease and Facility in the World makes a Breach as great as a Lover wou'd desire. *Lothario* was not unskilful or remiss in the Attack, but follow'd his Fire so close, that let *Camilla's* Integrity be built on never so obdurate a Rock, it must at last have fall'n. He wept, pray'd, flatter'd, promis'd, swore, vow'd, and shew'd so much Passion and Truth in what he said, that beating down the Care of her Honour, he, at last, triumph'd over what he scarce durst hope, tho' what he most of all desir'd; for she, at last, surrender'd, even *Camilla* surrender'd. Nor ought we to wonder if she yielded, since even *Lothario's* Friendship and Virtue were not able to withstand the terrible Assault; an evident Proof that Love is a Power too strong to be overcome by any thing but flying, and that no mortal Creature ought to be so presumptuous as to stand the Encounter, since there is need of something more than Human, and indeed a heavenly Force, to confront and vanquish that human Passion. *Leonela* was the only Confidant of this Amour, which these new Lovers and faithless Friends could not by any means conceal from her Knowledge. *Lothario* would not discover to *Camilla*, that her Husband, for her Trial, had designedly given him this Opportunity, to which he ow'd so extreme a Happiness; because she shou'd not think he wanted Love to solicit her himself with Importunity, or that she was gain'd on too easy Terms.

Anselmo came home in a few Days, but discover'd not what he had lost, tho' it was what he most valu'd and esteem'd: From thence he went to *Lothario*, and embracing him, begg'd of him to let him know his Fate. All I can tell you, my Friend, answer'd *Lothario*, is, that you may boast yourself the Husband of the best Wife in the World, the Ornament of her Sex, and the Pattern which all virtuous Women ought to follow. Words, Offers, Presents, all is ineffectual; the Tears I pretended to shed, mov'd only her Laughter. *Camilla* is not only Mistress of the greatest Beauty, but of Modesty, Discretion, Sweetness of Temper, and every other Virtue and Perfection that add to the Charms of a Woman of Honour. Therefore, my Friend, here take back your Money, I have had no Occasion to lay it out, for *Camilla's* Integrity cannot be corrupted by such base and mercenary things as Gifts and Promises. And now, *Anselmo*, be at last content with the Trial you have already made; and having so luckily got over the dangerous Quick-sands of Doubts and Suspicions that are to be met with in the Ocean of Matrimony, do not venture out again, with another Pilot, that Vessel, whose Strength you have sufficiently experienc'd; but believe yourself, as you are, securely anchor'd in a safe Harbour, at Pleasure and Ease, till Death, from whose Force, no Title, Power, nor Dignity can secure us, does come and cut the Cable. *Anselmo* was extremely satisfy'd with *Lothario's* Discourse, and believ'd it as firmly as if it had been an Oracle; yet desir'd him to continue his Pursuit, if it were but to pass away the Time: He did not require he shou'd press *Camilla* with those Importunities he had before us'd, but only make some Verses in her Praise, under the Name of *Cloris*; and he would make *Camilla* believe he celebrated a Lady he lov'd, under that Name, to secure her Honour and Reputation from the Censure which a more open Declaration would expose her to: He added, that if *Lothario* would not be at the expence of so much Trouble and Time, as to compose them himself, he would do it for him with a great deal of Pleasure. *Lothario* told him there was no need of that, since he himself was sometimes poetically given; do you but tell *Camilla* of my pretended Love, as you say you will, and I'll make the Verses as well as I can, tho' not so well as the Excellency of the Subject requires. The *Curious Impertinent*, and his treacherous Friend, having thus agreed the Matter, *Anselmo* went home, and then ask'd *Camilla* on what Occasion

333

she sent him the Letter? *Camilla*, who wonder'd that this Question had not been ask'd her before, reply'd, That the Motive that prevail'd with her to write in that Manner to him, was a Jealousy she had entertain'd, that *Lotario*, in his Absence, look'd on her with more criminal and desiring Eyes than he us'd to do when he was at home; but that since she had Reason to believe that Suspicion but weakly grounded, seeing he discover'd rather an Aversion than Love, as avoiding all Occasions of being alone with her. *Anselmo* told her she had nothing to apprehend from *Lotario* on that Account, since he knew his Affections engag'd on one of the noblest young Ladies of the City, whose Praise he writ under the Name of *Cloris*; but were he not thus engag'd, there was no Reason to suspect *Lotario's* Virtue and Friendship. *Camilla*, at this Discourse, without Doubt, would have been very jealous of *Lotario*, had he not told her his Design of abusing her Husband, with the Pretence of another Love, that he might, with the greater Liberty and Security, express her Praise and his Passion. The next Day, at Dinner, *Anselmo* desir'd him to read some of the Verses he had made on his beloved *Cloris*; telling him, he might say any thing of her before *Camilla*, since she did not know who the Lady was. Did *Camilla* know her, reply'd *Lotario*, that shou'd not make me pass over in Silence any Part of that Praise which was her due; for if a Lover complains of his Mistress's Cruelty, while he is praising her Perfections, she can never suffer in her Reputation. Therefore, without any Fear, I shall repeat a Sonnet which I made yesterday on the Ingratitude of *Cloris*.

A SONNET

At Dead of Night, when ev'ry troubled Breast
By balmy Sleep is eas'd of anxious Pain,
    When Slaves themselves, in pleasing Dreams are blest,
Of Heaven and Cloris, *restless I complain.*

The rosy Morn dispels the Shades of Night,
The Sun, the Pleasures, and the Day return;
    All Nature's chear'd with the reviving Light;
I, only I, can never cease to mourn.

> At *Noon*, in vain, I bid my *Sorrow cease*,
> The *Heat increases*, and my *Pains increase*,
>   And still my *Soul* in the mild *Evening* grieves:
> The *Night* returns, and my *Complaints* renew,
> No *Moment* sees me free; in vain I sue,
>   Heav'n ne'er relents, and *Cloris* ne'er relieves.

Camilla, was mightily pleas'd with the Sonnet, but *Anselmo* transported; he was lavish of his Commendation, and added that the Lady must be barbarously cruel that made no Return to so much Truth, and so violent a Passion. What, must we then believe all that a Poet in Love tells us for Truth? said *Camilla*. Madam, reply'd *Lothario*, tho' the *Poet* may exceed, yet the *Lover* corrects his Fondness for Fiction, and makes him speak Truth. *Anselmo*, to advance *Lothario's* Credit with *Camilla*, confirm'd whatever he said; but she not minding her Husband's Confirmations, was sufficiently persuaded, by her Passion for *Lothario*, to an implicit Faith in all he said; and therefore pleas'd with this Composition, and more satisfy'd in the Knowledge she had that all was address'd to herself, as the true *Cloris*, she desir'd him to repeat some other Verses he had made on that Subject, if he could remember any. I remember some, reply'd *Lothario*; but, Madam, in my Opinion, they are not so tolerable as the former; but you shall be Judge yourself.

A SONNET

1

> *I Die your Victim, cruel Fair,*
>   *And die without Reprieve,*
> *If you can think your Slave can bear*
>   *Your Cruelty, and live.*

2

> *Since all my Hopes of Ease are vain,*
>   *To die I now submit;*
> *And that you may not think I feign,*
>   *It must be at your Feet.*

335

3

Yet when my bleeding Heart you view,
  Bright Nymph, forbear to grieve;
For I had rather die for you,
  Than for another live.

4

In Death and dark Oblivion's Grave,
  Oh! let me lie forlorn,
For my poor Ghost wou'd pine and rave,
  Shou'd you relent and mourn.

Anselmo was not less profuse in his Praise of this Sonnet, than he had been of the other, and so added new Fuel to the Fire that was to consume his Reputation. He contributed to his own Abuse, in commending his false Friend's Attempts on his Honour, as the most important Service he could do it; and this made him believe, that every Step *Camilla* made down to Contempt and Disgrace, was a Degree she mounted towards that Perfection of Virtue which he desir'd she should attain.

Some time after, *Camilla* being alone with her Maid, I am asham'd, said she, my *Leonela*, that I gave *Lothario* so easy a Conquest over me, and did not know my own Worth enough to make him undergo some greater Fatigues, before I made him so entire a Surrender. I am afraid he will think my hasty Consent the Effect of the Looseness of my Temper, and not at all consider that the Force and Violence he us'd, depriv'd me of the Power of resisting. Ah! Madam, return'd *Leonela*, let not that disquiet you; for the speedy bestowing a Benefit of an intrinsick Value, and which you design to bestow at last, can never lessen the Favour; for according to the old Proverb, *He that gives quickly gives twice.* To answer your Proverb with another, reply'd *Camilla*, *That which cost little is less valued.* But this has nothing to do with you, answer'd *Leonela*, since 'tis said of Love that it sometimes goes, sometimes flies; runs with one, walks gravely with another; turns a third into Ice, and sets a fourth in a Flame: It wounds one, another it kills: like Lightning it begins and ends in the same Moment: It makes that Fort yield at Night which it besieg'd but in the Morning;

for there is no Force able to resist it. Since this is evident, what Cause have you to be surprized at your own Frailty? And why shou'd you apprehend any thing from *Lothario*, who has felt the same irresistable Power, and yielded to it as soon? For Love, to gain a Conquest, took the short Opportunity of my Master's Absence, which being so short and uncertain, Love, that had before determin'd this shou'd be done, added Force and Vigour to the Lover, not to leave any thing to Time and Chance, which might, by *Anselmo's* Return, cut off all Opportunities of accomplishing so agreeable a Work. The best and most officious Servant of Love's Retinue, is Occasion or Opportunity: This it is that Love improves in all its Progress, but most in the Beginning and first Rise of an Amour. I trust not in what I have said to the Uncertainty of Report, but to Experience, which affords the most certain and most valuable Knowledge, as I will inform You, Madam, some Day or other; for I am like you, made of frail Flesh and Blood, fir'd by Youth and youthful Desires. But, Madam, you did not surrender to *Lothario* till you had sufficient Proof of his Love, from his Eyes, his Vows, his Promises, and Gifts; till you had seen the Merit of his Person, and the Beauty of his Mind; all which convinc'd you how much he deserv'd to be lov'd. Then trouble yourself no more, Madam, with these Fears and Jealousies; but thank your Stars, that, since you were doom'd a Victim to Love, you fell by the Force of such Valour and Merit that cannot be doubted. You yielded to one who has not only the four S's,* which are requir'd in every good Lover, but even the whole *Alphabet*; as for Example, he is, in my Opinion, *Agreeable, Bountiful, Constant, Dutiful, Easy, Faithful, Gallant, Honourable, Ingenious, Kind, Loyal, Mild, Noble, Officious, Prudent, Quiet, Rich, Secret, True, Valiant, Wise;* the X indeed, is too harsh a Letter to agree with him, but he is *Young* and *Zealous* for your Honour and Service. *Camilla* laugh'd at her Woman's *Alphabet*, and thought her (as indeed she was) more learn'd in the practical Part of Love, than she had yet confess'd. She then inform'd her Mistress of an Affair that had been betwixt her and a young Man of the Town. *Camilla* was not a little concern'd at what she said, being apprehen-

* As if we shou'd say, *sightly, sprightly, sincere, and secret.*

sive that her Honour might suffer by her Woman's Indiscretion; and therefore ask'd her if the Amour had pass'd any
farther than Words? *Leonela*, without any Fear or Shame,
own'd her guilty Correspondence with all the Freedom in the
World; for the Mistress's Guilt gives the Servant Impudence;
and generally they imitate their Ladies Frailties, without any
fear of the publick Censure.

Camilla, finding her Error past Remedy, could only beg
Leonela to disclose nothing of her Affair to her Lover, and
manage her Amour with Secrecy and Discretion, for fear *Lothario* or *Anselmo* should hear of it. *Leonela* promis'd to obey
her; but she did it in such a Manner, that *Camilla* was perpetually in Fear of the loss of her Reputation by her Folly;
for she grew so confident on her Knowledge of her Lady's
Transgression, that she admitted the Gallant into the House,
not caring if her Lady knew it, being certain that she durst
not make any Discovery to her Master: For when once a Mistress has suffer'd her Virtue to be vanquish'd, and admits of
any criminal Correspondence, it subjects her to her own Servants, and makes her subservient to their leud Practices,
which she is slavishly bound to conceal. Thus it was with
Camilla, who was forc'd to wink at the visible Rendezvous,
which *Leonela* had with her Lover, in a certain Chamber of
the House which she thought proper for the Occasion; nor
was that all, she was constrain'd to give her the Opportunity
of hiding him, that he might not be seen by her Husband.

But all this Caution did not secure him from being seen by
Lothario one Morning, as he was getting out of the House by
break of Day. His Surprize had made him think it a Spirit,
had not his Haste away, and his muffling himself up as he did,
that he might not be known, convinc'd him of his Error, and
thrown him into a Fit of Jealousy, that had certainly undone
them all, had not *Camilla's* Wit and Address prevented it.
For *Lothario* concluded that *Camilla*, that had made no very
obstinate Resistance to him, had as easily surrender'd to some
other; and he fancy'd that the Person he saw come from her
House was the new-favour'd Lover; never remembring there
was such a Person as *Leonela* in the House, and that he might
be a Lover of hers. For when once a Woman parts with her

Virtue, she loses the Esteem even of the Man whose Vows and Tears won her to abandon it; and he believes she will with as little, if not less Difficulty, yield to Another; he perverts the least Suspicions into Reality, and takes the slightest Appearance for the most evident Matter of Fact.

Thus *Lothario*, distracted by the most violent Jealousy in the World, without allowing himself time to consider, gave way to the Transports of his Rage and Desire of Revenge on *Camilla*, who had not injur'd him; he goes immediately to *Anselmo*, and having found him abed: I have, my Friend, said he to him, these several Days undergone a most severe Conflict within my Mind, and us'd all the Force and Violence I was capable of to conceal an Affair from you, which I can no longer forbear discovering, without an apparent Wrong to Justice, and my Friendship. Know then that *Camilla* is now ready to do whatsoever I shall desire of her; and the Reason that most prevail'd with me to delay this Discovery, was, that I would be satisfy'd whether she were in earnest, or only pretended this Compliance to try me; but had she been so virtuous as You and I believ'd her, she would, by this time, have inform'd you of that Importunity which, by your Desire, I us'd; but finding that she is silent, and takes no notice of that to you, I have reason to believe that she is but too sincere in those guilty Promises she has made me, of meeting me to my Satisfaction in the Wardrobe, the next time your Absence from the Town should furnish her with an Opportunity. (This was true indeed, for that was the Place of their common Rendezvous) Yet I would not have you, continu'd he, take a rash and inconsiderate Revenge, since 'tis possible, before the time of Assignation, her Virtue may rally, and she repent her Folly. Therefore, as you have hitherto taken my Advice, be rul'd by me now, that you may not be impos'd on, but have a sufficient Conviction before you put your Resolves into Execution. Pretend two or three Days Absence, and then privately convey yourself behind the Hangings in the Wardrobe, as you easily may, whence you may, without Difficulty, be an Eye-Witness with me of *Camilla's* Conduct; and if it be as Criminal as we may justly fear, then you may with Secrecy and Speed punish her, as the Injury deserves.

Anselmo was extremely surpriz'd at so unexpected a Misfortune, to find himself deceiv'd in those imaginary Triumphs he pleas'd himself with, in *Camilla's* suppos'd Victory over all *Lothario's* Assaults. A great while he was in a silent Suspence, with his Eyes dejected, without Force, and without Spirit; but turning at last to his Friend, You have done all, said he, *Lothario*, that I could expect from so perfect a Friendship, I will therefore be entirely guided by your Advice; Do therefore what you please, but use all the Secrecy a Thing of this Nature requires. *Lothario*, assuring him of that, left him; but full of Repentance for the Rashness he had been guilty of in telling him so much as he had, since he might have taken a sufficient Revenge, by a less cruel and dishonourable way. He curs'd his want of Sense, and the Weakness of his Resolution, but could not find out any way to produce a less fatal Event of his Treachery, than he could justly expect from the Experiment. But at last he concluded to inform *Camilla* of all he had done; which his Freedom of Access gave him Opportunity to do that very Day, when he found her alone; and she began thus to him. I am so oppress'd, my *Lothario*, with a Misfortune which I lie under, that it will certainly for ever destroy my Quiet and Happiness, if there be not some speedy Remedy found for it: *Leonela* is grown so presumptuous, on her Knowledge of my Affairs, that she admits her Lover all Night to her Chamber, and so exposes my Reputation to the Censure of any that shall see him go out at unseasonable Hours from my House; and the greatest, and most remediless part of my Grief is, that I dare not correct or chide her for her Imprudence and Impudence; for being conscious of our Correspondence, she obliges me to conceal her Failings, which I am extremely apprehensive will in the end be very fatal to my Happiness. *Lothario* was at first jealous that *Camilla* design'd cunningly thus to impose her own Privado on him for *Leonela's*; but being convinc'd by her Tears, and the apparent Concern in her Face, he began to believe her, and at the same time to be infinitely confounded and griev'd for what he had done. Yet he comforted *Camilla*, assuring her he would take effectual Care for the future, that *Leonela's* Impudence should do her no Prejudice, and therefore begg'd her not to torment herself any more about it. Then he told all the unhappy Effects of his Jealous Rage, and that her Husband had agreed behind the Arras to be Witness of her Weakness. He ask'd her Pardon for the Folly, and her Counsel how to redress and prevent the ill Effect of it, and bring them out of those Difficulties into which his Madness had plung'd them.

Camilla express'd her Resentment and her Fears; and accus'd his Treachery, Baseness, and want of Consideration; yet her Anger and Fears being appeas'd, and a Woman's Wit being always more pregnant in Difficulties than a Man's, she immediately thought of a way to deliver them from Dangers that bore so dismal and helpless a Face. She therefore bid him engage *Anselmo* to be there the next Day, assuring him she did not question but by that means to get a more frequent, and secure Opportunity of enjoying one another than they hitherto had had. She would not make him privy to her whole Design, but bid him be sure to come after her Husband was hid, as soon as *Leonela* shou'd call him, and that he shou'd answer as directly to whatsoever she shou'd ask him, as if *Anselmo* were not within hearing. *Lothario* spar'd no Importunity to get from her her whole Design, that he might act his Part with the greater Assurance, and the better contribute to the Imposing on her Husband. All you have to do, reply'd *Camilla*, is to answer me directly what I shall demand; nor would she discover any more, for fear he should not acquiesce in her Opinion (which she was so well satisfy'd in) but raise Difficulties, and by Consequence, Obstacles, that might hinder her Design from having the desir'd Event, or run her upon some less successful Project. *Lothario* comply'd, and *Anselmo* in appearance left the Town to retire to his Friend in the Country, but secretly return'd to hide himself in the Wardrobe, which he did with the greater Ease, because *Camilla* and *Leonela* wilfully gave him Opportunity. We may easily imagine the Grief with which *Anselmo* hid himself, since it was to be a Spectator of his own Dishonour, and the Loss of all that Happiness he possessed in the Embraces of his beautiful and belov'd *Camilla*. On the other hand, she being now certain that *Anselmo* was hid, entered the Wardrobe with *Leonela*, and fetching a deep and piteous Sigh, thus adress'd herself to her: Ah! my *Leonela*!

would it not be much better that thou pierce this infamous Bosom with *Anselmo's* Dagger, before I execute what I design, which I have kept from thee that thou might'st not endeavour to disappoint me? Yet not so; for, where is the Justice that I should suffer for another's Offence? No, I will first know of *Lothario* what Action of mine has given him assurance to make me a Discovery of a Passion so injurious to his Friend, and my Honour. Go to the Window, *Leonela*, and call the wicked Man to me, who doubtless is waiting in the Street the Signal for his Admission to accomplish his villainous Design; yet first my Resolution shall be perform'd, which tho' it be cruel, is what my Honour strictly demands of me. Alas! my dear Lady, cry'd the cunning *Leonela*, alas! What do you intend to do with that Dagger? Is your fatal Design against yourself or *Lothario*? Alas! you can attack neither without the Ruin of your Fame and Reputation. You had better give no Opportunity to that bad Man by admitting him while we are thus alone in the House: Consider, Madam, we are but two weak and helpless Women, he a strong and resolute Man, whose Force is redoubled by the Passion and Desire that possess him; so that before you may be able to accomplish what you design, he may commit a Crime that will be more injurious to you than the Loss of your Life. We have reason to curse my Master *Anselmo*, who gives such frequent Opportunities to Impudence and Dishonesty to pollute our House. But, Madam, suppose you should kill him, as I believe you design, what shall we do with his dead Body? What! said *Camilla*, why we would leave him in this Place to be buried by *Anselmo*; for it must be a grateful Trouble to him to bury with his own Hand his own Infamy and Dishonour. Call him therefore quickly, for methinks every Moment my Revenge is deferr'd, I injure that Loyalty I owe to my Husband.

Anselmo gave great attention to all that was said, and every Word of *Camilla's* made a strange alteration in his Sentiments, so that he could scarce forbear coming out to prevent his Friend's Death, when he heard her desperate Resolution against his Life; but his Desire of seeing the end of so brave a Resolve withheld him, till he saw an absolute necessity of discovering himself to hinder the Mischief. Now *Camilla* put on a fear and weakness which resembled a Swoon; and having thrown herself on a Bed in the Room, *Leonela* began a most doleful Lamentation over her: Alas! said she, how unfortunate should I be, if my Lady, so eminent for Virtue and Chastity as well as Beauty, should thus perish in my Arms? This, and much more she utter'd with that force of perfect Dissimulation, that whoever had seen her would have concluded her one of the most innocent Virgins in the World, and her Lady a meer persecuted *Penelope*. *Camilla* soon came to herself, and cry'd to *Leonela*, why don't you call the most Treacherous and Unfaithful of Friends? Go, fly, and let not thy Delays waste my Revenge and Anger in meer Words and idle Threats and Curses. Madam, reply'd *Leonela*, I will go, but you must first give me that Dagger, lest you commit some Outrage upon your self in my Absence, which may give an eternal Cause of Sorrow to all your Friends that love and value you. Let not those Fears detain you, said *Camilla*, but assure yourself I will not do any thing till you return; for tho' I shall not fear to punish myself in the highest Degree, yet I shall not, like *Lucretia*, punish myself without killing him that was the principal cause of my Dishonour. If I must die, I shall not refuse it; but I will first satisfy my Revenge on him that has tempted me to come to this guilty Assignation, to make him lament his Crime without being guilty of any myself.

Camilla could scarce prevail with *Leonela* to leave her alone, but at last she obey'd her and withdrew, when *Camilla* entertain'd herself and her Husband with this following Soliloquy: Good Heav'n, said she, had I not better have continued my Repulses, than by this seeming Consent suffer *Lothario* to think Scandalously of me, till my Actions shall convince him of his Error? That indeed might have been better in some respects, but then I should have wanted this Opportunity of Revenge, and the Satisfaction of my Husband's injur'd Honour, if he were permitted without any Correction to go off with the Insolence of offering such Criminal Assaults to my Virtue. No, no, let the Traitor's Life atone for the Guilt of his false and unfaithful Attempts, and his Blood quench that leud Fire he was not content should burn in his own Breast. Let the World be Witness if it ever comes to know my Story, that *Camilla* thought it not enough to preserve her Virtue and Loyalty to her Husband entire, but also revenged the hateful Affront, and the intended Destruction of it. But it might be most convenient perhaps to let *Anselmo* know of this before I put my Revenge in Execution; yet on the first Attempt I sent him Word of it to the Village, and I can attribute his not resenting so notorious an Abuse to nothing but his generous Temper, and Confidence in his Friend, incapable of believing so try'd a Friend could be guilty of so much as a Thought against his Honour and Reputation; nor is this Incredulity so strange, since I for so long together could not perswade myself of the Truth of what my Eyes and Ears convey'd to me; and nothing could have convinc'd me of my generous Error, had his Insolence kept within any Bounds, and not dared to proceed to large Gifts, large Promises, and a Flood of Tears which he shed as the undissembled Testimony of his Passion. But to what Purpose are these Considerations? Or is there indeed any need of considering to perswade me to a brave Resolve? *Avaunt* false Thoughts. Revenge is now my Task, let the Treacherous Man approach, let him come, let him die, let him perish; let him but perish, no matter what's the fatal Consequence. My dear *Anselmo* receiv'd me to his Bosom Spotless and Chaste, and so shall the Grave receive me from his Arms. Let the Event be as fatal as it will, the worst Pollution I can this way suffer is of mingling my own Chaste Blood with the impure and corrupted Blood of the most False and Treacherous of Friends. Having said this, she travers'd the Room in so passionate a Manner, with the drawn Dagger in her Hand, and shew'd such an Agitation of Spirit in her Looks and Motion, that she appeared like one distracted, or more like a Murderer, than a tender and delicate Lady.

Anselmo, not a little to his Satisfaction, very plainly saw and heard all this from behind the Arras, which with the greatest Reason and Evidence in the World remov'd all his past Doubts and Jealousies, and he with abundance of Concern wished that *Lothario* would not come, that he might by that means escape the Danger that so apparently threatned him; to prevent which he had discover'd himself, had he not seen *Leonela* at that Instant bring *Lothario* into the Room. As soon

as *Camilla* saw him enter, she describ'd a Line with the Poniard on the Ground, and told him the Minute he presum'd to
pass that, she would strike the Dagger to his Heart: Hear me,
said she, and observe what I say without Interruption; when
I have done, you shall have Liberty to make what Reply you
please. Tell me first, *Lothario*, do you know my Husband,
and do you know Me? The Question is not so difficult but you
may give me immediate Answer: there is no need of considering, speak therefore without delay. *Lothario* was not so dull
as not to guess at her Design in having her Husband hid behind
the Hangings, and therefore adapted his Answers so well to
her Questions, that the Fiction was lost in the Appearance of
Reality. I did never imagine, fair *Camilla*, said *Lothario*, that
you would make this Assignation to ask Questions so distant
from the dear End of my Coming. If you had a Mind still to
delay my promis'd Happiness, you should have prepar'd me
for the Disappointment; for, the nearer the Hope of Possession
brings us to the Good we desire, the greater is the Pain to have
those Hopes destroy'd. But to answer your Demands, I must
own, Madam, that I do know your Husband, and he me; that
this Knowledge has grown up with us from our Childhood;
and, that I may be a Witness against my self of the Injury I am
compelled by Love to do him, I do also own, Divine *Camilla*,
that you too well know the Tenderness of our mutual Friendship: Yet Love is a sufficient Excuse for all my Errors, if they
were much more criminal than they are. And, Madam, that
I know you is evident, and love you equal to him, for nothing
but your Charms could have Power enough to make me forget
what I owe to my own Honour, and what to the holy Laws of
Friendship, all which I have been forc'd to break by the re-
sistless Tyranny of Love. Ah! had I known you less, I had been
more Innocent. If you confess all this, said *Camilla*, if you know
us both, how dare you violate so Sacred a Friendship, injure
so true a Friend, and appear thus confidently before me, whom
you know to be esteem'd by him the Mirror of his Love, in
which that Love so often views itself with Pleasure and Satisfaction; and in which you ought to have survey'd yourself so
far, as to have seen how small the Temptation is, that has prevail'd on you to wrong him. But alas! This points me to the

345

Cause of your Transgression, some suspicious Action of mine when I have been least on my Guard, as thinking myself alone; but assure yourself whatever it was, it proceeds not from Looseness or Levity of Principle, but a Negligence and Liberty which the Sex sometimes innocently fall into when they think themselves unobserv'd. If this were not the Cause, say, Tray-tor, when did I listen to your Prayers, or in the least regard your Tears and Vows, so that you might derive from thence the smallest Hope of accomplishing your infamous Desires? Did I not always with the last Aversion and Disdain reject your Criminal Passion? Did I ever betray a Belief in your lavish Promises? or admit of your prodigal Gifts? But since without some Hope no Love can long subsist, I will lay that hateful Guilt on some unhappy Inadvertency of mine; and therefore will inflict the same Punishment on myself, that your Crime deserves. And to shew you that I cannot but be cruel to you, who will not spare myself, I sent for you to be a Witness of that just Sacrifice I shall make to my dear Hus-band's injur'd Honour, on which you have fixed the blackest Mark of Infamy that your Malice could suggest, and which I alas! have sullied too by my thoughtless neglect of depriving you of the Occasion, if indeed I gave any, of nourishing your wicked Intentions. Once more I tell you, that the bare Sus-picion that my want of Caution, and setting so severe a Guard on my Actions as I ought, had made you harbour such wild and infamous Intentions, is the sharpest of my Afflictions, and what with my own Hands I resolve to punish with the utmost Severity. For, should I leave that Punishment to another, it would but increase my Guilt. Yes, I will die; but first to satisfy my Revenge, and impartial Justice, I will unmov'd, and un-relenting, destroy the fatal Cause that has reduc'd me to this desperate Condition.

At these Words she flew with so much Violence, and so well-acted a Fury on *Lothario* with her naked Dagger, that he could scarce think it feigned, and therefore secured him-self from her Blow by avoiding it, and holding her Hand. Thereupon, to give more Life to the Fiction, as in a Rage at her disappointed Revenge on *Lothario*, she cried out: Since my malicious Fortune denies a compleat Satisfaction to my just Desires, at least it shall not be in its Power entirely to defeat my Resolution. With that, drawing back her Dagger-Hand from *Lothario* who held it, she struck it into that part of her Body where it might do her the least damage, and then fell down, as fainting away with the Wound. *Lothario* and *Leonela* surpriz'd at the unexpected Event, knew not yet what to think, seeing her still lie all bloody on the Ground; *Lothario* pale and trembling ran to her to take out the Dagger, but was deliver'd of his Fears when he saw so little Blood follow it, and more than ever admir'd the Cunning and Wit of the Beautiful *Camilla*. Yet to play his Part as well, and shew himself a Friend, he lamented over *Camilla's* Body in the most pathetick Manner in the World, as if she had been really dead; he curs'd himself, and curs'd his Friend that had put him on that fatal Experiment; and knowing that *Anselmo* heard him, he said such things that were able to draw a greater Pity for him than even for *Camilla*, though she seem'd to have lost her Life in the unfortunate Adventure. *Leonela* remov'd her Body to the Bed, and begg'd *Lothario* to seek some Surgeon, that might with all the Secrecy in the World cure her Lady's Wound: She also ask'd his Advice, how to excuse it to her Master, if he should return before it was perfectly cur'd. He reply'd, they might say what they pleas'd, That he was not in a humour of advising, but bid her endeavour to stanch her Mistress's Blood, for he would go where they should never hear more of him; and so he left them, with all the Appearance of Grief and Concern that the Occasion required. He was no sooner gone, but he had leisure to reflect, with the greatest wonder imaginable, on *Camilla's* and her Woman's Conduct in this Affair, and on the Assurance which this Scene had given *Anselmo* of his Wife's Virtue; since now he could not but believe he had a second *Portia*, and he long'd to meet him, to rejoice over the best dissembled Imposture that ever bore away the Opinion of Truth. *Leonela* stanch'd the Blood, which was no more than necessary for covering the Cheat, and washing the Wound with Wine only as she bound it up, her Discourse was so moving, and so well acted, that it had been alone sufficient to have convinc'd *Anselmo* that he had the most virtuous Wife in the World. *Camilla* was not silent, but added fresh Confirmations; in every Word she spoke, she complain'd of her Cowardice and Baseness of Spirit, that deny'd her time and force to dispatch that Life, which was now so hateful to her. She ask'd her too, whether she shou'd inform her Husband of what had pass'd, or not? *Leonela* was for her concealing it, since the Discovery must infallibly engage her Husband in a Revenge on *Lothario*, which must as certainly expose Him too; for those things were never accomplish'd without the greatest Danger; and that a good Wife ought to the best of her Power prevent involving her Husband in Quarrels. *Camilla* yielded to her Reasons; but added, that they must find out some pretended cause of her Wound, which he would certainly see at his return. *Leonela* reply'd, that it was a difficult Task, since she was incapable even in Jest to dissemble the Truth. Am I not, answer'd *Camilla*, under the same difficulty, who cannot save my Life by the odious Refuge of a Falshood? Had we not better then confess the real Truth, than be caught in a Lye? Well, Madam, return'd *Leonela*, let this give you no farther Trouble, by to-morrow Morning I shall find out some Expedient or other; though I hope the Place were the Wound is, may conceal it enough from his Observation to secure us from all Apprehension; leave therefore the whole Event to Heaven, which always favours and assists the Innocent.

Anselmo saw and heard this formal Tragedy of his ruin'd Honour, with all the Attention imaginable, in which all the Actors perform'd their Parts so to the Life, that they seemed the Truth they represented; he wish'd with the last Impatience for the Night, that he might convey himself from his hiding Place to his Friend's House, and there rejoice for this happy Discovery of his Wife's experienc'd Virtue. *Camilla* and her Maid took care to furnish him with an Opportunity of departing, of which he soon took hold, for fear of losing it. 'Tis impossible to tell you all the Embraces he gave *Lothario*, and the Joy and extreme Satisfaction he express'd at his good Fortune, or the extravagant Praises he gave *Camilla*. *Lothario* heard all this without taking a Friend's Share in the Pleasure, for he was shock'd with the Concern he had to see his Friend so grosly impos'd on, and the Guilt of his own Treachery in injuring his Honour. Though *Anselmo* easily perceiv'd that *Lothario* was not touch'd with any Pleasure at his Relation, yet he believ'd *Camilla's* Wound, caus'd by him, was the true Motive of his not sharing his Joy; and therefore assur'd him, he need not too much trouble himself for it, since it could not be dangerous, she and her Woman having agreed to conceal it from him. This Cause of his Fear being remov'd, he desired him to put on a Face of Joy, since by his Means he should now possess a perfect Happiness and Content; and therefore he would spend the rest of his Life in conveying *Camilla's* Virtue to Posterity, by writing her Praise in Verse. *Lothario* approv'd his Resolution, and promis'd to do the same. Thus *Anselmo* remain'd the most delightfully deceiv'd of any Man alive. He therefore carried *Lothario* immediately to his House, as the Instrument of his Glory, though he was indeed the only Cause of his Infamy and Dishonour. *Camilla* receiv'd him with a Face, that ill express'd the Satisfaction of her Mind, being forc'd to put on Frowns in her Looks, while her Heart prompted nothing but Smiles of Joy for his Presence.

For some Months the Fraud was conceal'd; but then Fortune turning her Wheel, discover'd to the World the Wickedness they had so long and artificially disguis'd; and *Anselmo's* impertinent Curiosity cost him his Life.

VIII: THE CONCLUSION OF THE NOVEL OF THE CURIOUS IMPERTINENT; WITH THE DREADFUL BATTLE BETWIXT DON QUIXOTE, AND CERTAIN WINE-SKINS

THE Novel was come near a Conclusion, when *Sancho Panza* came running out of Don *Quixote's* Chamber in a terrible Fright, and crying out, Help, Help, good People, Help my Master, he's just now at it, Tooth and Nail, with that same Giant, the Princess *Micomicona's* Foe: I ne'er saw a more dreadful Battle in my born-days. He has lent him such a Sliver, that whip, off went the Giant's Head, as round as a Turnip. You're mad, *Sancho*, said the Curate, interrupted in his Reading; is thy Master such a Devil of a Heroe, as to fight a Giant at two thousand Leagues distance? Upon this, they presently heard a Noise and Bustle in the Chamber, and Don *Quixote* bawling out, Stay Villain, Robber, stay; since I have thee here, thy Scimitar shall but little avail thee; and with this, they heard him strike with his Sword, with all his Force, against the Walls. Good Folks, said *Sancho*, my Master does not want your hearkning; why don't you run in and help him? though I believe 'tis after Meat Mustard, for sure the Giant is by this Time gone to pot, and giving an Account of his ill Life: For I saw his Blood run all about the House, and his Head falling in the Middle on't: But such a Head! 'tis bigger than any Wine-skin* in *Spain*. Death and Hell (cries the Inn-keeper) I'll be cut like a Cucumber, if this Don *Quixote*, or Don Devil, has not been hacking my Wine-skins that stood fill'd at his Bed's-Head, and this Coxcomb has taken the spilt Liquor for Blood. Then running with the whole Company into the Room, they found the poor Knight in the most comical Posture imaginable.

He was standing in his Shirt, the fore-part of it scarcely reaching to the bottom of his Belly, and about a Span shorter behind; this added a very peculiar Air to his long lean Legs,

* *In Spain they keep their Wines in the Skin of a Hog, Goat, Sheep, or other Beast, pitch'd within and sew'd close without.*

as dirty and hairy as a Beast's. To make him all of a piece, he wore on his Head a little red greasy cast Nightcap of the Inn-keeper's; he had wrapp'd one of the best Blankets about his left Arm for a Shield; and wielded his drawn Sword in the Right, laying about him pell-mell; with now and then a Start of some military Expression, as if he had been really engag'd with some Giant. But the best Jest of all, he was all this Time fast asleep; for the Thoughts of the Adventure he had under-taken, had so wrought on his Imagination, that his depraved Fancy had in his Sleep represented to him the Kingdom of *Micomicon*, and the Giant; and dreaming that he was then fighting him, he assaulted the Wine-skins so desperately, that he set the whole Chamber a-float with good Wine. The Inn-keeper, enrag'd to see the Havock, flew at Don *Quixote* with his Fists; and had not *Cardenio* and the Curate taken him off, he had prov'd a Giant indeed against the Knight. All this could not wake the poor *Don*, till the Barber throwing a Bucket of cold Water on him, waken'd him from his Sleep, tho' not from his Dream.

The Shortness of her Champion's Shirt gave *Dorothea* a Surfeit of the Battle. *Sancho* ran up and down the Room searching for the Giant's Head, 'till finding his Labour fruit-less, Well, well, said he, now I see plainly that this House is haunted, for when I was here before, in this very Room was I beaten like any Stock-fish, but knew no more than the Man in the Moon Who struck me; and now the Giant's Head that I saw cut off with these Eyes, is vanish'd; and I'm sure I saw the Body spout Blood like a Pump. What a Prating and a Nonsense does this damn'd Son of Whore keep about Blood and a Pump, and I know not what, said the Inn-keeper; I tell you, Rascal, 'tis my Wine-skins that are slash'd, and my Wine that runs about the Floor here, and I hope to see the Soul of him that spilt it swimming in Hell for his Pains. Well, well, said *Sancho*, don't trouble me; I only tell you, that I can't find the Giant's Head, and my Earldom is gone after it, and so I'm undone, like Salt in Water. And truly *Sancho's* waking Dream was as pleasant as his Master's when asleep; the Inn-keeper was almost mad to see the foolish Squire harp so on the same String with his frantick Master, and swore they

351

should not come off now as before; that their Chivalry should
be no Satisfaction for his Wine, but that they should pay him
Sauce for the Damage, and for the very Leathern Patches
which the wounded Wine-skins would want.

Don *Quixote*, in the mean while, believing he had finish'd
his Adventure, and mistaking the Curate, that held him by
the Arms, for the Princess *Micomicona*, fell on his Knees before him, and with a Respect due to a Royal Presence; Now
may your Highness, said he, great and illustrious Princess, live
secure, free from any further Apprehensions from your conquer'd Enemy; and now am I acquitted of my Engagement,
since, by the Assistance of Heaven, and the Influence of Her
Favour, by whom I live and conquer, your Adventure is so
happily atchieved. Did not I tell you so Gentle-folks (said
Sancho) Who is drunk or mad Now? See if my Master has not
already put the Giant in Pickle? Here are the Bulls,* and I
am an Earl. The whole Company (except the Inn-keeper,
who gave himself to the Devil) were like to split at the Extravagancies of Master and Man. At last, the Barber, *Cardenio*,
and the Curate, having, with much ado, got Don *Quixote* to
Bed, he presently fell asleep, being heartily tir'd; and then
they left Him, to comfort *Sancho Panza* for the Loss of the
Giant's Head; but it was no easy Matter to appease the Inn-
keeper, who was at his Wit's End for the unexpected and
sudden Fate of his Wine-skins.

The Hostess, in the mean time, ran up and down the House
crying and roaring: In an ill Hour, said she, did this unlucky
Knight-Errant come into My House; I wish, for My Part, I had
never seen him, for he has been a dear Guest to Me. He and
his Man, his Horse and his Ass, went away last time without
paying me a Cross for their Supper, their Bed, their Litter
and Provender; and all, forsooth, because he was seeking Adventures. What in the Devil's Name have I to do with his
Statutes of Chivalry? if they oblige him not to pay, they shou'd
oblige him not to eat neither. 'Twas upon this Score that
t'other Fellow took away my good Tail; 'tis clear spoil'd, the
Hair is all torn off, and my Husband can never use it again.
And now to come upon me again, with destroying my Wine-

* *In allusion to the Joy of the Mob in Spain, when they see the Bulls coming.*

skins, and spilling my Liquor; may some body spill his Heart's
Blood for't for Me: But I will be paid, so I will, to the last
Maravedis, or I'll disown my Name, and forswear the Mother
that bore me. Her honest Maid *Maritornes* seconded her Fury;
But Mr Curate stopp'd their Mouths by promising that he
would see them satisfy'd for their Wine and their Skins, but
especially for the Tail which they kept such a Clutter about.
Dorothea comforted *Sancho*, assuring him, that whenever it
appear'd that his Master had kill'd the Giant, and restor'd
Her to her Dominions, he should be sure of the best Earldom
in her Disposal. With this he huckl'd up again, and swore
that he himself had seen the Giant's Head, by the same Token
that it had a Beard that reach'd down to his Middle; and if it
could not be found it must be hid by Witchcraft, for every
Thing went by Inchantment in that House, as he had found
to his Cost when he was there before. *Dorothea* answer'd,
That she believ'd him; and desir'd him to pluck up his Spirits,
for all Things would be well. All Parties being quieted, *Cardenio*, *Dorothea*, and the rest, intreated the Curate to finish
the Novel, which was so near a Conclusion; and he, in Obedience to their Commands, took up the Book and read on.

Anselmo grew so satisfy'd in *Camilla's* Virtue, that he liv'd
with all the Content and Security in the world; to confirm
which, *Camilla* ever in her Looks seem'd to discover her Aversion to *Lothario*, which made him desire *Anselmo* to dispense
with his coming to his House, since he found how averse his
Wife was to him, and how great a Disgust she had to his Company; but *Anselmo* would not be persuaded to yield to his
Request; and was so blind, that, seeking his Content, he perpetually promoted his Dishonour. He was not the only Person
pleas'd with the Condition he liv'd in; *Leonela* was so transported with her Amour, that, secur'd by her Lady's Connivance, she perfectly abandon'd herself to the indiscreet Enjoyment of her Gallant: So that one Night her Master heard some
Body in her Chamber, and coming to the Door to discover who
it was, he found it held fast against him; but at last forcing it
open, he saw one leap out of the Window the Instant he enter'd
the Room: He would have pursu'd him, but *Leonela* clinging
about him, begg'd him to appease his Anger and Concern, since

the Person that made his Escape was her Husband. *Anselmo* would not believe her, but drawing his Dagger, threatned to kill her if she did not immediately make full Discovery of the Matter. Distracted with Fear, she begg'd him to spare her Life, and she would discover Things that more nearly related to him than he imagin'd. Speak quickly then, reply'd *Anselmo*, or you die. 'Tis impossible, return'd she, that in this Confusion and Fright I should say any thing that can be understood; but give me but till to Morrow Morning, and I will lay such Things before you, as will surprize and amaze you: but believe me, Sir, the Person that leap'd out of the Window, is a young Man of this City, who is contracted to me. This something appeas'd *Anselmo*, and prevail'd with him to allow her till the next Morning to make her Confession; for he was too well assur'd of *Camilla's* Virtue, by the past Trial, to suspect that there could be any thing relating to Her in what *Leonela* had to tell him: Wherefore fastning her in her Room, and threatning that she should never come out till she had done what she had promis'd, he return'd to his Chamber to *Camilla*, and told her all that had pass'd, without omitting the Promise she had giv'n him to make some strange Discovery the next Morning. You may easily imagine the Concern this gave *Camilla*; she made no Doubt but that the Discovery *Leonela* had promis'd, was of her Disloyalty; and without waiting to know whether it were so or not, that very Night, as soon as *Anselmo* was asleep, taking with her all her Jewels, and some Money, she got undiscovered out of the House, and went to *Lothario*, inform'd him of all that had pass'd, and desir'd him either to put her in some Place of Safety, or to go with her where they might enjoy each other secure from the Fears of *Anselmo*. This surprizing Relation so confounded *Lothario*, that for some Time he knew not what he did, or what Resolution to take; but at last, with *Camilla's* Consent, he put her into a Nunnery where a Sister of his was Abbess, and immediately, without acquainting any body with his Departure, left the City.

Anselmo, as soon as it was Day, got up, without missing his Wife, and hurry'd away to *Leonela's* Chamber, to hear what she had to say to him; but he found no body there, only the Sheets ty'd together, and fasten'd to the Window, shew'd

which way she had made her Escape; on which he return'd
very sad to tell *Camilla* the Adventure, but was extremely
surpriz'd when he found her not in the whole House, nor could
hear any News of her from his Servants: But finding in his
Search her Trunks open, and most of her Jewels gone, he no
longer doubted of his Dishonour: So, pensive and half dress'd
as he was, he went to *Lothario's* Lodging, to tell him his Misfortune; but when his Servants inform'd him that he was gone
that very Night, with all his Money and Jewels, his Pangs were
redoubl'd, and his Grief increas'd almost to Madness. To conclude, he return'd home, found his House empty, for Fear had
driven away all his Servants. He knew not what to think, say,
or do; he saw himself forsaken by his Friend, his Wife, and
his very Servants, with whom he imagin'd that Heaven itself
had abandon'd him; but his greatest Trouble was to find himself robb'd of his Honour and Reputation, for *Camilla's* Crime
was but too evident from all these concurring Circumstances.
After a thousand distracting Thoughts, he resolv'd to retreat
to that Village whither he formerly retir'd to give *Lothario* an
Opportunity to ruin him; wherefore fastning up his Doors, he
took Horse, full of Despair and languishing Sorrow, the Violence of which was so great, that he had scarce rid half Way,
when he was forc'd to alight, and tying his Horse to a Tree,
he threw himself beneath it; and spent, in that melancholy
Posture, a thousand racking Reflections, most Part of the Day,
till a little before Night he discover'd a Passenger coming the
same Road, of whom he enquir'd what News at *Florence*? The
Traveller reply'd, that the most surprizing News that had
been heard of late, was now all the Talk of the City, which
was, that *Lothario* had that very Night carry'd away the
wealthy *Anselmo's* Wife *Camilla*, which was all confess'd by
Camilla's Woman, who was apprehended that Night as she
slipp'd from the Window of *Anselmo's* House by a Pair of
Sheets. The Truth of this Story I cannot affirm, continu'd the
Traveller; but every Body is astonish'd at the Accident; for
no Man could ever suspect such a Crime from a Person engag'd
in so strict a Friendship with *Anselmo*, as *Lothario* was; for
they were call'd the *Two Friends*. Is it yet known, reply'd
Anselmo, which way *Lothario* and *Camilla* are gone? No, Sir,

return'd the Traveller, tho' the Governor has made as strict a Search after them as is possible. *Anselmo* ask'd no more Questions, but after they had taken their Leaves of each other, the Traveller left him and pursued his Journey.

This mournful News so affected the unfortunate *Anselmo*, that he was struck with Death almost that very Moment; getting therefore on his Horse, as well as he could, he arriv'd at his Friend's House. He knew nothing yet of his Disgrace; but seeing him so pale and melancholy, concluded that some great Misfortune had befallen him. *Anselmo* desir'd to be immediately led to his Chamber, and furnish'd with Pen, Ink and Paper, and to be left alone with his Door locked: When finding that his End approach'd, he resolv'd to leave in Writing the Cause of his sudden and unexpected Death. Taking therefore the Pen, he began to write; but unable to finish what he design'd, he dy'd a Martyr to his impertinent Curiosity. The Gentleman finding he did not call, and that it grew late, resolv'd to enter his Chamber, and see whether his Friend were better or worse; he found him half out of Bed, lying on his Face, with the Pen in his Hand, and a Paper open before him. Seeing him in this Posture he drew near him, call'd and mov'd him, but soon found he was dead; which made him call his Servants to behold the unhappy Event, and then took up the Paper, which he saw was written in *Anselmo's* own Hand, and was to this Effect.

A Foolish and Impertinent Desire has robb'd me of Life. If Camilla *hear of my Death let her know that I forgive her; for she was not oblig'd to do Miracles, nor was there any Reason I should have desir'd or expected it; and since I contriv'd my own Dishonour, there is no Cause ——*

Thus far *Anselmo* writ, but Life wou'd not hold out till he could give the Reasons he design'd. The next Day the Gentleman of the House sent Word of *Anselmo's* Death to his Relations, who already knew his Misfortunes, as well as the Nunnery whither *Camilla* was retir'd. She herself was indeed very near that Death which her Husband had pass'd, though not for the Loss of him, but *Lothario*, of which she had lately heard a flying Report. But though she was a Widow now, she would neither take the Veil, nor leave the Nunnery, till in a few Days the News was confirm'd of his being slain in a Battle betwixt Monsieur *de Lautrec*, and that great General *Gonzalo Fernandez de Cordona*, in the Kingdom of *Naples*. This was the End of the Offending, and too late Penitent Friend; the News of which made *Camilla* immediately profess herself, and soon after, overwhelm'd with Grief and Melancholy, pay for her Transgression with the Loss of her Life. This was the unhappy End of them all proceeding from so impertinent a Beginning.

I like this Novel well enough, said the Curate; yet, after all, I cannot persuade myself, that there's any Thing of Truth in it; and if it be purely Invention, the Author was in the wrong; for 'tis not to be imagin'd there cou'd ever be a Husband so Foolish, as to venture on so dangerous an Experiment. Had he made his Husband and Wife, a Gallant and a Mistress, the Fable had appear'd more probable; but, as it is, 'tis next to impossible. However, I must confess, I have nothing to object against his manner of telling it.

IX: CONTAINING AN ACCOUNT OF MANY
SURPRIZING ACCIDENTS IN THE INN

AT the same Time the Inn-keeper, who stood at the Door seeing Company coming, More Guests, cry'd he, a brave jolly Troop, on my Word. If they stop here, we may sing *O be joyful*. What are they, said *Cardenio*? Four Men, said the Host, on horseback, *à la Gineta*,* with black Masks† on their Faces, and arm'd with Lances and Targets; a Lady too all in White, that rides single and mask'd; and two running Foot-men. Are they near, said the Curate? Just at the Door, reply'd the Inn-keeper. Hearing this, *Dorothea* veil'd herself, and *Cardenio* had just Time enough to step into the next Room, where Don *Quixote* lay, when the Strangers came into the Yard. The four Horse-men, who made a very genteel Appearance, dismounted and went to help down the Lady, whom one of them taking in his Arms, carry'd into the House; where he seated her in a Chair by the Chamber-door, into which *Cardenio* had withdrawn. All this was done without discovering their Faces, or speaking a Word; only the Lady, as she sat down in the Chair, breath'd out a deep Sigh, and let her Arms sink down, in a weak and fainting Posture. The Curate, marking their odd Behaviour, which rais'd in him a Curiosity to know who they were, went to their Servants in the Stable, and ask'd what their Masters were? *Indeed*,‡ Sir, said one of them, that's more than we can tell you; they seem of no mean Quality, especially that Gentleman who carry'd

---

* *A kind of Riding with short Stirrops, which the* Spaniards *took from the* Arabians, *and is still used by all the* African, *and* Eastern *Nations, with part of the* Northern, *such as the* Hungarians, *and is advantageous in Fight; for being ready to strike with their Sabres, they rise on their Stirrops, and, following as it were their blow, give more force to it.* † Antifaz: *a Piece of thin black Silk, which the* Spaniards *wear before their Faces in travelling, not for Disguise, but to keep off the Dust and Sun.* ‡ *It is in the Original* Par Diez *(i.e. By Ten) instead of* Par Dioz *(i.e. By G-d) thinking to cheat the Devil of an Oath, as when We say* y-cod *for by g-d. Tho' a certain Presbyter assur'd me, travelling together once upon the Road, That* y-cod *was an Oath. But when I catcht him saying* Odsooker's, *he excus'd himself, and said it was only a Contraction of* God succour us. *And consequently no Oath.*

the Lady into the House, for the rest pay him great Respect, and his Word is a Law to them. Who is the Lady, said the Curate? We know no more of her then of the rest, answer'd the Fellow, for we could never see her Face all the Time, and 'tis impossible we should know her or them any otherwise. They pick'd us up on the Road, my Comrade and myself, and prevailed with us to wait on them to *Andalusia*, promising to pay us well for our Trouble; so that bating the two Days Travelling in their Company, they are utter Strangers to us. Could you not hear them name one another all this Time, ask'd the Curate? No, truly, Sir, answer'd the Foot-man, for we heard them not speak a Syllable all the Way: The poor Lady, indeed, us'd to sigh and grieve so piteously, that we are perswaded she has no Stomach to this Journey: Whatever may be the Cause we know not; by her Garb she seems to be a Nun, but by her Grief and Melancholy, one might guess they are going to make her one, when perhaps the poor Girl has not a Bit of Nuns Flesh about her. Very likely, said the Cur-ate; and with that leaving them, he return'd to the Place where he left *Dorothea*, who, hearing the mask'd Lady sigh so frequently, mov'd by the natural Pity of the soft Sex, could not forbear enquiring the Cause of her Sorrow. Pardon me, Madam, said she, if I beg to know your Grief; and assure your-self, that my Request does not proceed from meer Curiosity, but an earnest Inclination to serve and assist you, if your Mis-fortune be any such as our Sex is naturally subject to, and in the Power of a Woman to cure. The melancholy Lady made no return to her Compliment, and *Dorothea* press'd her in vain with new Reasons, when the Gentleman, whom the Foot-boy signify'd to be the chief of the Company, interpos'd: Madam, said he, don't trouble yourself to throw away any generous Offer on that ungrateful Woman, whose Nature cannot re-turn an Obligation; neither expect any Answer to your De-mands, for her Tongue is a Stranger to Truth. Sir, said the disconsolate Lady, my Truth and Honour have made me thus miserable, and my Sufferings are sufficient to prove you the falsest and most base of Men. *Cardenio* being only parted from the Company by Don *Quixote's* Chamber-door, overheard these last Words very distinctly; and immediately cry'd out,

Good Heaven, what do I hear! What Voice struck my Ear just now? The Lady startl'd at his Exclamation, sprung from the Chair, and would have bolted into the Chamber whence the Voice came; but the Gentleman perceiving it, laid hold on her, to prevent her, which so disorder'd the Lady that her Mask fell off, and discover'd an incomparable Face, beautiful as an Angel's, tho' very pale, and strangely discompos'd, her Eyes eagerly rolling on every side, which made her appear distracted. *Dorothea* and the rest, not guessing what her Eyes sought by their violent Motion, beheld her with Grief and Wonder. She struggl'd so hard, and the Gentleman was so disorder'd by holding her, that his Mask dropp'd off too, and discover'd to *Dorothea*, who was assisting to hold the Lady, the Face of her Husband Don *Ferdinand*: Scarce had she known him, when with a long and dismal Oh! she fell in a Swoon, and would have reach'd the Floor with all her Weight, had not the Barber, by good Fortune, stood behind and supported her. The Curate ran presently to help her, and pulling off her Veil to throw Water in her Face, Don *Ferdinand* presently knew her, and was struck almost as dead as she at the Sight; nevertheless he did not quit *Lucinda*, who was the Lady that struggl'd so hard to get out of his Hands. *Cardenio* hearing *Dorothea's* Exclamation, and imagining it to be *Lucinda's* Voice, flew into the Chamber in great Disorder, and the first Object he met was Don *Ferdinand* holding *Lucinda*, who presently knew him. They were all struck dumb with Amazement: *Dorothea* gaz'd on Don *Ferdinand*; Don *Ferdinand* on *Cardenio*; and *Cardenio* and *Lucinda* on one another. At last *Lucinda* broke silence, and addressing Don *Ferdinand*, Let me go, said she; unloose your hold, my Lord: By the Generosity you shou'd have, or by your Inhumanity, since it must be so, I conjure you, leave me, that I may cling like Ivy to my only Support; and from whom, neither your Threats, nor Prayers, nor Gifts, nor Promises, could ever alienate my Love. Contend not against Heaven, whose Power alone could bring me to my dear Husband's Sight, by such strange and unexpected Means: You have a thousand Instances to convince you, that nothing but Death can make me ever forget him: Let this, at least, turn your Love into Rage, which may prompt you to end my Miseries with my Life, here before my dear Husband, where I shall be proud to lose it, since my Death may convince him of my unshaken Love and Honour, till the last Minute of my Life. *Dorothea*, by this Time had recover'd, and finding, by *Lucinda's* Discourse who she was, and that Don *Ferdinand* would not unhand her, she made a Virtue of Necessity, and falling at his Feet, My Lord, cry'd she, all bath'd in Tears, if that Beauty which you hold in your Arms, has not altogether dazzl'd your Eyes, you may behold at your Feet the once happy, but now miserable *Dorothea*. I am that poor and humble Villager, whom your generous Bounty, I dare not say your Love, did condescend to raise to the Honour of calling you her own: I am she, who, once confin'd to peaceful Innocence, led a contented Life, till Your Importunity, your Shew of Honour, and deluding Words, charm'd me from my Retreat, and made me resign my Freedom to your Power. How I am recompens'd, may be guess'd by my Grief, and my being found here in this strange Place, whither I was led, not through any Dishonourable Ends, but purely by Despair and Grief to be forsaken of You. 'Twas at your Desire I was bound to you by the strictest Tie, and whatever you do, you can never cease to be mine. Consider, my dear Lord, that my matchless Love may balance the Beauty and Nobility of the Person for whom you would forsake me; she cannot share your Love, for 'tis only mine; and *Cardenio's* Interest in her will not admit a Partner. 'Tis easier far, my Lord, to recall your wandring Desires, and fix them upon her that adores you, than to draw Her to love who hates you. Remember how you did sollicit my humble State, and conscious of my Meanness, yet paid a Veneration to my Innocence, which join'd with the honourable Condition of my yielding to your Desires, pronounce me free from ill Design or Dishonour. Consider these undeniable Truths: Have some Regard to your Honour! Remember you're a Christian! Why should you then make her Life end so miserably, whose Beginning your Favour made so happy? If I must not expect the Usage and Respect of a Wife, let me but serve you as a Slave; So I belong to you, tho' in the meanest Rank, I never shall complain: Let me not be expos'd to the slandring Reflections of the Censorious World by so cruel a Separation from my Lord:

361

Afflict not the declining Years of my poor Parents, whose faithful Services to You and Yours have merited a more suitable Return. If you imagine the Current of your noble Blood should be defil'd by mixing with mine, consider how many noble Houses have run in such a Channel; besides the Woman's Side is not essentially requisite to enoble Descent: But chiefly think on this, that Virtue is the truest Nobility, which if you stain by basely wronging me, you bring a greater Blot upon your Family than Marrying me could cause. In fine, my Lord, you cannot, must not disown me for your Wife: To attest which Truth, I call your own Words, which must be true, if you prize yourself for Honour, and that Nobility, whose want you so despise in Me; witness your Oaths and Vows, witness that Heaven which you so oft invok'd to ratify your Promises; and if all these should fail, I make my last Appeal to your own Conscience, whose Sting will always represent my Wrongs fresh to your Thoughts, and disturb your Joys amidst your greatest Pleasures.

These, with many such Arguments, did the mournful *Dorothea* urge, appearing so lovely in her Sorrow, that Don *Ferdinand's* Friends, as well as all the rest sympathiz'd with her, *Lucinda* particularly, as much admiring her Wit and Beauty, as mov'd by the Tears, the piercing Sighs and Moans that follow'd her Intreaties; and she wou'd have gone nearer to have comforted her, had not *Ferdinand's* Arms, that still held her, prevented it. He stood full of Confusion, with his Eyes fix'd attentively on *Dorothea* a great while; at last, opening his Arms, he quitted *Lucinda*, Thou hast Conquer'd, cry'd he, charming *Dorothea*, thou hast Conquer'd me, 'tis impossible to resist so many united Truths and Charms. *Lucinda* was still so disorder'd and weak, that she would have fall'n when *Ferdinand* quitted her, had not *Cardenio*, without regard to his Safety, leap'd forward and caught her in his Arms, and embracing her with Eagerness and Joy: Thanks, gracious Heaven, cry'd he aloud, my Dear, my faithful Wife, thy Sorrows now are ended; for where can'st thou rest more safe than in my Arms, which now support thee, as once they did when my bless'd Fortune first made thee mine? *Lucinda* then opening her Eyes, and finding herself in the Arms of her *Car-*

362

denio, without regard to Ceremony or Decency, threw her Arms about his Neck, and laying her Face to his, Yes, said she, thou art he, thou art my Lord indeed! 'Tis even you yourself the right Owner of this poor, harrass'd Captive. Now Fortune act thy worst, nor Fears nor Threats shall ever part me more from the sole Support and Comfort of my Life. This Sight was very surprizing to Don *Ferdinand* and the other Spectators. *Dorothea* perceiving, by Don *Ferdinand's* Change of Countenance, and laying his Hand to his Sword, that he prepared to assault *Cardenio*, fell suddenly on her Knees; and with an endearing Embrace, held Don *Ferdinand's* Legs so fast, that he could not stir. What means, cry'd she, all in Tears, the only Refuge of my Hope? see here thy own and dearest Wife at thy Feet, and her you would enjoy in her true Husband's Arms. Think then, my Lord, how unjust is your Attempt, to dissolve that Knot which Heaven has ty'd so fast. Can you e'er think or hope Success in your Design on her, who contemning all Dangers, and confirm'd in strictest Constancy and Honour, before your Face lies bath'd in Tears of Joy and Passion in her true Lover's Bosom? For Heaven's sake I intreat you, by your own Words I conjure you to mitigate your Anger, and permit that faithful Pair to consummate their Joys, and spend their remaining Days in Peace: Thus may you make it appear that you are generous and truly noble, giving the World so strong a Proof that you have your Reason at Command, and your Passion in Subjection. All this while, *Cardenio*, though he still held *Lucinda* in his Arms, had a watchful Eye on Don *Ferdinand*; resolving, if he had made the least Offer to his Prejudice, to make him repent it and all his Party, if possible, though at the Expence of his Life. But Don *Ferdinand's* Friends, the Curate, the Barber, and all the Company (not forgetting honest *Sancho Panza*) got together about Don *Ferdinand*, and intreated him to pity the Beautiful *Dorothea's* Tears; that, considering what she had said, the Truth of which was apparent, it would be the highest Injustice to frustrate her lawful Hopes; that their strange and wonderful Meeting could not be attributed to Chance, but the peculiar and directing Providence of Heaven; that nothing (as Mr Curate very well urg'd) but Death could part *Cardenio* from *Lucinda*; and that tho' the Edge of his Sword might separate them, he would make them happier by Death, than he could hope to be by surviving; that in irrecoverable Accidents, a Submission to Fate, and a Resignation of our Wills, shew'd not only the greatest Prudence, but also the highest Courage and Generosity; that he should not envy those happy Lovers what the Bounty of Heaven had conferr'd on them, but that he shou'd turn his Eyes on *Dorothea's* Grief, view her incomparable Beauty, which, with her true and unfeigned Love, made large Amends for the Meanness of her Parentage; but principally it lay upon him, if he glory'd in the Titles of Nobility and Christianity, to keep his Promise unviolated; that the more reasonable Part of Mankind could not otherwise be satisfied, or have any Esteem for him: Also that it was the special Prerogative of Beauty, if heightned by Virtue and adorned with Modesty, to lay claim to any Dignity, without Disparagement or Scandal to the Person that raises it; and that the strong Dictates of Delight having been once indulged, we are not to be blamed for following them afterwards, provided they be not unlawful. In short, to these Reasons they added so many enforcing Arguments, that Don *Ferdinand*, who was truly a Gentleman, could no longer resist Reason, but stooped down, and embracing *Dorothea*, Rise, Madam, said he, 'tis not proper that She should lie prostrate at my Feet, who triumphs over my Soul: If I have not hitherto paid you all the Respect I ought, 'twas perhaps so ordered by Heaven, that having by this a stronger Conviction of your Constancy and Goodness, I may henceforth set the greater Value on your Merit: Let the future Respects and Services I shall pay you, plead a Pardon for my past Transgressions; and let the violent Passions of my Love, that first made me Yours, be an Excuse for that which caus'd me to forsake you: View the now happy *Lucinda's* Eyes, and there read a thousand farther Excuses; but I promise henceforth never to disturb her Quiet; and may she live long and contented with her dear *Cardenio*; as I hope to do with my dearest *Dorothea*. Thus concluding, he embrac'd her again so lovingly, that it was with no small Difficulty that he kept in his Tears, which he endeavour'd to conceal, being asham'd to discover so effeminate a Proof of his Remorse.

Cardenio, *Lucinda*, and the greatest Part of the Company could not so well command their Passions, but all wept for Joy; even *Sancho Panza* himself shed Tears, though as he afterwards confess'd, it was not for downright Grief, but because he found not *Dorothea* to be the Queen of *Micomicona*, as he suppos'd, and of whom he expected so many Favours and Preferments. *Cardenio* and *Lucinda* fell at Don *Ferdinand's* Feet, giving him Thanks, with the strongest Expressions which Gratitude could suggest; he rais'd them up, and receiv'd their Acknowledgments with much Modesty; then begg'd to be inform'd by *Dorothea*, how she came to that Place. She related to him all she had told *Cardenio*, but with such a Grace, that what were Misfortunes to Her, prov'd an inexpressible Pleasure to those that heard her Relation. When she had done, Don *Ferdinand* told all that had befall'n him in the City, after he found the Paper in *Lucinda's* Bosom, which declared *Cardenio* to be her Husband; how he would have kill'd her, had not her Parents prevented him, how afterwards, mad with Shame and Anger, he left the City, to wait a more commodious Opportunity of Revenge; how in a short Time he learnt that *Lucinda* was fled to a Nunnery, resolving to end her Days there, if she could not spend them with *Cardenio*; that, having desired those three Gentlemen to go with him, they went to the Nunnery, and waiting till they found the Gate open, he left two of the Gentlemen to secure the Door, while he with the other enter'd the House, where they found *Lucinda* talking with a Nun in the Cloister; they forcibly brought her thence to a Village, where they disguis'd themselves for their more convenient Flight, which they more easily brought about, the Nunnery being situate in the Fields, distant a good Way from any Town. He likewise added, how *Lucinda* finding herself in his Power, fell into a Swoon, and that after she came to herself, she continually wept and sigh'd, but would not speak a Syllable; and that, accompanied with Silence only and Tears, they had Travelled till they came to that Inn, which proved to Him as his Arrival at Heaven, having put a happy Conclusion to all his earthly Misfortunes.

THE Joy of the whole Company was unspeakable
by the happy Conclusion of this perplex'd Business; *Dorothea*, *Cardenio*, and *Lucinda* thought
the sudden Change of their Affairs too surprizing
to be real; and through a Disuse of good Fortune,
could hardly be induced to believe their Happiness: Don *Ferdinand* thank'd Heaven a thousand Times for
its propitious Conduct in leading him out of a Labyrinth, in
which his Honour and Virtue were like to have been lost.
The Curate, as he was very instrumental in the general Re-
conciliation, had likewise no small share in the general Joy;
and that no Discontent might sour their universal Satisfaction,
Cardenio and the Curate engag'd to see the Hostess satisfied
for all Damages committed by Don *Quixote*: Only poor *Sancho* droop'd pitifully; he found his Lordship and his Hopes
vanish'd into Smoke, the Princess *Micomicona* was chang'd
to *Dorothea*, and the Giant to Don *Ferdinand*; thus very musty
and melancholy he slipp'd into his Master's Chamber, who
had slept on, and was just waken'd, little thinking of what
had happen'd.

I hope your early rising will do you no hurt, said he, Sir
Knight of the woful Figure; but you may now sleep on till
Doom's-day if you will; nor need you trouble your Head any
longer about killing any Giant, or restoring the Princess, for
all that is done to your Hand. That's more than probable,
answer'd the Knight, for I have had the most extraordinary,
the most prodigious and bloody Battle with the Giant, that I
ever had, or shall have during the whole Course of my Life; yet
with one cross stroke I laid his Head thwack on the Ground,
whence the great Effusion of Blood seem'd like a violent
Stream of Water. Of Wine you mean, said *Sancho*, for you
must know (if you know it not already) that your Worship's
dead Giant is a broach'd Wine-skin, and the Blood some thirty
Gallons of Tent which it held in its Belly, and your Head so
cleverly struck off, is the Whore my Mother; and so the Devil

366

take both Giant and Head, and all altogether, for *Sancho*.
What say'st thou, mad Man? said the Don, thou'rt frantick
sure. Rise, rise, Sir, said *Sancho*, and see what fine Work
you have cut out for yourself; here's the Devil-and-all to pay
for, and your great Queen is changed into a private Gentlewoman, call'd *Dorothea*, with some other such odd Matters,
that you will wonder with a Vengeance. I can wonder at nothing here, said Don *Quixote*, where you may remember I told
you all things are rul'd by Inchantment. I believe it, quoth
Sancho, had my tossing in a Blanket been of that kind; but
sure 'twas the likest a tossing in a Blanket of any thing I ever
knew in my Life. And this same Inn-keeper, I remember very
well, was one of those that toss'd me into the air, and as cleverly
and heartily he did it as a Man could wish, I'll say that for
him; so that after all I begin to smell a Rat, and do per'lously
suspect, that all our Inchantment will end in nothing but
Bruises and broken Bones. Heaven will retrieve all, said the
Knight; I will therefore dress, and march to the Discovery of
these wonderful Transformations. While *Sancho* made him
ready, the Curate gave Don *Ferdinand* and the rest an Account
of Don *Quixote's* Madness, and of the Device he used to draw
him from the *Poor Rock*, to which the suppos'd Disdain of his
Mistress had banish'd him in Imagination. *Sancho's* Adventures made also a Part in the Story, which prov'd very diverting to the Strangers. He added, that since *Dorothea's* Change
of Fortune had balkt their Design that way, some other Trick
should be found to decoy him home: *Cardenio* offer'd his
Service in the Affair, and that *Lucinda* should personate *Dorothea*: No, no (answer'd Don *Ferdinand*) *Dorothea* shall humour the Jest still, if this honest Gentleman's Habitation be
not very far off. Only two Days Journey said the Curate: I
would ride twice as far (said Don *Ferdinand*) for the Pleasure
of so good and charitable an Action. By this Don *Quixote* had
sally'd out Arm'd Cap-a-pee, *Mambrino's* Helmet (with a
great Hole in it) on his Head; his Shield on his left Arm, and
with his right he lean'd on his Lance. His meagre yellow
weather-beaten Face, of half a League in Length,* the un-

* Tho' Don *Quixote was very long-visag'd, yet to say his Face was half
a League in Length, is a most extravagant Hyperbole even for a* Spaniard

accountable Medley of his Armour, together with his grave and solemn Port, struck Don *Ferdinand* and his Companions dumb with Admiration, while the Champion casting his Eyes on *Dorothea*, with great Gravity and Solidity, broke silence with these Words.

I am inform'd by this my Squire, beautiful Lady, that your Greatness is annihilated, and your Majesty reduc'd to nothing, for of a Queen and mighty Princess, as you us'd to be, you are become a private Damsel. If any express Order from the Nec-romantic King your Father (doubting the Ability and Success of my Arm in the reinstating you) has occasioned this Change, I must tell him, that he is no Conjurer in these Matters, and does not know one half of his Trade;* nor is he skill'd in the Revolutions of Chivalry: For had he been conversant in the Study of Knight-Errantry as I have been, he might have found, that in every Age, Champions of less Fame than Don *Quixote de la Mancha* have finish'd more desperate Adventures; since the killing of a pitiful Giant, how arrogant soever he may be, is no such great Atchievement; for, not many Hours past, I en-counter'd one myself; the Success I will not mention, lest the Incredulity of some People might distrust the Reality; but Time, the Discoverer of all things, will disclose it, when least expected. Hold there, said the Host, 'twas with two Wine-skins, but no Giant that you fought. Don *Ferdinand* silenc'd the Inn-keeper, and bid him by no means interrupt Don *Quix-ote*, who thus went on. To conclude, most High and Disin-herited Lady, if your Father, for the Causes already men-tioned, has caus'd this Metamorphosis in your Person, believe him not; for there is no Peril on Earth, thro' which my Sword shall not open a way; and assure yourself that in a few Days, by the Overthrow of your Enemy's Head, it shall fix on yours that Crown, which is your lawful Inheritance. Here Don *Quixote* stopt, waiting the Princess's Answer; she, assur'd of Don *Fer-dinand's* Consent to carry on the Jest, 'till Don *Quixote* was got home, and assuming a Face of Gravity, Whosoever (answer'd

to make, but yet Cervantes *does actually say it;* Fernando viendo su rostro de media legua de andadura. Stevens *is egregiously mistaken here, he says,* Fernando *seeing his Countenance half a League off.* * *Literally,* one half of the Mass, *the saying of which is one great part of the Priestly Office.*

she) has inform'd you, Valorous Knight of the woful Figure,
that I have alter'd or chang'd my Condition, has impos'd upon
you; for I am just the same to Day as Yesterday; 'tis true some
unexpected, but fortunate Accidents, have varied some Circumstances of my Fortune, much to my Advantage, and far
beyond my Hopes; but I am neither chang'd in my Person, nor
alter'd in my Resolution of employing the Force of your re-
doubtable and invincible Arm in my Favour. I therefore apply
myself to your usual Generosity, to have those Words spoken
to my Father's Dishonour recall'd; and believe these easy and
infallible Means to redress my Wrongs, the pure effects of his
Wisdom and Policy, as the good Fortune I now enjoy, has been
the Consequence of your surprizing Deeds, as this Noble Presence can testify. What should hinder us then from setting
forward to Morrow Morning, depending for a happy and successful Conclusion on the Will of Heaven, and the Power of
your unparallell'd Courage?

The ingenious *Dorothea* having concluded, Don *Quixote*
turning to *Sancho*, with all the Signs of Fury imaginable; Now
must I tell thee, poor paultry Hang-dog (said he) thou art the
veryest Rascal in all *Spain*; tell me, Rogue, Scoundrel, did
not you just now inform me, that this Princess was chang'd into
a little private Damsel, call'd *Dorothea*, and the Head which
I lopp'd from the Giant's Shoulders, was the Whore your
Mother, with a thousand other Absurdities? Now, by all the
Powers of Heaven (looking up, and grinding his Teeth together) I have a Mind so to use thee, as to make thee appear
a miserable Example to all succeeding Squires, that shall dare
to tell a Knight-Errant a Lye. Good your Worship, cry'd *Sancho*, have Patience, I beseech you: Mayhap I am mistaken or
so, about my Lady Princess *Micomicona's* Concern there; but
that the Giant's Head came off the Wine-skins Shoulders, and
that the Blood was as good Tent as ever was tipt over Tongue,
I'll take my Corporal Oath on't; Gadzookers Sir, are not the
Skins all hack'd and slash'd within there at your Bed's-head,
and the Wine all in a Puddle in your Chamber? *But you'll guess
at the Meat presently, by the Sauce; the Proof of the Pudding
is in the eating, Master;** and if my Landlord here don't let

* *The Original runs*, it will be seen in the frying of the Eggs. *When Eggs*

1   24   369

you know it to your Cost, he's a very honest and civil Fellow, that's all. *Sancho*, said the Don, I pronounce thee *non Compos*, I therefore pardon thee, and have done. 'Tis enough, said Don *Ferdinand*, we therefore, in pursuance of the Princess's Orders, will this Night refresh ourselves, and to-morrow we will all of us set out to attend the Lord Don *Quixote*, in prosecution of this important Enterprize he has undertaken, being all impatient to be Eye-witnesses of his celebrated and matchless Courage. I shall be proud of the Honour of serving and waiting upon you, my good Lord, reply'd Don *Quixote*, and reckon myself infinitely oblig'd by the Favour and good Opinion of so honourable a Company; which I shall endeavour to improve and confirm, though at the Expence of the last drop of my Blood.

Many other Compliments had pass'd between Don *Quixote* and Don *Ferdinand*, when the Arrival of a Stranger interrupted them. His Dress represented him a Christian newly return'd from *Barbary*: He was clad in a short-skirted Coat of blue Cloth, with short Sleeves and no Collar, his Breeches were of blue Linen, with a Cap of the same Colour, a pair of Date-colour'd Stockings, and a *Turkish* Scimitar hung by a Scarf, in manner of a Shoulder Belt. There rode a Woman in his Company, clad in a *Moorish* Dress; her Face was cover'd with a Veil; she had on a little Cap of Gold-Tissue, and a *Turkish* Mantle that reach'd from her Shoulders to her Feet. The Man was well-shap'd and strong, his Age about Forty, his Face somewhat tann'd, his Mustachios long, and his Beard handsome: In short, his genteel Mien and Person were too distinguishable, to let the Gentleman be hid by the Meanness of his Habit. He call'd presently for a Room, and being answer'd that All were full, seem'd a little Troubl'd; however he went to the Woman who came along with him, and took her down from her Ass. The Ladies, being all surpriz'd at the oddness of the *Moorish* Dress, had the Curiosity to flock about the Stranger, and *Dorothea* very discreetly imagining that both

are to be fry'd, there is no knowing their goodness till they are broken, Royal Dict. Or, a Thief stole a Frying-pan, and the Woman, who own'd it, meeting him, askt him what he was carrying away: he answer'd, you will know when your Eggs are to be fry'd.

she and her Conductor were tir'd, and took it ill that they could not have a Chamber; I hope, Madam, you will bear your ill Fortune patiently, said she, For want of room is an Inconvenience incident to all publick Inns: But if you please, Madam, to take up with us, pointing to *Lucinda*, you may perhaps find that you have met with worse Entertainment on the Road, than what this Place affords. The unknown Lady made her no answer, but rising up, laid her Hands across her Breast, bow'd her Head, and inclin'd her Body, as a Sign that she acknowledg'd the Favour. By her Silence they conjectur'd her to be undoubtedly a *Moor*, and that she could not speak *Spanish*. Her Companion was now come back from the Stable, and told them; Ladies, I hope you will excuse this Gentlewoman from answering any Questions, for she is very much a Stranger to our Language. We are only, Sir, answer'd *Lucinda*, making her an Offer which Civility obliges us to make all Strangers, especially of our own Sex; that she would make us happy in her Company all Night, and fare as we do; we will make very much of her, Sir, and she shall want for nothing that the House affords. I return you humble Thanks, dear Madam, answer'd the Stranger, in the Lady's behalf and my own; and I infinitely prize the Favour, which the present Exigence and the Worth of the Donors, make doubly engaging. Is the Lady, pray Sir, a Christian or a *Moor*, ask'd *Dorothea*? Our Charity would make us hope she were the former; but by her Attire and Silence we are afraid she is the latter. Outwardly, Madam, answers he, she appears and is a *Moor*, but in her Heart a zealous Christian, which her longing Desires of being Baptiz'd have expresly testified. I have had no Opportunity of having her Christen'd since she left *Algiers*, which was her Habitation and Native Country; nor has any imminent danger of Death as yet oblig'd her to be brought to the Font, before she be better instructed in the Principles of our Religion; but, I hope by Heaven's Assistance, to have her shortly baptiz'd with all the Decency suiting her Quality, which is much above what her Equipage or mine seem to promise.

These Words rais'd in them all a Curiosity to be farther inform'd who the *Moor* and her Conductor were; but they thought it improper then to put them upon any more particu-

lar Relation of their Fortunes, because they wanted Rest and
Refreshment after their Journey. *Dorothea* placing the Lady
by her, begg'd her to take off her Veil. She look'd on her
Companion, as if she requir'd him to let her know what she
said; which, when he had let her understand in the *Arabian*
Tongue, joining his own Request also, she discover'd so charming a Face, that *Dorothea* imagin'd her more beautiful than
Lucinda; she on the other hand, fancy'd her handsomer than
Dorothea; and most of the Company believ'd her more beautiful than both of 'em. As Beauty has always a Prerogative, or
rather Charm, to attract Men's Inclinations, the whole Company dedicated their Desires to serve the lovely *Moor*. Don
Ferdinand ask'd the Stranger her Name, he answer'd *Lela
Zoraida*; she hearing him, and guessing what they ask'd,
suddenly reply'd with great Concern, tho' very gracefully, No,
no *Zoraida*, *Maria*, *Maria*; giving them to understand, that
her Name was *Maria* and not *Zoraida*. These Words, spoken
with so much eagerness, raised a Concern in every Body, the
Ladies especially, whose natural Tenderness shew'd itself by
their Tears; and *Lucinda* embracing her very lovingly, Ay,
ay, said she, *Maria*, *Maria*, which Words the *Moorish* Lady
repeated by way of Answer. *Zoraida Macange*, added she,
as much as to say, not *Zoraida*, but *Maria*, *Maria*. The Night
coming on, and the Inn-keeper, by order of Don *Ferdinand's*
Friends, having made haste to provide them the best Supper
he could, the Cloth was laid on a long Table, there being
neither round nor square in the House. Don *Quixote*, after
much Ceremony, was prevail'd upon to sit at the Head, he
desir'd the Lady *Micomicona* to sit next to him; and the rest
of the Company having placed themselves according to their
Rank and Convenience, they eat their Supper very heartily.
Don *Quixote*, to raise the Diversion, never minded his Meat,
but inspir'd with the same Spirit that mov'd him to preach
so much to the Goat-herds, he began to hold forth in this Manner. Certainly, Gentlemen, if we rightly consider it, those
who make Knight-Errantry their Profession, often meet with
most surprizing and stupendous Adventures. For what Mortal
in the World, at this Time entring within this Castle, and
seeing us sit together as we do, will imagine and believe us to

be the same Persons which in reality we are? Who is there
that can judge, that this Lady by my side is the great Queen
we all know her to be, and that I am that Knight of the woful
Figure, so universally made known by Fame? It is then no
longer to be doubted, but that this Exercise and Profession
surpasses all others that have been invented by Man, and is
so much the more honourable, as it is more expos'd to Dangers.
Let none presume to tell me that the Pen is preferable to the
Sword; for be they who they will, I shall tell them they know
not what they say: For the Reason they give, and on which
chiefly they rely, is, that the Labour of the Mind exceeds that
of the Body, and that the Exercise of Arms depends only on
the Body, as if the use of them were the Business of Porters,
which requires nothing but much Strength. Or, as if This,
which we who profess it call Chivalry, did not include the
Acts of Fortitude, which depend very much upon the Understanding. Or else, as if that Warriour, who commands an Army
or defends a City besieg'd, did not labour as much with the
Mind as with the Body. If this be not so, let Experience teach
us whether it be possible by bodily Strength to discover or
guess the Intentions of an Enemy. The forming Designs, laying of Stratagems, overcoming of Difficulties, and shunning of
Dangers, are all Works of the Understanding, wherein the
Body has no Share. It being therefore evident, that the Exercise of Arms requires the Help of the Mind as well as Learning, let us see in the next place, whether the Scholar or the
Soldier's Mind undergoes the greatest Labour. Now this may
be the better known, by regarding the End and Object each
of them aims at; for that Intention is to be most valued, which
makes the noblest End its Object. The Scope and End of
Learning, I mean, human Learning (in this Place I speak not
of Divinity, whose aim is to guide Souls to Heaven, for no
other can equal a Design so infinite as that) Is to give a Perfection to distributive Justice, bestowing upon every one his due,
and to procure and cause good Laws to be observ'd; an End
really Generous, Great, and worthy of high Commendation;
but yet not equal to that which Knight-Errantry tends to,
whose Object and End is Peace, which is the greatest Blessing
Man can wish for in this Life. And therefore the first good

News the World receiv'd, was That the Angels brought in
the Night, which was the Beginning of our Day, when they
sang in the Air, Glory to God on high, Peace upon Earth, and
to Men Good-will. And the only manner of Salutation taught
by the best Master in Heaven, or upon Earth, to his Friends
and Favourites, was, that entring any House they should say,
Peace be to this House. And at other times he said to them,
My Peace I give to you, My Peace I leave to you, Peace be
among you. A Jewel and Legacy worthy of such a Donor, a
Jewel so precious, that without it there can be no Happiness
either in Earth or Heaven. This Peace is the true End of War;
for Arms and War are one and the same thing. Allowing then
this Truth, that the End of War is Peace, and that in this it
excels the End of Learning, let us now weigh the Bodily Labours the Scholar undergoes, against those the Warriour suffers, and then see which are greatest. The Method and Language Don *Quixote* us'd in delivering himself were such, that
none of his Hearers at that time look'd upon him as a Mad-
man. But on the Contrary, most of them being Gentlemen,
to whom the use of Arms properly appertains, they gave him
a willing Attention; and he proceeded in this manner. These,
then, I say, are the Sufferings and Hardships a Scholar endures. First, Poverty, (not that they are all Poor, but to urge
the worst that may be in this Case) and having said he endures
Poverty, methinks nothing more need be urg'd to express his
Misery; for he that is Poor enjoys no Happiness, but labours
under this Poverty in all its Parts, at one time in Hunger, at
another in Cold, another in Nakedness, and sometimes in all
of them together; yet his Poverty is not so great, but still he
eats, though it be later than the usual Hour, and of the Scraps
of the Rich, or, which is the greatest of a Scholar's Misfortunes, what is call'd among them *going a Sopping*;* neither
can the Scholar miss of somebody's Stove or Fire-side to sit
by, where, though he be not thoroughly heated, yet he may
gather Warmth, and at last sleep away the Night under a
Roof. I will not touch upon other less material Circumstances,
as the want of Linen, and scarcity of Shoes, thinness and bald-
ness of their Clothes, and their Surfeiting when good Fortune

* *The Author means the Sops in porridge, giv'n at the Doors of Monasteries.*

throws a Feast in their Way: This is the difficult and uncouth Path they tread, often stumbling and falling, yet rising again and pushing on, till they attain the Preferment they aim at; whither being arriv'd, we have seen many of them, who, having been carried by a Fortunate Gale through all these Quicksands, from a *Chair* govern the World; their Hunger being chang'd into Satiety, their Cold into comfortable Warmth, their Nakedness into Magnificence of Apparel, and the Mat they us'd to lie upon, into stately Beds of costly Silks and softest Linen, a Reward due to their Virtue. But yet their Sufferings being compar'd with those the Soldier endures, appear much inferior, as I shall in the next Place make out.

SINCE, speaking of the Scholar, we began with his Poverty, and its several Parts, continu'd Don *Quixote*, let us now observe whether the Soldier be any Thing richer than he; and we shall find that Poverty it self is not poorer; for he depends on his miserable Pay, which he receives but seldom, or perhaps never; or else in that he makes by Marauding, with the Hazard of his Life, and Trouble of his Conscience. Such is sometimes his want of Apparel, that a slash'd Buff-Coat is all his Holiday Raiment and Shirt; and in the depth of Winter being in the open Field, he has nothing to cherish him against the sharpness of the Season, but the Breath of his Mouth, which issuing from an empty Place, I am persuaded is it self cold, though contrary to the Rules of Nature. But now see how he expects Night to make amends for all these Hardships in the Bed prepar'd for him, which, unless it be his own Fault, never proves too narrow; for he may freely lay out as much of the Ground as he pleases, and tumble to his content, without Danger of losing the Sheets. But above all, when the Day shall come, wherein he is to put in practice the Exercise of his Profession, and strive to gain some new Degree, when the Day of Battle shall come, then, as a Mark of his Honour, shall his Head be dignified with a Cap made of Lint, to stop a Hole made by a Bullet, or be perhaps carried off maim'd, at the Expence of a Leg or an Arm. And if this do not happen, but that merciful Heaven preserve his Life and Limbs, it may fall out that he shall remain as poor as before, and must run through many Encounters and Battles, nay always come off victorious, to obtain some little Preferment; and these Miracles too are rare: But, I pray tell me, Gentlemen, if ever you made it your Observation, how few are those who obtain due Rewards in War, in comparison of those Numbers that perish? Doubtless you will answer, that there is no parity between them; that the Dead cannot be reckon'd up, whereas, those who live and are rewarded, may be number'd with three figures.* It is quite otherwise with Scholars, not only those who fol-

* I.e. *Do not exceed* Hundreds.

low the Law, but others also, who all either by Hook or by
Crook get a Livelihood, so that tho' the Soldier's Sufferings
be much greater, yet his Reward is much less. To this it may
be answer'd, that it is easier to reward two thousand Scholars, than thirty thousand Soldiers, because the former are
recompens'd at the Expence of the Publick, by giving them
Employments, which of necessity must be bestow'd on those
of their Profession, but the latter cannot be gratified otherwise than at the Cost of the Master that employs them; yet
this very Difficulty makes good my Argument. But let us lay
this Matter aside, as a Point difficult to be decided, and let us
return to the Preference due to Arms above Learning, a Subject as yet in Debate, each Party bringing strong Reasons to
make out their Pretensions. Among others, Learning urges,
that without it Warfare itself could not subsist; because War,
as other Things, has its Laws, and is governed by them, and
Laws are the Province of Learning and Scholars. To this Objection the Soldiers make answer, that without Them the
Laws cannot be maintain'd, for it is by Arms that Commonwealths are defended, Kingdoms supported, Cities secur'd,
the High-way made safe, and the Sea deliver'd from Pirates.
In short, were it not for Them, Commonwealths, Kingdoms,
Monarchies, Cities, the Roads by Land, and the Waters of
the Sea, would be subject to the Ravages and Confusion that
attends War while it lasts and is at liberty to make use of
its unbounded Power, and Prerogative. Besides, it is past all
Controversy, that what costs dearest, is, and ought most to be
valu'd. Now for a Man to attain to an eminent degree in Learning costs him time, watching, hunger, nakedness, dizziness
in the Head, weakness in the Stomach, and other Inconveniences, which are the Consequences of these, of which I have
already in part made mention. But the rising gradually to be a
good Soldier, is purchas'd at the whole expence of all that is
requir'd for Learning, and that in so surpassing a Degree, that
there is no comparison betwixt them; because he is every
Moment in Danger of his Life. To what danger or distress
can a Scholar be reduc'd equal to that of a Soldier, who, being
besieg'd in some strong Place, and at his Post or upon Guard
in some Ravelin or Bastion, perceives the Enemy carrying on

a Mine under him, and yet must upon no account remove from thence, or shun the Danger which threatens him so near? All he can do, is, to give Notice to his Commander, that he may countermine, but must himself stand still, fearing and expecting when on a sudden he shall soar to the Clouds without Wings, and be again cast down headlong against his Will. If this Danger seem inconsiderable, let us see whether that be not greater when two Gallies shock one another with their Prows in the midst of the spacious Sea. When they have thus grappled, and are clinging together, the Soldier is confin'd to the narrow Beak, being a Board not above two Foot wide; and yet though he sees before him so many Ministers of Death threatning, as there are Pieces of Cannon on the other side pointing against him, and not half a Pike's Length from his Body; and being sensible that the first slip of his Feet sends him to the Bottom of *Neptune's* Dominions; still, for all this, inspir'd by Honour, with an undaunted Heart, he stands a Mark to so much Fire, and endeavours to make his way, by that narrow Passage, into the Enemy's Vessel. But what is most to be admir'd is, that no sooner one falls, where he shall never rise till the end of the World, than another steps into the same Place; and if he also drops into the Sea, which lies in wait for him like an Enemy, another, and after him another still fills up the Place, without suffering any Interval of Time to separate their Deaths; a Resolution and Boldness scarce to be parallell'd in any other Trials of War. Blessed be those happy Ages that were Strangers to the dreadful Fury of these devilish Instruments of Artillery, whose Inventor I am satisfy'd is now in Hell, receiving the Reward of his cursed Invention, which is the Cause that very often a cowardly base Hand takes away the Life of the bravest Gentleman, and that in the midst of that Vigour and Resolution which animates and inflames the Bold, a chance Bullet (shot perhaps by one that fled, and was frighted at the very Flash the mischievous Piece gave, when it went off) coming no Body knows how, or from whence, in a Moment puts a Period to the brave Designs, and the Life of one, that deserv'd to have surviv'd many Years. This consider'd, I could almost say, I am sorry at my Heart for having taken upon me this Profession of a Knight-Errant, in so detestable an Age; for tho' no Danger daunts me, yet it affects me to think, whether Powder and Lead may not deprive me of the Opportunity of becoming Famous, and making myself known throughout the World by the Strength of my Arm and Dint of my Sword. But let Heaven order Matters as it Pleases, for if I compass my Designs, I shall be so much the more honour'd by how much the Dangers I have expos'd myself to, are greater than those the Knights-Errant of former Ages underwent. All this long Preamble Don *Quixote* made, whilst the Company supp'd, never minding to eat a Mouthful, though *Sancho Panza* had several times advis'd him to mind his Meat, telling him there would be time enough afterwards to talk as he thought fit. Those who heard him were afresh mov'd with Compassion, to see a Man, who seem'd in all other Respects, to have a sound Judgment and clear Understanding, so absolutely mad and distracted, when any mention was made of his curs'd Knight-Errantry. The Curate told him, he was much in the right, in all he had said for the Honour of Arms; and that he, though a Scholar, and a Graduate, was of the same Opinion. Supper being ended and the Cloth taken away, whilst the Inn-keeper, his Wife, his Daughter, and *Maritornes*, fitted up Don *Quixote's* Loft for the Ladies, that they might lie by themselves that Night, Don *Ferdinand* intreated the Slave to give them an Account of his Life; conscious the Relation could not choose but be very delightful and surprizing, as might be guess'd by his coming with *Zoraida*. The Slave answer'd, He would most willingly comply with their Desires, and that he only fear'd the Relation would not give them all the Satisfaction he could wish; but that however rather than disobey, he would do it as well as he could. The Curate and all the Company thank'd him, and made fresh Instances to the same Effect. Seeing himself courted by so many, There is no need of Intreaties, said he, for what you may command; therefore, continu'd he, give me your Attention, and you shall hear a true Relation, perhaps not to be parallell'd by those fabulous Stories which are compos'd with much Art and Study. This caus'd all the Company to seat themselves, and observe a very strict Silence; and then with an agreeable and sedate Voice, he began in this manner.

379

IN the Mountains of *Leon* my Family had its first Original, and was more kindly dealt withal by Nature than by Fortune, though my Father might pass for Rich among the Inhabitants of those Parts who are but poorly provided for; to say Truth, he had been so, had he had as much Industry to preserve, as he had Inclination to dissipate his Income; but he had been a Soldier, and the Years of his Youth spent in that Employment, had left him in his old Age a Propensity to spend, under the Name of Liberality. War is a School where the Covetous grow free, and the Free prodigal: To see a Soldier a Miser, is a kind of Prodigy which happens but seldom. My Father was far from being one of them; for he pass'd the Bounds of Liberality, and came very near the Excesses of Prodigality; a Thing which cannot suit well with a marry'd Life, where the Children ought to succeed to the Estate, as well as Name of the Family. We were three of us, all at Man's Estate; and my Father, finding that the only Way (as he said) to curb his squandring Inclination, was, to dispossess himself of that which maintain'd it, his Estate, (without which *Alexander* himself must have been put to't) he call'd us one Day all three to him in his Chamber, and spoke to us in the following Manner.

My Sons, to persuade you that I love you, I need only tell you I am your Father, and you my Children; and on the other side, you have reason to think me unkind, considering how careless I am in preserving what should one Day be yours; but to convince you, however, that I have the Bowels of a Parent, I have taken a Resolution, which I have well weigh'd and consider'd for many Days. You are all now of an Age to chuse the kind of Life you each of you incline to; or, at least, to enter upon some Employment that may one Day procure you both Honour and Profit: Therefore I design to divide all I have into four Parts, of which I will give Three among You, and retain the Fourth for myself, to maintain me in my old Age, as long as it shall please Heaven to continue me in this Life. After that each of you shall have receiv'd his Part, I

could wish you would follow one of the Employments I shall
mention to you, every one as he finds himself inclin'd. There
is a Proverb in our Tongue, Which I take to contain a great
deal of Truth, as generally those sorts of Sayings do, being
short Sentences fram'd upon Observation and long Experience. This Proverb runs thus, *Either the Church, the Sea, or
the Court.* As if it should Plainly say, that whosoever desires
to thrive must follow one of these three; either be a Church-
man, or a Merchant and try his Fortune at Sea, or enter into
the Service of his Prince in the Court: For another Proverb
says, that *King's Chaff is better than other Mens Corn.* I say
this, because I would have one of you follow his Studies,
another I desire should be a Merchant, and the Third should
serve the King in his Wars; because it is a Thing of some
difficulty to get an entrance at Court; and though War does
not immediately procure Riches, yet it seldom fails of giving
Honour and Reputation. Within eight Days Time I will give
each of you your Portion, and not wrong you of a Farthing
of it, as you shall see by Experience. Now therefore tell me
if you are resolv'd to follow my Advice about your settling
in the World. And turning to me, as the Eldest, he bid me
answer first. I told him, that he ought not upon our Account
to divide or lessen his Estate, or way of Living; that we were
young Men and could shift in the World; and at last I concluded, that for my part I would be a Soldier, and serve God and
the King in that honourable Profession. My second Brother
made the same regardful Offer, and chose to go to the *Indies*;
resolving to lay out in Goods the Share that should be given
him here. The Youngest, and I believe, the wisest of us all,
said he would be a Church-man; and in order to it, go to *Salamanca*, and there finish his Studies. After this, my Father
embrac'd us all Three, and in a few Days perform'd what
he had promis'd; and, as I remember, it was three thousand
Ducats apiece, which he gave us in Money; for we had an
Uncle who bought all the Estate, and paid for it in ready
Money, that it might not go out of the Family. A little after,
we all took leave of my Father; and at parting I could not forbear thinking it a kind of Inhumanity to leave the old Gentleman in so straight a Condition: I prevail'd with him there-

fore to accept of two thousand of my three, the remainder being sufficient to make up a Soldier's Equipage. My Example work'd upon my other Brothers, and they each of them presented him with a thousand Ducats; so that my Father remain'd with four thousand Ducats in ready Money, and three thousand more in Land, which he chose to keep, and not sell out-right. To be short, we took our last leave of my Father and the Uncle I have mention'd, not without much Grief and Tears on all Sides. They particularly recommending to us to let them know, by all Opportunities, our good or ill Fortunes; We promis'd so to do, and having receiv'd the Blessing of our old Father, one of us went straight to *Salamanca*, the other to *Sevil*, and I to *Alicant*, where I was inform'd of a *Genoese* Ship, which was loading Wool for *Genoa*.

This Year makes two and twenty since I first left my Father's House, and in all that time, tho' I have writ several Letters I have not had the least News, either of Him, or of my Brothers. And now I will relate, in few Words, my own Adventures in all that course of Years. I took Shipping at *Alicant*, arriv'd safe and with a good Passage at *Genoa*, from thence I went to *Milan*, where I bought my Equipage, resolving to go and enter myself in the Army in *Piedmont*; but being come as far as *Alexandria de la Paille*, I was inform'd that the great Duke of *Alva* was passing into *Flanders* with an Army; this made me alter my first Resolution. I follow'd him, and was present at all his Engagements, as well as at the Deaths of the Counts *Egmont* and *Horne*; and at last I had a Pair of Colours under a famous Captain of *Guadalajara*, whose Name was *Diego de Urbina*. Some time after my Arrival in *Flanders*, there came News of the League concluded by Pope *Pius* V of happy Memory in Conjunction with *Spain*, against the common Enemy the *Turk*, who at that Time had taken the Island of *Cyprus* from the *Venetians*; which was an unfortunate and lamentable Loss to *Christendom*. It was also certain, that the General of this Holy League was the most Serene Don *Juan* of *Austria*, Natural Brother to our good King Don *Philip*. The great Fame of the Preparations for this War excited in me a vehement Desire of being present at the Engagement, which was expected to follow these Preparations; and although I

had certain Assurance, and, as it were, an Earnest of my being
advanc'd to be a Captain upon the first Vacancy: yet I resolved
to leave all those Expectations, and return, as I did, to *Italy*.
My good Fortune was such, that I arriv'd just about the same
Time that Don *Juan* of *Austria* landed at *Genoa*, in order to
go to *Naples*, and join the *Venetian* Fleet, as he did at *Messina*.
In short, I was at that great Action of the Battle of *Lepanto*,
being a Captain of Foot, to which Post my good Fortune, more
than my Desert, had now advanc'd me; and that Day, which
was so happy to all *Christendom* (because the World was then
disabus'd of the Error they had entertain'd, that the *Turk*
was Invincible by Sea) that Day, I say, in which the Pride of
the *Ottomans* was first broke, and which was so happy to all
Christians, even to those who dy'd in the Fight, who were
more so than those who remain'd alive and Conquerors, I alone
was the unhappy Man; since, instead of a Naval Crown, which
I might have hop'd for in the Time of the *Romans*, I found
myself that very Night a Slave, with Irons on my Feet, and
Manacles on my Hands. The thing happen'd thus: *Vehali*, King
of *Algiers*, a brave and bold Pirate, having boarded and taken
the *Capitana* Galley of *Malta*, in which only three Knights
were left alive, and those desperately wounded, the Galley
of *John Andrea Doria* bore up to succour them; in this Galley
I was embarqu'd with my Company, and doing my Duty on
this Occasion, I leap'd into the Enemy's Galley, which getting loose from ours, that intended to Board the *Algerine*, my
Soldiers were hindred from following me, and I remain'd alone
among a great Number of Enemies; whom not being able to
resist, I was taken after having receiv'd several Wounds; and
as you have heard already, *Vehali* having escap'd with all his
Squadron, I found myself his Prisoner; and was the only afflicted Man among so many joyful ones, and the only Captive
among so many Free; for on that Day above 15000 Christians,
who row'd in the *Turkish* Galleys, obtain'd their long-wish'd-
for Liberty. I was carry'd to *Constantinople*, where the Grand
Seignior *Selim* made *Vehali*, my Master, General of the Sea, he
naving behav'd himself very well in the Battle, and brought
away with him the great Flag of the Order of *Malta*, as a
Proof of his Valour.

The Second Year of my Captivity, I was a Slave in the *Capitana* Galley at *Navarino*; and I took Notice of the Christians Fault, in letting slip the Opportunity they had of taking the whole *Turkish* Fleet in that Port; and all the *Janisaries* and *Algerine* Pirates did so expect to be attack'd, that they had had all in readiness to escape on Shore without Fighting; so great was the Terror they had of our Fleet: But it pleas'd God to order it otherwise, not by any Fault of the Christian General, but for the Sins of Christendom, and because it is his Will we should always have some Enemies to chastise us. *Vehali* made his way to *Modon*, which is an Island not far from *Navarino*, and there landing his Men, fortify'd the Entrance of the Harbour, remaining in Safety there till *Don Juan* was forc'd to return home with his Fleet. In this Expedition, the Galley call'd *La Presa*, of which *Barbarossa's* own Son was Captain, was taken by the Admiral Galley of *Naples*, call'd the *Wolf*, which was commanded by that Thunder-bolt of War, that Father of the Soldiers, that happy and never-conquer'd Captain, Don *Alvaro de Baçan*, Marquis of *Santa Cruz*; and I cannot omit the manner of taking this Galley. The Son of *Barbarossa* was very cruel, and us'd his Slaves with great Inhumanity; they perceiving that the *Wolf*-Galley got of them in the Chace, all of a sudden laid by their Oars, and seizing on their Commander, as he was walking between them on the Deck, and calling to them to row hard; they pass'd him on from Hand to Hand to one another, from one End of the Galley to the other, and gave him such Blows in the handling him, that before he got back to the Main-Mast, his Soul had left his Body, and was fled to Hell. This, as I said, was the effect of His Cruelty, and Their Hatred.

After this we return'd to *Constantinople*; and the next Year, which was 1573, News came that Don *Juan* of *Austria* had taken *Tunis* and its Kingdom from the *Turks*, and given the Possession of it to *Muley Hamed*, having thereby defeated all the hopes of Reigning of *Muley Hamida*, one of the cruellest, and withal one of the bravest *Moors* in the World. The Grand Seignor was troubled at this Loss, and, using his wonted Artifices with the Christians, he struck up a Peace with the *Venetians*, who were much more desirous than he of it.

The Year after, which was 1574, he attack'd the *Goletta*, and the Fort which Don *Juan* had begun, but not above half finish'd, before *Tunis*. All this while I was a Galley-Slave, without any Hopes of Liberty; at least, I could not promise myself to obtain it by way of Ransom; for I was resolv'd not to write my Father the News of my Misfortune. *La Goletta** and the Fort were both taken, after some Resistance; the *Turkish* Army consisting of 75000 *Turks* in Pay, and above 400000 *Moors* and *Arabs* out of all *Africa* near the Sea; with such Provisions of War of all kinds, and so many Pioneers, that they might have cover'd the *Goletta* and the Fort with Earth by Handfuls. The *Goletta* was first taken, tho' always before reputed impregnable; and it was not lost by any Fault of its Defenders, who did all that could be expected from them; but because it was found by Experience, that it was practicable to make Trenches in that sandy Soil, which was thought to have Water under it within two Foot, but the *Turks* sunk above two Yards and found none; by which Means filling Sacks with Sand, and laying them on one another, they rais'd them so high, that they over-top't and commanded the Fort, in which none could be safe, nor shew themselves upon the Walls. It has been the Opinion of most Men, that we did ill to shut our selves up in the *Goletta*; and that we ought to have been drawn out to hinder their Landing; but they who say so, talk without Experience, and at Random, of such things; for if in all there were not above 7000 Men in the *Goletta* and the Fort, how could so small a Number, though never so brave, take the open Field against such Forces as those of the Enemies? And how is it possible that a Place can avoid being taken, which can have no Relief, particularly being besieg'd by such Numbers, and those in their own Country? But it seem'd to many others, and that is also my Opinion, that God Almighty favour'd *Spain* most particularly, in suffering that Sink of Iniquity and Misery, as well as that Spunge and perpetual Drain of Treasure to be destroy'd. For infinite Sums of Money were spent there to no purpose, without any other Design, than to preserve the Memory of one of the Emperor's (*Charles* the

* *The* Goletta *is a Fortress in the* Mediterranean; *between that Sea and the Lake of* Tunis: *In* 1535 *Charles* V. *took it by Storm.*

Fifth's) Conquests; as if it had been necessary to support the
Eternity of his Glory (which will be permanent) that those
Stones should remain in being. The Fort was likewise lost,
but the *Turks* got it Foot by Foot; for the Soldiers who defended it, sustain'd two and twenty Assaults, and in them
kill'd above 25000 of those *Barbarians*; and when it was
taken, of 300 which were left alive, there was not one Man
unwounded; a certain sign of the Bravery of the Garrison, and
of their Skill in defending Places. There was likewise taken,
by Composition, a small Fort in the midst of a Lake, which
was under the Command of Don *John Zanoguerra*, a Gentleman of *Valencia*, and a Soldier of great Renown. Don *Pedro
Puerto Carrero*, General of the *Goletta*, was taken Prisoner,
and was so afflicted at the Loss of the Place, that he dy'd of
Grief by the Way, before he got to *Constantinople*, whither
they were carrying him. They took also Prisoner the Commander of the Fort, whose Name was *Gabriel Cerbellon*, a
Milanese, and a great Ingineer, as well as a valiant Soldier.
Several Persons of Quality were killed in those two Fort-
resses, and amongst the rest was *Pagan Doria*, the Brother of
the Famous *John Andrea Doria*, a generous and noble-hearted
Gentleman, as well appear'd by his Liberality to that Brother;
and that which made his Death more worthy of Compassion,
was, that he receiv'd it from some *Arabs*, to whom he had
committed his Safety after the loss of the Fort, they having
promis'd to carry him disguis'd in a *Moor's* habit to *Tabarca*,
which is a small Fort held on that Coast by the *Genoeses*, for the
diving for Coral; but they cut off his Head, and brought it to
the *Turkish* General, who made good to them our *Spanish* Proverb, That the Treason pleases, but the Traitors are odious; for
he order'd them to be hang'd up immediately, for not having
brought him alive. Amongst the Christians which were taken
in the Fort, there was one Don *Pedro de Aguilar*, of some Place
in *Andalusia*, and who was an Ensign in the Place; a very
brave, and a very ingenious Man, and one who had a rare
Talent in Poetry. I mention him, because it was his Fortune
to be a Slave in the same Galley with Me, and chain'd to the
same Bench. Before he left the Port he made two Sonnets, by
way of Epitaph for the *Goletta* and the Fort, which I must

beg leave to repeat here, having learn'd them by heart, and I believe they will rather divert than tire the Company. When the Captive nam'd Don *Pedro de Aguilar*, Don *Ferdinand* look'd upon his Companions, and they all smil'd; and when he talk'd of the Sonnets, one of them said, Before you go on to repeat the Sonnets, I desire, Sir, you would tell me what became of that Don *Pedro de Aguilar*, whom you have mention'd. All that I know of him, answer'd the Slave, is, that after having been two Years in *Constantinople*, he made his Escape, disguis'd like an *Arnaut*,* and in company of a *Greek* Spy; but I cannot tell whether he obtain'd his Liberty or no, though I believe he did, because about a Year after I saw the same *Greek* in *Constantinople*, but had not an Opportunity to ask him about the Success of his Journey. Then I can tell you, reply'd the Gentleman, That the Don *Pedro* you speak of is my Brother, and is at present at Home, Marry'd, Rich, and has three Children. God be thanked, said the Slave, for the Favours he has bestow'd on him; for in my Mind there is no Felicity equal to that of recovering ones lost Liberty; and moreover, added the same Gentleman, I can say the Sonnets you mentioned, which my Brother made. Pray say them then, reply'd the Slave, for I question not but you can repeat them better than I. With all my Heart, answer'd the Gentleman. That upon the *Goletta* was thus.

* *A Trooper of* Epirus, Dalmatia, *or some of the adjacent Countries.*

XIII: THE STORY OF THE CAPTIVE CONTINU'D

A SONNET

> Blest Souls, discharg'd of Life's oppressive weight
>   Whose Virtue prov'd your Pass-port to the Skies:
> You there procur'd a more propitious Fate,
>   When for your Faith you bravely fell to rise.
>
> When Pious Rage, diffus'd thro' ev'ry Vein,
>   On this ungrateful Shore inflam'd your Blood;
> Each Drop you lost, was bought with Crowds of Slain,
>   Whose vital Purple swell'd the neighb'ring Flood.
>
> Tho' crush'd by Ruins, and by Odds, you claim
> That perfect Glory, that immortal Fame,
>   Which, like true Heroes, nobly you pursu'd;
> On these you seiz'd, even when of Life depriv'd,
> For still your Courage even your Lives surviv'd;
>   And sure 'tis Conquest thus to be subdu'd.

I know it's just as you repeat it, said the Captive: Well then, said the Gentleman, I'll give you now that which was made upon the Fort, if I can remember it.

A SONNET

> Amidst these barren Fields, and ruin'd Towers,
>   The Bed of Honour of the falling Brave,
> Three thousand Champions of the Christian Pow'rs
>   Found a new Life, and Triumph in the Grave.
>
> Long did their Arms their haughty Foes repel,
>   Yet strew'd the Fields with slaughter'd Heaps in vain;
> O'ercome by Toils, the pious Heroes fell,
>   Or but surviv'd more nobly to be slain.
>
> This dismal Soil, so fam'd in Ills of old,
> In ev'ry Age was fatal to the Bold,
>   The Seat of Horror, and the Warrior's Tomb!
> Yet hence to Heav'n more Worth was ne'er resign'd,
> Than these display'd; nor has the Earth combin'd,
>   Resum'd more noble Bodies in her Womb.

The Sonnets were applauded, and the Captive was pleas'd to hear such good News of his Friend and Companion: After that he pursu'd his Relation in these Terms; The *Turks* order'd the dismantling of the *Goletta*, the Fort being raz'd to their Hand by the Siege; and yet the Mines they made could not blow up the old Walls, which nevertheless were always thought the weakest Part of the Place; but the new Fortifications, made by the Ingineer *Fratin*, came easily down. In fine, the *Turkish* Fleet return'd in triumph to *Constantinople*, where not long after my Master *Vehali* dy'd, whom the *Turks* us'd to call *Vehali Fartax*, which in *Turkish* signifies the Scabby Renegade, as indeed he was; and the *Turks* give Names among themselves, either from some Virtue or some Defect that is in them; and this happens, because there are but four Families descended from the *Ottoman* Family; all the rest, as I have said, take their Names from some Defect of the Body, or some good Quality of the Mind. This Scabby Slave was at the Oar in one of the Grand Signior's Galleys for fourteen Years, till he was four and thirty Years old; at which time he turn'd Renegade, to be reveng'd of a *Turk* who gave him a Box on the Ear, as he was chain'd to the Oar, forsaking his Religion for his Revenge; after which he shew'd so much Valour and Conduct, that he came to be King of *Algiers*, and Admiral of the *Turkish* Fleet, which is the third Command in the whole Empire. He was a *Calabrian* by Birth, and of a mild Disposition towards his Slaves, as also of good Morals to the rest of the World. He had above 3000 Slaves of his own, all which after his Death were divided, as he had order'd by his Will, between the Grand Signior, his Sons and his Renegades. I fell to the Share of a *Venetian* Renegade, who was a Cabbin-boy in a *Venetian* Ship which was taken by *Vehali*, who lov'd him so, that he was one of his Favourite Boys; and he came at last to prove one of the cruelest Renegades that ever was known. His Name was *Azanaga*, and he obtain'd such Riches, as to rise by them to be King of *Algiers*; and with him I left *Constantinople*, with some Satisfaction to think, at least, that I was in a Place so near Spain, not because I could give Advice to any Friend of my Misfortunes, but because I hop'd to try whether I should succeed better in *Algiers* than I had done in *Constanti-*

nople, where I had try'd a thousand ways of running away, but could never execute any of them, which I hop'd I should compass better in *Algiers*, for Hopes never forsook me upon all the Disappointments I met with in the Design of recovering my Liberty. By this means I kept myself alive, shut up in a Prison or House, which the *Turks* call a *Bagnio*, where they keep their Christian Slaves, as well those of the King, as those who belong to private Persons, and also those who are call'd *El Almacen*, that is, who belong to the Publick, and are employ'd by the City in Works that belong to it. These latter do very difficultly obtain their Liberty; for having no particular Master, but belonging to the Publick, they can find no Body to treat with about their Ransom, though they have Money to pay it. The King's Slaves, which are ransomable, are not oblig'd to go out to work as the others do, except their Ransom stays too long before it comes; for then to hasten it, they make them work, and fetch Wood with the rest, which is no small Labour. I was one of those who were to be ransom'd; for when they knew I had been a Captain, though I told them the Impossibility I was in of being redeem'd, because of my Poverty, yet they put me among the Gentlemen that were to be ransom'd, and to that End they put me on a slight Chain, rather as a Mark of Distinction, than to restrain me by it; and so I pass'd my Life in that *Bagnio*, with several other Gentlemen of Quality, who expected their Ransom; and tho' Hunger and Nakedness might, as it did often, afflict us, yet nothing gave us such Affliction, as to hear and see the excessive Cruelties with which our Master us'd the other Christian Slaves; he would hang one one Day, then impale another, cut off the Ears of a third; and this upon such slight Occasions, that often the *Turks* would own, that he did it only for the Pleasure of doing it, and because he was naturally an Enemy to Mankind. Only one *Spanish* Soldier knew how to deal with him, his Name was *Saavedra*; who tho' he had done many things which will not easily be forgotten by the *Turks*, yet all to gain his Liberty, his Master never gave him a Blow, nor us'd him ill either in Word or Deed; and yet we were always afraid that the least of his Pranks would make him be impal'd; nay, he himself sometimes was afraid of it too; and if it were not for taking up too much of your Time, I could tell such Passages of him, as would divert the Company much better than the Relation of My Adventures, and cause more Wonder in them. But to go on; I say that the Windows of a very rich *Moor's* House look'd upon the Court of our Prison; which indeed, according to the Custom of the Country, were rather Peeping-holes than Windows, and yet they had also Lattices or Jealousies on the Inside. It happen'd one Day, that being upon a kind of Terras of our Prison, with only three of my Comrades, diverting ourselves as well as we could, by trying who could leap farthest in his Chains, all the other Christians being gone out to work, I chanc'd to look up to those Windows, and saw that out of one of them there appear'd a long Cane, and to it was a Bit of Linen ty'd, and the Cane was mov'd up and down, as if it had expected that some of us should lay hold of it. We all took notice of it, and one of us went and stood just under it, to see if they would let it fall; but just as he came to it, the Cane was drawn up, and shak'd to and fro sideways, as if they had made the same Sign, as People do with their Head when they deny. He retir'd upon that, and the same Motion was made with it as before. Another of my Comrades advanc'd, and had the same Success as the former; the third Man was us'd just as the rest; which I seeing, resolv'd to try my Fortune too; and as I came under the Cane, it fell at my Feet: Immediately I unty'd the Linen, within which was a Knot, which being open'd, shew'd us about ten *Zianins*, which is a sort of Gold of base Allay, us'd by the *Moors*, each of which is worth about two Crowns of our Money. 'Tis not to be much question'd, whether the Discovery was not as pleasant as surprizing; we were in Admiration, and I more particularly, not being able to guess whence this good Fortune came to us, especially to Me; for 'twas plain I was more meant than any of my Comrades, since the Cane was let go to Me when it was refus'd to Them. I took my Money, broke the Cane, and going upon the Terras saw a very fine white Hand that open'd and shut the Window with Haste. By this we imagin'd that some Woman who liv'd in that House had done us this Favour; and to return our Thanks, we bow'd ourselves after the *Moorish* Fashion, with our Arms cross our Breasts. A little after there appear'd out of the same Window, a little Cross made

of Cane, which immediately was pull'd in again. This confirm'd us in our Opinion, that some Christian Woman was a
Slave in that House, and that it was she that took Pity on us;
but the Whiteness of the Hand, and the Richness of the Bracelets upon the Arm, which we had a Glympse of, seem'd to destroy that Thought again; and then we believ'd it was some
Christian Woman turn'd *Mahometan*, whom their Masters
often marry, and think themselves very Happy; for Our Women are more valu'd by them than the Women of their own
Country. But in all this guessing we were far enough from
finding out the Truth of the Case; however, we resolv'd to be
very diligent in observing the Window, which was our North-
Star. There pass'd above fifteen Days before we saw either
the Hand or Cane, or any other Sign whatsoever; though in
all that time we endeavour'd to find out who liv'd in that
House, and if there were in it any Christian Woman who was
a Renegade; yet all we could discover amounted to only this,
that the House belong'd to one of the chief *Moors*, a very rich
Man, call'd *Agimorato*, who had been Alcayde of the *Pata*,
which is an Office much valu'd among them. But when we least
expected our golden Shower would continue, out of that Window we saw on a sudden the Cane appear again, with another
Piece of Linen, and a bigger Knot; and this was just at a time
when the *Bagnio* was without any other of the Slaves in it. We
all try'd our Fortunes as the first Time, and it succeeded accordingly, for the Cane was let go to none but me. I unty'd the Knot,
and found in it forty Crowns of *Spanish* Gold, with a Paper
written in *Arabick*, and at the Top of the Paper was a great
Cross. I kiss'd the Cross, took the Crowns, and returning to the
Terrass, we all made our *Moorish* Reverences; the Hand appear'd again, and I having made Signs that I would read the
Paper, the Window was shut. We remain'd all overjoy'd and
astonish'd at what had happen'd; and were extreme desirous
to know the Contents of the Paper; but none of us understood
Arabick, and it was yet more difficult to find out a proper Interpreter. At last I resolv'd to trust a Renegade, of *Murcia*, who
had shewn me great Proofs of his Kindness. We gave one another mutual Assurances, and on his Side he was oblig'd to
keep Secret all that I should reveal to him; for the Renegades,

who have thoughts of returning to their own Country, use to get Certificates from such Persons of Quality as are Slaves in *Barbary*, in which they make a sort of an Affidavit, that such a one, a Renegade, is an honest Man, and has always been kind to the Christians, and has a mind to make his Escape on the first Occasion. Some there are who procure these Certificates with an honest Design, and remain among Christians as long as they live; but others get them on purpose to make use of them when they go a Pirating on the Christian Shores; for then if they are shipwreck'd or taken, they shew these Certificates, and say, that thereby may be seen the Intention with which they came in the *Turks Company*; to wit, to get an Opportunity of returning to Christendom. By this means they escape the first Fury of the Christians, and are seemingly reconcil'd to the Church without being hurt; afterwards they take their Time, and return to *Barbary* to be what they were before.

One of these Renegades was my Friend, and he had Certificates from us all, by which we gave him much Commendation: But if the *Moors* had catch'd him with those Papers about him, they would have burnt him alive. I knew that not only he understood the *Arabick* Tongue, but also that he could both speak and write it currently. But yet before I resolv'd to trust him entirely, I bid him read me that Paper, which I had found by chance; he open'd it, and was a good while looking upon it, and construing it to himself. I ask'd him if he understood it; he said, Yes, very well; and that if I would give him Pen, Ink and Paper, he would translate it Word for Word. We furnish'd him with what he desir'd, and he went to work; having finish'd his Translation, he said, all that I have here put into *Spanish* is Word for Word what is in the *Arabick*; only observe, that wherever the Paper says *Lela Marien*, it means our Lady the Virgin *Mary*. The Contents were thus:

When I was a Child, my Father had a Slave, who taught me in my Tongue the Christian Worship, and told me a great many things of Lela Marien: The Christian Slave dy'd, and I am sure she went not to the Fire, but is with Alla, for I have seen her twice since; and she bid me go to the Land of the Christians to see Lela Marien, who had a great Kindness for

393

me. I do not know what is the matter; but tho' I have seen many Christians out of this Window, none has appear'd to me so much a Gentleman as thyself. I am very handsome and young, and can carry with me a great deal of Money, and other Riches; consider whether thou can'st bring it to pass that we may escape together, and thou shalt be my Husband in thy own Country, if thou art willing; but if thou art not, 'tis all one, Lela Marien will provide me a Husband. I wrote this my self; have a care to whom thou givest it to read, do not trust any Moor, because they are all treacherous; and in this I am much perplex'd, and could wish there were not a necessity of trusting any one; because if my Father should come to know it, he would certainly throw me into a Well, and cover me over with Stones. I will tie a Thread to the Cane, and with that thou may'st fasten thy Answer; and if thou can'st not find any one to write in Arabick, make me understand thy Meaning by Signs, for Lela Marien will help me to guess it. She and Alla keep thee, as well as this Cross, which I often kiss, as the Christian Slave bade me to do.

You may imagine, Gentlemen, that we were in admiration at the Contents of this Paper, and withal overjoy'd at them, which we express'd so openly, that the Renegade came to understand that the Paper was not found by chance, but that it was really writ to some one among us; and accordingly he told us his Suspicion, but desir'd us to trust him entirely, and that he would venture his Life with us to procure us our Liberty. Having said this, he pull'd a Brass Crucifix out of his Bosom, and with many Tears, swore by the God which it represented, and in whom he, though a wicked Sinner, did firmly believe, to be true and faithful to us with all Secrecy in what we should impart to him; for he guess'd, that by the means of the Woman who had writ that Letter, we might all of us recover our lost Liberty; and he, in particular, might obtain what he had so long wish'd for, to be receiv'd again into the Bosom of his Mother the Church, from whom, for his Sins, he had been cut off as a rotten Member. The Rene-gade pronounc'd all this with so many Tears, and such Signs of Repentance, that we were all of opinion to trust him, and tell him the whole Truth of the Business. We shew'd him the little Window out of which the Cane us'd to appear, and he from thence took good notice of the House, in order to inform himself who liv'd in it. We next agreed that it would be necessary to answer the *Moorish* Lady's Note; so immediately the Renegade writ down what I dictated to him; which was exactly as I shall relate, for I have not forgot the least material Circumstance of this Adventure, nor can forget them as long as I live. The Words then were these:

The true Alla *keep thee, my dear Lady, and that blessed Virgin, which is the true Mother of God, and has inspir'd thee with the Design of going to the Land of the Christians. Do thou pray her that she would be pleas'd to make thee understand how thou shalt execute what she has commanded thee; for she is so good that she will do it. On my part, and on that of the Christians who are with me, I offer to do for thee all we are able, even to the hazard of our Lives. Fail not to write to me, and give me notice of thy Resolution, for I will always answer thee: The* Great Alla *having given us a Christian Slave, who can read and write thy Language, as thou may'st perceive by this Letter; so that thou may'st, without Fear, give us notice of all thy Intentions. As for what thou say'st, that as soon as thou shalt arrive in the Land of the Christians, thou design'st to be my Wife, I promise thee on the Word of a good Christian, to take thee for my Wife, and thou may'st be assur'd that the* Christians *perform their Promises better than the* Moors. Alla, *and his Mother* Mary *be thy Guard, my dear Lady.*

Having writ and clos'd this Note, I waited two Days till the *Bagnio* was empty, and then I went upon the Terras, the ordinary place of our Conversation, to see if the Cane appear'd, and it was not long before it was stirring. As soon as it appear'd I shew'd my Note, that the Thread might be put to the Cane, but I found that was done to my Hand; and the Cane being let down I fastned the Note to it. Not long after the Knot was let fall, and I taking it up, found in it several Pieces of Gold and Silver, above fifty Crowns, which gave us infinite Content, and fortify'd our Hopes of obtaining at last our Liberty. That Evening our Renegade came to us, and told us, he had found out that the Master of that House was the same *Moor* we had been told of, call'd *Agimorato*, extremely rich, and who had one only Daughter to inherit all his Estate. That it was the Report of the whole City, that she was the handsomest Maid in all *Barbary*, having been demanded in Marriage by several Bassas and Viceroys, but that she had always refus'd to Marry; He also told us, that he had learnt she had had a Christian Slave who was dead, all which agreed with the Contents of the Letter. We immediately held a Council with the Renegade, about the Manner we shou'd use to carry off the *Moorish* Lady, and go all together to Christendom; when at last we agreed to expect the Answer of *Zoraida*, for that was the Name of the Lady who now desires to be call'd *Mary*; as well knowing she could best advise the overcoming all the Difficulties that were in our Way; and after this Resolution, the Renegade assur'd us again, that he would lose his Life, or deliver us out of Captivity.

The *Bagnio* was four Days together full of People, and all that time the Cane was invisible; but as soon as it return'd to its Solitude, the Cane appear'd, with a Knot much bigger than ordinary; Having unty'd it, I found in it a Letter, and a Hundred Crowns in Gold. The Renegade happen'd that Day to be with us, and we gave him the Letter to read; which he said contain'd these Words.

I Cannot tell, Sir, how to contrive that we may go together for Spain; *neither has* Lela Marien *told it me, tho' I have earnestly ask'd it of her; all I can do, is to furnish you out of this Window with a great deal of Riches, buy your Ransom and your Friends with that, and let one of you go to* Spain, *and buy a Bark there, and come and fetch the rest: As for me, you shall find me in my Father's Garden out of Town, by the Seaside, not far from* Babasso Gate; *where I am to pass all the Summer with my Father and my Maids, from which you may take me without Fear, in the Night time, and carry me to your Bark; but remember thou art to be my Husband: and if thou failest in that, I will desire* Lela Marien *to chastize thee. If thou can'st not trust one of thy Friends to go for the Bark, pay thy own Ransom and go thyself; for I trust thou wilt return sooner than another, since thou art a Gentleman and a Christian. Find out my Father's Garden, and I will take care to watch when the* Bagnio *is empty, and let thee have more Money.* Alla *keep my dear Lord.*

These were the Contents of the Second Letter we receiv'd. Upon the reading of it, every one of us offer'd to be the Man that should go and buy the Bark, promising to return with all Punctuality; but the Renegade oppos'd that Proposition, and said, he would never consent any one of us should obtain his Liberty before the rest, because Experience had taught him, that People once Free, do not perform what they promise when Captives; and that some Slaves of Quality had often us'd that Remedy, to send one either to *Valencia* or *Majorca*, with Money to buy a Bark, and come back and fetch the rest; but that they never return'd, because the Joy of having obtain'd their Liberty, and the Fear of losing it again, made them forget what they had promis'd, and cancell'd the Memory of all Obligations. To confirm which, he related to us a strange Story, which had happen'd in those Parts, as there often does among the Slaves. After this, he said that all that could be done, was for him to buy a Bark with the Money which should redeem one of us; that he could buy one in *Algiers*, and pretend to turn Merchant, and deal between *Algiers* and *Tetuan*; by which means, he being Master of the Vessel, might easily find out some way of getting us out of the *Bagnio*, and taking us on Board; and especially if the *Moorish* Lady did what she promis'd, and gave us Money to pay All our Ransoms; for being free, we might embark even at Noon-day: But the greatest Difficulty would be, that the *Moors* do not permit Renegades to keep any Barks, but large ones fit to cruize upon Christians, for they believe that a Renegade, particularly a *Spaniard*, seldom buys a Bark, but with a Design of returning to his own Country. That however, he knew how to obviate that Difficulty, by taking a *Tagarin Moor* for his Partner both in the Bark and Trade, by which means he should still be Master of her, and then all the rest would be easy. We durst not oppose this Opinion, tho' we had more Inclination every one of us to go to *Spain* for a Bark, as the Lady had advis'd; but we were afraid that if we contradicted him, as we were at his Mercy, he might betray us, and bring our Lives in Danger; particularly if the Business of *Zoraida* should be discover'd for whose

Liberty and Life we would have given all ours; so we determin'd to put ourselves under the Protection of God and the
Renegade. At the same time we answer'd *Zoraida*, telling
her, that we would do all she advis'd, which was very well,
and just as if *Lela Marien* herself had instructed her; and
that now it depended on her alone to give us the Means of
bringing this Design to pass. I promis'd her once more to be
her Husband. After this in two Days that the *Bagnio* happen'd to be empty, she gave us by the means of the Cane two
thousand Crowns of Gold; and withal a Letter in which she
let us know, that the next *Juma*, which is their *Friday*, she
was to go to her Father's Garden, and that before she went
she would give us more Money; and if we had not enough, she
would, upon our letting her know it, give us what we should
think sufficient; for her Father was so rich he would hardly
miss it; and so much the less, because he entrusted her with
the Keys of all his Treasure. We presently gave the Renegade
Five hundred Crowns to buy the Bark, and I paid my own Ransom with Eight hundred Crowns, which I put into the Hands
of a Merchant at *Valencia*, then in *Algiers*, who made the
Bargain with the King, and had me to his House upon parole,
to pay the Money upon the Arrival of the first Bark from *Valencia*; for if he had paid down the Money immediately, the King
might have suspected the Money had been ready, and lain
some time in *Algiers*, and that the Merchant for his own Profit
had conceal'd it; and in short, I durst not trust my Master with
ready Money, knowing his distrustful and malicious Nature.
The *Thursday* preceeding that *Friday* that *Zoraida* was to
go to the Garden, she let us have a thousand Crowns more;
desiring me at the same time, that if I paid my Ransom, I would
find out her Father's Garden, and contrive some way of seeing
her there. I answer'd in few Words, that I would do as she
desir'd, and she should only take care to recommend us to
Lela Marien, by those Prayers which the Christian Slave had
taught her. Having done this, Order was taken to have the
Ransom of my three Friends paid also; lest they seeing me at
Liberty, and themselves not so, though there was Money to
set them free, should be troubl'd in Mind, and give way to
the Temptation of the Devil, in doing something that might

redound to the Prejudice of *Zoraida*; for though the Consideration of their Quality ought to have given me Security of their Honour, yet I did not think it proper to run the least hazard in the Matter: So they were redeem'd in the same Manner, and by the same Merchant that I was, who had the Money beforehand; but we never discover'd to him the Remainder of our Intrigue, as not being willing to risque the Danger there was in so doing.

OUR Renegade had in a Fortnight's Time bought a very good Bark, capable of carrying above thirty People; and to give no Suspicion of any other Design, he undertook a Voyage to a Place upon the Coast call'd *Sargel*, about thirty Leagues to the Eastward of *Algiers* towards *Oran*, where there is a great Trade for dry'd Figs. He made this Voyage two or three Times in Company with the *Tagarin Moor* his Partner. Those *Moors* are call'd in *Barbary Tagarins*, who were driven out of *Arragon*; as they call those of *Granada*, *Mudajares*; and the same in the Kingdom of *Fez* are call'd *Elches*, and are the best Soldiers that Prince has.

Every Time he pass'd with his Bark along the Coast, he us'd to cast Anchor in a little Bay that was not above two Bow-shot from the Garden where *Zoraida* expected us; and there he us'd to exercise the *Moors* that row'd either in making the *Sala*, which is a Ceremony among them, or in some other Employment; by which he practis'd in Jest what he was re-solv'd to execute in Earnest. So sometimes he would go to the Garden of *Zoraida* and beg some Fruit, and her Father would give him some, though he did not know him. He had a Mind to find an Occasion to speak to *Zoraida*, and tell her, as he since own'd to me, that he was the Man who by my Order was to carry her to the Land of the Christians and that she might depend upon it; but he could never get an Opportunity of doing it, because the *Moorish* and *Turkish* Women never suffer themselves to be seen by any of their own Nation, but by their Husband, or by his or their Father's Command; but as for the Christian Slaves, they let them see them, and that more familiarly than perhaps could be wish'd. I should have been very sorry that the Renegade had seen or spoke to *Zoraida*, for it must needs have troubled her in-finitely to see that her Business was trusted to a Renegade; and God Almighty, who govern'd our Design, order'd it so, that the Renegade was disappointed. He in the mean time seeing how securely, and without Suspicion, he went and came along the Coast, staying where and when he pleas'd by the Way, and that his Partner the *Tagarin Moor* was of his Mind in all things; that I was at Liberty, and that there wanted nothing but some Christians to help us to row; bid me consider whom I intended to carry with me besides those who were ransom'd, and that I should make sure of them for the first *Friday*, because he had pitch'd on that Day for our Departure. Upon Notice of this Resolution, I spoke to twelve lusty *Spaniards*, good Rowers, and those who might easiliest get out of the City: it was a great Fortune that we got so many in such a Conjuncture, because there were above twenty Sail of Rovers gone out, who had taken aboard most of the Slaves fit for the Oar; and we had not had these, but that their Master happen'd to stay at Home that Summer, to finish a Galley he was building to cruize with, and was then upon the Stocks. I said no more to them, that only they should steal out of the Town in the Evening upon the next *Friday*, and stay for me upon the way that led to *Agimorato's* Garden. I spoke to every one by himself, and gave each of them order to say no more to any other Christian they should see, than that they staid for me there. Having done this, I had another thing of the greatest Importance to bring to pass, which was to give *Zoraida* Notice of our Design, and how far we had carry'd it, that she might be ready at a short Warning, and not be surpriz'd if we came upon the House on a sudden, and even before she could think that the Christian Bark could be come. This made me resolve to go to the Garden to try if it were possible to speak to her: So one Day, upon pretence of gathering a few Herbs, I enter'd the Garden, and the first Person I met was her Father, who spoke to me in the Language us'd all over the *Turkish* Dominions, which is a Mixture of all the *Christian* and *Moorish* Languages, by which we understand one another from *Constantinople* to *Algiers*, and ask'd me what I look'd for in his Garden, and who I belong'd to? I told him I was a Slave of *Arnaute Mami* (this Man I knew was his intimate Friend) and that I wanted a few Herbs to make up a Sallad. He then ask'd me if I were a Man to be redeem'd or no, and how much my Master ask'd for me? During these Questions, the beautiful *Zoraida* came out of the

Garden-house hard by, having descry'd me a good while before; and as the *Moorish* Women make no Difficulty of shewing themselves to the Christian Slaves, she drew near, without Scruple, to the Place where her Father and I were talking; neither did her Father shew any Dislike of her coming, but call'd to her to come nearer. It would be hard for me to express here the wonderful Surprize and Astonishment that the Beauty, the rich Dress, and the charming Air of my beloved *Zoraida* put me in: She was all bedeck'd with Pearls, which hung thick upon her Head and about her Neck and Arms. Her Feet and Legs were naked, after the Custom of that Country, and she had upon her Ancles a kind of Bracelet of Gold, and set with such rich Diamonds that her Father valu'd them, as she since told me, at ten thousand Pistoles a Pair; and those upon her Wrists were of the same value. The Pearls were of the best sort, for the *Moorish* Women delight much in them, and have more Pearls of all sorts than any Nation. Her Father was reputed to have the finest in *Algiers*, and to be worth besides, above two hundred thousand *Spanish* Crowns; of all which, the Lady you here see was then Mistress; but now is only so of Me. What she yet retains of Beauty after all her Sufferings, may help you to guess at her wonderful Appearance in the midst of her Prosperity. The Beauty of some Ladies has its Days and Times, and is more or less, according to Accidents or Passions, which naturally raise or diminish the Lustre of it, and sometimes quite extinguish it. All I can say, is, at that Time she appear'd to me the best-drest and most beautiful Woman I had ever seen; to which, adding the Obligations I had to her, she pass'd with me for a Goddess from Heaven, descended upon Earth for my Relief and Happiness. As she drew near, her Father told her, in his Country Language, that I was a Slave of his Friend *Arnaute Mami*, and came to pick a Sallad in his Garden. She presently took the Hint, and ask'd me in *Lingua Franca*, whether I was a Gentleman, and if I was, why I did not ransom myself? I told her I was already ransom'd, and that by the Price, she might guess the Value my Master set upon me, since he had bought me for 1500 Pieces of Eight: To which she reply'd: If thou hadst been my Father's Slave, I would not have let him part with thee for

twice as much; for, said she, You Christians never speak Truth
in any thing you say, and make yourselves poor to deceive the
Moors. That may be, Madam, said I, but in truth I have dealt
by my Master, and do intend to deal by all those I shall have
to deal with, sincerely and honourably. And when dost thou
go home? said she. To-morrow, Madam, said I, for here is a
French Bark that sails to-morrow, and I intend not to lose
that Opportunity. Is it not better, reply'd *Zoraida*, to stay
till there come some *Spanish* Bark, and go with them, and
not with the *French*, who, I am told, are no Friends of yours?
No; said I, yet if the Report of a *Spanish* Bark's coming should
prove true, I would perhaps stay for it, though 'tis more likely
I shall take the Opportunity of the *French*, because the Desire
I have of being at Home, and with those Persons I love, will
hardly let me wait for any other Conveniency. Without doubt,
said *Zoraida*, thou art Married in *Spain* and impatient to be
with thy Wife. I am not, said I, Marry'd, but I have given
my Word to a Lady, to be so as soon as I can reach my own
Country. And is the Lady handsome that has your Promise,
said *Zoraida*? She is so handsome, said I, that to describe her
rightly, and tell Truth, I can only say she is like you. At this
her Father laugh'd heartily, and said, On my word, Christian,
she must be very Charming if she be like my Daughter, who
is the greatest Beauty of all this Kingdom: Look upon her
well, and thou wilt say I speak Truth. *Zoraida's* Father was
our Interpreter for the most of what we talk'd, for though
she understood the *Lingua Franca*, yet she was not used to
speak it, and so explain'd herself more by Signs than Words.
While we were in this Conversation, there came a *Moor*
running hastily and cry'd aloud that four *Turks* had leap'd
over the Fence of the Garden, and were gathering the Fruit,
though it was not ripe. The old Man started at that, and so
did *Zoraida*, for the *Moors* do naturally stand in great Awe
of the *Turks* particularly of the Soldiers, who are so insolent
on their Side, that they treat the *Moors* as if they were their
Slaves. This made the Father bid his Daughter go in and shut
herself up close, whilst, said he, I go and talk with those
Dogs; and for thee, Christian, gather the Herbs thou want'st,
and go thy ways in Peace, and God conduct thee safe to thy

own Country. I bow'd to him, and he left me with *Zoraida*, to go and find out the *Turks*: She made also as if she were going away, as her Father had bid her; but she was no sooner hid from his Sight by the Trees of the Garden, but she turn'd towards me with her Eyes full of Tears, and said in her Language, *Amexi Christiano, Amexi,* which is, Thou art going away, Christian, thou art going: To which I answer'd, Yes, Madam, I am, but by no means without You; you may expect me next *Friday,* and be not surpriz'd when you see us, for we will certainly go to the Land of the Christians. I said this so passionately, that she understood me; and throwing one of her Arms about my Neck, she began to walk softly and with trembling towards the House. It pleas'd Fortune, that as we were in this Posture walking together (which might have prov'd very unlucky to us) we met *Agimorato* coming back from the *Turks,* and we perceiv'd he had seen us as we were; but *Zoraida,* very readily and discreetly, was so far from taking away her Arm from about my Neck, that drawing still nearer to me, she lean'd her Head upon my Breast, and letting her Knees give way, was in the Posture of one that swoons; I at the same time, made as if I had much ado to bear her up against my Will. Her Father came hastily to us, and seeing his Daughter in this Condition, ask'd her what was the Matter? But she not answering readily, he presently said, without doubt these *Turks* have frighted her, and she faints away; at which he took her in his Arms. She, as it were, coming to herself, fetch'd a deep Sigh, and with her Eyes not yet dry'd from Tears, she said *Amexi Christiano, Amexi,* be gone, Christian, be gone; to which her Father reply'd, 'Tis no Matter, Child, whether he go or no, he has done thee no Hurt, and the *Turks* at my Request are gone. 'Tis they who frighted her, said I; but since she desires I shou'd be gone, I'll come another time for my Sallad, by your Leave; for my Master says the Herbs of your Garden are the best of any he can have. Thou may'st have what, and when thou wilt, said the Father; for my Daughter does not think the Christians troublesome, she only wish'd the *Turks* away, and by Mistake bid thee be gone too, or make haste and gather thy Herbs. With this I immediately took leave of 'em both; and *Zoraida,* shewing great Trouble in her Looks, went away with her Father. I in the mean time, upon pretence of gathering my Herbs here and there, walk'd all over the Garden, observing exactly all the Places of coming in and going out, and every Corner fit for my Purpose, as well as what Strength there was in the House, with all other Conveniencies to facilitate our Business. Having done this I went my ways, and gave an exact Account of all that had happen'd, to the Renegade and the rest of my Friends, longing earnestly for the Time in which I might promise myself my dear *Zoraida's* Company, without any fear of Disturbance. At last the happy Hour came, and we had all the good Success, we could promise ourselves, of a Design so well laid; for the *Friday* after my Discourse with *Zoraida*, towards the Evening we came to an Anchor with our Bark, almost over-against the Place where my lovely Mistress liv'd; the Christians, who were to be employ'd at the Oar, were already at the Rendezvous, and hid up and down thereabouts. They were all in expectation of my coming, and very desirous to seize the Bark which they saw before their Eyes, for they did not know our Agreement with the Renegade, but thought they were by main Force to gain their Conveyance and their Liberty, by killing the *Moors* on Board. As soon as I and my Friends appear'd, all the rest came from their hiding-Places to us. By this time the City-Gates were shut, and no Soul appear'd in all the Country near us. When we were all together, it was a Question whether we should first fetch *Zoraida*, or make ourselves Masters of those few *Moors* in the Bark. As we were in this Consultation, the Renegade came to us, and asking what we meant to stand idle, told us his *Moors* were all gone to rest, and most of them asleep. We told him our Difficulty, and he immediately said, that the most important thing was to secure the Bark, which might easily be done, and without Danger, and then we might go for *Zoraida*.

We were all of his Mind, and so, without more ado, he march'd at the Head of us to the Bark, and leaping into it, he first drew a Scimitar, and cry'd aloud in the *Moorish* Language, let not a Man of you stir, except he means it shou'd cost him his Life; and while he said this, all the other Christians were got on Board. The *Moors*, who are naturally timorous, hearing the Master use this Language, were frighted, and without any Resistance, suffer'd themselves to be manacl'd, which was done with great expedition by the Christians, who told them at the same time, that if they made the least Noise, they would immediately cut their Throats. This being done, and half of our Number left to guard them, the Remainder, with the Renegade, went to *Agimorato's* Garden; and our good Fortune was such, that coming to force the Gate, we found it open with as much facility, as if it had not been shut at all. So we march'd on with great Silence to the House, without being perceiv'd by any Body. The lovely *Zoraida*, who was at the Window, ask'd softly, upon hearing us tread, whether we were *Nazarani*, that is Christians? I answer'd Yes; and desir'd her to come down. As soon as she heard my Voice, she staid not a Minute; but, without saying a Word, came down and open'd the Door, appearing to us all like a Goddess, her Beauty and the Richness of her Dress not being to be describ'd. As soon as I saw her, I took her by the Hand, which I kiss'd, the Renegade did the same, and then my Friends; the rest of the Company follow'd the same Ceremony; so that we all paid her a kind of Homage for our Liberty. The Renegade ask'd her in *Morisco*, whether her Father was in the Garden? She said Yes, and that he was asleep. Then said he, we must awake him, and take him with us, as also all that's valuable in the House. No, no, said *Zoraida*, my Father must not be touch'd, and in the House there is nothing so rich as what I shall carry with me, which is enough to make you all rich and content. Having said this she stept into the House, bid us be quiet, and she would soon return. I ask'd the Renegade what had pass'd between them, and he told me what he had said: To which I reply'd, that by no means any thing was to be done, otherwise than as *Zoraida* should please. She was already coming back with a small Trunk so full of Gold, that she could hardly carry it, when, to our great Misfortune, while this was doing, her Father awak'd, and hearing a Noise in the Garden, open'd a Window and look'd out: Having perceiv'd that there were Christians in it, he began to cry out in *Arabick*, Thieves, Thieves, Christians, Christians. These Cries

of his put us all into a terrible Disorder and Fear; but the
Renegade seeing our Danger, and how much it imported us to
accomplish our Enterprize before we were perceiv'd, he ran
up to the Place where *Agimorato* was, and took with him
some of our Company; for I durst by no means leave *Zoraida*,
who had swoon'd away in my Arms. Those who went up be-
stir'd themselves so well, that they brought down *Agimorato*
with his Hands ty'd behind him, and his Mouth stopp'd with
a Handkerchief, which hinder'd him from so much as speaking a Word; and threatning him besides, that if he made the
least Attempt to speak, it should cost him his Life. When his
Daughter, who was come to herself, saw him, she cover'd her
Eyes to avoid the Sight, and her Father remain'd the more
astonish'd, for he knew not how willingly she had put herself
into Our Hands. Diligence on our side being the chief thing
requisite, we us'd it so as we got to our Bark, when our Men
began to be in Pain for us, as fearing we had met with some
ill Accident: We got on Board about two Hours after it 'twas
dark; where the first thing we did was to unty the Hands of
Zoraida's Father, and to unstop his Mouth, but still with the
same Threatnings of the Renegade, in case he made any Noise.
When he saw his Daughter there, he began to sigh most passionately, and more when he saw me embrace her with Tenderness, and that she, without any Resistance or Struggling,
seem'd to endure it; he, for all this, was silent, for fear the
Threatnings of the Renegade should be put in Execution.
Zoraida seeing us a Board, and that we were ready to handle
our Oars to be gone, she bid the Renegade tell me, she desir'd
I would set her Father, and the other *Moors*, our Prisoners,
on Shore; for else she would throw herself into the Sea, rather
than see a Father, who had us'd her so tenderly, be carried
away Captive for her sake, before her Eyes. The Renegade
told me what she said, to which I agreed; but the Renegade
was of another Opinion; saying, that if we set them on shore
there, they would raise the Country, and give the Alarm to
the City, by which some light Frigates might be dispatch'd in
quest of us, and getting between us and the Sea, it would be
impossible for us to make our Escape; and that all that could
be done, was to set them at Liberty in the first Christian Land

we could reach. This seem'd so reasonable to us all, that *Zoraida* herself, being inform'd of the Motives we had Not to obey her at present, agreed to it. Immediately, with great Silence and Content, we began to ply our Oars, recommending ourselves to Providence with all our Hearts, and endeavour'd to make for *Majorca*, which is the nearest Christian Land; but the North Wind rising a little, and the Sea with it, we could not hold that Course, but were forc'd to drive along Shore towards *Oran*, not without great fear of being discover'd from *Sargel*, upon the Coast, about thirty Leagues from *Algiers*. We were likewise apprehensive of meeting some of those Galliots which came from *Tetuan* with Merchandize. Though, to say Truth, we did not so much fear these last; for except it were a cruizing Galliot, we all of us wish'd to meet such a one, which we shou'd certainly take, and so get a better Vessel to transport us in. *Zoraida* all this while hid her Face between my Hands, that she might not see her Father; and I could hear her call upon *Lela Marien* to help us. By that time we had got about Thirty Miles the Day broke, and we found our selves within a Mile of the Shore, which appear'd to us a desart solitary Place, but yet we row'd hard to get off to Sea, for fear of being discover'd by some body. When we were got about two Leagues out to Sea, we propos'd the Men shou'd row by turns, that some might refresh themselves; but the Men at the Oar said it was not time yet to rest, and that they could eat and row too, if those who did not row would assist them, and give them Meat and Drink; this we did, and a little while after the Wind blowing fresh, we ceas'd rowing and set sail for *Oran*, not being able to hold any other Course. We made above eight Miles an Hour, being in no fear of any thing but meeting some Cruizers. We gave Victuals to our *Moorish* Prisoners, and the Renegade comforted them, and told them they were not Slaves, but that they should be set at liberty upon the first Opportunity. The same was said to *Zoraida's* Father; who answer'd, I might expect from your Courtesy any thing else perhaps, O Christians; but that you should give me my Liberty, I am not simple enough to believe it; for you never would have run the Hazard of taking it from me, if you intended to restore it me so easily; especially since you know who I am, and what you may get for my Ransom, which if you will but name, I do from this Moment offer you all that you can desire for Me and for that unfortunate Daughter of mine, or for her alone, since she is the better part of me. When he had said this, he burst out into Tears so violently, that *Zoraida* could not forbear looking up at him, and indeed he mov'd Compassion in us all, but in her particularly; insomuch, as starting from my Arms, she flew to her Father's, and putting her Head to his, they began again so passionate and tender a Scene, that most of us could not forbear accompanying their Grief with our Tears; but her Father seeing her so richly dress'd, and so many Jewels about her, said to her, in his Language, What is the meaning of this, Daughter? for last Night before this Terrible Misfortune befel us, thou wert in thy ordinary Dress; and now, without scarce having had the Time to put on such things, I see thee adorn'd with all the Fineries that I could give thee, if we were at Liberty and in full Prosperity. This gives me more Wonder and Trouble than even our sad Misfortune; therefore answer me. The Renegade interpreted all that the *Moor* said, and we saw that *Zoraida* answer'd not one Word; but on a sudden, spying the little Casket in which she was us'd to put her Jewels, which he thought had been left in *Algiers*, he remain'd yet more astonish'd, and ask'd her how that Trunk could come into our Hands, and what was in it? To which the Renegade, without expecting *Zoraida's* Answer, reply'd, Do not trouble thyself to ask thy Daughter so many Questions, for with one Word I can satisfy them all. Know then that she is a Christian, and 'tis she that has filed off our Chains, and given us Liberty; she is with us by her own Consent, and I hope well pleas'd, as People should be who come from Darkness into Light, and from Death to Life. Is this true, Daughter? said the *Moor*. It is, reply'd *Zoraida*. How then, said the old Man, art thou really a Christian? and art thou she that has put thy Father into the Power of his Enemies? To which *Zoraida* reply'd, I am she that is a Christian, but not she that has brought thee into this Condition, for my Design never was to injure my Father, but only to do myself good. And what good hast thou done thyself? said the *Moor*. Ask that of *Lela*

Marien, reply'd *Zoraida*, for she can tell thee best. The old Man had no sooner heard this but he threw himself, with incredible Fury, into the Sea, where without doubt he had been drown'd, had not his Garments, which were long and wide, kept him some time above Water. *Zoraida* cry'd out to us to help him, which we all did so readily, that we pull'd him out by his Vest, but half drown'd, and without any Sense. This so troubl'd *Zoraida*, that she threw herself upon her Father and began to lament and take on as if he had been really dead. We turn'd his Head downwards, and by this means having disgorg'd a great deal of Water, he recover'd a little in about two Hours time. The Wind in the mean while was come about, and forc'd us toward the Shore, so that we were oblig'd to ply our Oars not to be driven upon the Land. It was our good Fortune to get into a small Bay, which is made by a Promontory, call'd the Cape of the *Caba Rumia*; which, in our Tongue, is the Cape of *The wicked Christian Woman*; and it is a Tradition among the *Moors*, that *Caba*, the Daughter of Count *Julian*, who was the Cause of the Loss of *Spain*, lies buried there; and they think it ominous to be forc'd into that Bay, for they never go in otherwise than by Necessity; but to us it was no unlucky Harbour, but a safe Retreat, considering how high the Sea went by this time. We posted our Centries on Shore, but kept our Oars ready to be ply'd upon Occasion, taking in the mean time some Refreshment of what the Renegade had provided, praying heartily to God and the Virgin *Mary*, to protect us, and help us to bring our Design to a happy Conclusion. Here, at the Desire of *Zoraida*, we resolv'd to set her Father on Shore, with all the other *Moors*, whom we kept fast bound; for she had not Courage, nor could her tender Heart suffer any longer, to see her Father and her Countrymen ill us'd before her Face; but we did not think to do it before we were just ready to depart, and then they could not much hurt us, the Place being a solitary one, and no Habitations near it. Our Prayers were not in vain; the Wind fell and the Sea became calm, inviting us thereby to pursue our intended Voyage: We unbound our Prisoners and set them on Shore, one by one, which they were mightily astonish'd at. When we came to put *Zoraida's*

Father on Shore, who by this time was come to himself, he said, Why do you think, Christians, that this wicked Woman desires I should be set at Liberty? Do you think it is for any Pity she takes of me? No certainly, but it is because she is not able to bear my Presence, which hinders the Prosecution of her ill Desires: I wou'd not have you think neither that she has embrac'd your Religion, because she knows the Difference between yours and ours, but because she has heard that she may live more loosely in your Country than at Home: and then turning himself to *Zoraida*, while I and another held him fast by the Arms, that he might commit no Extravagance, he said, O infamous and blind young Woman, where art thou going in the Power of these Dogs, our natural Enemies? Curs'd be the Hour in which I begot thee, and the Care and Affection with which I bred thee. But I, seeing he was not like to make an end of his Exclamations soon, made haste to set him on Shore, from whence he continu'd to give us his Curses and Imprecations; begging on his Knees of *Mahomet* to beg of God Almighty to confound and destroy us; and when being under Sail, we cou'd no longer hear him, we saw his Actions, which were tearing his Hair and Beard, and rolling himself upon the Ground; but he once strain'd his Voice so high, that we heard what he said, which was, Come back, my dear Daughter, for I forgive thee all; Let those Men have the Treasure which is already in their Possession, and do Thou return to comfort thy disconsolate Father, who must else lose his Life in these sandy Desarts. All this *Zoraida* heard, and shed abundance of Tears, but cou'd answer nothing, but beg that *Lela Marien*, who had made her a Christian, wou'd comfort him. God knows, said she, I cou'd not avoid doing what I have done; and that these Christians are not oblig'd to me, for I cou'd not be at rest till I had done this, which to thee, dear Father, seems so ill a Thing. All this she said, when we were got so far out of his Hearing, that we cou'd scarce so much as see him. So I comforted *Zoraida* as well as I cou'd, and we all minded our Voyage. The Wind was now so right for our Purpose, that we made no doubt of being the next Morning upon the *Spanish* Shore; but as it seldom happens that any Felicity comes so pure as not to be temper'd and allay'd by some mixture of Sorrow; either our ill Fortune, or the *Moor's* Curses had such an effect (for a Father's Curses are to be dreaded, let the Father be what he will) that about Midnight, when we were under full Sail, with our Oars laid by, we saw, by the Light of the Moon, hard by us, a round-stern'd Vessel with all her Sails out, coming a head of us, which she did so close to us, that we were forc'd to strike our Sail not to run foul of her; and the Vessel likewise seem'd to endeavour to let us go by; they had come so near us to ask from whence we came, and whither we were going? But doing it in *French*, the Renegade forbid us to answer, saying without doubt these are *French* Pirates, to whom every thing is Prize. This made us all be silent; and as we sail'd on, they being under the Wind, fir'd two Guns at us, both, as it appear'd, with Chain-shot, for one brought our Mast by the Board, and the other went thro' us, without killing any Body; but we, perceiving we were sinking, call'd to them to come and take us, for we were going to be drown'd; they then struck their own Sails, and putting out their Boat, there came about a dozen *French* on Board us, all well arm'd, and their Matches lighted. When they were close to us, seeing we were but few, they took us a-board their Boat, saying that this had happen'd to us for not answering their Questions. The Renegade had time to take the little Coffer or Trunk, full of *Zoraida's* Treasure, and heave it over-board, without being perceiv'd by any Body. When we were on Board their Vessel, after having learnt from us all they cou'd, they began to strip us, as if we had been their mortal Enemies: They plunder'd *Zoraida* of all the Jewels and Bracelets she had on her Hands and Feet; but that did not so much trouble me, as the Apprehension I was in for the rich Jewel of her Chastity, which she valu'd above all the rest. But that sort of People seldom have any Desires beyond the getting of Riches, which they saw in abundance before their Eyes; and their Covetousness was so sharpen'd by it, that even our Slaves Clothes tempted them. They consulted what to do with us; and some were of Opinion to throw us over-board, wrapt up in a Sail, because they intended to put into some of the *Spanish* Ports, under the Notion of being of *Britany*; and if they carry'd us with them, they

might be punish'd, and their Roguery come to light: But the
Captain, who thought himself rich enough with *Zoraida's*
Plunder, said he wou'd not touch at any Port of *Spain*, but
make his way through the *Straits* by Night, and so return to
Rochel, from whence he came. This being resolv'd, they bethought themselves of giving us their Long-boat, and what
Provision we might want for our short Passage. As soon as it
was Day, and that we descry'd the *Spanish* Shore (at which
Sight, so desirable a thing is Liberty, all our Miseries vanish'd
from our Thoughts in a Moment) they began to prepare things,
and about Noon they put us on Board, giving us two Barrels
of Water, and a small quantity of Bisket; and the Captain,
touch'd with some Remorse for the lovely *Zoraida*, gave her,
at parting, about forty Crowns in Gold, and would not suffer
his Men to take from her those Cloaths which now she has on.
We went a Board, shewing our selves rather thankful than
complaining. They got out to Sea, making for the *Straits*, and
we having the Land before us for our North Star, ply'd our
Oars, so that about Sunset we were near enough to have landed
before it was quite dark; but considering the Moon was hid
in Clouds, and the Heavens were growing dark, and we ignorant of the Shore, we did not think it safe to venture on it, tho'
many among us were so desirous of Liberty, and to be out of
all Danger, that they would have landed, though on a desart
Rock; and by that means, at least we might avoid all little
Barks of the Pirates of the *Barbary* Coast, such as those of
Tetuan, who come from Home when 'tis dark, and by Morning
are early upon the *Spanish* Coast; where they often make a
Prize, and go home to Bed the same Day. But the other Opinion
prevail'd, which was to row gently on, and if the Sea and
Shore gave leave, to land quietly where we cou'd. We did
accordingly, and about Midnight we came under a great Hill,
which had a sandy Shore, convenient enough for our landing.
Here we ran our Boat in as far as we cou'd, and being got on
Land, we all kiss'd it for joy, and thank'd God with Tears
for our Deliverance. This done, we took out the little Provision we had left, and climb'd up the Mountain, thinking ourselves more in Safety there, for we cou'd hardly persuade
ourselves, nor believe that the Land we were upon was the

Christian Shore. We thought the Day long a coming, and then we got to the top of the Hill, to see if we cou'd discover any Habitations; but we could no where discry either House, or Person, or Path. We resolv'd, however, to go further on, as thinking we could not miss at last of some Body to inform us where we were: That which troubl'd me most was, to see my poor *Zoraida* go on Foot among the sharp Rocks, and I would sometimes have carry'd her on my Shoulders; but she was as much concern'd at the Pains I took, as she cou'd be at what she endur'd; so leaning on me she went on with much Patience and Content. When we had gone about a quarter of a League, we heard the sound of a little Pipe, which we took to be a certain Sign of some Flock near us; and looking well about, we perceiv'd, at last, at the Foot of a Cork-tree a young Shepherd who was cutting a Stick with his Knife with great Attention and Seriousness. We call'd to him, and he having look'd up, ran away as hard as he could. It seems, as we afterwards heard, the first he saw were the Renegade and *Zoraida*, who being in the *Moorish* Dress, he thought all the *Moors* in *Barbary* were upon him; and running into the Wood, cry'd all the way as loud as he could, *Moors*, *Moors*, Arm, Arm, the *Moors* are landed. We hearing this Outcry, did not well know what to do: But considering that the Shepherd's Roaring wou'd raise the Country, and the Horse-guard of the Coast would be upon us, we agreed that the Renegade should pull off his *Turkish* Habit, and put on a Slave's Coat, which one of us lent him, though he that lent it him remain'd in his Shirt. Thus recommending ourselves to God, we went on by the same way that the Shepherd ran, still expecting when the Horse would come upon us; and we were not deceiv'd, for in less than two Hours, as we came down the Hills into a Plain, we discover'd about fifty Horse coming upon a half Gallop towards us; when we saw that, we stood still, expecting them. As soon as they came up, and, instead of so many *Moors*, saw so many poor Christian Captives, they were astonish'd. One of them ask'd us if We were the Occasion of the Alarm that a young Shepherd had given the Country? Yes, said I, and upon that began to tell him who we were, and whence we came; but one of our Company knew the Horse-man that had

414

ask'd us the Question, and without letting me go on, said, God be prais'd, Gentlemen, for bringing us to so good a part of the Country, for if I mistake not, we are near *Velez Malaga*; and if the many Years of my Captivity have not taken my Memory from me too, I think, that you, Sir, who ask us these Questions, are my Uncle *Don Pedro Bustamente*. The Christian Slave had hardly said this, but the Gentleman lighting from his Horse, came hastily to embrace the young Slave, saying, Dear Nephew, my Joy, my Life, I know thee, and have often lamented thy Loss, and so has thy Mother and thy other Relations, whom thou wilt yet find alive. God has preserv'd them, that they may have the Pleasure of seeing thee. We had heard thou wert in *Algiers*, and by what I see of thy Dress, and that of all this Company, you must all have had some miraculous Deliverance. It is so, reply'd the young Man, and we shall have time enough now to tell all our Adventures. The rest of the Horsemen hearing we were Christians escap'd from Slavery, lighted likewise from their Horses, offering them to us to carry us to the City of *Velez Malaga*, which was about a League and a half off. Some of them went where we had left our Boat, and got it into the Port, while others took us up behind them; and *Zoraida* rid behind the Gentleman, Uncle to our Captive. All the People, who had already heard something of our Adventure, came out to meet us; they did not wonder to see Captives at Liberty, nor *Moors* Prisoners; for in all that Coast they are us'd to it; but they were astonish'd at the Beauty of *Zoraida*, which at that Instant seem'd to be in its point of Perfection; for, what with the Agitation of Travelling, and what with the Joy of being safe in Christendom, without the terrible Thought of being retaken, she had such a beautiful Colour in her Countenance, that were it not for fear of being too partial, I durst say, there was not a more beautiful Creature in the World, at least that I had seen. We went straight to Church, to thank God for his great Mercy to us; and as we came into it, and that *Zoraida* had look'd upon the Pictures, she said there were several Faces there that were like *Lela Marien's*; we told her they were Her Pictures, and the Renegade explain'd to her as well as he could the Story of them, that she might adore them, as if in reality each of them had been the true *Lela Marien*, who had spoke to her; and she, who has a good and clear Understanding, comprehended immediately all that was said about the Pictures and Images. After this, we were dispers'd, and lodg'd in different Houses of the Town; but the young Christian Slave of *Velez* carry'd Me, *Zoraida*, and the Renegade to his Father's House, where we were accommodated pretty well, according to their Ability, and us'd with as much Kindness as their own Son. After six Days stay at *Velez*, the Renegade having inform'd himself of what was needful for him to know, went away to *Granada*, there to be re-admitted by the holy Inquisition into the Bosom of the Church. The other Christians, being at Liberty, went each whither he thought fit. *Zoraida* and I remain'd without other help than the forty Crowns the Pirate gave her, with which I bought the Ass she rides on, and since we landed, have been to her a Father and a Friend, but not a Husband: We are now going to see whether my Father be alive, or if either of my Brothers has had better Fortune than I; tho' since it has pleas'd Heaven to give me *Zoraida*, and make me Her Companion, I reckon no better Fortune could befall me. The Patience with which she bears the Inconvenience of Poverty, the Desire she shews of being made a Christian, do give me Subject of continual Admiration, and oblige me to serve and love her all the Days of my Life. I confess, the Expectation of being hers is not a little allay'd with the Uncertainties of knowing whether I shall find in my Country any one to receive us, or a Corner to pass my Life with her; and perhaps Time will have so alter'd the Affairs of our Family, that I shall not find any Body that will know me, if my Father and Brothers are dead.

This is, Gentlemen, the Sum of my Adventures, which whether or no they are entertaining, you are best Judges. I wish I had told them more compendiously; and yet, I assure you, the fear of being tedious has made me cut short many Circumstances of my Story.

XV: AN ACCOUNT OF WHAT HAPPEN'D AFTER-
WARDS IN THE INN, WITH SEVERAL OTHER
OCCURRENCES WORTH NOTICE

HERE the Stranger ended his Story, and Don *Ferdinand*, by way of Compliment in the be-half of the whole Company, said, Truly, Captain, the wonderful and surprizing Turns of your Fortune are not only entertaining, but the pleasing and graceful manner of your Relation is as extraordinary as the Adventures themselves: We are all bound to pay you our Acknowledgments; and I believe we could be delighted with a second Recital, though 'twere to last till to Morrow, provided it were made by You. *Cardenio* and the rest of the Company join'd with him in offering their utmost Service in the Re-establishment of his Fortune, and that with so much Sincerity and Earnestness, that the Captain had reason to be satisfy'd of their Affection. Don *Ferdinand* particularly propos'd to engage the Marquis his Brother to stand Godfather to *Zoraida*, if he would return with him; and farther, promis'd to provide him with all things necessary to support his Figure and Quality in Town; but the Captain making them a very handsome Compliment for their obliging Favours, excus'd himself from accepting those kind Offers at that time. It was now growing towards the dark of the Evening, when a Coach stopp'd at the Inn, and with it some Horse-men, who ask'd for a Lodging. The Hostess answer'd, they were as full as they could pack. Were you ten times fuller, answer'd one of the Horsemen, here must be room made for my Lord Judge, who is in this Coach. The Hostess hearing this was very much concern'd; said she, The Case, Sir, is plain, we have not one Bed empty in the House; but if his Lordship brings a Bed with him, as perhaps he may, he shall command my House with all my Heart, and I and my Husband will quit our own Chamber to serve him; Do so then, said the Man: and by this time a Gentleman alighted from the Coach, easily dis-tinguishable for a Man of Dignity and Office, by his long Gown and great Sleeves. He led a young Lady by the Hand, about sixteen Years of Age, dress'd in a riding Suit; her Beauty and charming Air attracted the Eyes of every Body with Admiration, and had not the other Ladies been present, any one might have thought it difficult to have match'd her outward Graces.

Don *Quixote* seeing them come near the Door, Sir, said he, you may enter undismay'd, and refresh yourself in this Castle, which though little and indifferently provided, must nevertheless allow Room and afford Accommodation to Arms and Learning; and more especially to Arms and Learning, that like yours, bring Beauty for their Guide and Conductor. For certainly at the approach of this lovely Damsel, not only Castles ought to open and expand their Gates, but even Rocks divide their solid Bodies, and Mountains bow their Ambitious Crests and stoop to entertain her. Come in therefore, Sir, enter this Paradise, where you shall find a bright Constellation, worthy to shine in conjunction with that Heaven of Beauty which you bring: Here shall you find Arms in their height, and Beauty in Perfection. Don *Quixote's* Speech, Mien, and Garb, put the Judge to a Strange Nonplus; and he was not a little surpriz'd on the t'other Hand at the sudden appearance of the Three Ladies, who being inform'd of the Judge's coming, and the young Lady's Beauty, were come out to see and entertain her. But Don *Ferdinand*, *Cardenio*, and the Curate, addressing him in a Stile very different from the Knight, soon convinc'd him that he had to do with Gentlemen, and Persons of Note, tho' Don *Quixote's* Figure and Behaviour put him to a stand, not being able to make any Reasonable Conjecture of his Extravagance. After the usual Civilities pass'd on both Sides, they found upon examination, that the Women must all lie together in Don *Quixote's* Apartment, and the Men remain without to guard them. The Judge consented that his Daughter shou'd go to the Ladies, and so what with his own Bed and what with the Inn-keeper's, He and the Gentlemen made a shift to pass the Night.

The Captain, upon the first sight of the Judge, had a strong Presumption that he was one of his Brothers, and presently ask'd one of his Servants his Name and Country. The Fellow told him, his Name was *Juan Perez de Viedma*, and that, as he was inform'd, he was born in the Highlands of *Leon*. This, with his own Observation, confirm'd his Opinion, that this was the Brother who had made Study his Choice; whereupon calling aside Don *Ferdinand*, *Cardenio*, and the Curate, he told them with great Joy what he had learn'd, with what the Servant further told him, that his Master being made a Judge of the Court of *Mexico*, was then upon his Journey to the *Indies*; that the young Lady was his only Daughter, whose Mother dying in Child-birth, settled her Dowry upon her Daughter for a Portion, and that the Father had still liv'd a Widower, and was very Rich. Upon the whole Matter, he ask'd their Advice, whether they thought it proper for him to discover himself presently to his Brother, or by some means try how his Pulse beat first in relation to his Loss, by which he might guess at his Reception. Why should you doubt of a kind one, Sir, said the Curate; Because I am poor, Sir, said the Captain, and would therefore by some Device fathom his Affections; for should he prove ashamed to own me, I should be more ashamed to discover myself. Then leave the Management to me, said the Curate; the Affable and Courteous Behaviour of the Judge seems to me so very far from Pride, that you need not doubt a welcome Reception; but however, because you desire it, I'll engage to find a way to sound him. Supper was now upon the Table, and all the Gentlemen sat down, but the Captain, who eat with the Ladies in the next Room; when the Company had half supp'd, My Lord-Judge, said the Curate, I remember about some Years ago, I was happy in the Acquaintance and Friendship of a Gentleman of your Name, when I was Prisoner in *Constantinople*; he was a Captain of as much Worth and Courage as any in the *Spanish* Infantry, but as unfortunate as brave. What was his Name, pray Sir, said the Judge? *Ruy Perez de Viedma*, answer'd the Curate, of a Town in the Mountains of *Leon*. I remember he told me a very odd Passage between his Father, his two Brothers, and himself; and truly had it come from any Man of less Credit and Reputation, I should have thought it no more than a Story: He said, that his Father made an equal Dividend of his Estate among his three Sons, giving them such Advice as might have fitted the Mouth of *Cato*; that He made Arms his choice, and with such success, that within a few

Years (by the pure Merit of his Bravery) he was made Captain of a Foot-Company, and had a fair prospect of being advanc'd to a Colonel; but his Fortune forsook him, where he had most reason to expect her Favour; for, in the memorable Battle of *Lepanto*, where so many Christians recover'd their Liberty he unfortunately lost his. I was taken at *Goletta*, and after different Turns of Fortune we became Companions at *Constantinople*; thence we were carry'd to *Algiers*, where one of the strangest Adventures in the World befel this Gentleman. The Curate then briefly ran though the whole Story of the Captain and *Zoraida* (the Judge sitting all the time more attentive than he ever did on the Bench) to their being taken and stripp'd by the *French*; and that he had hear'd nothing of them after that, nor could ever learn whether they came into *Spain*, or were carried Prisoners into *France*.

The Captain stood list'ning in a Corner and observ'd the Motions of his Brother's Countenance, while the Curate told his Story: Which, when he had finish'd, the Judge breathing out a deep Sigh, and the Tears standing in his Eyes: O Sir, said he, if you knew how nearly your Relation touches me, you would easily excuse the violent Eruption of these Tears. The Captain you spoke of is my eldest Brother, who, being of a stronger Constitution of Body, and more elevated Soul, made the Glory and Fame of War his Choice, which was one of the three Proposals made by my Father, as your Companion told you. I apply'd myself to Study, and my younger Brother has purchas'd a vast Estate in *Peru*, out of which he has transmitted to my Father enough to support his liberal Disposition; and to me, wherewithal to continue my Studies, and advance myself to the Rank and Authority which now I maintain. My Father is still alive, but dies daily for Grief he can learn nothing of his Eldest Son, and importunes Heaven incessantly, that he may once more see him before Death close his Eyes. 'Tis very strange, considering his Discretion in other Matters, that neither Prosperity nor Adversity could draw one Line from him, to give his Father an Account of his Fortunes. For had he or we had the least Hint of his Captivity, he needed not have staid for the Miracle of the *Moorish* Lady's Cane for his Deliverance. Now am I in the greatest uneasiness in the

World, lest the *French*, the better to conceal their Robbery, may have kill'd him; the Thoughts of this will damp the Pleasure of my Voyage, which I thought to prosecute so pleasantly. Could I but guess, dear Brother, continu'd he, where you might be found, I would hazard Life and Fortune for your Deliverance! Could our aged Father once understand you were alive, though hidden in the deepest and darkest Dungeon in *Barbary*, His Estate, mine, and my Brother's, all should fly for your Ransom! And for the Fair and Liberal *Zoraida*, what Thanks, what Recompence could we provide? O, might I see the happy Day of her Spiritual Birth and Baptism, to see her joined to him in Faith and Marriage, how should we all rejoice! These and such like Expressions the Judge utter'd with so much Passion and Vehemency, that he rais'd a Concern in every Body.

The Curate, foreseeing the happy Success of his Design, resolv'd to prolong the Discovery no farther; and to free the Company from suspence, he went to the Ladies Room, and leading out *Zoraida*, follow'd by the rest, he took the Captain by t'other Hand, and presenting them to the Judge; Suppress your Grief, my Lord, said he, and glut your Heart with Joy; behold what you so passionately desir'd, your dear Brother, and his fair Deliverer; this Gentleman is Captain *Viedma*, and this the Beautiful *Algerine*; the *French* have only reduc'd them to this low Condition, to make room for your Generous Sentiments and Liberality. The Captain then approaching to embrace the Judge, he held him off with both his Hands, to view him well, but once knowing him, he flew into his Arms with such Affection, and such abundance of Tears, that all the Spectators sympathiz'd in his Passions. The Brothers spoke so feelingly, and their mutual Affection was so moving, the Surprize so wonderful, and their Joy so transporting, that it must be left purely to Imagination to conceive. Now they tell one another the strange Turns and Mazes of their Fortunes, then renew their Caresses to the height of Brotherly Tenderness. Now the Judge embraces *Zoraida*, then makes her an offer of his whole Fortune; next makes his Daughter embrace her; then the sweet and innocent Converse of the beautiful Christian, and the lovely *Moor*, so touch'd the whole Company, that they all wept for Joy. In the mean time Don *Quixote* was very solidly attentive, and wond'ring at these strange Occurrences, attributed them purely to something answerable to the Chimerical Notions which are incident to Chivalry. The Captain and *Zoraida*, in concert with the whole Company, resolv'd to return with their Brother to *Sevil*, and thence to advise their Father of his Arrival and Liberty, that the old Gentleman should make the best shift he could to get so far to see the Baptism and Marriage of *Zoraida*, while the Judge took his Voyage to the *Indies*, being oblig'd to make no delay, because the *Indian* Fleet was ready at *Sevil*, to set sail in a Month for *New-Spain*.

Every thing being now settled, to the universal Satisfaction of the Company, and being very late, they all agreed for Bed, except Don *Quixote*, who would needs guard the Castle whilst They slept, lest some Tyrant or Giant, covetous of the great Treasure of Beauty which it inclosed, should make some dangerous Attempt. He had the Thanks of the House, and the Judge, being farther inform'd of his Humour, was not a little pleas'd. *Sancho Panza* was very uneasy and waspish for want of Sleep, tho' the best provided with a Bed, bestowing himself on his Pack-Saddle; but he paid dearly for it, as we shall hear presently. The Ladies being retir'd to their Chamber, and every Body else withdrawn to rest, and Don *Quixote* planted Centinel at the Castle Gate, a Voice was heard of a sudden singing so sweetly, that it allur'd all their Attentions, but chiefly *Dorothea's* with whom the Judge's Daughter Donna *Clara de Viedma* lay. None could imagine, who could make such pretty Musick without an Instrument; sometimes it sounded as from the Yard, sometimes as from the Stable. With this *Cardenio* knock'd softly at their Door, Ladies, Ladies, said he, are you awake? Can you sleep when so charmingly Serenaded? Don't you hear how sweetly one of the Footmen sings? Yes, Sir, said *Dorothea*, we hear him plainly. Then *Dorothea* hearkning as attentively as she could, heard this Song.

XVI: THE PLEASANT STORY OF THE YOUNG MULETEER WITH OTHER STRANGE ADVENTURES THAT HAPPEN'D IN THE INN

A SONG

I

Toss'd in Doubts and Fears I rove
On the Stormy Seas of Love;
Far from Comfort, far from Port,
Beauty's Prize, and Fortune's Sport:
Yet my Heart disclaims Despair,
While I trace my leading Star.

2

But Reserv'dness, like a Cloud,
Does too oft her Glories shroud.
Pierce the gloom, reviving Sight;
Be auspicious as you're bright.
As you hide or dart your Beams,
Your Adorer sinks or swims.

Dorothea thought it wou'd not be much amiss to give Donna *Clara* the Opportunity of hearing so excellent a Voice, wherefore jogging her gently, first on one side, and then on t'other, and the young Lady waking, I ask your Pardon, my Dear, cry'd *Dorothea*, for thus interrupting your Repose; and I hope you'll easily forgive me, since I only wake you that you may have the Pleasure of hearing one of the most charming Voices, that possibly you ever heard in your Life. Donna *Clara*, who was hardly awake, did not perfectly understand what *Dorothea* said, and therefore desired her to repeat what she had spoke to her. *Dorothea* did so; which then oblig'd Donna *Clara* also to listen; but scarce had she heard the early Musician sing two Verses, ere she was taken with a strange trembling, as if she had been seiz'd with a violent Fit of a Quartan Ague, and then closely embracing *Dorothea*, Ah! dear Madam, cry'd she, with a deep Sigh, why did you wake me? Alas! the greatest Happiness I cou'd now have expected, had been to have stopp'd my Ears: That unhappy Musician! How's this, my Dear, cry'd

Dorothea, have you not heard, that the young Lad who sung now is but a Muleteer? Oh no, he's no such thing, reply'd *Clara*, but a young Lord, Heir to a great Estate, and has such a full possession of my Heart, that if he does not slight it, it must be his for ever. *Dorothea* was strangely surpriz'd at the young Lady's passionate Expressions, that seem'd far to exceed those of Persons of her tender Years: You speak so mysteriously, Madam, reply'd she, that I can't rightly understand you, unless you will please to let me know more plainly, what you wou'd say of Hearts and Sighs, and this young Musician, whose Voice has caus'd so great an alteration in you. However, speak no more of 'em now; for I'm resolv'd I'll not lose the pleasure of hearing him sing. Hold, continu'd she, I fancy he's going to entertain us with another Song. With all my Heart, return'd *Clara*, and with that she stopt her Ears, that she might not hear him; at which again *Dorothea* cou'd not chuse but admire; but listening to his Voice, she heard the following Song.

HOPE

I

Unconquer'd Hope, thou Bane of Fear,
 And last Deserter of the Brave;
Thou soothing Ease of Mortal Care,
 Thou Traveller beyond the Grave;
Thou Soul of Patience, airy Food,
Bold Warrant of a distant Good,
Reviving Cordial, kind Decoy:
 Tho' Fortune frowns, and Friends depart,
 Tho' Silvia *flies me, flatt'ring Joy,*
  Nor Thou, nor Love, shall leave my doating Heart.

2

The Phœnix Hope can wing her flight
 Thro' the vast Desarts of the Skies,
And still defying Fortune's spight,
 Revive, and from her Ashes rise.
Then soar, and promise, tho' in vain,
What Reason's self despairs to gain,

Thou only, O presuming Trust,
  Can'st feed us still, yet never cloy:
And ev'n a Virtue when unjust,
  Postpone our Pain, and antedate our Joy.

3

No Slave, to lazy Ease resign'd,
  E'er triumph'd over noble Foes.
The Monarch Fortune most is kind
  To him who bravely dares oppose.
They say, Love sets his Blessings high;
  But who would prize an easy Joy!
Then I'll my Scornful Fair pursue,
  Tho' the coy Beauty still denies;
I grovel now on Earth 'tis true,
  But rais'd by her, the humble Slave may rise.

Here the Voice ended, and Donna *Clara's* Sighs began,
which caus'd the greatest Curiosity imaginable in *Dorothea*,
to know the Occasion of so moving a Song, and of so sad a
Complaint; wherefore she again intreated her to pursue the
Discourse she had begun before. Then *Clara* fearing *Lucinda*
wou'd over-hear her, getting as near *Dorothea* as was possible, laid her Mouth so close to *Dorothea's* Ear, that she was
out of Danger of being understood by any other; and began
in this manner. He who Sung is a Gentleman's Son of *Arragon*,
his Father is a great Lord, and dwelt just over-against my
Father's at *Madrid*; and tho' we had always Canvas Windows in Winter and Lattices in Summer,* yet, I can't tell by
what Accident, this young Gentleman, who then went to
School, had a Sight of me, and whether it were at Church,
or at some other Place, I can't justly tell you; but (in short)
he fell in love with me, and made me sensible of his Passion
from his own Windows, which were opposite to mine, with
so many Signs, and such Showers of Tears, that at once forc'd
me both to believe and to love him, without knowing for what
reason I did so. Amongst the usual Signs that he made me, one
was that of joining his Hands together, intimating by that his

* *Glass Windows are not us'd in* Spain, *at least they are not common, and
formerly there were none.*

Desire to marry me; which, tho' I heartily wish'd it, I could not communicate to any one, being Motherless, and having none near me whom I might trust with the Management of such an Affair; and was therefore constrain'd to bear it in Silence, without permitting him any other Favour, more than to let him gaze on me, by lifting up the Lattice or Oil'd-Cloth a little, when my Father and his were abroad. At which he wou'd be so transported with Joy, that you wou'd certainly have thought he had been distracted. At last my Father's Business call'd him away; yet not so soon, but that the young Gentleman had notice of it some time before his Departure; whence he had it I know not, for 'twas impossible for me to acquaint him with it. This so sensibly afflicted him, as far as I understand, that he fell sick; so that I cou'd not get a Sight of him all the Day of our Departure, so much as to look a Farewell on him. But after two Days Travel, just as we came into an Inn, in a Village a Day's journey hence, I saw him at the Inn-door, dress'd so exactly like a Muleteer, that it had been utterly impossible for me to have known him, had not his perfect Image been stamp'd in my Soul. Yes, yes, dear Madam, I knew him, and was amaz'd and overjoy'd at the Sight of him; and he saw me unknown to my Father, whose Sight he carefully avoids, when we cross the Ways in our Journey, and when we come to any Inn: And now, since I know who he is, and what Pain and Fatigue it must necessarily be to him to travel thus a-foot, I am ready to die myself with the Thought of what he suffers on My account; and wherever he sets his Feet, there I set my Eyes. I can't imagine what he proposes to himself in this Attempt; nor by what means he cou'd thus make his Escape from his Father, who loves him beyond Expression, both because he has no other Son and Heir, and because the young Gentleman's Merits oblige him to it; which you must needs confess when you see him: And I dare affirm, beside, that all he has sung was his own immediate Composition; for, as I have heard, he is an excellent Scholar, and a great Poet. And now whenever I see him, or hear him sing, I start and tremble, as at the sight of a Ghost, lest my Father shou'd know him, and so be inform'd of our mutual Affection. I never spoke one Word to him in my Life;

yet I love him so dearly, that 'tis impossible I should live without him. This, dear Madam, is all the Account I can give you of this Musician, with whose Voice you have been so well entertain'd, and which alone might convince you that he is no Muleteer, as you were pleas'd to say, but one who is Master of a great Estate, and of my poor Heart, as I have already told you.

Enough, dear Madam, reply'd *Dorothea*, kissing her a thousand times:'Tis very well, compose yourself till Day-light; and then I trust in Heaven I shall so manage your Affairs, that the End of them shall be as fortunate as the Beginning is innocent. Alas! Madam, return'd *Clara*, what End can I propose to myself; since his Father is so rich, and of so noble a Family, that he will hardly think me worthy to be his Son's Servant, much less his Wife? And then again, I would not marry without my Father's Consent for the Universe. All I can desire, is, that the young Gentleman would return home, and leave his Pursuit of me: Happily, by a long Absence, and the great Distance of Place, the Pain, which now so much afflicts me, may be somewhat mitigated; tho' I fear what I now propose as a Remedy, would rather increase my Distemper: Though I can't imagine whence, or by what means, this Passion for him seiz'd me, since we are both so young, being much about the same Age, I believe; and my Father says I shan't be Sixteen till next *Michaelmas. Dorothea* could not forbear laughing to hear the young Lady talk so innocently. My Dear (said *Dorothea*) let us repose ourselves the little remaining Part of the Night, and when Day appears, we will put a happy Period to your Sorrows, or my Judgment fails me. Then they address'd themselves again to Sleep, and there was a deep Silence through-out all the Inn; only the Inn-keeper's Daughter and *Maritornes* were awake, who knowing Don *Quixote's* Blind Side very well, and that he sat arm'd on Horse-back, keeping Guard without Doors, a Fancy took 'em, and they agreed to have a little Pastime with him, and hear some of his fine out-of-the-way Speeches.

You must know then, that there was but one Window in all the Inn that look'd out into the Field, and that was only a Hole out of which they us'd to throw their Straw: To this same

Hole then came these two demy-Ladies, whence they saw Don *Quixote* mounted, and leaning on his Lance, and often fetching such mournful and deep Sighs, that his very Soul seem'd to be torn from him at each of them: They observ'd besides, that he said in a soft amorous Tone, O my divine *Dulcinea del Toboso*! the Heaven of all Perfections! the End and Quintessence of Discretion! the Treasury of sweet Aspect and Behaviour! the Magazine of Virtue! and, in a Word, the Idea of all that is profitable, modest or delightful in the Universe! What noble Thing employs thy Excellency at this present? May I presume to hope that thy Soul is entertain'd with the Thoughts of thy Captive-Knight, who voluntarily exposes himself to so many Dangers for Thy sake? O thou Triformed Luminary, give me some Account of her! perhaps thou art now gazing with Envy on her, as she's walking either through some stately Gallery of her sumptuous Palaces, or leaning on her happy Window, there meditating how, with safety of her Honour and Grandeur, she may sweeten and alleviate the Torture which my poor afflicted Heart suffers for love of her; with what Glories she shall crown my Pains, what Rest she shall give to my Cares, what Life to my Death, and what Reward to my Services. And thou, more glorious Planet, which, by this time, I presume, art harnessing thy Horses to pay thy earliest Visit to my adorable *Dulcinea*; I entreat thee, as soon as thou dost see her, to salute her with my most profound Respects: But take heed, that when thou look'st on her, and addressest thyself to her, that thou dost not kiss her Face; for if thou dost, I shall grow more jealous of Thee, than ever Thou wert of the swift Ingrate, who made thee run and sweat so over the Plains of *Thessaly*, or the Banks of *Peneus*, I have forgotten through which of them thou ran'st so raging with Love and Jealousy. At these Words the Inn-keeper's Daughter began to call to him softly: Sir Knight, said she, come a little nearer this way, if you please. At these Words Don *Quixote* turn'd his Head, and the Moon shining then very bright, he perceiv'd somebody call'd him from the Hole, which he fancy'd was a large Window full of Iron-bars, all richly gilt, suitable to the stately Castle, for which he mistook the Inn; and all on a sudden, he imagin'd that the Beautiful Damsel, Daughter to the Lady of the Castle, overcome by the Charms of his Person, return'd to court him, as she did once before. In this Thought, that he might not appear uncivil or ungrateful, he turn'd *Rozinante* and came to the Hole; where seeing the two Lasses, Fair Damsels, said he, I cannot but pity you for your misplac'd Affection, since it is altogether impossible you should meet with any Return from the Object of your Wishes proportionable to your great Merits and Beauty; but yet you ought not by any means to condemn this unhappy Knight-Errant for his Coldness, since Love has utterly incapacitated him to become a Slave to any other but to her, who, at first Sight, made herself absolute Mistress of his Soul. Pardon me therefore, excellent Lady, and retire to your Apartment. Let not, I beseech you any farther Arguments of Love force me to be less grateful or civil than I would: But if in the Passion you have for me, you can bethink yourself of any thing else wherein I may do you any Service, Love alone excepted, command it freely; and I swear to you by my absent, yet most charming, Enemy, to sacrifice it to you immediately, though it be a Lock of *Medusa's* Hair, which are all Snakes, or the very Sun-beams enclos'd in a glass-Vial.

My Lady needs none of those things, Sir Knight, reply'd *Maritornes*. What then would she command? ask'd Don *Quixote*. Only the Honour of one of your fair Hands, return'd *Maritornes*, to satisfy, in some measure, that violent Passion which has obliged her to come hither with the great hazard of her Honour: For if my Lord, her Father, should know it, the cutting off one of her beautiful Ears were the least thing he would do to her. Oh! that he durst attempt it, cry'd Don *Quixote*; but I know he dare not, unless he has a mind to die the most unhappy Death that ever Father suffer'd, for sacrilegiously depriving his amorous Daughter of one of her delicate Members. *Maritornes* made no doubt that he would comply with her Desire, and having already laid her Design, got in a trice to the Stable, and brought *Sancho Panza's* Ass's Halter to the Hole, just as Don *Quixote* was got on his Feet upon *Rozinante's* Saddle, more easily to reach the barricado'd Window, where he imagin'd the enamour'd Lady staid; and lifting up his Hand to her, said, Here, Madam, take the Hand, or rather, as I may say, the Executioner of all earthly Miscreants; take, I say, that

Hand, which never Woman touch'd before; no, not even she herself who has intire Possession of my whole Body; nor do I hold it up to you that you may kiss it, but that you may observe the Contexture of the Sinews, the Ligament of the Muscles, and the Largeness and Dilatation of the Veins; whence you may conclude how strong that Arm must be, to which such a Hand is join'd. We shall see that presently, reply'd *Maritornes*, and cast the Noose she had made in the Halter on his Wrist; and then descending from the Hole, she ty'd the other end of the Halter very fast to the Lock of the Door. Don *Quixote* being sensible that the Bracelet she had bestow'd on him was very rough, cry'd, you seem rather to abuse than compliment my Hand; but I beseech you treat it not so unkindly, since that is not the Cause why I do not entertain a Passion for you; nor is it just or equal you should discharge the whole Tempest of your Vengeance on so small a Part. Consider, those who love truly, can never be so cruel in their Revenge. But not a Soul regarded what he said; for as soon as *Maritornes* had fasten'd him, she and her Confederate, almost dead with laughing, ran away, and left him so strongly oblig'd, that 'twas impossible he should disengage himself.

He stood then, as I said, on *Rozinante's* Saddle, with all his Arm drawn into the Hole, and the Rope fasten'd to the Lock, being under a fearful Apprehension, that if *Rozinante* mov'd but never so little on any side, he should slip and hang by the Arm, and therefore durst not use the least Motion in the World, tho' he might reasonably have expected from *Rozinante's* Patience and gentle Temper, that if he were not urg'd, he wou'd never have mov'd for a whole Age together of his own accord. In short, the Knight, perceiving himself fast, and that the Ladies had forsaken him, immediately concluded that all this was done by way of Enchantment, as in the last Adventure in the very same Castle, when the Inchanted *Moor* (the Carrier) did so damnably maul him. Then he began alone to curse his Want of Discretion and Conduct, since having once made his Escape out of that Castle in so miserable a Condition, he should venture into it a second time: For, by the way, 'twas an Observation among all Knights-Errant, that if they were once foil'd in an Adventure, 'twas a certain Sign it was not reserv'd for Them, but for some other to finish; wherefore they would never prove it again. Yet, for all this, he ventur'd to draw back his Arm, to try if he could free himself; but he was so fast bound, that his Attempt prov'd fruitless. 'Tis true 'twas with Care and Deliberation he drew it, for fear *Rozinante* should stir: And then fain would he have seated himself in the Saddle; but he found he must either stand, or leave his Arm for a Ransom. A hundred times he wish'd for *Amadis's* Sword, on which no Inchantment had Power; then he fell a cursing his Stars; then reflected on the great Loss the World would sustain all the Time he should continue under this Inchantment, as he really believ'd it; then his adorable *Dulcinea* came afresh into his Thoughts; many a time did he call to his trusty Squire *Sancho Panza*, who, bury'd in a profound Sleep, lay stretch'd at length on his Ass's Pannel, never so much as dreaming of the Pangs his Mother felt when she bore him; then the Aid of the Necromancers *Lirgandeo* and *Alquife* was invok'd by the unhappy Knight. And, in fine, the Morning surpriz'd him, rack'd with Despair and Confusion, bellowing like a Bull; for he cou'd not hope from Daylight any Cure, or Mitigation of his Pain, which he believ'd wou'd be eternal, being absolutely persuaded he was inchanted, since he perceiv'd that *Rozinante* mov'd no more than a Mountain; and therefore he was of Opinion, that neither He nor his Horse should eat, drink, or sleep, but remain in that State till the Malignancy of the Stars were o'er-past, or till some more powerful Magician should break the Charm.

But 'twas an erroneous Opinion; for it was scarce Daybreak, when four Horsemen, very well accoutred, their Firelocks hanging at the Pommels of their Saddles, came thither, and finding the Inn-Gate shut, call'd and knock'd very loud and hard; which Don *Quixote* perceiving from the Post where he stood Centinel, cry'd out with a rough Voice and a haughty Mien, Knights or Squires, or of whatsoever other Degree you are, knock no more at the Gates of this Castle, since you may assure yourselves, that those who are within at such an Hour as this, are either taking their Repose, or not accustom'd to open their Fortress, 'till *Phœbus* has display'd himself upon the Globe: Retire therefore, and wait till it is clear Day, and

431

then we will see whether 'tis just or no, that they shou'd open their Gates to you. What a Devil (cry'd one of them) what Castle or Fortress is this, that we shou'd be oblig'd to so long a Ceremony? Pr'ythee, Friend, if thou art the Inn-keeper, bid them open the Door to us; for we ride Post, and can stay no longer than just to bait our Horses. Gentlemen, said Don *Quixote*, do I look like an Inn-keeper then? I can't tell what thou'rt like, reply'd another, but I'm sure thou talk'st like a Mad-man, to call this Inn a Castle. It is a Castle, return'd Don *Quixote*, ay, and one of the best in the Province, and contains one who has held a Scepter in her Hand, and wore a Crown on her Head. It might more properly have been said exactly contrary, reply'd the Traveller, a Scepter in her Tail, and a Crown in her Hand: Yet 'tis not unlikely that there may be a Company of Strolers within, and those do frequently hold such Scepters, and wear such Crowns as thou pratest of: For certainly no Person worthy to sway a Scepter, or wear a Crown, would condescend to take up a Lodging in such a paltry Inn as this, where I hear so little Noise. Thou hast not been much conversant in the World (said Don *Quixote*) since thou art so miserably ignorant of Accidents so frequently met with in Knight-Errantry. The Companions of him that held this tedious Discourse with Don *Quixote*, were tired with their foolish Chattering so long together, and therefore they return'd with greater Fury to the Gate, where they knock'd so violently, that they wak'd both the Inn-keeper and his Guests; and so the Host rose to ask who was at the Door.

In the mean time *Rozinante*, pensive and sad, with Ears hanging down, and motionless, bore up his out-stretch'd Lord, when one of the Horses those Four Men rode upon, walk'd towards *Rozinante*, to smell him, and he truly being real Flesh and Blood, though very like a Wooden Block, cou'd not chuse but be sensible of it, nor forbear turning to smell the other, which so seasonably came to comfort and divert him; but he had hardly stir'd an Inch from his Place, when Don *Quixote's* Feet, that were close together, slipt asunder, and tumbling from the Saddle, he had inevitably fallen to the Ground, had not his Wrist been securely fasten'd to the Rope; which put him to so great a Torture, that he cou'd not imagine but that his hand was cutting off, or his Arm tearing from his Body; yet he hung so near the Ground, that he cou'd just reach it with the tips of his Toes, which added to his Torment; for perceiving how little he wanted to the setting his Feet wholly on the Ground, he strove and tugg'd as much as he cou'd to effect it; not much unlike those that suffer the Strapado, who put themselves to greater Pain in striving to stretch their Limbs, deluded by the hopes of touching the Ground, if they could but inch themselves out a little longer.

XVII: A CONTINUATION OF THE STRANGE
ADVENTURES IN THE INN

THE miserable Outcries of Don *Quixote* presently drew the Inn-keeper to the Door, which he hastily opening, was strangely affrighted to hear such a terrible roaring, and the Strangers stood no less surpriz'd. *Maritornes*, whom the Cries had also rouz'd, guessing the Cause, ran strait to the Loft, and slipping the Halter, releas'd the Don, who made her a very prostrate Acknowledgment, by an unmerciful Fall on the Ground. The Inn-keeper and Strangers crouded immediately round him to know the Cause of his Misfortune. He, without regard to their Questions, unmanacles his Wrist, bounces from the Ground, mounts *Rozinante*, braces his Target, couches his Lance, and taking a large Circumference in the Field, came up with a Hand-Gallop: Whoever, said he, dare affirm, assert, or declare that I have been justly enchanted, in case my Lady the Princess *Micomicona* will but give me Leave, I will tell him he lies, and will maintain my Assertion by immediate Combat. The Travellers stood amaz'd at Don *Quixote's* Words, till the Host remov'd their Wonder, by informing them of his usual Extravagancies in this kind, and that his Behaviour was not to be minded. They then ask'd the Inn-keeper if a certain Youth, near the Age of Fifteen, had set up at his House, clad like a Muleteer; adding withal some farther Marks and Tokens, denoting Donna *Clara's* Lover: He told them, that among the number of his Guests, such a Person might pass him undistinguish'd; but one of them accidentally spying the Coach which the Judge rid in, call'd to his Companions; O Gentlemen, Gentlemen, here stands the Coach which we were told my young Master follow'd, and here he must be, that's certain: Let's lose no time, one guard the Door, the rest enter the House to look for him— hold—stay—(continu'd he) ride one about to the other side o'th' House, lest he 'scape us through the Back-Yard. Agreed, says another; and they posted themselves accordingly. The Inn-keeper, though he might guess that they sought the young Gentleman whom they had describ'd, was nevertheless puz-

zl'd as to the Cause of their so diligent Search. By this time,
the Day-light and the Out-cries of Don *Quixote* had rais'd the
whole House, particularly the two Ladies, *Clara* and *Dorothea*, who had slept but little, the One with the Thoughts her
Lover was so near her, and the Other thro' an earnest Desire
she had to see him. Don *Quixote* seeing the Travellers neither
regard Him nor his Challenge, was ready to burst with Fury
and Indignation; and could he have dispens'd with the Rules
of Chivalry, which oblige a Knight-Errant to the finishing
one Adventure before his embarking in another, he had assaulted them all, and forc'd them to answer him to their Cost;
but being unfortunately engag'd to re-instate the Princess *Micomicona*, his Hands were ty'd up, and he was compell'd to
desist, expecting where the Search and Diligence of the four
Travellers would terminate: One of them found the young
Gentleman fast asleep by a Footman, little dreaming of being
follow'd or discover'd: The Fellow lugging him by the Arm,
cries out, Ay, Ay, Don *Lewis*, these are very fine Clothes you
have got on, and very becoming a Gentleman of Your Quality,
indeed; this Scurvy Bed too is very suitable to the Care and
Tenderness your Mother brought you up with. The Youth
having rub'd his drousy Eyes, and fixing them stedfastly on
the Man, knew him presently for one of his Father's Servants,
which struck him speechless with Surprize. The Fellow went
on; There is but one way, Sir, pluck up your Spirits, and return with us to your Father, who is certainly a dead Man unless you be recover'd. How came my Father to know, answer'd
Don *Lewis*, that I took this Way and this Disguise? One of
your Fellow Students, reply'd the Servant, whom you communicated your Design to, mov'd by your Father's Lamentation for your Loss, discover'd it; the good old Gentleman dispatch'd away four of his Men in search of you; and here we are
all at your Service, Sir, and the joyfullest Men alive; for our
old Master will give us a hearty Welcome, having so soon restor'd him what he lov'd so much. That, next to Heaven, is as
I please, said Don *Lewis*. What would You, or Heaven either,
please, Sir, but return to your Father? Come, come, Sir, talk
no more on't, home you must go, and home you shall go. The
Footman that lay with Don *Lewis*, hearing this Dispute, rose,

and related the Business to Don *Ferdinand*, *Cardenio*, and the rest that were now dress'd; adding withal, how the Man gave him the Title of Don, with other Circumstances of their Conference. They, being already charm'd with the Sweetness of his Voice, were curious to be inform'd more particularly of his Circumstances, and resolving to assist him, in case any Violence should be offer'd him, went presently to the Place where he was still contending with his Father's Servant.

By this *Dorothea* had left her Chamber, and with her Donna *Clara* in great Disorder. *Dorothea* beckoning *Cardenio* aside, gave him a short Account of the Musician and Donna *Clara*; and He told Her how that his Father's Servants were come for him. Donna *Clara* over-hearing him, was so exceedingly surpriz'd, that had not *Dorothea* run and supported her, she had sunk to the Ground. *Cardenio* promising to bring the Matter to a fair and successful End, advis'd *Dorothea* to retire with the indispos'd Lady to her Chamber. All the four that pursu'd Don *Lewis* were now come about him, pressing his Return without Delay, to comfort his poor Father; he answer'd 'Twas impossible, being engag'd to put a Business in Execution first, on which depended no less than his Honour, and his present and future Happiness. They urg'd, that since they had found him, there was no returning for them without Him, and if he would not go, he should be carry'd; Not unless you kill me, answer'd the Young Gentleman; upon which all the Company were join'd in the Dispute, *Cardenio*, Don *Ferdinand* and his Companions, the Judge, the Curate, the Barber, and Don *Quixote*, who thought it needless now to guard the Castle any longer. *Cardenio* who knew the young Gentleman's Story, ask'd the Fellows upon what Pretence, or by what Authority they could carry the Youth away against his Will: Sir, answer'd one of them, we have Reason good for what we do; no less than his Father's Life depends upon his return. Gentlemen, said Don *Lewis*, 'tis not proper perhaps to trouble you with a particular Relation of my Affairs; only thus much, I am a Gentleman, and have no Dependance that should force me to any thing beside my Inclination: Nay, but Sir, answer'd the Servant, Reason, I hope, will force you; and though it cannot move You, it must govern Us, who must execute our Orders, and force you back; we only act as we are order'd, Sir. Hold, said the Judge, and let us know the whole State of the Case. O Lord, Sir, answer'd one of the Servants that knew him, my Lord Judge, does not your Worship know your next Neighbour's Child? See here, Sir, he has run away from his Fathers House, and has put on these dirty tatter'd Rags to the Scandal of his Family, as your Worship may see. The Judge then viewing him more attentively knew him, and saluting him, What Jest is this, Don *Lewis*, cry'd he? What mighty Intrigue are you carrying on, young Sir, to occasion this Metamorphosis, so unbecoming your Quality? The Young Gentleman could not answer a Word, and the Tears stood in his Eyes; the Judge perceiving his Disorder, desir'd the four Servants to trouble themselves no farther, but leave the Youth to his Management, engaging his Word to act to their Satisfaction; and retiring with Don *Lewis*, he begg'd to know the Occasion of his Flight.

During their Conference, they heard a great Noise at the Inn-door, occasion'd by two Strangers, who, having lodg'd there over Night, and seeing the whole Family so busied in a curious Enquiry into the Four Horsemen's Business, thought to have made off without paying their Reckoning; but the Inn-keeper, who minded no Man's Business more than his own, stopp'd them in the nick, and demanding his Money, upbraided their ungenteel Design very sharply: They return'd the Compliment with Kick and Cuff so roundly, that the poor Host cry'd out for Help; his Wife and Daughter saw none so idle as Don *Quixote*, whom the Daughter addressing, I conjure you, Sir Knight, said she, by that Virtue deliver'd to you from Heaven, to succour my distress'd Father, whom two Villains are beating to Jelly. Beautiful Damsel, answer'd Don *Quixote* with a slow Tone and profound Gravity, your Petition cannot at the present Juncture prevail, I being withheld from undertaking any new Adventure, by Promise first to finish what I'm engag'd in; and all the Service you can expect, is only my Counsel in this important Affair; go with all speed to your Father, with Advice to continue and maintain the Battle with his utmost Resolution, till I obtain Permission from the Princess *Micomicona* to reinforce him, which once granted, you

437

need make no doubt of his Safety. Unfortunate Wretch that
I am, said *Maritornes*, who over-heard him, before you can
have this Leave, my Master will be sent to the other World.
Then, Madam, said he, procure me the Permission I mention'd,
and tho' he were sent into the other World, I'll bring him
back in Spite of Hell and the Devil, or at least so revenge his
Fall on his Enemies, as shall give ample Satisfaction to his
surviving Friends; whereupon breaking off the Discourse, he
went and threw himself prostrate before *Dorothea*, imploring
her, in Romantick Stile, to grant him a Commission to march
and sustain the Governor of that Castle, who was just fainting
in a dangerous Engagement. The Princess dispatch'd him very
willingly; whereupon presently buckling on his Target, and
taking up his Sword, he ran to the Inn-door, where the two
Guests were still handling their Landlord very unmercifully:
He there made a sudden Stop, tho' *Maritornes* and the Hostess
press'd him twice or thrice to tell the Cause of his Delay in his
promis'd Assistance to his Host. I make a Pause, said Don *Quixote*, because I am commanded by the Law of Arms to use my
Sword against none under the Order of Knighthood; but let my
Squire be call'd, this Affair is altogether His Province. In the
mean time Drubs and Bruises were incessant at the Inn-gate,
and the poor Host soundly beaten. His Wife, Daughter and
Maid, who stood by, were like to run mad at Don *Quixote's*
hanging back, and the Inn-keeper's unequal Combat; where
we shall leave him, with a Design to return to his Assistance
presently, tho' his Foolhardiness deserves a sound beating, for
attempting a thing he was not likely to go thro' with. We now
return to hear what Don *Lewis* answer'd the Judge, whom we
left retir'd with him, and asking the Reason of his travelling on
Foot, and in so mean a Disguise. The young Gentleman grasping his Hands very passionately, made this Reply, not without
giving a Proof of the Greatness of his Sorrow by his Tears.

Without Ceremony or Preamble, I must tell you, dear Sir,
that from the Instant that Heaven made us Neighbours, and I
saw Donna *Clara*, your Daughter and my Mistress, I resign'd
to her the whole Command of my Affections; and unless You,
whom I most truly call my Father, prevent it, she shall be my
Wife this very Day; for her sake I have abandon'd my Father's

438

House; for her have I thus disguis'd my Quality; her would I thus have follow'd thro' the World: She was the North-Star, to guide my wand'ring Course, and the Mark at which my Wishes flew. Her Ears indeèd are utter Strangers to my Passion; but yet her Eyes may guess, by the Tears she saw flowing from mine. You know my Fortune and my Quality; if these can plead Sir, I lay them at her Feet; then make me this Instant your happy Son; and if my Father, biass'd by contrary Designs should not approve my Choice, yet Time may produce some favourable Turn, and alter his Mind. The amorous Youth having done speaking, the Judge was much surpriz'd at the handsome Discovery he made of his Affections, but was not a little puzzled how to behave himself in so sudden and unexpected a Matter; he therefore, without any positive Answer, advis'd him only to compose his Thoughts, to divert himself with his Servants, and to prevail with them to allow him that Day to consider on what was proper to be done. Don *Lewis* express'd his Gratitude by forcibly kissing the Judge's Hands, and bathing them with his Tears, enough to move a Heart of Cannibal, much more a Judge's, who (being a Man o'th' World) had presently the Advantage of the Match and Preferment of his Daughter in the Wind; tho' he much doubted the Consent of Don *Lewis's* Father, who he knew design'd to match his Son into the Nobility.

By this time Don *Quixote's* Intreaties more than Threats had parted the Fray at the Inn-door; the Strangers paying their Reckoning went off, and Don *Lewis's* Servants stood expecting the Result of the Judge's Discourse with their young Master: When (as the Devil would have it) Who should come into the Inn but the Barber whom Don *Quixote* had robb'd of *Mambrino's* Helmet, and *Sancho* of the Pack-Saddle. As he was leading his Beast very gravely to the Stable, he spies *Sancho* mending something about the Pannel; he knew him presently, and setting upon him very roughly, Ay, Mr Thief, Mr Rogue, said he, have I caught you at last, and all my Ass's Furniture in your Hands too? *Sancho* finding himself so unexpectedly assaulted, and nettled at the dishonourable Terms of his Language, laying fast hold on the Pannel with one Hand, gave the Barber such a Douse on the Chops with t'other, as

439

set all his Teeth a bleeding; for all this the Barber stuck by his Hold, and cried out so loud, that the whole House was alarm'd at the Noise and Scuffle; I command you, Gentlemen, continu'd he, to assist me in the King's Name; for this Rogue has robb'd me on the King's High-way, and would now murder me, because I seize upon my Goods: That's a Lie, cry'd *Sancho*, 'twas no Robbery on the King's High-way, but lawful Plunder, won by my Lord Don *Quixote* fairly in the Field. The Don himself was now come up, very proud of his Squire's Behaviour on this Occasion, accounting him thenceforth a Man of Spirit, and designing him the Honour of Knighthood on the first Opportunity, thinking his Courage might prove a future Ornament to the Order. Among other things which the Barber urged to prove his Claim; Gentlemen, said he, this Pack-Saddle is as certainly my Pack-Saddle, as I hope to die in my Bed; I know it as well as if it had been bred and born with me; nay, my very Ass will witness for me; do but try the Saddle on him, and if it does not fit him as close as close can be, then call me a Liar—Nay more than that, Gentlemen, that very Day when they robb'd me of my Pack-Saddle, they took away a special new Bason which was never us'd, and which cost me a Crown. Here Don *Quixote* could no longer contain himself; but thrusting between them, he parted them; and having caus'd the Pack-Saddle to be deposited on the Ground to open View, till the Matter came to a final Decision: That this honourable Company may know, cry'd he, in what a manifest Error this honest Squire persists, take notice how he degrades That with the Name of Bason, which was, is, and shall be the Helmet of *Mambrino*, which I fairly won from him in the Field, and lawfully made myself Lord of by Force of Arms. As to the Pack-Saddle, 'tis a Concern that's beneath My Regard; all I have to urge in that Affair, is, That my Squire begg'd my Permission to strip that vanquish'd Coward's Horse of his Trappings to adorn his own; he had My Authority for the Deed, and he took them: And now for his converting it from a Horse's Furniture to a Pack-Saddle, no other Reason can be brought, but that such Transformations frequently occur in the Affairs of Chivalry. For a Confirmation of this, dispatch, run *Sancho* and produce the Helmet which this Squire would maintain to be a Bason.

O' my Faith, Sir, said *Sancho*, if this be all you can say for yourself, *Mambrino's* Helmet will prove as arrant a Bason, as this same Man's Furniture is a meer Pack-Saddle. Obey my Orders, said Don *Quixote*, I cannot believe that every thing in this Castle will be guided by Inchantment. *Sancho* brought the Bason, which Don *Quixote* holding up in his Hands, Behold, Gentlemen, continu'd he, with what Face can this impudent Squire affirm this to be a Bason, and not the Helmet I mention'd? Now I swear before you all, by the Order of Knighthood, which I profess, That this is the same individual Helmet which I won from him, without the least Addition or Diminution. That I'll swear, said *Sancho*; for since my Lord won it, he never fought but once in it, and that was the Battle wherein he freed those ungracious Gally-Slaves, who by the same Token would have knock'd out his Brains with a shower of Stones, had not this same honest Bason Helmet sav'd his Skull.

XVIII: THE CONTROVERSY ABOUT MAMBRINO'S HELMET AND THE PACK SADDLE, DISPUTED AND DECIDED; WITH OTHER ACCIDENTS, NOT MORE STRANGE THAN TRUE

PRAY good Gentlemen (said the Barber) let's have Your Opinion in this Matter, I suppose you will grant this same Helmet to be a Bason. He that dares grant any such thing, said Don *Quixote*, must know that he lies plainly, if a Knight; but if a Squire, he lies abominably. Our Barber (who was privy to the whole Matter) to humour the Jest, and carry the Diversion a little higher, took up t'other Shaver. Mr Barber, you must pardon me, Sir, if I don't give you your Titles, I must let you understand, said he, that I serv'd an Apprenticeship to Your Trade, and have been a Free Man in the Company these thirty Years, and therefore am not to learn what belongs to Shaving. You must likewise know that I have been a Soldier too in my younger Days, and consequently understand the Differences between a Helmet, a Morion, and a Close-Helmet, with all other Accoutrements belonging to a Man of Arms. Yet I say, with submission still to better Judgment, that this Piece, here in Dispute before us, is as far from being a Bason, as Light is from Darkness. Withal I affirm, on the other Hand, that altho' it be a Helmet, 'tis not a compleat one: Right (said the Don) for the lower Part and the Beaver are wanting. A clear Case, a clear Case, said the Curate, *Cardenio*, Don *Ferdinand* and his Companions, and the Judge himself (had not *Lewis's* Concern made him thoughtful) would have humour'd the Matter. Lord have mercy upon us now (said the poor Barber half distracted) is it possible that so many fine honourable Gentlemen should know a Bason or a Helmet no better than this comes to? Gadzookers, I defy the wisest University in all *Spain* with their Scholarship, to shew me the like. Well —— if it must be a Helmet, it must be a Helmet, that's all.—— And by the same Rule my Pack-Saddle must troop too, as this Gentleman says. I must confess, said Don *Quixote*, as to outward Appearance it is a Pack-Saddle; but as I have already said, I will not pretend to determine the Dispute as to that

442

Point. Nay, said the Curate, if Don *Quixote* speak not, the Matter will never come to a Decision; because in all Affairs of Chivalry, we must all give him the Preference. I swear, worthy Gentlemen, said Don *Quixote*, that the Adventures I have encounter'd in this Castle are so strange and super-natural, that I must infallibly conclude them the Effects of pure Magick and Inchantment. The first time I ever enter'd its Gates, I was strangely embarrass'd by an inchanted *Moor* that inhabited it, and *Sancho* himself had no better Enter-tainment from His Attendants; and last Night I hung sus-pended almost two Hours by this Arm, without the Power of helping myself, or of assigning any reasonable Cause of my Misfortune. So that for Me to meddle or give my Opinion in such confus'd and intricate Events, would appear Presump-tion; I have already given my final Determination as to the Helmet in Controversy, but dare pronounce no definitive Sen-tence on the Pack-Saddle, but shall remit it to the discerning Judgment of the Company; perhaps the Power of Inchant-ment may not prevail on You that are not dubb'd Knights, so that your Understandings may be free, and your judicial Faculties more piercing to enter into the true Nature of these Events, and not conclude upon them from their Appearances. Undoubtedly, answer'd Don *Ferdinand*, the Decision of this Process depends upon our Sentiments, according to Don *Quix-ote's* Opinion; that the Matter therefore may be fairly dis-cuss'd, and that we may proceed upon solid and firm Grounds, we'll put it to the Vote. Let every one give me his Suffrage in my Ear, and I will oblige myself to report them faithfully to the Board.

To those that knew Don *Quixote* this proved excellent Sport; but to others unacquainted with his Humour, as Don *Lewis* and his four Servants, it appeared the most ridiculous Stuff in Nature; three other Travellers too that happen'd to call in by the Way, and were found to be *Officers of the Holy Brotherhood*, or *Pursuivants*, thought the People were all be-witch'd in good earnest. But the Barber was quite at his Wit's end, to think that his Bason, then and there present before his Eyes, was become the Helmet of *Mambrino*; and that his Pack-Saddle was likewise going to be chang'd into rich Horse-

Furniture. Everybody laugh'd very heartily to see Don *Ferdinand* whispering each particular Person very gravely to have his Vote upon the important Contention of the Pack-Saddle. When he had gone the rounds among his own Faction, that were all privy to the Jest, Honest Fellow, said he very loudly, I grow weary of asking so many impertinent Questions; every Man has his Answer at his Tongue's-End, that 'tis meer Madness to call this a Pack-Saddle, and that 'tis positively, *Nemine Contradicente*, right Horse-Furniture, and great Horse-Furniture too; besides, Friend, your Allegations and Proofs are of no Force, therefore in spight of your Ass and you too, we give it for the Defendant, that this is, and will continue the Furniture of a Horse, nay and of a great Horse too. Now the Devil take me, said the Barber, *if you be not all damnably deceived; and may I be hang'd if my Conscience does not plainly tell me 'tis a down-right Pack-Saddle; but I have lost it according to Law, and so fare it well.——But I am neither mad nor drunk sure, for I am fresh and fasting this Morning from every thing but Sin.

The Barber's Raving was no less diverting than Don *Quixote's* Clamours; Sentence is pass'd, cry'd he; and let every Man take possession of his Goods and Chattels, and Heaven give him Joy. This is a Jest, a meer Jest, said one of the four Servants; certainly, Gentlemen, you can't be in earnest, you're too wise to talk at this rate: For my part, I say and will maintain it, for there's no Reason the Barber should be wrong'd, that This is a Bason, and That the Pack-Saddle of a He-Ass. Mayn't it be a She-Ass's Pack-Saddle, Friend, said the Curate? That's all one, Sir, said the Fellow, the Question is not whether it be a He or She-Ass's Pack-Saddle, but whether it be a Pack-saddle or not, that's the Matter, Sir. One of the Officers of the *Holy Brotherhood*, who had heard the whole Controversy, very angry to hear such an Error maintain'd: Gentlemen, said he, this is no more a Horse's Saddle than 'tis my Father, and he that says the contrary is drunk or mad. You lye like an unmannerly Rascal, said the Knight, and at the same time

* *In the Original it is* el sobrebarbero, *i.e. the Supernumerary or Additional Barber, in contradistinction to the other Barber who appears first in the History.*

with his Lance, which he had always ready for such Occasions, he offer'd such a Blow at the Officer's Head, that had
not the Fellow leap'd aside it would have laid him flat. The
Lance flew into pieces, and the rest of the Officers seeing their
Comrade so abus'd, cry'd out for Help, charging every one to
aid and assist the *Holy Brotherhood*. The Inn-keeper being
one of the Fraternity, ran for his Sword and Rod,* and then
joined his Fellows. Don *Lewis's* Servants got round their Master to defend him from Harm, and secure him lest he should
make his Escape in the Scuffle. The Barber seeing the whole
House turn'd topsy-turvy, laid hold again on his Pack-Saddle:
but *Sancho*, who watch'd his Motions, was as ready as He,
and secur'd t'other End of it.

Don *Quixote* drew and assaulted the Officers pell-mell.
Don *Lewis* call'd to his Servants to join Don *Quixote* and the
Gentlemen that sided with him; for *Cardenio*, Don *Ferdinand*
and his Friends had engag'd on his Side. The Curate cry'd
out, the Landlady shriek'd, her Daughter wept, *Maritornes*
howl'd, *Dorothea* was distracted with Fear, *Lucinda* could
not tell what to do, and Donna *Clara* was strangely frighted;
the Barber pommell'd *Sancho*, and *Sancho* belabour'd the
Barber. One of Don *Lewis's* Servants went to hold him, but
he gave him such a Rebuke on his Jaws, that his Teeth had
like to have forsook their Station; and then the Judge took
him into his Protection. Don *Ferdinand* had got one of the
Officers down, and laid him on Back and Side. The Inn-keeper
still cry'd out, Help the *Holy Brotherhood*; so that the whole
House was a Medley of Wailings, Cries, Shrieks, Confusions,
Fears, Terrors, Disasters, Slashes, Buffets, Blows, Kicks, Cuffs,
Battery, and Bloodshed.

In the greatest Heat of this Hurly-burly it came into Don
Quixote's Head, that he was certainly involv'd in the Disorder and Confusion of King *Agramant's* Camp; and calling
out with a Voice that shook the whole House; Hold, valorous
Knights, said he, all hold your furious Hands, sheath all your
Swords, let none presume to strike on pain of Death, but hear
me speak. The loud and monstrous Voice surpriz'd every Body

* *All these Troops of the* Holy Brotherhood *carry Wands or Rods as a
Mark of their Office.*

into Obedience, and the Don proceeded: I told you before, Gentlemen, that this Castle was inchanted, and that some Legion of Devils did inhabit it: Now let your own Eyes confirm my Words: Don't you behold the strange and horrid Confusion of King *Agramant's* Army remov'd hither, and put in execution among us? See, see how there they fight for the Sword, and yonder for the Horse; behold how some contend for the Helmet, and here others battle it for the Standard; and all fight we don't know how, nor can tell why. Let therefore my Lord Judge, and his Reverence Mr Curate, represent, one, King *Agramant*, and the other King *Sobrino*, and by their Wisdom and Conduct appease this Tumult; for, by the Powers Divine, 'twere a wrong to Honour, and a blot on Chivalry, to let so many Worthies, as are here met, kill one another for such Trifles.

Don *Quixote's* Words were *Hebrew* to the Officers, who having been roughly handled by *Cardenio*, *Ferdinand*, and his Friends, would not give it over so. But the Barber was content; for *Sancho* had demolish'd his Beard and Pack-Saddle both in the Scuffle: The Squire dutifully retreated at the first sound of his Master's Voice; Don *Lewis's* Servants were calm, finding it their best way to be quiet; but the Inn-keeper was refractory. He swore that Madman ought to be punished for his Ill-behaviour, and that every Hour he was making some Disturbance or another in his House. But at last, the Matter was made up, the Pack-Saddle was agreed to be Horse-Furniture, the Bason a Helmet, and the Inn a Castle, till the Day of Judgment, if Don *Quixote* would have it so. Don *Lewis's* Business came next in play. The Judge, in Concert with Don *Ferdinand*, *Cardenio*, and the Curate, resolv'd that Don *Ferdinand* should interpose his Authority on Don *Lewis's* behalf, and let his Servants know, That he would carry him to *Andalusia*, where he should be entertain'd according to his Quality by his Brother the Marquis; and they should not oppose this Design, seeing Don *Lewis* was positively resolv'd not to be forc'd to go back to his Father yet. Don *Ferdinand's* Quality, and Don *Lewis's* Resolution prevail'd on the Fellows to order Matters so, that three of them might return to acquaint their old Master, and the fourth wait on Don *Lewis*. Thus this monstrous heap of

Confusion and Disorder was digested into Form, by the Authority of *Agramant*, and Wisdom of King *Sobrino*.

But the Enemy of Peace, finding his Project of setting them all by the Ears so eluded, resolv'd once again to have another Trial of Skill, and play the Devil with them all the second Bout: For though the Officers, understanding the Quality of their Adversaries, were willing to desist, yet one of them, whom Don *Ferdinand* had kick'd most unmercifully, remembring that among other Warrants, he had one to apprehend Don *Quixote* for setting free the Gally-Slaves (which *Sancho* was sadly afraid would come about) he resolv'd to examine if the Marks and Tokens given of Don *Quixote* agreed with this Person; then drawing out a Parchment, and opening his Warrant, he made a shift to read it, at every other Word looking cunningly on Don *Quixote's* Face; whereupon having folded up the Parchment, and taking his Warrant in his left Hand, he clapt his right Hand fast in the Knight's Collar, crying You're the King's Prisoner: Gentlemen, I am an Officer, here's my Warrant. I charge you all to aid and assist the *Holy Brotherhood*. Don *Quixote*, finding himself us'd so rudely, by one whom he took to be a pitiful Scoundrel, kindl'd up into such a Rage, that he shook with Indignation, and catching the Fellow by the Neck with both his Hands, squeez'd him so violently, that if his Companions had not presently freed him, the Knight would certainly have throttled him before he had quitted his Hold.

The Inn-keeper being oblig'd to assist his Brother-Officer, presently join'd him: The Hostess seeing her Husband engaging a second time, rais'd a new Outcry, her Daughter and *Maritornes* bore the burden of the Song, sometimes praying, sometimes crying, sometimes scolding: *Sancho*, seeing what pass'd, By the Lord, said he, my Master is in the right; this Place is haunted, that's certain; there's no living quietly an Hour together. At last Don *Ferdinand* parted Don *Quixote* and the Officer, who were both pretty well pleas'd to quit their Bargain. However, the Officers still demanded their Prisoner, and to have him deliver'd bound into their Hands, commanding all the Company a second time to help and assist them in securing that publick Robber upon the King's high Road.

447

Don *Quixote* smil'd at the supposed Simplicity of the Fellows; at last, with solemn Gravity, Come hither, said he, you Offspring of Filth and Extraction of Dunghils, dare you call loosing the Fetter'd, freeing the Captiv'd, helping the Miserable, raising the Fall'n, and supplying the Indigent, dare you, I say, base-spirited Rascals, call these Actions Robbery? Your Thoughts, indeed, are too groveling and servile to understand, or reach the Pitch of Chivalry, otherwise you had understood, that even the Shadow of a Knight-Errant had Claim to your Adoration. You a Band of Officers; you're a Pack of Rogues, indeed, and Robbers on the Highway by Authority. What Blockhead of a Magistrate durst issue out a Warrant to apprehend a Knight-Errant like me? Could not his Ignorance find out that we are exempt from all Courts of Judicature? That our Valour is the Bench, our Will the Common Law, and our Sword the Executioner of Justice? Could not his Dulness inform him that no Rank of Nobility or Peerage enjoys more Immunities and Privileges? Has he any Precedent that a Knight-Errant ever paid Taxes, Subsidy, Poll-Money, or so much as Fare or Ferry? What Taylor ever had Money for his Cloaths, or what Constable ever made him pay a Reckoning for lodging in his Castle? What Kings are not proud of his Company; and what Damsels of his Love? And lastly, did you ever read of any Knight-Errant that ever was, is, or shall be, that could not, with his single Force, cudgel four hundred such Rogues as you to pieces, if they have the Impudence to oppose him?

XIX: THE NOTABLE ADVENTURE OF THE OFFI-CERS OF THE HOLY BROTHERHOOD, WITH DON QUIXOTE'S GREAT FEROCITY AND INCHANTMENT

WHILST Don *Quixote* talk'd at this rate, the Curate endeavour'd to persuade the Officers that he was distracted, as they might easily gather from his Words and Actions; and therefore, though they should carry him before a Magistrate, he would be presently acquitted, as being a Mad-man. He that had the Warrant made answer, That 'twas not his Business to examine whether he were mad or not? he was an Officer in Commission, and must obey Orders; and accord-ingly was resolv'd to deliver him up to the superior Power, which once done, they might acquit him five hundred times if they wou'd. But for all that, the Curate persisted they should not carry Don *Quixote* away with them this time, add-ing, that the Knight himself would by no means be brought to it; and in short, said so much, and the Knight did so much, that they had been greater Fools than he, could they not have plainly seen his Madness. They therefore not only desisted, but offer'd their Service in compounding the Difference be-tween *Sancho* and the Barber; their Mediation was accepted, they being Officers of Justice; and succeeded so well, that both Parties stood to their Arbitration, though not entirely satisfied with their Award, which order'd them to change their Pannels, but not their Halters nor the Girths. The Curate made up the Business of the Bason, paying the Barber, under-hand, eight Reals for it, and getting a general Release under his Hand of all Claims or Actions concerning it, and all things else. These two important Differences being so happily de-cided, the only Obstacles to a general Peace were Don *Lewis's* Servants and the Innkeeper; the first were prevail'd upon to accept the Proposals offer'd, which were, that three of them should go home, and the fourth attend Don *Lewis*, where Don *Ferdinand* should appoint. Thus this Difference was made up, to the unspeakable Joy of Donna *Clara*. *Zoraida* not well understanding any thing that past, was sad and chearful by turns, as she observ'd others to be by their Countenances, especially her beloved *Spaniard*, on whom her Eyes were more particularly fix'd. The Inn-keeper made a hideous Bawling; having discover'd that the Barber had receiv'd Money for his Bason, he knew no Reason, he said, why he should not be paid as well as other Folks, and swore that *Rozinante* and *Sancho's* Ass should pay for their Master's Extravagance before they should leave his Stable; The Curate pacify'd him, and Don *Ferdinand* paid him his Bill. All things thus accommodated, the Inn no longer resembled the Confusion of *Agramant's* Camp, but rather the universal Peace of *Augustus's* Reign: Upon which the Curate and Don *Ferdinand* had the Thanks of the House, as a just Acknowledgment for their so effectual Mediation.

Don *Quixote* being now free from the Difficulties and Delays that lately embarassed him, held it high time to prosecute his Voyage, and bring to some Decision the general Enterprize which he had the Voice and Election for. He therefore fully resolv'd to press his Departure, and fell on his Knees before *Dorothea*, but she would not hear him in that Posture, but prevail'd upon him to rise: He then addressing her in his usual Forms; Most beautiful Lady, said he, 'tis a known Proverb, *That Diligence is the Mother of Success*; and we have found the greatest Successes in War still to depend on Expedition and Dispatch, by preventing the Enemy's Design, and forcing a Victory before an Assault is expected. My Inference from this, most high and illustrious Lady, is, that our Residence in this Castle appears nothing conducive to our Designs, but may prove dangerous; for we may reasonably suppose that our Enemy the Giant may learn by Spies, or some other secret Intelligence, the Scheme of our Intentions, and consequently fortify himself in some inexpugnable Fortress, against the Power of our utmost Endeavours, and so the Strength of my invincible Arm may be ineffectual. Let us therefore, dear Madam, by our Diligence and sudden Departure hence, prevent any such his Designs, and force our good Fortune, by missing no Opportunity that we may lay hold of. Here he stopt, waiting the Princess's Answer. She, with a grave Aspect, and Style suiting his Extravagance, reply'd, The great Inclina-

tion and indefatigable Desire you shew, worthy Knight, in
assisting the Injur'd, and restoring the Oppress'd, lay a fair
Claim to the Praises and universal Thanks of Mankind; but
your singular Concern, and industrious Application in assisting me, deserve my particular Acknowledgments and Gratification; and I shall make it my peculiar Request to Heaven,
that your generous Designs, in my Favour, may be soon accomplish'd, that I may be enabled to convince you of the Honour
and Gratitude that may be found in some of our Sex. As to our
Departure, I shall depend upon your Pleasure, to whose Management I have not only committed the Care of my Person,
but also resign'd the whole Power of Command. Then, by the
Assistance of the Divine Power, answer'd he, I will lose no
Opportunity of re-instating your Highness, since you condescend to humble yourself to my Orders; let our March be
sudden, for the Eagerness of my Desires, the Length of the
Journey, and the Dangers of Delay, are great Spurs to my
Dispatch; since therefore Heaven has not created, nor Hell
seen the Man I ever fear'd; fly *Sancho*, saddle *Rozinante*, harness your Ass, and make ready the Lady's Palfry; let us take
leave of the Governor here, and these other Lords, and set
out from hence immediately.

Poor *Sancho* hearing all that pass'd, shook his Head. Lord,
Lord, Master, said he, there's always more Tricks in a Town
than are talk'd of (with Reverence be it spoken). Ho! Villain,
cry'd Don *Quixote*, what Tricks can any Town or City shew
to impair my Credit? Nay, Sir, quoth *Sancho*, if you grow
angry, I can hold my Tongue, if that be all; but there are some
things which you ought to hear, and I should tell as becomes
a trusty Squire and honest Servant. Say what thou wilt, said
the Knight, so it tend not to Cowardice; for if thou art afraid,
keep it to thyself, and trouble not me with the mention of
Fear, which my Soul abhors. Pshaw, hang Fear, answer'd
Sancho, that's not the matter; but I must tell you, Sir, that
which is as certain and plain as the Nose on your Face. This
same Madam here, that calls herself the Queen of the great
Kingdom of *Micomicon*, is no more a Queen than my Grandam.
For, do but consider, Sir, if she were such a fine Queen as you
believe, can you imagine she wou'd always be sucking of

Snouts,* and kissing and slabbering a certain Person, that shall be nameless in this Company? *Dorothea* blush'd at *Sancho's* Words, for Don *Ferdinand* had, indeed, sometimes, and in private, taken the Freedom with his Lips to reap some Part of the Reward his Affection deserv'd; which *Sancho* spying by chance made some Constructions upon it, very much to the Disadvantage of her Royalty; for, in short he concluded her no better than a Woman of Pleasure. She nevertheless wou'd take no Notice of his Aspersion, but let him go on; I say this, Sir, continu'd he, because after our trudging thro' all Weathers, fair after foul, Day after Night and Night after Day, this same Person in the Inn here, is like to divert himself at our Expence, and to gather the Fruit of our Labours. I think therefore, Master, there is no Reason, d'ye see, for saddling *Rozinante*, harnessing my Ass, or making ready the Lady's Palfrey; for we had better stay where we are; and let every Whore brew as she bakes, and every Man that is hungry go to Dinner.

Heavens! Into what a Fury did these disrespectful Words of *Sancho* put the Knight? his whole Body shook, his Tongue faulter'd, his Eyes glow'd. Thou Villanous, Ignorant, Rash, Unmannerly, Blasphemous Detractor, said he, how dar'st thou entertain such base and dishonourable Thoughts, much more utter thy rude and contemptible Suspicions before me and this Honourable Presence? Away from my Sight, thou Monster of Nature, Magazine of Lies, Cupboard of Deceits, Granary of Guile, Publisher of Follies, Foe of all Honour! Away, and never let me see thy Face again, on Pain of my most furious Indignation. Then bending his angry Brows, puffing his Cheeks, and stamping on the Ground, he gave *Sancho* such a Look as almost frighted the poor Fellow to Annihilation.

In the height of this Consternation, all that the poor Squire could do, was to turn his Back, and sneak out of the Room. But *Dorothea* knowing the Knight's Temper, undertook to mitigate his Anger, Sir Knight of the Woful Figure, said she, asswage your Wrath, I beseech you; 'tis below your Dignity to be offended at these idle Words of your Squire; and I dare

---

* Hocicando *in the Original, from* Hocico *the Snout of any Beast.* Hocico *quasi* Focico, *from the* Latin Fauces *Jaws. The* Spanish *form most* Latin *words by changing* F, *into* H; *thus* Fenum Hay *is* Heno, &c.

not affirm but that he has some colour of Reason for what
he said; for it were uncharitable to suspect his sincere Understanding, and honest Principles, of any false or malicious
Slanders or Accusation. We must therefore search deeper into
this Affair, and believe, That as you have found all Transactions in this Castle govern'd by Inchantment, so some diabol-
ical Illusion has appear'd to *Sancho*, and represented to his
Inchanted Sight what he asserts to my Dishonour. Now by
the Powers supreme, said the Knight, your Highness has cut
the Knot. The Misdemeanour of that poor Fellow must be
attributed purely to Inchantment, and the Power of some malicious Apparition; for the Good-nature and Simplicity of the
poor Wretch could never invent a Lye, or be guilty of an Aspersion to any one's Disadvantage. 'Tis evident, said Don *Ferdin-
and*, we therefore all intercede in behalf of honest *Sancho*,
that he may be again restor'd to your Favour, *sicut erat in
Principio*, before these Illusions had impos'd upon his Sense.
Don *Quixote* comply'd, and the Curate brought in poor *Sancho*
trembling, who on his Knees made an humble Acknowledgment of his Crime, and begg'd to have his Pardon confirm'd by
a gracious Kiss of his Master's Hand. Don *Quixote* gave him
his Hand and his Blessing. Now *Sancho*, said he, will you hereafter believe what I so often have told you, that the Power of
Inchantment over-rules every thing in this Castle? I will, and
like your Worship, quoth *Sancho*, all but my tossing in a Blanket; for really, Sir, that happen'd according to the ordinary
course of Things. Believe it not, *Sancho*, reply'd Don *Quixote*, for were I not convinc'd of the contrary, you should have
plentiful Revenge; but neither then, nor now, could I ever find
any Object to wreak my Fury or Resentment on. Every one
desir'd to know what was the Business in Question; whereupon the Inn-keeper gave them an Account of *Sancho's* tossing,
which set them all a laughing, and would have made *Sancho*
angry, had not his Master afresh assur'd him that 'twas only a
meer Illusion, which though the Squire believ'd not, he held
his Tongue. The whole Company having pass'd two Days in
the Inn, bethought themselves of departing; and the Curate
and Barber found out a Device to carry home Don *Quixote*,
without putting Don *Ferdinand* and *Dorothea* to the trouble

of humouring his Impertinence any longer. They first agreed with a Waggoner that went by with his Team of Oxen, to carry him home: Then had a kind of a wooden Cage made, so large that the Knight might conveniently sit, or lye in it. Presently after all the Company of the Inn disguis'd themselves, some with Masks, others by disfiguring their Faces, and the rest by Change of Apparel, so that Don *Quixote* shou'd not take them to be the same Persons. This done, they all silently enter'd his Chamber, where he was sleeping very soundly after his late Fatigues: They immediately laid hold on him so forcibly, and held his Arms and Legs so hard, that he was not able to stir, or do any thing but stare on those odd Figures which stood round him. This instantly confirm'd him in the strange Fancy that had so long disturb'd his craz'd Understanding, and made him believe himself undoubtedly inchanted; and those frightful Figures to be the Spirits and Demons of the inchanted Castle. So far the Curate's Invention succeeded to his Expectation. *Sancho* being the only Person there in his right Shape and Senses, beheld all this very patiently, and tho' he knew them all very well, yet was resolv'd to see the End on't ere he ventur'd to speak his Mind. His Master likewise said nothing, patiently expecting his Fate, and waiting the Event of his Misfortune. They had by this lifted him out of Bed, and placing him in the Cage, they shut him in, and nail'd the Bars of it so fast, that no small Strength could force them open. Then mounting him on their Shoulders, as they convey'd him out of the Chamber-Door, they heard as dreadful a Voice as the Barber's Lungs cou'd bellow, speak these Words:

Be not impatient, O Knight of the woful Figure, at your Imprisonment, since 'tis ordain'd by the Fates, for the more speedy Accomplishment of that most noble Adventure, which your incomparable Valour has intended. For accomplish'd it shall be, when the Rampant *Manchegan* Lion,* and the white *Tobosian* Dove shall be united, by humbling their lofty and erected Chests to the soft Yoke of Wedlock, from whose wonderful Coition shall be produc'd and spring forth brave

---

* *It may be translated the rampant* spotted *Lion as well as the rampant* Manchegan *Lyon: For the* Spanish *Word* Mancha *signifies both a* Spot *and the Country* La Mancha. *An untranslatable* Double Entendre.

Whelps which shall imitate the rampant Paws of their valorous Sire. And this shall happen before the bright Pursuer of the fugitive Nymph shall, by his rapid and natural Course, take a double Circumference in Visitation of the Luminous Signs. And thou, the most noble and faithful Squire that ever had Sword on Thigh, Beard on Face, or Sense of Smell in Nose, be not dispirited or discontented at this Captivity of the Flower of all Chivalry; for very speedily, by the eternal Will of the World's Creator, thou shalt find thyself enobled and exalted beyond the Knowledge of thy Greatness. And I confirm to thee, from the Sage *Mentironiana*,* that thou shalt not be defrauded of the Promises made by thy noble Lord. I therefore conjure thee to follow closely the Steps of the courageous and Inchanted Knight; for it is necessarily enjoin'd, that you both go where you both shall stay. The Fates have commanded me no more, farewell. For I now return, I well know whither.

The Barber manag'd the Cadence of his Voice so artificially towards the latter end of his Prophecy, that even those who were made acquainted with the Jest, had almost taken it for Supernatural.

Don *Quixote* was much comforted at the Prophecy, apprehending presently the Sense of it, and applying it to his Marriage with *Dulcinea del Toboso*, from whose happy Womb should issue the Cubs (signifying his Sons) to the eternal Glory of *La Mancha*; upon the Strength of which Belief raising his Voice, and heaving a profound Sigh; Whatsoever thou art, said he, whose happy Prognostication I own and acknowledge, I desire thee to implore (in my Name) the wise Magician, whose Charge I am, that his Power may protect me in this Captivity, and not permit me to perish before the Fruition of these grateful and incomparable Promises made to me; for the Confirmation of such Hopes, I wou'd think my Prison a Palace, my Fetters Freedom, and this hard Field-bed on which I lie, more easy than the softest Down, or most luxurious Lodgings. And as to the Consolation offer'd my Squire *Sancho Panza*, I am so convinc'd of his Honesty, and he has prov'd his Honour in so many Adventures, that I mistrust not his deserting me, through

* Mentironiana *is a fram'd Word from* Mentira *a Lye, as if we shou'd say* Fibberiana.

any Change of Fortune. And tho' his or my harder Stars shou'd disable me from bestowing on him the Island I have promis'd, or some Equivalent, his Wages at least are secur'd to him by my last Will and Testament, tho' what he will receive is more answerable, I confess, to my Estate and Ability, than to his Services and great Deserts. *Sancho Panza* made him three or four very respectful Bows, and kiss'd both his Hands (for one alone he cou'd not, being both ty'd together) and in an Instant the Demons hoisted up the Cage, and yoked it very handsomely to the Team of Oxen.

DON *Quixote* was not so much amaz'd at his Inchantment, as the Manner of it: Among all the Volumes of Chivalry that I have turn'd over, said he, I never read before of Knights-Errant drawn in Carts, or tugg'd along so leisurely, by such slothful Animals as Oxen. For they us'd to be hurry'd along with prodigious speed, invelop'd in some dark and dusky Cloud; or in some fiery Chariot drawn by winged Griffins, or some such expeditious Creatures; but I must confess, to be drawn thus by a Team of Oxen, staggers my Understanding not a little; tho' perhaps the Inchanters of our Times take a different Method from those in former Ages. Or rather the wise Magicians have invented some Course in their Proceedings for me, being the first Reviver and Restorer of Arms, which have so long been lost in Oblivion, and rusted thro' the Disuse of Chivalry. What is thy Opinion, my dear *Sancho*? Why truly, Sir, said *Sancho*, I can't tell what to think, being not so well read in these Matters as your Worship; yet for all that, I'm positive and can take my Oath on't, that these same Phantoms that run up and down here are not Orthodox. Orthodox, my Friend, said Don *Quixote*, how can they be Orthodox, when they are Devils, and have only assumed these Phantastical Bodies to surprize us into this Condition? To convince you, endeavour to touch them, and you will find, their Substances are not material, but only subtile Air, and outward Appearance. Gadzookers, Sir, said *Sancho*, I have touch'd them, and touch'd them again, Sir; and I find this same busy Devil here, that's fidling about, is as plump and fat as a Capon: Besides, he has another Property, very different from a Devil; for the Devils, they say, smell of Brimstone and other filthy Things, and this Spark has such a fine Scent of Essence about him, that you may smell him at least half a League. (Meaning Don *Ferdinand*, who, in all probability, like other Gentlemen of his Quality, had his Clothes perfum'd).

457

Alas, honest *Sancho*, answer'd Don *Quixote*, the Cunning of these Fiends is above the reach of thy Simplicity; for you must know, the Spirits, as Spirits, have no Scent at all; and if they shou'd, it must necessarily be some unsavoury Stench, because they still carry their Hell about them, and the least of a Perfume or grateful Odour were inconsistent with their Torments; so that this Mistake of yours must be attributed to some farther Delusion of your Sense. Don *Ferdinand* and *Cardenio*, upon these Discourses between Master and Man, were afraid that *Sancho* would Spoil all, and therefore or-der'd the Inn-keeper privately to get ready *Rozinante* and *Sancho's* Ass, while the Curate agreed with the Officers for so much a Day to conduct them home. *Cardenio* having hung Don *Quixote's* Target on the Pommel of *Rozinante's* Saddle, and the Bason on t'other side, he signify'd to *Sancho* by Signs, that he shou'd mount his Ass, and lead *Rozinante* by the Bridle; and lastly plac'd two Officers with their Fire-locks on each side of the Cart.

Being just ready to march, the Hostess, her Daughter, and *Maritornes*, came to the Door to take their Leave of the Knight, pretending unsupportable Grief for his Misfortune. Restrain your Tears, most honourable Ladies, said Don *Quix-ote*, for these Mischances are incident to those of my Profes-sion; and from these Disasters it is we date the Greatness of our Glory and Renown; they are the Effects of Envy, which still attends virtuous and great Actions, and brought upon us by the indirect means of such Princes and Knights as are emu-lous of our Dignity and Fame: but spite of all Oppression, spite of all the Magick, that ever its first Inventor *Zoroastres* un-derstood, Virtue will come off victorious; and triumphing over every Danger, will at last shine out in its proper Lustre like the Sun to enlighten the World. Pardon me, fair Ladies, if (thro' Ignorance or Omission of the Respects due to your Qualities) I have not behav'd myself to please you; for to the best of my Knowledge I never committed a wilful Wrong. And I crave the Assistance of your Prayers, towards my Enlarge-ment from this Prison, which some malicious Magician has confin'd me to; and the first Business of my Freedom, shall be a grateful Acknowledgment for the many and obliging Favours

458

confer'd upon me in this your Castle. Whilst the Ladies were thus entertain'd by Don *Quixote*, the Curate and Barber were busy taking their Leaves of their Company; and after mutual Compliments and Embraces, they engag'd to acquaint one another with their succeeding Fortunes. Don *Ferdinand* intreated the Curate to give him a Particular Relation of Don *Quixote's* Adventures, assuring him, that nothing would be a greater Obligation, and at the same time engag'd to inform him of his own Marriage and *Lucinda's* Return to her Parents; with an Account of *Zoraida's* Baptism, and Don *Lewis's* Success in his Amour.

The Curate having given his Word and Honour, to satisfy Don *Ferdinand*, and the last Compliments being past, was just going, when the Inn-keeper made him a proffer of a Bundle of Papers found in the Folds of the same Cloak-Bag, where he got *The Curious Impertinent*, telling him withal, That they were all at his Service; because since the Owner was not like to come and demand them, and he could not read, they cou'd not better be dispos'd of. The Curate thank'd him heartily, and opening the Papers, found them Entitl'd, *The Story of* Rinconete, *and* Cortadillo. The Title shewing it to be a Novel, and probably written by the Author of *The Curious Impertinent*, because found in the same Wallet, he put it in his Pocket, with a Resolution to peruse it the very first Opportunity: Then mounting with his Friend the Barber and both putting on their Masks, they follow'd the Procession, which march'd in this Order. The Carter led the Van, and next his Cart, flank'd on right and left with two Officers with their Firelocks; then follow'd *Sancho* on his Ass, leading *Rozinante*; and lastly the Curate and Barber on their mighty Mules brought up the Rear of the Body, all with a grave and solemn Air, marching no faster than the heavy Oxen allow'd. Don *Quixote* sat leaning against the Back of the Cage with his Hands ty'd and his Legs at length; but so silent and motionless, that he seem'd rather a Statue than a Man.

They had travell'd about two Leagues this slow and leisurely pace, when their Conductor stopping in a little Valley, propos'd it as a fit Place to bait in; but he was prevail'd upon to defer halting a little longer, being inform'd by the Barber

459

of a certain Valley beyond a little Hill in their View, better stor'd with Grass, and more convenient for their Purpose: They had not travell'd much farther when the Curate spy'd coming a round pace after them six or seven Men very well accoutred: They appear'd, by their brisk riding, to be mounted on Churchmens Mules, not carry'd, as the Don was, by a Team of sluggish Oxen: They endeavour'd before the Heat of the Day to reach their Inn, which was about a League farther. In short, they soon came up with our slow Itinerants; and one of them, that was a Canon of *Toledo*, and Master of those that came along with him, marking the formal Procession of the Cart, Guards, *Sancho*, *Rozinante*, the Curate, and the Barber, but chiefly the incag'd Don *Quixote*, cou'd not forbear asking what meant their strange Method of securing that Man; tho' he already believ'd (having observ'd the Guards) that he was some notorious Criminal in custody of the *Holy Brotherhood*. One of the Fraternity told him, That he cou'd not tell the Cause of that Knight's Imprisonment, but that he might answer for himself, because he best cou'd tell.

Don *Quixote* over-hearing their Discourse, Gentlemen, said he, if you are conversant and skill'd in Matters of Knight-Errantry, I will communicate my Misfortunes to you; if you are not, I have no reason to give myself the trouble. Truly, Friend, answer'd the Canon, I am better acquainted with Books of Chivalry than with *Villalpando's* Divinity; and if that be all your Objection, you may safely impart to me what you please. With Heaven's Permission be it so, said Don *Quixote*; you must then understand, Sir Knight, that I am borne away in this Cage by the force of Inchantments, thro' the envious Spight and Malice of some cursed Magicians; for Virtue is more zealously persecuted by Ill Men, than 'tis belov'd by the Good. I am by profession, a Knight-Errant, and none of those, I assure you, whose Deeds never merited a Place in the Records of Fame; but one, who in spight of Envy's self, in spight of all the Magi of *Persia*, the Brachmans of *India*, or the Gymnosophists of *Ethiopia*, shall secure to his Name a place in the Temple of Immortality, as a Pattern and Model to following Ages, that ensuing Knights-Errant, following my Steps, may be guided to the Top and highest Pitch of Heroick Honour. The noble

Don *Quixote de la Mancha* speaks truth, said the Curate, coming up to the Company, he is indeed inchanted in this Cart, not thro' his own Demerits or Offences, but the malicious Treachery of those whom Virtue displeases and Valour offends. This is, Sir, the Knight of the Woful Figure, of whom you have undoubtedly heard, whose mighty Deeds shall stand engrav'd in lasting Brass and time-surviving Marble, till Envy grows tir'd with labouring to deface his Fame, and Malice to conceal 'em.

The Canon hearing the Prisoner and his Guard talk thus in the same Stile, was in amaze, and bless'd himself for wonder, as did the rest of the Company, till *Sancho Panza* coming up, to mend the Matter, Look ye, Sirs, said he, I will speak the Truth, take it well, or take it ill. My Master here, is no more inchanted than my Mother: He's in his sober Senses, he eats and drinks, and does his Needs, like other Folks, and as he us'd to do; and yet they'll persuade me that a Man, who can do all this, is inchanted forsooth; he can speak too, for if they'll let him alone, he'll prattle you more than thirty Attorneys. Then turning towards the Curate, O Mr Curate, Mr Curate, continu'd he, do you think I don't know you, and that I don't guess what all these new Inchantments drive at! Yes I do know you well enough, for all you hide your Face; and understand your Design, for all your sly Tricks, Sir. But 'tis an old Saying, There's no striving against the Stream; and the Weakest still goes to the Wall. The Devil take the luck on't; had not your Reverence spoil'd our Sport, my Master had been marry'd before now to the Princess *Micomicona*, and I had been an Earl at least; nay, that I was sure of, had the worst come to the worst; but the old Proverb is true again, Fortune turns round like a Mill-wheel, and he that was yesterday at the Top, lies to day at the Bottom. I wonder Mr Curate, you that are a Clergyman should not have more Conscience; consider, Sir, that I have a Wife and Family who expect all to be great Folks, and my Master here is to do a World of good Deeds: And don't you think, Sir, that you won't be made to answer for all this one Day? Snuff me those Candles, said the Barber, hearing *Sancho* talk at this rate: What, Fool, are you brain-sick of your Masters Disease too? if you be, you're like to bear him Company in his Cage, I'll assure you, Friend. What inchanted Island is this that floats in your Scull, or what Succubus has been riding thy Fancy, and got it with Child of these Hopes? With Child! Sir, what d'ye mean, Sir? said *Sancho*, I scorn your Words, Sir; the best Lord in the Land shou'd not get Me with Child, no, not the King himself, Heaven bless him. For tho' I'm a poor Man, yet I'm an honest Man, and an old Christian, and don't owe any Man a Farthing; and tho' I desire Islands, there are other Folks, not far off that desire worse things. Every one is the Son of his own Works; I am a Man, and may be Pope of *Rome*, much more Governor of an Island; especially considering my Master may gain so many as he may want Persons to bestow 'em on. Therefore pray Mr Barber, take heed what you say; for all consists not in shaving of Beards, and there's some difference between a Hawk and a Hand-saw. I say so, because we all know one another, and no Body shall put a false Card upon Me. As to my Master's Inchantment, let it stand as it is, Heaven knows best: And a Stink is still worse for the stirring. The Barber thought Silence the best way to quiet *Sancho's* Impertinence; and the Curate, doubting that he might spoil all, intreated the Canon to put on a little before, and he would unfold the Mystery of the encag'd Knight, which perhaps he would find one of the pleasantest Stories he had ever heard: The Canon rid forward with him, and his Men follow'd, while the Curate made them a Relation of Don *Quixote's* Life and Quality, his Madness and Adventures, with the original Cause of his Distraction, and the whole Progress of his Affairs, till his being shut up in the Cage, to get him home, in order to have him cur'd. They all admired at this strange Account; and then the Canon turning to the Curate: Believe me, Mr Curate, said he, I am fully convinc'd, that these they call Books of Knight-Errantry are very prejudicial to the Publick. And tho' I have been led away with an idle and false Pleasure, to read the Beginnings of almost as many of 'em as have been Printed, I could never yet persuade myself to go through with any one to the End; for to me they all seem to contain one and the same thing; and there is as much in one of them as in all the rest. The whole Composition and Stile resemble that of the *Milesian* Fables, which are a sort of idle Stories, design'd only for Diversion, and not for Instruction. It is not so with those Fables which are call'd Apologues, that at once delight and instruct. But tho' the main Design of such Books is to please; yet I cannot conceive how it is possible they should perform it, being fill'd with such a Multitude of unaccountable Extravagancies. For the Pleasure which strikes the Soul, must be deriv'd from the Beauty and Congruity it sees or conceives in those things the Sight or Imagination lay before it; and nothing in itself deform'd or incongruous can give us any real Satisfaction. Now what Beauty can there be, or what Proportion of the Parts to the Whole, or of the Whole to the several Parts, in a Book, or Fable, where a Stripling of Sixteen Years of Age at one Cut of a Sword cleaves a Giant, as tall as a Steeple, through the Middle, as easily as if he were made of Paste-Board? Or when they give us the Relation of a Battle, having said the Enemy's Power consisted of a Million of Combatants, yet provided the Hero of the Book be against them, we must of necessity, tho' never so much against our Inclination, conceive that the said Knight obtain'd the Victory only by his own Valour, and the Strength of his Powerful Arm? And what shall we say of the great Ease and Facility with which an absolute Queen or Empress casts herself into the Arms of an Errant and unknown Knight? What Mortal, not altogether barbarous and unpolish'd, can be pleased to read, that a great Tower, full of armed Knights, cuts thro' the Sea like a Ship before the Wind, and setting out in the Evening from the Coast of *Italy*, lands by Break of Day in *Prestor John's* Country, or in some other, never known to *Ptolomy* or seen by *Marcus Paulus*?* If it shou'd be answer'd, That the Persons who compose these Books, write them as confess'd Lies; and therefore are not oblig'd to observe Niceties, or to have regard to Truth; I shall make this Reply, That Falshood is so much the more commendable, by how much it more resembles Truth; and is the more pleasing the more it is doubtful and possible. Fabulous Tales ought to be suited to the

---

* A Venetian, *and a very great Traveller. He liv'd in the* 13th Century, 1272. *He had travel'd over* Syria, Persia, *and the* Indies. *An Account of his Travels has been printed, and one of his Books is intitled* De Regionibus Orientis.

Reader's Understanding, being so contrived, that all Impossibilities ceasing, all great Accidents appearing feasible and the Mind wholly hanging in Suspence, they may at once surprize, astonish, please and divert; so that Pleasure and Admiration may go hand in hand. This cannot be performed by him that flies from Probability and Imitation, which is the Perfection of what is written. I have not seen any Book of Knight-Errantry that composes an entire Body of a Fable with all its Parts, so that the Middle is answerable to the Beginning, and the End to the Beginning and Middle; but on the contrary, they form them of so many Limbs, that they rather seem a Chimæra or Monster, than a well-proportion'd Figure. Besides all this, their Stile is uncouth, their Exploits incredible, their Love immodest, their Civility impertinent, their Battles tedious, their Language absurd, their Voyages preposterous; and in short, they are altogether void of solid Ingenuity, and therefore fit to be banish'd a Christian Commonwealth as useless and prejudicial. The Curate was very attentive, and believ'd him a Man of a sound Judgment, and much in the right in all he had urg'd; and therefore told him, That being of the same Opinion, and an Enemy to Books of Knight-Errantry, he had burnt all that belong'd to Don *Quixote*, which were a considerable Number. Then he recounted to him the Scrutiny he had made among them, what he had condemn'd to the Flames, and what spar'd; at which the Canon* laugh'd heartily, and said, That notwithstanding all he had spoken against those Books, yet he found one good thing in them, which was the Subject they furnish'd a Man of Understanding with to exercise his Parts, because they allow a large Scope for the Pen to dilate upon without any Check, describing Shipwrecks, Storms, Skirmishes and Battles; representing to us a brave Commander, with all the Qualifications, requisite in such a one, shewing his Prudence in disappointing the Designs of the Enemy, his Eloquence in persuading or dissuading his Soldiers, his Judgment in Council, his Celerity in Execution, and his Valour in assailing or repulsing an Assault; laying before us sometimes a dismal and melancholy Accident, sometimes a delightful and unexpected Adventure; in one Place, a beautiful,

* *This Canon of* Toledo *is Cervantes himself all along.*

modest, discreet and reserv'd Lady; in another, a Christian-
like, brave and courtcous Gentleman; here a boisterous, in-
human, boasting Ruffian; there an affable, warlike and wise
Prince; livelily expressing the Fidelity and Loyalty of Subjects, Generosity and Bounty of Sovereigns. He may no less,
at times, make known his Skill in Astrology, Cosmography,
Musick and Policy; and if he pleases, he cannot want an Opportunity of appearing knowing even in Necromancy. He may
describe the Subtilty of *Ulysses*, the Piety of *Æneas*, the Valour of *Achilles*, the Misfortunes of *Hector*, the Treachery of
Sinon, the Friendship of *Euryalus*, the Liberality of *Alexander*, the Valour of *Cæsar*, the Clemency and Sincerity of
Trajan, the Fidelity of *Zopyrus*, the Prudence of *Cato*; and
in fine, all those Actions that may make up a Compleat Hero,
sometimes attributing them all to one Person, and at other
times dividing them among many. This being so perform'd in
a grateful Stile, and with ingenious Invention, approaching
as much as possible to Truth, will doubtless compose so beautiful and various a Work, that, when finish'd, its Excellency
and Perfection must attain the best end of Writing, which is
at once to delight and instruct, as I have said before: For the
loose Method practis'd in these Books, gives the Author liberty
to play the Epick, the Lyrick, and the Dramatick Poet, and
to run through all the other Parts of Poetry and Rhetorick;
for Epicks may be as well writ in Prose* as in Verse.

* *The* Adventures of Telemachus *is a Proof of this.*

YOU are much in the right, Sir, reply'd the Curate; and therefore those who have hitherto publish'd Books of that Kind, are the more to be
blam'd, for having had no regard to good Sense,
Art or Rules, by the Observation of which they
might have made themselves as famous in Prose,
as the two Princes of *Greek* and *Latin* Poetry are in Verse.
I must confess, said the Canon, I was once tempted to write a
Book of Knight-Errantry myself, observing all those Rules;
and to speak the Truth, I writ above an hundred Pages, which,
for a better Tryal, whether they answer'd my Expectation, I
communicated to some learned and judicious Men fond of those
Subjects, as well as to some of those ignorant Persons, who
only are delighted with Extravagancies; and they all gave me
a satisfactory Approbation. And yet I made no farther Progress, as well in regard I look upon it to be a thing no way
agreeable with my Profession, as because I am sensible the
Illiterate are much more numerous than the Learned; and
tho' it were of more weight to be commended by the small
Number of the Wise, than scorn'd by the ignorant Multitude,
yet wou'd I not expose myself to the confus'd Judgment of the
giddy Vulgar, who principally are those who read such Books.
But the greatest Motive I had to lay aside, and think no more
of finishing it, was the Argument I form'd to myself deduc'd
from the Plays now usually acted: For, thought I, if Plays now
in use, as well those which are altogether of the Poet's Invention, as those that are grounded upon History, be All of them,
or, however, the greatest part, made up of most absurd Extravagancies and Incoherencies; Things that have neither head
nor foot, side nor bottom; and yet the Multitude sees them
with Satisfaction, esteems and approves them, tho' they are so
far from being good; and if the Poets who write, and the Players who act them, say they must be so contriv'd and no otherwise, because they Please the Generality of the Audience; and
if those which are regular and according to Art, serve only to

please half a score judicious Persons who understand them, whilst the rest of the Company cannot reach the Contrivance, nor know any thing of the Matter; and therefore the Poets and Actors say, they had rather get their Bread by the greater Number, than the Applause of the less: Then may I conclude the same will be the Success of this Book; so that when I have rack'd my Brains to observe the Rules, I shall reap no other Advantage, than to be laugh'd at for my Pains. I have sometimes endeavour'd to convince the Actors that they are deceiv'd in their Opinion, and that they will draw more Company and get more Credit by regular Plays, than by those preposterous Representations now in use; but they are so positive in their Humour, that no Strength of Reason, nor even Demonstration, can beat this Opinion into their Heads. I remember I once was talking to one of those obstinate Fellows; Do you not remember, said I, that within these few Years Three Tragedies were acted in *Spain*, written by a famous Poet of ours, which were so excellent, that they surpriz'd, delighted, and rais'd the Admiration of all that saw them, as well the Ignorant and Ordinary People as the Judicious and Men of Quality; and the Actors got more by those Three, than by Thirty of the best that have been writ since? Doubtless, Sir, said the Actor, you mean the Tragedies of *Isabella*, *Phillis*, and *Alexandra*? The very same, I reply'd, and do You judge whether they observ'd the Rules of the Drama; and whether by doing so, they lost any thing of their Esteem, or fail'd of pleasing all sorts of People. So that the Fault lies not in the Audience's desiring Absurdities, but in those who know not how to give 'em any thing else. Nor was there any thing preposterous in several other Plays, as for Example, *Ingratitude reveng'd*, *Numancia*, *the amorous Merchant*, *and the Favourable She-Enemy*; nor in some others, compos'd by judicious Poets to their Honour and Credit, and to the Advantage of those that acted them. Much more I added, which did indeed somewhat confound him, but no way satisfy'd or convinc'd him, so as to make him change his erroneous Opinion. You have hit upon a Subject, Sir, said the Curate, which has stir'd up in me an old Aversion I have for the Plays now in use, which is not inferior to that I bear to Books of Knight-Errantry. For whereas Plays, according to the Opinion of *Cicero*, ought to be Mirrors of Human Life, Patterns of good Manners, and the very Representatives of Truth; those now acted are Mirrors of Absurdities, Patterns of Follies, and Images of Ribaldry. For instance, what can be more absurd, than for the same Person to be brought on the Stage a Child in swadling-bands, in the first Scene of the first Act; and to appear in the second grown a Man? What can be more ridiculous than to represent to us a fighting old Fellow, a cowardly Youth, a rhetorical Footman, a politick Page, a churlish King, and an unpolish'd Princess? What shall I say of their Regard to the Time in which those Actions they represent, either might or ought to have happen'd, For I have seen a Play, in which the first Act began in *Europe*, the Second was in *Asia*, and the Third ended in *Africa*?* Probably, if there had been another Act, they would have carry'd it into *America*; and thus it would have been acted in the four Parts of the World. But if Imitation is to be a principal Part of the Drama, how can any tolerable Judgment be pleas'd, when representing an Action that happen'd in the time of King *Pepin* or *Charlemaign*, they shall attribute it to the Emperor *Heraclius*, and bring him in carrying the Cross into *Jerusalem*, and recovering the Holy Sepulchre, like *Godfrey* of *Boulogne*, there being a vast distance of Time betwixt these Actions? Thus they will clap together pieces of true History in a Play of their own framing, and grounded upon Fiction, mixing in it Relations of things that have happen'd to different People and in several Ages. This they do without any Contrivance that might make it appear probable, and with such visible Mistakes as are altogether inexcusable; but the worst of it is, that there are Idiots who look upon this as Perfection, and think every thing else to be mere Pedantry. But if we look into the Pious Plays, what a multitude of false Miracles shall we find in them? how many Errors and Contradictions, how often the Miracles wrought by one Saint attributed to another? Nay, even in the Profane Plays, they presume to work Miracles upon the bare Imagination and Conceit that such a supernatural Work, or a Machine, as they call it, will be Ornamental, and draw the common Sort to see the Play. These things are a Reflection upon Truth itself,

* *'Tis to be observ'd that the* Spanish *Plays have only three* Jornadas *or Acts*.

a less'ning and depreciating of History, and a Reproach to all *Spanish* Wits; because Strangers, who are very exact in observing the Rules of the Drama, look upon us as an ignorant and barbarous People, when they see the Absurdities and Extravagancies of our Plays. Nor would it be any Excuse to alledge, that the principal Design of all good Governments, in permitting Plays to be publickly acted, is to amuse the Commonalty with some lawful Recreation and so to divert those ill Humours which Idleness is apt to breed: And that since this End is attain'd by any sort of Plays, whether good or bad, it is needless to prescribe Laws to them, or oblige the Poets or Actors to compose and represent such as are strictly conformable to the Rules. To this I wou'd answer, that this End wou'd be infinitely better attain'd by good Plays, than by bad ones. He who sees a Play that is regular and answerable to the Rules of Poetry, is pleas'd with the Comic Part, inform'd by the serious, surpriz'd at the variety of Accidents, improv'd by the Language, warn'd by the Frauds, instructed by Examples, incens'd against Vice, and enamour'd with Virtue; for a good Play must cause all these Emotions in the Soul of him that sees it, tho' he were never so insensible and unpolish'd. And it is absolutely impossible, that a Play which has all these Qualifications, shou'd not infinitely divert, satisfy and please beyond another that wants them, as most of them do which are now usually acted. Neither are the Poets who write them in Fault, for some of them are very sensible of their Errors, and extremely capable of performing their Duty; but Plays being now altogether becoming Venal and a sort of Merchandize, they say, and with Reason, that the Actors would not purchase them, unless they were of that Stamp; and therefore the Poet endeavours to suit the Humour of the Actor, who is to pay him for his Labour. For proof of this let any Man observe that infinite number of Plays compos'd by an exuberant *Spanish* Wit,* so full of Gaiety and Humour, in such elegant Verse and choice Language, so sententious, and to conclude, in such a majestick Stile, that his Fame is spread through the Universe: Yet because he suited himself to the Fancy of the Actors, many of his Pieces have fallen short of their due Per-

* Lopes de Vega, *who writ an incredible Number of* Spanish *Plays.*

fection, tho' some have reach'd it. Others write Plays so inconsiderately, that after they have appear'd on the Stage, the Actors have been forc'd to fly and abscond, for fear of being punish'd, as it has often happen'd, for having affronted Kings, and dishonour'd whole Families. These, and many other ill Consequences, which I omit, would cease, by appointing an intelligent and judicious Person at Court to examine all Plays before they were acted, that is, not only those which are represented at Court, but throughout all *Spain*: so that, without His Licence, no Magistrate should suffer any Play to appear in Publick. Thus Players would be careful to send their Plays to Court, and might then act them with safety, and those who writ would be more circumspect, as standing in awe of an Examiner that could judge of their Works. By these means we should be furnish'd with good Plays, and the End they are design'd for would be attain'd, the People diverted, the *Spanish* Wits esteem'd, the Actors safe, and the Government spar'd the trouble of Punishing them. And if the same Person, or another, were intrusted to examine all new Books of Knight-Errantry, there is no doubt but some might be publish'd with all that Perfection you, Sir, have mention'd, to the Increase of Eloquence in our Language, to the utter Extirpation of the old Books, which would be borne down by the new; and for the innocent Pastime, not only of idle Persons, but even of those who have most Employment; for the Bow cannot always stand bent, nor can human Frailty subsist without some lawful Recreation.

The Canon and Curate were come to this Period, when the Barber, overtaking them, told the latter, that this was the Place he had pitch'd on for baiting, during the heat of the Day. The Canon, induc'd by the Pleasantness of the Valley, and the Satisfaction he found in the Curate's Conversation, as well as to be farther inform'd of Don *Quixote*, bore them Company, giving order to some of his Men to ride to the next Inn, and if his Sumpter-mule were arriv'd, to send him down Provisions to that Valley, where the Coolness of the Shade, and the Beauty of the Prospect gave him such a fair Invitation to dine; and that they should make much of themselves and their Mules with what the Inn cou'd afford.

In the mean time *Sancho* having disengag'd himself from the Curate and Barber, and finding an Opportunity to speak to his Master alone, he brush'd up to the Cage where the Knight sate. That I may clear my Conscience, Sir, said he, 'tis fitting that I tell you the plain Truth of your Inchantment here. Who, wou'd you think now, are these two Fellows that ride with their Faces cover'd? Even the Parson of our Parish and the Barber; none else I'll assure you, Sir. And they are in a Plot against you, out of meer Spite because your Deeds will be more famous than theirs: This being suppos'd, it follows, that you are not inchanted, but only cozen'd and abus'd; and if you'll but answer me one Question fairly and squarely, you shall find this out to be a palpable Cheat, and that there is no Inchantment in the Case, but merely your Senses turn'd topsy turvy.

Ask me what Questions you please, dear *Sancho*, said the Knight, and I will as willingly resolve them. But for thy Assertion, that those who guard us are my old Companions the Curate and Barber, 'tis Illusion all. The Power of Magick indeed, as it has an Art to clothe any thing in any Shape, may have dress'd these Demons in their Appearances to infatuate thy Sense, and draw thee into such a Labyrinth of Confusion, that even *Theseus's* Clue could not extricate thee out of it; and this with a Design, perhaps, to plunge me deeper into Doubts, and make me endanger my Understanding, in searching into the strange Contrivance of my Inchantment, which in every Circumstance is so different from all I ever read. Therefore rest satisfy'd that these are no more what thou imaginest, than I am a *Turk*. But now to thy Questions; propose them, and I will endeavour to answer.

Bless me, said *Sancho*, this is Madness upon Madness; but since 'tis so, answer me one Question. Tell me, as you hope to be deliver'd out of this Cage here, and as you hope to find yourself in my Lady *Dulcinea's* Arms when you least think on't; as you— Conjure me no more, answer'd Don *Quixote*, but ask freely, for I have promis'd to answer punctually. That's what I want, said *Sancho*, and you must tell me the Truth, and the whole Truth, neither more nor less, upon the Honour of your Knighthood. Pr'ythee no more of your Preliminaries or Preambles, cry'd Don *Quixote*, I tell thee I will answer to a tittle.

Then, said *Sancho*, I ask, with Reverence be it spoken, whether your Worship, since your being cag'd up, or inchanted, if you will have it so, has not had a Motion, more or less, as a Man may say? I understand not that Phrase, answer'd the Knight. Heigh-day! quoth *Sancho*, don't you know what I mean? Why there's ne'er a Child in our Country, that understands the Christ-cross-Row, but can tell you. I mean, have you a mind to do what another can't do for you? O now I understand thee, *Sancho*, said the Knight; and to answer directly to thy Question, positively yes, very often; and therefore pr'ythee help me out of this Strait; for, to be free with you, I am not altogether so sweet and clean as I cou'd wish.

XXII: A RELATION OF THE WISE CONFERENCE
BETWEEN SANCHO AND HIS MASTER

AH! Sir, said *Sancho*, have I caught you at last? This is what I wanted to know from my Heart and Soul. Come Sir, you can't deny, that when any Body is out of sorts, so as not to eat, or drink, or sleep, or do any natural Occasions that you guess, then we say commonly they're bewitch'd or so; from whence may be gather'd, that those who can eat their Meat, drink their Drink, speak when they're spoken to, and go to the Back-side when they have Occasion for't, are not bewitch'd or inchanted. Your Conclusion is good, answer'd Don *Quixote*, as to one sort of Inchantment; but as I said to thee, there's variety of Inchantments, and the Changes in them thro' the Alterations of Times and Customs branch them into so many Parts, that there's no arguing from what has been to what may be Now. For my Part I am verily persuaded of my Inchantment, and this suppresses any Uneasiness in my Conscience, which might arise upon any Suggestion to the contrary. To see myself thus idly and dishonourably borne about in a Cage, and withheld like a lazy idle Coward from the great Offices of my Function, when at this Hour perhaps Hundreds of Wretches may want my Assistance, wou'd be unsupportable, if I were not inchanted. Yet, for all that, your Worship shou'd try to get your Heels at Liberty, said *Sancho*. Come, Sir, let me alone, I'll set you free I warrant you; and then get you on your trusty *Rozinante's* Back, and a Fig for them all. The poor thing here jogs on as drooping and heartless, as if He were inchanted too. Take my Advice for once now, and if things don't go as your Heart cou'd wish, you have time enough to creep into your Cage again, and on the Word of a loyal Squire I'll go in with you, and be content to be inchanted as long as you please.

I commit the Care of thy Freedom to thy Management, said Don *Quixote*: Lay hold on the Opportunity, Friend *Sancho*, and thou shalt find me ready to be govern'd in all Particulars; tho' I am still afraid thou wilt find thy Cunning strangely over-reach'd in thy Pretended Discovery. The Knight and

473

Squire had laid their Plot, when they reach'd the Place that the Canon, Curate and Barber had pitch'd upon to alight in. The Cage was taken down, and the Oxen unyoak'd to graze; when *Sancho* addressing the Curate, Pray, said he, will you do so much, as let my Lord and Master come out a little to slack a Point, or else the Prison will not be so clean as the Presence of so worthy a Knight as my Masters requires. The Curate understanding him, answer'd that he would comply, but that he fear'd Don*Quixote*, finding himself once at Liberty, would give them the slip. I'll be Bail for him, said *Sancho*, Body for Body, Sir; and I, said the Canon, upon his bare Parole of Honour. That you shall have, said the Knight; besides, you need no Security beyond the Power of Art, for inchanted Bodies have no Power to dispose of themselves, nor to move from one Place to another, without Permission of the Necromancer, in whose Charge they are: The Magical Charms might rivet 'em for three whole Centuries to one Place, and fetch 'em back swift as the Wind, should the Inchanted have fled to some other Region. Lastly, as a most convincing Argument for his Release, he urg'd, that unless they would free him, or get farther off, he should be necessitated to offend their Sense of Smelling. They guess'd his meaning presently, and gave him his Liberty; and the first use he made of it, was to stretch his benumb'd Limbs three or four times; then marching up to *Rozinante*, he slap'd him twice or thrice on the Buttocks: I trust in Heaven, thou Flower and Glory of Horse-flesh, said he, that we shall soon be restor'd to our former Circumstances; I, mounted on thy Back, and thou between my Legs, while I exercise the Function for which Heaven has bestow'd me on the World. Then Walking a little aside with *Sancho*, he return'd, after a convenient Stay, much lighter in Body and Mind, and very full of his Squire's Project.

The Canon gaz'd on him, admiring his unparallell'd sort of Madness, the rather because in all his Words and Answers he display'd an excellent Judgment; and, as we have already observ'd, he only rav'd when the Discourse fell upon Knight-Errantry: Which moving the Canon to Compassion, when they had all seated themselves on the Grass, expecting the coming up of his Sumpter-Mule; Is it possible, Sir, said he, addressing himself to Don *Quixote*, that the unhappy reading of Books of Knight-Errantry should have such an Influence over you as to destroy your Reason, making you believe you are now inchanted, and many other such Extravagancies, as remote from Truth, as Truth itself is from Falshood? How is it possible that human Sense should conceive there ever were in the World such multitudes of famous Knights-Errant, so many Emperors of *Trebizond*, so many *Amadis's*, *Felixmartes* of *Hircania*, Palfrey's, rambling Damsels, Serpents, Monsters, Giants, unheard of Adventures, so many sorts of Inchantments, so many Battles, terrible Encounters, pompous Habits and Tournaments, amorous Princesses, Earls, Squires and jesting Dwarfs, so many Love-Letters and Gallantries, so many *Amazonian* Ladies, and, in short, such an incredible Number of extravagant Passages, as are contain'd in Books of Knight-Errantry? As for my own Particular, I confess, that while I read 'em, and do not reflect that they are nothing but Falshood and Folly, they give me some Satisfaction; but I no sooner remember what they are, but I cast the best of them from me, and wou'd deliver them up to the Flames if I had a Fire near me; as well deserving that Fate, because, like Impostors, they act contrary to the common Course of Nature. They are like Broachers of new Sects, and a new manner of Living, that seduce the ignorant Vulgar to give Credit to all their Absurdities: Nay, they presume to disturb the Brains of ingenious and well-bred Gentlemen, as appears by the Effect they have wrought on Your Judgment, having reduc'd you to such a Condition, that it is necessary to shut you up in a Cage, and carry you in a Cart drawn by Oxen, like some Lyon or Tyger that is carry'd about from Town to Town to be shewn. Have Pity on yourself, good Don *Quixote*, retrieve your lost Judgment, and make use of those Abilities Heav'n has blest you with, applying your excellent Talent to some other Study, which may be safer for your Conscience, and more for your Honour: But, if led away by your natural Inclination, you will read Books of Heroism and great Exploits, read in the Holy Scripture the Book of *Judges*, where you will find wonderful Truths and glorious Actions not to be question'd. *Lusitania* had a *Viriatus*, *Rome* a *Cæsar*, *Carthage* an *Hannibal*, *Greece* an *Alexander*, *Castile* a Count *Fernan Gonzalez*,* *Valencia* a *Cid*, *Andalusia* a *Gonzalo Fernandes*, *Estremadura* a *Diego Garcia de Peredez*, *Xerez* a *Garcia Perez de Vargas*, *Toledo* a *Garcilasso*, and *Sevil* a Don *Manuel de Leon*, the reading of whose brave Actions diverts, instructs, pleases, and surprizes the most judicious Readers. This will be a Study worthy your Talent, and by which you will become well read in History, in love with Virtue, knowing in Goodness, improv'd in Manners, brave without Rashness, and cautious without Cowardice; all which will redound to the Glory of God, your own Advancement, and the Honour of the Province of *La Mancha*, whence I understand you derive your Original. Don *Quixote* listen'd with great Attention to the Canon's Discourse, and perceiving he had done, after he had fix'd his Eyes on him for a considerable Space; Sir, said he, all your Discourse, I find, tends to signify to me, there never were any Knights-Errant; that all the Books of Knight-Errantry are false, fabulous, useless, and prejudicial to the publick; that I have done ill in reading, err'd in believing, and been much to blame in imitating them, by taking upon me the most painful Profession of Chivalry. And you deny that ever there were any *Amadis's* of *Gaul* or *Greece*, or any of those Knights mention'd in those Books. Even as you have said, Sir, quoth the Canon. You also were pleas'd to add, continu'd Don *Quixote*, that those Books had been very hurtful to me, having depriv'd me of my Reason and reduc'd me to be carry'd in a Cage; that therefore it would be for my Advantage to take up in Time, and apply myself to the reading of other Books, where I might find more Truth, more Pleasure, and better Instruction. You are in the right, said the Canon. Then I am satisfy'd, reply'd Don *Quixote*, you yourself are the Man that raves and is inchanted, since you have thus boldly blasphem'd against a Truth so universally receiv'd, that whosoever presumes to contradict it, as you have done, deserves the Punishment you would inflict on those Books, which in reading offend and tire you. For it were as easy to persuade the World that the Sun does not enlighten, the Frost cool, and

---

* Fernan Gonzales, Cid, *and the rest here mention'd, were* Spanish Commanders *of Note, of whom as many Fables have been written, as there ever were of Knights-Errant.*

476

the Earth bear us, as that there never was an *Amadis*, or any of the other adventurous Knights, whose Actions are the Subjects of so many Histories. What Mortal can persuade another, that there is no Truth in what is recorded of the Infanta *Floripes*, and *Guy* of *Burgundy*: as also *Fierabras* at the Bridge of *Mantible* in the Reign of *Charlemaign*? which Passages, I dare swear, are as true as that now it is Day. But if this be false, you may as well say there was no *Hector*, nor *Achilles*; nor a *Trojan* War, nor Twelve Peers of *France*, nor a King *Arthur* of *Britain*, who is now converted into a Crow, and hourly expected in his Kingdom. Some also may presume to say, that the History of *Guerino Meschino*, and that the attempt of St *Grial* are both false; that the Amours of Sir *Tristan* and Queen *Iseo* are Apocryphal, as well as those of Queen *Guinever* and Sir *Lancelot of the Lake*, whereas there are People living who can almost remember they have seen the old Lady *Quintanona*, who had the best Hand at filling a Glass of Wine of any Woman in all *Britain*. This I am so well assur'd of, that I can remember my Grandmother, by my Father's Side, whenever she saw an old Waiting-Woman with her Reverend Veil, us'd to say to me, Look yonder, Grandson, there's a Woman like the Old Lady *Quintanona*; whence I infer, she knew her, or at least had seen her Picture. Now, Who can deny the Veracity of the History of *Pierres* and the lovely *Malagona*, when to this Day the Pin, with which the brave *Pierres* turn'd his wooden Horse that carry'd him through the Air, is to be seen in the King's Armory? which Pin is somewhat bigger then the Pole of a Coach, by the same Token it stands just by *Babieca's* Saddle. At *Roncesvalles* they keep *Orlando's* Horn, which is as Big as a great Beam; whence it follows, that there were Twelve Peers, that there were such Men as *Pierres*, and the famous *Cid*, besides many other adventurous Knights, whose Names are in the Mouths of all People. You may as well tell me that the brave *Portuguese*, *John de Merlo*, was no Knight-Errant; that he did not go into *Burgundy*, where, in the City of *Ras*, he fought the famous *Moses Pierre*, Lord of *Charney*, and in the City of *Basil*, *Moses Henry de Ramestan*, coming off in both victorious, and loaded with Honour. You may deny the Adventures and Combats of the two heroick

477

Spaniards, *Pedro Barba* and *Gutierre Quixada* (from whose Male Line I am lineally descended) who in *Burgundy* overcame the Sons of the Earl of St *Paul*. You may tell me that Don *Ferdinand de Guevara* never went into *Germany* to seek Adventures, where he fought Sir *George*,* a Knight of the Duke of *Austria's* Court. You may say the Tilting of *Suero de Quinnones del Passo*, and the Exploits of *Moses Lewis de Falses*, against Don *Gonzalo de Guzman* a *Castilian* Knight, are meer Fables; and so of many other brave Actions perform'd by Christian Knights, as well *Spaniards* as Foreigners; which are so authentick and true, that I say it over again, he who denies them has neither Sense nor Reason. The Canon was much astonish'd at the Medley Don *Quixote* made of Truths and Fables, and no less to see how well read he was in all things relating to the Atchievements of Knights-Errant; and therefore I cannot deny Sir, answer'd he, but that there is some Truth in what you have said, especially in what relates to the *Spanish* Knights-Errant;† and I will grant there were Twelve Peers of *France*, yet I will not believe they perform'd all those Actions Archbishop *Turpin* ascribes to them: I rather imagine they were brave Gentlemen made Choice of by the Kings of *France*, and call'd Peers, as being all equal in Valour and Quality; or if they were not, at least they ought to have been so; and these compos'd a sort of military Order, like those of *Saint Jago*, or *Calatrava* among Us, into which all that are admitted, are suppos'd, or ought to be, Gentlemen of Birth and known Valour. And as now we say a Knight of St *John*, or of *Alcantara*, so in those Times they said, a Knight one of the Twelve Peers, because there were but Twelve of this military Order. Nor is it to be doubted but that there were such Men as *Bernardo del Carpio*‡ and the *Cid*, yet we have Reason to question whether ever they perform'd those great Exploits that are ascrib'd to them. As to the Pin, Count *Pierre's*

---

* *In the Original it is* Micer George. Oudin *says* Micer *is a corrupt* Spanish *way both of spelling and pronouncing* Messire, *an honourable Compellation in* French. † *The Author wou'd impose the belief of these Fabulous Stories as far as there are* Spaniards *concern'd in them; but they are ridiculous, and he that allows of* Spaniards, *must also allow of Knights-Errant of other Nations.* ‡ *'Tis a great Question, whether there ever was such a Man as* Bernard del Carpio.

Pin which you spoke of, and which you say stands by *Babieca's* Saddle, I own my Ignorance, and confess I was so short-sighted, that tho' I saw the Saddle, yet I did not perceive the Pin, which is somewhat strange, if it be so large as you describe it. 'Tis there without doubt, reply'd Don *Quixote*, by the same Token they say it is kept in a Leathern Case to keep it from rusting. That may very well be, said the Canon, but upon the Word of a Priest I do not remember I ever saw it: Yet grant it were there, That does not enforce the Belief of so many *Amadis's*, nor of such a Multitude of Knights-Errant as the World talks of; nor is there any Reason so worthy a Person, so judicious, and so well qualify'd as you are, shou'd imagine there is any Truth in the wild Extravagancies contain'd in all the fabulous nonsensical Books of Knight-Errantry.

VERY well, cry'd Don *Quixote*, then all those
Books must be Fabulous, tho' licens'd by Kings,
approv'd by the Examiners, read with general
Satisfaction, and applauded by the better Sort
and the Meaner, Rich and Poor, Learned and
Unlearned, Gentry and Commonalty; and, in
short, by all Sorts of Persons of what State and Condition
soever; and tho' they carry such an appearance of Truth, setting down the Father, Mother, Country, Kindred, Age, Place
and Actions to a tittle, and Day by Day, of the Knight and
Knights of whom they treat? For shame, Sir, continu'd he,
forbear uttering such Blasphemies; and believe me, in this I
advise you to behave yourself as becomes a Man of Sense, or
else read them and see what Satisfaction you will receive.
As for Instance, pray tell me, can there be any thing more
delightful, than to read a lively Description, which, as it were,
brings before your Eyes the following Adventure? A vast Lake
of boiling Pitch, in which an infinite Multitude of Serpents,
Snakes, Crocodiles, and other Sorts of fierce and terrible
Creatures, are swimming and traversing backwards and forwards, appears to a Knight-Errant's Sight. Then from the
midst of the Lake a most doleful Voice is heard to say these
Words: O Knight, whoever thou art, who gazest on this
dreadful Lake, if thou wilt purchase the Bliss conceal'd under
these dismal Waters, make known thy Valour, by casting thyself into the midst of these black burning Surges; for unless
thou dost so, thou art not worthy to behold the mighty Wonders enclos'd in the seven Castles of the Seven Fairies, that
are seated under these gloomy Waves. And no sooner have
the last Accents of the Voice reach'd the Knight's Ear, but
he, without making any further Reflection, or considering the
Danger to which he exposes himself, and even without laying
aside his ponderous Armour, only recommending himself to
Heaven and to his Lady, plunges headlong into the middle of
the burning Lake; and when least he imagines it, or can guess

where he shall stop, he finds himself on a sudden in the midst of verdant Fields, to which the *Elysian* bear no Comparison. There the Sky appears to him more transparent, and the Sun seems to shine with a redoubl'd Brightness. Next he discovers a most delightful Grove made up of beautiful shady Trees, whose Verdure and Variety regale his Sight, while his Ears are ravish'd with the wild and yet melodious Notes of an infinite Number of pretty painted Birds, that hop and bill and sport themselves on the twining Boughs. Here he spies a pleasant Rivulet, which, through its flow'ry Banks, glides along over the brightest Sand, and remurmurs over the whitest Pebbles that bedimple its smooth Surface, while That Other, through its liquid Crystal, feasts the Eye with a Prospect of Gold and Orient Pearl. There he perceives an artificial Fountain, form'd of party-colour'd Jasper and polish'd Marble; and hard by another, contriv'd in Grotesque, where the small Cockle-shells, plac'd in orderly Confusion among the white and yellow Shells, and mix'd with pieces of bright Crystal and counterfeit Emeralds, yield a delectable Sight; so that Art imitating Nature, seems here to out-do her. At a distance, on a sudden, he casts his Eyes upon a strong Castle, or stately Palace, whose Walls are of massy Gold, the Battlements of Diamonds, and the Gates of Hyacinths; in short, its Structure is so wonderful, that tho' all the Materials are no other than Diamonds, Carbuncles, Rubies, Pearls, Gold and Emeralds, yet the Workmanship exceeds them in Value. But having seen all this, can any thing be so charming as to behold a numerous Train of beautiful Damsels come out of the Castle in such glorious and costly Apparel, as would be endless for me to describe, were I to relate these things as they are to be found in History? Then to see the *Beauty* that seems the chief of all the Damsels, take the bold Knight, who cast himself into the burning Lake, by the Hand, and without speaking one Word, lead him into a most sumptuous Palace, where he is caused to strip as naked as he was born, then put into a delicious Bath, and perfum'd with precious Essences and odoriferous Oils; after which he puts on a fine Shirt, deliciously scented; and this done another Damsel throws over his Shoulders a magnificent Robe, worth at least a whole City, if not more. What a Sight

is it, when in the next Place they lead him into another Room
of State, where he finds the Tables so orderly cover'd, that
he is surpriz'd and astonish'd? There they pour over his Hands,
Water distill'd from Amber and odoriferous Flowers: He is
seated in an Ivory Chair; and while all the Damsels that attend him observe a profound Silence, such variety of Dainties
is serv'd up, and all so incomparably dress'd, that his Appetite
is at a stand, doubting on which to satisfy its Desire; at the
same time his Ears are sweetly entertain'd with Variety of
excellent Musick, none perceiving who makes it, or from
whence it comes. But above all, what shall we say to see,
after the Dinner is ended, and Tables taken away, the Knight
left leaning back in his Chair, perhaps picking his Teeth, as
is usual; and then another Damsel, much more beautiful than
any of the former, comes unexpectedly into the Room, and
sitting down by the Knight, begins to inform him what Castle
that is, and how she is inchanted in it; with many other Particulars, which surprize the Knight, and astonish those that
read his History. I will enlarge no more upon this Matter,
since from what has been said, it may sufficiently be infer'd,
that the reading of any Passage in any History of Knight-
Errantry, must be very delightful and surprizing to the Reader. And do you, good Sir, believe me, and as I said to you before, read these Books, which you may find will banish all
Melancholy, if you are troubl'd with it, and sweeten your Disposition if it be harsh. This I can say for myself, that since
my being a Knight-Errant, I am brave, courteous, bountiful,
well-bred, generous, civil, bold, affable, patient, a Sufferer of
Hardships, Imprisonment and Inchantments: And tho' I have
so lately been shut up in a Cage, like a Madman, I expect,
through the Valour of my Arm, Heaven favouring, and Fortune not opposing my Designs, to be a King of some Kingdom
in a very few Days, that so I may give Proofs of my innate
Gratitude and Liberality. For on my Word, Sir, a poor Man
is incapable of exerting his Liberality, tho' he be naturally
never so well inclined. Now That Gratitude which only consists in Wishes, may be said to be dead, as Faith without good
Works is dead. Therefore it is, I wish Fortune would soon
offer some Opportunity for me to become an Emperor, that

I might give Proofs of my Generosity, by advancing my Friends, but especially this poor *Sancho Panza* my Squire, who is the harmlessest Fellow in the World; and I would willingly give him an Earldom, which I have long since promis'd him, but that I fear he has not Sense and Judgment enough to manage it.

Sancho hearing his Master's last Words: Well, well, Sir, said he, never do you trouble your Head about that Matter; All you have to do is to get me this same Earldom, and let me alone to manage it: I can do as my Betters have done before me, I can put in a Deputy or a Servant, that shall take all Trouble off my Hands, while I, as a great Man should, loll at my Ease, receive my Rents, mind no Business, live merrily, and so let the World rub for *Sancho*. As to the Management of your Revenue, said the Canon, a Deputy or Steward may do well, Friend: But the Lord himself is oblig'd to stir in the Administration of Justice, to which there is not only an honest sincere Intention requir'd, but a judicious Head also to distinguish nicely, conclude justly, and chuse wisely; for if this be wanting in the Principal, all will be wrong in the Medium and End. I don't understand your Philosophy, quoth *Sancho*; all I said, and I'll say it again, is, That I wish I had as good an Earldom as I could govern; for I have as great a Soul as another Man, and as great a Body as most Men: And the first thing I wou'd do in my Government, I wou'd have no Body to controul me, I wou'd be absolute; and who but I; Now, he that's absolute, can do what he likes; he that can do what he likes, can take his Pleasure, he that can take his Pleasure, can be content, and he that can be content, has no more to desire; so the Matter's over, and come what will come I'm satisfied: If an Island, welcome; if no Island, fare it well; we shall see our selves in no worse a Condition, as one blind Man said to another. This is no ill reasoning of yours, Friend, said the Canon, tho' there is much more to be said upon this Topick of Earldoms, than you imagine. Undoubtedly, said Don *Quixote*; but I suit my Actions to the Example of *Amadis de Gaul*, who made his Squire *Gandalin* Earl of the Firm-Island; which is a fair Precedent for preferring *Sancho* to the same Dignity, to which his Merit also lays an unquestionable Claim. The Canon stood amaz'd at Don *Quixote's* methodical and orderly

Madness, in describing the Adventure of the *Knight of the Lake*, and the Impression made on him by the fabulous Conceits of the Books he had read; as likewise at *Sancho's* Simplicity in so eagerly contending for his Earldom, which made the whole Company very good Sport.

By this Time the Canon's Servants had brought the Provision, and spreading a Carpet on the Grass under the shady Trees, they sat down to Dinner; when presently they heard the Tinkling of a little Bell among the Copses close by them, and immediately afterwards they saw bolt out of the Thicket a very pretty She-Goat, speckled all over with black, white and brown Spots, and a Goat-herd running after it; who, in his familiar Dialect, call'd to it to stay and return to the Fold; but the Fugitive ran towards the Company frighted and panting, and stopt close by them, as if it had begg'd their Protection. The Goat-herd overtaking it, caught it by the Horns, and in a chiding way, as if the Goat understood his Resentments, you little wanton Nanny, said he, you spotted Elf, what has made you trip it so much of late? What Wolf has scar'd you thus, Huzzy? Tell me, little Fool, what is the matter? but the Cause is plain; thou art a Female, and therefore never can'st be quiet: Curse on thy freakish Humours, and all theirs whom thou so much resemblest; turn back, my Love, turn back, and tho' thou can'st not be content with thy Fold, yet there thou may'st be safe among the rest of thy Fellows; for if thou, that shou'dst guide and direct the Flock, lovest wandring thus, what must they do, what will become of them? The Goat-herd's Talk to his Goat was entertaining enough to the Company, especially to the Canon, who calling to him, Pr'ythee, honest Fellow, said he, have a little Patience, and let your Goat take its Liberty a while; for since it is a Female, as you say, she will follow her natural Inclination the more for your striving to confine it: Come then, and take a Bit, and a Glass of Wine with us, you may be better-humour'd after that. He then reach'd him the Leg of a Cold Rabbet, and, ordering him a Glass of Wine, the Goatherd drank it off, and returning Thanks, was pacify'd. Gentlemen, said he, I wou'd not have you think me a Fool, because I talk so seriously to this senseless Animal, for my Words bear a mysterious Meaning; I am indeed, as you see, Rustical and Unpolish'd; tho' not so ignorant, but that I can converse with Men, as well as Brutes. That is no Miracle, said the Curate, for I have known the Woods breed learned Men, and simple Sheepcotts contain Philosophers. At least, said the Goatherd, they harbour Men that have some Knowledge of the World: and to make good this Truth, if I thought not the Offer impertinent, or my Company trouble-some, you shou'd hear an Accident which but too well confirms what you have said. For my part, answer'd Don *Quixote*, I will hear you attentively, because, methinks, your coming has some-thing in it that looks like an Adventure of Knight-Errantry; and I dare answer, the whole Company will not so much bring their Parts in question, as to refuse to hear a Story so pleasing, surprizing and amusing, as I fancy yours will prove. Then pr'y-thee Friend begin, for we will all give you our Attention. You must excuse me for one, said *Sancho*, I must have a Word or two in private with this same Pasty at yon little Brook; for I design to fill my Belly for to morrow and next Day; having often heard my Master Don *Quixote* say, that whenever a Knight-Errant's Squire finds good Belly-timber, he must fall to and feed till his Sides are ready to burst, because they may happen to be bewilder'd in a thick Wood for five or six Days together; so that if a Man has not his Belly full beforehand, or his Wallet well provided, he may chance to be Crows-meat himself, as many Times it falls out. You're in the right, *Sancho*, said the Knight; but I have, for my part, satisfy'd my Bodily Appetite, and now want only Refreshment for my Mind, which I hope this honest Fellow's Story will afford me. All the Company agreed with Don *Quixote*: The Goatherd then stroaking his pretty Goat once or twice; Lie down thou speckl'd Fool, said he, lie by me here; for we shall have time enough to return home. The Creature seem'd to understand him, for as soon as her Master sat down, she stretch'd herself quietly by his Side, and look'd up in his Face as if she wou'd let him know that she minded what he said; and then he began thus.

XXIV: THE GOAT-HERD'S TALE

ABOUT three Leagues from this Valley, there is a
Village, which, though small, yet is one of the
richest hereabouts. In it there lived a Farmer
in very great Esteem; and tho' it's common for
the Rich to be respected, yet was this Person
more consider'd for his Virtue, than for the
Wealth he possess'd. But what he accounted himself happiest
in, was a Daughter of such extraordinary Beauty, Prudence,
Wit and Virtue, that all who knew or beheld her, cou'd not
but admire to see how Heaven and Nature had done their
utmost to embellish her. When she was but little she was
handsome, till at the Age of Sixteen she was most compleatly
beautiful. The Fame of her Beauty began to extend to the
neighbouring Villages; but why say I neighbouring Villages?
it extended to the remotest Cities, and enter'd the Palaces of
Kings, and the Ears of all manner of Persons, who from all
parts flock'd to see her, as something rare, or as a sort of Prodigy. Her Father was strictly careful of her, nor was she less
careful of herself; for there are no Guards, Bolts or Locks
which preserve a young Woman like her own Care and Caution————The Father's Riches and the Daughter's Beauty,
drew a great many, as well Strangers as Inhabitants of that
Country, to sue for her in Marriage; but such was the vast
number of the Pretenders, as did but the more confound and
divide the old Man in his Choice, upon whom to bestow so
valuable a Treasure. Among the Crowd of her Admirers, was
I; having good Reason to hope for Success, from the Knowledge her Father had of me, being a Native of the same Place,
of a good Family, and in the Flower of my Years, of a considerable Estate, and not to be despis'd for my Understanding.
With the very same Advantages, there was another Person of
our Village who made Court to her at the same time. This put
the Father to a stand, and held him in suspence, till his Daughter should declare in Favour of one of us: To bring this Affair
therefore to the speedier Issue, he resolv'd to acquaint *Leandra*, for so was this Fair-one call'd, that since we were Equals
in all things, he left her entirely free to chuse which of us was

486

most agreeable to herself. An Example worthy of being imitated by all Parents, who have any Regard for their Children.
I don't mean that they should be allow'd to chuse in things
mean or mischievous; but only that proposing to 'em ever
those things which are good, they should be allow'd in them
to gratify their Inclination. I don't know how *Leandra* approv'd this Proposal; this I only know, that her Father put us
both off, with the Excuse of his Daughter's being too young
to be yet dispos'd of; and that he treated us both in such general
Terms, as could neither well please nor displease us ————
My Rival's Name is *Anselmo*, mine *Eugenio*, for 'tis necessary
you shou'd know the Names of the Persons concern'd in this
Tragedy, the Conclusion of which, tho' depending yet, may
easily be perceiv'd likely to be unfortunate. About that time
there came to our Village one *Vincent de la Rosa*, the Son of a
poor labouring Man of the Neighbourhood. This *Vincent* came
out of *Italy*, having been a Soldier there, and in other foreign
Parts. When he was but twelve Years old, a Captain, that
happen'd to pass by here, with his Company, took him out of
this Country, and at the end of other twelve Years he return'd
hither, habited like a Soldier, all gay and glorious, in a thousand various Colours, bedeck'd with a thousand Toys of Crystal, and Chains of Steel. To day he put on one piece of Finery,
to morrow another; but all false, counterfeit and worthless.
The Country People, who by Nature are malicious, and who
living in Idleness are still more inclin'd to Malice, observ'd
this presently, and counting all his fine things, they found
that indeed he had but three Suits of Cloaths, which were of
a different Colour with the Stockings and Garters belonging
to 'em; yet did he manage 'em with so many Tricks and Inventions, that if one had not counted 'em, one wou'd have
sworn he had above ten Suits, and above twenty Plumes of
Feathers. ————Let it not seem impertinent that I mention
this Particular of his Cloaths and Trinkets, since so much of
the Story depends upon it. Seating himself upon a Bench, under a large spreading Poplar-tree, which grows in our Street,
he us'd to entertain us with his Exploits, while we stood gaping and listning at the Wonders he recounted: There was not
that Country, as he said, upon the Face of the Earth, which

he had not seen, nor Battle which he had not been engag'd
in; he had kill'd more *Moors*, for his own Share, than were
in *Morocco* and *Tunis* together; and had fought more Duels
than *Gante, Luna, Diego, Garcia de Peredez*,* or a thousand
others that he nam'd, yet in all of 'em had the better, and
never got a Scratch, or lost a Drop of Blood. Then again he
pretended to shew us the Scars of Wounds he had receiv'd,
which tho' they were not to be perceiv'd, yet he gave us to
understand they were so many Musket-shots, which he had
got in several Skirmishes and Rencounters. In short, he treated
all his Equals with an unparallel'd Arrogance; and even to
those who knew the Meanness of his Birth, he did not stick
to affirm, That his own Arm was his Father, his Actions were
his Pedigree, and that except as to his being a Soldier, he ow'd
no part of his Quality to the King himself, and that in being
a Soldier, he was as good as the King.

Besides these assum'd Accomplishments, he was a piece of
a Musician, and cou'd thrum a Guittar a little, but what his
Excellency chiefly lay in was Poetry; and so fond was he of
shewing his Parts that way, that upon every trifling Occasion,
he was sure to make a Copy of Verses a League and a half
long. This Soldier whom I have describ'd, this *Vincent de la
Rosa*, this Hero, this Gallant, this Musician, this Poet, was
often seen and view'd by *Leandra*, from a Window of her
House which look'd into the Street; she was struck with the
Tinsel of his Dress; she was charm'd with his Verses, of which
he took care to disperse a great many Copies; her Ears were
pleas'd with the Exploits he related of himself; and in short,
as the Devil wou'd have it, she fell in Love with him, before
ever he had the Confidence to make his Addresses to her:
And, as in all Affairs of Love, that is the most easily manag'd,
where, the Lady's Affection is pre-engag'd; so was it here no
hard thing for *Leandra* and *Vincent* to have frequent Meetings
to concert their Matters; and before ever any one of her many
Suitors had the least Suspicion of her Inclination, she had
gratify'd it; and leaving her Father's House (for she had no
Mother) had run away with this Soldier, who came off with
greater Triumph in this Enterprize, than in any of the rest

* Spaniards *famous for Duelling.*

he made his Boasts of. The whole Village was surpriz'd at this Accident, as was every one that heard it. I was amaz'd, *Anselmo* distracted, her Father in Tears, her Relations outrageous; Justice is demanded; a Party with Officers is sent out, who traverse the Roads, search every Wood, and, at three Days end, find the poor fond *Leandra* in a Cave of one of the Mountains, naked to her Shift, and robb'd of a great deal of Money and Jewels which she took from Home. They bring and present her to her Father; upon Enquiry made into the Cause of her Misfortune, she confess'd ingenuously, that *Vincent de la Rosa* had deceiv'd her, and upon promise of Marriage had prevail'd with her to leave her Father's House, with the Assurance of carrying her to the richest and most delicious City of the World, which was *Naples*; that she foolishly had given credit to him, and robbing her Father, had put herself into his Hands the first Night she was mist: That he carry'd her up a steep wild craggy Mountain, and put her in that Cave where she was found. In fine, she said, that tho' he had rifl'd her of all she had, yet he had never attempted her Honour; but leaving her in that manner he fled. It was no easy matter to make any of us entertain a good Opinion of the Soldier's Continence; but she affirm'd it with so many repeated Asseverations, that in some measure it serv'd to comfort her Father in his Affliction, who valu'd nothing so much as his Daughter's Reputation. The very same Day that *Leandra* appear'd again, she also disappear'd from us, for her Father immediately clapp'd her up in a Monastery, in a Town not far off, in hopes that Time might wear away something of her Disgrace. Those who were not interested in *Leandra*, excus'd her upon the account of her Youth. But those who were acquainted with her Wit and Sense, did not attribute her Miscarriage to her Ignorance, but to the Levity and Vanity of Mind, natural to Woman-kind. Since the Confinement of *Leandra*, *Anselmo's* Eyes cou'd never meet with an Object which cou'd give him either Ease or Pleasure; I too cou'd find nothing but what look'd sad and gloomy to me in the Absence of *Leandra*. Our Melancholy increas'd, as our Patience decreas'd: We curst a thousand times the Soldier's Finery and Trinkets, and rail'd at the Father's want of Precaution: At last we agreed, *Anselmo* and I, to leave the Village, and to retire to this Valley, where, He feeding a large Flock of Sheep, and I as large a Herd of Goats, all our own, we pass our time under the Trees, giving vent to our Passions, singing in Consort the Praises or Reproaches of the beauteous *Leandra*, or else sighing alone, make our Complaints to Heaven on our Misfortune. In imitation of us, a great many more of *Leandra's* Lovers have come hither into these steep and craggy Mountains, and are alike employ'd; and so many there are of 'em, that the Place seems to be turn'd to the old *Arcadia* we read of. On the top of that Hill there is such a number of Shepherds and their Cottages, that there is no part of it in which is not to be heard the Name of *Leandra*. This Man curses and calls her Wanton and Lascivious, another calls her Light and Fickle; one acquits and forgives her, another arraigns and condemns her; one celebrates her Beauty, another rails at her ill Qualities; in short, all blame, but all adore her: Nay, so far does this Extravagance prevail, that here are those who complain of her Disdain who never spoke to her; and others who are jealous of Favours which she never granted to any; for as I intimated before, her Inclination was not known before her Disgrace. There is not a hollow Place of a Rock, a Bank of a Brook, or a shady Grove, where there is not some or other of these amorous Shepherds telling their doleful Stories to the Air and Winds. Echo has learnt to repeat the Name of *Leandra*, *Leandra* all the Hills resound, the Brooks murmer *Leandra*, and 'tis *Leandra* that holds us all Inchanted, hoping without Hope, and fearing without knowing what we fear. Of all these foolish People, the Person who shews the least, and yet has the most Sense, is my Rival *Anselmo*, who forgetting all other Causes of Complaint, complains only of her Absence; and to his Lute, which he touches to Admiration, he joins his Voice in Verses of his own composing, which declare the Greatness of his Genius. For my part, I take another Course, I think a better, I'm sure an easier, which is to say all the ill things I can of Women's Levity, Inconstancy, their broken Vows and vain deceitful Promises, their Fondness of Show and Disregard of Merit. This, Gentlemen, was the Occasion of those Words, which, at my coming hither, I addrest to this Goat; for being a *she*, I hate her, tho' she is the best of my Herd. This is the Story which I promis'd to tell you; if you have thought it too long, I shall endeavour to requite your Patience in any thing I can serve you. Hard by is my Cottage, where I have some good fresh Milk and excellent Cheese, with several sorts of Fruits, which I hope you will find agreeable both to the Sight and Taste.

XXV: OF THE COMBAT BETWEEN DON QUIXOTE AND THE GOAT-HERD: WITH THE RARE ADVENTURE OF THE PENITENTS, WHICH THE KNIGHT HAPPILY ACCOMPLISH'D WITH THE SWEAT OF HIS BROWS

THE Goat-herd's Story was mightily lik'd by the whole Company, especially by the Canon, who particularly minded the manner of his relating it, that had more of a Scholar and Gentleman, than of a rude Goat-herd; which made him conclude the Curate had reason to say, that even the Mountains bred Scholars and Men of Sense. They all made large Proffers of their Friendship and Service to *Eugenio*, but Don *Quixote* exceeded 'em all, and addressing himself to him: Were I, said he, at this time in a capacity of undertaking any Adventure, I wou'd certainly begin from this very Moment to serve you; I wou'd soon release *Leandra* out of the Nunnery, where undoubtedly she is detain'd against her Will; and in spite of all the Opposition cou'd be made by the Lady Abbess and all her Adherents I wou'd return her to your Hands, that you might have the sole disposal of her, so far, I mean, as is consistent with the Laws of Knighthood, which expresly forbid that any Man shou'd offer the least Violence to a Damsel; yet (I trust in Heaven) that the Power of a friendly Magician will prevail against the force of a malicious Inchanter; and whenever this shall happen, you may assure yourself of my Favour and Assistance, to which I am oblig'd by my Profession, that injoins me to relieve the Oppress'd.

The Goat-herd, who till then had not taken the least notice of Don *Quixote* in particular, now looking earnestly on him, and finding his dismal Countenance and wretched Habit were no great Encouragement for him to expect a Performance of such mighty Matters, whisper'd the Barber who sat next him: Pray, Sir, said he, who is this Man that talks so extravagantly? For I protest I never saw so strange a Figure in all my Life. Whom can you imagine it shou'd be, reply'd the Barber, but the Famous Don *Quixote de la Mancha*, the Establisher of Justice, the Avenger of Injuries, the Protector of Damsels, the Terror of Giants, and the Invincible Gainer of Battles. The Account you give of this Person, return'd the Goatherd, is much like what we read in *Romances* and Books of Chivalry of those doughty Dons, who, for their mighty Prowess and Atchievements, were call'd Knights-Errant; and therefore I dare say you do but jest, and that this Gentleman's Brains have deserted their Quarters.

Thou art an impudent insolent Varlet, cry'd Don *Quixote*, 'tis Thy Paper-scull is full of empty Rooms; I have more Brains than the Prostitute thy Mother had about her when she carry'd thy Lump of Nonsense in her Womb. With that, snatching up a Loaf that was near him, he struck the Goat-herd so furious a Blow with it, that he almost level'd his Nose with his Face. T'other, not accustom'd to such Salutations, no sooner perceiv'd how scurvily he was treated, but without any Respect to the Table-cloth, Napkins, or to those who were eating, he leap'd furiously on Don *Quixote*, and grasping him by the Throat with both his Hands, had certainly strangl'd him, had not *Sancho Panza* come in that very nick of Time, and griping him fast behind, pull'd him backwards on the Table, bruising Dishes, breaking Glasses, spilling and overturning all that lay upon it. Don *Quixote* seeing himself freed, fell violently again upon the Goat-herd, who, all besmear'd with Blood, and trampl'd to pieces under *Sancho's* Feet, grop'd here and there for some Knife or Fork to take a fatal Revenge; but the Canon and Curate took care to prevent his Purpose, and in the mean while, by the Barber's Contrivance, the Goatherd got Don *Quixote* under him, on whom he let fall such a Tempest of Blows, as caus'd as great a Shower of Blood to pour from the poor Knight's Face as had stream'd from his own. The Canon and Curate were ready to burst with laughing, the Officers danc'd and jump'd at the Sport, every one cry'd Hallow! as Men use to do when two Dogs are snarling or fighting; *Sancho Panza* alone was vex'd, fretted himself to Death, and rav'd like a Madman because he cou'd not get from one of the Canon's Servingmen, who kept him from assisting his Master. In short, all were exceedingly merry, except the bloody Combatants, who had maul'd one another most miserably, when on a sudden they heard the Sound of a Trumpet so doleful, that it made 'em turn to listen towards that Part from whence it seem'd to come: But he who was most troubl'd at this dismal Alarm, was Don *Quixote*; therefore, tho' he lay under the Goat-herd, full sore against his Will, and was most lamentably bruis'd and batter'd, Friend Devil, cry'd he to him (for sure nothing less cou'd have so much Valour and Strength as to subdue my Forces) let us have a Cessation of Arms but for a single Hour; for the dolorous Sound of that Trumpet strikes my Soul with more Horror, than thy hard Fists do my Ears with Pain, and methinks excite me to some new Adventure. With that the Goat-herd, who was as weary of beating, as of being beaten, immediately gave him a Truce; and the Knight once more getting on his Feet, directed his then not hasty Steps to the Place whence the mournful Sound seem'd to come, and presently saw a number of Men all in White, like Penitents, descending from a rising Ground. The real Matter was this: The People had wanted Rain for a whole Year together, wherefore they appointed Rogations, Processions and Disciplines throughout all that Country, to implore Heaven to open its Treasury, and show'r down Plenty upon 'em; and to this End, the Inhabitants of a Village near that Place came in Procession to a devout Hermitage built on one of the Hills which surrounded that Valley.

Don *Quixote* taking notice of the strange Habit of the Penitents, and never reminding himself that he had often seen the like before, fancy'd immediately it was some new Adventure, and he alone was to engage in it, as he was oblig'd by the Laws of Knight-Errantry; and that which the more increas'd his Frenzy, was his mistaking an Image which they carry'd (all cover'd with Black) for some great Lady, whom these miscreant and discourteous Knights, he thought were carrying away against her Will. As soon as this Whimsy took him in the Head, he mov'd with what Expedition he cou'd towards *Rozinante*, who was feeding up and down upon the Plains, and whipping off his Bridle from the Pommel, and his Target which hung hard by, he bridl'd him in an Instant; then taking his Sword from *Sancho*, he got in a Trice on *Rozinante's* Back; where bracing his Target, and addressing himself aloud to all there present, O valorous Company, cry'd he, you shall now perceive of how great Importance it is to Mankind, that such illustrious Persons as those who profess the Order of Knight-Errantry shou'd exist in the World; now, I say, you shall see by my freeing that noble Lady, who is there basely and barbarously carry'd away Captive, that Knight Adventurers ought to be held in the highest and greatest Estimation. So saying, he punch't *Rozinante* with his Heels for want of Spurs; and forcing him to a Hand-gallop (for 'twas never read in any part of this true History that *Rozinante* did ever run full-speed) he posted to encounter the Penitents, in spite of all the Curate, Canon and Barber cou'd do to hinder him; much less cou'd *Sancho Panza's* Outcries detain him. Master! Sir! Don *Quixote*! baul'd out the poor Squire, whither are you posting? are you bewitch'd? does the Devil drive and set you on, thus to run against the Church? Ah Wretch that I am! ———— See, Sir? That is a Procession of Penitents, and the Lady they carry is the Image of the immaculate Virgin, our blessed Lady. Take heed what you do, for at this Time it may be certainly said you are out of your Wits.———— But *Sancho* might as well have kept his Breath for another use, for the Knight was urg'd with so vehement a Desire to encounter the White Men, and release the mourning Lady, that he heard not a Syllable he said, or if he had he wou'd not have turn'd back, even at the King's express Command. At last being come near the Procession, and stopping *Rozinante*, that already had a great Desire to rest a little, in a dismal Tone, and with a hoarse Voice, Ho! cry'd he, you there, who cover your Faces, perhaps because you are asham'd of yourselves, and of the Crime you are now committing, give Heed and Attention to what I have to say!———— The first who stop'd at this Alarm, were those who carry'd the Image; when one of the four Priests that sung the Litanies, seeing the strange Figure that Don *Quixote* made, and the Leanness of *Rozinante*, with other Circumstances which he observ'd in the Knight sufficient to have forc'd Laughter, presently made him this Answer; Good Sir! if you have any thing to say to us speak it quickly; for these poor Men whom you see are very much tir'd, therefore we neither can, nor is it reasonable we shou'd, stand thus in Pain to hear any thing that can't be deliver'd in two Words. I will say it in one, reply'd Don *Quixote*, which is this; I charge you immediately to release that beautiful Lady, whose Tears and Looks full of Sorrow evidently shew you carry her away by Violence, and have done her some unheard of Injury. This do, or I, who was born to punish such Outrages, will not suffer you to advance one Step with her, till she is entirely possess'd of that Liberty she so earnestly desires, and so justly deserves. This last Speech made 'em all conclude that the Knight was certainly distracted, and caus'd a general Laughter: But this prov'd like Oil to Fire, and so inflam'd Don *Quixote*, that laying his Hand on his Sword, without more Words, he presently assaulted those who carry'd the Image. At the same time one of them quitting his Post, came to encounter our Hero with a wooden Fork, on which he supported the Bier whenever they made a Stand, and warding with it a weighty Blow which Don *Quixote* design'd and aim'd at him, the Fork was cut in two; but the other who had the remaining Piece in his Hand, return'd the Knight such a Thwack on his left Shoulder, that his Target not being able to resist such rustick Force, the poor unfortunate Don *Quixote* was struck to the Ground and miserably bruis'd.

Sancho Panza, who had follow'd him as fast as his Breath and Legs wou'd permit, seeing him fall, cry'd out to his Adversary to forbear striking him, urging that he was a poor inchanted Knight, and one who in his whole Life had never done any Man Harm. But 'twas not *Sancho's* Arguments that held the Country Fellow's Hands, the only Motive was, that he fear'd he had kill'd him, since he cou'd not perceive he stir'd either Hand or Foot; wherefore tucking his Coat up to his Girdle, with all possible Expedition, he scour'd over the Fields like a Greyhound. Mean while Don *Quixote's* Companions hasten'd to the Place where he lay, when those of the Procession, seeing them come running towards them, attended by the Officers of the *Holy Brotherhood* with their Cross-bows along with them, began to have Apprehensions of some Disaster from the approaching Party, wherefore drawing up in a Body about the Image, the Disciplinants lifting up their Hoods, and grasping fast their Whips, as the Priest did their Tapers, they expected the Assault with the greatest Bravery, resolving to defend themselves and offend their Enemy as long and as much as possible: But Providence had order'd the Matter much better than they cou'd hope; for while *Sancho*, who had thrown himself on his Master's Body, was lamenting his Loss, and the suppos'd Death of so noble and generous a Lord, in the most ridiculous manner that e'er was heard, the Curate of the Knight's Party was come up with the other who came in the Procession, and was immediately known by him, so that their Acquaintance put an End to the Fears which both Sides where in of an Engagement. Don *Quixote's* Curate in few Words acquainted the other with the Knight's Circumstances; whereupon he and the whole Squadron of Penitents went over to see whether the unfortunate Knight were living or dead, and heard *Sancho Panza* with Tears in his Eyes bewailing over his Master; O Flower of Knighthood, cry'd he, that with one single Perilous Knock art come to an untimely End! Thou Honour of thy Family, and Glory of all *La Mancha*! nay, and of the whole varsal World beside; which, now it has lost thee, will be overrun by Miscreants and Outlaws, who will no longer be afraid to be maul'd for their Misdeeds. O bountiful above all the *Alexanders* in the World! thou who hast rewarded me but for poor eight Months Service with the best Island that is wash'd by Salt Water! Thou who wert humble to the Proud and haughty to the Humble! Thou who durst undertake Perils, and patiently endure Affronts! Thou who wert in love, no Body knows why! True Pattern of Good Men, and Scourge of the Wicked, sworn Foe to all Reprobates! and to say all at once that Man can say, thou Knight-Errant!

The woful Accents of the Squire's Voice at last recall'd Don *Quixote* to himself; when after a deep Sigh, the first thing he thought of was his absent *Dulcinea*. O charming *Dulcinea*, cry'd he, the Wretch that lingers banish'd from thy Sight, endures far greater Miseries than this! And then looking on his faithful Squire, Good *Sancho*, said he, help me once more into the Inchanted Carr: for I am not in a Condition to press the Back of *Rozinante*: This Shoulder is all broke to pieces. With all my Heart, my good Lord, reply'd *Sancho*, and pray let me advise you to go back to our Village with these Gentlemen who are your special Friends. At home we may think of some other Journey that may be more profitable and honourable than this. With reason hast thou spoken, *Sancho*, reply'd Don *Quixote*: It will become our Wisdom to be unactive, till the malevolent Aspects of the Planets, which now reign, be over. This grave Resolution was highly commended by the Canon, Curate, and Barber, who had been sufficiently diverted by *Sancho Panza's* ridiculous Lamentation. Don *Quixote* was plac'd in the Wagon as before, the Processioners recover'd their former Order, and past on about their Business. The Goat-herd took his Leave of the whole Company. The Curate satisfy'd the Officers for their Attendance, since they would stir no farther. The Canon desir'd the Curate to send him an Account of Don *Quixote's* Condition from that time forward, having a mind to know whether his Frenzy abated or increas'd; and then took his leave, to continue his Journey. Thus the Curate, the Barber, Don *Quixote*, and *Sancho Panza* were left together; as also the good *Rozinante*, that bore all these Passages as patiently as his Master. The Waggoner then yoak'd his Oxen, and having set Don *Quixote* on a Truss of Hay, jogg'd on after his slow accustom'd Pace that way the Curate had directed. In six Days time they reach'd the Knight's Village. 'Twas about Noon when they enter'd the Town; and as this happen'd to be on a *Sunday*, all the People were in the Market place, thro' the middle of which Don *Quixote's* Cart must of necessity pass. Every Body was curious to know what was in it; and the People were strangely surpriz'd when they saw and knew their Townsman. While they were gaping and wondring, a little Boy ran to the Knight's House, and gave Intelligence to the House-keeper and Niece, that their Master and Uncle was return'd, and very lean, pale and frightful as a Ghost, stretch'd out at length on a Bundle of Hay, in a Waggon, and drawn along by a Team of Oxen.

'Twas a piteous Thing to hear the Wailings of those two poor Creatures; the Thumps too which they gave their Faces, with the Curses and Execrations they thunder'd out against all Books of Chivalry, were almost as numerous as their Sighs and Tears: But the height of their lamenting was when Don *Quixote* enter'd the Door. Under the Noise of his Arrival *Sancho Panza's* Wife made haste thither to enquire after her good Man, who, she was inform'd, went a Squiring with the Knight. As soon as ever she set Eyes on him, the Question she ask'd him was this: Is the Ass in Health, or no? *Sancho* answer'd, he was come back in better Health than his Master. Well, said she, Heaven be prais'd for the good News. But hark you, my Friend, continu'd she, what have you got by this new Squireship? Have you brought me home e'er a Gown or Petticoat, or Shoes for my Children? In troth, sweet Wife, reply'd *Sancho*, I have brought thee none of those things; I am loaded with better things. Ay, said his Wife, that's well. Pr'ythee let me see some of them fine things; for I vow I've a hugeous Mind to see 'em; the Sight of 'em will comfort my poor Heart, which has been like to burst with Sorrow and Grief ever since thou went'st away. I'll shew 'em thee when we come Home, return'd *Sancho*; in the mean time rest satisfy'd; for if Heaven see good that we shou'd once again go abroad in search of other Adventures, within a little time after, at my return, thou shalt find me some Earl, or the Governor of some Island; ay, of one of the very best in the whole World. I wish with all my Heart this may come to pass, reply'd the good Wife; for, by my troth Husband, we want it sorely. But what do you mean by that same Word Island? for believe me I don't understand it. All in good time Wife, said *Sancho*; Honey is not made for an Ass's Mouth: I'll tell thee what 'tis hereafter. Thou will be amaz'd to hear all thy Servants and Vassals ne'er speak a Word to thee without, an't please you Madam, an't like your Ladyship, and your Honour. What dost thou mean, *Sancho*, by Ladyship, Islands and Vassals, quoth *Joan Panza*, for so she was call'd, tho' her Husband and she were nothing a-kin, only 'tis a Custom in *La Mancha* that the Wives are there call'd by their Husband's Sirnames. Pr'ythee *Joan*, said *Sancho*, don't trouble thy Head to know these Matters all at once, and in a heap, as a Body may say: 'Tis enough I tell thee the Truth, therefore hold thy Tongue.* Yet, by the way, one thing I will assure thee, That nothing in the varsal World is better for an honest Man, than to be Squire to a Knight-Errant while he's hunting of Adventures. 'Tis true, most Adventures he goes about do not answer a Man's Ex-

* Cose la boca, *i.e. Sew up thy Mouth.*

pectation so much as he cou'd wish; for of a Hundred that are met with, Ninety Nine are wont to be crabbed and unlucky ones. This I know to my cost: I myself have got well kick'd and toss'd in some of 'em, and soundly drubb'd and belabour'd in others; yet, for all that, 'tis rare Sport to be a watching for strange Chances, to cross Forests, to search and beat up and down in Woods, to scramble over Rocks, to visit Castles, and take up Quarters in an Inn at pleasure, and all the while the Devil a Cross to pay.

These were the Discourses with which *Sancho Panza* and his Wife *Joan* entertained one another, while the House-keeper and Niece undrest Don *Quixote* and put him into his Bed; where he lay looking asquint on 'em, but cou'd not imagine where he was. The Curate charg'd the Niece to be very careful and tender of her Uncle, and to be very watchful, lest he shou'd make another Sally; telling her the trouble and charge he had been at to get him home. Here the Women began their Out-cries again: Here the Books of Knight-Errantry were again execrated and damn'd to the bottomless Pit. Here they begg'd those cursed bewitching *Chimeras* and Lies might be thrown down into the very Centre, to the hellish Father of 'em: For, they were still almost distracted with the Fear of losing their Master and Uncle again, so soon as ever he recover'd; which indeed fell out according to their Fear. But tho' the Author of this History has been very curious and diligent in his Inquiry after Don *Quixote's* Atchievements in his third Expedition in quest of Adventures, yet he cou'd never learn a perfect Account of 'em, at least from any Author of Credit: Fame and Tradition alone have preserv'd some particulars of 'em in the Memoirs and Antiquities of *La Mancha*; as, that after the Knight's third Sally, he was present at certain famous Tilts and Tournaments made in the City of *Saragosa*, where he met with Occasions worthy the Exercise of his Sense and Valour: But how the Knight dy'd, our Author neither cou'd nor ever shou'd have learn'd, if by good Fortune he had not met with an antient Physician, who had a leaden Box in his Possession, which, as he averr'd, was found in the Ruins of an old Hermitage, as it was rebuilding. In this Box were certain Scrolls of Parchment written in *Gothic* Caracters, but containing Verses in the *Spanish* Tongue, in which many of his noble Acts were sung, and *Dulcinea del Toboso's* Beauty celebrated, *Rozinante's* Figure describ'd, and *Sancho Panza's* Fidelity applauded. They likewise gave an Account of Don *Quixote's* Sepulchre, with several Epitaphs and Encomiums on his Life and Conversation. Those that cou'd be throughly read and transcrib'd, are here added by the faithful Author of this new and incomparable History; desiring no other Recompence or Reward of the Readers, for all his Labour and Pains, in searching all the numerous and old Records of *La Mancha* to perfect this matchless Piece, but that they will be pleas'd to give it as much Credit as judicious Men use to give to Books of Knight-Errantry, which are now a-days so generally taking. This is the utmost of his Ambition, and will be sufficient Satisfaction for him, and likewise encourage him to furnish'em with other matter of Entertainment; which, tho' possibly not altogether so true as this, yet it may be as well contriv'd and diverting. The first Words in the Parchment found in the Leaden Box are these.

Monicongo, Academick of *Argamasilla*, on
Don *Quixote's* Monument

EPITAPH
Here lies a doughty Knight,
Who, bruis'd, and ill in plight,
Jogg'd over many a Track
On Rozinante's *Back.*
    Close by him Sancho's *laid*
Whereat let none admire:
    He was a Clown, 'tis said,
But ne'er the worse a Squire.

Paniaguado, Academick of *Argamasilla*, on
Dulcinea del Toboso's Monument

EPITAPH
Here Dulcinea *lies,*
    Once brawny, plump and lusty;
But now to Death a Prize,
    And somewhat lean and musty.

For her the Country-Fry,
Like Quixote, long stood steady.
Well might she carry't high;
Far less has made a Lady.

These were the Verses that cou'd be read: As for the rest, the Characters being defac'd, and almost eaten away, they were deliver'd to a University Student, in order that he might give us his Conjectures concerning their Meaning. And we are inform'd, that after many Lucubrations, and much Pains, he has effected the Work, and intends to oblige the World with it, giving us at the same time some hopes of Don *Quixote's* third Sally.

Por si altro cantera con miglior pletro.

THE END OF THE FIRST PART

VOLUME TWO

CONTENTS

Author's Preface, p. 1.

PART II · BOOK V

CONTENTS

CONTENTS

CONTENTS

PART II · BOOK VI (continued)

THE AUTHOR'S PREFACE

BLESS *me! Reader, gentle or simple, or whatever you be, how impatiently by this time must you expect this Preface, supposing it to be nothing but revengeful Invectives against the Author of the second Don Quixote.* But I must beg your Pardon: for I shall say no more of him than every Body says, That* Tordesillas *is the Place where he was Begotten, and* Tarragona *the Place where he was Born; and though it be universally said, that even a Worm when trod upon, will turn again, yet I'm resolv'd for once to cross the Proverb. You perhaps now would have me call him Coxcomb, Fool and Mad-man; but I'm of another Mind; and so let his Folly be its own Punishment. But there is something which I cannot so silently pass over: He is pleas'd to upbraid me with my Age: Indeed had it been in the Power of Man to stop the Career of Time, I would not have suffer'd the Old Gentleman to have laid his Fingers on me. Then he reflectingly tells me of the Loss of one of my Hands: as if that Maim had been got in a scandalous or Drunken Quarrel in some Tavern, and not upon the most memorable Occasion† that either past or present Ages have beheld, and which perhaps Futurity will never parallel. If my Wounds do not redound to my Honour in the Thoughts of some of those that look upon 'em, they will at least secure me the Esteem of those that know how they were gotten. A Soldier makes a nobler Figure as he lies Bleeding in the Bed of Honour, than safe in an Inglorious Flight; and I am so far from being asham'd of the Loss of my Hand, that were it possible to recal the same Opportunity, I should think my Wounds but a small Price for the Glory of sharing in that Prodigious Action. The Scars in a Soldier's Face and Breast, are the Stars that by a Laudable Imitation guide others to the Port of Honour and Glory. Besides, it is not the Hand, but the Understanding of a Man, that may be said to Write; and those Years that he is pleas'd to quarrel with, always improve the latter.*

* A Person, who wrote himself a Native of *Tordesillas*, Published an Impertinent Book by that Name, Printed at *Tarragona*, while our Author was preparing his second Part for the Press.   † The Battle of *Lepanto*.

I

I am not wholly insensible of his Epithets of Ignorant and Envious; but I take Heaven to Witness, I never was acquainted with any Branch of Envy beyond a sacred, generous and ingenuous Emulation, which could never engage me to abuse a Clergyman, especially if made the more Reverend by a Post in the Inquisition; And if any such Person thinks himself affronted, as that Author seems to hint, he is mightily mistaken; for I have a Veneration for his Parts,* admire his Works, and have an awful Regard for the efficacious Virtue of his Office.

I must return this fine Dogmatical Gentleman my hearty Thanks for his Criticism upon my Novels: *He is pleas'd very judiciously to say, that they have more of Satyr than of Morality; and yet owns, that the* Novels *are good. Now I thought that if a Thing was good, it must be so in every respect.*

Methinks, Reader, I hear you blame me for shewing so little Resentment, and using him so gently; but pray consider, 'tis not good to bear too hard upon a Man that is so over-modest and so much in Affliction: for certainly this must needs be a miserable Soul; He has not the Face, poor Man! to appear in Publick, but, conscious of his wretched Circumstances, conceals his Name, and counterfeits his Country, as if he had committed Treason, or some other punishable Crime: Well then, if ever you should happen to fall into his Company, pray in Pity tell him from me, that I have not the least Quarrel in the World with him: For I am not Ignorant of the Temptations of Satan; and of all his Imps, the Scribbling Devil is the most Irresistible. When that Demon is got into a Man's Head, he takes the Possession for Inspiration, and, full of his false Ability, falls slapdash to Writing and Publishing, which gets him as much Fame from the World as he has Money from the Booksellers, and as little Money from the Booksellers as he has Fame from the World. But if he won't believe what you say, and you be dispos'd to be merry, pray tell him this Story.

Once upon a time, there was a Mad-man in Sevil *that hit upon one of the prettiest out-of-the-way Whims that ever Mad-man in this World was possess'd withal. He gets him a hollow Cane, small at one end, and catching hold of a Dog in the Street, or any where else, he clapp'd his Foot on one of the Cur's Legs,*

* He means *Lopez de Vega.*

*and holding up his Hind-Legs in his Hand, he fitted his Cane
to the Dog's Back-side, and blew him up as round as a Ball:
Then giving him a Thump or two on the Guts, and turning to
the By standers, who are always a great many upon such Occasions: Well, Gentlemen, said he, What do you think, Is it
such an easy Matter to blow up a Dog? And what think You,
Sir, Is it such an easy Matter to write a Book? But if this Picture be not like him, pray, honest Reader, tell him this other
Story of a Dog and a Mad-man.*

*There was a Mad-man at Cordova, who made it his Business
to carry about the Streets upon his Head, a huge Stone of a
pretty Conscionable Weight; and whenever he met with a Dog
without a Master, especially such a surly Cur as would stalk
up to his Nose, he very fairly dropp'd his Load all at once,
souse upon him: The poor Beast would howl, and growl, and
clapping his Tail between his Legs, limp'd away without so
much as looking behind him, for two or three Streets length at
least. The Mad-man, mightily pleas'd with his new Device,
serv'd every Dog that had Courage to look him in the Face, with
the same Sauce; till one Day it was his Fortune to meet with
a Sportsman's Dog, a Capmaker by Trade, though that's
neither here nor there. The Dog was mightily valu'd by his
Master, but that was more than the Mad-man knew; so slap
went the Stone upon the poor Dog. The Animal being almost
crush'd to Death, set up his Throat, and yelp'd most piteously;
insomuch that his Master knowing it was his Dog by the Howl,
runs out, and, touch'd with the Injury, whips up a Stick that
was at Hand, lets drive at the Mad-man, and belabours him
to some Purpose, crying out at every Blow, You Son of a Bitch,
abuse my Spaniel! You inhumane Rascal, did not you know
that my Dog was a Spaniel! And so thwack'd the poor Luna-
tick, till he had not a whole Bone in his Skin. At last he crawl'd
from under his Clutches, and it was a whole Month before he
could lick himself whole again. Nevertheless out he came once
more with his Invention, and heavier than the former; but coming by the same Dog again, though he had a Month's Mind to
give him t'other Dab; yet recollecting himself, and shrugging
up his Shoulders: No quoth he, I must have a care, this Dog's*

a Spaniel. In short, all Dogs he met, whether Mastiffs or Hounds, were downright Spaniels to Him ever after. Now the Moral of the Fable is this: This Author's Wit is the Mad-man's Stone, and 'tis likely he will be cautious how he let's it fall for the future.

One Word more, and I have done with him. Pray tell the mighty Man, That as to his Menaces of taking the Bread out of my Mouth, I shall only Answer him with a piece of an Old Song, God prosper long our Noble King, our Lives and Safeties all, —— *and so Peace be with him. Long Live the great* Conde de Lemos, *whose Humanity and celebrated Liberality sustain me under the most severe Blows of Fortune! And may the eminent Charity of the Cardinal of* Toledo, *make an eternal Monument to his Fame! Had I never Publish'd a Word, and were as many Books Published against me, as there are Letters in* Mingo Revulgo's *Poems; yet the Bounty of these two Princes, that have taken Charge of me, without any Soliciting, or Adulation, were sufficient in my Favour: And I think myself Richer and Greater in Their Esteem, than I would in any profitable Honour that can be Purchas'd at the ordinary rate of Advancement. The Indigent Man may attain their Favour, but the Vicious cannot. Poverty may partly Eclipse a Gentleman, but cannot totally Obscure him; and those Glimmerings of Ingenuity that peep through the Chinks of a narrow Fortune, have always gain'd the Esteem of the truly Noble and Generous Spirits.*

Now Reader, I have done with him and you, only give me leave to tell you, that this Second Part of Don Quixote, *which I now present you, is cut by the same hand, and of the same Piece with the First. Here you have the Knight once more fitted out, and at last brought to his Death, and fairly laid in his Grave; that no Body may presume to raise any more Stories of him. He has committed Extravagancies enow already, he's sorry for't, and that's sufficient. Too much of one thing clogs the Appetite, but Scarcity makes every thing go down.*

I forgot to tell you, that my Persiles *is almost finish'd, and expects to kiss your Hands in a little time; and the Second Part of the* Galatea *will shortly put in for the same Honour.*

4

THE LIFE & ATCHIEVEMENTS OF THE RENOWN'D DON QUIXOTE DE LA MANCHA: PART II · BOOK V · I: WHAT PASS'D BETWEEN THE CURATE, THE BARBER AND DON QUIXOTE, CONCERNING HIS INDISPOSITION

CID *Hamet Benengeli* relates in the Second Part of this History, and Don *Quixote's* third Sally, that the Curate and the Barber were almost a whole Month without giving him a Visit; lest, calling to mind his former Extravagancies, he might take Occasion to renew them. However, they fail'd not every Day to see his Niece and his House-keeper, whom they charged to treat and cherish him with great Care, and to give him such Diet as might be most proper to chear his Heart, and comfort his Brain, whence in all likelihood his Disorder wholly proceeded. They answer'd, that they did so, and would continue it to their utmost power; the rather because they observed, that sometimes he seemed to be in his right Senses. This News was very welcome to the Curate and the Barber, who looked on this Amendment as an Effect of Their Contrivance, in bringing him home in the Inchanted Waggon, as 'tis Recorded in the last Chapter of the first Part of this most important, and no less punctual, History. There-upon they resolved to give him a Visit, and make trial them-selves of the Progress of a Cure, which they thought almost impossible. They also agreed not to speak a Word of Knight-Errantry, lest they should endanger a Wound so lately closed and so tender. In short, they went to see him, and found him sit-ting up in his Bed in a Wastecoat of green Bays, and a red *Toledo* Cap on his Head: But the poor Gentleman was so wither'd and wasted, that he look'd like a meer Mummy. He received them very civilly, and when they enquired of his Health, gave them an account of his Condition, expressing himself very handsomly, and with a great deal of Judgment. After they had discours'd a while of several Matters, they fell at last on State-Affairs and Forms of Government, Correcting this Grievance, and Condemning that, Reforming one Custom, Rejecting an-

5

other, and Establishing new Laws, as if they had been the *Lycurgus's* or *Solons* of the Age; till they had refined and new-modelled the Common-wealth at such a rate, that they seemed to have clapped it into a Forge, and drawn it out wholly different from what it was before. Don *Quixote* reasoned with so much Discretion on every Subject, that his two Visitors now undoubtedly believed him in his right Senses.

His Niece and House-keeper were present at these Discourses; and hearing him give so many Marks of a sound Understanding, thought they could never return Heaven sufficient Thanks for so extraordinary a Blessing. But the Curate, who wondered at this strange Amendment, being resolved to try whether Don *Quixote* was perfectly recovered, thought fit to alter the Resolution he had taken to avoid entring into any Discourse of Knight-Errantry; and therefore began to talk to him of News, and among the rest that it was credibly reported at Court, that the Grand Signior was advancing with a vast Army, and no Body knew where the Tempest would fall; that all *Christendom* was alarmed, as it used to be almost every Year; and that the King was providing for the Security of the Coasts of *Sicily* and *Naples*, and the Island of *Malta*. His Majesty, said Don *Quixote*, acts the part of a most prudent Warrior, in putting his Dominions betimes in a Possture of Defence; for by that Precaution he prevents the Surprizes of the Enemy: but yet if My Counsel were to be taken in this Matter, I would advise another sort of Preparation, which I fancy his Majesty little thinks of at present. Now Heaven assist thee, poor Don *Quixote*, (said the Curate to himself, hearing this,) I am afraid thou art now tumbling from the Top of thy Madness to the very Bottom of Simplicity. Thereupon the Barber, who had presently made the same Reflection, desired Don *Quixote* to communicate to them this mighty Project of his; for, said he, Who knows but, after all, it may be one of those that ought only to find a Place in the List of impertinent Admonitions usually given to Princes. No, good Mr Trimmer, answer'd Don *Quixote*, my Project is not impertinent, but highly adviseable. I meant no harm in what I said, Sir, replied the Barber, only we generally find, most of these Projects that are offered to the King, are either Impracticable or Whimsical, or

6

tend to the Detriment of the King or Kingdom. But mine, said Don *Quixote*, is neither impossible nor ridiculous; far from that,'tis the most easy, the most thoroughly weighed, and the most concise, that ever can be devis'd by Man. Methinks you are too long before you let us know it, Sir, said the Curate. To deal freely with you, reply'd Don *Quixote*, I should be loth to tell it you here Now, and have it reach the Ear of some Privy-Counsellor Tomorrow, and so afterwards see the Fruit of my Invention reap'd by somebody else. As for me, said the Barber, I give you my Word here, and in the Face of Heaven, never to tell it, either to King, Queen, Rook, Pawn,* or Knight, or any earthly Man: An Oath I learn'd out of the Romance of the *Curate*, in the Preface to which he tells the King, who it was that robb'd him of his hundred Doublons, and his Ambling Mule. I know nothing of the Story, said Don *Quixote*; but I have reason to be satisfied with the Oath, because I'm confident Master Barber is an honest Man. Tho' he were not, said the Curate, I'll be his Surety in this matter, and will engage for him, that he shall no more speak of it, than if he were dumb, under what Penalty you please. And who shall answer for You, Mr Curate, answer'd Don *Quixote*? My Profession, reply'd the Curate, which binds me to Secrecy. Body of me then! cry'd Don *Quixote*, what has the King to do more, but to cause publick Proclamation to be made, enjoining all the Knights-Errant that are disper'd in this Kingdom, to make their Personal Appearance at Court upon a certain Day. For though but half a Dozen should meet, there may be some One among them, who even alone might be able to destroy the whole united Force of *Turky*. For pray observe well what I say, Gentlemen, and take me along with ye. Do you look upon it as a new thing for one Knight-Errant alone to Rout an Army of Two Hundred Thousand Men, with as much ease as if all of 'em join'd together had but one Throat, or were made of Sugar-Paste? You know how many Histories are full of these Wonders. Were but the Renown'd Don *Belianis* living now, with a Vengeance on me, (for I'll curse no Body else) or some Knight of the innumerable Race of *Amadis de Gaul*, and he met with these *Turks*, what a woful Condition would they be in! However,

* *In Allusion to the Game at Chess, so common then in* Spain.

I hope Providence will in Pity look down upon his People, and raise up, if not so prevalent a Champion as those of former Ages, at least, some one who may perhaps rival them in Courage; Heaven knows my meaning; I say no more. Alas! said the Niece, hearing this, I'll lay my Life, my Uncle has still a hankring after Knight-Errantry. I will die a Knight-Errant, cry'd Don *Quixote*, and so let the *Turks* land where they please, how they please, and when they please, and with all the Forces they can Muster; once more I say, Heaven knows my Meaning. Gentlemen, said the Barber, I beg leave to tell you a short Story of somewhat that happened at *Sevil*: Indeed it falls out as pat as if it had been made for our present Purpose, and so I have a great Mind to tell it. Don *Quixote* gave Consent, the Curate and the rest of the Company were willing to hear; and thus the Barber begun.

A certain Person being Distracted, was put into the Mad-House at *Sevil* by his Relations. He had studied the Civil-Law, and taken his Degrees at *Ossuna*; tho', had he taken them at *Salamanca*, many are of Opinion he would have been mad too. After he had lived some Years in this Confinement, he was pleas'd to fancy himself in his right Senses, and upon this Conceit wrote to the Archbishop, beseeching him with great Earnestness, and all the Colour of Reason imaginable, to release him out of his Misery by his Authority, since by the Mercy of Heaven he was wholly freed from any Disorder in his Mind; only his Relations, he said, kept him in still to enjoy his Estate, and designed, in spight of Truth, to have him Mad to his dying Day. The Archbishop, persuaded by many Letters which he wrote to him on that Subject, all penn'd with Sense and Judgment, order'd one of his Chaplains to enquire of the Governor of the House, into the Truth of the Matter, and also to discourse with the Party, that he might set him at large, in case he found him free from Distraction. Thereupon the Chaplain went, and having ask'd the Governor what Condition the Graduate was in? Was answer'd, that he was still mad; that sometimes indeed he would talk like a Man of excellent Sense, but presently after he would relapse into his former Extravagancies, which at least ballanced all his rational Talk, as he himself might find, if he pleas'd to discourse him. The Chaplain, being resolv'd to make the Experiment, went to the Madman, and convers'd with him above an Hour, and in all that time could not perceive the least Disorder in his Brain; far from that, he deliver'd himself with so much Sedateness, and gave such direct and pertinent Answers to every Question, that the Chaplain was oblig'd to believe him sound in his Understanding: nay, he went so far, as to make a plausible Complaint against his Keeper, alledging, that, for the Lucre of those Presents which his Relations sent him, he represented him to those who came to see him, as one who was still distracted, and had only now and then lucid Intervals; but that after all, his greatest Enemy was his Estate, the Possession of which his Relations being unwilling to resign, they would not acknowledge the Mercy of Heaven, that had once more made him a rational Creature. In short, he pleaded in such a manner, that the Keeper was suspected, his Relations were censured as Covetous and Unnatural, and he himself was thought Master of so much Sense, that the Chaplain resolv'd to take him along with him, that the Archbishop might be able to satisfy himself of the Truth of the whole Business. In order to this, the credulous Chaplain desir'd the Governor to give the Graduate the Habit which he had brought with him at his first coming. The Governor us'd all the Arguments which he thought might dissuade the Chaplain from his Design, assuring him, that the Man was still frantick and disorder'd in his Brain. But he could not prevail with him to leave the Madman there any longer, and therefore was forced to comply with the Archbishop's Order, and returned the Man his Habit, which was neat and decent.

Having now put off his Madman's Weeds, and finding himself in the Garb of rational Creatures, he begg'd of the Chaplain, for Charity's sake, to permit him to take leave of his late Companions in Affliction. The Chaplain told him he would bear him Company, having a mind to see the Mad-folks in the House. So they went up Stairs, and with them some other People that stood by. Presently the Graduate came to a kind of a Cage, where lay a Man that was outrageously Mad, though at that Instant still and quiet; and addressing himself to him, Brother, said he, have you any Service to command me? I am just going to my own House, Thanks be to Heaven, which, of its infinite Goodness and Mercy, has restored me to my Senses. Be of good Comfort, and put your Trust in the Father of Wisdom, who will, I hope, be as Merciful to You as he has been to Me. I'll be sure to send you some choice Victuals, which I would have you eat by all means; for I must needs tell you, that I have Reason to imagine, from my own Experience, that all our Madness proceeds from keeping our Stomachs empty of Food, and our Brains full of Wind. Take heart then, my Friend, and be chearful; for, this desponding in Misfortunes impairs our Health, and hurries us to the Grave. Just over against that Room lay another Mad-man, who having listen'd with an envious Attention to all this Discourse, starts up from an old Mat on which he lay stark naked; Who's that, cry'd he aloud, that's going away so well recover'd and so wise? 'Tis I, Brother, that am going, reply'd the Graduate; I have now no need to stay here any longer; for which Blessing I can never cease to return my humble and hearty Thanks to the infinite Goodness of Heaven. Doctor, quoth the Madman, have a Care what you say, and let not the Devil delude you. Stir not a Foot, but keep snug in your old Lodging, and save your self the cursed Vexation of being brought back to your Kennel. Nay, answer'd the other, I'll warrant you there will be no Occasion for my coming hither again,* I know I am perfectly well. You well! cry'd the Madman, we shall soon see that. —— Farewel, but by the Sovereign *Jupiter*, whose Majesty I represent on Earth, for this very Crime alone that *Sevil* has committed in setting thee at large, affirming, that thou art sound in thy Intellects, I will take such a severe Revenge on the whole City, that it shall be remember'd with Terror from Age to Age, for ever and aye; Amen. Dost thou not know, my poor Brainless Thing in a Gown, that this is in My Power? I that am the Thundering *Jove*, that grasp in my Hands the red-hot Bolts of Heaven, with which I keep the threatned World in awe, and might reduce it all to Ashes. But stay, I will commute the fiery Punishment, which this ig-

---

* *In the Original*, tornar a andar estationes: *i.e. to visit the Station-Churches again: Certain Churches, with Indulgences, appointed to be visited, either for Pardon of Sins, or for procuring Blessings. Mad-men, probably in their lucid Intervals, were oblig'd to this Exercise.*

norant Town deserves, into another: I will only shut up the Flood-Gates of the Skies, so that there shall not fall a Drop of Rain upon this City, nor on all the neighbouring Country round about it, for three Years together, to begin from the very Moment that gives Date to this my inviolable Execration. Thou free! thou well, and in thy Senses! and I here mad, distemper'd, and confined! By my Thunder, I will no more indulge the Town with Rain, than I would hang my self. As every one there was attentive to these loud and frantick Threats, the Graduate turn'd to the Chaplain, and taking him by the Hand; Sir, said he, let not that Mad-man's Threats trouble you. Never mind him; for, if he be *Jupiter*, and will not let it Rain, I am *Neptune*, the Parent and God of the Waters, and it shall Rain as often as I please, where-ever Necessity shall require it. However, answer'd the Chaplain, good Mr *Neptune*, 'tis not convenient to provoke Mr *Jupiter*: Therefore be pleas'd to stay here a little longer, and some other Time at convenient Leisure, I may chance to find a better Opportunity to wait on you, and bring you away. The Keeper and the rest of the Company could not forbear Laughing, which put the Chaplain almost out of Countenance. In short, Mr *Neptune* was disrob'd again, stay'd where he was, and there's an end of the Story.

Well, Mr Barber, said Don *Quixote*, and this is your Tale which you said came so pat to the present purpose, that you could not forbear telling it! Ah, Good-man Cut-beard, Good-man Cut-beard! How blind must He be that can't see through a Sieve! Is it possible your pragmatical Worship should not know that the Comparisons made between Wit and Wit, Courage and Courage, Beauty and Beauty, Birth and Birth, are always odious and ill taken? I am not *Neptune*, the God of the Waters, good Mr Barber: neither do I pretend to set up for a wise Man when I am not so. All I aim at, is only to make the World sensible how much they are to blame, in not labouring to revive those most happy Times, in which the Order of Knight-Errantry was in its full Glory. But indeed, this degenerate Age of ours is unworthy the Enjoyment of so great a Happiness, which former Ages could boast, when Knights-Errant took upon themselves the Defence of Kingdoms, the Protection of Damsels, the Relief of Orphans, the Punishment of Pride and Oppression, and the Reward of Humility. Most of your Knights now-a-days, keep a greater Rustling with their Sumptuous Garments of Damask, Gold Brocade, and other costly Stuffs, than with the Coats of Mail, which they should glory to wear. No Knight Now will lie on the hard Ground in the open Field, expos'd to the injurious Air, from Head to Foot inclos'd in ponderous Armour: Where are those Now, who, without taking their Feet out of the Stirrups, and only leaning on their Lances, like the Knights-Errant of Old, strive to disappoint invading Sleep, rather than indulge it? Where is that Knight, who, having first travers'd a spacious Forest, climb'd up a steep Mountain, and journey'd over a dismal barren Shore, wash'd by a turbulent tempestuous Sea, and finding on the Brink a little Skiff, destitute of Sails, Oars, Mast, or any kind of Tackling, is yet so bold as to throw himself into the Boat with an undaunted Resolution, and resign himself to the implacable Billows of the Main, that now mount him to the Skies, and then hurry him down to the most profound Recesses of the Waters; till, with his insuperable Courage, surmounting at last the Hurricane, even in its greatest Fury, he finds himself above Three Thousand Leagues from the Place where he first imbark'd, and, leaping ashore in a remote and unknown Region, meets with Adventures that deserve to be recorded, not only on Parchment but on *Corinthian* Brass. But now, alas! Sloth and Effeminacy triumph over Vigilance and Labour; Idleness over Industry; Vice over Vertue; Arrogance over Valour, and the Theory of Arms over the Practice, that true Practice, which only liv'd and flourish'd in those Golden Days, and among those Professors of Chivalry. For, where shall we hear of a Knight more Valiant and more Honourable than the Renowned *Amadis de Gaul*? Who more discreet than *Palmerin of England*? Who more Affable and Complaisant than *Tirante the White*? Who more Gallant than *Lisuarte* of *Greece*? Who more Cut and Hack'd, or a greater Cutter and Hacker than Don *Belianis*? Who more Intrepid than *Perion* of *Gaul*? Who more Daring than *Felixmarte* of *Hyrcania*? Who more Sincere than *Esplandian*? Who more Courteous than *Ciriongilio* of *Thrace*? Who more Brave than *Rodomont*? Who more

Prudent than King *Sobrino*? Who more Desperate than *Rin-aldo*? Who more Invincible than *Orlando*? And who more Agreeable or more Affable than *Rogero*, from whom, (according to *Turpin* in his Cosmography) the Dukes of *Ferrara* are descended? All these Champions, Mr Curate, and a great many more that I could mention, were Knights-Errant, and the very Light and Glory of Chivalry; now, such as these are the Men I would advise the King to employ; by which means his Majesty would be effectually serv'd, and freed from a vast Expence, and the *Turk* would tear his very Beard for Madness. For my part, I don't design to stay where I am, because the Chaplain will not fetch me out; tho', if *Jupiter*, as Mr Barber said, will send no Rain, here stands one that will, and can Rain, when he pleases. This I say, that Goodman Bason here may know I understand his meaning. Truly, good Sir, said the Barber, I meant no ill, Heaven is my Witness, my Intent was good: and therefore I hope your Worship will take nothing amiss. Whether I ought to take it amiss or no, reply'd Don *Quixote*, is best known to myself. Well, said the Curate, I have hardly spoken a Word yet; and before I go, I would gladly be eas'd of a Scruple, which Don *Quixote's* Words have started within me, and which grates and gnaws my Conscience. Mr Curate may be free with me in greater Matters, said Don *Quixote*, and so may well tell his Scruple; for 'tis no Pleasure to have a Burden upon one's Conscience. With your leave then, Sir, said the Curate, I must tell you, that I can by no means prevail with myself to believe, that all this Multitude of Knights-Errant, which your Worship has mention'd, were ever real Men of this World, and true substantial Flesh and Blood; but rather, that whatever is said of them, is all Fable and Fiction, Lies and Dreams, related by Men rather half asleep than awake. This is indeed another Mistake, said Don *Quixote*, into which many have been led, who do not believe there ever were any of those Knights in the World. And in several Companies, I have many Times had occasion to vindicate that manifest Truth from the almost universal Error, that is entertained to its Prejudice. Sometimes my Success has not been answerable to the Goodness of my Cause, though at others it has; being supported on the Shoulders of Truth, which is so apparent, that I dare almost say, I have seen *Amadis de Gaul* with these very Eyes. He was a tall comely Personage, of a good and lively Complexion, his Beard well ordered tho' black, his Aspect at once awful and affable: A Man of few Words, slowly provoked, and quickly pacify'd. And, as I have given you the Picture of *Amadis*, I fancy I could readily delineate all the Knights-Errant that are to be met with in History: For once apprehending, as I do, that they were just such as their Histories report them, 'tis an easy matter to guess their Features, Statures and Complexions, by the Rules of ordinary Philosophy, and the Account we have of their Atchievements, and various Humours. Pray, good Sir, quoth the Barber, how tall then might the Giant *Morgante* be? Whether there ever were Giants or no, answer'd Don *Quixote*, is a Point much controverted among the Learned. However, the Holy Writ, that cannot deviate an Atome from Truth, informs us there were some, of which we have an Instance in the account it gives us of that huge *Philistine, Goliah*, who was seven Cubits and a half high; which is a prodigious Stature. Besides, in *Sicily* Thigh-bones and Shoulder-bones have been found of so immense a Size, that from thence of Necessity we must conclude by the certain Rules of Geometry, that the Men to whom they belong'd were Giants, as big as huge Steeples. But, for all this, I cannot positively tell you how big *Morgante* was; though I am apt to believe he was not very tall, and that which makes me inclinable to believe so, is, that in the History which gives us a particular Account of his Exploits, we read, that he often us'd to lie under a Roof. Now if there were any House that could hold him, 'tis evident he could not be of an immense Bigness. That must be granted, said the Curate, who took some Pleasure in hearing him talk at that strange Rate, and therefore ask'd him what his Sentiments were of the Faces of *Rinaldo* of *Montalban, Orlando*, and the rest of the Twelve Peers of *France*, who had all of 'em been Knights-Errant? As for *Rinaldo*, answer'd Don *Quixote*, I dare venture to say, he was broad-fac'd, of a ruddy Complexion, his Eyes sparkling and large, very Captious, extremely Cholerick, and a Favourer of Robbers and profligate Fellows. As for *Rolando, Rotolando*, or *Orlando*, (for all these several Names are given him in

14

History) I am of Opinion and assure myself, that he was of middling Stature, broad-shoulder'd, somewhat bandy-legg'd, brown-visag'd, red bearded, very hairy on his Body, surly-look'd, no Talker, but yet very civil and good-humour'd. If *Orlando* was no handsomer than you tell us, said the Curate, no wonder the fair *Angelica* slighted him, and preferr'd the brisk, pretty, charming, downy-chinn'd young *Moor* before him; neither was she to blame to neglect the Roughness of the one for the soft Embraces of the other. That *Angelica*, Mr Curate, said Don *Quixote*, was a dissolute Damsel, a wild flirting wanton Creature, and somewhat capricious to boot. She left the World as full of her Impertinencies as of the Fame of her Beauty. She despis'd a thousand Princes, a thousand of the most valiant and discreet Knights in the whole World, and took up with a paltry beardless Page, that had neither Estate nor Honour, and who could lay Claim to no other Reputation, but that of being grateful, when he gave a Proof of his Affection to his Friend *Dardinel*. And indeed, even that great Extoller of her Beauty, the celebrated *Ariosto*, either not daring, or rather not desiring to rehearse what happen'd to *Angelica*, after she had so basely prostituted herself (which Passages doubtless could not be very much to her Reputation) that very *Ariosto*, I say, dropp'd her Character quite, and left her with these Verses,

> *Perhaps some better Lyre shall sing,*
> *How Love and She made him* Cataya's *King:*

And without doubt that was a Kind of a Prophecy; for the Denomination of *Vates*, which signifies a Prophet, is common to those whom we otherwise call Poets. Accordingly indeed this Truth has been made evident; for in Process of Time, a famous *Andalusian* Poet* wept for her, and celebrated her Tears in Verse; and another eminent and choice Poet of *Castile*† made her Beauty his Theme. But, pray Sir, said the Barber, among so many Poets that have written in that Lady *Angelica's* Praise, did none of 'em ever write a Satyr upon her? Had *Sacripante*, or *Orlando* been Poets, answer'd Don *Quixote*, I make no Question but they would have handled her to some Purpose; for

* Luis Barahona de Solo.   † Lopez de Vega.

there's nothing more common than for cast Poets, when disdain'd by their feign'd or false Mistresses, to revenge themselves with Satyrs and Lampoons; a Proceeding certainly unworthy a generous Spirit. However, I never yet did hear of any Defamatory Verses on the Lady *Angelica*, tho' she made so much Mischief in the World. That's a Miracle indeed, cry'd the Curate. But here they were interrupted by a Noise below in the Yard, where the Niece and the House-keeper, who had left 'em some time before, were very Obstreperous, which made 'em all hasten to know what was the Matter.

II: OF THE MEMORABLE QUARREL BETWEEN
SANCHO PANZA, AND DON QUIXOTE'S NIECE
AND HOUSE-KEEPER; WITH OTHER
PLEASANT PASSAGES

THE History informs us, that the Occasion of the Noise which the Niece and House-keeper made, was *Sancho Panza's* endeavouring to force his way into the House, while they at the same time held the Door against him to keep him out. What have you to do in this House, ye Paunch-gutted Squob, cry'd one of 'em? Go, go, keep to your own home, Friend. 'Tis all along of You, and no body else, that my poor Master is distracted, debauch'd, and carry'd a Rambling all the Country over. Thou House-keeper for the Devil, reply'd *Sancho*, 'Tis I that am distracted, debauch'd, and carry'd a rambling, and not Your Master. 'Twas He led me the Jaunt; so you are wide of the Matter. 'Twas He that inveigled me from my House and Home with his Colloguing, and saying he would give me an Island; which is not come yet, and I still wait for. May'st thou be choak'd with thy plaguy Islands, cry'd the Niece, thou cursed Paunch! And what are your Islands! Any thing to eat, Good-man Greedy-gut, ha? Hold you there, answer'd *Sancho*! They are not to eat, but to govern; and better Governments than any four Cities, or as many Heads of the King's best Corporations. For all that, quoth the House-keeper, thou com'st not within these Doors, thou Bundle of Wickedness, and Sackful of Roguery! Go, govern your own House! Work, you lazy Rogue! To the Plough, and never trouble your Jolter-Head about Islands or Oylets. The Curate and the Barber took a great deal of Pleasure to hear this Dialogue. But Don *Quixote* fearing lest *Sancho* should not keep within Bounds, but blunder out some Discoveries prejudicial to his Reputation, while he ripped up a Pack of little foolish Slander, call'd him in, and enjoined the Women to be silent. *Sancho* enter'd, and the Curate and the Barber took leave of Don *Quixote*, despairing of his Cure, considering how deep his Folly was rooted in his Brain, and how bewitch'd he was with his silly Knight-Errantry.

Well, Neighbour, said the Curate to the Barber, now do I expect nothing better of our Gentleman, than to hear shortly he is gone upon another Ramble. Nor I neither, answer'd the Barber; but I don't wonder so much at the Knight's Madness as at the Silliness of the Squire, who thinks himself so sure of the Island, that I fancy all the Art of Man can never beat it out of his Skull. Heaven mend 'em, said the Curate! In the mean time let us observe 'em; we shall find what will be the Event of the Extravagance of the Knight, and the Foolishness of the Squire: One would think they had been cast in one Mould; and indeed the Master's Madness without the Man's Impertinence, were not worth a Rush. Right, said the Barber, and now they are together, methinks I long to know what passes between 'em. I don't doubt but the two Women will be able to give an Account of that, for they are not of a Temper to withstand the Temptation of List'ning. Mean while Don *Quixote* having lock'd himself up with his Squire, they had the following Colloquy. I take it very ill, said he, *Sancho*, that you should report, as you do, that I enticed you out of your paltry Hut, when you know, that I myself left my own Mansion-House. We set out together, continued together, and travel'd together. We ran the same Fortune, and the same Hazards together. If thou hast been toss'd in a Blanket once, I have been batter'd and bruis'd a hundred times; and that's all the Advantage I have had above thee. And reason good, answer'd *Sancho*; for you yourself use to say, that Ill-luck and Cross-bitings are oftner to light on the Knights than on their Squires. Thou art mistaken, *Sancho*, reply'd Don *Quixote*; for the Proverb will tell thee, that *Quando caput dolet*, &c. Nay, quoth *Sancho*, I understand no Language but my own. I mean, said Don *Quixote*, that when the Head akes, all the Members partake of the Pain: So then, as I am thy Master, I am also thy Head; and as thou art my Servant, thou art one of my Members; it follows therefore, that I cannot be sensible of Pain, but thou too ought'st to be affected with it; and likewise, that nothing of Ill can befal thee, but I must bear a Share. Right, quoth *Sancho*; but yet when I, as a Limb of you, was toss'd in a Blanket, my Head was pleas'd to stay a't'other side of the wall, and saw me frisking in the air, without going Snacks in my bodily Trouble. Thou art greatly mis-

18

taken, *Sancho*, answer'd Don *Quixote*, if thou think'st I was not sensible of thy Sufferings: For I was then more tortur'd in Mind, than thou wast tormented in Body; but let us adjourn this Discourse till some other time, which doubtless will afford us an Opportunity to redress past Grievances. I pray thee tell me now what does the Town say of me? What do the Neighbours, what do the People think of me? What say the Gentry, and the better Sort? How do the Knights discourse of my Valour, my high Feats of Arms, and my courteous Behaviour? What Thoughts do they entertain of my Design, to raise from the Grave of Oblivion the Order of Knight-Errantry, and restore it to the World? In short, tell me freely and sincerely whatever thou hast heard; neither enlarg'd with flattering Commendations, nor lessen'd by any Omission of my Dispraise; for 'tis the Duty of faithful Servants to lay Truth before their Masters in its honourable Nakedness. And I would have thee know, *Sancho*, that if it were to appear before Princes, in its native Simplicity, and disrobed of the odious Disguise of Flattery, we should see happier Days; this Age would be chang'd into an Age of Gold, and former Times compared to this, would be call'd the Iron Age. Remember this, and be advis'd, that I may hear thee impart a faithful Account of these Matters. That I will, with all my Heart, answer'd *Sancho*, so your Worship will not take it amiss, if I tell what I have heard, just as I heard it, and neither better nor worse. Nothing shall provoke me to Anger, answer'd Don *Quixote*; speak freely, and without any Circumlocution. Why then, quoth *Sancho*, first and foremost you are to know, that the common People take you for a downright Mad-man, and me for one that has not much Guts in his Brains. The Gentry say, that not being content to keep within the Bounds of Gentility, you have taken upon you to be a *Don*, and set up for a Knight, and a Right Worshipful, with a small Vineyard, and two acres of land, a Tatter before, and another behind. The Knights, forsooth, take Pepper i'th' nose, and say, they don't like to have your small Gentry think themselves as good as they, especially your old-fashion'd Country Squires that mend and lamp-black their own Shoes, and darn ye their old black stockings themselves with a needleful of green silk. All this does not affect me, said Don *Quixote*, for I always wear good Clothes, and never have 'em patch'd. 'Tis true, they may be a little torn sometimes, but that's more with my armour than my long Wearing. As for what relates to your Prowess, (said *Sancho* proceeding) together with your Feats of Arms, your courteous Behaviour, and your Undertaking, there are several Opinions about it. Some say he's mad, but a pleasant Sort of a Madman; others say, he's Valiant, but his Luck is naught; others, he's courteous, but damn'd impertinent. And thus they spend so many Verdicts upon you, and take us both so to Pieces, that they leave neither you nor me a sound Bone in our Skins. Consider, *Sancho*, said Don *Quixote*, that the more eminently Virtue shines, the more 'tis expos'd to the Persecution of Envy. Few or none of those famous Heroes of Antiquity, could escape the venomous Arrows of Calumny. *Julius Cæsar*, that most courageous, prudent, and valiant Captain, was mark'd, as being Ambitious, and neither so clean in his Apparel, nor in his Manners, as he ought to have been. *Alexander*, whose mighty Deeds gain'd him the Title of the Great, was charg'd with being addicted to Drunkenness. *Hercules*, after his many heroick Labours, was accus'd of Voluptuousness and Effeminacy. Don *Galaor*, the Brother of *Amadis de Gaul*, was taxed with being Quarrelsome, and his Brother himself with being a Whining, Blubbering Lover. And therefore, my *Sancho*, since so many Worthies have not been free from the Assaults of Detraction, well may I be content to bear my Share of that Epidemical Calamity, if it be no more than thou hast told me now. Body of my Father! quoth *Sancho*, there's the Business; you say well, if this were all: But they don't stop here. Why, said Don *Quixote*, what can they say more? More, cry'd *Sancho*, Oddsnigs! we are still to flea the Cat's Tail. You have had nothing yet but Apple-pies and Sugar-plumbs. But if you have a Mind to hear all those Slanders and Backbitings that are about Town concerning your Worship, I'll bring you one anon that shall tell you every kind of thing that's said of you, without baiting you an ace on't! *Bartholomew Carrasco's* Son I mean, who has been a Scholard at the Versity of *Salamanca*, and is got to be a Batchelor of Arts. He came last Night, you must know, and as I went to bid him welcome Home, he told me, that your Worship's History is already in Books, by the Name of the most Renowned Don *Quixote de la Mancha*. He says I am in too, by my own Name of *Sancho Pança*, and eke also my Lady *Dulcinea del Toboso*; nay, and many things that pass'd betwixt nobody but us two, which I was amaz'd to hear, and could not for my Soul imagine, how the Devil he that set 'em down cou'd come by the Knowledge of 'em. I dare assure thee, *Sancho*, said Don *Quixote*, that the Author of our History must be some Sage In-chanter, and one of those from whose universal Knowledge, none of the things which they have a Mind to record can be conceal'd. How should he be a Sage and an Inchanter, quoth *Sancho*? The Batchelor *Sampson Carrasco*, for that's the Name of my Tale's Master, tells me, he that wrote the History is call'd *Cid Hamet Berengenas*.* That's a *Moorish* Name, said Don *Quixote*. Like enough, quoth *Sancho*; your *Moors* are main Lovers of *Berengenas*. Certainly, *Sancho*, said Don *Quix-ote*, thou art mistaken in the Surname of that *Cid*, that Lord, I mean; for *Cid* in *Arabic* signifies Lord. That may very well be, answer'd *Sancho*. But if you'll have me fetch you the young Scholard, I'll fly to bring him hither. Truly, Friend, said Don *Quixote*, thou wilt do me a particular Kindness; for what thou hast already told me, has so fill'd me with Doubts and Expecta-tions, that I shall not eat a Bit that will do me good till I am in-form'd of the whole Matter. I'll go and fetch him, said *Sancho*. With that, leaving his Master, he went to look for the Batche-lor, and having brought him along with him a-while after, they all had a very pleasant Dialogue.

* *A Sort of Fruit in Spain, which they boil with or without Flesh, it was brought over by the* Moors. *Sancho makes this Blunder, being more us'd to this Fruit than hard Names. He meant* Benengeli.

III: THE PLEASANT DISCOURSE BETWEEN DON QUIXOTE, SANCHO PANÇA, AND THE BATCHELOR SAMPSON CARRASCO

DON *Quixote* remain'd strangely pensive, expecting the Batchelor *Carrasco*, from whom he hop'd to hear News of himself, recorded and printed in a Book, as *Sancho* had informed him: He could not be persuaded that there was such a History extant, while yet the Blood of those Enemies he had cut off, had scarce done reeking on the Blade of his Sword; so that they could not have already finish'd and printed the History of his mighty Feats of Arms. However, at last he concluded, that some learned Sage had, by the way of Inchantment, been able to commit them to the Press, either as a Friend, to extol his heroick Atchievements above the noblest Performances of the most famous Knights-Errant; or as an Enemy, to sully and annihilate the Lustre of his great Exploits, and debase 'em below the most inferior Actions that ever were mention'd of any of the meanest Squires. Though (thought he to himself) the Actions of Squires were never yet recorded; and after all, if there were such a Book printed, since it was the History of a Knight-Errant, it could not choose but be Pompous, Lofty, Magnificent, and Authentick. This Thought yielded him a-while some small Consolation; but then he relaps'd into melancholick Doubts and Anxieties, when he consider'd that the Author had given himself the Title of *Cid*, and consequently must be a *Moor*. A Nation from whom no Truth could be expected, they all being given to impose on others with Lies and fabulous Stories, to falsify and counterfeit, and very fond of their own Chimera's. He was not less uneasy, lest that Writer should have been too lavish in treating of his Amours, to the Prejudice of his Lady *Dulcinea del Toboso's* Honour. He earnestly wish'd, that he might find his own inviolable Fidelity celebrated in the History, and the Reservedness and Decency which he had always so religiously observed in his Passion for her; slighting Queens, Empresses, and Damsels of every Degree for her Sake, and suppressing the dangerous Impulses of natural Desire. *Sancho* and *Carrasco* found him thus agitated and perplex'd with a thousand melancholick Fancies, which yet did not hinder him from receiving the Stranger with a great deal of Civility.

This Batchelor, though his Name was *Sampson*, was none of the biggest in Body, but a very great Man at all manner of Drollery; he had a pale and bad Complexion, but good Sense. He was about four and twenty Years of Age, round Visag'd, flat Nos'd, and wide Mouth'd, all Signs of a malicious Disposition, and of one that would delight in nothing more than in making Sport for himself, by ridiculing others; as he plainly discover'd when he saw Don *Quixote*. For, falling on his Knees before him, admit me to kiss your Honour's Hand, cry'd he, most noble Don *Quixote*; for by the Habit of St *Peter*, which I wear, (though indeed I have as yet taken but the Four first of the Holy Orders) you are certainly one of the most renowned Knights-Errant that ever was, or ever will be, through the whole Extent of the habitable Globe. Blest may the Sage *Cid Hamet Benengeli* be, for enriching the World with the History of your mighty Deeds; and more than blest, that curious Virtuoso, who took care to have it translated out of the *Arabick* into our vulgar Tongue, for the universal Entertainment of Mankind! Sir, said Don *Quixote*, making him rise, is it then possible that my History is extant, and that is was a *Moor*, and one of the Sages that penn'd it? 'Tis so notorious a Truth, said the Batchelor, that I do not in the least doubt but at this Day there have already been published above twelve thousand Copies of it. *Portugal*, *Barcelona*, and *Valencia*, where they have been printed, can witness that, if there were Occasion. 'Tis said, that 'tis also now in the Press at *Antwerp*. And I verily believe there's scarce a Language into which it is not to be translated. Truly, Sir, said Don *Quixote*, one of the things that ought to yield the greatest Satisfaction to a Person of eminent Virtue, is to live to see himself in good Reputation in the World, and his Actions published in Print. I say, in good Reputation, for otherwise there's no Death but would be preferable to such a Life. As for a good Name and Reputation, reply'd *Carrasco*, your Worship has gain'd the Palm from all the Knights-Errant that ever liv'd: For, both the *Arabian* in his

History, and the Christian in his Version, have been very industrious to do Justice to your Character: your peculiar Galantry; your Intrepidity and Greatness of Spirit in confronting Danger; your Constancy in Adversities, your Patience in suffering Wounds and Afflictions, your Modesty and Continence in that Amour, so very *Platonick*, between your Worship and my Lady *Donna Dulcinea del Toboso*. Odsbobs! cry'd *Sancho*, I never heard her call'd so before; that *Donna* is a new Kick; for she us'd to be call'd only my Lady *Dulcinea del Toboso*; in that, the History is out already. That's no material Objection, said *Carrasco*. No, certainly, added Don *Quixote*: But pray, good Mr Batchelor, on which of all my Adventures does the History seem to lay the greatest Stress of Remark? As to that, answer'd *Carrasco*, the Opinions of Men are divided according to their Tastes: Some cry up the Adventure of the Windmills, which appear'd to your Worship so many *Briareus's* and Giants. Some are for that of the Fulling-mills: Others stand up for the Description of the two Armies, that afterwards prov'd two Flocks of Sheep. Others prize most the Adventure of the dead Corps that was carrying to *Segovia*. One says, that none of them can compare with that of the Galley-Slaves; another, that none can stand in Competition with the Adventure of the *Benedictine* Giants, and the Valorous *Biscayner*. Pray, Mr Batchelor, quoth *Sancho*, is there nothing said of that of the *Yanguesians*, an't please you, when our precious *Rozinante* was so maul'd for offering to take a little carnal Recreation with the Mares? There's not the least thing omitted, answer'd *Carrasco*; the Sage has inserted all with the nicest Punctuality imaginable; so much as the Capers which honest *Sancho* fetch'd in the Blanket. I fetch'd none in the Blanket, quoth *Sancho*, but in the Air; and that too, oftner than I cou'd ha' wish'd, the more my Sorrow. In my Opinion, said Don *Quixote*, there is no manner of History in the World, where you shall not find Variety of Fortune, much less any Story of Knight-Errantry, where a Man cannot always be sure of good Success. However, said *Carrasco*, some who have read your History, wish that the Author had spar'd himself the Pains of registering some of that infinite Number of Drubs which the Noble Don *Quixote* receiv'd. There lies the Truth of the History, quoth *Sancho*.

Those things in human Equity, said Don *Quixote*, might very well have been omitted; for Actions that neither impair nor alter the History, ought rather to be bury'd in Silence than related, if they redound to the Discredit of the Hero of the History. Certainly *Æneas* was never so pious as *Virgil* represents him, nor *Ulysses* so prudent as he is made by *Homer*. I am of your Opinion, said *Carrasco*; but 'tis one thing to write like a Poet, and another thing to write like an Historian. 'Tis sufficient for the first to deliver Matters as they ought to have been, whereas the last must relate 'em as they were really transacted, without adding or omitting any thing, upon any Pretence whatever. Well, quoth *Sancho*, if this same *Moorish* Lord be once got into the Road of Truth, a hundred to one but among my Master's Rib-roastings he has not forgot mine: for they never took Measure of his Worship's Shoulders, but they were pleas'd to do as much for my whole Body: But 'twas no Wonder; for 'tis his own Rule, that if once his Head akes, every Limb must suffer too. *Sancho*, said Don *Quixote*, you are an arch unlucky Knave; upon my Honour you can find Memory when you have a Mind to have it. Nay, quoth *Sancho*, though I were minded to forget the Rubs and Drubs I ha' suffer'd, the Bumps and Tokens that are yet fresh on my Ribs would not let me. Hold your Tongue, said Don *Quixote*, and let the Learned Batchelor proceed, that I may know what the History says of me. And of me too quoth *Sancho*, for they tell me I am one of the top Parsons in't. Persons, you should say, *Sancho*, said *Carrasco*, and not Parsons. Hey-day! quoth *Sancho*, have we got another Corrector of hard Words. If this be the Trade, we shall never ha' done. May I be curs'd, said *Carrasco*, if you be not the second Person in the History, honest *Sancho*; nay, and some there are who had rather hear you talk than the best there; though some there are again that will say, you were horribly credulous, to flatter yourself with having the Government of that Island, which your Master here present promis'd you. While there's Life there's Hope, said Don *Quixote*: When *Sancho* is grown mature with Time and Experience, he may be better qualify'd for a Government than he is yet. Odsbodikins! Sir, quoth *Sancho*, if I ben't fit to govern an Island at these Years, I shall never be a Governor, though I live to the

Years of *Methusalem*; but there the Mischief lies, we have Brains enough, but we want the Island. Come *Sancho*, said Don *Quixote*, hope for the best; trust in Providence; all will be well, and perhaps better than you imagine: But know, there's not a Leaf on any Tree that can be moved without the Permission of Heaven. That's very true, said *Carrasco*; and I dare say, *Sancho* shall not want a Thousand Islands to govern, much less one; that is, if it be Heaven's Will. Why not, quoth *Sancho*? I ha' seen Governors in my time, who, to my thinking, could not come up to me passing the Sole of my Shoes, and yet forsooth, they call'd them Your Honour, and they eat their Victuals all in Silver. Ay, said *Carrasco*, but these were none of your Governors of Islands, but of other easy Governments: Why, Man, these ought, at least, to know their Grammar. *Gramercy*, for that, quoth *Sancho*, give me but a *Grey Mare** once, and I shall know her well enough, I'll warrant ye. But leaving the Government in the Hands of him that will best provide for me, I must tell you, Master Batchelor *Sampson Carrasco*, I am huge glad, that as your Author has not forgot me, so he has not given an ill character of me; for by the Faith of a trusty Squire, had he said any thing that did not become an *Old Christian*† as I am, I had rung him such a Peal, that the Deaf should have heard me. That were a Miracle, said Carrasco. Miracle me no Miracles, cry'd *Sancho*; let every Man take care how he talks, or how he writes of other Men, and not set down at random, higgle-de piggledy, whatever comes into his Noddle. One of the Faults found with this History, said *Carrasco*, is, that the Author has thrust into't a Novel, which he calls, *The Curious Impertinent*; not that 'tis ill writ; or the Design of it to be mislik'd; but because it is not in its right Place, and has no Coherence with the Story of Don *Quixote*. I'll lay my Life, quoth *Sancho*, the Son of a Mungrel has made a Gallimawfry of it all. Now, said Don *Quixote*, I perceive that he who attempted to write my History, is not one of the Sages, but some ignorant prating Fool, who would needs

---

* *This Gingle of the Words* Grammar, Gramercy, *and* Grey Mare, *is done in Conformity to the Original, which wou'd not admit of a literal Translation.*   † *A Name by which the* Spaniards *desire to be distinguish'd from the* Jews *and* Moors.

be meddling and set up for a Scribbler, without the least Grain of Judgment to help him out; and so he has done like *Orbaneja*, the Painter of *Ubeda*; who being ask'd what he painted, answer'd, As it may hit; and when he had scrawl'd out a mis-shapen Cock, was forc'd to write underneath in *Gothick* Letters, *This is a Cock*. At this rate, I believe he has perform'd in my History, so that it will require a Commentary to explain it. Not at all, answer'd *Carrasco*; for he has made every thing so plain, that there's not the least thing in't but what any one may understand. Children handle it, Youngsters read it, grown Men understand it, and old People applaud it. In short, 'tis universally so thumb'd, so glean'd, so studied, and so known, that if the People do but see a Lean Horse, they presently cry, There goes *Rozinante*. But none apply themselves to the reading of it more than your Pages: There's ne'er a Nobleman's Anti-chamber where you shan't find a Don *Quixote*. No sooner has one laid it down, but another takes it up. One asks for it here, and there 'tis snatch'd up by another. In a Word, 'tis esteem'd the most pleasant and least dangerous Diversion that ever was seen, as being a Book that does not betray the least indecent Expression, nor so much as a profane Thought. To write after another Manner, said Don *Quixote*, were not to write Truth but Falshood; and those Historians who are guilty of that, should be punish'd like those who counterfeit the Lawful Coin.* But I cannot conceive what could move the Author to stuff his History with foreign Novels and Adventures, not at all to the Purpose; while there was a sufficient Number of my own to have exercis'd his Pen. But without doubt we may apply the Proverb, *With Hay or with Straw*,† &c. for verily, had he altogether confin'd himself to my Thoughts, my Sighs, my Tears, my laudable Designs, my Adventures, he might yet have swell'd his Book to as great a Bulk, at least, as all *Tostatus's*‡ Works. I have also Reason to believe, Mr Batchelor, that to compile a History, or write any Book whatsoever, is a more difficult Task than Men imagine. There's need of a vast

* *Clippers and Coiners in* Spain, *are burnt.*   † *The Proverb entire is,* De Paja o de heno el jergon lleno, *i.e.* The Bed *or* Tick full of Hay or Straw, *so it be fill'd, no matter with what.*   ‡ *A famous* Spaniard *who wrote many Volumes of Divinity.*

Judgment, and a ripe Understanding. It belongs to none but great Genius's to express themselves with Grace and Elegance, and draw the Manners and Actions of others to the Life. The most artful Part in a Play is the Fool's, and therefore a Fool must not pretend to write it. On the other Side, History is in a Manner a sacred Thing, so far as it contains Truth; for where Truth is, the Supreme Father of it may also be said to be, at least, in as much as concerns Truth. However, there are Men that will make you Books, and turn 'em loose into the World, with as much Dispatch as they would do a Dish of Fritters. There's no Book so bad, said the Batchelor, but something good may be found in it. That's true, said Don *Quixote*; yet 'tis a common thing for Men, who have gain'd a very great Reputation by their Writings, before they printed them, to lose it afterwards quite, or, at least, the greatest Part. The Reason's plain, said *Carrasco*; their Faults are more easily discover'd, after their Books are printed, as being then more read, and more narrowly examin'd, especially if the Author had been much cry'd up before, for then the Severity of the Scrutiny is so much the greater. All those that have rais'd themselves a Name by their Ingenuity, great Poets and celebrated Historians, are most commonly, if not always, envy'd by a Sort of Men, who delight in censuring the Writings of others, though they never publish any of their own. That's no Wonder, said Don *Quixote*, for there are many Divines, that could make but very dull Preachers, and yet are very quick at finding Faults and Superfluities in other Mens Sermons. All this is Truth, reply'd *Carrasco*; and therefore I could wish these Censurers would be more merciful and less scrupulous, and not dwell ungenerously upon small Spots, that are in a Manner but so many Atoms on the Face of the clear Sun which they murmur at. And if *aliquando bonus dormitat Homerus*, let 'em consider how many Nights he kept himself awake to bring his noble Works to Light, as little darken'd with Defects as might be. Nay, many times it may happen that what is censur'd for a Fault, is rather an Ornament, like Moles that sometimes add to the Beauty of the Face. And when all is said, he that publishes a Book runs a very great Hazard, since nothing can be more impossible than to compose one that may secure the Approbation of every

Reader. Sure, said Don *Quixote*, that which treats of me can have pleas'd but few. Quite contrary, said *Carrasco*; for as *Stultorum infinitus est numerus*, so an infinite Number has admir'd your History. Only some there are who have tax'd the Author with want of Memory or Sincerity; because he has forgot to give an Account who it was that stole *Sancho's* Dapple; for that Particular is not mention'd there; only we find by the Story that it was stol'n; and yet, by and by, we find him riding the same Ass again, without any previous Light given us into the Matter. Then they say, that the Author forgot to tell the Reader, what *Sancho* did with those Hundred Pieces of Gold he found in the Portmanteau in *Sierra Morena*; for there's not a Word said of 'em more; and many People have a great mind to know what he did with 'em, and how he spent 'em; which is one of the most material Points in which the Work is defective. Master *Sampson*, quoth *Sancho*, I an't now in a Condition to cast up the Accompts, for I'm taken ill of a sudden with such a Wambling in the Stomach, and find myself so maukish, that if I don't see and fetch it up with a Sup or two of good old Bub, I shall waste like the Snuff of a farthing Candle.* I have that Cordial at home, and my Chuck stays for me. When I have had my Dinner, I am for you, and will satisfy you, or any Man that wears a Head, about any thing in the World, either as to the Loss of the Ass, or the laying out of those same Pieces of Gold. This said, without a Word more, or waiting for a Reply, away he went. Don *Quixote* desir'd, and intreated the Batchelor to stay and do Penance with him. The Batchelor accepted his Invitation, and stay'd. A Couple of Pigeons were got ready to mend their Commons. All Dinner-time they discours'd about Knight-Errantry, *Carrasco* humouring him all the while. After they had slept out the Heat of the Day, *Sancho* came back, and they renew'd their former Discourse.

* I shall be stuck upon St Lucia's Thorn, *suppos'd to be a Cant Phrase for the* Rack; *for which the Royal* Spanish *Dictionary produces no other Voucher but this Passage.*

IV: SANCHO PANÇA SATISFIES THE BATCHELOR SAMPSON CARRASCO IN HIS DOUBTS AND QUERIES: WITH OTHER PASSAGES FIT TO BE KNOWN AND RELATED

SANCHO return'd to Don *Quixote's* House, and beginning again where he left off; Now, quoth he, as to what Master *Sampson* wanted to know; that is, when, where, and by whom my Ass was stol'n: I answer, That the very Night that we march'd off to the *Sierra Morena*, to avoid the Hue and Cry of the Holy Brotherhood, after the rueful Adventure of the Galley Slaves, and that of the dead Body that was carrying to *Segovia*, my Master and I slunk into a Wood; where he leaning on his Lance and I, without alighting from *Dapple*, both sadly bruis'd and tir'd with our late Skirmishes, fell fast asleep, and slept as soundly as if we had had Four Feather-beds under us; but I especially was as serious at it as any Dormouse; so that the Thief, whoever he was, had Leisure enough to clap four Stakes under the four Corners of the Pack-Saddle, and then leading away the Ass from between my Legs, without being perceiv'd by me in the least, there he fairly left me mounted. This is no new thing, said Don *Quixote*, nor is it difficult to be done: With the same Stratagem *Sacripante* had his Steed stol'n from under him by that notorious Thief *Brunelo* at the Siege of *Albraca*. It was broad Day, said *Sancho*, going on, when I, half awake and half asleep, began to stretch myself in my Pack-Saddle; but with my stirring, down came the Stakes, and down came I souse, with a confounded Squelch on the Ground. Presently I look'd for my Ass, but no Ass was to be found. O how thick the Tears trickled from my Eyes, and what a piteous Moan I made! If he that made our History has forgot to set it down Word for Word, I wou'd not give a Rush for his Book, I'll tell him that. Some time after, I can't just tell you how long it was, as we were going with my Lady the Princess *Micomicona*, I knew my Ass again, and he that rid him, though he went like a Gipsy; and who shou'd it be, d'ye think, but *Gines de Passamonte*, that Son of Mischief, that Crack-

Rope, whom my Master and I sav'd from the Galleys. The Mistake does not lie there, said *Carrasco*; but only that the Author sets you upon the same Ass that was lost, before he gives an Account of his being found. As to that, reply'd *Sancho*, I don't know very well what to say. If the Man made a Blunder, who can help it? But mayhaps 'twas a Fault of the Printer. I make no question of that, said *Carrasco*; but pray, what became of the Hundred Pieces? Were they sunk? I fairly spent 'em on myself, quoth *Sancho*, and on my Wife and Children; they help'd me to lay my Spouse's Clack, and made her take so patiently my rambling and trotting after my Master Don *Quixote*; for had I come back with my Pockets empty, and without my Ass, I must have look'd for a rueful Greeting. And now if you have any more to say to me, here am I, ready to answer the King himself; for what has any Body to meddle or make whether I found or found not, or spent or spent not? If the Knocks and Swadlings that have been bestow'd on my Carcase in our Jaunts, were to be rated but at Three *Maravedis* a piece, and I to be satisfy'd Ready Cash for every one, a Hundred Pieces of Gold more would not pay for half of them; and therefore let every Man lay his Finger on his Mouth, and not run hand over head, and mistake Black for White, and White for Black; for every Man is as Heaven made him, and sometimes a great deal worse. Well, said the Batchelor, if the Author print another Edition of the History, I'll take special Care he shan't forget to insert what honest *Sancho* has said, which will make the Book as good again. Pray, good Mr Batchelor, ask'd Don *Quixote*, are there any other Emendations requisite to be made in this History? Some there are, answer'd *Carrasco*, but none of so much Importance as those already mention'd. Perhaps the Author promises a Second Part, said Don *Quixote*? He does, said *Carrasco*; but he says he cannot find it, neither can he discover who has it: So that we doubt whether it will come out or no, as well for this Reason, as because some People say that *Second Parts* are never worth any thing; others cry, there's enough of Don *Quixote* already: However, many of those that love Mirth better than Melancholy, cry out, Give us more *Quixotery*; let but Don *Quixote* appear, and *Sancho* talk, be it what it will, we are satisfy'd. And how stands the

Author affected? said the Knight. Truly, answered *Carrasco*,
as soon as ever he can find out the History, which he is now
looking for with all imaginable Industry, he is resolved to send
it immediately to the Press, though more for his own Profit
than through any Ambition of Applause. What, quoth *Sancho*, does he design to do it to get a Penny by it? nay, then we
are like to have a rare History indeed; we shall have him botch
and whip it up, like your Taylors on *Easter-Eve*, and give us
a Huddle of Flim-flams that will never hang together; for your
hasty Work can never be done as it should be. Let Mr *Moor*
take care how he goes to work; for, my Life for his, I and my
Master will stock him with such a Heap of Stuff in Matter of
Adventures and odd Chances, that he'll have enough not only
to write a Second Part, but an Hundred. The poor Fellow, belike, thinks we do nothing but sleep on a Hay-mow; but let
us once put Foot into the Stirrup, and he'll see what we are
about: This at least I'll be bold to say, that if my Master would
be rul'd by me, we had been in the Field by this time, undoing
of Misdeeds and righting of Wrongs, as good Knights-Errant
use to do. Scarce had *Sancho* made an end of his Discourse,
when *Rozinante's* Neighing reach'd their Ears. Don *Quixote*
took it for a lucky Omen, and resolv'd to take another Turn
within three or four Days. He discover'd his Resolutions to the
Batchelor, and consulted him to know which way he shou'd
steer his Course. The Batchelor advis'd him to take the Road
of *Saragosa* in the Kingdom of *Arragon*, a solemn Tournament
being shortly to be perform'd at that City on St *George's* Festival; where by worsting all the *Arragonian* Champions he
might win immortal Honour, since to out-tilt them would be
to out-rival all the Knights in the Universe. He applauded his
noble Resolution, but withal admonish'd him not to be so desperate in exposing himself to Dangers, since his Life was not
his own, but theirs who in Distress stood in want of his Assistance and Protection. That's it now, quoth *Sancho*, that
makes me sometimes ready to run mad, Mr Batchelor, for my
Master makes no more to set upon an Hundred armed Men,
than a young hungry Taylor to guttle down half a Dozen of
Cucumbers. Body of me! Master Batchelor, there's a Time
to retreat as well as a Time to advance; *Saint Jago* and *Close*

Spain,* must not always be the Cry: For I've heard somebody say, and, if I an't mistaken, 'twas my Master himself, That Valour lies just half way between Rashness and Cowheartedness; and if it be so, I would not have him run away without there's a Reason for't, nor would I have him fall on when there's no Good to be got by't. But above all things I wou'd have him to know, if he has a mind I shou'd go with him, that the Bargain is, He shall fight for us both, and that I am ty'd to nothing but to look after him and his Victuals and Clothes: So far as this comes to, I will fetch and carry like any Water-Spaniel; but to think I'll lug out my Sword, though it be but against poor Rogues, and sorry Shirks, and Hedge-birds, y'troth I must beg his Diversion. For my part, Mr Batchelor, 'tis not the Fame of being thought Valiant that I aim at, but that of being deem'd the very best and trustiest Squire that ever follow'd the Heels of a Knight-Errant: And if, after all my Services, my Master Don *Quixote* will be so kind as to give me one of those many Islands which his Worship says he shall light on, I shall be much beholden to him; but if he does not, why then I am born, d'ye see, and one Man must not live to rely on another, but on his Maker. Mayhaps the Bread I shall eat without Government, will go down more savourily than if I were a Governor; and what do I know but that the Devil is providing me one of these Governments for a Stumbling-block, that I may stumble and fall, and so break my Jaws, and ding out my Butter-Teeth. I was born *Sancho*, and *Sancho* I mean to die; and yet for all that, if fairly and squarely, with little Trouble and less Danger, Heaven would bestow on me an Island, or some such-like Matter, I'm no such Fool neither, d'ye see, as to refuse a good thing when 'tis offer'd me. No, I remember the old Saying, When the Ass is given thee, run and take him by the Halter; and when good Luck knocks at the Door let him in, and keep him there. My Friend *Sancho*, said *Carrasco*, you have spoken like any University-Professor: However, trust in Heaven's Bounty, and the noble Don *Quix-*

---

* Santiago cierra Espana, *is the Cry of the* Spanish *Soldiers when they fall on in Battle, encouraging one another to* close *with the Enemy;* Cerrár con el enemigo. *It is likewise an Exhortation to the* Spaniards *to keep themselves compact and* close *together.*

ote, and he may not only give thee an Island, but even a Kingdom. One as likely as the other, quoth *Sancho*; and yet let me
tell you, Mr Batchelor, the Kingdom which my Master is to
give me, you shan't find it thrown into an old Sack; for I have
felt my own Pulse, and find myself sound enough to rule Kingdoms and govern Islands; I ha' told my Master as much before
now. Have a care *Sancho*, said *Carrasco*, Honours change
Manners; perhaps when you come to be a Governor, you will
scarce know the Mother that bore ye. This, said *Sancho*, may
happen to those that were born in a Ditch, but not to those
whose Souls are cover'd, as mine is, four Fingers thick with
good old Christian Fat.* No, do but think how good-condition'd I be, and then you need not fear I shou'd do dirtily by
any one. Grant it, good Heaven, said Don *Quixote*! we shall
see when the Government comes, and methinks I have it already before my Eyes. After this he desir'd the Batchelor, if
he were a Poet, to oblige him with some Verses on his design'd
Departure from his Mistress *Dulcinea del Toboso*. Every Verse
to begin with one of the Letters of her Name, so that joining
every first Letter of every Verse together, they might make
Dulcinea del Toboso. The Batchelor told him, that though he
were none of the famous Poets of *Spain*, who, they say, were
but three and a half,† he would endeavour to make that Ac-
rostick; though he was sensible this would be no easy Task,
there being Seventeen Letters in the Name; so that if he made
four Stanza's of four Verses apiece, there wou'd be a Letter
too much; and if he made his Stanza's of five Lines, so as to
make a double *Decima* or a *Redondilla*, there would be three
Letters too little; however, he wou'd strive to drown a Letter,
and so take in the whole Name in sixteen Verses. Let it be so
by any means, said Don *Quixote*; for no Woman will believe
that those Verses were made for her where her Name is not
plainly to be discern'd. After this, 'twas agreed they should

* *A Spanish way of expressing he was not of the Jewish or Moorish Race.*
† *The first* Alonzo de Ercilla, *Author of the* Araucana: *(an Epic Poem,
which I have read with a great deal of Pleasure, nor did it cost me a little
Money to purchase it of the late Mr* Rymer,) *the second,* Juan Rufo *of*
Cordova, *Author of the* Austriada; *and the third,* Christopher Verves *of*
Valentia, *Author of the* Montserrate. *By the Half-Poet Don* Gregorio
thinks Cervantes *means himself.*

set out within a Week. Don *Quixote* charg'd the Batchelor not
to speak a word of all this, especially to the Curate, Mr *Nicolas*
the Barber, his Niece, and his House-keeper, lest they shou'd
obstruct his honourable and valorous Design. *Carrasco* gave
him his Word, and having desir'd Don *Quixote* to send an Account of his good or bad Success at his Conveniency, took his
Leave, and left him; and *Sancho* went to get every thing ready
for his Journey.

V: THE WISE AND PLEASANT DIALOGUE BETWEEN SANCHO PANZA, AND TERESA PANZA HIS WIFE: TOGETHER WITH OTHER PASSAGES WORTHY OF HAPPY MEMORY

THE Translator of this History, being come to this Fifth Chapter, thinks fit to inform the Reader, that he holds it to be Apocryphal; because it introduces *Sancho* speaking in another Style than could be expected from his slender Capacity, and saying things of so refin'd a Nature, that it seems impossible he cou'd do it. However, he thought himself oblig'd to render it into our Tongue, to maintain the Character of a faithful Translator, and therefore he goes on in this manner.

Sancho came home so chearful and so merry, that his Wife read his Joy in his Looks as far as she cou'd see him. Being impatient to know the Cause, My Dear, cry'd she, what makes you so merry? I shou'd be more merry, my Chuck, quoth *Sancho*, wou'd but Heaven so order it, that I were not so well pleas'd as I seem to be. You speak Riddles, Husband, quoth she; I don't know what you mean by saying, You shou'd be more merry if you were not so well pleased; for, tho' I am silly enough, I can't think a Man can take pleasure in not being pleas'd. Look ye, *Teresa*, quoth *Sancho*, I am merry because I am once more going to serve my Master Don *Quixote*, who is resolv'd to have t'other Frolick, and go a hunting after Adventures, and I must go with him; for he needs must, whom the Devil drives. What should I lie starving at home for? The Hopes of finding another Parcel of Gold like that we spent, rejoices the Cockles of my Heart: But then it grieves me to leave thee, and those sweet Babes of ours; and wou'd Heaven but be pleas'd to let me live at home dry-shod, in Peace and Quietness, without gadding over Hill and Dale, thro' Brambles and Briars (as Heaven might well do with small Cost, if it wou'd, and with no manner of Trouble, but only to be willing it should be so) why then 'tis a clear Case that my Mirth wou'd be more firm and sound, since my present Gladness is mingl'd with a Sorrow to part with thee. And so I think I have made

36

out what I have said, that I should be merrier if I did not seem
so well pleas'd. Look you, *Sancho*, quoth the Wife, ever since
you have been a Member of a Knight-Errant, you talk so round
about the Bush, that no body can understand you. 'Tis enough,
quoth *Sancho*, that he understands me who understands all
things; and so scatter no more Words about it, Spouse. But be
sure you look carefully after *Dapple* for these three Days,
that he may be in good Case, and fit to bear Arms; double his
Pittance, look out his Pannel and all his Harness, and let every
thing be set to rights; for we are not going to a Wedding, but
to roam about the World, and to make our Party good with
Giants, and Dragons, and Hobgoblins, and to hear nothing but
hissing, and yelling, and roaring, and howling and bellowing;
all which wou'd yet be but Sugar-plumbs, if we were not to
meet with the *Yanguesian* Carriers,* and Inchanted *Moors*.
Nay, as for that Husband, quoth *Teresa*, I am apt enough to
think you Squires-Errant don't eat their Master's Bread for
nothing; and therefore it shall be my daily Prayer, that you
may quickly be freed from that plaguy Trouble. Troth, Wife,
quoth *Sancho*, were not I in hopes to see myself, ere it be long,
Governor of an Island, o' my Conscience I shou'd drop down
dead on the Spot. Not so, my Chicken, quoth the Wife, *Let
the Hen live, though it be with Pip.* Do thou live, and let all
the Governments in the World go to the Devil. Thou cam'st
out of thy Mother's Belly without Government, thou hast
liv'd hitherto without Government, and thou may'st be carried to thy long home without Government, when it shall
please the Lord. How many People in this World live without
Government, yet do well enough, and are well look'd upon?
There's no Sauce in the World like Hunger, and as the Poor
never want that, they always eat with a good Stomach. But
look ye, my Precious, if it shou'd be thy good Luck to get a
Government, prithee don't forget your Wife and Children.
Take notice that little *Sancho* is already full Fifteen, and 'tis
high time he went to School, if his Uncle the Abbot mean to
leave him something in the Church. Then there's *Mary Sancha*, your Daughter; I dare say the Burden of Wedlock will
never be the Death of her, for I shrewdly guess, she longs as

* *Who beat the Master and Man before in the preceeding Vol.*

37

much for a Husband, as you do for a Government; and when all comes to all, better my Daughter ill married, then well kept. I' good sooth! Wife, quoth *Sancho*, if it be Heaven's blessed Will that I get any thing by Government, I'll see and match *Mary Sancha* so well, that she shall, at least, be call'd my Lady. By no means, Husband, cry'd the Wife, let her match with her Match: If from clouted Shoes you set her upon high Heels, and from her coarse Russet Coat you put her into a Fardingale, and from plain *Moll* and *Thee* and *Thou*, go to call her Madam, and your Ladyship, the poor Girl won't know how to behave herself, but will every Foot make a Thousand Blunders, and shew her homespun Country Breeding. Tush! Fool, answer'd *Sancho*, 'twill be but two or three Years Prentiship; and then you'll see how strangely she'll alter; your Ladyship and keeping of State will become her, as if they had been made for her; and suppose they should not, what is it to any body? Let her but be a Lady, and let what will happen. Good *Sancho*, quoth the Wife, don't look above yourself; I say, keep to the Proverb, that says, Birds of a Feather flock together.* 'Twould be a fine thing, e'trow! for us to go and throw away our Child on one of your Lordlings, or Right Worshipfuls, who when the Toy shou'd take him in the Head, wou'd find new Names for her, and call her Country *Joan*, Plough Jobber's Bearn, and Spinner's Web. No, no, Husband, I han't bred the Girl up as I ha' done, to throw her away at that rate I'll assure ye. Do thee but bring home Money, and leave me to get her a Husband. Why there's *Lope Tocho*, old *Joan Tocho's* Son, a hale jolly young Fellow, and one whom we all know; I have observ'd he casts a Sheep's Eye at the Wench, he's one of our Inches, and will be a good Match for her; then we shall always have her under our Wings, and be all as one, Father and Mother, Children and Grandchildren, and Heaven's Peace and Blessing will always be with us. But ne'er talk to me of marrying her at your Courts, and Great Men's Houses, where she'll understand no Body, and no Body

---

* *In the Original, it is,* Wipe your Neighbour's Son's Nose, and take him into your House, *i.e.* Marry him to your Daughter. *You had better take a Neighbour you know with his Faults, than a Stranger you don't know.* Stevens's Dict. *under the Word* Hijo.

will understand her. Why, thou Beast, cry'd *Sancho*, thou
Wife for *Barabbas*, why dost thou hinder me from marrying
my Daughter to one that will get me Grandchildren that may
be called your Honour and your Lordship? Han't I always
heard my Betters say, That he who will not when he may,
when he will he shall have nay: When good Luck is knocking
at our Door, is it fit to shut him out? No, no, let us make Hay
while the Sun shines, and spread our Sails before this prosperous Gale. [This Mode of Locution, and the following Huddle of Reflections and Apothegms, said to have been spoken
by *Sancho*, made the Translator of this History say, he held
this Chapter Apocryphal.] Can'st thou not perceive, thou
senseless Animal, said *Sancho* going on, that I ought to venture
over Head and Ears to light on some good gainful Government,
that may free our Ancles from the Clogs of Necessity, and
marry *Mary Sancha* to whom we please? Then thou'lt see
how Folks will call thee my Lady *Teresa Panza*, and thou'lt
sit in the Church with thy Carpets and Cushions, and lean
and loll in State, though the best Gentlewoman in the Town
burst with Spight and Envy. No, no, remain as you are, still
in the same Posture, neither higher nor lower, like a Picture
in the Hangings. Go to, let's have no more of this, little *Sancha* shall be a Countess in spight of thy Teeth, I say. Well,
well, Husband, quoth the Wife, have a care what you say,
for I fear me these high Kicks will be my *Molly's* Undoing.
Yet do what you will, make her a Dutchess or a Princess, but
I'll never give my Consent. Look ye, Yoke-Fellow, for my
part, I ever lov'd to see every thing upon the Square, and can't
abide to see Folks take upon them when they should not. I
was christen'd plain *Teresa*, without any Fiddle-faddle, or
Addition of Madam, or your Ladyship. My Father's Name
was *Cascajo*; and because I married you, they call me *Teresa
Panza*, though indeed by right I should be call'd *Teresa Cascajo.** But where the Kings are, there are the Laws, and I am
e'en contented with that Name without a Flourish before it,
to make it longer and more tedious than 'tis already; neither
will I make myself any body's Laughing-stock. I'll give 'em

* *The Custom of* Spain, *is ever to call Women, tho' married, by their Maiden
Names, which makes* Teresa *say what she does.*

no Cause to cry (when they see me go like a Countess, or a Governor's Madam,) Look, look, how Madam Hog-wash struts along! 'Twas but t'other Day she'd tug ye a Distaff, capp'd with Hemp, from Morning till Night, and would go to Mass with her Coat over her Head for want of a Hood; yet now look how she goes in her Fardingale, and her rich Trimmings and Fallals, no less than a whole Tradesman Shop about her mangy Back, as if every Body did not know her. No, Husband, if it please Heaven but to keep me in my Seven Senses, or my Five, or as many as I have, I'll take care to tie up People's Tongues from setting me out at this rate. You may go, and be a Governor, or an Islander, and look as big as Bull-Beef an you will; but by my Grand-mother's Daughter, neither I nor my Girl will budge a Foot from our Thatch'd House. For the Proverb says:

> The Wife that expects to have a good Name,
> Is always at home as if she were lame:
> And the Maid that is honest, her cheifest Delight,
> Is still to be doing from Morning to Night.*

March you and your Don *Quixote* together, to your Islands and Adventures, and leave us here to our sorry Fortune: I'll warrant you Heaven will better it, if we live as we ought to do. I wonder tho' who made him a Don; neither his Father nor his Grandsire ever had that Feather in their Caps. The Lord help thee, Woman! quoth *Sancho*, what a Heap of Stuff hast thou twisted together without Head or Tail! What have thy *Cascajo's*, thy Fardingales and Fallals, thy old Saws, and all this Tale of a roasted Horse, to do with what I have said? Hark thee me, Gammar Addlepate, (for I can find no better Name for thee, since thou'rt such a blind Buzzard as to miss my Meaning, and stand in thy own Light) should I ha' told thee that my Girl was to throw herself Head foremost from the Top of some Steeple, or to trot about the World like a Gipsy, or, as

---

* La Muger honrada,
La pierna quebrada,
y en casa;
La Donzella honesta
El hazer algo es su fiesta.

the Infanta *Donna Urraca** did, then thou might'st have some Reason not to be of my Mind. But if in the twinkling of an Eye, and while one might toss a Pancake, I clap you a Don and a Ladyship upon the Back of her; if I fetch her out of her Straw, to sit under a stately Bed's Tester; and squat her down on more Velvet-Cushions, than all the *Almohada's*† of *Morocco* had *Moors* in their Generation, why should'st thou be against it, and not be pleas'd with what pleases me? Shall I tell you why, Husband, answer'd *Teresa*? 'tis because of the Proverb, *He that covers thee, discovers thee*. A poor Man is scarce minded, but every one's Eyes will stare upon the Rich; and if that rich Man has formerly been Poor, this sets others a grumbling and backbiting; and your evil Tongues will ne'er ha' done, but swarm about the Streets like Bees, and buz their Stories into People's Ears. Look you, *Teresa*, said *Sancho*, mind what I say to thee, I'll tell thee things that perhaps thou ne'er heard'st of in thy Life: Nor do I speak of my own Head, but what I heard from that good Father who preach'd in our Town all last *Lent*. He told us, if I an't mistaken, that all those things which we see before our Eyes, do appear, hold and exist in our Memories much better, and with a greater Stress than things pass'd. [All these Reasons which are here offer'd by *Sancho*, are another Argument to persuade the Translator to hold this Chapter for Apocryphal, as exceeding the Capacity of *Sancho*.] From thence it arises, said *Sancho*, going on, that when we happen to see a Person well dress'd, richly equipp'd, and with a great Train of Servants, we find ourselves mov'd and prompted to pay him Respect, in a manner, in spite of our Teeth, tho' at that very Moment our Memory makes us call to remembrance some low Circumstances, in which we had seen that Person before. Now this Ignominy, be it either by reason of his Poverty, or mean Parentage, as 'tis already pass'd, is no more, and only that which we see before our Eyes remains. So then, if this Person, whom Fortune has rais'd to that Height out of his former Obscurity, by his Father's Means, be well-bred, Generous and

---

* *A Spanish Princess.* † Almohada, *signifies a Cushion, and was also the surname of a famous Race of the* Arabs *in* Africk, *and from thence introduced among the* Moors *in* Spain. *So that here's a sort of Pun or Allusion to the Name, and the Women in* Spain *sit all upon Cushions on the Ground, which is the Cause there is so much mention made of them.*

Civil to all Men, and does not affect to vye with those that are of noble Descent; assure thy self, *Teresa*, no body will remember what he was, but look upon him as what he is, unless it be your envious Spirits, from whose Taunts no prosperous Fortune can be free. I don't understand you, Husband, quoth *Teresa*, even follow your own Inventions, and don't puzzle my Brains with your Harangues and Retricks. If y'are so devolv'd to do as ye say—*Resolv'd* you should say, Wife, quoth *Sancho*, and not *devolv'd*. Pry'thee, Husband, said *Teresa*, let's ha' no Words about that Matter: I speak as Heaven's pleas'd I should; and for hard Words, I give my Share to the Curate. All I have to say now, is this: If you hold still in the Mind of being a Governor, pray e'en take your Son *Sancho* along with you; and henceforth train him up to your Trade of Governing; for 'tis but fitting that the Son should be brought up to the Father's Calling. When once I am Governor, quoth *Sancho*, I'll send for him by the Post, and I'll send thee Money withal; for I dare say, I shall want none; there never wants those that will lend Governors Money when they have none. But then be sure you clothe the Boy so, that he may look, not like what he is, but like what he is to be. Send you but Money, quoth *Teresa*, and I'll make him as fine as a *May-day* Garland.* So then, Wife, quoth *Sancho*, I suppose we are agreed that our *Moll* shall be a Countess. The Day I see her a Countess, quoth *Teresa*, I reckon I lay her in her Grave. However, I tell you again, e'en follow your own Inventions; you Men will be Masters, and we poor Women are born to bear the Clog of Obedience, though our Husbands have no more Sense than a Cuckoo. Here she fell a weeping as heartily as if she had seen her Daughter already Dead and Buried. *Sancho* comforted her, and promis'd her, that tho' he was to make her a Countess, yet he would see and put it off as long as he cou'd. Thus ended their Dialogue, and he went back to Don *Quixote*, to dispose every thing for a March.

* Como un palmito, *in the Original: i.e.* as fine as a Palm-Branch. *In Italy and* Spain *they carry in Procession, on* Palm-Sunday, *a Palm-branch, the Leaves of which are platted and interwoven with great Art and Nicety.*

VI: WHAT PASS'D BETWEEN DON QUIXOTE, HIS NIECE, AND THE HOUSE-KEEPER: BEING ONE OF THE MOST IMPORTANT CHAPTERS IN THE WHOLE HISTORY

WHILE *Sancho Pança*, and his Wife *Teresa Cascajo*, had the foregoing impertinent* Dialogue, Don *Quixote's* Niece and House-keeper were not idle, guessing by a thousand Signs that the Knight intended a Third Sally. Therefore they endeavour'd by all possible Means to divert him from his foolish Design; but all to no purpose; for this was but preaching to a Rock, and hammering cold stubborn Steel. But among other Arguments; in short, Sir, quoth the House-keeper, if you will not be rul'd, but will needs run wandring over Hill and Dale, like a stray Soul between Heaven and Hell, seeking for Mischief, for so I may well call the hopeful Adventures which you go about, I'll never leave complaining to Heaven and the King, till there's a Stop put to't some way or other. What Answer Heaven will vouchsafe to give thee, I know not, answer'd Don *Quixote*: neither can I tell what Return his Majesty will make to thy Petition; this I know, that were I King, I would excuse my self from answering the infinite Number of impertinent Memorials that disturb the Repose of Princes. I tell thee, Woman, among the many other Fatigues which Royalty sustains, 'tis one of the greatest to be oblig'd to hear every one, and to give Answer to all People. Therefore pray trouble not his Majesty with any thing concerning me. But, pray, Sir, tell me, reply'd she, are there not a many Knights in the King's Court? I must confess, said Don *Quixote*, that for the Ornament, the Grandeur, and the Pomp, of Royalty, many Knights are, and ought to be maintained there. Why then, said the Woman, would it not be better for your Worship to be one of

---

* *So it is in the Original* viz. impertinente platica: *but Mr* Jarvis, *very justly, suspects the Irony to be here broke by the Transcriber or Printer, and not by the Author himself, and that it should be* (importante) important, *which carries on the grave Ridicule of the History.*

those brave Knights, who serve the King their Master on Foot in his Court? Hear me, Sweet-heart, answer'd Don *Quixote*, all Knights cannot be Courtiers, nor can all Courtiers be Knights-Errant. There must be of all Sorts in the World; and though we were all to agree in the common Appellation of Knights, yet there would be a great Difference between the one and the other. For your Courtiers, without so much as stirring out of their Chambers, or the Shade and Shelter of the Court, can journey over all the Universe in a Map, without the Expence and Fatigue of Travelling, without suffering the Inconveniencies of Heat, Cold, Hunger, and Thirst; while we who are the true Knight-Errants, expos'd to those Extremities, and all the Inclemencies of Heaven, by Night and by Day, on Foot as well as on Horseback, measure the whole Surface of the Earth with our own Feet. Nor are we only acquainted with the Pictures of our Enemies, but with their very Persons, ready upon all Occasions and at all times to engage 'em, without standing upon Trifles, or the Ceremony of measuring Weapons, stripping, or examining whether our Opponents have any holy Relicks, or other secret Charms about 'em, whether the Sun be duly divided, or any other Punctilio's and Circumstances observ'd among private Duelists; Things which thou understandest not, but I do: And must further let thee know, that the true Knight-Errant, tho' he meet Ten Giants, whose tall aspiring Heads not only touch but over-top the Clouds, each of them stalking with prodigious Legs like huge Towers, their sweeping Arms like Masts of Mighty Ships, each Eye as large as a Mill-Wheel, and more fiery than a Glass-Furnace; yet he is so far from being afraid to meet them, that he must encounter them with a gentle Countenance, and an undaunted Courage, assail them, cloze with them, and if possible vanquish and destroy 'em all in an Instant; nay, though they came arm'd with the Scales of a certain Fish, which they say is harder than Adamant, and instead of Swords had dreadful Sabres of keen *Damascan* Steel, or mighty Maces with Points of the same Metal, as I have seen them more than a Dozen times. I have condescended to tell thee thus much, that thou may'st see the vast Difference between Knights and Knights; and I think 'twere to be wish'd that all Princes knew so far how to make the Distinction, as to give the Pre-eminence to this first Species of Knights-Errant, among whom there have been some whose Fortitude has not only been the Defence of our Kingdom, but of many more, as we read in their Histories. Ah! Sir, said the Niece, have a care what you say; all the Stories of Knights-Errant, are nothing but a Pack of Lies and Fables, and if they are not burnt, they ought at least to wear a *Sanbenito*,* the Badge of Heresy, or some other Mark of Infamy, that the World may know 'em to be wicked, and Perverters of good Manners. Now by the Powerful Sustainer of my Being, cry'd Don *Quixote*, wert thou not so nearly related to me, wert thou not my own Sister's Daughter, I would take such Revenge for the Blasphemy thou hast uttered, as would resound through the whole Universe. Who ever heard of the like Impudence? That a young Baggage, who scarce knows her Bobbins from a Bodkin, should presume to put in her Oar, and censure the Histories of Knights-Errant! What would Sir *Amadis* have said, had he heard this! But he undoubtedly would have forgiven thee, for he was the most Courteous and Complaisant Knight of his Time, especially to the Fair Sex, being a great Protector of Damsels; but thy Words might have reach'd the Ears of some, that would have sacrific'd thee to their Indignation; for all Knights are not possess'd of Civility or Good-nature; some are Rough and Revengeful; and neither are all those that assume the Name, of a Disposition suitable to the Function; some indeed were of the right Stamp, but others are either Counterfeit, or of such an Allay as cannot bear the Touch-stone, though they deceive the Sight. Inferior Mortals there are, who aim at Knight-hood, and strain to reach the Height of Honour; and High-born Knights there are, who seem fond of groveling in the Dust, and being lost in the Crowd of inferior Mortals. The first raise themselves by Ambition or by Virtue; the last debase themselves by Negligence or by Vice; so that there is need of a distinguishing Understanding to judge between these two Sorts of Knights, so near ally'd in Name, and so different in Actions. Bless me! dear Uncle, cry'd the Niece, that you should know so much, as to be able, if there was Occasion, to get up

* A Coat of black Canvass, painted over with Flames and Devils, worn by Hereticks when going to be burnt, by Order of the Inquisition.

into a Pulpit, or preach in the Streets,* and yet be so strangely mistaken, so grosly blind of Understanding, as to fancy a Man of your Years and Infirmity can be strong and valiant; that you can set every thing right, and force stubborn Malice to bend, when you yourself stoop beneath the Burden of Age; and what's yet more odd, that you are a Knight, when 'tis well known you are none? For tho' some Gentlemen may be Knights, a poor Gentleman can hardly be so, because he can't buy it. You say well, Niece, answer'd Don *Quixote*; and as to this last Observation, I could tell you things that you would admire at, concerning Families; but because I will not mix Sacred Things with Profane, I wave the Discourse. However, listen both of you, and for your farther Instruction know, that all the Lineages and Descents of Mankind, are reduceable to these four Heads: First, Of those, who from a very small and obscure Beginning, have rais'd themselves to a spreading and prodigious Magnitude. Secondly, Of those who deriving their Greatness from a noble Spring, still preserve the Dignity and Character of their original Splendor. A Third, Are those who, though they had large Foundations, have ended in a Point like a Pyramid, which by little and little dwindle as it were into nothing, or next to nothing, in comparison of its Basis. Others there are (and those are the Bulk of Mankind) who have neither had a good Beginning, nor a rational Continuance, and whose Ending shall therefore be obscure; such are the common People, the *Plebeian* Race. The *Ottoman* Family is an Instance of the first Sort, having deriv'd their present Greatness from the poor Beginning of a base-born Shepherd. Of the second Sort, there are many Princes who being born such, enjoy their Dominions by Inheritance, and leave them to their Successors without Addition or Diminution. Of the third Sort, there is an infinite Number of Examples; for all the *Pharaohs* and *Ptolomies* of *Egypt*, your *Cæsars* of *Rome*, and all the Swarm (if I may use that Word) of Princes, Monarchs, Lords, *Medes*, *Assyrians*, *Persians*, *Greeks* and *Barbarians*: All these Families and Empires have ended in a Point, as well as those who gave rise to 'em:

---

* *A common thing in* Spain *and* Italy, *for the Fryars and young Jesuits, in an extraordinary Fit of Zeal, to get upon a Bulk, and hold forth in the Streets or Market-Place.*

for it were impossible at this Day to find any of their Descendants, or if we cou'd find 'em, it would be in a poor groveling Condition. As for the Vulgar, I say nothing of 'em, more than that they are thrown in as Cyphers to increase the Number of Mankind, without deserving any other Praise. Now, my good-natur'd Souls, you may at least draw this reasonable Inference from what I have said of this promiscuous Dispensation of Honours, and this Uncertainty and Confusion of Descent, That Virtue and Liberality in the present Possessor, are the most just and undisputable Titles to Nobility; for the Advantages of Pedigree, without these Qualifications, serve only to make Vice more conspicuous. The great Man that is Vicious will be greatly Vicious, and the rich Miser is only a covetous Beggar; for, not he who possesses, but that spends and enjoys his Wealth, is the rich and the happy Man; nor he neither who barely spends, but who does it with Discretion. The poor Knight indeed cannot shew he is one by his Magnificence; but yet by his Virtue, Affability, Civility, and courteous Behaviour, he may display the chief Ingredients that enter into the Composition of the Knighthood; and tho' he can't pretend to Liberality, wanting Riches to support it, his Charity may recompence that Defect; for an Alms of two *Maravedis* chearfully bestow'd upon an indigent Beggar, by a Man in poor Circumstances, speaks him as liberal as the larger Donative of a vain-glorious rich Man before a fawning Crowd. These Accomplishments will always shine thro' the Clouds of Fortune, and at last break through 'em with Splendor and Applause. There are two Paths to Dignity and Wealth; Arts and Arms. Arms I have chosen, and the Influence of the Planet *Mars* that presided at my Nativity, led me to that adventurous Road. So that all your Attempts to shake my Resolution are in vain: for in spite of all Mankind, I will pursue what Heaven has fated, Fortune ordain'd, what Reason requires, and (which is more) what my Inclination demands. I am sensible of the many Troubles and Dangers that attend the Prosecution of Knight-Errantry, but I also know what infinite Honours and Rewards are the Consequences of the Performance. The Path of Virtue is narrow, and the Way of Vice easy and open; but their Ends and Resting-places are very different. The latter is a broad

Road indeed, and down-hill all the way, but Death and Contempt are always met at the End of the Journey; whereas the former leads to Glory and Life, not a Life that soon must have an End, but an immortal Being. For I know, as our great *Castilian* Poet* expresses it, that

Thro' steep Ascents, thro' strait and rugged Ways,
Our selves to Glory's lofty Seats we raise:
In vain he hopes to reach the bless'd Abode,
Who leaves the narrow Path, for the more easy Road.

Alack a-day! cry'd the Niece, my Uncle is a Poet too! He knows every thing. I'll lay my Life he might turn Mason in case of Necessity. If he would but undertake it, he could build a House as easy as a Bird-cage. Why truly, Niece, said Don *Quixote*, were not my Understanding wholly involv'd in Thoughts relating to the Exercise of Knight-Errantry, there is nothing which I durst not engage to perform, no Curiosity should escape my Hands, especially Bird-cages and Tooth-pickers.† By this some body knock'd at the Door and being ask'd who it was, *Sancho* answer'd, 'twas he. Whereupon the House-keeper slipp'd out of the way, not willing to see him, and the Niece let him in. Don *Quixote* receiv'd him with open Arms; and locking themselves both in the Closet, they had another Dialogue as pleasant as the former.

* Boscan, *one of the first Reformers of the* Spanish *Poetry*. † Palillo de dientes, *i.e. a little Stick for the Teeth. Tooth-pickers in* Spain *are made of long shavings of Boards, split and reduc'd to a Straw's Breadth, and wound up like small Wax-lights.*

VII: AN ACCOUNT OF DON QUIXOTE'S CON-FERENCE WITH HIS SQUIRE, AND OTHER MOST FAMOUS PASSAGES

THE House-keeper no sooner saw her Master and *Sancho* lock'd up together, but she presently sur-mis'd the Drift of that close Conference, and con-cluding that no less than Villanous Knight-Erran-try and another Sally would prove the Result of it, she flung her Veil over her Head, and quite cast down with Sorrow and Vexation, trudg'd away to seek *Sampson Carrasco*, the Batchelor of Arts; depending on his Wit and Eloquence, to dissuade his Friend Don *Quixote* from his frantick Resolution. She found him walking in the Yard of his House, and fell presently on her Knees before him in a cold Sweat, and with all the Marks of a disorder'd Mind. What's the matter, Woman, said he, (somewhat surpriz'd at her Pos-ture and Confusion) what has befallen you, that you look as if you were ready to give up the Ghost; Nothing, said she, dear Sir, but that my Master's departing, he's departing, that's most certain. How! cry'd *Carrasco*. What d'you mean? Is his Soul departing out of his Body? No, answer'd the Woman, but all his Wits are quite and clean departing. He means to be Gad-ding again into the wide World, and is upon the Spur now the third time to hunt after Ventures, as he calls 'em,* tho' I don't know why he calls those Chances so. The first time he was brought home, was athwart an Ass, and almost cudgel'd to pieces. T'other Bout he was forc'd to ride home in a Waggon, coup'd up in a Cage, where he would make us believe he was inchanted; and the poor Soul look'd so dismally, that the Mother that bore him would not have known the Child of her Bowels; so meagre, wan, and wither'd, and his Eyes so sunk and hid in the utmost Nook and Corner of his Brain, that I am sure I spent about Six Hundred Eggs to cocker him up again; ay, and more too, as Heaven and all the World's my Witness, and the Hens that laid 'em can't deny it. That I believe, said the Batchelor, for your Hens are so well-bred, so fat, and so

* *Ventura, signifies both* good Luck, *and also* Adventures.

good, that they won't say one thing and think another for the
World. But is this all? Has no other ill Luck befall'n you,
besides this of your Master's intended Ramble? No other, Sir,
quoth she. Then trouble your Head no farther, said he, but
get you home, and as you go, say me the Prayer of St *Apollonia*, if you know it: then get me some warm Bit for Breakfast, and I'll come to you presently, and you shall see Wonders.
Dear me, quoth she, the Prayer of St *Polonia*! Why, 'tis only
good for the Tooth-ach; but his Ailing lies in his Skull. Mistress, said he, don't dispute with me: I know what I say. Have
I not commenc'd Batchelor of Arts at *Salamanca*, and do you
think there's any *Batcherlorizing* beyond that? With that
away she goes, and he went presently to find the Curate, to
consult with him about what shall be declar'd in due time.

When *Sancho* and his Master were lock'd up together
in the Room, there pass'd some Discourse between them, of
which the History gives a very punctual and impartial Account. Sir, quoth *Sancho* to his Master, I have at last reluc'd
my Wife, to let me go with your Worship where-ever you'll
have me. *Reduc'd* you would say, *Sancho*, said Don *Quixote*,
and not *reluc'd*.★ Look you, Sir, quoth *Sancho*, If I an't mistaken, I have wish'd you once or twice not to stand correcting my Words, if you understand my Meaning: If you don't,
why then do but say to me, *Sancho*, Devil, or what you please,
I understand thee not; and if I don't make out my Meaning
plainly, then take me up; for I am so focible —— I understand
you not, said Don *Quixote* interrupting him, for I can't guess
the Meaning of your *Focible*. Why, so Focible, quoth *Sancho*,
is as much as to say, Focible. That is, I am so and so, as it were.
Less and less do I understand thee, said the Knight. Why then,
quoth *Sancho*, there's an end of the Matter, it must e'en stick
there for me, for I can speak no better. O! now, quoth Don
Quixote, I fancy I guess your Meaning, you mean *docible*, I
suppose, implying that you are so ready and apprehensive,
that you will presently observe what I shall teach you. I'll lay
any even Wager now, said the 'Squire, you understood me
well enough at first, but you had a Mind to put me out, merely

---

★ *But just now* Sancho *corrected his Wife for saying* devolv'd, *instead of*
resolv'd.

to hear me put your fine Words out-a-joint. That may be, said
Don *Quixote*, but pr'ythee tell me, what says *Teresa*? Why,
an't please you, quoth *Sancho*, *Teresa* bids me make sure Work
with your Worship, and that we may have less Talking and
more Doing; that a Man must not be his own Carver; that he
who Cuts does not Shuffle; that 'tis good to be certain; that
Paper speaks when Beards never wag; that a Bird in Hand is
worth two in the Bush. One *Hold-fast* is better than two *I'll
give thee*. Now, I say, a Woman's Counsel is not worth much,
yet he that despises it, is no wiser than he shou'd be—I say so
too, said Don *Quixote*; but pray, good *Sancho*, proceed; for
thou art in an excellent Strain; thou talk'st most sententiously
to Day. I say, quoth *Sancho*, as you better know yourself than
I do, that we're all mortal Men, here to Day and gone to Morrow; as soon goes the young Lamb to the Spit, as the old Weather; no Man can tell the Length of his Days; for Death is deaf,
and when he knocks at the Door, Mercy on the Porter. He's
in Post-haste, neither fair Words nor foul, Crowns nor Mitres
can stay him, as the Report goes, and as we are told from the
Pulpit. All this I grant, said Don *Quixote*: But what would you
infer from hence? Why, Sir, quoth *Sancho*, all I wou'd be at is,
that your Worship allow me so much a Month* for my Wages,
whilst I stay with you, and that the aforesaid Wages be paid
me out of your Estate. For I'll trust no longer to Rewards, that
mayhaps may come late, and mayhaps not at all. I'd be glad to
know what I get, be't more or less. A little in one's own Pocket,
is better than much in another Man's Purse. 'Tis good to keep
a Nest-Egg. Every little makes a mickle; while a Man gets he
never can lose. Should it happen indeed, that your Worship
should give me this same Island, which you promis'd me, though
'tis what I dare not so much as hope for, why then I an't such
an ungrateful, nor so unconscionable a Muck-worm, but that
I am willing to strike off upon the Income, for what Wages I
receive, Cantity for Cantity. Would not Quantity have been
better than Cantity, ask'd Don *Quixote*? Ho! I understand you
now, cry'd *Sancho*: I dare lay a Wager I should have said Quantity and not Cantity: but no matter for that, since you knew
what I meant. Yes, *Sancho*, quoth the Knight, I have div'd to

* *The Custom of* Spain *is to pay their Servants Wages by the Month.*

the very Bottom of your Thought, and understand now the Aim of all your numerous Shot of Proverbs. Look you, Friend *Sancho*, I shou'd never scruple to pay thee Wages, had I any Example to warrant such a Practice. Nay, could I find the least glimmering of a Precedent thro' all the Books of Chivalry that ever I read, for any yearly or monthly Stipend, your Request should be granted. But I have read all, or the greatest Part of the Histories of Knights-Errant, and find that all their 'Squires depended purely on the Favour of their Masters for a Subsistence; till by some surprizing Turn in the Knight's Fortune, the servants were advanced to the Government of some Island, or some equivalent Gratuity; at least, they had Honour and a Title conferred on them as a Reward. Now, Friend *Sancho*, if you will depend on these Hopes of Preferment, and return to my Service, 'tis well; if not, get you home, and tell your impertinent Wife, that I will not break through all the Rules and Customs of Chivalry, to satisfy her sordid Diffidence and yours; and so let there be no more Words about the matter, but let us part Friends; and remember this, that if there be Vetches in my Dove-House, it will want no Pigeons. Good Arrears are better than ill Pay; and a Fee in Reversion is better than a Farm in Possession. Take notice too, there's Proverb for Proverb, to let you know that I can pour out a Volley of 'em as well as you. In short, if you will not go along with me upon Courtesy, and run the same Fortune with me, Heaven be with you, and make you a Saint; I do not question but I shall get me a 'Squire, more Obedient, more Careful, and less Saucy and Talkative than you.

Sancho hearing his Master's firm Resolution, 'twas cloudy Weather with him in an Instant; he was struck dumb with Disappointment, and down sunk at once his Heart to his Girdle; for he verily thought he could have brought him to any Terms, through a vain Opinion, that the Knight would not for the World go without him. While he was thus dolefully bury'd in Thought, in came *Sampson Carrasco*, and the Niece, very eager to hear the Batchelor's Arguments to dissuade Don *Quixote* from his intended Sally. But *Sampson*, who was a rare Comedian, presently embracing the Knight, and beginning in a high Strain, soon disappointed her. O Flower of Chivalry, cry'd he, refulgent Glory of Arms, living Honour and Mirror of our *Spanish* Nation, may all those who prevent the Third Expedition which thy heroick Spirit meditates, be lost in the Labyrinth of their perverse Desires, and find no Thread to lead 'em to their Wishes. Then turning to the House-keeper, You have no need now to say the Prayer of St *Apollonia*, said he, for I find it written in the Stars, that the Illustrious Champion must no longer delay the Prosecution of Glory; and I should injure my Conscience, should I presume to dissuade him from the Benefits that shall redound to Mankind, by exerting the Strength of his formidable Arm, and the innate Virtues of his heroick Soul. Alas! his Stay deprives the oppressed Orphans of a Protector, Damsels of a Deliverer, Champions of their Honour, Widows of an obliging Patron, and marry'd Women of a vigorous Comforter, nay, also delays a Thousand other important Exploits and Atchievements, which are the Duty and necessary Consequences of the honourable Order of Knight-Errantry. Go on then, my graceful, my valorous Don *Quixote*, rather this very Day than the next; let your Greatness be upon the Wing, and if any thing be wanting towards the compleating of your Equipage, I stand forth to supply you with my Life and Fortune, and ready, if it be thought expedient, to attend your Excellence as a 'Squire, an Honour which I am ambitious to attain. Well, *Sancho*, (said Don *Quixote*, hearing this, and turning to his 'Squire) did not I tell thee I should not want 'Squires; behold who offers me his Service, the most excellent Batchelor of Arts, *Sampson Carrasco*, the perpetual Darling of the Muses, and Glory of the *Salamanca*-Schools, sound and active of Body, patient of Labour, inur'd to Abstinence, silent in Misfortune, and in short, endow'd with all the Accomplishments that constitute a 'Squire. But forbid it Heav'n, that to indulge my private Inclinations I should presume to weaken the whole Body of Learning, by removing from it so substantial a Pillar, so vast a Repository of Sciences, and so eminent a Branch of the Liberal Arts. No, my Friend, remain thou another *Sampson* in thy Country, be the Honour of *Spain*, and the Delight of thy ancient Parents; I shall content myself with any 'Squire, since *Sancho* does not vouchsafe to go with me. I do, I do, (cry'd *Sancho*, relenting with Tears in his Eyes) I do vouchsafe; it

53

shall never be said of *Sancho Pança*, no longer Pipe no longer
Dance. Nor have I Heart of Flint, Sir; for all the World knows,
and especially our Town, what the whole Generation of the
Pança's has ever been: Besides, I well know, and have already
found by a many good Turns, and more good Words, that your
Worship has had a good Will towards me all along; and if I have
done otherwise than I should, in standing upon Wages, or so,
it were merely to humour my Wife, who, when once she's set
upon a thing, stands digging and hammering at a Man like a
Cooper at a Tub, till she clinches the Point. But hang it, I am
the Husband, and will be her Husband, and she's but a Wife,
and shall be a Wife. None can deny but I am a Man every Inch
of me, where-ever I am, and I will be a Man at home in spite
of any Body; so that you've no more to do, but to make your
Will and Testament; but be sure you make the Conveyance
so firm, that it can't be rebuk'd, and then let's be gone as soon
as you please, that Master *Sampson's* Soul may be at rest; for
he says his Conscience won't let him be quiet, till he has set
you upon another Journey thro' the World; and I here again
offer myself to follow your Worship, and promise to be Faithful and Loyal, as well, nay, and better than all the 'Squires
that ever waited on Knights-Errant. The Batchelor was a-
maz'd to hear *Sancho Pança* express himself after that manner; and though he had read much of him in the first Part of
his History, he could not believe him to be so pleasant a Fellow
as he is there represented. But hearing him now talk of *rebuk-
ing* instead of revoking Testaments and Conveyances, he was
induc'd to credit all that was said of him, and to conclude him
one of the oddest Compounds of the Age; nor could he imagine
that the World ever saw before so extravagant a Couple as the
Master and the Man.

Don *Quixote* and *Sancho* embrac'd, becoming as good
Friends as ever, and so with the Approbation of the Grand
Carrasco, who was then the Knight's Oracle, it was decreed,
that they should set out at the Expiration of three Days; in
which time all Necessaries should be provided, especially a
whole Helmet, which Don *Quixote* said he was resolv'd by
all means to purchase. *Sampson* offer'd him one which he
knew he could easily get of a Friend, and which look'd more

dull with the Mold and Rust, than bright with the Lustre of
the Steel. The Niece and the House-keeper made a woful Outcry; they tore their Hair, scratch'd their Faces, and howl'd
like common Mourners at Funerals, lamenting the Knight's
Departure, as it had been his real Death; and cursing *Carrasco*
most unmercifully, though his Behaviour was the Result of
a Contrivance plotted between the Curate, the Barber, and
himself. In short, Don *Quixote* and his 'Squire having got all
things in a Readiness, the one having pacify'd his Wife, and
the other his Niece and House-keeper; towards the Evening
without being seen by any Body but the Batchelor, who would
needs accompany them about half a League from the Village,
they set forward for *Toboso*. The Knight mounted his *Rozinante*, and *Sancho* his trusty *Dapple*, his Wallet well stuff'd
with Provisions, and his Purse with Money, which Don *Quixote* gave him to defray Expences. At last *Sampson* took his
Leave, desiring the Champion to give him from time to time,
an Account of his Success, that according to the Laws of Friendship, he might sympathize in his good or evil Fortune. Don
Quixote made him a Promise, and then they parted; *Sampson*
went home, and the Knight and 'Squire continu'd their Journey for the great City of *Toboso*.

VIII: DON QUIXOTE'S SUCCESS IN HIS JOURNEY TO VISIT THE LADY DULCINEA DEL TOBOSO

BLESSED be the mighty *Alla*,* says *Hamet Benengeli*, at the Beginning of his Eighth Chapter; blessed be *Alla*! Which Ejaculation he thrice repeated, in Consideration of the Blessing that Don *Quixote* and *Sancho* had once more taken the Field again; and that from this Period the Readers of their delightful History may date the Knight's Atchievements, and the 'Squire's Pleasantries; and he intreats 'em to forget the former heroical Transactions of the wonderful Knight, and fix their Eyes upon his future Exploits, which take Birth from his setting out for *Toboso*, as the former began in the Fields of *Montiel*. Nor can so small a Request be thought unreasonable, considering what he promises, which begins in this manner.

Don *Quixote* and his 'Squire were no sooner parted from the Batchelor, but *Rozinante* began to neigh, and *Dapple* to bray; which both the Knight and the 'Squire interpreted as good Omens, and most fortunate Presages of their Success; tho' the Truth of the Story is, that as *Dapple's* Braying exceeded *Rozinante's* Neighing, *Sancho* concluded that his Fortune should out-rival and eclipse his Master's; which Inference I will not say he drew from some Principles in Judicial Astrology, in which he was undoubtedly well-grounded, though the History is silent in that Particular; however, 'tis recorded of him, that oftentimes upon the falling or stumbling of his Ass, he wish'd he had not gone abroad that Day, and from such Accidents prognosticated nothing but Dislocation of Joints, and breaking of Ribs; and notwithstanding his foolish Character, this was no bad Observation. Friend *Sancho*, said Don *Quixote* to him, I find the approaching Night will overtake us, ere we can reach *Toboso*, where, before I enter upon any Expedition, I am resolv'd to pay my Vows, receive my Benediction, and take my Leave of the Peerless *Dulcinea*; being assured after that of happy Events, in the most dangerous Adventures; for nothing in this World inspires a Knight Errant with so much Valour, as the Smiles and favourable Aspects

* *The* Moors *call God* Alla.

of his Mistress. I am of your Mind, quoth *Sancho*; but I am afraid, Sir, you will hardly come at her, to speak with her, at least not to meet her in a Place where she may give you her Blessing, unless she throw it you over the Mud-Wall of the Yard, where I first saw her, when I carried her the News of your mad Pranks in the midst of *Sierra Morena*. Mud-Wall, dost thou say, cry'd Don *Quixote*! Mistaken Fool, that Wall could have no Existence but in thy muddy Understanding: 'Tis a mere Creature of thy dirty Fancy; for that never-duly-celebrated Paragon of Beauty and Gentility, was then un-doubtedly in some Court, in some stately Gallery, or Walk, or as 'tis properly called, in some Sumptuous and Royal Palace. It may be so said *Sancho*, though so far as I can remember, it seem'd to me neither better nor worse than a Mud-Wall. 'Tis no matter, reply'd the Knight, let us go thither; I will visit my dear *Dulcinea*; let me but see her, though it be over a Mud-Wall, through a Chink of a Cottage, or the Pales of a Garden, at a Lattice, or any where; which way soever the least Beam from her bright Eyes reaches mine, it will so enlighten my Mind, so fortify my Heart, and invigorate every Faculty of my Being, that no Mortal will be able to rival me in Prudence and Valour. Troth! Sir, quoth *Sancho*, when I beheld that same Sun of a Lady, methought it did not shine so bright, as to cast forth any Beams at all; but mayhaps the Reason was, that the Dust of the Grain she was winnowing rais'd a Cloud about her Face, and made her look somewhat dull. I tell thee again, Fool, said Don *Quixote*, thy Imagination is dusty and foul; will it never be beaten out of thy stupid Brain, that my Lady *Dulcinea* was winnowing? Are such Exercises us'd by Persons of Her Quality, whose Recreations are always noble, and such as display an Air of Greatness suitable to their Birth and Dignity? Can'st thou not remember the Verses of our Poet, when he recounts the Employments of the four Nymphs at their Crystal Mansions, when they advanc'd their Heads above the Streams of the lovely *Tagus*, and sat upon the Grass, working those rich Embroideries, where Silk and Gold, and Pearl emboss'd, were so curiously interwoven, and which that ingenious Bard so artfully describes? So was my Princess em-ploy'd when she blessed thee with her Sight; but the envious

Malice of some base Necromancer fascinated thy Sight, as it represents whatever is most grateful to me in different and displeasing Shapes. And this makes me fear, that if the History of my Atchievements, which they tell me is in Print, has been written by some Magician who is no Well-wisher to my Glory, he has undoubtedly deliver'd many things with Partiality, misrepresented my Life, inserting a hundred Falshoods for one Truth, and diverting himself with the Relation of idle Stories, foreign to the Purpose, and unsuitable to the Continuation of a true History. O Envy! Envy! Thou gnawing Worm of Virtue, and Spring of infinite Mischiefs! There is no other Vice, my *Sancho*, but pleads some Pleasure in its Excuse; but Envy is always attended by Disgust, Rancour, and distracting Rage. I am much of your Mind, said *Sancho*, and I think, in the same Book which Neighbour *Carrasco* told us he had read of our Lives, the Story makes bold with my Credit, and has handled it at a strange Rate, and has dragg'd it about the Kennels, as a Body may say. Well, now as I am an honest Man, I never spoke an ill Word of a Magician in my born Days; and I think they need not envy my Condition so much. The Truth is, I am somewhat malicious; I have my roguish Tricks now and then; but I was ever counted more Fool than Knave for all that, and so indeed I was bred and born; and if there were nothing else in me but my Religion (for I firmly believe whatever our Holy *Roman* Catholick Church believes, and I hate the *Jews* mortally) these same Historians should take pity o' me, and spare me a little in their Books. But let 'em say on to the End of the Chapter; naked I came into the World, and naked must go out. 'Tis all a Case to *Sancho*, I can neither win nor lose by the Bargain; and so my Name be in Print, and handed about, I care not a Fig for the worst they can say of me. What thou say'st, *Sancho*, answer'd Don *Quixote*, puts me in mind of a Story. A celebrated Poet of our Time wrote a very scurrilous and abusive Lampoon upon all the intriguing Ladies of the Court, forbearing to name one, as not being sure whether she deserv'd to be put into the Catalogue or no; but the Lady not finding herself there, was not a little affronted at the Omission, and made a great Complaint to the Poet, asking him what he had seen in her, that he shou'd leave her out of his List; desiring him at the same time to enlarge his Satire, and put her in, or expect to hear farther from her. The Author obeyed her Commands, and gave her a Character with a Vengeance, and, to her great Satisfaction, made her as famous for Infamy as any Woman about the Town. Such another Story is that of *Diana's* Temple, one of the Seven Wonders of the World, burnt by an obscure Fellow merely to eternize his Name; which, in spite of an Edict that enjoin'd all People never to mention it, either by Word of Mouth, or in Writing, yet is still known to have been *Erostratus*. The Story of the great Emperor *Charles* the Fifth, and a *Roman* Knight, upon a certain Occasion, is much the same. The Emperor had a great Desire to see the famous Temple once called the *Pantheon*, but now more happily, the Church of *All Saints*. 'Tis the only entire Edifice remaining of Heathen *Rome*, and that which best gives an Idea of the Glory and Magnificence of its great Founders. 'Tis built in the Shape of a half Orange, of a vast Extent and very lightsome, tho' it admits no Light, but at one Window, or to speak more properly, at a round Aperture on the Top of the Roof. The Emperor being got up thither, and looking down from the Brink upon the Fabrick, with a *Roman* Knight by him, who shew'd all the Beauties of that vast Edifice: after they were gone from the Place, says the Knight, addressing the Emperor, It came into my Head a thousand times, Sacred Sir, to embrace your Majesty, and cast myself with you, from the Top of the Church to the Bottom, that I might thus purchase an immortal Name. I thank you said the Emperor, for not doing it; and for the future, I will give you no Opportunity to put your Loyalty to such a Test. Therefore I banish you my Presence for ever; which done, he bestow'd some considerable Favour on him. I tell thee, *Sancho*, this Desire of Honour is a strange bewitching thing. What dost thou think made *Horatius*, arm'd at all Points, plunge headlong from the Bridge into the rapid *Tyber*? What prompted *Curtius* to leap into the profound flaming Gulph? What made *Mutius* burn his Hand? What forc'd *Cæsar* over the *Rubicon*, spite of all the Omens that dissuaded his Passage? And to instance a more modern Example, what made the undaunted *Spaniards* sink their Ships, when under the most courteous

Cortez, but that scorning the stale Honour of this so often con-quer'd World, they sought a Maiden Glory in a new Scene of Victory? These and a Multiplicity of other great Actions, are owing to the immediate Thirst and Desire of Fame, which Mortals expect as the proper Price and immortal Recompence of their great Actions. But we that are Christian Catholick Knights-Errant must fix our Hopes upon a higher Reward, plac'd in the Eternal and Celestial Regions, where we may expect a permanent Honour and compleat Happiness; not like the Vanity of Fame, which at best is but the Shadow of great Actions, and must necessarily vanish, when destructive Time has eat away the Substance which it follow'd. So, my *Sancho*, since we expect a Christian Reward, we must suit our Actions to the Rules of Christianity. In Giants we must kill Pride and Arrogance: But our greatest Foes, and whom we must chiefly combat, are within. Envy we must overcome by Generosity and Nobleness of Soul; Anger, by a repos'd and easy Mind; Riot and Drowsiness, by Vigilance and Temperance; Lascivi-ousness, by our inviolable Fidelity to those who are Mistresses of our Thoughts; and Sloth, by our indefatigable Peregrina-tions through the Universe, to seek Occasions of Military, as well as Christian Honours. This, *Sancho*, is the Road to lasting Fame, and a good and honourable Renown. I understand pass-ing well every Tittle you have said, answer'd *Sancho*; but pray now, Sir, will you dissolve me of one Doubt, that's just come into my Head. Resolve thou would'st say, *Sancho*, re-ply'd Don *Quixote*: Well, speak, and I will endeavour to satis-fy thee. Why then, quoth *Sancho*, pray tell me, these same *Julys*, and these *Augusts*, and all the rest of the famous Knights you talk of that are dead, where are they now? Without doubt, answer'd Don *Quixote*, the Heathens are in Hell. The Chris-tians, if their Lives were answerable to their Profession, are either in Purgatory, or in Heaven. So far so good, said *Sancho*; but pray tell me, the Tombs of these Lordlings, have they any Silver Lamps still burning before 'em, and are their Chapel-Walls hung about with Crutches, Winding-sheets, old Peri-wigs, Legs and Wax-Eyes, or with what are they hung? The Monuments of the dead Heathens, said Don *Quixote*, were for the most Part sumptuous Pieces of Architecture. The Ashes of

Julius Cæsar were deposited on the Top of an Obelisk, all of one Stone of a prodigious Bigness, which is now called *Aguglia di San Pietro*, St *Peter's* Needle. The Emperor *Adrian's* Sepulchre was a vast Structure as big as an ordinary Village, and called *Moles Adriani*, and now the Castle of St *Angelo* in *Rome*. Queen *Artemisia* buried her Husband *Mausolus* in so curious and magnificent a Pile, that his Monument was reputed one of the seven Wonders of the World. But none of these, nor any other of the Heathen Sepulchres, were adorn'd with any Winding-sheets, or other Offering, that might imply the Persons interred were Saints. Thus far we are right, quoth *Sancho*; now, Sir, pray tell me, which is the greatest Wonder, to raise a dead Man, or kill a Giant? The Answer is obvious, said Don *Quixote*; to raise a dead Man certainly. Then, Master, I have nick'd you, saith *Sancho*, for he that raises the Dead, makes the Blind see, the Lame walk, and the Sick healthy, who has Lamps burning Night and Day before his Sepulchre, and whose Chapel is full of Pilgrims, who adore his Relicks on their Knees; that Man, I say, has more Fame in this World and in the next, than any of your Heathenish Emperors or Knights-Errant e'er had, or will ever have. I grant it, said Don *Quixote*. Very good, quoth *Sancho*, I'll be with you anon. This Fame, these Gifts, these Rights, Privileges, and what d'ye call 'em, the Bodies and Relicks of these Saints have; so that by the Consent and Good-liking of our Holy Mother the Church, they have their Lamps, their Lights, their Winding-sheets, their Crutches, their Pictures, their Heads of Hair, their Legs, their Eyes, and the Lord knows what, by which they stir up People's Devotion, and spread their Christian Fame. Kings will vouchsafe to carry the Bodies of Saints or their Relicks on their Shoulders, they'll kiss you the Pieces of their Bones, and spare no Cost to set off and deck their Shrines and Chapels. And what of all this, said Don *Quixote*? What's your Inference? Why, truly, Sir, quoth *Sancho*, that we turn Saints as fast as we can, and that's the readiest and cheapest way to get this same Honour you talk of. 'Twas but Yesterday or t'other Day, or I can't tell when, I'm sure 'twas not long since, that two poor bare-footed Friars were Sainted; and you can't think what a Crowd of People there is to kiss the Iron

61

Chains they wore about their Wastes instead of Girdles, to humble the Flesh. I dare say, they are more reverenc'd than *Orlando's* Sword, that hangs in the Armory of our Sovereign Lord the King, whom Heaven grant long to reign! So that for ought I see, better it is to be a Friar, tho' but of a beggarly Order, than a valiant Errant Knight; and a Dozen or two of sound Lashes, well meant, and as well laid on, will obtain more of Heaven than two thousand Thrusts with a Lance; tho' they be given to Giants, Dragons, or Hobgoblins. All this is very true, reply'd Don *Quixote*, but all Men cannot be Friars; we have different Paths allotted us, to mount to the high Seat of Eternal Felicity. Chivalry is a Religious Order, and there are Knights in the Fraternity of Saints in Heaven. However, quoth *Sancho*, I have heard say, there are more Friars there than Knights-Errant. That is, said Don *Quixote*, because there is a greater Number of Friars than of Knights. But are there not a great many Knights-Errant too? said *Sancho*. There are many indeed, answer'd Don *Quixote*, but very few that deserve the Name. In such Discourses as these, the Knight and Squire pass'd the Night, and the whole succeeding Day, without encountring any Occasion to signalize themselves; at which Don *Quixote* was very much concern'd. At last, towards Evening the next Day, they discover'd the goodly City of *Toboso*, which reviv'd the Knight's Spirits wonderfully, but had a quite contrary Effect on his Squire, because he did not know the House where *Dulcinea* liv'd, no more than his Master. So that the one was mad till he saw her, and the other very melancholick and disturb'd in Mind, because he had never seen her; nor did he know what to do, shou'd his Master send him to *Toboso*. However, as Don *Quixote* would not make his Entry in the Day-time, they spent the Evening among some Oaks not far distant from the Place, till the prefix'd Moment came; then they enter'd the City, where they met with Adventures indeed.

IX: THAT GIVES AN ACCOUNT OF THINGS
WHICH YOU'LL KNOW WHEN
YOU READ IT

THE sable Night had spun out half her Course, when Don *Quixote* and *Sancho* descended from a Hill, and enter'd *Toboso*. A profound Silence reign'd over all the Town, and all the Inhabitants were fast asleep, and stretch'd out at their Ease. The Night was somewhat clear, though *Sancho* wish'd it dark, to hide his Master's Folly and his own. Nothing disturb'd the general Tranquility, but now and then the barking of Dogs, that wounded Don *Quixote's* Ears, but more poor *Sancho's* Heart. Sometimes an Ass bray'd, Hogs grunted, Cats mew'd; which jarring Mixture of Sounds was not a little augmented by the Stillness and Serenity of the Night, and fill'd the enamour'd Champion's Head with a thousand inauspicious Chimera's. However, turning to his Squire, My dear *Sancho*, said he, shew me the Way to *Dulcinea's* Palace, perhaps we shall find her still awake. Body on me, cry'd *Sancho*, what Palace do you mean? When I saw her Highness, she was in a little paltry Cot. Perhaps, reply'd the Knight, she was then retir'd into some corner of the Palace, to divert her self in private with her Damsels, as great Ladies and Princesses sometimes do. Well, Sir, said *Sancho*, since it must be a Palace whether I will or no, yet can you think this is a Time of Night to find the Gates open, or a seasonable Hour to thunder at the Door, till we raise the House and alarm the whole Town? Are we going to a Bawdy-house, think you, like your Wenchers, that can rap at a Door any Hour of the Night, and knock People up when they list? Let us once find the Palace, said the Knight, and then I'll tell thee what we ought to do: But stay, either my Eyes delude me, or that lofty gloomy Structure which I discover yonder, is *Dulcinea's* Palace. Well, lead on, Sir, said the Squire; and yet though I were to see it with my Eyes, and feel it with my ten Fingers, I shall believe it e'en as much as I believe 'tis now Noon-day. The Knight led on, and having rode about two hundred Paces, came at last to the Building which he took for

63

Dulcinea's Palace; but found it to be the great Church of the Town. We are mistaken, *Sancho*, said he, I find this is a Church. I see it is, said the Squire; and I pray the Lord we have not found our Graves; for 'tis a plaguy ill Sign to haunt Churchyards at this Time of Night, especially when I told you, if I an't mistaken, that this Lady's House stands in a little blind Alley, without any Thorough-fair. A Curse on thy distemper'd Brain! cry'd Don *Quixote*; where, Blockhead, where didst thou ever see Royal Edifices and Palaces built in a blind Alley, without a Thorough-fair? Sir, said *Sancho*, every Country has its several Fashions; and for ought you know, they may build their great Houses and Palaces in blind Alleys at *Toboso*: And therefore, good your Worship, let me alone to hunt up and down in what By-Lanes and Allies I may strike into; mayhap in some Nook or Corner we may light upon this same Palace: Wou'd Old Nick had it for me, for leading us such a Jaunt, and plaguing a body at this rate. *Sancho*, said Don *Quixote*, speak with greater Respect of my Mistress's Concerns; be merry and wise, and do not throw the Helve after the Hatchet. Cry Mercy, Sir, quoth *Sancho*, but wou'd it not make any Man mad, to have you put me upon finding readily our Dame's House at all times, which I never saw but once in my Life? nay, and to find it at Midnight, when you your self can't find it, that have seen it a thousand times! Thou wilt make me desperately angry, said the Knight: Hark you, Heretick, have I not repeated it a thousand times, that I never saw the peerless *Dulcinea*, nor ever enter'd the Portals of her Palace; but that I am in Love with her purely by Hear-say, and upon the great Fame of her Beauty and rare Accomplishments? I hear you say so now, quoth *Sancho*; and since you say you never saw her, I must needs tell you I never saw her neither. That's impossible, said Don *Quixote*; at least you told me you saw her winnowing Wheat, when you brought me an Answer to the Letter which I sent by you. That's neither here nor there, Sir, reply'd *Sancho*; for to be plain with you, I saw her but by Hear-say too, and the Answer I brought you was by Hear-say as well as the rest, and I know the Lady *Dulcinea* no more than the Man in the Moon. *Sancho*, *Sancho*, said Don *Quixote*, there's a Time for all Things; unseasonable Mirth

64

always turns to Sorrow. What, because I declare that I have never seen nor spoken to the Mistress of my Soul, is it for you to trifle and say so too, when you're so sensible of the contrary?

Here their Discourse was interrupted, a Fellow with two Mules happening to pass by them, and by the Noise of the Plough which they drew along they guess'd it might be some Country Labourer going out before Day to his Husbandry; and so indeed it was. He went singing the doleful Ditty of the Defeat of the *French* at *Roncesvalles*;* *Ye* Frenchmen *all must rue the woful Day*. Let me die (said Don *Quixote*, hearing what the Fellow sung) if we have any good Success to Night; dost thou hear what this Peasant sings, *Sancho*? Ay marry do I, quoth the Squire; but what's the Rout at *Roncesvalles* to us? it concerns us no more than if he had sung the Ballad of *Colly my Cow*; we shall speed neither the better nor the worse for it. By this Time the Ploughman being come up to them; Good-morrow, honest Friend, cry'd Don *Quixote* to him; pray can you inform me which is the Palace of the peerless Princess, the Lady *Dulcinea del Toboso*? Sir, said the Fellow, I am a Stranger, and but lately come into this Town; I'm Ploughman to a rich Farmer: But here, right over-against you, lives the Curate and the Sexton, they're the likeliest to give you some Account of that Lady-Princess, as having a List of all the Folks in Town, though I fancy there's no Princess at all lives here; there be indeed a power of Gentle-folk, and each of them may be a Princess in her own House for ought I know. Perhaps, Friend, said Don *Quixote*, we shall find the Lady for whom I enquire among those. Why truly Master, answer'd the Plough-man, as you say, such a Thing may be, and so speed you well! 'Tis Break of Day. With that, switching his Mules, he stay'd for no more Questions.

Sancho perceiving his Master in Suspence, and not very well satisfy'd; Sir, said he, the Day comes on apace, and I think 'twill not be very handsome for us to stay to be star'd at, and sit sunning our selves in the Street. We had better slip out of Town again, and betake our selves to some Wood hard by, and

---

* *The Battle of* Roncesvalles *is a doleful melancholy Song like our* Chevy-Chase, *which is the Reason why it is look'd upon as Ominous, by super-stitious People*.

then I will come back, and search every Hole and Corner in Town for this same House, Castle, or Palace of my Lady's, and 'twill go hard if I don't find it out at long run; then will I talk to her Highness, and tell her how you do, and how I left you hard by, waiting her Orders and Instructions about talking with her in private, without bringing her Name in question. Dear *Sancho*, said the Knight, thou hast spoke and included a thousand Sentences in the Compass of a few Words; I approve, and lovingly accept thy Advice. Come, my Child, let us go, and in some neighbouring Grove find out a convenient Retreat; then, as thou say'st, thou shalt return to seek, to see, and to deliver my Embassy to my Lady, from whose Discretion and most courteous Mind I hope for a thousand Favours, that may be counted more than wonderful. *Sancho* sat upon Thorns till he had got his Master out of Town, lest he shou'd discover the Falshood of the Account he brought him in *Sierra Morena*, of *Dulcinea's* answering his Letter; So hast'ning to be gone, they were presently got two Miles from the Town into a Wood, where Don *Quixote* took Covert, and *Sancho* was dispatch'd to *Dulcinea*. In which Negotiation some Accidents fell out, that require new Attention and a fresh Belief.

X: HOW SANCHO CUNNINGLY FOUND OUT A WAY TO INCHANT THE LADY DULCINEA; WITH OTHER PASSAGES NO LESS CERTAIN THAN RIDICULOUS

THE Author of this important History being come to the Matters which he relates in this Chapter, says he would willingly have left 'em buried in Oblivion, in a manner despairing of his Reader's Belief: For Don *Quixote's* Madness flies here to so extravagant a Pitch, that it may be said to have out-stripp'd, by two Bow-shots, all imaginable Credulity. However, notwithstanding this Mistrust, he has set down every Particular, just as the same was transacted, without adding or diminishing the least Atom of Truth through the whole History; not valuing in the least such Objections as may be rais'd to impeach him of Breach of Veracity. A Proceeding which ought to be commended; for Truth indeed rather alleviates than hurts, and will always bear up against Falshood, as Oil does above Water. And so continuing his Narration, he tells us, That when Don *Quixote* was retir'd into the Wood or Forest, or rather into the Grove of Oaks near the Grand *Toboso*, he order'd *Sancho* to go back to the City, and not to return to his Presence till he had had Audience of his Lady; beseeching her that it might please her to be seen by her captive Knight, and vouchsafe to bestow her Benediction on him, that by the Virtue of that Blessing he might hope for a prosperous Event in all his Onsets and perilous Attempts and Adventures. *Sancho* undertook the Charge, engaging him as successful a Return of this as of his former Message.

Go then, Child, said the Knight, and have a care of being daunted when thou approachest the Beams of that refulgent Sun of Beauty. Happy, thou, above all the Squires of the Universe! Observe and engrave in thy Memory the Manner of thy Reception; mark whether her Colour changes upon the Delivery of thy Commission; whether her Looks betray any Emotion or Concern when she hears my Name; whether she does not seem to sit on her Cushion with a strange Uneasiness, in case thou happen'st to find her seated on the pompous Throne

of her Authority. And if she be standing, mind whether she
stands sometimes upon one Leg, and sometimes on another;
whether she repeats three or four times the Answer which
she gives thee, or changes it from kind to cruel, and then again
from cruel to kind; whether she does not seem to adjust her
Hair, though every Lock appears in perfect Order. In short,
observe all her Actions, every Motion, every Gesture; for by
the accurate Relation which thou giv'st of these things, I shall
divine the Secrets of her Breast, and draw just Inferences in
relation to my Amour. For I must tell thee, *Sancho*, if thou dost
not know it already, that the outward Motions of Lovers are
the surest Indications of their inward Affections, they are the
most faithful Intelligencers in an amorous Negociation. Go
then, my trusty Squire, thy own better Stars, not mine, attend
thee; and meet with a more prosperous event, than that which
in this doleful Desert, toss'd between Hopes and Fears, I dare
expect. I'll go, Sir, quoth *Sancho*, and I'll be back in a trice:
Mean while cheer up, I beseech you; come Sir, comfort that
little Heart of yours, no bigger than a Hazle-Nut! Don't be
cast down, I say; remember the old Saying, *Faint Heart ne'er
won fair Lady*: Where there's no Hook, to be sure there will
hang no Bacon: The Hare leaps out of the Bush where we least
look for her. I speak this, to give you to understand, that
though we could not find my Lady's Castle in the Night, I may
light on it when I least think on it now 'tis Day; and when I
have found it, let me alone to deal with her. Well, *Sancho*,
said the Knight, thou hast a rare Talent in applying thy Proverbs; Heaven give thee better Success in thy Designs! This
said, *Sancho* turn'd his Back, and switching his *Dapple*, left
the Don on Horseback, leaning on his Lance, and resting on his
Stirrups, full of melancholy and confus'd Imaginations. Let us
leave him too, to go along with *Sancho*, who was no less uneasy
in his Mind. No sooner was he got out of the Grove, but turning about, and perceiving his Master quite out of Sight, he dismounted, and laying himself down at the Foot of a Tree, thus
began to hold a Parley with himself. Friend *Sancho*, quoth he,
pray let me ask you whither your Worship is going? Is it to
seek some Ass you have lost? No by my Troth. What is't then
thou art hunting after? Why I am looking, you must know, for

a thing of nothing, only a Princess, and in her the Sun of Beauty, forsooth, and all Heaven together. Well, and where dost thou think to find all this, Friend of mine? Where! why in the great City of *Toboso*. And pray, Sir, who set you to work? Who set me to work! There's a Question! Why, who but the most renowned Don *Quixote de la Mancha*, he that rights the Wrong'd, that gives Drink to the Hungry, and Meat to those that are a Dry. Very good, Sir, but pray dost know where she lives? Not I, efackins! but my Master says 'tis somewhere in a King's Palace, or stately Castle. And hast thou ever seen her trow? No marry han't I: Why, my Master himself ne'er sat Eyes on her in his Life. But tell me, *Sancho*, what if the People of *Toboso* should know that you are come to inviegle their Princesses, and make their Ladies run astray, and should baste your Carcase handsomely, and leave you ne'er a sound Rib, do you not think they would be mightily in the Right on't? Why, troth, they would not be much in the wrong; tho' me-thinks they should consider too, that I am but a Servant, and sent on another body's Errand, and so I am not at all in Fault. Nay, never trust to that, *Sancho*, for your People of *la Man-cha*, are plaguy hot and toucheous, and will endure no Tricks to be put upon 'em: Body of me! if they but smoke thee, they'll mawl thee after a strange rate. No, no, fore-warn'd fore-armed: Why do I go about to look for more Feet than a Cat has, for another Man's Maggot! Besides, when all's done, I may perhaps as well look for a Needle in a Bottle of Hay, or for a Scholar at *Salamanca*, as for *Dulcinea* all over the Town of *Toboso*. Well, 'tis the Devil, and nothing but the Devil, has put me upon this troublesome Piece of Work. This was the Dialogue *Sancho* had with himself; and the Consequence of it was the following Soliloquy. Well, there's a Remedy for all things but Death, which will be sure to lay us flat one time or other. This Master of mine, by a thousand Tokens I ha' seen, is a downright Madman, and I think I come within an Inch of him; nay, I am the greatest Cod's-head of the Two, to serve and follow him as I do, if the Proverb ben't a Lyar, Shew me thy Company, I'll tell thee what thou art; and t'other old Saw, Birds of a Feather flock together. Now then my Master being mad, and so very mad as to mistake sometimes one thing for

another, Black for White, and White for Black; as when he
took the Wind-Mills for Giants, the Friar's Mules for Dromedaries, and the Flocks of Sheep for Armies, and much more to
the same Tune; I guess 'twill be no hard matter to pass upon
him the first Country-Wench I shall meet with, for the Lady
Dulcinea. If he won't believe it, I'll swear it; if he swear again,
I'll out-swear him; and if he be positive, I'll be more positive
than he; and stand to't, and out-face him in't, come what will
on't: So that when he finds I won't flinch, he'll either resolve
never to send me more of his sleeveless Errands, seeing what
a lame Account I bring him, or he'll think some one of those
wicked Wizards, who, he says, owes him a Grudge, has transmogrify'd her into some other Shape out of spite. This happy
Contrivance help'd to compose *Sancho's* Mind, and now he
look'd on his grand Affair to be as good as done. Having therefore staid till the Evening, that his Master might think he had
employ'd so much Time in going and coming, things fell out
very luckily for him; for as he arose to mount his *Dapple*, he
spy'd three Country-Wenches coming towards him from *Toboso*, upon three young Asses; whether Male or Female, the
Author has left undetermined, tho' we may reasonably suppose they were She-Asses, such being most frequently us'd to
ride on by Country-Lasses in those Parts. But this being no
very material Circumstance, we need not dwell any longer
upon the Decision of that Point. 'Tis sufficient they were Asses,
and discover'd by *Sancho*; who thereupon made all the haste
he could to get to his Master, and found him breathing out a
Thousand Sighs and amorous Lamentations. Well, my *Sancho*, said the Knight immediately upon his Approach, what
News? Are we to mark this Day with a white or a black Stone?
Ev'n mark it rather with Red Oker, answer'd *Sancho*, as they
do Church-Chairs, that every body may know who they belong to. Why then, said Don *Quixote*, I suppose thou bringest
good News. Ay, marry do I, quoth *Sancho*, you have no more
to do but to clap Spurs to *Rozinante*, and get into the open
Fields, and you'll see my Lady *Dulcinea del Toboso*, with a
Brace of her Damsels, coming to see your Worship. Blessed
Heaven! cry'd Don *Quixote*, what art thou saying, my dear
Sancho? Take heed, and do not presume to beguile my real

Grief with a delusive Joy. Adsookers! Sir, said *Sancho*, what shou'd I get by putting a Trick upon you, and being found out the next Moment? Seeing is believing all the World over. Come, Sir, put on, put on, and you'll see our Lady Princess coming, dress'd up and bedeck'd like her own sweet self indeed. Her Damsels and she are all one Spark of Gold; all Pearls, all Diamonds, all Rubies, all Cloth of Gold above ten Inches high. Their Hair spread over their Shoulders like so many Sunbeams, and dangling and dancing in the Wind; and what's more, they ride upon three Flea-bitten gambling Hags; there's not a Piece of Horse-flesh can match 'em in three Kingdoms. Ambling Nags thou meanest, *Sancho*, said Don *Quixote*. Gambling Hags or Ambling Nags, quoth *Sancho*, there's no such Difference methinks; but be they what they will, I'm sure, I ne'er sat Eyes on finer Creatures than those that ride upon their Backs, especially my Lady *Dulcinea*; 'twould make one swoon away but to look upon her. Let us move then, my *Sancho*, said Don *Quixote*; and as a Gratification for these unexpected happy Tidings, I freely bestow on thee the best Spoils the next Adventure we meet with shall afford; and if that content thee not, take the Colts which my three Mares thou know'st of, are now ready to foal on our town-common. Thank you for the Colts, said *Sancho*; but as for the Spoils, I am not sure they'll be worth any thing. They were now got out of the Wood, and discover'd the three Country-Lasses at a small Distance. Don *Quixote* casting his Eyes towards *Toboso*, and seeing no body on the Road but the three Wenches, was strangely troubled in Mind, and turning to *Sancho*, ask'd him whether the Princess and her Damsels were come out of the City when he left 'em? Out of the City cry'd *Sancho*! Why where are your Eyes? Are they in your Heels, in the Name of Wonder, that you can't see 'em coming towards us, shining as bright as the Sun at Noon Day? I see nothing, return'd Don *Quixote*, but three Wenches upon as many Asses. Now Heaven deliver me from the Devil, quoth *Sancho*! Is't possible your Worship shou'd mistake Three what d'ye-call-ems, Three Ambling Nags I mean, as white as driven Snow, for Three ragged Ass-Colts! Body of me! I'll e'en peel off my Beard by the Roots an't be so. Take it from me, Friend *Sancho*, said the Knight,

71

they are either He or She-Asses, as sure as I am Don *Quixote*, and thou *Sancho Pança*; at least, they appear to be such. Come Sir, quoth the Squire, don't talk at that rate, but snuff your Eyes, and go pay your Homage to the Mistress of your Soul; for she's near at hand; and so saying, *Sancho* hastens up to the three Country Wenches, and alighting from *Dapple*, took hold of one of the Asses by the Halter, and falling on his Knees, Queen, and Princess, and Dutchess of Beauty, quoth he, an't please your Haughtiness, and Greatness, vouchsafe to take into your good Grace and Liking, yonder Knight, your Prisoner and Captive, who's turn'd of a sudden into cold Marble-Stone, and struck all of a heap, to see himself before your High and Mightiness. I am *Sancho Pança*, his Squire, and he himself the wand'ring Weather-beaten Knight, Don *Quixote de la Mancha*, otherwise call'd the Knight of the Woful Figure. By this time, Don *Quixote* having plac'd himself down on his Knees by *Sancho*, gaz'd with dubious and disconsolate Eyes on the Creature, whom *Sancho* call'd Queen and Lady; and perceiving her to be no more than a plain Country-Wench, so far from being well-favour'd that she was blubber-cheek'd, and flat-nos'd, he was lost in Astonishment, and cou'd not utter one Word. On the other side, the Wenches were no less surpriz'd, to see themselves stopp'd by two Men in such different Out-sides, and on their Knees. But at last she whose Ass was held by *Sancho* took Courage, and broke Silence in an angry Tone. Come, cry'd she, get out of our way with a Murrain, and let us go about our Business; for we are in haste. O Princess! and Universal Lady of *Toboso*, answer'd *Sancho*, why does not that great Heart of yours melt, to see the Post and Pillar of Knight-Errantry fall down before your high and mighty Presence! Hey-day, (quoth another of the Females, hearing this) What's here to do! Look how your small Gentry come to jeer and flout poor Country Girls, as if we could not give 'em as good as they bring. Go, get about your Business, and let us go about ours, and speed you well. Rise, *Sancho*, said Don *Quixote*, hearing this, for I am now convinc'd, that my malicious Stars, not yet satisfy'd with my past Misfortunes, still shed their baleful Influence, and have barr'd all the Passages that could convey Relief to my miserable Soul, in this frail Habitation of Animated Clay. O! thou Extremity of all that's valuable, Master-piece of all human Perfection, and only Comfort of this afflicted Heart, thy adorer; though now a spiteful Inchanter persecutes me, and fascinates my Sight, hiding with Mists and Cataracts from me, and me alone, those Peerless Beauties under the foul Disguise of rustick Deformity, if he has not transform'd thy faithful Knight into some ugly Shape to make me loathsome to thy Sight, look on me with a smiling amorous Eye; and in the Submission and Genuflexion which I pay to thy Beauty, even under the fatal Cloud that obscures it, read the Humility with which my Soul adores thee. Tittle-tattle, quoth the Country-Wench, Spare your Breath to cool your Porridge, and rid me of your idle Gibberish. Get you on, Sir, and let us go; and we shall think it a Kindness. This said, *Sancho* made way for her, and let her pass, overjoy'd his Plot had succeeded so well. The imaginary *Dulcinea* was no sooner at Liberty, but punching her Ass with the End of a Staff which she had in her Hand, she began to scour along the Plain: But the angry Beast not being us'd to such smart Instigations, fell a kicking and wincing at such a rate, that down came my Lady *Dulcinea*. Presently Don *Quixote* ran to help her up, and *Sancho* to re-settle and gird her Pack-Saddle, that hung under the Ass's Belly. Which being done, the Knight very courteously was going to take his Inchanted Mistress in his Arms, to set her on her Saddle; but she being now got on her Legs, took a run, and clapping her Hands upon the Ass's Crupper, at one Jump leap'd into her Pannel, as swift as a Hawk, and there she sate with her Legs astride like a Man. By the Lord *Harry*! quoth *Sancho*, our Lady Mistress is as nimble as an Eel. Let me be hang'd, if I don't think she might teach the best Jocky in *Cordova* or *Mexico*, to mount a Horseback. At one Jump she was vaulted into the Saddle, and, without Spurs, makes her Nag smoke it away like a Greyhound; her Damsels are notable Whipsters too; adad! they don't come much short of her, for they fly like the Wind. Indeed, he said true, for when *Dulcinea* was once mounted, they all made after her full speed, without so much as looking behind 'em for above half a League. Don *Quixote* follow'd 'em as far as he cou'd with his Eyes; and when they were quite out of Sight, turning to his Squire, Now *Sancho*, saith he, What thinkest thou of this Matter? Are not these base Inchanters Inexorable; How extensive is their Spite, thus to deprive me of the Happiness of seeing the Object of my Wishes in her natural Shape and Glory. Sure I was doom'd to be an Example of Misfortunes, and the Mark against which those Caitiffs are employ'd to shoot all the Arrows of their Hatred. Note, *Sancho*, that these Traytors were not content to turn and transform my *Dulcinea*, but they must do it into the vile and deform'd Resemblance of that Country-Wench; nay, they even took from her that sweet Scent of fragrant Flowers and Amber, those grateful Odours, so essential to Ladies of her Rank; for, to tell the Truth, when I went to help her upon her Nag, as thou call'st it, (for to me it seem'd nothing but an Ass) such a Whiff, such a rank Hogo of raw Garlick invaded my Nostrils, as had like to have overcome me, and put me into a Convulsion. O ye vile Wretches, cry'd *Sancho*! O ye wicked and ill-minded Inchanters: O that I might but once see the whole Nest of ye threaded together on one String, and hung up a smoaking by the Gills like so many *Pilchards*! You know a deal, you can do a deal, and you make a deal of Mischief. One would have thought you might have been contented, like a Pack of Rogues as you are, with having chang'd the Pearls of my Lady's Eyes into Gall-nuts, and her most pure Golden Locks into a Red Cow's Tail; but you must be meddling with her Breath, by which we might have guess'd what lay hid under that coarse Disguise; though for my Part I must needs own, she did not appear to be Deform'd at all, but rather Fair and Beautiful; by the same Token that she had a Mole on the Side of the Upper Lip, like a Whisker, whence sprouted Seven or Eight red Hairs, each about a Span in Length, looking like so many Threads of Gold Wire. As the Moles on the Body, said Don *Quixote*, are generally answerable to those on the Face, *Dulcinea* should have such another Mole on the Brawn of her Thigh, opposite to that Side of her Face where that Beauty-spot is seated: But methinks, *Sancho*, the Hairs thou talkest of, are of a Length somewhat extraordinary for Moles. That's neither here nor there, quoth *Sancho*; there they were I'll assure you, and they look'd too as if she had brought 'em with her into the World.

That I believe, said Don *Quixote*, for every Part of *Dulcinea* must be naturally perfect and compleat; so that though a hundred Moles were scatter'd over her fair Outside, and as conspicuous too as that which thou didst see, they would be no Deformities in her; but so many Moons and Stars, an additional Lustre to her Beauty. But tell me *Sancho*, that Saddle which appear'd to me to be the Pannel of an Ass, was it a Pillion or Side-Saddle? It was a Pad-Saddle, answer'd *Sancho*, with a Field-covering, and so rich that it might purchase half a Kingdom. And could not I see all this, cry'd Don *Quixote*? Well, I have said it, and must repeat it a thousand times, I am the most unfortunate Man in the Universe. The cunning Rogue of a Squire, hearing his Master talk at that rate, could hardly keep his Countenance, and refrain from laughing, to see how admirably he had fool'd him. At last, after a great deal of Discourse of the same Nature they both mounted again, and took the Road for *Saragossa*, designing to be present at the most celebrated Festivals and Sports that are solemnized every Year in that noble City. But they met with many Accidents by the Way, and those so extraordinary, and worthy the Reader's Information, that they must not be pass'd over unrecorded nor unread; as shall appear from what follows.

XI: OF THE STUPENDOUS ADVENTURE THAT BEFEL THE VALOROUS DON QUIXOTE, WITH THE CHARIOT OR CART OF THE COURT OR PARLIAMENT OF DEATH

DON *Quixote* rode on very melancholick; the Malice of the Magicians, in transforming his Lady *Dulcinea*, perplex'd him strangely, and set his Thoughts upon the Rack, how to dissolve the Inchantment, and restore her to her former Beauty. In this disconsolate Condition, he went on abandon'd to Distraction, carelessly giving *Rozinante* the Reins: And the Horse finding himself at Liberty, and tempted by the Goodness of the Grass, took the Opportunity to feed very heartily. Which *Sancho* perceiving, Sir, (said he, rouzing him from his waking Dream) Sorrow was never design'd for Beasts, but Men; but yet let me tell you, if Men give way to't too much, they make Beasts of themselves. Come, Sir, awake, awake by any means, pull up the Reins, and ride like a Man; cheer up, and shew yourself a Knight-Errant. What the Devil ails you? Was ever a Man so mop'd? Are we here, or are we in *France*, as the Saying is? Let all the *Dulcineas* in the World be doom'd to the Pit of Hell, rather than one single Knight-Errant be cast down at this rate. Hold, *Sancho*, cry'd Don *Quixote*, with more Spirit than one would have expected; hold, I say; not a blasphemous Word against that beauteous inchanted Lady; for all her Misfortunes are chargeable on the unhappy Don *Quixote*, and flow from the Envy which those Necromancers bear to me. So say I, Sir, reply'd the Squire; for would it not vex any one that had seen her before, to see her now as you saw her? Ah, *Sancho*, said the Knight, thy Eyes were bless'd with a View of her Perfections in their entire Lustre, thou hast Reason to say so. Against Me, against My Eyes only is the Malice of her Transformation directed. But now I think on't, *Sancho*, thy Description of her Beauty was a little absurd in that Particular, of comparing her Eyes to Pearls; sure such Eyes are more like those of a Whiting or a Sea-Bream, than those of a fair Lady; and in my Opinion,

Dulcinea's Eyes are rather like two verdant Emeralds rail'd in with two Celestial Arches, which signify her Eye-brows. Therefore, *Sancho*, you must take your Pearls from her Eyes, and apply 'em to her Teeth, for I verily believe you mistook the one for the other. Troth! Sir, it might be so, reply'd *Sancho*, for her Beauty confounded me, as much as her Ugliness did you. But let us leave all to Heaven, that knows all things that befal us in this Vale of Misery, this wicked troublesome World, where we can be sure of nothing without some Spice of Knavery or Imposture. In the mean time, there's a thing comes into my Head that puzzles me plaguily. Pray, Sir, when you get the better of any Giant or Knight, and send 'em to pay Homage to the Beauty of your Lady and Mistress, how the Devil will the poor Knight or Giant be able to find this same *Dulcinea*. I can't but think how they'll be to seek, how they'll saunter about, gaping and staring all over *Toboso* Town, and if they should meet her full butt in the Middle of the King's Highway, yet they'll know her no more than they knew the Father that begot me. Perhaps, *Sancho*, answer'd Don *Quixote*, the Force of her Inchantment does not extend so far as to debar Vanquish'd Knights and Giants from the Privilege of seeing her in her unclouded Beauties; I will try the Experiment on the first I conquer, and will command them to return immediately to me, to inform me of their Success. I like what you say main well, quoth *Sancho*; we may chance to find out the Truth by this means; and if so be my Lady is only hid from your Worship, she has not so much Reason to complain as you may have; but when all comes to all, so our Mistress be safe and sound, let us make the best of a bad Market, and e'en go seek Adventures. The rest we'll leave to Time, which is the best Doctor in such Cases, nay, in worse Diseases. Don *Quixote* was going to return an Answer, but was interrupted by a Cart that was crossing the Road. He that drove it was a hideous Devil, and the Cart being open, without either Tilt or Boughs, expos'd a Parcel of the most surprizing and different Shapes imaginable. The first Figure that appear'd to Don *Quixote*, was no less than Death itself, though with a human Countenance; on the one Side of Death stood an Angel with large Wings of different Colours; on the other Side was plac'd an Emperor

77

with a Crown that seem'd to be of Gold; at the Feet of Death lay *Cupid* with his Bow, Quiver, and Arrows, but not blindfold. Next to these a Knight appear'd compleatly arm'd except his Head, on which, instead of a Helmet, he wore a Hat; whereon was mounted a large Plume of Party-colour'd Feathers. There were also several other Persons in strange and various Dresses. This strange Appearance at first somewhat surpriz'd Don *Quixote*, and frighted the poor Squire out of his Wits; but presently the Knight clear'd up on second Thoughts, imagining it some rare and hazardous Adventure that call'd on his Courage. Pleas'd with this Conceit, and arm'd with a Resolution able to confront any Danger, he plac'd himself in the Middle of the Road, and with a loud and menacing Voice, You Carter, Coachman, or Devil, cry'd he, or whatever you be, let me know immediately whence you come, and whither you go, and what strange Figures are those which load that Carriage, which by the Freight rather seems to be *Charon's* Boat, than any terrestrial Vehicle. Sir, answer'd the Devil very civilly, stopping his Cart, we are strolling Players, that belong to *Angulo's* Company, and it being *Corpus-Christi-Tide*, we have this Morning acted a Tragedy, call'd *The Parliament of Death*, in a Town yonder behind the Mountain, and this Afternoon we are to play it again in the Town you see before us, which being so near, we travel to it in the same Cloaths we act in, to save the Trouble of new dressing ourselves. That young Man plays Death; that other an Angel: This Woman, Sir, our Poet's Bedfellow, plays the Queen; there is one acts a Soldier; he next to him an Emperor; and I myself play the Devil; and you must know, the Devil is the best Part in the Play. If you desire to be satisfy'd in any thing else, do but ask and I'll resolve you, for the Devil knows every thing. Now by the Faith of my Function, said Don *Quixote*, I find we ought not to give Credit to Appearances, before we have made the Experiment of feeling them; for at the Discovery of such a Scene, I would have sworn some strange Adventure had been approaching. I wish you well good People; drive on to act your Play, and if I can be serviceable to you in any Particular, believe me ready to assist you with all my Heart; for in my very Childhood I lov'd Shows, and have been a great Admirer of Dramatick Representations

78

from my youthful Days. During this friendly Conversation, it unluckily fell out, that one of the Company antickly dress'd, being the Fool of the Play, came up frisking with his Morrice Bells, and three full blown Cow's Bladders fasten'd to the End of a Stick. In this odd Appearance he began to flourish his Stick in the Air, and bounce his Bladders against the Ground just at *Rozinante's* Nose. The Jingling of the Bells, and the rattling Noise of the Bladders so startl'd and affrighted the quiet Creature, that Don *Quixote* could not hold him in; and having got the Curb betwixt his Teeth, away the Horse hurried his unwilling Rider up and down the Plain, with more Swiftness than his feeble Bones seemed to promise. *Sancho* considering the Danger of his Master's being thrown, presently alighted, and ran as fast he cou'd to his Assistance; but before he cou'd come up to him, *Rozinante* had made a false Step, and laid his Master and himself on the Ground; which was indeed the common End of *Rozinante's* mad Tricks and presumptuous Racing. On the other Side, the Fool no sooner saw *Sancho* slide off to help his Master, but he leap'd upon poor *Dapple*, and rattling his Bladders over the terrify'd Animal's Head, made him fly thro' the Field towards the Town where they were to Play. *Sancho* beheld his Master's Fall, and his Ass's Flight at the same time, and stood strangely divided in himself, not knowing which to assist first, his Master or his Beast. At length the Duty of a good Servant and a faithful Squire prevailing, he ran to his Master, tho' every obstreperous Bounce with the Bladders upon *Dapple's* Hind-quarters, struck him to the very Soul, and he could have wish'd every Blow upon his own Eye-Balls, rather than on the least Hair of his Ass's Tail. In this Agony of Spirits, he came to Don *Quixote*, whom he found in far worse Circumstances than the poor Knight could have wish'd; and helping him to remount; O! Sir, cry'd he, the Devil is run away with *Dapple*. What Devil, ask'd Don *Quixote*? The Devil with the Bladders, answer'd *Sancho*. No matter, said Don *Quixote*, I'll force the Traytor to restore him, though he were to lock him up in the most profound and gloomy Caverns of Hell. Follow me, *Sancho*; We may easily overtake the Waggon, and the Mules shall atone for the Loss of the Ass. You need not be in such haste now, quoth *Sancho*, for I perceive the Devil has left

79

Dapple already, and is gone his ways. What *Sancho* said was true, for both Ass and Devil tumbled for Company, in Imitation of Don *Quixote* and *Rozinante*; and *Dapple* having left his new Rider to walk on foot to the Town, now came himself running back to his Master. All this, said Don *Quixote*, shall not hinder me from revenging the Affront put upon us by that unmannerly Devil, at the Expence of some of his Companions, though it were the Emperor himself. O good your Worship! cry'd *Sancho*, never mind it; I beseech you take my Counsel, Sir; never meddle with Players, there's never any thing to be got by't; they are a Sort of People that always find a many Friends. I have known one of 'em taken up for two Murders, yet 'scape the Gallows. You must know, that as they are a Parcel of merry Wags, and make Sport where-ever they come, every body is fond of 'em, and is ready to stand their Friend, especially if they be the King's Players, or some of the noted Gangs, who go at such a tearing Rate, that one might mistake some of 'em for Gentlemen or Lords. I care not, said Don *Quixote*, tho' all Mankind unite to assist 'em, that buffooning Devil shall never 'scape unpunish'd, to make his Boast that he has affronted me. Whereupon, riding up to the Waggon, which was now got pretty near the Town, Hold, hold, he cry'd; stay, my pretty Sparks, I'll teach you to be civil to the Beasts that are intrusted with the honourable Burden of a Squire to a Knight-Errant. This loud Salutation having reach'd the Ears of the Strolling Company, tho' at a good Distance, they presently understood what it imported; and resolving to be ready to entertain him, Death presently leap'd out of the Cart; the Emperor, the Devil-driver, and the Angel immediately follow'd; and even the Queen, and the God *Cupid*, as well as the rest, having taken up their Share of Flints, stood rang'd in Battle-Array ready to receive their Enemy, as soon as he should come within Stone-shot. Don *Quixote* seeing them drawn up in such excellent Order, with their Arms lifted up, and ready to let fly at him a furious Volley of Shot, made a Halt to consider in what Quarter he might attack this dreadful Batallion with least Danger to his Person. Thus pausing, *Sancho* overtook him, and seeing him ready to charge, For Goodness Sake, Sir, cry'd he, what d'ye mean? Are you mad, Sir? There's no Fence against the Beggar's Bullets, unless you could fight with a Brazen Bell over you. Is it not rather Rashness than true Courage, think you, for one Man to offer to set upon a whole Army? where Death is too, and where Emperors fight in Person; nay, and where good and bad Angels are against you? But if all this weighs nothing with you, consider I beseech you, that though they seem to be Kings, Princes, and Emperors, yet there's not so much as one Knight-Errant among 'em all. Now thou hast hit upon the only Point, said Don *Quixote*, that could stop the Fury of my Arm: For indeed, as I have often told thee, *Sancho*, I am bound up from drawing my Sword against any below the Order of Knighthood. 'Tis thy Business to fight in this Cause, if thou hast a just Resentment of the Indignities offer'd to thy Ass; and I from this Post will encourage and assist thee with salutary Orders and Instructions. No, I thank you, Sir, quoth *Sancho*, I hate Revenge; a true Christian must forgive and forget; and as for *Dapple*, I don't doubt but to find him willing to leave the Matter to me, and stand to my Verdict in the Case, which is to live peaceably and quietly as long as Heaven is pleas'd to let me. Nay then, said Don *Quixote*, if that be thy Resolution, Good *Sancho*, Prudent *Sancho*, Christian *Sancho*, Downright *Sancho*, let us leave these idle Apparitions, and proceed in Search of more substantial and honourable Adventures, of which, in all Probability, this Part of the World will afford us a wonderful Variety. So saying, he wheel'd off, and *Sancho* follow'd him. On the other side, Death with all his flying Squadron return'd to their Cart, and went on their Journey. Thus ended the most dreadful Adventure of the Chariot of Death, much more happily than could have been expected, Thanks to the laudable Counsels which *Sancho Pança* gave his Master; who the Day following had another Adventure no less remarkable, with One that was a Knight-Errant and a Lover too.

XII: THE VALOROUS DON QUIXOTE'S STRANGE
ADVENTURE WITH THE BOLD KNIGHT
OF THE MIRRORS

DON *Quixote* pass'd the Night, that succeeded his Encounter with Death, under the Covert of some lofty Trees; where, at *Sancho's* Persuasion, he refresh'd himself with some of the Provisions which *Dapple* carried. As they were at Supper, Well, Sir, quoth the Squire, what a rare Fool I had been, had I chosen for my good News the Spoils of your first Venture, instead of the Breed of the three Mares! Troth! commend me to the Saying, *A Bird in Hand is worth two in the Bush*. However, answer'd Don *Quixote*, had'st thou let me fall on, as I wou'd have done, thou might'st have shar'd, at least, the Emperor's Golden Crown, and *Cupid's* painted Wings; for I wou'd have pluck'd 'em off, and put 'em into thy Power. Ah, but says *Sancho*, your strolling Emperor's Crowns and Sceptres are not of pure Gold, but Tinsel and Copper. I grant it, said Don *Quixote*; nor is it fit the Decorations of the Stage should be real, but rather Imitations, and the Resemblance of Realities, as the Plays themselves must be; which, by the way, I wou'd have you love and esteem, *Sancho*, and consequently those that write, and also those that act 'em; for they are all instrumental to the Good of the Commonwealth, and set before our eyes those Looking-glasses that reflect a lively Representation of human Life; nothing being able to give us a more just Idea of Nature, and what we are or ought to be, than Comedians and Comedies. Prithee tell me, Hast thou never seen a Play acted, where Kings, Emperors, Prelates, Knights, Ladies, and other Characters, are introduced on the Stage? One acts a Ruffian, another a Soldier; this Man a Cheat, and that a Merchant; one plays a designing Fool, and another a foolish Lover: But the Play done, and the Actors undress'd, they are all equal, and as they were before. All this I have seen, quoth *Sancho*. Just such a Comedy, said Don *Quixote*, is acted on the great Stage of the World, where some play the Emperors, others the Prelates, and, in short, all the Parts that can be brought into a Dramatick Piece; till Death, which is the Catastrophe and End of the Action, strips the Actors of all their Marks of Distinction, and levels their Quality in the Grave. A rare Comparison, quoth *Sancho*, though not so new, but that I have heard it over and over. Just such another is that of a Game at Chess, where while the Play lasts, every Piece has its particular Office; but when the Game's over, they are all mingl'd and huddled together, and clapp'd into a Bag, just as when Life's ended we are laid up in the Grave. Truly, *Sancho*, said Don *Quixote*, thy Simplicity lessens, and thy Sense improves every Day. And good Reason why, quoth *Sancho*; some of your Worship's Wit must needs stick to me; for your dry unkindly Land, with good dunging and tilling, will in time yield a good Crop. I mean, Sir, that the Dung and Muck of your Conversation being thrown on the barren Ground of my Wit, together with the Time I ha' served your Worship, and kept you Company; which is, as a body may say, the Tillage; I must needs bring forth blessed Fruit at last, so as not to shame my Master, but keep in the Paths of good Manners, which you have beaten into my sodden Understanding. *Sancho's* affected Stile made Don *Quixote* laugh, tho' he thought his Words true in the main; and he could not but admire at his Improvement. But the Fellow never discover'd his Weakness so much as by endeavouring to hide it, being most apt to tumble when he strove to soar too high. His Excellence lay chiefly in a Knack at drawing Proverbs into his Discourse, whether to the Purpose or not, as any one that has observ'd his manner of Speaking in this History, must have perceived.

In such Discourses they passed a great part of the Night, till *Sancho* wanted to drop the Portcullices of his Eyes, which was his way of saying he had a mind to go to sleep. Thereupon he unharness'd *Dapple*, and set him a grazing: But poor *Rozinante* was condemn'd to stand saddled all Night, by his Master's Injunction and Prescription, us'd of old by all Knights-Errant, who never unsaddled their Steeds in the Field, but took off their Bridles, and hung 'em at the Pummel of the Saddle. However, he was not forsaken by faithful *Dapple*, whose Friendship was so unparallel'd and inviolable, that unquestion'd Tradition has handed it down from Father to Son, that the Author of this true History compos'd particular Chapters of the united Affection of these two Beasts; tho', to preserve the Decorum due to so heroick a History, he wou'd not insert 'em in the Work. Yet sometimes he cannot forbear giving us some new Touches on that Subject; as when he writes, That the two friendly Creatures took a mighty Pleasure in being together to scrub and lick one another; and when they had had enough of that Sport, *Rozinante* would gently lean his Head at least half a Yard over *Dapple's* Neck, and so they wou'd stand very lovingly together, looking wistly on the Ground for two or three Days; except Somebody made 'em leave that contemplative Posture, or Hunger compell'd them to a Separation. Nay, I cannot pass by what is reported of the Author, how he left in Writing, That he had compar'd their Friendship to that of *Nysus* and *Euryalus*, and that of *Pylades* and *Orestes*, which if it were so, deserves universal Admiration; the sincere Affection of these quiet Animals being a just Reflection on Men, who are so guilty of breaking their Friendship to one another. From hence came the Saying, *There's no Friend; all Friendship's gone: Now Men hug, then fight anon.* And that other, *Where you see your Friend, trust to your self.* Neither shou'd the World take it ill, that the cordial Affection of these Animals was compar'd by our Author to that of Men; since many important Principles of Prudence and Morality, have been learnt from irrational Creatures; as, the Use of Clysters from the Stork, and the Benefit of Vomiting from the Dog. The Crane gave Mankind an Example of Vigilance, the Ant of Providence, the Elephant of Honesty, and the Horse of Loyalty. At last, *Sancho* fell asleep at the Root of a Cork-tree, and his Master fetch'd a Slumber under a spacious Oak. But it was not long e'er he was disturb'd by a Noise behind him, and starting up, he look'd and hearken'd on the Side whence he thought the Voice came, and discover'd two Men on Horse-back; one of whom letting himself carelesly slide down from the Saddle, and calling to the other, Alight, Friend, said he, and unbridle the Horse; for methinks this Place will supply them plentifully with Pasture, and me with Silence and Solitude to Indulge my amorous Thoughts. While he said this, he laid himself down on the Grass; in doing which, the Armour he had on made a Noise, a sure Sign, that gave Don *Quixote* to understand he was some Knight-Errant. Thereupon going to *Sancho*, who slept on, he pluck'd him by the Arm; and having wak'd him with much ado, Friend *Sancho*, said he, whispering him in his Ear, here's an Adventure. Heaven grant it be a good one! quoth *Sancho*. But where's that same Lady Adventure's Worship? Where! dost thou ask, *Sancho*? Why, turn thy Head, Man, and look yonder. Dost thou not see a Knight-Errant there lying on the Ground? I have Reason to think he is in melancholy Circumstances, for I saw him fling himself off from his Horse, and stretch himself on the Ground in a disconsolate manner, and his Armour clash'd as he fell. What of all that, quoth *Sancho*? How do you make this to be an Adventure? I will not yet affirm, answer'd Don *Quixote*, that 'tis an Adventure; but a very fair Rise to one as ever was seen. But hark! he's tuning some Instrument, and by his coughing and spitting he's clearing his Throat to sing. Troth now, Sir, quoth *Sancho*, 'tis e'en so in good earnest; and I fancy 'tis some Knight that's in Love. All Knights-Errant must be so, answer'd Don *Quixote*: But let us hearken, and if he sings, we shall know more of his Circumstances presently, for out of the Abundance of the Heart the Mouth speaketh. *Sancho* wou'd have answer'd, but that the Knight of the Wood's Voice, which was but indifferent, interrupted him with the following

SONG

1

Bright Queen, how shall your loving Slave
  Be sure not to displease?
Some Rule of Duty let him crave;
  He begs no other Ease.

2

Say, must I die, or hopeless live?
  Ill Act as you Ordain:
Despair a silent Death shall give,
  Or Love himself complain.

3

My Heart, tho' soft as Wax, will prove
  Like Diamonds firm and true:
For, what th' Impression can remove,
  That's stamp'd by Love and you?

85

The Knight of the Wood concluded his Song with a Sigh, that seem'd to be fetch'd from the very Bottom of his Heart; and after some Pause, with a mournful and disconsolate Voice: O the most Beautiful, but most Ungrateful of Womankind, cry'd he, how is it possible, most serene *Casildea de Vandalia*, your Heart shou'd consent that a Knight who idolizes your Charms, shou'd waste the Flower of his Youth, and kill himself with continual Wandrings and hard Fatigues? Is it not enough, that I have made you to be acknowledg'd the greatest Beauty in the World, by all the Knights of *Navarre*, all the Knights of *Leon*, all the *Tartesians*, all the *Castilians*, and, in fine, by all the Knights of *La Mancha*? Not so neither, said Don *Quixote* then; for I my self am of *La Mancha*, and never acknowledg'd, nor ever could, nor ought to acknowledge a Thing so injurious to the Beauty of my Mistress; therefore, *Sancho*, 'tis a plain Case, this Knight is out of his Senses. But let us hearken, perhaps we shall discover something more. That you will, I'll warrant you, quoth *Sancho*, for he seems in Tune to hoan a Month together. But it happen'd otherwise; for the Knight of the Wood over-hearing them, ceas'd his Lamentation, and raising himself on his Feet, in a loud but courteous Tone called to them, Who's there? What are ye? Are ye of the Number of the Happy or the Miserable? Of the Miserable, answer'd Don *Quixote*. Repair to me then, said the Knight of the Wood, and be assur'd you have met Misery and Affliction itself. Upon so moving and civil an Invitation, Don *Quixote* and *Sancho* drew near him; and the mournful Knight taking Don *Quixote* by the Hand, Sit down, said he, Sir Knight; for that your Profession is Chivalry, I need no other Conviction than to have found you in this Retirement, where Solitude and the cold Night-Dews are your Companions, and the proper Stations and reposing Places of Knights-Errant. I am a Knight, answer'd Don *Quixote*, and of the Order you mention; and though my Sorrows, and Disasters, and Misfortunes usurp the Seat of my Mind, I have still a Heart dispos'd to entertain the Afflictions of others. Yours, as I gather by your Complaints, is derived from Love, and, I suppose, owing to the Ingratitude of that Beauty you now mention'd. While they were thus parleying together, they sat close by one another on the hard Ground, very peaceably and lovingly, and not like Men that by Break of Day were to break one another's Heads. And is it your Fortune to be in Love, ask'd the Knight of the Wood? 'Tis my Misfortune, answer'd Don *Quixote*; though the pleasant Reflection of having plac'd our Affections Worthily, sufficiently balances the Weight of our Disasters, and turns them to a Blessing. This might be true, reply'd the Knight of the Wood, if the Disdain of some Mistresses were not often so galling to our Tempers, as to inspire us with something like the Spirit of Revenge. For my part, said Don *Quixote*, I never felt my Mistress's Disdain. No truly, quoth *Sancho*, who was near them, for my Lady is as gentle as a Lamb, and as soft as Butter. Is that your Squire, said the Knight of the Wood? It is, answer'd Don *Quixote*. I never saw a Squire, said the Knight of the Wood, that durst presume to interrupt his Master, when he was speaking himself. There's my Fellow yonder; he's as big as his Father, and yet no Man can say, he was ever so saucy as to open his Lips when I spoke. Well, well, quoth *Sancho*, I have talk'd, and may talk again, and before as, and perhaps —but I have done—The more ye stir, the more 'twill stink. At the same time the Squire of the Wood pulling *Sancho* by the Arm, Come Brother, said he, let us two go where we may chat freely by ourselves, like downright Squires as we are, and let our Masters get over Head and Ears in the Stories of their Loves: I'll warrant ye they'll be at it all Night, and won't have done by that time 'tis Day. With all my Heart, quoth *Sancho*; and then I'll tell you who I am, and what I am, and you shall judge if I am not fit to make one among the talking Squires. With that the two Squires withdrew, and had a Dialogue, as comical as that of their Masters was serious.

XIII: THE ADVENTURE WITH THE KNIGHT OF THE WOOD CONTINU'D; WITH THE WISE, RARE AND PLEASANT DISCOURSE THAT PASS'D BETWEEN THE TWO SQUIRES

THE Knights and their Squires thus divided, the latter to tell their Lives, and the former to relate their Amours; the Story begins with the Squire of the Wood. Sir, said he to *Sancho*, this is a troublesome Kind of Life, that we Squires of Knights-Errant lead: Well may we say, we eat our Bread with the Sweat of our Brows; which is one of the Curses laid on our first Parents. Well may we say too, quoth *Sancho*, we eat it with a cold Shivering of our Bodies; for there are no poor Creatures that suffer more by Heat or Cold, than We do. Nay, if we cou'd but eat at all, 'twou'd never vex one; for good Fare lessens Care; but sometimes we shall go ye a Day or two, and never so much as breakfast, unless it be upon the Wind that blows. After all, said the Squire of the Wood, we may bear with this, when we think of the Reward we are to expect; for that same Knight-Errant must be excessively Unfortunate, that has not some time or other the Government of some Island, or some good handsome Earldom, to bestow on his Squire. As for me, quoth *Sancho*, I have often told my Master, I wou'd be contented with the Government of any Island; and he is so Noble and Free-hearted, that he has promis'd it me over and over. For my part, quoth the other Squire, I shou'd think myself well paid for my Services with some good Canonry, and I have my Master's Word for it too. Why then, quoth *Sancho*, belike your Master is some Church-Knight, and may bestow such Livings on his good Squires. But mine is purely Laic; some of his wise Friends indeed (no Thanks to them for it) once upon a time counsell'd him to be an Archbishop: I fancy they wish'd him no good, but he wou'd not; for he'll be nothing but an Emperor. I was plaguily afraid he might have had a hankering after the Church, and so have spoil'd My Preferment, I not being gifted that way; for between You and I, though I look like a Man in a Doublet, I shou'd make but an

Ass in a Cassock. Let me tell you, Friend, quoth the Squire of the Wood, that you are out in your Politicks; for these Island-Governments bring more Cost than Worship; there's a great Cry, but little Wool; the best will bring more Trouble and Care than they are worth, and those that take 'em on their Shoulders are ready to sink under 'em. I think it were better for us to quit this confounded Slavery, and e'en jog Home, where we may entertain our selves with more delightful Exercises, such as Fishing, and Hunting, and the like; for he's a sorry Country Squire indeed, that wants his Horse, his Couple of Hounds, or his Fishing-Tackle, to live pleasantly at Home. All this I can have at Will, quoth *Sancho*: Indeed I have ne'er a Nag; but I have an honest Ass here, worth two of my Master's Horses any Day in the Year. A bad *Christmas* be my Lot, and may it be the next, if I wou'd swop Beasts with him, tho' he gave me four Bushels of Barley to boot, no marry wou'd not I: Laugh as much as you will at the Value I set on my *Dapple*; for *Dapple*, you must know, is his Colour. Now as for Hounds, we have enough to spare in our Town; and there's no Sport like Hunting at another Man's Cost. Faith and Troth! Brother Squire, quoth the Squire of the Wood, I am fully set upon't. These Vagrant Knights may e'en seek their mad Adventures by themselves for me, I'll Home, and breed up my Children as it behoves me; for I have Three, as Precious as three Orient Pearls. I have but two, quoth *Sancho*; but they might be presented to the Pope himself, especially my Girl, that I breed up to be a Countess (Heaven bless her) in spight of her Mother's Teeth. And how old, pray said the Squire of the Wood, may this same Young Lady Countess be? Why, she's about Fifteen, answer'd *Sancho*, a little over or a little under; but she's as tall as a Pike, as fresh as an *April*-Morning, and strong as a Porter. With these Parts, quoth the other, she may set up not only for a Countess, but for one of the Wood-Nymphs! Ah, the Young Buxsome Whore's Brood! What a Spring the Mettlesome Quean will have with her! My Daughter's no Whore, quoth *Sancho*, in a grumbling Tone, and her Mother was an honest Woman before her: and they shall be Honest, by Heaven's Blessing, while I live and do well: So, Sir, pray keep your Tongue between your Teeth, or speak as you ought. Methinks your Master shou'd have taught you better Manners; for Knights-Errant are the very pink of Courtesy. Alas, quoth the Squire of the Wood, how you're mistaken! how little you know the way of praising People now-a-days; Have you never observ'd when any Gentleman at a Bull-Feast gives the Bull a home Thrust with his Lance, or when any Body behaves himself cleverly upon any Occasion, the People will cry out, What a brisk Son of a Whore that is! a clever Dog, I'll warrant him. So what seems to be Slander, in that Sense is notable Commendation: And be advis'd by me, don't think those Children worth the owning, who won't do that which may make their Parents be commended in that Fashion. Nay, if it be so, quoth *Sancho*, I'll disown 'em if they don't, and henceforth you may call my Wife and Daughter all the Whores and Bawds you can think on, and welcome; for they do a thousand things that deserve all these fine Names. Heaven send me once more to see them, and deliver me out of this mortal Sin of Squire-Erranting, which I have been drawn into a second time, by the wicked Bait of a hundred Ducats, which the Devil threw in my own way in *Sierra Morena*, and which he still haunts me with, and brings before my Eyes here and there and every where. Oh that plaguy Purse, 'tis still running in my Head; methinks I am counting such another over and over! Now I hug it, now I carry it home, now I am buying Land with it; now I let Leases, now I'm receiving my Rents, and live like a Prince! Thus I pass away the Time, and this lulls me on to drudge on to the end of the Chapter, with this Dunder-headed Master of mine, who to my knowledge is more a Madman than a Knight. Truly, said the Squire of the Wood, this makes the Proverb true, Covet-ousness breaks the Sack. And now you talk of Madmen, I think my Master is worse than yours; for he is one of those, of whom the Proverb says, Fools will be meddling; and, who meddles with another Man's Business, Milks his Cows into a Sieve. In searching after another Knight's Wits, he loses his own; and hunts up and down for that, which may make him rue the find-ing. And is not the poor Man in Love, quoth *Sancho*? I marry, said t'other, and with one *Casildea de Vandalia*, one of the oddest Pieces in the World; she'll neither Roast nor Boil, and is neither Fish, Flesh, nor good Red-Herring. But that's not the

Thing that plagues his Noddle now. He has some other Crot-
chets in his Crown, and you'll hear more of it ere long. There
is no way so smooth, quoth *Sancho*, but it has a Hole or Rub
in't to make a Body stumble. In some Houses they boil Beans,
and in mine are whole Kettles full. So Madness has more need
of good Attendants than Wisdom. But if this old saying be true,
that it lightens Sorrow to have Companions in our Grief, you
are the fittest to comfort me; you serve one Fool and I another.
My Master, quoth the Squire of the Wood, is more stout than
foolish, but more Knave than either. Mine is not like yours
then, quoth *Sancho*, he has not one Grain of Knavery in him;
he's as dull as an old crack'd Pitcher, hurts no Body, does all
the Good he can to every Body; a Child may persuade him it
is Night at Noon-Day, and he is so simple, that I can't help
loving him, with all my Heart and Soul, and can't leave him,
in spite of all his Follies. Have a care, Brother, said the Squire
of the Wood, when the Blind leads the Blind both may fall into
the Ditch. 'Tis better to wheel about fair and softly, and steal
home again to our own Fire-sides; for those who follow their
Nose are often led into a Stink. Here the Squire of the Wood
observing that *Sancho* spit very often and very dry, I fancy,
Brother, said he, that our Tongues stick to the Palates of our
Mouths with Talking, but to cure that Disease I have something that hangs to the Pommel of my Saddle, as good as ever
was tipp'd over Tongue. Then he went and took down a
Leather Bottle of Wine, and a cold Pye, at least half a Yard
long; which is no Fiction, for *Sancho* himself, when he laid
his Hands on it, took it rather for a bak'd Goat than a Kid,
though it was indeed but an over-grown Rabbit. What! said
Sancho at the Sight, did you bring this too abroad with you?
What d'ye think, said t'other? Do you take me for one of your
Fresh-Water Squires? I'd have you know, I carry as good Provision at my Horse's Crupper, as any General upon his March.
Sancho did not stay for an Invitation, but fell to in the Dark,
cramming down Morsels as big as his Fist. Ay marry, Sir, said
he, you are a Squire every Inch of you, a true and trusty, round
and sound, noble and free hearted Squire. This good Cheer is
a Proof of it, which I don't say jump'd hither by Witchcraft;
but one would almost think so. Now here sits poor wretched

I, that have nothing in my Knapsack but a Crust of Cheese, so hard, a Giant might break his Grinders in't, and a few Acorns, Walnuts and Filberds; a shame on my Masters Nigardly Temper, and his cursed Maggot, in fancying that all Knights-Errant must live on a little dry'd Fruit and Sallads. Well, well, Brother reply'd the Squire of the Wood, our Masters may Diet themselves by Rules of Chivalry, if they please; your Thistles, and your Herbs and Roots don't at all agree with my Stomach, I must have good Meat, I faith! and this Bottle here still at Hand at the Pommel of my Saddle. 'Tis my Joy, my Life, the Comfort of my Soul, I hug and kiss it every Moment, and now recommend it to you as the best Friend in the World. *Sancho* took the Bottle, and rearing it to his thirsty Lips, with his Eyes fix'd upon the Stars, kept himself in that happy Contemplation for a Quarter of an Hour together. At last, when he had taken his Draught, with a deep Groan, a Nod on one side, and a cunning Leer, O! the Son of a Whore! What a rare and Catholick Bub this is! Oh ho! quoth the Squire of the Wood, have I caught you at your Son of a Whores! Did not I tell you, that it was a way of commending a thing? I knock under, quoth *Sancho*, and own 'tis no Dishonour to call one a Son of a Whore, when we mean to praise him. But now, by the Remembrance of her you love best, prithee tell me, is not this your right *Ciudad Real** Wine? Thou hast a rare Palate, answer'd the Squire of the Wood, 'tis the very same, and of a good Age too. I thought, said *Sancho*, but is it not strange now? that turn me but loose among a Parcel of Wines I shall find the Difference: Adad! Sir, I no sooner clap my Nose to a Taster of Wine, but I can tell the Place, the Grape, the Flavour, the Age, the Strength, and all the Qualities of the Parcel: And all this is natural to me, Sir, for I had two Relations by the Father's-side that were the nicest Tasters that were known of a long time in *La Mancha*; of which two I'll relate you a Story that makes good what I said, It fell out on a time, that some Wine was drawn fresh out of a Hogshead, and given to these same Friends of mine to Taste; and they were ask'd their Opinions of the Condition, the Quality, the Goodness, the Badness of the Wine, and all that. The one try'd it with the Tip of his Tongue, the

* Ciudad Real, *is a City of* Spain, *noted for good Wine.*

92

other only smell'd it; the first said the Wine tasted of Iron; the second said, it rather had a Tang of Goats Leather. The Vintner swore his Vessel was clean, and the Wine neat, and so Pure that it could have no Taste of any such Thing. Well, Time ran on, the Wine was Sold, and when the Vessel came to be empty'd, what do you think Sir, was found in the Cask? A little Key, with a bit of Leathern Thong ty'd to't; Now, judge you by this, whether he that comes of such a Generation, has not reason to understand Wine? More reason than to understand Adventures, answer'd the other: Therefore since we have enough, let's not trouble ourselves to look after more, but e'en jog home to our little Cots, where Heaven will find us, if it be its Will. I intend, said *Sancho*, to wait on my Master till we come to *Saragosa*, but then I'll turn over a new Leaf. To conclude: The two friendly Squires having talk'd and drank, and held out almost as long as their Bottle, it was high time that Sleep should lay their Tongues, and asswage their Thirst, for to quench it was impossible. Accordingly they had no sooner fill'd their Bellies, but they fell fast asleep, both keeping their Hold on their almost empty Bottle. Where we shall for a while leave 'em to their rest, and see what pass'd between their Masters.

XIV: A CONTINUATION OF THE ADVENTURE
OF THE KNIGHT OF THE WOOD

MANY were the Discourses that pass'd between Don *Quixote* and the Knight of the Wood: Amongst the rest, You must know, Sir Knight, said the latter, that by the Appointment of Fate, or rather by my own Choice, I became enamour'd of the Peerless *Casildea de Vandalia*. I call her Peerless, because she is singular in the Greatness of her Stature, as well as in that of her State and Beauty. But this Lady has been pleas'd to take no other Notice of my honourable Passion, than employing me in many perilous Adventures, like *Hercules's* Step-mother: still promising me, after I had put an happy end to one, that the Performance of the next should put me in Possession of my Desires. But after a Succession of numberless Labours, I do not know which of her Commands will be the last, and will crown my Lawful Wishes. Once by her particular Injunction, I challeng'd that famous Giantess *La Giralda* of *Sevil*,* who is as strong and undaunted as one that is made of Brass, and who, without changing Place, is the most changeable and unconstant Woman in the World; I went, I saw, and overcame: I made her stand still, and fix'd her in a constant Point, for the Space of a whole Week; no Wind having blown in the Skies during all that time but the North. Another time she enjoin'd me to remove the ancient Stones of the sturdy Bulls of *Guisando*;† a Task more suitable to the Arms of Porters than those of Knights. Then she commanded me to descend and dive into the Cavern or Den of *Cabra*,‡ (a terrible and unheard of Attempt) and to bring her an Account of all the Wonders in that dismal Profundity. I stopp'd the Motion of *La Giralda*, I weigh'd the Bulls of *Guisando*, and with a precipitated Fall plung'd and brought to light the darkest Secrets of *Cabra's* black Abyss. But still, ah! still my Hopes are dead. How dead? How, because

---

* Giralda, *is a Brass Statue, on a Steeple* in Seville; *which serves instead of a Weathercock.*   † *The Bulls of* Guisando *are two vast Statues remaining in that Town ever since the Time of the* Romans. *Suppos'd to be set up by* Metellus.   ‡ *A Place like some of the Caverns in the Peak in Derbyshire.*

her Disdain still lives, lives to injoin me new Labours, new Exploits. For, lastly, She has order'd me to traverse the remotest Provinces of *Spain*, and exact a Confession from all the Knights-Errant that roam about the Land, that her Beauty alone excels that of all other Women, and that I am the most valiant and most enamour'd Knight in the World. I have already journey'd over the greatest Part of *Spain* on this Expedition, and overcome many Knights who had the Temerity to contradict my Assertion: But the Perfection of my Glory, is the Result of my Victory over the renown'd Don *Quixote de la Mancha*, whom I conquer'd in single Combat, and compell'd to submit his *Dulcinea's* to my *Casildea's* Beauty. And now I reckon the wandring Knights of the whole Universe, all vanquish'd by My Prowess: Their Fame, their Glory, and their Honours being all vested in this great Don *Quixote*, who had before made them the Spoils of his Valorous Arm; though now they must attend the Triumphs of my Victory, which is the greater, since the Reputation of the Victor rises in Proportion to that of the Vanquish'd; and all the latter's Laurels are transferr'd to me.

Don *Quixote* was amaz'd to hear the Knight run on at this rate, and had the Lye ready at his Tongue's-end to give him a thousand times; but designing to make him own his Falsity with his own Mouth he strove to contain his Choler; and arguing the Matter very calmly, Sir Knight, said he, That your Victories have extended over all the Knights in *Spain*, and perhaps over the whole World, I will not dispute; but that you have vanquish'd Don *Quixote de la Mancha*, you must give me leave to doubt: It might be some body like him; though he is a Person whom but very few can resemble. What d'ye mean? Answer'd the Knight of the Wood: By yon spangled Canopy of the Skies I fought Don *Quixote* Hand to Hand, vanquish'd him, and made him submit; he is a tall wither-faced, leathern-jaw Fellow, scragg'd, grizzle-hair'd, Hawk-nos'd, and wears long, black, lank Mustachios: He is distinguish'd in the Field by the Title of the Knight of the *Woful Figure*: He has for his Squire one *Sancho Pança*, a labouring Man; he bestrides and manages that far-fam'd Courser *Rozinante*; and has for the Mistress of his Affection, one *Dulcinea del Toboso*, sometimes called *Al-*

donsa Lorenzo; as mine, whose Name was *Casildea*, and who is of *Andalusia*, is now distinguish'd by the Denomination of *Casildea de Vandalia*; and if all these convincing Marks be not sufficient to prove this Truth, I wear a Sword that shall force even Incredulity to credit it. Not so fast, good Sir Knight, said Don *Quixote*; pray attend to what I shall deliver upon this Head: You must know that this same Don *Quixote* is the greatest Friend I have in the World; insomuch that I may say I love him as well as I do my self. Now the Tokens that you have describ'd him by, are so agreeable to his Person and Circumstances, that one would think he should be the Person you subdu'd. On the other hand, I am convinc'd by the more powerful Argument of undeniable Sense, that it cannot be he. But thus far I will allow you, as there are many Inchanters that are his Enemies, especially one whose Malice hourly persecutes him, perhaps one of them has assumed his Likeness, thus by a Counterfeit Conquest, to defraud him of the Glory contracted by his signal Chivalry over all the Universe. In Confirmation of which I can farther tell you, 'tis but two Days ago that these envious Magicians transform'd the Figure and Person of the Beautiful *Dulcinea del Toboso* into the base and sordid Likeness of a Rustic Wench. And if this will not convince you of your Error, behold Don *Quixote* himself in Person, that here stands ready to maintain his Words with his Arms, either a Foot or on Horseback, or in what other manner you may think convenient. As he said this, up he started, and laid his Hand to his Sword, expecting the Motions and Resolutions of the Knight of the Wood. But with a great deal of Calmness, Sir, said he, A good Paymaster grudges no Surety; He that could once vanquish Don *Quixote* when transform'd, needs not fear him in his proper Shape. But since Darkness is not proper for the Atchievements of Knights, but rather for Robbers and Ruffians, let us expect the Morning-light, that the Sun may be Witness of our Valour. The Conditions of our Combat shall be, That the Conquer'd shall be wholly at the Mercy of the Conqueror, who shall dispose of him at Discretion; provided always he abuses not his Power, by commanding any thing unworthy the Honour of Knighthood. Content, said Don *Quixote*, I like these Terms very well. With that they both went to

look out their Squires whom they found snoring very soundly
in just the same Posture as when they first fell asleep. They
rouz'd them up; and order'd them to get their Steeds ready;
for the first Rays of the rising Sun must behold them engage in
a bloody and unparallel'd single Combat. This News thunder-struck *Sancho*, and put him to his Wits-end for his Master's Danger; having heard the Knight of the Wood's Courage strangely magnified by his Squire. However, without the
least Reply, he went with his Companion to seek their Beasts,
who by this time had smelled out one another, and were got
lovingly both together. Well Friend, said the Squire to *Sancho* as they went, I find our Masters are to fight; so You and I
are like to have a Brush too; for 'tis the way among us *Andalu-
sians*, not to let the Seconds stand idly by, with Arms across,
while their Friends are at it. This, said *Sancho*, may be a Custom in Your Country; but let me tell you, 'tis a damn'd Custom, Sir Squire, and none but Ruffians and Bloody-minded Fellows would stand up for't. But there's no such Practice among
Squires-Errant, else my Master would have minded me of it ere
this; for he has all the Laws of Knight-Errantry by Heart. But
suppose there be such a Law, I will not obey it, that's flat: I'll
rather pay the Penalty that's laid on such peaceable Squires:
I don't think the Fine can be above two Pounds of Wax,* and
that will cost me less than the Lint would to make Tents for
my Scull, which methinks is already cleft down to my Chin.
Besides, how would you have me fight? I have ne'er a Sword,
nor ever wore any. No matter, quoth the Squire of the Wood,
I've a Cure for that Sore. I ha' got here a Couple of Linen-Bags,
both of a Size, you shall take one, and I t'other, and so we'll let
drive one at one another with these Weapons and fight at Bag-
blows. Ay, ay, with all my Heart, quoth *Sancho*; this will dust
our Jackets purely, and won't hurt our Skins. Not so neither,
reply'd the Squire of the Wood; for we'll put half a dozen of
smooth Stones into each Bag, that the Wind mayn't blow 'em
to and fro, and they may play the better, and so we may brush
one another's Coats cleverly, and yet do our selves no great
hurt. Body of my Father! quoth *Sancho*, what soft sable Fur,

* A Custom in Spain, *of fining small Offenders to pay a small Quantity of
Wax for the Use of some Church.*

what dainty carded Cotton and Lamb's-Wool he crams into the Bags, to hinder our making Pap of our Brains, and Touch-Wood of our Bones: But I say again and again, I am not in a Humour to fight, though they were only full of Silk Balls. Let our Masters fight, and hear on't in another World; but let us drink and live while we may, for why should we strive to end our Lives before their Time and Season; and be so eager to gather the Plumbs that will drop of themselves when they're ripe? Well, said the Squire of the Wood, for all that, we must fight half an Hour or so. Not a Minute, reply'd *Sancho*: I han't the Heart to quarrel with a Gentleman with whom I have been eating and drinking. I an't angry with you in the least, and were I to be hang'd for't, I could never fight in cold Blood. Nay, if that be all, said the Squire of the Wood, you shall be angry enough, I'll warrant you; for, before we go to't, d'ye see, I'll walk up very handsomly to you, and lend your Worship three or four sound Slaps o' the Chaps, and knock you down; which will be sure to waken your Choler, though it slept as sound as a Dormouse. Nay then, quoth *Sancho*, I have a Trick for your Trick, if that be all, and you shall have as good as you bring, for I will take me a pretty middling Leaver, (you understand me) and before you can awaken My Choler, will I lay Yours asleep so fast, that it shall never wake more, unless in t'other World; where 'tis well known, I am one who will let no Man's Fist dust My Nose. Let every Man look before he leaps. Many come for Wool, that go home shorn. No Man knows what another can do: So Friend, let every Man's Choler sleep with him: Blessed are the Peace-makers, and cursed are the Peace-breakers. A baited Cat may turn as fierce as a Lion. Who knows then what I that am a Man may turn to, if I'm provok'd. Take it therefore for a Warning from me, Squire, that all the Mischief you may be hatching in this manner shall lie at your Door. Well, said t'other, 'twill be Day anon, and then we shall see what's to be done.

And now a thousand Sorts of pretty Birds began to warble in the Trees, and with their various chearful Notes seem'd to salute the fresh *Aurora*, who then display'd her rising Beauties through the Gates and Arches of the East, and gently shook from her dewy Locks a Shower of liquid Pearls, sprinkling and enriching the verdant Meads with that reviving Treasure, which seemed to spring and drop from the bending Leaves. The Willows distill'd their delicious Manna, the Rivulets fondly murmur'd, the Fountains smil'd, the Woods were cheer'd, the Fields enrich'd at her Approach. But no sooner the dawning Light recall'd Distinction, than the first thing that presented itself to *Sancho's* View, was the Squire of the Wood's Nose, which was so big that it overshadow'd almost his whole Body. In short, 'tis said to have been of a monstrous Size, crooked in the middle, studded with Warts and Carbuncles, tawny as a Russet-Pippin, and hanging down some two Fingers below his Mouth. The unreasonable Bulk, dismal Hue, Protuberancy, and Crookedness of that Nose so disfigur'd the Squire, that *Sancho* was seiz'd with a Trembling at the Sight, like a Child in Convulsions, and resolved now to take two hundred Cuffs, before his Choler should awaken to encounter such a Hobgoblin. As for Don *Quixote*, he fix'd his Eyes upon his Antagonist; but as his Helmet was on, and he had pull'd down the Bever, his Face could not be seen, however, he observ'd him to be strong-limb'd, though not very tall. Over his Armour he wore a Coat that look'd like Cloth of Gold, overspread with Looking-glasses (Mirrors) cut into Half-Moons, which made a very glittering Show: A large Plume of yellow, green, and white Feathers waved about his Helmet; and his Lance, which he had set up against a Tree, was very thick and long, with a Steel Head a Foot in Length. Don *Quixote* survey'd every Particular, and from his Observations, judged him to be a Man of great Strength. But all this was so far from daunting his Courage, like *Sancho*, that, with a gallant Deportment, Sir Knight of the Mirrors, said he, if your eager Desire of Combat has not made you deaf to the Intreaties of Civility, be pleas'd to lift up your Bever a-while, that I may see whether the Gracefulness of your Face equals that of your Body. Whether you be Vanquish'd or Victorious in this Enterprize, answer'd the Knight of the Mirrors, you shall have Leisure enough to see my Face: I cannot at present satisfy your Curiosity; for every Moment of Delay from Combat is, in my Thoughts, a Wrong done to the Beautiful *Casildea de Vandalia*. However, reply'd Don *Quixote*, while we get a Horse-

7-2

back, you may tell me whether I be the same Don *Quixote*
whom you pretend to have overcome? To this I answer you,
said the Knight of the Mirrors, you are as like the Knight I
vanquish'd as one Egg is like another. But considering what
you tell me, that you are persecuted by Inchanters, I dare not
affirm that you are the same. 'Tis enough for me, said Don
Quixote, that you believe you may be in Error; but that I may
entirely rid your Doubts, let's to Horse; for if Providence, my
Mistress, and my Arm assist me, I will see your Face in less
time than it would have cost you to have lifted up your Bever,
and make you know that I am not that Don *Quixote* whom
you talk'd of having vanquished. This said, without any more
Words they mounted. Don *Quixote* wheel'd about with *Rozinante*, to take Ground for the Career; The Knight of the Mirrors did the like. But before Don *Quixote* had rid twenty Paces,
he heard him call to him: So meeting each other half way,
Remember Sir Knight, cry'd he, the Conditions on which we
fight; the Vanquish'd, as I told you before, shall be at the
Mercy of the Conqueror. I grant it, answer'd Don *Quixote*,
provided the Victor imposes nothing on him that derogates
from the Laws of Chivalry. I mean no otherwise, reply'd the
Knight of the Mirrors. At the same time Don *Quixote* happen'd
to cast his Eye on the Squire's strange Nose, and wonder'd no
less at the Sight of it than *Sancho*, taking him to be rather a
Monster than a Man. *Sancho* seeing his Master set out to take
so much Distance as was fit to return on his Enemy with greater
Force, would not trust himself alone with Squire *Nose*, fearing the greater should be too hard for the less, and either that
or Fear should strike him to the Ground. This made him run
after his Master, till he had taken hold of *Rozinante's* Stirrup
Leathers; and when he thought him ready to turn back to
take his Career, Good your Worship, cry'd he, before you run
upon your Enemy, help me to get up into yon Cork-tree, where
I may better, and much more to my liking, see your brave Battle
with the Knight. I rather believe, said Don *Quixote*, thou
wantest to be pearched up yonder as on a Scaffold, to see the
Bull-baiting without Danger. To tell you the Truth, quoth
Sancho, that Fellow's unconscionable Nose has so frighted
me, that I dare not stay within his Reach. It is indeed such a

Sight, said Don *Quixote*, as might affect with Fear, any other
but my self; and therefore come, I'll help thee up. Now while
Sancho was climbing up the Tree, with his Master's Assistance, the Knight of the Mirrors took as much Ground as he
thought proper for his Career; and imagining Don *Quixote* had
done the same, he faced about, without expecting the Trumpet's Sound, or any other Signal for a Charge, and with his
Horse's full Speed, which was no more than a middling Trot,
(for he was neither more promising, nor a better Performer
than *Rozinante*) he went to encounter his Enemy. But seeing
him busy in helping up his Squire, he held in his Steed, and
stopped in the middle of the Career, for which the Horse was
mightily oblig'd to him, being already scarce able to stir a Foot
farther. Don *Quixote*, who thought his Enemy was flying upon
him, set spurs to *Rozinante's* hinder Flank vigorously, and so
waken'd his Mettle, that the Story says, this was the only
Time he was known to gallop a little, for at all others, downright Trotting was his best. With this unusual Fury, he soon
got to the Place where his Opponent was striking his Spurs
into his Horse's Sides up to the very Rowels, without being
able to make him stir an Inch from the Spot. Now while he
was thus goading him on, and at the same time encumber'd
with his Lance, either not knowing how to set it in the Rest,
or wanting Time to do it, Don *Quixote*, who took no notice
of his Disorder, encounter'd him without Danger so furiously,
that the Knight of the Mirrors was hurry'd, in spite of his
Teeth, over his Horse's Crupper, and was so hurt with falling
to the Ground, that he lay without Motion, or any Sign of Life.
Sancho no sooner saw him fallen, but down he comes sliding
from the Tree, and runs to his Master; who having dismounted,
was got upon the Knight of the Mirrors, and was unlacing his
Helmet, to see if he were dead or alive, and give him Air. But
who can relate what he saw, when he saw the Face of the
Knight of the Mirrors, without raising Wonder, Amazement,
or Astonishment in those that shall hear it? He saw, says the
History, in that Face, the very Visage, the very Aspect, the
very Physiognomy, the very Make, the very Features, the
very Effigy of the Batchelor *Sampson Carrasco*. Come *Sancho*, cry'd he, as he saw it, come hither, look and admire what

thou may'st see, yet not believe. Haste, my Friend, and mark the Power of Magick; What Sorcerers and Inchanters can do! *Sancho* drew near, and seeing the Batchelor *Sampson Carrasco's* Face, began to cross himself a thousand times, and bless himself as many more. The poor defeated Knight all this while gave no Sign of Life: Sir, quoth *Sancho* to his Master, if you'll be rul'd by me, make sure work: Right or wrong, e'en thrust your Sword down this Fellow's Throat that's so like the Batchelor *Sampson Carrasco*; and so mayhaps in him you may chance to murder one of those bitter Dogs, those Inchanters that haunt you so. That Thought's not amiss, said Don *Quixote*; and with that drawing his Sword, he was going to put *Sancho's* Advice in Execution, when the Knight's Squire came running without the Nose that so disguised him before; and calling to Don *Quixote*, Hold, Noble Don *Quixote*, cry'd he! Take heed! Beware! 'Tis your Friend *Sampson Carrasco*, that now lies at your Worship's Mercy, and I am his Squire. And where's your Nose, quoth *Sancho*, seeing him now without Disguise? Here in my Pocket answer'd the Squire, and so saying, he pull'd out the Nose of a Varnish'd Paste-board Vizard, such as it has been describ'd. *Sancho* having more and more star'd him in the Face with great Earnestness, Blessed Virgin defend me, quoth he! Who's this? *Thomas Cecial*, my Friend and Neighbour? The same, Friend *Sancho*, quoth the Squire! I'll tell you anon by what Tricks and Wheedles he was inveigl'd to come hither. Mean while desire your Master not to misuse, nor slay, nor meddle in the least with the Knight of the Mirrors, that now lies at his Mercy; for there's nothing more sure than that 'tis our ill-advis'd Countryman *Sampson Carrasco*, and no body else.

By this time the Knight of the Mirrors began to come to himself; which when Don *Quixote* observ'd, setting the Point of his Sword to his Throat, Thou dy'st, Knight, cry'd he, if thou refuse to confess that the peerless *Dulcinea del Toboso* excels thy *Casildea de Vandalia* in Beauty. Besides this, thou shalt promise (if thou escape with Life from this Combat) to go to the City of *Toboso*; where, as from Me, thou shalt present thy self before the Mistress of my Desires, and resign thy Person to her Disposal: If she leaves thee to thy own, then

thou shalt come back to me, (for the Track of my Exploits
will be thy Guide) and thou shalt give me an Account of the
Transaction between her and thee. These Conditions are conformable to our Agreement before the Combat, and do not
transgress the Rules of Knight-Errantry. I do confess, said
the discomfited Knight, that the Lady *Dulcinea del Toboso's*
ripp'd and dirty Shoe is preferable to the clean, though ill-
comb'd Locks of *Casildea*; and I promise to go to her, and come
from her Presence to yours, and bring you a full and true Relation of all you have enjoin'd me. You shall also confess and
believe, added Don *Quixote*, that the Knight you vanquish'd
neither was nor could be Don *Quixote de la Mancha*, but some
body else in his Likeness; as I on the other side do confess and
believe, that though you seem to be the Batchelor *Sampson
Carrasco*, you are not he, but some other whom my Enemies
have transformed into his Resemblance, to assuage the Violence of my Wrath, and make me entertain with Moderation
the Glory of my Victory. All this I confess, believe and allow,
said the Knight; and now I beseech you let me rise, if the Hurt
I have receiv'd by my Fall will give me leave, for I find myself
very much bruis'd. Don *Quixote* help'd him to rise by the Aid
of his Squire *Thomas Cecial*, on whom *Sancho* fixed his Eyes
all the while, asking him a thousand Questions; the Answers
to which convinced him, that he was the real Thomas *Cecial*,
as he said, though the Conceit of what was told him by his
Master, that the Magicians had transform'd the Knight of the
Mirrors into *Sampson Carrasco*, had made such an Impression
on his Fancy, that he could not believe the Testimony of His
own Eyes. In short, the Master and the Man persisted in their
Error. The Knight of the Mirrors and his Squire, much out of
Humour, and much out of Order, left Don *Quixote*, to go to
some Town where he might get some Ointments and Plaisters
for his Ribs. Don *Quixote* and *Sancho* continued their Progress
for *Saragosa*; where the History leaves them, to relate who
the Knight of the Mirrors and his Squire were.

DON *Quixote* went on extremely pleas'd, and joyful, priding himself and glorifying in the Victory he had got over so valiant a Knight, as the Knight of the Mirrors, and relying on his Parole of Honour, which he could not violate, without forfeiting his Title to Chivalry, that he would return to give him an Account of his Reception, by which means he expected to hear whether his Mistress continued under the Bonds of Inchantment. But Don *Quixote* dream'd of one thing, and the Knight of the Mirrors thought of another. His only Care for the present was how to get cur'd of his Bruises.

Here the History relates, That when the Batchelor *Carrasco*, advised Don *Quixote* to proceed in his former Profession of Knight-Errantry; it was the Result of a Conference which he had with the Curate and the Barber, about the best means to prevail with Don *Quixote* to stay quietly at Home, and desist from rambling after his unlucky Adventures. For *Carrasco* thought, and so did the rest, that it was in vain to pretend to hinder him from going abroad again, and therefore the best way would be to let him go, and that he should meet him by the Way, equipped like a Knight-Errant, and should take an Opportunity to Fight, and overcome him, which he might easily do; first making an Agreement with him, that the Vanquished should submit to the Victor's Discretion: so that after the Batchelor had Vanquished him, he should command him to return to his House and Village, and not offer to depart thence in two Years, without Permission; which it was not doubted but Don *Quixote* would religiously observe, for fear of infringing the Laws of Chivalry; and in this Time they hoped he might be weaned of his Frantick Imaginations, or they might find some means to cure him of his Madness. *Carrasco* undertook this Task, and *Thomas Cecial*, a brisk, pleasant Fellow, *Sancho's* Neighbour and Gossip, proffered to be his Squire. *Sampson* equipped himself, as you have heard, and *Thomas Cecial* fitted a huge Paste-board-Nose to his own, that his Gossip *Sancho* might not know him when they met. Then they follow'd

Don *Quixote* so close, that they had like to have overtaken him in the midst of his Adventure with the Chariot of Death; and at last, they found him in the Wood, that happened to be the Scene of their Encounter, which might have proved more fatal to the Batchelor, and had spoiled him for ever from taking another Degree, had not Don *Quixote* been so obstinate, in not believing him to be the same Man.

And now *Thomas Cecial*, seeing the ill Success of their Journey; by my Troth! said he, Master *Carrasco*, we have been served well enough. 'Tis easy to begin a Business, but a hard matter to go through. Don *Quixote* is Mad, and we think our selves Wise; yet he is gone away sound, and laughing in his Sleeve; and your Worship is left here well bang'd, and in the Dumps: Now pray who is the greatest Madman, he that is so because he cannot help it, or he that is so for his Pleasure? The Difference is, answer'd the Batchelor, that he that can't help being Mad, will always be so; but he that only plays the Fool for his Fancy, may give over when he pleases. Well then, quoth *Cecial*, I, who was pleased to play the Fool in going a Squire-Erranting with your Worship, for the self-same Reason will give it over now, and even make the best of my way home again. Do as you will, replied *Carrasco*, but it is a Folly to think I ever will go home, till I have swingeingly paid that unaccountable Madman. It is not that he may recover his Wits neither: No, it is pure Revenge now, for the Pain in my Bones won't give me leave to have any manner of Charity for him. Thus they went on Discoursing, till at last they got to a Town, where, by good Fortune, they met with a Bone-setter, who gave the bruised Batchelor some Ease. *Thomas Cecial* left him, and went Home, while the other staid to meditate Revenge. In due time the History will speak of him again, but must not now forget to entertain you with Don *Quixote's* Joy.

XVI: WHAT HAPPEN'D TO DON QUIXOTE, WITH A SOBER GENTLEMAN OF LA MANCHA

DON *Quixote* pursued his Journey, full, as we said before, of Joy and Satisfaction; his late Victory made him esteem himself the most Valiant Knight-Errant of the Age. He counted all his future Adventures as already finish'd and happily atchiev'd. He defy'd all Inchantments and Inchanters. No longer did he remember the innumerable Blows he had receiv'd in the Course of his Errantry, nor the Shower of Stones that had dash'd out half of his Teeth, nor the Ingratitude of the Galley-Slaves, nor the Insolence of the *Yanguesian* Carriers, that had so abominably batter'd his Ribs with their Pack staves. In short, he concluded with himself, that if he cou'd but by any manner of Means dissolve the Inchantment of his adored *Dulcinea*, he should have no need to envy the greatest Felicity that ever was, or ever could be attained by the most fortunate Knight in the habitable Globe. While he was wholly employ'd in these pleasing Imaginations; Sir, quoth *Sancho* to him, is it not a pleasant thing that I can't for the Blood of me, put out of my Mind that huge unconscionable Nose, and whapping Nostrils of *Thomas Cecial* my Gossip? How *Sancho*, answer'd Don *Quixote*, do'st thou still believe, that the Knight of the Mirrors was the Batcheler *Carrasco*, and that *Thomas Cecial* was his Squire? I don't know what to say to't, quoth *Sancho*, but this I'm sure of, that no body but He cou'd give me those Items of my House, and of my Wife and Children as he did. Besides when his hugeous Nose was off, he had *Tom. Cecial's* Face to a Hair. I ought to know it I think: I have seen it a Hundred and a Hundred times, for we are but next-door Neighbours; and then he had his Speech to a Tittle. Come on, return'd Don *Quixote*; let us reason upon this Business. How can it enter into any one's Imagination, that the Batchelor *Sampson Carrasco* shou'd come Arm'd at all Points like a Knight-Errant, on purpose to Fight with Me? Have I ever been his Enemy, or given him any Occasion to be mine? Am I his Rival? Or has he taken up the Profession of Arms, in

Envy of the Glory which I have purchas'd by my Sword? Ay,
but then, reply'd *Sancho*, what shall we say to the Resemblance between this same Knight, whoever he be, and the
Batchelor *Carrasco*, and the Likeness between his Squire and
my Gossip? If 'tis an Inchantment, as your Worship says, were
there no other People in the World but they two, to make 'em
like? All, all, cry'd Don *Quixote*, is the Artifice and Delusion of
those malevolent Magicians that persecute me, who, foreseeing that I shou'd get the Victory, disguised their Vanquish'd
Property under the Resemblance of my Friend the Batchelor;
that at the Sight, my Friendship might interpose between the
Edge of my Sword, and moderate my just Resentment, and so
rescue him from Death, who basely had attempted on my Life.
But thou, *Sancho*, by Experience, which cou'd not deceive
thee, know'st how easy a Matter 'tis for Magicians to trans-
mute the Face of any one into another Resemblance, fair into
foul, and foul again into fair; since not two Days ago, with thy
own Eyes thou beheld'st the Peerless *Dulcinea* in her natural
State of Beauty and Proportion: when I, the Object of their
Envy, saw her in the homely Disguise of a Blear-ey'd, Fetid,
Ugly Country-Wench. Why then should'st thou wonder so
much at the frightful Transformation of the Batchelor and thy
Neighbour *Cecial*? But however, this is a Comfort to me, that
I got the better of my Enemy, whatsoever Shape he assum'd.
Well, quoth *Sancho*, Heaven knows the Truth of all things.
This was all the Answer he thought fit to make; for as he knew
that the Transformation of *Dulcinea* was only a Trick of his
own, he was willing to wave the Discourse, though he was the
less satisfy'd in his Master's Chimeras; but fear'd to drop some
Word that might have betray'd his Roguery.

While they were in this Conversation, they were overtaken by a Gentleman, mounted on a very fine Flea-bitten
Mare. He had on a Riding-Coat of fine Green Cloth, fac'd with
Murry-colour'd Velvet, a Hunter's Cap of the same. The Furniture of his Mare was Country-like, and after the Jennet-
fashion, and also Murry and Green. By his Side hung a *Moorish*
Scimitar, in a large Belt of Green and Gold. His Buskins were
of the same Work with his Belt: His Spurs were not Gilt, but
Burnish'd so well with a certain green Varnish, that they

look'd better, to suit with the rest of his Equipage, than if they had been of pure Gold. As he came up with them, he very civilly saluted them, and clapping Spurs to his Mare, began to leave 'em behind him. Thereupon Don *Quixote* call'd to him: Sir, cry'd he, if you are not in too much haste, we should be glad of the Favour of your Company, so far as you Travel this Road. Indeed, answer'd the Gentleman, I had not thus Rid by you, but that I'm afraid your Horse may prove unruly with my Mare. If that be all, Sir, quoth *Sancho*, you may hold in your Mare; for our Horse here is the Honestest and Soberest Horse in the World; he is not in the least given to do any naughty thing on such Occasions. Once upon a time indeed, he happen'd to forget himself, and go astray; but then He, and I, and my Master ru'd for't, with a Vengeance. I tell you again, Sir, you may safely stay if you please, for if your Mare were to be serv'd up to him in a Dish, I'll lay my Life he would not so much as touch her. Upon this, the Traveller stopp'd his Mare, and did not a little gaze at the Figure and Countenance of our Knight, who rode without his Helmet, which, like a Wallet, hung at the Saddle-bow of *Sancho's* Ass. If the Gentleman in green gaz'd on Don *Quixote*, Don *Quixote* look'd no less upon him, judging him to be some Man of Consequence. His Age seem'd about Fifty; he had some gray Hairs, a sharp Look, and a grave yet pleasing Aspect. In short, his Mien and Appearance spoke him a Man of Quality. When he look'd on Don *Quixote*, he thought he had never beheld before such a strange appearance of a Man. He could not but admire at the Lankness of his Horse; he consider'd then the Long-back'd, Raw-bon'd Thing that bestrid him; His wan, meagre Face, his Air, his Gravity, his Arms and Equipage; such a Figure, as perhaps had not been seen in that Country time out of mind. Don *Quixote* observed how intent the travelling Gentleman had been in surveying him, and reading his Desire in his Surprize, as he was the very Pink of Courtesy and fond of pleasing every one, without staying till he should question him, he thought fit to prevent him. Sir, said he, that you are surpriz'd at this Figure of mine, which appears so new and exotick, I do not wonder in the least; but your Admiration will cease when I have inform'd you, that I am one of those Knights who go in quest of Adventures. I have left my Country, Mortgaged my Estate, quitted my Pleasures, and thrown myself into the Arms of Fortune. My design was to give a new Life to Knight-Errantry, that so long has been lost to the World; and thus, after infinite Toils and Hardships; sometimes stumbling, sometimes falling; casting myself headlong in one place, and rising again in another, I have compass'd a great part of my Desire, relieving Widows, protecting Damsels, assisting Marry'd Women and Orphans, the proper and natural Office of Knights-Errant; and so by many Valorous and Christian-like Atchievements, I have merited the Honour of the Press in almost all the Nations of the World. Thirty thousand Volumes of my History have been printed already, and thirty thousand Millions more are like to be printed, if Heaven prevent not. In short, to sum up all in one Word, know, I am Don *Quixote de la Mancha*, otherwise call'd, The Knight of the Woful Figure; I own it lessens the value of Praise to be the Publisher of its own self; yet 'tis what I am sometimes forc'd to, when there is none present to do me Justice. And now, good Sir, no longer let this Steed, this Lance, this Shield, this Armour, nor this Squire, nor the Paleness of my Looks, nor my exhausted Body, move your Admiration, since you know who I am, and the Profession I follow. Having said this, Don *Quixote* was silent, and the Gentleman in Green, by his delaying to answer him, seem'd as if he did not intend to make any Return. But at last, after some pause; Sir Knight, said he, you were sensible of my Curiosity by my Looks, and were pleas'd to say my Wonder wou'd cease when you had inform'd me who you was; but I must confess, since you have done that, I remain no less surpriz'd and amaz'd than ever. For is it possible there should be at this time any Knights-Errant in the World, or that there shou'd be a true History of a living Knight-Errant in Print? I cannot persuade myself there is any body now upon Earth that relieves Widows, protects Damsels, or assists Married Women and Orphans; and I should still have been of the same Mind, had not my Eyes afforded me a sight of such a Person as yourself. Now Heaven be prais'd, for this History of your true and noble Feats of Arms, which you say is in Print, will blot out the Memory of all those idle Romances of pretended Knights-Errant that have so fill'd and pester'd the World, to the detriment of good Education, and the Prejudice and Dishonour of true History. There is a great deal to be said, answer'd Don *Quixote*, for the Truth of Histories of Knight-Errantry, as well as against it. How, return'd the Gentleman in Green! Is there any Body living who makes the least Scruple but that they are false. Yes, Sir, myself for one, said Don *Quixote*; But let that pass: If we continue any time together on the Road, I hope to convince you that you have been to blame in suffering yourself to be carry'd away with the Stream of Mankind that generally disbelieves 'em. The Traveller at this Discourse, began to have a Suspicion that Don *Quixote* was distracted, and expected the next Words would confirm him in that Opinion: But before they enter'd into any further Conversation, Don *Quixote* begg'd him to acquaint him who he was, since he had given him some Account of his own Life and Condition. Sir Knight of the Woful Figure, answer'd the other, I am a Gentleman, born at a Village, where God willing, we shall dine by and by. My Name is Don *Diego de Miranda*. I have a reasonable Competency, I pass my time contentedly with my Wife, my Children and my Friends; My usual Diversions are Hunting and Fishing; yet I keep neither Hawks nor Hounds, but some tame Partridges and a Ferret. I have about Three or Fourscore Books, some *Spanish*, some *Latin*; some of History, and others of Divinity. But for Books of Knight-Errantry; none ever came within my Doors. I am more inclinable to read those that are Profane than those of Devotion, if they be such as yield an innocent Amusement, and are agreeable for their Style, and surprizing for their Invention, tho' we have but few of 'em in our Language. Sometimes I eat with my Neighbours and Friends, and often I invite 'em to do the like with me. My Treats are clean and handsome, neither penurious nor superfluous. I am not given to murmur and backbite, nor do I love to hear others do it. I am no curious Inquirer into the Lives and Actions of other People. Every Day I hear Divine Service, and give to the Poor, without making a Shew of it, or presuming on my good Deeds, lest I should give way to Hypocrisy and Vain-glory; Enemies that too easily possess themselves of the best guarded Hearts. I endeavour to reconcile those that are at Variance. I pay my Devotions to

the Blessed Virgin, and ever trust in Heaven's infinite Mercy.
Sancho listen'd with great Attention to this Relation of the
Gentleman's way of Living; and believing that a Person who
had led so good and pious a Life, was able to work Miracles,
he jump'd in haste from his Ass, and catching hold of his right
Stirrup, with Tears in his Eyes and Devotion in his Heart,
fell a kissing his Foot. What's the Matter, Friend, cry'd the
Gentleman, wondring at his proceeding? What is the meaning
of this Kissing? Oh! good Sir, quoth *Sancho*, Let me kiss that
dear Foot of yours, I beseech you; for you are certainly the
first Saint on Horse-back I ever saw in my born Days. Alas!
replied the Gentleman, I am no Saint but a great Sinner: You
indeed, Friend, I believe are a good Soul, as appears by your
Simplicity. With that *Sancho* return'd to his Pack-Saddle,
having by this Action provok'd the profound Gravity of his
Master to smile, and caused new Admiration in Don *Diego*.
And now Don *Quixote* enquires of him, how many Children
he had, telling him at the same time, that among the things in
which the Ancient Philosophers, who had not the true Knowledge of God, made Happiness consist, as the Advantages of
Nature and Fortune, one was, to have many Friends and a
numerous and Vertuous Offspring. I have a Son, Sir Knight,
answer'd the Gentleman; and perhaps if I had him not, I shou'd
not think myself the more unhappy; not that he is so bad
neither; but because he is not so good as I wou'd have him.
He is Eighteen Years of Age; the last Six he has spent at *Salamanca* to perfect himself in his *Latin* and *Greek*. But, when I
wou'd have had him to have proceeded to the Study of other
Sciences, I found him so engag'd in that of Poetry, if it may
be call'd a Science, that 'twas impossible to make him look
either to the Study of the Law, which I intended him for, or
of Divinity, the noblest Part of all Learning. I was in hopes
he might have become an honour to his Family, living in an
Age in which good and vertuous Literature is highly favour'd
and rewarded by Princes; for Learning without Vertue, is like
a Pearl upon a Dunghill. He now spends whole Days in examining, whether *Homer* in such a Verse of his *Iliads*, says
well or no? Whether such an Epigram in *Martial* ought not
to be expung'd for Obscenity? And whether such and such

Verses in *Virgil* are to be taken in such a Sense, or otherwise. In short, his whole Converse is with the celebrated Poets, with *Horace* and *Persius*, *Juvenal*, and *Tibullus*. But as for modern Rhimers, he has but an indifferent Opinion of 'em. And yet for all this Disgust of *Spanish* Poetry, he is now breaking his Brain upon a Paraphrase or Gloss on four Verses that were sent him from the University, and which I think are design'd for a Prize. Sir, reply'd Don *Quixote*, Children are the Flesh and Blood of their Parents, and, whether good or bad, are to be cherish'd as part of ourselves. 'Tis the Duty of a Father to train 'em up from their tenderest Years in the Paths of Vertue, in good Discipline and Christian Principles, that when they advance in Years they may become the Staff and Support of their Parents Age, and the Glory of their Posterity. But as for forcing them to this or that Study, 'tis a thing I don't so well approve. Persuasion is all, I think, that is proper in such a case; especially when they are so Fortunate as to be above studying for Bread, as having Parents that can provide for their future Subsistence, they ought in my Opinion to be indulged in the Pursuit of that Science to which their own Genius gives them the most Inclination. For though the Art of Poetry is not so profitable as delightful, yet it is none of those that disgrace the ingenious Professor. Poetry, Sir, in my Judgment, is like a tender Virgin in her Bloom, Beautiful and Charming to Amazement: All the other Sciences are so many Virgins, whose Care it is to Enrich, Polish and Adorn her, and as she is to make use of them all, so are they all to have from her a grateful Acknowledgment. But this Virgin must not be roughly handl'd, nor dragg'd along the Street, nor expos'd to every Market-place, and Corner of great Men's Houses. A good Poet is a kind of an Alchymist, who can turn the Matter he prepares into the purest Gold and an inestimable Treasure. But he must keep his Muse within the Rules of Decency, and not let her prostitute her Excellency in lewd Satires and Lampoons, nor in licentious Sonnets. She must not be Mercenary, though she need not give away the Profits she may claim from Heroick Poems, deep Tragedies, and Pleasant and Artful Comedies. She is not to be attempted by Buffoons, nor by the Ignorant Vulgar, whose Capacity can never reach to a due Sense of the

Treasures that are lock'd up in her. And know, Sir, that when I mention the Vulgar, I don't mean only the common Rabble; for whoever is ignorant, be he Lord or Prince, is to be listed in the Number of the Vulgar. But whoever shall apply himself to the Muses with those Qualifications, which, as I said, are essential to the Character of a good Poet, his Name shall be Famous, and valu'd in all the polish'd Nations of the World. And as to what you say, Sir, that your Son does not much esteem our Modern Poetry; in my Opinion, he is somewhat to blame; and my Reason is this: *Homer* never wrote in *Latin*, because he was a *Grecian*; nor did *Virgil* write in *Greek*, because *Latin* was the Language of his Country. In short, all your Ancient Poets wrote in their Mother-Tongue, and did not seek other Languages to express their lofty Thoughts. And thus, it wou'd be well *that* Custom shou'd extend to every Nation; there being no Reason that a *German* Poet shou'd be despised, because he writes in his own Tongue; or a *Castilian* or *Biscayner*, because they write in theirs. But I suppose, your Son does not mislike Modern Poetry, but such Modern Poets as have no Tincture of any other Language or Science, that may adorn, awaken, and assist their Natural Impulse. Though even in this too there may be Error. For, 'tis believ'd, and not without Reason, that a Poet is naturally a Poet from his Mother's Womb, and that, with the Talent which Heaven has infus'd into him, without the Help of Study or Art, he may produce these Compositions that verify that Saying, *Est Deus in nobis, &c.* Not but that a natural Poet, that improves himself by Art, shall be much more accomplish'd, and have the Advantage of him that has no Title to Poetry but by his Knowledge in the Art; because Art cannot go beyond Nature, but only adds to its Perfection. From which it appears, that the most perfect Poet is he whom Nature and Art combine to qualify. Let then your Son proceed and follow the Guidance of his Stars, for being so good a Student as I understand he is, and already got up the first Step of the Sciences, the Knowledge of the Learned Tongues, he will easily ascend to the Pinacle of Learning, which is no less an Honour and an Ornament to a Gentleman, than a Mitre is to a Bishop, or the long Robe to the Civilian. Shou'd your Son write Satires to lessen the Reputation of any Person, you wou'd do well to take him to Task, and tear his defamatory Rhimes; but if he studies to write such Discourses in Verse, to ridicule and explode Vice in general, as *Horace* so elegantly did, then encourage him: For a Poet's Pen is allow'd to inveigh against Envy and Envious Men, and so against other Vices, provided it aim not at particular Persons. But there are Poets so abandon'd to the Itch of Scurrility, that rather than lose a villanous Jest, they'll venture being banish'd to the Islands of *Pontus*.* If a Poet is modest in his Manners, he will be so in his Verses. The Pen is the Tongue of the Mind; the Thoughts that are formed in the one, and those that are traced by the other, will bear a near Resemblance. And when Kings and Princes see the wonderful Art of Poetry shine in prudent, virtuous, and solid Subjects, they honour, esteem, and enrich them, and even crown them with Leaves of that Tree, which is ne'er offended by the Thunderbolt, as a Token that nothing shall offend those whose Brows are honour'd and adorn'd with such Crowns. The Gentleman hearing Don *Quixote* express himself in this manner, was struck with so much Admiration, that he began to lose the bad Opinion he had conceiv'd of his Understanding. As for *Sancho*, who did not much relish this fine Talk, he took an Opportunity to slink aside in the Middle of it, and went to get a little Milk of some Shepherds that were hard by keeping their Sheep. Now when the Gentleman was going to renew his Discourse, mightily pleas'd with these judicious Observations, Don *Quixote* lifting up his Eyes, perceiv'd a Waggon on the Road, set round with little Flags, that appear'd to be the King's Colours; and believing it to be some new Adventure, he call'd out to *Sancho* to bring him his Helmet. *Sancho* hearing him call aloud, left the Shepherds, and clapping his Heels vigorously to *Dapple's* Sides, came trotting up to his Master, to whom there happen'd a most terrifying and desperate Adventure.

* *As* Ovid *was.*

THE History relates, that *Sancho* was chaffering
with the Shepherds for some Curds, when Don
Quixote called to him; and finding that his Master
was in haste, he did not know what to do with
'em, nor what to bring 'em in; yet loth to lose his
Purchase (for he had already paid for 'em,) he bethought himself at last of clapping 'em into the Helmet, where
having 'em safe, he went to know his Master's Pleasure. As
soon as he came up to him, Give me that Helmet, Friend, said
the Knight, for if I understand any thing of Adventures, I descry one yonder that obliges me to Arm. The Gentleman in Green
hearing this, look'd about to see what was the Matter, but
could perceive nothing but a Waggon, which made towards
'em, and by the little Flags about it, he judg'd it to be one of
the King's Carriages, and so he told Don *Quixote*. But his Head
was too much possess'd with Notions of Adventures to give
any Credit to what the Gentleman said; Sir, answer'd he,
Fore-warn'd, fore-arm'd; a Man loses nothing by standing on
his Guard. I know by Experience, that I have Enemies visible
and invisible, and I cannot tell when, nor where, nor in what
Shape they may attack me. At the same time he snatch'd the
Helmet out of *Sancho's* Hands, before he could discharge it
of the Curds, and clapp'd it on his Head, without examining
the Contents. Now the Curds being squeezed between his bare
Crown and the Iron, the Whey began to run all about his Face
and Beard; which so surpriz'd him, that calling to *Sancho* in
great Disorder, What's this, cry'd he, *Sancho*! What's the
matter with me! Sure my Scull is growing soft, or my Brains
are melting, or else I sweat from Head to Foot! But if I do, I'm
sure 'tis not for Fear. This certainly must be a very dreadful
Adventure that's approaching. Give me something to wipe me
if thou can'st, for I'm almost blinded with the Torrent of

Sweat. *Sancho* did not dare to say a Word, but giving him a Cloth, bless'd his Stars that his Master had not found him out. Don *Quixote* dry'd himself, and taking off the Helmet to see what it should be that felt so cold on his Head, perceiving some white Stuff, and putting it to his Nose, soon found what it was. Now, by the Life of my Lady *Dulcinea del Toboso*, cry'd he, thou hast put Curds in my Helmet, vile Traytor and unmannerly Squire. Nay, reply'd *Sancho* cunningly, and keeping his Countenance, if they be Curds, good your Worship give 'em me hither, and I'll eat 'em: But hold, now I think on't, the Devil eat 'em for me; for he himself must have put 'em there. What! I offer to do so beastly a Trick! Do you think I have no more Manners? As sure as I'm alive, Sir, I have got my Inchanters too that owe me a Grudge, and plague me as a Limb of your Worship; and I warrant have put that nasty Stuff there on Purpose to set you against me, and make you fall foul on my Bones. But I hope they've miss'd their aim this time, i'troth! My Master is a wise Man, and must needs know that I had neither Curds nor Milk, nor any thing of that Kind; and if I had met with Curds, I should sooner have put 'em in my Belly than his Helmet. Well, said Don *Quixote*, there may be something in that. The Gentleman had observed these Passages, and stood amaz'd, but especially at what immediately follow'd; for the Knight-Errant having put on the Helmet again, fixed himself well in the Stirrups, try'd whether his Sword were loose enough in his Scabboard, and rested his Lance, Now, cry'd he, come what will come; here am I, who dare encounter the Devil himself in *propria Persona*. By this time the Waggon was come up with them, attended only by the Carter, mounted on one of the Mules, and another Man that sat on the forepart of the Waggon. Don *Quixote* making up to 'em, Whither go ye, Friends, said he, What Waggon is this? What do you convey in it? And what is the Meaning of these Colours? The Waggon is mine, answer'd the Waggoner: I have there two brave Lions, which the General of *Oran* is sending to the King our Master, and these Colours are to let People understand that what goes here belongs to Him. And are the Lions large, enquir'd Don *Quixote*? Very large, answer'd the Man in the fore-part of the Waggon: There never came bigger from *Africk* into *Spain*. I am their Keeper, added he, and have had charge of several others, but I never saw the like of these before. In the foremost Cage is a He-Lion, and in the other behind, a Lioness. By this time they are cruel hungry, for they have not eaten to Day; therefore pray, good Sir, ride out of the Way, for we must make haste to get to the Place where we intend to feed 'em. What! said Don *Quixote*, with a scornful Smile, Lion-Whelps against Me! Against Me those puny Beasts! And at this time of Day? Well, I'll make those Gentlemen that sent their Lions this Way, know whether I am a Man to be scar'd with Lions. Get off, honest Fellow; and since you are the Keeper, open their Cages, and let 'em both out; for maugre and in despite of those Inchanters that have sent 'em to try me, I'll make the Creatures know in the midst of this very Field, who Don *Quixote de la Mancha* is. So thought the Gentleman to himself, now has our poor Knight discover'd what he is; the Curds, I find, have soften'd his Scull, and mellow'd his Brains. While he was making this Reflection, *Sancho* came up to him, and begg'd him to dissuade his Master from his rash Attempt. O good dear Sir! cry'd he, for Pity-sake hinder my Master from falling upon these Lions, by all means, or we shall be torn a-pieces. Why, said this Gentleman, is your Master so arrant a Madman then, that you should fear he would set upon such furious Beasts? Ah Sir! said *Sancho*, he is not mad, but woundy ventursome. Well, reply'd the Gentleman, I'll take care there shall be no harm done; and with that advancing up to Don *Quixote*, who was urging the Lion-Keeper to open the Cage; Sir, said he, Knights-Errant ought to engage in Adventures, from which there may be some Hopes of coming off with Safety, but not in such as are altogether desperate; for that Courage which borders on Temerity, is more like Madness than true Fortitude. Besides, these Lions are not come against You, but sent as a Present to the King, and therefore 'tis not the best way to detain 'em, or stop the Waggon. Pray, sweet Sir, reply'd Don *Quixote*, go and amuse yourself with your tame Partridges and your Ferrets, and leave every one to his own Business. This is mine, and I know best whether these worthy Lions are sent against me or no. Then turning about to the Keeper, Sirrah! you Rascal you, said he, either open the Cages immediately, or

I vow to*—I'll pin thee to the Waggon with this Lance. Good Sir, (cry'd the Waggoner, seeing this strange Apparition in Armour so resolute) for Mercy's-sake do but let me take out our Mules first, and get out of harm's way with 'em as fast as I can, before the Lions get out; for if they should once set upon the poor Beasts, I should be undone for ever; for alas! that Cart and they are all I have in the World to get a Living with. Thou Man of little Faith, said Don *Quixote*, take 'em out quickly then, and go with 'em where thou wilt; though thou shalt presently see that thy Precaution was needless, and thou might'st have spared thy Pains. The Waggoner upon this made all the haste he could to take out his Mules, while the Keeper cry'd out as loud as he was able, Bear witness, all ye that are here present, that 'tis against my Will I'm forc'd to open the Cages and let loose the Lions; and that I protest to this Gentleman here, that he shall be answerable for all the Mischief and Damage they may do; together with the Loss of my Salary and Fees. And now, Sirs, shift for yourselves as fast as you can, before I open the Cages: For, as for myself, I know the Lions will do me no harm. Once more the Gentleman try'd to dissuade Don *Quixote* from doing so mad a thing; telling him, that he tempted Heaven, in exposing himself without Reason to so great a Danger. To this Don *Quixote* made no other Answer, but that he knew what he had to do. Consider however what you do, reply'd the Gentleman, for 'tis most certain that you are very much mistaken. Well, Sir, said Don *Quixote*, if you care not to be Spectator of an Action, which you think is like to be tragical, e'en set Spurs to your Mare, and provide for your Safety. *Sancho* hearing this, came up to his Master with Tears in his Eyes, and begg'd him not to go about this fearful Undertaking, to which the Adventure of the Wind-Mills, and the Fulling-Mills, and all the Brunts he had ever born in his Life, were but Childrens Play. Good your Worship, cry'd he, do but mind, here's no Inchantment in the Case, nor any thing like it. Alack-a-day! Sir, I peep'd even now through the Grates of the Cage, and I'm sure I saw the Claw of a true Lion, and such a Claw as makes me think the Lion that owns it must be as big as a Moun-

* *In* Spanish, *it is* Voto a tal, *which is an* Offer *to swear, but our* Knight *stops without going on with the* Oath.

tain. Alas poor Fellow! said Don *Quixote*, thy Fear will make him as big as half the World. Retire, *Sancho*, and leave me, and if I chance to fall here, thou know'st our old Agreement; repair to *Dulcinea*, I say no more. To this he added some Expressions, which cut off all Hopes of his giving over his mad Design. The Gentleman in the Green would have oppos'd him, but considering the other was much better arm'd, and that it was not Prudence to encounter a Madman, he even took the Opportunity while Don *Quixote* was storming at the Keeper, to march off with his Mare, as *Sancho* did with *Dapple*, and the Carter with his Mules, every one making the best of their way to get as far as they could from the Waggon, before the Lions were let loose. Poor *Sancho* at the same time made sad Lamentations for his Master's Death; for he gave him for lost, not questioning but the Lions had already got him into their Clutches. He curs'd his ill Fortune, and the Hour he came again to his Service; but for all his Wailing and Lamenting, he punch'd on poor *Dapple*, to get as far as he could from the Lions. The Keeper, perceiving the Persons who fled to be at a good Distance, fell to arguing and intreating Don *Quixote* as he had done before. But the Knight told him again, that all his Reasons and Intreaties were but in vain, and bid him say no more, but immediately dispatch. Now while the Keeper took time to open the foremost Cage, Don *Quixote* stood debating with himself, whether he had best make his Attack on Foot or on Horseback; and upon mature Deliberation, he resolved to do it on Foot, lest *Rozinante*, not us'd to Lions, should be put into Disorder. Accordingly he quitted his Horse, threw aside his Lance, grasp'd his Shield, and drew his Sword; then advancing with a deliberate Motion, and an undaunted Heart, he posted himself just before the Door of the Cage, commending himself to Heaven, and afterwards to his Lady *Dulcinea*. Here the Author of this faithful History could not forbear breaking the Thread of his Narration, and, rais'd by Wonder to Rapture and Enthusiasm, makes the following exclamation. O thou most magnanimous Hero! Brave and unutterably Bold Don *Quixote de la Mancha*! Thou Mirror and grand Exemplar of Valour! Thou Second, and New Don *Emanuel de Leon*, the late Glory and Honour of all *Spanish* Cavaliers; What Words, what Colours shall I use to express, to paint in equal Lines, this astonishing Deed of thine! What Language shall I employ to convince Posterity of the Truth of this thy more than human enterprize! What Praises can be coined, and Elogies invented, that will not be outvied by thy superior Merit, though Hyperboles were piled on Hyperboles! Thou, Alone, on Foot, Intrepid and Magnanimous, with nothing but a Sword, and that none of the sharpest, with thy single Shield, and that none of the brightest, stood'st ready to receive and encounter the savage Force of two vast Lions, as fierce as ever roared within the *Lybian* Desarts. Then let thy own unrival'd Deeds, that best can speak thy Praise, amaze the World, and fill the Mouth of Fame, brave Champion of *la Mancha*: while I'm obliged to leave off the high Theme, for want of Vigor to maintain the Flight. Here ended the Author's Exclamation, and the History goes on.

The Keeper observing the Posture Don *Quixote* had put himself in, and that it was not possible for him to prevent letting out the Lions, without incurring the Resentment of the desperate Knight, set the Door of the foremost Cage wide open; where, as I have said, the Male Lion lay, who appeared of a monstrous Bigness, and of a hideous frightful Aspect. The first thing he did was to roll and turn himself round in his Cage; in the next Place he stretch'd out one of his Paws, put forth his Claws, and rouz'd himself. After that he gap'd and yawn'd for a good while, and shew'd his dreadful Fangs, and then thrust out half a Yard of Broad Tongue, and with it lick'd the Dust out of his Eyes and Face. Having done this, he thrust his Head quite out of the Cage, and star'd about with his Eyes that look'd like two live Coals of Fire; a Sight and Motion, enough to have struck Terror into Temerity itself. But Don *Quixote* only regarded it with Attention, wishing his grim Adversary would leap out of his Hold, and come within his reach, that he might exercise his Valour, and cut the Monster piece-meal. To this Height of Extravagance had his Folly transported him; but the generous Lion, more gentle than arrogant, taking no notice of his Vapouring and Bravadoos, after he had look'd about him a while, turn'd his Tail, and having shew'd Don *Quixote* his Posteriors, very contentedly lay down again in his Apartment.

Don *Quixote* seeing this, commanded the Keeper to rouze him with his Pole, and force him out whether he would or no. Not I, indeed Sir, answer'd the Keeper; I dare not do it for my Life; for if I provoke him, I'm sure to be the first he'll tear to Pieces. Let me advise you, Sir, to be satisfy'd with your Day's Work. 'Tis as much as the bravest He that wears a Head can pretend to do. Then pray go no farther, I beseech you: The Door stands open, the Lion is at his Choice, whether he will come out or no. You have waited for him, you see he does not care to look you in the Face, and since he did not come out at the first, I dare engage he will not stir out this Day. You have shewn enough the Greatness of your Courage. No man is obliged to do more than challenge his Enemy, and wait for him in the Field. If he comes not, that's his own Fault, and the Scandal is his, as the Honour the Challenger's. 'Tis true, reply'd Don *Quixote*. Come, shut the Cage-Door, Honest Friend, and give me a Certificate under thy Hand in the amplest Form thou can'st devise, of what thou hast seen me perform; how thou did'st open the Cage for the Lion; how I expected his coming, and he did not come out. How, upon his not coming out then, I stay'd his own Time, and instead of meeting me, he turned Tail and lay down. I am oblig'd to do no more. So, Inchantments avant! and Heaven prosper Truth, Justice, and Knight-Errantry! Shut the Door, as I bid thee, while I make Signs to those that ran away from us, and get 'em to come back, that they may have an Account of this Exploit from thy own Mouth. The Keeper obey'd, and Don *Quixote* clapping on the Point of his Lance, the Handkerchief with which he had wip'd off the Curds from his Face, wav'd it in the Air, and call'd as loud as he was able to the Fugitives, who fled nevertheless, looking behind 'em all the way, and troop'd on in a Body with the Gentleman in Green at the Head of 'em. At last, *Sancho* observ'd the Signal of the white Flag, and calling out to the rest, Hold, cry'd he, my Master calls to us, I'll be hang'd if he has not got the better of the Lions. At this they all faced about, and perceiv'd Don *Quixote* flourishing his Ensign; whereupon recovering a little from their Fright, they leisurely rode back, till they could plainly distinguish Don *Quixote's* Voice; and then they came up to the Waggon. As soon as they were got near it, Come on Friend, said he to the Carter; put thy Mules to the Waggon again, and pursue thy Journey; and *Sancho* do thou give him two Ducats for the Lion-keeper and himself, to make them amends for the Time I have detained them. Ay, that I will with all my Heart, quoth *Sancho*; but what's become of the Lions? Are they dead or alive? Then the Keeper very formally related the whole Action, not failing to exaggerate, to the best of his Skill, Don *Quixote's* Courage; how at his Sight alone the Lion was so terrify'd, that he neither would nor durst quit his strong Hold, tho' for that end his Cage-Door was kept open for a considerable Time; and how at length upon his remonstrating to the Knight, who would have had the Lion forced out, that it was presuming too much upon Heaven, he had permitted, though with great Reluctancy, that the Lion should be shut up again. Well, *Sancho*, said Don *Quixote* to his Squire, what dost thou think of this? Can Inchantment prevail over true Fortitude? No, these Magicians may perhaps rob me of Success, but never of my invincible Greatness of Mind. In short, *Sancho* gave the Waggoner and the Keeper the two Pieces. The first harness'd his Mules, and the last thank'd Don *Quixote* for his Noble Bounty, and promis'd to acquaint the King himself with his Heroick Action when he came to Court. Well, said Don *Quixote*, if his Majesty should chance to enquire who the Person was that did this thing, tell him 'twas *The Knight of the Lions*; a Name I intend henceforth to take up, in lieu of that which I hitherto assum'd, of *The Knight of the Woful Figure*; in which Proceeding I do but conform to the ancient Custom of Knights-Errant, who changed their Names as often as they pleas'd, or as it suited with their Advantage. After this, the Waggon made the best of its way, as Don *Quixote*, *Sancho*, and the Gentleman in Green did of theirs. The latter for a great while was so taken up with making his Observations on Don *Quixote*, that he had not Time to speak a Syllable; not knowing what opinion to have of a Person, in whom he discover'd such a Mixture of good Sense and Extravagance. He was a Stranger to the first Part of his History; for had he read it, he could not have wonder'd either at his Words or Actions: But not knowing the Nature of his Madness, he took him to be wise and distracted by Fits; since in his Discourse he still express'd himself justly and handsomely enough; but in his Actions all was wild, extravagant and unaccountable. For, said the Gentleman to himself, can there be any thing more foolish, than for this Man to put on his Helmet full of Curds, and then believe 'em convey'd there by Inchanters; or any thing more extravagant than forcibly to endeavour to fight with Lions? In the midst of this Soliloquy, Don *Quixote* interrupted him. Without doubt, Sir, said he, you take me for a downright Madman, and indeed my Actions may seem to speak me no less. But for all that, give me leave to tell you, I am not so mad, nor is my Understanding so defective, as I suppose you may fancy. What a noble Figure does the gallant Knight make, who in the midst of some spacious Place transfixes a furious Bull* with his Lance in the View of his Prince! What a noble Figure makes the Knight, who before the Ladies at a harmless Tournament, comes prancing through the Lists inclos'd in shining Steel; or those Court-Champions, who in Exercises of Martial Kind, or that at least are such in Appearance, shew their Activity: and though all they do is nothing but for Recreation, are thought the Ornament of a Prince's Court! But a much nobler Figure is the Knight-Errant, who fir'd with the Thirst of a glorious Fame, wanders through Desarts, through solitary Wildernesses, through Woods, through Cross-ways, over Mountains and Valleys, in quest of perilous adventures, resolv'd to bring them to a happy Conclusion. Yes, I say, a nobler Figure is a Knight-Errant succouring a Widow in some depopulated Place, than the Court-Knight making his Addresses to the City Dames. Every Knight has his particular Employment. Let the Courtier wait on the Ladies; let him with splendid Equipage adorn his Prince's Court, and with a magnificent Table support poor Gentlemen. Let him give Birth to Feasts and Tournaments, and shew his Grandeur, Liberality, and Munificence, and especially his Piety; in all these things he fulfils the Duties of his Station. But as for the Knight-Errant, let him search into all the Corners of the World, enter into the most intricate Labyrinths, and every Hour be ready to attempt Impossibility itself. Let him in desolate Wilds baffle the Rigor of the Weather, the scorching Heat of the Sun's fiercest Beams, and the Inclemency of Winds and

* *The manner of riding at and killing Bulls in the Bull-Feasts in* Spain.

Snow: Let Lions never fright him, Dragons daunt him, nor evil
Spirits deter him. To go in Quest of these, to meet, to dare, to
conflict, and to overcome 'em all, is his principal and proper
Office. Since then my Stars have decreed me to be one of those
Adventurous Knights, I think my self obliged to attempt every
thing that seems to come within the Verge of my Profession.
This, Sir, engag'd me to encounter those Lions just now, judging it to be my immediate Business, tho' I was sensible of the
extreme Rashness of the Undertaking. For well I know, that
Valour is a Virtue situate between the two vicious Extremes
of Cowardice and Temerity. But certainly 'tis not so ill for a
Valiant Man to rise to a Degree of Rashness, as 'tis to fall short
and border upon Cowardice. For as 'tis easier for a Prodigal to
become Liberal, than a Miser; so 'tis easier for the hardy and
rash Person to be reduced to true Bravery, than for the Coward
ever to rise to that Virtue: And therefore in thus attempting
Adventures, believe me, Signor Don *Diego*, 'tis better to exceed the Bounds a little, and over-do, rather than under-do the
thing; because it sounds better in People's Ears to hear it said,
how that such a Knight is Rash and Hardy, than such a Knight
is Dastardly and Timorous. For my part, Sir, answer'd Don
Diego, I think all you have said and done is agreeable to the ex-
actest Rules of Reason; and I believe, if the Laws and Ordinances of Knight-Errantry were lost, they might be all recover'd from you, your Breast seeming to be the safe Repository and Archive where they are lodg'd. But it grows late, let
us make a little more haste to get to our Village, and to my
Habitation, where you may rest your self after the Fatigues,
which doubtless you have sustain'd, if not in Body, at least in
Mind, whose Pains often afflict the Body too. Sir, answer'd
Don *Quixote*, I esteem your Offer as a singular Favour; and so
putting on a little faster than they had done before, about two
in the Afternoon they reached the Village, and got to the
House of Don *Diego*, whom now Don *Quixote* called the
Knight of the *Green Coat*.

XVIII: HOW DON QUIXOTE WAS ENTERTAINED AT THE CASTLE OR HOUSE OF THE KNIGHT OF THE GREEN COAT, WITH OTHER EXTRA-VAGANT PASSAGES

DON *Quixote* found, that Don *Diego de Miranda's* House was spacious after the Country manner; the Arms of the Family were over the Gate in rough Stone, the Buttery in the Fore-yard, the Cellar under the Porch, and all around several great Jars of that Sort commonly made at *Toboso*; the Sight of which bringing to his Remembrance his Inchanted and Transform'd *Dulcinea*, he heav'd a deep Sigh, and neither minding what he said, nor who was by, broke out into the following Exclamation.

> O! Pledges, once my Comfort and Relief,*
> Though pleasing still, discover'd now with Grief.

O ye *Tobosian* Urns, that awaken in my Mind the Thoughts of the sweet Pledge of my most bitter Sorrows! Don *Diego's* Son, who, as it has been said, was a Student, and poetically inclin'd, heard these Words as he came with his Mother to welcome him home; and, as well as she, was not a little surpriz'd to see what a strange Creature his Father had brought with him. Don *Quixote* alighted from *Rozinante*, and very courteously desiring to kiss her Ladyship's Hands, Madam, said Don *Diego*, this Gentleman is the Noble Don *Quixote de la Mancha*, the Wisest, and most Valiant Knight-Errant in the World; pray let him find a Welcome suitable to his Merit, and your usual Civility. Thereupon Donna *Christina* (for that was the Lady's Name) receiv'd him very kindly, and with great Marks of Respect; to which Don *Quixote* made a proper and handsome Return; and then almost the same Compliments pass'd between him and the young Gentleman, whom Don *Quixote* judg'd by his Words to be a Man of Wit and Sense.

Here the Author inserts a long Discription of every Particular in Don *Diego's* House, giving us an Inventory of all the

---

* O dulces prendas, *the Beginning of a Sonnet in the* Diana *of* Montemayor.

Goods and Chattels, and every Circumstance peculiar to the House of a rich Country Gentleman: But the Translator presum'd that it would be better to omit these little things, and such like insignificant Matters, being foreign to the main Subject of this History, which ought to be more grounded on material Truth, than cold and insipid Digressions.

Don *Quixote* was brought into a fair Room, where *Sancho* took off his Armour, and then the Knight appeared in a pair of close Breeches, and a Doublet of Shamoy-Leather, all besmear'd with the Rust of his Armour. About his Neck he wore a plain Band, unstarch'd, after the manner of a Student; about his Legs sad-colour'd Spatter-dashes, and on his Feet a pair of Wax-leather Shoes. He hung his trusty Sword by his Side in a Belt of a Sea-Wolf's Skin; which makes many of Opinion he had been long troubled with a Pain in the Kidneys. Over all this he clapp'd on a long Cloak of good Russet-Cloth: But first of all he wash'd his Head and Face in five Kettle-fulls of Water, if not in six: for as to the exact Number there is some Dispute. And 'tis observable, that the Water still retain'd a Tincture of Whey: Thanks to *Sancho's* Gluttony, that had made him clap into his Master's Helmet those dismal Curds, that so contaminated his awful Head and Face. In this Dress the Knight with a graceful and sprightly Air, walk'd into another Room, where Don *Lorenzo*, the young Gentleman whom we have already mention'd, waited his coming, to keep him Company till the Cloth was laid; the Mistress of the House being gone in the mean time to provide a handsome Entertainment, that might convince her Guest she understood how to make those welcome that came to her House. But before the Knight was ready, Don *Lorenzo* had Leisure to discourse his Father about him. Pray, Sir, said he, who is this Gentleman you have brought with you? Considering his Name, his Aspect, and the Title of Knight-Errant, which you give him, neither my Mother nor I can tell what to think of him. Truly, Son, answer'd Don *Diego*, I don't know what to say to you; all that I can inform you of, is, that I have seen him play the maddest Pranks in the World, and yet say a thousand sensible things that contradict his Actions. But discourse him yourself, and feel the Pulse of his Understanding; make use of Your Sense to judge of His;

though to tell you the Truth, I believe his Folly exceeds his Discretion. Don *Lorenzo* then went to entertain Don *Quixote*, and after some Discourse had pass'd between 'em, Sir, said the Knight, I am not wholly a Stranger to your Merit; Don *Diego de Miranda*, your Father, has given me to understand you are a Person of excellent Parts, and especially a great Poet. Sir, answer'd the young Gentleman, I may perhaps pretend to Poetry, but never to be a great Poet: 'Tis true, I am somewhat given to Rhiming, and love to read good Authors; but I am very far from deserving to be thought one of their Number. I do not mislike your Modesty, reply'd Don *Quixote*; 'tis a Virtue not often found among Poets, for almost every one of them thinks himself the greatest in the World. There is no Rule without an Exception, said Don *Lorenzo*; and 'tis not impossible but there may be one who may deserve the Name, tho' he does not think so himself. That's very unlikely, reply'd Don *Quixote*. But pray, Sir, tell me what Verses are those that your Father says you are so puzzled about? If it should be what we call a Gloss or a Paraphrase, I understand something of that way of Writing, and should be glad to see it. If the Composition be design'd for a Poetical Prize, I would advise you only to put in for the second; for the first always goes by Favour, and is rather granted to the great Quality of the Author than to his Merit; but as to the next, 'tis adjudg'd to the most deserving; so that the third may in a manner be esteem'd the second, and the first no more than the third, according to the Methods us'd in our Universities of giving Degrees. And yet, after all, 'tis no small matter to gain the honour of being call'd the first. Hitherto all's well, thought Don *Lorenzo* to himself, I can't think thee mad yet; let's go on—With that addressing himself to Don *Quixote*, Sir, said he, you seem to me to have frequented the Schools; pray what Science has been your particular Study? That of Knight-Errantry, answer'd Don *Quixote*, which is as good as that of Poetry, and somewhat better too. I don't know what sort of a Science that is, said Don *Lorenzo*, nor indeed did I ever hear of it before. 'Tis a Science answer'd Don *Quixote*, that includes in itself all the other Sciences in the World, or at least the greatest Part of them: Whoever professes it, ought to be learned in the Laws, and understand distributive and commutative Justice, in order to right all Mankind. He ought to be a Divine, to give a Reason of his Faith, and vindicate his Religion by Dint of Argument. He ought to be skill'd in Physick, especially in the Botanick Part of it, that he may know the Nature of Simples, and have recourse to those Herbs that can cure Wounds; for a Knight-Errant must not expect to find Surgeons in the Woods and Desarts. He must be an Astronomer, to understand the Motions of the Celestial Orbs, and find out by the Stars the Hour of the Night, and the Longitude and Latitude of the Climate on which Fortune throws him: and he ought to be well instructed in all the other Parts of the Mathematicks, that Science being of constant use to a Professor of Arms, on many Accounts too numerous to be related. I need not tell you, that all the divine and moral Virtues must center in his Mind. To descend to less material Qualifications; he must be able to swim like a Fish, know how to shooe a Horse, mend a Saddle or Bridle: and returning to higher Matters, he ought to be inviolably devoted to Heaven and his Mistress, Chaste in his Thoughts, Modest in Words, and Liberal and Valiant in Deeds; Patient in Afflictions, Charitable to the Poor; and finally a Maintainer of Truth, though it cost him his Life to defend it. These are the Endowments to constitute a good Knight-Errant; and now, Sir, be you a Judge, whether the Professors of Chivalry have an easy Task to perform, and whether such a Science may not stand in Competition with the most celebrated and best of those that are taught in Colleges? If it be so, answer'd Don *Lorenzo*, I say it deserves the preheminence over all other Sciences. What do you mean, Sir, by that, *If it be so*, cry'd Don *Quixote*? I mean, Sir, reply'd Don *Lorenzo*, that I doubt whether there are now, or ever were, any Knights-Errant, especially with so many rare Accomplishments. This makes good what I have often said, answer'd Don *Quixote*; most People will not be persuaded there ever were any Knights-Errant in the World. Now Sir, because I verily believe, that unless Heaven will work some Miracle to convince them that there have been, and still are Knights-Errant, those incredulous Persons are too much Wedded to their Opinion to admit such a Belief; I will not now lose Time to endeavour to let you see how much you and they are mistaken; all I design to do, is

only to beseech Heaven to convince you of your being in an
Error, that you may see how useful Knights-Errant were in
former Ages, and the vast Advantages that would result in ours
from the Assistance of Men of that Profession. But now Effeminacy, Sloth, Luxury, and ignoble Pleasures, triumph, for the
Punishment of our Sins. Now, said Don *Lorenzo* to himself, our
Gentleman has already betray'd his blind side; but yet he gives
a Colour of Reason to his Extravagance, and I were a Fool
should I think otherwise. Here they were called to Dinner
which ended the Discourse: And at that time Don *Diego* taking
his Son aside, ask'd him what he thought of the Stranger? I
think, Sir said Don *Lorenzo*, that 'tis not in the Power of all the
Physicians in the World to cure his Distemper. He is Mad past
Recovery, but yet he has lucid Intervals. In short, they Din'd,
and their Entertainment prov'd such as the old Gentleman had
told the Knight he us'd to give his Guests, neat, plentiful, and
well-order'd. But that which Don *Quixote* most admir'd, was,
the extraordinary Silence he observ'd through the whole
House, as if it had been a Monastery of mute *Carthusians*. The
Cloth being remov'd, Grace said, and Hands wash'd, Don *Quixote* earnestly desir'd Don *Lorenzo* to shew him the Verses he
had wrote for the Poetical Prize. Well, Sir, answer'd he, because I will not be like those Poets that are unwilling to shew
their Verses when intreated to do it, but will tire you with
them when no Body desires it, I'll shew you my Gloss or Paraphrase, which I did not Write with a Design to get a Prize, but
only to exercise my Muse. I remember said Don *Quixote*, a
Friend of mine, a Man of Sense, once told me, he wou'd not advise any one to break his Brains about that sort of Composition;
and he gave me this Reason for't, That the Gloss or Comment
cou'd never come up to the Theme; so far from it, that most commonly it left it altogether, and run contrary to the Thought
of the Author. Besides he said, that the Rules to which Custom
ties up the Composers of those elaborate Amusements are too
strict, allowing no Interrogations, no such Interjections as *said
he*, or *shall I say*; no changing of Nouns into Verbs; nor any
altering of the Sense: Besides several other Confinements that
cramp up those who puzzle their Brains with such a crabbed
way of Glossing, as you yourself, Sir, without doubt must

know. Really, Signior Don *Quixote*, said Don *Lorenzo*, I wou'd fain catch you Tripping, but you still slip from me like an Eel. I don't know, Sir, reply'd Don *Quixote*, what you mean by your *slipping*? I'll tell you another Time, answer'd the young Gentleman; in the mean while be pleas'd to hear the Theme and Paraphrase, which is this:

THE THEME

Cou'd I recall departed Joy,
 Though barr'd the Hopes of greater Gain,
Or now the future Hours employ,
 That must succeed my pleasant Pain!

The Gloss or Paraphrase

1

All Fortune's Blessings disappear,
 She's fickle as the Wind;
And now I find her as severe,
 As once I thought her kind.
How soon the fleeting Pleasure's past?
How long the ling'ring Sorrows last!
 Unconstant Goddess, thro' thy Hate,
Do not thy prostrate Slave destroy,
 I'd ne'er complain, but bless my Fate,
Could I recall departed Joy.

2

Of all thy Gifts I beg but this,
 Glut all Mankind with more;
Transport 'em with redoubled Bliss,
 But only mine restore.
With Thought of Pleasure once possess'd,
I'm now as curst as I was bless'd;
 Oh wou'd the charming Hour return,
How pleas'd I'd live, how free from Pain!
 I ne'er wou'd pine, I ne'er wou'd mourn,
Tho' barr'd the Hopes of greater Gain.

3

But Oh the Blessing I implore,
 Not Fate itself can give!

Since Time elaps'd exists no more,
  No Pow'r can bid it live.
Our Days soon vanish into nought,
And have no Being but in Thought.
  Whate'er began must end at last;
In vain we twice wou'd Youth enjoy;
  In vain would we recall the past,
Or Now the future Hours employ.

4

Deceiv'd by Hope, and rack'd by Fear,
  No longer Life can please.
I'll then no more its Torments bear,
  Since Death so soon can ease.
This Hour I'll die——But let me pause—
A rising Doubt my Courage awes.
  Assist ye Pow'rs, that rule my Fate,
Alarm my Thoughts, my Rage refrain,
  Convince my Soul there's yet a State
That must succeed my present Pain.

As soon as Don *Lorenzo* had read over his Paraphrase, Don *Quixote* rose from his Seat, and taking him by the Hand, By the highest Mansions in the Skies, cry'd the Knight aloud, Noble Youth, you're the best Poet in the World, and deserve to be crown'd with Laurel, not at *Cyprus* or *Gaeta*, as a certain Poet said, whom Heaven forgive, but at the University of *Athens*, were it still in being, and at those of *Paris*, *Bologna* and *Salamanca*. May those Judges that deny you the Honour of the first Prize, be shot with Arrows by the God of Verse, and may the Muses abhor to come within their Houses. Pray, Sir, if I may beg that Favour, let me hear you read one of your loftiest Productions, for I desire to have a full Taste of your admirable Genius. I need not tell you that Don *Lorenzo* was mightily pleas'd to hear himself prais'd by Don *Quixote*, tho' he believ'd him to be Mad. So bewitching and welcome a thing is Adulation, even from those we at other times despise. Don *Lorenzo* verify'd this Truth, by his ready Compliance with Don *Quixote's* Request, and recited to him the following Sonnet, on the Story of *Pyramus* and *Thisbe*.

Pyramus and *Thisbe*. A Sonnet.

See how, to bless the loving Boy,
The Nymph for whom he burns with equal Fires
Pierces the Wall that parts 'em from their Joy,
While hovering Love prompts, gazes, and admires.

The trembling Maid in Whispers and in Sighs
Dares hardly breathe the Passion she betrays:
But Silence speaks, and Love thro' ravish'd Eyes,
Their Thoughts, their Flames, their very Souls conveys.

Wild with Desires, they sally out at last,
But quickly find their Ruin in their Haste:
    And rashly lose all Pleasure in Despair.

Oh strange Mischance! But do not Fortune blame;
Love joyn'd 'em first, then Death, the Grave, and Fame:
    What loving Wretch a Nobler Fate would share!

Now Heaven be prais'd, said Don *Quixote*, when Don *Lorenzo* had made an end! Among the infinite Number of insipid Men of Rhime, I have at last found a Man of Rhime and Reason, and, in a word, an absolute Poet.

Don *Quixote* stay'd four Days at Don *Diego's* House, and during all that time, met with a very generous Entertainment. However, he then desired his leave to go, and return'd him a Thousand Thanks for his kind Reception; letting him know, that the Duty of his Profession did not admit of his staying any longer out of Action; and therefore he design'd to go in quest of Adventures, which he knew were plentifully to be found in that Part of *Spain*; and that he would employ his Time in that, till the Tilts and Tournaments began at *Saragosa*, to which Place 'twas now his chief Intent to go. However, he would first go to *Montesino's* Cave, about which so many wonderful Stories were told in those Parts; and there he would endeavour to explore and discover the Source and original Springs of the Seven Lakes, commonly called the Lakes of *Ruydera*. Don *Diego* and his Son highly commended his noble Resolution, and desired him to command whatever their House afforded, assuring him he was sincerely Welcome to do it; the

Respect they had for his Honourable Profession, and his particular Merit, obliging them to do him all manner of Service. In short, the Day of his Departure came, a Day of Joy and Gladness to Don *Quixote*, but of Grief and Sadness to poor *Sancho*, who had no mind to change his Quarters, and liked the good Cheer and Plenty at Don *Diego's* House, much better than his short hungry Commons in Forests and Desarts, the sorry Pittance of his ill-stored Wallets, which he however crammed and stuffed with what he thought could best make the change of his Condition tolerable. And now Don *Quixote* taking his leave of Don *Lorenzo*, Sir, said he, I don't know whether I have already said it to you, but if I have, give me leave to repeat it once more, that if you are Ambitious of climbing up to the difficult, and in a manner inaccessible, Summit of the Temple of Fame, your surest way is to leave on one hand the narrow Path of Poetry, and follow the narrower Track of Knight-Errantry, which in a trice may raise you to an Imperial Throne. With these Words, Don *Quixote* seemed to have summed up the whole Evidence of his Madness. However, he could not conclude without adding something more: Heaven knows, said he, how willingly I would take Don *Lorenzo* with me, to instruct him in those Virtues that are annexed to the Employment I profess, to spare the Humble, and crush the Proud and Haughty. But since his tender Years do not qualify him for the Hardships of that Life, and his Laudable Exercises detain him, I must rest contented with letting you know, That one way to acquire Fame in Poetry, is, to be govern'd by other Men's Judgment more than your own: For it is natural to Fathers and Mothers not to think their own Children ugly; and this Error is no where so common as in the Off-spring of the Mind. Don *Diego* and his Son were again surprized to hear this Medley of good Sense and Extravagance, and to find the poor Gentleman so strongly bent on the quest of his unlucky Adventures, the only Aim and Object of his Desires. After this, and many Compliments, and mutual Reiterations of Offers of Service, Don *Quixote* having taken leave of the Lady of the Castle, he on *Rozinante*, and *Sancho* on *Dapple*, set out, and pursued their Journey.

XIX: THE ADVENTURE OF THE AMOROUS
SHEPHERD, AND OTHER TRULY
COMICAL PASSAGES

DON *Quixote* had not travelled far, when he was
overtaken by two Men that looked like Students or Ecclesiasticks, with two Farmers, all
mounted upon Asses. One of the Scholars had
behind him a small Bundle of Linen, and two
pair of Stockings, trussed up in green Buckram
like a Portmanteau; the other had no other Luggage but a
Couple of Foils and a Pair of Fencing-Pumps. And the Husbandmen had a Parcel of other things, which shew'd, that having
made their Market at some adjacent Town, they were now
returning home with their Ware. They all admir'd (as indeed
all others did that ever beheld him) what kind of a Fellow Don
Quixote was, seeing him make a Figure so different from any
thing they had ever seen. The Knight saluted them, and perceiving their Road lay the same way, offer'd them his Company, intreating them however to move an easier Pace, because
their Asses went faster than his Horse; and to engage them
the more, he gave them a Hint of his Circumstances and Profession; that he was a Knight-Errant travelling round the World
in Quest of Adventures, that his proper Name was Don *Quixote de la Mancha*; but his Titular Denomination, *The Knight of
the Lions*. All this was *Greek*, or Pedlar's *French* to the Countrymen; but the Students presently found out his Blind-side. However, with a respectful Distance, Sir Knight, said one of them,
if you are not fix'd to any set Stage, as Persons of your Function
seldom are, let us beg the Honour of your Company; and you
shall be entertain'd with one of the finest and most sumptuous
Weddings, that ever was seen, either in *la Mancha*, or many
Leagues round it. The Nuptials of some young Prince, I presume, said Don *Quixote*? No, Sir, answered the other, but of a
Yeoman's Son, and a Neighbour's Daughter; he the richest in
all this Country, and she the handsomest you ever saw. The
Entertainment at the Wedding will be New and Extraordinary, 'tis to be kept in a Meadow near the Village where the

134

Bride lives. They call her *Quiteria the Handsome,* by reason of her Beauty; and the Bridegroom *Camacho the Rich,* on account of his Wealth. They are well match'd as to Age, for she draws towards Eighteen, and he is about Two and Twenty, though some nice Folks that have all the Pedigrees in the World in their Heads, will tell ye, that the Bride comes of a better Family than he; but that's not minded now-a-days, for Money you know will hide many Faults. And indeed, this same *Camacho* is as free as a Prince, and designs to spare no Cost upon his Wedding. He has taken a Fancy to get the Meadow shaded with Boughs, that are to cover it like an Arbor, so that the Sun will have much ado to peep thro', and visit the green Grass underneath. There are also provided for the Diversion of the Company several Sorts of Anticks and Morrice-Dancers, some with Swords, and some with Bells; for there are young Fellows in his Village can manage 'em cleverly. I say nothing of those that play Tricks with the Soles of their Shoes when they dance, leaving that to the Judgment of the Guests. But nothing that I've told or might tell you of this Wedding, is like to make it so remarkable as the things which I imagine poor Basil's Despair will do. This Basil is a young Fellow, that lives next Door to *Quiteria's* Father. Hence Love took occasion to give Birth to an Amour, like that of old, between *Pyramus* and *Thisbe;* for *Basil's* Love grew up with him from a Child, and she encourag'd his Passion with all the kind Return that Modesty could grant; insomuch, that the mutual Affection of the two little ones was the common Talk of the Village. But *Quiteria* coming to Years of Maturity, her Father began to deny *Basil* the usual Access to his House; and to cut off his farther Pretences, declared his Resolution of marrying her to *Camacho,* who is indeed his Superior in Estate, though far short of him in all other Qualifications; for *Basil,* to give the Devil his Due, is the cleverest Fellow we have; he'll pitch ye a Bar, Wrestle or play at Tennis with the best He in the Country; he runs like a Stag, leaps like a Buck, plays at Nine-pins so well, you'd think he tips 'em down by Witchcraft; sings like a Lark; touches a Guitar so rarely, he even makes it speak; and to compleat his Perfections, he handles a Sword like a Fencer. For that very single Qualification, said Don *Quixote,* he deserves not only

135

Quiteria the Handsome, but a Princess; nay, Queen *Guinever* herself, were she now living, in spight of Sir *Lancelot* and all that would oppose it. Well, quoth *Sancho*, who had been silent, and list'ning all the while, my Wife us'd to tell me, she would have every one marry with their Match. Like to like, quoth the Devil to the Collier, and every Sow to her own Trough, as t'other Saying is: As for my part, all I would have is, that honest *Basil* e'en marry her! for methinks I have a huge liking to the young Man, and so Heaven bless them together, say I, and a Murrain seize those that will spoil a good Match between those that love one another! Nay, said Don *Quixote*, if Marriage should be always the Consequence of mutual Love, what would become of the Prerogative of Parents, and their Authority over their Children? If young Girls might always chuse their own Husbands, we should have the best Families intermarry with Coachmen and Grooms; and young heiresses would throw themselves away upon the first wild young Fellows, whose promising Out-sides and Assurance makes 'em set up for Fortunes, though all their Stock consists in Impudence. For the Understanding which alone should distinguish and chuse in these Cases as in all others, is apt to be blinded or biass'd by Love and Affection; and Matrimony is so nice and critical a Point, that it requires not only our own cautious Management, but even the Direction of a superior Power to chuse right. Whoever undertakes a long Journey, if he be wise, makes it his Business to find out an agreeable Companion. How cautious then should He be, who is to take a Journey for Life, whose Fellow-Traveller must not part with him but at the Grave; his Companion at Bed and Board and Sharer of all the Pleasures and Fatigues of his Journey; as the Wife must be to the Husband! She is no such Sort of Ware, that a Man can be rid of when he pleases: When once that's purchas'd, no Exchange, no Sale, no Alienation can be made: She is an inseparable Accident to Man: Marriage is a Noose, which, fasten'd about the Neck, runs the closer, and fits more uneasy by our struggling to get loose: 'Tis a *Gordian* Knot which none can unty, and being twisted with our Thread of Life, nothing but the Scythe of Death can cut it. I could dwell longer on this Subject, but that I long to know from the Gentleman, whether he can tell us any thing more of

Basil? All I can tell you, said the Student, is, that he's in the Case of all desperate Lovers; since the Moment he heard of this intended Marriage, he has never been seen to smile or talk rationally; he is in a deep Melancholy, that might indeed rather be call'd a dozing Frenzy; he talks to himself, and seems out of his Senses; he hardly eats or sleeps, and lives like a Savage in the open Fields; his only Sustenance a little Fruit, and his only Bed the hard Ground; sometimes he lifts up his Eyes to Heaven, then fixes them on the Ground, and in either Posture stands like a Statue. In short, he is reduc'd to that Condition, that we who are his Acquaintance verily believe, that the Consummation of this Wedding to Morrow will be attended by his Death. Heav'n forbid; Marry and Amen, cry'd *Sancho*! Who can tell what may happen? He that gives a broken Head can give a Plaister. This is one Day, but to Morrow is another, and strange things may fall out in the roasting of an Egg. After a Storm comes a Calm. Many a Man that went to Bed well, has found himself dead in the Morning when he awak'd. Who can put a Spoke in Fortune's Wheel? No body here I am sure. Between a Woman's Yea and Nay, I would not engage to put a Pin's-point, so close they be one to another. If Mrs *Quiteria* love Master *Basil*, she'll give *Camacho* the Bag to hold; for this same Love, they say, looks through Spectacles, that makes Copper look like Gold, a Cart like a Coach, and a Shrimp like a Lobster. Whither in the name of Ill-luck art thou running now *Sancho*, said Don *Quixote*? When thou fall'st to threading thy Proverbs and old Wives Sayings, the Devil (who I wish had thee) can't stop thee. What dost Thou know, poor Animal, of Fortune, or her Wheel, or any thing else? Why truly, Sir, quoth *Sancho*, if you don't understand me, no wonder if my Sentences be thought Nonsense. But let that pass, I understand myself; and I'm sure I han't talk'd so much like a Ninny. But you forsooth are so sharp a Cricket. A Critick, Blockhead, said Don *Quixote*, thou confounded Corrupter of human Speech? By yea, and by nay, quoth *Sancho*, what makes you so angry, Sir? I was never brought up at School nor Varsity, to know when I murder a hard Word. I was never at Court to learn to spell, Sir. Some are born in one Town, some in another; one at St *Jago*, another at *Toledo*; and even There all are not

137

so nicely spoken. You are in the right, Friend, said the Student: Those Natives of that City, who live among the Tanners, or about the Market of *Zocodover*, and are confin'd to mean Conversation, cannot speak so well as those that frequent the polite Part of the Town, and yet they are all of *Toledo*. But Propriety, Purity, and Elegance of Style, may be found among Men of Breeding and Judgment; let 'em be born where they will, for Their Judgment is the Grammar of good Language, though Practice and Example will go a great way. As for my part, I have had the Happiness of good Education; it has been my Fortune to study the Civil Law at *Salamanca*, and I have made it my Business all along to express myself properly, neither like a Rustick nor a Pedant. Ay, ay, Sir, said the other Student, your Parts might have qualify'd you for a Master of Arts Degree, had you not misemploy'd 'em in minding so much those foolish Foils you carry about with you, and that make you lag behind your Juniors. Look you good Sir Batchelor, said the other, your mean Opinion of these Foils is erroneous and absurd; for I can deduce the Usefulness of the Art of Fencing from several undeniable Axioms: Pshaw, said *Corchuelo*, for so was the other called, don't tell me of Axioms: I'll fight you, Sir, at your own Weapons. Here am I that understand neither Quart, nor Tierce; but I have an Arm, I have Strength, and I have Courage. Give me one of your Foils, and in spight of all your Distances, Circles, Falsifies, Angles, and all other Terms of your Art, I'll shew you there's nothing in't, and will make Reason glitter in your Eyes. That Man breathes not Vital Air, that I will turn my Back on. And he must have more than human Force, that can stand his Ground against me. As for standing Ground, said the Artist, I won't be oblig'd to't. But have a care, Sir, how you press upon a Man of Skill, for ten to one, at the very first Advance, but he's in your Body up to the Hilt. I'll try that presently, said *Corchuelo*; and springing briskly from his Ass, snatch'd one of the Foils which the Student carry'd. Hold, hold, Sir, said Don *Quixote* I will stand Judge of the Field, and see fair Play on both Sides; and interposing with his Lance, he alighted, and gave the Artist time to put himself in his Posture, and take his Distance. Then *Corchuelo* flew at him like a Fury, helter skelter, cut and thrust, backstroke and forestroke, single

and double, and laid on like any Lion. But the Student stopp'd
him in the middle of his Career with such a Dab in the Teeth,
that he made *Corchuelo* foam at the Mouth. He made him kiss
the Button of his Foil, as if it had been a Relick, though not
altogether with so much Devotion. In short, he told all the
Buttons of his short Cassock with pure clean Thrusts, and made
the Skirts of it hang about him in Rags like Fish-tails. Twice
he struck off his Hat, and in fine, so maul'd and tir'd him, that
through perfect Vexation *Corchuelo* took the Foil by the Hilt,
and hurl'd it from him with such Violence, that one of the
Countrymen that were by, happening to be a Notary-Publick,
has it upon Record to this Day, that he threw it almost three
quarters of a League; which Testimony has serv'd, and yet
serves to let Posterity know that Strength is overcome by Art.
At last *Corchuelo*, puffing and blowing, sat down to rest himself, and *Sancho*, coming up to him, Mr Batchelor, quoth he,
henceforwards take a Fool's Advice, and never challenge a
Man to Fence, but to Wrestle or pitch the Bar; you seem cut
out for those Sports: But this Fencing is a ticklish Point, Sir,
meddle no more with it; for I have heard some of your Masters
of the Science say, they can hit the Eye of a Needle with the
Point of a Sword. *Corchuelo* acknowledg'd himself convinc'd
of an Error by Experience, and embracing the Artist, they became the better Friends for this Tilting. So, without staying
for the Notary that went for the Foil, and could not be back in
a great while, they put on to the Town where *Quiteria* liv'd,
they all dwelling in the same Village. By the way, the Student
held forth upon the Excellency of the Noble Science of Defence, with so many plain and convincing Reasons, drawn from
expressive Figures and Mathematical Demonstrations, that
all were satisfy'd of the Excellency of the Art, and *Corchuelo*
was reclaim'd from his Incredulity. 'Twas now pretty dark;
but before they got to the Village, there appear'd an entire
blazing Constellation: Their Ears were entertain'd with the
pleasing, but confus'd Sounds of several Sorts of Musick, Drums,
Fiddles, Pipes, Tabors and Bells; and as they approached nearer
still, they found a large Arbour at the Entrance of the Town,
stuck full of lights, which burnt undisturb'd by the least Breeze
of Wind. The Musicians, which are the Life and Soul of Di-

139

version at a Wedding, went up and down in Bands about the
Meadow. In short, some danc'd, some sung, some play'd, and
Mirth and Jollity revell'd through that delicious Seat of Plea-
sure. Others were employ'd in raising Scaffolds for the better
View of the Shows and Entertainments prepar'd for the happy
Camacho's Wedding, and likewise to solemnize poor *Basil's*
Funeral. All the Persuasions and Endeavours of the Students
and Countrymen could not move Don *Quixote* to enter the
Town; urging for his Reason the Custom of Knights-Errant,
who chose to lodge in Fields and Forests under the Canopy
of Heaven, rather than in soft Beds under a gilded Roof; and
therefore he left 'em, and went a little out of the Road, full sore
against *Sancho's* Will, who had not yet forgot the good Lodging
and Entertainment he had at Don *Diego's* House or Castle.

XX: AN ACCOUNT OF RICH CAMACHO'S
WEDDING, AND WHAT BEFEL
POOR BASIL

SCARCE had the fair *Aurora* given place to the refulgent Ruler of the Day, and given him time, with the
Heat of his prevailing Rays, to dry the liquid Pearls
on his Golden Locks, when Don *Quixote*, shaking off
sluggish Sleep from his drowsy Limbs, arose and
call'd his Squire: But finding him still Snoring, O thou
most happy Mortal upon Earth, said he, how sweet is thy Repose; Envy'd by none, and envying no Man's Greatness, secure
thou sleep'st, thy Soul compos'd and calm! No Power of Magick
persecutes Thee, nor are thy Thoughts affrighted by Inchantments. Sleep on, sleep on, a hundred times, sleep on. Those
jealous Cares that break a Lover's Heart, do not extend to
Thee; neither the Dread of craving Creditors, nor the dismal
Foresight of inevitable Want, or Care of finding Bread for a
helpless starving Family, keep thee waking. Ambition does
not make thee uneasy, the Pomp and Vanity of this World do
not perplex thy Mind; for all thy Care's Extent reaches but to
thy Ass. Thy Person and thy Welfare thou hast committed to
My Charge, a Burden impos'd on Masters by Nature and Custom, to weigh and counterpoise the Offices of Servants. Which
is the greatest Slave? The Servant's Business is perform'd by
a few Manual Duties, which only reconcile him more to rest,
and make him sleep more sound; while the anxious Master has
not leisure to close his Eyes, but must labour Day and Night to
make Provision for the Subsistence of his Servant; not only in
time of Abundance, but even when the Heavens deny those
kindly Showers that must supply this Want. To all this fine
Expostulation *Sancho* answer'd not a word; but slept on, and
was not to be wak'd by his Master's calling, or otherwise,
till he prick'd him in the Buttocks with the sharp End of his
Lance. At length opening his Eye-lids half way, and rubbing
them, after he had gap'd and yawn'd, and stretch'd his drowsy
Limbs, he look'd about him, and snuffing up his Nose, I'm much
mistaken quoth he, if from this same Arbour there come not a

pure Steam of a good broil'd Rasher, that comforts my Nostrils more than all the Herbs and Rushes hereabouts. And by my Holy Dame, a Wedding that begins so savourly must be a dainty one. Away Cormorant, said Don *Quixote*, rouze and let's go see it, and learn how it fares with the disdain'd *Basil*. Fare? quoth *Sancho*; why if he be poor, he must e'en be so still, and not think to marry *Quiteria*. 'Tis a pretty Fancy, i'faith! For a Fellow who has not a Cross, to run madding after what is Meat for his Betters. I'll lay my Neck that *Camacho* covers this same *Basil* from Head to Foot with white Six-pences, and will spend ye more at a Breakfast than t'other's worth, and be ne'er the worse. And d'ye think that Madam *Quiteria* will quit her fine rich Gowns and Petticoats, her Necklaces of Pearl, her Jewels, her Finery and Bravery, and all that *Camacho* has given her, and may afford to give her, to marry a Fellow with whom she must knit or spin for her Living? What signifies His Bar-pitching and Fencing? Will that pay for a Pint of Wine at the Tavern? If all those rare Parts won't go to Market, and make the Pot boil, the duce take 'em for me: tho' where they light on a Man that has wherewithal, may I never stir, if they don't set him off rarely. With good Materials on a good Foundation, a Man may build a good House, and Money is the best Foundation in the World. For Heaven's Sake, dear *Sancho*, said Don *Quixote*, bring thy tedious Harangue to a Conclusion. For my part, I believe, were't thou let alone when thy Clack is once set a going, thou would'st scarce allow thyself time to eat or sleep, but would'st prate on to the End of the Chapter. Troth Master! reply'd *Sancho*, your Memory must be very short, not to remember the Articles of our Agreement before I came this last Journey with you. I was to speak what I would, and when I would, provided I said nothing against my Neighbour, or your Worship's Authority; and I don't see that I have broken my Indentures yet. I remember no such Article, said Don *Quixote*; and though it were so, 'tis my Pleasure you now be silent and attend me; for the Instruments we heard last Night begin to chear the Vallies, and doubtless the Marriage will be solemnized this Morning, ere the Heat of the Day prevent the Diversion. Thereupon *Sancho* said no more but saddled *Rozinante*, and clapp'd his Pack-saddle on *Dapple's* back; then

142

both mounting, away they rode fair and softly into the Arbour. The first thing that bless'd *Sancho's* Sight there, was a whole Steer spitted on a large Elm, before a mighty Fire made of a Pile of Wood, that seemed a flaming Mountain. Round this Bonfire were placed six capacious Pots, cast in no common Mould, or rather six ample Coppers, every one containing a whole Shamble of Meat, and entire Sheep were sunk and lost in them, and soak'd as conveniently as Pigeons. The Branches of the Trees round were all garnish'd with an infinite Number of cas'd Hares, and pluck'd Fowl of several Sorts: And then for Drink, *Sancho* told above threescore Skins of Wine, each of which contained above two *Arrobas*,* and as it afterwards prov'd, sprightly Liquor. A goodly Pile of white Loaves made a large Rampart on the one side, and a stately Wall of Cheeses set up like Bricks made a comely Bulwark on the other. Two Pans of Oil, each bigger than a Dyer's Fat, serv'd to fry their Pancakes, which they lifted out with two strong Peels when they were fry'd enough, and then they dipp'd 'em in as large a Kettle of Honey prepar'd for that purpose. To dress all this Provision, there were above fifty Cooks, Men and Women, all cleanly, diligent and chearful. In the ample Belly of the Steer they had sew'd up twelve little sucking Pigs embowell'd, to give it the more savoury Taste. Spices of all Sorts lay about in such Plenty, that they appear'd to be bought by Wholesale. In short, the whole Provision was indeed Country-like, but plentiful enough to feast an Army. *Sancho* beheld all this with Wonder and Delight. The first Temptation that captivated his Senses was the goodly Pots; his Bowels yearn'd, and his Mouth water'd at the dainty Contents: By and by he falls desperately in Love with the Skins of Wine; and lastly, his Affections were fix'd on the Frying-pans, if such honourable Kettles may accept of the Name. The Scent of the fry'd Meat put him into such a commotion of spirit that he could hold out no longer, but accosting one of the busy Cooks with all the smooth and hungry Reasons he was Master of, he begg'd his Leave to sop a Luncheon of Bread in one of the Pans. Friend, quoth the Cook, no Hunger must be felt near us to Day (Thanks to the Founder)

* *In Spain they reckon the Quantity of Wine by the Weight, an Arroba being 28 Pounds, so that two of 'em make Seven Gallons.*

'Light, 'light Man, and if thou can'st find ever a Ladle there, skim out a Pullet or two, and much good may do you. Alack-a-day, quoth *Sancho*, I see no Ladle, Sir. Blood and Suet, cry'd the Cook, what a silly helpless Fellow thou art! Let me see. With that he took a Kettle, and sowsing into one of the Pots, he fish'd out three Hens and a couple of Geese at one heave. Here, Friend, said he to *Sancho*, take this, and make shift to stay your stomach with that *Scum* till dinner be ready. Heaven reward you, cry'd *Sancho*, but where shall I put it! Here, answer'd the Cook, take Ladle and all, and thank the Founder, once more I say; no Body will grudge it thee. While *Sancho* was thus employ'd, Don *Quixote* saw twelve young Farmers Sons, all dress'd very Gay, enter upon stately Mares, as richly and gaudily equipp'd as the Country could afford, with little Bells fasten'd to their Furniture. These in a close Body made several Careers up and down the Meadow, merrily shouting and crying out, Long live *Camacho*, and *Quiteria*, He as rich as She fair, and She the fairest in the World! Poor Ignorants (thought Don *Quixote*, over-hearing them) you speak as you know; but had you ever seen my *Dulcinea del Toboso*, you would not be so lavish of your Praises here. In a little while, at several other parts of the spacious Arbour enter'd a great Number of Dancers, and among the rest twenty four young active Country-Lads in their fine Holland-Shirts, with their Handkerchiefs wrought with several Colours of fine Silk, wound about their Heads, each of 'em with Sword in Hand. They Danc'd a Military Dance, and skirmish'd with one another, mixing and intermixing with their naked Swords, with wonderful sleight and activity, without hurting each other in the least. This Dance pleas'd Don *Quixote* mightily, and though he was no Stranger to such sort of Dances, he thought it the best he had ever seen. There was another he also liked very well, perform'd all by most Beautiful young Maids, between fourteen and eighteen Years of Age, clad in slight Green, with their Hair partly filletted up with Ribbons, and partly hanging loose about their Shoulders, as bright and lovely as the Sun's Golden Beams. Above all they wore Garlands of Roses, Jasmine, Amaranth, and Honey-suckles. They were led up by a Reverend Old Man, and a Matronly Woman, both much

more light and active than their Years seemed to promise.
They danc'd to the Musick of *Zamora* Bagpipes; and such
was the Modesty of their Looks, and the Agility of their Feet,
that they appear'd the prettiest Dancers in the World. After
these, came in an artificial Dance or Masque, consisting of
Eight Nymphs, cast into two Divisions, of which *Love* led one,
and *Wealth* the other; one with his Wings, his Bow, his Arrows, and his Quiver; the other array'd in several gaudy Colours of Gold and Silk. The Nymphs of *Cupid's* Party had their
Names inscribed in large Characters behind their Backs. The
first was *Poesy*, *Prudence* was the next, the third *Nobility*, and
Valour was the fourth. Those that attended *Wealth* were
Liberality, *Reward*, *Treasure*, and *Peaceable Possession*. Before 'em came a Pageant representing a Castle, drawn by four
Savages, clad in green, cover'd over with Ivy, and grim surly
Vizards on their Faces, so to the Life that they had almost
frighted *Sancho*. On the Frontispiece and on every Quarter of
the Edifice was inscrib'd, the Castle of *Wise Reservedness*.
four expert Musicians play'd to them on Pipe and Tabor. *Cupid*
began the Dance, and after two Movements, he cast up his
Eyes, and bent his Bow against a Virgin that stood upon the
Battlements of the Castle, addressing himself in this manner.

The Masque

LOVE

My Name is Love, *supreme my Sway,*
  The greatest Good and greatest Pain.
Air, Earth, and Seas my Power obey,
  And Gods themselves must drag my Chain.
In every Heart my Throne I keep,
  Fear ne'er could daunt my daring Soul:
I fire the Bosom of the Deep,
  And the profoundest Hell controul.

Having spoken these Verses, *Cupid* shot an Arrow over the
Castle, and retir'd to his Station. Then *Wealth* advanc'd, and
perform'd two Movements; after which the Musick stopp'd,
and he express'd himself thus:

WEALTH

Love's my Incentive and my End,
But I'm a greater Power than Love;
Tho' Earthly Born, I Earth transcend,
For Wealth's a Blessing from above.
Bright Maid, with me receive and bless
The surest Pledge of all Success;
Desir'd by All, us'd right by Few,
But best bestow'd, when grac'd by you.

Wealth withdrew, and *Poesy* came forward, and after she had performed her Movements like the rest, fixing her Eyes upon the Lady of the Castle, repeated these Lines:

POESY

Sweet Poesy in moving Lays
Love into Hearts, Sense into Souls conveys;
With Sacred Rage can tune to Bliss or Woe,
Sways all the Man, and gives him Heaven below.

Bright Nymph, with ev'ry Grace adorn'd,
Shall noble Verse by Thee be scorn'd?
'Tis Wit can best thy Beauty prize;
Then raise the Muse, and thou by her shalt rise.

Poesy retir'd, and *Liberality* advanced from *Wealth's* side, and after the Dance spoke thus:

LIBERALITY

Behold that noble golden Mean
Betwixt the Sparing and Profuse!
Good Sense and Merit must be seen
Where Liberality's in Use.

But I for Thee will lavish seem;
For Thee Profuseness I'll approve:
For, where the Merit is extreme,
Who'd not be prodigal of Love?

In this manner all the Persons of each Party advanc'd and spoke their Verses, of which some were pretty and some foolish enough. Among the rest, Don *Quixote*, tho' he had a good Memory, remember'd only these here set down. Then the two Divisions join'd into a very pretty Country-Dance; and still as *Cupid* pass'd by the Castle he shot a Flight of Arrows, and *Wealth* batter'd it with Golden-Balls; then drawing out a great Purse of *Roman* Cat's-Skin that seem'd full of Money, he threw it against the Castle, the Boards of which were presently disjointed, and fell down, leaving the Virgin discover'd without any Defence. Thereupon *Wealth* immediately enter'd with his Party, and throwing a Gold Chain about her Neck, made a shew of leading her Prisoner: But then *Cupid* with his Attendants came to her Rescue; and both Parties engaging, were parted by the Savages, who joining the Boards together, inclos'd the Virgin as before; and all was perform'd with Measure, and to the Musick, that played all the while; and so the Show ended, to the great Content of the Spectators. When all was over, Don *Quixote* ask'd one of the Nymphs, who it was that compos'd the Entertainment? She answer'd, that it was a certain Clergyman who liv'd in their Town, that had a rare Talent that way. I dare lay a Wager, said Don *Quixote*, he was more a Friend to *Basil* than to *Camacho*, and knows better what belongs to a Play than a Prayer-Book: He has express'd *Basil's* Parts and *Camacho's* Estate very naturally in the Design of your Dance. God bless the King and *Camacho* say I, quoth *Sancho*, who heard this. Well! *Sancho*, says Don *Quixote*, thou art a white-liver'd Rogue to change Parties as thou dost; thou'rt like the Rabble, which always cry, Long live the Conqueror. I know not what I'm like, reply'd *Sancho*; but this I know, that this Kettle-full of Geese and Hens, is a Bribe for a Prince. *Camacho* has fill'd my Belly, and therefore has won my Heart. When shall I ladle out such dainty *Scum* out of *Basil's* Porridge-Pots (added he, shewing his Master the Meat, and falling on lustily); therefore a Fig for his Abilities say I. As he sows so let him reap, and as he reaps so let him sow. My old Grannum (rest her Soul) was wont to say, there were but two Families in the World, *Have-much* and *Have-little*; and she had ever a great Kindness for the Family of the *Have-much*. A Doctor gives his Advice by the Pulse of your Pocket; and an Ass cover'd with Gold, looks better than an

Horse with a Pack-Saddle; so once more I say, *Camacho* for My Money. Hast thou not done yet? said Don *Quixote*. I must have done, answer'd *Sancho*, because I find you begin to be in a Passion, else I had Work cut out for Three Days and a Half. Well! said Don *Quixote*, thou wilt never be silent till thy Mouth's full of Clay; when thou'rt dead, I hope I shall have some Rest. Faith and Troth now Master, quoth *Sancho*, you did ill to talk of Death, Heaven bless us, 'tis no Child's Play; you've e'en spoil'd my Dinner; the very Thought of raw Bones and lanthorn Jaws makes me sick. Death eats up all Things, both the young Lamb and old Sheep; and I have heard our Parson say, Death values a Prince no more than a Clown; all's Fish that comes to his Net; he throws at all, and sweeps Stakes; he's no Mower that takes a Nap at Noon-Day, but drives on, fair Weather or foul, and cuts down the green Grass as well as the ripe Corn: He's neither squeamish nor queesy-stomach'd, for he swallows without chewing, and crams down all things into his ungracious Maw; and tho' you can see no Belly he has, he has a confounded Dropsy, and thirsts after Men's Lives, which he guggles down like Mother's Milk. Hold, hold, cry'd the Knight, go no further, for thou art come to a very hand-some Period; thou hast said as much of Death in thy home-spun Cant, as a good Preacher could have done: Thou hast got the Knack of Preaching, Man! I must get thee a Pulpit and Bene-fice, I think. He preaches well that lives well, quoth *Sancho*, that's all the Divinity I understand. Thou hast Divinity enough, said the Don; only I wonder at one thing, 'tis said the Beginning of Wisdom proceeds from the Fear of Heaven; how happens it then, that thou, who fearest a Lizard more than Omnipotence, should'st be so wise? Pray, Sir, reply'd *Sancho*, judge You of your Knight-Errantry, and don't meddle with other Men's Fears, for I am as pretty a Fearer of Heaven as any of my Neighbours; and so let me dispatch this *Scum*, (and much Good may't do thee honest *Sancho*;) Consider, Sir, we must give an Account for our idle Words, another Day; I must have t'other Pluck at the Kettle. With that he attack'd it with so couragious an Appetite, that he sharpen'd his Master's, who would certainly have kept him company, had he not been pre-vented by that which necessity obliges me to relate this instant.

XXI: THE PROGRESS OF CAMACHO'S WEDDING, WITH OTHER DELIGHTFUL ACCIDENTS

WHILE Don *Quixote* and *Sancho* were discoursing, as the former Chapter has told you, they were interrupted by a great Noise of Joy and Acclamations rais'd by the Horsemen, who shouting and galloping, went to meet the young Couple, who, surrounded by a thousand Instruments and Devices, were coming to the Arbour, accompany'd by the Curate, their Relations, and all the better sort of the Neighbourhood, set out in their Holiday Cloaths. Hey-day! quoth *Sancho*, as soon as he saw the Bride, what have we here? Adzookers, this is no Country-Lass, but a fine Court-Lady, all in her Silks and Sattins, by the Mass! Look, look ye, Master, see if instead of Glass Necklaces, she have not on Fillets of rich Coral; and instead of green Serge of *Cuencha*, a thirty-pil'd Velvet. I'll warrant her Lacing is white Linnen too; but hold, may I never squint if it ben't Sattin. Bless us! see what Rings she has on her Fingers, no Jet, no Pewter Bawbles, pure beaten Gold, as I'm a Sinner, and set with Pearls too! If every Pearl ben't as white as a Syllabub, and each of them as precious as an Eye! How she's bedizon'd, and glistens from Top to Toe! And now yonder agin, what fine long Locks the young Slut has got? If they ben't false, I ne'er saw longer in my born Days. Ah Jade! what a fine stately Person she is! What a many Trinkets and glaring Gugaws are dangling in her Hair and about her Neck! Cuds-niggers! she puts me in mind of an over-loaden Date-Tree. I'my Conscience! she's a juicy Bit, a mettl'd Wench, and might well pass Muster in *Flanders*. Well! I say no more, but happy is the Man that has thee! Don *Quixote* could not help smiling to hear *Sancho* set forth the Bride after his Rustick way, though at the same time he beheld her with admiration, thinking her the most beautiful Woman he had ever seen, except his Mistress *Dulcinea*. However, the fair *Quiteria* appear'd somewhat pale, probably with the ill Rest which Brides commonly have the Night before their Marriage, in order to Dress themselves to Advantage. There was a large Scaffold

149

erected on one side of the Meadow, and adorn'd with Carpets and Boughs for the Marriage-Ceremony, and the more convenient Prospect of the Shows and Entertainments. The Procession was just arriv'd to this Place, when they heard a piercing Outcry, and a Voice calling out, Stay, rash and hasty People, stay: Upon which all turning about, they saw a Person coming after them in a black Coat border'd with Crimson powder'd with Flames of Fire. On his Head he wore a Garland of mournful Cypress, and a large Truncheon in his Hand, headed with an Iron Spike. As soon as he drew near, they knew him to be the gallant *Basil*, and the whole Assembly began to fear some Mischief would ensue, seeing him come thus unlook'd for, and with such an Outcry and Behaviour. He came up tir'd and panting before the Bride and Bridegroom; then leaning on his Truncheon, he fix'd his Eyes on *Quiteria*, turning pale and trembling at the same time, and with a fearful hollow Voice, Too well you know, cry'd he, unkind *Quiteria*, that, by the Ties of Truth, and Law of that Heaven which we all revere, while I have Life you cannot be marry'd to another. You may remember too, that all the while I stay'd, hoping that Time and Industry might better my Fortune, and render me a Match more equal to you, I never offer'd to transcend the Bounds of honourable Love, by soliciting Favours to the Prejudice of your Virtue. But you, forgetting all the Ties between us, are going now to break 'em, and give my Right to another, whose large Possessions, though they can procure him all other Blessings, I had never envy'd, could they not have purchased You. But no more, the Fates have ordained it, and I will further their Design, by removing this unhappy Obstacle out of your Way. Live, rich *Camacho*, live happy with the ungrateful *Quiteria* many Years, and let the poor, the miserable *Basil* die, whose Poverty has clipped the Wings of his Felicity, and laid him in the Grave! Saying these last Words, he drew out of his supposed Truncheon a short Tuck that was concealed in it, and setting the Hilt of it to the Ground, he fell upon the Point in such a Manner that it came out all bloody at his Back, the poor Wretch weltring on the Ground in Blood. His Friends, strangely confounded by this sad Accident, ran to help him, and Don *Quixote* forsaking *Rozinante* made Haste to his Assistance, and taking him

150

up in his Arms, found there was still Life in him. They would
fain have drawn the Sword out of his Body, but the Curate
urged it was not convenient till he had made Confession, and
prepared himself for Death, which would immediately attend
the Effusion of Blood, upon pulling the Tuck out of his Body.
While they were debating this Point, *Basil* seemed to come a
little to himself, and calling on the Bride: Oh! *Quiteria* (said
he, with a faint and doleful Voice) now, now, in this last and
departing Minute of my Life, even in this dreadful Agony of
Death, would you but vouchsafe to give me your Hand, and
own yourself my Wife, I should think myself rewarded, for
the Torments I endure; and, pleased to think this desperate
Deed made me Yours, though but for a Moment, I would die
contented. The Curate hearing this, very earnestly recommended to him the Care of his Soul's Health, which at the
present Juncture was more proper than any Gratification of
his outward Man; that his Time was but short, and he ought
to be very earnest with Heaven, in imploring its Mercy and
Forgiveness for all his Sins, but especially for this last desperate
Action. To which *Basil* answer'd, That he could think of no
Happiness till *Quiteria* yielded to be his; but if she would do
it, that Satisfaction would calm his Spirits, and dispose him
to confess himself heartily. Don *Quixote* hearing this, cry'd
out aloud, That *Basil's* Demand was just and reasonable, and
that Signior *Camacho* might as honourably receive her as
the worthy *Basil's* Widow, as if he had received her at her
Father's Hands. Say but the Word, Madam, continu'd he, pronounce it once to save a Man from Despair and Damnation;
you will not be long bound to it, since the nuptial Bed of this
Bridegroom must be the Grave. *Camacho* stood all this while
strangely confounded, till at last he was prevail'd on by the
repeated Importunities of *Basil's* Friends, to consent that *Quiteria* should humour the dying Man, knowing her own Happiness would thereby be deferr'd but a few Minutes longer.
Then they all bent their Intreaties to *Quiteria*, some with
Tears in their Eyes, others with all the engaging Arguments
their Pity could suggest. She stood a long Time inexorable,
and did not return any Answer, till at last the Curate came to
her, and bid her resolve what she would do; for *Basil* was just

ready to give up the Ghost. But then the poor Virgin, trembling and dismay'd, without speaking a Word, came to poor *Basil*, who lay gasping for Breath, with his Eyes fix'd in his Head as if he were just expiring; she kneel'd down by him, and with the most manifest Signs of Grief beckon'd to him for his Hand. Then *Basil* opening his Eyes, and fixing them in a languishing Posture on hers, Oh *Quiteria*, said he, your Heart at last relents when your Pity comes too late. Thy Arms are now extended to relieve me, when those of Death draw me to their Embraces; and they alas! are much too strong for thine. All I desire of thee, O fatal Beauty, is this, let not that fair Hand deceive me now, as it has done before, but confess, that what you do is free and voluntary, without Constraint, or in Compliance to any one's Commands; declare me openly thy true and lawful Husband: Thou wilt not sure dissemble with one in Death, and deal falsly with his departing Soul, that all his Life has been true to thee. In the midst of all this Discourse he fainted away, and all the Bystanders thought him gone. The poor *Quiteria*, with a blushing Modesty, a kind of Violence upon herself, took him by the Hand, and with a great deal of Emotion, No Force, said she, could ever work upon my Will to this Degree, therefore believe it purely my own free Will and Inclination, that I here publickly declare you my only lawful Husband: Here's my Hand in Pledge, and I expect yours as freely in return, if your Pains and this sudden Accident have not yet bereft you of all Sense. I give it you, said *Basil*, with all the Presence of Mind Imaginable, and here I own myself thy Husband. And I thy Wife, said she, whether thy Life be long, or whether from my Arms they bear thee this Instant to the Grave. Methinks, quoth *Sancho*, this young Man talks too much for a Man in his Condition; pray advise him to leave off his Wooing, and mind his Soul's Health. I'm afraid his Death is more in his Tongue than between his Teeth. Now when *Basil* and *Quiteria* had thus plighted their Faith to each other, while yet their Hands were join'd together, the tender-hearted Curate, with Tears in his Eyes, poured on 'em both the nuptial Blessing, beseeching Heaven at the same Time, to have Mercy on the new-marry'd Man's Soul, and in a Manner mixing the Burial Service with the Matrimonial. As soon as the Benediction was pronounc'd, up starts *Basil* briskly from the Ground, and with an unexpected Activity whips the Sword out of his Body, and caught his dear *Quiteria* close in his Arms. All the Spectators stood amaz'd, and some of the simpler Sort stuck not to cry out, A Miracle, a Miracle! No, no, cry'd *Basil*, no Miracle, no Miracle, but a Stratagem, a Stratagem. The Curate, more astonish'd and concern'd than all the rest, came with both his Hands to feel the Wound, and discover'd that the Sword had no where pass'd through the cunning *Basil's* Body, but only through a Tin Pipe full of Blood artfully fitted to his Body, and, as it was afterwards known, so prepar'd that the Blood could not congeal. In short, the Curate, *Camacho*, and the Company, found they had all been egregiously impos'd upon. As for the Bride, she was so far from being displeas'd, that hearing it urg'd that the Marriage could not stand good in Law, because it was fraudulent and deceitful, she publickly declar'd that she again confirm'd it to be just, and by the free Consent of both Parties. *Camacho* and his Friends judging by this that the Trick was premeditated, and that she was privy to the Plot, enrag'd at this horrid Disappointment, had Recourse to a stronger Argument, and drawing their Swords set furiously on *Basil*, in whose Defence almost as many were immediately unsheathed. Don *Quixote* immediately mounting with his Lance couch'd, and cover'd with his Shield, led the Van of *Basil's* Party, and falling in with the Enemy, charg'd clear thro' the Gross of their Battalia. *Sancho*, who never lik'd any dangerous Work, resolv'd to stand Neuter, and so retired under the Walls of the mighty Pot whence he had got the precious Skimmings, thinking That would be respected whatever Side gain'd the Battle. Don *Quixote*, addressing himself to *Camacho's* Party, Hold, Gentlemen, cry'd he, 'tis not just thus with Arms to redress the Injuries of Love. Love, and War are the same thing, and Stratagems and Policy are as allowable in the one as in the other. *Quiteria* was design'd for *Basil*, and He for Her, by the unalterable Decrees of Heaven. *Camacho's* Riches may purchase him a Bride, and more Content elsewhere, and those whom Heav'n has join'd let no Man put asunder. *Basil* had but this one Lamb, and the Lamb of his Bosom, let none therefore offer to take his single Delight from

him, though presuming on his Power; for here I solemnly declare, that he who first attempts it must pass through me, and
this Lance through him. At which he shook his Lance in the
Air with so much Vigor and Dexterity, that he cast a sudden
Terror into those that beheld him, who did not know the
threatning Champion. In short, Don *Quixote's* Words, the
good Curate's diligent Mediation, together with *Quiteria's*
Inconstancy, brought *Camacho* to a Truce; and he then discreetly consider'd, that since *Quiteria* lov'd *Basil* before
Marriage, 'twas probable she would love him afterwards, and
that therefore he had more Reason to thank Heaven for so
good a Riddance, than to repine at losing her. This Thought,
improv'd by some other Considerations, brought both Parties
to a fair Accommodation; and *Camacho*, to shew he did not
resent the Disappointment, blaming rather *Quiteria's* Levity
than *Basil's* Policy, invited the whole Company to stay, and
take Share of what he had provided. But *Basil*, whose Virtues, in spight of his Poverty, had secured him many Friends,
drew away Part of the Company to attend him and his Bride
to her own Town; and among the rest Don *Quixote*, whom
they all honour'd as a Person of extraordinary Worth and
Bravery. Poor *Sancho* followed his Master with a heavy
Heart! he could not be reconcil'd to the Thoughts of turning
his Back so soon upon the good Cheer and Jollity at *Camacho's*
Feast, that lasted till Night; and had a strange Hankering
after those dear Flesh-Pots of *Egypt*, which though he left
behind in Reality, he yet carry'd along with him in Mind. The
beloved *Scum* which he had, that was nigh guttl'd already,
made him view with Sorrow the almost empty Kettle, the
dear Casket where his Treasure lay: So that stomaching
mightily his Master's Defection from *Camacho's* Feast, he
sullenly pac'd on after *Rozinante*, very much out of Humour,
though he had just fill'd his Belly.

XXII: AN ACCOUNT OF THE GREAT ADVENTURE OF MONTESINO'S CAVE, SITUATED IN THE HEART OF LA MANCHA, WHICH THE VALOROUS DON QUIXOTE SUCCESSFULLY ATCHIEV'D

THE new married Couple entertained Don *Quixote* very nobly, in Acknowledgment of his Readiness to defend their Cause; they esteem'd his Wisdom equal to his Valour, and thought him both a *Cid* in Arms, and a *Cicero* in Arts. Honest *Sancho* too recruited himself to the Purpose, during the three Days his Master stay'd, and so came to his good Humour again. *Basil* then inform'd them, that *Quiteria* knew nothing of his Stratagem: but being a pure Device of his own, he had made some of his nearest Friends acquainted with it, that they should stand by him if occasion were, and bring him off upon the Discovery of the Deceit. It deserves a handsomer Name, said Don *Quixote*, since conducive to so good and honourable an End, as the Marriage of a Loving Couple. By the way, Sir, you must know, that the greatest Obstacle to Love, is Want, and a narrow Fortune: For the continual Bands and Cements of mutual Affection are Mirth, Content, Satisfaction, and Jollity. These manag'd by skilful Hands, can make Variety in the Pleasures of Wedlock, preparing the same thing always with some additional Circumstance, to render it new and delightful. But when pressing Necessity and Indigence deprive us of those Pleasures that prevent Satiety, the Yoke of Matrimony is often found very galling, and the Burden intolerable. These Words were chiefly directed by Don *Quixote* to *Basil*, to advise him by the way to give over those airy Sports and Exercises, which indeed might feed his Youth with Praise, but not his Old Age with Bread, and to bethink himself of some grave and substantial Employment, that might afford him a Competency, and something of a Stock for his declining Years. Then pursuing his Discourse: The Honourable Poor Man, said he, if the Poor can deserve that Epithet, when he has a Beautiful Wife, is bless'd with a Jewel: He that deprives him of her, robs him of his Honour, and may be said to deprive him of his

Life. The Woman that is Beautiful, and keeps her Honesty when her Husband is Poor, deserves to be Crown'd with Laurel, as the Conquerors were of Old. Beauty is a tempting Bait, that attracts the Eyes of all Beholders, and the Princely Eagles, and the most high-flown Birds stoop to its pleasing Lure. But when they find it in Necessity, then Kites and Crows, and other ravenous Birds will all be grappling with the alluring Prey. She that can withstand these dangerous Attacks, well deserves to be the Crown of her Husband. However, Sir, take this along with you, as the Opinion of a Wise Man, whose Name I have forgot; he said, there was but one good Woman in the World, and his Advice was, that every Married Man should think his own Wife was She, as being the only way to live contented. For my own part, I need not make the Application to myself, for I am not Married, nor have I as yet any Thoughts that way; but if I had, 'twould not be a Woman's Fortune, but her Character should recommend her; for publick Reputation is the Life of a Lady's Vertue, and the outward Appearance of Modesty is in one Sense as good as the Reality; since a private Sin is not so prejudicial in this World, as a publick Indecency. If you bring a Woman honest to your Bosom, 'tis easy keeping her so, and perhaps you may improve her Vertues. If you take an unchaste Partner to your Bed, 'tis hard mending her; for the Extremes of Vice and Vertue are so great in a Woman, and their Points so far asunder, that 'tis very improbable, I won't say impossible, they should ever be reconcil'd. *Sancho*, who had patiently listen'd so far, could not forbear making some Remarks on his Master's Talk. This Master of mine, thought he to himself, when I am talking some good Things, full of Pith and Marrow, as He may be now, was wont to tell me that I should tie a Pulpit at my Back, and stroll with it about the World to retail my Rarities; but I might as well tell Him, that when once he begins to tack his Sentences together, a single Pulpit is too little for him; he had need have two for every Finger, and go pedling about the Market and cry, Who buys my Ware? Old Nick take him for a Knight-Errant! I think he's one of the seven wise Masters. I thought he knew nothing but his Knight-Errantry, but now I see the Devil a thing can scape him; he has an Oar in every Man's Boat, and a Finger in every Pye. As he mutter'd this somewhat loud his Master over-heard him. What's that thou'rt Grumbling about, *Sancho*, said he? Nothing, Sir, nothing quoth *Sancho*. I was only wish-ing I had heard your Worship Preach this Doctrine before I Married, then mayhap I might have with the old Proverb said, A sound Man needs no Physician. What, is *Teresa* so bad then, ask'd Don *Quixote*? Not so very bad neither, answer'd *Sancho*; nor yet so good as I would have her. Fie, *Sancho*, said Don *Quix-ote*, thou dost not do well to speak ill of thy Wife, who is a good Mother to thy Children. There is no Love lost, Sir, quoth *San-cho*, for she speaks as ill of me, when the Fit takes her, especi-ally when she's in one of her Jealous Moods, for then Old Nick himself cou'd not bear her Maundring.

Don *Quixote* having tarried three Days with the young Couple, and been entertain'd like a Prince, he intreated the Student, who fenced so well, to help him to a Guide that might conduct him to *Montesino's* Cave, resolving to go down into it, and prove by his own Eye-sight the Wonders that were re-ported of it round the Country. The Student recommended a Cousin-German of his for his Conductor, who, he said, was an Ingenious Lad, a pretty Scholar, and a great Admirer of Books of Knight-Errantry, and cou'd shew him the famous Lake of *Ruydera* too: adding, that he would be very good Company for the Knight, as being one that wrote Books for the Booksellers, in order to Dedicate 'em to Great Men. Accordingly, the Learn-ed Cousin came, mounted on an Ass with Foal; his Pack-saddle cover'd with an old Carpet, or coarse Packing-Cloth. There-upon *Sancho* having got ready *Rozinante* and *Dapple*, well stuffed his Wallet, and the Student's Knapsack to boot, they all took their leave, steering the nearest Course to *Montesino's* Cave. To pass the Time on the Road, Don *Quixote* ask'd the Guide, To what Course of Study he chiefly apply'd himself? Sir, answer'd the Scholar, my Business is Writing, and Copy-Money my chief Study. I have publish'd some Things with the general Approbation of the World, and much to my own Ad-vantage. Perhaps, Sir, you may have heard of one of my Books call'd, *The Treatise of Liveries and Devices*; in which I have obliged the Publick with no less than seven Hundred and three sorts of Liveries and Devices, with their Colours, Mottos, and

Cyphers; so that any Courtier may furnish himself there upon any Extraordinary Appearance, with what may suit his Fancy or Circumstances, without racking his own Invention to find what is agreeable to his Inclination. I can furnish the Jealous, the Forsaken, the Disdain'd, the Absent, with what will fit 'em to a Hair. Another Piece which I now have on the Anvil, I design to call the *Metamorphosis*, or *The* Spanish *Ovid*; an Invention very new and extraordinary. 'Tis in short, *Ovid Burlesqu'd*; wherein I discover who the *Giralda** of *Sevil* was; who the Angel of the *Magdalen*; I tell ye what was the Pipe of *Vecinguerra* of *Cordova*, what the Bulls of *Guisando*, the *Sierra Morena*, the Fountains of *Laganitos*, and *Lavapies* at *Madrid*; not forgetting that of *Piojo*, nor those of the Golden Pipe, and the Abbey; and I embellish the Fables with Allegories, Metaphors, and Translations, that will both delight and instruct. Another Work, which I soon design for the Press, I call a Supplement to *Polydore Virgil*, concerning the Invention of Things; A Piece, I'll assure you, Sir, that shews the great Pains and Learning of the Compiler, and perhaps in a better Stile than the old Author. For Example, he has forgot to tell us, who was the first that was troubl'd with a Catarrh in the World; and who was the first that was Flux'd for the *French Disease*. Now, Sir, I immediately resolve it, and confirm my Assertion by the Testimony of at least four and twenty Authentick Writers; By which Quotations alone, you may guess, Sir, at what Pains I have been to instruct and benefit the Publick.

Sancho having hearkened with great Attention all this while, Pray, Sir, quoth he to him, so Heaven guide your Right-hand in all you Write, let me ask you, Who was the first Man that scratch'd his Head? Scratch'd his Head, Friend, answer'd the Author? Ay, Sir, scratch'd his Head, quoth *Sancho*: Sure you that know all things, can tell me that, or the Devil's in't! What think you of old Father *Adam*? Old Father *Adam*, answer'd the Scholar! Let me see—Father *Adam* had a Head, he had Hair, he had Hands, and he cou'd scratch: But Father *Adam* was the first Man; *Ergo*, Father *Adam* was the first Man that scratch'd his Head. 'Tis plain you are in the right. O ho,

---

* *All these are noted Things, or Places in Spain, on which many fabulous Stories are grounded.*

am I so, Sir, quoth *Sancho*? Another Question, by your Leave, Sir, Who was the first Tumbler in the World? Truly Friend, answer'd the Student, that's a Point I cannot resolve you without consulting my Books; but as soon as ever I get home, I will study Night and Day to find it out. For two fair Words, quoth *Sancho*, I'll save you that Trouble. Can you resolve that Doubt, ask'd the Author? Ay, marry, can I, said *Sancho*: The first Tumbler in the World was *Lucifer*; when he was cast out of Heaven he tumbled into Hell. You are positively in the right, said the Scholar. Where did you get that, *Sancho*, said Don *Quixote*? For I dare swear 'tis none of your own. Mum! quoth *Sancho*. In asking of foolish Questions, and selling of Bargains, let *Sancho* alone, quo' I; I don't want the help of my Neighbours. Truly, said Don *Quixote*, thou hast given thy Question a better Epithet than thou art aware of: For there are some Men who busy their Heads, and lose a World of Time in making Discoveries, the Knowledge of which is good for nothing upon the Earth, unless it be to make the Discoverers laugh'd at.

With these, and such diverting Discourses they pass'd their Journey, till they came to the Cave the next Day, having lain the Night before in an inconsiderable Village on the Road. There they bought a hundred Fathom of Cordage to hang Don *Quixote* by, and let him down to the lowest part of the Cave; he being resolved to go to the very Bottom, were it as deep as Hell. The Mouth of it was inacessible, being quite stopp'd up with Weeds, Bushes, Brambles, and wild Fig-Trees, though the Entrance was wide and spacious. Don *Quixote* was no sooner come to the Place, but he prepared for his Expedition into that Under-World, telling the Scholar, that he was resolved to reach the Bottom, though deep as the profound Abyss; and all having alighted, his Squire and his Guide accordingly girt him fast with a Rope. While this was doing, good sweet Sir, quoth *Sancho*, consider what you do. Don't venture into such a cursed black Hole! Look before you Leap, Sir, and be not so wilful as to bury your self alive. Don't hang your self like a Bottle or a Bucket, that is let down to be soused in a Well. Alack-a-day, Sir, it is none of Your Business to pry thus into every Hole, and go down to the Pit of Hell for the nonce? Peace Coward, said the Knight, and bind me fast; for surely for Me such an Enterprize as this is reserved. Pray Sir, said the Student, when you are in, be very Vigilant in exploring and observing all the Rarities in the Place. Let nothing escape your Eyes, perhaps you may discover there some things worthy to be inserted in my Metamorphosis. Let him alone, quoth *Sancho*, he will go thro' stitch with it: He'll make a Hog or a Dog of it, I'll warrant you. Don *Quixote* being well bound, not over his Armour, but his Doublet, bethought himself of one thing they had forgot. We did ill, said he, not to provide our selves of a little Bell, that I should have carried down with me, to Ring for more or less Rope as I may have occasion for, and inform you of my being Alive. But since there is no Remedy, Heaven prosper me. Then Kneeling down, he in a low Voice recommended himself to the Divine Providence for Assistance and Success in an Adventure so strange, and in all appearance so dangerous. Then raising his Voice, O thou Mistress of my Life and Motions, cry'd he, most Illustrious and Peerless *Dulcinea del Toboso*, if the Prayers of an adventurous absent Love may reach the Ears of the far-distant Object of his Wishes, by the Power of thy unspeakable Beauty I conjure thee to grant me thy Favour and Protection, in this Plunge and Precipice of my Fortune. I am now going to Ingulph, and cast my self into this dismal Profundity, that the World may know nothing can be impossible to Him, who influenc'd by thy Smiles, attempts under the Banner of thy Beauty, the most difficult Task. This said, he got up again, and approaching the Entrance of the Cave, he found it stopp'd up with Brakes and Bushes, so that he must be obliged to make his Way by Force. Whereupon, drawing his Sword, he began to cut and slash the Brambles that stopp'd up the Mouth of the Cave, when presently an infinite Number of over-grown Crows and Daws came rushing and fluttering out of the Cave about his Ears, so thick, and with such an Impetuosity, as over-whelm'd him to the Ground. He was not superstitious enough to draw any ill Omen from the Flight of the Birds; besides, 'twas no small Encouragement to him, that he spy'd no Bats nor Owls, nor other ill-boding Birds of Night among them: He therefore rose again with an undaunted Heart, and committed himself to the black and dreadful Abyss. But *Sancho* first gave him his Benediction, and making a Thousand Crosses over him, Heaven be thy Guide, quoth he, and our Lady of the Rock in *France*, with the Trinity of *Gaeta*,* thou Flower and Cream, and Scum of all Knights-Errant. Go thy Ways, thou Hackster of the World, Heart of Steel, and Arms of Brass! And may'st thou come back Sound, Wind and Limb, out of this dreadful Hole, which thou art running into, once more to see the warm Sun, which thou art now leaving.

The Scholar too pray'd to the same Effect for the Knight's happy Return. Don *Quixote* then call'd for more Rope, which they gave him by Degrees, till his Voice was drown'd in the Windings of the Cave, and their Cordage was run out. That done they began to consider whether they should hoist him up again immediately or no; however, they resolv'd to stay half an Hour, and then they began to draw up the Rope, but were strangely surpriz'd to find no Weight upon it; which made 'em conclude, the poor Gentleman was certainly lost. *Sancho* bursting out in Tears, made a heavy Lamentation, and fell a hawling up the Rope as fast as he cou'd, to be thoroughly satisfy'd. But after they had drawn up about fourscore Fathoms, they felt a Weight again, which made 'em take Heart; and at length they plainly saw Don *Quixote*. Welcome, cry'd *Sancho* to him, as soon as he came in Sight; Welcome dear Master, I'm glad you're come again; we were afraid you had been Pawn'd for the Reckoning. But *Sancho* had no Answer to this Compliment; and when they had pull'd the Knight quite up, they found that his Eyes were clos'd as if he had been fast asleep. They laid him on the Ground, and unbound him: Yet he made no sign of Waking, and all their turning and shaking was little enough to make him come to himself. At last he began to stretch his Limbs, as if he had waken'd out of the most profound Sleep, and staring wildly about him, Heaven forgive you, Friends, cry'd he; for you have rais'd me from one of the sweetest Lives that ever Mortal led, and most delightful Sights that ever Eyes beheld. Now I perceive how fleeting are all the Joys of this Transitory Life; They are but an imperfect Dream, they fade like a Flower, and vanish like a Shadow. Oh ill-fated *Montesinos*! Oh *Durandarte* unfortunately Wounded! Oh unhappy *Belerma*! Oh deplorable *Guadiana*! And you the distress'd Daugh-

* *Particular Places of Devotions.*

ters of *Ruydera*, whose flowing Waters shew what Streams of
Tears once trickl'd from your Lovely Eyes! These Expressions,
utter'd with great Passion and Concern, surpriz'd the Scholar
and *Sancho*, and they desir'd to know his meaning, and what
he had seen in that Hell upon Earth. Call it not Hell, answer'd
Don *Quixote*, for it deserves a better Name, as I shall soon let
you know. But first give me something to Eat, for I am prodigi-
ously hungry. They then spread the Scholar's coarse Saddle-
cloath for a Carpet; and examining their old Cupboard, the
Knapsack, they all three sat down on the Grass, and eat heartily together, like Men that were a Meal or Two behind-hand.
When they had done, Let no Man stir, said Don *Quixote*, sit
still, and hear me with Attention.

XXIII: OF THE WONDERFUL THINGS WHICH THE UNPARALLEL'D DON QUIXOTE DECLAR'D HE HAD SEEN IN THE DEEP CAVE OF MONTESINOS, THE GREATNESS AND IMPOSSIBILITY OF WHICH MAKES THIS ADVENTURE PASS FOR APOCRYPHAL

IT was now past Four in the Afternoon, and the Sun was opportunely hid behind the Clouds, which, interposing between his Rays, invited Don *Quixote*, without Heat or Trouble, to relate to his Illustrious Auditors the Wonders he had seen in *Montesino's* Cave.

About twelve or fourteen Men's depth, said he, in the Profundity of this Cavern, on the Right Hand, there is a Concavity wide enough to contain a large Waggon, Mules and all. This Place is not wholly dark, for thro' some Chinks and narrow Holes, that reach to the distant Surface of the Earth, there comes a glimmering Light. I discover'd this Recess, being already weary of hanging by the Loins, discourag'd by the profound Darkness of the Region below me, destitute of a Guide, and not knowing whither I went: Resolving therefore to rest my self there a while, I call'd to you to give me no more Rope, but it seems you did not hear me. I therefore enter'd, and coiling up the Cord, sat upon it very melancholy, and thinking how I shou'd most conveniently get down to the Bottom, having no body to guide or support me. While thus I sat pensive, and lost in Thought, insensibly, without any previous Drowsiness, I found my self surpriz'd by Sleep; and after that, not knowing how, nor which way I waken'd, I unexpectedly found my self in the finest, the sweetest, and most delightful Meadow, that ever Nature adorn'd with her Beauties, or the most inventive Fancy could ever imagine. Now that I might be sure this was neither a Dream nor an Illusion, I rubb'd my Eyes, blow'd my Nose, and felt several Parts of my Body, and convinced my self, that I was really awake, with the use of all my Senses, and all the Faculties of my Understanding sound and active as at this Moment.

Presently I discover'd a Royal and Sumptuous Palace, of

which the Walls and Battlements seem'd all of clear and transparent Crystal. At the same time, the Spacious Gates opening, there came out towards me a venerable old Man, clad in a sad-colour'd Robe, so long that it swept the Ground; on his Breast and Shoulders he had a Green-Sattin-Tippit after the manner of those worn in Colleges. On his Head he wore a black *Milan* Cap, and his broad hoary Beard reach'd down below his Middle. He had no kind of Weapon in his Hands, but a Rosary of Beads about the bigness of Walnuts, and his *Credo* Beads appear'd as large as ordinary Ostrich-Eggs. The Aweful and Grave Aspect, the Pace, the Port and goodly Presence of this old Man, each of 'em apart, and much more all together, struck me with Veneration and Astonishment. He came up to me, and without any previous Ceremony, embracing me close: 'Tis a long time, said he, most Renown'd Knight, Don *Quixote de la Mancha*, that We who dwell in this inchanted Solitude have hop'd to see you here; that you may inform the upper World of the surprizing Prodigies concealed from Human Knowledge in this Subterranean Hollow, call'd the Cave of *Montesinos*: An Enterprize reserv'd alone for your insuperable Heart, and stupendous Resolution. Go with me then, thou most illustrious Knight, and behold the Wonders inclos'd within this transparent Castle, of which I am the perpetual Governour and chief Warden, being the same individual *Montesinos*, from whom this Cavern took its Name.

No sooner had the reverend old Man let me know who he was, but I entreated him to tell me, whether it was true or no, that at his Friend *Durandarte's* Dying Request he had taken out his Heart with a small Dagger, the very moment he expir'd, and carry'd it to his Mistress *Belerma*, as the Story was current in the World? 'Tis Literally true, answer'd the Old Gentleman, except that single Circumstance of the Dagger; for I us'd neither a small nor a large Dagger on this occasion, but a well polish'd Poniard, as sharp as an Awl. I'll be hang'd, quoth *Sancho*, if it was not one of your *Sevil* Poniards of *Raymond de Hoze's* making. That can't be, said Don *Quixote*, for that Cutler liv'd but t'other Day, and the Battle of *Roncesvalles*, where this Accident happened, was fought many Ages ago: But this is of no importance to the Story. You are in the right, Sir, said the Student, and pray go on, for I hearken to your Relation with the greatest Satisfaction imaginable. That, Sir, said the Knight, increases my Pleasure in telling it. But to proceed: The Venerable *Montesinos*, having conducted me into the Crystal-Palace, led me into a spacious Ground-Room, exceeding cool, and all of Alabaster. In the middle of it stood a stately Marble Tomb, that seem'd a Master-piece of Art; upon which lay a Knight extended all at length, not of Stone or Brass, as on other Monuments, but pure Flesh and Bones. He covered the Region of his Heart with his Right-Hand, which seemed to me somewhat hairy, and very full of Sinews, a sign of the great Strength of the Body to which it belonged. *Montesinos*, observing that I viewed this Spectacle with Surprize, Behold, said he, the Flower and Mirror of all the amorous and valiant Knights of his Age, my Friend *Durandarte*, who, together with Me and many others of both Sexes, are kept here inchanted by *Merlin* that *British* Magician, who, they say, was the Son of the Devil; though I cannot believe it, only his Knowledge was so great, that he might be said to know more than the Devil. Here I say we are inchanted, but how and for what cause no Man can tell, though Time I hope will shortly reveal it. But the most wonderful part of my Fortune is this, I am as certain, as that the Sun now shines, that *Durandarte* dy'd in My Arms, and that with these Hands I took out his Heart, by the same Token that it weigh'd above two Pounds, a sure Mark of his Courage; for, by the Rules of Natural Philosophy, the most Valiant Men have still the biggest Hearts. Nevertheless, tho' this Knight really dy'd, he still complains and sighs sometimes as if he were alive. Scarce had *Montesinos* spoke these Words, but the miserable *Durandarte* cry'd out aloud, Oh! Cousin *Montesinos*, the last and dying Request of your departing Friend, was to take my Heart out of my Breast with a Poniard or a Dagger, and carry it to *Belerma*. The Venerable *Montesinos* hearing this fell on his Knees before the afflicted Knight, and with Tears in his Eyes, Long, long ago, said he, *Durandarte*, thou dearest of my Kinsmen, have I perform'd what you enjoin'd me on that bitter fatal Day when you expired. I took out your Heart with all imaginable Care, not leaving the least Particle of it in your Breast: I gently

165

wiped it with a Lac'd Handkerchief, and posted away with it to *France*, as soon as I had committed your dear Remains to the Bosom of the Earth, having shed Tears enough to have wash'd my Hands clear of the Blood they had gather'd by plunging in your Entrails. To confirm this Truth yet farther, at the first place where I stopp'd from *Roncesvalles*, I laid a little Salt upon your Heart, to preserve it from Putrefaction, and keep it, if not fresh, at least free from any ill Smell, till I presented it into the Hands of *Belerma*, who with you and me, and *Guadiana** your Squire, as also *Ruydera* (the Lady's Woman) with her seven Daughters, her two Nieces, and many others, of your Friends and Acquaintance, is here confined by the Necromantick Charms of the Magician *Merlin*; and though it be now above five hundred Years since we were first convey'd to this Inchanted Castle, we are all still alive, except *Ruydera*, her Daughters and Nieces, who by the favour of *Merlin*, that pity'd their Tears, were turned into so many Lakes, still extant in the World of the Living, and in the Province of *La Mancha*, distinguish'd by the Names of the Lakes of *Ruydera*; seven of 'em belonging to the Kings of *Spain*, and the two Nieces to the Knights of the most Holy Order of St *John*. Your Squire *Guadiana*, lamenting his hard Fate, was in like manner Metamorphosed into a River that bears his Name; yet still so sensible of your Disaster, that when he first arose out of the Bowels of the Earth to flow along its Surface, and saw the Sun in a strange Hemisphere, he plunged again under Ground, striving to hide his melting Sorrows from the World; but the natural Current of his Waters forcing a Passage up again, he is compell'd to appear where the Sun and Mortals may see him. Those Lakes mixing their Waters in his Bosom, he swells, and glides along in sullen State to *Portugal*, often expressing his deep Melancholy by the muddy and turbid Colour of his Streams; which, as they refuse to please the Sight, so likewise deny to indulge mortal Appetite by breeding such fair and savoury Fish as may be found in the Golden *Tagus*. All this I have often told you, my dearest *Durandarte*; and since you return me no Answer, I must conclude you believe me not, or

---

* Guadiana *a River in* Spain, *that sinks into the Earth and rises again a great distance off.*

that you do not hear me; for which (Witness it Heaven) I am
extremely griev'd. But now I have other News to tell ye, which,
though perhaps it may not asswage your Sorrows, yet I am sure
it will not increase 'em. Open your Eyes, and behold in your
Presence that mighty Knight, of whom *Merlin* the Sage has
foretold so many Wonders: That Don *Quixote de la Mancha*,
I mean, who has not only restor'd to the World the Function
of Knight-Errantry, that has lain so long in Oblivion, but advanc'd it to greater Fame than it could boast in former Ages,
the Nonage of the World. 'Tis by His Power we may expect to
see the fatal Charm dissolv'd, that keeps us here confin'd; for
great Performances are properly reserv'd for great Personages.
And shou'd it not be so, answer'd the grieving *Durandarte*,
with a faint and languishing Voice? Shou'd it not be so, I say,
Oh Cousin! *Patience, and Shuffle the Cards.* * Then turning on
one side, without speaking a Word more, he relaps'd into his
usual Silence. After this, I was alarm'd with piteous howling
and crying, which, mix'd with lamentable Sighs and Groans,
oblig'd me to turn about, to see whence it proceeded. Then
thro' the Crystal-Wall I saw a mournful Procession of most
Beautiful Damsels, all in black, marching in two Ranks, with
Turbans on their Heads after the *Turkish* Fashion; and last
of all came a Majestick Lady, dress'd also in Mourning, with
a long White Veil, that reach'd from her Head down to the
Ground. Her Turban was twice as big as the biggest of the rest:
She was somewhat beetle-browed, her Nose was flattish, her
Mouth wide, but her Lips Red; her Teeth, which she some-
times discover'd, seem'd to be thin and snaggy, but indeed as
White as blanch'd Almonds. She held a fine Handkerchief,
and within it I cou'd perceive a Heart of Flesh, so dry and
wither'd that it look'd like Mummy. *Montesinos* inform'd me,
that the Procession consisted of *Durandarte's* and *Belerma's*
Servants, who were inchanted there with their Master and
Mistress: but that the last was *Belerma* her self, who with her
Attendants used four Days in the Week constantly thus to sing,
or rather howl their Dirges over the Heart and Body of his

* Patience and Shuffle, *is a Spanish Proverb, like our* Patience per force;
*used by them, because those that lose at Cards commonly use to shuffle them
afterwards very much.*

Cousin; and that though *Belerma* appear'd a little haggard at that Juncture, occasioned by the Grief she bore in her own Heart, for that which she carried in her Hand, yet had I seen her before her Misfortunes had sunk her Eyes and tarnished her Complexion, worse than the Diseases of her Sex, from which she was free, I must have owned, that even the celebrated *Dulcinea del Toboso*, so famous in *La Mancha*, and over the whole Universe, could scarce have vyed with her in Gracefulness and Beauty. Hold there, good Signior Don *Montesinos*, said I. You know that Comparisons are odious, therefore no more comparing, I beseech you; but go on with your Story. The Peerless *Dulcinea del Toboso* is what she is, and the Lady *Belerma* is what she is, and has been: so no more upon that Subject. I beg your Pardon, answered *Montesinos*, Signior Don *Quixote*, I might have guess'd indeed that you were the Lady *Dulcinea's* Knight, and therefore I ought to have bit my Tongue off, sooner than to have compared her to any thing lower than Heaven itself. This Satisfaction, which I thought sufficient from the great *Montesinos*, stifled the Resentment I else had shewn, for hearing my Mistress compared to *Belerma*. Nay, marry, quoth *Sancho*, I wonder you did not catch the old doating Huncks by the Weasond, and maul, and thresh him thick and three-fold! How could you leave one Hair on his Chin? No, no, *Sancho*, answer'd Don *Quixote*, there is always a Respect due to our Seniors, tho' they be no Knights; but most when they are such, and under the Oppression of Inchantment. However, I am satisfied, that in what Discourse pass'd between us, I took care not to have any thing that look'd like an Affront fixed upon me. But Sir, ask'd the Scholar, how cou'd you see and hear so many strange things in so little Time? I can't conceive how you could do it. How long, said Don *Quixote*, do you reckon that I have been in the Cave? A little above an Hour, answered *Sancho*. That's impossible, said Don *Quixote*, for I saw Morning and Evening, and Evening and Morning, three times since; so that I could not be absent less than three Days from this upper World. Ay, ay, quoth *Sancho*, my Master's in the Right; for these Inchantments, that have the greatest Share in all his Concerns, may make That seem three Days and three Nights to him, which is but an Hour to other People. It

must be so, said Don *Quixote*. I hope, Sir, said the Scholar, you
have eaten something in all that time. Not one Morsel, reply'd
Don *Quixote*, neither have had the least desire to Eat, or so
much as thought of it all the while. Do not they that are Inchanted sometimes Eat? ask'd the Scholar. They never do, answered Don *Quixote*, and consequently they are never troubled
with exonerating the Dregs of Food; tho' 'tis not unlikely that
their Nails, their Beards and Hair still grow. Do they never
sleep neither, said *Sancho*? Never, said Don *Quixote*; at least
they never clos'd their Eyes while I was among 'em, nor I
neither. This makes good the Saying, quoth *Sancho*, *Tell me
thy Company, and I'll tell thee what thou art*. Troth! you have
all been inchanted together. No wonder if you neither eat nor
slept, since you were in the Land of those that always watch
and fast. But Sir, would you have me speak as I think; and pray
don't take it in ill part, for if I believe one Word of all you have
said―― What do you mean, Friend, said the Student? Do
you think the Noble Don *Quixote* would be guilty of a Lye? and
if he had a mind to stretch a little, could he, think you, have
had leisure to frame such a number of Stories in so short a time?
I don't think that my Master would lye neither, said *Sancho*.
What d'ye think then, Sir, said Don *Quixote*? Why truly, Sir,
quoth *Sancho*, I do believe that this same cunning Man, this
Merlin, that bewitched, or inchanted, as you call it, all that
Rabble of People you talk of, may have crammed and inchanted
some way or other, all that you have told us, and have yet to
tell us, into your Noddle. It is not impossible but such a thing
may happen, said Don *Quixote*, tho' I am convinced it was
otherwise with me; for I am positive that I saw with these
Eyes, and felt with these Hands, all I have mentioned. But
what will you think when I tell you, among many wonderful
things, that I saw three Country-Wenches leaping and skipping about those pleasant Fields like so many wild Goats; and
at first Sight knew one of them to be the Peerless *Dulcinea*, and
the other Two the very same we spoke to not far from *Toboso*.
I ask'd *Montesinos* if he knew them? He answered in the Neg-
ative; but imagined them some Inchanted Ladies, who were
newly come, and that the Appearance of strange Faces was no
Rarity among 'em, for many of the past Ages and the present

were inchanted there, under several Disguises; and that, among the rest he knew Queen *Guinever* and her Woman *Quintaniona*, that officiated as Sir *Lancelot's* Cup-bearer, as he came from *Britain. Sancho*, hearing his Master talk at that Rate, had like to have forgot himself, and burst out a laughing; for he well knew that *Dulcinea's* Inchantment was a Lye, and that he himself was the chief Magician and Raiser of the Story; and thence concluding his Master stark mad: In an ill Hour, quoth he, dear Master of mine, and in a woful Day, went your Worship down to the other World, and in a worse Hour met you with that plaguy *Montesinos*, that has sent you back in this rueful Pickle. You went hence in your right Senses; cou'd talk prettily enough now and then; had your handsome Proverbs and wise Sayings every Foot, and would give wholesome Counsel to all that would take it: But now, bless me! you talk as if you had left your Brains in the Devil's Cellar. I know thee, *Sancho*, said Don *Quixote*, and therefore I regard thy Words as little as possible. And I yours, reply'd *Sancho*. Nay, you may cripple, lame, or kill me, if you please, either for what I've said, or mean to say, I must speak my Mind tho' I die for't. But before your Blood's up, pray Sir, tell me, how did you know it was your Mistress? Did you speak to her? What did she say to you? And what did you say to her? I knew her again, said Don *Quixote*, by the same Cloaths she wore when thou shew'd'st her to me. I spoke to her; but she made no Answer, but suddenly turn'd away, and fled from me like a Whirlwind. I intended to have followed her, had not *Montesinos* told me 'twou'd be to no Purpose; warning me besides, that 'twas high time to return to the upper Air: And changing the Discourse, he told me that I shou'd hereafter be made acquainted with the Means of disinchanting them all. But while *Montesinos* and I were thus talking together, a very odd Accident, the Thoughts of which trouble me still, broke off our Conversation. For as we were in the height of our Discourse, who shou'd come to me but one of the unfortunate *Dulcinea's* Companions, and before I was aware, with a faint and doleful Voice, Sir, said she, my Lady *Dulcinea del Toboso* gives her Service to you, and desires to know how you do; and being a little short of Money at present, she desires you of all Love and Kindness, to lend her six Reals upon this New-Fustian-Petticoat, or more or less as you can spare it, Sir, and she'll take care to redeem it very honestly in a little time. The Message surpriz'd me strangely, and therefore turning to *Montesinos*, Is it possible, Sir, said I, that Persons of Quality, when inchanted, are in Want? Oh! very possible, Sir, said he; Poverty ranges every where, and spares neither Quality inchanted nor uninchanted; and therefore since the Lady *Dulcinea* desires you to lend her these six Reals, and the Pawn is a good Pawn, let her have the Money; for sure it is very low with her at this time. I scorn to take Pawns, said I, but my Misfortune is, that I can't answer the full Request; for I have but four Reals about me, and that was the Money thou gavest me t'other Day, *Sancho*, to dis- tribute among the Poor. However, I gave her all I had, and desired her to tell her Mistress, I was very sorry for her Wants; and that if I had all the Treasures which *Cræsus* possess'd, they shou'd be at her Service; and withal, that I dy'd every Hour for want of her reviving Company; and made it my humble and earnest Request, that she wou'd vouchsafe to see and converse with her Captive Servant, and weather-beaten Knight: Tell her, continu'd I, when she least expects it, she will come to hear how I made an Oath, as the Marquess of *Mantua* did when he found his Nephew *Baldwin* ready to ex- pire on the Mountain, never to eat upon a Table-cloth, and several other Particulars which he swore to observe, till he had revenged his Death; So in the like solemn manner will I swear, never to desist from traversing the habitable Globe, and ranging through all the seven Parts of the World, more indefatigable than ever was done by Prince *Pedro* of *Portugal*,* till I have freed her from her Inchantment. All this and more you owe my Mistress, said the Damsel; and then, having got the four Reals, instead of dropping me a Curtesy, she cut me a Caper in the Air two Yards high. Now Heaven defend us, cry'd *Sancho*! Who cou'd ever have believ'd that these Devil- ish Inchanters and Inchantments shou'd have so much Power,

---

* *Prince* Pedro *of* Portugal *was a great Traveller for the Time he liv'd in, which gave occasion to the spreading of many Fables concerning him, and which made the ignorant vulgar say, He travel'd over the* Seven *Parts of the* World.

as to bewitch my Master at this rate, and craze his sound Understanding in this manner. Alas! Sir, for the love of Heaven take care of yourself. What will the World say of you? Rouse up your dozing Senses, and don't dote upon those Whimsies, that have so wretchedly crack'd that rare Head-piece of yours. Well, said Don *Quixote*, I cannot be angry at thy ignorant Tittle-tattle, because it proceeds from thy Love towards me. Thou think'st, poor Fellow, that whatever is beyond the Sphere of thy narrow Comprehension must be impossible: But, as I have already said, there will come a Time, when I shall give thee an account of some Things I have seen below, that will convince thee of the Reality of those I told thee now, the Truth of which admits of no Dispute.

XXIV: WHICH GIVES AN ACCOUNT OF A THOU-
SAND FLIM-FLAMS AND STORIES, AS IMPERTINENT
AS NECESSARY TO THE RIGHT UNDERSTANDING
OF THIS GRAND HISTORY

THE Translator of this famous History, declares, that at the beginning of the Chapter, which treats of the Adventure of *Montesino's* Cave, he found a Marginal Annotation, written with the *Arabian* Author's own Hand in these Words:

I cannot be perswaded, nor believe, that all the wonderful Accidents said to have happened to the Valorous Don Quixote *in the Cave, so punctually befel him as he relates them: For, the Course of his Adventures hitherto has been very Natural, and bore the Face of Probability; but in This there appears no Coherence with Reason, and nothing but monstrous Incongruities. But on the other hand, if we consider the Honour, Worth, and Integrity of the Noble Don* Quixote, *we have not the least Reason to suspect he would be guilty of a Lye; but rather that he would sooner have been Transfix'd with Arrows. Besides, he has been so particular in his Relation of that Adventure, and given so many Circumstances, that I dare not declare it absolutely Apocryphal; especially when I consider, that he had not time enough to invent such a Cluster of Fables. I therefore insert it among the rest, without offering to determine whether it is true or false; leaving it to the Discretion of the Judicious Reader. Though I must acquaint him by the way; that Don* Quixote, *upon his Death-bed, utterly disowned this Adventure, as a perfect Fable, which he said, he had invented purely to please his Humour, being suitable to such as he had formerly read in Romances:* And so much by way of Digression.

The Scholar thought *Sancho* the most saucy Servant, and his Master the calmest Madman that ever he saw; tho' he attributed the Patience of the latter to a certain good Humour and easiness of Temper infus'd into him by the Sight of his Mistress *Dulcinea*, even under Inchantment. Otherwise he wou'd have thought his not checking *Sancho* a greater sign of Madness than his Discourse. Noble Don *Quixote*, said he, for four principal Reasons I am extremely pleased with having taken this Journey with you. First, it has procur'd me the Honour of your Acquaintance, which I shall always esteem a singular Happiness. In the second Place, Sir, the Secrets of *Montesino's* Cave, and the Transformations of *Guadiana*, and *Ruydera's* Lakes, have been reveal'd to me, which may look very great in my *Spanish Ovid*. My third Advantage is, to have discover'd the Antiquity of Card-playing, which I find to have been a Pastime in use even in the Emperor *Charles* the Great's time, as may be collected from the Words of *Durandarte*, who, after a long *Speech* of *Montesino's*, said as he wak'd, *Patience & shuffle the cards,* * which vulgar expression he could never have learn'd in his Inchantment: It follows therefore that he must have heard it when he liv'd in *France*, which was in the Reign of that Emperor; which Observation is nick'd, I think, very opportunely for my Supplement to *Polydore Virgil*, who, as I remember, has not touch'd upon Card-playing; I will insert it into my Work, I'll assure you, Sir, as a matter of great Importance, having the Testimony of so Authentick and Ancient an Author as Sir *Durandarte*. The fourth part of my good Fortune, is to know the certain and true Source of the River *Guadiana*, which has hitherto disappointed all Human Enquiries. There is a great deal of Reason in what you say, answer'd Don *Quixote*: But, under favour, Sir, pray tell me, should you happen to get a License to publish your Book, which I somewhat doubt, whom you will pitch upon for your Patron? Oh, Sir, answer'd the Author, there are Grandees† enough in *Spain*, sure, that I may Dedicate to. Truly, not many, said Don *Quixote*; there are indeed, several whose Merits deserve the Praise of a Dedication, but very few whose Generosity will reward the Pains and Civility of the Author. I must confess, I know a Prince whose Generosity may make amends for what is wanting in the rest; and that to such a Degree, that should I make bold to come to Particulars, and speak of his great Merits, 'twould be enough to stir up a noble Emulation in above four generous Breasts; but more of this some other time, 'tis late now, and therefore convenient to think of a Lodging. Hard by

* *See this Proverb explain'd in the preceding Chapter.*   † *Grandees are such of the Nobility, as have the Privilege of being Cover'd before the King.*

us here, Sir, said the Author, is an Hermitage, the Retirement of a Devout Person, who, as they say, was once a Soldier, and is look'd upon as a good Christian, and so charitable, that he has built there a little House at his own expence, purely for the Entertainment of Strangers. But does he keep Hens there trow! ask'd *Sancho*? Few Hermits in this Age are without 'em, said Don *Quixote*; for their way of Living now falls short of the Strictness and Austerity of those in the Desarts of *Egypt*, who went clad only with Palm-leaves, and fed on the Roots of the Earth. Now because I speak well of those of old, I would not have you think I reflect on the others. No, I only mean that their Penances are not so severe as in former Days; yet this does not hinder but that the Hermits of the present Age may be good Men. I look upon them to be such; at least, their Dissimulation secures them from Scandal; and the Hypocrite that puts on the Form of Holiness, does certainly less harm than the barefac'd Sinner. As they went on in their Discourse, they saw a Man following them a great Pace on Foot, and switching up a Mule laden with Lances and Halberds. He presently overtook 'em, gave them the time of the Day, and pass'd by. Stay, honest Fellow, cry'd Don *Quixote*, seeing him go so fast, make no more hast than is consistent with good speed. I can't stay, Sir, said the Man, for these Weapons that you see, must be used To-morrow Morning; So, Sir, I am in haste, good-by, I shall lodge to Night at the Inn beyond the Hermitage; if you chance to go that Way, there you may find me, and I'll tell you strange News: so fare ye well. Then whipping his Mule, away he mov'd forwards, so fast that Don *Quixote* had not leisure to ask him any more Questions. The Knight who had always an itching Ear after Novelties, to satisfy his Curiosity immediately propos'd their holding straight on to the Inn without stopping at the Hermitage, where the Scholar design'd to have stay'd all Night. Well, they all consented, and made the best of their Way: however, when they came near the Hermitage, the Scholar desir'd Don *Quixote* to call with him for a Moment, and drink a Glass of Wine at the Door. *Sancho* no sooner heard this propos'd, but he turn'd *Dapple* that way, and rode thither before; but to his great Grief, the hospitable Hermit was abroad, and nobody at home but the Hermit's Companion, who being ask'd whether he had any *strong* Liquor within? made answer, that he cou'd not come at any, but as for *small* Water he might have his Belly-full. Body of me! quoth *Sancho*, were mine a Water-Thirst, or had I liking to your cold Comfort, there are Wells enough upon the Road, where I might have swill'd my Skin full: Oh, the good Cheer at Don *Diego's* House, and the savoury Scum at *Camacho's* Wedding, when shall I find your Fellow! They now spurr'd on towards the Inn, and soon overtook on the Road a young Fellow beating it on the Hoof pretty leisurely. He carry'd his Sword over his Shoulder with a Bundle of Cloaths hanging upon it; which, to all outward Appearance, consisted of a pair of Breeches, a Cloak, and a Shirt or two. He had on a tatter'd Velvet-Jerkin, with a ragged Sattin-Lining; his Shirt hung out, his Stockings were of Silk, and his Shooes square at the Toes, after the Court-Fashion. He seem'd about Eighteen or Nineteen Years of Age, a good pleasant-look'd Lad, and of a lively and active Disposition. To pass the Fatigue of his Journey the best he cou'd, he Sung all the Way, and as they came near him, was just ending the last Words of a Ballad which the Scholar got by Heart, and were these.

> *A plague on ill Luck! Now my Ready's all gone,*
> *To the Wars poor Pilgarlick must trudge:*
> *Tho' had I but Money, to Rake as I've done,*
> *The Devil a Foot wou'd I budge.*

So, young Gentleman, said Don *Quixote* to him, methinks you go very light and airy. Whither are you bound, I pray you, if a Man may be so bold? I'm going to the Wars, Sir, answer'd the Youth; and for my Travelling thus, Heat and Poverty will excuse it. I admit the Heat, replied Don *Quixote*; but why Poverty, I beseech you? Because I have no cloaths to put on, reply'd the Lad, but what I carry in this Bundle; and if I should wear them out upon the Road, I should have nothing to make a handsome Figure with in any Town; for I have no Money to buy new ones, till I overtake a Regiment of Foot that lies about some twelve Leagues off, where I design to list my self, and then I shall not want a Conveniency to ride with the Baggage till we come to *Carthagena*, where, I hear, they are to em-

bark; for I had rather serve the King abroad, than any beggarly Courtier at home. But pray, said the Scholar, have not you
laid up something while you were there? Had I served any of
your Grandees or great Persons, said the young Man, I might
have done well enough, and have had a Commission by this
time, for their Foot-boys are presently advanced to Captains
and Lieutenants, or some other good Post: But a Plague on it,
Sir, it was always my ill Fortune to serve pitiful Upstarts and
Younger Brothers, and my Allowance was commonly so ill
paid, and so small, that the better half was scarce enough to
wash my Linen; how then should a poor Devil of a Page, who
would make his Fortune, come to any good in such a miserable
Service? But, said Don *Quixote*, how comes it about that in all
this time you could not get yourself a whole Livery? Alack-a-
day, Sir, answer'd the Lad, I had a couple: but my Masters
dealt with me as they do with Novices in Monasteries, if they
go off before they Profess, the fresh Habit is taken from them,
and they return them their own Cloaths. For you must know,
that such as I served, only buy Liveries for a little Ostentation;
so when they have made their Appearance at Court, they
sneak down into the Country, and then the poor Servants are
stripp'd and must even betake themselves to their Rags again.
A sordid Trick, said *Quixote*, or as the *Italians* call it, a notorious *Espilorcheria*.* Well, you need not repine at leaving the
Court, since you do it with so good a Design; for there is nothing in the World more commendable than to serve God in the
first Place, and the King in the next, especially in the Profession of Arms, which if it does not procure a Man so much Riches
as Learning, may at least intitle him to more Honour. It is true,
that more Families have been advanced by the Gown, but yet
your Gentlemen of the Sword, whatever the Reason of it is,
have always I know not what Advantage above the Men of
Learning; and something of Glory and Splendor attends 'em,
that makes them out-shine the rest of Mankind. But take my
Advice along with you, Child; if you intend to raise your self
by Military Employment, I would not have you be uneasy with
the Thoughts of what Misfortunes may befal you; the worst
can be but to Die, and if it be a good Honourable Death, your

* Espilorcheria, *a beggarly mean Action.*

Fortune's made; and you're certainly happy. *Julius Cæsar*, that valiant *Roman* Emperor, being ask'd what kind of Death was best? That which is sudden and unexpected, said he; and tho' his Answer had a relish of Paganism, yet with respect to Human Infirmities, 'twas very Judicious: for, suppose you should be cut off at the very first Engagement by a Cannon Ball, or the spring of a Mine; what matters it? 'Tis all but Dying, and there's an end of the Business. As *Terence* says, a Soldier makes a better Figure Dead in the Field of Battle, than Alive and safe in Flight. The more likely he is to rise in Fame and Preferment, the better Discipline he keeps; the better he Obeys, the better he will know how to Command: And pray observe, my Friend, that 'tis more Honourable for a Soldier to smell of Gun-powder than of Musk and Amber; or if Old Age overtakes you in this noble Employment, though all over Scars, though Maim'd and Lame, you will still have Honour to support you, and secure you from the Contempt of Poverty; nay, from Poverty it self; for there is Care taken, that Veteran and disabled Soldiers may not want: Neither are they to be used as some Men do their Negro Slaves, who, when they are old, and past Service, are turn'd Naked out of Doors, under Pretence of Freedom, to be made greater Slaves to Cold and Hunger; a Slavery from which nothing but Death can set the Wretches free. But I'll say no more to you on this Subject at this time. Get up behind me, and I'll carry you to the Inn, where you shall sup with me, and to morrow Morning make the best of your way; and may Heaven prosper your good Designs.

The Page excus'd himself from riding behind the Knight, but accepted of his Invitation to Supper very willingly. *Sancho*, who had all the while given Ear to his Master's Discourse, is said to have been more than usually surpriz'd, hearing him talk so wisely. Now Blessing on thee, Master of mine, thought he to himself; how comes it about that a Man who says so many good things, should relate such ridiculous Stories and Whimsies, as he would have us believe of *Montesino's* Cave. Well, Heaven knows best, and the Proof of the Pudding is in the Eating. By this time, it began to grow dark, and they arrived at the Inn, where, Don *Quixote* alighting, ask'd presently for the Man with the Lances and Halbards. The Inn-keeper

178

answer'd, that he was rubbing down his Mule in the Stable. *Sancho* was very well pleas'd to be at his Journey's end, and the more, that his Master took the House for a real Inn, and not for a Castle, as he us'd to do. He and the Scholar then set up the Asses, giving *Rozinante* the best Manger and Standing in the Stable.

XXV: WHERE YOU FIND THE GROUNDS OF THE BRAYING ADVENTURE, THAT OF THE PUPPET-PLAYER, AND THE MEMORABLE DIVINING OF THE FORTUNE-TELLING APE

DON Quixote was on Thorns to know the strange Story that the Fellow upon the Road engag'd to tell him; so that going into the Stable he minded him of his Promise, and press'd him to relate the whole matter to him that Moment. My Story will take up some time, quoth the Man, and is not to be told standing; have a little Patience, Master of mine, let me make an end of serving my Mule, then I'll serve your Worship, and tell you such things as will make you stare. Don't let that hinder, reply'd Don Quixote, for I'll help you my self; and so saying, he lent him a helping Hand, cleansing the Manger, and sifting the Barley; which humble compliance oblig'd the Fellow to tell his Tale the more willingly: So that seating himself upon a Bench with Don Quixote, the Scholar, the Page, Sancho, and the Inn-keeper about him, for his full Auditory, he began in this manner.

It happen'd on a time, that in a Borough about some four Leagues and a half from this Place, one of the Aldermen* lost his Ass: They say 'twas by the Roguery of a waggish Jade that was his Maid; but that's neither here nor there, the Ass was lost and gone, that's certain; and what's more, it could not be found neither high nor low. This same Ass had been missing about a fortnight, some say more, some less, when another Alderman of the same Town meeting this same losing Alderman in the Market-place, Brother, quoth he, pay me well, and I'll tell you news of your Ass. Troth! quoth the other, that I will; but then let me know where the poor Beast is? Why, answer'd the other, this Morning what should I meet upon the Mountains yonder but he, without either Pack-Saddle or Furniture, and so lean that it griev'd my Heart to see him; but yet so wild and skittish, that when I would have driven him home before me, he ran away as the Devil were in him, and got into

* Regidor.

180

the thickest of the Wood. Now if you please, we'll both go to-gether and look for him; I'll but step home first and put up this Ass, then I'll come back to you, and we'll about it out of hand. Truly, Brother, said the other, I'm mightily beholden to you, and will do as much for You another time. The Story happen'd neither more nor less, but such as I tell you, for so all that know it relate it word for word. In short, the two Aldermen, hand in hand, a-foot trudg'd up the Hills, and hunted up and down; but after many a weary Step, no Ass was to be found. Upon which, quoth the Alderman, that had seen him, to t'other, hark you me, Brother, I have a Device in my Noddle to find out this same Ass of yours, though he were under Ground, as you shall hear. You must know I can Bray to Admiration, and if you can but Bray never so little, the Job's done. Never so little, cry'd t'oth-er, Body of me! I won't vail my Bonnet at Braying to e'er an Ass or Alderman in the Land. Well, we shall try That, quoth the other, for my Contrivance is that you shall go on one side of the Hill, and I on the other; sometimes You shall Bray, and sometimes I; so that, if your Ass be but thereabouts, My Life for Yours, he'll be sure to answer his Kind, and Bray again. Gramercy, Brother, quoth the other! A rare Device, i'fack! let You alone for Plotting. At the same time they parted accord-ing to Agreement, and when they were far enough off, they both fell a Braying so perfectly well, that they cheated one an-other; and meeting, each in hopes to find the Ass; is it possible, Brother, said the Owner of the Ass, that it was not my Ass that Bray'd? No, marry, that it wasn't, 'twas I, answer'd the other Alderman. Well, Brother, cry'd the Owner, then there's no manner of difference between You and an Ass, as to matter of Braying; I never heard any thing so natural in my Life. Oh fye! Sir, quoth the other, I am nothing to You: You shall lay two to one against the best Brayer in the Kingdom, and I'll go your halves. Your Voice is lofty, and of a great Compass; you keep excellent Time, and hold out a Note rarely, and your Cadence is full and ravishing. In short, Sir, I knock under the Table, and yield you the Bays. Well then, Brother, answer'd the Owner, I shall always have the better Opinion of my self for this one good Quality; for though I knew I Bray'd pretty well, I never thought my self so great a Master before. Well, quoth the other, thus you see what rare Parts may be lost for want of being known, and a Man never knows his own Strength, till he puts it to a Trial. Right, Brother, quoth the Owner, for I should never have found out this wonderful Gift of mine, had it not been for this Business in hand, and may we speed in't, I pray! After these Compliments they parted again, and went Braying, this on one side of the Hill, and that on t'other. But all to no purpose, for they still deceiv'd one another with their Braying, and, running to the Noise, met one another as before.

At last they agreed to Bray twice one after another, that by That Token they might be sure 'twas not the Ass, but They that bray'd. But all in vain, they almost Bray'd their Hearts out, but no answer from the Ass. And indeed, how could it, poor Creature! when they found him at last in the Wood half eaten by the Wolves. Alack-a-day poor *Grizzle*, cry'd the Owner, I don't wonder now he took so little notice of his loving Master! Had he been alive, as sure as he was an Ass he would have Bray'd again. But let him go, this Comfort I have at least Brother; though I have lost him, I've found out that rare Talent of yours, that has hugely solac'd me under this Affliction. The Glass is in a good Hand, Mr Alderman, quoth the other, and if the Abbot sings well, the young Monk is not much behind him.

With this, these same Aldermen, very much down i'th' Mouth, and very hoarse, went home and told all their Neighbours the whole Story word for word; one praising t'other's Skill in Braying, and t'other returning the Compliment. In short, one got it by the end, and t'other got it by the end; the Boys got it, and all the idle Fellows got it, and there was such a Brawling, and such a Braying in our Town, that one would have thought Hell broke loose among us. But to let you see now how the Devil never lies dead in a Ditch, but catches at every foolish thing to set People by the Ears; our Neighbouring Towns had it up, and when they saw any of our Townsfolks they fell a Braying, hitting us in the Teeth with the Braying of our Aldermen. This made ill Blood between us; for we took it in mighty Dudgeon, as well we might, and came to Words upon't, and from Words to Blows; for the People of our Town, are well known by this, as the Beggar knows his Dish, and are apt to be jeer'd wheresoever they go; and then to't they go, Ding Dong, Hand over Head, in spight of Law or Gospel. And they've carry'd the Jest so far, that I believe to morrow or next day, the Men of our Town, to wit, The Brayers, will be in the Field against those of another Town about two Leagues off, that are always plaguing us. Now, that we should be well provided, I have brought these Lances and Halberds that ye saw me carry. So this is my Story, Gentlefolks, and if it ben't a strange one, I'm woundily mistaken.

Here the honest Man ended; when presently enters a Fellow dress'd in Trowsers and Doublet all of Shammy-Leather, and calling out, as if he were some-body: Landlord, cry'd he, have you any Lodgings? For here comes the Fortune-telling Ape, and the Puppet-shew of *Melisandra's* Deliverance. Body of me! cry'd the Inn-keeper, who's here? Master *Peter*? We shall have a merry Night, Faith! Honest Master *Peter*, you're welcome with all my Heart! But where's the Ape, and the Show, that I can't see them. They'll be here presently, said *Peter*. I only came before to see if you had any Lodgings. Lodging, Man, said the Inn-keeper, Zookers! I would turn out the Duke of *Alva* himself, rather than Master *Peter* should want room. Come, come, bring in your things, for here are Guests in the House to Night that will be good Customers to you, I warrant you. That's a good Hearing, said *Peter*; and to encourage them I'll lower my Prices, and if I can but get my Charges to Night, I'll look for no more; so I will hasten forward the Cart. This said, he ran out of the Door again.

I had forgot to tell you, that this same Master *Peter* wore over his left Eye and half his Cheek a Patch of Green Taffata, by which it was to be supposed that something ailed that side of his Face. Don *Quixote* enquired who this Master *Peter* was, and what his Ape and his Show! Why, Sir, answer'd the Inn-keeper, he has strolled about the Country here this great while with a curious Puppet-show, which represents the Play of *Melisandra* and Don *Gayferos*, one of the best Shows that has been acted time out of mind in this Kingdom. Then he has an Ape! Bless us, Sir, it is such an Ape! But I will say no more; you shall see, Sir: It will tell you every thing you ever did in your Life. The like was never seen before. Ask him a Quest-

ion, it will listen to you, and then, whip, up it leaps on its Master's Shoulder, and whispers first in his Ear what it knows,
and then Master *Peter* tells you. He tells you what is to come,
as well as what is passed; it is true, he does not always hit so pat
as to what is to come; but after all, he is seldom in the wrong;
which makes us apt to think, the Devil helps him at a dead lift.
Two Reals is the Price for every Question he answers, or his
Master for him, which is all one, you know; and that will
mount to Money at the Year's end, so that 'tis thought the
Rogue is well to pass; and indeed much good may it do him, for
he is a notable Fellow, and a boon Companion, and leads the
merriest Life in the World, talks for six Men, and drinks for a
dozen, and all this he gets by his Tongue, his Ape, and his Show.

By this time, Master *Peter* came back with his Puppet-
Show, and his Ape in a Cart. The Ape was pretty lusty, without any Tail, and his Buttocks bare as a Felt. Yet he was not
very ugly neither. Don *Quixote* no sooner saw him, but coming
up to him, Mr Fortune-teller, said he, will you be pleased to
tell us, what Fish we shall catch, and what will become of us,
and here's your Fee? saying this, he order'd *Sancho* to deliver
Mr *Peter* two Reals. Sir, answer'd *Peter*, this Animal gives no
Account of Things to come; he knows something indeed of
Matters past, and a little of the present. Odds bobs! quoth *Sancho*, I would not give a brass Jack to know what's past; for who
knows that better than my self; I'm not so foolish as to pay for
what I know already: But since you say he has such a knack at
guessing the present, let Goodman Ape tell me what my Wife
Teresa is doing, and what she is about, and here's my two
Reals. I'll have nothing of you before-hand, said Master *Peter*;
so clapping himself on his Left Shoulder, up skipp'd the Ape
thither at one frisk, and laying his Mouth to his Ear grated his
Teeth: and having made Apish Grimaces and a chattering
Noise for a Minute or two, with another skip down he leap'd
on the Ground. Immediately upon this, Master *Peter* ran to
Don *Quixote*, and fell on his Knees, and embracing his Legs,
Oh glorious Restorer of Knight-Errantry, cry'd he, I embrace
these Legs, as I would the Pillars of *Hercules*. Who can sufficiently extol the great Don *Quixote de la Mancha*, the Reviver
of drooping Hearts, the Prop and Stay of the Falling, the Raiser

184

of the Fallen, and the Staff of Comfort to the Weak and Afflicted! At these Words Don *Quixote* stood amaz'd, *Sancho* quak'd, the Page wonder'd, the Brayer bless'd himself, the Inn-keeper star'd, and the Scholar was in a brown Study, all astonish'd at Master *Peter's* Speech; who then turning to *Sancho*, And thou honest *Sancho Pancho*, said he, the best Squire to the best Knight in the World, bless thy kind Stars; for thy good Spouse *Teresa* is a good House-wife, and is at this instant dressing a Pound of Flax; by the same Token, she has standing by her, on her left Hand, a large broken-mouth Jug, which holds a pretty scantling of Wine, to cheer up her Spirits. By yea, and nay, quoth *Sancho*, that's likely enough, for she's a true Soul, and a jolly Soul: were it not for a Spice of Jealousy that she has now and then, I would not change her for the Giantess *Andondona* herself, who, as my Master says, was as clever a piece of Woman's Flesh as ever went upon two Legs. Well, much good may't do thee, honest *Teresa*; Thou art resolv'd to provide for one, I find, though thy Heirs starve for it. Well! said Don *Quixote*, great is the Knowledge procur'd by Reading, Travel and Experience! What on Earth but the Testimony of my own Eyes could have persuaded me that Apes had the Gift of Divination! I am indeed the same Don *Quixote de la Mancha*, mention'd by this ingenious Animal, though I must confess somewhat undeserving of so great a Character as it has pleas'd him to bestow on me: But nevertheless I am not sorry to have Charity and Compassion bear so great a Part in my Commendation, since my Nature has always dispos'd me to do good to all Men, and hurt to none.

Now had I but Money, said the Page, I would know of Mr Ape what Luck I shall have in the Wars. I have told you already, (said Master *Peter*, who was got up from before Don *Quixote*) that this Ape does not meddle with what is to come; but if he could, it should cost you nothing, for Don *Quixote's* sake, whom to oblige, I would sacrifice all the Interest I have in the World; and as a Mark of it, Gentlemen, I freely set up my Show, and give all the Company in the House some Diversion *gratis*. The Inn-keeper hearing this, was over-joy'd, and order'd Master *Peter* a convenient Room to set up his Motion, and he immediately went about it.

In the mean time Don *Quixote*, who could not bring himself
to believe that an Ape could do all this, taking *Sancho* to a Corner of the Stable; Look ye, *Sancho*, said he, I have been weigh-
ing and considering the wonderful Gifts of this Ape, and find
in short, Master *Peter* must have made a secret Compact with
the Devil. Nay, quoth *Sancho*, (misunderstanding the word
Compact) if the Devil and he have pack'd any thing together
in hugger-mugger, 'tis a pack of Roguery to be sure, and they
are a pack of Knaves for their pains, and let 'em e'en pack together, say I. Thou dost not apprehend me, said Don *Quixote*;
I mean, the Devil and He must have made an agreement together, that Satan should infuse this Knowledge into the Ape,
to purchase the Owner an Estate; and in return, the last has
certainly engag'd his Soul to this destructive Seducer of Mankind. For the Ape's Knowledge is exactly of the same proportion with the Devil's, which only extends to the Discovery of
things past and present, having no Insight into Futurity, but
by such probable Conjectures and Conclusions as may be deduc'd from the former working of antecedent Causes; true Pre-
science and Prediction being the Sacred Prerogative of God,
to whose all-seeing Eyes, all Ages, past, present, and to come,
without the Distinction of Succession and Termination, are
always present. From this, I say, 'tis apparent this Ape is but
the Organ through which the Devil delivers his Answers to
those that ask it Questions; and this same Rogue should be put
into the Inquisition, and have the Truth press'd out of his
Bones. For sure neither the Master nor his Ape can lay any
Pretence to Judicial Astrology; nor is the Ape so conversant in
the Mathematicks, I suppose, as to erect a Scheme. Though I
must confess, that Creatures of less Parts, as foolish illiterate
Women, Footmen and Coblers, pretend now-a-days to draw
Certainties from the Stars, as easily and readily as they shuffle
a Pack of Cards, to the Disgrace of the Sublime Science, which
they have the Impudence to profess. I knew a Lady that ask'd
one of these Figure-casters, if a little foisting Bitch she had
should have Puppies, and how many, and of what Colour?
My Conjurer, after he had scrawl'd out his Scheme, very judiciously pronounc'd, that the pretty Creature should have
Three delicate Puppies, one Green, one Red, and another

Mix'd-colour'd, provided she would take Dog between Eleven and Twelve at Night or Noon, either on a *Monday* or a *Saturday*; and the Success happen'd as exactly as could be expected from his Art; for the Bitch some Days after, dy'd very fairly of a Surfeit, and Master Figure-flinger was reputed a special Conjurer all the Town over, as most of these Fellows are. For all that, said *Sancho*, I would have you ask Master *Peter's* Ape, whether the Passages you told us concerning *Montesinos's* Cave be true or no; for saving the Respect I owe your Worship, I take them to be no better than Fibbs, and idle Stories, or Dreams at least. You may think what you will, answer'd Don *Quixote*, however I'll do as you would have me, though I confess my Conscience somewhat scruples to do such a thing. While they were thus engag'd in Discourse, Master *Peter* came and told Don *Quixote*, the Show was ready to begin, and desired him to come and see it, for he was sure his Worship would like it. The Knight told him, he had a Question to put to his Ape first, and desired he might tell him, whether certain things that happen'd to him in *Montesinos's* Cave were Dreams or Realities, for he doubted they had something of both in them. Master *Peter* fetched his Ape immediately, and placing him just before the Knight and his Squire; Look you, says he, Mr Ape, this worthy Knight would have you tell him whether some things which happened to him in *Montesinos's* Cave were true or no? Then upon the usual Signal, the Ape jumping upon Master *Peter's* left Shoulder, chattered his Answer into his Ear, which the Interpreter delivered thus to the Enquirer. The Ape, Sir, says, That part of those things are false, and part of them true, which is all he can resolve ye, as to this Question; and now his Virtue has left him, and won't return till *Friday* next. If you would know any more, you must stay till then, and he'll answer as many Questions as you please. Lawk you there now, quoth *Sancho*, did not I tell you, that all you told us of *Montesinos's* Cave would not hold Water? That the Event will determine, reply'd the Knight, which we must leave to Process of Time to produce; for it brings every thing to light, tho' buried in the Bowels of the Earth. No more of this at present: let us now see the Puppet-show; I fancy we shall find something in it worth seeing. Something! said Master *Peter*,

187

Sir, you shall see a Thousand things worth Seeing. I tell you, Sir, I defy the World to shew such another. I say no more: *Operibus credite & non verbis.* But now let us begin, for it grows late, and we have much to do, say, and show. Don *Quixote* and *Sancho* comply'd, and went into the Room where the Show stood, with a good Number of small Wax-Lights glimmering round about, that made it shine gloriously. Master *Peter* got to his Station within, being the Man that was to move the Puppets; and his Boy stood before to tell what the Puppets said, and with a White Wand in his Hand, to point at the several Figures as they came in and out, and explain the Mystery of the Show. Then all the Audience having taken their Places, Don *Quixote*, *Sancho*, the Scholar, and the Page, being preferr'd to the rest; the Boy, who was the Mouth of the Motion, began a Story, that shall be heard or seen by those, who will take the Pains to read or hear the next Chapter.

XXVI: A PLEASANT ACCOUNT OF THE
PUPPET-PLAY, WITH OTHER VERY
GOOD THINGS TRULY

THE *Tyrians* and the *Trojans* were all silent; that is, the Ears of all the Spectators hung on the Mouth of the Interpreter of the Show, when in the first Place they had a loud Flourish of Kettle-Drums and Trumpets within the Machine, and then several Discharges of Artillery; which Prelude being soon over, Gentlemen, cry'd the Boy, raising his Voice, We present you here with a true History taken out of the Chronicles of *France*, and the *Spanish* Ballads, sung even by the Boys about the Streets, and in every Body's Mouth; it tells you how Don *Gayferos* deliver'd his Wife *Melisandra*, that was a Prisoner among the *Moors* in *Spain*, in the City of *Sansuena*, now call'd *Saragosa*. Now, Gallants, the first Figure we present you with, is Don *Gayferos* playing at Tables according to the Ballad,

> *Now* Gayferos *the live-long Day,*
> *Oh errant Shame, at Draughts does play;*
> *And, as at Court, most Husbands do,*
> *Forgets his Lady Fair and True.*

Gentlemen, in the next Place, mark that Personage that peeps out there with a Crown on his Head, and a Sceptre in his Hand. 'Tis the Emperor *Charlemain*, the fair *Melisandra's* reputed Father, who, vex'd at the Idleness and Negligence of his Son-in-Law, comes to chide him; and pray observe with what Passion and Earnestness he rates him, as if he had a Mind to lend him half a Dozen sound Raps over the Pate with his Sceptre. Nay, some Authors don't stick to tell ye, he gave him as many, and well laid on too; and after he had told him how his Honour lay a Bleeding, till he had deliver'd his Wife out of Durance, among many other Pithy Sayings, look to it (quoth he to him as he went) I'll say no more. Mind how the Emperor turns his Back upon him, and how he leaves Don *Gayferos* nettl'd and in the Dumps. Now see how he starts up, and in a Rage dings the Tables one way, and whirls the Men another;

189

and calling for his Arms with all haste, borrows his Cousin-German *Orlando's* Sword *Durindana*, who withal offers to go along with him in this difficult Adventure, but the valorous enrag'd Knight will not let him, and says, he's able to deliver his Wife himself, without His help, though they kept her down in the very Center of the Earth. And now he's going to put on his Armour, in order to begin his Journey.

Now, Gentlemen, cast your Eyes upon yon Tower; you are to suppose it one of the Towers of the Castle of *Saragosa*, now call'd the *Aljaferia*. That Lady, whom you see in the Balcony there in a *Moorish* Habit, is the peerless *Melisandra*, that casts many a heavy Look towards *France*, thinking of *Paris* and her Husband, the only Comfort in her Imprisonment. But now! Silence, Gentlemen, pray Silence! here is an Accident wholly new, the like perhaps never heard of before: Don't you see that *Moor* who comes a Tiptoe creeping and stealing along with his Finger in his Mouth behind *Melisandra*? Hear what a Smack he gives on her sweet Lips, and see how she spits and wipes her Mouth with her white Smock-Sleeve! See how she takes on, and tears her lovely Hair for very Madness, as if 'twere to blame for this Affront. Next pray observe that grave *Moor* that stands in the open Gallery! That's *Marsilius* the King of *Sansuena*, who having been an Eye-Witness of the Sauciness of the *Moor*, order'd him immediately to be apprehended, tho' his Kinsman and great Favourite, to have two hundred Lashes given him, then to be carried thro' the City, with Criers before to proclaim his Crime, the Rods of Justice behind. And look how all this is put in Execution sooner almost than the Fact is committed. For your *Moors*, ye must know, don't use any Form of Indictment as We do, neither have they any Legal Trials. Child, Child, said Don *Quixote*, go on directly with your Story, and don't keep us here with your Excursions and Ramblings out of the Road: I tell you there must be a formal Process and Legal Trial to prove Matters of Fact. Boy, said the Master from behind the Show, do as the Gentleman bids you. Don't run so much upon Flourishes, but follow your plain Song, without venturing on Counter-Points, for fear of spoiling all. I will, Sir, quoth the Boy, and so proceeding: Now, Sirs, he that you see there a Horse-back wrapt up in the *Gascoign-*

Cloak, is Don *Gayferos* himself whom his Wife, now reveng'd on the *Moor* for his Impudence, seeing from the Battlements of the Tower, takes him for a Stranger, and talks with him as such, according to the Ballad;

> *Quoth* Melisandra, *if per Chance,*
> *Sir Traveller, you go for France,*
> *For Pity's Sake, ask when you're there,*
> *For* Gayferos, *my Husband dear.*

I omit the rest, not to tire you with a long Story. 'Tis sufficient that he makes himself known to her, as you may guess by the Joy she shews; and accordingly now see how she lets herself down from the Balcony, to come at her loving Husband, and get behind him. But unhappily, alas! one of the Skirts of her Gown is caught upon one of the Spikes of the Balcony, and there she hangs and hovers in the Air miserably, without being able to get down. But see how Heaven is merciful, and sends Relief in the greatest Distress! Now Don *Gayferos* rides up to her, and not fearing to tear her rich Gown, lays hold on't, and at one pull brings her down; and then at one lift, sets her astride upon his Horse's Crupper, bidding her to sit fast, and clap her Arms about him, that she might not fall; for the Lady *Melisandra* was not us'd to that kind of Riding.

Observe now, Gallants, how the Horse neighs, and shews how proud he is of the Burden of his brave Master and fair Mistress. Look now, how they turn their Backs, and leave the City, and gallop it merrily away towards *Paris*. Peace be with you, for a peerless Couple of true Lovers! May ye get safe and sound into your own Country, without any Let or ill Chance in your Journey, and live as long as *Nestor* in Peace and Quietness among your Friends and Relations: Plainness, Boy, cry'd Master *Peter*, none of your Flights, I beseech you, for Affectation is the Devil. The Boy answer'd nothing, but going on; Now, Sirs, quoth he, some of those idle People, that love to pry into every thing, happen'd to spy *Melisandra* as she was making her Escape, and ran presently and gave *Marsilius* notice of it: whereupon he straight commanded to sound an Alarm; and now mind what a Din and Hurly-burly there is, and how the City shakes with the Ring of the Bells backwards in all the

Mosques! There you are out, Boy, said Don *Quixote*: The *Moors* have no Bells, they only use Kettle-Drums, and a kind of Shaulms like our Waits or Hautboys; so that your Ringing of Bells in *Sansuena* is a meer Absurdity, good Master *Peter*. Nay, Sir, said Master *Peter*, giving over Ringing; if you stand upon these Trifles with us, we shall never please you. Don't be so severe a Critick: Are there not a thousand Plays that pass with great Success and Applause, though they have many greater Absurdities, and Nonsense in abundance? On, Boy, on, let there be as many Impertinencies as Moats in the Sun; no matter, so I get the Money. Well said, answer'd Don *Quixote*. And now, Sirs, quoth the Boy, observe what a vast Company of glittering Horse comes pouring out of the City, in pursuit of the Christian Lovers; what a dreadful Sound of Trumpets, and Clarions, and Drums, and Kettle-Drums there's in the Air. I fear they will overtake them, and then will the poor Wretches be dragg'd along most barbarously at the Tails of their Horses, which wou'd be sad indeed. Don *Quixote*, seeing such a Number of *Moors*, and hearing such an Alarm, thought it high time to assist the flying Lovers; and starting up, It shall never be said while I live, cry'd he aloud, that I suffer'd such a Wrong to be done to so famous a Knight and so daring a Lover as Don *Gayferos*. Forbear then your unjust Pursuit, ye base-born Rascals: Stop, or prepare to meet my furious Resentment. Then drawing out his Sword, to make good his Threats, at one Spring he gets to the Show, and with a violent Fury lays at the *Moorish* Puppets, cutting and slashing in a most terrible Manner; some he overthrows, and beheads others; maims this, and cleaves that in pieces. Among the rest of his merciless Strokes, he thunder'd one down with such a mighty Force, that had not Master *Peter* luckily duck'd and squatted down, it had certainly chopp'd off his Head as easily as one might cut an Apple. Hold, hold, Sir, cry'd the Puppet-Player, after the narrow Escape, hold for Pity's Sake. What do you mean, Sir? These are no real *Moors* that you cut and hack so, but poor harmless Puppets made of Pasteboard. Think o' what you do, you ruin me for ever. Oh that ever I was born! you've broke me quite. But Don *Quixote*, without minding his Words, doubl'd and redoubl'd his Blows so thick, and laid about him so outrageously, that in less than two *Credo's* he had cut all the Strings and Wires, mangl'd the Puppets, and spoil'd and demolish'd the whole Motion. King *Marsilius* was in a grievous Condition. The Emperor *Charlemain's* Head and Crown were cleft in two. The whole Audience was in a sad Consternation. The Ape scamper'd off to the Top of the House. The Scholar was frighted out of his Wits; the Page was very uneasy, and *Sancho* himself was in a terrible Fright; for, as he swore after the Hurricane was over, he had never seen his Master in such a Rage before.

The general Rout of the Puppets being over, Don *Quixote's* Fury began to abate; and with a more pacify'd Countenance turning to the Company, Now, said he, cou'd I wish all those incredulous Persons here who slight Knight-Errantry might receive Conviction of their Error, and behold undeniable Proofs of the Benefit of that Function: For how miserable had been the Condition of poor Don *Gayferos* and the fair *Melisandra* by this Time, had I not been here and stood up in their Defence! I make no Question but those Infidels wou'd have apprehended 'em, and us'd 'em barbarously. Well, when all's done, long live Knight-Errantry, long let it live, I say, above all things whatsoever in this World. Ay, ay, said Master *Peter* in a doleful Tone, let it live long for Me, so I may die; for why should I live so unhappy, as to say with King *Rodrigo*,* *Yesterday I was Lord of* Spain, *to Day have not a Foot of Land I can call mine* ? 'Tis not Half an Hour, nay scarce a Moment, since I had Kings and Emperors at Command. I had Horses in Abundance, and Chests and Bags full of fine things; but now you see me a poor sorry undone Man, quite and clean broke and cast down, and in short a meer Beggar. What's worst of all, I've lost my Ape too, who I'm sure will make me sweat ere I catch him again; and all through the rash Fury of this Sir Knight here, who they say protects the Fatherless, redresses Wrongs, and does other charitable Deeds, but has fail'd in all these good Offices to miserable me, Heaven be prais'd for't: Well may I call him the Knight of the Woful Figure, for he has put me and all that belongs to Me in a woful Case. The Puppet-player's Lamentations moving *Sancho's* Pity, Come, quoth he, don't cry, Master *Peter*,

* *The last King of the* Goths *that reign'd in* Spain, *conquer'd by the* Moors.

thou break'st my Heart to hear thee take on so; Don't be cast down, Man, for my Master's a better Christian, I'm sure, than to let any poor Man come to Loss by him: When he comes to know he's done you Wrong, he'll pay you for every Farthing of Damage, I'll engage. Truly, said Master *Peter*, if his Worship wou'd but pay me for the Fashion of my Puppets he has spoil'd, I'll ask no more, and he'll discharge a good Conscience; for he that wrongs his Neighbour, and does not make Restitution, can never hope to be sav'd, that's certain. I grant it, said Don *Quixote*; but I am not sensible how I have in the least injur'd you, good Master *Peter*! No, Sir! not injur'd me, cry'd Master *Peter*! Why these poor Relicks that lie here on the cold Ground, cry out for Vengeance against you. Was it not the invincible Force of that powerful Arm of yours that has scatter'd and dismember'd them so? And whose were those Bodies, Sir, but mine? and by whom was I maintain'd, but by them? Well, said Don *Quixote*, now I am thoroughly convinc'd of a Truth, which I have had Reason to believe before, that those cursed Magicians that daily persecute me, do nothing but delude me, first drawing me into dangerous Adventures by the Appearances of them as really they are, and then presently after changing the Face of things as they please. Really and truly Gentlemen, I vow and protest before ye all that hear me, that all that was acted here, seem'd to be really transacted *ipso facto* as it appear'd. To Me *Melisandra* appear'd to be *Melisandra*, Don *Gayferos* was Don *Gayferos*, *Marsilius Marsilius*, and *Charlemain* was the real *Charlemain*. Which being so, I could not contain my Fury, and acted according to the Duties of my Function, which obliges me take the injured Side. Now, tho' what I have done proves to be quite contrary to my good Design, the Fault ought not to be imputed to Me, but to my persecuting Foes; yet I own myself sorry for the Mischance, and will condemn myself to pay the Costs. Let Master *Peter* see what he must have for the Figures that are damag'd, and I will pay it him now in good and lawful Money on the Nail. Heaven bless your Worship, cry'd Master *Peter*, with a profound Cringe; I cou'd expect no less from the wonderful Christianity of the valorous Don *Quixote de la Mancha*, the sure Relief and Bulwark of all miserable Wanderers. Now let my Landlord and the great *Sancho* be Mediators and Appraisers between your Worship and my self, and I'll stand to their Award: They agreed: and presently Master *Peter* taking up *Marsilius* King of *Saragossa*, that lay by on the Ground with his Head off: You see Gentlemen, said he, 'tis impossible to restore this King to his former Dignity; and therefore with Submission to your better Judgments, I think that for his Destruction, and to get him a Successor, seven and twenty Pence* is little enough o'Conscience. Proceed, said Don *Quixote*. Then for this that is cleft in two, said Master *Peter*, taking up the Emperor *Charlemain*, I think he's richly worth One and Thirty Pence Half Penny.† Not so richly neither, quoth *Sancho*. Truly, said the Inn-keeper, I think, 'tis pretty reasonable; but we'll make it even Money, let the poor Fellow have Half a Crown. Come, said Don *Quixote*, let him have his full Price; we'll not stand haggling for so small a Matter in a Case like this: So make haste Master *Peter*, for 'tis near Supper-time, and I have some strong Presumptions that I shall eat heartily. Now, said Master *Peter*, for this Figure here that's without a Nose and blind of one Eye, being the fair *Melisandra*, I'll be reasonable with you; give me Fourteen Pence,‡ I wou'd not take less from my Brother. Nay, said Don *Quixote*, the Devil's in't if *Melisandra* ben't by this time with her Husband, upon the Frontiers of *France* at least; for the Horse that carry'd 'em seem'd to me rather to fly than to gallop; and now you tell me of a *Melisandra* here without a Nose forsooth, when 'tis Ten to One but she's now in her Husband's Arms in a good Bed in *France*. Come, come Friend, God help ev'ry Man to his own; let us have fair Dealing, so proceed. Master *Peter* finding that the Knight began to harp upon the old String, was afraid he would fly off; and making as if he had better consider'd of it, Cry y'e Mercy, Sir, said he, I was mistaken; this cou'd not be *Melisandra* indeed, but one of the Damsels that waited on her; and so I think Five Pence will be fair enough for her. In this manner he went on, setting his Price upon the Dead and Wounded, which the Arbitrators moderated to the content of both Parties; and the whole Sum amounted to Forty Reals and Three Quarters, which *Sancho* paid him

* *Four Reals and a half.* † *Five Reals and a Quarter.* ‡ *Two Reals and Twelve Maravedis.*

13-2

195

down; and then Master *Peter* demanded Two Reals more, for the Trouble of catching his Ape. Give it him, said Don *Quixote*, and set the Monkey to catch the Ape; and now wou'd I give Two Hundred more to be assured that Don *Gayferos* and the Lady *Melisandra* were safely arrived in *France* among their Friends. No Body can better tell than my Ape, said Master *Peter*, though the Devil himself will hardly catch him, if Hunger, or his Kindness for me, don't bring us together again to Night. However to Morrow will be a new Day, and when 'tis light we'll see what's to be done.

The whole Disturbance being appeas'd, to Supper they went lovingly together, and Don *Quixote* treated the whole Company, for he was Liberality itself. Before Day the Man with the Lances and Halbards left the Inn, and some Time after the Scholar and the Page came to take Leave of the Knight; the First to return Home, and the Second to continue his Journey, towards whose Charges Don *Quixote* gave him Twelve Reals. As for Master *Peter*, he knew too much of the Knight's Humour to desire to have any thing to do with him, and therefore having pick'd up the Ruins of the Puppet Show, and got his Ape again, by break of day he pack'd off to seek his fortune. The Inn-keeper, who did not know Don *Quixote*, was as much surpriz'd at his Liberality as at his Madness. In fine, *Sancho* paid him very honestly by his Master's Order, and mounting a little before Eight a Clock, they left the Inn, and proceeded on their Journey; where we will leave 'em, that we may have an Opportunity to relate some other Matters very requisite for the better understanding of this famous History.

XXVII: WHEREIN IS DISCOVER'D WHO MASTER PETER WAS, AND HIS APE; AS ALSO DON QUIX-OTE'S ILL SUCCESS IN THE BRAYING ADVENTURE, WHICH DID NOT END SO HAPPILY AS HE DESIR'D AND EXPECTED

ID *Hamet*, the Auther of this celebrated History, begins this Chapter with this Asseveration, *I swear as a true Catholick*; which the Translator illustrates and explains in this manner: That Historian's swearing like a true Catholick, though he was a Mahometan *Moor*, ought to be receiv'd in no other Sense, than that, As a true Catholick, when he affirms any thing with an Oath, does or ought to swear Truth, So would he relate the Truth as impartially as a Christian would do, if he had taken such an Oath, in what he design'd to write of Don *Quixote*; especially as to the Account that is to be given us of the Person who was known by the Name of Master *Peter*, and the Fortune-telling Ape, whose Answers occasion'd such a Noise, and created such an Amazement all over the Country. He says then, that any one who has read the foregoing Part of this History, cannot but remember one *Gines de Passamonte*, whom Don *Quixote* had rescu'd, with several other Galley-Slaves, in *Sierra Morena*; a Piece of Service for which the Knight was not over-burden'd with Thanks, and which that ungrateful Pack of Rogues repaid with a Treatment altogether unworthy such a Deliverance. This *Gines de Passamonte*, or, as Don *Quixote* call'd him, *Ginesillo de Parapilla*, was the very Man that stole *Sancho's* Ass; the manner of which Robbery, and the Time when it was committed, being not inserted in the first Part, has been the Reason that some People have laid that, which was caus'd by the Printer's Neglect, to the Inadvertency of the Author. But 'tis beyond all question, that *Gines* stole the Ass while *Sancho* slept on his Back, making use of the same Trick and Artifice which *Brunelo* practis'd when he carry'd off *Sacripante's* Horse from under his Legs, at the Siege of *Albraca*. However, *Sancho* got Possession again, as has been told you before.

Gines it seems being obnoxious to the Law, was apprehensive of the strict Search that was made after him, in order to bring him to Justice for his repeated Villanies, which were so great and numerous, that he himself had wrote a large Book of 'em; and therefore he thought it advisable to make the best of his Way into the Kingdom of *Arragon*, and having clapp'd a Plaister over his Left Eye, resolv'd in that Disguise to set up a Puppet-Show, and stroll with it about the Country; for you must know, he had not his Fellow at any thing that could be done by Sleight of Hand. Now it happen'd, that in his Way he fell into the Company of some Christian Slaves who came from *Barbary*, and struck a Bargain with 'em for this Ape, whom he taught to leap on his Shoulder at a certain Sign, and to make as if he whisper'd something in his Ear. Having brought his Ape to this, before he enter'd into any Town he inform'd himself in the adjacent Parts as well as he could, of what particular Accidents had happen'd to this or that person; and having a very retentive Memory, the first thing he did was to give 'em a Sight of his Show, that represented sometimes one Story and sometimes another, which were generally well known and taking among the Vulgar. The next thing he had to do, was to commend the wonderful Qualities of his Ape, and tell the Company, That the Animal had the Gift of revealing Things past and present; but that in Things to come, he was altogether uninstructed. He ask'd Two Reals* for every Answer, tho' now-and-then he lower'd his Price as he felt the Pulse of his Customers. Sometimes when he came to the Houses of People, of whose Concerns he had some Account, and who wou'd ask the Ape no Questions, because they did not care to part with their Money, he wou'd notwithstanding be making Signs to his Ape, and tell 'em, the Animal had acquainted him with this or that Story, according to the Information he had before; and by that means he got a great Credit among the common People, and drew a mighty Crowd after him. At other Times, though he knew nothing of the Person, the Subtilty of his Wit supply'd his want of Knowledge, and brought him handsomly off: and no Body being so inquisitive or pressing as to make him declare by what Means his Ape attain'd to this Gift of Divination, he impos'd

* *About a Shilling.*

198

on every one's Understanding, and got almost what Money he pleas'd.

He was no sooner come to the Inn, but he knew Don *Quixote*, *Sancho*, and the rest of the Company: But he had like to have paid dear for his Knowledge, had the Knight's Sword fallen but a little lower when he made King *Marsilius's* Head fly and routed all his *Moorish* Horse, as the Reader may have observ'd in the foregoing Chapter. And this may suffice in relation to Mr *Peter* and his Ape.

Now let us overtake our Champion of *la Mancha*. After he had left the Inn, he resolv'd to take a Sight of the River *Ebro*, and the Country about it, before he went to *Saragossa*, since he was not straiten'd for Time, but might do that, and yet arriv'd soon enough to make one at the Justs and Tournaments at that City. Two Days he travel'd without meeting with any thing worth his Notice or the Reader's, when on the third, as he was riding up a Hill, he heard a great Noise of Drums, Trumpets, and Guns. At first he thought some Regiment of Soldiers was on its March that Way, which made him spur up *Rozinante* to the Brow of the Hill, that he might see 'em pass by; and then he saw in a Bottom above two hundred Men, as near as he cou'd guess, arm'd with various Weapons, as Lances, Crossbows, Partisans, Halberds, Pikes, some few Fire-locks, and a great many Targets. Thereupon he descended into the Vale, and made his Approaches towards the Battalion so near as to be able to distinguish their Banners, judge of their Colours, and observe their Devices; more especially one that was to be seen on a Standard of white Sattin, on which was represented to the Life a little Jack-Ass, much like a *Sardinian* Ass Colt, holding up his Head, stretching out his Neck, and thrusting out his Tongue, in the very Posture of an Ass that is braying, with this Distich written in fair Characters about it:

> 'Twas something more than Nothing which one Day
> Made one and t'other worthy Bailiff bray.

Don *Quixote* drew this Inference from the Motto, That those were the Inhabitants of the braying Town, and he acquainted *Sancho* with what he had observ'd, giving him also to understand, that the Man who told 'em the Story of the two braying Aldermen was apparently in the Wrong, since according to the Verses on the Standard, they were two Bailiffs and not two Aldermen.* It matters not one Rush what you call them, quoth *Sancho*; for those very Aldermen that bray'd might in Time come to be made Bailiffs of the Town, and so both those Titles might have been given 'em well enough. But what is it to you, or me, or the Story, whether the two Brayers were Aldermen or Bailiffs, so they but bray'd as we are told? As if a Bailiff were not as likely to bray as an Alderman?

In short, both Master and Man plainly understood, that the Men who were thus up in Arms, were those that were jeer'd for Braying, got together to fight the People of another Town, who had indeed abus'd them more than was the part of good Neighbours; thereupon Don *Quixote* advanc'd towards them, to *Sancho's* great Grief, who had no manner of liking to such kind of Adventures. The Multitude soon got about the Knight, taking him for some Champion, who was come to their Assistance. But Don *Quixote*, lifting up his Vizor, with a graceful Deportment, rode up to the Standard, and there all the chief Leaders of the Army got together about him, in order to take a Survey of his Person, no less amaz'd at this strange Appearance than the rest. Don *Quixote* seeing 'em look so earnestly on him, and no Man offer so much as a Word or Question, took Occasion from Their Silence to break his Own; and raising his Voice, Good Gentlemen, cry'd he, I beseech you with all the Endearments imaginable, to give no Interruption to the Discourse I am now delivering to you, unless you find it distasteful or tedious; which if I am unhappy enough to occasion, at the least hint you shall give me, I will clap a Seal on my Lips, and a Padlock on my Tongue. They all cry'd that he might speak what he pleas'd, and they would hear him with all their Hearts. Having this License, Don *Quixote* proceeded. Gentlemen, said he, I am a Knight-Errant: Arms are my Exercise; and my Profession is to shew Favour to those that are in Necessity of Favour, and to give Assistance to those that are in Distress. I have for some time been no Stranger to the Cause of your Uneasiness, which excites you to take Arms to be reveng'd on your Insult-

* *The* Spanish *Word* Alcalde *answers nearly to our Bailiff of a Corporation, as* Regidor *does to that of* Alderman.

ing Neighbours; and having often busied my Intellectuals, in making Reflections on the Motives which have brought you together, I have drawn this Inference from it, That according to the Laws of Arms, you really injure yourselves, in thinking yourselves affronted; for no particular Person can give an Affront to a whole Town and Society of Men, except it be by accusing 'em all of High-Treason in general, for want of knowing on which of them to fix some Treasonable Action, of which he supposes some of them to be guilty. We have an Instance of this Nature in Don *Diego Ordonnez De Lara*, who sent a Challenge to all the Inhabitants of *Zamora*, not knowing that *Vellido de Olfos* had Assassinated the King his Master in that Town, without any Accomplices; and so accusing and defying 'em all, the Defence and Revenge belong'd to 'em all in general. Though it must be own'd, that Don *Diego* was somewhat unreasonable in his Defiance, and strain'd the Point too far: For, it was very little to the Purpose to defy the Dead, the Waters, the Bread, those that were yet unborn, with many other trifling Matters mentioned in the Challenge. But let That pass; for when once the Choler boils over, the Tongue grows unruly, and knows no Moderation. Taking it for granted then, that no particular Person can affront a whole Kingdom, Province, City, Commonwealth, or Body Politick, it is but just to conclude, That 'tis needless to revenge such a pretended Affront; since such an Abuse is no sufficient Provocation, and indeed, positively no Affront. It would be a pretty Piece of Wisdom, truly, should those out of the Town of *Reloxa* sally out every Day on those who spend their ill-natur'd Breaths miscalling 'em every where. 'Twould be a fine Business indeed, if the Inhabitants of those several famous Towns that are nick-nam'd by our Rabble, and call'd the one Cheese-mongers, the other Coster-mongers, these Fish-mongers, and those Soap-boilers, should know no better than to think themselves Dishonour'd, and in revenge, be always drawing out their Swords at the least Word, for every idle insignificant Quarrel. No, no, Heaven forbid! Men of Sagacity and Wisdom, and well-govern'd Commonwealths are never induc'd to take up Arms, nor endanger their Persons, and Estates, but on the four following Occasions. In the first Place, to defend the Holy Catholick Faith. Secondly, for the Security of their Lives, which they are commanded to preserve by the Laws of God and Nature. Thirdly, the Preservation of their good Name, the Reputation of their Family, and the Conservation of their Estates. Fourthly, the Service due to their Prince in a just War; and if we please, we may add a Fifth, which indeed may be referr'd to the Second, the Defence of our Country. To these five Capital Causes may be subjoin'd several others, which may induce Men to vindicate themselves, and have Recourse even to the way of Arms: But to take 'em up for meer Trifles, and such Occasions as rather challenge our Mirth and contemptuous Laughter, than Revenge, shews the Person who is guilty of such Proceedings, to labour under a Scarcity of Sense Besides, to seek after an unjust Revenge (and indeed no Human Revenge can be just) is directly against the Holy Law we profess, which commands us to forgive our Enemies, and to do good to those that hate us. An Injunction, which though it seems difficult in the Implicit Obedience we shou'd pay to it, yet is only so to those who have less of Heaven than of the World, and more of the Flesh than of the Spirit. For, the Redeemer of Mankind, whose Words never could deceive, said, *That his Yoke was easy, and his Burden light*; and according to that, he could prescribe nothing to our Practice which was impossible to be done. Therefore, Gentlemen, since Reason and Religion recommend Love and Peace to you, I hope you will not render your selves obnoxious to all Laws, both Human and Divine, by a Breach of the publick Tranquility—The Devil fetch me, quoth *Sancho* to himself, if this Master of mine must not have been bred a Parson, if not, he's as like one as one Egg is like another. Don *Quixote* paus'd a while, to take Breath; and perceiving his Auditory still willing to give him Attention, had proceeded in his Harangue, had not *Sancho's* good Opinion of his Parts, made him lay hold on this Opportunity to talk in *his* Turn. Gentlemen, quoth he, my Master Don *Quixote de la Mancha*, once call'd the Knight of the Woful Figure, and now the Knight of the Lions, is a very judicious Gentleman, and talks Latin and his own Mother-Tongue as well as any of your Varsity-Doctors. Whatever Discourse he takes in hand, he speaks ye to the purpose, and like a Man of Mettle; he has ye all the Laws and Rules of that same thing you call Duel and

Punctilio of Honour, at his Fingers Ends; so that you have no more to do but to do as He says, and if in taking his Counsel you ever tread awry, let the Blame be laid on My Shoulders. And indeed, as you've already been told, 'tis a very silly Fancy to be asham'd to hear one Bray; for I remember when I was a Boy, I could Bray as often as I listed, and no body went about to hinder me; and I could do it so rarely, and to the Life, without Vanity be it spoken, that all the Asses in our Town would fall a Braying when they heard Me Bray; yet for all this, I was an honest Body's Child, and came of good Parentage, d'ye see; 'tis true, indeed, four of the best young Men in our Parish envy'd me for this great Ability of mine; but I car'd not a Rush for their Spite. Now, that you mayn't think I tell you a Flam, do but hear me, and then judge; for this rare Art is like Swimming, which, when once learn'd, is never to be forgotten. This said, he clapp'd both the Palms of his Hands to his Nose, and fell a Braying so obstreperously, that it made the neighbouring Valleys ring again. But while he was thus Braying, one of those that stood next to him, believing he did it to mock them, gave him such a hearty Blow with a Quarter-Staff on his Back, that down he brought him to the Ground. Don *Quixote* seeing what a rough Entertainment had been given to his Squire, mov'd with his Lance in a threatning Posture towards the Man that had us'd poor *Sancho* thus; but the Crowd thrust themselves in such a manner between them, that the Knight found it impracticable to pursue the Revenge he design'd. At the same time, finding that a Shower of Stones began to rain about his Ears, and a great Number of Cross-Bows and Muskets were getting ready for his Reception, he turn'd *Rozinante's* Reins, and Gallop'd from 'em as fast as four Legs would carry him, sending up his hearty Prayers to Heaven to deliver him from this Danger, and, being under grievous Apprehensions at every Step, that he should be shot through the Back, and have the Bullet come out at his Breast, he still went fetching his Breath, to try if it did any ways fail him. But the Country-Battalion were satisfy'd with seeing him fly, and did not offer to shoot at him.

As for *Sancho*, he was set upon his Ass before he had well recover'd his Senses, which the Blow had taken from him, and then they suffer'd him to move off; not that the poor Fellow had Strength enough to guide him, but *Dapple* naturally follow'd *Rozinante* of his own accord, not being able to be a Moment from him. The Don being at a good Distance from the arm'd Multitude, fac'd about, and seeing *Sancho* pacing after him without any troublesome Attendants, stay'd for his coming up. As for the Rabble, they kept their Posts till it grew dark, and their Enemies having not taken the Field to give 'em Battle, they march'd Home, so overjoy'd to have shewn their Courage, without Danger, that had they been so well bred, as to have known the antient Custom of the *Greeks*, they would have erected a Trophy in that Place.

XXVIII: OF SOME THINGS WHICH BENENGELI TELLS US HE THAT READS SHALL KNOW, IF HE READS 'EM WITH ATTENTION

WHEN the Valiant Man flies, he must have discover'd some foul Play, and 'tis the part of prudent Persons to reserve themselves for more favourable Opportunities. This Truth is verified in Don *Quixote*, who, rather than expose himself to the Fury of an incens'd and ill-designing Multitude, betook himself to Flight, without any Thoughts of *Sancho*, till he found himself beyond the reach of those Dangers in which he had left his trusty Squire involv'd. *Sancho* came after him, as we have told you before, laid a-cross his Ass, and having recover'd his Senses, overtook him at last, and let himself drop from his Pack-saddle at *Rozinante's* Feet, all Batter'd and Bruis'd, and in a sorrowful Condition. Don *Quixote* presently dismounted to search his Wounds, and finding no Bones broken, but his Skin whole from Head to Feet; You must Bray, cry'd he angrily, you must Bray, with a Pox, must you! 'Tis a piece of excellent Discretion to talk of Halters in the House of a Man whose Father was Hang'd. What Counterpart could you expect to your Musick, Blockhead, but a Thorough-Bass of Bastinadoes? Thank Providence, Sirrah! that as they gave you a dry Benediction with a Quarter-Staff, they did not cross you with a Cutlas. I han't Breath to answer you at present, quoth *Sancho*, but my Back and Shoulders speak enough for me. Pray let's make the best of our way from this cursed Place, and whene'er I Bray again, may I get such another Pult, on my Kidneys. Yet I can't help saying, that your Knights-Errant can betake themselves to their Heels to save *one* upon Occasion, and leave their trusty Squires to be beaten like Stock-fish, in the midst of their Enemies. A Retreat is not to be accounted a Flight, reply'd Don *Quixote*; for know, *Sancho*, that Courage which has not Wisdom for its Guide, falls under the Name of Temerity; and the rash Man's successful Actions are rather owing to his good Fortune, than to his Bravery. I own I did retire, but I deny that I fled; and in such a Retreat I did but imitate many Valiant Men who, not to hazard their Persons indiscreetly, reserv'd themselves for a more fortunate Hour. Histories are full of Examples of this nature, which I do not care to relate at present, because they would be more tedious to Me, than profitable to Thee.

By this time Don *Quixote* had help'd *Sancho* to bestride his Ass, and being himself Mounted on *Rozinante*, they Pac'd softly along, and got into a Grove of Poplar-Trees, about a Quarter of a League from the Place where they Mounted. Yet as softly as they rid, *Sancho* could not help now and then heaving up deep Sighs and lamentable Groans. Don *Quixote* ask'd him, why he made such a heavy Moan? *Sancho* told him, That from his Rump to his Pole, he felt such grievous Pains, that he was ready to sink. Without doubt, said Don *Quixote*, the Intense-ness of thy Torments, is by reason the Staff with which thou wert struck, was broad and long, and so having fallen on those Parts of thy Back, caused a Contusion there, and affects them all with Pain; and had it been of a greater Magnitude, thy Grievances had been so much the greater. Truly, quoth *Sancho*! you've clear'd that in very pithy Words, of which no Body made any doubt. Body of me! was the Cause of my Ailing so hard to be guess'd, that you must tell me that so much of me was sore as was hit by the Weapon? Should my ankle-bone ake, and you scratch your Head till you had found out the Cause of it, I would think that something. But for you to tell me that Place is sore where I was Bruis'd, every Fool could do as much. Faith and Troth, Sir Master of mine, I grow Wiser and Wiser every Day: I find you're like all the World, that lay to Heart no Body's Harms but their own. I find whereabouts we are, and what I'm like to get by you; for e'en as you left me now in the Lurch to be well belabour'd and rib-roasted, and t'other Day to dance the Caper-Galliard in the Blanket you wot of; so I must expect a Hundred and a Hundred more of these good Vails in your Service; and as the Mischief has now lighted on my Shoulders, next Bout I look for it to fly at my Eyes. A Plague of my Jolter head, I have been a Fool and Sot all along, and am never like to be Wiser while I live. Would it not be better for Me to trudge home to my Wife and Children, and look after my House with that little Wit that Heaven has given me, without galloping after your Tail high and low, through confounded cross-Roads and By-ways, and wicked and crooked Paths, that the Ungodly themselves can't find out! And then most commonly to have nothing to moisten one's Weasand that's fitting for a Christian to drink, nothing but meer Element and Dog's Porridge! And nothing to stuff one's Puddings that's worthy of a Catholick Stomach? Then after a Man has tir'd himself off his Legs, when he'd be glad of a good Bed, to have a Master cry, Here, are you sleepy? Lie down Mr Squire, your Bed's made: Take six Foot of good hard Ground, and measure your Corps there; and if that won't serve, take as much more and welcome: You're at Rack and Manger, spare not, I beseech your Dogship; there's Room enough. Old Nick roast and burn to a Cinder that unlucky Son of Mischief that first set People a madding after this Whim of Knight-Errantry, or at least the first Ninny-hammer that had so little Forecast as to turn Squire to such a Parcel of Mad-men as were your Knights-Errant—in the Days of Yore I mean; I am better bred than to speak ill of those in Our Time; no, I honour them, since your Worship has taken up this blessed Calling; for you've a long Nose, the Devil himself could not out-reach you, you can see farther into a Milstone than He. I durst lay a Wager, said Don *Quixote*, that now thou art suffered to prate without Interruption, thou feel'st no manner of Pain in thy whole Body. Pr'ythee talk on, my Child, say any thing that comes uppermost to thy Mouth, or is burdensome to thy Brain; so it but alleviates thy Pain, thy Impertinencies will rather please than offend me; and if thou hast such a longing Desire to be at home with thy Wife and Children, Heaven forbid I should be against it. Thou hast Money of mine in thy Hands: See how long 'tis since we sallied out last from Home, and cast up the Wages by the Month, and pay thy self. An't like your Worship, quoth *Sancho*, when I serv'd my Master *Carrasco*, Father to the Batchelor, your Worship's Acquaintance, I had two Ducats a Month, besides my Victuals: I don't know what You'll give me; tho' I'm sure there's more Trouble in being Squire to a Knight-Errant, than in being Servant to a Farmer; for truly we that go to Plough and Cart in a Farmer's Service, though we moil and sweat so-a-days as not to have a dry Thread to our Backs, let the worst come to the worst, are sure of a Bellyful at Night out of the Pot, and to snore in a Bed. But I don't know when I have had a good Meal's Meat or a good Night's Rest in all your whole Service, unless it were that short time when we were at Don *Diego's* House, and when I made a Feast on the savoury Skimming of *Camacho's* Cauldron, and Eat, Drank, and Lay at Master *Basil's*. All the rest of my time I have had my Lodging on the cold Ground, and in the open Fields, subject to the Inclemency of the Sky, as you call it; living on the Rinds of Cheese, and Crusts of mouldy Bread; drinking sometimes Ditch water, sometimes Spring, as we chanc'd to light upon't in our way. Well, said Don *Quixote*, I grant all this, *Sancho*; then how much more dost thou expect from Me, than thou hadst from thy Master *Carrasco*? Why, truly, quoth *Sancho*, if your Worship will pay me Twelve-pence a Month more than *Thomas Carrasco* gave me, I shall think it very fair, and tolerable Wages; but then instead of the Island which you know you promis'd me, I think you can't in Conscience give me less than six and thirty Pence a Month more, which will make in all Thirty Reals, neither more nor less. Very well, said Don *Quixote*, let's see then, 'tis now twenty-five Days since we set out from home, reckon what this comes to, according to the Wages thou hast allowed thy self, and be thy own Pay-master. Odsdiggers! quoth *Sancho*, we are quite out in our Account; for as to the Governor of an Island's Place, which you promised to help me to, we ought to reckon from the time you made the Promise, to this very Day. Well, and pray how long is it, ask'd Don *Quixote*? If I remember rightly, quoth *Sancho*, 'tis about some twenty Years ago, Two or Three Days more or less. With that Don *Quixote*, hitting himself a good clap on the Forehead, fell a Laughing heartily. Why, cry'd he, we have hardly been out two Months from the very beginning of our first Expedition, and in all the time we were in *Sierra Morena*, and our whole Progress: And hast thou the Impudence to affirm it's twenty Years since I promis'd the Grant of the Island? I am now convinc'd thou hast a mind to make all the Money which thou hast of mine in thy Keeping, go for the Payment of thy Wages. If this be thy meaning, well and good, e'en take it, and much Good may it do thee; for rather than be troubled any longer with such a Varlet, I would contentedly see my self without a Penny. But tell me, thou Perverter of the Laws of Chivalry that relate to Squires, where didst thou ever see or read, that any Squire to a Knight-Errant stood capitulating with his Master, as thou hast done with Me, for so much or so much a Month? Launch, unconscionable Wretch, thou Cut-Throat Scoundrel; launch, launch, thou base Spirit of Mammon, into the vast Ocean of their Histories; and if thou canst shew me a Precedent of any Squire that ever dar'd to say, or but to think as much as thou hast presum'd to tell me, then will I give thee leave to affix it on my Forehead, and hit me four Fillips on the Nose. Away then, pack off with thy Ass this Moment, and get thee Home, for thou shalt never stay in my Service any longer. Oh how much Bread, how many Promises have I now ill bestow'd on thee! Vile groveling Wretch, that hast more of the Beast than of the Man! When I was just going to prefer thee to such a Post, that in spight of thy Wife thou had'st been call'd my Lord, thou sneak'st away from me. Thou'rt leaving me, when I had fully resolv'd, without any more Delay, to make thee Lord of the best Island in the World, Sordid Clod! Well might'st thou say indeed, that Honey is not for the Chaps of an Ass. Thou art indeed a very Ass, an Ass thou wilt live, and an Ass thou wilt die; for I dare say, thou'lt never have Sense enough while thou liv'st, to know thou art a Brute. While Don *Quixote* thus up-braided and rail'd at *Sancho*, the poor Fellow, all dismay'd, and touch'd to the quick, beheld him with a wistful Look; and the Tears standing in his Eyes for Grief, Good sweet Sir, cry'd he, with a doleful and whining Voice, I confess I want nothing but a Tail to be a perfect Ass; if your Worship will be pleas'd but to put one to my Back-side, I shall deem it well set on, and be your most faithful Ass all the Days of my Life: But forgive me, I beseech you, and take pity on my Youth. Consider I've but a dull Head-piece of my own; and if my Tongue runs at ran-dom sometimes, 'tis because I'm more Fool than Knave, Sir: Who errs and mends, to Heaven himself commends. I shou'd wonder much, said Don *Quixote*, if thou shouldst not interlard thy Discourse with some pretty Proverb. Well, I will give thee my Pardon for this once, provided thou correct those Imperfections that offend me, and shew'st thy self of a less craving Temper. Take Heart then, and let the Hopes which thou may'st entertain of the Performance of my Promise, raise in thee a nobler Spirit. The Time will come, do not think it impossible because delayed. *Sancho* promised to do his best, though he could not rely on his own Strength.

Matters being thus amicably adjusted, they put into the Grove, where the Don laid himself at the Foot of an Elm, and his Squire at the Foot of a Beech; for every one of those Trees, and such others, has always a Foot, though never a Hand. *Sancho* had but an ill Night's Rest of it, for his Bruises made his Bones more than ordinarily sensible of the Cold. As for Don *Quixote*, he entertain'd himself with his usual Imaginations. However, they both slept, and by Break of Day continu'd their Journey towards the River *Ebro*, where they met—what shall be told in the next Chapter.

XXIX: THE FAMOUS ADVENTURE OF
THE INCHANTED BARK

FAIR and softly, Step by Step, Don *Quixote* and his Squire got in Two Days Time to the Banks of the River *Ebro*, which yielded a very entertaining Prospect to the Knight. The Verdure of its Banks, and the abounding Plenty of the Water, which clear like liquid Crystal, flow'd gently along within the spacious Channel, awaked a thousand amorous Chimeras in his roving Imagination, and more especially the Thoughts of what he had seen in *Montesino's* Cave; for tho' Master *Peter's* Ape had assured him, that it was partly false as well as partly true, he was rather inclined to believe it all true; quite contrary to *Sancho*, who thought it every Tittle as false as Hell.

While the Knight went on thus agreeably amused, he spied a little Boat without any Oars or Tackle, moor'd by the River-Side to the Stump of a Tree: Thereupon looking round about him, and discovering no body, he presently alighted, and ordered *Sancho* to do the like, and tie their Beasts fast to some of the Elms or Willows thereabouts. *Sancho* ask'd him what was the Meaning of all this? Thou art to know, answer'd Don *Quixote*, that most certain this Boat lies here for no other Reason but to invite me to embark in it, for the Relief of some Knight or other Person of high Degree that is in great Distress: For thus, according to the Method of Inchanters, in the Books of Chivalry, when any Knight whom they protect, happens to be involv'd in some very great Danger, from which none but some other valorous Knight can set him free; then though they be two or three thousand Leagues at least distant from each other, up the Magician snatches the auxiliary Champion in a Cloud, or else provides him a Boat, and in the Twinkling of an Eye, in either Vehicle, through the airy Fluid or the liquid Plain, he wafts him to the Place where his Assistance is wanted. Just to the same Intent does this very Bark lie here; 'tis as clear as the Day, and therefore, before it be too late, *Sancho*, tie up *Rozinante* and *Dapple*, let us commit our selves to the Guidance of Providence; for embark I will, though barefooted Friars should beg me to desist. Well, well, quoth *Sancho*, if I

must, I must. Since you will every Foot run haring into these—
I don't know how to call them, these confounded Vagaries, I
have no more to do but to make a Leg, and submit my Neck to
the Collar; for, as the Saying is, *Do as thy Master bids thee,
though it be to sit down at his Table*. But for all that, fall Back
fall Edge, I must and will discharge my Conscience, and tell
you plainly, that as blind as I am, I can see with Half an Eye,
that it is no inchanted Bark, but some Fisherman's Boat; for
there are many in this River, whose Waters afford the best
Shads in the World. This Caution did *Sancho* give his Master
while he was tying the Beasts to a Tree, and going to leave
them to the Protection of Inchanters, full sore against his will.
Don *Quixote* bid him not be concern'd at leaving them there,
for the Sage who was to carry 'em through in a Journey of such
an Extent and Longitude, would be sure to take care of the
Animals. Nay, nay, as for that Matter, quoth *Sancho*, I don't
understand your Longitude, I never heard such a cramp Word
in my Born-days. Longitude, said Don *Quixote*, is the same as
Length: I don't wonder that thou dost not understand the
Word, for thou'rt not oblig'd to understand *Latin*. Yet you
shall have some forward Coxcombs pretend to be knowing
when they are ignorant. Now the Beasts are fast Sir, quoth
Sancho, what's next to be done? Why now, answer'd Don
Quixote, let us recommend our selves to Providence and weigh
Anchor, or to speak plainly, embark and cut the Cable. With
that, leaping in, and *Sancho* following, he cut the Rope, and so
by Degrees the Stream carry'd the Boat from the Shore. Now
when *Sancho* saw himself towards the Middle of the River, he
began to quake for fear; but nothing griev'd his Heart so much
as to hear *Dapple* bray, and to see *Rozinante* struggle to get
loose. Sir, quoth he, hark how my poor *Dapple* brays, to bemoan our leaving of him; and see how poor *Rozinante* tugs hard
to break his Bridle, and is e'en wild to throw himself after us.
Alack and alack! my poor dear Friends, Peace be with you
where you are, and when this mad Freak, the Cause of our
doleful parting, is ended in Repentance, may we be brought
back to your sweet Company again. This said, he fell a blubbering, and set up such a Howl, that Don *Quixote* had no Patience with him, but looking angrily on him, What dost fear,

cry'd he, thou great white-liver'd Calf? What dost thou cry for? Who pursues thee? Who hurts thee, thou dastardly Craven, thou Cowardly Mouse, thou Soul of a Milk-sop, thou Heart of Butter? Dost want for any thing, base unsatisfy'd Wretch? What would'st thou say, wert thou to climb barefoot the rugged *Riphean* Mountains? Thou that sittest here in State like an Archduke, Plenty and Delight on each side of thee, while thou glidest gently down the calm current of this delightful River, which will soon convey us into the Main Ocean? We have already flow'd down some seven or eight hundred Leagues. Had I but an Astrolabe here to take the Altitude of the Pole, I could easily tell thee how far we have proceeded to an Inch: Tho' either I know but little, or we have just pass'd, or shall presently pass, the *Equinoctial Line*, that divides and cuts the two opposite Poles at equal distances.

And when we come to this same *Line* you speak of, quoth *Sancho*, how far have we gone then? A mighty way, answered Don *Quixote*. When we come under the Line I spoke of, we shall have measured the other half of the Terraqueous Globe, which according to the *System* and *Computation* of *Ptolomy*, who was the greatest Cosmographer in the World, contains three hundred and sixty Degrees. Odsbodikins quoth *Sancho*, you've brought me now a notable Fellow to be your Voucher, Goodman *Tollme*, with his *Amputation* and *Cistern*, and the rest of your Gibberish! Don *Quixote* smil'd at *Sancho's* Blunders, and going on, The *Spaniards*, said he, and all those that Embark at *Cadiz* for the *East-Indies*, to know whether they have pass'd the *Equinoctial-Line*, according to an Observation that has been often experienc'd, need do no more than look whether there be any Lice left alive among the Ship's Crew; for if they have pass'd it, not a Louse is to be found in the Ship, though they would give his weight in Gold for him. Look therefore, *Sancho*, and if thou find'st any such Vermin still creeping about thee, then we have not yet pass'd the Line; but if thou do'st not, then we have surely pass'd it. The Devil a Word I believe of all this, quoth *Sancho*. However, I'll do as you bid me. But hark you me, Sir, now I think on't again, where's the need of trying these Quirks; Don't I see with my two Eyes that we are not five Rods length from the Shore?

Look you there stands *Rozinante* and *Dapple*, upon the very spot where we left them; and now I look closely into the Matter, I will take my Corporal Oath that we move no faster than a Snail can Gallop, or an Ant can Trot. No more Words, said Don *Quixote*, but make the Experiment as I bid you, and let the rest alone. Thou dost not know what belongs to Colures, Lines, Parallels, Zodiacks, Eclipticks, Poles, Solstices, Equinoctials, Planets, Signs, Points, and Measures, of which the Spheres Celestial and Terrestrial are compos'd; for did'st thou know all these Things, or some of them at least, thou mightest plainly perceive what Parallels we have cut, what Signs we have pass'd and what Constellations we have left, and are now leaving behind us. Therefore I would wish thee once again to search thy self; for I cannot believe but thou art as clear from Vermin as a Sheet of white Paper. Thereupon *Sancho* advancing his Hand very gingerly towards the left side of his Neck, after he had grop'd a while, lifted up his Head; and staring in his Master's Face, look you, Sir, quoth he, pulling out something, either your Rule is not worth this, or we are many a fair League from the Place you spoke of. How! answer'd Don *Quixote*, hast thou found something then, *Sancho*? Ay, marry have I, quoth *Sancho*; and more things than one too, and so saying he shook and snapp'd his Fingers, and then wash't his whole Hand in the River; down whose Stream the Boat drove gently along, without being mov'd by any secret Influence or hidden Inchantment, but only by the help of the Current, hitherto calm and smooth.

By this time they descry'd two great Water-mills in the middle of the River, which Don *Quixote* no sooner spy'd, but calling to his Squire, Look, look, my *Sancho*, cry'd he! see'st thou yon City or Castle there! This is the Place where some Knight lies in Distress, or some Queen or Princess is detain'd, for whose Succour I am convey'd hither. What a Devil do you mean with your City or Castle, cry'd *Sancho*? Body of me! Sir, don't you see as plain as the Nose on your Face, they are nothing but Water-mills, in the midst of the River, to grind Corn. Peace, *Sancho*, reply'd Don *Quixote*, they look like Water-mills I grant you, but they are no such things: How often, have I not told thee already, do these Magicians change and over-

turn every Thing as they please; not that they can change their
very Being, but they disguise and alter the Appearances of
them; of which we have an Instance in the unhappy Transformation of *Dulcinea*, the only Refuge of my Hope.

The Boat being now got into the very strength of the Stream
began to move less slowly than it did before. The People in the
Mills perceiving the Boat to come a-drift full upon the Mill-
wheels, came running out with their long Poles to stop it; and
as their Faces and Cloaths were powder'd all over with Meal-
dust, they made a very odd Appearance. So-ho! there, cry'd
they as loud as they could bawl, is the Devil in the Fellows?
Are ye mad in the Boat there? Hold! You'll be drown'd, or
ground to pieces by the Mill-wheels. Don *Quixote* having cast
his Eyes on the Millers, Did I not tell thee, *Sancho*, said he,
that we should arrive where I must exert the strength of my
Arm? Look what Hang-dogs, what horrid Wretches come
forth to make Head against me! How many Hobgoblins oppose
my Passage! Do but see what deform'd Physiognomies they
have: Meer Bug-bears! But I shall make ye know, Scoundrels,
how insignificant all your Efforts must prove. Then standing
up in the Boat, he began to threaten the Millers in a haughty
Tone: Ye paltry Slaves, cry'd he, base and ill-advis'd Scum of
the World, release instantly the Captive Person who is injur-
iously detain'd and oppress'd within your Castle or Prison, be
they of high or low Degree; for I am Don *Quixote de la Mancha*,
otherwise call'd the Knight of the Lions, for whom the happy
Atchievement of this Adventure is reserv'd, by the Decree of
Heaven. This said, he unsheath'd his Sword, and began to
fence with the Air, as if he had been already engaging the Millers; who hearing, but not understanding, his mad Words,
stood ready with their Poles to stop the Boat, which was now
near the Mill-dam and just entring the rapid Stream and narrow Channel of the Wheels.

In the mean time, *Sancho* was devoutly fallen on his Knees,
praying Heaven for a happy Deliverance out of this mighty
Plunge, but this one time. And indeed his Prayers met with
pretty good Success; for the Millers so bestirr'd themselves
with their Poles that they stopp'd the Boat, yet not so cleverly
but they overset it, tipping Don *Quixote* and *Sancho* over into

the River. 'Twas well for the Knight that he could swim like a Duck; and yet the weight of his Armour sunk him twice to the Bottom; and had it not been for the Millers, who jump'd into the Water, and made a shift to pull out both the Master and the Man, in a manner Craning them up, there had been an end of them both.

When they were both hawl'd ashore, more over-drench'd than thirsty, *Sancho* betook himself to his Knees again, and with up-lifted Hands and Eyes made a long and hearty Prayer, that Heaven might keep him from this time forwards clear of his Master's rash Adventures.

And now came the Fishermen who own'd the Boat, and finding it broken to pieces, fell upon *Sancho*, and began to strip him, demanding Satisfaction both of him and his Master for the Loss of their Bark. The Knight with a great deal of Gravity and Unconcern, as if he had done no manner of Harm, told both the Millers and the Fishermen, that he was ready to pay for the Boat, provided they would fairly surrender the Persons that were detain'd unjustly in their Castle. What Persons, or what Castle, you mad Oaf, said one of the Millers? Marry guep, would you carry away the Folk that come to grind their Corn at Our Mills? Well, said Don *Quixote* to himself, Man had as good preach to a Stone-wall, as to expect to persuade with In-treaties such Dregs of Human Kind to do a good and generous Action. Two Sage Inchanters certainly clash in this Adventure, and the one thwarts the other: One provided me a Bark, t'other overwhelm'd me in it. Heaven send us better Times! There is nothing but Plotting and Counter-plotting, Undermining and Counter-mining in this World. Well, I can do no more. Then raising his Voice, and casting a fix'd Eye on the Water-mills, My dear Friends, cry'd he, whoever you are that are immur'd in this Prison, pardon me, I beseech ye; for so my ill Fate and yours ordains, that I cannot free you from your Confinement: The Adventure is reserv'd for some other Knight. This said, he came to an Agreement with the Fisher-men, and order'd *Sancho* to pay them fifty Reals for the Boat. *Sancho* pull'd out the Money with a very ill Will, and parted with it with a worse, muttering between his Teeth, that two Voyages like that would sink their whole Stock.

The Fisher-men and the Millers could not forbear admiring at two such Figures of Human Offspring, that neither spoke nor acted like the rest of Mankind: for they could not so much as guess what Don *Quixote* meant by all his extravagant Speeches; so taking them for Mad-men, they left 'em, and went the Millers to their Mills, and the Fisher-men to their Huts. Don *Quixote* and *Sancho* return'd to their Beasts like a Couple of as sense-less Animals; and thus ended the Adventure of the Inchanted Bark.

XXX: WHAT HAPPEN'D TO DON QUIXOTE
WITH THE FAIR HUNTRESS

WITH wet Bodies and melancholy Minds, the Knight and Squire went back to *Rozinante* and *Dapple*; though *Sancho* was the more cast down and out of Sorts of the Two; for it griev'd him to the very Soul to see the Money dwindle; being as chary of that as of his Heart's Blood, or the Apples of his Eyes. To be short, to Horse they went, without speaking one Word to each other, and left the famous River: Don *Quixote* bury'd in his amorous Thoughts and *Sancho* in those of his Preferment, which he thought far enough off yet; for, as much a Fool as he was, he plainly perceiv'd that all, or most of his Master's Actions tended only to Folly: Therefore he but waited an Opportunity to give him the Slip and go home, without coming to any farther Reckoning, or taking a formal Leave. But Fortune provided for him much better than he expected.

It happen'd that the next Day about Sun-set, as they were coming out of a Wood, Don *Quixote* cast his Eyes round a Verdant Meadow, and at the farther End of it descry'd a Company, whom upon a nearer View he judg'd to be Persons of Quality, that were taking the Diversion of Hawking; approaching nearer yet, he observ'd among 'em a very fine Lady upon a white pacing Mare, in green Trappings, and a Saddle of Cloth of Silver. The Lady her self was dress'd in Green, so Rich and so Gay, that nothing could be finer. She rode with a Goss-Hawk on her left Fist, by which Don *Quixote* judg'd her to be of Quality, and Mistress of the Train that attended; as indeed she was. Thereupon calling to his Squire, Son *Sancho*, cry'd he, run and tell that Lady on the Palfry with the Goss-Hawk on her Fist, that I the *Knight of the Lions* humbly salute her Highness; and that if she pleases to give me leave, I should be proud to receive her Commands, and have the Honour of waiting on her, and kissing her fair Hands. But take special Care, *Sancho*, how thou deliverest thy Message, and be sure don't lard My Compliments with any of Thy Proverbs. Why this to me, quoth *Sancho*? Marry, you need not talk of Larding, as if I had never went Ambassador before to a High and Mighty Dame. I don't know that ever thou did'st, reply'd Don *Quixote*, at least on My Account, unless it were when I sent thee to *Dulcinea*. It may be so, quoth *Sancho*: But a good Pay-master needs no Surety; and where there's Plenty the Guests can't be empty: That is to say, I need none of your telling nor tutoring about that matter: for, as silly as I look, I know something of every thing. Well, well, I believe it, said Don *Quixote*. Go then in a good Hour, and Heaven inspire and guide thee.

Sancho put on, forcing *Dapple* from his old Pace to a Gallop; and approaching the fair Huntress, he alighted, and falling on his Knees: Fair Lady, quoth he, that Knight yonder, call'd the *Knight of the Lions*, is my Master; I am his Squire, *Sancho Pança* by Name. This same *Knight of the Lions*, who but t'other Day was call'd *The Knight of the Woful Figure*, has sent me to tell you, That so please your Worship's Grace to give him leave with your good Liking, to do as he has a mind; which as he says and as I believe, is only to serve your high-flown Beauty, and be your eternal Vassal; you may chance to do a thing that would be for your own good, and he would take it for a hugeous Kindness at your Hands. Indeed, honest Squire, said the Lady, you have acquitted your self of your Charge with all the graceful Circumstances which such an Embassy requires: Rise, pray rise, for 'tis by no means fit the Squire to so great a Knight, as *The Knight of the Woful Figure*, to whose Name and Merit we are no Strangers, should remain on his Knees. Rise then, and desire your Master, by all means to honour us with his Company, that my Lord Duke and I may pay him our Respects at a House we have hard by.

Sancho got up, no less amaz'd at the Lady's Beauty than at her Affability, but much more because she told him they were no Strangers to his Master, *The Knight of the Woful Figure*. Nor did he wonder why she did not call him by his Title of *Knight of the Lions*; considering, he had but lately assumed it.

Pray, said the Dutchess, (whose particular Title we don't yet know) Is not this Master of yours the Person, whose History came out in Print, by the Name of *the Renown'd* Don *Quixote de la Mancha*, the Mistress of whose Affections is a certain Lady call'd *Dulcinea del Toboso*? The very same, an't please your Worship, said *Sancho*; and that Squire of his that is, or should be in the Book, *Sancho Pança* by Name, is my own self, if I was not chang'd in my Cradle; I mean, chang'd in the Press. I am mighty glad to hear all this, said the Dutchess. Go then, Friend *Pança*, and tell your Master, That I congratulate him upon his Arrival in our Territories, to which he is Welcome; and assure him from me, that this is the most agreeable News I could possibly have heard.

Sancho, overjoy'd with this gracious Answer, return'd to his Master, to whom he repeated all that the great Lady had said to him; praising to the Skies, in his clownish Phrase, her great Beauty and courteous Nature.

Don *Quixote*, pleas'd with this good beginning, seated himself handsomely in the Saddle, fix'd his Toes in his Stirrups, set the Bever of his Helmet as he thought best became his Face, rous'd up *Rozinante's* Mettle, and with a graceful Assurance mov'd forwards to kiss the Dutchess's Hand. As soon as *Sancho* went from her, she sent for the Duke her Husband, and gave him an Account of Don *Quixote's* Embassy. Thereupon they both attended his coming with a pleasant Impatience; for, having read the first Part of his History, they were no less desirous to be acquainted with his Person; and resolv'd, as long as he staid with them, to give him his own Way, and humour him in all things, treating him still with all the Forms essential to the Entertainment of a Knight-Errant; which they were the better able to do, having been much conversant with Books of that kind.

And now Don *Quixote* drew nigh with his Vizor up; and *Sancho* seeing him offer to alight, made all the haste he could to be ready to hold his Stirrup: But as Ill-luck would have it, as he was throwing his Leg over his Pack-Saddle to get off, he entangl'd his Foot so strangely in the Rope that serv'd him instead of a Stirrup, that not being able to get it out, he hung by the Heel with his Nose to the Ground. On the other Side Don *Quixote*, who was us'd to have his Stirrup held when he dismounted, thinking *Sancho* had hold of it already, lifted up his right Leg over the Saddle to alight; but as it happened to be ill-girt, down he brought it with himself to the Ground, confounded with Shame, and muttering between his Teeth many a hearty Curse against *Sancho*, who was all the while with his Foot in the Stocks. The Duke seeing them in that Condition, order'd some of his People to help them; and they rais'd Don *Quixote*, who was in no very good Case with his Fall; however, limping, as well as he could, he went to pay his Duty to the Lady, and would have fall'n on his Knees at her Horse's Feet: But the Duke alighting, would by no means permit it; and embracing Don *Quixote*, I am sorry, said he, Sir Knight *of the Woful Figure*, that such a Mischance should happen to you at your first Appearance on My Territories, but the Negligence of Squires is often the Cause of worse Accidents. Most generous Prince, said Don *Quixote*, I can think nothing bad that could befal me here, since I have had the Happiness of seeing your Grace: For though I had fallen low as the very Center, the Glory of this Interview would raise me up again. My Squire indeed, a Vengeance seize him for't, is much more apt to give his saucy Idle Tongue a Loose, than to gird a Saddle well; but Prostrate or Erect, on Horseback or on Foot, in any Posture I shall always be at your Grace's Command, and no less at her Grace's, your worthy Consort's Service. Worthy did I say, yes, she is worthy to be call'd the Queen of Beauty and Sovereign Lady of all Courtesy. Pardon me there, said the Duke, Noble Don *Quixote de la Mancha*; where the Peerless *Dulcinea* is remember'd, the Praise of all other Beauties ought to be forgot.

Sancho was now got clear of the Noose, and standing near the Dutchess, an't please your Worship's Highness, quoth he, before his Master could answer, it can't be deny'd, nay, I dare vouch it in any Ground in *Spain*, that my Lady *Dulcinea del Toboso* is woundy handsome and fair: But *where we least think, there starts the Hare*. I've heard your great Scholards say, That she you call Dame Nature, is like a Potter, and he that makes one handsome Pipkin may make two or three Hundred. And so, d'ye see, you may understand by this, that my Lady Dutchess here does not a jot come short of my Lady *Dulcinea del Toboso*. Don *Quixote*, upon this, addressing himself to the Dutchess, Your Grace must know, said he, that no Knight-Errant ever had such an eternal Babler, such a bundle of Conceit for a Squire, as I have; and if I have the honour to continue for some

221

time in your Service, your Grace will find it true. I am glad, answer'd the Dutchess, that honest *Sancho* has his Conceits, it's a shrewd sign he is wise; for merry Conceits, you know, Sir, are not the Offspring of a dull Brain, and therefore if *Sancho* be jovial and jocose, I'll warrant him also a Man of Sense: And a Prater, Madam, added Don *Quixote*. So much the better, said the Duke; for a Man that talks well, can never talk too much. But not to lose our time here, Come on, Sir Knight of the Woful Figure,———Knight of the Lions, your Highness should say, quoth *Sancho*: The Woful Figure is out of Date; and so pray let the Lions come in play. Well then, said the Duke, I intreat the Knight of the Lions to vouchsafe us his Presence at a Castle I have hard by, where he shall find such Entertainment as is justly due to so eminent a Personage, such Honours as the Dutchess and my self are wont to pay to all Knights-Errant that travel this Way.

Sancho having by this got *Rozinante* ready, and girded the Saddle tight, Don *Quixote* mounted his Steed, and the Duke a stately Horse of his own; and the Dutchess riding between 'em both, they mov'd towards the Castle: She desir'd that *Sancho* might always attend near her, for she was extremely taken with his notable Sayings; *Sancho* was not hard to be intreated, but crowded in between 'em, and made a fourth in their Conversation, to the great Satisfaction both of the Duke and Dutchess, who esteem'd themselves very fortunate in having an Opportunity to entertain at their Castle such a Knight-Errant and such an Erring Squire.

XXXI: WHICH TREATS OF MANY
AND GREAT MATTERS

SANCHO was overjoy'd to find himself so much in the
Dutchess's Favour, flattering himself that he shou'd
fare no worse at her Castle than he had done at Don
Diego's and *Basil's* Houses; for he was ever a Cordial
Friend to a plentiful way of Living, and therefore
never fail'd to take such Opportunities by the Fore-
top, where-ever he met them. Now the History tells us, that
before they got to the Castle, the Duke rode away from them,
to instruct his Servants how to behave themselves toward Don
Quixote; so that no sooner did the Knight come near the Gates,
but he was met by two of the Duke's Lacquies or Grooms in
long Vests, like Night-Gowns, of fine Crimson Sattin. These
suddenly took him in their Arms, and lifting him from his Horse
without any further Ceremony, Go great and mighty Sir, said
they, and help my Lady Dutchess down. Thereupon Don *Quixote* went and offer'd to do it; and many Compliments, and much
Ceremony pass'd on both sides: but in Conclusion, the Dutchess's Earnestness prevail'd; for she would not alight from her
Palfry but in the Arms of her Husband, excusing her self from
incommoding so great a Knight with so insignificant a Burden.
With that the Duke took her down. And now, being enter'd
into a large Court-yard, there came two Beautiful Damsels,
who threw a long Mantle of fine Scarlet over Don *Quixote's*
Shoulders. In an Instant, all the Galleries about the Court-yard
were crouded with Men and Women, the Domesticks of the
Duke, who cry'd out, Welcome, Welcome, the Flower and
Cream of Knight-Errantry! Then most, if not all of them,
sprinkl'd whole Bottles of sweet Water upon Don *Quixote*, the
Duke and the Dutchess: All which agreeably surpriz'd the
Don, and this was indeed the first Day he knew and firmly believ'd himself to be a Real Knight-Errant, and that his Knighthood was more than Fancy; finding himself treated just as
he had read the Brothers of the Order were entertain'd in
former Ages.

Sancho was so transported, that he even forsook his beloved
Dapple, to keep close to the Dutchess, and enter'd the Castle

with the Company: But his Conscience flying in his Face for leaving that dear Companion of his alone, he went to a Reverend old Waiting-Woman, who was one of the Dutchess's Retinue, and whispering her in the Ear, Mrs *Gonsales*, or Mrs —— Pray forsooth may I crave your Name? *Donna Rodriguez de Grijalva* is my Name, said the old *Duenna*; What is your Business with me, Friend? Pray now, Mistress, quoth *Sancho*, do so much as go out at the Castle-Gate, where you'll find a *Dapple* Ass of mine; see him put into the Stable, or else put him in your self; for poor thing, 'tis main fearful and timersome, and can't abide to be alone in a strange Place. If the Master, said she pettishly, has no more Manners than the Man, we shall have a fine time on't. Get you gone, you saucy Jack, the Devil take thee and him that brought you hither to affront me. Go seek somewhere else for Ladies to look to your Ass, you Lolpoop! I'd have you to know, that Gentlewomen like me are not us'd to such Drudgeries. Don't take Pepper in your Nose at it, reply'd *Sancho*, you need not be so frumpish, Mistress. As good as you have done it. I have heard my Master say (and he knows all the Histories in the World) that when Sir *Lancelot* came out of *Britain*, Damsels look'd after him, and Waiting-women after his Horse. Now by my Troth! whether you believe it or no, I would not swop my Ass for Sir *Lancelot's* Horse, I'll tell you that. I think the Fool rides the Fellow, quoth the Waiting-woman: Hark you, Friend, if you be a Buffoon, keep your Stuff for those Chapmen that will bid you fairer. I would not give a Fig for all the Jests in Your Budget. Well enough yet, quoth *Sancho*, and a Fig for you too, an' you go to that: Adad! should I take thee for a Fig, I might be sure of a ripe one, your Fig is rotten Ripe, forsooth; say no more: if Sixty is the Game, you're a Peep out. You Rascally Son of a Whore, cried the Waiting-woman, in a pelting Chafe, whether I am Old or no, Heaven best knows, I shall not stand to give an Account to such a Ragamuffin as thou, thou Garlick-eating Stinkard. She spoke this so loud, that the Dutchess over-heard her; and seeing the Woman so altered and as red as Fire, asked what was the Matter? Why, Madam, said the Waiting-woman, here's a Fellow would have me put his Ass in the Stable; telling me an idle Story of Ladies that looked after one *Lancelot*, and Waiting-women after his Horse; and because I won't be his Ostler, the Rake-shame very civilly calls me Old. Old, said the Dutchess, that's an Affront no Woman can well bear. You are mistaken, honest *Sancho*, *Rodriguez* is very Young, and the long Veil she wears, is more for Authority and Fashion-sake, than upon account of her Years. May there be ne'er a good one in all those I've to live, quoth *Sancho*, if I meant her any Harm, only I've such a natural Love for my Ass, an't like your Worship, that I thought I cou'd not recommend the poor Titt to a more charitable Body than this same Madam *Rodriguez*. *Sancho*, said Don *Quixote*, with a sour Look, do's this Talk befit this Place? D'you know where you are? Sir, quoth *Sancho*, every Man must tell his Wants, be he where he will. Here I bethought my self of *Dapple*, and here I spoke of him: Had I call'd him to mind in the Stable, I wou'd have spoken of him there.

Sancho has Reason on his side, said the Duke; and no Body ought to chide him for it. But let him take no further care, *Dapple* shall have as much Provender as he will eat, and be us'd as well as *Sancho* himself.

These small Jars being over, which yielded Diversion to all the Company, except Don *Quixote*, he was led up a stately Stair-Case, and then into a noble Hall, sumptuously hung with rich Gold Brocade. There his Armour was taken off by Six young Damsels, that serv'd him instead of Pages, all of 'em fully instructed by the Duke and Dutchess how to behave themselves so towards Don *Quixote*, that he might look on his Entertainment as conformable to those which the famous Knights-Errant receiv'd of Old.

When he was unarm'd, he appear'd in his close Breeches and Shamoy-doublet, raw-boned and meagre, tall and lank, with a pair of Lantern-Jaws that met i' the middle of his Mouth; in short, he made so very odd a Figure, that notwithstanding the strict Injunction the Duke had laid on the Young Females who waited on him, to stifle their Laughter, they were hardly able to contain. They desir'd he would give 'em leave to take off his Cloaths, and put him on a clean Shirt. But he would by no Means permit it, giving 'em to understand, That Modesty was as commendable a Vertue in a Knight as Valour; and therefore he desir'd them to leave the Shirt with *Sancho*; and

then retiring to an adjacent Chamber, where there was a rich
Bed, he lock'd himself up with his Squire, pull'd of his Cloaths,
shifted himself, and then while they were alone he began to
take him to Task.

Now said he, modern Buffoon and Jolter-head of old, what
can'st thou say for thy self? Where learned you to abuse such
a Venerable Ancient Gentlewoman, one so worthy of Respect
as *Donna Rodriguez*? Was that a proper time to think of your
Dapple? Or can you think Persons of Quality, who nobly entertain the Masters, forget to provide for their Beasts? For
Heaven's sake, *Sancho*, mend thy Behaviour, and don't betray
thy home-spun Breeding, lest thou be thought a Scandal to thy
Master. Dost not thou know, saucy Rustick, that the World
often makes an Estimate of the Master's Discretion by that of
his Servant, and that one of the most considerable Advantages the Great have over their Inferiors, is to have Servants as
good as themselves? Art thou not sensible, pitiful Fellow as
thou art, the more unhappy I, that if they find thee a gross
Clown, or a mad Buffoon, they will take me for some Hedge-
Knight or paltry shifting Rook? Pr'ythee, therefore, dear *Sancho*, shun these Inconveniencies; for he that aims too much at
Jests and Drolling, is apt to trip and tumble, and is at last despis'd as an insipid ridiculous Buffoon. Then curb thy Tongue,
think well, and ponder thy Words before they get loose; and
take notice, we are come to a Place, whence by the Assistance
of Heaven and the Force of this puissant Arm, we may depart
better five to one in Fortune and Reputation. *Sancho* promis'd
him to behave himself better for the future, and to sew up his
Mouth or bite out his Tongue, rather than speak one Word
which was not duly consider'd, and to the purpose; so that his
Master need not fear any one shou'd find out what they were.
Don *Quixote* then dress'd himself, put on his Belt and Sword,
threw his Scarlet Cloak over his Shoulders, and clapt on a Mon-
teer Cap of Green Velvet, which had been left him by the Damsels. Thus accoutred he enter'd the State-Room, where he
found the Damsels rang'd in two Rows, attending with Water,
and all Necessaries to wash him in State; and having done him
that Office, with many humble Curt'sies, and solemn Ceremonies, immediately twelve Pages with the Gentleman-Sewer

at the Head of 'em, came to conduct him to Supper, letting him know that the Duke and Dutchess expected him. Accordingly, they led 'em in great Pomp, some walking before and some behind, into another Room, where a Table was magnificently set out for four People.

As soon as he approach'd, the Duke and the Dutchess came as far as the Door to receive him, and with them a grave Clergyman, one of those that assume to govern Great Men's Houses, and who, not being nobly born themselves, don't know how to instruct those that are, but would have the Liberality of the Great measur'd by the Narrowness of their own Souls, making those whom they govern Stingy, when they pretend to teach 'em Frugality. One of these in all likelihood was this grave Ecclesiastick, who came with the Duke to receive Don *Quixote.*

After a thousand courtly Compliments on all sides, Don *Quixote* at last approach'd the Table, between the Duke and the Dutchess, and here arose a fresh Contest; for the Knight, being offer'd the Upper End of the Table, thought himself oblig'd to decline it. However, he cou'd not withstand the Duke's pressing Importunities, but was forced at last to comply. The Parson sat right against him, and the Duke and the Dutchess on each Side.

Sancho stood by all the while, gaping with wonder to see the Honour done his Master; and observing how many Ceremonies pass'd, and what Intreaties the Duke us'd to prevail with him to sit at the Upper End of the Table: With your Worship's good Leave, quoth he, I'll tell you what happen'd once in our Town, in reference to this stir and ado that you've had now about Places. The Words were scarce out of his Mouth, when Don *Quixote* began to tremble, as having reason to believe he was going to throw up some impertinent thing or other. *Sancho* had his Eyes upon him, and presently understanding his Motions, Sir, quoth he, don't fear; I won't be Unmannerly, I warrant you. I'll speak nothing, but what shall be pat to the purpose: I han't so soon forgot the Lesson you gave me about talking Sense or Nonsense, little or much. I don't know what thou mean'st, said Don *Quixote*; say what thou wilt, so thou do it quickly. Well, quoth *Sancho*, turning to the Duke, what I am going to tell you is every tittle true. Should I trip never so little in my Story, my Master is here to take me up, and give me the Lye. Pr'ythee, said Don *Quixote*, lie as much as thou wilt, for all Me; I won't be thy hindrance. But take heed however what thou say'st. Nay, nay, quoth *Sancho*, let me alone for that: I have heeded it and reheeded it over and over, and that you shall see——I warrant you. Truly, my Lord, said Don *Quixote*, it were convenient, that your Grace should order this Fellow to be turned out of the Room; for he will plague you with a thousand Impertinences. Oh! as for that you must excuse us, said the Dutchess, for by the Duke's Life I swear, * *Sancho* must not stir a step from me; I'll engage for him, he shall say nothing, but what's very proper. Many and many proper Years, quoth *Sancho* may your Holiness live, Madam Dutchess, for your good Opinion of me; though 'tis more your Goodness than my Desert. Now then for my Tale.

Once upon a Time a Gentleman in our Town, of a good Estate, and Family, for he was of the Blood of the *Alamos* of *Medina del Campo*, and married one *Donna Mencia de Quinones*, who was the Daughter of Don *Alonzo de Maranon*, a Knight of the Order of St *Jago*, the very same that was drown'd in the *Herradura*, about whom that Quarrel happen'd formerly in our Town, in which I heard say, that my Master Don *Quixote* was embroil'd, and little *Tom*, the Madcap, who was the Son of Old *Balvastro* the Farrier, happen'd to be sorely hurt——Is not all this true now, Master? Speak the Truth and shame the Devil, that their Worships Graces may know that I am neither a Prater nor a Liar. Thus far, said the Clergyman, I think thou art the first rather than the latter; I can't tell what I shall make of thee by and by. Thou producest so many Witnesses, *Sancho*, said Don *Quixote*, and mention'st so many Circumstances, that I must needs own, I believe what thou say'st to be true. But go on, and shorten the Story; for as thou beginnest, I am afraid thou'lt not have done these two Days. Pray don't let him shorten it, said the Dutchess: Let him go on his own way, tho' he were not to make an end these six Days; I shall hear him with Pleasure, and think the Time as pleasantly employ'd as any I ever pass'd in my Life——I say

* *A Custom in Spain to swear by the Life of those they love and honour.*

228

then, my Masters, quoth *Sancho*, that this same Gentleman I told you of at first, and I know him as well as I know my Right-Hand from my Left, for 'tis not a Bow-shot from my House to his; this Gentleman invited a Husbandman to Dine with him, who was a poor Man, but main Honest——On, Friend, said the Chaplain, at the rate you proceed you won't have made an end before you come to t'other World. I shall stop short of half Way, quoth *Sancho*, and it be Heaven's blessed Will: A little more of your Christian Patience, good Doctor! Now this same Husbandman, as I said before, coming to this same Gentleman's House, who had given him the Invitation, Heaven rest his Soul, poor Heart! for he's now dead and gone; and more than that, they say, he dy'd the Death of an Angel. For my part, I was not by him when he dy'd; for I was gone to Harvest-Work, at that very Time, to a Place call'd *Temblique*. Prithee, honest Friend, said the Clergyman, leave your Harvest Work and come back quickly from *Temblique*, without staying to bury the Gentleman, unless you've a Mind to occasion more Funerals; therefore pray make an end of your Story.—You must know then, quoth *Sancho*, that as they two were ready to sit down at Table,—I mean, the Husbandman and the Gentleman——Methinks I see them now before my Eyes plainer than ever I did in my born Days. The Duke and the Dutchess were infinitely pleas'd to find how *Sancho* spun out his Story, and how the Clergyman fretted at his Prolixity, and Don *Quixote* spent himself with Anger and Vexation. Well, quoth *Sancho*, to go on with my Story, when they were going to sit down, the Husbandman wou'd not sit till the Gentleman had taken his place; but the Gentleman made him a Sign to put himself at the Upper-end. *By no means*, Sir, quoth the Husbandman. *Sit down*, said t'other. *Good your Worship*, quoth the Husbandman—— *Sit where I bid thee*, said the Gentleman. Still the other excus'd himself, and would not; and the Gentleman told him, he should, as meaning to be Master in his own House. But the over-mannerly Looby, fancying he should be huge well-bred and civil in it, scrap'd and cring'd, and refus'd; till at last the Gentleman, in a great Passion, e'en took him by the Shoulders and forc'd him into the Chair. Sit there, clod-pate, cry'd he, for let Me sit where-ever I will, That still will be the Upper-end, and the

Place of Worship to thee. And now you have my Tale, and I think I ha' spoke nothing but what's to the Purpose.

Don *Quixote's* Face was in a thousand Colours that speckl'd its natural Brown; so that the Duke and Dutchess were oblig'd to check their Mirth, when they perceiv'd *Sancho's* Roguery, that Don *Quixote* might not be put too much out of Countenance. And therefore to turn the Discourse, that *Sancho* might not run into other Fooleries, the Dutchess ask'd Don *Quixote*, what News he had of the Lady *Dulcinea*, and how long it was since he had sent her any Giants or Robbers for a Present, not doubting but that he had lately subdu'd many such? Alas! Madam, answer'd he, my Misfortunes have had a Beginning, but, I fear, will never have an End. I have vanquished Giants, Elves, and Cut-throats, and sent them to the Mistress of my Soul, but where shall they find her? She is Inchanted, Madam, and transform'd to the ugliest Piece of Rusticity that can be imagin'd. I don't know, Sir, quoth *Sancho*, when I saw her last she seem'd to be the finest Creature in the Varsal World; thus far, at least, I can safely vouch for her upon my own Knowledge, that for Activity of Body, and Leaping, the best Tumbler of 'em all does not go beyond her. Upon my honest Word, Madam Dutchess, she'll Vault from the Ground upon her Ass like a Cat. Have you seen her Inchanted, said the Duke? Seen her, quoth *Sancho*? And who the Devil was the first that hit upon this Trick of her Inchantment, think you, but I? She is as much Inchanted as my Father.

The Churchman hearing 'em talk of Giants, Elves, and Inchantments, began to suspect this was Don *Quixote de la Mancha*, whose History the Duke so often us'd to read, tho' he had several times reprehended him for it; telling him, 'twas a Folly to read such Follies. Being confirm'd in his Suspicion, he address'd himself very angrily to the Duke. My Lord, said he, your Grace will have a large Account to give one Day, for Soothing this poor Man's Follies. I suppose this same Don *Quixote*, or Don *Quite Sot*, or whatever you are pleas'd to call him, cannot be quite so besotted as you endeavour to make him, by giving him such Opportunities to run on in his fantastical Humours. Then directing his Discourse to Don *Quixote*, Hark ye, said he, Goodman Addlepate, who has put it into your Crown that

230

you are a Knight-Errant, that you vanquish Giants and Robbers? Go, go, get you Home again, look after your Children, if you have any, and what honest Business you have to do, and leave wandering about the World, building Castles in the Air, and making yourself a Laughing-stock to all that know you, or know you not. Where have you found, in the Name of Mischief, that there ever has been or are now any such Things as Knights-Errant? Where will you meet with Giants in *Spain*, or Monsters in *La Mancha*? Where shall one find your inchanted *Dulcinea's* and all those Legions of Whimsies and Chimera's that are talk'd of on your Account, but in your own empty Skull?

Don *Quixote* gave this reverend Person the hearing with great Patience. But at last, seeing him Silent, without minding his Respect to the Duke and Dutchess, up he started with Indignation and Fury in his Looks, and said——But his Answer deserves a Chapter by itself.

XXXII: DON QUIXOTE'S ANSWER TO HIS REPROVER, WITH OTHER GRAVE AND MERRY ACCIDENTS

DON *Quixote* being thus suddenly got up, shaking from Head to Foot for Madness, as if he had Quick-silver in his Bones, cast an angry Look on his indiscreet Censor, and with an eager Delivery, sputtering and stammering with Choler: This Place, cry'd he, the Presence of these noble Persons, and the Respect I have always had for your Function, check my just Resentment, and tie up my Hands from taking the Satisfaction of a Gentleman. For these Reasons, and since every one knows that you Gown-men, as well as Women, use no other Weapon but your Tongues, I'll fairly engage you upon equal Terms, and combat you at your own Weapon. I should rather have expected sober Admonitions from a Man of our Cloth, than infamous Reproaches. Charitable and wholesome Correction ought to be manag'd at another rate, and with more Moderation, The least that can be said of this Reproof which you've given me here so bitterly, and in Publick, is, that it has exceeded the Bounds of Christian Correction, and a gentle one had been much more becoming. Is it fit, that without any Insight into the Offence which you reprove, you should without any more ado, call the Offender, Fool, Sot, and Addle pate? Pray Sir, what foolish Action have you seen me do, that should provoke you to give me such ill Language, and bid me so Magisterially go Home to look after my Wife and Children, before you know whether I have any? Don't you think those deserve as severe a Censure, who screw themselves into other Men's Houses, and pretend to Rule the Master? A fine World 'tis truly, when a poor Pedant, who has seen no more of it than lies within twenty or thirty Leagues about him, shall take upon him to prescribe Laws to Knight-Errantry and judge of those who profess it! You, forsooth, esteem it an idle Undertaking, and Time lost to wander through the World, though scorning its Pleasures, and sharing the Hardships and Toils of it, by which the Vertuous aspire to the high Seat of Immortality. If Persons of Honour, Knights, Lords, Gentlemen, or

Men of any Birth, should take me for a Fool or a Coxcomb, I should think it an irreparable Affront. But for mere Scholars, that never trod the Paths of Chivalry, to think me mad, I despise and laugh at it. I am a Knight, and a Knight will I die, if so it please Omnipotence. Some chuse the high Road of haughty Ambition; others the low Ways of base servile Flattery; a third sort take the crooked Path of deceitful Hypocrisy; and a few, very few, that of true Religion. I for my own Part, guided by my Stars, follow the narrow Track of Knight-Errantry; and for the Exercise of it, I despise Riches, but not Honour. I have redress'd Grievances, and righted the Injur'd, chastis'd the Insolent, vanquish'd Giants, and trod Elves and Hobgoblins under my Feet! I am in Love, but no more than the Profession of Knight-Errantry obliges me to be; yet I am none of this Age's vicious Lovers, but a chaste Platonick. My Intentions are all directed to vertuous Ends, and to do no Man Wrong, but Good to all the World. And now let your Graces judge, most excellent Duke and Dutchess, whether a Person who makes it his only Study to practise all this, deserves to be upbraided for a Fool.

Well said, I'faith! quoth *Sancho*; say no more for yourself, my good Lord and Master, stop when you're weil; for there's not the least matter to be added more on your side, either in Word, Thought, or Deed. Besides, since Mr Parson has had the Face to say point-blank, as one may say, that there neither are, nor ever were any Knights-Errant in the World, no mar'l he does not know what he says. What! said the Clergyman, I warrant, You are that *Sancho Pança*, to whom they say your Master has promis'd an Island? Ay, marry am I, answer'd *Sancho*; and I am he that deserves it as well as another Body; and I am one of those of whom they say, *Keep with good Men and thou shalt be one of them*; and of those of whom 'tis said again, *Not with whom thou wert bred, but with whom thou hast fed*; as also *lean against a good Tree, and it will shelter thee*. I have lean'd and stuck close to my good Master, and kept him Company this many a Month; and now He and I are all one; and I must be as He is, an't be Heaven's blessed Will; and so He live and I live, He will not want Kingdoms to Rule, nor shall I want Islands to Govern.

That thou shalt not, honest *Sancho*, said the Duke; for I, on the great Don *Quixote's* Account, will now give thee the Government of an odd one of my own of no small Consequence. Down, down on thy Knees, *Sancho*, cry'd Don *Quixote*, and kiss his Grace's Feet for this Favour. *Sancho* did accordingly: But when the Clergyman saw it, he got up in a great Heat. By the Habit which I wear, cry'd he, I can scarce forbear telling your Grace, that you are as mad as these Sinful Wretches. Well may they be mad, when such Wise Men as you humour and authorize their Frenzy; you may keep 'em here and stay with 'em yourself, if your Grace pleases; but for my part I'll leave you and go home, to save myself the labour of reprehending what I can't mend. With that, leaving the rest of his Dinner behind him, away he flung; the Duke and the Dutchess not being able to pacify him: Though indeed the Duke could not say much to him, for Laughing at his impertinent Passion. When he had done Laughing, Sir Knight of the Lions, said he, you have answer'd so well for yourself and your Profession, that you need no farther Satisfaction of the angry Clergyman; especially if you consider, that whatever he might say, it was not in his Power to fix an Affront on a Person of your Character, since Women and Churchmen cannot give an Affront. Very true, my Lord, said Don *Quixote*; and the Reason is, because he that cannot receive an Affront, consequently can give none. Women, Children and Churchmen, as they cannot vindicate themselves when they are injur'd, so neither are they capable of receiving an Affront. For there is this difference betwixt an *Affront* and *Injury*, as your Grace very well knows; an *Affront* must come from a Person that is both able to give it, and maintain it when he has given it. An *Injury* may be done by any sort of People whatsoever. For Example, a Man walking in the Street about his Business is set upon by Ten arm'd Men, who cudgel him; he draws his Sword to revenge the Injury, but the Assailants overpowering him, he cannot have the Satisfaction he desir'd. This Man is injur'd, but not affronted. But to confirm it by another Instance; Suppose a Man comes behind another's Back, hits him a Box o'the Ear, and then runs away, the other follows him, but can't overtake him. He that has received the Blow has received an Injury, 'tis true, but not an

Affront; because to make it an Affront, it should have been justify'd. But if he that gave it, though he did it basely, stands his Ground, and faces his Adversary, then he that receiv'd is both Injur'd and Affronted: Injur'd, because he was struck in a cowardly manner; Affronted, because he that struck him stood his Ground to maintain what he had done. Therefore according to the settled Laws of Duelling, I may be Injured but am not Affronted. Children can have no Resentment, and Women can't Fly, nor are they oblig'd to stand it out, and 'tis the same thing with the Clergy, for they carry no Arms either Offensive or Defensive. Therefore though they are naturally bound by the Laws of Self-preservation to defend themselves, yet are they not oblig'd to offend others. Upon second Thoughts then, though I said just now, I was Injur'd; I think now, I am not; for he that can receive no Affront, can give none. Therefore I ought not to have any Resentment for what that good Man said, neither indeed have I any. I only wish he would have staid a little longer, that I might have convinc'd him of his Error, in believing there were never any Knights-Errant in the World. Had *Amadis* or any one of his innumerable Race, but heard him say any thing like this, I can assure his Reverence, it would have gone hard with him. I'll be sworn it would, quoth *Sancho*; they would have undone him, as you would undo an Oyster; and have cleft him from Head to Foot, as one would slice a Pomegranate, or a ripe Muskmelion; take my word for't. They were a Parcel of tough Blades, and would not have swallow'd such a Pill. By the Mackins I verily believe, had *Rinaldo* of *Montalban* but heard the poor Toad talk at this rate, he would have laid him on such a Poult over the Chaps with his Shoulder o'Mutton Fist, as would have secur'd him from prating these three Years. Ay, ay, if he had fallen into their Clutches, see how he would have got out again!

The Dutchess was ready to die with laughing at *Sancho*, whom she thought a more pleasant Fool, and a greater Madman than his Master; and she was not the only Person at that time of this Opinion. In short, Don *Quixote* being pacify'd, they made an end of Dinner, and then while some of the Servants were taking away, there came in four Damsels, one carrying a Silver Bason, another an Ewer of the same Metal; a third two

235

very fine Towels over her Arm, and the fourth with her Sleeves tuck'd above her Elbows, held in her Lilly-white Hand (for exceeding white it was) a large Wash-ball of *Naples*-Soap. Presently she that held the Bason, went very civilly, and clapped it under Don *Quixote's* Chin, while he, wondring at this extraordinary Ceremony, yet fancying it was the Custom of the Country to wash the Face instead of the Hands, thrust out his long Chin, without speaking a Word; and then the Ewer began to rain on his Face, and the Damsel that brought the Wash-ball fell to Work, and belather'd his Beard so effectually, that the Suds, like huge Flakes of Snow, flew all over the passive Knight's Face; insomuch, that he was forc'd to shut his Eyes.

The Duke and Dutchess, who knew nothing of the matter, stood expecting where this extraordinary Scouring would end. The Female Barber, having thus laid the Knight's Face a soaking a handful high in Suds, pretended she wanted Water, and sent another with the Ewer for more, telling her the Gentleman would stay for it. She went and left him in one of the most odd ridiculous Figures that can be imagined. There he sat expos'd to all the Company, with half a yard of Neck stretch'd out, his bristly Beard and Chaps all in a white Foam, which did not at all mend his Walnut Complexion, insomuch that 'tis not a little strange how those that had so comical a Spectacle before 'em could forbear laughing out-right. The Malicious Damsels, who had a Hand in the Plot, did not dare to look up, nor let their Eyes meet those of their Master or Mistress, who stood strangely divided between Anger and Mirth, not knowing what to do in the Case, whether they should punish the Girls for their Boldness, or reward 'em for the Diversion they took in seeing the Knight in that Posture.

At last the Maid came back with the Water, and the other having rins'd off the Soap, she that held the Linen, gently wip'd and dry'd the Knight's Beard and Face; after which all four dropping a low Curt'sy, were going out of the Room. But the Duke, that Don *Quixote* might not smell the Jest, call'd to the Damsel that carried the Bason, and order'd her to come and wash Him too, but be sure she had Water enough. The Wench being sharp and cunning, came and put the Bason under the Duke's Chin, as she had done to Don *Quixote*, but with a quicker

Dispatch; and then having dry'd him clean, they all made their Honours, and went off. It was well they understood their Master's meaning, in serving him as they did the Knight; for as it was afterwards known, had they not done it, the Duke was resolv'd to have made 'em pay dear for their Frolick.

Sancho took great Notice of all the Ceremonies at this Washing. S'Life! quoth he, I'd fain know whether 'tis not the Custom of this Country to scrub the Squire's Beard, as wel as the Knight's. For o' my Conscience mine wants it not a little. Nay, if they would run it over with a Razor too, so much the better. What art thou talking to thy self *Sancho*, said the Dutchess? Why an't like your Grace's Worship, quoth *Sancho*, I'm only saying, that I've been told how in other great Houses, when the Cloth is taken away, they use to give Folks Water to wash their Hands, and not Suds to scour their Beards. I see now 'tis good to Live and Learn. There's a Saying indeed, He that lives long, suffers much. But I have a huge Fancy, that to suffer one of these same Scourings is rather a Pleasure than a Pain. Well, *Sancho*, said the Dutchess, trouble thy self no farther, I'll see that one of my Maids shall wash thee, and if there be occasion, lay thee a Bucking too. My Beard is all I want to have scrubb'd at present, quoth *Sancho*: As for the rest we'll think on it another time. Here, Steward, said the Dutchess, see that *Sancho* has what he has a mind to, and be sure do just as he would have you. The Steward told her Grace, that Signior *Sancho* shou'd want for nothing; and so he took *Sancho* along with him to Dinner.

Mean while Don *Quixote* stay'd with the Duke and Dutchess, talking of several Matters, but all relating to Arms and Knight-Errantry. The Dutchess then took an Opportunity to desire the Knight to give a particular Description of the Lady *Dulcinea del Toboso*'s Beauty and Accomplishments, not doubting but his good Memory would enable him to do it well; adding withal, that according to the Voice of Fame, she must needs be the finest Creature in the whole World, and consequently in all *La Mancha*.

With that, Don *Quixote*, fetching a deep Sigh, Madam, said he, cou'd I rip out my Heart, and expose it to your Grace's View in a Dish on this Table, I might save my Tongue the Labour of attempting that which it cannot express, and you can scarce believe; for there your Grace would see her Beauty depainted to the Life. But why should I undertake to delineate, and copy one by one each several Perfection of the Peerless *Dulcinea*! That Burden must be sustain'd by stronger Shoulders than mine: That Task were worthy of the Pencils of *Parrhasius*, *Timantes*, and *Apelles*, or the Graving-tools of *Lysippus*. The Hands of the best Painters and Statuaries shou'd indeed be employ'd to give in Speaking Paint, in Marble and *Corinthian* Brass, an exact Copy of her Beauties; while *Ciceronian* and *Demosthenian* Eloquence labour'd to reach the Praise of her Endowments. Pray, Sir, ask'd the Dutchess, what do you mean by that Word *Demosthenian*? *Demosthenian* Eloquence, Madam, said Don *Quixote*, is as much as to say, the Eloquence of *Demosthenes*, and the *Ciceronian* that of *Cicero*, the two greatest Orators that ever were in the World. 'Tis true, said the Duke; and you but shew'd your Ignorance, my Dear, in asking such a Question. Yet the Noble Don *Quixote* would highly oblige us, if he would but be pleas'd to attempt her Picture now; for even in a rude Draught of her Lineaments, I question not but she will appear so Charming, as to deserve the Envy of the Brightest of her Sex. Ah! my Lord, said Don *Quixote*, it would be so indeed, if the Misfortune which not long since befel her, had not in a Manner raz'd the Idea out of the Seat of my Memory; and as it is, I ought rather to bewail her Change, than describe her Person: For your Grace must know that as I lately went to Kiss her Hands, and obtain her Benediction and Leave for my intended Absence in quest of new Adventures, I found her quite another Creature than I expected. I found her Inchanted, Transform'd from a Princess to a Country-Wench, from Beauty to Ugliness, from Courtliness to Rusticity, from a Reserv'd Lady to a Jumping Joan, from Sweetness itself to the Stench of a Pole-cat, from Light to Darkness, from an Angel to a Devil; in short, from *Dulcinea del Toboso*, to a Peasantess of *Sayago*.* Bless us! cry'd the Duke with a loud Voice, What

---

* Villanos de Sayago *are properly Peasants of* Galicia, *which are accounted the most uncouth in all* Spain, *whence all rude People come to be compar'd with them. Here* Stevens *mistakes; for* Sayago *is a Territory about* Zamora, *in the Kingdom of* Leon (*not* Galicia) *as he himself says in his Dictionary*

Villain has done the World such an Injury? Who has robb'd it not only of the Beauty that was its Ornament, but of those charming Graces that were its Delight, and that Virtue which was its Living Honour? Who should it be, reply'd Don *Quixote*, but one of those damn'd Inchanters, one of those numerous Envious Fiends, that without Cessation persecute me? That wicked Brood of Hell, spawn'd into the World to Eclipse the Glory of Good and Valiant Men, and Blemish their Exploits, while they labour to Exalt and Magnify the Actions of the Wicked. These Cursed Magicians have Persecuted me, and Persecute me now, and will continue till they have sunk me and my lofty Deeds of Chivalry into the Profound Abyss of Oblivion. Yes, yes, they chuse to Wound me in that Part which they well know is most sensible: Well knowing, that to deprive a Knight-Errant of his Lady, is to rob him of those Eyes with which he sees, of the Sun that enlightens him, and the Food that sustains him. For as I have often said, a Knight-Errant without a Lady, is like a Tree without Leaves, a Building without Mortar, or a Shadow without a Body that causes it.

I grant all this, said the Dutchess; yet if we may believe the History of your Life, which was lately Publish'd with Universal Applause, it seems to imply, to the best of my Remembrance, that you never saw the Lady *Dulcinea*, and that there is no such Lady in the World; but rather that she is a meer Notional Creature, engender'd and brought forth by the Strength and Heat of your Fancy, and there Endow'd with all the Charms and good Qualifications, which you are pleas'd to ascribe to her.

Much may be said upon this Point, said Don *Quixote*; Heaven knows whether there be a *Dulcinea* in the World or not, and whether she be a Notional Creature or not. These are Mysteries not to be so narrowly enquir'd into. Neither have I Engender'd, or Begot that Lady. I do indeed make her the Object of my Contemplations, and as I ought, look on her as a Lady en-

the same says Sobrino *in his Dictionary too. The poor Country-People about* Zamora *are call'd* Sayagos *from* Sayal, *a coarse Sackcloth, their usual Cloathing, hence any poor People, especially Mountaineers, are call'd* Sayagos.

239

dow'd with all those Qualifications that may raise the Character of a Person to Universal Fame. She is to me beautiful without Blemish, reserv'd without Pride, amorous with Modesty,
agreeable for her Courteous Temper, and courteous, as an
Effect of her generous Education, and, in short, of an illustrious
Parentage. For Beauty displays its Lustre to a higher Degree
of Perfection when join'd with Noble Blood, than it can in those
that are meanly Descended.

The Observation is just, said the Duke; but give me leave,
Sir, to propose to you a Doubt, which the Reading of that History hath started in my Mind: 'Tis, that allowing there be a
Dulcinea at *Toboso*, or elsewhere, and as Beautiful as you describe her, yet I do not find she can any way equal in Greatness
of Birth the *Oriana's*,* the *Alastrajarea's*, the *Madasima's*,
and a thousand others of whom we read in those Histories,
with which you have been so Conversant, To this, said Don
Quixote, I Answer, that *Dulcinea* is the Daughter of her own
Actions, and that Virtue enobles the Blood. A Virtuous Man of
mean Condition, is more to be esteem'd than a Vicious Person
of Quality. Besides, *Dulcinea* is possess'd of those other Endowments that may entitle her to Crowns and Scepters, since
Beauty alone has rais'd many of her Sex to a Throne. Where
Merit has no Limits, Hope may well have no Bounds; and to
be Fair and Virtuous is so Extensive an Advantage, that it gives,
tho' not a *Formal*, at least a *Virtual* Claim to larger Fortunes. I
must own, Sir, said the Dutchess, that in all your discourse, you,
as we say, proceed with the Plummet of Reason, and Fathom
all the Depths of Controversy. Therefore, I submit, and from
this time I am resolv'd to believe, and will make all my Domesticks, nay, my Husband too, if there be Occasion, believe and
maintain, that there is a *Dulcinea del Toboso* extant, and living
at this Day; that she is Beautiful and of good Extraction; and
to sum up all in a Word, altogether deserving the Services of so
great a Knight as the Noble Don *Quixote*; which I think is the
highest Commendation I can bestow on her. But yet I must confess, there is still one Scruple that makes me uneasy, and causes
me to have an ill Opinion of *Sancho*. 'Tis that the History tells
us, that when *Sancho Pança* carried your Letter to the Lady

* *The Names of great Ladies in Romances.*

Dulcinea, he found her Winnowing a Sack of Corn, by the same Token that it was the worst sort of Wheat, which makes me much doubt her Quality.

Your Grace must know, answer'd Don *Quixote*, that almost every thing that relates to Me, is manag'd quite contrary to what the Affairs of other Knights-Errant us'd to be. Whether it be the unfathomable Will of Destiny, or the Implacable Malice of some envious Inchanter orders it so, or no, I can't well tell. For 'tis beyond all doubt, that most of us Knights-Errant still have had something peculiar in our Fates. One has had the Privilege to be above the Power of Inchantments, another Invulnerable, as the famous *Orlando*, one of the twelve Peers of *France*, whose Flesh, they tell us, was impenetrable every where but in the Sole of his left Foot, and even there too he cou'd be Wounded with no other Weapon than the Point of a great Pin; so that when *Bernardo del Carpio* deprived him of Life at *Roncesvalles*, finding he cou'd not Wound him with his Sword, he lifted him from the Ground, and squeez'd him to Death in his Arms; remembring how *Hercules* kill'd *Antæus*, that cruel Giant, who was said to be the Son of the Earth. Hence I infer, that probably I may be secur'd in the same manner, under the Protection of some particular Advantage, tho' 'tis not that of being Invulnerable; for I have often found by Experience, that my Flesh is tender, and not impenetrable. Nor does any private Prerogative free me from the Power of the Inchantment; for I have found myself clapp'd into a Cage, where all the World cou'd not have Lock'd me up, but the Force of Necromantick Incantations. But since I got free again, I believe that even the Force of Magick will never be able to confine me thus another time. So that these Magicians finding they cannot work their wicked Ends directly on me, revenge themselves on what I most esteem, and endeavour to take away my Life by persecuting that of *Dulcinea*, in whom, and for whom I live. And therefore I believe, when my Squire deliver'd my Embassy to her, they Transform'd her into a Country-Dowdy, poorly busied in the low and base Employment of Winnowing Wheat. But I do aver, that it was neither Rye, nor Wheat, but Oriental Pearl: and to prove this, I must acquaint your Graces, that passing t'other Day by *Toboso*, I could not so much as find *Dulcinea's* Palace; whereas my Squire went the next Day, and saw her in all her native Charms, the most beautiful Creature in the World! yet when I met her presently after, she appear'd to me in the Shape of an Ugly, Coarse, Country-Mawkin, Boorish, and Ill-bred, though she really is Discretion itself. And therefore, because I myself cannot be Inchanted, the unfortunate Lady must be thus Inchanted, Misus'd, Disfigur'd, Chopp'd and Chang'd. Thus my Enemies wreaking their Malice on Her, have reveng'd themselves on Me, which makes me abandon my self to Sorrow, till she be restor'd to her former Perfections.

I have been the more large in this Particular, that no Body might insist on what *Sancho* said, of her sifting of Corn: For if she appear'd chang'd to Me, what Wonder is it if she seem'd so to Him. In short, *Dulcinea* is both Illustrious and well-born, being descended of the most ancient and best Families in *Toboso*, of whose Blood I am positive she has no small Share in her Veins; and now that Town will be no less famous in After-Ages for being the Place of her Nativity, than *Troy* for *Helen*, or *Spain* for *Cava*,* though on a more honourable Account.

As for *Sancho Pança's* part, I assure your Grace he is one of the most pleasant Squires that ever waited on a Knight-Errant. Sometimes he comes out with such sharp Simplicities, that one is pleasantly puzzl'd to judge, whether he be more Knave or Fool. The Varlet, indeed, is full of Roguery enough to be thought a Knave; but then he has yet more Ignorance, and may better be thought a Fool. He doubts of every thing, yet believes every thing; and when one would think he had entangl'd himself in a piece of downright Folly beyond Recovery, he brings himself off of a sudden so cleverly, that he is applauded to the Skies. In short, I would not change him for the best Squire that wears a Head, tho' I might have a City to boot, and therefore I don't know whether I had best let him go to the Government which your Grace has been pleas'd to promise him. Though, I

---

* *The Nick-name of Count* Julian's *Daughter, who having been Ravish'd by King* Rodrigo, *occasion'd the bringing in of the* Moors *into* Spain. *Her true Name was* Florinda, *but as she was the occasion of* Spain's *being betray'd to the* Moors, *the Name is left off among the Women and commonly given to Bitches.*

must confess, his Talent seems to lie pretty much that way:
For, give never so little a whet to his Understanding, he will
manage his Government as well as the King does his Customs.
Then Experience convinces us, that neither Learning nor any
other Abilities, are very material to a Governor. Have we not
a Hundred of them that can scarce read a Letter, and yet they
govern as sharp as so many Hawks. Their main Business is only
to mean well, and to be resolv'd to do their best; for they can't
want able Counsellors to Instruct them. Thus those Governors
who are Men of the Sword, and no Scholars, have their Asses-
sors on the Bench to direct them. My Counsel to *Sancho* shall
be, that he neither take Bribes, nor lose his Privileges, with
some other little Instructions, which I have in my Head for
him, and which at a proper time I will communicate, both for
his private Advantage, and the publick Good of the Island he
is to Govern.

So far had the Duke, the Dutchess, and Don *Quixote* been
discoursing together, when they heard a great Noise in the
House, and by and by *Sancho* came running in unexpectedly
into the Room where they sate, in a terrible Fright, with a
Dish-clout before him instead of a Bib. The Scullions, and other
greasy Rabble of the Kitchen were after him, one of them pursuing him with a little Kneading-Trough full of Dish-water,
which he endeavour'd by any Means to put under his Chin,
while another stood ready to have wash'd the poor Squire
with it. How now, Fellow, said the Dutchess! What's the
Matter here? What would you do with this good Man? Don't
you consider he's a Governor Elect? Madam, quoth the Barber-
Scullion, the Gentleman won't let us wash him according to
Custom, as my Lord Duke and his Master were. Yes marry but
I will, quoth *Sancho*, in a mighty Huff, but then it shall be with
cleaner Sudds, cleaner Towels, and not quite so slovenly Paws;
for there's no such Difference between my Master and me
neither, that he must be wash'd with *Angel-Water*, and I with
the Devil's Lye: So far the Customs of great Men's Houses are
good as they give no Offence. But this same Beastly washing in
a Puddle, is worse Penance than a Friar's Flogging. My Beard
is clean enough, and wants no such refreshing. Stand clear,
you had best; for the first that comes to wash me, or touch a

Hair of my Head (my Beard I would say) Sir Reverence of the
Company, I'll take him such a Dowse o' the Ear, he shall feel
it a Twelve-month after: For these kind of Ceremonies and
Soapings, d'ye see, look more like Flouts and Jeers, than like a
civil Welcome to Strangers! The Dutchess was like to have
burst her Sides with Laughing, to see *Sancho's* Fury, and hear
how he argu'd for himself. But Don *Quixote* did not very well
like to see him with such a nasty Dish-clout about his Neck,
and made the Sport of the Kitchen-Pensioners. Therefore after
he had made a deep Bow to the Duke, as it were desiring leave
to speak, looking on the Scullions: Hark ye, Gentlemen, cry'd
he, very gravely, Pray let the Young Man alone, and get you
gone as you came, if you think fit. My Squire is as cleanly as another Man; that Trough won't do; you had better have brought
him a Dram-Cup. Away; he advis'd by me, and leave him: For
neither he nor I can abide such slovenly Jestings. No, no, quoth
Sancho, taking the Words out of his Master's Mouth, let them
stay, and go on with their Show. I'll pay my Barbers, I'll warrant ye. They had as good take a Lion by the Beard as meddle
with mine. Let 'em bring a Comb hither, or what they will,
and Curry-comb it, and if they find any thing there that should
not be there, I'll give 'em leave to cut and mince me as small as
a Horse. *Sancho* is in the right, said the Dutchess, still Laughing, and will be in the right, in all he says; he is as clean and
neat as can be, and needs none of your scouring, and if he does
not like our way of Washing, let him do as he pleases. Besides,
you who pretend to make others clean, have shewn yourselves
now very Careless and Idle, I don't know whether I mayn't
say Impudent too, to offer to bring your Kneading-Trough and
your Dish-Clouts to such a Person, and such a Beard, instead of
a golden Bason and Ewer, and fine Diaper-Towels. But you are
a Pack of unmannerly Varlets, and like saucy Rascals as you
are, can't help shewing your Spight to the Squires of Knights-
Errant.

The greasy Regiment, and even the Steward, who was with
them, thought verily the Dutchess had been in earnest. So they
took the Cloth from *Sancho's* Neck, and sneaked off quite out
of Countenance. *Sancho* seeing himself delivered from his Apprehension of this Danger, ran and threw himself on his Knees

before the Dutchess. Heaven bless your Worship's Grace, quoth he, Madam Dutchess. Great Persons are able to do great Kindnesses. For my Part, I don't know how to make your Worship amends for this you've done me now. I can only wish I might see myself an arm'd Knight-Errant for your sake, that I might spend all the Days of my Life in the Service of so high a Lady. I am a poor Country-Man, my Name is *Sancho Pança*, Children I have, and serve as a Squire. If in any of these Matters, I can do you any good, you need but speak; I'll be nimbler in doing than your Worship shall be in ordering. 'Tis evident *Sancho*, said the Dutchess, that you have learn'd Civility in the School of *Courtesy* itself, and have been bred up under the Wings of Don *Quixote*, who is the very Cream of Compliment, and the Flower of Ceremonies. All Happiness attend such a Knight and such a Squire; the one the *North Star* of Chivalry-Errant, the other the bright Luminary of Squire-like Fidelity. Rise, my Friend *Sancho*, and assure yourself, that for the Recompence of your Civilities, I will persuade my Lord Duke to put you in Possession of the Government he promis'd you, as soon as he can. After this, Don *Quixote* went to take his Afternoon's Sleep. But the Dutchess desir'd *Sancho*, if he were not very sleepy, he would pass the Afternoon with her and her Woman in a cool Room. *Sancho* told her Grace, that indeed he did use to take a good sound Nap, some four or five Hours long in a Summer's Afternoon; but to do her good Honour a Kindness, he would break an old Custom for once, and do his best to hold up that Day, and wait on her Worship. The Duke on his Side gave fresh Orders, that Don *Quixote* should be entertain'd exactly like a Knight-Errant, without deviating the least step from the Road of Chivalry, such as is observable in Books of that kind.

XXXIII: THE SAVOURY CONFERENCE WHICH THE DUTCHESS AND HER WOMEN HELD WITH SANCHO PANZA, WORTH YOUR READING AND OBSERVATION

THE Story afterwards informs us, that *Sancho* slept not a Wink all that Afternoon, but waited on the Dutchess as he had promised. Being mightily taken with his comical Discourse, she order'd him to take a low Chair and sit by her; but *Sancho*, who knew better things, absolutely declin'd it, till she press'd him again to sit as he was a Governor, and speak as he was a Squire; in both which Capacities he deserv'd the very Seat of *Cid Ruy Diaz*, the famous Champion. *Sancho* shrugg'd up his Shoulders and obey'd, and all the Dutchess's Women standing round about her to give her silent Attention, she began the Conference.

Now that we are private, said she, and no Body to over-hear us, I would desire you, my Lord Governor, to resolve me of some Doubts in the printed History of the great Don *Quixote*, which puzzle me very much. First, I find that the good *Sancho* had never seen *Dulcinea*, the Lady *Dulcinea del Toboso*, I should have said, nor carried her his Master's Letter, as having left the Table-Book behind him in *Sierra Morena*; how then durst he feign an Answer, and pretend he found her winnowing Wheat? A Fiction and Banter so injurious to the Reputation of the peerless *Dulcinea*, and so great a Blemish on the Character of a faithful Squire! Here *Sancho* got up without speaking a Word, laid his Finger on his Lips, and with his Body bent, crept cautiously round the Room, lifting up the Hangings, and peeping in every Hole and Corner: At last, finding the Coast clear, he return'd to his Seat. Now, quoth he, Madam Dutchess, since I find there's no Body here but ourselves, you shall e'en hear, without Fear or Favour, the Truth of the Story, and what else you'll ask me; but not a Word of the Pudding. First and Foremost I must tell you, I look on my Master Don *Quixote* to be no better than a down-right Madman, tho' sometimes he'll stumble on a Parcel of Sayings so quaint and so tightly put together, that the Devil himself could not mend 'em; but in the main, I can't beat it out of my Noddle but that he's as Mad as a *March* Hare. Now, because I'm pretty confident of knowing his blind Side, whatever Crotches comes into my Crown, though with-out either Head or Tail, yet can I make them pass upon him for Gospel. Such was the Answer to his Letter, and another Sham that I put upon him but t'other Day, and is not in Print yet, touching my Lady *Dulcinea's* Inchantment; for you must know, between you and I, she's no more inchanted than the Man in the Moon. With that, at the Dutchess's Request, he related the whole Passage of the late pretended Inchantment very faithfully, to the great Diversion of the Hearers. But Sir, said the Dutchess, I have another Scruple in this Affair no less unaccountable than the former; for I think I hear something whisper me in the Ear, and say, if Don *Quixote de la Mancha* be such a Shallow-brains, why does *Sancho Pança*, who knows him to be so, wait upon this Madman, and rely thus upon his vain extravagant Promises? I can only infer from this, that the Man is more a Fool than the Master; and if so, will not Madam Dutchess be thought as Mad as either of 'em, to bestow the Government of an Island, or the Command of others, on one who can't govern himself? By'r Lady, quoth *Sancho*, your Scruple comes in Pudding-time. But it need not whisper in your Ear, it may e'en speak plain, and as loud as it will. I am a Fool that's certain, for if I'd been wise, I had left my Master many a fair Day since; but it was my Luck and my vile Errantry, and that's all can be said on't. I must follow him through Thick and Thin. We are both Townsborn Children; I have eaten his Bread, I love him well, and there's no Love lost between us. He pays me very well, he has given me three Colts, and I am so very true and trusty to him, that nothing but Death can part us. And if your High and Mightiness does not think fit to let me have this same Government, why so be it; with less was I born, and with less shall I die; it may be for the Good of my Conscience to go without it. I am a Fool 'tis true, but yet I understand the Meaning of the Saying, the Pismire had Wings to do her Hurt; and *Sancho* the Squire may sooner get to Heaven than *Sancho* the Governor. There's as good Bread baked here as in *France*, and *Joan's* as good as my Lady in the Dark. In the Night all

247

Cats are gray. Unhappy's he that wants his Breakfast at Two in the Afternoon. 'Tis always good Fasting after a good Breakfast. There's no Man has a Stomach a Yard bigger than another, but let it be never so big, there will be Hay and Straw enough to fill it. A Belly full's a Belly full. The Sparrow speeds as well as the Sparrow-Hawk. Good Serge is fine, but coarse Cloth is warm; and four Yards of the one are as long as four Yards of the other. When the Hour is come we must all be pack'd off; the Prince and the Prick-Louse go the same Way at last: the Road is no fairer for the one than the other. The Pope's Body takes up no more room than the Sexton's, tho' one be taller; for when they come to the Pit, all are alike, or made so in spite of our Teeth,* and so good-night or good-morrow, which you please. And let me tell you again, if you don't think fit to give me an Island, cause I'm a Fool, I'll be so wise not to care whether you do or no. 'Tis an old Saying, the Devil lurks behind the Cross. All is not Gold that glisters. From the Tail of the Plough, *Bamba* was made King of *Spain*; and from his Silks and Riches was *Rodrigo* cast to be devoured by the Snakes, if the old Ballads say true; and sure they are too old to tell a Lye. That they are indeed, said *Donna Rodriguez*, the old Waiting-woman, who listen'd among the rest; for I remember one of the Ballads tells us, how Don *Rodrigo* was shut up alive in a Tomb full of Toads, Snakes and Lizards; and how after two Days, he was heard to cry out of the Tomb in a low and doleful Voice, Now they eat me, now they gnaw me in the Part where I sinn'd most: And according to this, the Gentleman is in the Right, in saying, He had rather be a poor Labourer, than a King, to be gnaw'd to Death by Vermin.

Sancho's proverbial Aphorisms, and the simple Waiting-woman's Comment upon the Text, were no small Diversion to the Dutchess. You know, said she, honest *Sancho*, that the Promise of a Gentleman or Knight, must be as precious and sacred to him as his Life; I make no Question then, but that my Lord Duke, who is also a Knight, though not of your Master's Order, will infallibly keep his Word with you in respect of

* *The common Sort in* Spain *are bury'd without Coffins, which is the Reason* Sancho *is made to suppose, if the Grave be not long enough they bow the Body, and cram it in: A clownish ignorant Notion, but never practiced.*

your Government. Take Courage then *Sancho*, for when you least dream on't, in spite of all the Envy and Malice of the World, you will suddenly see yourself in full Possession of your Government, and seated in your Chair of State in your rich Robes, with all your Marks and Ornaments of Power about you. But be sure to administer true Justice to your Vassals, who by their Loyalty and Discretion will merit no less at your Hands.

As for the governing Part, quoth *Sancho*, let me alone. I was ever charitable and good to the Poor, and scorn to take the Bread out of another Man's Mouth. On the other side, by'r Lady, they shall play me no foul Play. I'm an old Cur at a Crust, and can sleep Dog-sleep when I list. I can look sharp as well as another, and let me alone to keep the Cobwebs out of my Eyes. I know where the Shoe wrings me; I'll know who and who's together. Honesty's the best Policy. I'll stick to that. The Good shall have my Hand and Heart, but the Bad neither Foot nor Fellowship. And in my Mind, the main Point in this point of Governing, is to make a good Beginning. I'll lay my Life, that as simple as *Sancho* sits here, in a Fortnight's Time he'll manage ye this same Island as rightly as a Sheaf of Barly. You say well *Sancho*, said the Dutchess, for Time ripens all things. No Man's born wise; Bishops are made of Men, and not of Stones. But to return once more to the Lady *Dulcinea*; I am more than half persuaded that *Sancho's* Design of putting the Trick upon his Master, was turn'd into a greater Cheat upon himself: For I am well assured, that the Creature whom you fancy'd to be a Country-Wench, and took so much pains to persuade your Master that she was *Dulcinea del Toboso*, was really the same *Dulcinea del Toboso*, and really inchanted, as Don *Quixote* thought; and the Magicians that persecute your Master first invented that Story, and put it into your Head. For you must know, that we have our Inchanters here that have a Kindness for us, and give us an Account of what happens in the World faithfully and impartially, without any Tricks or Equivocations; and take my Word for't the jumping Country-Wench was and is still *Dulcinea del Toboso*, who is as certainly Inchanted as the Mother that bore her; and when we least expect it, we shall see her again in her true Shape and in all her native Lustre, and then *Sancho* will find 'twas he himself was bubbled. Troth Madam, quoth *Sancho*, all this might well be: And now I'm apt to believe what my Master tells me of *Montesino's* Cave; where, as he says, he saw my Lady *Dulcinea del Toboso* in the self same Garb, and as handsome as I told him I had seen her when it came into my Noddle to tell him she was inchanted. Ay, my Lady, it must be quite contrary to what I ween'd, as your Worship's Grace well observes; for, Lord bless us! who the Devil can imagine that such a Numskul as I should have it in him to devise so cunning a Trick of a sudden? Besides, who can think that my Master's such a Goose, as to believe so unlikely a Matter upon the single Vouching of such a dunder-headed Fellow as I? But for all that, my good Lady, I hope you know better things than to think me a Knave; alack-a-day, it can't be expected that such an Ignoramus as I am, shou'd be able to divine into the Tricks and Wiles of wicked Magicians. I invented that Flam only because my Master wou'd never leave teizing me; but I had no Mind to abuse him, not I; and if it fell out otherwise than I meant, who can help it? Heaven knows my Heart. That's honestly said, answered the Dutchess, but pray tell me, *Sancho*, What was it you were speaking of *Montesino's* Cave? I've a great Mind to know that Story. Thereupon *Sancho* having related the whole Matter to the Dutchess; Look you, said she, this exactly makes out what I said to you just now; for since the great Don *Quixote* affirms he saw there the same Country-Wench that *Sancho* met coming from *Toboso*, 'tis past all doubt 'twas *Dulcinea*; and this shews the Inchanters are a subtil sort of People that will know every thing, and give a quick and sure Information. Well, quoth *Sancho*, if my Lady *Dulcinea del Toboso* be inchanted, 'tis the worse for her: What have I to do to Quarrel with all my Master's Enemies? They can't be few for ought I see, and they are plaguy Fellows to deal withal. Thus much I dare say, She I saw was a Country-Wench; a Country-Wench I took her to be, and a Country-Wench I left her. Now if that same Dowdy was *Dulcinea* in good Earnest, how can I help it? I ought not to be call'd to an Account for't. No, let the Saddle be set upon the right Horse, or we shall ne'er ha' done. *Sancho* told me this, cries one, *Sancho* told me that, cries t'other; *Sancho* o'this Side, *Sancho* o'that Side; *Sancho* did this, and *Sancho* did that: as if *Sancho* were I don't know who, and not the same *Sancho* that goes already far and near thro' the World in Books, as *Sampson Carrasco* tells me, and he's no less than a Batchelor of Arts at *Salamanca* Varsity, and such Folks as he can't tell a Lye, unless they be so disposed, or it stands them in good stead. So let no Body meddle or make, nor offer to pick a Quarrel with me about the Matter, since I'm a Man of Reputation; and, as my Master says, a good Name is better than Riches. Clap me but into this same Government* once, and you shall see Wonders. He that has been a good Servant, will make a good Master; a trusty Squire will make a rare Governour I'll warrant you. *Sancho* speaks like an Oracle, said the Dutchess; every thing he says is a Sentence like those of *Cato*, or at least the very Marrow of *Michael Verino*:† *Florentibus occidit annis*; that is, he died in his *Spring*: In short, to speak after his Way, *Under a bad Cloke look for a good Drinker*.

Faith and Troth Madam Dutchess, quoth *Sancho*, I never drank out of Malice in my born Days; for Thirst perhaps I may; for I ha'nt a Bit of Hypocrisy in me, I drink when I have Occasion, and sometimes when I have no Occasion: I'm no proud Man, d'ye see, and when the Liquor's offer'd me I whip it off, that they mayn't take me for a Churl or a Sneaksby, or think I don't understand my self nor good Manners; for when a Friend or a good Fellow drinks and puts the Glass to one, who can be so hard-hearted as to refuse to pledge him, when it costs nothing but to open one's Mouth? However, I commonly look before I leap, and take no more than needs must.

* *In the Original* encaxenme esse govierno, *i.e.* case me but in this same Government. † *A young* Florentine *of exceeding great Hopes, who dy'd young, and whose Loss was lamented by all the Poets of his Time. His Fables and Distichs, in imitation of* Cato's, *are preserved and esteemed. He dy'd at Seventeen, rather than take his Physician's Advice, which was a Wife.* Politian *made the following Epitaph on this very learned Youth and excellent moral Poet of* Florence:

Sola *Venus* poterat lento succurrere morbo:
Ne se pollueret, maluit ille Mori.

Venus *alone his slow Disease cou'd cure:*
But He chose Death, rather than Life not pure.

And truly there's no fear we poor Squires to Knights-Errant should be great Trespassers that way. Alack-a-day! mere Element must be our daily Beveridge, Ditch-water, for want of better, in Woods and Desarts, on Rocks and Mountains, without lighting on the Blessing of one merciful Drop of Wine, though you'd give one of your Eyes for a single Gulp.

I believe it, *Sancho*, said the Dutchess; but now it grows late, and therefore go and take some Rest; after that we'll have a longer Conversation, and will take Measures about *clapping* you suddenly into this same Government, as you're pleas'd to word it. *Sancho* kiss'd the Dutchess's Hand once more, and begg'd her Worship's Grace that special Care might be taken of his *Dapple*, for that he was the Light of his Eyes. What is that *Dapple*, ask'd the Dutchess? My Beast, a'nt like your Honour, answer'd *Sancho*; my Ass I would say, saving your Presence; but because I won't call him Ass, which is so common a Name among Men, I call him *Dapple*. 'Tis the very same Beast I wou'd have given Charge of to that same Gentlewoman when I came first to this Castle; but her Back was up presently, and she flew out as if I had call'd her ugly Face, old Witch, and what not. However, I'll be judged by any one, whether such like sober grave Bodies as she and other *Duenas* are, be not fitter to look after Asses, than to sit with a prim Countenance to grace a fine State-Room? Passion o' my Heart! What a deadly Grudge a certain Gentleman of our Town, that shall be nameless, had to these Creatures! I mean these old waiting Gentlewomen.* Some filthy Clown I dare engage, said Donna *Rodriguez* the *Duena*; had he been a Gentleman, or a Person of good Breeding, he wou'd have prais'd them up to the Skies. Well, said the Dutchess, let's have no more of that; let Donna *Rodriguez* hold her Tongue, and Signior *Sancho Pança* go to his Repose, and leave me to take care of his *Dapple's* good Entertainment; for since I find him to be one of *Sancho's* Moveables, I'll place him in my Esteem above

* *The* Spanish Word is Duennas, *which are old Women, kept by Ladies for State only, and to make up the Number of their Attendants, as likewise to have an Eye over the young Maids, for Women of Quality keep many. By the Maids they are hated as Spies on their Actions, and by others are accounted no better than Bawds, so that by this means they become odious to all.*

the Apple of my Eye. Place him in the Stable, my good Lady, reply'd *Sancho*, that's as much as he deserves; neither he nor I are worthy of being placed a Minute of an Hour where you said: Odsbobs! I'd sooner be stuck in the Guts with a Butcher's Knife, than you should be served so; I am better bred than that comes to; for tho' my Lord and Master has taught me, that in Point of Haviour one ought rather to over-do than under-do, yet when the Case lies about an Ass and the Ball of one's Eye, 'tis best to think twice, and go warily about the Matter. Well, said the Dutchess, your Ass may go with you to the Government, and there you may feed him, and pamper him, and make as much of him as you please. Adad! my Lady, quoth *Sancho*, don't let your Worship think this will be such a strange Matter neither. I have seen more Asses than one go to a Government before now; and if mine goes too, 'twill be no new thing e'trow.

Sancho's Words again set the Dutchess a Laughing; and so sending him to take his Rest, she went to the Duke, and gave him an Account of the pleasant Discourse between Her and the Squire. After this they resolved to have some notable Contrivance to make Sport with Don *Quixote*, and of such a romantick Cast as should humour his Knight-Errantry. And so successful they were in their Management of that Interlude, that it may well be thought one of the best Adventures in this famous History.

Part II Book VI

I: CONTAINING WAYS AND MEANS FOR DIS-INCHANTING THE PEERLESS DULCINEA DEL TOBOSO, BEING ONE OF THE MOST FAMOUS ADVENTURES IN THE WHOLE BOOK

THE Duke and Dutchess were extremely diverted with the Humours of their Guests: Resolving therefore to improve their Sport, by carrying on some pleasant Design, that might bear the Appearance of an Adventure, they took the Hint from Don *Quixote's* Account of *Montesinos's* Cave, as a Subject from which they might raise an extraordinary Entertainment: The rather, since, to the Dutchess's Amazement, *Sancho's* Simplicity was so great, as to believe that *Dulcinea del Toboso* was really inchanted, though he himself had been the first Contriver of the Story, and her only Inchanter.

Accordingly, having given Directions to their Servants that nothing might be wanting, and propos'd a Day for Hunting the Wild Boar, in five or six Days they were ready to set out, with a Train of Huntsmen and other Attendants not unbecoming the greatest Prince. They presented Don *Quixote* with a Hunting-Suit, but he refus'd it, alledging it superfluous, since he was in a short Time to return to the hard Exercise of Arms, and could carry no Sumpters or Wardrobes along with him: But *Sancho* readily accepted one of fine green Cloth, with Design to sell it the first Opportunity.

The Day prefix'd being come, Don *Quixote* arm'd, and *Sancho* equipp'd himself in his new Suit, and mounting his Ass, which he would not quit for a good Horse that was offer'd him, he crowded in among the Train of Sportsmen. The Dutchess also in a Dress both odd and gay, made one of the Company. The Knight, who was Courtesy it self, very gallantly would needs hold the Reins of her Palfrey, though the Duke seem'd very unwilling to let him. In short, they came to the Scene of their Sport, which was in a Wood between two very high Mountains, where alighting, and taking their several Stands, the Dutchess with a pointed Javelin in her Hand, attended by the Duke and Don *Quixote*, took her Stand in a Place where they knew the Boars were used to pass through. The Hunters posted themselves in several Lanes and Paths as they most conveniently could: But as for *Sancho*, he chose to stay behind 'em all with his *Dapple*, whom he would by no means leave a Moment, for fear the poor Creature should meet with some sad Accident.

And now the Chace began with full Cry, the Dogs open'd, the Horns sounded, and the Huntsmen hollow'd in so loud a Consort, that there was no hearing one another. Soon after, a hideous Boar, of a monstrous Size, came on, gnashing his Teeth and Tusks, and foaming at the Mouth; and being baited hard by the Dogs, and follow'd close by the Huntsmen, made furiously towards the Pass which Don *Quixote* had taken. Whereupon the Knight grasping his Shield, and drawing his Sword, mov'd forward to receive the raging Beast. The Duke join'd him with a Boar-Spear, and the Dutchess would have been foremost, had not the Duke prevented her. *Sancho* alone, seeing the furious Animal, resolv'd to shift for one, and leaving *Dapple*, away he scudded as fast as his Legs would carry him towards an high Oak, to the Top of which he endeavour'd to clamber: But as he was getting up, one of the Boughs unluckily broke, and down he was tumbling, when a Snag or Stump of another Bough caught hold of his new Coat, and stopp'd his Fall, slinging him in the Air by the Middle, so that he could neither get up nor down. His fine green Coat was torn, and he fancy'd every Moment the wild Boar was running that way with foaming Chaps and dreadful Tusks to tear him to pieces; which so disturb'd him, that he roar'd and bellow'd for Help, as if some wild Beast had been devouring him in good earnest.

At last the Tusky Boar was laid at his Length with a Number of pointed Spears fix'd in him; and Don *Quixote* being alarm'd by *Sancho's* Noise, which he could distinguish easily, look'd about, and discover'd him swinging in the Tree with his Head downwards, and close by him poor *Dapple*, who like a true Friend never forsook him in his Adversity; for *Cid Hamet* observes, that they were such true and inseparable Friends, that *Sancho* was seldom seen without *Dapple*, or *Dapple* without *Sancho*. Don *Quixote* went and took down his Squire, who, as soon as he was at Liberty, began to examine the Damage his fine Hunting-Suit had receiv'd, which griev'd him to the Soul, for he priz'd it as much as if it had made him Heir to an Estate.

Mean while the Boar being laid across a large Mule, and cover'd with Branches of Rosemary and Myrtle, was carry'd in Triumph by the victorious Huntsmen to a large Field-Tent, pitch'd in the middle of the Wood, where an excellent Entertainment was provided suitable to the Magnificence of the Founder.

Sancho drew near the Dutchess, and shewing her his torn Coat, Had we been hunting the Hare now, or catching of Sparrows, quoth he, my Coat might have slept in a whole Skin. For my part, I wonder what Pleasure there can be in beating the Bushes for a Beast, which if it does but come at you, will run it's plaguy Tushes in your Guts, and be the Death of you: I han't forgot an old Song to this Purpose;

> *May Fate of* Fabila *be thine,*
> *And make thee Food for Bears or Swine.*

That *Fabila*, said Don *Quixote*, was a King of the *Goths*, who going a Hunting once, was devoured by a Bear. That's it I say, quoth *Sancho*; and therefore why should Kings and other great Folks run themselves into Harm's Way, when they may have Sport enough without it: Mercy on me! what Pleasure can you find, any of ye all, in killing a poor Beast that never meant any Harm! You are mistaken, *Sancho*, said the Duke, Hunting wild Beasts is the most proper Exercise for Knights and Princes; for in the Chace of a stout noble Beast, may be represented the whole Art of War, Stratagems, Policy and Ambuscades, with all other Devices usually practised to overcome an Enemy with Safety. Here we are expos'd to the Extremities of Heat and Cold; Ease and Laziness can have no Room in this Diversion: By this we are inur'd to Toil and Hardship, our Limbs are strengthen'd, our Joints made supple, and our whole Body hale and active: In short, it is an Exercise that may be beneficial to many, and can be prejudicial to none; and the most enticing Property is it's Rarity, being plac'd above the Reach of the Vulgar, who may indeed enjoy the Diversion of other Sorts of Game, but not this nobler Kind, nor that of Hawking, a Sport also reserv'd for Kings and Persons of Quality. Therefore, *Sancho*, let me advise you to alter your Opinion, against you become a Governor; for then you'll find the great Advantage of these Sports and Diversions. You're out, far wide, Sir, quoth *Sancho*, 'twere better that a Governor had his Legs broken, and be laid up at home, than to be gadding abroad at this Rate. 'Twould be a pretty Business, forsooth, when poor People come weary and tir'd to wait on the Governor about Business, that he should be rambling about the Woods for his Pleasure! There would be a sweet Government truly! Good faith, Sir, I think these Sports and Pastimes are fitter for those that have nothing to do than for Governors. No, I intend my Recreation shall be a Game at Whisk at *Christmas*, and Nine-pins on *Sundays* and Holidays; but for your Hunting, as you call it, it goes mightily against my Calling and Conscience. I wish with all my Heart, said the Duke, that you prove as good as you promise; but saying and doing are different Things. Well, well, quoth *Sancho*, be it how it will, I say that an honest Man's Word is as good as his Bond. Heaven's Help is better than early rising. 'Tis the Belly makes the Feet amble, and not the Feet the Belly. My Meaning is, that with Heaven's Help, and my honest Endeavours, I shall govern better than any Goshawk. Do but put your Finger in my Mouth, and try if I can't bite. A Curse on thee, and thy impertinent Proverbs, said Don *Quixote*: Shall I never get thee to talk Sense without a Sting of that disagreeable Stuff? I beseech your Graces, do not countenance this eternal Dunce, or he will teize your very Souls with a thousand unseasonable and insignificant old Saws, for which I wish his Mouth stitch'd up, and my self a Mischief, if I hear him. Oh, Sir, said the Dutchess, *Sancho's* Proverbs will always please for their sententious Brevity, though they were as numerous as a printed Collection; and I assure you, I relish 'em more than I would do others, that might be better, and more to the Purpose.

After this, and such like diverting Talk, they left the Tent, and walk'd into the Wood to see whether any Game had fall'n into their Nets. Now, while they were thus intent upon their Sport, the Night drew on apace, and more cloudy and overcast than was usual at that Time of the Year, which was about Mid-summer; but it happen'd very critically for the better carrying on the intended Contrivance. A little while after the Close of the Evening, when it grew quite dark, in a Moment the Wood seem'd all on Fire, and blaz'd in every Quarter. This was attended by an alarming Sound of Trumpets, and other warlike Instruments, answering one another from all Sides, as if several Parties of Horse had been hastily marching through the Wood: Then presently was heard a confus'd Noise of *Moorish* Cries, such as are us'd in joining Battle, which together with the Rattling of the Drums, the loud Sound of the Trumpets, and other Instruments of War, made such a hideous and dreadful Consort in the Air, that the Duke was amaz'd, the Dutchess astonish'd, Don *Quixote* was surpriz'd, and *Sancho* shook like a Leaf, and even those that knew the Occasion of all this were affrighted.

This Consternation caus'd a general Silence, and by and by one riding Post, equipp'd like a Devil, pass'd by the Company, winding a huge hollow Horn, that made a horrible hoarse Noise. Hark you, Post, said the Duke, whither so fast? What are you? and what Parties of Soldiers are these that march across the Wood? I am the Devil, cry'd the Post in a horrible Tone, and go in Quest of Don *Quixote de la Mancha*; and those that are coming this Way, are six Bands of Necromancers, that conduct the Peerless *Dulcinea del Toboso*, inchanted in a triumphant Chariot. She is attended by that gallant *French* Knight, *Montesinos*, who comes to give Information how she may be freed from Inchantment. Wer't thou as much a Devil, said the Duke, as thy horrid Shape speaks thee to be, thou wouldst have known this Knight here before thee to be that Don *Quixote de la Mancha* whom thou seekest. Before Heaven, and on my Conscience, reply'd the Devil, I never thought on't; for I have so many Things in my Head, that it almost distracts me; I had quite and clean forgot my Errand. Surely, quoth *Sancho*, this Devil must be a very honest Fellow, and a good Christian; for he swears as devoutly by Heaven and his Conscience, as I should do; and now I am apt to believe there be some good People even in Hell. At the same time, the Devil directing himself to Don *Quixote*, without dismounting; To thee, O Knight of the Lions, cry'd he, (and I wish thee fast in their Claws) to thee am I sent by the valiant, but unfortunate *Montesinos*, to bid thee attend his Coming in this very Place, whither he brings one whom they call *Dulcinea del Toboso*, in order to give thee Instructions touching her Disinchantment. Now I have deliver'd my Message, I must fly, and the Devils that are like me be with thee, and Angels guard the rest. This said, he winded his monstrous Horn, and, without staying for an Answer, disappear'd.

This increas'd the general Consternation, but most of all surpriz'd Don *Quixote* and *Sancho*; the latter, to find that, in Spite of Truth, they still would have *Dulcinea* to be inchanted; and the Knight to think that the Adventures of *Montesinos's* Cave were turn'd to Reality. While he stood pondering these Things in his Thoughts; Well, Sir, said the Duke to him, what do you intend to do? Will you stay? Stay! cry'd Don *Quixote*, shall I not? I will stay here, intrepid and couragious, though all the infernal Powers inclos'd me round. So you may if you will, quoth *Sancho*, but if any more Devils or Horns come hither, they shall as soon find me in *Flanders* as here.

Now the Night grew darker and darker, and several shooting Lights were seen glancing up and down the Wood, like Meteors or glaring Exhalations from the Earth. Then was heard an horrid Noise, like the Creaking of the ungreas'd Wheels of heavy Waggons, from which piercing ungrateful Sound, Bears and Wolves themselves are said to fly. This odious Jarring was presently seconded by a greater, which seem'd to be the dreadful Din and Shocks of four several Engagements in each Quarter of the Wood, with all the Sounds and Hurry of so many join'd Battles. On one Side were heard several Peals of Cannon; on the other the Discharging of numerous Vollies of small Shot; here the Shouts of the engaging Parties that seem'd to be near at hand; there Cries of the *Moors* that seem'd at a great Distance. In short, the strange confus'd Intermixture of Drums, Trumpets, Cornets, Horns, the Thund'ring of the Cannon, the Rattling of the small Shot, the Creaking of the Wheels, and the Cries of the Combatants, made the most dismal Noise imaginable, and try'd Don *Quixote's* Courage to the uttermost. But poor *Sancho* was annihilated, and fell into a

Swoon upon the Dutchess's Coats, who taking Care of him,
and ordering some Water to be sprinkled in his Face, at last
recover'd him, just as the foremost of the creaking Carriages
came up, drawn by four heavy Oxen cover'd with Mourning,
and carrying a large lighted Torch upon each Horn. On the Top
of the Cart or Waggon was an exalted Seat, on which sate a
venerable old Man, with a Beard as white as Snow, and so
long that it reach'd down to his Girdle. He was clad in a long
Gown of black Buckram, as were also two Devils that drove
the Waggons, both so very monstrous and ugly, that *Sancho*
having seen 'em once, was forc'd to shut his Eyes, and would
not venture upon a second Look. The Cart, which was stuck
full of Lights within, being approach'd to the Standing, the
reverend old Man stood up, and cry'd with a loud Voice, *I am
the Sage* Lirgander; and the Cart pass'd on without one Word
more being spoken. Then follow'd another Cart with another
grave old Man, who making the Cart stop at a convenient Distance, rose up from his high Seat, and in as deep a Tone as the
first, cry'd, *I am the Sage* Alquif, *great Friend to* Urganda *the
unknown*; and so went forward. He was succeeded by a third
Cart, that mov'd in the same solemn Pace, and bore a Person
not so ancient as the rest, but a robust and sturdy, sour-look'd,
ill-favour'd Fellow, who rose up from his Throne like the rest,
and with a more hollow and Devil-like Voice, cry'd out, *I am*
Archelaus *the Inchanter, the mortal Enemy of* Amadis de Gaul,
and all his Race; which said, he pass'd by, like the other Carts;
which taking a short Turn, made a Halt, and the grating Noise
of the Wheels ceasing, an excellent Consort of sweet Musick
was heard, which mightily comforted poor *Sancho*, and passing with him for a good Omen, My Lady, (quoth he to the
Dutchess, from whom he would not budge an Inch) there can
be no Mischief sure where there's Musick. Very true, said the
Dutchess, especially when there is Brightness and Light. Ay,
but there's no Light without Fire, reply'd *Sancho*, and Brightness comes most from Flames; who knows but those about us
may burn us? But Musick I take to be always a Sign of Feasting
and Merriment. We shall know presently what this will come
to, said Don *Quixote*; and he said right, for you will find it in
the next Chapter.

260

II: WHEREIN IS CONTINU'D THE INFORMATION GIVEN TO DON QUIXOTE HOW TO DISINCHANT DULCINEA, WITH OTHER WONDERFUL PASSAGES

WHEN the pleasant Musick drew near, there appear'd a stately triumphant Chariot drawn by six dun Mules cover'd with white, upon each of which sat a Penitent clad also in white, and holding a great lighted Torch in his Hand. The Carriage was twice or thrice longer than any of the former, twelve other Penitents being plac'd at the Top and Sides all in white, and bearing likewise each a lighted Torch, which made a dazling and surprizing Appearance. There was a high Throne erected at the further End, on which sat a Nymph array'd in Cloth of Silver, with many golden Spangles glittering all about her, which made her Dress, though not rich, appear very glorious: Her Face was cover'd with transparent Gauze, through the flowing Folds of which might be descry'd a most beautiful Face; and by the great Light which the Torches gave, it was easy to discern, that as she was not less than seventeen Years of Age, neither could she be thought above twenty. Close by her was a Figure clad in a long Gown like that of a Magistrate, reaching down to it's Feet, and it's Head cover'd with a black Veil. When they came directly opposite to the Company, the Shawms or Hautboys that play'd before, immediately ceas'd, and the *Spanish* Harps and Lutes, that were in the Chariot, did the like; then the Figure in the Gown stood up, and opening it's Garments, and throwing away it's mourning Veil, discover'd a bare and frightful Skeleton, that represented the deform'd Figure of Death; which startl'd Don *Quixote*, made *Sancho's* Bones rattle in his Skin for Fear, and caus'd the Duke and the Dutchess to seem more than commonly disturb'd. This living Death being thus got up, in a dull heavy sleeping Tone, as if it's Tongue had not been well awake, began in this Manner.

THE DECREE OF MERLIN

MERLIN'S SPEECH

Behold old Merlin, *in Romantick Writ,*
Miscall'd the spurious Progeny of Hell;
A Falshood current with the Stamp of Age:
I reign the Prince of Zoroastic Science,
That oft evokes and rates the rigid Pow'rs:
Archive of Fate's dread Records in the Skies,
Coevous with the Chivalry of Yore;
All brave Knights-Errant still I've deem'd my Charge,
Heirs of my Love, and Fav'rites of my Charms.

While other magick Seers, averse from Good,
Are dire and baleful like the Seat of Woe,
My nobler Soul, where Pow'r and Pity join,
Diffuses Blessings, as They scatter Plagues.

Deep in the nether World, the dreary Caves
Where my retreated Soul in silent State,
Forms mystick Figures and tremendous Spells,
I heard the peerless Dulcinea's *Moans.*

Appriz'd of her Distress, her frightful Change,
From princely State, and Beauty near divine,
To the vile Semblance of a rustick Quean,
The dire Misdeed of Necromantick Hate:
I sympathiz'd, and awfully revolv'd
Twice fifty thousand Scrolls, occult and loath'd,
Sum of my Art, Hell's black Philosophy;
Then clos'd my Soul within this bony Trunk,
This ghastly Form, the Ruins of a Man;
And rise in Pity to reveal a Cure
To Woes so great, and break the cursed Spell.

O Glory thou of all that e'er could grace
A Coat of Steel, and Fence of Adamant!
Light, Lanthorn, Path, and Polar Star and Guide
To all who dare dismiss ignoble Sleep
And downy Sloth, for Exercise of Arms,
For Toils continual, Perils, Wounds and Blood!
Knight of unfathom'd Worth, Abyss of Praise,
Who blend'st in one the Prudent and the Brave!
To thee, great Quixote, *I this Truth declare;*

That to restore her to her State and Form,
Toboso's *Pride, the peerless* Dulcinea,
'Tis Fate's Decree, That Sancho, *thy good Squire,*
On his bare brawny Buttocks should bestow
Three thousand Lashes, and eke three hundred more,
Each to afflict, and sting, and gall him sore.
So shall relent the Authors of her Woes,
Whose awful Will I for her Ease disclose.

Body o'me, quoth *Sancho*, three thousand Lashes! I won't give my self three; I'll as soon give my self three Stabs in the Guts. May you and your disinchanting go to the Devil. What a Plague have my Buttocks to do with the Black-Art? Passion of my Heart! Master *Merlin*, if you have no better Way for disinchanting the Lady *Dulcinea*, she may e'en lie bewitch'd to her dying Day for me.

How now, opprobrious Rascal! cry'd Don *Quixote*, stinking Garlick-eater! Sirrah, I will take you and tie your Dogship to a Tree, as naked as your Mother bore you; and there I will not only give you three thousand three hundred Lashes, but six thousand six hundred, ye Varlet, and so smartly, that you shall feel 'em still though you rub your Backside three thousand Times, Scoundrel. Answer me a Word, you Rogue, and I'll tear out your Soul. Hold, hold, cry'd *Merlin*, hearing this, this must not be; the Stripes inflicted on honest *Sancho* must be voluntary, without Compulsion, and only laid on when he thinks most convenient. No set Time is for the Task prefix'd, and if he has a Mind to have abated one half of this Atonement, 'tis allow'd; provided the remaining Stripes be struck by a strange Hand, and heavily laid on.

Hold you there, quoth *Sancho*, neither a strange Hand nor my own, neither heavy nor light shall touch my Bum. What a Pox, did I bring Madam *Dulcinea del Toboso* into the World, that my hind Parts should pay for the Harm her Eyes have done; Let my Master Don *Quixote* whip himself, he's a Part of her; he calls her, every foot, my Life, my Soul, my Sustenance, my Comfort, and all that. So e'en let him jirk out her Inchantment at his own Bum's Cost; but as for any whipping of me, I deny and pronounce* it flat and plain.

* A *Blunder of* Sancho's, *for* renounce.

No sooner had *Sancho* thus spoke his Mind, but the Nymph that sat by *Merlin's* Ghost in the glittering Apparel, rising, and lifting up her thin Veil, discover'd a very beautiful Face; and with a masculine Grace, but no very agreeable Voice, addressing *Sancho*; O thou disastrous Squire, said she, thou Lump with no more Soul than a broken Pitcher, Heart of Cork, and Bowels of Flint! Hadst thou been commanded, base Sheepstealer, to have thrown thy self headlong from the Top of a high Tower to the Ground; hadst thou been desir'd, Enemy of Mankind, to have swallow'd a dozen of Toads, two dozen of Lizards, and three dozen of Snakes; or hadst thou been requested to have butcher'd thy Wife and Children, I should not wonder that it had turn'd thy squeamish Stomach: But to make such a Hesitation at three thousand three hundred Stripes, which every puny School-boy makes nothing of receiving every Month, 'tis amazing, nay astonishing to the tender and commiserating Bowels of all that hear thee, and will be a Blot in thy Scutcheon to all Futurity. Look up, thou wretched and marble-hearted Animal; look up, and fix thy huge louring goggle Eyes upon the bright Luminaries of my Sight: Behold these briny Torrents, which, streaming down, furrow the flowery Meadows of my Cheeks: Relent, base and inexorable Monster, relent; let thy savage Breast confess at last a Sense of my Distress; and, mov'd with the Tenderness of my Youth, that consumes and withers in this vile Transformation, crack this sordid Shell of Rusticity that invelopes my blooming Charms. In vain has the Goodness of *Merlin* permitted me to reassume a while my native Shape, since neither that nor the Tears of Beauty in Affliction, which are said to reduce obdurate Rocks to the Softness of Cotton, and Tigers to the Tenderness of Lambs, are sufficient to melt thy haggard Breast. Scourge that brawny Hide of thine, stubborn and unrelenting Brute, that coarse Inclosure of thy coarser Soul, and rouse up thus thy self from that base Sloth, that makes thee live only to eat and pamper thy lazy Flesh, indulging still thy voracious Appetite. Restore me the Delicacy of my Skin, the Sweetness of my Disposition, and the Beauty of my Face. But if my Intreaties and Tears cannot work thee into a reasonable Compliance, if I am not yet sufficiently wretched to move thy Pity, at least let the Anguish of that miserable Knight, thy tender Master, mollify thy Heart. Alas! I see his very Soul just at his Throat, and sticking not ten Inches from his Lips, waiting only thy cruel or kind Answer, either to fly out of his Mouth, or return into his Breast.

Don *Quixote* hearing this, clapp'd his Hand upon his Gullet, and turning to the Duke; By Heavens, my Lord, said he, *Dulcinea* is in the right; for I find my Soul travers'd in my Windpipe like a Bullet in a Cross-bow. What's your Answer now, *Sancho*, said the Dutchess? I say, as I said before, quoth *Sancho*; as for the flogging, I pronounce it flat and plain. Renounce, you mean, said the Duke. Good your Lordship, quoth *Sancho*, this is no Time for me to mind Niceties, and spelling of Letters: I have other Fish to fry. This plaguy Whipping-bout makes me quite distracted. I don't know what I say or do —— But I would fain know of my Lady *Dulcinea del Toboso*, where she pick'd up this kind of Breeding, to beg thus like a sturdy Beggar? Here she comes to desire me to lash my Backside, as raw as a piece of Beef, and the best Word she can give, is, Soul of a broken Pitcher, Monster, Brute, Sheep-stealer, with a ribble rabble of saucy Nick-names, that the Devil himself would not bear. Do you think, Mistress of mine, that my Skin is made of Brass? Or shall I get any thing by your Disinchantment? Beshrew her Heart, where's the fine Present she has brought along with her to soften me? A Basket of fine Linen, Holland-Shirts, Caps and Socks (though I wear none) had been somewhat like. But to fall upon me, and bespatter me thus with dirty Names, d'ye think that will do? No, i'fackins: Remember the old Sayings, a golden Load makes the Burden light; Gifts will enter Stone-Walls; Scratch my Breech, and I'll claw your Elbow; a Bird in Hand is worth two in the Bush. Nay, my Master too, who, one would think, should tell me a fine Story, and coax me up with dainty Sugar-plumb Words, talks of tying me to a Tree, forsooth, and of doubling the whipping. Odsbobs! methinks those troublesom People should know who they prate to. 'Tis not only a Squire Errant they would have to whip himself, but a Governor; and there is no more to do, think they, but up and ride? Let 'em e'en learn Manners, with a Pox. There's a Time for some Things, and a Time for all Things; a

Time for great Things, and a Time for small Things. Am I now in the Humour to hear Petitions, d'ye think? just when my Heart's ready to burst, for having torn my new Coat; they would have me tear my own Flesh too, in the Devil's Name, when I have no more Stomach to it, than *to be among the Men-eaters.** Upon my Honour, *Sancho*, said the Duke, if you don't relent, and become as soft as a ripe Fig, you shall have no Government. 'Twould be a fine Thing indeed, that I should send among my Islanders a merciless hard-hearted Tyrant, whom neither the Tears of distress'd Damsels, nor the Admonitions of wise, ancient, and powerful Inchanters, can move to Compassion. In short, Sir, no Stripes, no Government. But, quoth *Sancho*, mayn't I have a Day or two to consider on't? Not a Minute, cry'd *Merlin*, you must declare now, and in this very Place, what you resolve to do, for *Dulcinea* must be again transform'd into a Country-Wench, and carried back immediately to *Montesinos's* Cave; or else she shall go as she is now to the *Elysian Fields*, there to remain till the Number of the Stripes be made out. Come come, honest *Sancho*, said the Dutchess, pluck up a good Courage, and shew your Gratitude to your Master, whose Bread you have eaten, and to whose generous Nature, and high Feats of Chivalry we are all so much oblig'd: Come, Child, give your Consent, and make a Fool of the Devil: Hang Fear, faint Heart ne'er won fair Lady; Fortune favours the brave, as you know better than I can tell you. Hark you, Master *Merlin*, (quoth *Sancho*, without giving the Dutchess an Answer) pray will you tell me one Thing. How comes it about, that this same Post-Devil that came before you, brought my Master Word from Signior *Montesinos* that he would be here, and give him Directions about this Disinchantment, and yet we hear no News of *Montesinos* all this while? Pshaw, answer'd *Merlin*, the Devil's an Ass, and a lying Rascal; he came from me, and not from *Montesinos*, for he, poor Man, is still in his Cave, expecting the Dissolution of the Spell that confines him there yet, so that he is not quite ready to be free, and the worst is still behind.† But if he owes you any Money, or you

* *In the original*, To turn Cacique; Bolverme Cazique. Caciques *are petty Kings in the* West-Indies.   † Aun le falta la cola por desollar, *i.e.* The Tail still remains to be flay'd: *Which is the most troublesom and hard to be done.*

have any Business with him, he shall be forth-coming, when, and where you please. But now pray make an End, and under-go this small Penance, 'twill do you a World of good; for 'twill not only prove beneficial to your Soul, as an Act of Charity, but also to your Body, as a healthy Exercise; for you are of a very sanguine Complexion, *Sancho*, and losing a little Blood will do you no Harm. Well, quoth *Sancho*, there is like to be no Want of Physicians in this World, I find; the very Conjurers set up for Doctors too. Well then, since every body says as much, (though I can hardly believe it) I am content to give my self the three thousand three hundred Stripes, upon Condition that I may be paying 'em off as long as I please; observe, that though I will be out of Debt as soon as I can, that the World mayn't be with-out the pretty Face of the Lady *Dulcinea del Toboso*, which, I must own, I could never have believ'd to have been so hand-som. *Item*, I shall not be bound to fetch Blood, that's certain; and if any Stroke happen to miss me, it shall pass for one how-ever. *Item*, Master *Merlin* (because he knows all Things) shall be oblig'd to reckon the Lashes, and take Care I don't give my self one more than the Tale. There's no Fear of that, said *Merlin*; for at the very last Lash the Lady *Dulcinea* will be disin-chanted, come straight to you, make you a Courtsy, and give you Thanks. Heaven forbid, I should wrong any Man of the least Hair of his Head. Well, quoth *Sancho*, what must be, must be: I yield to my hard Luck, and on the aforesaid Terms, take up with my Penance.

Scarce had *Sancho* spoke, when the Musick struck up again, and a congratulatory Volley of small Shot was immediately discharg'd. Don *Quixote* fell on *Sancho's* Neck, hugging and kissing him a thousand Times. The Duke, the Dutchess, and the whole Company seem'd mightily pleased. The Chariot mov'd on, and, as it pass'd by, the fair *Dulcinea* made the Duke and Dutchess a Bow, and *Sancho* a low Courtsy.

And now the jolly Morn began to spread her smiling Looks in the Eastern Quarter of the Skies, and the Flowers of the Field to disclose their bloomy Folds, and raise their fragrant Heads. The Brooks now cool and clear, in gentle Murmurs, play'd with the grey Pebbles, and flow'd along to pay their liquid crystal Tribute to the expecting Rivers. The Sky was clear, the Air serene, swept clean by brushing Winds for the Reception of the shining Light, and every Thing, not only jointly, but in it's separate Gaiety, welcom'd the fair *Aurora*, and, like her, foretold a fairer Day. The Duke and Dutchess, well pleased with the Management and Success of the Hunting, and the counterfeit Adventure, return to the Castle; resolving to make a second Essay of the same Nature, having receiv'd as much Pleasure from the first, as any Reality could have produced.

III: THE STRANGE AND NEVER-THOUGHT-OF AD-VENTURE OF THE DISCONSOLATE MATRON, ALIAS, THE COUNTESS TRIFALDI, WITH SANCHO PANZA'S LETTER TO HIS WIFE TERESA PANZA

THE whole Contrivance of the late Adventure was plotted by the Duke's Steward, a Man of Wit, and of a facetious and quick Fancy: He made the Verses, acted *Merlin* himself, and instructed a Page to personate *Dulcinea*: And now by his Master's Appointment, he prepar'd another Scene of Mirth, as pleasant and as artful, and surprizing as can be imagin'd.

The next Day, the Dutchess ask'd *Sancho* whether he had begun his penitential Task, to disinchant *Dulcinea*? Ay, marry have I, quoth *Sancho*, for I have already lent my self five Lashes on the Buttocks. With what, Friend, ask'd the Dutchess? With the Palm of my Hand, answer'd *Sancho*. Your Hand! said the Dutchess, those are rather Claps than Lashes, *Sancho*; I doubt Father *Merlin* won't be satisfied at so easy a Rate; for the Liberty of so great a Lady is not to be purchased at so mean a Price. No, you should lash yourself with something that may make you smart: A good Frier's Scourge, a Cat of Nine tails, or Penitent's Whip, would do well; for Letters written in Blood, stand good; but Works of Charity faintly and coldly done, lose their Merit, and signify nothing. Then, Madam, quoth he, will your Worship's Grace do so much as help me to a convenient Rod, such as you shall think best; though it must not be too smarting neither; for Faith, though I am a Clown, my Flesh is as soft as any Lady's in the Land, no Disparagement to any body's Buttocks. Well, well, *Sancho*, said she, it shall be my Care to provide you a Whip that shall suit your soft Constitution, as if they were Twins. But now, my dear Madam, quoth he, you must know I have written a Letter here to my Wife *Teresa Panza*, to give her to understand how Things are with me. I have it in my Bosom, and 'tis just ready to send away; it wants nothing but the Direction on the outside. Now I would have your Wisdom to read it, and see if it be not written like a

Governor; I mean, in such a Stile as Governors should write. And who penn'd it, ask'd the Dutchess? What a Question there is now, quoth *Sancho*? Who should pen it but my self, Sinner as I am? And did you write it too, said the Dutchess? Not I, quoth *Sancho*, for I can neither write, nor read; though I can make my Mark. Let's see the Letter, said the Dutchess, for I dare say, your Wit is set out in it to some Purpose. *Sancho* pull'd the Letter out of his Bosom unseal'd, and the Dutchess, having taken it, read what follows.

SANCHO PANÇA
to his wife
TERESA PANÇA

If I am well Lash'd, yet I am Whipp'd into a Government: I've got a good Government, it cost me many a good Lash. Thou must know, my Teresa, that I am resolv'd thou shalt ride in a Coach; for now any other Way of going, is to me, but creeping on all Fours, like a Kitten. Thou art now a Governor's Wife, guess whether any one will dare to tread on thy Heels. I have sent thee a Green Hunting-Suit of Reparel, which my Lady Dutchess gave me. Pray see and get it turn'd into a Petticoat and Jacket for our Daughter. The Folks in this Country are very ready to talk little Good of my Master, Don Quixote. They say he is a mad Wise-man, and a pleasant Mad-man, and that I an't a jot behindhand with him. We have been in Montesinos's *Cave, and* Merlin *the Wizard has pitch'd on me to disinchant* Dulcinea del Toboso, *the same who among you is call'd* Aldonsa Lorenzo. *When I have given my self three Thousand three Hundred Lashes, lacking five, she will be as disinchanted as the Mother that bore her. But not a Word of the Pudding; for if you tell your Case among a parcel of tattling Gossips, you'll ne'er have done; one will cry 'tis White, and others 'tis Black. I am to go to my Government very suddenly, whither I go with a huge Mind to make Money, as I am told all new Governors do. I'll first see how Matters go, and then send thee Word whether thou hadst best come or no.* Dapple *is well, and gives his humble Service to you. I won't part with him, though I were to be made the* Great Turk. *My Lady Dutchess kisses thy Hands a Thousand times over; pray return her two Thousand for her one; for there's nothing cheaper than fair Words, as my Master says. Heaven has not been pleased to make me light on another Cloak-Bag, with a hundred Pieces of Gold in it, like those you wot of. But all in good time; don't let that vex thee, my Jugg, the Government will make it up, I'll warrant thee. Though after all, one thing sticks plaguily in my Gizzard: They tell me, that when once I have tasted on't, I shall be ready to eat my very Fingers after it, so savoury is the Sauce. Should it fall out so, I should make but an ill hand of it; and yet your maim'd and crippl'd Alms-folks pick up a pretty Livelihood, and make their Begging as good as a Prebend. So that one way or other, Old Girl, matters will go swimmingly, and thou'lt be Rich and Happy. Heaven make thee so, as well it may; and keep me for thy Sake. From this Castle, the Twentieth of June, 1614.*

Thy Husband, the Governor,

Sancho Pança.

Methinks, Mr *Governor,* said the Dutchess (having read the Letter) you are out in two Particulars; first, when you intimate that this Government was bestow'd on you for the Stripes you are to give yourself; whereas you may remember, it was allotted you before this Dis-inchantment was dreamt of. The second Branch that you fail'd in, is the Discovery of your Avarice, which is the most detestable Quality in Governors; because their Self-Interest is always indulg'd at the Expence of Justice. You know the Saying, Covetousness breaks the Sack, and that Vice always prompts a Governor to fleece and oppress the Subject. Truly, my good Lady, quoth *Sancho,* I meant no harm, I did not well think of what I wrote, and if your Grace's Worship does not like this Letter, I'll tear it, and have another; but remember the old Saying, seldom comes a better. I shall make but sad Work on't, if I must pump my Brains for't. No, no, said the Dutchess, this will do well enough, and I must have the Duke see it.

They went then into the Garden, where they were to dine that Day, and there she shew'd the Duke the learn'd Epistle, which he read over with a great deal of Pleasure.

After Dinner, *Sancho* was entertaining the Company very pleasantly, with some of his savoury Discourse, when suddenly they were surpriz'd with the mournful Sound of a Fife, which play'd in Consort with a hoarse unbrac'd Drum. All the Company seem'd amaz'd and discompos'd at the unpleasing Noise, but Don *Quixote* especially was so alarm'd with this solemn Martial Harmony, that he could not compose his Thoughts. *Sancho's* Fear undoubtedly wrought the usual Effects, and carried him to crouch by the Dutchess.

During this Consternation, two Men in deep Mourning Cloaks trailing on the Ground, enter'd the Garden, each of 'em beating a large Drum cover'd also with Black, and with these a third playing on a Fife, in Mourning like the rest. They usher'd in a Person of a Gigantick Stature, to which the long black Garb in which he was wrapp'd up, was no small Addition: It had a Train of a prodigious Length, and over the Cassock was girt a broad black Belt, which slung a Scimitar of a mighty Size. His Face was cover'd with a thin black Veil, through which might be discern'd a Beard of vast Length, as white as Snow. The Solemnity of his Pace kept exact Time to the Gravity of the Musick: In short, his Stature, his Motion, his black Hue, and his Attendance, were every way surprizing and astonishing. With this State and Formality he approach'd, and fell on his Knees at a convenient distance, before the Duke; who not suffering him to speak till he arose, the monstrous Spectre erected his Bulk, and throwing off his Veil, discover'd the most terrible, hugeous, white, broad, prominent, bushy Beard, that ever mortal Eyes were frighted at. Then fixing his Eyes on the Duke, and with a deep sonorous Voice, roaring out from the ample Cavern of his spreading Lungs, *Most High and Potent Lord*, cry'd he, *my Name is* Trifaldin *with the white Beard, Squire to the Countess* Trifaldi, otherwise yclep'd, *the Disconsolate Matron*, from whom I am Ambassador to your Grace, begging Admittance for her Ladyship to come and relate, before your Magnificence, the unhappy and wonderful Circumstances of her Misfortune. But first, she desires to be inform'd whether the Valorous and Invincible Knight, Don *Quixote de la Mancha*, resides at this Time in your Castle; for 'tis in Quest of him that my Lady has travell'd without Coach or Palfrey, Hungry and thirsty, and, in short, without breaking her Fast, from the Kingdom of *Candaya*, all the Way to these your Grace's Territories: A thing incredibly miraculous, if not wrought by Inchantment. She is now without the Gate of this Castle, waiting only for your Grace's Permission to enter. This said, the Squire cough'd, and with both his Hands, stroak'd his unwieldy Beard from the top to the bottom, and with a formal Gravity expected the Duke's Answer.

Worthy Squire *Trifaldin with the white Beard*, said the Duke, long since have we heard of the Misfortunes of the Countess *Trifaldi*, whom Inchanters have occasion'd to be call'd the *Disconsolate Matron*; and therefore, most stupendious Squire, you may tell her that she may make her Entry, and that the Valiant Don *Quixote de la Mancha* is here present, on whose generous Assistance she may safely rely for Redress. Inform her also from me, That, if she has Occasion for my Aid, she may depend on my Readiness to do her Service, being oblig'd, as I am a Knight, to be aiding and assisting, to the utmost of my Power, to all Persons of her Sex, in Distress, especially widow'd Matrons, like her Ladyship.

Trifaldin, hearing this, made his Obeisance with the Knee, and beckoning to the Fife and Drums to observe his Motion, they all march'd out in the same solemn Procession as they enter'd, and left all the Beholders in a deep Admiration of his Proportion and Deportment.

Then the Duke turning to Don *Quixote*, Behold, Sir Knight, said he, how the Light and Glory of Virtue dart their Beams through the Clouds of Malice and Ignorance, and shine to the remotest Parts of the Earth: 'Tis hardly six Days since you have vouchsafed to honour this Castle with your Presence, and already the Afflicted and Distress'd flock hitherto from the uttermost Regions, not in Coaches, or on Dromedaries, but on Foot, and without eating by the Way; such is their Confidence in the Strength of that Arm, the Fame of whose great Exploits flies and spreads every where, and makes the whole World acquainted with your Valour.

What would I give, my Lord, said Don *Quixote*, that the same Holy Pedant were here now, who t'other Day at your Table would have run down Knight-Errantry at such a Rate; that the Testimony of his own Eyes might convince him of the Absurdity of his Error, and let him see, that the Comfortless, and Afflicted, do not in enormous Misfortunes, and uncommon Adversity, repair for Redress to the Doors of droning Church-men, or your little Sacristans of Villages; nor to the Fire-side of your Country Gentleman, who never travels beyond his Land-mark; nor to the lolling, lazy Courtier, who rather hearkens after News, which he may relate, than endeavours to perform such Deeds as may deserve to be recorded and re-lated. No, the Protection of Damsels, the Comfort of Widows, the Redress of the Injur'd, and the Support of the Distress'd, are no where so perfectly to be expected as from the generous Professors of Knight-Errantry. Therefore I thank Heaven a thousand Times, for having qualify'd me to answer the Neces-sities of the Miserable by such a Function. As for the Hard-ships and Accidents that may attend me, I look on 'em as no Discouragements, since proceeding from so noble a Cause. Then let this Matron be admitted to make known her Request, and I will refer her for Redress, to the Force of my Arm, and the Intrepid Resolution of my Couragious Soul.

IV: THE FAMOUS ADVENTURE OF THE DIS-CONSOLATE MATRON* CONTINU'D

THE Duke and Dutchess were mightily pleas'd to find Don *Quixote* wrought up to a Resolution so agreeable to their Design. But *Sancho*, who made his Observations, was not so well satisfy'd. I am in a bodily Fear, quoth he, that this same Mistress Waiting-Woman will be a Balk to my Preferment. I remember I once knew a *Toledo* Pothecary that talk'd like a Canary-Bird, and us'd to say, where-ever come old Waiting-Women, good Luck can happen there to no Man. Body of me, he knew 'em too well, and therefore valu'd 'em accordingly. He could have eaten 'em all with a Grain of Salt. Since then the best of 'em are so plaguy troublesom and impertinent, what will those be that are in doleful Dumps, like this same Countess Three Folds, Three Skirts, or Three Tails,† what d'ye call her? Hold your Tongue *Sancho*, said Don *Quixote*: This Matron that comes so far in Search of me, lives too remote to lie under the Lash of the Apothecary's Satire. Besides, you are to remember she's a Countess, and when Ladies of that Quality become *Governantes*; or Waiting-Women, 'tis only to Queens or Empresses; and in their own Houses they are as absolute Ladies as any others, and attended by other Waiting-Women. Ay, ay, (cry'd Donna *Rodriguez*, who was present) there are some that serve my Lady Dutchess here in that Capacity, that might have been Countesses too had they had better Luck. But we are not all born to be rich, though we are all born to be honest. Let no Body then speak ill of Waiting-Gentlewomen, especially of those that are ancient and Maidens; for though I am none of those, I easily conceive the Advantage that a Waiting-Gentlewoman, who is a Maiden, has over one that is a Widow. When all's said, whoever will offer to meddle with Waiting-Women will get little by't. Many go out for Wooll, and come home shorn themselves. For all that, quoth *Sancho*, your Waiting-Women are not so bare, but that they may be shorn, if my Bar-

---

* *The* Spanish *is* Duena, *which signifies an old Waiting-Woman, or* Governante, *as it is render'd in* Quevedo's Visions.   † Trifaldi, *the Name of the* Countess, *signifies* Three Skirts, *or* Three Tails.

ber spoke Truth: So that they had best not stir the Rice, though it sticks to the Pot. These Squires, forsooth, answer'd Donna *Rodriguez*, must be always cocking up their Noses against us: As they are always haunting the Anti-Chambers, like a Parcel of evil Sprights as they are, they see us whisk in and out at all Times; so when they are not at their Devotion, which Heaven knows, is almost all the Day long, they can find no other Pastime than to abuse us, and tell idle Stories of us, unburying our Bones, and burying our Reputation. But their Tongues are no Slander, and I can tell those silly Rakeshames, that, in spite of their Flouts, we shall keep the upper Hand of 'em, and live in the World in the better Sort of Houses, though we starve for't, and cover our Flesh, whether delicate or not, with black Gowns, as they cover a Dunghil with a Piece of Tapistry when a Procession goes by. S'Life, Sir, were this a proper Time, I would convince you and all the World, that there's no Virtue but is inclos'd within the Stays of a Waiting-Woman. I fancy, said the Dutchess, that honest *Rodriguez* is much in the Right: But we must now choose a fitter Time for this Dispute, to confound the ill Opinion of that wicked Apothecary, and to root out that which the great *Sancho Pança* has fix'd in his Breast. For my Part, quoth *Sancho*, I won't dispute with her; for since the Thoughts of being a Governor have steam'd up into my Brains, all my Concern for the Squire is vanish'd into Smoke; and I care not a wild Fig for all the Waiting-Women in the World.

This Subject would have engag'd 'em longer in Discourse, had they not been cut short by the Sound of the Fife and Drums, that gave 'em Notice of the *disconsolate Matron's* Approach. Thereupon the Dutchess ask'd the Duke, how it might be proper to receive her? And how far Ceremony was due to her Quality as a Countess? Look you (quoth *Sancho*, striking in before the Duke could answer) I would advise ye to meet her Countess-ship half way, but for the Waiting-Womanship don't stir a Step. Who bids you trouble your self? said Don *Quixote*. Who bid me! answer'd *Sancho*, why I my self did. Han't I been Squire to your Worship, and thus serv'd a 'Prenticeship to good Manners? And han't I had the Flower of Courtesy for my Master, who has often told me, A Man may as well lose at *One and Thirty*, with a Card too much, as a Card too little? Good

Wits jump; a Word to the wise is enough. *Sancho* says well, said the Duke: To decide the Matter, we will first see what Kind of a Countess she is, and behave our selves accordingly.

Now the Fife and the Drums enter'd as before—But here the Author ends this short Chapter, and begins another, prosecuting the same Adventure, which is one of the most notable in the History.

V: THE ACCOUNT WHICH THE DISCONSOLATE MATRON GIVES OF HER MISFORTUNE

THE doleful Drums and Fife were follow'd by twelve elderly Waiting-Women that enter'd the Garden, rank'd in Pairs, all clad in large mourning Habits, that seem'd to be of mill'd Serge, over which they wore Veils of white Calicoe, so long, that nothing could be seen of their black Dress, but the very Bottom. After them came the Countess *Trifaldi*, handed by her Squire *Trifaldin*, *with the white Beard*. The Lady was dress'd in a Suit of the finest Bays; which, had it been nap'd, would have had Tufts as big as Rouncival Pease. Her Train, or Tail, which you will, was mathematically divided into three equal Skirts or Angles, and born up by three Pages in mourning; and from this pleasant triangular Figure of her Train, as every one conjectur'd, was she call'd *Trifaldi*; as who should say, the Countess of *Threefolds*, or *Three Skirts*. *Ben-engeli* is of the same Opinion, though he affirms that her true Title was the Countess of *Lobuna*,* or of *Wolf-Land*, from the Abundance of Wolves bred in her Country; and had they been Foxes, she had, by the same Rule, been call'd the Countess *Zorruna*,† or of *Fox-Land*; it being a Custom in those Nations, for great Persons to take their Denominations from the Commodity with which their Country most abounds. However, this Countess chose to borrow her Title from this new Fashion of her own Invention, and leaving her Name of *Lobuna*, took that of *Trifaldi*.

Her twelve female Attendants approach'd with her in a Procession-pace, with black Veils over their Faces, not transparent, like that of *Trifaldin*, but thick enough to hinder altogether the Sight of their Countenances. As soon as the whole Train of Waiting-Women was come in, the Duke and the Dutchess, and Don *Quixote* stood up, and so did all those who were with 'em. Then the twelve Women, ranging themselves in two Rows, made a Lane for the Countess to march up between 'em, which she did, still led by *Trifaldin*, her Squire. The

* Lobo *is Spanish for a* Wolf.   † Zorro *is Spanish for a* He-Fox; *whence these two Words are deriv'd.*

Duke, the Dutchess, and Don *Quixote*, advancing about a dozen
Paces to meet her, she fell on her Knees, and with a Voice,
rather hoarse and rough, than clear and delicate, May it please
your Highnesses, said she, to spare your selves the Trouble
of receiving with so much Ceremony and Compliment a Man
(Woman I would say) who is your devoted Servant. Alas! the
Sense of my Misfortunes has so troubl'd my Intellectuals, that
my Responses cannot be suppos'd able to answer the critical
Opinion of your Presence. My Understanding has forsook me,
and is gone a Wool-gathering, and sure 'tis far remote; for the
more I seek it, the more unlikely I am to find it again. The
greatest Claim, Madam, answer'd the Duke, that we can lay
to Sense, is a due Respect, and decent Deference to the Worthi-
ness of your Person, which, without any further View, sufficiently bespeaks your Merit and excellent Qualifications.
Then begging the Honour of her Hand, he led her up, and
plac'd her in a Chair by his Dutchess, who receiv'd her with
all the Ceremony suitable to the Occasion.

Don *Quixote* said nothing all this while, and *Sancho* was
sneaking about, and peeping under the Veils of the Lady's
Women; but to no purpose; for they kept themselves very
close and silent, till she at last thus began. Confident* I am,
thrice potent Lord, thrice beautiful Lady, and thrice intelligent Auditors, that my most unfortunate Miserableness shall
find in your most generous and compassionate Bowels, a most
misericordial Sanctuary; my Miserableness, which is such as
would liquify Marble, malleate Steel, and mollify adamantine
Rocks. But before the Rehearsal of my ineffable Misfortunes
enter, I won't say your Ears, but the publick Mart of your hearing Faculties, I earnestly request, that I may have Cognizance,
whether the Cabal, Choir, or Conclave of this illustrissimous
Appearance, be not adorn'd with the Presence of the adjutori-
ferous Don *Quixote de la Manchissima*, and his squirissimous
Pança? *Pança* is at your *Elbowissimous* (quoth *Sancho*, before
any body else could answer) and Don *Quixotissimo* likewise:
Therefore, most dolorous *Medem*, you may tell out your Teale;
for we are all ready to be your Ladyship's *Servitorissimous* to
the best of our *Cepecities*, and so forth. Don *Quixote* then ad-

* *A Fustian Speech contriv'd on purpose, and imitated by* Sancho.

vanced, and, addressing the Countess, if your Misfortunes, embarrass'd Lady, said he, may hope any Redress from the Power
and Assistance of Knight-Errantry, I offer you my Force and
Courage, and, such as they are, I dedicate 'em to your Service.
I am Don *Quixote de la Mancha*, whose Profession is a sufficient
Obligation to succour the Distress'd, without the Formality
of Preambles, or the Elegance of Oratory to circumvent my
Favour. Therefore, pray, Madam, let us know, by a succinct
and plain Account of your Calamities, what Remedies should
be apply'd; and, if your Griefs are such as do not admit of a
Cure, assure your self at least, that we will comfort you in your
Afflictions, by sympathizing in your Sorrow.

The Lady, hearing this, threw her self at Don *Quixote's*
Feet, in spite of his kind Endeavours to the contrary; and striving to embrace 'em, Most invincible Knight, said she, I prostrate my self at these Feet, the Foundations and Pillars of
Chivalry-Errant, the supporters of my drooping spirits, whose
indefatigable Steps alone can hasten my Relief, and the Cure
of my Afflictions. O valorous Knight-Errant, whose real Atchievements eclipse and obscure the fabulous Legend of the
Amadises, *Esplandians*, and *Belianises*! Then, turning from
Don *Quixote*, she laid hold on *Sancho*, and squeezing his Hands
very hard, And thou, the most loyal Squire, that ever attended
on the Magnanimity of Knight-Errantry, whose Goodness is
more extensive than the Beard of my Usher *Trifaldin*! How
happily have thy Stars plac'd thee, under the Discipline of the
whole martial College of Chivalry Professors, center'd and
epitomiz'd in the single Don *Quixote*! I conjure thee, by thy
Love of Goodness, and thy unspotted Loyalty to so great a Master, to employ thy moving and interceding Eloquence in my
Behalf, that eftsoons his Favour may shine upon this humble,
and most disconsolate Countess.

Look you, Madam Countess, quoth *Sancho*, as for measuring
my Goodness by your Squire's Beard, that's neither here nor
there; so my Soul go to Heav'n when I depart this Life, I don't
matter the rest; for, as for the Beards of this World, 'tis not
what I stand upon; so that, without all this pawing and wheed-
ling, I'll put in a Word for you to my Master. I know he loves
me, and besides, at this Time, he stands in need of me about a

certain Business, and he shall do what he can for you. But pray discharge your burthen'd Mind; unload, and let us see what Griefs you bring, and then leave us to take Care of the rest.

The Duke and Dutchess were ready to burst with Laughing, to find the Adventure run in this pleasant Strain; and they admir'd, at the same Time, the rare Cunning and Management of *Trifaldi*, who, re-assuming her Seat, thus began her Story.

The famous Kingdom of *Candaya*, situated between the great *Taprobana* and the South Sea, about two Leagues beyond *Cape Comorin*, had, for it's Queen, the Lady *Donna Maguntia*, whose Husband King *Archipielo* dying, left the Princess *Antonomasia*, their only Child, Heiress to the Crown. This Princess was educated, and brought up under my Care and Direction; I being the eldest, and first Lady of the Bed-Chamber to the Queen, her Mother. In Process of Time, the young Princess arriv'd at the Age of fourteen Years, and appear'd so perfectly beautiful, that it was not in the Power of Nature to give any Addition to her Charms: What's yet more, her Mind was no less adorn'd than her Body. Wisdom itself was but a Fool to her: She was no less discreet than fair, and the fairest Creature in the World; and so she is still, unless the fatal Knife, or unrelenting Sheers of the envious and inflexible Sisters have cut her Thread of Life. But sure the Heavens would not permit such an Injury to be done to the Earth, as the untimely lopping off the loveliest Branch that ever adorn'd the Garden of the World.

Her Beauty, which my unpolish'd Tongue can never sufficiently praise, attracting all Eyes, soon got her a World of Adorers, many of 'em Princes, who were her Neighbours, and more distant Foreigners. Among the rest, a private Knight, who resided at Court, was so audacious as to raise his Thoughts to that Heaven of Beauty. This young Gentleman was indeed Master of all Gallantries that the Air of his courtly Education cou'd inspire; and so confiding on his Youth, his handsom Mien, his agreeable Air and Dress, his graceful Carriage, and the Charms of his easy Wit, and other Qualifications, he follow'd the Impulse of his inordinate and most presumptuous Passion. I must needs say, that he was an extraordinary Person, he play'd to a Miracle on the Guittar, and made it speak not only to the Ears, but to the very Soul. He danc'd to Admiration, and had such a rare Knack at making of Bird-Cages, that he might have got an Estate by that very Art; and, to sum up all his Accomplishments, he was a Poet. So many Parts and Endowments were sufficient to have mov'd a Mountain, and much more the Heart of a young tender Virgin. But all his fine Arts and soothing Behaviour had prov'd ineffectual against the Virtue and Reservedness of my beautiful Charge, if the damn'd cunning Rogue had not first conquer'd me. The deceitful Villain endeavour'd to seduce the Keeper, so to secure the Keys of the Fortress: In short, he so ply'd me with pleasing Trifles, and so insinuated himself into my Soul, that at last he perfectly bewitch'd me, and made me give Way before I was aware, to what I should never have permitted. But that which first wrought me to his Purpose, and undermin'd my Virtue, was a cursed Copy of Verses he sung one Night under my Window, which, if I remember right, began thus.

A SONG

A Secret Fire consumes my Heart;
And, to augment my raging Pain,
The charming Foe that rais'd the Smart,
Denies me Freedom to complain.
But sure 'tis just, we should conceal
The Bliss and Woe in Love we feel;
For, oh! what human Tongue can tell
The Joys of Heaven, or Pains of Hell!

The Words were to me so many Pearls of Eloquence, and his Voice sweeter to my Ears than Sugar to the Taste. The Reflection on the Misfortune which these Verses brought on me, has often made me applaud *Plato's* Design of banishing all Poets from a good and well-govern'd Commonwealth, especially those who write wantonly or lasciviously. For, instead of composing lamentable Verses, like those of the Marquiss of *Mantua*, that make Women and Children cry by the Fireside, they try their utmost Skill on such soft Strokes as enter the Soul, and wound it, like that Thunder which hurts and consumes all within, yet leaves the Garment sound. Another Time he entertain'd me with the following Song.

A SONG

Death, put on some kind Disguise,
And at once my Heart surprize:
For 'tis such a Curse to live,
And so great a Bliss to die;
Should'st thou any Warning give,
I'd relapse to Life for Joy.

Many other Verses of this Kind he ply'd me with, which charm'd when read, but transported when sung. For you must know, that when our eminent Poets debase themselves to the writing a Sort of Composure call'd *Love-Madrigals*, and *Roundelays*, now much in Vogue in *Candaya*, those Verses are no sooner heard, but they presently produce a Dancing of Souls, Tickling of Fancies, Emotion of Spirits, and, in short, a pleasing Distemper in the whole Body, as if Quicksilver shook it in every Part.

So that once more I pronounce those Poets very dangerous, and fit to be banish'd to the Isles of *Lizards*. Though truly, I must confess, the Fault is rather chargeable on those foolish People that commend, and the silly Wenches that believe 'em. For had I been as cautious as my Place requir'd, his amorous Serenades could never have mov'd me, nor would I have believed his poetical Cant, such as, *I dying live, I burn in Ice, I shiver in Flames, I hope in Despair, I go, yet stay,* with a thousand such Contradictions, which make up the greatest Part of those Kind of Compositions. As ridiculous are their Promises of the Phœnix of *Arabia*, *Ariadne's* Crown, the Coursers of the Sun, the Pearls of the Southern Ocean, the Gold of *Tagus*, the Balsam of *Panchaya*, and Heaven knows what! By the way, 'tis observable, that these Poets are very liberal of their Gifts, which they know they never can make good.

But whither, woe's me, whither do I wander, miserable Woman? What Madness prompts me to accuse the Faults of others, having so long a Score of my own to answer for! Alas! not his Verses, but my own Inclination: Not his Musick, but my own Levity; not his Wit, but my own Folly open'd a Passage, and levell'd the Way for Don *Clavijo* (for that was the Name of the Knight). In short, I procur'd him Admittance, and by my

Connivance, he very often had natural Familiarity with *Antonomasia*, who, poor Lady, was rather deluded by me, than by him. But, wicked as I was, 'twas upon the honourable Score of Marriage; for had he not been engag'd to be her Husband, he shou'd not have touch'd the very Shadow of her Shoe-string. No; no; Matrimony, Matrimony, I say; for without that, I'll never meddle in any such Concern. The greatest Fault in this Business, was the Disparity of their Conditions; he being but a private Knight, and she Heiress to the Crown. Now this Intrigue was kept very close for some Time by my cautious Management; but at last a certain Kind of Swelling in *Antonomasia's* Belly began to tell Tales; so that, consulting upon the Matter, we found there was but one Way; Don *Clavijo* should demand the young Lady in Marriage before the Curate,* by Virtue of a Promise under her Hand, which I dictated for the Purpose, and so binding, that all the Strength of *Sampson* himself could not have broke the Tie. The Business was put in Execution, the Note was produc'd before the Priest, who examin'd the Lady, and, finding her Confession to agree with the Tenor of the Contract, put her in Custody of a very honest Serjeant. Bless us, quoth *Sancho*, Serjeants too; and Poets, and Songs, and Verses in Your Country! O' my Conscience, I think the World's the same all the World over! But, go on, Madam *Trifaldi*, I beseech you, for 'tis late, and I am upon Thorns till I know the End of this long-winded Story. I will, answer'd the Countess.

* *In* Spain, *when a young Couple have promis'd each other Marriage, and the Parents obstruct it, either Party may have Recourse to the* Vicar, *who, examining the Case, has full Power to bring them together; and this it is the Countess ridiculously alludes to in her Story.*

IF every Word that *Sancho* spoke gave the Dutchess new Pleasure, every Thing he said put Don *Quixote* to as much Pain; so that he commanded him Silence, and gave the Matron Opportunity to go on. In short, said she, the Business was debated a good while, and after many Questions and Answers, the Princess firmly persisting in her first Declaration, Judgment was given in favour of Don *Clavijo*, which Queen *Maguntia*, her Mother, took so to Heart, that we bury'd her about three Days after. Then without doubt she dy'd, quoth *Sancho*. That's a clear Case, reply'd *Trifaldin*, for in *Candaya* they don't use to bury the living, but the dead. But with your good Leave, Mr *Squire*, answer'd *Sancho*, People that were in a Swoon have been bury'd alive before now, and methinks Queen *Maguntia* should only have swoon'd away, and not have been in such Haste to have dy'd in good Earnest; for while there's Life there's Hopes, and there's a Remedy for all Things but Death. I don't find the young Lady was so much out of the Way neither, that the Mother should lay it so grievously to Heart. Indeed had she marry'd a Footman, or some other Servant in the Family, as I am told many others have done, it had been a very bad Business, and past curing; but for the Queen to make such a heavy Outcry when her Daughter marry'd such a fine-bred young Knight, Faith and Troth, I think the Business had been better made up. 'Twas a Slip, but not such a heinous one, as one would think: For as my Master here says, and he won't let me tell a Lye, as of Scholars they make Bishops, so of your Knights (chiefly if they be Errant) one may easily make Kings and Emperors.

That's most certain, said Don *Quixote*, turn a Knight-Errant loose into the wide World with two pennyworth of good Fortune, and he is in *potentia propinqua* (*proxima* I would say) the greatest Emperor in the World. But let the Lady proceed, for hitherto her Story has been very pleasant, and I doubt the most bitter Part of it is still untold. The most bitter truly, Sir, answer'd she; and so bitter, that Wormwood, and every bitter Herb, compared to it, are as sweet as Honey.

The Queen being really dead, continu'd she, and not in a Trance, we bury'd her, and scarce had we done her the last Offices, and taken our last Leaves, when (*Quis talia fando temperet à Lachrymis*? Who can relate such Woes, and not be drown'd in Tears?) the Giant *Malambruno*, Cousin-german to the deceas'd Queen, who, besides his native Cruelty, was also a Magician, appear'd upon her Grave, mounted on a wooden Horse, and, by his dreadful angry Looks, shew'd he came thither to revenge the Death of his Relation, by punishing Don *Clavijo* for his Presumption, and *Antonomasia* for her Over-sight. Accordingly, he immediately inchanted them both upon the very Tomb, transforming her into a brazen female Monkey, and the young Knight into a hideous Crocodile of an unknown Metal; and between them both he set an Inscription in the *Syriack* Tongue, which we have got since translated into the *Candayan*, and then into *Spanish*, to this Effect.

These two presumptuous Lovers shall never recover their natural Shapes till the valorous Knight of la Mancha *enter into a single Combat with me: For, by the irrevocable Decrees of Fate, this unheard of Adventure is reserv'd for his unheard of Courage.*

This done, he drew a broad Scimitar of a monstrous Size, and, catching me fast by the Hair, made an Offer to cut my Throat, or to whip off my Head. I was frighted almost to Death, my Hair stood on end, and my Tongue cleav'd to the Roof of my Mouth. However, recovering myself as well as I could, trembling and weeping, I begg'd Mercy in such a moving Accent, and in such tender melting Words, that at last my Intreaties prevail'd on him to stop the cruel Execution. In short, he order'd all the Waiting-women at Court to be brought before him, the same that you see here at present; and after he had aggravated our Breach of Trust, and rail'd against the deceitful Practices, mercenary Procuring, and what else he could urge in Scandal of our Profession, and it's very Being, reviling us for the Fact of which I alone stood guilty; I will not punish you with instant Death, said he, but inflict a Punishment which shall be a lasting and eternal Mortification. Now, in the very Instant of his denouncing our Sentence, we felt the Pores of our Faces to open, and all about 'em perceiv'd an itching Pain, like the pricking of Pins and Needles. Thereupon, clapping our Hands to our Faces, we found 'em as you shall see 'em immediately; saying this, the *disconsolate Matron* and her Attendance, throwing off their Veils, expos'd their Faces all rough with bristly Beards; some red, some black, some white, and others motley. The Duke and Dutchess admir'd, Don *Quixote* and *Sancho* were astonish'd, and the Standers-by were Thunder-struck. Thus, said the Countess, proceeding, has that murdering and bloody-minded *Malambruno* serv'd us, and planted these rough and horrid Bristles on our Faces, otherwise most delicately smooth. Oh! that he had chopp'd off our Heads with his monstrous Sci-mitar, rather than to have disgraced our Faces with these Brushes upon 'em! For, Gentlemen, if you rightly consider it, and truly, what I have to say should be attended with a Flood of Tears; but such Rivers and Oceans have fallen from me al-ready upon this doleful Subject, that my Eyes are as dry as Chaff; and therefore pray let me speak without Tears at this Time. Where, alas! shall a Waiting-woman dare to shew her Head with such a Furz-bush upon her Chin? What charitable Person will entertain her? What Relations will own her? At the best, we can scarcely make our Faces passable, though we torture 'em with a thousand Slops and Washes, and even thus we have much ado to get the Men to care for us. What will be-come of her then that wears a Thicket upon her Face! Oh Ladies, and Companions of my Misery! In an ill Hour were we begot, and in a worse came we into the World! With these Words the *disconsolate Matron* seem'd to faint away.

VII: OF SOME THINGS THAT RELATE TO THIS ADVENTURE, AND APPERTAIN TO THIS MEMORABLE HISTORY

ALL Persons that love to read Histories of the Nature of this, must certainly be very much obliged to *Cid Hamet*, the original Author, who has taken such Care in delivering every minute Particular distinctly entire, without concealing the least Circumstances that might heighten the Humour, or, if omitted, have obscur'd the Light and Truth of the Story. He draws lively Pictures of the Thoughts, discovers the Imaginations, satisfies Curiosity in Secrets, clears Doubts, resolves Arguments, and, in short, makes manifest the least Atoms of the most inquisitive Desire! O most famous Author! O fortunate Don *Quixote*! O renown'd *Dulcinea*! O facetious *Sancho*! jointly and severally may you live and continue to the latest Posterity, for the general Delight and Recreation of Mankind—but the Story goes on—

Now, on my honest Word, quoth *Sancho*, when he saw the Matron in a Swoon, and by the Blood of all the *Pança's*, my Forefathers, I never heard nor saw the like, neither did my Master ever tell me, or so much as conceit in that working Head-piece of his, such an Adventure as this. Now all the Devils in Hell (and I would not curse any body) run away with thee for an inchanting Son of a Whore, thou damn'd Giant *Malambruno*! Couldst thou find no other Punishment for these poor Sinners, but by clapping Scrubbing-Brushes about their Muzzles, with a Pox to you? Had it not been much better to slit their Nostrils half way up their Noses, though they had snuffl'd for it a little, than to have planted these quick-set Hedges o'er their Chaps? I'll lay any Man a Wager now, the poor Devils have not Money enough to pay for their shaving.

'Tis but too true, Sir, said one of them, we have not wherewithal to pay for taking our Beards off; so that some of us, to save Charges, are forc'd to lay on Plaisters of Pitch that pull away Roots and all, and leave our Chins as smooth as the Bot-

288

tom of a Stone-Mortar. There is indeed a Sort of Women in *Candaya*, that go about from House to House, to take off the Down or Hairs that grown about the Face,* trim the Eyebrows, and do twenty other little private Jobs for the Women; but we here, who are my Lady's *Duennas*, wou'd never have any thing to do with them, for they have got ill Names; for though formerly they got free Access, and pass'd for Relations, now they are look'd upon to be no better than Bawds. So if my Lord Don *Quixote* do not relieve us, our Beards will stick by us as long as we live. I'll have mine pluck'd off Hair by Hair among the *Moors*, answer'd Don *Quixote*, rather than not free you from yours. Ah, valorous Knight! (cry'd the Countess *Trifaldi*, recovering that Moment from her Fit) the sweet Sound of your Promise reach'd my Hearing in the very midst of my Trance, and has perfectly restor'd my Senses. I beseech you therefore, once again, most illustrious Sir, and invincible Knight-Errant, that your gracious Promise may soon have the wish'd-for Effect. I'll be guilty of no Neglect, Madam, answer'd Don *Quixote*: Point out the Way, and you shall soon be convinc'd of my Readiness to serve you.

You must know then, Sir, said the disconsolate Lady, from this Place to the Kingdom of *Candaya*, by Computation, we reckon five thousand Leagues, two or three more or less: But if you ride through the Air in a direct Line, 'tis not above three thousand two hundred and twenty-seven. You are likewise to understand that *Malambruno* told me, that when Fortune should make me find out the Knight who is to dissolve our Inchantment, he would send him a famous Steed, much easier and less resty and full of Tricks, than those Jades that are commonly let out to hire, as being the same wooden Horse that carry'd the valorous *Peter* of *Provence*, and the fair *Magalona*, when he stole her away. 'Tis manag'd by a wooden Peg in it's Forehead, instead of a Bridle, and flies as swiftly through the

---

* *There are a Sort of Women-Barbers in* Spain, *that take the Down off Womens Faces, and sell them Washes, and these are commonly reputed to be giv'n to Bawding. This* Down *the* Spaniards *call* Bello, *from the* Latin Vellus (*I suppose*) *which means a* Fleece, (*or* Fell, *from the same* Vellus). Bello *is also* Spanish *for handsom, from* Bellus, Latin. *In old* Spanish *Books* Bello *is* Riches; *to intimate there's nothing* handsom, *without being* rich. *Accordingly* Horace *says*—Formam Regina Pecunia donat.

Air, as if all the Devils in Hell were switching him, or blowing Fire in his Tail. This Courser, Tradition delivers, to have been the Handy-work of the sage *Merlin*, who never lent him to any but particular Friends, or when he was paid Sauce for him. Among others, his 'Friend *Peter* of *Provence* borrow'd him, and by the Help of his wonderful Speed, stole away the fair *Magalona*, as I said, setting her behind on the Crupper; for you must know he carries double, and so tow'ring up in the Air, he left the People that stood near the Place whence he started, gaping, staring, and amaz'd.

Since that Journey, we have heard of no body that has back'd him. But this we know, that *Malambruno* since that got him by his Art; and has us'd him ever since, to post about to all Parts of the World. He's here to day, and to morrow in *France*, and the next Day in *America*: And one of the best Properties of the Horse is, that he costs not a Farthing in keeping; for he neither eats nor sleeps, neither needs he any shoeing; besides, without having Wings, he ambles so very easy through the Air, that you might carry in your Hand a Cup full of Water a thousand Leagues, and not spill a Drop; so that the fair *Magalona* lov'd mightily to ride him.

Nay, quoth *Sancho*, as for an easy Pacer, commend me to my *Dapple*. Indeed he's none of your High-Flyers, he can't gallop in the Air; but on the King's Highway, he shall pace ye with the best Ambler that ever went on four Legs. This set the whole Company a laughing. But then the disconsolate Lady going on; This Horse, said she, will certainly be here within half an Hour after 'tis dark, if *Malambruno* designs to put an End to our Misfortunes, for that was the Sign by which I should discover my Deliverer. And pray, forsooth, quoth *Sancho*, how many will this same Horse carry upon Occasion? Two, answer'd she, one in the Saddle, and t'other behind on the Crupper; and those two are commonly the Knight and the Squire, if some stolen Damsel be not to be one. Good disconsolate Madam, quoth *Sancho*, I'd fain know the Name of this same Nag. The Horse's Name, answer'd she, is neither *Pegasus*, like *Bellephoron's*; nor *Bucephalus*, like *Alexander's*; nor *Brilladoro*, like *Orlando's*; nor *Bayard*, like *Rinaldo's*; nor *Frontin*, like *Rogero's*; nor *Bootes*, nor *Pyrith-*

ous, like the Horses of the Sun; neither is he call'd *Orelia*, like the Horse which *Rodrigo*, the last King of *Spain*, of the *Gothick* Race, bestrid that unfortunate Day, when he lost the Battle, the Kingdom and his Life. I'll lay you a Wager, quoth *Sancho*, since the Horse goes by none of those famous Names, he does not go by that of *Rosinante* neither, which is my Master's Horse, and another-guess Beast than any you've reckon'd up. 'Tis very right, answer'd the bearded Lady: However, he has a very proper and significant Name; for he is call'd *Clavileno*, or *Wooden-Peg* the *Swift*, from the Wooden-Peg in his Forehead; so that for the Significancy of Name at least he may be compared with *Rosinante*. I find no Fault with his Name, quoth *Sancho*; but what kind of Bridle or Halter do you manage him with? I told you already, reply'd she, that he is guided with the Peg, which being turn'd this way or that way, he moves accordingly, either mounting aloft in the Air, or almost brushing and sweeping the Ground, or else flying in the middle Region, the Way which ought indeed most to be chosen in all Affairs of Life. I should be glad to see this notable Tit, quoth *Sancho*, but don't design to get on his Back, either before or behind. No, by my holy Dame, you may as well expect Pears from an Elm. 'Twere a pretty Jest, I trow, for me that can hardly sit my own *Dapple*, with a Pack-Saddle as soft as Silk, to suffer my self to be hors'd upon a hard wooden Thing, without either Cushion or Pillow under his Buttocks. Before *George*! I won't gall my Backside to take off the best Lady's Beard in the Land. Let them that have Beards wear 'em still, or get them whip'd off as they think best; I'll not take such a long Jaunt with my Master, not I. There is no need of me in this shaving of Beards, as there was in *Dulcinea's* Business. Upon my Word, dear Sir, but there is, reply'd *Trifaldi*, and so much, that without You nothing can be done. God save the King! cry'd *Sancho*, what have we Squires to do with our Masters Adventures? We must bear the Trouble forsooth, and they run away with the Credit! Body o'me, 'twere something, would those that write their Stories, but give the Squires their due Share in their Books; as thus, *Such a Knight ended such an Adventure; but it was with the Help of such a one his Squire, without which the Devil a bit could he ever have done it*. But they shall barely tell you in their Histories, *Sir* Para-lipomenon, *Knight of the three Stars, ended the Adventure of the six Hobgoblins*; and not a Word all the while of his Squire's Person, as if there were no such Man, though he was by all the while, poor Devil. In short, good People, I don't like it; and once more I say, my Master may e'en go by himself for *Sancho*, and Joy betide him. I'll stay and keep Madam Dutch-ess Company here, and mayhap by that Time he comes back, he'll find his Lady *Dulcinea's* Business pretty forward; for I mean to give my bare Breech a Jirking till I brush off the very Hair, at idle Times, that is, when I've nothing else to do.

Nevertheless, honest *Sancho*, said the Dutchess, if your Company be necessary in this Adventure, you must go; for all good People will make it their Business to intreat you; and 'twou'd look very ill, that through your vain Fears, these poor Gentlewomen should remain thus with rough and bristly Faces. God save the King, I cry again, said *Sancho*, were it a piece of Charity for the Relief of some good sober Gentle-women, or poor innocent Hospital-Girls, something might be said: But to gall my Backside, and venture my Neck, to unbeard a Pack of idling trolloping Chamber-jades, with a Murrain! not I, let them go elsewhere for a Shaver; I wish I might see the whole Tribe of 'em wear Beards from the highest to the lowest, from the proudest to the primest, all hairy like so many She-goats. You are very angry with Waiting-women, *Sancho*, said the Dutchess: That 'Pothecary has inspir'd you with this bit-ter Spirit. But you're to blame, Friend, for I'll assure you there are some in my Family, that may serve for Patterns of Discretion to all those of their Function; and Donna *Rodriguez* here will let me say no less. Ay, ay, Madam, said Donna *Rodriguez*, your Grace may say what you please: This is a censorious World we live in, but Heaven knows all; and whether good or bad, beard-ed or unbearded, we Waiting-Gentlewomen had Mothers as well as the rest of our Sex; and since Providence has made us as we are, and plac'd us in the World, it knows wherefore, and so we trust in it's Mercy, and no body's Beard. Enough, Donna *Rodriguez*, said Don *Quixote*; as for you, Lady *Trifaldi*, and other distressed Matrons, I hope that Heaven will speedily look with a pitying Eye on your Sorrows, and that *Sancho* will do as I shall desire. I only wish *Clavileno* would once come, that I may encounter *Malambruno*, for I am sure no Razor should be more expeditious in shaving your Ladyship's Beard, than my Sword to shave that Giant's Head from his Shoulders: Heaven may a while permit the wicked, but not for ever.

Ah! most valorous Champion, said the disconsolate Matron, may all the Stars in the celestial Regions shed their most propitious Influence on your generous Valour, which thus supports the Cause of our unfortunate Office, so expos'd to the poisonous Rancour of Apothecaries, and so revil'd by saucy Grooms and Squires. Now all ill Luck attend the low-spirited Quean, who, in the Flower of her Youth, will not rather choose to turn Nun, than Waiting-woman! poor forlorn contemn'd Creatures as we are! though descended in a direct Line from Father to Son, from *Hector* of *Troy* himself, yet would not our Ladies find a more civil Way to speak to us, than *Thee* and *Thou*, though it were to gain 'em a Kingdom. O Giant *Malambruno*! thou, who though an Inchanter, art always most faithful to thy Word, send us the peerless *Clavileno*, that our Misfortunes may have an End. For if the Weather grows hotter than it is, and these shaggy Beards still sprout about our Faces, what a sad Pickle will they be in!

The disconsolate Lady utter'd these Lamentations in so pathetick a manner, that the Tears of all the Spectators waited on her Complaints; and even *Sancho* himself began to water his Plants, and condescend at least to share in the Adventure, and attend his Master to the very fag-end of the World, so he might contribute to the clearing away the Weeds that overspread those venerable Faces.

VIII: OF CLAVILENO'S* (ALIAS WOODEN-PEG'S) ARRIVAL, WITH THE CONCLUSION OF THIS TEDIOUS ADVENTURE

THESE Discourses brought on the Night, and with it the appointed Time for the famous *Clavileno's* Arrival. Don *Quixote*, very impatient at his Delay, began to fear, that either he was not the Knight for whom this Adventure was reserv'd, or else that the Giant *Malambruno* had not Courage to enter into a single Combat with him. But, unexpectedly, who should enter the Garden but four Savages cover'd with green Ivy, bearing on their Shoulders a large wooden Horse, which they set upon his Legs before the Company; and then one of them cry'd out, Now let him that has the Courage, mount this Engine—I am not he, quoth *Sancho*, for I have no Courage, nor am I a Knight—And let him take his Squire behind him, if he has one (continu'd the Savage) with this Assurance from the valorous *Malambruno*, that no foul Play shall be offer'd, nor will he use any thing but his Sword to offend him. 'Tis but only turning the Peg before him, and the Horse will transport him through the Air to the Place where *Malambruno* attends their Coming. But let them blindfold their Eyes, lest the dazzling and stupendious Height of their Career should make 'em giddy; and let the Neighing of the Horse inform 'em that they are arriv'd at their Journey's End. Thus having made his Speech, the Savage turned about with his Companions, and, leaving *Clavileno*, march'd out handsomly the same Way they came in.

The Disconsolate Matron seeing the Horse, almost with Tears address'd Don *Quixote*; Valorous Knight, cry'd she, *Malambruno* is a Man of his Word, the Horse is here, our Beards bud on; therefore I and every one of us conjure you by all the Hairs on our Chins, to hasten our Deliverance; since there needs no more but that you and your Squire get up, and give a happy Beginning to your intended Journey. Madam, answer'd Don *Quixote*, I'll do't with all my Heart, I will not so

* *A Name compounded of the two* Spanish *Words*, Clavo *a* Nail *or* Pin, *and* Leno, *Wood.*

much as stay for a Cushion, or to put on my Spurs, but mount instantly; such is my Impatience to disbeard your Ladyship's Face, and restore ye all to your former Gracefulness. That's more than I shall do, quoth *Sancho*, I an't in such plaguy Haste, not I; and if the quickset Hedges on their Snouts can't be lopp'd off without my riding on that hard Crupper, let my Master furnish himself with another Squire, and these Gentlewomen get some other Barber. I'm no Witch sure, to ride through the Air at this rate upon a Broomstick! What will my Islanders say, think ye, when they hear their Governor is flying like a Paper-Kite? Besides, 'tis three or four thousand Leagues from hence to *Candaya*, and what if the Horse should tire upon the Road? Or the Giant grow humoursom? What would become of us then? We may be seven Years a getting home again; and Heaven knows by that Time what would become of my Government: Neither Island nor Dryland would know poor *Sancho* agen. No, no, I know better Things; what says the old Proverb? Delays breed Danger; and when a Cow's given thee, run and halter her! I am the Gentlewoman's humble Servant, but they and their Beards must excuse me, Faith! St *Peter* is well at *Rome*, that is to say, here I'm much made of, and by the Master of the House's Good-Will, I hope to see my self a Governor. Friend *Sancho*, said the Duke, as for your Island it neither floats nor stirs, so there's no Fear it should run away before you come back; the Foundations of it are fix'd and rooted in the profound Abyss of the Earth. Now because you must needs think I cannot but know, that there is no Kind of Office of any Value that is not purchas'd with some Sort of Bribe or Gratification, of one Kind or other, all that I expect for advancing you to this Government, is only that you wait on your Master in this Expedition, that there may be an End of this memorable Adventure: And I here engage my Honour, that whether you return on *Clavileno* with all the Speed his Swiftness promises, or that it should be your ill Fortune to be oblig'd to Foot it back like a Pilgrim, begging from Inn to Inn, and Door to Door, still whenever you come, you will find your Island where you left it, and your Islanders as glad to receive you for their Governor as ever. And for my own Part, Signior *Sancho*, I'll assure you, you'd very much wrong my Friendship, should you in the least doubt my Readiness to serve you. Good your Worship say no more, cry'd *Sancho*, I am but a poor Squire, and your Goodness is too great a Load for my Shoulders. But hang Baseness; Mount, Master, and blindfold me, somebody; wish me a good Voyage, and pray for me—But hark ye, good Folks, when I am got up, and fly in the Skies, mayn't I say my Prayers, and call on the Angels my self to help me, trow? Yes, yes, answer'd *Tri-faldi*; for *Malambruno*, though an Inchanter, is nevertheless a Christian, and does all Things with a great deal of Sagacity, having nothing to do with those he should not meddle with. Come on then, quoth *Sancho*, God and the most Holy Trinity of *Gaeta** help me! Thy Fear, *Sancho*, said Don *Quixote*, might by a superstitious Mind be thought ominous: Since the Adven-ture of the Fulling-Mills, I have not seen thee possess'd with such a panick Terror. But, hark ye, begging this noble Com-pany's Leave, I must have a Word with you in private. Then withdrawing into a distant Part of the Garden among some Trees; My dear *Sancho*, said he, thou seest we are going to take a long Journey; thou art no less sensible of the Uncertainty of our Return, and Heaven alone can tell what Leisure or Con-veniency we may have in all that Time: Let me therefore beg thee to slip aside to thy Chamber, as if it were to get thy self ready for our Journey; and there presently dispatch me only some 500 Lashes on the Account of the 3300 thou standest en-gag'd for; 'twill soon be done, and a Business well begun, you know, is half ended. Stark mad, before *George*, cry'd *Sancho*. I wonder you are not asham'd, Sir. This is just as they say, you see me in Haste, and ask me for a Maidenhead? I am just going to ride the wooden Horse, and you would have me flay my Backside. Truly, truly, you're plaguily out this Time. Come, come, Sir, let's do one Thing after another; let us get off these Women's Whiskers, and then I'll feague it away for *Dulcinea*: I have no more to say on the Matter at present. Well, honest *Sancho*, reply'd Don *Quixote*, I'll take thy Word for once, and I hope thou'lt make it good; for I believe thou art more Fool than Knave. I am what I am, quoth *Sancho*; but whatever I be, I'll keep my Word, ne'er fear it.

Upon this they return'd to the Company; and just as they

---

* *A Church in Italy of special Devotion to the Blessed Trinity.*

were going to mount, Blind thy Eyes, *Sancho*, said Don *Quixote*, and get up. Sure he that sends so far for us, can have no Design to deceive us! since 'twould never be to his Credit to delude those that rely on his Word of Honour; and though the Success should not be answerable to our Desires, still the Glory of so brave an Attempt will be ours, and 'tis not in the Power of Malice to eclipse it. To horse then, Sir, cry'd *Sancho*, to horse: The Tears of those poor bearded Gentlewomen have melted my Heart, and methinks I feel their Bristles sticking in it. I shan't eat a Bit to do me good, till I see them have as pretty dimpled smooth Chins and soft Lips as they had before. Mount then, I say, and blindfold your self first; for, if I must ride behind, 'tis a plain Case you must get up before me. That's right, said Don *Quixote*; and with that, pulling a Handkerchief out of his Pocket, he gave it to the Disconsolate Matron to hoodwink him close. She did so; but presently after, uncovering himself, if I remember right, said he, We read in *Virgil* of the *Trojan Palladium*, that wooden Horse which the *Greeks* offer'd *Pallas*, full of arm'd Knights, who afterwards prov'd the total Ruin of that famous City. 'Twere prudent therefore, before we got up, to probe this Steed, and see what he has in his Guts. You need not, said the Countess *Trifaldi*, I dare engage there's no ground for any such Surmise; for *Malambruno* is a Man of Honour, and would not so much as countenance any base or treacherous Practice; and whatever Accident befals ye, I dare answer for. Upon this Don *Quixote* mounted without any Reply, imagining that what he might further urge concerning his Security, would be a Reflexion on his Valour. He then began to try the Pin, which was easily turn'd; and as he sat with his long Legs stretch'd at Length for want of Stirrups, he look'd like one of those antique figures in a *Roman* Triumph, woven in some old Piece of Arras.

Sancho very leisurely and unwillingly was made to climb up behind him; and fixing himself as well as he could on the Crupper, felt it somewhat hard and uneasy. With that, looking on the Duke, good my Lord, quoth he, will you lend me something to clap under me; some Pillow from the Page's Bed, or the Dutchess's Cushion of State, or any thing; for this Horse's Crupper is so confounded hard, I fancy 'tis rather Marble than

Wood. 'Tis needless, said the Countess, for *Clavileno* will bear no Kind of Furniture upon him; so that for your greater Ease, you had best sit Sideways like a Woman. *Sancho* took her Advice; and then, after he had taken his Leave of the Company, they bound a Cloth over his Eyes. But presently after uncovering his Face, with a pitiful Look on all the Spectators, Good tender-hearted Christians, (cry'd he, with Tears in his Eyes) bestow a few *Pater-Nosters* and *Ave-Mary's* on a poor departing brother, and pray for my soul, as you expect the like charity your selves in such a Condition. What! you Rascal, said Don *Quixote*, d'ye think your self at the Gallows, and at the Point of Death, that you hold forth in such a lamentable Strain? Dastardly Wretch without a Soul, dost thou not know that the fair *Magalona* once sat in thy Place, and alighted from thence, not into the Grave, thou Chicken-hearted Varlet, but into the Throne of *France*, if there's any Truth in History? And do not I sit by thee, that I may vie with the valorous *Peter* of *Provence*, and press the Seat that was once press'd by him? Come, blindfold thy Eyes, poor spiritless Animal, and let me not know thee betray the least Symptom of Fear, at least not in my Presence. Well, quoth *Sancho*, hoodwink me then among ye: But 'tis no Mar'l one should be afraid, when you won't let one say his Prayers, nor be pray'd for, though for ought I know we may have a Legion of Imps about our Ears, to clap us up in the Devil's Pound* presently.

Now both being hoodwink'd, and Don *Quixote* perceiving every Thing ready for their setting out, began to turn the Pin; and no sooner had he set his Hand to it, but the Waiting-Women and all the Company set up their Throats, crying out, Speed you, speed you well, valorous Knight, Heaven be your Guide, undaunted Squire! Now, now, you fly aloft. See how they cut the Air more swiftly than an Arrow! now they mount, and tower, and soar, while the gazing World wonders at their Course. Sit fast, sit fast, couragious *Sancho*; you don't sit

* *In the Original it is*, To carry us to Peralvillo, *i.e.* To hang us first, and try us afterwards, *as* Jarvis *translates it.* Stevens's *Dictionary says*, Peralvillo *is a Village near* Ciudad-Real *in Castile, where the holy Brotherhood, or Officers for apprehending Highwaymen, dispatch those they take in the Fact, without bringing 'em to Trial; like what we call, Hanging a Man first, and trying him afterwards.*

steady; have a Care of falling; for should you now drop from that amazing Height, your Fall would be greater than the aspiring Youths, that misguided the Chariot of the Sun his Father. All this *Sancho* heard; and girting his Arms fast about his Master's Waist, Sir, quoth he, why do they say we are so high, since we can hear their Voices? Troth I hear 'em so plainly, that one would think they were close by us. Ne'er mind that, answer'd Don *Quixote*; for in these extraordinary Kind of Flights, we must suppose our hearing and seeing will be extraordinary also. But don't hold me so hard, for you'll make me tumble off. What makes thee tremble so? I'm sure I never rid easier in all my Life; our Horse goes as if he did not move at all. Come then, take Courage; we make swinging Way, and have a fair and merry Gale. I think so too, quoth *Sancho*, for I feel the Wind puff as briskly upon me here, as if I don't know how many Pair of Bellows were blowing Wind in my Tail. *Sancho* was not altogether in the Wrong; for two or three Pair of Bellows were indeed levell'd at him then, which gave Air very plentifully; so well had the Plot of this Adventure been laid by the Duke, the Dutchess, and their Steward, that nothing was wanting to further the Diversion.

Don *Quixote* at last feeling the Wind, Sure, said he, we must be risen to the middle Region of the Air, where the Winds, Hail, Snow, Thunder, Lightning, and other Meteors are produc'd; so that if we mount at this rate, we shall be in the Region of Fire presently, and what's worst, I don't know how to manage this Pin, so as to avoid being scorch'd and roasted alive. At the same Time some Flax, with other combustible Matter, which had been got ready, was clapp'd at the End of a long Stick, and set on Fire at a small Distance from their Noses, and the Heat and Smoke affecting the Knight and the Squire; May I be hang'd, quoth *Sancho*, if we ben't come to this Fire-Place you talk of, or very near it; for the half of my Beard is sing'd already. I have a huge Mind to peep out, and see whereabouts we are. By no Means, answer'd Don *Quixote*; I remember the strange but true Story of Doctor *Torralva*, whom the Devils carry'd to *Rome* hoodwink'd, and bestriding a Reed, in twelve Hours Time, setting him down on the Tower of *Nona*, in one of the Streets of that City. There he saw the dreadful Tumult,

299

Assault, and Death of the Constable of *Bourbon*; and the next Morning he found himself at *Madrid*, where he related the whole Story. Among other Things, he said, as he went through the Air, the Devil bid him open his Eyes, which he did, and then he found himself so near the Moon, that he could touch it with his Finger; but durst not look toward the Earth, lest the Distance should make his Brains turn round. So *Sancho*, we must not unveil our Eyes, but rather wholly trust to the Care and Providence of him that has Charge of us; and fear nothing, for we only mount high, to come souse down like a Hawk, upon the Kingdom of *Candaya*, which we shall reach presently: For though it appears not half an Hour to us since we left the Garden, we have, nevertheless, travell'd over a vast Tract of Air. I know nothing of the Matter, reply'd *Sancho*, but this I am very certain, that if your Madam *Magulane*, or *Magalona* (what d'ye call her) could sit this damn'd wooden Crupper without a good Cushion under her Tail, she must have a harder Pair of Buttocks than mine.

This Dialogue was certainly very pleasant all this while to the Duke, and Dutchess, and the rest of the Company; and now at last resolving to put an End to this extraordinary Adventure, which had so long entertain'd them successfully, they order'd one of their Servants to give fire to *Clavileno's* Tail; and the Horse being stuft full of squibs, crackers, and other fire-works, burst presently into Pieces, with a mighty Noise, throwing the Knight one Way, and the Squire another, both sufficiently sing'd. By this Time, the Disconsolate Matron, and bearded Regiment, were vanish'd out of the Garden, and all the rest counterfeiting a Trance, lay flat upon the Ground; Don *Quixote* and *Sancho* sorely bruis'd, made shift to get up, and looking about, were amaz'd to find themselves in the same Garden whence they took Horse, and see such a Number of People lie dead, as they thought, on the Ground. But their Wonder was diverted by the Appearance of a large Lance stuck in the Ground, and a Scroll of white Parchment fasten'd to it by two green silken Strings, with the following Inscription upon it in golden Characters.

The Renowned Knight, Don Quixote de la Mancha, *atchiev'd the Adventure of the Countess* Trifaldi, *otherwise call'd the Dis-*

consolate Matron, *and her Companions in Distress, by barely attempting it. Malambruno is fully satisfy'd. The Waiting-Gentlewomen have lost their Beards: King Clavijo and Queen Antonomasia have resum'd their pristine Shapes; and when the Squire's Penance shall be finish'd, the white Dove shall 'scape the Pounces of the pernicious Hawks that pursue her, and her pining Lover shall lull her in his Arms. This is pre-ordain'd by the sage Merlin, Proto-inchanter of Inchanters.*

Don *Quixote* having read this Oracle, and construing it to refer to *Dulcinea's* Disinchantment, render'd Thanks to Heaven for so great a Deliverance; and approaching the Duke and Dutchess, who seem'd as yet in a Swoon, he took the Duke by the Hand: Courage, Courage, Noble Sir, cry'd he, there's no Danger; the Adventure is finish'd without Bloodshed, as you may read it register'd in that Record.

The Duke, yawning and stretching, as if he had been wak'd out of a sound Sleep, recover'd himself by Degrees, as did the Dutchess, and the rest of the Company; all of them acting the Surprize so naturally, that the Jest could not be discover'd. The Duke, rubbing his Eyes, made a shift to read the Scroll; then embracing Don *Quixote*, he extoll'd his Valour to the Skies, assuring him, he was the bravest Knight the Earth had ever possess'd. As for *Sancho*, he was looking up and down the Garden for the Disconsolate Matron, to see what Sort of a Face she had got, now her Furz-bush was off. But he was inform'd, that as *Clavileno* came down flaming in the Air, the Countess, with her Women, vanish'd immediately, but not one of 'em Chinbristled, nor so much as a Hair upon their Faces.

Then the Dutchess ask'd *Sancho*, how he had far'd in his long Voyage? Why truly, Madam, answer'd he, I have seen Wonders; for you must know, that though my Master would not suffer me to pull the Cloth from my Eyes, yet as I have a Kind of Itch to know every Thing, and a Spice of the Spirit of Contradiction, still hankering after what's forbidden me; so when, as my Master told me, we were flying through the Region of Fire, I shov'd my Handkerchief a little above my Nose, and look'd down; and what d'you think I saw? I spy'd the Earth a hugeous Way afar off below me (Heaven bless us!) no bigger than a Mustard Seed; and the Men walking to and fro upon't, not much larger than Hazle-Nuts. Judge now if we were not got up woundy high! Have a Care what you say, my Friend, said the Dutchess; for if the Men were bigger than Hazle-Nuts, and the Earth no bigger than a Mustard-seed, one Man must be bigger than the whole Earth, and cover it so that you could not see it. Like enough, answer'd *Sancho*; but for all that, d'you see, I saw it with a Kind of a Side-Look upon one Part of it, or so. Look you, *Sancho*, reply'd the Dutchess, that won't bear; for Nothing can be wholly seen by any Part of it. Well, well, Madam, quoth *Sancho*, I don't understand your Parts and Wholes! I saw it, and there's an End of the Story. Only you must think, that as we flew by Inchantment, so we saw by Inchantment; and thus I might see the Earth, and all the Men, which Way soever I look'd. I'll warrant, you won't believe me neither when I tell you, that when I thrust up the Kerchief above my Brows, I saw my self so near Heaven, that between the Top of my Cap and the main Sky, there was not a Span and a half. And, Heaven bless us! forsooth, what a huge-ous great Place it is! And we happen'd to travel that Road where the seven She-Goatstars* were: And Faith and Troth, I had such a Mind to play with 'em (having been once a Goatherd my self) that I fancy I'd have cry'd my self to Death, had I not done it. So soon as I spy'd 'em, what does me I, but sneaks down very soberly from behind my Master, without telling any living Soul, and play'd, and leap'd about for three quarters of an Hour by the Clock, with the pretty Nanny-Goats, who are as sweet and fine as so many Marigolds or Gilly-flowers; and honest *Wooden Peg* stirr'd not one Step all the while. And while *Sancho* employ'd himself with the Goats, ask'd the Duke, how was Don *Quixote* employ'd? Truly, answer'd the Knight, I am sensible all Things were alter'd from their natural Course; therefore what *Sancho* says, seems the less strange to me. But for my own Part, I neither saw Heaven nor Hell, Sea nor Shore. I perceiv'd indeed we pass'd through the middle Region of the Air, and were pretty near that of Fire, but that we came so near Heaven, as *Sancho* says, is altogether incredible; because we then must have pass'd quite through the fiery Region, which lies between the Sphere of the Moon and the

* *The* Pleiades, *vulgarly call'd in* Spanish, *the Seven Young She-Goats.*

upper Region of the Air. Now it was impossible for us to reach that Part, where are the *Pleiades*, or the *Seven Goats*, as *Sancho* calls 'em, without being consum'd in the elemental Fire; and therefore since we escaped those Flames, certainly we did not soar so high, and *Sancho* either lies or dreams. I neither lie nor dream, reply'd *Sancho*. Uds Precious! I can tell you the Marks and Colour of every Goat among 'em. If you don't believe me, do but ask and try me. You'll easily see whether I speak Truth or no. Well, said the Dutchess, prithee tell them me, *Sancho*. Look you, answer'd *Sancho*, there were two of 'em green, two carnation, two blue, and one party-colour'd. Truly, said the Duke, that's a new Kind of Goats you have found out, *Sancho*, we have none of those Colours upon Earth. Sure, Sir, reply'd *Sancho*, you'll make some Sort of Difference between heavenly She-Goats, and the Goats of this World? But *Sancho*, said the Duke, among those She-Goats did you see never a He?* not one horn'd Beast of the masculine Gender? Not one, Sir, I saw no other horn'd Thing but the Moon; and I have been told, that neither He-Goats, nor any other cornuted Tups are suffer'd to lift their Horns beyond those of the Moon.

They did not think fit to ask *Sancho* any more Questions about his airy Voyage, for, in the Humour he was in, they judg'd he would not stick to ramble all over the Heavens, and tell 'em News of whatever was doing there, though he had not stirr'd out of the Garden all the while.

Thus ended, in short, the Adventure of the Disconsolate Matron, which afforded sufficient Sport to the Duke and Dutchess, not only for the present, but for the rest of their Lives; and might have supply'd *Sancho* with Matter of Talk from Generation to Generation, for many Ages, could he have liv'd so long. *Sancho* (said Don *Quixote*, whispering him in the Ear) since thou wou'dst have us believe what thou hast seen in Heaven, I desire thee to believe what I saw in *Montesinos's* Cave. Not a Word more.

* Cabron: *A Jest on the double Meaning of that Word, which signifies both* a He-Goat *and a* Cuckold. Sancho, *by his Answer, seems to take, or hit by Chance on the Jest.*

IX: THE INSTRUCTIONS WHICH DON QUIXOTE GAVE SANCHO PANÇA, BEFORE HE WENT TO THE GOVERNMENT OF HIS ISLAND, WITH OTHER MATTERS OF MOMENT

THE Satisfaction which the Duke and Dutchess receiv'd by the happy Success of the Adventure of the Disconsolate Matron, encourag'd 'em to carry on some other pleasant Project, since they could with so much Ease impose on the Credulity of Don *Quixote*, and his Squire. Having therefore given Instructions to their Servants and Vassals how to behave themselves towards *Sancho* in his Government; the Day after the Scene of the Wooden-Horse, the Duke bid *Sancho* prepare, and be in a Readiness to take Possession of his Government; for now his Islanders wish'd as heartily for him, as they did for Rain in a dry Summer. *Sancho* made an humble Bow, and looking demurely on the Duke, Sir, quoth he, since I came down from Heaven, whence I saw the Earth so very small, I an't half so hot as I was for being a Governor. For what Greatness can there be in being at the Head of a puny Dominion, that's but a little Nook of a tiny Mustard-seed? And what Dignity and Power can a Man be reckon'd to have, in governing half a dozen Men no bigger than Hazle-Nuts? For I could not think there were any more in the whole World. No, if your Grace would throw away upon me never so little a Corner in Heaven, though it were but half a League, or so, I would take it with better Will than I would the largest Island on Earth. Friend *Sancho*, answer'd the Duke, I can't dispose of an Inch of Heaven; for that's the Province of God alone; but what I am able to bestow, I give you; that is, an Island tight and clever, round and well proportion'd, fertile and plentiful to such a Degree, that if you have but the Art and Understanding to manage Things right, you may make Hoard there both of the Treasure of this World and the next.

Well then, quoth *Sancho*, let me have this Island, and I'll do my best to be such a Governor, that, in spite of Rogues, I shan't want a small Nook in Heaven one Day or other. 'Tis not out of

Covetousness neither, that I'd leave my little Cott, and set up for somebody, but meerly to know what Kind of Thing it is to be a Governor. Oh! *Sancho*, said the Duke, when once you've had a Taste of it, you'll never leave licking your Fingers, 'tis so sweet and bewitching a Thing to command and be obey'd. I am confident, when your Master comes to be an Emperor (as he cannot fail to be, according to the Course of his Affairs) he will never by any Consideration be persuaded to Abdicate; his only Grief will be, that he was one no sooner.

Troth, Sir, reply'd *Sancho*, I am of your Mind; 'tis a dainty Thing to command, though 'twere but a Flock of Sheep. Oh! *Sancho*, cry'd the Duke, let me live and die with thee; for thou hast an Insight into every Thing. I hope thou'lt prove as good a Governor as thy Wisdom bespeaks thee. But no more at this Time,—to Morrow, without further Delay, you set forward to your Island, and shall be furnish'd this Afternoon with Equipage and Dress answerable to your Post, and all other Necessaries for your Journey.

Let 'em dress me as they will, quoth *Sancho*, I shall be the same *Sancho Pança* still. That's true, said the Duke, yet every Man ought to wear Clothes suitable to his Place and Dignity; for a Lawyer should not go dress'd like a Soldier, nor a Soldier like a Priest. As for you, *Sancho*, you are to wear the Habit both of a Captain and a Civil Magistrate; so your Dress shall be a Compound of those two; for in the Government that I bestow on you, Arms are as necessary as Learning, and a Man of Letters as requisite as a Swordsman.—Nay, as for Letters, quoth *Sancho*, I can't say much for my self: For as yet I scarce know my A, B, C; but yet, if I can but remember my *Christ's-Cross*,* 'tis enough to make me a good Governor: As for my Arms, I'll not quit my Weapon as long as I can stand, and so Heaven be our Guard. *Sancho* can't do amiss, said the Duke, while he remembers these Things.

By this Time Don *Quixote* arriv'd, and hearing how suddenly *Sancho* was to go to his Government, with the Duke's Permission, he took him aside to give him some good Instructions for his Conduct in the Discharge of his Office.

* *He means the* Christ-cross-Row; *so call'd from the* Cross *being put at the Beginning of the* A, B, C.

Being enter'd Don *Quixote's* Chamber, and the Door shut, he almost forcibly oblig'd *Sancho* to sit by him; and then with a grave deliberate Voice he thus began.

I give Heaven infinite Thanks, Friend *Sancho*, that before I have the Happiness of being put in Possession of my Hopes, I can see thine already crown'd: Fortune hastening to meet thee with thy Wishes. I, who had assign'd the Reward of thy Services upon my happy Success, am yet but on the Way to Preferment; and thou, beyond all reasonable Expectation, art arriv'd at the Aim and End of thy Desires. Some are assiduous, solicitous, importunate, rise early, bribe, intreat, press, will take no Denial, obstinately persist in their Suit, and yet at last never obtain it. Another comes on, and by a lucky Hit or Chance, bears away the Prize, and jumps into the Preferment which so many had pursu'd in vain; which verifies the Saying, *The Happy have their Days, and those they choose; The Unhappy have but Hours, and those they lose.* Thou, who seem'st to me a very Blockhead, without sitting up late, or rising early, or any manner of Fatigue or Trouble, only the Air of Knight-Errantry being breath'd on thee, art advanc'd to the Government of an Island in a trice, as if it were a Thing of no Moment, a very Trifle. I speak this, my dear *Sancho*, not to upbraid thee, nor out of Envy, but only to let thee know, thou art not to attribute all this Success to thy own Merit, while 'tis entirely owing to the kind heavenly Disposer of human Affairs, to whom thy Thanks ought to be return'd. But, next to Heaven, thou art to ascribe thy Happiness to the Greatness of the Profession of Knight-Errantry, which includes within it self such Stores of Honour and Preferment.

Being convinc'd of what I have already said, be yet attentive, O my Son, to what I, thy *Cato*, have further to say: Listen, I say, to my Admonitions, and I will be thy North-Star, and Pilot to steer and bring thee safe into the Port of Honour, out of the tempestuous Ocean, into which thou art just going to launch; for Offices and great Employments are no better than profound Gulphs of Confusion.

First of all, O my Son, fear God; for the Fear of God is the beginning of Wisdom, and Wisdom will never let thee go astray.

Secondly, Consider what thou wert, and make it thy Business to know thy self, which is the most difficult Lesson in the World. Yet from this Lesson thou wilt learn to avoid the Frog's foolish Ambition of Swelling to rival the Bigness of the Ox; else the Consideration of your having been a Hog-driver, will be, to the Wheel of your Fortune, like the Peacock's ugly Feet.*

True, quoth *Sancho*, but I was then but a little Boy; for when I grew up to be somewhat bigger, I drove Geese, and not Hogs. But methinks that's nothing to the Purpose; for all Governors can't come from Kings and Princes.

Very true, pursu'd Don *Quixote*; therefore those who want a noble Descent, must allay the Severity of their Office with Mildness and Civility, which, directed by Wisdom, may secure 'em from the Murmurs and Malice, from which no State nor Condition is exempt.

Be well pleased with the Meanness of thy Family, *Sancho*; nor think it a Disgrace to own thy self deriv'd from Labouring Men; for, if thou art not ashamed of it thy self, no body else will strive to make thee so. Endeavour rather to be esteem'd humble and virtuous, than proud and vicious. The Number is almost infinite, of those who, from low and vulgar Births, have been rais'd to the highest Dignities, to the Papal Chair, and the Imperial Throne; and this I could prove by Examples enough to tire thy Patience.

Make Virtue the Medium of all thy Actions, and thou wilt have no Cause to envy those whose Birth gives 'em the Titles of great Men, and Princes; for Nobility is inherited, but Virtue acquir'd: And Virtue is worth more in it self, than Nobleness of Birth.

If any of thy poor Relations come to see thee, never reject nor affront 'em; but, on the contrary, receive and entertain 'em with Marks of Favour; in this thou wilt display a Generosity of Nature, and please Heaven, that would have no body despise what it has made.

If thou send'st for thy Wife, as 'tis not fit a man in thy station should be long without his Wife, and she ought to partake of her Husband's good Fortune, teach her, instruct her, polish

---

* *The Peacock, in the Fable, prided herself in her Beauty, till she was put in Mind of her ugly Feet.*

her the best thou canst, till her native rusticity is refin'd to a handsomer Behaviour: For often an ill-bred Wife throws down all that a good and discreet Husband can build up.

Should'st thou come to be a Widower (which is not impossible) and thy Post recommended thee to a Bride of a higher Degree, take not one that shall, like a Fishing-Rod, only serve to catch Bribes. For, take it from me, the Judge must, at the general and last Court of Judicature, give a strict account of the Discharge of his Duty, and must pay severely at his dying Day for what he has suffered his Wife to take.

Let never obstinate Self-conceit be thy Guide; 'tis the Vice of the ignorant, who vainly presume on their Understanding.

Let the Tears of the Poor find more Compassion, though not more Justice, than the Informations of the Rich.

Be equally solicitous to find out the Truth, where the Offers and Presents of the Rich, and the Sobs and Importunities of the Poor, are in the Way.

Where ever Equity should, or may take Place, let not the Extent or Rigour of the Law bear too much on the Delinquent; for 'tis not a better Character in a Judge to be rigorous, than to be indulgent.

When the Severity of the Law is to be softned, let Pity, not Bribes, be the Motive.

If thy Enemy has a Cause before thee, turn away thy Eyes from thy Prejudice, and fix them on the Matter of Fact.

In another Man's Cause, be not blinded by thy own Passions, for those Errors are almost without Remedy; or their Cure will prove expensive to thy Wealth and Reputation.

When a beautiful Woman comes before thee, turn away thy Eyes from her Tears, and thy Ears from her Lamentations; and take Time to consider sedately her Petition, if thou would'st not have thy Reason and Honesty lost in her Sighs and Tears.

Revile not with Words those whom their Crimes oblige thee to punish in Deed; for the Punishment is enough to the Wretches, without the Addition of ill Language.

In the Trial of Criminals, consider as much as thou canst without Prejudice to the Plaintiff, how defenceless and open the miserable are to the Temptations of our corrupt and deprav'd Nature, and so far shew thy self full of Pity and Clemency; for though God's Attributes are equal, yet his Mercy is more attractive and pleasing in our Eyes, than his Justice.

If thou observ'st these Rules, *Sancho*, thy Days shall be long, thy Fame eternal, thy Recompence full, and thy Felicity unspeakable. Thou shalt marry thy Children and Grand-Children to thy Heart's Desire; they shall want no Titles: Belov'd of all Men, thy Life shall be peaceable, thy Death in a good and venerable old Age, and the Off-spring of thy Grand-Children, with their soft youthful Hands, shall close thy Eyes.

The Precepts I have hitherto given thee, regard the Good and Ornament of thy Mind. Now give Attention to those Directions that relate to the adorning of thy Body.

X: THE SECOND PART OF DON QUIXOTE'S
ADVICE TO SANCHO PANÇA

WHO would not have taken Don *Quixote* for a Man of extraordinary Wisdom, and as excellent Morals, having heard him documentize his Squire in this Manner; only, as we have often observ'd in this History, the least Talk of Knight-Errantry spoil'd all, and made his Understanding muddy; but in every Thing else, his Judgment was very clear, and his Apprehension very nice, so that every Moment his Actions us'd to discredit his Judgment, and his Judgment his Actions. But in these œconomical Precepts which he gave *Sancho*, he shew'd himself Master of a pleasant Fancy, and mingled his Judgment and Extravagance in equal Proportions. *Sancho* lent him a great deal of Attention, in hopes to register all those good Counsels in his Mind, and put them in Practice; not doubting but by their Means he should acquit himself of his Duty like a Man of Honour.

As to the Government of thy Person and Family (pursu'd Don *Quixote*) my first Injunction is Cleanliness. Pare thy Nails, nor let 'em grow as some do, whose Folly persuades them, that long Nails add to the Beauty of the Hand; till they look more like *Castril's* Claws, than a Man's Nails. 'Tis foul and unsightly.

Keep thy Clothes tight about thee; for a slovenly Looseness is an Argument of a careless Mind; unless such a Negligence, like that of *Julius Cæsar*, be affected for some cunning Design.

Prudently examine what thy Income may amount to in a Year: And if sufficient to afford thy Servants Liveries, let them be decent and lasting, rather than gaudy and for Show; and for the Over-plus of thy good Husbandry, bestow it on the Poor. That is, if thou canst keep six Footmen, have but three; and let what would maintain three more, be laid out in charitable Uses. By that Means thou wilt have Attendants in Heaven as well as on Earth, which our vainglorious great ones, who are Strangers to this Practice, are not like to have.

Lest thy Breath betray thy Peasantry, defile it not with Onions and Garlick.

Walk with Gravity, and speak with Deliberation, and yet not as if thou didst hearken to thy own Words; for all Affectation is a Fault.

Eat little at Dinner, and less at Supper; for the Stomach is the Storehouse, whence Health is to be imparted to the whole Body.

Drink moderately; for Drunkenness neither keeps a Secret, nor observes a Promise.

Be careful not to chew on both Sides, that is, fill not thy Mouth too full, and take heed not to eruct before Company.

Eruct, quoth *Sancho*, I don't understand that cramp Word. To eruct, answer'd Don *Quixote*, is as much as to say, *to belch*; but this being one of the most disagreeable and beastly Words in our Language, though very expressive and significant, the more polite, instead of *belching*, say *eructing*, which is borrow'd from the *Latin*. Now though the vulgar may not understand this, it matters not much; for Use and Custom will make it familiar and understood. By such Innovations are Languages enrich'd, when the Words are adopted by the Multitude, and naturaliz'd by Custom.

Faith and Troth, quoth *Sancho*, of all your Counsels, I'll be sure not to forget this, for I've been mightily given to *belching*. Say eructing, reply'd Don *Quixote*, and leave off belching. Well, quoth *Sancho*, be it as you say, eruct, I'll be sure to remember.

In the next place, *Sancho*, said the Knight, do not overlard your common Discourse with that glut of Proverbs, which you mix in it continually; for though Proverbs are properly concise and pithy Sentences, yet as thou bring'st 'em in, in such a huddle, by the Head and Shoulders, thou makest 'em look like so many Absurdities. Alas! Sir, quoth *Sancho*, this is a Disease that Heaven alone can cure; for I've more Proverbs than will fill a Book; and when I talk, they crowd so thick and fast to my Mouth, that they quarrel which shall get out first; so that my Tongue is forc'd to let 'em out as fast, first come first serv'd, though nothing to my Purpose. But henceforwards I'll set a Watch on my Mouth, and let none fly out, but such as shall befit the Gravity of my Place. For in a rich Man's House the Cloth is soon laid; where there's Plenty the Guests can't be empty. A Blot's no Blot till 'tis hit. He's safe who stands under the Bells; you can't eat your Cake and have your Cake; and Store's no Sore.

Go on, go on, Friend, said Don *Quixote*, thread, tack, stitch on, heap Proverb on Proverb, out with 'em Man, spew them out! There's no body coming. My Mother whips me, and I whip the Gigg. I warn thee to forbear foisting in a Rope of Proverbs every where, and thou blunder'st out a whole Litany of old Saws, as much to the Purpose as *the last Year's Snow*. Observe me, *Sancho*, I condemn not the Use of Proverbs; but 'tis most certain, that such a Confusion and Hodge-podge of 'em, as thou throw'st out and dragg'st in by the Hair together, make Conversation fulsom and poor.

When thou do'st ride, cast not thy Body all on the Crupper, nor hold thy Legs stiff down, and straddling from the Horse's Belly; nor yet so loose, as if thou wert still on *Dapple*; for the Air and Gracefulness of sitting a Horse, distinguishes sometimes a Gentleman from a Groom. Sleep with Moderation; for he that rises not with the Sun, loses so much Day. And remember this, *Sancho*, that Diligence is the Mother of good Fortune: Sloth, on the contrary, never effected any thing that sprung from a good and reasonable Desire.

The Advice which I shall conclude with, I would have thee be sure to fix in thy Memory, though it relate not to the adorning thy Person; for I am persuaded, it will redound as much to thy Advantage, as any I have yet given thee: And this it is:

Never undertake to dispute, or decide any Controversies, concerning the Pre-eminence of Families; since in the Comparison, one must be better than the other; for he that is lessen'd by thee will hate thee, and the other whom thou preferrest will not think himself obliged to thee.

As for thy Dress, wear close Breeches and Hose, a long Coat, and a Cloak a little longer. I don't advise thee to wear wide-kneed'd Breeches, or Trunk-Hose, for they become neither Swordsmen, nor Men of Business.

This is all the Advice, Friend *Sancho*, I have to give thee at present. If thou takest Care to let me hear from thee hereafter, I shall give thee more, according as the Occasions and Emergencies require.

Sir, said *Sancho*, I see very well that all you've told me is mighty good, wholesom, and to the Purpose: But what am I the better, if I cannot keep it in my Head? I grant you, I shan't easily forget That about paring my Nails, and marrying again, if I should have the Luck to bury my Wife. But for all that other Gallimaufry, and Heap of Stuff, I can no more remember one Syllable of it, than the Shapes of last Year's Clouds. Therefore let me have it in black and white, I beseech you. 'Tis true, I can neither write nor read, but I'll give it to my Father Confessor, that he may beat and hammer it into my Noddle, as Occasion serves. O Heaven, cry'd Don *Quixote*, how scandalous it looks in a Governor not to be able to write or read! I must needs tell thee, *Sancho*, that for a Man to be so illiterate, or to be left-handed, implies that either his Parents were very poor and mean, or that he was of so perverse a Nature, he could not receive the Impressions of Learning, or any Thing that is good. Poor Soul, I pity thee! This is indeed a very great Defect. I would have thee at least learn to write thy Name. Oh! as for that, quoth *Sancho*, I can do well enough: I can set my Name; for when I serv'd Offices in our Parish, I learnt to scrawl a Sort of Letters, such as they mark Bundles of Stuff with, which they told me spelt my Name. Besides, I can pretend my right Hand is lame, and so another shall sign for me; for there's a Remedy for all Things but Death. And since I've the Power, I'll do what I list; for as the Saying is, *He whose Father is Judge, goes safe to his Trial.** And as I am a Governor, I hope I am somewhat higher than a Judge. New Lords, new Laws. Ay, ay, any, let them come as they will, and play at Bo-peep. Let 'em backbite me to my Face, I'll bite-back the Biters. Let 'em come for Wool, and I'll send 'em home shorn. Whom God loves, his House happy proves. The rich Man's Follies pass for wise Sayings in this World. So I, being

* *The new Translation has it*, He whose Father is Mayor——*with a Break, and this Note at bottom*, viz.

Sancho *hints at* some well known Proverb.

The Proverb may be found in Stevens's *Dictionary:* Quien padre tiene Alcalde seguro va al juicio. *The Original indeed does break off in the Middle, as being a well known Proverb, applicable to all that have powerful Friends.*

rich, d'you see, and a Governor, and free-hearted too into the
Bargain, as I intend to be, I shall have no Faults at all. 'Tis
so, daub your self with Honey, and you'll never want Flies.
What a Man has, so much he's sure of, said my old Grannam;
and who shall hang the Bell about the Cat's Neck?

Confound thee, cry'd Don *Quixote*, for an eternal Proverb-
voiding Swag-belly. Threescore thousand *Belzebubs* take
thee, and thy damn'd nauseous Rubbish. Thou hast been this
Hour stringing them together, like so many Ropes of Onions,
and poisoning and racking* me with 'em. I dare say, these
wicked Proverbs will one Day bring thee to the Gallows;
they'll provoke thy Islanders to pull thee down, or at least
make 'em shun thee like a common Nuisance. Tell me, thou
Essence of Ignorance, where dost thou rake 'em up? And who
taught thy Cods-head to apply 'em? For it makes me sweat,
as if I were delving and threshing, to speak but one, and apply
it properly.

Udsprecious! my good Master, quoth *Sancho*, what a small
Matter puts you in a pelting Chase! Why the Devil should you
grudge me the Use of my own Goods and Chattels? I have no
other Estate. Proverbs on Proverbs are all my Stock. And now
I have four ready to pop out, as pat to the Purpose as Pears to
a Panier.† But mum for that. Now Silence is my Name.‡ No,
reply'd Don *Quixote*, rather Prate-roast and Sauce-box I should
call thee; for thou art all Tittle-tattle and Obstinacy. Yet
methinks I'd fain hear these four notable Proverbs that come
so pat to the Purpose. I thank Heaven I have a pretty good
Memory, and yet I can't for my Soul call one to Mind. Why,
Sir, quoth *Sancho*, what Proverbs would you have better than
these? Between two Cheek Teeth never clap thy Thumbs.
And when a Man says, get out of my House; what would you

---

* *The Original is*, Draughts of the Rack. *It alludes to a particular Kind
of Torture in* Spain; *namely, a thin Piece of Gauze, moisten'd, and put to
the Lips of a Person dying with Thirst, who swallows it down by Degrees,
and then it is pull'd up again by the End the Executioner holds in his
Hand.*   † *Pears sent to* Madrid, *from* Daroca, *in March, when they are
scarce, and made up nicely, to prevent bruising.*   ‡ *In the Original,* To
keep Silence well is call'd *Sancho. The Proverb is,* To keep Silence well
is called (*Santo*) Holy: *But* Sancho, *out of Archness or Ignorance, changes*
Santo *to his own Name* Sancho.

with my Wife? There's no Answer to be made. And again, whether the Pitcher hit the Stone, or the Stone the Pitcher, 'tis bad for the Pitcher. All these fit to a Hair, Sir; That is, let no body meddle with his Governor, or his Betters, or he'll rue for it, as sure as a Gun; as he must expect who runs his Finger between two Cheek-Teeth (and though they were not Cheek-Teeth, if they be but Teeth, that's enough.) In the next Place, let the Governor say what he will, there's no gainsaying him; 'tis as much as when one says, get out of my House; what would you with my Wife? And as for the Stone and the Pitcher, a blind Man may see through it. And so he that sees a Mote in another Man's Eye, should do well to take the Beam out of his own; that People mayn't say, the Pot calls the Kettle black-arse, and the dead Woman's afraid of her that's flea'd. Besides, your Worship knows, that a Fool knows more in his own House, than a wise body in another Man's. That's a Mistake, *Sancho*, reply'd Don *Quixote*; for the Fool knows nothing, neither in his own House, nor in another Man's; for no substantial Knowledge can be erected on so bad a Foundation as Folly. But let's break off this Discourse: If thou dost not discharge the Part of a good Governor, thine will be the Fault, though the Shame and Discredit will be mine. However, this is my Comfort, I've done my Duty in giving thee the best and most wholesom Advice I could: And so Heaven prosper and direct thee in thy Government, and disappoint my Fears of thy turning all Things upside down in that poor Island; which I might indeed prevent, by giving the Duke a more perfect Insight into thee, and discovering to him, that all that gor-belly'd paunch-gutted little Corps of thine, is nothing but a Bundle of Proverbs, and Sack-full of Knavery.

Look you, Sir, quoth *Sancho*, if you think me not fit for this Government I'll think no more on't. Alas! the least Snip of my Soul's Nails (as a Body may say) is dearer to me than my whole Body: And I hope I can live plain *Sancho* still, upon a Luncheon of Bread and a Clove of Garlick, as contented as Governor *Sancho* upon Capons and Partridges. Death and Sleep makes us all alike, Rich and Poor, High and Low. Do but call to mind what first put this Whim of Government into my Noddle, you'll find 'twas your own self; for as for me, I know no more what belongs to Islands and Governors than a blind Buzzard.

So if you fancy the Devil will have me for being a Governor, let me be plain *Sancho* still, and go to Heaven; rather than my Lord Governor, and go to Hell.

These last Words of thine, *Sancho*, said Don *Quixote*, in my Opinion, prove thee worthy to govern a thousand Islands. Thou hast naturally a good Disposition, without which all Knowledge is insufficient. Recommend thy self to the Divine Providence, and be sure never to depart from Uprightness of Intention; I mean, have still a firm Purpose and Design to be thoroughly inform'd in all the Business that shall come before thee, and act upon just Grounds, for Heaven always favours good Desires: And so let's go to Dinner, for I believe now the Duke and Dutchess expect us.

XI: HOW SANCHO PANÇA WAS CARRIED TO HIS GOVERNMENT, AND OF THE STRANGE ADVENTURE THAT BEFEL DON QUIXOTE IN THE CASTLE

WE have it from the traditional Account of this History, that there is a manifest Difference between the Translation and the *Arabick* in the Beginning of this Chapter; *Cid Hamet* having in the Original taken an Occasion of criticizing on himself, for undertaking so dry and limited a Subject, which must confine him to the bare History of Don *Quixote* and *Sancho*, and debar him the Liberty of launching into Episodes and Digressions that might be of more Weight and Entertainment. To have his Fancy, his Hand and Pen bound up to a single Design, and his Sentiments confin'd to the Mouths of so few Persons, he urg'd as an insupportable Toil, and of small Credit to the Undertaker; so that, to avoid this Inconveniency, he has introduc'd into the first Part, some Novels, as *The Curious Impertinent*, and that of the *Captive*, which were in a manner distinct from the Design, though the rest of the Stories which he brought in there, fall naturally enough in with Don *Quixote's* Affairs, and seem of Necessity to claim a Place in the Work. It was his Opinion likewise, as he has told us, that the Adventures of Don *Quixote*, requiring so great a Share of the Reader's Attention, his *Novels*, must expect but an indifferent Reception, or, at most, but a cursory View, not sufficient to discover their artificial Contexture, which must have been very obvious had they been publish'd by themselves, without the Interludes of Don *Quixote's* Madness, or *Sancho's* Impertinence. He has therefore in this second Part avoided all distinct and independent Stories, introducing only such as have the Appearance of Episodes, yet flow naturally from the Design of the Story, and these but seldom, and with as much Brevity as they can be express'd. Therefore since he has ty'd himself up to such narrow Bounds, and confin'd his Understanding and Parts, otherwise capable of the most copious Subjects, to the pure Matter of this present Undertaking, he begs it may add a Value to his Work; and that he may be commended, not so much for what he has writ, as for what he has forborn to write. And then he proceeds in his History as follows.

After Dinner Don *Quixote* gave *Sancho* in Writing the Copy of his verbal Instructions, ordering him to get some Body to read 'em to him. But the Squire had no sooner got them, but he dropt the Paper, which fell into the Duke's Hands; who communicating the same to the Dutchess, they found a fresh Occasion of admiring the Mixture of Don *Quixote's* good Sense and Extravagance: And so carrying on the Humour, they sent *Sancho* that Afternoon with a suitable Equipage to the Place he was to govern, which, where-ever it lay, was to be an Island to him.

It happen'd that the Management of this Affair was committed to a Steward of the Duke's, a Man of a facetious Humour, and who had not only Wit to start a pleasant Design, but Discretion to carry it on; two Qualifications which make an agreeable Consort when they meet, nothing being truly agreeable without good Sense. He had already personated the Countess *Trifaldi* very successfully, and, with his Master's Instructions, in relation to his Behaviour towards *Sancho*, could not but discharge his Trust to a Wonder. Now it fell out, that *Sancho* no sooner cast his Eyes on the Steward, but he fancy'd he saw the very Face of *Trifaldi*; and turning to his Master, The Devil fetch me, Sir, quoth he, if you don't own that this same Steward of the Duke's here has the very Phiz of my Lady *Trifaldi*. Don *Quixote* look'd very earnestly on the Steward; and having perus'd him from Top to Toe, *Sancho*, said he, thou need'st not give thy self to the Devil to confirm this Matter: I see their Faces are the very same; yet for all that the Steward and the Disconsolate Lady cannot be the same Person; for that would imply a very great Contradiction, and might involve us in more abstruse and difficult Doubts, than we have Conveniency now to discuss or examine. Believe me, Friend, our Devotion cannot be too earnest, that we may be deliver'd from the Power of these cursed Inchantments. Adad, Sir, quoth *Sancho*, you may think I'm in Jest; but I heard him open just now, and I thought the very Voice of Madam *Trifaldi* sounded in my Ears:

But Mum's the Word: I say nothing, though I shall watch his Waters to find out whether I am right or wrong in my Suspicion. Well, do so, said Don *Quixote*; and fail not to acquaint me with all the Discoveries thou canst make in this Affair, and other Occurrences in thy Government.

At last *Sancho* set out, with a numerous Train. He was dress'd like a Man of the long Robe, and wore over his other Clothes a wide sad-colour'd Coat or Gown of water'd Camblet, and a Cap of the same Stuff. He was mounted on a He-Mule, and rid short after the Gennet Fashion. Behind him, by the Duke's Order, was led his *Dapple*, bridl'd and saddl'd like a Horse of State, in gaudy Trappings of Silk; which so delighted *Sancho*, that every now and then he turn'd his Head about to look upon him, and thought himself so happy, that now he would not have chang'd Fortunes with the Emperor of *Germany*. He kiss'd the Duke and Dutchess's Hand at parting, and receiv'd his Master's Benediction, while the Don wept, and *Sancho* blubber'd abundantly.

Now, Reader, let the noble Governor depart in Peace, and speed him well. His Administration in his Government may perhaps make you laugh to some Purpose, when it comes in play. But in the mean time let us observe the Fortune of his Master the same Night; for though it don't make you laugh outright, it may chance to make ye draw in your Lips, and shew your Teeth like a Monkey; for 'tis the Property of his Adventures, to create always either Surprize or Merriment.

'Tis reported then, that immediately upon *Sancho's* Departure, Don *Quixote* found the want of his Presence; and had it been in his Power, he wou'd have revok'd his Authority, and depriv'd him of his Commission. The Dutchess perceiving his Disquiet, and desiring to understand the Cause of his Melancholy, told him, that if it was *Sancho's* Absence made him uneasy, she had Squires enough and Damsels in her House, that should supply his Place in any Service he wou'd be pleas'd to command 'em. 'Tis true, Madam, answer'd Don *Quixote*, I am somewhat concern'd for the Absence of *Sancho*; but there is a more material Cause of my present Uneasiness; and I must beg to be excus'd, if among the many Obligations your Grace is pleas'd to confer on me, I decline all but the good Intention that has offer'd 'em. All I have further to crave, is your Grace's Permission to be alone in my Apartment, and to be my own Servant. Your Pardon, Sir, reply'd the Dutchess; I can't consent you shou'd be alone: I have four Damsels, blooming as so many Roses, that shall attend you. They will be no Roses to me, return'd Don *Quixote*, but so many Prickles to my Conscience; and if they come into my Chamber, they must fly in at the Window. If your Grace would crown the many Favours you have heap'd on this worthless Person, I beseech you to leave him to himself, and the Service of his own Hands. No Desires, Madam, must enter my Doors; for the Walls of my Chamber have always been a Bulwark to my Chastity, and I shall not infringe my Rule for all the Bounty you can lavish on me. In fine, rather than think of being undress'd by any Mortal, I would lie rough the whole Night. Enough, enough, noble Sir, said the Dutchess; I desist, and will give Orders that not so much as the Buzzing of a Fly, much less the Impertinence of a Damsel, shall disturb your Privacy. I am far from imposing any thing, Sir, that should urge Don *Quixote* to a Transgression in Point of Decency; for if I conjecture right, among the many Virtues that adorn him, his Modesty is the most distinguishable. Dress therefore and undress by your self, how you please, when you will, and no body shall molest you: Nay, that you may not be obliged to open your Doors upon the Account of any natural Necessity, Care shall be taken that you may find in your Room whatever you may have Occasion for in the Night. And may the great *Dulcinea del Toboso* live a thousand Ages, and her Fame be diffus'd all over the habitable Globe, since she has merited the Love of so valorous, so chaste, and loyal a Knight; and may the indulgent Heavens incline the Heart of our Governor *Sancho Pança*, to put a speedy End to his Discipline, that the Beauties of so great a Lady may be restor'd to the View of the admiring World! Madam, return'd Don *Quixote*, your Grace has spoken like your self; so excellent a Lady could utter nothing but what denotes the Goodness and Generosity of her Mind: And certainly 'twill be *Dulcinea's* peculiar Happiness to have been prais'd by you; for 'twill raise her Character more to have had your Grace for her Panegyrist, than if the best Orators in the World had labour'd to set it forth. Sir, said the Dutchess, waving this Discourse, 'tis Supper-time, and my Lord expects us: Come then, let's to Supper, that you may go to Bed betimes; for you must needs be weary still with the long Journey you took to *Candaya* Yesterday. Indeed, Madam, answer'd Don *Quixote*, I feel no Manner of Weariness, for I can safely swear to your Grace, that I never rid an easier Beast, nor a better Goer than *Clavileno*. For my Part, I can't imagine what could induce *Malambruno* to part with so swift and gentle a Horse, nay, and to burn him too in such a Manner. 'Tis to be suppos'd, said the Dutchess, that being sorry for the Harm he had done, not only to the Countess *Trifaldi* and her Attendants, but to many others, and repenting of the bad Deeds which, as a Wizzard and a Necromancer, he doubtless had committed, he had a Mind to destroy all the Instruments of his wicked Profession, and accordingly he burn'd *Clavileno* as the chief of 'em, that Engine having serv'd him to rove all over the World: Or perhaps he did not think any Man worthy of bestriding him after the great Don *Quixote*, and so with his Destruction, and the Inscription which he has caus'd to be set up, he has eterniz'd your Valour.

Don *Quixote* return'd his Thanks to the Dutchess, and after Supper retir'd to his Chamber, not suffering any Body to attend him; so much he fear'd to meet some Temptation that might endanger the Fidelity which he had consecrated to his *Dulcinea*, keeping always the Eyes of his Mind fix'd on the Constancy of *Amadis*, the Flower and Mirror of Knight-Errantry. He therefore shut the Door of his Chamber after him, and undress'd himself by the Light of two Wax-Candles. But oh! the Misfortune that befell him, unworthy such a Person. As he was straining to pull off his Hose, there fell, not Sighs, or any thing that might disgrace his decent Cleanliness, but about four and twenty Stitches of one of his Stockings, which made it look like a Lattice-Window. The good Knight was extremely afflicted, and would have given then an Ounce of Silver for a Dram of green Silk; green Silk, I say, because his Stockings were green.

Here *Benengeli* could not forbear exclaiming: O Poverty! Poverty! What could induce that great *Cordova* Poet to call thee a holy thankless Gift! Even I that am a *Moor*, have learn'd

by the Converse I have had with Christians, that Holiness con-
sists in Charity, in Humility, in Faith, in Obedience, and in
Poverty: But sure he who can be contented when Poor, had
need to be strengthen'd by God's peculiar Grace; unless the
Poverty which is included among these Virtues, be only that
Poorness in Spirit, which teaches us to use the things of this
World as if we had 'em not. But thou, second Poverty, fatal
Indigence, of which I now am speaking, why dost thou intrude
upon Gentlemen, and affect well-born Souls more than other
People? Why dost thou reduce them to cobble their Shoes,
and wear some Silk, some Hair, and some Glass Buttons on the
same tatter'd Waistcoat, as if it were only to betray Variety of
Wretchedness? Why must their Ruffs be of such a dismal Hue,
in Rags, dirty, rumpl'd, and ill starch'd? (and by this you may
see how ancient is the use of Starch and Ruffs). How miserable
is a poor Gentleman, who to keep up his Honour, starves his
Person, fares sorrily, or fasts unseen within his solitary narrow Apartment; then putting the best Face he can upon the
Matter, comes out picking his Teeth, though 'tis but an honourable Hypocrisy, and though he has eaten nothing that requires that nice Exercise! Unhappy he, whose Honour is in
continual Alarms, who thinks that at a Mile's Distance every
one discovers the Patch in his Shoe, the Sweat of his Forehead
soak'd through his old rusty Hat, the Bareness of his Clothes,
and the very Hunger of his famish'd Stomach.

All these melancholy Reflections were renew'd on Don
Quixote's Mind by the Rent in his Stocking. However, for his
Consolation, he bethought himself that *Sancho* had left him a
Pair of light Boots, which he design'd to put on the next Day.

In short, to Bed he went, with a pensive heavy Mind, the
thoughts of *Sancho's* Absence, and the irreparable Damage
that his Stocking had receiv'd, made him uneasy: He would
have darn'd it, though it had been with Silk of another Colour,
one of the greatest Tokens of Want a poor Gentleman can shew,
during the course of his tedious Misery.

At last he put out the Lights, but 'twas sultry hot, and he
could not compose himself to Rest. Getting up therefore, he
open'd a little Shutter of a barr'd Window that look'd into a
fine Garden, and was presently sensible that some People were

walking and talking there: He listen'd, and as they rais'd their Voices, he easily overheard their Discourse.

No more, dear *Emerenia*, said one to the other: Do not press me to sing; you know that from the first Moment this Stranger came to the Castle, and my unhappy Eyes gaz'd on him, I have been too conversant with Tears and Sorrow, to sing or relish Songs. Alas! all Musick jars when the Soul's out of Tune. Besides, you know the least thing wakens my Lady, and I would not for the World she should find us here. But grant she might not wake, what will my Singing signify, if this new *Æneas*, who is come to our Habitation to make me wretched, should be asleep, and not hear the Sound of my Complaints? Pray, my dear *Altisidora*, said the other, do not make your self uneasy with those Thoughts; for without doubt the Dutchess is fast asleep, and every Body in the House but We, and the Lord of thy Desires; He is certainly awake, I heard him open his Window just now; then sing, my poor grieving Creature, sing and join the melting Musick of thy Lute to the soft Accents of thy Voice. If my Lady happens to hear us, we'll pretend we came out for a little Air. The Heat within Doors will be our Excuse. Alas! my dear, reply'd *Altisidora*, 'tis not that frights me most: I would not have my Song betray my Thoughts; for those that do not know the mighty force of Love, will be apt to take me for a light and indiscreet Creature—But yet since it must be so, I'll venture: Better Shame on the Face, than Sorrow in the Heart! This said, she began to touch her Lute so sweetly, that Don *Quixote* was ravish'd. At the same Time an infinite Number of Adventures of this Nature, such as he had read of in his idle Books of Knight-Errantry, Windows, Grates, Gardens, Serenades, amorous Meetings, Parleys and Fopperies, all crowded into his Imagination, and he presently fancied, that one of the Dutchess's Damsels was fallen in Love with him, and struggl'd with her Modesty to conceal her Passion. He began to be apprehensive of the Danger to which his Fidelity was exposed, but yet firmly determin'd to withstand the powerful Allurement; and so recommending himself with a great deal of Fervency to his Lady *Dulcinea del Toboso*, he resolv'd to hear the Musick; and, to let the Serenading Ladies know he was awake, he feign'd a kind of a Sneeze, which did not a little please 'em; for 'twas the only thing they wanted, to be assured their Jest was not lost. With that, *Altisidora* having tun'd her Lute afresh, after a Flourish, began the following Song.

THE MOCK SERENADE

Wake, Sir Knight, now Love's invading,
  Sleep in Holland Sheets no more;
When a Nymph is Serenading,
  'Tis an errant Shame to snore.

Hear a Damsel, tall and tender,
  Honing in most rueful Guise,
With Heart almost burn'd to Cinder,
  By the Sun-beams of thy Eyes.

To free Damsels from Disaster,
  Is, they say, your daily Care:
Can you then deny a Plaister,
  To a Wounded Virgin here?

Tell me, Doughty Youth, Who curs'd thee
  With such Humours and ill Luck?
Was't some sullen Bear dry-nurs'd thee,
  Or She-Dragon gave thee suck?

Dulcinea, that Virago,
  Well may brag of such a Kid:
Now her Name is up, and may go
  From Toledo to Madrid.

Would she but her Prize surrender,
  (Judge how on thy Face I doat!)
In exchange I'd gladly send her
  My best Gown and Petticoat.

Happy I, would Fortune doom thee
  But to have me near thy Bed,
Stroak thee, Pat thee, Curry-Comb thee,
  And hunt o'er thy solid Head.

But I ask too much sincerely,
  And I doubt I ne'er must do't,
I'd but kiss thy Toe, and fairly
  Get the Length thus of thy Foot.

How I'd Rig thee, and what Riches
Should be heap'd upon thy Bones;
Caps and Socks, and Cloaks and Breeches,
Matchless Pearls, and Precious Stones.

Do not from above, like Nero,
See me burn, and slight my Woe!
But to quench my Fires, my Hero,
Cast a pitying Eye below.

I'm a Virgin-Pullet truly;
One more tender ne'er was seen,
A meer Chicken, fledg'd but newly;
Hang me if I'm yet fifteen.

Wind and Limb, all's tight about me,
My Hair dangles to my Feet.
I am straight too, if you doubt me,
Trust your Eyes, come down and see't.

I've a Bob Nose has no Fellow,
And a Sparrow's Mouth as rare,
Teeth like Topazes all Yellow;
Yet I'm deem'd a Beauty here.

You know what a rare Musician,
    (If you hearken) courts your Choice:
I can say my Disposition
    Is as taking as my Voice.

These and such like Charms I've Plenty,
    I'm a Damsel of this Place:
Let Altisidora *tempt ye;*
    Or she's in a woful Case.

Here the courting Damsel ended her Song, and the courted
Knight began his Expostulation. Why (said he, with a Sigh
heav'd from the Bottom of his Heart) why must I be so unhappy
a Knight, that no Damsel can gaze on me without falling in
Love? Why must the peerless *Dulcinea del Toboso* be so unfortunate, as not to be permitted the single Enjoyment of my transcendent Fidelity? Queens, why do you envy her? Empresses,
why do you persecute her? Damsels of fifteen, why do you
attempt to deprive her of her Right? Leave! oh, leave the un-

fortunate Fair! Let her Triumph, Glory, and Rejoice in the quiet Possession of the Hearts which Love has allotted her, and the absolute Sway which she bears over my yielding Soul. Away, unwelcome Crowd of Loving Impertinents; *Dulcinea* alone can soften my manly Temper, and mould me as she pleases. For her I am all Sweetness, for you I'm Bitterness it self. There is to me no Beauty, no Prudence, no Modesty, no Gaity, no Nobility among your Sex, but in *Dulcinea* alone. All other Women seem to me deform'd, silly, wanton, and base-born, when compar'd with Her. Nature brought me forth only that I might be devoted to Her Service. Let *Altisidora* weep or sing: Let the Lady despair on whose Account I have received so many Blows in the disastrous Castle of the inchanted *Moor*;* still I am *Dulcinea's*, and hers alone, dead or alive, dutiful, unspotted, and unchang'd, in spight of all the Necromantick Powers in the World. This said, he hastily clapp'd to the Window, and flung himself into his Bed, with as high an Indignation, as if he had receiv'd some great Affront. There let us leave him a while, in regard the great *Sancho Pança* calls upon us to see him commence his famous Government.

* *Alluding to the Story of* Maritornes *and the Carrier, in the former Part of the History.*

XII: HOW THE GREAT SANCHO PANÇA TOOK POSSESSION OF HIS ISLAND, AND IN WHAT MANNER HE BEGAN TO GOVERN

O THOU perpetual Surveyor of the *Antipodes*, bright Luminary of the World, and Eye of Heaven, sweet Fermenter of Liquids,* here *Timbrius* call'd, there *Phœbus*, in one place an Archer, in another a Physician! Parent of Poesy, and Inventer of Musick, perpetual Mover of the Universe, who, though thou seem'st sometimes to set, art always rising! O Sun, by whose assistance Man begets Man, on thee I call for help! Inspire me, I beseech thee, warm and illumine my gloomy Imagination, that my Narration may keep pace with the Great *Sancho Pança's* Actions throughout his Government; for without thy powerful Influence, I feel my self benum'd, dispirited and confus'd——Now I proceed.

Sancho, with all his Attendants, came to a Town that had about a Thousand Inhabitants, and was one of the best where the Duke had any Power: They gave him to understand that the Name of the Place was the Island of *Barataria*, either because the Town was called *Baratario*, or because the Government cost him so cheap.† As soon as he came to the Gates, (for it was Wall'd) the chief Officers and Inhabitants in their Formalities came out to receive him, the Bells rung, and all the People gave general Demonstrations of their Joy. The new Governor was then carry'd in mighty Pomp to the Great Church, to give Heaven Thanks; and after some ridiculous Ceremonies, they deliver'd him the Keys of the Gates, and receiv'd him as a perpetual Governor of the Island of *Barataria*. In the mean time, the Garb, the Port, the huge Beard, and the short and thick Shape of the new Governor, made every

---

* Sweet Motive of Wine-cooling Bottles, *so* Jarvis *has it, with the following Note, viz.* Cantimplora *is a Sort of Bottle for keeping Wine cool, with a very long Neck, and very broad and flat below, that the Ice may lie conveniently upon it in the Pail, and a broad Cork fitted to the Pail, with a Hole in the middle to let the Neck of the Bottle through.*   † Barato, *signifies cheap.*

one who knew nothing of the Jest wonder, and even those who were privy to the Plot, who were many, were not a little surpriz'd.

In short, from the Church they carry'd him to the Court of Justice; where, when they had plac'd him in his Seat, My Lord Governor, said the Duke's Steward to him, 'tis an ancient Custom here, that he who takes Possession of this famous Island, must answer to some difficult and intricate Question that is propounded to him; and by the Return he makes, the People feel the Pulse of his Understanding, and by an Estimate of his Abilities, judge whether they ought to rejoice or to be sorry for his Coming.

All the while the Steward was speaking, *Sancho* was staring on an Inscription in large characters on the wall over against his Seat, and as he could not read, he ask'd, what was the Meaning of that which he saw painted there upon the Wall? Sir, said they, 'tis an account of the Day when your Lordship took Possession of this Island: And the Inscription runs thus: *This Day, being such a Day of this Month, in such a Year, the Lord Don* Sancho Pança *took Possession of this Island, which may he long enjoy.* And who is he, ask'd *Sancho*, whom they call Don *Sancho Pança*? Your Lordship, answer'd the Steward; for we know of no other *Pança* in this Island but your self, who now sits in this Chair. Well, Friend, said *Sancho*, pray take notice, that *Don* does not belong to me, neither was it borne by any of my Family before me. Plain *Sancho Pança* is my Name: My Father was call'd *Sancho*, my Grand-father *Sancho*; and all of us have been *Pança's*, without any Don or Donna added to our Name. Now do I already guess your *Dons* are as thick as Stones in this Island. But 'tis enough that Heaven knows my Meaning; if my Government happens but to last four Days to an end, it shall go hard but I'll clear the Island of those swarms of *Dons* that must needs be as troublesom as so many Flesh-flies.* Come, now for your Question, good Mr Steward, and I'll answer it as well as I can, whether the Town be sorry or pleased.

---

* *A severe Satire on the* Spanish *Pride and Affectation of Gentility.* Don *is a Title properly belonging to only Families of Note, but of late 'tis grown very common, which is the Abuse which* Sancho *would here redress.*

At the same Instant two Men came into the Court, the one dress'd like a Country Fellow, the other look'd like a Taylor, with a pair of Sheers in his Hand. An't please you, my Lord, cry'd the Taylor, I and this Farmer here are come before your Worship. This honest Man came to my Shop Yesterday; for, saving your Presence, I am a Taylor, and Heaven be prais'd free of my Company: So my Lord, he shew'd me a piece of Cloth: Sir, quoth he, is there enough of this to make me a Cap?* Whereupon I measur'd the Stuff, and answer'd him, yes, an't like your Worship. Now as I imagin'd, d'ye see, he could not but imagine (and perhaps he imagin'd right enough) that I had a mind to cabbage some of his Cloth; judging hard of us honest Taylors. Prithee, quoth he, look whether there ben't enough for two Caps? Now I smelt him out, and told him there was. Whereupon the old Knave (an't like your Worship) going on to the same Tune, bid me look again and see whether it would not make three? And at last if it wou'd not make five? I was resolv'd to humour my Customer, and said it might. So we struck a Bargain; just now the Man is come for his Caps, which I gave him, but when I ask him for my Money, he'll have me give him his Cloth again, or pay him for't. Is this true, honest Man, said *Sancho* to the Farmer? Yes, an't please you, answer'd the Fellow; but pray let him shew the five Caps he has made me. With all my Heart, cry'd the Taylor; and with that, pulling his Hand from under his Cloak, he held up five little tiny Caps, hanging upon his four Fingers and Thumb, as upon so many Pins. There, quoth he, you see the five Caps this good Gaffer asks for; and may I never whip a stich more, if I have wrong'd him of the least snip of his Cloth, and let any Workman be Judge. The fight of the Caps, and the oddness of the Cause set the whole Court a laughing. Only *Sancho* sat gravely considering a while, and then, Methinks, said he, this Suit here needs not be long depending, but may be decided without any more ado, with a great deal of Equity; and therefore the Judgment of the Court is, That the Taylor shall lose his Making, and the Country Man his Cloth, and that the Caps be given to the poor Prisoners, and so let there be an end of the Business.

* Caperuza *in the Original, which means a Country-man's Cap: Though* Stevens *translates it in this Place, a* Cloak: *But he's mistaken, as the Reader will soon see.*

If this Sentence provok'd the Laughter of the whole Court, the next no less rais'd their Admiration. For after the Gover, nor's Order was executed, two old Men appeared before him, one of 'em with a large Cane in his Hand, which he us'd as a Staff. My Lord, said the other, who had none, some time ago I lent this Man ten Gold Crowns to do him a kindness; which Money he was to repay me on Demand. I did not ask him for it again in a good While, lest it should prove a greater Inconveniency to him to repay me than he labour'd under when he borrow'd it: However, perceiving that he took no care to pay me, I have ask'd him for my Due; nay, I have been forc'd to dun him hard for it. But still he did not only refuse to pay me again, but deny'd he ow'd me any Thing, and said, that if I lent him so much Money, he certainly return'd it. Now, because I have no Witnesses of the Loan, nor he of the pretended Payment, I beseech your Lordship to put him to his Oath; and if he will swear he has paid me, I'll freely forgive him before God and the world. What say you to this, old Gentleman with the Staff, ask'd *Sancho*? Sir, answer'd the old Man, I own he lent me the Gold; and since he requires my Oath, I beg you'll be pleas'd to hold down your Rod of Justice,* that I may swear upon't, how I have honestly and truly return'd him his Money. Thereupon the Governor held down his Rod, and in the mean time the Defendant gave his Cane to the Plaintiff to hold, as if it hinder'd him, while he was to make a Cross, and swear over the Judge's Rod: This done, he declar'd, That 'twas true the other had lent him the ten Crowns; but that he had really return'd him the same Sum into his own Hands; and that because he supposed the Plaintiff had forgot it, he was continually asking him for it. The great Governor hearing this, ask'd the Creditor what he had to reply? He made Answer, That since his Adversary had sworn it, he was satisfy'd; for he believ'd him to be a better Christian than to offer to forswear himself, and that perhaps he had forgot he had been repaid. Then the Defendant took his Cane again, and having made a low Obeisance to the Judge, was immediately leaving the Court. Which when *Sancho* perceiv'd, reflecting on the Passage of the Cane, and admiring the

* *The way of swearing in* Spain *in some Cases, is to hold down the Rod of Justice, and making a Cross on it, swear by that.*

Creditor's Patience, after he had study'd a while with his Head leaning over his Stomach, and his Fore-finger on his Nose, on a sudden he order'd the old Man with the Staff to be called back. When he was return'd, Honest Man, said *Sancho*, let me see that Cane a little; I have a Use for't. With all my Heart, answer'd the other; Sir, here it is; and with that he gave it him. *Sancho* took it; and giving it the other old Man, There, said he, go your ways, and Heaven be with you; for now you're paid. How so, my Lord, cry'd the old Man? Do you judge this Cane to be worth ten Gold Crowns? Certainly, said the Governor, or else I am the greatest Dunce in the World. And now you shall see whether I have not a Head-piece fit to govern a whole Kingdom upon a shift. This said, he order'd the Cane to be broken in open Court, which was no sooner done, but out dropp'd the ten Crowns. All the Spectators were amaz'd, and began to look on their Governor as a second *Solomon*. They ask'd him how he could conjecture that the ten Crowns were in the Cane? He told 'em, that having observ'd how the Defendant gave it to the Plaintiff to hold while he took his Oath, and then swore he had truly return'd him the Money in his own Hands, after which he took his cane again from the Plaintiff; this consider'd, it came into his Head, that the Money was lodg'd within the Reed. From whence may be learn'd, that though sometimes those that govern are destitute of Sense, yet it often pleases God to direct 'em in their Judgments. Besides, he had heard the Curate of his Parish tell of such another Business; and he had so special a Memory, that were it not that he was so unlucky as to forget all he had a mind to remember, there could not have been a better in the whole Island. At last the two old Men went away, the one to his Satisfaction, the other with eternal Shame and Disgrace, and the Beholders were astonish'd: Insomuch that the Person, who was commission'd to register *Sancho's* Words and Actions, and observe his Behaviour, was not able to determine, whether he should not give him the Character of a wise Man, instead of that of a Fool, which he had been thought to deserve.

No sooner was this Trial over, but in came a Woman, haling along a Man that look'd like a good substantial Grasier. Justice, my Lord Governor, Justice! cry'd she aloud; and if I can-

not have it on Earth, I'll have it from Heaven! Sweet Lord
Governor, this wicked Fellow met me in the Middle of a Field,
and has had the full Use of my Body; he has handled me like a
Dishclout. Woe's me, he has robbed me of that which I had
kept these three and twenty Years. Wretch that I am, I had
guarded it safe from Natives and Foreigners, Christians and
Infidels! I have been always as tough as Cork; no Salimander
ever kept it self more entire in Fire, nor no Wool among the
Briers, than did poor I, till this lewd Man, with nasty Fists,
handled me at this rate. Woman, Woman, quoth *Sancho*, no
Reflections yet; whether your Gallant's Hands were nasty or
clean, that's not to the Purpose. Then turning to the Grasier,
Well, Friend, said he, what have you to say to this Woman's
Complaint? My Lord, (answer'd the Man, looking as if he had
been frighted out of his Wits) I am a poor Drover, and deal in
Swine; so this Morning I was going out of this Town, after I
had sold (under Correction be it spoken) four Hogs, and what
with the Duties and the sharping Tricks of the Officers, I hardly clear'd any Thing by the Beasts. Now as I was trudging
Home, whom should I pick up by the Way, but this Hedge-
Madam here; and the Devil, who has a Finger in every Pye,
being powerful, forc'd us to yoke together. I gave her that
which would have contented any reasonable Woman; but she
was not satisfied, and wanted more Money; and would never
leave me, till she had dragg'd me hither. She'll tell ye I ravish'd
her; but, by the Oath I have taken, or mean to take, she lies
like a Drab as she is, and this is every Tittle true. Fellow, quoth
Sancho, hast thou any Silver about thee? Yes, an't like your
Worship, answer'd the Drover, I have some twenty Ducats in
Silver in a leathern Purse here in my Bosom. Give it the Plaintiff, Money and all, quoth *Sancho*. The Man, with a trembling
Hand, did as he was commanded: The Woman took it, and
dropp'd a thousand Courtesies to the Company, wishing on her
Knees as many Blessings to the good Governor, who took such
special Care of poor fatherless and motherless Children, and
abus'd Virgins; and then she nimbly tripp'd out of Court, holding the Purse fast in both her Hands; though first she took Care
to peep into it, to see whether the Silver were there. Scarce
was she gone, when *Sancho* turning to the Fellow, who stood

332

with the Tears in his Eyes, and look'd as if he had parted with his Blood as well as his Money; Friend, said he, run and over-take the Woman, and take the Purse from her, whether she will or no, and bring it hither. The Drover was neither so deaf nor so mad as to be twice bid; away he flew like Lightning after his Money. The whole Court was in mighty Expectation, and could not tell what could be the End of the Matter. But a while after the Man and the Woman came back, he pulling, and she tugging; she with her Petticoat tuck'd up, and the Purse in her Bosom, and he using all the Strength he had to get it from her. But it was to no Purpose; for the Woman defended her Prize so well, that all his Manhood little avail'd. Justice, cry'd she, for Heaven's Sake, Justice, Gentlemen! Look you, my Lord, see this impudent Ruffian, that on the King's Highway, nay, in the Face of the Court, would rob me of my Purse, the very Purse you condemn'd him to give me. And has he got it from you? ask'd the Governor. Got it! quoth the Woman, I'll lose my Life be-fore I'll lose my Purse. I were a pretty Baby then, to let him wipe my Nose thus? No, you must set other Dogs upon me than this sorry sneaking mangy Whelp; Pincers, Hammers, Mallets, and Chizzels shan't wrench it out of my Clutches; no, not the claws of a lion; they shall sooner have my Soul than my Money. She says the Truth, my Lord, said the Fellow, for I am quite spent: The Jade is too strong for me; I cannot grapple with her. *Sancho* then call'd to the Female. Here, quoth he, Honesty! You She-Dragon, let me see the Purse. The Woman deliver'd it to him; and then he return'd it to the Man; Hark you, Mis-tress, said he to her, had you shew'd your self as stout and vali-ant to defend your Body, (nay, but half so much) as you've done to defend your Purse, the Strength of *Hercules* could not have forc'd you. Hence Impudence, get out of my Sight. Away, with a Pox to you; and do not offer to stay in this Island, nor within six Leagues of it, on Pain of two hundred Lashes. Out, as fast as you can, you tricking, brazen-fac'd, Brimstone, Hedge-Drab, away. The Wench was in a terrible Fright, and sneak'd away, hanging down her Head as shamefully as if she had been catch'd in the Deed of Darkness. Now Friend, said the Governor to the Man, get you home with your Money, and Heaven be with you: But another Time, if you han't a Mind to come off worse, be

sure you don't yoke with such Cattle. The Drover thank'd him
as well as he could, and away he went; and all the People admir'd afresh their new Governor's Judgment and Sentences.
An Account of which was taken by him that was appointed to
be his historiographer, and forthwith transmitted to the Duke,
who expected it with Impatience. Now let us leave honest
Sancho here; for his Master, with great Earnestness, requires
our Attendance, *Altisidora's* Serenade having strangely discompos'd his Mind.

XIII: OF THE DREADFUL ALARMS GIVEN TO DON QUIXOTE BY THE BELLS AND CATS, DURING THE COURSE OF ALTISIDORA'S AMOURS

E left the great Don *Quixote* profoundly buried in the Thoughts into which the enamour'd *Altisidora's* Serenade had plung'd him. He threw himself into his Bed; but the Cares and Anxieties which he brought thither with him, like so many Fleas, allow'd him no Repose, and the Misfortune of his torn Stocking, added to his Affliction. But as Time is swift, and no Bolts nor Chains can bar his rapid Progress, posting away on the Wings of the Hours, the Morning came on apace. At the return of Light, Don *Quixote*, more early than the Sun, forsook his downy Bed, put on his Shamoy-Apparel, and drawing on his walking Boots, conceal'd in one of 'em the Disaster of his Hose: He threw his Scarlet Cloke over his Shoulder, and clapp'd on his valiant Head his Cap of green Velvet edg'd with Silver Lace. Over his right Shoulder he hung his Belt,* the Sustainer of his trusty executing Sword. About his Wrist he wore the Rosary, which he always carry'd about him. And thus accoutred, with a great deal of State and Majesty, he moved towards the Anti-Chamber, where the Duke and Dutchess were ready dress'd, and, in a manner, expecting his Coming. As he went through a Gallery he met *Altisidora* and her Companion, who waited for him in the Passage; and no sooner did *Altisidora* espy him, but she dissembled a swooning Fit, and immediately dropp'd into the Arms of her Friend, who presently began to unlace her Stays. Which Don *Quixote* perceiving, he approach'd, and turning to the Damsel, I know the Meaning of all this, said he, and whence these Accidents proceed. You know more than I do, answer'd the assisting Damsel: But this I am sure of, that hitherto there's not a Damsel in this House, that has enjoy'd her Health better than *Altisidora*; I never knew her make the least Complaint before. A

* *Here his Belt, according to the true Signification of* Tahali, *is one hung on his Shoulders: At* Diego de Mirandas *it seem'd to be a Belt girded about his Loins, and was made of a Skin proper for the Weakness he was suppos'd to have in them.*

335

Vengeance seize all the Knights-Errant in the World, if they are all so ungrateful. Pray, my Lord Don *Quixote*, retire, for this poor young Creature will not come to herself as long as you are by. Madam, answer'd the Knight, I beg that a Lute may be left in my Chamber this Evening, that I may asswage this Lady's Grief as well as I can; for in the Beginning of an Amour, a speedy and free Discovery of our Aversion or Pre-engagement, is the most effectual Cure. This said, he left 'em, that he might not be found alone with them by those that might happen to go by. He was scarce gone, but *Altisidora's* counterfeited Fit was over, and turning to her Companion, By all means, said she, let him have a Lute; for without doubt the Knight has a Mind to give us some Musick, and we shall have Sport enough. Then they went and acquainted the Dutchess with their Proceed-ing, and Don *Quixote's* desiring a Lute. Whereupon, being overjoy'd at the Occasion, she plotted with the Duke and her Women a new Contrivance to have a little harmless Sport with the Don. After this, they expected, with a pleasing Impatience, the Return of Night, which stole upon them as fast as had done the Day, which the Duke and Dutchess pass'd in agreeable Converse with Don *Quixote*. The same Day she dispatch'd a trusty Page of hers, who had personated *Dulcinea* in the Wood, to *Teresa Pança*, with her Husband's Letter, and the Bundle of Clothes which he had left behind, charging him to bring her back a faithful Account of every Particular between 'em.

At last, it being eleven a Clock at Night, Don *Quixote* retir'd to his Apartment, and finding a Lute there, he tun'd it, open'd the Window, and perceiving there was somebody walking in the Garden, he ran over the Strings of the Instrument, and having tun'd it again as nicely as he could, he cough'd and clear'd his Throat, and then with a Voice somewhat hoarse, yet not unmusical, he sung the following Song, which he had compos'd himself that very Day.

THE ADVICE

Love, a strong designing Foe,
    Careless Hearts with Ease deceives;
Can that Breast resist his Blow,
    Which your Sloth unguarded leaves?

If you're idle, you're destroy'd,
 All his Art on you he tries;
But be watchful and employ'd,
 Straight the baffled Tempter flies.

Maids, for modest Grace admir'd,
 If they would their Fortunes raise,
Must in Silence live retir'd,
 'Tis their Virtue speaks their Praise.

Prudent Men in this agree,
 Whether Arms or Courts they use;
They may trifle with the Free,
 But for Wives the Virtuous chuse.

Wanton Loves, which in their Way
 Roving Travellers put on,
In the Morn are fresh and gay,
 In the Evening cold and gone.

Loves that come with eager Haste,
 Still with equal Haste depart;
For an Image ill imprest,
 Soon is vanish'd from the Heart.

On a Picture fair and true,
 Who wou'd paint another Face?
Sure no Beauty can subdue,
 While a greater holds the Place.

The Divine Tobosan, *Fair*
 Dulcinea, *claims me whole;*
Nothing can her Image tear;
 'Tis one Substance with my Soul.

Then let Fortune smile or frown,
 Nothing shall my Faith remove;
Constant Truth, the Lover's Crown,
 Can work Miracles in Love.

No sooner had Don *Quixote* made an End of his Song, to which the Duke, Dutchess, *Altisidora,* and almost all the People in the Castle listen'd all the while, but on a sudden, from an open Gallery, that was directly over the Knight's Window, they let down a Rope, with at least a hundred little tinkling Bells hanging about it. After that came down a great Number of Cats, pour'd out of a huge Sack, all of 'em with smaller Bells ty'd to their Tails. The Jangling of the Bells, and the Squawling of the Cats made such a dismal Noise, that the very Contrivers of the Jest themselves were scar'd for the present, and Don *Quixote* was strangely surpris'd and quite dismay'd. At the same Time, as ill Luck would have it, two or three frighted Cats leap'd in through the Bars of his Chamber-Window, and running up and down the Room like so many evil Spirits, one would have thought a whole Legion of Devils had been flying about the Chamber. They put out the Candles that stood lighted there, and endeavoured to get out. Mean while the Rope with the bigger Bells about it was pull'd up and down, and those who knew nothing of the Contrivance were greatly surpriz'd. At last, Don *Quixote*, recovering from his Astonishment, drew his Sword, and fenc'd and laid about him at the Window, crying aloud, Avaunt ye wicked Inchanters! hence Infernal Scoundrels! for I am Don *Quixote de la Mancha*, and all your damn'd Devices cannot work their Ends against me. And then running after the Cats that frisk'd about the Room, he began to thrust and cut at them furiously, while they strove to get out. At last they made their Escape at the Window, all but one of 'em, who finding himself hard put to it, flew in his Face; and laying hold on his Nose with his Claws and Teeth, put him to such Pain, that the Don began to roar out as loud as he could. Thereupon the Duke and the Dutchess, imagining the Cause of his Outcry, ran to his Assistance immediately; and having opened the Door of his Chamber with a Master-Key, found the poor Knight struggling hard with the Cat, that would not quit it's Hold. By the Light of the Candles which they had with them, they saw the unequal Combat: The Duke offer'd to interpose, and take off the Animal; but Don *Quixote* would not permit him. Let no body take him off, cry'd he; let me alone Hand to Hand with this Devil, this Sorcerer, this Necromancer! I'll make him know what it is to deal with Don *Quixote de la Mancha*. But the Cat, not minding his Threats, growl'd on, and still held fast; till at length the Duke got it's Claws unhook'd from the Knight's Flesh, and flung the Beast out at the

Window. Don *Quixote's* Face was hideously scratch'd, and his Nose in no very good Condition: Yet nothing vex'd him so much as that they had rescu'd out of his Hands that villainous Necromancer. Immediately some Ointment was sent for, and *Altisidora* her self, with her own Lily-white Hands, apply'd some Plaisters to his Sores, and whispering him in the Ear, as she was dressing him, Cruel hard-hearted Knight, said she, all these Disasters are befallen thee, as a just Punishment for thy obdurate Stubbornness and Disdain. May thy Squire *Sancho* forget to whip himself, that thy Darling *Dulcinea* may never be deliver'd from her Inchantment, nor thou ever be bless'd with her Embraces, at least so long as I thy neglected Adorer live. Don *Quixote* made no Answer at all to this, only he heav'd up a profound Sigh, and then went to take his Repose, after he had return'd the Duke and Dutchess Thanks, not so much for their Assistance against that rascally Crew of catter-wauling and jangling Inchanters, for he defy'd them all, but for their Kindness and good Intent. Then the Duke and the Dutchess left him, not a little troubled at the Miscarriage of their Jest, which they did not think would have prov'd so fatal to the Knight, as to oblige him, as it did, to keep his Chamber five Days. During which Time, there happen'd to him another Adventure, more pleasant than the last; which, however, cannot be now related; for the Historian must return to *Sancho Pança*, who was very busy, and no less pleasant in his Government.

XIV: A FURTHER ACCOUNT OF SANCHO
PANÇA'S BEHAVIOUR IN HIS
GOVERNMENT

THE History informs us, that *Sancho* was conducted from the Court of Justice to a sumptuous Palace; where, in a spacious Room, he found the Cloth laid, and a most neat and magnificent Entertainment prepar'd. As soon as he enter'd, the Wind-Musick play'd, and four Pages waited on him, in order to the washing his Hands; which he did with a great deal of Gravity. And now the Instruments ceasing, *Sancho* sat down at the upper End of the Table; for there was no Seat but there, and the Cloth was only laid for one. A certain Personage, who afterwards appear'd to be a Physician, came and stood at his Elbow, with a Whalebone Wand in his Hand. Then they took off a curious white Cloth that lay over the Dishes on the Table, and discover'd great Variety of Fruit, and other Eatables. One that look'd like a Student, said Grace; a Page put a lac'd Bib under *Sancho's* Chin; and another, who did the Office of Sewer, set a Dish of Fruit before him.* But he had hardly put one Bit into his Mouth, before the Physician touch'd the Dish with his Wand, and then it was taken away by a Page in an Instant. Immediately another with Meat was clapp'd in the Place; but *Sancho* no sooner offer'd to taste it, but the Doctor with the Wand conjur'd it away as fast as the Fruit. *Sancho* was amaz'd at this sudden Removal, and looking about him on the Company, ask'd them whether they us'd to tantalize People at that rate, feeding their Eyes, and starving their Bellies? My Lord Governor, answer'd the Physician, you are to eat here no otherwise than according to the Use and Custom of other Islands where there are Governors. I am a Doctor of Physick, my Lord, and have a Salary allow'd me in this Island, for taking Charge of the Governor's Health, and I am more careful of it than of my own; studying Night and Day his Constitution, that I may the better know what to prescribe when he falls sick. Now the chief Thing I do, is to attend him always

* *The* Spaniards *and* Italians *begin Dinner with Fruit, as we end it.*

340

at his Meals, to let him eat what I think convenient for him, and to prevent his eating what I imagine to be prejudicial to his Health, and offensive to his Stomach. Therefore I now order'd the Fruit to be taken away, because 'tis too cold and moist; and the other Dish, because 'tis as much too hot, and overseason'd with Spices, which are apt to increase Thirst; and he that drinks much, destroys and consumes the radical Moisture, which is the Fuel of Life. So then, quoth *Sancho*, this Dish of roasted Partridges here can do me no manner of Harm. Hold, said the Physician, the Lord Governor shall not eat of 'em, while I live to prevent it. Why so? cry'd *Sancho*: Because, answer'd the Doctor, our great Master *Hippocrates*, the North-Star, and Luminary of Physick, says in one of his Aphorisms, *Omnis Saturatio mala, perdicis autem pessima*: That is, all Repletion is bad, but that of Partridges is worst of all. If it be so, said *Sancho*, let Mr Doctor see which of all these Dishes on the Table will do me most Good and least Harm, and let me eat my Belly-full of that, without having it whisk'd away with his Wand. For, by my Hopes, and the Pleasures of Government, as I live, I am ready to die with Hunger; and not to allow me to eat any Victuals (let Mr Doctor say what he will) is the Way to shorten my Life, and not to lengthen it. Very true, my Lord, reply'd the Physician, however, I am of Opinion, you ought not to eat of these Rabbets, as being a hairy, furry Sort of Food; nor would I have you taste of that Veal: Indeed if it were neither roasted nor pickled, something might be said; but as it is, it must not be. Well then, said *Sancho*, what think you of that huge Dish yonder that smokes so? I take it to be an *Olla Podrida*;* and that being a Hodge-podge of so many Sorts of Victuals, sure I can't but light upon something there that will nick me, and be both wholesom and toothsom. *Absit*, cry'd the Doctor, far be such an ill Thought from us; no Diet in the World yields worse Nutriment than those Mishmashes do. No, leave that luxurious Compound to your rich Monks and Prebendaries, your Masters of Colleges, and lusty Feeders at Country-Weddings: But let them not incumber the Tables of Governors, where nothing but delicate unmix'd Viands in their Prime ought to make their Appearance. The Reason is, that simple

* *'Tis what we corruptly call an* Olio, *all Sorts of Meat stew'd together.*

Medicines are generally allow'd to be better than Compounds; for in a Composition there may happen a Mistake by the unequal Proportion of the Ingredients; but Simples are not subject to that Accident. Therefore what I would advise at present, as a fit Diet for the Governor, for the Preservation and Support of his Health, is a hundred of small Wafers, and a few thin Slices of Marmalade, to strengthen his Stomach and help Digestion. *Sancho* hearing this, lean'd back upon his Chair, and looking earnestly in the Doctor's Face, very seriously ask'd him what his Name was, and where he had studied? My Lord, answer'd he, I am call'd Doctor *Pedro Rezio de Aguero*. The Name of the Place where I was born, is *Tirteafuera*, and lies between *Caraquel* and *Almodabar del Campo*, on the Right-hand; and I took my Degree of Doctor in the University of *Osuna*.* Hark you, said *Sancho*, in a mighty Chafe, Mr Dr *Pedro Rezio de Aguero*, born at *Tirteafuera*, that lies between *Caraquel* and *Almodabar del Campo*, on the Right-hand, and who took your Degrees of Doctor at the University of *Osuna*, and so forth, Take your self away! avoid the Room this Moment, or by the Sun's Light, I'll get me a good Cudgel, and beginning with your Carcase, will so be-labour and rib-roast all the Physick-mongers in the Island, that I will not leave therein one of the Tribe of those, I mean that are ignorant Quacks; for as for learned and wise Physicians, I'll make much of 'em, and honour 'em like so many Angels. Once more *Pedro Rezio*, I say, get out of my Presence. Avaunt! or I'll take the Chair I sit upon, and comb your Head with it to some Purpose; and let me be call'd to an Account about it when I give up my Office; I don't care, I'll clear my self by saying, I did the World good Service, in ridding it of a bad Physician, the Plague of a Commonwealth. Body of me! let me eat, or let 'em take their Government again; for an Office that won't afford a Man his Victuals, is not worth two Horse-Beans. The Physician was terrify'd, seeing the Governor in such a Heat, and wou'd that Moment have slunk out of the Room, had not the Sound of a Post-Horn in the Street been heard that Moment; whereupon the Steward immediately looking out at the Window, turn'd back, and said, there was

* *The Doctor's Name and Birth-place are fictitious;* Rezio de Aguero *signifies,* Positive of the Omen; *and* Terteafuera, Take your self away.

an Express come from the Duke, doubtless with some Dispatch of Importance.

Presently the Messenger enter'd sweating, with Haste and Concern in his Looks, and pulling a Packet out of his Bosom, deliver'd it to the Governor. *Sancho* gave it to the Steward, and order'd him to read the Direction, which was this: *To Don* Sancho Pança, *Governor of the Island* Barataria, *to be deliver'd into his own Hands, or those of his Secretary.* Who is my Secretary? cry'd *Sancho.* 'Tis I, my Lord, (answer'd one that was by) for I can write and read, and am a *Biscayner.* That last Qualification is enough to make thee set up for Secretary to the Emperor himself, said *Sancho.* Open the Letter then, and see what it says. The new Secretary did so, and having perus'd the Dispatch by himself, told the Governor, that 'twas a Business that was to be told only in private: *Sancho* order'd every one to leave the Room, except the Steward and the Carver, and then the Secretary read what follows.

I Have receiv'd Information, My Lord Don Sancho Pança, *that some of our Enemies intend to attack your Island with great Fury, one of these Nights: You ought therefore to be watchful, and stand upon your Guard, that you may not be found unprovided. I have also had Intelligence from faithful Spies, that there are four Men got into the Town in Disguise, to murder you; your Abilities being regarded as a great Obstacle to the Enemy's Designs. Look about you, take heed how you admit Strangers to speak with you, and eat nothing that is laid before you. I will take care to send you Assistance, if you stand in need of it: And in every Thing I rely on your Prudence. From our Castle, the 16th of August, at four in the Morning.*

Your Friend,
The Duke.

Sancho was astonish'd at the News, and those that were with him seem'd no less concern'd. But at last turning to the Steward, I'll tell you, said he, what is first to be done in this Case, and that with all Speed; Clap me that same Doctor *Rezio* in a Dungeon; for if any Body has a Mind to kill me, it must be he, and that with a lingring Death, the worst of Deaths, Hunger-starving. However, said the Carver, I am of Opinion, your

Honour ought not to eat any of the Things that stand here before ye; for they were sent in by some of the Convents; and 'tis a common Saying, *The Devil lurks behind the Cross*: Which no body can deny, quoth *Sancho*; and therefore let me have for the present but a Luncheon of Bread, and some four Pound of Raisins; there can be no Poison in that: For, in short, I cannot live without eating; and if we must be in a Readiness against these Battles, we had need be well victuall'd; for 'tis the Belly keeps up the Heart, and not the Heart the Belly. Mean while, Secretary, do you send my Lord Duke an Answer, and tell him, his Order shall be fulfill'd in every Part without fail. Remember me kindly to my Lady Dutchess, and beg of her not to forget to send one on purpose, with my Letter and Bundle, to *Teresa Pança* my Wife; which I shall take as a special Favour; and I will be mindful to serve her to the best of my Power: And when your Hand's in, you may crowd in my Service to my Master Don *Quixote de la Mancha*, that he may see I am neither forgetful nor ungrateful; the rest I leave to you; put in what you will, and do your Part like a good Secretary, and a stanch *Biscayner*. Now take away here, and bring me something to eat; and then you shall see I am able to deal with all the Spies, Wizzards, and cut-throat Dogs that dare to meddle with me and my Island.

At that Time a Page entring the Room; My Lord, said he, there's a Countryman without desires to speak with your Lordship about Business of great Consequence. 'Tis a strange Thing, cry'd *Sancho*, that one must still be plagu'd with these Men of Business! Is it possible, they should be such Sots, as not to understand this is not a Time for Business? Do they fancy, that we Governors and Distributers of Justice are made of Iron and Marble, and have no need of Rest and Refreshment like other Creatures of Flesh and Blood. Well, before Heaven, and o'my Conscience, if my Government does but last, as I shrewdly guess it will not, I'll get some of these Men of Business laid by the Heels. Well, for once let the Fellow come in——But first take heed he ben't one of the Spies or Ruffian-Rogues that would murder me. As for that, said the Page, I dare say he had no Hand in the Plot; poor Soul, he looks as if he could not help it; there's no more Harm in him to see to, than in a Piece of good

Bread.*There's no need to fear, said the Steward, since we are all here by you. But hark you, quoth *Sancho*, now Dr *Rezio's* gone, might not I eat something that has some Substance in it, though it were but a Crust and an Onion? At Night, answer'd the Carver, your Honour shall have no Cause to complain: Supper shall make Amends for the Want of your Dinner. Heaven grant it may, said *Sancho*.

Now the Countryman came in, and by his Looks seem'd to be a good harmless silly Soul. As soon as he enter'd the Room, Which is my Lord Governor, quoth he? Who but he that sits in the Chair, answer'd the Secretary! I humble my self to his Worship's Presence, quoth the Fellow; and with that, falling on his Knees, begg'd to kiss his Hand; which *Sancho* refus'd, but bid him rise and tell him what he had to say. The Countryman then got up; My Lord, quoth he, I am a Husbandman of *Miguel Turra*, a Town some two Leagues from *Ciudadreal*. Here's another *Tirte a fuera*, quoth *Sancho*; Well, go on Friend; I know the Place full well; 'tis not far from our Town. An't please you, said the Countryman, my Business is this: I was marry'd by Heaven's Mercy in the Face of our Holy Mother the *Roman* Catholick Church; and I have two Boys that take their Learning at the College; the youngest studies to become a *Batchelor*, and the eldest to be a *Master*, of Arts. I am a Widower, because my Wife is dead; she dy'd, an't please you, or to speak more truly, she was kill'd, as a body may say, by a damn'd Doctor, that gave her a Purge when she was with Child. Had it been Heaven's blessed Will that she had been brought to Bed of a Boy, I would have sent him to study, to have been a *Doctor*, that he might have had no Cause to envy his Brothers. So then, quoth *Sancho*, had not your Wife died, or had they not made her die, you had not been a Widower. Very true, answer'd the Man. We are much the nearer, cry'd *Sancho*; go on, honest Friend, and prithee dispatch; for 'tis rather Time to take an Afternoon's Nap than to talk of Business. Now, Sir, I must tell you, continu'd the Farmer, that that Son of mine the Batchelor of Art that is to be, fell in Love with a Maiden of our Town, *Clara Perlerina* by Name, the Daughter of *Andrew Perlerino*,

---

* Bueno como el Pan. *When the Country People wou'd define an honest good natured Man, they say,* He is as good as Bread it self.

a mighty rich Farmer; and *Perlerino* is not their right Name neither; but because the whole Generation of 'em is troubled with the Palsy,* they us'd to be call'd from the Name of that Ailing, *Perlaticos*; but now they go by that of *Perlerino*; and truly it fits the young Woman rarely, for she is a precious Pearl for Beauty, especially if you stand on her right Side, and view her, she looks like a Flower in the Fields. On the left indeed she does not look altogether so well; for there she wants an Eye, which she lost by the Small-Pox, that has digg'd a many Pits somewhat deep all over her Face; but those that wish her well, say, that's nothing; and that those Pits are but so many Graves to bury Lovers Hearts in. She is so cleanly, that because she will not have her Nose drop upon her Lips, she carries it cock'd up, and her Nostrils are turn'd up upon each Side, as if they shunn'd her Mouth, that is somewhat of the widest; and for all that she looks exceeding well; and were it not for some ten or dozen of her Butter Teeth and Grinders, which she wants, she might set up for one of the cleverest Lasses in the Country. As for her Lips, I don't know what to say of 'em, for they are so thin and so slender, that were it the Fashion to wind Lips as they do Silk, one might make a Skain of hers; besides, they are not of the ordinary Hue of common Lips; no, they are of the most wonderful Colour that ever was seen, as being speckled with Blue, Green, and Orange-Tawny. I hope my Lord Governor will pardon me, for dwelling thus on the Picture and several rare Features of her that is one Day to be my Daughter, seeing 'tis meerly out of my hearty Love and Affection for the Girl. Prithee paint on as long as thou wilt, said *Sancho*; I am mightily taken with this Kind of Painting, and if I had but dined, I would not desire a better Desert than thy Original. Both my self and that are at your Service, quoth the Fellow; or at least we may be in Time, if we are not now. But, alas! Sir, that is nothing; could I set before your Eyes her pretty Carriage, and her Shape, you would admire. But that's not to be done; for she is so crooked and crumpled up together, that her Knees and her Chin meet, and yet any one may perceive that if she could but stand upright, her Head would touch the very

---

* Perlesia, *in Spanish, is the Palsy; and those who have it, the* Spaniards *call* Perlaticos; *whence this Name.*

Cieling; and she would have given her Hand to my Son, the
Batchelor, in the Way of Matrimony before now, but that
she's not able to stretch it forth, the Sinews being quite shrunk
up: However, the broad long-gutter'd Nails add no small Grace
to it, and may let you know what a well-made Hand she has.

So far so good, said *Sancho*; but let us suppose you have
drawn her from Head to Foot: What is it you'd be at now?
Come to the Point, Friend, without so many Windings and
Turnings, and going round about the Bush. Sir, said the Farmer,
I would desire your Honour to do me the Kindness to give me
a Letter of Accommodation to the Father of my Daughter-in-
Law, beseeching him to be pleas'd to let the Marriage be fulfill'd; seeing we are not unlike, neither in Estate, nor in bodily
Concerns. For, to tell you the Truth, my Lord Governor, my
Son is bewitch'd, and there is not a Day passes over his Head
but the foul Fiends torment him three or four Times; and having once had the ill Luck to fall into the Fire, the Skin of his
Face is shrivell'd up like a Piece of Parchment, and his Eyes
are somewhat sore and full of Rheum. But when all is said, he
has the Temper of an Angel; and were he not apt to thump and
belabour himself now and then in his Fits, you would take him
to be a Saint.

Have you any thing else to ask, honest Man, said *Sancho*?
Only one Thing more, quoth the Farmer; but I am somewhat
afraid to speak it: Yet I cannot find in my Heart to let it rot
within me; and therefore, fall Back fall Edge, I must out with
it. I would desire your Worship to bestow on me some three
hundred or six hundred Ducats towards my Batchelor's Portion, only to help him to begin the World, and furnish him a
House; for, in short, they wou'd live by themselves, without
being subject to the Impertinencies of a Father-in-Law. Well,
said *Sancho*, see if you would have any Thing else; if you
would, don't let Fear or Bashfulness be your Hindrance: Out
with it Man. No truly, quoth the Farmer; and he had hardly
spoke the Words, when the Governor starting up, and laying
hold of the Chair he sat on: You brazen-fac'd silly impudent
Country-Booby, cry'd he, get out of my Presence this Moment,
or, by the Blood of the *Panças*, I'll crack your Jolter-head with
this Chair, you whoreson Raggamuffin, Painter for the Devil;

347

Dost thou come at this Time of Day to ask me for six hundred Ducats? Where should I have 'em, mangy Clod-pate? And if I had 'em, why should I give 'em thee, thou old doating Scoundrel? What a Pox care I for *Miguel Turra*, or all the Generation of the *Perlerinos*? Avoid the Room, I say, or by the Life of the Duke, I'll be as good as my Word, and ding out thy Cookoo-Brains. Thou art no Native of *Miguel Turra*, but some Imp of the Devil, sent on his Master's Errand to tempt my Patience. 'Tis not a Day and half that I have been Governor, and thou would'st have me have six hundred Ducats already, Dunder-headed Sot.

The Steward made Signs to the Farmer to withdraw, and he went out accordingly, hanging down his Head, and to all Appearance very much afraid lest the Governor should make good his angry Threats; for the cunning Knave knew very well how to act his Part. But let us leave *Sancho* in his angry Mood, and let there be Peace and Quietness, while we return to Don *Quixote*, whom we left with his Face cover'd over with Plaisters; the Scratches which he had got when the Cat so clapperclaw'd him, having obliged him to no less than eight Days Retirement; during which Time there happen'd that to him, which *Cid Hamet* promises to relate with the same Punctuality and Veracity with which he delivers the Particulars of this History, how trivial soever they may be.

XV: WHAT HAPPEN'D TO DON QUIXOTE WITH DONNA RODRIGUEZ THE DUTCHESS'S WOMAN; AS ALSO OTHER PASSAGES WORTHY TO BE RECORDED, AND HAD IN ETERNAL REMEMBRANCE

DON *Quixote*, thus unhappily hurt, was extremely sullen, and melancholy, his Face wrapp'd up and mark'd, not by the Hand of a Superior Being, but the Paws of a Cat, a Misfortune incident to Knight-Errantry. He was six Days without appearing in Publick; and one Night when he was thus confined to his Apartment, as he lay awake, reflecting on his Misfortunes, and *Altisidora's* Importunities, he perceived some Body was opening his Chamber-Door with a Key, and presently imagin'd that the amorous Damsel was coming to make an Attempt on his Chastity, and expose him to the Danger of forfeiting that Loyalty which he had vow'd to his Lady *Dulcinea del Toboso*. Prepossess'd with that Conceit, No, (said he loud enough to be heard) the greatest Beauty in the Universe shall never remove the dear Idea of the charming Fair, that is engrav'd and stamp'd in the very Center of my Heart, and the most secret Recesses of my Breast. No, thou only Mistress of my Soul, whether transform'd into a rank Country Wench, or into one of the Nymphs of the golden *Tagus*, that weave Silk and Gold in the Loom: Whether *Merlin* or *Montesinos* detain thee where they please, be where thou wilt, thou still art mine; and where-ever I shall be, I must and will be thine. Just as he ended his Speech, the Door opened. Up he got in the Bed, wrapp'd from Head to Foot in a yellow Satin Quilt, with a Woollen Cap on his Head, his Face and his Mustachio's bound up; his Face to heal it's Scratches, and his Mustachio's, to keep them from hanging down: In which Posture, he look'd like the strangest Apparition that can be imagin'd. He fix'd his Eyes towards the Door, and when he expected to have seen the yielding and doleful *Altisidora*, he beheld a most Reverend Matron approaching in a white Veil, so long that it cover'd her from Head to Foot. Betwixt her

349

Left-hand Fingers she carried half a Candle lighted, and held her Right-hand before her Face to keep the Blaze of the Taper from her Eyes, which were hidden by a huge Pair of Spectacles. All the way she trod very softly, and mov'd a very slow Pace. Don *Quixote* watch'd her Motions, and observing her Garb and her Silence, took her for some Witch or Inchantress, that came in that Dress to practise her wicked Sorceries upon him; and began to make the Sign of the Cross as fast as he cou'd. The Vision advanc'd all the while, and being got to the middle of the Chamber, lifted up it's Eyes, and saw Don *Quixote* thus making a thousand Crosses on his Breast. But if he was astonish'd at sight of such a Figure, she was no less affrighted at his; so that as soon as she spy'd him thus wrapp'd up in yellow, so lank, be-patch'd and muffled up; Bless me, cry'd she, what's this! With the sudden fright, she dropp'd the Candle, and now being in the Dark, as she was running out, the Length of her Coats made her stumble, and down she fell in the Middle of the Chamber: Don *Quixote* at the same Time was in great Anxiety: Phantom, cry'd he, or whatever thou art, I conjure thee to tell me who thou art, and what thou requir'st of me? If thou art a Soul in Torment, tell me, and I will endeavour thy Ease to the utmost of my Power; for I am a Catholick Christian, and love to do good to all Mankind; for which Reason I took upon me the Order of Knight-Errantry, whose extensive Duties engage me to relieve the Souls in Purgatory. The poor old Woman hearing her self thus conjur'd, judg'd Don *Quixote's* Fears by her own; and therefore with a low and doleful Voice, My Lord Don *Quixote*, said she, (if you are he) I am neither a Phantom nor a Ghost, nor a Soul in Purgatory, as I suppose you fancy; but *Donna Rodriguez*, my Lady Dutchess's Matron of Honour, who come to you about a certain Grievance, of the Nature of those which you use to redress. Tell me *Donna Rodriguez*, said Don *Quixote*, are not you come to manage some Love Intrigue? If you are, take it from me, you'll lose your Labour: 'Tis all in vain, Thanks to the peerless Beauty of my Lady *Dulcinea del Toboso*. In a Word, Madam, provided you come not on some such Embassy you may go light your Candle and return, and we will talk of any Thing you please; but remember I bar all dangerous Insinua-

tions, all amorous Enticements: What! I procure for others,
cry'd the Matron! I find you don't know me, Sir. I am not so
stale yet, to be reduc'd to such poor Employments. I have
good Flesh still about me, Heaven be praised, and all my Teeth
in my Head, except some few, which the Rheums, so rife in
this Country of *Arragon*, have robb'd me of. But stay a little,
I'll go light my Candle, and then I'll tell you my Misfortunes,
for 'tis You that set to rights every Thing in the World. This
said, away she went, without staying for an Answer.

Don *Quixote* expected her a while quietly, but his working
Brain soon started a thousand Chimera's concerning this new
Adventure; and he fancied he did ill in giving Way, though
but to a Thought of endangering his Faith to his Mistress.
Who knows, said he to himself, but that the Devil is now endeavouring to circumvent me with an old Governante, though
it has not been in his Power to do it with Countesses, Mar-
chionesses, Dutchesses, Queens, nor Empresses. I have often
heard say, and that by Persons of great Judgment, that if he
can, he will rather tempt a Man with an ugly Object, than
with one that's Beautiful.* Who knows but this Solitude, this
Occasion, the Stillness of the Night, may rouze my sleeping
Desires, and cause me in my latter Age to fall, where I never
stumbled before? In such Cases 'tis better to fly than to stay
to face the Danger. But why do I argue so foolishly? Sure 'tis impossible that an antiquated Waiting-Matron, in a long White
Veil, like a Winding-sheet, with a Pair of Spectacles over her
Nose, should create, or waken, an unchaste Thought in the
most abandon'd Libertine in the World. Is there any of these
Duena's or Governante's that has good Flesh? Is there one of
those Implements of Antichambers that is not impertinent,
affected, and intolerable? Avaunt then, all ye idle Crowd of
wrinkl'd Female Waiters, unfit for any human Recreation!
How is that Lady to be commended, who, they tell us, set up
only a couple of Mawkins in her Chamber, exactly representing two Waiting-Matrons, with their Work before 'em! The
State and Decorum of her Room was as well kept with those
Statues, as it would have been with real *Duena's*. So saying,
he started from the Bed, to lock the Door, and shut out *Donna*

* *In the Original, with a flat-nosed rather than a Hawk-nosed Woman.*

Rodriguez; but in that very Moment she happen'd to come in with a Wax-Candle lighted; at what Time spying the Knight near her, wrapp'd in his Quilt, his Face bound up and a woollen Cap on his Head; she was frighted again, and started two or three Steps back. Sir Knight, said she, is my Honour safe? for I don't think it looks handsomly in you to come out of your Bed? I ought to ask you the same Question, Madam, said Don *Quixote*; and therefore tell me whether I shall be safe from being assaulted and ravish'd. Whom are you afraid of, Sir Knight, cry'd she? Of you, reply'd Don *Quixote*: for, in short, I am not made of Marble, nor you of Brass; neither is it now the Noon of Day, but that of Night; and a little later too, if I am not mistaken; beside, we are in a Place more close and private than the Cave must have been, where the false and presumptuous *Æneas* enjoy'd the beautiful and tender-hearted *Dido*. However, give me your Hand, Madam; for I desire no greater Security than that of my own Continence and Circumspection. This said, he kiss'd his own Right-hand, and with it took hold of hers, which she gave him with the same Ceremony.

Here *Cid Hamet* (making a Parenthesis) swears by *Mahomet*, he would have given the best Coat of two that he had, only to have seen the Knight and the Matron walk thus Hand in Hand from the Chamber-Door to the Bed-side. To make short, Don *Quixote* went to Bed again, and *Donna Rodriguez* sat down in a Chair at some Distance, without taking off her Spectacles, or setting down the Candle. Don *Quixote* crouded up together, and cover'd himself close, all but his Face, and after they had both remain'd a while in Silence, the first that broke it was the Knight. Now, Madam, said he, you may freely unburden your Heart, sure of Attention to your Complaints, from chaste Ears, and Assistance in your Distress from a compassionate Heart. I believe as much, said the Matron, and promised my self no less charitable an Answer from a Person of so graceful and pleasing a Presence. The Case then is, noble Sir, that though you see me sitting in this Chair, in the middle of *Arragon*, in the Habit of an insignificant unhappy *Duenna*, I am of *Asturias de Oviedo*, and one of the best Families in that Province. But my hard Fortune, and the Neglect of my Parents, who fell to Decay, too soon, I can't tell how, brought me to *Madrid*; where, because they cou'd do no better, for fear of the worst, they plac'd me with a Court-Lady, to be her Chamber-Maid. And though I say it, for all manner of Plain-Work, I was never out-done by any one in all my Life. My Father and Mother left me at Service, and return'd home; and some few Years after, they both dy'd, and went to Heaven, I hope; for they were very good and religious Catholicks. Then was I left an Orphan, and wholly reduc'd to the sorrow-ful Condition of such Court-Servants, wretched Wages, and a slender Allowance. About the same time the Gentleman-Usher fell in Love with me, before I dreamt of any such Thing, Heaven knows. He was somewhat stricken in Years, had a fine Beard, was a personable Man, and what's more, as good a Gentle-man as the King; for he was of the Mountains. We did not carry Matters so close in our Love, but it came to my Lady's Ears; and so to hinder Peoples Tongues, without any more ado, she caus'd us to be marry'd in the Face of our Holy Mother the Catholick Church; which Matrimony produc'd a Daughter, that made an End of my good Fortune, if I had any. Not that I died in Childbed; for I went my full Time, and was safely de-liver'd; but because my Husband (rest his Soul) dy'd a while after of a Fright; and had I but Time to tell you how it hap-pen'd, I dare say you wou'd wonder. Here she began to weep piteously; Good Sir, cry'd she, I must beg your Pardon, for I can't contain myself. As often as I think of my poor Husband, I can't forbear shedding of Tears. Bless me, how he look'd! and with what Stateliness he would ride, with my Lady be-hind him, on a stout Mule as black as Jet (for Coaches and Chairs were not us'd then as they are now a-days, but the Ladies rode behind their Gentlemen-Ushers.) And now my Tongue's in, I can't help telling you the whole Story, that you may see what a fine well-bred Man my dear Husband was, and how nice in every Punctilio.

One Day, at *Madrid*, as he came in to St *James's-Street*, which is somewhat narrow, with my Lady behind him, he met a Judge of the Court, with two Officers before him: Where-upon, as soon as he saw him, to shew his Respect, my Husband turn'd about his Mule, as if he design'd to have waited on him. But my Lady whispering him in the Ear, What d'ye mean,

said she, Blockhead! Don't you know I am here? The Judge on
his side was no less civil, and stopping his Horse, Sir, said he,
pray keep your Way; you must not wait on me, it becomes me
rather to wait on my Lady *Casilda*, (for that was the Lady's
Name.) However my Husband with his Hat in his Hand, persisted in his civil Intentions. But at last, my Lady being very
angry with him for it, took a great Pin, or rather, as I am apt
to believe, a Bodkin out of her Case, and run it into his Back;
upon which my Husband suddenly starting, and crying out,
fell out of the Saddle, and pull'd down my Lady after him.
Immediately two of her Footmen ran to help her, and the
Judge and his Officers did the like. The Gate of *Guadalajara*
was presently in a Hubbub (the idle People about the Gate I
mean.) In short, my Lady return'd home a-foot, and my Husband went to a Surgeon, complaining that he was prick'd
through the Lungs. And now this Civility of his was talk'd
of every where, insomuch that the very Boys in the Streets
would flock about him and jeer him; for which Reason, and
because he was somewhat short-sighted, my Lady dismiss'd
him her Service; which he took so to Heart, poor Man, that
it cost him his Life soon after. Now was I left a poor helpless
Widow, and with a Daughter to keep, who still increas'd in
Beauty as she grew up, like the Foam of the Sea. At length,
having the Name of an Excellent Work-woman at my Needle,
my Lady Dutchess, who was newly marry'd to his Grace, took
me to live with her here in *Arragon*, and my Daughter, as well
as my self. In time the Girl grew up, and became the most
accomplish'd Creature in the World. She Sings like a Lark,
Dances like a Fairy, Trips like a wild Buck, Writes and Reads
like a School-master, and casts Accompts like an Usurer. I say
nothing of her Neatness; but certainly the purest Spring-water
that runs is not more cleanly; and then for her Age, she is now,
if I mistake not, just Sixteen Years, Five Months, and Three
Days old. Now who shou'd happen to fall in Love with this
Daughter of mine, but a mighty rich Farmer's Son, that lives
in one of my Lord Duke's Villages not far off; and indeed, I
can't tell how he manag'd Matters, but he plyd her so close,
that upon a Promise of Marriage he wheedled her into a Consent, and in short, got his Will of her, and now refuses to make

354

his Word good. The Duke is no stranger to the Business; for I have made my Complaint to him about it many and many times, and begg'd of him to enjoin the young Man to wed my Daughter; but he turns his deaf Ear to me, and can't endure I shou'd speak to him of it, because the young Knave's Father is rich, and lends the Duke Money, and is bound for him upon all Occasions, so that he would by no means disoblige him.

Therefore, Sir, I apply my self to your Worship, and beseech you to see my Daughter righted, either by Intreaties, or by Force, seeing every Body says you were sent into this World to redress Grievances, and assist those in Adversity. Be pleas'd to cast an Eye of Pity on my Daughter's Orphan-state, her Beauty, her Youth, and all her other good Parts; for, o'my Conscience, of all the Damsels my Lady has, there is not one can come up to her by a Mile; no, not she that's cry'd up as the airiest and finest of 'em all, whom they call *Altisidora*: I am sure she is not to be nam'd the same Day: For, let me tell you, Sir, all is not Gold that glisters. This same *Altisidora* after all, is a Hoity-toity, that has more Vanity than Beauty, and less Modesty than Confidence: Besides, she is none of the soundest neither, for her Breath is so strong, that no body can endure to stand near her for a Moment. Nay, my Lady Dutchess too—but I must say no more, for as they say, Walls have Ears. What of my Lady Dutchess? said Don *Quixote*. By all that's dear to you, *Donna Rodriguez*, tell me, I conjure you. Your Intreaties, said the Matron, are too strong a Charm to be resisted, dear Sir, and I must tell you the Truth. Do you observe, Sir, that Beauty of my Lady's, that Softness, that Clearness of Complexion, smooth and shining like a polish'd Sword; those Cheeks, all Milk and Vermilion, fair like the Moon, and glorious like the Sun; that Air when she treads, as if she disdain'd to touch the Ground, and in short, that Look of Health that enlivens all her Charms; let me tell you, Sir, she may thank Heaven for't in the first Place, and next to that, two Issues in both her Legs, which she keeps open to carry off the ill Humours, with which the Physicians say her Body abounds. Bless'd Virgin, cry'd Don *Quixote*! Is it possible the Dutchess should have such Drains! I shou'd not have believ'd it from any Body but you, though a Barefoot Friar had sworn it. But yet certainly from so much Perfection,

23-2

no ill Humours can flow, but rather liquid Amber. Well, I am now persuaded such Sluices may be of Importance to Health.

Scarce had Don *Quixote* said those Words, when at one Bounce the Chamber-door flew open; whereupon *Donna Rodriguez* was seiz'd with such a terrible Fright, that she let fall her Candle, and the Room remain'd as dark as a Wolf's Mouth,* as the Saying is; and presently the poor *Duenna* felt some body hold her by the Throat, and squeeze her Weasand so hard, that it was not in her Power to cry out. And another having pull'd up her Coats, laid her on so unmercifully upon her bare Buttocks with a Slipper, or some such Thing, that it wou'd have mov'd any one but those that did it, to Pity. Don *Quixote* was not without Compassion, yet he did not think fit to stir from the Bed, but lay snug and silent all the while, not knowing what the meaning of this Bustle might be, fearing lest the Tempest that pour'd on the Matron's Posteriors, might also light upon his own; and not without Reason; for indeed, after the mute Executioners had well curried the old Gentlewoman (who durst not cry out) they came to Don *Quixote*, and turning up the Bed-Clothes, pinch'd him so hard, and so long, that in his own Defence, he cou'd not forbear laying about him with his Fists as well as he cou'd; 'till at last, after the Scuffle had lasted about half an Hour, the invisible Phantoms vanish'd. *Donna Rodriguez* set her Coats to rights, and lamenting her hard Fortune, left the Room, without speaking a Word to the Knight. As for him, he remain'd where he was, sadly pinch'd and tir'd, and very moody and thoughtful, not knowing who this wicked Inchanter shou'd be, that had us'd him in that manner: but we shall know that in it's proper Time. Now let us leave him, and return to *Sancho Pança*, who calls upon us, as the Order of our History requires.

* *Because a Wolf's Mouth is black, say the Dictionaries.*

XVI: WHAT HAPPEN'D TO SANCHO PANÇA, AS HE WENT THE ROUNDS IN HIS ISLAND

WE left our mighty Governor much out of Humour, and in a pelting Chafe with that saucy Knave of a Countryman, who, according to the Instructions he had receiv'd from the Steward, and the Steward from the Duke, had banter'd his Worship with his impertinent Description. Yet as much a Dunce and a Fool as he was, he made his Party good against them all. At last, addressing himself to those about him, among whom was Doctor *Pedro Rezio*, who had ventur'd into the Room again, after the Consult about the Duke's Letter was over; Now, said he, do I find in good earnest that Judges and Governors must be made of Brass, or ought to be made of Brass, that they may be Proof against the Importunities of those that pretend Business, who at all Hours, and at all Seasons would be heard and dispatch'd, without any Regard to any body but themselves, let what will come of the rest, so their turn is serv'd. Now if a poor Judge does not hear and dispatch them presently, either because he is otherways busy and cannot, or because they don't come at a proper Season, then do they grumble, and give him their Blessing backwards, rake up the Ashes of his Forefathers, and would gnaw his very Bones. But with your Leave, good Mr *Busy-Body*, with all your Business you are too hasty, pray have a little Patience, and wait a fit Time to make your Application. Don't come at Dinner-time, or when a Man is going to sleep, for we Judges are Flesh and Blood, and must allow Nature what she naturally requires; unless it be poor I, who am not to allow mine any Food, Thanks to my Friend, Master Doctor *Pedro Rezio Tirteafuera* here present, who is for starving me to Death, and then swears 'tis for the Preservation of my Life. Heaven grant him such a Life, I pray, and all the Gang of such Physickmongers as he is; for the good Physicians deserve Palms and Laurels.

All that knew *Sancho* wonder'd to hear him talk so sensibly, and began to think that Offices and Places of Trust inspir'd some Men with understanding, as they stupify'd and confound-

ed others. However, Doctor *Pedro Rezio Aguero de Tirteafuera*
promis'd him he should sup that Night, though he trespass'd
against all the Aphorisms of *Hippocrates*. This pacify'd the
Governor for the present, and made him wait with a mighty
Impatience for the Evening, and Supper. To his thinking the
Hour was so long a coming, that he fancy'd Time stood still, but
yet at last the wish'd for Moment came, and they serv'd him
up some minc'd Beef with Onions, and some Calves-feet somewhat stale. The hungry Governor presently fell to with more
Eagerness and Appetite than if they had given him *Milan* God-
wits, *Roman* Pheasants, *Sorrentum* Veal, *Moron* Partridges,
or *Lavajos* Green Geese. And after he had pretty well taken
off the sharp Edge of his Stomach, turning to the Physician,
Look you, quoth he, Mr Doctor, hereafter never trouble your
self to get me Dainties or Tid-bits to humour my Stomach; that
would but take it quite off the Hinges; by Reason it has been
us'd to nothing but good Beef, Bacon, Pork, Goats-flesh, Turnips
and Onions; and if you ply me with your Kick-shaws, your nice
Courtiers Fare, 'twill but make my Stomach squeamish and
untoward, and I should perfectly loath them one Time or other.
However, I shall not take it amiss, if Master Sewer will now
and then get me one of those *Ollas Podrida's*, and the stronger
they are the better;*where all Sorts of good Things are rotten
stew'd, and as if it were lost in one another: and the more they
are thus rotten, and like their Name, the better the Smack;
and there you may make a Jumble of what you will, so it be
eatable, and I shall remember him, and make him Amends
one of these Days. But let no body put Tricks upon Travellers,
and make a Fool of me; for either we are, or we are not. Let's
be merry and wise; when God sends his Light he sends it to
all; I'll govern this Island fair and square, without underhand
Dealings, or taking of Bribes; but take notice, I won't bate an
Inch of my Right; and therefore let every one carry an even

---

* *A Dish consisting of a great Number of Ingredients, as Flesh, Fowl,* &c.
all stew'd together. Olla *signifies a* Pot, *and* Podrida, *putrify'd, rotten; as
if the stewing them together was suppos'd to have the same Effect, as to
making 'em tender, as Rottenness wou'd have. But* Covarruvius, *in his
Etymologies, derives it from* Poderoso, *powerful; because all the Ingredients are substantial and nourishing; and this is confirm'd by* Sancho's
adding, the stronger *they are the better.*

Hand, and mind their Hits, or else I'd have them to know there's Rods in Piss for 'em. They that urge me too far shall rue for it; make your self Honey, and the Flies will eat you. Indeed, my Lord Governor, said the Steward, your Lordship is much in the right in all you have said; and I dare engage for the Inhabitants of this Island, that they will obey and observe your Commands, with Diligence, Love, and Punctuality; for your gentle way of governing in the Beginning of your Administration, does not give them the least Opportunity to act, or but to design any thing to your Lordship's disadvantage. I believe as much, answer'd *Sancho*, and they would be silly Wretches, should they offer to do or think otherwise. Let me tell you too, 'tis my Pleasure you take care of me, and my *Dapple*, that we may both have our Food as we ought, which is the most material Business. Next, let us think of going the Rounds, when 'tis Time for me to do it; for I intend to clear this Island of all Filth and Rubbish, of all Rogues and Vagrants, idle Lusks and sturdy beggars. For I would have you to know, my good friends, that your slothful, lazy, lewd People in a Commonwealth, are like Drones in a Bee-hive, that waste and devour the Honey which the labouring Bees gather. I design to encourage Husbandmen, preserve the Privileges of the Gentry, reward virtuous Persons, and above all Things reverence Religion, and have regard to the Honour of religious Men. What think you of this, my good Friends? do I talk to the Purpose, or do I talk idly? You speak so well, my Lord Governor, answer'd the Steward, that I stand in Admiration to hear a Man so unletter'd as you are (for I believe your Lordship can't read at all) utter so many notable Things, and in every Word a Sentence; far from what they who sent you hither, and they who are here present, ever expected from your Understanding. But every Day produces some new Wonder, Jests are turn'd into Earnest, and those who design'd to laugh at others, happen to be laugh'd at themselves.

It being now Night, and the Governor having supp'd, with Doctor *Rezio's* Leave, he prepar'd to walk the Rounds, and set forward, attended by the Steward, the Secretary, the Gentleman-Waiter, the Historiographer who was to register his Acts, several Sergeants and other Limbs of the Law, so many in Number that they made a little Battalion, in the Middle of which

359

the great *Sancho* march'd with his Rod of Justice in his Hand,
in a notable Manner. They had not walk'd far in the Town,
before they heard the clashing of Swords, which made 'em
hasten to the Place whence the Noise came. Being come thither,
they found only two Men a fighting, who gave over, perceiving
the Officers. What (cry'd one of them at the same Time) do they
suffer Folks to be robb'd in this Town in Defiance of Heaven and
the King? Do they let Men be stripp'd in the Middle of the
Street? Hold, honest Man, said *Sancho*, have a little Patience,
and let me know the Occasion of this Fray, for I am the Governor. My Lord, said the other Party, I'll tell you in few Words:
Your Lordship must know, that this Gentleman, just now,
at a Gaming-Ordinary over the Way, won above a thousand
Reals, Heaven knows how: I stood by all the while, and gave
Judgment for him in more than one doubtful Cast, though I
could not well tell how to do it in Conscience. He carried off
his Winnings, and when I expected he would have given me
a Crown Gratuity,* as it is a Claim among Gentlemen of my
Fashion, who frequent Gaming-Ordinaries, from those that
play high and win, for preventing Quarrels, being at their
Backs, and giving Judgment right or wrong, nevertheless he
went away without giving me any Thing: I ran after him, not
very well pleased with his Proceeding, yet very civilly desir'd
him to consider I was his Friend, that he knew me to be a Gentleman, though fallen to Decay, that had nothing to live upon,
my Friends having brought me up to no Employment; and therefore I intreated him to be so kind as to give me eight Reals; but
the stingy Soul, a greater Thief than *Cacus*, and a worse Sharper
than *Andradilla*, would give me but sneaking four Reals. And
now, my Lord, you may see how little Shame and Conscience
there's in him. But 'ifaith, had not your Lordship come just in
the Nick, I would have made him bring up his Winnings, and
taught him the Difference between a Rook and a Jack-daw.
What say you to this, cry'd *Sancho* to the other? The other

* Barato; *it originally signifies* Cheap; *but, amongst Gamesters,* dar barato
*is, when a winning Gamester, by Way of Courtesy, or for some other Reason,
gives something to a Stander-by. And this in Spain is a common Practice
among all Ranks of People, and many live upon it; for it is expected as
Due, and sometimes, to make the Reward the greater, these Rascals give
Judgment wrongfully for the Winner.*

made Answer, that he could not deny what his Antagonist had said, that he would give him but four Reals, because he had given him Money several Times before; and they who expect the Benevolence, shou'd be mannerly, and be thankful for what is given them, without haggling with those that have won, unless they know 'em to be common Cheats, and the Money not won fairly; and that to shew he was a fair Gamester, and no Sharper, as the other said, there needed no better Proof than his Refusal to give him any Thing, since the Sharpers are always in Fee with these Bully-Rocks who know 'em, and wink at their Cheats. That's true, said the Steward: Now what would your Lordship have us to do with these Men? I'll tell you, said *Sancho*, First, you that are the Winner, whether by fair Play or by foul, give your Bully-back here a hundred Reals immediately, and thirty more for the poor Prisoners: And you that have nothing to live on, and were brought up to no Employment, and go sharping up and down from Place to Place, pray take your hundred Reals, and be sure by to Morrow to go out of this Island, and not to set Foot in it again these Ten Years and a Day, unless you have a Mind to make an End of your Banishment in another World; for if I find you here I will make you swing on a Gibbet, with the Help of the Hangman; away, and let no body offer to reply, or I'll lay him by the Heels. Thereupon the one disburs'd, and the other receiv'd; the first went Home, and the last went out of the Island; and then the Governor going on, either I shall want of my Will, said he, or I'll put down these disorderly Gaming-Houses; for I have a Fancy they are highly prejudicial. As for this House in Question, said one of the Officers, I suppose it will be a hard Matter to put it down, for it belongs to a Person of Quality, who loses a great deal more by Play at the Year's End, than he gets by his Cards. You may shew your Authority against other Gaming-Houses of less Note, that do more Mischief, and harbour more dangerous People than the Houses of Gentlemen and Persons of Quality, where your notorious Sharpers dare not use their Slights of Hand. And since Gaming is a Vice that is become a common Practice, 'tis better to play in good Gentlemens Houses, than in those of Under Officers, where they shall draw you in a poor Bubble, and after they have kept him playing all the Night long, send him away stripp'd naked to the Skin. Well, all in good Time, said *Sancho*: I know there's a great deal to be said in this Matter. At the same Time one of the Officers came holding a Youth, and having brought him before the Governor; An't please your Worship, said he, this young Man was coming towards us, but as soon as he perceiv'd it was the Rounds, he sheer'd off, and set a running as fast as his Legs would carry him; a Sign he's no better than he should be. I ran after him, but had not he happen'd to fall, I had never come up with him. What made you run away, Friend? said *Sancho*. Sir, answer'd the young Man, 'twas only to avoid the Questions one is commonly teiz'd with by the Watch. What Business d'you follow? ask'd *Sancho*. I am a Weaver by Trade, answer'd the other. A Weaver of what? ask'd the Governor. Of Steel Heads for Lances, with your Worship's good Leave, said t'other. Oh hoh, cry'd *Sancho*, you are a Wag I find, and pretend to pass your Jests upon us: Very well. And pray whither are you going at this Time of Night? To take the Air, an't like your Worship, answer'd the other. Good, said *Sancho*, and where do they take the Air in this Island? Where it blows, said the Youth. A very proper Answer, cry'd *Sancho*. You are a very pretty impudent Fellow, that's the Truth on't. But pray make Account that I am the Air, or the Wind, which you please, and that I blow in your Poop, and drive you to the Round-house.—Here—take him and carry him away thither to rights: I'll take care the Youngster shall sleep out of the Air to Night; he might catch Cold else by lying abroad. Before *George*, said the young Man, you shall as soon make me a King as make me sleep out of the Air to Night. Why, you young Slip-string, said *Sancho*, is it not in my Power to commit thee to Prison, and fetch thee out again, as often as 'tis my Will and Pleasure? For all your Power, answer'd the Fellow, you shan't make me sleep in Prison. Say you so, cry'd *Sancho*, Here, away with him to Prison, and let him see to his Cost who is mistaken, he or I; and lest the Jaylor should be greas'd in the Fist to let him out, I'll fine him two thousand Ducats if he let thee stir a Foot out of Prison. All that's a Jest, said the other; for I defy all Mankind to make me sleep this Night in a Prison. Tell me, Devil incarnate, said *Sancho*, hast thou some Angel to take off the Irons which I'll have thee

362

clapp'd in, and get thee out? Well, now my good Lord Governor (said the young Man very pleasantly) let us talk Reason, and come to the Point. Suppose your Lordship should send me to Jail, and get me laid by the Heels in the Dungeon, shackled and manacled, and lay a heavy Penalty on the Jaylor in Case he let me out; and suppose your Orders be strictly obey'd; yet for all that, if I have no Mind to sleep, but will keep awake all Night without so much as shutting my Eyes, pray can You, with all the Power you have, make me sleep whether I will or no? No certainly, said the Secretary, and the young Man has made out his Meaning. Well, said *Sancho*, but I hope you mean to keep your self awake, and only forbear sleeping to please your own Fancy, and not to thwart my Will. I mean nothing else indeed, my Lord, said the Lad. Why then go Home and sleep, quoth *Sancho*, and Heaven send thee good Rest. I'll not be thy Hind-'rance. But have a Care another Time of sporting with Justice; for you may meet with some Men in an Office, that may chance to break your Head, while you are breaking your Jest. The Youth went his Way, and the Governor continu'd his Rounds.

A while after came two of the Officers, bringing a Person along with them. My Lord Governor, said one of 'em, we have brought here one that's dress'd like a Man, yet is no Man, but a Female, and no ugly one neither. Thereupon they lifted up to her Eyes two or three Lanthorns, and by their Light discovered the Face of a Woman about Sixteen Years of Age, beautiful to Admiration, with her Hair put up in a Network Caul of Gold and green Silk. They examin'd her Dress from Head to Foot, and found that her Stockings were of Carnation Silk, and her Garters of white Taffeta, fring'd with Gold and Pearls. Her Breeches were of Gold Tissue, upon a green Ground, and her Coat of the same Stuff; under which she wore a Doublet of very fine Stuff gold and white. Her Shoes were white, and made like Mens. She had no Sword, but only a very rich Dagger, and several costly Rings on her Fingers. In a Word, the young Creature seem'd very lovely to 'em all, but not one of 'em knew her. Those of the Company who liv'd in the Town, could not imagine who she was; and those who were privy to all the Tricks that were to be put upon *Sancho*, were more at a Loss than the rest, well knowing that this Adventure was not of their own contriving; which put them in great Expectation of the Event. *Sancho* was surpriz'd at her Beauty, and ask'd her who she was, whither she was going, and on what Account she had put on such a Dress? Sir, said she (casting her Eyes on the Ground with a decent Bashfulness) I can't tell you before so many People what I have so much Reason to wish may be kept secret. Only this one Thing I do assure you, I am no Thief, nor evil-minded Person; but an unhappy Maid, whom the Force of Jealousy has constrain'd to transgress the Laws of Maiden Decency. The Steward hearing this, My Lord Governor, said he, be pleas'd to order your Attendants to retire, that the Gentle-woman may more freely tell her Mind. The Governor did accordingly, and all the Company remov'd at a Distance, except the Steward, the Gentleman-Waiter, and the Secretary; and then the young Lady thus proceeded.

I am the Daughter of *Pedro Perez Mazorca*, Farmer of the Wool in this Town, who comes very often to my Father's House. This will hardly pass, Madam, said the Steward, for I know *Pedro Perez* very well, and I am sure he has neither Son nor Daughter: Besides, you tell us he's your Father, and at the same Time that he comes very often to your Father's House. I observ'd as much, said *Sancho.* Indeed, Gentlemen, said she, I am now so troubl'd in Mind, that I know not what I say, but the Truth is, I am the Daughter of *Diego de la Llana*, whom I suppose you all know. Now this may pass, said the Steward, for I know *Diego de la Llana*, who is a very considerable Gentle-man, has a good Estate, and a Son and a Daughter. But since his Wife dy'd, no body in this Town can say he ever saw that Daughter, for he keeps her so close, that he hardly suffers the Sun to look on her; though indeed the common Report is, that she is an extraordinary Beauty. You say very true, Sir, reply'd the young Lady; and I am that very Daughter; as for my Beauty, if Fame has given a wrong Character of it, you will now be undeceiv'd, since you have seen my Face; and with this she burst out into Tears. The Secretary perceiving this, whisper'd the Gentleman-Waiter in the Ear: Sure, said he, some extra-ordinary Matter must have happen'd to this poor young Lady, since it could oblige one of her Quality to come out of Doors in this Disguise, and at this unseasonable Hour. That's without

Question, answer'd the other; for her Tears too confirm the Suspicion. *Sancho* comforted her with the best Reasons he could think on; and bid her not be afraid, but tell 'em what had befal'n her, for they would all really do whatever lay in their Power to make her easy.

You must know, Gentlemen, said she, that 'tis now ten Years that my Father has kept me close, ever since my Mother dy'd. We have a small Chapel richly adorn'd in the House, where we hear Mass; and in all that Time I have seen nothing but the Sun by Day, and the Moon and Stars by Night; neither do I know what Streets, Squares, Market-places and Churches are, no nor Men, except my Father, my Brother, and that *Pedro Perez* the Wool-Farmer, whom I at first would have pass'd upon you for my Father, that I might conceal the right. This Confinement (not being allow'd to stir abroad, though but to go to Church) has made me uneasy this great while, and made me long to see the World, or at least the Town where I was born, which I thought was no unlawful or unseemly Desire. When I heard 'em talk of Bull-Feasts, Prizes, acting of Plays, and other publick Sports, I ask'd my Brother, who is a Year younger than I, what they meant by those Things, and a World of others, which I have not seen; and he inform'd me as well as he could: But that made me but the more eager to be satisfy'd by my own Eyes. In short, I begg'd of my Brother—I wish I never had done it—and here she relaps'd into Tears. The Steward perceiving it; Come, Madam, said he, pray proceed, and make an End of telling us what has happen'd to you; for your Words and your Tears keep us all in Suspence. I have but few Words more to add, answer'd she, but many more Tears to shed; for they are commonly the Fruit of such imprudent Desires.

That Gentleman of the Duke's, who acted the Part of *Sancho's* Sewer, or Gentleman-Waiter, and was smitten with the young Lady's Charms, could not forbear lifting up his Lanthorn to get another Look; and as he view'd her with a Lover's Eyes, the Tears that trickled down her Cheeks seem'd to him so many Pearls, or some of the heavenly Dew on a fair drooping Flower, precious as oriental Gems. This made him wish that the Misfortune might not be so great as her Sighs and Tears bespoke it. As for the Governor, he stood fretting to hear her hang so long upon her Story; and therefore bid her make an End, and keep 'em no longer thus, for it was late, and they had a great deal of Ground to walk over yet. Thereupon, with broken Sobs, and half-fetch'd Sighs, Sir, said she, all my Misfortune is, that I desir'd my Brother to lend me some of his Clothes, and that he would take me out some Night or other to see all the Town, while our Father was asleep. Importun'd by my Intreaties, he consented, and having lent me his Clothes, he put on mine, which fit him as if they had been made for him; for he has no Beard at all, and makes a mighty handsom woman. So this very Night, about an Hour ago, we got out, and being guided by my Father's Footboy, and our own unruly Desires, we took a Ramble over the whole Town; and as we were going Home, we perceiv'd a great Number of People coming our Way; whereupon, said my Brother, Sister, this is certanly the Watch; follow me, and let us not only run, but fly as fast as we can, for if we should be known, 'twould be the worse for us. With that he fell a running as fast as if he had Wings to his Feet. I fell a running too, but was so frighted, that I fell down before I had gone half a dozen Steps; and then a Man overtook me, and brought me before you, and this Crowd of People, by whom, to my Shame, I am taken for an ill Creature; a bold indiscreet Night-walker. And has nothing befallen you but this, cry'd *Sancho*? You talk'd at first of some Jealousy, that had set you a gadding. Nothing else indeed, answer'd the Damsel; though I pretended Jealousy; I ventur'd out on no other Account but a little to see the World, and that too no further than the Streets of this Town. All this was afterwards confirm'd by her Brother, who now was brought by some of the Watch, one of whom had at last overtaken him, after he had left his Sister. He had nothing on but a very rich Petticoat, and a blue Damask Manteau, with a gold Galloon; his Head without any Ornament but his own Hair that hung down in natural Curls like so many Rings of Gold. The Governor, the Steward, and the Gentleman-Waiter took him aside, and after they had examined him apart, why he had put on that Dress, he gave the same Answer his Sister had done, and with no less Bashfulness and Concern, much to the Satisfaction of the Gentleman-Waiter, who was much smitten with the young Lady's Charms.

366

As for the Governor, after he had heard the whole Matter, Truly, Gentlefolks, said he, here's a little Piece of childish Folly: And to give an Account of this wild Frolick, and slip of Youth, there needed not all these Sighs and Tears, nor these Hems and Haughs, and long Excuses. Could not you, without any more ado, have said, Our Names are so and so, and we stole out of our Father's House for an Hour or two, only to ramble about the Town, and satisfy a little Curiosity, and there had been an end of the Story, without all this weeping and wailing? You say very well, said the young Damsel, but you may imagine that in the Trouble and Fright I was in, I could not behave my self as I should have done. Well, said *Sancho*, there's no Harm done; go along with us, and we'll see you home to your Father's, perhaps you mayn't yet be miss'd. But have a Care how you gad Abroad to see Fashions another Time. Don't be too venturesom. An honest Maid should be still at Home, as if she had one Leg broken. A Hen and a Woman are lost by rambling; and she that longs to see, longs also to be seen. I need say no more.

The young Gentleman thank'd the Governor for his Civility, and then went Home under his Conduct. Being come to the House, the young Spark threw a little Stone against one of the Iron-barr'd Windows; and presently a Maid Servant, who sat up for 'em, came down, open'd the Door, and let him and his Sister in.

The Governor with his company then continu'd his Rounds, talking all the Way they went of the genteel Carriage and Beauty of the Brother and Sister, and the great Desire these poor Children had to see the World by Night.

As for the Gentleman-Waiter, he was so passionately in Love, that he resolved to go the next Day, and demand her of her Father in Marriage, not doubting but the old Gentleman would comply with him, as he was one of the Duke's principal Servants. On the other Side, *Sancho* had a great Mind to strike a Match between the young Man and his Daughter *Sanchica*; and he resolved to bring it about as soon as possible; believing no Man's Son could think himself too good for a Governor's Daughter. At last his Round ended for that Night, and his Government two or three Days after; which also put an End to all his great Designs and Expectations, as shall be seen hereafter.

XVII: WHO THE INCHANTERS AND EXECUTIONERS WERE THAT WHIPP'D THE DUENNA, AND PINCH'D AND SCRATCH'D DON QUIXOTE; WITH THE SUC-CESS OF THE PAGE THAT CARRIED SANCHO'S LETTER TO HIS WIFE TERESA PANÇA

CID *Hamet*, the most punctual Enquirer into the minutest Particles of this authentick History, relates, that when *Donna Rodriguez* was going out of her Chamber to Don *Quixote's* Apart-ment, another old Waiting-woman that lay with her perceiv'd it: And as one of the chief Pleasures of all those female Implements consists in enquiring, prying, and running their Noses into every Thing, she pres-ently watch'd her Fellow-Servant's Motions, and follow'd her so cautiously, that the good Woman did not discover it. Now *Donna Rodriguez* was no sooner got into the Knight's Cham-ber, but the other, lest she should forfeit her Character of a true tattling Waiting-woman, flew to tell the Dutchess in her Ear, that *Donna Rodriguez* was in Don *Quixote's* Chamber. The Dutchess told the Duke, and having got his Leave to take *Altisidora* with her, and go to satisfy her Curiosity about this Night-Visit, they very silently crept along in the Dark, till they came to Don *Quixote's* Door, and as they stood listening there, overheard very easily every Word they said within. So that when the Dutchess heard her leaky Woman expose the Fountains* of her Issues, she was not able to contain, nor was *Altisidora* less provok'd. Full of Rage and greedy Revenge, they rush'd into the Chamber, and beat the *Duenna*, and claw'd the Knight, as has been related. For those affronting Expressions that are levell'd against the Beauty of Women, or the good Opinion of themselves, raise their Anger and Indig-nation to the highest Degree, and incense them to a Desire of Revenge.

The Dutchess diverted the Duke with an Account of what had pass'd; and having a mighty Mind to continue the Merri-

* El Aranjuez, *in the Original. It is a Royal Garden, near* Madrid, *famous for it's Fountains and Water-works. The Metaphor is too far fetch't for an* English *Translation.*

ment which Don *Quixote's* Extravagancies afforded 'em, the Page that acted the Part of *Dulcinea* when 'twas propos'd to end her Inchantment, was dispatch'd away to *Teresa Pança*, with a Letter from her Husband, (for *Sancho* having his Head full of his Government, had quite forgot to do it) and at the same time the Dutchess sent another from herself, with a large costly String of Coral, as a Present.

Now the Story tells us, that the Page was a sharp and ingenious Lad, and being very desirous to please his Lord and Lady, made the best of his way to *Sancho's* Village. When he came near the Place, he saw a Company of Females washing at a Brook, and ask'd 'em, whether they could inform him, if there liv'd not in that Town a Woman whose Name was *Teresa Pança*, Wife to one *Sancho Pança*, Squire to a Knight call'd Don *Quixote de la Mancha*? He had no sooner ask'd the Question, but a young Wench, that was washing among the rest, stood up: That *Teresa Pança* is my Mother, quoth she; That Gaffer *Sancho* is my own Father, and that same Knight our Master. Well then, Damsel, said the Page, pray go along with me, and bring me to your Mother; for I have a Letter and a Token here for her from your Father. That I will with all my Heart, Sir, said the Girl, who seem'd to be about fourteen Years of Age, little more or less; and with that leaving the Clothes she was washing to one of her Companions, without staying to dress her Head or put on her Shoes, away she sprung before the Page's Horse, bare-legg'd, and with her Hair about her Ears. Come along, an't please you, quoth she, our House is hard by; 'tis but just as you come into the Town, and my Mother's at Home, but brim-full of Sorrow, poor Soul, for she has not heard from my Father I don't know how long. Well, said the Page, I bring those Tidings that will chear her Heart, I warrant her. At last, what with Leaping, Running, and Jumping, the Girl being come to the House, Mother, Mother, (cry'd she as loud as she could, before she went in) come out, Mother, come out! here's a Gentleman has brought Letters and Tokens from my Father. At that Summons, out came the Mother, spinning a Lock of coarse Flax, with a Russet Petticoat about her, so short that it look'd as if it had been cut off at the Placket; a Waistcoat of the same, and her Smock hanging loose about it.

Take her otherwise, she was none of the oldest, but look'd somewhat turn'd of Forty, strong built, sinewy, hale, vigorous, and in good Case. What's the Matter, Girl? (quoth she, seeing her Daughter with the Page) What Gentleman is that? A Servant of your Ladyship's, my Lady *Teresa Pança*, answer'd the Page; and at the same Time alighting, and throwing himself at her Feet with the most humble Submission, My noble Lady *Donna Teresa*, said he, permit me the Honour to kiss your Ladyship's Hand, as you are the only legitimate Wife of my Lord Don *Sancho Pança*, proper Governor of the Island of *Barataria*. Alack-a-day, good Sir, quoth *Teresa*, what d'you do? By no means: I am none of your Court-Dames, but a poor silly Country Body, a Plough man's Daughter, the Wife indeed of a Squire-Errant, but no Governor. Your Ladyship, reply'd the Page, is the most worthy Wife of a thrice-worthy Governor; and for Proof of what I say, be pleased to receive this Letter, and this Present: With that he took out of his Pocket a String of Coral Beads set in Gold, and putting it about her Neck: This Letter, said he, is from his Honour the Governor, and another that I have for you, together with these Beads, are from her Grace the Lady Dutchess, who sends me now to your Ladyship.

Teresa stood amaz'd, and her Daughter was transported. Now I'll be hang'd, quoth the young Baggage, if our Master, Don *Quixote*, be not at the Bottom of this. Ay, this is his doing. He has given my Father that same Government or Earldom he has promis'd him so many times. You say right, answer'd the Page: 'Tis for the Lord Don *Quixote's* sake that the Lord *Sancho* is now Governor of the Island of *Barataria*, as the Letter will inform you. Good Sir, quoth *Teresa*, read it me, an't like your Worship; for tho' I can spin, I can't read a Jot: Nor I neither, e'fackins, cry'd *Sanchica*; but do but stay a little, and I'll go fetch one that shall, either the Batchelor *Sampson Carrasco*, or our Parson himself, who'll come with all their Hearts, to hear news of my father. You may save your self the trouble, said the Page; for though I cannot spin, yet I can read; and I'll read it to ye: With that he read the Letter which is now omitted, because it has been inserted before. That done, he pull'd out another from the Dutchess, which runs as follows.

370

Friend Teresa,

Your Husband Sancho's *good Parts, his Wit and Honesty, oblig'd me to desire the Duke my Husband to bestow on him the Government of one of his Islands. I am inform'd he is as sharp as a Hawk in his Office; for which I am very glad, as well as my Lord Duke, and return Heaven many Thanks, that I have not been deceiv'd in making Choice of him for that Preferment. For you must know,* Signiora Teresa, *'tis a difficult Thing to meet with a good Governor in this World; and may Heaven make me as good as* Sancho *proves in his Government.*

I have sent you, my Dear Friend, a String of Coral Beads, set in Gold; I could wish they were Oriental Pearls for your Sake; but a small Token may not hinder a great one. The Time will come when we shall be better acquainted; and when we have convers'd together, who knows what may come to pass? Commend me to your Daughter Sanchica, *and bid her from me to be in a Readiness; for I design to marry her greatly when she least thinks of it.*

I understand you have fine large Acorns in your Town; pray send me a Dozen or two of 'em; I shall set a greater Value upon 'em, as coming from your Hands. And pray let me have a good long Letter, to let me know how you do; and if you have Occasion for any Thing, 'tis but ask and have; I shall even know your Meaning by your Gaping. So Heaven preserve you.

From this
    Castle.

Your Loving Friend,

The Dutchess.

Bless me, quoth *Teresa,* when she had heard the Letter, what a good Lady's this! Not a Bit of Pride in her! Heaven grant me to be buried with such Ladies, and not with such proud Madams as we have in our Town, who because they are Gentlefolks forsooth, think the Wind must not blow upon 'em, but come flaunting to Church, as stately as if they were Queens. It seems they think it Scorn to look on a poor Country Woman: But la you here's a good Lady, who, though she be a Dutchess, calls me her Friend, and uses me as if I were as high as her self. Well, may I see her as high as the highest Steeple in the whole Country! As for the Acorns she writes for, Master o'mine, I'll send her good Ladyship a whole Peck, and such swindgeing Acorns, that every Body shall come to admire 'em far and near. And now, *Sanchica*, see that the Gentleman be made welcome, and want for nothing. Take Care of his Horse. Run to the Stable, get some Eggs, cut some Bacon; he shall fare like a Prince: The rare News he has brought us, and his good Looks deserve no less. Mean while I'll among my Neighbours; I can't hold. I must run and tell 'em the News; our good Curate too shall know it, and Master *Nicholas* the Barber; for they have all along been thy Father's Friends. Ay, do, Mother, said the Daughter; but hark you, you must give me half the Beads; for I dare say the great Lady knows better Things than to give 'em all to you. 'Tis all thy own, Child, cry'd the Mother; but let me wear it a few Days about my Neck; for thou canst not think how it rejoices the very Heart of me. You will rejoice more presently, said the Page, when you see what I have got in my Portmantle; a fine Suit of Green Cloth, which the Governor wore but one Day a Hunting, and has here sent to my Lady *Sanchica*. Oh the Lord love him, cry'd *Sanchica*, and the fine Gentleman that brings it me!

Presently, away ran *Teresa* with the Beads about her Neck, and the Letters in her Hand, all the while playing with her Fingers on the Papers, (as if they had been a Timbrel) and meeting by chance the Curate and the Batchelor *Carrasco*, she fell a dancing and frisking about; Faith and Troth, cry'd she, we are all made now. Not one small Body in all our Kindred. We have got a poor Thing call'd a Government. And now let the proudest of 'em all toss up her Nose at me, and I'll give her as good as she brings, I'll make her know her Distance. How now, *Teresa*, said the Curate? What mad Fit is this? What Papers are those in your Hand? No mad Fit at all, answer'd *Teresa*; but these are Letters from Dutchesses and Governors, and these Beads about my Neck are right Coral, the *Ave-Maries* I mean; and the *Pater-Nosters* are of beaten Gold, and I'm a Madam Governess I'll assure ye. Verily, said the Curate, there's no understanding you, *Teresa*, we don't know what you mean. There's what will clear the Riddle, quoth *Teresa*, and with that she gave 'em the Letters. Thereupon the Curate having read 'em aloud, that *Sampson Carrasco* might also be inform'd, they both stood and look'd on one another, and were more at a Loss than before. The Batchelor ask'd her who brought the letter? *Teresa* told them they might go home with her and see: 'twas a sweet handsom young Man, as fine as any Thing; and that he had brought her another Present worth twice as much. The Curate took the String of Beads from her Neck, and view'd it several times over, and finding that it was a Thing of Value, he could not conceive the Meaning of all this. By the Habit that I wear, cry'd he, I cannot tell what to think of this Business. In the first Place, I am convinc'd these Beads are right Coral and Gold; and in the next, here's a Dutchess sends to beg a Dozen or two of Acorns. Crack that Nut if you can, said *Sampson Carrasco*. But come, let's go to see the Messenger, and probably he'll clear our Doubts.

Thereupon going with *Teresa*, they found the Page sifting a little Corn for his Horse, and *Sanchica* cutting a Rasher of Bacon* to be fry'd with Eggs for his Dinner. They both lik'd the Page's Mien and his Garb, and after the usual Compliments, *Sampson* desir'd him to tell 'em some News of Don *Quixote* and *Sancho Pança*; for though they had read a Letter from the latter to his Wife, and another from the Dutchess, they were no better than Riddles to 'em, nor could they imagine how *Sancho* should come by a Government, especially of an Island, well knowing that all the Islands in the *Mediterranean*, or the greatest Part of 'em, were the King's.

Gentlemen, answer'd the Page, 'tis a certain Truth, that Signior *Sancho Pança* is a Governor, but whether it be of an Island or not, I do not pretend to determine: But this I can assure you, that he commands in a Town that has above a Thousand Inhabitants. And as for my Lady Dutchess's sending to a Country-Woman for a few Acorns, that's no such Wonder; for she is so free from Pride, that I have known her send to borrow a Comb of one of her Neighbours. You must know, our Ladies of *Arragon*, though they are as Noble as those of *Castile*, do not stand so much upon Formalities and Punctilio's; neither do they take so much State upon 'em, but treat People with more Familiarity.

While they were thus discoursing, in came *Sanchica* skip-

---

* *In the Original it is, cutting a Rasher to fry, and to pave it with Eggs, i.e. Eggs laid as close together in the Frying-Pan as Pebbles in a Pavement.*

ping, with her Lap full of Eggs; and turning to the Page, Pray Sir, said she, tell me, does my Father wear Trunk-Breeches* now he's a Governor? Truly, said the Page, I never minded it, but without doubt he does. O Gemini! cry'd the young wench, what would not I give to see my Father in his Trunk-Breeches! Is it not a strange Thing, that ever since I can remember my self, I have wish'd to see my Father in Trunk-Breeches. You'll see him as you'd have him, said the Page, if your Ladyship does but live. Odsfish, if his Government holds but two months, you'll see him go with an Umbrella over his Head.

The Curate and the Batchelor plainly perceiv'd that the Page did but laugh at the Mother and the Daughter; but yet the costly String of Beads and the Hunting Suit, which by this time *Teresa* had let 'em see, confounded 'em again. In the mean while they could not forbear smiling at *Sanchica's* odd Fancy, and much less at what her Mother said. Good Master Curate, quoth she, do so much as inquire whether any of our Neighbours are going to *Madrid* or *Toledo*. I'd have 'em buy me a hugeous Farthingale, of the newest and most courtly Fashion, and the very finest that can be got for Money; for by my Holy Dame, I mean to credit my Husband's Government as much as I can; and if they vex me, I'll hie me to that same Court, and ride in my Coach too as well as the best of 'em; for she that is a Governor's Lady may very well afford to have one. O rare Mother, cry'd *Sanchica*, would 'twere to Night before to Morrow. May hap, when they saw me sitting in our Coach by my Lady Mother, they would jeer and flout; Look, look, would they say, yonder's Goody Trollop, the Plough-jobber's Bearn! How she flaunts it, and goes ye lolling in her Coach like a little Pope *Joan*.† But what would I care? Let 'em trudge on in the Dirt, while I ride by in my Coach. Shame and ill-Luck go along with all your little backbiting scrubs. Let them laugh that win; the curs'd fox thrives the better. Am I not in the right, Mother? Ay, marry art thou, Child, quoth *Teresa*; and indeed my good

* In the Original Calças atacadas. *They are Breeches and Stockings all in one, and laced, or clasp'd, or tied to the* Girdle.   † Papesa. *A she Pope. Our Translators, says* Jarvis, *have render'd this* Pope Joan. *But adds he, there is more humour in making the Country People so ignorant as to believe the Pope had, if not a Wife, a Concubine, as many of the great Clergy had, than in supposing they had ever heard of* Pope Joan.

Honey *Sancho* has often told me, all these good Things, and many more would come to pass; and thou shalt see, Daughter, I'll never rest till I get to be a Countess. There must be a Beginning in all Things, as I have heard it said by thy Father, who's also the Father of Proverbs, when a Cow's given thee, run and take her with a Halter. When they give thee a Government take it; when an Earldom, catch it; and when they whistle* to thee with a good Gift, snap at it. That which is good to give is good to take, Girl. 'Twere a pretty Fancy, trow, to lie snoring a Bed, and when Good-Luck knocks, not to rise and open the Door. Ay, quoth *Sanchica*, what is't to me, though they should say all they've a mind to say. When they see me so tearing fine, and so woundy great, let 'em spit their Venom, and say, set a Beggar on Horseback, and so forth. Who would not think, said the Curate, hearing this, but that the whole Race of the *Pança's* came into the World with their Paunches stuff'd with Proverbs. I never knew one of the Name but threw 'em out at all Times, let the Discourse be what it would. I think so too, said the Page; for his Honour the Governor blunders 'em out at every Turn, many Times indeed wide from the Purpose; however, always to the Satisfaction of the Company, and with high Applause from my Lord and my Lady. Then, Sir, you assure us still, said *Carrasco*, that *Sancho* is really a Governor; and that a Dutchess sends these Presents and Letters upon his Account; for tho' we see the Things, and read the Letters, we can scarce prevail with our selves to believe it; but are apt to run into our Friend Don *Quixote's* Opinion, and look on all this as the Effect of some Inchantment: So that I could find in my Heart to feel and try whether you are a visionary Messenger, or a Creature of Flesh and Blood. For my Part, Gentlemen, answer'd the Page, all I can tell ye, is, that I am really the Messenger I appear to be, that the Lord *Sancho Pança* is actually a Governor, and that the Duke and the Dutchess, to whom I belong, are able to give, and have given him that Government, where I am credibly inform'd he behaves himself most worthily. Now if there be any Inchantment in the Matter, I leave You to examine that; for by the Life of my

* *In the Original, when they cry, Tus, Tus, i.e. as people call Dogs to their Porridge.*

375

Parents, one of the greatest Oaths I can utter, for they are both alive, and I love 'em dearly, I know no more of the Business. That may be, said the Batchelor, but yet *dubitat Augustinus*. You may doubt if you please, reply'd the Page; but I have told you the Truth; which will always prevail over Falshood, and rise uppermost, as Oil does above Water. But if you will *operibus credere, & non verbis*, let one of ye go along with me, and you shall see with your Eyes what you will not believe by the Help of your Ears. I'll go with all my Heart, quoth *Sanchica*; take me up behind ye, Sir; I've a huge mind to see my Father. The Daughters of Governors, said the Page, must not travel thus unattended, but in Coaches or Litters, and with a handsom Train of Servants. Cud's my Life, quoth *Sanchica*, I can go a Journey as well on an Ass as in one of your Coaches. I am none of your tender squeamish Things, not I. Peace, Chicken, quoth the Mother, thou dost not know what thou say'st, the Gentleman is in the right: Times are alter'd. When 'twas plain *Sancho*, 'twas plain *Sanchica*; but now he's a Governor, thou'rt a Lady. I can't well tell whether I am right or no. My Lady *Teresa* says more than she is aware of, said the Page. But now, continu'd he, give me a Mouthful to eat as soon as you can, for I must go back this Afternoon. Be pleas'd then, Sir, said the Curate, to go with me, and partake of a slender Meal at my House; for my Neighbour *Teresa* is more willing than able to entertain so good a Guest. The Page excus'd himself a while, but at last comply'd, being persuaded 'twould be much for the better; and the Curate on his Side was glad of his Company, to have an Opportunity to inform himself at large about Don *Quixote* and his Proceedings. The Batchelor proffer'd *Teresa* to write her Answers to her Letters; but as she look'd upon him to be somewhat waggish, she would not permit him to be of her Counsel; so she gave a Rowl, and a couple of Eggs, to a young Acolyte of the Church, who could write, and he wrote two Letters for her; one to her Husband, and the other to the Dutchess, all of her own inditing, and perhaps not the worst in this famous History, as hereafter may be seen.

XVIII: A CONTINUATION OF SANCHO PANÇA'S GOVERNMENT, WITH OTHER PASSAGES, SUCH AS THEY ARE

THE Morning of that Day arose, which succeeded the Governor's rounding Night, the Remainder of which the Gentleman-Waiter spent not in Sleep, but in the pleasing Thoughts of the lovely Face, and charming Grace of the disguis'd Virgin; on the other Side, the Steward bestow'd that Time in Writing to his Lord and Lady what *Sancho* did and said; wondering no less at his Actions than at his Expressions, both which display'd a strange Intermixture of Discretion and Simplicity.

At last the Lord Governor was pleas'd to rise; and, by Dr *Pedro Rezio's* Order, they brought him for his Breakfast a little Conserve, and a Draught of fair Water, which he would have exchang'd with all his Heart for a good Luncheon of Bread, and a Bunch of Grapes; but seeing he could not help himself, he was forc'd to make the best of a bad Market, and seem to be content, though full sore against his Will and Appetite; for the Doctor made him believe, that to eat but little, and that which was dainty, enliven'd the Spirits, and sharpen'd the Wit, and consequently such a Sort of Diet was most proper for Persons in Authority and weighty Employments, wherein there is less need of the Strength of the Body than of that of the Mind. This Sophistry serv'd to famish *Sancho*, who, half dead with Hunger, curs'd in his Heart both the Government and him that had given it him. However, hungry as he was, by the Strength of his slender Breakfast, he fail'd not to give Audience that Day; and the first that came before him was a Stranger, who put the following Case to him, the Steward and the rest of the Attendants being present.

My Lord, said he, a large River divides in two Parts one and the same Lordship. I beg your Honour to lend me your Attention, for 'tis a Case of great Importance, and some Difficulty— Upon this River there is a Bridge; at one End of which there stands a Gallows, and a kind of Court of Justice, where four

377

Judges use to sit, for the Execution of a certain Law made by the Lord of the Land and River, which runs thus.

Whoever intends to pass from one End of this Bridge to the other, must first upon his Oath declare whither he goes, and what his Business is. If he swear Truth, he may go on; but if he swear false, he shall be hang'd, and die without Remission upon the Gibbet at the End of the Bridge.

After due Promulgation of this Law, many People, notwithstanding it's Severity, adventur'd to go over this Bridge, and as it appear'd they swore true, the Judges permitted 'em to pass unmolested. It happen'd one Day that a certain Passenger being sworn, declar'd, that by the Oath he had taken, he was come to die upon that Gallows, and that was all his Business.

This put the Judges to a Nonplus; for, said they, If we let this Man pass freely, he is forsworn, and according to the Letter of the Law he ought to die: If we hang him, he has sworn Truth, seeing he swore he was to die on that Gibbet; and then by the same Law we should let him pass.

Now your Lordship's Judgment is desir'd what the Judges ought to do with this Man? For they are still at a stand, not knowing what to determine in this Case; and having been inform'd of your sharp Wit, and great Capacity in resolving difficult Questions, they sent me to beseech your Lordship in their Names, to give your Opinion in so intricate and knotty a Case.

To deal plainly with you, answer'd *Sancho*, those worshipful Judges that sent you hither, might as well have spar'd themselves the Labour; for I am more inclin'd to Dulness I assure you than Sharpness: However, let me hear your Question once more, that I may thoroughly understand it, and perhaps I may at last hit the Nail o'the Head. The Man repeated the Question again and again; and when he had done, To my thinking, said *Sancho*, this Question may be presently answer'd, as thus; The Man swore he came to die on the Gibbet, and if he dies there, he swore true, and according to the Law he ought to be free, and go over the Bridge. On the other Side, if you don't hang him, he swore false, and by the same Law he ought to be hang'd. 'Tis as your Lordship says, reply'd the Stranger, you have stated the Case right. Why then, said *Sancho*, ev'n let that Part of the Man that swore true, freely pass; and hang the

378

other Part of the Man that swore false, and so the Law will be fulfill'd. But then my Lord, reply'd the Stranger, the Man must be divided into two Parts, which if we do, he certainly dies, and the Law, which must every tittle of it be observ'd, is not put in Execution.

Well, hark you me, honest Man, said *Sancho*, either I am a Codshead, or there is as much Reason to put this same Person you talk of to Death as to let him live and pass the Bridge; for if the Truth saves him, the Lye condemns him. Now the Case stands thus, I would have you tell those Gentlemen that sent you to me, since there's as much Reason to bring him off, as to condemn him, that they e'en let him go free; for 'tis always more commendable to do Good than Hurt. And this I would give you under my own Hand, if I could write. Nor do I speak this of my own Head; but I remember one Precept, among many others, that my Master Don *Quixote* gave me the Night before I went to govern this Island, which was, that when the Scale of Justice is even, or a Case is doubtful, we should prefer Mercy before Rigour; and it has pleas'd God I should call it to Mind so luckily at this Juncture. For my Part, said the Steward, this Judgment seems to me so equitable, that I do not believe *Lycurgus* himself, who gave Laws to the *Lacedæmonians*, could ever have decided the Matter better than the great *Sancho* has done.

And now, Sir, sure there's enough done for this Morning; be pleas'd to adjourn the Court, and I'll give Order that your Excellency may dine to your Heart's Content. Well said, cry'd *Sancho*, that's all I want, and then a clear Stage, and no Favour. Feed me well, and then ply me with Cases and Questions thick and threefold; you shall see me untwist 'em, and lay 'em open as clear as the Sun.

The Steward was as good as his Word, believing it would be a Burden to his Conscience to famish so wise a Governor; besides, he intended the next Night to put into Practice the last Trick which he had Commission to pass upon him.

Now *Sancho* having plentifully din'd that Day, in spite of all the Aphorisms of Doctor *Tirte a fuera*, when the Cloth was remov'd, in came an Express with a Letter from Don *Quixote* to the Governor. *Sancho* order'd the Secretary to read it to

379

himself, and if there were nothing in it for secret Perusal, then to read it aloud. The Secretary having first run it over accordingly, My Lord, said he, the Letter may not only be publickly read, but deserves to be engraved in Characters of Gold; and thus it is.

DON QUIXOTE DE LA MANCHA
to
SANCHO PANÇA
Governor of the Island of Barataria

When I expected to have had an Account of thy Carelessness and Impertinencies, Friend Sancho, I was agreeably disappointed with News of thy wise Behaviour; for which I return particular Thanks to Heaven, that can raise the lowest from their Poverty, and turn the Fool into a Man of Sense. I hear thou governest with all the Discretion of a Man; and that, while thou approv'st thyself one, thou retainest the Humility of the meanest Creature. But I desire thee to observe, Sancho, that 'tis many Times very necessary and convenient to thwart the Humility of the Heart, for the better Support of the Authority of a Place. For the Ornament of a Person that is advanc'd to an eminent Post, must be answerable to it's Greatness, and not debas'd to the Inclination of his former Meanness. Let thy Apparel be neat and handsom; even a Stake well dress'd does not look like a Stake. I would not have thee wear foppish, gaudy Things; nor affect the Garb of a Soldier, in the Circumstances of a Magistrate; but let thy Dress be suitable to thy Degree, and always clean and decent.

To gain the Hearts of thy People, among other Things, I have two chiefly to recommend: One is, to be affable, courteous, and fair to all the World; I have already told thee of that: And the other, to take Care that Plenty of Provisions be never wanting, for nothing afflicts or urges more the Spirits of the Poor, than Scarcity and Hunger.

Do not put out many new Orders, and if thou dost put out any, see that they be wholesom and good, and especially that they be strictly observ'd; for Laws not well obey'd, are no better than if they were not made, and only shew that the Prince who had the Wisdom and Power to make 'em, had not resolution to see 'em executed; and Laws that only threaten, and are not kept, become like the Log that was given to the Frogs to be their King, which they fear'd at first, but soon scorn'd and trampled on.

Be a Father to Virtue, but a Father-in-Law to Vice. Be not always severe, nor always merciful; chuse a Mean between these two Extremes; for that middle Point is the Center of Discretion.

Visit the Prisons, the Shambles, and the publick Markets, for the Governor's Presence is highly necessary in such Places.

Comfort the Prisoners that hope to be quickly dispatch'd.

Be a Terror to the Butchers, that they may be fair in their Weights, and keep Hucksters and fraudulent Dealers in Awe, for the same Reason.

Should'st thou unhappily be inclin'd to be covetous, given to Women, or a Glutton, as I hope thou art not, avoid shewing thy self guilty of those Vices; for when the Town, and those that come near thee have discover'd thy Weakness, they'll be sure to try thee on that Side, and tempt thee to thy everlasting Ruin.

Read over and over, and seriously consider the Admonitions and Documents I gave thee in Writing before thou went'st to thy Government, and thou wilt find the Benefit of it, in all those Difficulties and Emergencies that so frequently attend the Function of a Governor.

Write to thy Lord and Lady, and shew thy self grateful; for Ingratitude is the Offspring of Pride, and one of the worst Corruptions of the Mind; whereas he that is thankful to his Benefactors, gives a Testimony that he will be so to God, who has done, and continually does him so much good.

My Lady Dutchess dispatch'd a Messenger on purpose to thy Wife Teresa, with thy Hunting Suit, and another Present. We expect his Return every Moment.

I have been somewhat out of Order, by a certain Cat-Encounter I had lately, not much to the Advantage of my Nose; but all that's nothing, for if there are Necromancers that misuse me, there are others ready to defend me.

Send me Word whether the Steward that is with thee had any Hand in the Business of the Countess of Trifaldi, as thou wert once of Opinion; and let me also have an Account of whatever befals thee, since the Distance between us is so small. I have Thoughts of leaving this idle Life 'ere long; for I was not born for Luxury and Ease.

A Business has offer'd, that I believe will make me lose the Duke and Dutchess's Favour; but though I am heartily sorry for't, that does not alter my Resolution; for, after all, I owe more to my Profession than to Complaisance; and as the Saying is, Amicus Plato, sed magis amica Veritas. I send thee this Scrap of Latin, flattering my self that since thou cam'st to be a Governor, thou may'st have learn'd something of that Language. Farewel, and Heaven keep thee above the Pity of the World.

Thy Friend,

Don Quixote de la Mancha.

Sancho gave great Attention to the Letter, and it was highly applauded both for Sense and Integrity, by every Body that heard it. After that he rose from Table, and calling the Secretary, went without any further Delay, and lock'd himself up with him in his Chamber to write an Answer to his Master Don *Quixote.* He order'd the Scribe to set down Word for Word what he dictated, without adding or diminishing the least Thing. Which being strictly observ'd, this was the Tenor of the Letter.

SANCHO PANÇA

to

DON QUIXOTE *DE LA MANCHA*

I Am so taken up with Business, that I han't Time to scratch my Head, or pare my Nails, which is the Reason they are so long. God help me! I tell you this, dear Master of mine, that you may not marvel, why I han't yet let you know whether it goes well or ill with me in this same Government, where I am more Hunger-starv'd than when you and I wandered through Woods and Wildernesses.

My Lord Duke wrote to me t'other Day, to inform me of some Spies that were got into this Island to kill me: But as yet I have discover'd none but a certain Doctor, hir'd by the Islanders to kill all the Governors that come near it. They call him Dr Pedro Rezio de Aguero, and he was born at Tirte a fuera, his Name is enough to make me fear he'll be the Death of me. This same Doctor says of himself, that he does cure Diseases when you have 'em; but when you have 'em not, he only pretends to keep 'em from coming. The Physick he uses, is Fasting upon Fasting,

382

till he turns a Body to a meer Skeleton; as if to be wasted to Skin and Bones were not as bad as a Fever. In short, he starves me to Death; so that when I thought, as being a Governor, to have my Belly full of good hot Victuals, and cool Liquor, and to refresh my Body in Holland Sheets, and on a soft Feather-Bed, I am come to do Penance like a Hermit; and as I do it unwillingly, I am afraid the Devil will have me at last.

All this while I have not so much as finger'd the least Penny of Money, either for Fees, Bribes, or any Thing; and how it comes to be no better with me, I can't for my Soul imagine; for I have heard by the bye, that the Governors who come to this Island are wont to have a very good Gift, or at least a very round Sum lent 'em by the Town before they enter: And they say too, that this is the usual Custom, not only here, but in other Places.

Last Night going my Rounds, I met with a mighty handsom Damsel in Boy's Clothes, and a Brother of her's in Woman's Apparel. My Gentleman-Waiter fell in Love with the Girl, and intends to make her his Wife, as he says. As for the Youth I have pitch'd upon him to be my Son-in-Law. To Day we both design to discourse the Father, one Diego de la Liana, who's a Gentleman, and an old Christian every Inch of him.

I visit the Markets, as you advis'd me, and Yesterday found one of the Hucksters selling Hazle-Nuts; she pretended they were all new, but I found she had mix'd a whole Bushel of old, empty, rotten Nuts among the same Quantity of new. With that I judg'd them to be given to the Hospital-Boys, who knew how to pick the good from the bad, and gave Sentence against her that she should not come into the Market in fifteen Days; and People said, I did well. What I can tell you, is, that if you'll believe the Folks of this Town, there's not a more rascally Sort of People in the World than these Market-Women, for they are all a saucy, foul-mouth'd, impudent, hellish Rabble; and I judge 'em to be so, by those I have seen in other Places.

I am mighty well pleas'd that my Lady Dutchess has writ to my Wife Teresa Pança, and sent her the Token you mention. It shall go hard but I will requite her Kindness one Time or other. Pray give my Service to her, and tell her from me, she has not cast her Gift in a broken Sack, as something more than Words shall shew.

If I might advise you, and had my Wish, there shou'd be no falling out between your Worship and my Lord and Lady; for, if You quarrel with 'em, 'tis I must come by the worst for't. And since you mind me of being grateful, it won't look well in you not to be so to those who have made so much of you at their Castle.

As for your Cat-Affair I can make nothing of it, only I fancy you are still haunted after the old Rate. You'll tell me more when we meet.

I would fain have sent you a Token, but I do not know what to send, unless it were some little Glister-Pipes, which they make here very curiously, and fix most cleverly to the Bladders. But if I stay in my Place, it shall go hard but I'll get something worth the sending, be it what it will.

If my Wife Teresa Pança writes to me, pray pay the Postage, and send me the Letter; for I mightily long to hear how it is with her, and my House and Children.

So Heaven preserve you from ill-minded Inchanters, and send me safe and sound out of this Government, which I am much afraid of, as Doctor Pedro Rezio *diets me.*

Your Worship's Servant

Sancho Pança, *the Governor.*

The Secretary made up the Letter, and immediately dispatch'd the Express. Then those who carry'd on the Plot against *Sancho*, combin'd together, and consulted how to remove him from the Government: And *Sancho* pass'd that Afternoon in making several Regulations, for the better Establishment of that which he imagin'd to be an Island. He publish'd an Order against the Higlers and Forestallers of the Markets; and another to encourage the bringing in of Wines from any Part whatever, provided the Owners declar'd of what Growth they were, that they might be rated according to their Value and Goodness; and that they who should adulterate Wine with Water, or give it a wrong Name, should be punish'd with Death. He lower'd the Price of all Kind of Apparel, and particularly that of Shoes, as thinking it exorbitant. He regulated Servants Wages, that were unlimited before, and proportion'd 'em to the Merit of their Service. He laid severe Penalties up-

on all those that should sing or vend lewd and immoral Songs
and Ballads, either in the open Day, or in the Dusk of the Evening; and also forbid all blind People the singing about Miracles
in Rhimes, unless they produc'd authentick Testimonies of
their Truth; for it appear'd to him, that most of those that
were sung in such Manner were false, and a Disparagement
to the true.

He appointed a particular Officer to inspect the Poor, not to
persecute, but to examine 'em, and know whether they were
truly such; for under Pretence of counterfeit Lameness, and
artificial Sores, many canting Vagabonds impudently rob the
true Poor of Charity, to spend it in Riot and Drunkenness.

In short, he made so many wholesom Ordinances, that to
this Day they are observ'd in that Place, and call'd, *The Con-
stitutions of the Great Governor* Sancho Pança.

XIX: A RELATION OF THE ADVENTURES OF THE SECOND DISCONSOLATE OR DISTREST MATRON, OTHERWISE CALL'D DONNA RODRIGUEZ

CID *Hamet* relates, that Don *Quixote's* Scratches being heal'd, he began to think the Life he led in the Castle not suitable to the Order of Knight-Errantry which he profess'd; he resolv'd therefore to take Leave of the Duke and Dutchess, and set forwards for *Saragosa*; where, at the approaching Tournament, he hop'd to win the Armour, the usual Prize at the Festivals of that Kind. Accordingly, as he sat at Table with the Lord and Lady of the Castle, he began to acquaint 'em with his Design, when behold two Women entred the great Hall, clad in deep Mourning from Head to Foot: One of 'em approaching Don *Quixote*, threw herself at his Feet, where lying prostrate, and in a manner kissing 'em, she fetch'd such deep and doleful Sighs, and made such sorrowful Lamentations, that all those who were by, were not a little surpriz'd. And though the Duke and the Dutchess imagin'd it to be some new Device of their Servants against Don *Quixote*, yet perceiving with what Earnestness the Woman sigh'd and lamented, they were in doubt, and knew not what to think; till the compassionate Champion raising her from the Ground, engag'd her to lift up her Veil, and discover, what they least expected, the Face of *Donna Rodriguez*, the *Duenna* of the Family: And the other Mourner prov'd to be her Daughter, whom the rich Farmer's Son had deluded. All those that knew 'em were in great Admiration, especially the Duke and the Dutchess; for though they knew her Simplicity and Indiscretion, they did not believe her to be so far gone in Madness. At last the sorrowful Matron addressing her self to the Duke and Dutchess; May it please your Graces, said she, to permit me to direct my Discourse to this Knight, for it concerns me to get out of an unlucky Business, into which the Impudence of a treacherous Villain has brought us. With that the Duke gave her Leave to say what she would; Then applying herself to Don *Quixote*; 'Tis not long, said she, valorous Knight, since I gave your Worship an Account how basely and treacherously a graceless young Farmer had us'd my dear Child, the poor undone Creature here present; and you then promis'd me to stand up for her, and see her righted; and now I understand you are about to leave this Castle, in quest of the good Adventures Heaven shall send you. And therefore before you are gone no body knows whither, I have this Boon to beg of your Worship, that you would do so much as challenge this sturdy Clown, and make him marry my Daughter, according to his Promise before he was concern'd with her. For, as for my Lord Duke, 'tis a Folly to think he'll ever see me righted, for the Reason I told you in private. And so Heaven preserve your Worship, and still be our Defence. Worthy Matron (answer'd Don *Quixote*, with a great deal of Gravity and solemn Form) moderate your Tears, or to speak more properly, dry 'em up, and spare your Sighs; for I take upon me to see your Daughter's Wrongs redress'd; though she had done much better, had not her too great Credulity made her trust the Protestations of Lovers, which generally are readily made, but most uneasily perform'd. Therefore, with my Lord Duke's Permission, I will instantly depart, to find out this ungracious Wretch, and as soon as he is found, I will challenge him, and kill him if he persists in his Obstinacy; for the chief End of my Profession is to pardon the submissive, and to chastise the stubborn; to relieve the miserable, and destroy the cruel. Sir Knight, said the Duke, you need not give your self the Trouble of seeking the Fellow, of whom that good Matron complains; nor need you ask me Leave to challenge him; for I already engage, that he shall meet you in Person to answer it here in this Castle, where safe Lists shall be set up for you both, observing all the Laws of Arms that ought to be kept in Affairs of this Kind, and doing each Party Justice, as all Princes ought to do, that admit of single Combats within their Territories. Upon that Assurance, said Don *Quixote*, with your Grace's Leave, I for this Time wave my Punctilio's of Gentility, and debasing my self to the Meanness of the Offender, qualify him to measure Lances with me; and so let him be absent or present, I challenge and defy him, as a Villain, that has deluded this poor Creature, that was a Maid, and now, through his Baseness, is none; and he shall either perform his Promise of making her his lawful Wife, or die in the Contest. With that, pulling off his Glove, he flung it down into the Middle of the Hall, and the Duke took it up, declaring, as he had already done, that he accepted the Challenge in the Name of his Vassal; fixing the Time for Combat to be six Days after, and the Place to be the Castle-Court. The Arms to be such as are usual among Knights, as Lance, Shield, Armour of Proof, and all other Pieces, without Fraud, Advantage or Inchantment, after Search made by the Judges of the Field.

But in the first Place, added the Duke, 'tis requisite, that this true Matron, and this false Virgin, commit the Justice of their Cause into the Hands of their Champion, for otherwise there will be nothing done, and the Challenge is void in course. I do, answer'd the Matron; and so do I, added the Daughter, all asham'd, blubbering, and in a crying Tone. The Preliminaries being adjusted, and the Duke having resolv'd with himself what to do in the Matter, the mourning Petitioners went away, and the Dutchess order'd they should no longer be look'd upon as her Domesticks, but as Ladies Errant, that came to demand Justice in her Castle; and accordingly there was a peculiar Apartment appointed for 'em, where they were serv'd as Strangers, to the Amazement of the other Servants, who could not imagine what would be the End of *Donna Rodriguez* and her forsaken Daughter's ridiculous and confident Undertaking.

Presently after this, to complete their Mirth, and as it were for the last Course, in came the Page that had carry'd the Letters and the Presents to *Teresa Pança*. The Duke and Dutchess were overjoy'd to see him return'd, having a great Desire to know the Success of his Journey. They enquir'd of him accordingly, but he told 'em, that the Account he had to give 'em could not well be deliver'd in publick, nor in few Words; and therefore begg'd their Graces would be pleas'd to take it in private, and in the mean time entertain themselves with those Letters. With that, taking out two, he deliver'd 'em to her Grace. The Superscription of the one was, *These for my Lady Dutchess of I don't know what Place:* and the Direction on the other, thus, *To my Husband* Sancho Pança, *Governor of the Island* Barataria, *whom Heaven prosper as many or more Years than me.*

The Dutchess sat upon Thorns till she had read her Letter;

so having open'd it, and run it over to her self, finding there was nothing of Secrecy in it, she read it out aloud, that the whole Company might hear what follows.

TERESA PANÇA'S *LETTER TO THE DUTCHESS*

My Lady,

The Letter your Honour sent me pleased me hugeously; for Troth 'tis what I heartily long'd for. The String of Coral is a good Thing, and my Husband's Hunting Suit may come up to it. All our Town takes it mighty kindly, and is very glad that your Honour has made my Spouse a Governor, though no body will believe it, especially our Curate, Master Nicholas the Barber, and Sampson Carrasco the Batchelor. But what care I, whether they do or no? So it be true, as it is, let every one have their Saying. Though 'tis a Folly to lye, I had not believed it neither, but for the Coral and the Suit; for every body here takes my Husband to be a Dolt, and can't for the Blood of 'em imagine what he can be fit to govern, unless it be a Herd of Goats. Well! Heaven be his Guide, and speed him as he sees best for his Children. As for me, my dear Lady, I am resolv'd, with your good liking, to make Hay while the Sun shines, and go to Court, to loll it along in a Coach, and make a World of my Back Friends, that envy me already, stare their Eyes out. And therefore, good your Honour, pray bid my Husband send me store of Money; for I believe 'tis dear living at Court; one can have but little Bread there for Six-pence, and a Pound of Flesh is worth thirty Maravedies, which would make one stand amaz'd. And if he is not for my coming, let him send me word in Time, for my Feet itch to be jogging; for my Gossips and Neighbours tell me, that if I and my Daughter go about the Court as we should, spruce and fine, and at a tearing Rate, my Husband will be better known by me, than I by him; for many can't chuse but ask what Ladies are those in the Coach? With that one of my Servants answers, The Wife and Daughter of Sancho Pança, Governor of the Island of Barataria; and thus shall my Husband be known, and I honour'd far and near; and so have at all; Rome has every Thing. *

You can't think how I am troubl'd that we have gather'd no

* *As Head of the World, formerly in Temporals, as now in Spirituals.*

Acorns here-away this Year; however, I send your Highness about half a Peck, which I have cull'd one by one: I went to the Mountains on purpose, and got the biggest I could find; I wish they had been as big as Ostrich Eggs.

Pray let not your Pomposity forget to write to me, and I'll be sure to send you an Answer, and let you know how I do, and send you all the News in our Village, where I am waiting and praying the Lord to preserve your Highness, and not to forget me. My Daughter Sanchica, and my Son, kiss your Worship's Hands.

She that wishes rather to see you than write to you.

Your Servant, Teresa Pança.

This Letter was very entertaining to all the Company, especially to the Duke and Dutchess; insomuch that her Grace asked Don *Quixote*, whether it would be amiss to open the Governor's Letter, which she imagin'd was a very good one? The Knight told her, that, to satisfy her Curiosity, he would open it; which being done, he found what follows.

TERESA PANÇA'S *LETTER TO HER HUSBAND* SANCHO PANÇA

I Receiv'd thy Letter, dear Honey Sancho, and I vow and swear to thee, as I am a Catholick Christian, I was within two Fingers Breadth of running mad for Joy. Look you, my Chuck, when I heard thou wert made a Governor, I was so transported, I had like to have fallen down dead with meer Gladness; for thou knowest sudden Joy is said to kill as soon as great Sorrow. As for thy Daughter Sanchica, she scatter'd her Water about, before she was aware, for very Pleasure. I had the suit thou sent'st me before my Eyes, and the Lady Dutchess's Corals about my Neck, held the Letter in my Hands, and had him that brought 'em standing by me; and for all that, I thought what I saw and felt was but a Dream. For who could have thought a goatherd should ever come to be a Governor of Islands? But what said my Mother, Who a great deal would see, a great while must live. I speak this because if I live longer, I mean to see more; for I shall ne'er be at Rest till I see thee a Farmer or Receiver of the Customs; for though they be offices that send many to the Devil,

*for all that, they bring Grist to the Mill. My Lady Dutchess
will tell thee how I long to go to Court. Pray think on't, and let
me know thy Mind; for I mean to credit thee there, by going
in a Coach.*

*Neither the Curate, the Barber, the Batchelor, nor the Sexton
will believe thou art a Governor; but say 'tis all Juggling or
Inchantment, as all thy Master Don Quixote's Concerns use to
be; and Sampson threatens to find thee out, and put this Maggot of a Government out of thy Pate, and Don Quixote's Madness out of his Coxcomb. For my Part I do but laugh at 'em,
and look upon my String of Coral, and contrive how to fit up the
Suit thou sent'st me into a Gown for thy Daughter.*

*I sent my Lady the Dutchess some Acorns; I would they were
beaten Gold; I prithee send me some Strings of Pearl, if they be
in Fashion in thy Island.*

*The News here is, that Berrueca has married her Daughter
to a sorry Painter, that came hither, pretending to paint any
Thing. The Township set him to paint the King's Arms over
the Town-Hall: He ask'd 'em two Ducats for the Job, which
they paid him; so he fell to Work; and was eight Days a daub-
ing, but could make nothing on't at last; and said he could not
hit upon such pidling Kind of Work, and so gave 'em their
Money again. Yet for all this he marry'd with the Name of a
good Workman. The Truth is, he has left his Pencil upon't,
and taken the Spade, and goes to the Field like a Gentleman.
Pedro de Lobo's Son has taken Orders, and shav'd his Crown,
meaning to be a Priest. Minguilla, Mingo Silvato's Grand-
Daughter, heard of it, and sues him upon a Promise of Marriage: Ill Tongues do not stick to say she has been with Child by
him, but he stiffly denies it. We have no Olives this Year, nor is
there a Drop of Vinegar to be got for Love or Money. A Company of Soldiers went through this Place, and carry'd along
with them three Wenches out of the Town: I don't tell thee their
Names, for mayhaps they will come back, and there will not
want some that will marry 'em, for better for worse. Sanchica
makes Bone-Lace, and gets her three Half-pence a Day clear,
which she saves in a Box with a Slit, to go towards buying
Houshold-stuff. But now she's a Governor's Daughter, she has
no Need to work, for thou wilt give her a Portion. The Fountain*

in the Market is dry'd up. A Thunderbolt lately fell upon the Pillory: There may they all light. I expect thy Answer to this, and thy Resolution concerning my going to Court: So Heaven send thee long to live, longer than my self, or rather, as long; for I would not willingly leave thee behind me in this World.

Thy Wife,

Teresa Pança.

These Letters were admir'd, and caus'd a great deal of Laughter and Diversion; and to complete the Mirth, at the same Time the Express return'd that brought *Sancho's* Answer to Don *Quixote*, which was likewise publickly read, and startl'd all the Hearers, who took the Governor for a Fool! Afterwards the Dutchess withdrew, to know of the Page what he had to relate of his Journey to *Sancho's* Village; of which he gave her a full Account, without omitting the least Particular. He also brought her the Acorns, and a Cheese, which *Teresa* had given him for a very good one, and better than those of *Troncheon*, and which the Dutchess gratefully accepted. Now let us leave her, to tell the End of the Government of Great *Sancho Pança*, the Flower and Mirror of all Island-Governors.

XX: THE TOILSOM END AND CONCLUSION OF
SANCHO PANÇA'S GOVERNMENT

TO think the Affairs of this Life are always to remain in the same State, is an erroneous Fancy. The Face of Things rather seems continually to change and roll with a circular Motion; Summer succeeds the Spring; Autumn the Summer; Winter the Autumn; and then Spring again: So Time proceeds in this perpetual Round; only the Life of Man is ever hastening to it's End, swifter than Time it self, without Hopes to be renew'd, unless in the next, that is unlimited and infinite. This says *Cid Hamet*, the *Mahometan* Philosopher. For even by the Light of Nature, and without that of Faith, many have discover'd the Swiftness and Instability of this present Being, and the Duration of the Eternal Life which is expected. But this moral Reflection of our Author is not here to be suppos'd as meant by him in it's full Extent; for he intended it only to shew the Uncertainty of *Sancho's* Fortune, how soon it vanish'd like a Dream, and how from his high Preferment he return'd to his former low Station.

It was now but the seventh Night, after so many Days of his Government, when the careful Governor had betaken himself to his Repose, sated not with Bread and Wine, but cloy'd with hearing Causes, pronouncing Sentences, making Statutes, and putting out Orders and Proclamations: Scarce was Sleep, in spite of wakeful Hunger, beginning to close his Eyes, when of a sudden he heard a great Noise of Bells, and most dreadful Out-cries, as if the whole Island had been sinking. Presently he started, and sat up in his Bed, and listen'd with great Attention, to try if he could learn how far this Uproar might concern Him. But while he was thus hearkening in the Dark, a great Number of Drums and Trumpets were heard, and that Sound being added to the Noise of the Bells and the Cries, gave so dreadful an Alarm, that his Fear and Terror increas'd, and he was in a sad Consternation. Up he leap'd out of his Bed, and put on his Slippers, the Ground being damp, and without any Thing else in the World on but his Shirt, ran and open'd his Chamber-door, and saw above twenty Men come running along the Galleries with lighted Links in one Hand, and drawn Swords in the other, all crying out, Arm! my Lord Governor, Arm! a World of Enemies are got into the Island, and we are undone, unless your Valour and Conduct relieve us. Thus bawling and running with great Fury and Disorder, they got to the Door where *Sancho* stood quite scar'd out of his Senses. Arm, Arm, this Moment, my Lord! cry'd one of 'em, if you have not a mind to be lost with the whole Island. What would ye have me Arm for? quoth *Sancho*. Do I know any thing of Arms or Fighting, think ye? Why don't ye rather send for Don *Quixote*, my Master, he'll dispatch your Enemies in a trice. Alas! as I am a Sinner to Heaven, I understand nothing of this hasty Service. For Shame, my Lord Governor, said another, what a Faintheartedness is this? See! we bring you here Arms offensive and defensive; arm your self, and march to the Market Place. Be our Leader and Captain as you ought, and shew your self a Governor. Why then arm me, and good Luck attend me, quoth *Sancho*; with that they brought him two large Shields, which they had provided, and without letting him put on his other Clothes, clapp'd 'em over his Shirt, and ty'd the one behind upon his Back, and the other before upon his Breast, having got his Arms through some Holes made on Purpose. Now the Shields being fasten'd to his Body, as hard as Cords could bind 'em, the poor Governor was cas'd up and immur'd as straight as an Arrow, without being able so much as to bend his Knees, or stir a Step. Then having put a Lance into his Hand for him to lean upon, and keep himself up, they desir'd him to march, and lead 'em on, and put Life into 'em all, telling him, that they did not doubt of Victory, since they had him for their Commander. March! quoth *Sancho*, how do you think I am able to do it, squeez'd as I am? These Boards stick so plaguy close to me, I can't so much as bend the Joints of my Knees; You must e'en carry me in your Arms, and lay me across, or set me upright before some Passage, and I'll make good that Spot of Ground, either with this Lance or my Body. Fie, my Lord Governor, said another, 'tis more your Fear than your Armour that stiffens your Legs, and hinders you from moving. Move, move, march on, 'tis high Time, the Enemy grows stronger, and the Danger presses. The poor Governor thus urg'd and upbraided, endeavoured to go forwards; but the first Motion he made, threw him to the Ground at his full Length, so heavily, that he gave over all his Bones for broken; and there he lay like a huge Tortoise in his Shell, or a Flitch of Bacon clapp'd between two Boards, or like a Boat overturn'd upon a Flat, with the Keel upwards. Nor had those drolling Companions the least Compassion upon him as he lay; quite contrary, having put out their Lights, they made a terrible Noise, and clatter'd with their Swords, and trampl'd too and again upon the poor Governor's Body, and laid on furiously with their Swords upon his Shields, insomuch, that if he had not shrunk his Head into 'em for Shelter, he had been in a woful Condition. Squeez'd up in his narrow Shell, he was in a grievous Fright, and a terrible Sweat, praying from the Bottom of his Heart for Deliverance from the cursed Trade of governing Islands. Some kick'd him, some stumbl'd and fell upon him, and one among the rest jump'd full upon him, and there stood for some Time, as on a Watch-Tower, like a General encouraging his Soldiers, and giving Orders, crying out, There Boys, there! the Enemies charge most on that Side, make good that Breach, secure that Gate, down with those Scaling-Ladders, fetch Fire-balls, more Grenadoes, burning Pitch, Rosin, and Kettles of scalding Oil. Intrench your selves, get Beds, Quilts, Cushions, and barricadoe the Streets; in short, he call'd for all the Instruments of Death, and all the Engines us'd for the Defence of a City that is besieg'd and storm'd. *Sancho* lay snug, though sadly bruis'd, and while he endur'd all quietly, Oh that it would please the Lord, quoth he to himself, that this Island were but taken, or that I were fairly dead, or out of this Peck of Troubles. At last Heaven heard his Prayers, and when he least expected it, he heard 'em cry, Victory, Victory! The Enemy's routed. Now my Lord Governor, rise, come and enjoy the Fruits of Conquest, and divide the Spoils taken from the Enemy, by the Valour of your invincible Arms. Help me up, cry'd poor *Sancho* in a doleful Tone; and when they had set him on his Legs, let all the Enemy I have routed, quoth he, be nail'd to my Forehead: I'll divide no Spoils of Enemies: But if I have one Friend here, I only beg he would give me a Draught of Wine to comfort me, and help to dry up the Sweat that I am in; for I am all over Water.

Thereupon they wip'd him, gave him Wine, and took off his Shields: after that, as he sat upon his Bed, what with his Fright, and what with the Toil he had endur'd, he fell into a Swoon, insomuch, that those who acted this Scene, began to repent they had carry'd it so far. But *Sancho* recovering from his Fit in a little time, They also recover'd from their Uneasiness. Being come to himself, he ask'd what 'twas a Clock? They answer'd, 'twas now break of Day. He said nothing, but, without any Words, began to put on his Clothes. While this was doing, and he continu'd seriously silent, all the Eyes of the Company were fix'd upon him, wondring what could be the meaning of his being in such haste to put on his Clothes. At last he made an End of dressing himself, and creeping along softly, (for he was too much bruis'd to go along very fast) he got to the Stable, follow'd by all the Company, and coming to *Dapple*, he embrac'd the quiet Animal, gave him a loving Kiss on the Forehead, and, with Tears in his Eyes, Come hither, said he, my Friend, thou faithful Companion, and Fellow-sharer in my Travels and Miseries; when thee and I consorted together, and all my Cares were but to mend thy Furniture, and feed thy little Carcase, then happy were my Days, my Months, and Years. But since I forsook Thee, and clamber'd up the Towers of Ambition and Pride, a thousand Woes, a thousand Torments, and four thousand Tribulations have haunted and worry'd my Soul. While he was talking thus, he fitted on his Pack-Saddle, no Body offering to say any thing to him. This done, with a great deal of Difficulty he mounted his Ass, and then addressing himself to the Steward, the Secretary, the Gentleman-waiter, and Doctor *Pedro Rezio*, and many others that stood by; Make Way, Gentlemen, said he, and let me return to my former Liberty. Let me go that I may seek my old Course of Life, and rise again from that Death that buries me here alive. I was not born to be a Governor, nor to defend Islands nor Cities from Enemies that break in upon 'em. I know better what belongs to Ploughing, Delving, Pruning and Planting of Vineyards, than how to make Laws, and defend Countries and Kingdoms. St *Peter* is very well at *Rome*: Which is as much as to say, let every one stick to the Calling he was born to. A Spade does better in My Hand than a Governor's Truncheon; and I had

396

rather fill my Belly with a Mess of plain Porridge,* than lie at the Mercy of a Coxcombly Physick-monger that starves me to Death. I had rather solace my self under the Shade of an Oak in Summer, and wrap my Corps up in a double Sheep-skin in the Winter at my Liberty, than lay me down with the Slavery of a Government in fine Holland Sheets, and case my Hide in Furs and richest Sables. Heaven be with you, Gentlefolks, and pray tell my Lord Duke from me, that naked I was born, and naked I am at present. I have neither won nor lost, which is as much as to say, without a penny I came to this Government, and without a Penny I leave it, quite contrary to what other Governors of Islands use to do, when they leave 'em. Clear the Way then, I beseech you, and let me pass; I must get my self wrapp'd up all over in Cere-cloth; for I don't think I've a sound Rib left, thanks to the Enemies that have walk'd over me all Night long. This must not be, my Lord Governor, said Doctor *Rezio*, for I will give your Honour a Balsamick Drink, that is a Specifick against falls, dislocations, contusions, and all manner of Bruises, and that will presently restore you to your former Health and Strength. And then for your Diet, I promise to take a new Course with you, and to let you eat abundantly of what-soever you please. 'Tis too late, Mr Doctor, answer'd *Sancho*; you shall as soon make me turn *Turk*, as hinder me from going. No, no, these Tricks shan't pass upon me again, you shall as soon make me fly to Heaven without Wings, as get me to stay here, or ever catch me nibbling at a Government again, though it were serv'd up to me in a cover'd Dish. I am of the Blood of the *Pança's*, and we are all wilful and positive. If once we cry odd, it shall be odd in spite of all Mankind, though it be even. Go to then: Let the Pismire leave behind him in this Stable those Wings that lifted him up in the Air to be a Prey to Mart-lets and Sparrows. Fair and Softly. Let me now tread again on plain ground; though I mayn't wear pink'd Cordovan Leather-Pumps, I shan't want a Pair of Sandals† to my Feet. Every Sheep to her Mate. Let not the Cobler go beyond his Last; and so

---

* Gazpacho: *It is made of Oil, Vinegar, Water, Salt, and Spice, with toasted Bread. A sort of Soupe Maigre, says* Steven's Dict.   † *A sort of flat Sandal or Shoe made of Hemp, or of Bull-rushes, artfully platted, and fitted to the Foot; worn by the poor People in* Spain *and* Italy.

let me go, for 'tis late. My Lord Governor, said the Steward, though it grieves us to part with your Honour, your Sense and Christian Behaviour engaging us to covet your Company, yet we would not presume to stop you against your Inclination: But you know that every Governor, before he leaves the Place he has govern'd, is bound to give an Account of his Administration. Be pleas'd therefore to do so for the ten Days* you have been among us, and then Peace be with you. No Man has Power to call me to an Account, reply'd *Sancho*, unless it be by my Lord Duke's Appointment. Now to Him it is that I am going, and to Him I'll give a fair and square Account. And indeed, going away so bare as I do, there needs no greater Signs that I have govern'd like an Angel. In truth, said Dr *Rezio*, the great *Sancho* is in the right; and I am of Opinion, we ought to let him go; for certainly the Duke will be very glad to see him. Thereupon they all agreed to let him pass, offering first to attend him, and supply him with whatever he might want in his Journey, either for Entertainment or Conveniency. *Sancho* told 'em, that all he desir'd was a little Corn for his Ass, and half a Cheese, and half a Loaf for himself; having Occasion for no other Provisions in so short a Journey. With that they all embrac'd him, and he embrac'd them all, not without Tears in his Eyes, leaving 'em in Admiration of the good Sense which he discover'd both in his Discourse and unalterable Resolution.

* *How comes the Steward to say* ten Days, *when it is plain* Sancho *govern'd only* seven Days! *It is, says* Jarvis, *either owing to Forgetfulness in the Author, or perhaps is a new Joke of the Steward's, imagining* Sancho *to be as ignorant of Reckoning as of Writing. And in Effect* Sancho, *by not denying it, allows the ten Days.*

XXI: WHICH TREATS OF MATTERS THAT RELATE TO THIS HISTORY, AND NO OTHER

THE Duke and Dutchess resolv'd that Don *Quix-ote's* Challenge against their Vassal should not be ineffectual; and the young Man being fled into *Flanders*, to avoid having *Donna Rodriguez* to his Mother-in-law, they made choice of a *Gascoin* Lacquey, nam'd *Tosilos*, to supply his Place, and gave him Instructions how to act his Part. Two Days after, the Duke acquainted Don *Quixote*, that within four days his anta-gonist would meet him in the Lists, arm'd at all Points like a Knight, to maintain that the Damsel ly'd through the Throat, and through the Beard, to say that he had ever promis'd her Marriage. Don *Quixote* was mightily pleas'd with this News, promising himself to do Wonders on this Occasion; and esteem-ing it an extraordinary Happiness to have such an Opportunity to shew before such Noble Spectators how extensive were his Valour and his Strength. Cheer'd and elevated with these Hopes, he waited for the End of these four Days, which his eager Impatience made him think so many Ages.

Well, now letting them pass, as we do other Matters, let us a while attend *Sancho*, who, divided betwixt Joy and Sorrow, was now on his *Dapple*, making the best of his Way to his Master, whose Company he valu'd more than the Government of all the Islands in the World. He had not gone far from his Island, or City, or Town (or whatever you will please to call it, for he never troubl'd himself to examine what it was) be-fore he met upon the Road six Pilgrims, with their Walking-Staves, Foreigners as they prov'd, and such as us'd to beg Alms singing. As they drew near him, they plac'd themselves in a Row, and fell a singing all together in their Language some-thing that *Sancho* could not understand, unless it were one Word, which plainly signify'd Alms; by which he guess'd that Charity was the Burden and Intent of their Song. Being exceed-ing charitable, as *Cid Hamet* reports him, he open'd his Wal-let, and having taken out the Half-Loaf and Half-Cheese, gave 'em them, making Signs withal, that he had nothing else to give 'em. They took the Dole with a good Will, but yet, not satisfy'd, they cry'd, *Guelt, Guelt.* * Good People, quoth *Sancho*, I don't understand what you would have. With that, one of them pull'd out a Purse that was in his Bosom, and shew'd it to *Sancho*, by which he understood, that 'twas Money they wanted. But he, putting his Thumb to his Mouth, and wagging his Hand with his four Fingers upwards, made a Sign that he had not a Cross; and so clapping his Heels to *Dapple's* Sides, he began to make way through the Pilgrims; but at the same time one of 'em, who had been looking on him very earnestly, laid hold on him, and throwing his Arms about his Middle, Bless me! (cry'd he in very good *Spanish*) what do I see? Is it possible? Do I hold in my Arms my dear Friend, my good Neighbour *Sancho Pança*? Yes, sure, it must be he, for I am neither drunk nor dreaming. *Sancho* wondring to hear himself call'd by his Name, and to see himself so lovingly hugg'd by the Pilgrim, star'd upon him without speaking a Word; but, though he look'd seriously in his Face a good while, he could not guess who he was. The Pilgrim observing his Amazement, What, said he, Friend *Sancho*, don't you know your old Acquaintance, your Neighbour *Ricote* the *Morisco*, that kept a Shop in your Town? Then *Sancho* looking wistly on him again, began to call him to mind, at last he knew him again perfectly, and clipping him about the Neck without alighting, *Ricote*, cry'd he, who the Devil could ever have known thee transmogrify'd in this Mumming Dress! Pr'ythee who has franchify'd thee at this rate? and how durst thou offer to come again into *Spain*? Should'st thou come to be known, adad I would not be in thy Coat for all the World. If thou dost not betray me, said the Pilgrim, I am safe enough, *Sancho*; for no Body can know me in this Disguise. But let us get out of the Road, and make to yonder Elm-Grove; my Comrades and I have agreed to take a little Refreshment there, and thou shalt dine with us. They are honest Souls, I'll assure thee. There I shall have an Opportunity to tell thee how I have pass'd my Time since I was forc'd to leave the Town in Obedience to the King's Edict, which, as thou knowest, so severely threatens those of our unfortunate Nation. *Sancho* consented, and *Ricote* having spoke to the rest of the Pilgrims, they went all together to the

* Guelte *in Dutch is Money.*

Grove, at a good Distance from the Road. There they laid by their Staves, and taking off their Pilgrims Weeds, remain'd in *Cuorpo*; all of 'em young handsom Fellows, except *Ricote*, who was somewhat stricken in Years. Every one carry'd his Wallet, which seem'd well furnish'd, at least with savoury and high-season'd Bits, the Provocative to the turning down good Liquor. They sat down on the Ground, and making the green Grass their Tablecloth, presently there was a comfortable Appearance of Bread, Salt, Knives, Nuts, Cheese, and some Bacon Bones, on which there were still some good Pickings left, or which at least might be suck'd. They also had a kind of black Meat call'd *Caveer*, made of the Roes of Fish, a certain Charm to keep Thirst awake. They also had good Store of Olives, though none of the moistest; but the chief Glory of the Feast, was six Leather Bottles of Wine, every Pilgrim exhibiting one for his Share; even honest *Ricote* himself was now transform'd from a *Morisco* to a *German*, and clubb'd his Bottle, his Quota making as good a Figure as the rest. They began to eat like Men that lik'd mighty well their savoury Fare; and as it was very Relishing, they went leisurely to work, to continue the longer, taking but a little of every one at a time on the point of a Knife. Then all at once they lifted up their Arms, and applying their own Mouths to the Mouths of the Bottles, and turning up their Bottoms in the Air, with their Eyes fix'd on Heaven, like Men in an Extasy, they remain'd in that Posture a good while, transfusing the Blood and Spirit of the Vessels into their Stomachs, and shaking their Heads, as in a Rapture, to express the Pleasure they receiv'd. *Sancho* admir'd all this extremely; he cou'd not find the least Fault with it; quite contrary, he was for making good the Proverb, *When thou art at* Rome, *do as they do at* Rome; so he desir'd *Ricote* to lend him his Bottle, and taking his Aim as well as the rest, and with no less Satisfaction, shew'd 'em he wanted neither Method nor Breath. Four times they caress'd the Bottles in that manner, but there was no doing it the Fifth; for they were quite exhausted, and the Life and Soul of 'em departed, which turn'd their Mirth into Sorrow. But while the Wine lasted, all was well. Now and then one or other of the Pilgrims would take *Sancho* by the right Hand, *Spaniard* and

German all one now, and cry'd, *Bon Campagno*. Well said, i'faith, answer'd *Sancho*; *Bon Campagno, Perdie*. And then he would burst out a laughing for half an Hour together, without the least Concern for all his late Misfortunes, or the Loss of his Government; for Anxieties use to have but little Power over the Time that Men spend in Eating or Drinking. In short, as their Bellies were full, their Bones desir'd to be at Rest, and so five of 'em dropp'd asleep, only *Sancho* and *Ricote* who had indeed eat more, but drank less, remain'd awake, and remov'd under the Cover of a Beech at a small Distance, where, while the other slept, *Ricote* in good *Spanish* spoke to *Sancho* to this Purpose.

Thou well, knowest Friend *Sancho Pança*, how the late Edict, that injoin'd all those of our Nation to depart the Kingdom, alarm'd us all; at least me it did; insomuch that the Time limited for our going was not yet expir'd, but I thought the Law was ready to be executed upon me and my Children. Accordingly I resolv'd to provide betime for their Security and mine, as a Man does that knows his Habitation will be taken away from him, and so secures another before he is obliged to remove. So I left our Town by my self, and went to seek some Place beforehand, where I might convey my Family, without exposing my self to the Inconveniency of a Hurry, like the rest that went; for the wisest among us were justly apprehensive, that the Proclamations issued out for the Banishment of our *Moorish* Race, were not only Threats, as some flatter'd themselves, but would certainly take Effect at the Expiration of the limited Time. I was the rather inclin'd to believe this, being conscious that our People had very dangerous Designs; so that I could not but think the King was inspir'd by Heaven to take so brave a Resolution, and expel those Snakes out of the Bosom of the Kingdom: Not that we were all guilty, for there were some sound and real Christians among us; but their Number was so small, that they could not be oppos'd to those that were otherwise, and it was not safe to keep Enemies within Doors. In short, it was necessary we should be banish'd; but though some might think it a mild and pleasant Fate, to us it seems the most dreadful Thing that could befal us: Wherever we are, we bemoan with Tears our Banishment from *Spain*; for, after

all, there we were born, and 'tis our Native Country. We find
no where the Entertainment our Misfortune requires; and
even in *Barbary* and all other Parts of *Africk*, where we expected to have met with the best Reception and Relief, we find
the greatest Inhumanity, and the worst Usage. We did not
know our Happiness till we had lost it; and the Desire which
most of us have to return to *Spain*, is such, that the greatest
Part of those that speak the Tongue as I do, who are many,
come back hither, and leave their Wives and Children there
in a forlorn Condition; so strong is their Love for their native
Place; and now I know by Experience the Truth of the Saying
Sweet is the Love of one's own Country. For my Part, having
left our Town, I went into *France*, and though I was very
well receiv'd there, yet I had a mind to see other Countries;
and so passing through it, I travell'd into *Italy*, and from thence
into *Germany*, where methought one might live with more
Freedom, the Inhabitants being a good-humour'd sociable
People, that love to live easy with one another, and every Body
follows his own Way: for there's Liberty of Conscience allow'd in the greatest Part of the Country. There, after I had
taken a Dwelling in a Village near *Augsburgh*, I struck into the
Company of these Pilgrims, and got to be one of their Number,
finding they were some of those who make it their Custom to
go to *Spain*, many of 'em every Year to visit the Places of Devotion, which they look upon as their *Indies*, and best Market,
and surest Means to get Money. They travel almost the whole
Kingdom over, nor is there a Village where they are not sure
to get Meat and Drink, and six Pence at least in Money. And
they manage Matters so well, that at the End of their Pilgrimage they commonly go off with about a hundred Crowns clear
Gains, which they change into Gold, and hide either in the
Hollow of their Staves, or the Patches of their Clothes, and
either thus, or some other private Way convey it usually into
their own Country, in spite of all Searches at their going out
of the Kingdom. Now, *Sancho*, my Design in returning hither
is to fetch the Treasure that I left bury'd when I went away,
which I may do with the less Inconveniency, by reason it lies
in a Place quite out of the Town. That done, I intend to write
or go over my self from *Valencia* to my Wife and Daughter,

who I know are in *Algiers*, and find one Way or other to get 'em over to some Port of *France*, and from thence bring 'em over into *Germany*, where we will stay, and see how Providence will dispose of us: For I am sure my Wife *Francisca* and my Daughter are good Catholick Christians; and though I can't say I am as much a Believer as they are, yet I have more of the Christian than of the Mahometan, and make it my constant Prayer to the Almighty to open the Eyes of my Understanding, and let me know how to serve him. What I wonder at, is, that my Wife and Daughter should rather chuse to go for *Barbary* than for *France*, where they might have liv'd like Christians.

Look you, *Ricote*, answer'd *Sancho*, may-haps, that was none of their Fault, for to my Knowledge *John Tiopieyo*, thy Wife's Brother, took 'em along with him, and he, be-like, being a rank *Moor*, would go where he thought best. And I must tell thee further, Friend, that I doubt thou'lt lose thy Labour in going to look after thy hidden Treasure; for the Report was hot among us, that thy Brother-in-law and thy Wife had a great many Pearls, and a deal of Gold taken away from 'em, which should have been interr'd. That may be, reply'd *Ricote*, but I am sure, Friend of mine, they have not met with my hoard; for I never would tell 'em where I had hid it, for fear of the worst: And therefore, if thou wilt go along with me, and help me carry off this Money, I will give thee two hundred Crowns, to make thee easier in the World. Thou know'st I can tell 'tis but low with thee. I would do it, answer'd *Sancho*, but I an't at all covetous. Were I in the least given to it, this Morning I quitted an Employment, which had I but kept, I might have got enough to have made the Walls of my House of beaten Gold; and before six Months had been at an End, I might have eaten my Victuals in Plate. So that as well for this Reason, as because I fancy it would be a Piece of Treason to the King, in abetting his Enemies, I would not go with thee, though thou wouldst lay me down twice as much. And pr'ythee, said *Ricote*, what Sort of Employment is it thou hast left? Why, quoth *Sancho*, I have left the Government of an Island, and such an Island as i'faith you'll scarce meet with the like in haste within a Mile of an Oak. And where is this Island, said *Ricote*? Where, quoth

Sancho, why some two Leagues off, and it is call'd the Island of *Barataria*. Pr'ythee don't talk so, reply'd *Ricote*; Islands lie a great Way off in the Sea; there are none of 'em on the main Land. Why not, quoth *Sancho*? I tell thee, Friend *Ricote*, I came from thence but this Morning, and Yesterday I was there governing it at my Will and Pleasure like any Dragon; yet for all that I e'en left it, for this same Place of a Governor seem'd to me but a ticklish and perilous kind of an Office. And what didst thou get by thy Government, ask'd *Ricote*? Why, answer'd *Sancho*, I have got so much Knowledg, as to understand that I am not fit to govern any Thing, unless it be a Herd of Cattle; and that the Wealth that's got in these Kind of Governments, costs a Man a deal of Labour and Toil, Watching and Hunger; for in your Islands, Governors must eat next to nothing; especially if they have Physicians to look after their health. I can make neither Head nor Tail of all this, said *Ricote*; it seems to me all Madness; for who would be such a Simpleton as to give Thee Islands to govern? Was the World quite bare of abler Men, that they could pick out no body else for a Governor? Pr'ythee say no more, Man, but come to thy Senses, and consider whether thou wilt go along with me and help me to carry off my hidden Wealth, my Treasure, for I may well give it that Name, considering how much there is of it, and I'll make a Man of thee, as I have told thee. Hark you me, *Ricote*, answered *Sancho*, I've already told thee my Mind: Let it suffice that I will not betray thee, and so a God's Name go thy Way, and let me go mine; for full well I wot, *That what's honestly got may be lost, but what's ill got will perish and the Owner too*. Well, *Sancho*, said *Ricote*, I'll press thee no further. Only pr'ythee tell me, wert thou in the Town when my Wife and Daughter went away with my Brother-in-law? Ay marry was I, quoth *Sancho*, by the same Token, thy Daughter look'd so woundy handsom, that there was old crouding to see her, and every Body said she was the finest Creature o'God's Earth. She wept bitterly all the Way, poor Thing, and embrac'd all her She-Friends and Acquaintance, and begg'd of all those that flock'd about her to pray for her, and that in so earnest and piteous a manner, that she e'en made me shed Tears, though I am none of the greatest Blubberers. Faith and Troth, many there had a good Mind to have got her away from her Uncle upon the Road, and have hid her; but the Thoughts of the King's Proclamation kept 'em in Awe. But he that shew'd himself the most concern'd, was Don *Pedro de Gregorio*, that young rich Heir that you know. They say he was up to the Ears in Love with her, and has never been seen in the Town since she went. We all thought he was gone after her, to steal her away, but hitherto we have heard no more of the Matter. I have all along had a Jealousy, said *Ricote*, that this Gentleman lov'd my Daughter: But I always had too good Opinion of my *Ricote's* Virtue, to be uneasy with his Passion; for thou know'st, *Sancho*, very few, and hardly any of our Women of *Moorish* Race, ever marry'd with the old Christians on the Account of Love; and so I hope, that my Daughter, who, I believe, minds more the Duties of Religion than any Thing of Love, will but little regard this young Heir's Courtship. Heaven grant she may, quoth *Sancho*, for else 'twould be the worse for 'em both. And now, honest Neighbour, I must bid thee good bye, for I have a mind to be with my Master Don *Quixote* this Evening. Then Heaven be with thee, Friend *Sancho*, said *Ricote*: I find my Comrades have fetch'd out their Naps, and 'tis time we should make the best of our Way. With that, after a kind Embrace, *Sancho* mounted his *Dapple*, *Ricote* took his Pilgrims Staff, and so they parted.

XXII: WHAT HAPPEN'D TO SANCHO BY THE WAY, WITH OTHER MATTERS, WHICH YOU WILL HAVE NO MORE TO DO THAN TO SEE

SANCHO staid so long with *Ricote*, that the Night over-took him within half a League of the Duke's Castle. It grew dark; however as it was Summer Time, he was not much uneasy, and chose to go out of the Road, with a Design to stay there till the Morning. But as ill Luck wou'd have it, while he was seeking some Place where he might rest himself, he and *Dapple* tumbled of a sudden into a very deep Hole, which was among the Ruins of some old Buildings. As he was falling, he pray'd with all his Heart, fancying himself all the while sinking down into the bottomless Pit; but he was in no such Danger, for by that time he had descended somewhat lower than eighteen Foot, *Dapple* made a full Stop at the Bottom, and his Rider found himself still on his Back, without the least Hurt in the World. Presently *Sancho* began to consider the state of his Bones, held his Breath, and felt all about him, and finding himself sound Wind and Limb, and in a whole Skin, he thought he could never give Heaven sufficient Thanks for his wondrous Preservation; for at first he gave himself over for lost, and broke into a thousand Pieces. He grop'd with both Hands about the Walls of the Pit, to try if it were possible to get out without Help; but he found 'em all so plain, and so steep, that there was not the least Hold or Footing to get up. This griev'd him to the Soul, and to increase his Sorrow, *Dapple* began to raise his Voice in a very piteous and doleful Manner, which pierc'd his Master's very Heart; nor did the poor Beast make such Moan without Reason; for, to say the Truth, he was but in a woeful Condition. Woe's me, cry'd *Sancho*, what sudden and unthought-of Mischances every Foot befal us poor Wretches that live in this miserable World! Who would have thought that He, who but Yesterday saw himself seated in the Throne of an Island-Governor, and had Servants and Vassals at his Beck, should to Day find himself buried in a Pit, without the least Soul to help him, or come to his Relief! Here we are like to perish with deadly Hunger,

I and my Ass, if we don't die before, he of his Bruises, and I of Grief and Anguish: at least, I shan't be so lucky as was my Master Don *Quixote*, when he went down into the Cave of the Inchanter *Montesinos*. He found better Fare there than he could have at his own House, the Cloth was laid, and his Bed made, and he saw nothing but pleasant Visions: But I am like to see nothing here but Toads and Snakes. Unhappy Creature that I am! What have my foolish Designs and Whimsies brought me to? If ever 'tis Heaven's blessed Will that my Bones be found, they'll be taken out of this dismal Place bare, white and smooth, and those of my poor *Dapple* with 'em, by which, perhaps, it will be known whose they are, at least by those who shall have taken notice that *Sancho Pança* never stirred from his Ass, nor his Ass from *Sancho Pança*. Unhappy Creatures that we are, I say again! Had we dy'd at Home among our Friends, though we had miss'd of Relief, we should not have wanted Pity and some to close our Eyes at the last Gasp. Oh! my dear Companion and Friend, said he to his Ass, how ill have I requited thy faithful Services? Forgive me, and pray to Fortune the best thou canst to deliver us out of this Plunge, and I here promise thee to set a Crown of Laurel on thy Head, that thou may'st be taken for no less than a Poet Laureat, and thy Allowance of Provender shall be doubled. Thus *Sancho* bewail'd his Misfortune, and his Ass hearken'd to what he said, but answer'd not a Word, so great was the Grief and Anguish which the poor Creature endur'd at the same time.

At length, after a whole Night's lamenting and complaining at a miserable Rate, the Day came on, and it's Light having confirm'd *Sancho* in his Doubts of the Impossibility of getting out of that Place without Help, he set up his Throat again, and made a vigorous Outcry, to try whether any Body might not hear him. But alas! all his Calling was in vain,* for all around there was no Body within hearing; and then he gave himself over for dead and buried. He cast his Eyes on *Dapple*, and seeing him extended on the Ground, and sadly down in the Mouth,

---

* *In the Original*, All his Cries were in the Desert, *i.e. thrown away; alluding, perhaps, to the Scripture Character of* John Baptist, *that he was* Vox clamantis in Deserto, *the Voice of one crying in the Wilderness, or* Desert.

he went to him, and try'd to get him on his Legs, which with much ado, by means of his assistance, the poor Beast did at last, being hardly able to stand. Then he took a Luncheon of Bread out of his Wallet, that had run the same Fortune with 'em, and giving it to the Ass, who took it not at all amiss, and made no Bones of it, Here, said *Sancho*, as if the Beast had understood him, a fat Sorrow is better than a lean. At length he perceiv'd on one Side of the Pit a great Hole wide enough for a Man to creep through stooping: He drew to it, and having crawl'd through on all Four, found that it led into a Vault that enlarg'd it self the further it extended, which he could easily perceive, the Sun shining in towards the Top of the Concavity. Having made this Discovery, he went back to his Ass, and like one that knew what belong'd to digging, with a Stone, began to remove the Earth that was about the Hole, and labour'd so effectually, that he soon made a Passage for his Companion. Then taking him by the Halter, he led him along fair and softly through the Cave, to try if he cou'd not find a Way to get out on the other Side. Sometimes he went in the Dark, and sometimes without Light, but never without Fear. Heaven defend me, said he to himself, what a Heart of a Chicken have I! This now, which to me is a sad Disaster, to my Master, Don *Quixote*, would be a rare Adventure. He would look upon these Caves and Dungeons as lovely Gardens, and glorious Palaces, and hope to be led out of these dark narrow Cells into some fine Meadow; while I, luckless, helpless, heartless Wretch that I am, every Step I take, expect to sink into some deeper Pit than this, and go down I don't know whither. Welcome ill Luck, when it comes alone. Thus he went on, lamenting and despairing, and thought he had gone somewhat more than half a League, when, at last, he perceiv'd a Kind of a confus'd Light, like that of Day-break in at some open Place, but which, to poor *Sancho*, seem'd a Prospect of a Passage into another World.

But here *Cid Hamet Benengeli* leaves him a while, and returns to Don *Quixote*, who entertain'd and pleas'd himself with the Hopes of a speedy Combat between him and the Dishonourer of Donna *Rodriguez's* Daughter, whose Wrongs he design'd to see redress'd on the appointed Day.

It happen'd one Morning, as he was riding out to prepare

and exercise against the Time of Battle, as he was practising
with *Rosinante*, the Horse, in the Middle of his Manage,
pitch'd his Feet near the Brink of a deep Cave; insomuch that
if Don *Quixote* had not us'd the best of his Skill, he must infallibly have tumbled into it. Having scap'd that Danger, he was
tempted to look into the Cave without alighting, and wheeling about, rode up to it. Now while he was satisfying his Curiosity, and seriously musing, he hought the heard a noise within,
and thereupon list'ning, he could distinguish these Words,
which in a doleful Tone arose out of the Cavern; Ho! above
there! Is there no good Christian that hears me, no charitable
Knight or Gentleman that will take Pity of a Sinner buried
alive, a poor Governor without a Government. Don *Quixote*
fancy'd he heard *Sancho's* Voice, which did not a little surprise
him, and for his better Satisfaction, raising his Voice as much as
he could, Who's that below, cry'd he? Who's that complains?
Who shou'd it be, to his Sorrow, cry'd *Sancho*, but the most
wretched *Sancho Pança*, Governor, for his Sins and for his unlucky Errantry, of the Island of *Barataria*, formerly Squire to
the famous Knight, Don *Quixote de la Mancha*? These Words
redoubl'd Don *Quixote's* Admiration, and increas'd his Amazement; for he presently imagin'd that *Sancho* was dead, and
that his Soul was there doing Penance. Possess'd with that
Fancy, I conjure thee, said he, by all that can conjure thee, as
I am a Catholick Christian, to tell me who thou art? and, if thou
art a Soul in Pain, let me know what thou would'st have me do
for thee; for since my Profession is to assist and succour all that
are afflicted in this World, it shall also be so to relieve and help
those who stand in need of it in the other, and who cannot help
themselves. Surely, Sir, answer'd he from below, you that
speak to me should be my Master Don *Quixote*: By the Tone of
your Voice it can be no Man else. My Name is Don *Quixote*, reply'd the Knight, and I think it my Duty to assist not only the
Living but the Dead in their Necessities. Tell me then who
thou art, for thou fill'st me with Astonishment? and if thou art
my Squire, *Sancho Pança*, and dead, if the Devil have not got
thee, and through Heaven's Mercy thou art in Purgatory, our
Holy Mother, the *Roman* Catholick Church, has sufficient Suf-
frages to redeem thee from the Pains thou endur'st, and I my

self will solicite her on thy behalf as far as my Estate will go; therefore proceed, and tell me quickly who thou art? Why then, reply'd the Voice, by whatever you'll have me swear by, I make Oath that I am *Sancho Pança*, your Squire, and that I never was dead yet in my Life. But only having left my Government, for Reasons and Causes which I han't leisure yet to tell you, last Night unluckily I fell into this Cave, where I am still, and *Dapple* with me, that will not let me tell a Lye; for, as a farther Proof of what I say, he is here. Now what's strange, immediately, as if the Ass had understood what his Master said, to back his Evidence, he fell a braying so obstreperously, that he made the whole Cave ring again. A worthy Witness, cry'd Don *Quixote*! I know his Bray, as if I were the Parent of him, and I know thy Voice too, my *Sancho*. I find thou art my real Squire; stay therefore till I go to the Castle, which is hard by, and fetch more Company to help thee out of the Pit into which thy Sins, doubtless, have thrown thee. Make haste, I beseech you, Sir, quoth *Sancho*, and for Heaven's Sake come again as fast as you can, for I can no longer endure to be here buried alive, and I am e'en dying with Fear.

Don *Quixote* went with all Speed to the Castle, and gave the Duke and Dutchess an Account of *Sancho's* Accident, whilst they did not a little wonder at it, though they conceiv'd he might easily enough fall in at the Mouth of the Cave, which had been there Time out of Mind. But they were mightily surpriz'd to hear he had abdicated his Government before they had an Account of his coming away.

In short, they sent Ropes, and other Conveniencies by their Servants to draw him out, and at last with much Trouble and Labour, both he and his *Dapple* were restored from that gloomy Pit, to the full Enjoyment of the Light of the Sun. At the same time a certain Scholar standing by, and seeing him hois'd up; just so, said he, should all bad Governors come out of their Governments; just as this Wretch is dragg'd out of this profound Abyss, pale, half-starv'd, famish'd, and, as I fancy, without a Cross in his Pocket. Hark you, Goodman Slander, reply'd *Sancho*, 'tis now eight or ten Days since I began to govern the Island that was given me, and in all that Time I never had my Belly-full but once; Physicians have persecuted me,

411

Enemies have trampl'd over me, and bruised my Bones, and I
have had neither Leisure to take Bribes, nor to receive my just
Dues. Now all this considered, in my Opinion I did not deserve
to come out in this Fashion. But Man appoints, and God disap-
points. Heaven knows best what's best for us all. We must take
Time as it comes, and our Lot as it falls. Let no Man say, I'll
drink no more of this Water. Many count their Chickens before they are hatch'd, and where they expect Bacon meet with
Broken Bones. Heaven knows my Mind, and I say no more,
though I might. Ne'er trouble thy self, *Sancho*, said Don *Quixote*, nor mind what some will say, for then thou wilt never have
done. So thy Conscience be clear, let the World talk at random,
as it uses to do. One may as soon tie up the Winds, as the
tongues of Slanderers. If a Governor comes rich from his Government, they say he has fleec'd & robb'd the People; if poor,
then they call him idle Fool, and ill Husband. Nothing so sure,
then, quoth *Sancho*, but this Bout they'll call me a shallow
Fool, but for a Fleecer or a Robber, I scorn their Words, I defy
all the World. Thus discoursing as they went, with a Rabble
of Boys and idle People about 'em, they at last got to the Castle,
where the Duke and the Dutchess waited in the Gallery for
the Knight and Squire. As for *Sancho*, he would not go up to
see the Duke, till he had seen his Ass in the Stable, and provided for him; for he said, the poor Beast had but sorry Entertainment in his last Night's Lodging: This done, away he went
to wait on his Lord and Lady, and throwing himself on his
Knees, My Lord and Lady, said he, I went to govern your Island
of *Barataria*, such being your Will and Pleasure, though 'twas
your Goodness more than my Desert. Naked I entered into it,
and naked I came away, I neither won nor lost. Whether I govern'd well or ill, there are those not far off can tell, and let them
tell, if they please, that can tell better than I. I have resolv'd
doubtful Cases, determined Law-suits, and all the while ready
to die with Hunger, such was the Pleasure of Doctor *Pedro
Rezio* of *Tirte a fuera*, that Physician in Ordinary to Island-
Governors. Enemies set upon us in the Night, and after they
had put us in great Danger, the People of the Island say they
were deliver'd, and had the Victory by the Strength of my
Arm, and may Heaven prosper 'em as they speak Truth, say I.

In short, in that time, I experienced all the Cares & Burthens
this Trade of Governing brings along with it, and I found 'em
too heavy for My Shoulders. I was never cut out for a Ruler,
and I am too clumsy to meddle with Edge-Tools, and so before
the Government left me, I e'en resolv'd to leave the Government; and, accordingly, yesterday Morning I quitted the Island
as I found it, with the same Streets, the same Houses, and the
same Roofs to them, as when I came to it. I have ask'd for nothing by Way of Loan, and made no Hoard against a rainy Day.
I design'd, indeed, to have issu'd out several wholesom Orders,
but did not, for fear they should not be kept, in which Case it
signifies no more to make 'em than if one made 'em not. So, as
I said before, I came away from the Island without any Company but my *Dapple*. I fell into a Cave, and went a good Way
through it, till this Morning by the Light of the Sun, I spy'd
the Way out, yet not so easy, but that had not Heaven sent my
Master Don *Quixote* to help me, there I might have staid till
Doom's-day. And now, my Lord Duke, and my Lady Dutchess,
here's your Governor *Sancho Pança* again, who by a ten Days
Government has only pick'd up so much Experience, as to
know he would not give a Straw to be Governor not only of an
Island, but of the versal World. This being allow'd, kissing
your Honours Hands, and doing like the Boys when they play
at *Trusse* or *Faile*, who cry, Leap you, and then let me leap; so
I leap from the Government to my old Master's Service again.
For after all, though with Him I often eat my Bread in bodily
Fear, yet still I fill my Belly; and, for my Part, so I have but
that well stuff'd, no matter whether it be with Carrots or with
Partridge.

Thus *Sancho* concluded his long Speech, and Don *Quixote*,
who all the while dreaded he would have said a thousand Impertinencies, thank'd Heaven in his Heart, finding him end
with so few. The Duke embrac'd *Sancho*, and told him, he was
very sorry he had quitted his Government so soon, but that he
would give him some other Employment that should be less
troublesom, and more profitable. The Dutchess was no less
kind, giving Order he should want for nothing, for he seem'd
sadly bruis'd and out of Order.

XXIII: OF THE EXTRAORDINARY AND UNACCOUNT-ABLE COMBAT BETWEEN DON QUIXOTE DE LA MANCHA, AND THE LACQUEY TOSILOS, IN VINDICATION OF THE MATRON DONNA RODRIGUEZ'S DAUGHTER

THE Duke and Dutchess were not sorry that the Interlude of *Sancho's* Government had been play'd, especially when the Steward, who came that very Day, gave 'em a full and distinct Account of every Thing the Governor had done and said, during his Administration, using his very Expressions, and repeating almost every Word he had spoke, concluding with a Description of the Storming of the Island, and *Sancho's* Fear and Abdication, which proved no unacceptable Entertainment.

And now the History relates, that the Day appointed for the Combat was come, nor had the Duke forgot to give his Lacquey, *Tosilos*, all requisite Instructions how to vanquish Don *Quixote*, and yet neither kill nor wound him; to which Purpose he gave Orders that the Spears or Steel heads of their Lances should be taken off, making Don *Quixote* sensible that Christianity, for which he had so great a Veneration, did not admit that such Conflicts should so much endanger the Lives of the Combatants, and that it was enough he granted him free Lists in his Territories, though it was against the Decree of the Holy Council, which forbids such Challenges; for which Reason he desir'd him not to push the Thing to the utmost Rigour. Don *Quixote* reply'd, that his Grace had the sole Disposal of all Things, and it was only his Duty to obey.

And now the dreadful Day being come, the Duke caus'd a spacious Scaffold to be erected for the Judges of the Field of Battle, and for the Matron and her Daughter, the Plaintiffs.

An infinite Number of People flock'd from all the neighbouring Towns and Villages to behold this wonderful new kind of Combat, the like to which had never been seen or so much as heard of in those Parts, either by the Living or the Dead. The first that made his Entrance at the Barriers, was the Marshal of the Field, who came to survey the Ground, and rode all over it, that there might be no foul Play, nor private Holes, or Contrivance to make one stumble or fall. After that enter'd the Matron and her Daughter, who seated themselves in their Places, all in deep Mourning, their Veils close to their Eyes, and over their Breasts, with no small Demonstrations of Sorrow. Presently at one End of the listed Field appeared the peerless Champion, Don *Quixote de la Mancha*: A while after, at the other, enter'd the grand Lacquey, *Tosilos*, attended with a great Number of Trumpets, and mounted on a mighty Steed, that shook the very Earth. The Visor of his Helmet was down, and he was arm'd Cap-a-pée in shining Armour of Proof. His Courser was a Flea-bitten Horse, that seem'd of *Friesland* Breed, and had a Quantity of Wool about each of his Fetlocks. The valorous Combatant came on, well tutor'd by the Duke his Master how to behave himself towards the valorous Don *Quixote de la Mancha*, being warn'd to spare his Life by all Means, and therefore to avoid a Shock in his first Career, that might otherwise prove fatal, should he encounter him directly. *Tosilos* fetch'd a Compass about the Barrier, and at last made a Stop right against the two Women, casting a leering Eye upon her that had demanded him in Marriage. Then the Marshal of the Field call'd to Don *Quixote*, and in the Presence of *Tosilos*, ask'd the Mother and the Daughter, whether they consented that Don *Quixote de la Mancha* should vindicate their Right, and whether they would stand or fall by the Fortune of their Champion? They said they did, and allow'd of whatever he should do in their behalf, as good and valid. The Duke and Dutchess by this Time were seated in a Gallery that was over the Barriers, which were surrounded by a vast Throng of Spectators, all waiting to see the vigorous and never-before-seen Conflict. The Conditions of the Combat were these, That if Don *Quixote* were the Conqueror, his Opponent should marry *Donna Rodriguez's* Daughter; but if the Knight were overcome, then the Victor should be discharg'd from his Promise, and not bound to give her any other Satisfaction. Then the Marshal of the Field placed each of them on the Spot whence they should start, dividing equally between them the Advantage of the Ground, that neither of them might have the Sun in his Eyes. And now the Drums beat, and the Clangor of the Trumpets resounded through the Air; the Earth shook under 'em, and the Hearts of the numerous Spectators were in Suspense, some fearing, others expecting the good or bad Issue of the Battle. Don *Quixote* recommending himself with all his Soul to Heaven, and his Lady *Dulcinea del Toboso*, stood expecting when the precise Signal for the Onset should be given.—But our Lacquey's Mind was otherwise employ'd, and all his Thoughts were upon what I am going to tell you.

It seems, as he stood looking on his Female Enemy, she appear'd to him the most beautiful Woman he had ever seen in his whole Life; which being perceiv'd by the little blind Archer, to whom the World gives the Name of Love, he took his Advantage, and fond of improving his Triumphs, though it were but over the Soul of a Lacquey;* he came up to him softly, and without being perceived by any one, he shot an Arrow two Yards long into the poor Footman's Side so smartly, that his Heart was pierc'd through and through: A thing which the mischievous Boy could easily do; for Love is invisible, and has free Ingress or Egress where he pleases, at a most unaccountable Rate. You must know then, that when the Signal for the Onset was given, our Lacquey was in an Extasy, transported with the Thoughts of the Beauty of his lovely Enemy, insomuch that he took no manner of Notice of the Trumpet's Sound; quite contrary to Don *Quixote*, who no sooner heard it, but clapping Spurs to his Horse, be began to make towards his Enemy with *Rosinante's* best Speed. At the same time his good Squire *Sancho Pança* seeing him start, Heaven be thy Guide, cry'd he aloud, thou Cream and Flower of Chivalry-Errant, Heaven give thee the Victory, since thou hast Right on thy Side. *Tosilos* saw Don *Quixote* coming towards him, yet instead of taking his Career to encounter him; without leaving the Place, he call'd as loud as he could to the Marshal of the Field, who thereupon rode up to him to see what he would have. Sir, said *Tosilos*, is not this Duel to be fought, that I may marry yonder young Lady, or let it alone? Yes, answer'd the Marshal. Why then, said the Lacquey, I feel a Burden upon my Conscience, and am sensible I should have a great deal to

* Lacayuna. A Lacqueyan Soul. *A Word made for the Purpose.*

answer for, should I proceed any further in this Combat; and therefore I yield myself vanquish'd, and desire I may marry the Lady this Moment. The Marshal of the Field was surpriz'd, and, as he was privy to the Duke's Contrivance of that Business, the Lacquey's unexpected Submission put him to such a Nonplus, that he knew not what to answer. On the other Side, Don Quixote stopt in the middle of his Career, seeing his Adversary did not put himself in a Posture of Defence. The Duke could not imagine why the Business of the Field was at a Stand, but the Marshal having inform'd him, he was amaz'd and in a great Passion. In the mean time, *Tosilos* approaching Donna *Rodriguez*, Madam, cry'd he, I am willing to marry your Daughter, there's no need of Law-Suits, nor of Combats in the Matter, I had rather make an end of it peaceably, and without the hazard of Body and Soul. Why then, said the valorous Don *Quixote*, hearing this, since 'tis so, I am discharg'd of my Promise; let them e'en marry a God's Name, and Heaven bless 'em, and give 'em Joy. At the same time the Duke coming down within the Lists, and applying himself to *Tosilos*, Tell me Knight, said he, is it true, that you yield without Fighting, and that at the Instigation of your timorous Conscience, you are resolv'd to marry this Damsel? Yes, an't please your Grace, answer'd *Tosilos*. Marry, and I think 'tis the wisest Course, quoth *Sancho*; for what says the Proverb, what the Mouse would get, give the Cat, and keep thy self out of Trouble. In the mean while *Tosilos* began to unlace his Helmet, and call'd out that somebody might help him off with it quickly, as being so chok'd with his Armour, that he was scarce able to breathe. With that they took off his Helmet with all Speed, and then the Lacquey's Face was plainly discover'd. Donna *Rodriguez* and her Daughter perceiving it, presently, a Cheat! a Cheat! cry'd they: They have got *Tosilos*, my Lord Duke's Lacquey to counterfeit my lawful Husband; Justice of Heaven and the King! This is a Piece of Malice and Treachery not to be endur'd. Ladies, said Don *Quixote*, don't vex your selves, there's neither Malice nor Treachery in the Case, or if there be, the Duke is not in the Fault: No, those evil-minded Necromancers that persecute me, are the Traitors, who envying the Glory I should have got by this Combat, have transformed the Face of my Adversary into this, which you see is the Duke's Lacquey. But take my Advice, Madam, added he to the Daughter, and in spite of the Baseness of my Enemies, marry him, for I dare engage 'tis the very Man you claim as your Husband. The Duke hearing this, angry as he was, could hardly forbear losing all his Indignation in Laughter. Truly, said he, so many extraordinary Accidents every Day befal the great Don *Quixote*, that I am inclinable to believe this is not my Lacquey, though he appears to be so. But for our better Satisfaction, let us defer the Marriage but a Fortnight, and in the mean while keep in close Custody this Person that has put us into this Confusion; perhaps by that time he may resume his former Looks, for doubtless the Malice of these mischievous Magicians against the noble Don *Quixote* cannot last so long, especially when they find all these Tricks and Transformations so little avail. Alack-a-day! Sir, quoth *Sancho*, those plaguy Imps of the Devil are not so soon tir'd as you think; for where my Master is concern'd they us'd to form and deform, and chop and change this into that, and that into t'other. 'Tis but a while ago that they transmography'd the *Knight of the Mirrors*, whom he had overcome, into a special Acquaintance of ours, the Batchelor *Sampson Carrasco* of our Village; and as for the Lady *Dulcinea del Toboso*, our Mistress, they have bewitch'd and be devil'd her into the Shape of a meer Country-Blouze, and so I verily think this saucy Fellow here is like to die a Footman, and will live a Footman all the Days of his Life. Well, cry'd the Daughter, let him be what he will, if he'll have me, I'll have him. I ought to thank him, for I had rather be a Lacquey's Wife, than a Gentleman's cast-off mistress; besides, he that deluded me is no Gentleman neither. To be short, the Sum of the Matter was, that *Tosilos* should be confin'd to see what his Transformation would come to. Don *Quixote* was proclaim'd Victor by general Consent; and the People went away, most of 'em very much out of Humour, because the Combatants had not cut one another to pieces to make 'em Sport; according to the Custom of the young Rabble, to be sorry, when, after they have staid, in hopes to see a Man hang'd, he happens to be pardon'd, either by the Party he had wrong'd, or the Magistrate. The Crowd being dispers'd, the Duke and Dutchess return'd with Don *Quixote* into the Castle;

Tosilos was secur'd, and kept close: As for Donna *Rodriguez* and her Daughter, they were very well pleas'd to see, one Way or other that the Business would end in Marriage; and *Tosilos* flattered himself with the like Expectation.

XXIV: HOW DON QUIXOTE TOOK HIS LEAVE OF THE DUKE, AND WHAT PASS'D BETWEEN HIM AND THE WITTY WANTON ALTISIDORA THE DUTCHESS'S DAMSEL

DON *Quixote* thought it now time to leave the idle Life he led in the Castle, believing it a mighty Fault, thus to shut himself up, and indulge his sensual Appetite among the tempting Varieties of Dainties and Delights, which the Lord and Lady of the Place provided for his Entertainment, as a Knight-Errant; and he thought he was to give a strict Account to Heaven for a Course of Life so opposite to his active Profession. Accordingly, one Day he acquainted the Duke and Dutchess with his Sentiments, and begg'd their Leave to depart. They both seem'd very unwilling to part with him, but yet, at last, yielded to his Intreaties. The Dutchess gave *Sancho* his Wife's Letters, which he could not hear read without weeping. Who would have thought, cry'd he, that all the mighty Hopes with which my Wife swell'd her self up at the News of my Preferment, should come to this at last, and now I should be reduced again to trot after my Master Don *Quixote de la Mancha*, in Search of Hunger and broken Bones! However, I am glad to see my *Teresa* was like her self, in sending the Dutchess the Acorns; which if she had not done, she had shew'd herself a dirty ungrateful Sow, and I should have been confounded mad with her. My Comfort is, that no Man can say the Present was a Bribe; for I had my Government before she sent it, and 'tis fit those who have a Kindness done 'em, should shew themselves grateful, though it be with a small Matter. In short, naked I came into the Government, and naked I went out of it; and so I may say for my Comfort with a safe Conscience, naked I came into the World, and naked I am still; I neither won nor lost, that's no easy Matter, as Times go, let me tell you. These were *Sancho's* Sentiments at his Departure.

Don *Quixote* having taken his solemn Leave of the Duke and Dutchess over-night, left his Apartment the next Morning, and appear'd in his Armour in the Court-yard, the Galleries all

round about being fill'd at the same Time with the People of
the House; the Duke and Dutchess being also got thither to see
him: *Sancho* was upon his *Dapple*, with his Cloak-bag, his
Wallet, and his Provision, very brisk and chearful; for the
Steward that acted the Part of *Trifaldi*, had given him a Purse,
with two hundred Crowns in Gold to defray Expences, which
was more than Don *Quixote* knew at that Time. And now while
every Body look'd to see 'em set forward, on a sudden the arch
and witty *Altisidora* started from the rest of the Dutchess's
Damsels and Attendants that stood by among the rest, and in
a doleful Tone, address'd her self to him in the following
Doggrel Rhimes.

THE MOCK FAREWELL

I

> Stay, cruel Don,
> Do not be gone,
> Nor give thy Horse the Rowels:
> For every Jag
> Thou giv'st thy Nag,
> Does prick me to the Bowels.

> Thou dost not shun
> Some butter'd Bun,
> Or Drab without a Rag on:
> Alas! I am
> A very Lamb,
> Yet love like any Dragon.

> Thou didst deceive
> And now dost leave
> A Lass, as tight as any
> That ever stood,
> In Hill or Wood
> Near Venus and Diana.

> Since thou, false Fiend,
> When Nymph's thy Friend,
> Æneas like dost bob her;
> Go rot and die,
> Boil, roast, or fry,
> With Barrabas the Robber.

2

Thou tak'st thy Flight,
Like ravenous Kite,
That holds within his Pounces
A tender Bit,
A poor Tom-tit,
Then whist away he flounces.

The Heart of me,
And Night-Coifs three
With Garters twain you plunder,
From Legs of hue,
White, black, and blue,
So marbl'd o'er you'd wonder.

Two thousand Groans,
And warm Ahones,
Are stuff'd within thy Pillion:
The least of which,
Like flaming Pitch,
Might have burn'd down old Ilion.

Since thou, false Fiend,
When Nymph's thy Friend,
Æneas like dost bob her;
Go, rot, and die,
Boil, roast, or fry,
With Barrabas the Robber.

3

As sour as Crab
Against thy Drab,
May be thy Sancho's Gizzard:
And he ne'er thrum
His brawny Bum,
To free her from the Wizard.

May all thy Flouts,
And sullen Doubts,
Be scor'd upon thy Dowdy;

And she ne'er freed,
For thy Misdeed,
From rusty Phiz, and cloudy.

May Fortune's Curse
From bad to worse,
Turn all thy best Adventures;
Thy Joys to Dumps,
Thy Brags to Thumps,
And thy best Hopes to Banters.

Since thou, false Fiend,
When Nymph's thy Friend,
Æneas like dost bob her:
Go, rot, and die,
Boil, roast, or fry,
With Barrabas the Robber.

4

May'st thou Incog
Sneak like a Dog,
And o'er the Mountains trudge it;
From Spain to Cales,*
From Usk to Wales:
Without a Cross in Budget.

If thou'rt so brisk
To play at Whisk,
In hopes of winning Riches;
For want of Trump,
Stir ev'n thy Rump,
And lose thy very Breeches.

May thy Corns ake,
Then Pen-knife take,
And cut thee to the Raw-bone:
With Tooth-ach mad,
No ease be had,
Tho' Quacks pull out thy Jaw-bone.

* Good Spanish Geography.

423

> *Since thou, false Fiend,*
> *When Nymph's thy Friend,*
> *Æneas like dost bob her;*
> *Go, rot, and die,*
> *Boil, roast, or fry,*
> *With* Barrabas *the Robber.*

Thus *Altisidora* express'd her Resentments, and Don *Quix-ote*, who look'd on her seriously all the while, would not an-swer a Word; but turning to *Sancho*, Dear *Sancho*, said he, by the Memory of thy Fore-Fathers, I conjure thee to tell me one Truth: Say, hast thou any Night-Coifs or Garters that belong to this Love-sick Damsel? The three Night-Coifs I have, quoth *Sancho*; but as for the Garters I know no more of 'em than the Man in the Moon. The Dutchess being wholly a Stranger to this Part of *Altisidora's* Frolick, was amaz'd to see her proceed so far in it, though she knew her to be of an arch and merry Disposition. But the Duke being pleased with the Humour, resolv'd to carry it on. Thereupon addressing himself to Don *Quixote*, Truly Sir Knight, said he, I do not take it kindly, that after such civil Entertainment as you have had here in my Castle, you should offer to carry away three Night-Coifs, if not a pair of Garters besides, the proper Goods and Chattels of this Damsel here present. This was not done like a Gentleman, and does not make good the Character you would maintain in the World; Therefore restore her Garters, or I challenge you to a mortal combat, without being afraid that your evil-minded Inchanters should alter my Face, as they did my Footman's. Heaven forbid, said Don *Quixote*, that I should draw my Sword against your most illustrious Person, to whom I stand indebted for so many Favours. No, my Lord, as for the Night-Coifs I will cause 'em to be restor'd, for *Sancho* tells me he has 'em; but as for the Garters, 'tis impossible, for neither he nor I ever had 'em; and if this Damsel of yours will look carefully among her Things, I dare say she'll find 'em. I never was a Pilferer, my Lord, and while Heav'n forsakes me not, I never shall be guilty of such Baseness. But this Damsel, as you may perceive, talks like one that is in Love, and accuses me of that whereof I am innocent; so that not regarding her little Revenge, I have no need to ask Pardon either of her or your Grace. I only beg you'll be pleased to entertain a better Opinion of me and once more permit me to depart. Farewel, noble Don *Quixote*, said the Dutchess; may Providence so direct your Course, that we may always be bless'd with the good News of your Exploits; and so Heaven be with you, for the longer you stay, the more you increase the Flames in the Hearts of the Damsels that gaze on you. As for this young indiscreet Creature, I'll take her to task so severely, she shall not misbehave her self so much as in a Word or Look for the future. One Word more, I beseech you, O valorous Don *Quixote*, cry'd *Altisidora*: I beg your Pardon for saying you had stol'n my Garters, for i' my Conscience I have 'em on: But my Thoughts ran a Wool-gathering; and I did like the Countryman, who look'd for his Ass while he was mounted on his Back. Marry come up, cry'd *Sancho*, whom did they take me for, trow? A Concealer of stoln Goods, no indeed; had I been given that Way, I might have had Opportunities enough in my Government.

Then Don *Quixote* bow'd his Head, and after he had made a low Obeisance to the Duke, the Dutchess, and all the Company, he turn'd about with *Rosinante*; and *Sancho* following him on *Dapple*, they left the Castle, and took the Road for *Saragossa*.

DON *Quixote* no sooner breath'd the Air in the open Field, free from *Altisidora's* amorous Importunities, but he fancy'd himself in his own Element; he thought he felt the Spirit of Knight-Errantry reviving in his Breast; and turning to *Sancho*, Liberty, said he, Friend *Sancho*, is one of the most valuable Blessings that Heaven has bestow'd on Mankind. Not all the Treasures conceal'd in the Bowels of the Earth, nor those in the Bosom of the Sea, can be compared with it. For Liberty, a Man may, nay ought to hazard, even his Life, as well as for Honour, accounting Captivity the greatest Misery he can endure. I tell thee this, my *Sancho*, because thou wert a Witness of the good Cheer and Plenty which we met with in the Castle; yet in the midst of those delicious Feasts, among those tempting Dishes, and those Liquors cool'd with Snow, methought I suffer'd the Extremity of Hunger, because I did not enjoy them with that Freedom as if they had been my own: For the Obligations that lie upon us to make suitable Returns for Kindnesses receiv'd, are Ties that will not let a generous Mind be free. Happy the Man, whom Heaven has bless'd with Bread, for which he is oblig'd to thank kind Heaven alone! For all these fine Words, quoth *Sancho*, 'tis not proper for us to be unthankful for two hundred good Crowns in Gold, which the Duke's Steward gave me in a little Purse, which I have here, and cherish in my Bosom, as a Relique against Necessity, and a comforting Cordial next my Heart against all Accidents; for we are not like always to meet with Castles, where we shall be made much of. A Peasecods on't! we are more like to meet with damn'd Inns, where we shall be rib-roasted.

As the wandring Knight and Squire went discoursing of this and other Matters, they had not rode much more than a League, ere they espy'd about a dozen Men, who look'd like Country-Fellows sitting at their Victuals, with their Cloaks under them, on the green Grass, in the middle of a Meadow.

Near 'em they saw several white Clothes or Sheets spread out and laid close to one another, that seem'd to cover something. Don *Quixote* rode up to the People, and after he had civilly saluted 'em, ask'd what they had got under that Linen? Sir, answer'd one of the Company, they are some carv'd Images that are to be set up at an Altar we are erecting in our Town. We cover 'em, lest they should be sullied, and carry 'em on our Shoulders for fear they should be broken. If you please, said Don *Quixote*, I should be glad to see 'em; for considering the Care you take of 'em, they should be Pieces of Value. Ay, marry are they, quoth another, or else we're damnably cheated; for there's ne'er an Image among 'em that does not stand us in more than fifty Ducats; and, that you may know I'm no Liar, do but stay, and you shall see with your own Eyes. With that, getting up on his Legs, and leaving his Victuals, he went and took off the Cover from one of the Figures, that happen'd to be St *George* on Horseback, and under his Feet a Serpent coil'd up, his Throat transfix'd with a Lance, with the Fierceness that is commonly represented in the Piece; and all, as they use to say, spick and span new, and shining like beaten Gold. Don *Quixote* having seen the Image, This, said he, was one of the best Knights-Errant the Divine Warfare or Church-Militant ever had: His Name was Don St *George*, and he was an extraordinary Protector of Damsels. What's the next? The Fellow having uncover'd it, it proved to be St *Martin* on Horseback. This Knight too, said Don *Quixote* at the first sight, was one of the Christian Adventurers, and I am apt to think he was more liberal than valiant; and thou may'st perceive it, *Sancho*, by his dividing his Cloak with a poor Man; he gave him half, and doubtless 'twas Winter time, or else he would have giv'n it him whole, he was so charitable. Not so neither, I fancy, quoth *Sancho*, but I guess he stuck to the Proverb: *To Give and Keep what's fit, Requires a Share of Wit*. Don *Quixote* smil'd, and desir'd the Men to shew him the next Image; which appear'd to be that of the Patron of *Spain* a Horse-back, with his Sword bloody, trampling down *Moors*, and treading over Heads. Ay, this is a Knight indeed, (cry'd Don *Quixote*, when he saw it) one of those that fought in the Squadrons of the Saviour of the World: He is call'd Don *Sant-Jago, Mata Moros*, or Don St *James the Moor-killer*, and may be reckon'd one of the most valorous Saints and Professors of Chivalry that the Earth then enjoy'd, and Heaven now possesses. Then they uncover'd another Piece, which shew'd St *Paul* falling from his Horse, with all the Circumstances usually express'd in the Story of his Conversion, and represented so to the Life, that he look'd as if he had been answering the Voice that spoke to him from Heaven. This, said Don *Quixote*, was the greatest Enemy the Church Militant had once, and prov'd afterwards the greatest Defender it will ever have. In his Life a true Knight-Errant, and in Death a stedfast Saint; an indefatigable Labourer in the Vineyard of the Lord, a Teacher of the *Gentiles*, who had Heaven for his School, and Christ him self for his Master and Instructor. Then Don *Quixote* perceiving there were no more Images, desir'd the Men to cover those he had seen: And now, my good Friends, said he to 'em, I cannot but esteem the Sight that I have had of these Images as a happy Omen; for these Saints and Knights were of the same Profession that I follow, which is that of Arms: The Difference only lies in this Point, that They were Saints, and fought according to the Rules of holy Discipline; and I am a Sinner, and fight after the manner of Men. They conquer'd Heaven by Force, for Heaven is taken by Violence; but I, alas, cannot yet tell what I gain by the Force of my Labours! Yet were my *Dulcinea del Toboso* but free from her Troubles, by a happy Change in my Fortune, and an Improvement in my Understanding, I might perhaps take a better Course than I do. Heaven grant it, quoth *Sancho*, and let the Devil do his worst.

All this while the Men wonder'd at Don *Quixote's* Figure as well as his Discourse; but could not understand one Half of what he meant. So that after they had made an end of their Dinner, they got up their Images, took their Leaves of Don *Quixote*, and continu'd their Journey.

Sancho remain'd full of Admiration, as if he had never known his Master; he wonder'd how he should come to know all these Things; and fancy'd there was not that History or Adventure in the World, but he had it at his Fingers Ends. Faith and Troth, Master of mine, quoth he, if what has happen'd to us to Day may be call'd an Adventure, it is one of

the sweetest and most pleasant we ever met with in all our
Rambles; for we are come off without a Dry-basting, or the
least bodily Fear. We have not so much as laid our Hands upon
our Weapons, nor have we beaten the Earth with our Car-
cases; but here we be safe, and sound, neither a-dry nor
a-hungry. Heaven be prais'd, that I have seen all this with
my own Eyes! Thou say'st well, *Sancho*, said Don *Quixote*,
but I must tell thee, that Seasons and Times are not always
the same, but often take a different Course! and what the Vulgar call Forebodings and Omens, for which there are no rational
Grounds in Nature, ought only to be esteem'd happy Encounters
by the Wise. One of these superstitious Fools, going out of his
House betimes in the Morning, meets a Friar of the Blessed
Order of St *Francis*, and starts as if he had met a Griffin, turns
back, and runs home again. Another Wise-acre happens to
throw down the Salt on the Tablecloth, and thereupon is sadly
cast down himself, as if Nature were oblig'd to give Tokens of
ensuing Disasters, by such slight and inconsiderable Accidents
as these. A wise and truly religious Man ought never to pry
into the Secrets of Heaven. *Scipio*, landing in *Africa*, stumbl'd
and fell down as he leap'd ashore: Presently his Soldiers took
this for an ill Omen, but He, embracing the Earth, cry'd, I have
thee fast, *Africa*; thou shalt not 'scape me. In this manner,
Sancho, I think it a very happy Accident, that I met these Images. I think so too, quoth *Sancho*; but I would fain know why
the *Spaniards* call upon that same St *James* the Destroyer of
Moors, just when they are going to give Battle, they cry, Sant-
Jago, and close Spain. Pray is *Spain* open, that it wants to be
clos'd up? What do you make of that Ceremony? Thou art a
very simple Fellow, *Sancho*, answer'd Don *Quixote*. Thou
must know that Heaven gave to *Spain* this mighty Champion
of the Red-Cross for it's Patron and Protector, especially in the
desperate Engagements which the *Spaniards* had with the
Moors; and therefore they invoke him in all their martial
Encounters, as their Protector; and many times he has been
personally seen cutting and slaying, overthrowing, trampling
and destroying the *Hagarene* Squadrons;* of which I could

* *Hagarene Squadrons, i.e. Moorish, because they have a Tradition, that
the* Moors *are descended from* Hagar.

give thee many Examples deduc'd from authentick *Spanish* Histories.

Here *Sancho* changing the Discourse, Sir, quoth he, I can't but marvel at the Impudence of *Altisidora*, the Dutchess's Damsel. I warrant you, that same Mischief-monger they call Love has plaguily maul'd her, and run her through without Mercy. They say he's a little blind Urchin, and yet the dark Youth, with no more Eye-sight than a Beetle, will hit you a Heart as sure as a Gun, and bore it through and through with his Dart, if he undertakes to shoot at it. However, I have heard say, that the Shafts of Love are blunted and beaten back by the modest and sober Carriage of young Maidens. But upon this *Altisidora* their Edge seems rather to be whetted than made blunt. You must observe *Sancho*, said Don *Quixote*, that Love is void of Consideration, and disclaims the Rules of Reason in his Proceedings. He is like Death, and equally assaults the lofty Palaces of Kings, and the lowly Cottages of Shepherds. Wherever he takes entire Possession of a Soul, the first Thing he does, is to banish thence all Bashfulness and Shame. So these being banish'd from *Altisidora's* Breast, she confidently discover'd her loose Desires, which, alas! rather fill'd me with Confusion than Pity. If so, quoth *Sancho*, you are confoundedly cruel; how could you be so hard-hearted and ungrateful? Had the poor Thing but made Love to me, I dare say, I should have come to at the first Word, and have been at her Service. Beshrew my Midriff, what a Heart of Marble, Bowels of Brass, and Soul of Plaster you have! But I can't for the Blood of me imagine, what the poor Creature saw in your Worship, to make her doat on you and play the Fool at this Rate! Where the Devil was the sparkling Appearance, the Briskness, the fine Carriage, the sweet Face that bewitch'd her? Indeed and indeed, I often survey your Worship from the Tip of your Toe to the topmost Hair on your Crown; and not to flatter you, I can see nothing in you, but what's more likely to scare one, than to make one fall in Love. I've heard that Beauty is the first and chief Thing that begets Love; now you not having any, an't like your Worship, I can't guess what the poor Soul was smitten with. Take notice, *Sancho*, answer'd Don *Quixote*, that there are two Sorts of Beauty, the one of the Soul, and the other of the

Body. That of the Soul lies and displays it self in the Understanding, in Principles of Honour and Virtue, in a handsom Behaviour, in Generosity and good Breeding; all which Qualities
may be found in a Person not so accomplish'd in outward Features. And when this Beauty, and not that of the Body, is the
Object of Love, then the Assaults of that Passion are much more
fierce, more surprising and effectual. Now, *Sancho*, though I
am sensible I am not handsom, I know at the same Time I'm
not deform'd; and provided an honest Man be possessed of the
Endowments of the Mind which I have mentioned, and nothing
appears monstrous in him, 'tis enough to entitle him to the Love
of a reasonable Creature.

Thus discoursing they got into a Wood quite out of the Road,
and on a sudden Don *Quixote*, before he knew where he was,
found himself entangled in some Nets of green Thread, that
were spread across among the Trees. Not being able to imagine
what it was, Certainly, *Sancho*, cried he, this Adventure of the
Nets must be one of the most unaccountable that can be imagined. Let me die now if this be not a Stratagem of the evil-minded
Necromancers that haunt me, to entangle me so that I may not
proceed, purely to revenge my Contempt of *Altisidora's* Addresses. But let them know, that though these Nets were Adamantine Chains, as they are only made of green Thread, and
though they were stronger than those in which the jealous God
of Blacksmiths caught *Venus* and *Mars*, I would break them
with as much Ease as if they were weak Rushes, or fine Cotton-
Yarn. With that the Knight put briskly forwards, resolved to
break through, and make his Words good; but in the very Moment there sprung from behind the Trees two most beautiful
Shepherdesses, at least they appeared to be so by their Habits,
only with this Difference, that they were richly dressed in Gold
Brocade. Their flowing Hair hung down about their Shoulders
in Curls, as charming as the Sun's Golden Rays, and circled on
their Brows with Garlands of green Bays and Red-flower-
gentle interwoven. As for their Age, it seemed not less than
fifteen, nor more than eighteen Years. This unexpected Vision
dazzled and amazed *Sancho*, surprized Don *Quixote*, made
even the gazing Sun stop short in his Career, and held the surprized Parties a while in the same Suspence and Silence; till at

last one of the Shepherdesses opening her Coral Lips, Hold, Sir, she cried; pray do not tear those Nets which we have spread here, not to offend you, but to divert ourselves; and because 'tis likely you'll enquire, why they are spread here, and who we are, I shall tell you in few Words.

About two Leagues from this Place lies a Village, where there are many People of Quality and good Estates; among these, several have made up a Company, all of Friends, Neighbours and Relations, to come and take their Diversion in this Place, which is one of the most delightful in these Parts. To this Purpose we design to set up a new *Arcadia*. The young Men have put on the Habit of Shepherds, and Ladies the Dress of Shepherdesses. We have got two Eclogues by Heart; one out of the famous *Garcilasso*, and the other out of *Camoens*, that most excellent *Portugueze* Poet; though the Truth is, we have not yet repeated them, for Yesterday was but the first Day of our coming hither. We have pitched some Tents among the Trees, near the Banks of a large Brook that waters all these Meadows. And last Night we spread these Nets, to catch such simple Birds as our Calls should allure into the Snare. Now, Sir, if you please to afford us your Company, you shall be made very welcome, and handsomly entertained; for we are all disposed to pass the Time agreeably, and for a while banish Melancholy from this Place. Truly, fair Lady, answered Don *Quixote*, *Actæon* could not be more lost in Admiration and Amazement, at the Sight of *Diana* bathing herself, than I have been at the Appearance of your Beauty. I applaud the Design of your Entertainment and return you Thanks for your obliging Offers; assuring you, that if it lies in my Power to serve you, you may depend on my Obedience to your Commands: For my Profession is the very Reverse of Ingratitude, and aims at doing Good to all Persons, especially those of your Merit and Condition; so that were these Nets spread over the Surface of the whole Earth, I would seek out a Passage through new Worlds, rather than I would break the smallest Thread that conduces to your Pastime: And that you may give some Credit to this seeming Exaggeration, know that he who makes this Promise is no less than Don *Quixote de la Mancha*, if ever such a Name has reached your Ears. Oh, my Dear, cried the other Shepherdess, what good Fortune this is! You see this Gentleman before us: I must tell you, he is the most valiant, the most amorous, and the most complaisant Person in the World, if the History of his Exploits already in Print, does not deceive us. I have read it, my Dear, and I hold a Wager, that honest Fellow there by him is one *Sancho Pança*, his Squire, the most comical Creature that ever was. You have nicked it, quoth *Sancho*, I am that comical Creature, and that very Squire you wot of, and there's my Lord and Master, the self-same hist'ri-fy'd, and aforesaid Don *Quixote de la Mancha*. Oh pray, my Dear, said the other, let us intreat him to stay; our Father, and our Brothers will be mighty glad of it; I have heard of his Valour and his Merit, as much as you now tell me; and what's more, they say he is the most constant and faithful Lover in the World; and that his Mistress, whom they call *Dulcinea del Toboso*, bears the Prize from all the Beauties in *Spain*. 'Tis not without Justice, said Don *Quixote*; if your peerless Charms do not dispute her that Glory. But, Ladies, I beseech ye do not endeavour to detain me; for the indispensable Duties of my Profession will not suffer me to rest in one Place.

At the same Time came the Brother of one of the Shepherdesses, clad like a Shepherd, but in a Dress as splendid and gay as those of the young Ladies. They told him that the Gentleman whom he saw with them was the valorous Don *Quixote de la Mancha*, and that other, *Sancho Pança*, his Squire, of whom he had read the History. The gallant Shepherd having saluted him, begged of him so earnestly to grant them his Company, to their Tents, that Don *Quixote* was forced to comply, and go with them.

About the same Time the Nets were drawn and filled with divers little Birds, who being deceived by the Colour of the Snare, fell into the Danger they would have avoided. Above thirty Persons, all gaily dressed like Shepherds and Shepherdesses, got together there, and being informed who Don *Quixote* and his Squire were, they were not a little pleased, for they were already no Strangers to his History. In short, they carried 'em to their Tents, where they found a clean, sumptuous, and plentiful Entertainment ready. They obliged the Knight to take the Place of Honour, and while they sat at Table, there was not one that did not gaze on him, and wonder at so strange a Figure. At last, the Cloth being removed, Don *Quixote*, with a great deal of Gravity, lifting up his Voice; Of all the Sins that Men commit, said he, none, in my Opinion, is so great as Ingratitude, though some think Pride a greater; and I ground my Assertion on this, That Hell is said to be full of the Ungrateful. Ever since I have had the Use of Reason, I have employ'd my utmost Endeavours to avoid this Crime; and if I am not able to repay the Benefits I receive in their Kind, at least I am not wanting in real Intentions of making suitable Returns; and if that be not sufficient, I make my Acknowledgments as publick as I can; for he that proclaims the Kindnesses he has receiv'd, shews his Disposition to repay 'em if he could; and those that receive are generally inferior to those that give. The Supreme Being, that is infinitely above all Things, bestows his Blessings on us so much beyond the Capacity of all other Benefactors, that all the Acknowledgments we can make can never hold Proportion with his Goodness. However, a thankful Mind in some measure supplies it's want of Power with hearty Desires, and unfeign'd Expressions of a Sense of Gratitude and Respect. I am in this Condition as to the Civilities I have been treated with here; for I am unable to make an Acknowledgment equal to the Kindnesses I have receiv'd. I shall therefore only offer ye what is within the narrow Limits of my own Abilities; which is to maintain, for two whole Days together, in the middle of the Road that leads to *Saragosa*, that these Ladies here disguis'd in the Habit of Shepherdesses, are the fairest and most courteous Damsels in the World, excepting only the peerless *Dulcinea del Toboso*, sole Mistress of my Thoughts, without Offence to all that hear me be it spoken.

Here *Sancho*, who had with an uncommon Attention all the while given Ear to his Master's Compliment, thought fit to put in a Word or two. Now in the Name of Wonder, quoth he, can there be any Body in the world so impudent as to offer to swear or but to say, this Master of mine is a Mad-man? Pray tell me, ye Gentlemen Shepherds, did you ever know any of your Country Parsons, though never so wise, or so good Scholars, that cou'd deliver themselves so finely? Or is there any of your Knights-Errant, though never so fam'd for Prowess, that can make such an Offer as he here has done. Don *Quixote* turn'd towards *Sancho*, and beholding him with Eyes full of fiery Indignation: Can there be any Body in the World, cry'd he, that can say thou art not an incorrigible Blockhead, *Sancho*, a Compound of Folly and Knavery, wherein Malice also is no small Ingredient? Who bids thee meddle with my Concerns, Fellow, or busy thy self with my Folly or Discretion? Hold your saucy Tongue, Scoundrel! Make no Reply, but go and saddle *Rosinante*, if he is unsaddled, that I may immediately perform what I have offer'd; for in so noble and so just a Cause, thou may'st reckon all those who shall presume to oppose me, subdu'd and overthrown. This said, up he started, in a dreadful Fury, and with Marks of Anger in his Looks, to the Amazement of all the Company, who were at a Loss whether they should esteem him a Mad-man or a Man of Sense: They endeavoured to prevail with him to lay aside his Challenges, telling him, they were sufficiently assur'd of his grateful Nature, without exposing him to the Danger of such Demonstrations; and as for his Valour, they were so well inform'd by the History of his numerous Atchievements, that there was no need of any new Instance to convince 'em of it. But all these Representations could not dissuade him from his Purpose; and therefore having mounted *Rosinante*, brac'd his Shield, and grasp'd his Lance, he went and posted himself in the Middle of the High-way, not far from the verdant Meadow, follow'd by *Sancho* on his *Dapple*, and all the pastoral Society, who were desirous to see the Event of that arrogant and unaccountable Resolution. And now the Champion having taken his Ground, made the neighbouring Air ring with the following Challenge. O ye, whoe'er you are, Knights, 'Squires, a foot or o'Horseback, that now pass, or shall pass this Road within these two Days, know that Don *Quixote de la Mancha*, Knight-Errant, stays here, to assert and maintain, that the Nymphs, who inhabit these Groves and Meadows, surpass in Beauty and courteous Disposition, all those in the Universe, setting aside the Sovereign of my Soul, the Lady *Dulcinea del Toboso*. And he that dares uphold the contrary, let him appear, for here I expect his coming. Twice he repeated these lofty Words, and twice they were repeated in vain, not being heard by any Adventurer. But his old Friend,

Fortune, that had a strange Hand at managing his Concerns, and always mended upon it, shew'd him a jolly Sight; for by and by he discover'd on the Road a great Number of People a Horseback, many of 'em with Lances in their Hands, all trooping together very fast. The Company that watch'd Don *Quixote*'s Motions, no sooner spy'd such a Squadron, driving the Dust before 'em, but they got out of Harm's way, not judging it safe to be so near Danger: And as for *Sancho*, he shelter'd himself behind *Rosinante*'s Crupper; only Don *Quixote* stood fix'd with an undaunted Courage. When the Horsemen came near, one of the foremost bawling to the Champion, So hey! cry'd he! get out of the Way, and be hang'd. The Devil's in the Fellow! Stand off, or the Bulls will tread thee to Pieces. Go to, ye Scoundrels, answer'd Don *Quixote*, none of your Bulls are any Thing to Me, tho' the fiercest that ever were fed on the Banks of *Xarama*.* Acknowledge, Hang-dogs, all in a Body, what I have proclaim'd here to be Truth, or else stand Combat with me. But the Herds-men had not Time to answer, neither had Don *Quixote* any to get out of the Way, if he had been inclin'd to it; for the Herd of wild Bulls were presently upon him, as they pour'd along, with several tame Cows,† and a huge Company of Drivers and People, that were going to a Town where they were to be baited the next Day. So bearing down all before 'em, Knight and 'Squire, Horse and Man, they trampled 'em under Foot at an unmerciful Rate. There lay *Sancho* maul'd, Don *Quixote* stunn'd, *Dapple*, bruis'd, and *Rosinante* in very indifferent Circumstances. But for all this, after the whole Rout of Men and Beasts were gone by, up started Don *Quixote*, ere he was throughly come to himself; and staggering, and stumbling, falling, and getting up again, as fast as he could, he began to run after them: Stop Scoundrels, stop, cry'd he aloud, stay, 'tis a single Knight defies ye all, one who scorns the Humour of making a Golden Bridge for a flying Enemy. But the hasty Travellers did not stop nor slacken their Speed for all his loud Defiance; and minded it no more than the last Year's Snow.

---

* *The Bulls of* Xarama *are accounted the fiercest in* Spain. † Mansos Cabestros. *According to the Royal Dictionary, they are old tame Oxen with Bells about their Necks.*

At last Weariness stopp'd Don *Quixote*; so that with all his Anger, and no Prospect of Revenge, he was forc'd to sit down in the Road till *Sancho* came up to him with *Rosinante* and *Dapple*. Then the Master and Man made a shift to remount, and, ashamed of their bad Success, hasten'd their Journey, without taking Leaving of their Friends of the *New Arcadia*.

A CLEAR Fountain, which Don *Quixote* and *Sancho* found among some verdant Trees, serv'd to refresh 'em, besmear'd with Dust, and tir'd as they were, after the rude Encounter of the Bulls. There by the Brink, leaving *Rosinante* and *Dapple*, unbridl'd and unhalter'd, to their own liberty, the two forlorn Adventurers sat down. *Sancho* wash'd his Mouth, and Don *Quixote* his Face. The 'Squire then went to his old Cupboard, the Wallet; and having taken out of it what he us'd to call Belly Timber, laid it before the Knight: But Don *Quixote* would eat nothing for pure Vexation, and *Sancho* durst not begin for pure good Manners, expecting that he would first shew him the Way. However, finding him so wrapp'd in his Imaginations, as to have no Thoughts of lifting his Hand up to his Mouth, the Squire, without letting one Word come out of his, laid aside all Kind of good Breeding, and began to stuff his hungry Maw with what Bread and Cheese he had before him: Eat, Friend *Sancho*, cry'd Don *Quixote*, repair the Decays of Nature, and sustain Life, which thou hast more Reason to cherish than I; leave me to die abandon'd to my Sorrows, and the Violence of my Misfortunes. I was born, *Sancho*, to Live Dying, and thou to Die Eating. And that thou may'st be convinc'd I tell thee Truth, do but reflect upon Me, famous in Histories, dignify'd with the Honour of the Press, renown'd for Feats of Arms, courteous in Behaviour, respected by Princes, belov'd and importun'd by Damsels; yet after all this, when I at last flatter'd my self with Hopes of Laurels, Triumphs and Crowns, the Reward merited by my valorous Atchievements, behold me trod under Foot, trampl'd like the Highway Dirt, kick'd and bruis'd by the Hoofs of vile and filthy Beasts. The Thought dulls the Edge of my Teeth, and my Appetite; unhinges my Jaws, benums my Hands, and stupifies my Senses; and fearing more to live than to die, I am resolv'd almost to starve my self; though to die with Hunger be the most cruel of all Deaths. So that belike, quoth *Sancho* (without losing any Time in Chewing) you will not make good the Saying, '*Tis good to die with a full Belly*. For my Part, I am not so simple yet as to kill my self. No, I am like the Cobler, that stretches his Leather with his Teeth: I am for lengthning my Life by Eating; and I'll stretch it with my Grinders as far as Heaven will let it run. Faith and Troth, Master, there's no greater Folly in the World than for a Man to despair, and throw the Helve after the Hatchet. Therefore take my Advice, fall to, and eat as I do, and when you have done, lie down and take a Nap; the fresh Grass here will do as well as a Feather-bed. I dare say, by that Time you 'wake you'll find your self better in Body and Mind.

Don *Quixote* follow'd *Sancho's* Counsel; for he was convinc'd the Squire spoke good Natural Philosophy at that time. However, in the mean while a Thought coming into his Mind, Ah! *Sancho*, said he, if thou would'st but do something that I am now going to desire thee, my Cares wou'd sit more easy on me, and my Comfort wou'd be more certain. 'Tis only this; while, according to thy Advice, I try to compose my Thoughts with Sleep, do thou but step aside a little, and exposing thy Back Parts bare in the open Air, take the Reins of *Rosinante's* Bridle, and give thy self some three or four Hundred smart Lashes, in Part of the three Thousand and odd thou art to receive to dis-enchant *Dulcinea*; for, in Truth, 'tis a Shame, and a very great Pity That poor Lady should remain inchanted all this while, through Thy Carelessness and Neglect. There's a great deal to be said, as to that, quoth *Sancho*; but that will keep cold, first let's go to Sleep, and then come what will come: Heaven knows what will be done. Do you think, Sir, 'tis nothing for a man to flog himself in cold blood? I'd have you to know, 'tis a cruel Thing, especially when the Lashes must light upon a Body, so weak and horribly lin'd within as mine is. Let my Lady *Dulcinea* have a little Patience; one of these Days, when she least dreams on't, she'll see my Skin pink'd and jagg'd like a slashed Doublet with Lashes. There's nothing lost that comes at last; while there's Life there's Hopes; which is as good as to say, I live with an intent to make good my Promise. Don *Quixote* gave him Thanks, eat a little, and *Sancho* a great deal; and then both betook themselves to their Rest, leaving those constant Friends and Companions, *Rosinante* and *Dapple*, to their own Discretion, to repose or feed at Random on the Pasture that abounded in that Meadow.

The Day was now far gone when the Knight and the Squire wak'd: they mounted, and held on their Journey, making the best of their Way to an Inn, that seem'd to be about a League distant. I call it an Inn, because Don *Quixote* himself call'd it so, contrary to his Custom, it being a common Thing with him to take Inns for Castles.

Being got thither, they ask'd the Inn-keeper whether he had got any Lodgings? Yes, answer'd he, and as good Accommodation as you cou'd expect to find even in the City of *Saragosa*. They alighted, and *Sancho* put up his Baggage in a Chamber, of which the Landlord gave him the Key; and after he had seen *Rosinante* and *Dapple* well provided for in the Stable, he went to wait on his Master, whom he found sitting upon a Seat made in the Wall, the Squire blessing himself more than once, that the Knight had not taken the Inn for a Castle. Supper-time approaching, Don *Quixote* retir'd to his Apartment, and *Sancho* staying with the Host, ask'd him what he had to give 'em for Supper? What you will, answer'd he, you may pick and choose, Fish or Flesh, Butcher's Meat or Poultry, Wild-Fowl, and what not: Whatever Land, Sea, and Air afford for Food, 'tis but ask and have, every Thing is to be had in this Inn. There's no need of all this, quoth *Sancho*, a Couple of roasted Chickens will do our Business; for my Master has a nice Stomach, and eats but little; and as for me, I am none of your unreasonable Trencher-men. As for Chickens, reply'd the Inn-keeper, truly we have none, for the Kites have devour'd 'em. Why then quoth *Sancho*, Roast us a good handsom Pullet with Eggs, so it be young and tender. A Pullet, Master! answer'd the Host, Faith and Troth, I sent above fifty yesterday to the City to sell; but setting aside Pullets, you may have any thing else. Why then, quoth *Sancho*, e'en give us a good Joint of Veal or Kid: Cry Mercy, reply'd the Inn Keeper, now I remember me, we have none left in the House, the last Company that went clear'd me quite, but by next Week we shall have enough and to spare. We are finely holp'd up quoth *Sancho*!

Now, will I hold a good Wager, all these Defects must be made up with a Dish of Eggs and Bacon. Hey day! cry'd the Host, my Guest has a rare Knack at guessing 'efaith, I told him I had no Hens nor Pullets in the House, and yet he would have me to have Eggs! Think on something else, I beseech you, and let's talk no more of that. Body of me, cry'd *Sancho*, let's come to something; tell me what thou hast, good Mr Landlord, and don't put me to trouble my Brains any longer. Why then, d'ye see, quoth the Host, to deal plainly with you, I have a delicate Pair of Cow-heels that look like Calves Feet, or a Pair of Calves Feet that look like Cow-heels, dress'd with Onions, Pease and Bacon; a Dish for a Prince, they are just ready to be taken off, and by this Time they cry, come eat me, come eat me. Cow-heels! cry'd *Sancho*, I set my Mark upon 'em: Let no body touch 'em. I'll give more for 'em than any other shall. There's nothing I love better. No body else shall have 'em, answer'd the Host; you need not fear, for all the Guests I have in the House besides your selves, are Persons of Quality, that carry their Steward, their Cook, and their Provisions along with 'em. As for Quality, quoth *Sancho*, my Master's a Person of as good Quality as the proudest he of 'em all, an' you go to that; but his Profession allows of no Larders nor Butteries. We commonly clap us down in the midst of a Field, and fill our Bellies with Acorns or Medlars. This was the Discourse that pass'd betwixt *Sancho* and the Inn-keeper; for as to the Host's Interrogatories, concerning his Master's Profession, *Sancho* was not then at Leisure to make him any Answer.

In short, Supper-time came, Don *Quixote* went to his Room, the Host brought the Dish of Cow-heels, such as it was, and sat him down fairly to Supper——But at the same Time, in the next Room, which was divided from that where they were by a slender Partition, the Knight overheard somebody talking. Dear Don *Jeronimo*, said the unseen Person, I beseech you, 'till Supper's brought in, let us read another Chapter of the Second Part of Don *Quixote*. The Champion no sooner heard himself nam'd, but up he started, and listen'd with attentive Ears to what was said of him, and then he heard that Don *Jeronimo* answer, Why would you have us read Nonsense, Signior Don *John*? Methinks any one that has read the first Part of Don

441

Quixote, should take but little Delight in reading the Second. That may be, reply'd Don *John*; however, it mayn't be amiss to read it; for there is no Book so bad, as not to have something that's good in it. What displeases me most in this Part, is, that it represents Don *Quixote* no longer in Love with *Dulcinea del Toboso*. Upon these Words, Don *Quixote*, burning with Anger and Indignation, cry'd out: Whoever says that Don *Quixote de la Mancha* has forgot, or can forget *Dulcinea del Toboso*, I will make him know with equal Arms, that he departs wholly from the Truth; for the peerless *Dulcinea del Toboso* cannot be forgotten, nor can Don *Quixote* be guilty of Forgetfulness. *Constancy* is his Motto; and to preserve his Fidelity with Pleasure, and without the least Constraint, is his Profession. Who's that answers us? Cries one of those in the next Room. Who should it be, quoth *Sancho*, but Don *Quixote de la Mancha* his own self, the same that will make good all he has said, and all that he has to say, take my Word for't: For a good Pay-master ne'er grudges to give Security.

Sancho had no sooner made that Answer, but in came the two Gentlemen (for they appear'd to be no less) and one of 'em throwing his Arms about Don *Quixote's* Neck, Your Presence, Sir Knight, said he, does not belye your Reputation, nor can your Reputation fail to raise a Respect for your Presence. You are certainly the true Don *Quixote de la Mancha*, the North-Star, and Luminary of Chivalry-Errant in despight of him that has attempted to usurp your Name, and annihilate your At-chievements, as the Author* of this Book, which I here deliver into your Hand, has presumed to do. With that he took the Book from his Friend, and gave it to Don *Quixote*. The Knight took it, and without saying a Word, began to turn over the Leaves; and then returning it a while after; In the little I have seen, said he, I have found three Things in this Author, that deserve Reprehension. First, I find fault with some Words in his Preface. In the second Place, his Language is *Arragonian*, for sometimes he writes without Articles: And the third Thing

---

* An Arragonian *publish'd a Book, which he called the Second Part of Don* Quixote, *before our Author had printed this. See the Preface of this Second Part, and the Account of the Life of* Cervantes; *who brings this in by way of Invective against that* Arragonian.

I have observ'd, which betrays most his Ignorance, is, he's out of the Way in one of the principal Parts of the History: For there he says, that the Wife of my Squire *Sancho Pança*, is called *Mary Gutierrez*, which is not true; for her Name is *Teresa Pança*; and he that errs in so considerable a Passage, may well be suspected to have committed many gross Errors through the whole History. A pretty impudent Fellow, is this same History Writer, cried *Sancho*! Sure he knows much what belongs to our Concerns, to call my Wife *Teresa Pança, Mary Gutierrez*! Pray take the Book again, an't like your Worship, and see whether he says any Thing of Me, and whether he has not changed My Name too. Sure by what you've said, honest Man, said Don *Jeronimo*, you should be *Sancho Pança*, Squire to Signior Don *Quixote*? So I am, quoth *Sancho*, and I am proud of the Office. Well, said the Gentleman, to tell you Truth, the last Author does not treat you so civilly as you seem to deserve. He represents you as a Glutton, and a Fool, without the least Grain of Wit or Humour, and very different from the *Sancho* we have in the first Part of your Master's History. Heaven forgive him, quoth *Sancho*; he might have left me where I was, without offering to meddle with me. Every Man's Nose won't make a Shoeing-Horn. Let's leave the World as it is. St *Peter* is very well at *Rome*. Presently the two Gentlemen invited Don *Quixote* to sup with 'em in their Chamber; for they knew there was nothing to be got in the Inn fit for his Entertainment. Don *Quixote*, who was always very complaisant, could not deny their Request, and went with 'em. *Sancho* staid behind with the Flesh-pot, *cum mero mixto imperio*: * He placed himself at the upper End of the Table, with the Inn-keeper for his Mess-Mate; for he was no less a Lover of Cow-heels than the Squire.

While Don *Quixote* was at Supper with the Gentlemen, Don *John* asked him, when he heard of the Lady *Dulcinea del Toboso*? Whether she were married? Whether she had any Children, or were with Child or no? Or whether, con-

---

* *That is, with a deputed or subordinate power.* Merum imperium, *according to the Civilians, is that residing in the Sovereign:* Merum mixtum imperium *is that delegated to Vassals or Magistrates in Causes Civil or Criminal.*

443

tinuing still in her Maiden State, and preserving her Honour and Reputation unstained, she had a grateful Sense of the Love and Constancy of Signor Don *Quixote*? *Dulcinea* is still a Virgin, answered Don *Quixote*, and my amorous Thoughts more fixed than ever; our Correspondence after the old Rate, not frequent, but her Beauty transformed into the homely Appearance of a Female Rustick. And with that, he told the Gentlemen the whole Story of her being inchanted, what had befallen him in the Cave of *Montesinos*, and the Means that the Sage *Merlin* had prescribed to free her from Inchantment, which was *Sancho's* Penance of three thousand three hundred Lashes. The Gentlemen were extremely pleased to hear from Don *Quixote's* own Mouth the strange Passages of his History, equally wondering at the Nature of his Extravagancies, and his elegant Manner of relating 'em. One Minute they looked upon him to be in his Senses, and the next, they thought he had lost 'em all; so that they could not resolve what Degree to assign him between Madness and sound Judgment.

By this Time *Sancho* having eat his Supper, and left his Landlord, mov'd to the Room where his Master was with the two Strangers, and as he bolted in, Hang me, quoth he, Gentlemen, if he that made the Book your Worships have got, could have a Mind that he and I should ever take a loving Cup together: I wish, as he calls me Greedy-gut, he does not set me out for a Drunkard too. Nay, said Don *Jeronimo*, he does not use you better as to that Point; though I cannot well remember his Expressions. Only this I know, they are scandalous and false, as I perceived by the Physiognomy of sober *Sancho* here present. Take my Word for't, Gentlemen, quoth the Squire, the *Sancho* and the Don *Quixote* in your Book, I don't know who they be, but they are not the same Men as those in *Cid Hamet Benengeli's* History, for we two are they, just such as *Benengeli* makes us; my Master valiant, discreet, and in Love; and I a plain, merry-conceited Fellow, but neither a Glutton, nor a Drunkard. I believe you, said Don *John*, and I could wish, were such a Thing possible, that all other Writers whatsoever were forbidden to record the Deeds of the great Don *Quixote*, except *Cid Hamet*, his first Author; as *Alexander* forbad all other Painters to draw his Picture, except *Apelles*. Let any one

444

draw Mine, if he pleases, said Don *Quixote*; but let him not abuse the Original; for when Patience is loaded with Injuries, many times it sinks under it's Burden. No Injury, reply'd Don *John*, can be offer'd to Signor Don *Quixote* but what he is able to revenge, or at least ward off with the Shield of his Patience, which, in my Opinion, is very great and powerful.

In such Discourse they spent a good Part of the Night; and though Don *John* endeavour'd to persuade Don *Quixote* to read more of the Book, to see how the Author had handled his Subject, he could by no means prevail with him, the Knight giving him to understand, he had enough of it, and as much as if he had read it throughout, concluding it to be all of a Piece, and Nonsense all over; and that he would not encourage the Scribbler's Vanity so far as to let him think he had read it, should it ever come to his Ears that the Book had fallen into his Hands; well knowing we ought to avoid defiling our Thoughts, and much more our Eyes, with vile and obscene Matters.

They asked him, which Way he was travelling? He told 'em he was going for *Saragosa*, to make one at the Tournaments held in that City once a Year, for the Prize of Armour. Don *John* acquainted him, that the pretended second Part of his History gave an Account how Don *Quixote*, whoever he was, had been at *Saragosa* at a publick Running at the Ring, the Description of which was wretched and defective in the Contrivance, mean and low in the Stile and Expression, and miserably poor in Devices, all made up of foolish idle Stuff. For that Reason, said Don *Quixote*, I will not set a Foot in *Saragosa*, and so the World shall see what a notorious Lie this new Historian is guilty of, and all Mankind shall perceive I am not the Don *Quixote* he speaks of. You do very well, said Don *Jeronimo*, besides, there is another Tournament at *Barcelona*, where you may signalize your Valour. I design to do so, replied Don *Quixote*: And so Gentlemen, give me Leave to bid you good Night, and permit me to go to Bed, for 'tis Time; and pray place me in the Number of your best Friends, and most faithful Servants. And me too, quoth *Sancho*; for mayhap you may find me good for something.

Having taken Leave of one another, Don *Quixote* and *Sancho* retired to their Chamber, leaving the two Strangers in

445

Admiration, to think what a Medley the Knight had made of good Sense and Extravagance: But fully satisfied however, that these two Persons were the true Don *Quixote* and *Sancho*, and not those obtruded upon the Publick by the *Arragonian* Author.

Early in the Morning Don *Quixote* got up, and knocking at the thin Wall that parted his Chamber from that of the Gentlemen, he took his Leave of 'em. *Sancho* pay'd the Host nobly, but advis'd him either to keep better Provision in his Inn, or to commend it less.

THE Morning was cool, and seem'd to promise a temperate Day, when Don *Quixote* left the Inn, having first inform'd himself, which was the readiest Way to *Barcelona*; for he was resolved he would not so much as see *Saragosa*, that he might prove that new Author a Liar, who (as he was told) had so misrepresented him in the pretended second Part of his History. For the Space of six Days he travelled without meeting any Adventure worthy of Memory; but the seventh, having lost his Way, and being overtaken by the Night, he was obliged to stop in a Thicket, either of Oaks or Cork-trees, for in This *Cid Hamet* does not observe the same Punctuality he has kept in other Matters. There both Master and Man dismounted, and laying themselves down at the Foot of the Trees; *Sancho*, who had handsomly filled his Belly that Day, easily resigned himself into the Arms of Sleep. But Don *Quixote*, whom his Chimeras kept awake much more than Hunger, could not so much as close his Eyes; his working Thoughts being hurried to a thousand several Places. This Time he fancied himself in *Montesinos's* Cave; fancied he saw his *Dulcinea* perverted as she was into a Country Hoyden jump at a single Leap upon her Ass-Colt. The next Moment he thought he heard the sage *Merlin's* Voice, heard him in awful Words relate the Means required to effect her Dis-inchantment. Presently a Fit of Despair seiz'd him: He was stark mad to think on *Sancho's* Remissness and Want of Charity; the Squire having not given himself above five Lashes, a small and inconsiderable Number in Proportion to the Quantity of the Penance still behind. This Reflection so nettled him, and so aggravated his Vexation, that he could not forbear thinking on some extraordinary Methods. If *Alexander* the Great, thought he, when he could not unty the *Gordian* Knot, said, 'tis the same Thing to cut, or to undo, and so slashed it asunder, and yet became the Sovereign of the World; why may not I free *Dulcinea* from Inchantment, by whipping *Sancho* myself, whether he will or no? For if the Condition of this Remedy consist in *Sancho's* receiving three thousand and odd Lashes, what does it signify

447

to me, whether he gives himself those Blows, or another gives 'em him, since the Stress lies upon his receiving 'em, by what Means soever they are given? Full of that Conceit he came up to *Sancho*, having first taken the Reins of *Rosinante's* Bridle, and fitted 'em to his Purpose of lashing him with 'em. He then began to untruss *Sancho's* Points, and 'tis a received Opinion, he had but one that was us'd before and held up his Breeches; but he no sooner fell to work, but *Sancho* started out of his Sleep, and was thoroughly awake in an Instant. What's here, cried he? Who's that fumbles about me, and untrusses my Points? 'Tis I, answer'd Don *Quixote*, I am come to repair thy Negligence, and to seek the Remedy of my Torments. I come to whip thee, *Sancho*, and to discharge, in Part at least, that Debt for which thou stand'st engaged. *Dulcinea* perishes, while thou livest careless of her Fate, and I die with Desire. Untruss therefore freely and willingly: For I am resolv'd, while we are here alone in this Recess, to give thee at least two thousand Stripes.

Hold you there, quoth *Sancho*. Pray be quiet, will you. Body of me, let me alone, or I protest deaf Men shall hear us. The Jirks I am bound to give myself, are to be voluntary, and not forced; and at this Time I have no Mind to be whipped at all: Let it suffice, that I promise you to firk and scourge myself, when the Humour takes me. No, said Don *Quixote*, there's no standing to thy Courtesy, *Sancho*; for thou art hard-hearted; and, though a Clown, yet thou art tender of thy Flesh; and so saying, he strove with all his Force to untie the Squire's Points. Which, when *Sancho* perceiv'd, he started up on his Legs, and setting upon his Master, closed with him, tripped up his Heels, threw him fairly upon his Back; and then set his Knee upon his Breast, and held his Hands fast, so that he could hardly stir, or fetch his Breath. Don *Quixote*, overpowered thus, cried, How now, Traitor! What, rebel against thy Master, against thy natural Lord, against him that gives thee Bread! I neither mar King, nor make King,* quoth *Sancho*, I do but defend my-

---

* Henry *the Bastard, afterwards King of* Castile, *being about to murder* Pedro *the lawful King; as they struggled, he fell under him, when* Bertran Cla-quin, *a* Frenchman *that served* Henry, *coming to his Assistance, turned him a-top of* Pedro, *speaking at the same Time those Words that* Sancho *repeats.*

self, that am naturally my own Lord. If your Worship will promise to let me alone, and give over the Thoughts of Whipping me at this Time, I'll let you rise, and will leave you at Liberty; if not, here thou diest, Traitor to Donna *Sancha*. Don *Quixote* gave his Parole of Honour, and swore by the Life of his best Thoughts, not to touch so much as a Hair of *Sancho's* Coat,* but intirely leave it to his Discretion to whip himself when he thought fit. With that, *Sancho* got up from him, and removed his Quarters to another Place at a good Distance, but as he went to lean against another Tree, he perceived something bobbing at his Head, and lifting up his Hands, found it to be a Man's Feet with Shoes and Stockings on: Quaking for Fear, he moved off to another Tree, where the like impending Horror dangl'd over his Head. Straight he call'd out to Don *Quixote* for Help. Don *Quixote* came, and inquiring into the Occasion of his Fright, *Sancho* answer'd, that all those Trees were full of Men's Feet and Legs. Don *Quixote* began to search and grope about, and falling presently into the Account of the Business; Fear nothing, *Sancho*, said he, there's no Danger at all; for what thou feel'st in the Dark are certainly the Feet and Legs of some Banditti and Robbers, that have been hang'd up on these Trees; for here the Officers of Justice hang 'em up by Twenties and Thirties in Clusters, by which I suppose we cannot be far from *Barcelona*; and indeed he guess'd right.

And now Day breaking, they lifted up their Eyes and saw the Bodies of the Highway-men hanging on the Trees: But if the Dead surpriz'd 'em, how much more were they disturb'd at the Appearance of above forty live Banditti, who pour'd upon 'em, and surrounded 'em on a sudden, charging 'em in the *Catalan* Tongue, to stand till their Captain came.

Don *Quixote* found himself on foot, his Horse unbridl'd, his Lance against a Tree at some Distance, and, in short, void of all Defence; and therefore he was forc'd to put his Arms across, hold down his Head, and shrug up his Shoulders, reserving

---

* Ropa in the Original, which signifies all that belongs to a Man's Cloathing. Stevens translates it Hair of his Head. The French Translator has it right, Poil de la Robe. How Jarvis's Translation has it, I know not; but I make no Doubt of it's being right, as having been supervis'd by the learn'd and polite Dr O—d, and Mr P——.

himself for a better Opportunity. The Robbers presently fell to Work, and began to rifle *Dapple*, leaving on his Back nothing of what he carry'd, either in the Wallets or the Cloke-bag; and 'twas very well for *Sancho*, that the Duke's pieces of gold, and those he brought from home, were hid in a Girdle about his Waist; though for all that, those honest Gentlemen would certainly have taken the Pains to have search'd and survey'd him all over, and would have had the Gold, though they had stripp'd him of his Skin to come at it; but by good Fortune their Captain came in the Interim. He seem'd about four and thirty Years of Age, his Body robust, his Stature tall, his Visage aus- tere, and his Complexion swarthy. He was mounted on a strong Horse, wore a Coat of Mail, and no less than two Pistols on each Side. Perceiving that his Squires (for so they call Men of that Profession in those Parts) were going to strip *Sancho*, he order'd 'em to forbear, and was instantly obey'd, by which means the Girdle escap'd. He wonder'd to see a Lance rear'd up against a Tree, a Shield on the Ground, and Don *Quixote* in Armour and pensive, with the saddest, most melancholy Coun- tenance that Despair it self could frame. Coming up to him, be not so sad, honest Man, said he; you have not fall'n into the Hands of some cruel *Busiris*, but into those of *Roque Guinart*, a Man rather compassionate than severe. I am not sad, answer'd Don *Quixote*, for having fall'n into thy Power, valorous *Roque*, whose boundless Fame spreads through the Universe, but for having been so remiss as to be surpriz'd by thy Soldiers with my Horse unbridl'd; whereas, according to the Order of Chivalry- Errant, which I profess, I am oblig'd to live always upon my Guard, and at all Hours be my own Centinel; for let me tell thee, great *Roque*, had they met me mounted on my Steed, arm'd with my Shield and Lance, they would have found it no easy Task to make me yield; for, know, I am Don *Quixote de la Mancha*, the same whose Exploits are celebrated through all the habitable Globe.

Roque Guinart found out immediately Don *Quixote's* blind Side, and judg'd there was more Madness than Valour in the Case: Now, though he had several Times heard him mention'd in Discourse, he could never believe what was related of him to be true, nor could he be persuaded that such a Humour should reign in any Man; for which Reason he was very glad to have met him, that Experience might convince him of the Truth. Therefore addressing himself to him, Valorous Knight, said he, vex not your self, nor tax Fortune with Unkindness, for it may happen, that what you look upon now as a sad Accident, may redound to your Advantage; for Heaven, by strange and unaccountable Ways, beyond the Reach of human Imagination, uses to raise up those that are fall'n, and fill the Poor with Riches. Don *Quixote* was going to return him Thanks, when from behind 'em they heard a Noise like the trampling of several Horses, though it was occasion'd but by one, on which came full speed a Person that look'd like a young Gentleman about twenty Years of Age. He was clad in green Damask edg'd with Gold Galloon suitable to his Waistcoat, a Hat turn'd up behind, strait Wax'd-leather Boots, his Spurs, Sword and Dagger gilt, a light Bird-piece in his Hand, and a Case of Pistols before him. *Roque* having turn'd his Head at the Noise, discover'd the handsom Apparition, which approaching nearer, spoke to him in this manner.

You are the Gentleman I look'd for, valiant *Roque*; for with You I may perhaps find some Comfort, though not a Remedy, in my Affliction. In short, not to hold you in Suspence (for I am sensible you don't know me) I'll tell you who I am. My Name is *Claudia Jeronima*; I am the Daughter of your particular Friend *Simon Forte*, sworn Foe to *Clauquel Torrelas*, who is also your Enemy, being one of your adverse faction. You already know, this *Torrelas* had a Son whom they call Don *Vincente Torrelas*, at least he was call'd so within these two Hours. That Son of his, to be short in my sad Story, I'll tell you in four Words what Sorrow he has brought me to. He saw me, courted me, was heard, and was belov'd. Our Amour was carry'd on with so much Secrecy, that my Father knew nothing of it; for there is no Woman, though ever so retir'd and closely look'd to, but can find Time enough to compass and fulfil her unruly Desires. In short, he made me a Promise of Marriage, and I the like to him, but without proceeding any further. Now Yesterday I understood, that, forgetting his Engagements to me, he was going to wed another, and that they were to be marry'd this Morning; a Piece of News that quite distracted me, and made me lose all Patience. Therefore, my Father being out of Town, I took the Opportunity of equipping my self as you see, and by the Speed of this Horse overtook Don *Vincente* about a League hence, where, without urging my Wrongs, or staying to hear his Excuses, I fir'd at him, not only with this Piece, but with both my Pistols, and, as I believe, shot him through the Body, thus with his Heart's-Blood washing away the Stains of my Honour. This done, there I left him to his Servants, who neither dar'd nor could prevent the sudden Execution; and came to seek your Protection, that by your Means I may be conducted into *France*, where I have Relations to entertain me; and withal to beg of you to defend my Father from Don *Vincente's* Party, who might otherwise revenge his Death upon our Family.

Roque admiring at once the Resolution, agreeable Deportment, and handsom Figure of the beautiful *Claudia*; Come, Madam, said he, let us first be assur'd of your Enemy's Death, and then consider what is to be done for you: Hold, cry'd Don *Quixote*, who had hearken'd with great Attention to all this Discourse, none of you need trouble yourselves with this Affair, the Defence of the Lady is My Province. Give me my Horse and Arms, and stay for me here, I will go and find out this Knight, and, dead or alive, force him to perform his Obligations to so great a Beauty. Ay, ay, quoth *Sancho*, you may take his Word for't, my Master has a rare Stroke at making Matches; 'tis but t'other Day he made a young Rogue yield to marry a Maid whom he would have left in the Lurch, after he was promis'd to her; and had it not been for the Inchanters, that plague his Worship, who transmogrify'd the Bridegroom into a Footman, and broke off the Match, the said Maid had been none by this Time.

Roque was so much taken up with the thought of *Claudia's* Adventure, that he little minded either Master or Man; but ordering his Squires to restore what they had taken from *Dapple* to *Sancho*, and to retire to the Place where they had quarter'd the Night before, he went off upon the Spur with *Claudia*, to find the expiring Don *Vincente*. They got to the Place where *Claudia* met him, and found nothing but the Marks of Blood newly spilt; but looking round about 'em, they discover'd a Company of People at a Distance on the Side of a Hill, and presently judg'd 'em to be Don *Vincente* carry'd by his Servants either to his Cure or Burial. They hasted to overtake 'em, which they soon effected, the others going but slowly; and they found the young Gentleman in the Arms of his Servants, desiring 'em with a spent and fainting Voice to let him die in that Place, his Wounds paining him so that he could not bear going any further. *Claudia* and *Roque* dismounting, hastily came up to him. The Servants were startl'd at the Appearance of *Roque*, and *Claudia* was troubl'd at the Sight of Don Vincente, and, divided between Anger and Compassion, Had you given me this, and made good your Promise, said she to him, laying hold of his Hand, you had never brought this Misfortune upon your self. The wounded Gentleman lifting up his languishing Eyes, and knowing *Claudia*, Now do I see, said he, my fair deluded Mistress, 'tis You that have given me the fatal Blow, a Punishment never deserv'd by the innocent unfortunate *Vincente*, whose Actions and Desires had no other End but that of Serving his *Claudia*. What, Sir, answer'd she presently, can you deny that you went this Morning to marry *Leonora*, the Daughter of wealthy *Belvastro*? 'Tis all a false Report, answer'd he, rais'd by my evil Stars to spur up your Jealousy to take my Life, which since I leave in your fair Hands, I reckon well dispos'd of; and to confirm this Truth, give me your Hand, and receive mine, the last Pledge of Love and Life, and take me for your Husband; 'tis the only Satisfaction I have to give for the imaginary Wrong you suspect I have committed. *Claudia* press'd his Hand, and being pierc'd at once to the very Heart, dropp'd on his bloody Breast into a Swoon, and Don *Vincente* fainted away into a deadly Trance.

Roque's Concern struck him senseless, and the Servants ran for Water to throw in the Faces of the unhappy Couple; by which at last *Claudia* came to herself again, but Don *Vincente* never wak'd from his Trance, but breath'd out the last Remainder of his Life. When *Claudia* perceiv'd this, and could no longer doubt but that her dear Husband was irrecoverably dead, she burst the Air with her Sighs, and wounded the Heavens with her Complaints. She tore her Hair, scatter'd it in the Wind, and with her merciless Hands disfigur'd her Face,

shewing all the lively Marks of Grief that the first Sallies of
Despair can discover. O cruel and inconsiderate Woman, cry'd
she, how easily wast thou set on this barbarous Execution! Oh,
madding Sting of Jealousy, how desperate are thy Motions, and
how tragick the Effects! Oh my unfortunate Husband, whose
sincere Love and Fidelity to me have thus for his nuptial Bed
brought him to the cold Grave! Thus the poor Lady went on
in so sad and moving a Strain, that even *Roque's* rugged Temper now melted into Tears, which on all Occasions had still
been Strangers to his Eyes. The Servants wept and lamented,
Claudia relaps'd into her Swooning as fast as they found means
to bring her to Life again; and the whole Appearance was a
most moving Scene of Sorrow. At last *Roque Guinart* bid Don
Vincente's Servants carry his Body to his Father's House,
which was not far distant, in order to have it buried. *Claudia*
communicated to *Roque* her Resolution of retiring into a Monastery, where an Aunt of hers was Abbess, there to spend the
rest of her Life, wedded to a better and an immortal Bridegroom. He commended her pious Resolution, offering to conduct her whither she pleas'd, and to protect her Father and
Family from all Assaults and Practices of their most dangerous
Enemies. *Claudia* made a modest Excuse for declining his Company, and took leave of him weeping. Don *Vincente's* Servants
carry'd off the dead Body, and *Roque* return'd to his Men. Thus
ended *Claudia Jeronima's* Amour, brought to so lamentable a
Catastrophe by the prevailing Force of a cruel and desperate
Jealousy.

 Roque Guinart found his Crew where he had appointed,
and Don *Quixote* in the Middle of 'em, mounted on *Rosinante*,
and declaiming very copiously against their Way of Living, at
once dangerous to their Bodies, and destructive to their Souls;
but his Auditory being chiefly compos'd of *Gascoigners*, a wild
unruly kind of People, all his Morality was thrown away upon
'em. *Roque* upon his Arrival ask'd *Sancho* if they had restor'd
him all his Things; every Thing, Sir, answer'd *Sancho*, but
three Night-Caps, that are worth a King's Ransom. What
says the Fellow, cry'd one of the Robbers? Here they be, and
they are not worth three Sices. As to the intrinsick Value,
reply'd Don *Quixote*, they may be worth no more, but 'tis

the Merit of the Person that gave 'em me that raises their Value to that Price.

Roque order'd 'em to be restor'd immediately; and commanding his Men to draw up in a Line, he caus'd all the Clothes, Jewels, Money, and all the other Booty they had got since the last Distribution, to be brought before him; then readily appraising every Particular, and reducing into Money what cou'd not be divided, he cast up the Account of the Whole, and then made a just Dividend into Parts, paying to every Man his exact and due Proportion with so much Prudence and Equity, that he fail'd not in the least Point of distributive Justice. The Booty thus shar'd to the general Satisfaction, if it were not for this punctual Management (said Roque, turning to Don Quixote) there would be no living among us. Well, quoth Sancho, Justice must needs be a good Thing, and the old Proverb still holds good, Thieves are never Rogues among themselves. One of the Banditti over-hearing him, cock'd his Gun, and would certainly have shot him through the Head, had not the Captain commanded him to hold. Poor Sancho was struck as mute as a Fish, and resolv'd not to open his Lips once more, till he got into better Company.

By this Time, came one or two of their Scouts that lay perdu on the Road, and inform'd their Captain, that they had discover'd a great Company of Travellers on the Way to Barcelona. Are they such as we look for, ask'd Roque, or such as look for us ? Such as we look for, Sir, answer'd the Fellow; away then, cry'd Roque, all of ye, my Boys, and bring 'em me hither straight, let none escape. The Squires presently obey'd the Word of Command, and left Don Quixote, Roque and Sancho to wait their Return. In the mean time Roque entertain'd the Knight with some Remarks on his Way of Living. I should not wonder, said he, Signor Don Quixote, that our Life should appear to you a restless Complication of Hazards and Disquiets; for 'tis no more than what daily Experience has made me sensible of. You must know, that this Barbarity and austere Behaviour which I affect to shew is a pure Force upon my Nature, being urg'd to this Extremity by the Resentment of some severe Injuries, which I could not put up without a satisfactory Revenge, and now I am in, I must go through; one Sin draws on another, in spight of my better Designs; and I am now involv'd in such a Chain of Wrongs, Factions, Abetters, and Engagements, that no less than the Divine Power of Providence can free me from this Maze of Confusion: Nevertheless I despair not still of a successful End of my Misfortunes.

Don *Quixote*, being surpriz'd to hear such sound Sense and sober Reflection come from one, whose disorderly Profession was so opposite to Discretion and Politeness; Signor *Roque*, said he, 'tis a great Step to Health for a Man to understand his Distemper, and the Compliance of the Patient to the Rules of Physick is reckon'd half the Cure. You appear sensible of the Malady, and therefore may reasonably expect a Remedy, though your Disease being fix'd by a long Inveteracy, must subject you (I'm afraid) to a tedious Course. The Almighty Physician will apply effectual Medicines: Therefore be of good Heart, and do your Part towards the Recovery of your sick Conscience. If you have a Mind to take the shortest Road to Happiness, immediately abandon the fatal Profession you now follow, and come under my Tuition, to be instructed in the Rules of Knight-Errantry, which will soon expiate your Offences, and intitle you to Honour, and true Felicity. *Roque* smil'd to hear Don *Quixote's* serious Advice, and changing the Discourse, gave him an Account of *Claudia Jeronima's* tragical Adventure, which griev'd *Sancho* to the Heart; for the Beauty, Life and Spirit of the young Damsel, had not a little wrought upon his Affections.

By this Time *Roque's* Party had brought in their Prize, consisting of two Gentlemen on Horseback, and two Pilgrims on Foot, and a Coach full of Women, attended by some half a dozen Servants a-foot and a Horseback, besides two Muleteers that belong'd to the two Gentlemen. They were all conducted in solemn Order, surrounded by the Victors, both they and the vanquish'd being silent, and expecting the definitive Sentence of the Grand *Roque*. He first ask'd the Gentlemen who they were? Whither bound? And what Money they had about 'em? They answer'd, that they were both Captains of *Spanish* Foot, and their Companies were at *Naples*; and they design'd to embark on the four Gallies, which they heard were bound for *Sicily*, and their whole Stock amounted to two or three hundred Crowns, which they thought a pretty Sum of Money for Men of their Profession, who seldom use to hoard up Riches. The Pilgrims being examin'd in like manner, said, they intended to embark for *Rome*, and had about some threescore Reals between 'em both. Upon examining the Coach, he was informed by one of the Servants, that my Lady Donna *Guiomar de Quinonnes*, Wife to a Judge of *Naples*, with her little Daughter, a Chambermaid, and an old *Duena*, together with six other Servants, had among 'em all about six hundred Crowns. So then, said *Roque*, we have got here in all nine hundred Crowns and sixty Reals; I think I have got about threescore Soldiers here with me. Now among so many Men how much will fall to each particular Share? Let me see, for I am none of the best Accomptants. Cast it up, Gentlemen. The Highwaymen hearing this, cry'd, long live *Roque Guinart*, and damn the Dogs that seek his Ruin. The Officers look'd simply, the Lady was sadly dejected, and the Pilgrims were no less cast down, thinking this a very odd Confiscation of their little Stock. *Roque* held 'em a while in suspence to observe their Humours, which he found all very plainly to agree in that Point, of being melancholy for the Loss of their Money: Then turning to the Officers, do me the favour, Captains, said he, to lend me threescore Crowns; and you, Madam, if your Ladyship pleases, shall oblige me with fourscore, to gratify these honest Gentlemen of my Squadron; 'tis our whole Estate and Fortune; and you know, the Abbot dines, of what he sings for. Therefore I hope you will excuse our Demands, which will free you from any more Disturbance of this Nature, being secur'd by a Pass, which I shall give you, directed to the rest of my Squadrons that are posted in these Parts, and who, by virtue of my Order, will let you go unmolested; for I scorn to wrong a Soldier, and I must not fail in my Respects, Madam, to the fair Sex, especially to Ladies of your Quality.

The Captains with all the Grace they could, thank'd him for his great Civility and Liberality, for so they esteem'd his letting them keep their own Money. The Lady would have thrown herself out of the Coach at his Feet, but *Roque* would not suffer it, rather excusing the Presumption of his Demands, which he was forc'd to, in pure Compliance with the Necessity

457

of his Fortune. The Lady then order'd one of her Servants to pay immediately the fourscore Crowns. The Officers disburs'd their *Quota*, and the Pilgrims made an oblation of their mite; but *Roque* ordering 'em to wait a little, and turning to his Men, Gentlemen, said he, here are two Crowns a piece for each of you, and twenty over and above. Now let us bestow ten of 'em on these poor Pilgrims, and the other ten on this honest Squire, that he may give us a good Word in his Travels. So calling for Pen, Ink and Paper, of which he always went provided, he wrote a Passport for 'em, directed to the Commanders of his several Parties, and taking his Leave, dismiss'd them, all wondring at his Greatness of Soul, that spoke rather an *Alexander* than a profess'd Highwayman. One of his Men began to mutter in his *Catalan* Language: This Captain of ours is plaguy charitable, he would make a better Friar than a Pad; come, come, if he has a Mind to be so liberal forsooth, let his own Pocket, not ours, pay for it. The Wretch spoke not so low, but he was overheard by *Roque*, who whipping out his Sword, with one Stroke almost cleft his Skull in two. Thus it is I punish Mutiny, said he. All the rest stood motionless, and durst not mutter one Word, so great was the Awe they bore him. *Roque* then withdrew a little, and wrote a Letter to a Friend of his in *Barcelona*, to let him know that the famous Knight-Errant Don *Quixote*, of whom so many strange Things were reported, was with him; that he might be sure to find him on *Midsummer-day* on the great Key of that City, arm'd at all Points, mounted on *Rosinante*, and his Squire on an Ass; that he was a most pleasant ingenious Person, and would give great Satisfaction to him and his Friends the *Niarros*, for which Reason he gave them this Notice of the Don's coming; adding, that he should by no Means let the *Cadells*, his Enemies, partake of this Pleasure, as being unworthy of it: But how was it possible to conceal from them, or any Body else, the Folly and Discretion of Don *Quixote*, and the Buffoonery of *Sancho Pança*. He deliver'd the Letter to one of his Men, who changing his Highway Clothes to a Countryman's Habit, went to *Barcelona*, and gave it as directed.

458

XXVIII: DON QUIXOTE'S ENTRY INTO BARCE-LONA, WITH OTHER ACCIDENTS THAT HAVE LESS INGENUITY THAN TRUTH IN 'EM

DON *Quixote* stay'd three Days and three Nights with *Roque*, and had he tarried as many hundred years, he might have found subject enough for Admiration in that Kind of Life. They slept in one Place, and eat in another, sometimes fearing they knew not what, then laying in wait for they knew not whom. Sometimes forc'd to steal a Nap standing, never enjoying a sound Sleep. Now in this Side the Country, then presently in another Quarter; always upon the Watch, Spies hearkning, Scouts listening, Carbines presenting; though of such heavy Guns they had but few, being arm'd generally with Pistols. *Roque* himself slept apart from the rest, making no Man privy to his Lodgings; for so many were the Proclamations against him from the Viceroy of *Barcelona*, and such were his Disquiets and Fears of being betray'd by some of his Men for the Price of his Head, that he durst trust no Body. A Life most miserable and uneasy.

At length, by Cross-roads, and By-ways, *Roque*, Don *Quixote* and *Sancho*, attended by six other Squires, got to the Strand of *Barcelona* on *Midsummer-Eve* at Night; where *Roque*, having embrac'd Don *Quixote*, and presented *Sancho* with the ten Crowns he had promis'd him, took his Leave of 'em both, after many Compliments on both Sides. *Roque* return'd to his Company, and Don *Quixote* stay'd there waiting the Approach of Day, mounted as *Roque* left him. Not long after the fair *Aurora* began to peep through the Balconies of the East, cheering the Flowry Fields, while at the same Time a melodious Sound of Hautboys and Kettle-Drums cheer'd the Ears, and presently was join'd with jingling of Morrice-Bells and the Trampling and Cries of Horsemen coming out of the City. Now *Aurora* usher'd up the jolly Sun, who look'd big on the Verge of the Horizon, with his broad Face as ample as a Target. Don *Quixote* and *Sancho*, casting their Looks abroad, discover'd the Sea, which they had never seen before. To them it made a noble and spacious Appearance, far bigger than the Lake *Ruydera*, which they saw in *la Mancha*. The Gallies in the Port taking in their Awnings, made a pleasant Sight with their Flags and Streamers, that wav'd in the Air, and sometimes kiss'd and swept the Water. The Trumpets, Hautboys, and other warlike Instruments that resounded from on board, fill'd the Air all round with reviving and martial Harmony. A while after, the Gallies moving, began to join on the calm Sea in a counterfeit Engagement; and at the same Time a vast Number of Gentlemen march'd out of the City nobly equipp'd with rich Liveries, and gallantly mounted, and in like manner did their Part on the Land, to compleat the warlike Entertainment. The Marines discharg'd numerous Vollies from the Gallies, which were answer'd by the great Guns from the Battlements of the Walls and Forts about the City, and the mighty Noise echo'd from the Gallies again by a Discharge of the long Pieces of Ordnance in their Fore-castles. The Sea smil'd and danc'd, the Land was gay, and the Sky serene in every Quarter, but where the Clouds of Smoke dimm'd it a while: Fresh Joy sat smiling in the Looks of Men, and Gladness and Pomp were display'd in their Glory. *Sancho* was mightily puzzled though, to discover how these huge bulky Things that mov'd on the Sea cou'd have so many Feet.

By this Time the Gentlemen that maintain'd the Sports on the Shore, galloping up to Don *Quixote* with loud Acclamations, the Knight was not a little astonish'd: One of 'em amongst the rest, who was the Person to whom *Roque* had written, cry'd out aloud; Welcome, the Mirror, the Light, and North-Star of Knight-Errantry! Welcome, I say, Valorous Don *Quixote de la Mancha*, not the Counterfeit and Apocryphal, shewn us lately in false Histories, but the true, legitimate, and identick He, describ'd by *Cid Hamet*, the Flower of Historiographers! Don *Quixote* made no Answer, nor did the Gentleman stay for any, but wheeling about with the rest of his Companions, all prancing round him in token of Joy, they encompass'd the Knight and the Squire. Don *Quixote* turning about to *Sancho*, It seems, said he, these Gentlemen know us well. I dare engage they have read our History, and that which the *Arragonian* lately publish'd. The Gentleman that spoke to the Knight, returning, Noble Don *Quixote*, said he, we intreat you to come along with the Company, being all your humble Servants, and Friends of *Roque Guinart*. Sir, answer'd Don *Quixote*, your Courtesy bears such a Likeness to the great *Roque's* Generosity, that could Civility beget Civility, I should take yours for the Daughter or near Relation of his. I shall wait on you where you please to command, for I am wholly at your Devotion: The Gentleman return'd his Compliment, and so all of 'em inclosing him in the Middle of their Brigade, they conducted him towards the City, Drums beating, and Hautboys playing before 'em all the Way. But as the Devil and ill Luck would have it, or the Boys, who are more unlucky than the Devil himself, two mischievous young Bastards made a shift to get through the Crowd of Horsemen, and one of 'em lifting up *Rosinante's* Tail, and the other that of *Dapple*, they thrust a Handful of Briars under each of 'em. The poor Animals feeling such unusual Spurs apply'd to their Posteriors, clapp'd their Tails close, and increas'd their Pain, and began to wince, and flounce and kick so furiously, that at last they threw their Riders, and laid both Master and Man sprawling in the Street. Don *Quixote*, out of Countenance, and nettl'd at his Disgrace, went to dis-engage his Horse from his new Plumage, and *Sancho* did as much for *Dapple*, while the Gentlemen turn'd to chastise the Boys for their Rudeness. But the young Rogues were safe enough, being presently lost among a huge Rabble that follow'd. The Knight and Squire then mounted again, and the Musick and Procession went on, till they arriv'd at their Conductor's House, which, by it's Largeness and Beauty, bespoke the Owner Master of a great Estate; where we leave him for the present, because 'tis *Cid Hamet's* Will and Pleasure it should be so.

THE Person who entertain'd Don *Quixote*, was call'd Don *Antonio Moreno*, a Gentleman of good Parts, and plentiful Fortune, loving all those Diversions that may innocently be obtain'd without Prejudice to his Neighbours, and not of the Humour of those, who wou'd rather lose their friend than their Jest. He therefore resolv'd to make his Advantage of Don *Quixote's* Follies without Detriment to his Person.

In order to this, he persuaded the Knight to take off his Armour, and in his strait-lac'd Chamois-Clothes (as we have already shewn him) to stand in a Balcony that look'd into one of the principal Streets of the City, where he stood expos'd to the Rabble that were got together, especially the Boys, who gap'd and star'd on him, as if he had been some overgrown Baboon. The several Brigades of Cavaliers in their Liveries, began afresh to fetch their Careers about him, as if the Ceremony were rather perform'd in Honour of Don *Quixote* than any Solemnity of the Festival. *Sancho* was hugely pleas'd, fancying he had chopp'd upon another *Camachio's* Wedding, or another House like that of Don *Diego de Miranda*, or some Castle like the Duke's.

Several of Don *Antonio's* Friends din'd with him that Day, and all of 'em honouring and respecting Don *Quixote* as a Knight-Errant, they puff'd up his Vanity to such a Degree, that he could scarce conceal the Pleasure he took in their Adulation. As for *Sancho*, he made such Sport to the Servants of the House, and all that heard him, that they watch'd every Word that came from his Mouth. Being all very merry at Table, Honest *Sancho*, said Don *Antonio*, I am told you admire Capons and Sausages so much, that you can't be satisfied with a Belly-full, and when you can eat no more, you cram the rest into your Breeches against the next Morning. No, Sir, an't like you, answer'd *Sancho*, 'tis all a Story, I am more cleanly than greedy, I'd have you to know; here's my Master can tell you, that many Times he and I use to live for a Week together upon a handful of Acorns and Walnuts. Truth is, I am not overnice; in such a Place as this, I eat what's given me; for a Gift-Horse should not be look'd into the Mouth. But whosoever told you I was a Greedy-Gut and a Sloven, has told you a Fib, and were it not for Respect to the Company, I would tell him more of my Mind, so I would. Verily, said Don *Quixote*, the manner of *Sancho's* Feeding ought to be deliver'd to succeeding Ages on brazen Monuments, as a future Memorial of his Abstinence and Cleanliness, and an Example to Posterity. 'Tis true, when he satisfies the Call of Hunger, he seems to do it somewhat ravenously; indeed he swallows apace, uses his Grinders very notably, and chews with both Jaws at once. But in spite of the Charge of Slovenliness now laid upon him, I must declare, he is so nice an Observer of Neatness, that he ever makes a clear Conveyance of his Food; when he was Governor, his Nicety in Eating was remarkable, for he wou'd eat Grapes and ev'n Pomegranate-Seeds with the Point of his Fork. How, cry'd Don *Antonio*, has *Sancho* then been a Governor? Ay, marry has he, answer'd *Sancho*, Governor of the Island of *Barataria*. Ten Days I govern'd, and who but I! But I was so broken of my Rest all the Time, that all I got by't was to learn to hate the Trade of Governing from the Bottom of my Soul. So that I made such Haste to leave it, I fell into a deep Hole, where I was buried alive, and should have lain till now, had not Providence pull'd me out. Don *Quixote* then related the Circumstances of *Sancho's* Government; and the Cloth being taken away, Don *Antonio* took the Knight by the Hand, and carried him into a private Chamber, wherein there was no kind of Furniture, but a Table that appear'd to be of Jasper, supported by Feet of the same, with a brazen Head set upon it, from the Breast upwards, like the Effigies of one of the *Roman* Emperors. Don *Antonio* having walk'd with Don *Quixote* several Turns about the Room, Signor Don *Quixote*, said he, being assur'd that we are very private, the Door fast, and no Body listning, I shall communicate to you one of the most strange and wonderful Adventures that ever was known, provided you treasure it up as a Secret in the closest Apartment of your Breast. I shall be as secret as the Grave, answer'd the Knight, and will clap a Tombstone over your Secret, for farther Security; besides, assure your self, Don *Antonio*, continu'd he, (for by this Time he had learn'd the Gentleman's Name) you converse with a Person whose Ears are open to receive what his Tongue never betrays. So that whatever you commit to My Trust, shall be buried in the Depth of bottomless Silence, and lie as secure as in your own Breast.

In Confidence of your Honour, said Don *Antonio*, I doubt not to raise your Astonishment, and disburden my own Breast of a Secret, which has long lain upon my Thoughts, having never found hitherto any Person worthy to be made a Confident in Matters to be conceal'd. This cautious Proceeding rais'd Don *Quixote's* Curiosity strangely; after which Don *Antonio* led him to the Table, and made him feel and examine all over the Brazen Head, the Table, and the Jasper Supporters. Now, Sir, said he, know that this Head was made by one of the greatest Inchanters or Necromancers in the World. If I am not mistaken, he was a *Polander* by Birth, and the Disciple of the celebrated *Escotillo*,* of whom so many Prodigies are related. This wonderful Person was here in my House, and by the Intercession of a thousand Crowns, was wrought upon to frame me this Head, which has the wonderful Property of answering in your Ear to all Questions. After long Study, erecting of Schemes, casting of Figures, Consultations with the Stars, and other Mathematical Operations, this Head was brought to the aforesaid Perfection, and to morrow (for on *Fridays* it never speaks) it shall give you Proof of it's Knowledge, till when you may consider of your most puzzling and important Doubts, which will have a full and satisfactory Solution. Don *Quixote* was amaz'd at this strange Virtue of the Head, and could hardly credit Don *Antonio's* Account; but considering the shortness of the time that deferr'd his full Satisfaction in the Point, he was content to suspend his Opinion till next Day; and only thank'd the Gentleman for making him so great a Dis-

---

* *Or*, Little Scot. Cervantes *means* Michael Scotus, *who, being more knowing in natural and experimental Philosophy than was common in the dark Ages of Ignorance, pass'd for a Magician; as* Friar Bacon *and* Albert the Great *did; of the first of whom* (Friar Bacon) *a like Story of a Brazen Head is told.*

covery. So out of the Chamber they went, and Don *Antonio* having lock'd the Door very carefully, they return'd into the Room where the rest of the Company were diverted by *Sancho's* relating to 'em some of his Master's Adventures.

That Afternoon they carry'd Don *Quixote* abroad, without his Armour, mounted, not on *Rosinante*, but on a large easy Mule, with genteel Furniture, and himself dress'd after the City Fashion, with a long Coat of Tawny-colour'd Cloth, which with the present Heat of the Season, was enough to put Frost it self into a Sweat. They gave private Orders that *Sancho* should be entertain'd within Doors all that Day, lest he should spoil their Sport by going out. The Knight being mounted, they pinn'd to his Back without his Knowledge a Piece of Parchment, with these Words written in large Letters; This is Don *Quixote de la Mancha*. As soon as they began their Walk, the Sight of the Parchment drew the Eyes of every Body to read the Inscription; so that the Knight hearing so many People repeat the Words, *This is Don* Quixote *de la* Mancha, wonder'd to hear himself nam'd and known by every one that saw him: Thereupon turning to Don *Antonio*, that rode by his Side: How great, said he, is this single Prerogative of Knight-Errantry, by which it's Professors are known and distinguish'd through all the Confines of the Universe. Don't you hear, Sir, continu'd he, how the very Boys in the Street, who have never seen me before, know me? 'Tis very true, Sir, answer'd Don *Antonio*, like Fire that always discovers it self by it's own Light, so Virtue has that Lustre that never fails to display it self, especially that Renown which is acquir'd by the Profession of Arms.

During this Procession of the Knight and his applauding Followers, a certain *Castilian* reading the Scroll at Don *Quixote's* Back, cry'd out aloud, Now the Devil take thee for Don *Quixote de la Mancha*! Who would have thought to have found thee here, and still alive, after so many hearty Drubbings that have been laid about thy Shoulders. Can't you be mad in private, and among your Friends, with a Pox to you, but you must run about the World at this Rate, and make every Body that keeps you Company as Errant-Coxcombs as your self? Get you home to your Wife and Children, Blockhead,

look after your House, and leave playing the Fool and distracting thy Senses at this Rate, with a Parcel of nonsensical Whimsies. Friend, said Don *Antonio*, go about your Business, and
keep your Advice for them that want it. Signor Don *Quixote* is
a Man of too much Sense, not to be above your Counsel, and we
know our Business without your intermeddling. We only pay
the Respect due to Virtue. So, in the Name of ill-luck, go your
Ways, and don't meddle where you have no Business. Truly
now, said the *Castilian*, you're in the Right, for 'tis but striving against the Stream to give him Advice, though it grieves
me to think this Whim of Night-Errantry should spoil all the
good Parts which they say this Madman has. But ill-luck light
on me, as you'd have it, and all my Generation, if e'er you catch
me advising him or any one else again, though I were desired,
and were to live the Years of *Methusalem*. So saying, the Ad-
viser went his Ways, and the Cavalcade continu'd; but the
Rabble press'd so very thick to read the Inscription, that Don
Antonio was forc'd to pull it off, under Pretence of doing something else.

Upon the Approach of Night they return'd home, where
Don *Antonio's* Wife, a Lady of Quality, and every way accomplish'd, had invited several of her Friends to a Ball, to honour
her Guest, and share in the Diversion his Extravagances afforded. After a noble Supper, the Dancing begun about ten
o'Clock at Night. Among others, were two Ladies of an airy
waggish Disposition, such as though virtuous enough at the
Bottom, would not stick to strain a Point of Modesty for the
Diversion of good Company. These two made their Court
chiefly to Don *Quixote*, and ply'd him so with Dancing one
after another, that they tir'd not only his Body but his very
Soul. But the best was to see what an unaccountable Figure
the grave Don made, as he hopp'd and stalk'd about, a long
sway-back'd, starv'd-look'd, thin-flank'd, two-legg'd Thing,
Wainscot-Complexion'd, stuck up in's close Doublet, auk-
ward enough a-conscience, and certainly none of the lightest
at a Saraband. The Ladies gave him several private Hints of
their Inclination to his Person, and he was not behind-hand in
intimating to them as secretly, that they were very indifferent
to him; till at last being almost teiz'd to Death, *Fugite partes*

adversæ, cry'd he aloud, and avaunt Temptation! Pray Ladies, play your amorous Pranks with somebody else, leave me to the Enjoyment of my own Thoughts, which are employ'd and taken up with the peerless *Dulcinea del Toboso*, the sole Queen of my Affection; and so saying, he sat himself down on the Ground in the Midst of the Hall to rest his wearied Bones. Don *Antonio* gave Order that he should be taken up and carry'd to Bed; and the first who was ready to lend a helping Hand was *Sancho*, and as he was lifting him up, By'r Lady, Sir Master of mine, you have shook your Heels most fetiously. Do you think we who are stout and valiant must be Caperers, and that every Knight-Errant must be a Snapper of Castinets? If you do, you're woundily deceiv'd, let me tell you. Gadzookers, I know those who wou'd sooner cut a Giant's Wind-pipe, than a Caper. Had you been for the Shoe-Jig,* I had been your Man; for I slap it away like any Jer-faulcon; but as for regular Dancing, I can't work a Stitch at it. This made Diversion for the Company, till *Sancho* led out his Master, in order to put him to Bed, where he left him cover'd over Head and Ears that he might sweat out the Cold he had caught by Dancing.

The next Day Don *Antonio* resolving to make his intended Experiment on the inchanted Head, conducted Don *Quixote* into the Room where it stood, together with *Sancho*, a Couple of his Friends, and the two Ladies that had so teaz'd the Knight at the Ball, and who had staid all Night with his Wife; and having carefully lock'd the Door, and enjoin'd them Secrecy, he told them the Virtue of the Head, and that this was the first Time he ever made Proof of it; and except his two Friends, no body did know the Trick of the Inchantment, and, had not they been told of it before, they had been drawn into the same Error with the rest; for the Contrivance of the Machine was so artful and so cunningly manag'd, that it was impossible to discover the Cheat. Don *Antonio* himself was the first that made his Application to the Ear of the Head, close to which, speaking in a Voice just loud enough to be heard by the Company; Tell me, O Head, said he, by that mysterious Virtue wherewith thou art endu'd, what are my Thoughts at present?

* *Shoe Jig, in which the Dancers slap the Sole of their Shoe with the Palm of their Hand in Time and Measure.*

The Head in a distinct and intelligible Voice, though without moving the Lips, answer'd, *I am no Judge of Thoughts*. They were all astonish'd at the Voice, being sensible no Body was in the Room to answer. How many of us are there in the Room, said Don *Antonio* again? The Voice answer'd in the same Key, Thou and thy Wife, two of thy Friends, and two of hers, a famous Knight call'd Don *Quixote de la Mancha*, and his Squire *Sancho Pança* by Name. Now their Astonishment was greater than before, now they wonder'd indeed, and the Hair of some of 'em stood on end with Amazement. 'Tis enough, said *Antonio*, stepping aside from the Head, I am convinc'd, 'twas no Impostor sold thee to me, Sage Head, discoursing Head, Oraculous, Miraculous Head! Now let some Body else try their Fortunes. As Women are generally most curious and inquisitive, one of the Dancing Ladies venturing up to it, Tell me, Head, said she, what shall I do to be truly beautiful. *Be honest*, answer'd the Head. I have done, reply'd the Lady. Her Companion then came on, and with the same Curiosity, I would know, said she, whether my Husband loves me or no? The Head answer'd, *Observe his Usage, and that will tell thee*. Truly (said the marry'd Lady to her self as she withdrew) that Question was needless; for indeed a Man's Actions are the surest Tokens of the Dispositions of his Mind. Next came up one of Don *Antonio's* Friends and ask'd, Who am I? The Answer was, *Thou knowest*; That's from the Question, reply'd the Gentleman, I would have thee tell me whether Thou know'st me: *I do*, answer'd the Head, *thou art Don* Pedro Norris. 'Tis enough, O Head, said the Gentleman, thou hast convinc'd me, that thou knowest all Things. So making Room for some Body else, his Friend advanc'd, and ask'd the Head what his eldest Son and Heir desir'd? I have already told thee, said the Head, that I was no Judge of Thoughts; however, I will tell thee, that what thy Heir desires, is to bury thee. 'Tis so, reply'd the Gentleman, What I see with my Eye, I mark with my Finger; I know enough.

Don *Antonio's* Lady ask'd the next Question: I don't well know what to ask thee, said she to the Head, only tell me whether I shall long enjoy my dear Husband? Thou shalt, answer'd the Head, for his healthy Constitution and Temperance promise Length of Days, while those who live too fast, are not like to live long. Next came Don *Quixote*: Tell me thou Oracle, said he, was what I reported of my Adventures in *Montesinos's* Cave, a Dream or Reality? Will *Sancho* my Squire fulfil his Promise, and scourge himself effectually? And shall *Dulcinea* be dis-inchanted? As for the Adventures in the Cave, answer'd the Head, there's much to be said; they have something of both; *Sancho's* Whipping shall go on but leisurely; however, *Dulcinea* shall at last be really freed from Inchantment. That's all I desire to know, said Don *Quixote*, for the whole Stress of my good Fortune depends on *Dulcinea's* Dis-inchantment. Then *Sancho* made the last Application, An't please you, Mr Head, quoth he, shall I chance to have another Government? Shall I ever get clear of this starving Squire-Erranting? And shall I ever see my own fire-side again? The Head answer'd, thou shalt be a Governor in thine own House; if thou go'st home, thou may'st see thy own Fire-side again; and if thou leav'st off thy Service, thou shalt get clear of thy Squireship. Gadzookers, cry'd *Sancho*, that's a very good one, I vow! a Horse-head might ha' told all this; I could have prophesied thus much my self. How now, Brute, said Don *Quixote*, what Answers would'st thou have but what are pertinent to thy Questions? Nay, quoth *Sancho*, since you'll have it so, it shall be so; I only wish Mr Head would have told me a little more concerning the Matter.

Thus the Questions propos'd, and the Answers return'd were brought to a Period, but the Amazement continu'd among all the Company except Don *Antonio's* two Friends, who understood the Mystery, which *Benengeli* is resolv'd now to discover, that the World should be no longer amaz'd with an erroneous Opinion of any Magick or Witch-craft operating in the Head. He therefore tells you, that Don *Antonio Moreno*, to divert himself, and surprise the Ignorant, had this made in imitation of such another Device, which he had seen contriv'd by a Statuary at *Madrid*.

The manner of it was thus: The Table and the Frame on which it stood, the Feet of which resembl'd four Eagles Claws, were of Wood, painted and varnish'd like Jasper. The Head, which look'd like the *Bust* of a *Roman* Emperor, and of a Brass

Colour, was all hollow, and so were the Feet of the Table, which answer'd exactly to the Neck and Breast of the Head; the whole so artificially fix'd, that it seem'd to be all of a Piece; through this Cavity ran a Tin Pipe, convey'd into it by a Passage through the Cieling of the Room under the Table. He that was to answer set his Mouth to the End of the Pipe in the Chamber underneath, and by the Hollowness of the Trunk receiv'd their Questions, and deliver'd his Answers in clear and articulate Words, so that the Imposture could scarcely be discover'd. The Oracle was manag'd by a young ingenious Gentleman, Don *Antonio's* Nephew, who having his Instructions before-hand from his Uncle, was able to answer readily and directly to the first Questions, and by Conjectures or Evasions, make a Return handsomly to the rest, with the help of his Ingenuity. *Cid Hamet* informs us further, that during ten or twelve Days after this the wonderful Machine continu'd in mighty Repute, but at last the Noise of Don *Antonio's* having an inchanted Head in his House, that gave Answers to all Questions, began to fly about the City; and as he fear'd, this would reach the Ears of the watchful Centinels of our Faith, he thought fit to give an Account of the whole Matter to the Reverend Inquisitors, who order'd him to break it to Pieces, lest it should give Occasion of Scandal among the ignorant Vulgar. But still the Head pass'd for an Oracle and a Piece of Inchantment with Don *Quixote* and *Sancho*, though the Truth is, the Knight was much better satisfied in the Matter than the Squire.

The Gentry of the City in Complaisance to Don *Antonio*, and for Don *Quixote's* more splendid Entertainment, or rather to make his Madness a more publick Diversion, appointed a Running at the Ring about six Days after, but this was broken off upon an Occasion that afterwards happen'd.

Don *Quixote* had a mind to take a Turn in the City on Foot, that he might avoid the Crowd of Boys that follow'd him when he rode. He went out with *Sancho* and two of Don *Antonio's* Servants, that attended him by their Master's Order; and passing thro' a certain Street, Don *Quixote* look'd up, and spy'd written over a Door in great Letters these Words, *Here is a Printing-House*. This Discovery pleas'd the Knight extremely, having now an Opportunity of seeing a Printing-Press, a Thing he had never seen before; and therefore to satisfy his Curiosity, in he went with all his Train. There he saw some working off the Sheets, others correcting the Forms, some in one Place picking of Letters out of the Cases, in another some looking over a Proof; in short, all the Variety that is to be seen in great Printing-Houses. He went from one Workman to another, and was very inquisitive to know what every Body had in Hand; and they were not backward to satisfy his Curiosity. At length coming to one of the Compositors, and asking him what he was about? Sir, said the Printer, this Gentleman here (shewing a likely sort of a Man, something grave, and not young) has translated a Book out of *Italian* into *Spanish*, and I am setting some of it here for the Press. What is the Name of it pray? Said Don *Quixote*: Sir, answer'd the Author, the Title of it in *Italian* is *Le Bagatele*. And pray, Sir, ask'd Don *Quixote*, what's the Meaning of that Word in *Spanish*? Sir, answer'd the Gentleman, *Le Bagatele* is as much to say *Trifles*; but though the Title promises so little, yet the Contents are Matters of Importance. I am a little conversant in the *Italian*, said the Knight, and value my self upon singing some Stanzas of *Ariosto*; therefore, Sir, without any Offence, and not doubting of your Skill, but meerly to satisfy my Curiosity, pray tell me, have you ever met with such a Word as *Pignata* in *Italian*? Yes, very often, Sir, answer'd the Author. And how do you render it pray? said Don *Quixote*. How should I render it, Sir, reply'd the Translator, but by the Word *Porridge-Pot*? Body of me, cried Don *Quixote*, you are Master of the *Italian* Idiom? I dare hold a good Wager, that where the *Italian* says *Piace*, you translate it *Please*; where it says *Piu* you render it *More*; *Su*, *Above*, and *Giu*, *Beneath*. Most certainly, Sir, answer'd t'other, for such are their proper Significations. What rare Parts, said Don *Quixote*, are lost to Mankind for want of their being exerted and known! I dare swear, Sir, that the World is backward in encouraging your Merit. But 'tis the Fate of all ingenious Men: How many of 'em are crampt up and discountenanc'd by a narrow Fortune! And how many, in spite of the most laborious Industry, discourag'd; Though, by the way, Sir, I think this kind of Version

471

from one Language to another, except it be from the noblest of Tongues, the *Greek* and *Latin*, is like viewing a Piece of *Flemish* Tapistry on the wrong Side, where, though the Figures are distinguishable, yet there are so many Ends and Threads, that the Beauty and Exactness of the Work is obscur'd, and not so advantageously discern'd as on the right Side of the Hangings. Neither can this barren Employment of translating out of easy Languages shew either Wit or Mastery of Stile, no more than copying a Piece of Writing by a Precedent; though still the Business of Translating wants not it's Commendations, since Men very often may be worse employ'd. As a further Proof of it's Merits, we have Doctor *Christoval de Figuero's* Translation of *Pastor Fido*, and Don *Juan de Xaurigui's Aminta*, Pieces so excellently well done, that they have made 'em purely their own, and left the Reader in Doubt which is the Translation and which the Original. But tell me, pray Sir, do you print your Book at your own Charge, or have you sold the Copy to a Bookseller? Why truly, Sir, answer'd the Translator, I publish it upon my own Account, and I hope to clear at least a thousand Crowns by this first Edition; for I design to print off two thousand Books, and they will go off at six Reals apiece in a Trice. I'm afraid you'll come short of your Reckoning, said Don *Quixote*; 'tis a sign you are still a Stranger to the Tricks of these Booksellers and Printers, and the Juggling there is among them. I dare engage you will find two thousand Books lie very heavy upon your Hands, especially if the Piece be somewhat tedious, and wants Spirit. What, Sir, reply'd the Author, would you have me sell the Profit of my Labour to a Bookseller for three Maravedis a Sheet? For that's the most they will bid, nay, and expect too I should thank them for the Offer. No, no, Sir, I print not my Works to get Fame in the World, my Name is up already; Profit, Sir, is my End, and without it What signifies Reputation? Well, Sir, go on and prosper, said Don *Quixote*, and with that moving to another Part of the Room, he saw a Man correcting a Sheet of a Book call'd, *The Light of the Soul*. Ay, now this is something, cry'd the Knight, these are the Books that ought to be printed, though there are a great many of that Kind; for the Number of Sinners is prodigious in this Age, and there is Need of an infinite quantity of Lights for so many dark Souls as we have among us. Then passing on, and inquiring the Title of a Book of which another Workman was correcting a Sheet, they told him 'twas the Second Part of that ingenious Gentleman Don *Quixote de la Mancha*, written by a certain Person, a Native of *Tordesillas*. I have heard of that Book before, said Don *Quixote*, and really thought it had been burnt, and reduc'd to Ashes for a foolish impertinent Libel; but all in good time. Execution-day will come at last.* For made Stories are only so far good and agreeable as they are profitable, and bear the Resemblance of Truth; and true History the more valuable, the farther it keeps from the fabulous. And so saying, he flung out of the Printing-house in a Huff.

That very Day Don *Antonio* would needs shew Don *Quixote* the Gallies in the Road, much to *Sancho's* Satisfaction, because he had never seen any in his Life. Don *Antonio* therefore gave Notice to the Commander of the Gallies, that in the Afternoon he would bring his Guest, Don *Quixote de la Mancha*, to see them, the Commander and all the People of the Town being by this Time no Strangers to the Knight's Character. But what happen'd in the Gallies, must be the Subject of the next Chapter.

* But it's Martinmass will come, as it does to every Hog. Martinmass, *or about the Feast of St* Martin, *is the Time for making Bacon for Winter, which gave occasion to this* Spanish *Proverb, as is observ'd by* Sobrino *in his* Spanish *and* French *Dictionary. A cada puerco le viene su san Martin; and, adds he, it is applicable to sensual voluptuous Men who fatten themselves as Hogs to die like them at God's appointed Time.*

XXX: OF SANCHO'S MISFORTUNE ON BOARD THE GALLIES, WITH THE STRANGE ADVENTURES OF THE BEAUTIFUL MORISCA (MOORISH LADY)

MANY and serious were Don *Quixote's* Reflections on the Answer of the inchanted Head, though none hit on the Deceit, but center'd all in the Promise of *Dulcinea's* Disinchantment; and expecting it would speedily be effected, he rested joyfully satisfy'd. As for *Sancho*, though he hated the Trouble of being a Governor, yet still he had an itching Ambition to rule, to be obey'd, and appear great; for even Fools love Authority.

In short, that Afternoon Don *Antonio*, his two Friends, Don *Quixote*, and *Sancho*, set out for the Gallies. The Commander being advertis'd of their coming, upon their Appearance on the Key, order'd all the Gallies to strike Sail; the Musick play'd, and a Pinnace spread with rich Carpets and Crimson Velvet Cushions was presently hoisted out, and sent to fetch 'em aboard. As soon as Don *Quixote* set his Foot into it, the Admiral Galley discharg'd her Forecastle-Piece, and the rest of the Gallies did the like. When Don *Quixote* got over the Gunnel of the Galley on the Starboard-side, the whole Crew of Slaves, according to their Custom of saluting Persons of Quality, welcom'd him with three *hu, hu, huz*, or *huzzah's*. The General (for so we must call him) by Birth a *Valencian*, and a Man of Quality, gave him his Hand, and embrac'd him. This Day, said he, will I mark as one of the happiest I expect to see in all my Life, since I have the Honour now to see Senior Don *Quixote de la Mancha*; this Day, I say, that sets before my Eyes the Summary of wandring Chivalry collected in one Person. Don *Quixote* return'd his Compliment with no less Civility, and appeared overjoy'd to see himself so treated like a Grandee. Presently they all went into the State-Room, which was handsomly adorn'd, and there they took their Places. The Boatswain went to the Forecastle, and with his Whistle or Call gave the Sign to the Slaves to strip, which was obey'd in a Moment. *Sancho* was scar'd to see so many Fellows in their naked Skins, but most of all when he saw 'em hoist up the sails so incredibly fast, as he thought could never have been done but by so many Devils. He had plac'd himself a Mid-ship, next the aftmost Rower on the Starboard-side; who being instructed what to do, caught hold of him, and giving him a Hoist, handed him to the next Man, who toss'd him to a third; and so the whole Crew of Slaves, beginning on the Starboard-side, made him fly so fast from Bench to Bench, that poor *Sancho* lost the very Sight of his Eyes, and verily believed all the Devils in Hell were carrying him away to rights. Nor did the Slaves give over bandying him about, till they had handed him in the same man-ner over all the Larboard-side; and then they set him down where they had taken him up, but strangely disordered, out of Breath, in a cold Sweat, and not truly sensible what it was that had happen'd to him.

Don *Quixote* seeing his Squire fly at this Rate without Wings, ask'd the General if that were a Ceremony us'd to all Strangers aboard the Gallies; for, if it were, he must let him know, that as he did not design to take up his Residence there, he did not like such Entertainment; and vow'd to Heaven, that if any of 'em came to lay hold on him to toss him at that Rate, he would spurn their Souls out of their Bodies; and with this, starting up, he lays his Hand on his Sword.

At the same Time they lower'd their Sails, and with a dread-ful Noise let down the Main-yard; which so frighted *Sancho*, who thought the Sky was flying off it's Hinges, and falling upon him, that he duck'd and thrust his Head between his Legs for Fear. Don *Quixote* was a little out of Sorts too, he began to shiver, and shrug up his Shoulders, and chang'd Colour. The Slaves hoisted the Main-yard again with the same Force and Noise that they had lower'd it withal. But all this with such Silence on their Parts, as if they had neither Voice nor Breath. The Boatswain then gave the Word to weigh Anchor; and leap-ing a Top of the Fore-castle among the Crew, with his Whip or Bull's-Pizzle, he began to dust and fly-flap their Shoulders, and by little and little to put off to Sea.

When *Sancho* saw so many colour'd Feet moving at once, for he took the Oars to be such; Beshrew my Heart, quoth he, here is Inchantment in good Earnest; all our Adventures and Witchcrafts have been nothing to this. What have these poor

Wretches done, that their Hides must be curry'd at this Rate? And how dares this plaguy Fellow go whistling about here by himself, and maul thus so many People? Well, I say, this is Hell, or Purgatory at least.

Don *Quixote* observing how earnestly *Sancho* look'd on these Passages; Ah! dear *Sancho*, said he, what an easy Matter now were it for you to strip to the Waist, and clap your self among these Gentlemen, and so complete *Dulcinea's* Disinchantment; among so many Companions in Affliction, you wou'd not be so sensible of the Smart; and besides, the sage *Merlin* perhaps might take every one of these Lashes, being so well laid on, for ten of those which you must certainly one Day inflict on your self. The General of the Gallies was going to ask what he meant by these Lashes, and *Dulcinea's* Disinchantment, when a Mariner cry'd out, they make Signs to us from *Monjoui*,* that there's a Vessel standing under the Shore to the Westward. With that the General leaping upon the Coursey, cry'd, pull away my Hearts, let her not escape us; this Brigantine is an *Algiereen*, I warrant her. Presently the three other Gallies came up with the Admiral to receive Orders, and he commanded two of 'em to stand out to Sea, while he with the other would keep along the Shore, that so they might be sure of their Prize.

The Rowers tugg'd so hard that the Gallies scudded away like Lightning, and those that stood to Sea, discover'd about two Miles off, a Vessel with fourteen or fifteen Oars, which, upon Sight of the Gallies, made the best of her Way off, hoping by her Lightness to escape; but all in vain, for the Admiral's Galley being one of the swiftest Vessels in those Seas, gain'd so much Way upon her, that the Master of the *Brigantine* seeing his Danger, was willing the Crew should quit their Oars, and yield, for Fear of exasperating their General. But Fate order'd it otherwise; for upon the Admiral's coming up with the *Brigantine* so near as to hale her, and bid them strike, two *Toraquis*, that is, two drunken *Turks*, among twelve others that were on Board the Vessel, discharg'd a couple of Muskets, and kill'd two Soldiers that were upon the Wale of the Galley. The

* Monjoui *is a high Tower at* Barcelona, *on which always stands a Centinel, who by Signs gives Notice what Vessels he discovers at Sea.*

General seeing this, vow'd he would not leave a Man of them alive; and coming up with great Fury to grapple with her, she slipp'd away under the Oars of the Galley. The Galley ran a-head a good Way, and the little Vessel finding her self clear for the present, though without Hopes to get off, crouded all the Sail she could, and with Oars and Sails began to make the best of her Way, while the Galley tack'd about. But all their Diligence did not do 'em so much Good as their Presumption did 'em Harm; for the Admiral coming up with her after a short Chace, clapp'd his Oars in the Vessel, and so took her and every Man in her alive.

By this Time the other Gallies were come up, and all four return'd with their Prize into the Harbour, where great Numbers of People stood waiting, to know what Prize they had taken. The General came to an Anchor near the Land, and perceiving the Vice-Roy was on the Shore, he mann'd his Pinnace to fetch him aboard, and gave Orders to lower the Main-yard, to hang up the Master of the *Brigantine*, with the rest of the Crew, which consisted of about six and thirty Persons, all proper lusty Fellows, and most of 'em *Turkish* Musqueteers. The General ask'd, Who commanded the Vessel; whereupon one of the Prisoners, who was afterwards known to be a *Spaniard*, and a Renegado, answer'd him in *Spanish*, This was our Master, my Lord, said he, shewing him a young Man not twenty Years of Age, and one of the handsomest Persons that could be imagin'd. You inconsiderate Dog, said the General, What made you kill my Men, when you saw 'twas not possible for you to escape? Is this the Respect due to an Admiral? Don't you know that Rashness is no Courage? While there is any Hope, we are allow'd to be bold, but not to be desperate. The Master was offering to reply, but the General could not stay to hear his Answer, being oblig'd to go and entertain the Vice-Roy, who was just come aboard with his Retinue, and others of the Town. You have had a lucky Chace, my Lord, said the Vice-Roy: What have you got? Your Excellency shall see presently, answer'd the General, I'll shew them you immediately hanging at the Main-yard-Arm. How so, reply'd the Vice-Roy? Because, said he, they have kill'd me, contrary to all Law of Arms, Reason and Custom of the Sea, two of the best Soldiers I had on board; for which I have sworn to hang them every Mother's Son, especially this young Rogue, the Master. Saying thus, he shew'd him a Person with his Hands already bound, and the halter about his neck, expecting nothing but death. His youth, beauty, and resignation began to plead much in his behalf with the Vice-Roy, and made him inclinable to save him; Tell me, Captain, said he, art thou born a *Turk*, or a *Moor*, or art thou a Renegado? None of all these, answered the Youth in good *Spanish*. What then, said the Vice-Roy? A Christian Woman, reply'd the Youth; a Woman, and a Christian, though in these Clothes, and in such a Post; but 'tis a Thing rather to be wonder'd at, than believ'd. I humbly beseech ye, my Lords, continu'd the Youth, to defer my Execution till I give you the History of my Life, and I can assure ye the Delay of your Revenge will be but short. This Request was urg'd so piteously, that no Body could deny it; whereupon the General bade him proceed, assuring him, nevertheless, that there was no Hopes of Pardon for an Offence so great as was that of which he was guilty. Then the Youth began.

I am one of that unhappy and imprudent Nation, whose Miseries are fresh in your Memories. My Parents being of the *Morisco* Race: the Current of their Misfortunes, with the Obstinacy of two Uncles, hurried me out of *Spain* into *Barbary*. In vain I profess'd my self a Christian, being really one, and not such a secret *Mahometan* as too many of us were; this could neither prevail with my Uncles to leave me in my native Country, nor with the Severity of those Officers that had Orders to make us evacuate *Spain*, to believe it was not a Pretence. My Mother was a Christian, my Father, a Man of Discretion, professed the same Belief, and I suck'd the Catholick Faith with my Milk. I was handsomly educated, and never betray'd the least Mark of the *Morisco* Breed, either in Language or Behaviour. With these Endowments, as I grew up, that little Beauty I had, if ever I had any, began to increase; and for all my retir'd Life, and the Restraint upon my appearing abroad, a young Gentleman, call'd Don *Gaspar Gregorio*, got a Sight of me: He was Son and Heir to a Knight that liv'd in the next Town: 'Twere tedious to relate, how he got an Opportunity to converse with me, fell desperately in Love,

478

and affected me with a Sense of his Passion. I must be short, lest this Halter cut me off in the Middle of my Story. I shall only tell you, that he would needs bear me Company in my Banishment, and accordingly, by the Help of the *Morisco* Language, of which he was a perfect Master, he mingl'd with the Exiles, and getting acquainted with my two Uncles that conducted me, we all went together to *Barbary*, and took up our Residence at *Algiers*, or rather Hell it self.

My Father, in the mean Time, had very prudently, upon the first News of the Proclamation to banish us, withdrawn to seek a Place of Refuge for us in some Foreign Country, leaving a considerable Stock of Money and Jewels hidden in a private Place, which he discover'd to no Body but me, with Orders not to move it till his Return.

The King of *Algiers*, understanding I had some Beauty, and also that I was Rich, which afterwards turn'd to my Advantage, sent for me, and was very inquisitive about my Country, and what Jewels and Gold I had got. I satisfied him as to the Place of my Nativity, and gave him to understand, that my Riches were buried in a certain Place where I might easily recover 'em, were I permitted to return where they lay.

This I told him, that in Hopes of sharing in my Fortune, his Covetousness should divert him from injuring my Person. In the midst of these Questions, the King was inform'd, that a certain Youth, the handsomest and loveliest in the World, had come over in Company with us. I was presently conscious that Don *Gregorio* was the Person, his Beauty answering so exactly their Description. The Sense of the young Gentleman's Danger was now more grievous to me than my own Misfortunes, having been told that those barbarous *Turks* are much fonder of a handsom Youth, than the most beautiful Woman. The King gave immediate Orders he shou'd be brought into his Presence, asking me whether the Youth deserv'd the Commendations they gave him? I told him, inspir'd by some good Angel, that the Person they so much commended was no Man, but of my own Sex, and withal begg'd his Permission to have her dress'd in a Female Habit, that her Beauty might shine in it's natural Lustre, and so prevent her Blushes, if she should appear before his Majesty in that unbecoming Habit. He consented, promising withal, to give Order next Morning for my Return to *Spain*, to recover my Treasure. I spoke with Don *Gaspar*, represented to him the Danger of appearing a Man, and prevail'd with him to wait on the King that Evening in the Habit of a *Moorish* Woman. The King was so pleas'd with her Beauty, that he resolv'd to reserve her as a Present for the *Grand Signior*; and fearing the Malice of his Wives in the *Seraglio*, and the Solicitations of his own Desires, he gave her in Charge to some of the principal Ladies of the City, to whose House she was immediately conducted.

This Separation was grievous to us both, for I cannot deny that I love him. Those who have ever felt the Pangs of a parting Love can best imagine the Affliction of our Souls. Next Morning, by the King's Order, I embark'd for *Spain* in this Vessel, accompany'd by these two *Turks* that kill'd your Men, and this *Spanish* Renegado that first spoke to you, who is a Christian in his Heart, and came along with me with a greater Desire to return to *Spain* than to go back to *Barbary*. The rest are all *Moors* and *Turks*, who serve for Rowers. Their Orders were to set me on Shore with this Renegado, in the Habits of Christians, on the first *Spanish* Ground they should discover; but these two covetous and insolent *Turks*, would needs, contrary to their Order, first cruise upon the Coast, in Hopes of taking some Prize; being afraid, that if they should first set us ashore, some Accident might happen to us, and make us discover that the Brigantine was not far off at Sea, and so expose 'em to the Danger of being taken, if there were Gallies upon the Coast. In the Night we made this Land, not mistrusting any Gallies lying so near, and so we fell into your Hands.

To conclude, Don *Gregorio* remains in Womens Habit among the *Moors*, nor can the Deceit long protect him from Destruction; and here I stand expecting, or rather fearing my Fate, which yet cannot prove unwelcome, I being now weary of living. Thus, Gentlemen, you have heard the unhappy Passages of my Life; I have told you nothing but what is true, and all I have to beg is, that I may die as a Christian, since I am innocent of the Crimes of which my unhappy Nation is accus'd. Here she stopp'd, and with her Story and her Tears melted the Hearts of many of the Company.

The Vice-Roy, being mov'd with a tender Compassion, was the first to unbind the Cords that manacl'd her fair Hands, when an ancient Pilgrim, who came on Board with the Vice-Roy's Attendants, having with a fix'd Attention minded the Damsel during her Relation, came suddenly, and throwing himself at her Feet, Oh! *Anna Felix*, cry'd he, my dear unfortunate Daughter! Behold thy Father *Ricote*, that return'd to seek thee, being unable to live without thee, who art the Joy and Support of my Age. Upon this, *Sancho*, who had all this while been sullenly musing, vex'd at the Usage he had met with so lately, lifting up his Head, and staring the Pilgrim in the Face, knew him to be the same *Ricote* he had met on the Road the Day he left his Government, and was likewise fully persuaded, that this was his Daughter, who being now unbound, embrac'd her Father, and join'd with him in his Joy and Grief. My Lords, said the old Pilgrim, this is my Daughter, *Anna Felix*, more unhappy in Fortune than in Name, and fam'd as much for her Beauty as for her Father's Riches. I left my Country to seek a Sanctuary for my Age, and having fix'd upon a Residence in *Germany*, return'd in this Habit with other Pilgrims to dig up and regain my Wealth, which I have effectually done; but I little thought thus unexpectedly to have found my greatest Treasure, my dearest Daughter. My Lords, if it can consist with the Integrity of your Justice, to pardon our small Offence, I join my Prayers and Tears with hers, to implore your Mercy on our Behalf; since we never design'd you any Injury, and are innocent of those Crimes for which our Nation has justly been banish'd. Ay, ay, cry'd *Sancho* (putting in) I know *Ricote* as well as the Beggar knows his Dish; and so far as concerns *Anna Felix's* being his Daughter, I know that's true too; but for all the Story of his Goings-out and Comings-in, in his Intentions, whether they were good, or whether they were bad, I'll neither meddle nor make, not I.

So uncommon an Accident fill'd all the Company with Admiration; so that the General turning to the fair Captain, Your Tears, said he, are so prevailing, Madam, that they compel me now to be forsworn. Live, lovely *Anna Felix*, live as many Years as Heaven has decreed you; and let those rash and insolent Slaves, who alone committed the Crimes, bear the Punish-

ment of it. With that he gave Order to have the two delinquent
Turks hang'd up at the Yard-Arm: But at the Intercession of
the Vice-Roy, their Fault shewing rather Madness than Design, the fatal Sentence was revok'd; the General considering
at the same time, that their Punishment in cold Blood would
look more like Cruelty than Justice.

Then they began to consider how they might retrieve Don
Gaspar Gregorio from the Danger he was in; to which purpose
Ricote offer'd to the Value of above a Thousand Ducats, which
he had about him in Jewels, to purchase his Ransom. But the
readiest Expedient was thought to be the Proposal of the
Spanish Renegado, who offer'd, with a small Bark and half a
dozen Oars mann'd by Christians, to return to *Algiers*, and set
him at Liberty, as best knowing when and where to land,
and being acquainted with the Place of his Confinement. The
General and the Vice-Roy demurr'd to this Motion, thro' a
Distrust of the Renegado's Fidelity, since he might perhaps
betray the Christians that were to go along with him. But
Anna Felix engaging for his Truth, and *Ricote* obliging himself
to ransom the Christians if they were taken, the Design was
resolv'd upon.

The Vice-Roy went ashore, committing the *Morisca* and
her Father to Don *Antonio Moreno's* Care, desiring him at the
same time to command his House for any thing that might
conduce to their Entertainment; such Sentiments of Kindness
and Good-nature had the Beauty of *Anna Felix* infus'd into
his Breast.

XXXI: OF AN UNLUCKY ADVENTURE, WHICH DON QUIXOTE LAID MOST TO HEART OF ANY THAT HAD YET BEFALLEN HIM

DON *Antonio's* Lady was extremely pleas'd with the Company of the fair *Morisca*, whose Sense being as exquisite as her Beauty, drew all the most considerable Persons in the City to visit her. Don *Quixote* told Don *Antonio* that he could by no means approve the Method they had taken to release Don *Gregorio*, it being full of Danger, with little or no Probability of Success; but that their surest Way would have been to set *Him* ashore in *Barbary*, with his Horse and Arms, and leave it to *Him* to deliver the Gentleman in spite of all the *Moorish* Power, as Don *Gayferos* had formerly rescu'd his Wife *Melissandra*. Good your Worship, quoth *Sancho*, hearing this, look before you leap. Don *Gayferos* had nothing but a fair Race for't on dry Land, when he carried her to *France*. But here, an't please you, though we should deliver Don *Gregorio*, how the Devil shall we bring him over to *Spain* cross the broad Sea? There's a Remedy for all Things but Death, answer'd Don *Quixote*, 'tis but having a Bark ready by the Sea-side, and then let me see what can hinder our getting into it. Ah Master, Master, quoth *Sancho*, there's more to be done than a Dish to wash: Saying is one Thing, and Doing is another, and for my Part, I like the Renegado very well, he seems to me a good honest Fellow, and cut out for the Business. Well, said Don *Antonio*, if the Renegado fails, then the Great Don *Quixote* shall embark for *Barbary*.

In two Days the Renegado was dispatch'd away in a fleet Cruiser of six Oars o'side, mann'd with brisk lusty Fellows, and two Days after that, the Gallies with the General left the Port, and steer'd their Course Eastwards. The General having first engag'd the Vice-Roy to give him an Account of Don *Gregorio's* and *Anna Felix's* Fortune.

Now it happen'd one Morning that Don *Quixote* going abroad to take the Air upon the Sea shore, arm'd at all Points, according to his Custom (his Arms, as he said, being his best

Attire, as Combat was his Refreshment) he spy'd a Knight riding towards him, arm'd like himself from Head to Foot, with a bright Moon blazon'd on his Shield, who coming within Hearing, call'd out to him, Illustrious, and never-sufficiently-extoll'd Don *Quixote de la Mancha*, I am the Knight of the *White Moon*, whose incredible Atchievements, perhaps, have reach'd thy Ears. Lo, I am come to enter into Combat with thee, and to compel thee by Dint of Sword, to own and acknowledge my Mistress, by whatever Name and Dignity she be distinguish'd, to be, without any Degree of Comparison, more beautiful than thy *Dulcinea del Toboso*. Now if thou wilt fairly confess this Truth, thou freest thy self from certain Death, and me from the Trouble of taking or giving thee thy Life. If not, the Conditions of our Combat are these: If Victory be on my Side, thou shalt be oblig'd immediately to forsake thy Arms, and the Quest of Adventures, and to return to thy own Home, where thou shalt engage to live quietly and peaceably for the Space of one whole Year, without laying Hand on thy Sword, to the Improvement of thy Estate, and the Salvation of thy Soul. But if thou com'st off Conqueror, my Life is at thy Mercy, my Horse and Arms shall be thy Trophy, and the Fame of all my former Exploits, by the lineal Descent of Conquest, be vested in thee as Victor. Consider what thou hast to do, and let thy Answer be quick, for my Dispatch is limited to this very Day.

Don *Quixote* was amaz'd and surpriz'd as much at the Arrogance of the Knight of the *White Moon's* Challenge, as at the Subject of it; so with a solemn and austere Address, Knight of the *White Moon*, said he, whose Atchievements have as yet been kept from my Knowledge, 'tis more than probable, that you have never seen the illustrious *Dulcinea*; for had you ever view'd her Perfections, you had there found Arguments enough to convince you, that no Beauty past, present, or to come, can parallel hers; and therefore without giving you directly the Lye, I only tell thee, Knight, thou art mistaken, and this Position I will maintain by accepting your Challenge on your Conditions, except that Article of your Exploits descending to Me; for, not knowing what Character your Actions bear, I shall rest satisfied with the Fame of my own, by which, such as they are, I am willing to abide. And since your Time is so limited, chuse your Ground, and begin your Career as soon as you will, and expect to be met with: A fair Field, and no Favour: *To whom God shall give her*,* St Peter *give his Blessing*.

While the two Knights were thus adjusting the Preliminaries of Combat, the Vice-Roy, who had been inform'd of the Knight of the *White Moon's* Appearance near the City Walls, and his parlying with Don *Quixote*, hasten'd to the Scene of Battle, not suspecting it to be any thing but some new Device of Don *Antonio Moreno*, or somebody else. Several Gentlemen, and Don *Antonio* among the rest, accompany'd him thither. They arriv'd just as Don *Quixote* was wheeling *Rosinante* to fetch his Career; and seeing 'em both ready for the Onset, he interpos'd, desiring to know the Cause of the sudden Combat. The Knight of the *White Moon* told him there was a Lady in the Case, and briefly repeated to his Excellency what pass'd between him and Don *Quixote*. The Vice-Roy whisper'd Don *Antonio*, and ask'd him whether he knew that Knight of the *White Moon*, and whether their Combat was not some jocular Device to impose upon Don *Quixote*? Don *Antonio* answer'd positively, that he neither knew the Knight, nor whether the Combat were in Jest or Earnest. This put the Vice-Roy to some Doubt whether he should not prevent their Engagement; but being at last persuaded that it must be a Jest at the Bottom, he withdrew. Valorous Knights, said he, if there be no *Medium* between Confession and Death, but Don *Quixote* be still resolv'd to deny, and you, the Knight of the *White Moon*, as obstinately to urge, I have no more to say; the Field is free, and the Lord have Mercy on ye.

The Knights made their Compliments to the Vice-Roy for his gracious Consent; and Don *Quixote* making some short *Ejaculations* to Heaven and his Mistress, as he always us'd upon these Occasions, began his Career, without either Sound of Trumpet or any other Signal. His Adversary was no less forward; for setting Spurs to his Horse, whch was much the swifter, he met Don *Quixote* before he had ran half his Career, so forcibly, that without making use of his Lance, which 'tis

* *Meaning* Victory. *These are Words used at the Marriage Ceremony.*

thought he lifted up on Purpose, he overthrew the Knight of *la Mancha* and *Rosinante*, both coming to the Ground with a terrible Fall.

The Knight of the *White Moon* got immediately upon him, and clapping the Point of his Lance to his Face, Knight, cry'd he, you are vanquish'd, and a dead Man, unless you immediately fulfil the Conditions of your Combat. Don *Quixote*, bruis'd and stunn'd with his Fall, without lifting up his Beaver, answer'd in a faint hollow Voice, as if he had spoke out of a Tomb, *Dulcinea del Toboso* is the most beautiful Woman in the World, and I the most unfortunate Knight upon the Earth. 'Twere unjust that such Perfection should suffer through my Weakness. No, pierce my Body with thy Lance, Knight, and let my Life expire with my Honour. Not so rigorous neither, reply'd the Conqueror, let the Fame of the Lady *Dulcinea del Toboso* remain entire and unblemish'd: provided the Great Don *Quixote* return home for a Year, as we agreed before the Combat, I am satisfied. The Vice-Roy and Don *Antonio* with many other Gentlemen were Witnesses to all these Passages, and particularly to this Proposal, to which Don *Quixote* answer'd, that upon Condition he should be enjoin'd nothing to the Prejudice of *Dulcinea*, he would, upon the Faith of a true Knight, be punctual in the Performance of every Thing else. This Acknowledgment being made, the Knight of the *White Moon* turn'd about his Horse, and saluting the Vice-Roy, rode at a Hand-Gallop into the City, whither Don *Antonio* follow'd him, at the Vice-Roy's Request, to find who he was, if possible.

Don *Quixote* was lifted up, and upon taking off his Helmet, they found him pale, and in a cold Sweat. As for *Rosinante*, he was in so sad a Plight, that he could not stir for the present. Then as for *Sancho*, he was in so heavy a taking, that he knew not what to do, nor what to say; he was sometimes persuaded he was in a Dream, sometimes he fancy'd this rueful Adventure was all Witchcraft and Inchantment. In short, he found his Master discomfited in the Face of the World, and bound to good Behaviour, and to lay aside his Arms for a whole Year. Now he thought his Glory eclips'd, his Hopes of Greatness vanish'd into Smoke, and his Master's Promises, like his Bones,

486

put out of Joint by that cursed Fall, which he was afraid had at
once crippl'd *Rosinante* and his Master. At last the vanquish'd
Knight was put into a Chair, which the Vice-Roy had sent for,
for that Purpose, and they carry'd him into Town, accompany'd likewise by the Vice-Roy, who had a great Curiosity
to know who this Knight of the *White Moon* was, that had
left Don *Quixote* in so sad a Condition.

XXXII: AN ACCOUNT OF THE KNIGHT OF THE WHITE MOON, DON GREGORIO'S ENLARGE‑ MENT, AND OTHER PASSAGES

DON *Antonio Moreno* follow'd the Knight of the *White Moon* to his Inn, whither he was attended by a troublesom Rabble of Boys. The Knight being got to his Chamber, where his Squire waited to take off his Armour, Don *Antonio* came in, declaring he would not be shook off, till he had discover'd who he was. The Knight finding that the Gentleman would not leave him; Sir, said he, since I lie under no Obligation of concealing my self, if you please, while my Man disarms me, you shall hear the whole Truth of the Story.

You must know, Sir, I am call'd the Batchelor *Carrasco*; I live in the same Town with this Don *Quixote*, whose unac‑ countable Phrenzy has mov'd all his Neighbours, and me among the rest, to endeavour by some Means to cure his Madness; in order to which, believing that Rest and Ease would prove the surest Remedy, I bethought my self of this present Stratagem; and about three Months ago, in all the Equipage of a Knight‑ Errant, under the Title of the Knight of the *Mirrours*, I met him on the Road, fix'd a Quarrel upon him, and the Conditions of our Combat were as you have heard already. But Fortune then declar'd for Him, for he unhors'd and vanquish'd me, and so I was disappointed: He prosecuted his Adventures, and I return'd home shamefully, very much hurt with my Fall. But willing to retrieve my Credit, I made this second Attempt, and now have succeeded. For I know him to be so nicely punctual in whatever his Word and Honour is engag'd for, that he will undoubtedly perform his Promise. This, Sir, is the Sum of the whole Story, and I beg the Favour of you to conceal me from Don *Quixote*, that my Project may not be ruin'd the second Time, and that the honest Gentleman, who is naturally a Man of good Parts, may recover his Understanding. Oh! Sir, re‑ ply'd Don *Antonio*, what have you to answer for, in robbing the World of the most diverting Folly, that ever was expos'd among Mankind? Consider, Sir, that his Cure can never bene‑

fit the Publick half so much as his Distemper. But I am apt to believe, Sir Batchelor, that his Madness is too firmly fix'd for your Art to remove, and (Heaven forgive me) I can't forbear wishing it may be so; for by Don *Quixote's* Cure we not only lose his good Company, but the Drolleries and comical Humours of *Sancho Pança* too, which are enough to cure Melancholy it self of the Spleen. However, I promise to say nothing of the Matter, though I confidently believe, Sir, your Pains will be to no Purpose. *Carrasco* told him, that having succeeded so far, he was obliged to cherish better Hopes; and asking Don *Antonio* if he had any farther Service to command him, he took his Leave, and packing up his Armour on a Carriage-Mule, presently mounted his Charging-Horse, and leaving the City that very Day, posted homewards, meeting no Adventure on the Road worth a Place in this faithful History.

Don *Antonio* gave an Account of the Discourse he had had with *Carrasco* to the Vice-Roy, who was vex'd to think that so much pleasant Diversion was like to be lost to all those that were acquainted with the Don's Follies.

Six Days did Don *Quixote* keep his Bed, very dejected, sullen, and out of Humour, and full of severe and black Reflections on his fatal Overthrow. *Sancho* was his Comforter, and among other his Crumbs of Comfort, My dear Master, quoth he, chear up, come pluck up a good Heart, and be thankful for coming off no worse. Why, a Man has broke his Neck with a less Fall, and you han't so much as a broken Rib. Consider, Sir, that they that game, sometimes must lose; we must not always look for Bacon where we see the Hooks. Come, Sir, cry a Fig for the Doctor, since you won't need him this Bout; let us jog home fair and softly, without thinking any more of sauntring up and down no Body knows whither in Quest of Adventures and bloody Noses. Why, Sir, I am the greatest Loser, an you go to that, though 'tis you that are in the worst Pickle. 'Tis true, I was weary of being a Governor, and gave over all Thoughts that Way; but yet I never parted with my Inclination of being an Earl; and now if you miss being a King, by casting off your Knight-Errantry, poor I may go whistle for my Earldom. No more of that, *Sancho*, said Don *Quixote*; I shall only retire for a Year, and then re-assume my honourable Profession, which

489

will undoubtedly secure Me a Kingdom, and Thee an Earl-dom. Heav'n grant it may, quoth *Sancho*, and no Mischief betide us: Hope well, and have well, says the Proverb.

Don *Antonio* coming in, broke off the Discourse, and with great Signs of Joy calling to Don *Quixote*, Reward me, Sir, cry'd he, for my good News; Don *Gregorio* and the Renegado are safe arriv'd, they are now at the Vice-Roy's Palace, and will be here this Moment. The Knight was a little reviv'd at this News; Truly, Sir, said he to Don *Antonio*, I could almost be sorry for his good Fortune, since he has forestall'd the Glory I should have acquir'd, in releasing, by the Strength of my Arm, not only him, but all the Christian Slaves in *Barbary*. But whither am I transported, Wretch that I am! Am I not miserably conquered, shamefully overthrown! forbidden the Paths of Glory for a whole long tedious Year? What, should I boast, who am fitter for a Distaff than a Sword! No more of that, quoth *Sancho*: Better my Hog dirty at Home, than no Hog at all. Let the Hen live, though she have the Pip. To Day for thee, and to Morrow for me. Never lay this ill Fortune to Heart; he that's down to Day, may be up to Morrow, unless he has a Mind to lie a Bed. Hang Bruises; so rouse, Sir, and bid Don *Gregorio* welcome to *Spain*; for by the Hurry in the House, I believe he's come; and so it happen'd, for Don *Gregorio* having paid his Duty to the Vice-Roy, and given him an Account of his Delivery, was just arriv'd at Don *Antonio's* with the Renegado, very impatient to see *Anna Felix*. He had chang'd the Female Habit he wore when he was freed, for one suitable to his Sex, which he had from a Captive who came along with him in the Vessel, and appear'd a very amiable and handsom Gentle-man, though not above eighteen Years of Age. *Ricote* and his Daughter went out to meet him, the Father with Tears, and the Daughter with a joyful Modesty. Their Salutation was reserv'd, without an Embrace, their Love being too refin'd for any loose Behaviour: But their Beauties surpriz'd every Body: Silence was emphatical in their Joys, and their Eyes spoke more Love than their Tongues could express. The Renegado gave a short Account of the Success of his Voyage, and Don *Gregorio* briefly related the Shifts he was put to among the Women in his Confinement, which shew'd his Wit and Discretion to be much above his Years. *Ricote* gratify'd the Ship's Crew very nobly, and particularly the Renegado, who was once more receiv'd into the Bosom of the Church, having with due Penance and sincere Repentance purify'd himself from all his former Uncleanness.

Some few Days after, the Vice-Roy, in concert with Don *Antonio*, took such Measures as were expedient, to get the Banishment of *Ricote* and his Daughter repeal'd, judging it no Inconvenience to the Nation, that so just and orthodox Persons should remain among 'em. Don *Antonio* being oblig'd to go to Court about some other Matters, offer'd to sollicit in their Behalf, hinting to him, that, through the Intercession of Friends, and more powerful Bribes, many difficult Matters were brought about there to the Satisfaction of the Parties. There is no relying upon Favour and Bribes in our Business, said *Ricote*, who was by, for the great Don *Bernardino de Velasco*, Count *de Salazar*, to whom the King gave the Charge of our Expulsion, is a Person of too strict and rigid Justice, to be mov'd either by Money, Favour, or Affection; and though I cannot deny him the Character of a merciful Judge in other Matters, yet his piercing and diligent Policy finds the Body of our *Moriscan* Race to be so corrupted, that Amputation is the only Cure. He is an *Argus* in his Ministry, and by his watchful Eyes has discover'd the most secret Springs of their Machinations, and resolving to prevent the Danger which the whole Kingdom was in, from such a powerful Multitude of inbred Foes, he took the most effectual Means; for after all, lopping off the Branches may only prune the Tree, and make the poisonous Fruit spring faster; but to overthrow it from the Root, proves a sure Deliverance; nor can the Great *Philip* the Third be too much extoll'd; first, for his Heroick Resolution in so nice and weighty an Affair, and then for his Wisdom in intrusting Don *Bernardino de Velasco* with the Execution of this Design. Well, when I come to Court, said Don *Antonio* to *Ricote*, I will however use the most advisable Means, and leave the rest to Providence. Don *Gregorio* shall go with me to comfort his Parents, that have long mourn'd for his Absence. *Anna Felix* shall stay here with my Wife, or in some Monastery; and as for honest *Ricote*, I dare engage the Vice-Roy will be satisfy'd to let him remain under his Protection till he sees how I succeed. The Vice-Roy consented to all this; but Don *Gregorio* fearing the worst, was unwilling to leave his fair Mistress; however, considering that he might return to her after he had seen his Parents, he yielded to the Proposal, and so *Anna Felix* remain'd with Don *Antonio's* Lady, and *Ricote* with the Vice-Roy.

Two Days after, Don *Quixote*, being somewhat recover'd, took his Leave of Don *Antonio*, and having caus'd his Armour to be laid on *Dapple*, he set forwards on his Journey home: *Sancho* thus being forc'd to trudge after him on Foot. On the other Side, Don *Gregorio* bid adieu to *Anna Felix*, and their Separation, though but for a while, was attended with Floods of Tears, and all the Excess of passionate Sorrow. *Ricote* offer'd him a thousand Crowns, but he refus'd them, and only borrow'd five of Don *Antonio*, to repay him at Court.

XXXIII: WHICH TREATS OF THAT WHICH SHALL BE SEEN BY HIM THAT READS IT, AND HEARD BY HIM THAT LISTENS WHEN 'TIS READ

DON *Quixote*, as he went out of *Barcelona*, cast his Eyes on the Spot of Ground where he was overthrown. Here once *Troy* stood, said he; here my unhappy Fate, and not my Cowardice, depriv'd me of all the Glories I had purchas'd. Here Fortune, by an unexpected Reverse, made me sensible of her Unconstancy and Fickleness. Here my Exploits suffer'd a total Eclipse; and, in short, here fell my Happiness, never to rise again. *Sancho* hearing his Master thus dolefully paraphrasing on his Misfortune, Good Sir, quoth he, 'tis as much the Part of great Spirits to have Patience when the World frowns upon 'em, as to be joyful when all goes well: And I judge of it by my self; for if when I was a Governor I was merry, now I am but a poor Squire afoot I am not sad. And indeed I have heard say, that this same She Thing they call Fortune, is a whimsical freakish drunken Quean, and blind into the Bargain; so that she neither sees what she does, nor knows whom she raises, nor whom she casts down. Thou art very much a Philosopher, *Sancho*, said Don *Quixote*, thou talk'st very sensibly. I wonder how thou cam'st by all this; but I must tell thee there is no such Thing as Fortune in the World; nor does any Thing that happens here below of Good or Ill come by Chance, but by the particular Providence of Heaven; and this makes good the Proverb, That every Man may thank himself for his own Fortune. For my Part, I have been the Maker of mine, but for want of using the Discretion I ought to have us'd, all my presumptuous Edifice sunk, and tumbl'd down at once. I might well have consider'd, that *Rosinante* was too weak and feeble to withstand the Knight of the *White Moon's* huge and strong-built Horse. However, I would needs adventure; I did the best I could, and was overcome. Yet though it has cost me my Honour, I have not lost, nor can I lose, my Integrity to perform my Promise. When I was a Knight-Errant, valiant and bold, the Strength of my Hands and my Actions gave a Reputation to my Deeds; and now I am no more than a dismounted Squire, the Performance of my Promise shall give a Reputation to my Words. Trudge on then, Friend *Sancho*, and let us get home, to pass the Year of our Probation. In that Retirement we shall recover new Vigour to return to that, which is never to be forgotten by me, I mean the Profession of Arms. Sir, quoth *Sancho*, 'tis no such Pleasure to beat the Hoof as I do, that I shou'd be for large Marches. Let us hang up this Armour of yours upon some Tree, in the room of one of those Highwaymen that hang hereabouts in Clusters; and when I am got upon *Dapple's* Back, we will ride as fast as you please: For to think I can mend my Pace, and foot it all the Way, is what you must excuse me in. Thou hast spoken to Purpose, *Sancho*, said Don *Quixote*; let my Arms be hung for a Trophy, and underneath, or about 'em, we will carve on the Bark of the Trees the same Inscription, which was written near the Trophy of *Orlando's* Arms:

> *Let none but he these Arms displace,*
> *Who dares* Orlando's *Fury face.*

Why, this is as I'd have it, quoth *Sancho*; and were it not that we shall want *Rosinante* upon the Road, 'twere not amiss to leave him hanging too. Now I think better on't, said Don *Quixote*, neither the Armour nor the Horse shall be serv'd so. It shall never be said of me, *For good Service, bad Reward*. Why that's well said, quoth *Sancho*, for indeed 'tis a Saying among Wise Men, that the Fault of the Ass must not be laid on the Packsaddle; and therefore, since in this last Job You your self were in Fault, even punish your self, and let not your Fury wreak it self upon your poor Armour, bruis'd and battered with doing you Service, nor upon the Tameness of *Rosinante*, that good-condition'd Beast, nor yet upon the Tenderness of my Feet, requiring them to travel more than they ought.

They pass'd that Day, and four more after that, in such kind of Discourse, without meeting any Thing that might interrupt their Journey; but on the fifth Day, as they enter'd into a Country Town, they saw a great Company of People at an Inn-Door, being got together for Pastime, as being a Holiday. As soon as Don *Quixote* drew near, he heard one of the Country-

494

men cry to the rest, look ye now, we'll leave it to one of these two Gentlemen that are coming this Way, they know neither of the Parties: Let either of 'em decide the Matter. That I will with all my Heart, said Don *Quixote*, and with all the Equity imaginable, if you'll but state the Case right to me. Why, Sir, said the Countryman, the Business is this; One of our Neigh-bours here in this Town, so fat and so heavy, that he weighs eleven *Arrobas*,* or eleven Quarters of a Hundred, (for that's the same Thing) has challeng'd another Man o' this Town, that weighs not half so much, to run with him a hundred Paces with equal Weight. Now he that gave the Challenge, being ask'd how they should make equal Weight, demands that the other who weighs but five Quarters of a hundred, should carry a hundred and an half of Iron, and so the Weight, he says, will be equal. Hold, Sir, cry'd *Sancho* before Don *Quixote* cou'd answer, this Business belongs to me, that come so lately from being a Governor, and a Judge, as all the World knows; I ought to give Judgment in this doubtful Case. Do then, with all my Heart, Friend *Sancho*, said Don *Quixote*, for I am not fit to give Crumbs to a Cat,† my Brain is so disturb'd, and out of Order. *Sancho* having thus got Leave, and all the Countrymen stand-ing about him, gaping to hear him give Sentence, Brothers, quoth he, I must tell you, that the fat Man is in the wrong Box, there's no manner of Reason in what he asks; for if, as I always heard say, he that is challeng'd may chuse his Weapons, there's no Reason that he should chuse such as may incumber him, and hinder him from getting the better of him that defy'd him. Therefore 'tis my Judgment, that he who gave the Chal-lenge, and is so big and so fat, shall cut, pare, slice, or shave off a hundred and fifty Pounds of his Flesh, here and there, as he thinks fit; and then being reduc'd to the Weight of t'other, both Parties may run their Race upon equal Terms. By fore *George*, quoth one of the Country-People that had heard the Sentence, this Gentleman has spoken like one of the Saints in Heaven; he has given Judgment like a Casuist; but I warrant

---

* *An* Arroba *is a quarter of an Hundred Weight.* † *Alluding to the Custom in* Spain, *of an old or disabled Soldier's carrying Offals of Tripe or Liver about the Streets to feed the Cats.——Poor* Quixote's *Arrogance is mightily abated by his being vanquish'd.*

the fat Squab loves his Flesh too well to part with the least
Sliver of it, much less will he part with a Hundred and Half.
Why then, quoth another Fellow, the best Way will be not to
let 'em run at all; for then *Lean* need not venture to sprain his
Back by running with such a Load; and *Fat* need not cut out
his pamper'd Sides into Collops: So let half the Wager be spent
in Wine, and let's take these Gentlemen to the Tavern that
has the best, *and lay the Cloak upon me when it rains.* I return
ye Thanks, Gentlemen, said Don *Quixote,* but I cannot stay a
Moment, for dismal Thoughts and Disasters force me to appear
unmannerly, and to travel at an uncommon Rate; and so saying,
he clapp'd Spurs to *Rosinante,* and mov'd forwards, leaving
the People to descant on his strange Figure, and the rare Parts
of his Groom, for such they took *Sancho* to be. If the Man be so
wise, quoth another of the Country-Fellows to the rest, bless
us! what shall we think of the Master! I'll hold a Wager, if
they be going to study at *Salamanca,* they will come to be Lord
Chief-Justices in a trice; for there's nothing more easy, 'tis but
studying and studying again, and having a little Favour and
good Luck; and when a Man least dreams of it, slap, he shall
find himself with a Judge's Gown upon his Back, or a Bishop's
Mitre upon his Head.

That Night the Master and the Man took up their Lodging
in the Middle of a Field, under the Roof of the open Sky; and
the next Day, as they were on their Journey, they saw coming
towards 'em, a Man a-foot with a Wallet about his Neck, and
a Javelin or Dart in his Hand, just like a Foot-Post: The Man
mended his Pace when he came near Don *Quixote,* and almost
running, came, with a great deal of Joy in his Looks, and embrac'd Don *Quixote's* right Thigh, for he cou'd reach no
higher. My Lord Don *Quixote de la Mancha,* cry'd he, oh!
how heartily glad my Lord Duke will be when he understands
you are coming again to his Castle, for there he is still with my
Lady Dutchess. I don't know you, Friend, answer'd Don *Quixote,* nor can I imagine who you shou'd be, unless you tell me
yourself. My Name is *Tosilos,* an't please your Honour; I am
my Lord Duke's Footman, the same who wou'd not fight with
you about *Donna Rodriguez's* Daughter. Bless me! cry'd Don
Quixote, is it possible you should be the Man whom those

Enemies of mine, the *Magicians*, transform'd into a Lacquey, to deprive me of the Honour of that Combat? Softly, good Sir, reply'd the Footman, there was neither Inchantment nor Transformation in the Case. I was as much a Footman when I enter'd the Lists, as when I went out; and it was because I had a Mind to marry the young Gentlewoman, that I refus'd to fight. But I was sadly disappointed; for when you were gone, my Lord Duke had me soundly bang'd, for not doing as he order'd me in that Matter; and the Upshot was this, *Donna Rodriguez* is pack'd away to seek her Fortune, and the Daughter is shut up in a Nunnery. As for me I am going to *Barcelona*, with a Packet of Letters from my Lord to the Vice-Roy. However, Sir, if you please to take a Sup, I have here a Calabash full of the best. 'Tis a little hot, I must own, but 'tis neat, and I have some excellent Cheese, that will make it go down, I'll warrant ye. I take you at your Word, quoth *Sancho*, I am no proud Man, leave Ceremonies to the Church, and so let's drink, honest *Tosilos*, in spite of all the Inchanters in the *Indies*. Well, *Sancho*, said Don *Quixote*, thou art certainly the veriest Glutton that ever was, and the silliest Blockhead in the World, else thou wouldst consider that this Man thou seest here, is inchanted, and a Sham-Lacquey. Then stay with him if thou thinkest fit, and gratify thy voracious Appetite; for my Part, I'll ride softly on before. *Tosilos* smil'd, and laying his Bottle and his Cheese upon the Grass, he and *Sancho* sat down there, and like sociable Messmates, never stirr'd till they had quite clear'd the Wallet of all that was in it fit for the Belly; and this with such an Appetite, that when all was consum'd, they lick'd the very Packet of Letters, because it smelt of Cheese. While they were thus employ'd, hang me, quoth *Tosilos*, if I know what to make of this Master of yours: doubtless he ought to be reckon'd a Madman. Why *ought*?* reply'd *Sancho*; he *owes* nothing to any Body; for he pays for every Thing, especially where Madness is current: There he might be the richest Man in the Kingdom, he has such a Stock of it. I see it full well, and full well I tell him of it: but what boots it? especially now that he's all in the Dumps, for having

---

* A double entendre *upon the Word* deve, *which is put for* must, *the Sign of a Mood, or* for owing a Debt.

been worsted by the Knight of the *White Moon*. *Tosilos* beg-
g'd of *Sancho* to tell him that Story; but *Sancho* said it would
not be handsom to let his Master stay for him, but that next
time they met he'd tell him the whole Matter. With that they
got up, and after the Squire had brush'd his Cloaths, and
shaken off the Crumbs from his Beard, he drove *Dapple* along;
and with a *good by t'ye*, left *Tosilos*, in order to overtake his
Master, who staid for him under the Cover of a Tree.

XXXIV: HOW DON QUIXOTE RESOLV'D TO TURN SHEPHERD, AND LEAD A RURAL LIFE, FOR THE YEAR'S TIME HE WAS OBLIG'D NOT TO BEAR ARMS; WITH OTHER PASSAGES TRULY GOOD AND DIVERTING

IF Don *Quixote* was much disturb'd in Mind before his Overthrow, he was much more disquieted after it. While he stay'd for his Squire under the Tree, a thousand Thoughts crowded into his Head, like Flies into a Honey-Pot; sometimes he ponder'd on the Means to free *Dulcinea* from Inchantment, and at others, on the Life he was to lead during his involuntary Retirement. In this brown Study, *Sancho* came up to him, crying up *Tosilos* as the honestest Fellow and the most Gentleman-like Footman in the World. Is it possible, *Sancho*, said Don *Quixote*, thou should'st still take that Man for a real Lacquey? Hast thou forgot how thou saw'st *Dulcinea* converted and transformed into the Resemblance of a rustick Wench, and the Knight of the *Mirrours* into the Batchelor *Carrasco*; and all this by the Necromantick Arts of those evil-minded Magicians, that persecute me? But laying this aside, pr'ythee tell me, did'st thou not ask *Tosilos* what became of *Altisidora*: Whether she bemoan'd my Absence, or dismiss'd from her Breast those amorous Sentiments that disturb'd her when I was near? Faith and Troth, quoth *Sancho*, my Head ran on something else, and I was too well employ'd to think of such foolish Stuff. Body of me! Sir, are you now in a Mood to ask about other Folks Thoughts, especially their Love-Thoughts too? Look you, said Don *Quixote*, there's a great deal of Difference between those Actions that proceed from Love, and those that are the Effect of Gratitude. It is possible a Gentleman should not be at all amorous, but strictly speaking, he cannot be ungrateful. 'Tis very likely that *Altisidora* lov'd me well; she presented me, as thou know'st, with three Night-Caps; she wept and took on when I went away; curs'd me, abus'd me, and in spite of Modesty, gave a Loose to her Passion; all Tokens that she was deeply in Love with me, for the Anger of Lovers commonly vents it self in Curses. It was not in my Power to give her any Hopes, nor had I any costly Present to bestow on her; for all I have reserv'd is for *Dulcinea*; and the Treasures of a Knight-Errant are but Fairy-Gold, and a delusive Good: So all I can do, is only to remember the unfortunate Fair, without Prejudice however to the Rights of my *Dulcinea*, whom thou greatly injur'st, *Sancho*, by delaying the Accomplishment of the Penance that must free the poor Lady from Misery. And since thou art so ungenerously sparing of that pamper'd Hide of thine, may I see it devour'd by Wolves, rather than see it kept so charily for the Worms. Sir, quoth *Sancho*, to deal plainly with you, it can't for the Blood of me, enter into my Head, that jirking my Back-side will signify a Straw to the Dis-inchanting of the Inchanted. Sir, 'tis as if we shou'd say, If your Head akes, anoint your Shins. At least, I dare be sworn that in all the Stories of Knight-Errantry you have thumb'd over, you never knew Flogging unbe-witch'd any Body. However, when I can find my self in the Humour, d'ye see, I'll about it; when Time serves, I'll chastise my self, ne'er fear. I wish thou would'st, answer'd Don *Quix-ote*, and may Heaven give thee Grace at last to understand how much 'tis thy Duty to relieve thy Mistress; for as she is mine, by Consequence she is thine, since thou belong'st to me.

Thus they went on talking, till they came near the Place where the Bulls had run over 'em; and Don *Quixote* knowing it again, *Sancho*, said he, yonder's that Meadow where we met the fine Shepherdesses, and the gallant Shepherds, who had a Mind to renew or imitate the pastoral *Arcadia*. 'Twas certainly a new and ingenious Conceit. If thou think'st well of it, we'll follow their Example, and turn Shepherds too, at least for the Time I am to lay aside the Profession of Arms; I'll buy a Flock of Sheep, and every thing that's fit for a pastoral Life, and so calling my self the Shepherd *Quixotis*, and thee the Shepherd *Pansino*, we'll range the Woods, the Hills and Meadows, singing and versifying. We'll drink the liquid Crys-tal, sometimes out of the Fountains, and sometimes from the purling Brooks, and the swift gliding Streams. The Oaks, the Cork-Trees, and Chesnut-Trees will afford us both Lodging and Diet; the Willows will yield us their Shade; the Roses present us their inoffensive Sweets; and the spacious Meads will be our Carpets, diversify'd with Colours of all Sorts: Bless'd with the purest Air, and unconfin'd alike, we shall breathe that and Freedom. The Moon and Stars, our Tapers of the Night, shall light our Evening Walks. Light Hearts will make us merry, and Mirth will make us sing. Love will inspire us with a Theme and Wit, and *Apollo* with harmonious Lays. So shall we become famous, not only while we live, but make our Loves eternal as our Songs. As I live, quoth *Sancho*, this Sort of Life nicks me to an Hair,* and I fancy, that if the Batchelor *Samson Carrasco* and Master *Nicholas* have but once a Glimpse of it, they'll e'en turn Shepherds too; nay, 'tis well if the Curate does not put in for one among the rest, for he's a notable Joker, and merrily inclined. That was well thought on, said Don *Quixote*: And then if the Batchelor will make one among us, as I doubt not but he will, he may call himself the Shepherd *Samsonino*, or *Carrascon*; and Master *Nicholas Niculoso*, as formerly old *Boscan* call'd himself *Nemoroso*.† For the Curate, I don't well know what Name we shall give him, unless we should call him the Shepherd *Curiambro*. As for the Shepherdesses with whom we must fall in Love, we can't be at a Loss to find 'em Names, there are enough for us to pick and chuse; and since my Mistress's Name is not improper for a Shepherdess, any more than for a Princess, I will not trouble myself to get a better; thou mayst call thine as thou pleasest. For my Part, quoth *Sancho*, I don't think of any other Name for mine, but *Teresona*, that will fit her fat Sides full well, and is taken from her Christian Name too: so when I come to mention her in my Verses, every Body will know her to be my Wife, and commend my Honesty, as being one that is not for picking another Man's Lock: As for the Curate, he must be contented without a Shepherdess, for good Example's sake. And for the Batchelor, let him take his own Choice, if he means to have one. Bless me! said Don *Quixote*, what a Life shall we lead! What a Melody of Oaten Reeds,

---

* *This kind of Life squares and corners with me exactly.* Quadrado y es-quinado: *Alluding to the Corner-Stone of a Building, which answers both Ways.* † *In plain* English, *as if Mr Wood (for so* Bosque *signifies), should call himself Mr* Grove, *(so* Nemus *signifies in* Latin).

and *Zamora** Bag-Pipes shall we have resounding in the Air!
What Intermixture of Tabors, Morrice Bells, and Fiddles! and
if to all the different Instruments we add the *Albogues*, we
shall have all Manner of Pastoral Musick. What are the
Albogues? quoth *Sancho*: For I don't remember I've ever seen
or heard of 'em in my Life. They are, said Don *Quixote*, a
Sort of Instruments made of Brass-Plates, rounded like Candlesticks: The one shutting into the other, there arises through
the Holes or Stops, and the Trunk or Hollow, an odd Sound,
which if not very grateful, or harmonious, is however not altogether disagreeable, but does well enough with the Rusticity
of the Bag-Pipe and Tabor. You must know the Word is *Moorish*, as indeed are all those in our *Spanish*, that begin with
an *Al*, as *Almoaza*, *Almorsar*, *Alhombra*, *Alguasil*, *Alucema*,
Almacen, *Alcanzia*, and the like, which are not very many.
And we have also but three *Moorish* Words in our Tongue that
end in *I*; and they are *Borcequi*, *Zaquicami* and *Maravedi*; for
as to *Alheli* and *Alfaqui*, they are as well known to be *Arabick*
by their beginning with *Al*, as their ending in *I*. I cou'd not forbear telling thee so much by the Bye, thy *Quere* about *Albogue*
having brought it into my Head. There is one Thing more that
will go a great Way towards making us compleat in our new
Kind of Life, and that's Poetry; thou know'st I am somewhat
given that Way, and the Batchelor *Carrasco* is a most accom-
plished Poet, to say nothing of the Curate; though I'll hold a
Wager he is a Dabbler in it too, and so is Master *Nicholas*,
I dare say; for all your Barbers are notable Scrapers and
Songsters. For my Part, I'll complain of Absence, thou shalt
celebrate thy own Loyalty and Constancy; the Shepherd
Carrascon shall expostulate on his Shepherdesses Disdain,
and the Pastor *Curiambro* chuse what Subject he likes best,
and so all will be managed to our Hearts Content. Alas! quoth
Sancho, I am so unlucky, that I fear me, I shall never live to see
these blessed Days. How shall I lick up the curds & cream! I'll
ne'er be without a wooden Spoon in my Pocket. Oh, how many
of them will I make! What Garlands and what pretty pastoral
Fancies will I contrive! which though they mayn't recommend

* *Zamorra is a City in* Spain, *famous for that Sort of Musick, as* Lanca-
shire *is in* England *for the Horn-pipe.*

me for Wisdom, will make me pass at least for an ingenious Fellow. My Daughter *Sanchica* shall bring us our Dinner a Field. But hold, have a Care of that! she's a young likely Wench, and some Shepherds are more Knaves than Fools; and I would not have my Girl go out for Wool, and come home shorn; for Love and wicked Doings, are to be found in the Fields, as well as in Cities; and in a Shepherd's Cot, as well as in a King's Palace. Take away the Cause, and the Effect ceases; what the Eye ne'er sees, the Heart ne'er rues. One Pair of Heels is worth two Pair Hands; and we must watch as well as pray. No more Proverbs, good *Sancho*, cry'd Don *Quixote*; any one of these is sufficient to make us know thy Meaning. I have told thee often enough not to be so lavish of thy Proverbs; but 'tis all lost upon thee: I preach in a Desert: my Mother whips me, and I whip the Top. Faith and Troth, quoth *Sancho*, this is just as the Saying is, the Porridge-Pot calls the Kettle Black-Arse——You chide me for speaking Proverbs, and yet you bring 'em out two at a Time. Look you, *Sancho*, those I speak, are to the Purpose, but thou fetchest thine in by Head and Shoulders, to their utter Disgrace, and thy own. But no more at this Time, it grows late, let us leave the Road a little, and take up our Quarters yonder in the Fields; to Morrow will be a new Day. They did accordingly, and made a slender Meal, as little to *Sancho's* liking as his hard Lodging; which brought the Hardships of Knight-Erranting fresh into his Thoughts, and made him wish for the better Entertainment he had sometimes found, as at Don *Diego's*, *Camacho's*, and Don *Antonio's* Houses; but he consider'd after all, that it cou'd not be always fair Weather, nor was it always foul; so he betook himself to his Rest till Morning, and his Master to the usual Exercise of his roving Imaginations.

XXXV: THE ADVENTURE OF THE HOGS

THE Night was pretty dark, though the Moon still kept her Place in the Sky; but it was in such a Part, as oblig'd her to be invisible to us; for now and then Madam *Diana* takes a Turn to the *Antipodes*, and then the Mountains in Black, and the Valleys in Darkness, mourn her Ladyship's Absence. Don *Quixote*, after his first Sleep, thought Nature sufficiently refresh'd, and would not yield to the Temptations of a second. *Sancho* indeed did not enjoy a *second*, but from a different Reason: for he usually made but one Nap of the whole Night, which was owing to the Soundness of his Constitution, and his Unexperience of Cares, that lay so heavy upon Don *Quixote*.

Sancho, said the Knight, after he had pull'd the Squire till he had waked him too, I am amaz'd at the Insensibility of thy Temper. Thou art certainly made of Marble or solid Brass, thou liest so without either Motion or Feeling: Thou sleep'st while I wake; thou sing'st while I mourn; and while I am ready to faint for want of Sustenance, thou art lazy and unwieldy with mere Gluttony. It is the Part of a good Servant, to share in the Afflictions of his Master. Observe the Stillness of the Night, and the solitary Place we are in. 'Tis Pity such an Opportunity should be lost in Sloth and unactive Rest; Rouse for Shame, step a little aside, and with a good Grace, and a cheerful Heart, score me up some three or four Hundred Lashes upon thy Back, towards the Disinchanting of *Dulcinea*. This I make my earnest Request, being resolv'd never to be rough with thee again upon this Account; for I must confess thou can'st lay a heavy Hand on a Man upon Occasion. When that Performance is over, we'll pass the Remainder of the Night in Chanting, I of Absence, and thou of Constancy, and so begin those Pastoral Exercises, which are to be our Employment at Home. Sir, answer'd *Sancho*, do you take me for a Monk or Friar, that I should start up in the middle of the Night, and discipline myself at this rate? Or, do you think it such an easy Matter to scourge and clapper-claw my Back one Moment, and fall a singing the next? Look you, Sir, say not a Word more of this Whipping; for as I love my Flesh, you'll put me upon making some rash Oath or other that you won't like, and then if the bare brushing of my Coat would do you any Good, you shou'd not have it, much less the currying of my Hide, and so let me go to sleep again. Oh obdurate Heart! cry'd Don *Quixote*; Oh, impious Squire! Oh Nourishment and Favours ill bestow'd! Is this my Reward for having got thee a Government, and my good Intentions to get thee an Earldom, or an Equivalent at least, which I dare engage to do when this Year of our Obscurity is elaps'd; for, in short, *Post tenebras spero lucem*. That I don't understand, quoth *Sancho*, but This I very well know, that while I am asleep, I feel neither Hope nor Despair; I am free from Pain and insensible of Glory. Now Blessings light on him that first invented this same Sleep: It covers a Man all over, Thoughts and all, like a Cloak; 'tis Meat for the Hungry, Drink for the Thirsty, Heat for the Cold, and Cold for the Hot. 'Tis the current Coin that purchases all the Pleasures of the World cheap; and the Balance that sets the King and the Shepherd, the Fool and the Wise-man even. There is only one Thing, which somebody once put into my Head, that I dislike in Sleep; 'tis, that it resembles Death; there's very little Difference between a Man in his first Sleep, and a Man in his last Sleep. Most elegantly spoken, said Don *Quixote*! Thou hast much outdone any Thing I ever heard thee say before, which confirms me in the Truth of one of thy own Proverbs; *Birth is much, but Breeding more*. Cod's me! Master of mine, cry'd *Sancho*, I'm not the only He now that threads Proverbs, for you tack 'em together faster than I do, I think: I see no Difference, but that yours come in Season, mine out of Season; but for all that, they are all but Proverbs.

Thus they were employ'd, when their Ears were alarm'd with a kind of a hoarse and grunting Noise, that spread it self over all the adjacent Valleys. Presently Don *Quixote* started up on his Legs, and laid his Hand to his Sword: As for *Sancho*, he immediately set up some Intrenchments about him, clapping the Bundle of Armour on one Side, and fortifying the other with the Ass's Pack-saddle, and then gathering himself up of a Heap, squatted down under *Dapple's* Belly, where he lay panting, as full of Fears as his Master of Surprize; while

every Moment the Noise grew louder, as the Cause of it approach'd, to the Terror of the one, at least; for as for t'other,
'tis sufficiently known what his Valour was.

Now the Occasion was this: Some Fellows were driving a
Herd of above six hundred Swine to a certain Fair; and with
their grunting and squeaking, the filthy Beasts made such a
horrible Noise, that Don *Quixote* and *Sancho* were almost
stunn'd with it, and could not imagine whence it proceeded.
But at length the Knight and Squire standing in their Way, the
rude Bristly Animals came thronging up all in a Body, and without any Respect of Persons, some running between the Knight's
Legs, and some between the Squire's, threw down both Master and Man, having not only insulted *Sancho's* Intrenchments,
but also thrown down *Rosinante*: And having thus broke in
upon 'em, on they went, and bore down all before 'em, overthrowing Pack-saddle, Armour, Knight, Squire, Horse and all;
crowding, treading and trampling over them all at a horrid
Rate. *Sancho* was the first that made a shift to recover his
Legs; and having by this time found out what the Matter was,
he call'd to his Master to lend him his Sword, and swore he
would stick at least half a dozen of those rude Porkers immediately. No, no, my Friend, said Don *Quixote*, let 'em e'en
go; Heaven inflicts this Disgrace upon my guilty Head; for 'tis
but a just Punishment that Dogs should devour, Hornets sting,
and vile Hogs trample on a vanquish'd Knight-Errant. And
belike, quoth *Sancho*, that Heaven sends the Fleas to sting,
the Lice to bite, and Hunger to famish us poor Squires, for
keeping these vanquish'd Knights Company. If we Squires
were the Sons of those Knights, or any ways related to 'em,
why then, something might be said for our bearing a Share of
their Punishment, though it were to the third and fourth Generation. But what have the *Panças* to do with the *Quixotes*?
Well, let's to our old Places again, and sleep out the little that's
left of the Night. To Morrow is a new Day. Sleep, *Sancho*,
cry'd Don *Quixote*, sleep, for thou wert born to sleep; but I,
who was design'd to be still waking, intend before *Aurora*
ushers in the Sun, to give a Loose to my Thoughts, and vent my
Conceptions in a Madrigal, that I made last Night unknown to
thee. Methinks, quoth *Sancho*, a Man can't be in great Afflic-

tion, when he can turn his Brain to the making of Verses. Therefore, you may versify on as long as you please, and I'll sleep it out as much as I can. This said, he laid himself down on the Ground, as he thought best, and hunching himself close together, fell fast asleep, without any Disturbance from either Debts, Suretiship, or any Care whatsoever. On the other side, Don *Quixote* leaning against the Trunk of a Beech, or a Cork-Tree (for 'tis not determin'd by *Cid Hamet* which it was) sung in Consort with his Sighs, the following Composition:

A SONG TO LOVE

Whene'er I think what mighty Pain,
The Slave must bear who drags thy Chain,
Oh! Love, for Ease to Death I go,
The Cure of Thee, the Cure of Life and Woe.

But when, alas! I think I'm sure
Of that which must by killing cure,
The Pleasure that I feel in Death,
Proves a strong Cordial to restore my Breath.

Thus Life each Moment makes me die,
And Death it self new Life can give:
I Hopeless and Tormented lie,
And neither truly Die nor Live.

The many Tears as well as Sighs that accompany'd this musical Complaint, were a Sign that the Knight had deeply laid to Heart his late Defeat, and the Absence of his *Dulcinea*.

Now Day came on, and the Sun darting his Beams on *Sancho's* Face, at last awak'd him: whereupon, rubbing his Eyes, and yawning and stretching his drowsy Limbs, he perceived the Havock that the Hogs had made in his Baggage, which made him wish, not only the Herd, but somebody else too at the Devil for Company. In short, the Knight and the Squire both set forward on their Journey, and about the Close of the Evening, they discovered some half a Score Horsemen, and four or five Fellows on Foot, making directly towards them. Don *Quixote* at the Sight, felt a strange Emotion in his Breast, and *Sancho* fell a shivering from Head to Foot; for they perceiv'd that these Strangers were provided with Spears and Shields, and other warlike Implements: Whereupon the Knight turning to the Squire, Ah! *Sancho*, said he, were it lawful for me at this Time to bear Arms, and had I my Hands at Liberty and not ty'd up by my Promise, what a joyful Sight should I esteem this Squadron that approaches! But perhaps, notwithstanding my present Apprehensions, Things may fall out better than we expect.

By this Time the Horsemen with their Lances advanc'd, came close up to them without speaking a Word, and encompassing Don *Quixote* in a menacing Manner, with their Points levell'd to his Back and Breast, one of the Footmen, by laying his Finger upon his Mouth, signify'd to Don *Quixote*, that he must be mute; then taking *Rosinante* by the Bridle, he led him out of the Road, while the rest of the Footmen secured *Sancho* and *Dapple*, and drove them silently after Don *Quixote*, who attempted twice or thrice to ask the Cause of this Usage; but he no sooner began to open, but they were ready to run the Heads of their Spears down his Throat. Poor *Sancho* far'd worse yet; for as he offer'd to speak, one of the Foot-Guards gave him a Jagg with a Goad, and serv'd *Dapple* as bad, though the poor Beast had no Thought of saying a Word.

As it grew Night, they mended their Pace, and then the Darkness increas'd the Fears of the Captive Knight and Squire, especially when every Minute their Ears were tormented with these or such like Words: On, on, ye *Troglodytes*; Silence, ye *Barbarian* Slaves; Vengeance, ye *Anthropophagi*; Grumble not, ye *Scythians*; Be blind, ye murdering *Polyphemes*, ye devouring Lions. Bless us (thought *Sancho*) what Names do they call us here! *Trollopites*, *Barber's Slaves*, and *Andr'w Hodgepodgy*, *City-Cans*, and *Burframes*; I don't like the Sound of 'em. Here's one Mischief on the Neck of another. When a Man's down, down with him: I would compound for a good dry Beating, and glad to 'scape so too. Don *Quixote* was no less perplex'd, not being able to imagine the Reason either of their hard Usage or scurrilous Language, which hitherto promis'd but little Good. At last, after they had rode about an Hour in the Dark, they came to the Gates of a Castle, which Don *Quixote* presently knowing to be the Duke's, where he had so lately been; Heaven bless me, cry'd he, what do I see! Was not this

the Mansion of Civility and Humanity! But thus the Vanquish'd are doom'd to see every Thing frown upon 'em. With
that the two Prisoners were led into the great Court of the
Castle, and found such strange Preparations made there, as
increas'd at once their Fear, and their Amazement; as we shall
find in the next Chapter.

XXXVI: OF THE MOST SINGULAR AND STRANGEST ADVENTURE THAT BEFEL DON QUIXOTE IN THE WHOLE COURSE OF THIS FAMOUS HISTORY

ALL the Horse-men alighted, and the Footmen snatching up Don *Quixote* and *Sancho* in their Arms, hurry'd them into the Court-Yard, that was illuminated with above a hundred Torches, fix'd in huge Candlesticks; and about all the Galleries round the Court, were placed above five hundred Lights; insomuch, that all was Day in the Midst of the Darkness of the Night. In the Middle of the Court there was a Tomb, rais'd some two Yards from the Ground, with a large Pall of black Velvet over it, and round about it a hundred Tapers of Virgins-Wax, stood burning in Silver Candlesticks. Upon the Tomb lay the Body of a young Damsel, who, though to all Appearance dead, was yet so beautiful, that Death it self seem'd lovely in her Face. Her Head was crown'd with a Garland of fragrant Flowers, and supported by a Pillow of Cloth of Gold, and in her Hands, that were laid across her Breast, was seen a Branch of that yellow Palm, that us'd of old to adorn the Triumphs of Conquerors. On one Side of the Court there was a Kind of a Theatre erected, on which two Personages sat in Chairs, who by the Crowns upon their Heads, and Scepters in their Hands were, or at least appeared to be Kings. By the Side of the Theatre, at the Foot of the Steps by which the Kings ascended, two other Chairs were plac'd, and thither Don *Quixote* and *Sancho* were led, and caus'd to sit down; the Guards that conducted 'em continuing silent all the while, and making their Prisoners understand, by awful Signs, that They must also be silent. But there was no great Occasion for that Caution; for their Surprize was so great, that it had ty'd up their Tongues without it.

At the same Time two other Persons of Note ascended the Stage with a numerous Retinue, and seated themselves on two stately Chairs by the two Theatrical Kings. These Don *Quixote* presently knew to be the Duke and Dutchess, at whose Palace he had been so nobly entertained. But what he discover'd as the greatest Wonder, was, that the Corpse upon the Tomb was the Body of the fair *Altisidora*.

As soon as the Duke and Dutchess had ascended, Don *Quix-ote* and *Sancho* made 'em a profound Obeisance, which they returned with a short inclining of their Heads. Upon this a certain Officer enter'd the Court, and coming up to *Sancho*, he clapp'd over him a black Buckram Frock, all figur'd over with Flames of Fire, and taking off his Cap, he put on his Head a Kind of Mitre, such as is worn by those who undergo publick Penance by the Inquisition; whispering him in the Ear at the same Time, that if he did but offer to open his Lips, they would put a Gag in his Mouth, or murder him to rights. *Sancho* viewed himself over from Head to Foot, and was a little startl'd to see himself all over in Fire and Flames: but yet since he did not feel himself burn, he car'd not a Farthing. He pull'd off his Mitre, and found it pictured over with Devils; but he put it on again, and bethought himself, that since neither the Flames burn'd him, nor the Devils ran away with him, 'twas well enough. Don *Quixote* also stedfastly survey'd him, and in the midst of all his Apprehensions, could not forbear smiling to see what a strange Figure he made. And now in the midst of that profound Silence, while every thing was mute, and Expectation most attentive, a soft and charming Symphony of Flutes, that seemed to issue from the Hollow of the Tomb, agreeably fill'd their Ears. Then there appeared at the Head of the Monument, a young Man extremely handsom, and dress'd in a *Roman* Habit, who to the Musick of a Harp, touch'd by himself, sung the following Stanza's with an excellent Voice:

ALTISIDORA'S DIRGE

While slain, the fair Altisidora *lies*
  A Victim to Don Quixote's *cold Disdain;*
Here all Things mourn, all Pleasure with her dies,
  And Weeds of Woe disguise the Graces Train.

I'll sing the Beauties of her Face and Mind,
  Her hopeless Passion, her unhappy Fate;
Not Orpheus *self in Numbers more refin'd,*
  Her Charms, her Love, her Suff'rings could relate.

Nor shall the Fair alone in Life be sung,
Her boundless Praise in my immortal Choice;
In the cold Grave, when Death benums my Tongue,
For thee, bright Maid, my Soul shall find a Voice.

When from this narrow Cell my Spirit's free,
And wanders grieving with the Shades below,
Ev'n o'er Oblivion's Waves I'll sing to Thee;
And Hell it self shall sympathize in Woe.

Enough, cry'd one of the two Kings; no more, Divine Musician; it were an endless Task to enumerate the Perfections
of *Altisidora*, or give us the Story of her Fate. Nor is she dead,
as the ignorant Vulgar surmises; no, in the Mouth of Fame she
lives, and once more shall revive, as soon as *Sancho* has undergone the Penance that is decreed to restore her to the World.
Therefore, O *Rhadamanthus*! thou who sittest in joint Commission with Me in the opacous Shades of *Dis*, tremendous
Judge of Hell! Thou to whom the Decrees of Fate, inscrutable
to Mortals, are reveal'd, in order to restore this Damsel to
Life, open and declare 'em immediately, nor delay the promised Felicity of her Return, to comfort the drooping World.

Scarce had *Minos* finish'd his Charge, but *Rhadamanthus*
starting up; Proceed, said he, ye Ministers and Officers of the
Houshold, superior and inferior, high and low; proceed one
after another, and mark me *Sancho's* Chin with twenty-four
Twitches, give him twelve Pinches, and run six Pins into his
Arms and Backside; for *Altisidora's* Restoration depends on
the Performance of this Ceremony. *Sancho* hearing this, could
hold out no longer, but bawling out, Body of me! cry'd he, I'll
as soon turn *Turk*, as give you Leave to do all this. You shall
put no Chin or Countenance of mine upon any such Mortification. What the Devil can the spoiling of My Face signify to the
restoring of this Damsel? I may as soon turn up my broad End,
and awaken her with a Gun. *Dulcinea* is bewitch'd and I forsooth must flog my self, to free her from Witchcraft! And
here's *Altisidora* too, drops off of one Distemper or other, and
presently poor *Sancho* must be pull'd by the Handle of his
Face, his Skin fill'd with Oilet holes, and his Arms pinch'd
Black and Blue, to save Her from the Worms! No, no, you must

not think to put Tricks upon Travellers. An old Dog understands Trap.* Relent, cry'd *Rhadamanthus* aloud, thou Tyger, submit proud *Nimrod*, suffer and be silent, or thou dy'st: No Impossibility is required from thee; and therefore pretend not to expostulate on the Severity of thy Doom. Thy Face shall receive the Twitches, thy Skin shall be pinch'd, and thou shalt groan under the Penance. Begin, I say, ye Ministers of Justice, execute my Sentence, or, as I'm an honest Man, ye shall curse the Hour ye were born. At the same Time six old *Duena's*, or Waiting-women, appear'd in the Court, marching in a formal Procession one after another four of 'em wearing Spectacles, and all with their Right Hands held aloft, and their Wrists, according to the Fashion, about four Inches bare, to make their Hands seem the longer. *Sancho* no sooner spy'd them, but, roaring out like a Bull, Do with me what you please, cry'd he, let a Sackful of mad Cats lay their Claws on me, as they did on my Master in this Castle, drill me through with sharp Daggers, tear the Flesh from my Bones with red-hot Pincers, I'll bear it with Patience, and serve your Worships: But the Devil shall run away with me at once, before I'll suffer old Waiting-women to lay a Finger upon me. Don *Quixote* upon this broke Silence; Have Patience, my Son, cry'd he, and resign thy self to these Potentates, with Thanks to Heaven, for having endow'd thy Person with such a Gift, as to release the Inchanted, and raise the Dead from the Grave.

By this the Waiting-women were advanced up to *Sancho*, who, after much Persuasion, was at last wrought upon to settle himself in his Seat, and submit his Face and Beard to the Female Executioners; the first that approach'd gave him a clever Twitch, and then dropp'd him a Courtesy. Less Courtesy, and less Sauce, good Mrs Governante, cry'd *Sancho*; for, by the Life of *Pharaoh*, your Fingers stink of Vinegar. In short, all the Waiting-women, and most of the Servants came and twitch'd and pinch'd him decently, and he bore it all with unspeakable Patience. But when they came to prick him with Pins, he could contain no longer; but starting up in a pelting Chase, snatch'd up one of the Torches that stood near him, and swinging it round, put all the Women and the rest of his

* Tus, Tus, *in the Original. See this explain'd elsewhere.*

Tormentors to their Heels. Avaunt, cry'd he, ye Imps of the Devil, d'ye think my Backside is made of Brass, or that I intend to be your Master's Martyr, with a Horse-pox t'ye?

At the same Time *Altisidora*, who could not but be tired with lying so long upon her Back, began to turn herself on one Side, which was no sooner perceiv'd by the Spectators, but they all set up the Cry, *She lives, she lives!* Altisidora *lives!* And then *Rhadamanthus* addressing himself to *Sancho*, desir'd him to be pacify'd, for now the wonderful Recovery was effected. On the other Side Don *Quixote*, seeing *Altisidora* stir, went and threw himself on his Knees before *Sancho*; My dear Son, cry'd he, for now I will not call thee Squire, now is the Hour for thee to receive some of the Lashes that are incumbent upon thee for the Disinchanting of *Dulcinea*. This, I say, is the auspicious Time, when the Virtue of thy Skin is most mature and efficacious for working the Wonders that are expected from it. Out of the Frying-pan into the Fire, quoth *Sancho*; I have brought my Hogs to a fair Market truly; after I have been twing'd and tweak'd by the Nose, and every where, and my Buttocks stuck all over, and made a Pin-cushion of, I must be now whipp'd like a Top, must I? If you've a Mind to get rid of me, can't you as well tie a good Stone about my Neck, and tip me into a Well. Better make an End of me at once, than have me loaded so every foot like a Pack-horse with other Folks Burdens. Look ye, say but one Word more to me of any such Thing, and on my Soul, all the Fat shall be in the Fire.

By this Time *Altisidora* sat on the Tomb, and presently the Musick struck up, all the Instruments being join'd with the Voices of the Spectators, who cry'd aloud, Live, live, *Altisidora, Altisidora* live! The Duke and Dutchess got up, and with *Minos* and *Rhadamanthus*, accompany'd by Don *Quixote* and *Sancho*, went all in a Body to receive *Altisidora*, and hand her down from the Tomb. She pretending to faint, bow'd to the Duke and Dutchess, and also to the two Kings; but casting a skew Look upon Don *Quixote*, Heaven forgive that hardhearted lovely Knight, said she, whose Barbarity has made me an Inhabitant of the other World for ought I know a thousand Years. But to thee, said she, turning to *Sancho*, to thee, the most compassionate Squire that the World contains,

I return my Thanks for my Change from Death to Life; in Acknowledgment of which, six of the best Smocks I have shall be chang'd into Shirts for thee; and if they are not spick and span new, yet they are all as clean as a Peny. *Sancho* pull'd off his Mitre, put his Knee to the Ground, and kiss'd her Hand. The Duke commanded, that they should return him his Cap, and instead of his flaming Frock, to give him his Gaberdine; but *Sancho* begg'd of his Grace, that he might keep the Frock and Mitre, to carry into his own Country, as a Relick of that wonderful Adventure. The Dutchess said, he should have 'em, for he knew she was always one of his best Friends. Then the Duke order'd the Company to clear the Court, and retire to their respective Lodgings, and that Don *Quixote* and *Sancho* should be conducted to their Apartments.

XXXVII: WHICH COMES AFTER THE THIRTY-SIXTH, AND CONTAINS SEVERAL PARTICULARS, NECESSARY FOR THE ILLUSTRATION OF THIS HISTORY

THAT Night *Sancho* lay in a Truckle-bed in Don *Quixote's* Chamber, a Lodging not much to the Squire's liking, being very sensible that his Master would disturb him with impertinent Chat all Night long; and this Entertainment he found himself not rightly dispos'd for, his late Penance having taken him quite off the talking Pin; and a Hovel, with good sound Sleep, had been more agreeable to his Circumstances, than the most stately Apartments in such troublesom Company; and indeed his Apprehensions prov'd so right, that his Master was scarcely laid when he began to open:

Sancho, said he, what is your opinion of this night's adventure? Great and mighty is the Force of Love when heighten'd by Disdain, as the Testimony of your own Eyes may convince you in the Death of *Altisidora*. 'Twas neither a Dart, a Dagger, nor any Poison that brought her to her End, but she expir'd through the meer Sense of my Disdain of her Affection. I had not car'd a Pin, answer'd *Sancho*, though she had dy'd of the Pip, so she had but let Me alone; I never courted her, nor slighted her in my born Days; and for my Part, I must still think it strange, that the Life and Well-doing of *Altisidora*, a whimsical, maggotty Gentlewoman, should depend upon the plaguing of *Sancho Pança*. But there are such Things as Inchanters and Witchcrafts that's certain, from which good Heaven deliver me! for 'tis more than I can do my self. But now, Sir, let me sleep, I beseech you; for if you trouble me with any more Questions, I'm resolv'd to leap out of the Window. I'll not disturb thee, honest *Sancho*, said Don *Quixote*, sleep, if the Smart of thy late Torture will let thee. No Pain, answer'd *Sancho*, can be compar'd to the Abuse my Face suffer'd, because 'tis done by the worst of ill-natur'd Creatures, I mean old Waiting-women; The Devil take 'em, quo' I, and so good Night! I want a good Nap to set me to rights, and so once again, pray let me sleep. Do so, said Don *Quixote*, and Heaven be with thee. Thereupon they both fell asleep, and while they are asleep, *Cid Hamet* takes the Opportunity to tell us the Motives that put the Duke and Dutchess upon this odd Compound of Extravagancies, that has been last related. He says, that the Batchelor *Carrasco* meditating Revenge for having been defeated by Don *Quixote* when he went by the Title of the Knight of the *Mirrors*, resolv'd to make another Attempt in Hopes of better Fortune; and therefore having understood where Don *Quixote* was, by the Page that brought the Letters and Present to *Sancho's* Wife, he furnish'd himself with a fresh Horse and Arms, and had a White Moon painted on his Shield; his Accoutrements were all pack'd up on a Mule, and, lest *Thomas Cecial* his former Attendant should be known by Don *Quixote* or *Sancho*, he got a Country-Fellow to wait on him as a Squire. Coming to the Duke's Castle, he was inform'd that the Knight was gone to the Tournament at *Saragosa*, the Duke giving the Batchelor an Account also how pleasantly they had impos'd upon him with the Contrivance for *Dulcinea's* Disinchantment, to be effected at the Expence of *Sancho's* Posteriors. Finally, he told him how *Sancho* had made his Master believe that *Dulcinea* was transform'd into a Country-Wench by the Power of Magick; and how the Dutchess had persuaded *Sancho* that he was deluded himself, and *Dulcinea* inchanted in good earnest. The Batchelor, though he could not forbear laughing, was nevertheless struck with Wonder at this Mixture of Cunning and Simplicity in the Squire, and the uncommon Madness of the Master. The Duke then made it his Request, that if he met with the Knight, he should call at the Castle as he return'd, and give him an Account of his Success, whether he vanquish'd him or not. The Batchelor promis'd to obey his Commands; and, departing in Search of Don *Quixote*, he found him not at *Saragosa*, but travelling farther, met him at last, and had his Revenge as we have told you. Then taking the Duke's Castle in his Way home, he gave him an Account of the Circumstances and Conditions of the Combat, and how Don *Quixote* was repairing homewards, to fulfil his Engagement of returning to and remaining in his Village for a Year, as it was incumbent on the Honour of Chivalry to perform, and in this Space, the Batchelor said, he hop'd the poor Gentleman might recover his Senses, declaring withal, that the Concern he had upon him, to see a Man of his Parts in such a distracted Condition, was the only Motive that could put him upon such an Attempt. Upon this he return'd home, there to expect Don *Quixote*, who was coming after him. This Information engag'd the Duke, who was never to be tir'd with the Humours of the Knight and the Squire, to take this Occasion to make more Sport with 'em; he order'd all the Roads thereabouts, especially those that Don *Quixote* was most likely to take, to be laid by a great many of his Servants, who had Orders to bring him to the Castle, right or wrong.

They met him accordingly, and sent their Master an Account of it; whereupon all Things being prepar'd against his coming, the Duke caus'd the Torches and Tapers to be all lighted round the Court, and *Altisidora's* Tragi-comical Interlude was acted, with the Humours of *Sancho Pança*, the whole so to the Life, that the Counterfeit was hardly discernable. *Cid Hamet* adds, that he believ'd those that play'd all these Tricks were as mad as those they were impos'd upon: And that the Duke and Dutchess were within a Hair's Breadth of being thought Fools themselves, for taking so much Pains to make Sport with the Weakness of two poor silly Wretches.

Now to return to our two Adventurers; the Morning found one of them fast asleep, and the other broad awake, transported with his wild Imaginations. They thought it Time to rise, especially the Don, for the Bed of Sloth was never agreeable to him, whether vanquish'd or victorious.

Altisidora, whom Don *Quixote* suppos'd to have been rais'd from the Dead, did that Day (to humour her Lord and Lady) deck her Head with the same Garland she wore upon the Tomb, and in a loose Gown of white Taffaty flower'd with Gold, her dishevel'd Locks flowing negligently on her Shoulders, she enter'd Don *Quixote's* Chamber, supporting herself with an Ebony Staff.

The Knight was so surpriz'd and amaz'd at this unexpected Apparition, that he was struck dumb; and not knowing how to behave himself, he slunk down under the Bed-Clothes, and

518

cover'd himself over Head and Ears. However, *Altisidora* plac'd her self in a Chair close by his Bed's-head, and after a profound Sigh: To what an Extremity of Misfortune and Distress, said she in a soft and languishing Voice, are young Ladies of my Virtue and Quality reduc'd, when they thus trample upon the Rule of Modesty, and without regard to Virgin-Decency, are forc'd to give their Tongues a Loose, and betray the Secrets of their Hearts! Alas! Noble Don *Quixote de la Mancha,* I am one of those unhappy Persons over-rul'd by my Passion, but yet so reserv'd and patient in my Sufferings, that Silence broke my Heart, and my Heart broke in Silence. 'Tis now two Days, most inexorable and marble-hearted Man, since the Sense of your severe Usage and Cruelty brought me to my Death, or something so like it, that every one that saw me, judg'd me to be dead. And had not Love been compassionate, and assign'd my Recovery on the Sufferings of this kind Squire, I had ever remain'd in the other World. Truly, quoth *Sancho,* Love might e'en as well have made Choice of my Ass for that Service, and he would have obliged me a great deal more. But pray, good Mistress, tell me one Thing now, and so Heaven provide you a better natur'd Sweet-heart than my Master, What did you see in the other World? What Sort of Folks are there in Hell? For There I suppose you have been; for those that die of Despair, must needs go to that Summer-house. To tell you the Truth, reply'd *Altisidora,* I fancy I could not be dead out-right, because I was not got so far as Hell; for had I been once in, I'm sure I should ne'er have been allow'd to have got out again. I got to the Gates indeed, where I found a round Dozen of Devils in their Breeches and Waistcoats, playing at Tennis with flaming Rackets; they wore flat Bands with scollop'd Flanders Lace and Ruffles of the same; four Inches of their Wrists bare,* to make their Hands look the longer; in which they held Rackets of Fire. But what I most wonder'd at, was, that instead of Tennis-balls, they made use of Books that were every whit as light, and stuff'd with Wind and Flocks, or such Kind of Trumpery. This was indeed most strange and wonderful; but, what still amaz'd me more, I found, that con-

---

* *It was so strange and impudent a Sight for Women or Men to shew their naked Wrists or Arms, that the Author puts the Devils in that Fashion.*

trary to the Custom of Gamesters, among whom the winning Party at least is in good Humour, and the Losers only angry, these Hellish Tossers of Books of both Sides did nothing but fret, fume, stamp, curse and swear most horribly, as if they had been all Losers.

That's no Wonder at all, quoth *Sancho*; for your Devils, whether they play or no, win or lose, they can never be contented. That may be, said *Altisidora*, but another Thing that I admire (I then admir'd I would say) was, that the Ball would not bear a second Blow, but at every Stroke they were oblig'd to change Books, some of 'em new, some old, which I thought very strange. And one Accident that happen'd upon this I can't forget: They toss'd up a new Book fairly bound, and gave it such a smart Stroke, that the very Guts flew out of it, and all the Leaves were scatter'd about. Then cry'd one of the Devils to another, look, look, what Book is that? 'Tis the Second Part of the History of Don *Quixote*, said the other; not that which was compos'd by *Cid Hamet*, the Author of the first, but by a certain *Aragonian*, who professes himself a Native of *Tordesillas*. Away with it, cry'd the first Devil, down with it, plunge it to the lowest Pit of Hell, where I may never see it more. Why, is it such sad Stuff, said the other? Such intolerable Stuff, cry'd the first Devil, that if I and all the Devils in Hell should set our Heads together to make it worse, it were past our Skill. The Devils continu'd their Game, and shatter'd a World of other Books, but the Name of Don *Quixote*, that I so passionately ador'd, confin'd my Thoughts only to that Part of the Vision which I have told you. It could be nothing but a Vision to be sure, said Don *Quixote*, for I am the only Person of the Name now in the Universe, and that very Book is toss'd about here at the very same Rate, never resting in a Place, for every Body has a Fling at it. Nor am I concern'd that any Phantom assuming My Name, should wander in the Shades of Darkness, or in the Light of this World, since I am not the Person of whom that History treats. If it be well writ, faithful and authentick, it will live Ages; but if it be bad, 'twill have a quick Journey from it's Birth to the Grave of Oblivion. *Altisidora* was then going to renew her Expostulations and Complaints against Don *Quixote*, had not he thus interrupted her: I have often caution'd you, Madam, said he, of fixing your Affections upon a Man who is absolutely uncapable of making a suitable Return. It grieves me to have a Heart obtruded upon me, when I have no Entertainment to give it, but bare cold Thanks. I was only born for *Dulcinea del Toboso*, and to Her alone the Destinies (if such there be) have devoted my Affection: So 'tis Presumption for any other Beauty to imagine she can displace her, or but share the Possession she holds in my Soul. This I hope may suffice to take away all Foundation from your Hopes, to recal your Modesty, and re-instate it in it's proper Bounds, for Impossibilities are not to be expected from any Creature upon Earth.

At hearing this, Death of my Life! cry'd *Altisidora*, putting on a violent Passion, thou Lump of Lead, who hast a Soul of Morter, and a Heart as little and as hard as the Stone of an Olive, more stubborn than a sullen Plough-jobber, or a Carrier's Horse that will never go out of his Road, I have a good Mind to tear your Eyes out, as deep as they are in your Head. Why, thou beaten Swash-buckler, thou Rib-roasted Knight of the Cudgel, hast thou the Impudence to think that I dy'd for Love of thy Lanthorn-Jaws? No, no, Sir Tiffany, all that you have seen this Night has been Counterfeit, for I would not suffer the Pain of a Flea-bite, much less that of dying, for such a Dromedary as thou art. Troth! Lass, I believe thee, quoth *Sancho*; for all these Stories of People dying for Love are meer Tales of a roasted Horse. They tell you they'll die for Love, but the Devil a-bit. Trust to that and be laugh'd at.

Their Discourse was interrupted by the coming in of the Harper, Singer, and Composer of the Stanzas that were perform'd in the Court the Night before. Sir Knight, said he to Don *Quixote*, making a profound Obeisance, let me beg the Favour of being number'd among your most humble Servants; 'tis an Honour which I have long been ambitious to receive, in regard of your great Renown, and the Value of your Atchievements. Pray Sir, said Don *Quixote*, let me know who you are, that I may proportion my Respects to your Merits. The Spark gave him to understand, he was the Person that made and sung the Verses he heard the last Night. Truly, Sir, said Don *Quixote*, you have an excellent Voice; but I think your Poetry was little to the Purpose; for what Relation pray have the Stanzas of *Garcilasso* to this Lady's Death? Oh! Sir, never wonder at that, reply'd the Musician, I do but as other Brothers of the Quill: All the upstart Poets of the Age do the same, and every one writes what he pleases, how he pleases, steals and from whom he pleases, whether it be to the Purpose or no; for let 'em write and set to Musick what they will, though never so impertinent and absurd, there is a Thing call'd poetical Licence, that is our Warrant, and a Safeguard and Refuge for Nonsense, among all the Men of Jingle and Metre.

Don *Quixote* was going to answer, but was interrupted by the coming in of the Duke and Dutchess, who improving the Conversation, made it very pleasant for some Hours; and *Sancho* was so full of his odd Conceits and arch Wipes, that the Duke and Dutchess were at a Stand which to admire most, his Wit, or his Simplicity. After that, Don *Quixote* beg'd Leave for his Departure that very Day, alledging that Knights in his unhappy Circumstances were rather fitter to inhabit an humble Cottage than a Kingly Palace. They freely comply'd with his Request, and the Dutchess desir'd to know if *Altisidora* had yet attain'd to any Share of his Favour. Madam, answer'd Don *Quixote*, I must freely tell your Grace, that I am confident all this Damsel's Disease proceeds from nothing else in the World but Idleness. So nothing in Nature can be better Physick for her Distemper, than to be continually employ'd in some innocent and decent Things. She has been pleas'd to inform me, that Bone-lace is much worn in Hell; and since, without doubt, she knows how to make it, let that be her Task, and I'll engage the tumbling of her Bobbins to and again will soon toss her Love out of her Head. Now this is my Opinion, Madam, and my Advice. And mine too, quoth *Sancho*, for I never knew any of your Bone-lace-makers die for Love, nor any other young Wench, that had any Thing else to do; I know it by my self: When I am hard at Work, with a Spade in my Hand, I no more think of Pig'snyes (my own dear Wife I mean) than I do of my dead Cow, though I love her as the Apple of my Eye. You say well, *Sancho*, answer'd the Dutchess, and I'll take care that *Altisidora* shall not want Employment for the future; she understands her Needle, and I'm resolv'd she shall make use on't. Madam, said *Altisidora*, I shall have no Occasion for any Remedy of that Nature; for the Sense of the Severity and ill Usage that I have met with from that Vagabond Monster, will, without any other Means, soon raze him out of my Memory. In the mean Time, I beg your Grace's Leave to retire, that I may no longer behold, I won't say his woful Figure, but his ugly and abominable Countenance. These Words, said the Duke, put me in Mind of the Proverb, *After railing, comes forgiving*. *Altisidora* putting her Handkerchief to her Eyes, as it were to dry her Tears, and then making her Honours to the Duke and Dutchess, went out of the Room. Alack-a-day! Poor Girl, cry'd *Sancho*; I know what will be the End of Thee, since thou art fall'n in the Hands of that sad Soul, that merciless Master of mine, with a Crab-tree Heart, as tough as any Oak. Woe be to thee, a'faith! Hadst thou fall'n in Love with this sweet Face of mine, Body of me, thou hadst met with a Cock of the Game. The Discourse ended here. Don *Quixote* dress'd, din'd with the Duke and Dutchess, and departed that Afternoon.

XXXVIII: WHAT HAPPEN'D TO DON QUIXOTE, AND HIS SQUIRE, IN THEIR WAY HOME

THE vanquish'd Knight-Errant continu'd his Journey, equally divided between Grief and Joy; the Thought of his Overthrow sometimes sunk his Spirits, but then the Assurance he had of the Virtue lodg'd in *Sancho*, by *Altisidora's* Resurrection, rais'd them up again; and yet, after all, he had much ado to persuade himself that the amorous Damsel was really dead. As for *Sancho*, his Thoughts were not at all of the pleasing Kind; on the contrary, he was mightily upon the Sullen, because *Altisidora* had bilk'd him of the Smocks she promis'd him; and his Head running upon that, Faith and Troth, Sir, quoth he, I have the worst Luck of any Physician under the Cope of Heaven; other Doctors kill their Patients, and are paid for it too and yet they are at no farther Trouble than scrawling two or three cramp Words for some physical Slip-slop, which the 'Pothecaries are at all the Pains to make up. Now here am I, that save People from the Grave at the Expence of my own Hide, pinch'd, clapper-claw'd, run through with Pins, and whipp'd like a Top, and yet the Devil a Cross I get by the Bargain. But if ever they catch me a curing any Body o' this Fashion, unless I have my Fee beforehand, may I be serv'd as I have been for nothing. Odsdiggers! they shall pay Sauce for't; no Money, no Cure; the Monk lives by his singing; and I can't think Heaven would make me a Doctor, without allowing me my Fees. You're in the right, *Sancho*, said Don *Quixote*, and *Altisidora* has done unworthily in disappointing you of the Smocks. Though you must own, that the Virtue by which thou workest these Wonders was a free Gift, and cost thee nothing to learn, but the Art of Patience. For my Part, had you demanded your Fees for disinchanting *Dulcinea*, you should have receiv'd 'em already; but I am afraid there can be no Gratuity proportionable to the Greatness of the Cure; and therefore I wou'd not have the Remedy depend upon a Reward; for Who knows whether my proffering it, or thy Acceptance of it, might not hinder the Effect of the Penance? However, since we've gone so far, we'll put it to a Trial: Come,

Sancho, name your Price, and down with your Breeches. First pay your Hide, then pay your self out of the Money of mine that you have in your Custody. *Sancho* opening his Eyes and Ears above a Foot wide at this fair Offer, leap'd presently at the Proposal. Ay, ay, Sir, now you say something, quoth he, I'll do't with a Jirk now, since you speak so feelingly: I have a Wife and Children to maintain, Sir, and I must mind the main Chance. Come then, how much will you give me by the Lash? Were your Payment, said Don *Quixote*, to be answerable to the Greatness and Merits of the Cure, not all the Wealth of *Venice*, nor the *Indian* Mines were sufficient to reward thee. But see what Cash you have of mine in your Hands, and set what Price you will on every Stripe. The Lashes, quoth *Sancho*, are in all three thousand three hundred and odd, of which I have had five; the rest are to come, let those five go for the odd ones, and let's come to the three thousand three hundred. At a *Quartillo*, or three half-Pence a-Piece (and I wou'd not bate a Farthing, if 'twere to my Brother) they will make three thousand three hundred three Half-pences. Three thousand three Half-pences make fifteen hundred three Pences, which amounts to seven hundred and fifty Reals, or Six-pences. Now the three hundred remaining three Half-pences make an hundred and fifty three Pences, and threescore and fifteen Six-pences; put that together, and it comes just to eight hundred and twenty five Reals, or Six-pences, to a Farthing. This Money, Sir, if you please, I'll deduct from yours that I have in my Hands, and then I'll reckon my self well paid for my Jirking, and go home well pleas'd, though well whipp'd; but that's nothing, something has some Savour; he must not think to catch Fish, who is afraid to wet his Feet. I need say no more. Now Blessings on thy Heart, my dearest *Sancho*, cry'd Don *Quixote*! Oh! my Friend, how shall *Dulcinea* and I be bound to pray for thee, and serve thee while it shall please Heaven to continue us on Earth! If she recover her former Shape and Beauty, as now she infallibly must, her Misfortune will turn to her Felicity, and I shall triumph in my Defeat. Speak, dear *Sancho*, when wilt thou enter upon thy Task, and a hundred Reals more shall be at thy Service, as a Gratuity for thy being expeditious? I'll begin this very Night, answer'd *Sancho*, do you but order it so that we may lie in the Fields, and you shall see how I'll lay about me; I shan't be sparing of my Flesh, I'll assure you.

Don *Quixote* long'd for Night so impatiently, that like all eager expecting Lovers, he fancy'd *Phœbus* had broke his Chariot-Wheels, which made the Day of so unusual a Length; but at last it grew dark, and they went out of the Road into a shady Wood, where they both alighted, and being sat down upon the Grass, they went to Supper upon such Provision as *Sancho's* Wallet afforded.

And now having satisfy'd himself, he thought it Time to satisfy his Master, and earn his Money. To which Purpose he made himself a Whip of *Dapple's* Halter, and having stripp'd himself to the Waist, retir'd farther up into the Wood at a small Distance from his Master. Don *Quixote*, observing his Readiness and Resolution, could not forbear calling after him; Dear *Sancho*, cry'd he, be not too cruel to thy self neither: have a care, do not hack thy self to Pieces: make no more Haste than good Speed; go more gently to Work, soft and fair goes farthest; I mean, I would not have Thee kill thy self before thou gettest to the End of the Tally; and that the Reckoning may be fair on both Sides, I will stand at a Distance, and keep an Account of the Strokes by the Help of my Beads; and so Heaven prosper thy pious Undertaking. He's an honest Man, quoth *Sancho*, who pays to a Farthing; I only mean to give my self a handsom Whipping, for don't think I need kill my self to work Miracles. With that he began to exercise the Instrument of Penance, and Don *Quixote* to tell the Strokes. But by that Time *Sancho* had apply'd seven or eight Lashes on his bare Back, he felt the Jest bite him so smartly, that he began to repent him of his Bargain: Whereupon, after a short Pause, he call'd to his Master, and told him, that he would be off with him, for such Lashes as these, laid on with such a confounded Lick-back, were modestly worth three Pence a-piece of any Man's Money; and truly he could not afford to go on at three Half-pence a Lash. Go on, Friend *Sancho*, answer'd Don *Quixote*, take Courage and proceed, I'll double thy Pay, if that be all. Say you so, quoth *Sancho*, then have at all; I'll lay it on thick and threefold. Do but listen ———— With that,

Slap went the Scourge; but the cunning Knave left persecuting his own Skin, and fell foul o' the Trees, fetching such dismal Groans every now and then, that one would have thought he had been giving up the Ghost. Don *Quixote*, who was naturally tender-hearted, fearing he might make an End of himself before he could finish his Penance, and so disappoint the happy Effects of it: Hold, cry'd he, hold my Friend, as thou lovest thy Life, hold, I conjure thee, no more at this Time. This seems to be a very sharp Sort of Physick. Therefore pray don't take it all at once, make two Doses of it. Come, come, all in good Time, *Rome* was not built in a Day. If I have told right, thou hast given thy self above a thousand Stripes; that's enough for one Beating; for, to use a homely Phrase, The Ass will carry his Load, but not a double Load; Ride not a free Horse to Death. No, no, quoth *Sancho*, it shall ne'er be said of me, the eaten Bread is forgotten, or that I thought it working for a dead Horse, because I am paid before-hand. Therefore stand off, I beseech you; get out of the Reach of my Whip, and let me lay on t'other Thousand, and then the Heart of the Work will be broke: such another flogging Bout, and the Job will be over. Since thou art in the Humour, reply'd Don *Quixote*, I will withdraw, and Heaven strengthen and reward thee! With that, *Sancho* fell to work afresh, and beginning upon a new Score, lash'd the Trees at so unconscionable a Rate, that he fetch'd off their Skins most unmercifully. At length, raising his Voice, seemingly resolved to give himself a sparring Blow, he lets drive at a Beech-Tree with might and main: There! cry'd he, down with Thee, *Sampson*, and all that are about Thee! This dismal Cry, with the Sound of the dreadful Strokes that attended it, made Don *Quixote* run presently to his Squire, and laying fast hold on the Halter, which *Sancho* had twisted about and manag'd like a Bull's Pizzle, Hold, cry'd he, Friend *Sancho*, stay the Fury of thy Arm: Do'st thou think I will have thy Death, and the Ruin of thy Wife and Children to be laid at my Door? Forbid it Fate! Let *Dulcinea* stay a While, till a better Opportunity offers it self. I my self will be contented to live in Hopes, that when thou hast recover'd new Strength, the Business may be accomplish'd to every Body's Satisfaction. Well, Sir, quoth *Sancho*, if it be your Worship's

Will and Pleasure it should be so, so let it be, quo' I. But for Goodness-sake, do so much as throw your Cloak over my Shoulders; for I am all in a muck-Sweat, and I've no Mind to catch Cold; we Novices are somewhat in Danger of that when we first undergo the Discipline of *Flogging*. With that, Don *Quixote* took off his Cloak from his own Shoulders, and putting it over those of *Sancho*, chose to remain in Cuerpo; and the crafty Squire being lapp'd up warm, fell fast asleep, and never stirr'd till the Sun wak'd him.

In the Morning they went on their Journey, and after three Hours riding, alighted at an Inn, for it was allow'd by Don *Quixote* himself to be an Inn, and not a Castle, with Moats, Towers, Portcullices and Draw-Bridges, as he commonly fancy'd; for now the Knight was mightily off the romantick Pin, to what he us'd to be, as shall be shew'd presently more at large. He was lodg'd in a Ground-Room, which instead of Tapistry, was hung with a coarse painted Stuff, such as is often seen in Villages. One of the Pieces had the Story of *Helen* of *Troy*, when *Paris* stole her away from her Husband *Menelaus*, but scrawl'd out after a bungling Rate by some wretched Dauber or other. Another had the Story of *Dido* and *Æneas*, the Lady on the Top of a Turret, waving a Sheet to her fugitive Guest, who was in a Ship at Sea, crowding all the Sails he could to get from her. Don *Quixote* made this Observation upon the two Stories, that *Helen* was not at all displeas'd at the Force put upon her, but rather leer'd and smil'd upon her Lover: Whereas on the other Side, the fair *Dido* shew'd her Grief by her Tears, which, because they should be seen, the Painter had made as big as Walnuts. How unfortunate, said Don *Quixote*, were these two Ladies, that they liv'd not in This Age, or rather how much more unhappy am I, for not having liv'd in Theirs! I would have met and stopp'd those Gentlemen, and sav'd both *Troy* and *Carthage* from Destruction; nay, by the Death of *Paris* alone, all these Miseries had been prevented. I'll lay you a Wager, quoth *Sancho*, that before we be much older, there will not be an Inn, a Hedge-Tavern, a blind Victualling-House, nor a Barber's Shop in the Country, but what will have the Story of Our Lives and Deeds pasted and painted along the Walls. But I could wish with all

my Heart though, that they may be done by a better Hand
than the bungling Son of a Whore that drew these. Thou art
in the Right, *Sancho*; for the Fellow that did these, puts me
in Mind of *Orbaneja* the Painter of *Uveda*, who as he sat at
Work, being ask'd what he was about? made Answer, any
Thing that comes uppermost; and if he chanc'd to draw a
Cock, he underwrit, *This is a Cock*, lest People should take
it for a Fox. Just such a one was he that painted, or that wrote
(for they are much the same) the History of this new Don
Quixote, that has lately peep'd out, and ventur'd to go a
Strolling; for his Painting or Writing is all at Random, and any
Thing that comes uppermost. I fancy he's also not much unlike
one *Mauleon*, a certain Poet, who was at Court some Years ago,
and pretended to give Answer *ex tempore* to any Manner of
Questions: Some Body ask'd him what was the Meaning of
Deum de Deo? whereupon my Gentleman answer'd very pertly
in *Spanish, De donde diere*, that is, *Hab nab at a Venture*.

But to come to our own Affairs. Hast thou an Inclination to
have t'other Brush to night? What think you of a warm House?
Would it not do better for that Service than the open Air?
Why truly, quoth *Sancho*, a Whipping is but a Whipping
either Abroad or within Doors, and I could like a close warm
Place well enough, so it were among Trees; for I love Trees
hugely, d'ye see, methinks they bear me Company, and have a
sort of fellow-feeling of my Sufferings. Now I think on't, said
Don *Quixote*, it shall not be to Night, honest *Sancho*, you shall
have more Time to recover, and we'll let the rest alone till we
get Home; 'twill not be above two Days at most. E'en as your
Worship pleases, answer'd *Sancho*; but if I might have my
Will, it were best making an End of the Job, now my Hand's
in, and my Blood up. There's nothing like striking while the
Iron is hot, for Delay breeds Danger: 'Tis best Grinding at the
Mill before the Water is past: Ever take while you may have
it: A Bird in Hand is worth two in the Bush. For Heaven's
sake, good *Sancho*, cry'd Don *Quixote*, let alone thy Proverbs;
if once thou go'st back to *Sicut erat*, or, as it was in the Begin-
ning, I must give thee over. Can'st thou not speak as other
Folks do, and not after such a tedious round-about manner.
How often have I told thee of This? Mind what I tell you, I'm

sure you'll be the better for it. 'Tis an unlucky Trick I've got, reply'd *Sancho*, I can't bring you in three Words to the Purpose without a Proverb, nor bring you in any Proverb but what I think to the Purpose; but I'll mend if I can. And so for this Time their Conversation broke off.

XXXIX: HOW DON QUIXOTE AND
SANCHO GOT HOME

THAT whole Day Don *Quixote* and *Sancho* continu'd in the Inn, expecting the Return of Night,
the one to have an Opportunity to make an End
of his Penance in the Fields, and the other to see
it fully perform'd, as being the most material Pre-
liminary to the Accomplishment of his Desires.

In the mean Time, a Gentleman with three or four Servants
came riding up to the Inn, and one of 'em calling him that
appear'd to be the Master, by the Name of Don *Alvaro Tarfe*,
your Worship, said he, had as good stop here till the Heat of
the Day be over. In my Opinion, the House looks cool and
cleanly. Don *Quixote* over-hearing the Name of *Tarfe*, and
presently turning to his Squire, *Sancho*, said he, I am much
mistaken if I had not a Glimpse of this very Name of Don
Alvaro Tarfe, in turning over that pretended second Part of
my History. As likely as not, quoth *Sancho*; but first let him
alight, and then we'll question him about the Matter.

The Gentleman alighted, and was shew'd by the Landlady
into a Ground-Room that fac'd Don *Quixote's* Apartment, and
was hung with the same Sort of coarse painted Stuff. A while
after the Stranger had undress'd for Coolness, he came out to
take a Turn, and walked into the Porch of the House, that was
large and airy: There he found Don *Quixote*, to whom addressing himself, Pray, Sir, said he, which Way do you travel? To a
Country-Town not far off, answer'd Don *Quixote*, the Place of
my Nativity. And pray, Sir, which Way are You bound? To
Granada, Sir, said the Knight, the Country where I was born.
And a fine Country it is, reply'd Don *Quixote*. But pray, Sir,
may I beg the Favour to know your Name, for the Information
I am persuaded will be of more Consequence to My Affairs than
I can well tell you. They call me Don *Alvaro Tarfe*, answer'd
the Gentleman. Then without Dispute, said Don *Quixote*, you
are the same Don *Alvaro Tarfe*, whose Name fills a Place in the
second Part of Don *Quixote de la Mancha's* History, that was
lately publish'd by a new Author? The very Man, answer'd
the Knight; and that very Don *Quixote*, who is the principal

Subject of that Book, was my intimate Acquaintance; I am the Person that intic'd him from his Habitation so far at least, that he had never seen the Tournament at *Saragosa*, had it not been through my Persuasions, and in my Company; and indeed, as it happen'd, I prov'd the best Friend he had, and did him a singular Piece of Service; for had I not stood by him, his intolerable Impudence had brought him to some shameful Punishment. But pray, Sir, said Don *Quixote*, be pleas'd to tell me one Thing; Am I any thing like that Don *Quixote* of yours? The farthest from it in the World, Sir, reply'd the other. And had he, said our Knight, one *Sancho Pança* for his Squire? Yes, said Don *Alvaro*, but I was the most deceiv'd in him that could be; for by common Report that same Squire was a comical, witty Fellow, but I found him a very great Blockhead. I thought no less, quoth *Sancho*; for it is not in every Body's Power to crack a Jest, or say pleasant Things; and that *Sancho* you talk of must be some paltry Raggamuffin, some guttling Mumper, or pilfering Crack-Rope, I warrant him. For 'tis I that am the true *Sancho Pança*; 'tis I that am the Merry-conceited Squire, that have always a Tinker's Budget full of Wit and Waggery, that will make Gravity grin in Spite of it's Teeth. If you won't believe me, do but try me; keep me Company but for a Twelve-Month, or so, you'll find what a Shower of Jokes and notable Things drop from me every Foot. Adad! I set every Body a laughing, many Times, and yet I wish I may be hang'd, if I design'd it in the least. And then for the true Don *Quixote de la Mancha*, here you have him before you. The Stanch, the Famous, the Valiant, the Wise, the Loving Don *Quixote de la Mancha*, the Righter of Wrongs, the Punisher of Wickedness, the Father to the Fatherless, the Bully-rock of Widows, the Murderer* of Damsels and Maidens; he whose only Dear and Sweet-heart is the peerless *Dulcinea del Toboso*; here he is, and here am I his Squire. All other Don *Quixote's*, and all *Sancho Pança's*, besides us two, are but Shams, and Tales of a Tub. Now by the Sword of St *Jago*, honest Friend, said Don *Alvaro*, I believe as much; for the little thou hast utter'd Now, has more of Humour than all I ever heard come from the other.

* *In the Original*, el Matador de las Donzellas. *A Blunder of* Sancho's Murderer *of Damsels, instead of* Maintainer.

The Blockhead seem'd to carry all his Brains in his Guts, there's nothing a Jest with him but filling his Belly, and the Rogue's too heavy to be diverting. For my Part, I believe the Inchanters that persecute the good Don *Quixote*, sent the bad one to persecute Me too. I can't tell what to make of this Matter; for though I can take my Oath, I left one Don *Quixote* under the Surgeon's Hands at the Nuncio's House in *Toledo*, yet here starts up another Don *Quixote* quite different from Mine. For my Part, said our Knight, I dare not avow my self the good, but I may venture to say, I am not the bad one; and as a Proof of it, Sir, be assur'd, that in the whole Course of my Life, I never saw the City of *Saragosa*; and so far from it, that hearing this Usurper of my Name had appear'd there at the Tournament, I declin'd coming near it, being resolv'd to convince the World that he was an Impostor. I directed my Course to *Barcelona*, the Seat of Urbanity, the Sanctuary of Strangers, the Refuge of the Distress'd, the Mother of Men of Valour, the Redresser of the Injur'd, the Residence of true Friendship, and the first City of the World for Beauty and Situation. And though some Accidents that befel me there, are so far from being grateful to my Thoughts, that they are a sensible Mortification to me, yet in my Reflection of having seen that City, I find Pleasure enough to alleviate my Misfortune: In short, Don *Alvaro*, I am that Don *Quixote de la Mancha*, whom Fame has celebrated, and not the pitiful Wretch who has usurp'd my Name, and would arrogate to himself the Honour of my Designs. Sir, you are a Gentleman, and I hope will not deny me the Favour to depose before the Magistrate of this Place, that you never saw me in all your Life 'till this Day, and that I am not the Don *Quixote* mention'd in that second Part, nor was this *Sancho Pança* my 'Squire, the Person you knew formerly. With all my Heart, said Don *Alvaro*, though I must own my self not a little confounded to find at the same time two Don *Quixote's*, and two *Sancho Pança's*, as different in their Behaviour as they are alike in Name; for my Part, I don't know what to think on't, and I'm sometimes apt to fancy my Senses have been impos'd upon.* Ay, ay, quoth *Sancho*, there has been

* *In the Original, it is,* I am now assur'd that I have not seen what I have seen, nor, in respect to Me, has that happen'd which has happen'd.

533

foul Play to be sure. The same Trick that serv'd to bewitch my Lady *Dulcinea del Toboso* has been play'd You; and if three Thousand and odd Lashes laid on by me on the hind Part of my Belly, wou'd dis-inchant your Worship as well as her, they shou'd be at your Service with all my Heart; and what's more, they should not cost you a Farthing. I don't understand what you mean by those Lashes, said Don *Alvaro*. Thereby hangs a Tale, quoth *Sancho*, but that's too long to relate at a Minute's Warning; but if it be our Luck to be Fellow-Travellers, you may chance to hear more of the Matter.

Dinner-time being come, Don *Quixote* and Don *Alvaro* din'd together; and the Mayor, or Bailiff, of the Town happening to come into the Inn with a Publick-Notary, Don *Quixote* desir'd him to take the Deposition which Don *Alvaro Tarfe* there present was ready to give, confessing and declaring, That the said Deponent had not any Knowledge of the Don *Quixote* there present, and that the said Don *Quixote* was not the same Person that he this Deponent had seen mention'd in a certain printed History, intituled, or call'd the Second Part of Don *Quixote de la Mancha*, written by *Avellaneda*, a Native of *Tordesillas*. In short, the Magistrate drew up, and engross'd the Affidavit in due Form, and the Testimonial wanted nothing to make it answer all the Intentions of Don *Quixote* and *Sancho*, who were as much pleas'd as if it had been a Matter of the last Consequence, and that their Words and Behaviour had not been enough to make the Distinction apparent between the two Don *Quixote's* and the two *Sancho's*.

The Compliments and Offers of Service that pass'd after that between Don *Alvaro* and Don *Quixote* were not a Few, and our Knight of *La Mancha* behav'd himself therein with so much Discretion, that Don *Alvaro* was convinc'd he was mistaken; for he thought there was some Inchantment in the Case, since he had thus met with two Knights and two Squires of the same Names and Professions, and yet so very different.

They set out towards the Evening, and about half a League from the Town, the Road parted into two, one Way led to Don *Quixote's* Habitation, and the other was that which Don *Alvaro* was to take. Don *Quixote* in that little Time let him understand the Misfortune of his Defeat, with *Dulcinea's* Inchantment, and the Remedy prescrib'd by *Merlin*; all which was new Matter of Wonder to Don *Alvaro*, who having embrac'd Don *Quixote* and *Sancho*, left them on their Way, and He followed his own.

Don *Quixote* pass'd that Night among the Trees, to give *Sancho* a fair Occasion to make an End of his Discipline, when the cunning Knave put it in Practice just after the same manner as the Night before. The Bark of the Trees paid for all, and *Sancho* took such care of his Back, that a Fly might have rested there without any Disturbance.

All the while his abus'd Master was very punctual in telling the Strokes, and reckon'd, that with those of the foregoing Night, they amounted just to the Sum of three Thousand and twenty-nine. The Sun, that seem'd to have made more than ordinary Haste to rise and see this Human Sacrifice, gave 'em Light however to continue their Journey; and as they went on, they descanted at large upon Don *Alvaro's* Mistake, and their own Prudence, in relation to the Certificate before the Magistrate, in so full and authentick a Form.

Their Travels all that Day, and the ensuing Night, afforded no Occurrence worth mentioning, except that *Sancho* that Night put the last Hand to his Whipping-work, to the inexpressible Joy of Don *Quixote*, who waited for the Day with as great Impatience, in hopes he might light on his Lady *Dulcinea* in her disinchanted State; and all the Way he went, he made up to every Woman he spy'd, to see whether she were *Dulcinea del Toboso* or not; for he so firmly rely'd on *Merlin's* Promises, that he did not doubt of the Performance.

He was altogether taken up with these Hopes and Fancies, when they got to the Top of a Hill, that gave 'em a Prospect of their Village. *Sancho* had no sooner bless'd his Eyes with the Sight, but down he fell on his Knees, and O, my long, long wish'd-for Home! cry'd he, open thy Eyes, and here behold thy Child, *Sancho Pança*, come back to thee again, if not very full of Money, yet very full of Whipping: Open thy Arms, and receive thy Son Don *Quixote* too, who, though he got the worst on't with another, he ne'ertheless got the better of himself, and that's the best kind of Victory one can wish for; I have his own Word for it. However, though I have been swingingly flog'd, yet I han't lost all by the Bargain, for I have whipp'd some Money into my Pocket. Forbear thy Impertinence, said Don *Quixote*, and let us now in a decent manner make our Entry into the Place of our Nativity, where we will give a Loose to our Imaginations, and lay down the Plan that is to be follow'd in our intended Pastoral Life. With these Words they came down the Hill, and went directly to their Village.

XL: OF THE OMINOUS ACCIDENTS THAT CROSS'D DON QUIXOTE AS HE ENTERED HIS VILLAGE, WITH OTHER TRANSACTIONS THAT ILLUS-TRATE AND ADORN THIS MEMORABLE HISTORY

WHEN they were entring into the Village, as *Cid Hamet* relates, Don *Quixote* observ'd two little Boys contesting together, in an adjoining Field; and says one to the other: Never fret thy Gizzard about it, for thou shalt never see her while thou hast Breath in thy Body. Don *Quixote* over-hearing this, *Sancho*, said he, did you mind the Boy's Words, *Thou shalt never see her while thou hast Breath in thy Body*. Well, answer'd *Sancho*, and what's the great Business though the Boy did say so? How! reply'd Don *Quixote*, dost thou not perceive, that applying the Words to My Affairs, they plainly imply that I shall never see my *Dulcinea. Sancho* was about to answer again, but was hindred by a full Cry of Hounds and Huntsmen pursuing a Hare, which was put so hard to her Shifts, that she came and squatted down for Shelter just between *Dapple's* Feet. Immediately *Sancho* laid hold of her without Difficulty, and presented her to Don *Quixote*; but he, with a dejected Look, refusing the Present, cry'd out aloud, *Malum signum, Malum signum*, An ill Omen, An ill Omen, A Hare runs away, Hounds pursue her, and *Dulcinea* is not started. You are a strange Man, quoth *Sancho*. Can't we suppose now, that poor Puss here is *Dulcinea*, the Grey-hounds that followed her are those Dogs the Inchanters, that made her a Country Lass. She scours away, I catch her by the Scut, and give her safe and sound into your Worship's Hands; and pray make much of her now you have her; for my Part, I can't, for the Blood of me, see any Harm nor any ill Luck in this Matter.

By this Time the two Boys that had fallen out came up to see the Hare; and *Sancho* having ask'd the Cause of their Quarrel, he was answer'd by the Boy that spoke the Ominous

Words, that he had snatch'd from his Play-fellow a little Cage full of Crickets, which he would not let him have again. Upon that *Sancho* put his Hand in his Pocket, and gave the Boy a Three-penny Piece for his Cage, and, giving it to Don *Quixote*, There, Sir, quoth he, here are all the Signs of ill Luck come to nothing. You have them in your own Hands; and though I am but a Dunder-head, I dare swear these Things are no more to Us than the Rain that fell at *Christmas*. I am much mistaken if I ha'n't heard the Parson of our Parish advise all sober Catholicks against heeding such Fooleries; and I have heard you your self, my dear Master, say, that all such Christians as troubl'd their Heads with these Fortune-telling Follies, were neither better nor worse than downright Numskulls: So let us e'en leave Things as we found 'em, and get Home as fast as we can.

By this time the Sportsmen were come up, and demanding their Game, Don *Quixote* deliver'd them their Hare. They pass'd on, and just at their coming into the Town, they perceiv'd the Curate and the Batchelor *Carrasco* at their Devotions in a small Field adjoining. But we must observe by the Way, that *Sancho Pança*, to cover his Master's Armour, had by way of a Sumpter-Cloth, laid over *Dapple's* Back the Buckram Frock figur'd with Flames of Fire, which he wore at the Duke's the Night that *Altisidora* rose from the Dead, and he had no less judiciously clapp'd the Mitre on the Head of the Ass, which made so odd and whimsical a Figure, that it might be said, never four-footed Ass was so bedizen'd before. The Curate and the Batchelor presently knowing their old Friends, ran to meet 'em with open Arms; and while Don *Quixote* alighted and return'd their Embraces, the Boys, who are ever so quick-sighted that nothing can 'scape their Eyes, presently spying the mitred Ass, came running and flocking about 'em; Oh law! cry'd they to one another, look a' there Boys! Here's Gaffer *Sancho Pança's* Ass as fine as a Lady! and Don *Quixote's* Beast leaner than ever. With that they ran hooping and hollowing about 'em through the Town, while the two Adventurers, attended by the Curate and the Batchelor, mov'd towards Don *Quixote's* House, where they were receiv'd at the Door by his House-keeper and his Niece, that had already had Notice of their Arrival. The News having also reach'd *Teresa Pança*, *Sancho's* Wife, she came running half naked, with her Hair about her Ears, to see him; leading by the Hand all the Way her Daughter *Sanchica*, who hardly wanted to be lug'd along. But when she found that her Husband looked a little short of the State of a Governor, Mercy o' me, quoth she, what's the Meaning of this, Husband! You look as though you had come all the Way on Foot, nay, and tir'd off your Legs too! Why, you come liker a Shark than like a Governor. Mum, *Teresa*, quoth *Sancho*, 'tis not all Gold that glisters, and every Man was not born with a Silver Spoon in his Mouth. First let's go Home, and then I'll tell thee Wonders. I've taken Care of the main Chance. Money I have, old Girl, and I came honestly by it, without wronging any Body. Hast got Money, old Boy, nay then 'tis well enough, no Matter which Way, let it come by Hook or by Crook, 'tis but what your Betters have done afore you. At the same Time *Sanchica* hugging her Father, ask'd him what he had brought Her Home, for she had gap'd for him as the Flowers do for the Dew in *May*. Thus *Sancho* leading *Dapple* by the Halter on one Side, his Wife taking him under the Arm on the other, and his Daughter fastning upon the Waist-band of his Breeches, away they went together to his Cottage, leaving Don *Quixote* at his own House, under the Care of his Niece and House-keeper, with the Curate and Batchelor to keep him Company.

That very Moment Don *Quixote* took the two last aside, and without mincing the Matter, gave 'em a short Account of his Defeat, and the Obligation he lay under of being confin'd to his Village for a Year, which, like a true Knight-Errant, he was resolv'd punctually to observe: He added, that he intended to pass that Interval of Time in the Innocent Functions of a Pastoral Life; and therefore he would immediately commence Shepherd, and entertain his amorous Passion solitarily in Fields and Woods; and beg'd if Business of greater Importance were not an Obstruction, that they wou'd both please to be his Companions, assuring them he would furnish them with such a Number of Sheep, as might entitle them to such a Profession. He also told 'em, that he had already in a Manner fitted them for the Undertaking, for he had provided them all with

539

Names the most pastoral in the World. The Curate being desirous to know the Names, Don *Quixote* told him he would himself be called the Shepherd *Quixotis*, that the Batchelor shou'd be called the Shepherd *Carrascone*, the Curate Pastor *Curiambro*, and *Sancho Pança, Pansino* the Shepherd.

They were struck with Amazement at this new Strain of Folly; but considering this might be a Means of keeping him at Home, and hoping at the same Time, that within the Year he might be cur'd of his mad Knight-Errantry, they came into his Pastoral Folly, and with great Applause to his Project, freely offer'd their Company in the Design. We shall live the most pleasant life imaginable, said *Sampson Carrasco*; for, as every Body knows, I am a most celebrated Poet, and I'll write Pastorals in abundance. Sometimes too I may raise my Strain, as Occasion offers, to divert us as we range the Groves and Plains. But one Thing, Gentlemen, we must not forget, 'tis absolutely necessary that each of us chuse a Name for the Shepherdess he means to celebrate in his Lays, nor must we forget the Ceremony us'd by the amorous Shepherds, of Writing, Carving, Notching, or Engraving on every Tree the Names of such Shepherdesses, though the Bark be ever so hard. You are very much in the Right, reply'd Don *Quixote*, though for my Part, I need not be at the Trouble of devising a Name for an imaginary Shepherdess, being already captivated by the peerless *Dulcinea del Toboso*, the Nymph of these Streams, the Ornament of these Meads, the Primrose of Beauty, the Cream of Gracefulness, and in short, the Subject that can merit all the Praises that hyperbolical Eloquence can bestow. We grant all this, said the Curate, but we who can't pretend to such Perfections, must make it our Business to find out some Shepherdesses of a lower Form, that will be good-natur'd, and meet a Man half-way upon occasion. We shall find enow, I'll warrant you, reply'd *Carrasco*: And though we meet with none, yet will we give those very Names we find in Books, such as *Phillis, Amarillis, Diana, Florinda, Galatea, Belisarda,* and a thousand more, which are to be dispos'd of publickly in the open market; and when we have purchas'd 'em, they are our own. Besides, if my Mistress (my Shepherdess I should have said) be called *Ann*, I will name her in my Verses *Anarda*; if *Frances*, I'll call her *Francenia*; and if *Lucy* be her Name, then *Lucinda* shall be my Shepherdess, and so forth; and if *Sancho Pança* makes one of our Fraternity, he may celebrate his Wife *Teresa* by the Name of *Teresania*. Don *Quixote* could not forbear smiling at the Turn given to that Name. The Curate again applauded his laudable Resolution, and repeated his Offer of bearing him Company all the Time that his other Employment wou'd allow him; and then they took their Leaves, giving him all the good Advice that they thought might conduce to his Health and Welfare.

No sooner were the Curate and Batchelor gone, but the House-keeper and Niece, who, according to Custom, had been listening to all their Discourse, came both upon Don *Quixote*; Bless me, Uncle, cry'd the Niece, what's here to do! What New Maggot's got into your Head? When we thought you were come to stay at home, and live like a sober honest Gentleman in your own House, are you hearkning after new Inventions, and running a Wool-gathering after Sheep, forsooth! By my troth, Sir, you're somewhat of the latest: The Corn is too old to make Oaten Pipes of. Lord, Sir, quoth the House-keeper, how will your Worship be able to endure the Summer's Sun, and the Winter's Frost in the open Fields? And then the Howlings of the Wolves, Heaven bless us! Pray, good Sir, don't think on't: 'Tis a Business fit for no Body but those that are bred and born to it, and as strong as Horses. Let the Worst come to the Worst, better be a Knight-Errant still, than a Keeper of Sheep. Troth, Master, take my Advice; I am neither drunk nor mad, but fresh and fasting from every Thing but Sin, and I have fifty Years over my Head; be rul'd by me; stay at home, look after your Concerns, go often to Confession, do good to the Poor, and if ought goes ill with you, let it lie at My Door. Good Girls, said Don *Quixote*, hold your prating: I know best what I have to do: Only help to get me to Bed, for I find my self somewhat out of Order. However, don't trouble your Heads, whether I be a Knight-Errant, or an Errant-Shepherd, you shall always find that I will provide for you. The Niece and Maid, who without Doubt were good-natur'd Creatures, undress'd him, put him to Bed, brought him something to eat, and tended him with all imaginable Care.

XLI: HOW DON QUIXOTE FELL SICK, MADE
HIS LAST WILL, AND DIED

As all human Things, especially the Lives of Men, are transitory, their very beginnings being but steps to their Dissolution; so Don *Quixote*, who was no way exempted from the common Fate, was snatch'd away by Death when he least expected it. Whether his Sickness was the Effect of his melancholy Reflections, or whether it was so pre-ordain'd by Heaven, most certain it is, he was seiz'd with a violent Fever, that confined him to his Bed six Days.

All that Time his good Friends, the Curate, Batchelor, and Barber came often to see him, and his trusty 'Squire *Sancho Pança* never stirr'd from his Bed-side.

They conjectur'd that his Sickness proceeded from the Regret of his Defeat, and his being disappointed of *Dulcinea's* Dis-inchantment; and accordingly they left nothing unessay'd to divert him. The Batchelor beg'd him to pluck up a good Heart, and rise, that they might begin their Pastoral Life, telling him, that he had already writ an Eclogue to that Purpose, not inferior to those of *Sanazaro*, and that he had bought with his own Money, of a Shepherd of *Quintanar* two tearing Dogs to watch their Flock, the one call'd *Barcino*, and the other *Butron*; but this had no Effect on Don *Quixote*, for he still continu'd dejected. A Physician was sent for, who, upon feeling his Pulse, did not very well like it; and therefore desir'd him of all Things to provide for his Soul's Health, for that of his Body was in a dangerous Condition. Don *Quixote* heard this with much more Temper than those about him; for his Niece, his House-keeper, and his 'Squire fell a weeping as bitterly as if he had been laid out already. The Physician was of Opinion, that mere Melancholy and Vexation had brought him to his approaching End. Don *Quixote* desir'd them to leave him a little, because he found himself inclinable to Rest; they retir'd, and he had a hearty Sleep of about Six Hours, which the Maid and Niece were afraid had been his last.

At length he wak'd, and with a loud Voice, Blessed be the

Almighty, cry'd he, for this great Benefit he has vouchsafed to do me! Infinite are his Mercies; they are greater, and more in Number than the Sins of Men. The Niece hearkening very attentively to these Words of her Uncle, and finding more Sense in them than there was in his usual Talk, at least since he had fallen ill; What do you say, Sir, said she, has any Thing extraordinary happen'd? What Mercies are these you mention? Mercies, answer'd he, that Heaven has this Moment vouchsafed to shew me, in spite of all my Iniquities. My Judgment is return'd clear and undisturb'd, and that Cloud of Ignorance is now remov'd, which the continual Reading of those damnable Books of Knight-Errantry had cast over my Understanding. Now I perceive their Nonsense and Impertinence, and am only sorry the Discovery happens so late, when I want Time to make Amends by those Studies that shou'd enlighten my Soul, and prepare me for Futurity. I find, Niece, my End approaches; but I wou'd have it such, that though my Life has got me the Character of a Mad-man, I may deserve a better at my Death. Dear Child, continu'd he, send for my honest Friend the Curate, the Batchelor *Carrasco*, and Master Nicholas the Barber, for I intend to make my Confession, and my Will. His Niece was sav'd the Trouble of sending, for presently they all three came in; which Don *Quixote* perceiving, My good Friends, said he, I have happy News to tell you; I am no longer Don *Quixote de la Mancha*, but *Alonso Quixano*, the same whom the World for his fair Behaviour has been formerly pleas'd to call *the Good*. I now declare my self an Enemy to *Amadis de Gaul*, and his whole Generation; all profane Stories of Knight Errantry, all Romances I detest. I have a true Sense of the Danger of reading them, and of all my pass'd Follies, and through Heaven's Mercy, and my own Experience, I abhor them. His three Friends were not a little surprized to hear him talk at this rate, and concluded some new Frenzy had possess'd him. What now, said *Sampson* to him? What's all this to the Purpose, Signor Don *Quixote*? We have just had the News that the Lady *Dulcinea* is dis-inchanted; and now we are upon the point of turning Shepherds, to sing, and live like Princes, you are dwindl'd down to a Hermit.

No more of that, I beseech you, reply'd Don *Quixote*; all the

543

Use I shall make of these Follies at present, is to heighten my Repentance; and though they have hitherto prov'd prejudicial, yet by the Assistance of Heaven, they may turn to my Advantage at my Death: I find it comes fast upon me, therefore, pray Gentlemen, let us be serious. I want a Priest to receive my Confession, and a Scrivener to draw up my Will. There's no trifling at a Time like this; I must take Care of my Soul; and therefore pray let the Scrivener be sent for, while Mr Curate prepares me by Confession.

Don *Quixote's* Words put them all into such Admiration, that they stood gazing upon one another; they thought they had Reason to doubt of the Return of his Understanding, and yet they cou'd not help believing him. They were also apprehensive he was near the Point of Death, considering the sudden Recovery of his Intellects; and he deliver'd himself after that with so much Sense, Discretion and Piety, and shew'd himself so resign'd to the Will of Heaven, that they made no Scruple to believe him restor'd to his perfect Judgment at last. The Curate thereupon clear'd the Room of all the Company but himself and Don *Quixote*, and then confess'd him. In the mean time the Batchelor ran for the Scrivener, and presently brought him with him; and *Sancho Pança* being inform'd by the Batchelor how ill his Master was, and finding his Niece and House-keeper all in Tears, began to make wry Faces, and fall a crying. The Curate having heard the sick Person's Confession, came out, and told them, that the good *A¹onso Quixano* was very near his End, and certainly in his Senses; and therefore they had best go in, that he might make his Will. These dismal Tidings open'd the Sluices of the House-keeper's, the Niece's, and the good Squire's swollen Eyes, so that a whole Inundation of Tears burst out of those Flood Gates, and a thousand Sighs from their Hearts; for indeed, either as *Alonso Quixano*, or as Don *Quixote de la Mancha*, as it has been observ'd, the sick Gentleman had always shew'd himself such a good natur'd Man, and of so agreeable a Behaviour, that he was not only belov'd by his Family, but by every one that knew him.

The Scrivener, with the rest of the Company, then went into the Chamber, and the Preamble and former Part of the Will being drawn, and the Testator having recommended his

Soul to Heaven, and bequeath'd his Body to the Earth, according to Custom, he came to the Legacies as follows.

Item, I give and bequeath to *Sancho Pança*, whom in my Madness I made my 'Squire, whatever Money he has, or may have of mine in his Hands; and whereas there are Reckonings and Accounts to be adjusted between us, for what he has received and disburs'd; my Will and Pleasure is, That whatever may remain due to Me, which can be but small, be enjoyed by him as my free Gift, without any Let or Molestation, and much Good may it do him. And as, when I was mad, he was, through my Means made Governor of an Island, I wou'd now, in my right Senses, give him the Government of a Kingdom, were it in my Power, in Consideration of his Integrity and Faithfulness. And now, my Friend, said he, turning to *Sancho*, pardon me that I have brought upon thee, as well as my self, the Scandal of Madness, by drawing thee into my own Errors, and persuading thee that there have been and still are Knights-Errant in the World. Woe is me, my dear Master's Worship! cry'd *Sancho*, all in Tears, don't die this Bout, but e'en take My Counsel, and live on a many Years; 'tis the maddest Trick a Man can ever play in his whole Life, to let his Breath sneak out of his Body without any more ado, and without so much as a Rap o'er the Pate, or a Kick of the Guts; to go out *like the Snuff of a Farthing-Candle*, and die merely of the Mulligrubs, or the Sullens. For Shame, Sir, don't give way to Sluggishness, but get out of your doleful Dumps, and rise. Is this a Time to lie honing and groaning a Bed, when we shou'd be in the Fields in our Shepherd's Cloathing, as we had resolv'd? Ten to one but behind some Bush, or under some Hedge, we may find the Lady Madam *Dulcinea*, strip'd of her inchanted Rags, and as fine as a Queen. Mayhaps you take it to Heart, that you were unhors'd, and a little Crupper-scratched t'other Day; but if that be all, lay the Blame upon Me, and say 'twas My Fault, in not girting *Rosinante* tight enough. You know too, there's nothing more common in your Errantry-Books, than for the Knights to be every Foot jostl'd out of the Saddle. There's nothing but Ups and Downs in this World, and he that's cast down to Day, may be a cock-a-hoop to Morrow. Even so, said *Sampson*, honest *Sancho* has a right Notion of the Matter.

Soft and fair, Gentleman, reply'd Don *Quixote*, ne'er look for Birds of this Year in the Nests of the last: I was mad, but I am now in my Senses; I was once Don *Quixote de la Mancha*, but am now (as I said before) the plain *Alonso Quixano*, and I hope the Sincerity of my Words, and my Repentance, may restore me the same Esteem you have had for me before, and so Mr Scrivener pray go on.

Item, I constitute and appoint *Antonia Quixano*, my Niece here present, sole Heiress of all my Estate, both Real and Personal, after all my just Debts and Legacies bequeath'd by these Presents, shall have been pay'd, satisfy'd, and deducted out of the best of my Goods and Chattels; and the first of that Kind to be discharg'd, shall be the Salary due to my House-keeper, together with twenty Ducats over and above her Wages; which said Sum I leave and bequeath her to buy her Mourning.

Item, I appoint Mr Curate, and Mr *Sampson Carrasco* the Batchelor, here present, to be the Executors of this my last Will and Testament.

Item, It is my Will, that if my Niece *Antonia Quixano* be inclinable to marry, it be with none but a Person, who, upon strict Enquiry, shall be found never to have read a Book of Knight-Errantry in his Life; and in case it appears, that he has been conversant in such Books, and that she persists in her Resolution to marry him, she is then to forfeit all Right and Title to my Bequest, which in such Case, my Executors are hereby impower'd to dispose of to pious Uses, as they shall think most proper.

Item, I intreat the said Executors, that if at any time they happen to meet with the Author of a Book now extant, en-titl'd, *The Second Part of the Atchievements of Don* Quixote de la Mancha, they wou'd from Me most heartily beg his Pardon for my being undesignedly the Occasion of his writing such a Parcel of Impertinences as is contain'd in that Book; for it is the greatest Burthen to my departing Soul, that ever I was the Cause of his making such a Thing publick.

Having finish'd the Will he fell into a swooning Fit, and extended his Body to the full Length in the Bed. All the Company were troubled and alarm'd, and ran to his Assistance: However, he came to himself at last; but relaps'd into the like Fits almost every Hour, for the Space of three Days that he liv'd after he had made his Will.

The whole Family was in Grief and Confusion; and yet, after all, the Niece continued to eat, the House-keeper drank, and wash'd down Sorrow; and *Sancho Pança* made much of himself: For there is a strange Charm in the Thoughts of a good Legacy, or the Hopes of an Estate, which wondrously removes or at least alleviates the Sorrow that Men would otherwise feel for the Death of Friends.

In short, Don *Quixote's* last Day came, after he had made those Preparations for Death, which good Christians ought to do; and by many fresh and weighty Arguments, shew'd his Abhorrence of Books of Knight-Errantry. The Scrivener, who was by, protested he had never read in any Books of that kind of any Knight-Errant who ever dy'd in his Bed so quietly, and like a good Christian, as Don *Quixote* did. In short, amidst the Tears and Lamentations of his Friends, he gave up the Ghost, or to speak more plainly, died; which, when the Curate perceiv'd, he desir'd the Scrivener to give him a Certificate, how *Alonso Quixano*, commonly call'd *The Good*, and sometimes known by the Name of Don *Quixote de la Mancha*, was departed out of this Life into another, and died a natural Death. This he desired, lest any other Author but *Cid Hamet Benengeli* should take Occasion to raise him from the Dead, and presume to write endless Histories of his pretended Adventures.

Thus dy'd that ingenious Gentleman Don *Quixote de la Mancha*, whose Native Place *Cid Hamet* has not thought fit directly to mention, with design that all the Towns and Villages in *La Mancha* should contend for the Honour of giving him Birth, as the Seven Cities of *Greece* did for *Homer*. We shall omit *Sancho's* Lamentations, and those of the Niece and the House keeper, as also several Epitaphs that were made for his Tomb, and will only give you this which the Batchelor *Carrasco* caused to be put over it.

DON QUIXOTE'S EPITAPH

The Body of a Knight lies here,
  So brave, that to his latest Breath,
Immortal Glory was his Care,
  And makes him triumph over Death.

His Looks spread Terror every Hour;
  He strove Oppression to controul;
Nor cou'd all Hell's united Pow'r
  Subdue or daunt his Mighty Soul,

Nor has his Death the World deceiv'd
  Less than his wondrous Life surpriz'd;
For if he like a Madman liv'd,
  At least he like a Wise One dy'd.

Here the sagacious *Cid Hamet* addressing himself to his Pen, O thou my slender Pen, says he, thou, of whose Knib, whether well or ill cut, I dare not speak my Thoughts! Suspended by this Brass-wire, remain upon this Spit-Rack where I lodge thee. There may'st thou claim a Being many Ages, unless presumptuous and wick'd Historians take thee down to profane thee. But e're they lay their heavy Hands on thee, bid 'em beware, and, as well as thou can'st, in their own Stile, tell 'em,

  Avaunt,* *ye Scoundrels, all and some!*
  I'm kept for no such Thing.
  Defile me not; but hang yourselves;
  And so God save the King!

For Me alone was the great *Quixote* born, and I alone for Him. Deeds were his Task, and to record 'em, Mine. *We two, like Tallies for each other struck, are nothing when apart.* In vain the spurious Scribe of *Tordesillas* dared with his blunt and bungling Ostridge-Quill invade the Deeds of my most valorous Knight: His Shoulders are unequal to th' Attempt: The Task's superior to his frozen Genius.

And thou, Reader, if ever thou can'st find him out in his

* Tatè, tatè, Sollonzicos, &c. *Words borrow'd from an old Romance, says Don* Gregorio *in the Author's Life.*

Obscurity, I beseech thee advise him likewise to let the wearied, mouldring Bones of Don *Quixote*, rest quiet in the Earth that covers 'em. Let him not expose 'em in *Old Castile*, against the Sanctions of Death, impiously raking him out of the Vault where he really lies stretch'd out beyond a Possibility of taking a third Ramble through the World. The two Sallies that he has made already (which are the Subject of these two Volumes, and have met with such universal Applause in this and other Kingdoms) are sufficient to ridicule the pretended Adventures of Knights-Errant. Thus advising him for the best, thou shalt discharge the Duty of a Christian, and do good to him that wishes thee Evil. As for me, I must esteem my self happy, to have been the first that render'd those fabulous, nonsensical Stories of Knight-Errantry, the Object of the publick Aversion. They are already going down, and I do not doubt but they will drop and fall altogether in good Earnest, never to rise again.
Adieu.

FINIS

ABOUT THE TRANSLATOR

P. A. MOTTEUX (1660–1718) was born in Rouen and moved to England after the revocation of the Edict of Nantes (1685). He edited the periodical *The Gentleman's Journal* (1692–4), completed Sir Thomas Urquhart's translation of Rabelais (1693), and published his classic translation of *Don Quixote* between 1700 and 1703.

ABOUT THE INTRODUCER

A. J. CLOSE is Lecturer in Spanish at Cambridge University and the author of *The Romantic Approach to Don Quixote* and various writings on Cervantes, the Spanish Golden Age and modern critical theory.

This book is set in Monotype Goudy Modern. The American
type-designer and printer F.W. Goudy redrew this typeface
after a caption he saw in Alfred Pollard's *Fine books* from
1912. Called Goudy Open, it was characterized by
delicate, open letters. After the first proofs
he filled in the open spaces and called it
Goudy Modern. Around 1928
the typeface was recut
by the Monotype
Corporation.